D1386219

THE

STAR TREK®
ENCYCLOPEDIA

A Reference Guide to the Future

By

MICHAEL OKUDA
DENISE OKUDA
DEBBIE MIREK

Illustrations by
DOUG DREXLER

S I M O N & S C H U S T E R

LONDON·SYDNEY·NEW YORK·TOKYO·SINGAPORE·TORONTO

For our parents.

First published in Great Britain by Simom & Schuster Ltd, 1994
A Paramount Communications Company

Simon & Schuster Ltd
West Garden Place
Kendal Street
London W2 2AQ

Simon & Schuster of Australia Pty Ltd
Sydney

A CIP catalogue record for this book is available from the British Library.
ISBN 0-671-71834-7

Printed in the U.S.A.

INTRODUCTION

The *Star Trek* saga now spans three television series and six feature films produced over nearly three decades. At this writing, there are over 263 hours of *Star Trek* in existence, and a fourth series and a seventh movie are already in the works. *Star Trek* has indeed become an icon of 20th-century popular culture. Yet with this extraordinary success, It is increasingly difficult for those involved with the show (either as viewers or as production staff) to remember the enormous body of details that has been created for the show. This book has been created to help keep track of all that stuff.

In writing this volume, we have assumed editorially that both authors and readers are residents of the late 24th century, a number of years after the current *Star Trek* adventures. This is our attempt to place everything in a historical perspective. This edition includes material up through the sixth season of *Star Trek: The Next Generation* and the first year of *Star Trek: Deep Space Nine*. Although that is our official cut-off point, we've snuck in a few data points from the following season's episodes that were in production as this book was being finished. Dates indicated in this volume are drawn from our own *Star Trek Chronology: The History of the Future* (Pocket Books, 1993).

We have stayed fairly strictly with material only from finished, aired versions of episodes and released versions of films. We have not used any material from the *Star Trek* novels or other publications. This isn't because we don't like those works (we're quite fond of many of them, and we hope this book will be useful to our writer friends), but as with the Chronology, we wanted to create a reference to the source material itself — that is, the episodes and the movies. This way, anyone building on this encyclopedia can be reasonably sure that his or her work is directly based on actual *Star Trek* source material. In a related vein, this book adheres to Paramount studio policy that regards the animated *Star Trek* series as not being part of the "official" *Star Trek* universe, even though we count ourselves among that show's fans. For those desiring reference material on the animated series, we refer you to Bjo Trimble's updated *Star Trek Concordance*.

Episode numbers. In the main listing for each episode (listed under the episodes' titles), we have indicated an episode number. These are *not* Paramount's internal production numbers (which are sometimes confusing), but are simply the number of that episode within that series in order of production. In other words, "The Cage" (TOS), "Encounter at Farpoint, Part I" (TNG), and "Emissary, Part I" (DS9) are all episode #1 of their respective series. The suffix (TOS) indicates an episode of The Original Series, while (TNG) denotes an episode of *The Next Generation*, and a title labeled (DS9) is from *Deep Space Nine*. (For those who

simply *must* know: Episode numbers assigned to episodes of the Original Series are indeed the internal Desilu/Paramount numbers. Studio production numbers for *Next Generation* episodes can be determined by adding 100 to our episode number, so that "Encounter at Farpoint, Part I" is production number 101. Add 400 to our episode numbers to get production numbers for *Deep Space Nine* episodes, so that "Emissary, Part I" is production number 401.)

Mistakes. We have no doubt that a few errors have made their way into this volume, despite many, many hours spent researching and checking things. We hope to eventually do a second edition to this book, and we would very much like to correct as many of them as possible. If you find a blooper and would like to help in our quest, please drop us a brief note in care of Pocket Books, 1230 Avenue of the Americas, New York, NY 10020. *Please be sure to include the page number on which you noticed the inaccuracy, and mention the episode or movie in which the correct information appears.* Note that we're *only* interested in errors arising from contradictions or significant omissions from final aired versions of episodes and released versions of the movies. We're *not* looking for dialog that may have been cut from a script, or for any other supplemental or purely conjectural information. (Because there are frequently significant differences between a script and a finished episode, we are not using scripts as final references, except for spelling of names.) Also, please understand that despite Pocket Books' considerable generosity in giving us more than twice as many pages as we had for the Chronology, we still had to select material on the basis of what we felt would be of the most interest to the greatest number of readers. If you are the *first* person to tell us about a particular error, and if we use your suggestion, we'll mention your name in the acknowledgments of the next edition.

Using this book: Entries are listed alphabetically in the body of the encyclopedia. Within an entry, any term **bold-faced** indicates that there is a separate entry under that name with further information. Entries preceeded with a • bullet are episode titles. *Italic type* indicates behind-the-scenes information in which we briefly step out of the fictional *Star Trek* universe to discuss the show itself. Character name entries generally include the actor's name in parentheses, where applicable. Appendices A and B at the back of this book contain chronological information on *Star Trek* history and *Star Trek* production. Appendix C contains lists of episode titles and writers in production order.

ACKNOWLEDGMENTS

We would like to acknowledge Bjo Trimble and Larry Nemecek for serving as research consultants on this book. They have graciously permitted us to take advantage of background work they have done for their own projects. We are grateful for all the help we could get, especially with the compressed schedule on which this book was produced.

The monumental task of proofreading and editing this manuscript could not have been completed without Suzie Miller, Jim Van Over, Keith Holt, Nancy Ohlson, Kurt Hanson, Leslie Blitman, D. K. Heller, and René Zajac. Assistance in research was lent by Rick Sternbach, Jeff Erdmann, Tom Mirek, Terry Erdmann, Midge Gerhardt, Paul Frenczli, Suzanne Gibsmn, Warren James, Wes Yokoyama, David Alexander, and Shirley Maiewski of the *Star Trek* Welcommittee.

At Paramount Pictures, our thanks to: Rick Berman, Michael Piller, Jeri Taylor, Ira Steven Behr, Bob Justman, David Livingston, Merri Howard, Peter Lauritson, Bobby della Santina, Brad Yacobian, Ronald D. Moore, Brannon Braga, Peter Allan Fields, Naren Shankar, Jim Crocker, Robert Wolfe, René Echevarria, Wendy Neuss, Steve Oster, Paula Block, Dan Curry, Gary Hutzel, Ronald B. Moore, Judy Elkins, Marvin Rush, Jonathan West, Andre Bormanis, Joe Longo, Alan Sims, Susan Sackett, Steve Frank, Kathy Slechta, Fred Seibly, Guy Vardaman, Kristine Fernandez, Kim Fitzgerald, Heidi Smothers, Dawn Velazquez, Lolita Fatjo, Jana Wallace, Mary Allen, Robbin Slocum, Cheryl Gluckstern, Zayra Cabot, Dave Rossi, and Diane Castro.

Our colleagues and friends at the *Star Trek* art departments: Casey Cannon, Sharon Davis, Ricardo Delgado, Wendy Drapanas, Doug Drexler, John Eaves, Anthony Fredrickson, Scott Herbertson, Richard James, Alan Kobayashi, Jim Magdaleno, Randy McIlvain, Jim Martin, Karl Martin, Jim Mees, Andy Neskoronmy, Louise Nielsen, Alex Perez, Laura Richarz, Eugene W. Roddenberry, Jr., Gary Speckman, Rick Sternbach, Sandy Veneziano, Ron Wilkinson, and Herman Zimmerman. At Pocket Books, Kevin Ryan, Scott Shannon, John Ordover, Tyya Turner, and James Wang.

Thanks to Greg Jein for helping us track down many reference photos of props from the original *Star Trek* series and the *Star Trek* movies. Additional photos were provided by Richard Barnett, Bill George, and Paula Block. Thanks to Anthony Fredrickson and Ed Miarecki for building the *Enterprise* models used on the cover.

As with the *Star Trek Chronology*, many photographs in this volume were directly taken from film and video frames of the actual episodes and movies. As a result, the directors of photography of the shows should be credited: Jerry Finnerman and Al Francis (original *Star Trek* series), Richard H. Kline *(Star Trek: The Motion Picture)*, Gayne Rescher *(Star Trek II: The Wrath of Khan)*, Charles Correll *(Star Trek III: The Search for Spock)*, Don Peterman *(Star Trek IV: The Voyage Home)*, Andrew Laszlo *(Star Trek V: The Final Frontier)*, Hiro Narita *(Star Trek VI: The Undiscovered Country)*, Ed Brown, Jr. *(Star Trek: The Next Generation*, years 1 and 2), Marvin Rush *(Star Trek: The Next Generation,* years 3-6, and *Star Trek: Deep Space Nine,* year 1), and Jonathan West *(Star Trek: The Next Generation*, year 6). Production stills by: Mel Traxel *(Star Trek I)*, Bruce Birmelin *(Star Trek II, IV, and V)*, John Shannon *(Star Trek III)*, and Gregory Schwartz *(Star Trek VI)*. *Star Trek: The Next Generation* and *Star Trek: Deep Space Nine* still photographers have included Kim Walker, Julie Dennis, Robbie Robinson, Fred Sabine, and Michael Paris. (We apologize in advance because we know this is not a complete list of unit still photographers.) ILM effects stills by Terry Chostner and Kerry Nordquist. Additional prop photos by Anthony Fredrickson. Author photos by Robbie Robinson and Richard Barnett. Isaac Asimov photograph by Alex Gotfryd, courtesy of Doubleday Books. Photo retouching by Doug Drexler.

This book was written on Apple Macintosh PowerBook computers using Microsoft Word software. Page layout was done with Aldus PageMaker, video frame captures were done with Radius VideoVision, photo retouching was done with Adobe Photoshop, and drawings were done with Adobe Illustrator and Adobe Dimensions. Charts were built with Microsoft Excel. We salute everyone who helped make these wonderful tools available to the rest of us.

Special thanks to Miriam Mita, Ralph Winter, Tom Mirek, George Wright, Pat Packard, Jim Kraxberger, Peter Kahl, Teri Mirek-Kahl, Peter Mirek, Amanda Mirek, Caitlin Mirek, Dorothy Fontana, Donna Drexler, Geoffrey Mandel, Steve Horch, K. M. "Killer" Fish, Moja Richarz, Russ Galen, Van Ling, Helen Cohen, Bob Levinson, Mark Young, Robert Hess, Pat Repalone, Larry Yaeger, Peter Kavanagh, Steve Capps, Michael Tchao, Maurice Naragon, Juan Lopez, Richard Arnold, Ernie Over, Dorothy Duder, Tamara Haack, Craig Okuda, Judy Saul, Todd Tathwell, Annie Yokoyama, Alice P. Liddell, Ford Prefect, Susan Calvin, Heywood Floyd, Jonas Grumby, Kermit the Frog, Luke Skywalker, Cosmic Osmo, Max Headroom, and everyone at the Banzai Institute. Extra-special thanks to Gary Monak, R.J. Hohman, Mike Deken, and "Danger" Madalone for letting Denise fly like Peter Pan.

Once again, our thanks and love to Gene Roddenberry, who created a universe and let us all play in it.

A&A officer. Abbreviation for archaeology and anthropology specialist, a staff officer aboard the original *Starship Enterprise*. **Lieutenant Carolyn Palamas** was the A&A officer when the *Enterprise* visited planet **Pollux IV** in 2267. ("Who Mourns for Adonais" [TOS]).

A.F. An old aquaintance of Jean-Luc Picard. While Picard was at the Academy, he carved A.F.'s initials into **Boothby's** prized elm tree on the parade grounds. Picard failed Organic Chemistry because of A.F. ("The Game" [TNG]).

AU. Abbreviation for Astronomical Unit,a measure of length equal to the distance from the Earth to the Sun, some 150 million kilometers. The **V'Ger** cloud was described as being over 82 AUs in diameter, which is pretty darned big. (*Star Trek: The Motion Picture*).

Aaron, Admiral. (Ray Reinhardt). Stationed at **Starfleet Headquarters** in San Francisco, Aaron had been taken over by the unknown alien intelligence that infiltrated Starfleet Command in 2364. ("Conspiracy" [TNG]).

Abrom. (William Wintersole). **Zeon** member of the underground on planet **Ekos** fighting against the Nazi oppression in 2268. Abrom, his brother Isak, and other members of the underground aided Kirk and Spock in locating Federation cultural observer **John Gill**. ("Patterns of Force" [TOS]).

absorbed. Term used to describe members of the society on planet **Beta III** who were controlled by the computer known as **Landru**. When a person was absorbed, their individual will was stripped and the person was forced to behave in a manner that the computer prescribed as being beneficial to society. ("Return of the Archons" [TOS]).

Academy Flight Range. Located near **Saturn** in the Sol System, an area reserved for flight exercises by cadets from the **Starfleet Academy**. An accident at the Academy Flight Range in 2368 took the life of cadet Joshua Albert. ("The First Duty" [TNG]). SEE: **Crusher, Wesley; Kolvoord Starburst; Locarno, Cadet First Class Nicholas.**

Academy Range Officer. Starfleet officer in charge of the **Academy Flight Range**, located near Saturn. ("The First Duty" [TNG]).

Academy. SEE: **Starfleet Academy.**

Acamar III. Home planet of the **Acamarian** race. The *Enterprise*-D met Sovereign **Marouk**, an Acamarian leader, and her attendants there. ("The Vengeance Factor" [TNG]).

Acamar System. The location of the planet **Acamar III**. ("The Vengeance Factor" [TNG]).

Acamarians. Humanoid race from planet **Acamar III**. The Acamarians had enjoyed peace for the past century, with the exception of Acamar's nomadic **Gatherers**, who left their homeworld to become interstellar marauders. These races appeared largely human with the exception of a facial cleft in their foreheads and the use of individualized decorative facial tattooing. Acamarian blood is based on an unusual iron and copper composite, making it readily identifiable. Within Acamarian culture, membership in a clan is considered of great social and political importance, and conflicts between the various clans often became violent. One such feud, between the **Lornaks** and the **Tralestas**, lasted some three centuries, and ended only after the last Tralesta was dead.

The Acamarian government, headed by Soverign **Marouk**, extended an offer of reconciliation to the renegade Gatherers in 2366. The negotiations, mediated by Jean-Luc Picard, were eventually successful. ("The Vengeance Factor" [TNG]). SEE: **Yuta.** *Photo: Sovereign Marouk.*

ACB. SEE: **Annular Confinement Beam.**

access terminal. Systems connector port used aboard **Borg** ships to allow individual Borg to link to their collective. ("I, Borg" [TNG]).

access tunnel. Series of passageways traversing Deep Space 9, filled with circuitry and other utilities that may be accessed for repairs. The device responsible for the **aphasia virus** was located in one of the access tunnels containing the food-replicator circuitry. ("Babel" [DS9]). *Similar to the Jefferies tubes used aboard Federation starships.*

Accolan. (Dan Mason). Citizen and artist on planet **Aldea** who would have helped raise **Harry Bernard, Jr.**, child of an *Enterprise*-D crew member, had Harry and other children remained on Aldea in 2364. ("When the Bough Breaks" [TNG]).

aceton assimilators. Weapon used by the **Menthars** in their war with the **Promellians** a thousand years ago. Aceton assimilators could drain power from distant sources (such as an enemy ship), then use that power to generate deadly radiation to kill the ship's crew.

The Menthars placed hundreds of thousands of these devices in the asteroid field near **Orelious IX,** thus trapping the Promellian cruiser *Cleponji* a millennium ago. The devices remained active and trapped *Enterprise*-D there in 2366. ("Booby Trap" [TNG]).

acetylcholine. Biochemical substance, a neurotransmitter that promotes the propagation of electrical impulses from one nerve cell to another in carbon-based life. Spock performed an acetylcholine test on a huge spaceborne **amoeba** creature that destroyed the **Gamma 7A System** in 2268, although McCoy felt the test was improperly done. ("The Immunity Syndrome" [TOS]).

Achilles. Popular gladiator who fought McCoy and Spock in the televised arena on planet 892-IV in 2267. ("Bread and Circuses" [TOS]). SEE: **892, Planet IV**.

actinides. Radioactive compounds often found in uranium ore. Actinides in the **Ikalian asteroid belt** made it difficult for sensors to determine the location of **Kriosian** rebels in the area in 2367. ("The Mind's Eye" [TNG]).

active tachyon beam. SEE: **tachyon detection grid**.

Adam. (Charles Napier). Follower of **Dr. Sevrin** who sought the mythical planet **Eden** in 2269. The musically inclined Adam died when he ate an acid-saturated fruit on a world he thought was Eden. ("The Way to Eden" [TOS]). *Charles Napier also played country-and-western singer Tucker McElroy in* The Blues Brothers.

Adams, Dr. Tristan. (James Gregory). Assistant director of the **Tantalus V** penal colony in 2266. Adams seized control of the colony after director **Simon Van Gelder** became insane from testing a neural neutralizer device. Adams later died from exposure to the unit. ("Dagger of the Mind" [TOS]).

adaptive interface link. Computer connection used to exchange information between two computer systems of totally alien origin. An adaptive interface link was used to download information from an alien space probe of unknown origin to station Deep Space 9's computers on stardate 46925. ("The Forsaken" [DS9]). SEE: **Pup**.

Adele, Aunt. Jean-Luc Picard's relative, who taught him a number of home remedies for common ailments. These included ginger tea for the common cold ("Ensign Ro" [TNG]) and steamed milk with nutmeg to treat sleeplessness. ("Cause and Effect" [TNG]). *Aunt Adele was also mentioned in "Schisms" (TNG). She was named for* Star Trek *assistant director Adele Simmons (pictured).*

Adelman Neurological Institute. Biomedical research facility where **Dr. Toby Russell** served on staff in 2368. ("Ethics" [TNG]).

Adelphi, U.S.S. Federation starship, *Ambassador* class, Starfleet registry NCC-26849 that conducted the disastrous first contact with the planet Ghorusda. Forty-seven people, including *Adelphi* **captain Darson**, were killed in the incident, which later became known as the **Ghorusda disaster**. ("Tin Man" [TNG]).

Adelphous IV. Destination of the *Enterprise*-D following its encounter with the Romulan Warbird *Devoras* in 2367. ("Data's Day" [TNG]).

adrenaline. Pharmaceutical based on the humanoid hormone epinephrine. Adrenaline was the accepted treatment

for radiation illness right after the Atomic Age but was replaced as the preferred treatment after **hyronalyn** was developed. In 2267, Dr. Leonard McCoy found adrenaline to be the only cure for a radiation-induced hyperaccelerated aging disease that affected several *Enterprise* crew members. ("The Deadly Years" [TOS]). SEE: **polyadrenaline**.

Agamemnon, U.S.S. Federation starship. The *Agamemnon* was part of task force three, under Captain Picard's indirect command during an expected **Borg** invasion of 2369. ("Descent, Part I" [TNG]). *The* Agamemnon *was named for the Greek mythological figure who was commander of the Greek forces during the Trojan War.*

Age of Ascension. A Klingon rite of passage, marking a new level of spiritual attainment for a Klingon warrior. The ritual involves a recitation by the ascendee, proclaiming *"DaHjaj Suvwl'e' jIH. tlgwlj Sa'angNIS. Iw bIQtlqDaq jIjaH."* ("Today I am a Warrior. I must show you my heart. I travel the river of blood.") The warrior then strides between two lines of other Klingons, who subject him or her to painstiks while the warrior is expected to express his or her most profound feelings while under this extreme duress. **Worf** underwent his Age of Ascension ritual at age 15 in 2355. Ten years later, in 2365, Worf celebrated the anniversary of his Age of Ascension with his *Enterprise*-D crewmates ("The Icarus Factor" [TNG]). Worf's brother, **Kurn**, was not told that he was the son of **Mogh** until Kurn reached his Age of Ascension in 2360. Until that point, Kurn believed he was the son of **Lorgh** ("Sins of the Father" [TNG]).

Age of Decision. A **Talarian** rite of passage signaling the age of majority for a Talarian male at 14 years. SEE: **Jono**. ("Suddenly Human" [TNG]).

Agents 201 and 347. Humans raised on an unknown alien planet, then returned to Earth in the 1960s with a mission to protect humanity from its own self-destructive nature. Both agents were killed in an automobile accident before they could complete their task, so their mission fell to Supervisor 194, also known as **Gary Seven**. ("Assignment: Earth" [TOS]).

agonizer. Small device worn by each crew member on the *I.S.S. Enterprise* in the **mirror universe**. This device was used for punishment and was extremely painful. ("Mirror, Mirror" [TOS]).

agony booth. Method of torture in the **mirror universe** on board the *I.S.S. Enterprise*. The mirror Chekov was subjected to the booth after an assassination attempt on Captain Kirk. ("Mirror, Mirror" [TOS]).

Ah-Kel. (Randy Ogelsby). Humanoid of the **Miradorn** species. Ah-Kel's twin, **Ro-Kel**, was killed by the fugitive **Croden** during a robbery in 2369. Ah-Kel's symbiotic relationship with his twin was severed and he vowed to kill Croden in retaliation. ("Vortex" [DS9]).

ahn-woon. Vulcan weapon made of a single leather strip that could be used as a whip or noose. Spock appeared to strangle Kirk with the *ahn-woon* at the conclusion of their fight on **Vulcan** in 2267. ("Amok Time" [TOS]).

air police sergeant. (Hal Lynch). Security officer of Earth's 20th-century United States Air Force who was beamed aboard the *Enterprise* in 1969. Lipton apprehended Kirk and Sulu trying to remove data from the **Omaha Air Base**, but was beamed up to the *Enterprise*, where he was detained under the watchful eye of Transporter Chief Kyle. ("Tomorrow is Yesterday" [TOS]).

air tram. Transit vehicle used in the San Francisco Bay area in the 23rd century. Admiral Kirk rode an air tram to Starfleet Headquarters prior to his meeting with Admiral Nogura regarding the **V'Ger** threat. (*Star Trek: The Motion Picture*).

airlock. Aboard a spaceship or space station, an airlock is a passageway that permits personnel to pass from an area in which an atmosphere is maintained, into an area where no atmosphere, or a different atmosphere, exists. Typically, airlocks are used to exit a vehicle into the vacuum of space. Aboard station Deep Space 9, airlocks are also used as passageways to docked spacecraft. ("Captive Pursuit" [DS9]).

Ajax, U.S.S. Federation starship, *Apollo* class, Starfleet registry number NCC-11574. In 2327, the *Ajax* was Ensign Cortin Zwellers' first assignment after his graduation from Starfleet Academy ("Tapestry" [TNG]). In 2364, Starfleet propulsion specialist **Kosinski** tested an experimental warp drive upgrade on the *Ajax*, although it was later discovered that Kosinski's theories were baseless. ("Where No One Has Gone Before." [TNG]). In 2368, the *Ajax* served as part of the **tachyon detection grid**, part of Picard's blockade against Romulan interference during the **Klingon civil war**. ("Redemption, Part II" [TNG]). *Named for two heroes from Greek mythology who fought in the Trojan War, Ajax of Salamis and Ajax of Locris.*

Ajur. (Karen Landry). Twenty seventh-century **Vorgon** criminal who traveled backward in time to locate Captain Picard and the *Tox Uthat*. ("Captain's Holiday" [TNG]).

Akaar, Leonard James. Son of **Eleen** and **Teer Akaar** on planet **Capella IV**, born 2267. Leonard James Akaar was hereditary leader, or **teer**, of the Ten Tribes on that planet, and was named after Captain James Kirk and Chief Surgeon Leonard McCoy. Akaar's mother, Eleen, ruled as regent during his childhood. ("Friday's Child" [TOS]).

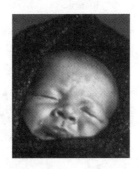

Akaar, Teer. (Ben Gage). High **teer** or leader of the Ten Tribes of planet **Capella IV**. Akaar was killed in 2267 by rival **Maab** in a power struggle for leadership of the ten tribes. Akaar was succeeded by his son, **Leonard James Akaar**, born of his widow **Eleen** shortly after the elder Akaar's death. ("Friday's Child" [TOS]).

Akadar, Temple of. Ancient ceremonial temple from which, centuries ago, the brothers **Krios** and **Valt** ruled a vast interstellar empire. In 2368, a holodeck re-creation of the temple served as the location of a **Ceremony of Reconciliation** between the peoples of two star systems that had taken the names of each of the brothers. ("The Perfect Mate" [TNG]).

Akagi, U.S.S. Federation starship, *Rigel* class, Starfleet registry number NCC-62158. The *Akagi* served in Picard's armada to blockade Romulan supply ships supplying the **Duras** family forces during the **Klingon civil war** in 2368. ("Redemption, Part II" [TNG]). *The Akagi was named for the Japanese carrier that fought the U.S.S. Hornet in the bitter Battle of Midway in World War II. Episode writer Ron Moore thought it fitting that in Star Trek's future, the Akagi would be serving alongside the* **Hornet**.

Aktuh and Melota. A Klingon opera, a favorite of *Enterprise*-D lieutenant Worf. ("Unification, Part II" [TNG]).

Akuta. (Keith Andes). Leader of the race that inhabited planet **Gamma Trianguli VI**. As leader of his people, he wore antennae so he could hear commands from **Vaal**, their god. Vaal felt that the *Enterprise* landing party was a threat and instructed Akuta how to kill them. Among his people, Akuta was known as "the eyes of Vaal." ("The Apple" [TOS]).

Al-Leyan transport. Professor **Richard Galen** had hoped to gain passage on an Al-Leyan transport from **Deep Space 4** to Caere as part of his quest in 2369 to learn about the first humanoids to live in our galaxy. ("The Chase" [TNG]).

Alameda. Location of a 20th-century American naval base near San Francisco, on Earth. The American aircraft carrier *U.S.S. Enterprise* was docked there in 1986, and Starfleet officers Chekov and Uhura broke into the facility to obtain high-energy photons. (*Star Trek IV: The Voyage Home*).

Alan-a-Dale. (LeVar Burton). In Earth mythology, a minstrel who was a member of **Robin Hood**'s band of outlaws in ancient England. Geordi La Forge was cast in this part by **Q** during a fantasy crafted for Captain Picard in 2367. Unfortunately, Geordi's musical skills were not up to the part. ("QPid" [TNG]).

Alans. (Whitney Rydbeck). Specialist in volcanology and geomechanics aboard the *Enterprise*-D. Alans assisted in the geological survey of planets in the **Selcundi Drema** sector in 2365. ("Pen Pals" [TNG]).

Alawanir Nebula. Nebula investigated by the *Enterprise*-D in 2369. ("Rightful Heir" [TNG]).

Alba Ra. A contemporary (24th-century) **Talarian** music form. Electronic, discordant and very loud, it was a favorite listening pleasure of **Jono.** ("Suddenly Human" [TNG]).

Albeni meditation crystal. A colorless sphere about 10 cm in diameter, producing a warm glow and a soft hum. Used as an aid to meditation. Riker presented an Albeni meditation crystal to **Beata** of planet **Angel One**. ("Angel One" [TNG]).

Albert, Joshua. Starfleet Academy cadet and part of the Academy's **Nova Squadron**, killed in a flight accident in 2368. Although preliminary testimony pointed to pilot error on the part of Albert as the cause of his death, Cadet **Wesley Crusher** later testified that the squadron was attempting to perform a **Kolvoord Starburst** at the time of the accident. The attempt at the prohibited maneuver was blamed for the cadet's death. ("The First Duty" [TNG]).

Albert, Lieutenant Commander. (Ed Lauter). Starfleet officer and father of Cadet **Joshua Albert**. Commander Albert was present at the inquiry into his son's death in 2368. ("The First Duty" [TNG]).

Alcyones. Race that destroyed the last **Tarellian** plague vessel in 2358. ("Haven" [TNG]).

Aldabren Exchange. A strategy in **three-dimensional chess**. Commander Riker used this exchange to defeat the Ferengi, **Nibor**, during the **Trade Agreements Conference** in 2366. ("Ménage à Troi" [TNG]).

Aldara. Cardassian *Galor*-class warship commanded by **Gul Danar**. The *Aldara* pursued **Tahna Los** after the Bajoran terrorist stole an antimatter converter from the Cardassians in 2369. ("Past Prologue" [DS9]).

Aldea. Long thought to be mere legend, Aldea was held to be a peaceful, advanced world where technology provided for every citizen to pursue intellectual and artistic endeavors. The legends had a basis in truth.

The **Aldeans** had indeed achieved an idyllic existence, then used a powerful cloaking device to mask their planet from potential intruders. Over the centuries, the planet, located in the **Epsilon Mynos System**, faded into the obscurity of legend. Unfortunately, the planet's cloaking and shielding systems caused damage to the planet's **ozone** layer, resulting in widespread radiation poisoning to the Aldeans. Eventually, the Aldeans became sterile, unable to bear children. In an effort to perpetuate their people, they attempted to kidnap children from the *Enterprise*-D crew. After the attempt failed, starship personnel assisted the Aldeans in dismantling their shielding systems so that the planet's ozone layer would have a chance to return to normal. ("When the Bough Breaks" [TNG]).

Aldeans. Humanoid inhabitants of planet **Aldea**. The Aldeans suffered long-term chromosomal damage from radiation exposure when their cloaking device caused a breakdown in the planet's **ozone** layer. ("When the Bough Breaks" [TNG]).

Aldebaran III. Planet where **Janet Wallace** and her husband, Theodore, performed experiments that used various carbohydrate compounds to slow the degeneration of plant life. Dr. Wallace suggested those experiments might be used to find a cure to the aging disease that afflicted several of the *Enterprise* crew in 2267. ("The Deadly Years" [TOS]).

Aldebaron. Psychologist Dr. **Elizabeth Dehner** joined the *Enterprise* crew at the Aldebaron colony in 2265. ("Where No Man Has Gone Before" [TOS]).

Aldebaran serpent. A three-headed reptile from Aldeberan. **Q** appeared briefly in the form of such an animal during his second visit to the *Enterprise*-D. ("Hide and "Q" [TNG]).

Aldebaran whiskey. A green-colored alcoholic beverage of considerable potency. Although most intoxicating beverages served aboard the *Enterprise*-D used synthehol instead of alcohol, Picard gave Guinan a bottle of Aldeberan whiskey that she kept behind the bar. ("Relics" [TNG]). *Data served some Aldeberan whiskey to Scotty after Scotty expressed displeasure with synthehol-based scotch. Data must have been unfamiliar with Aldeberan whiskey, because he described the drink by simply noting that "it is green," an homage by episode writer Ron Moore to Scotty's delivery of the same line in "By Any Other Name" (TOS).*

Aldorian ale. Beverage served in the Ten-Forward Lounge of the *Enterprise*-D at the request of the **Harodian miners** who were guests aboard the ship in 2368. ("The Perfect Mate" [TNG]).

Alexander. (Michael Dunn). Platonian citizen who, unlike other **Platonians,** lacked telekinetic powers. Alexander had a pituitary hormone deficiency, resulting in his short stature and his inability to absorb the chemical **kironide** from his planet's native food. Because he had no telekinetic powers, Alexander was forced to act as court buffoon to his fellow Platonians. Alexander befriended the *Enterprise* landing party in 2268 and eventually left with them. ("Plato's Stepchildren" [TOS]).

Alexander. SEE: **Rozhenko, Alexander.**

Alfa 117. Class-M planet, the site of a geological survey mission during which a transporter malfunction created a partial duplicate of Captain Kirk in 2266. The transporter malfunction also stranded remaining members of the landing party on the planet's surface, threatening their survival when nighttime temperatures dropped to 120 degrees below zero.

The survey team survived in part by using their phasers to heat rocks, which then served to warm team personnel. ("The Enemy Within" [TOS]).

Algeron. SEE: **Treaty of Algeron.**

Algolian ceremonial rhythms. A musical style played during the closing reception of the **Trade Agreements Conference** on board the *Enterprise*-D. Commander Riker later imitated the rhythms by modifying the warp field phase adjustment of the Ferengi ship *Krayton*'s warp engines, thereby making it possible for Enterprise-D personnel to determine that he, Deanna Troi, and Lwaxana Troi were being held aboard the *Krayton*. ("Ménage à Troi" [TNG]).

Alice in Wonderland. Old Earth children's story written by 19th-century English author Lewis Carroll. Two characters from this book, the **White Rabbit** and **Alice**, appeared on the **amusement park planet** during an *Enterprise* landing party's visit in 2267. ("Shore Leave" [TOS]).

Alice series. (#1-250: Alyce Andrece. #251-500: Rhae Andrece). One of the many models of **androids** who populated the planet controlled by **Harry Mudd** in 2267. This brunette model was a particular favorite of Mudd's, who had 500 Alices made. ("I, Mudd" [TOS]).

Alice. Character from the children's story, *Alice in Wonderland*. Alice appeared on the **amusement park planet** after Dr. McCoy, on a landing party there in 2267, mentioned the world looked like something out of that fanciful book. ("Shore Leave" [TOS]).

Alkar, Ambassador Ves. (Chip Lucia). Federation mediator. A Lumerian, Alkar had empathic powers, and used those abilities to surreptitiously transfer his negative emotions into another person, giving him the emotional strength to handle even the most difficult disputes. These "receptacles" (as Alkar described them) suffered from greatly accelerated aging and severe personality disorders, eventually dying. Alkar continued this practice for many years before Dr. Beverly Crusher discovered it during an investigation into the death of **Sev Maylor** in 2369. Maylor had been a victim of Alkar's abuse. He was in the process of subjecting Deanna Troi to the same treatment when he died after being cut off from access to her mind. ("Man of the People" [TNG]).

• **"All Our Yesterdays."** Original Series episode #78. Written by Jean Lisette Aroeste. Directed by Marvin Chomsky. Stardate 5943.7. *First aired in 1969. Spock and McCoy are trapped in a planet's distant past, where Spock finds love with an exiled woman.* SEE: **atavachron; Atoz, Mr.; Beta Niobe; Sarpeidon; Vulcans; Zarabeth; Zor Khan.**

allamaraine. Word shouted by **Falow** each time the players in the **Chula** game moved to another **shap**, or level. Also the basis of a nursery rhyme recited by a little girl named **Chandra** as part of the game. ("Move Along Home" [DS9]).

allasomorph. Shape-shifting species of intelligent life with the power to alter its molecular structure into that of other life-forms. **Salia** and **Anya** of planet **Daled IV** were both allasomorphs. ("The Dauphin" [TNG]). SEE: **shape-shifter.**

• **"Allegiance."** *Next Generation* episode #66. Written by Richard Manning & Hans Beimler. Directed by Winrich Kolbe. Stardate 43714.1. *First aired in 1990. Picard is kidnapped by unknown aliens, who lock him in a room with other humanoids in an effort to study the concept of authority. The aliens that kidnapped Picard are given no name or homeworld, so those life-forms are described under* **Haro, Mitena**, *the identity they assumed in the episode.* SEE: **Bolarus IX; Bolians; Browder IV; Chalna; Chalnoth; Cor Caroli V; Esoqq; Haro, Mitena; Hood, U.S.S.; Lonka Pulsar; Mizar II; Mizarians; Moropa; Ordek Nebula; Phyrox Plague; Stargazer, U.S.S.; Tholl, Kova; Wogneer creatures.**

Allenby, Ensign Tess. (Mary Kohnert). Flight Control officer aboard the *Enterprise*-D, she piloted the ship during the mission at **Gamelan V** in 2367 ("Final Mission" [TNG]). Allenby was at the conn when the ship encountered a school of two-dimensional creatures while en route to planet **T'lli Beta** ("The Loss" [TNG]).

Alliance. One of the two main rival factions in control of the colony on planet **Turkana IV** following the collapse of the colonial government in the 2350s. In bitter competition with the **Coalition**, the Alliance captured the crew of the Federation freighter *Arcos*, crashed on the planet in 2367. The Alliance hoped to trade the *Arcos* crew members for weapons from the *Enterprise*-D to use in their ongoing battle with the **Coalition**. ("Legacy" [TNG]).

Alpha Carinae II. Class-M planet with two major land masses used in 2268 to test the **M-5** computer's performance in conducting routine planetary contact and survey operations. ("The Ultimate Computer" [TOS]). SEE: **Canopus Planet.**

Alpha Carinae V. Planet origin of the **Drella**, a creature that derives its energy from the emotion of love. ("Wolf in the Fold" [TOS]).

Alpha Centauri. One of the nearest stars to Earth's Solar system, some 4.3 light-years from Sol. In Earth's past, Kirk told United States Air Force officer **Fellini** that he was a little green man from Alpha Centauri and that it was a beautiful place to visit ("Tomorrow Is Yesterday" [TOS]). Alpha Centauri was home to noted scientist **Zefram Cochrane**, who invented warp drive in the 21st century ("Metamorphosis" [TOS]).

Alpha Cygnus IX. Federation Ambassador **Sarek** was credited for a treaty with this planet, one of the many triumphs of his distinguished career. ("Sarek" [TNG]).

Alpha III, Statutes of. Landmark document in the protection of individual civil liberties, cited by **Samuel Cogley** when James Kirk was accused of murder in 2267 but denied the opportunity to face his accuser. ("Court Martial" [TOS]).

Alpha Majoris I. Planet origin of the Mellitus, a creature that is gaseous when moving and becomes solid when it ceases movement. ("Wolf in the Fold" [TOS]).

Alpha Moon. One of two satellites orbiting planet **Peliar Zel**. The inhabitants of Alpha Moon devised an ingenious system to generate power by tapping into the magnetic field of Peliar Zel. While this was of great benefit to the people on Alpha Moon, it had detrimental environmental effects on nearby **Beta Moon**, also orbiting Peliar Zel. The two moons, historically at odds, sought the mediation services of Ambassador **Odan** to resolve the conflict in 2367. ("The Host" [TNG]).

Alpha Omicron System. An uncharted system that the *Enterprise*-D passed en route to a mission in the Guernica System in 2367. A previously unknown life-form was discovered in the Alpha Omicron system, living in the vacuum of space. SEE: **Junior** (Galaxy's Child" [TNG]).

Alpha Onias III. An uninhabited class-M planet, listed by Federation survey teams as barren and inhospitable. Subspace fluctuations detected in the system in 2367 suggested a possible Romulan base. While on Alpha Onias III to investigate this possibility, Commander Riker experienced an elaborate holodeck-type virtual reality devised by **Barash**. ("Future Imperfect" [TNG]).

Alpha Proxima II. Planet where several women were knifed to death. The murders were reminiscent of those committed by Jack the Ripper. ("Wolf in the Fold" [TOS]).

Alpha Quadrant. One quarter of the entire Milky Way galaxy. The region in which most of the **United Federation of Planets**, including **Earth**, is located. The galaxy is so huge that the majority of the Alpha Quadrant remains unexplored, even in the 24th century. Station **Deep Space 9** is located in Alpha Quadrant. ("Captive Pursuit" [DS9]). *The reason for splitting the Federation between Alpha and Beta Quadrants was to rationalize Kirk's line in* Star Trek II *that the* Enterprise *was the only starship in the quadrant.*

Alpha V, Colony. A human settlement where **Charles Evans**' nearest living relatives lived. ("Charlie X" [TOS]).

alpha-wave inducer. Device used to enhance sleep in humanoids, but only meant for occasional use. **Kajada** told Dr. Bashir she was having difficulty sleeping so she used an alpha-wave inducer. ("The Passenger" [DS9]).

alpha-currant nectar. Priceless **Wadi** beverage offered by **Falow** as a wager in a **Dabo** game at Deep Space 9 in 2369. Quark declined the bid after taking a drink of the nectar and finding it distasteful. ("Move Along Home" [DS9]).

Alrik, Chancellor. (Mickey Cottrell). The head of the government of the **Valt Minor** system who, in 2368, conducted the historic **Ceremony of Reconciliation** between his star system and the **Krios** system, ending centuries of war. A stern and humorless man, Alrik was concerned only with the matters of the treaty between the two systems, and not with the ceremony or with the gift of the **empathic metamorph** named **Kamala**. ("The Perfect Mate" [TNG]).

Altair III. Planet at which *Starship* **Hood** executive officer **William Riker** refused to allow *Hood* captain **DeSoto** to transport to the surface. Riker felt the mission was too dangerous to expose the ship's captain to risk. The incident took place prior to Riker's assignment to the *Enterprise*-D. *The star Altair, also known as Alpha Aquila, is the brightest star in the constellation Aquila the Eagle, visible from Earth.* ("Encounter at Farpoint, Part I" [TNG]).

Altair VI. Planet whose people ended a long interplanetary conflict in 2267. The *Starship Enterprise* was scheduled to attend the inauguration of their new president shortly after the end of that war, but the visit was postponed when Spock diverted the ship to planet **Vulcan** because he was undergoing *Pon farr* ("Amok Time" [TOS]). Altair VI was mentioned in Starfleet Academy's notorious *Kobayashi Maru* training simulation. The incident involved a damaged ship near that planet. (*Star Trek II: The Wrath of Khan*).

Altair water. Beverage that Dr. McCoy ordered at a bar on Earth just before trying to book passage to the **Genesis Planet**. (*Star Trek III: The Search for Spock*).

Altairian Conference. Meeting at which Picard met **Captain Rixx** prior to 2364. ("Conspiracy" [TNG]).

Altarian encephalitis. A retrovirus that incorporated its DNA directly into the cells of its host. The virus could lie dormant for years, but activate without warning. Victims would be pyrexic and comatose and would suffer from widespread synaptic degradation. Long-term memory, usually from the moment of the infection, would be destroyed. In a virtual reality created by **Barash** on **Alpha Onias III**, Commander Riker was told he had contracted Altarian encephalitis in 2367, thus explaining a significant memory loss. ("Future Imperfect" [TNG]).

Altec. Class-M planet; along with **Straleb**, part of the **Coalition of Madena**. Although Altec was technically at peace with Straleb, relations between the two planets had been strained to the point that an interplanetary incident was created when it was revealed that **Benzan** of Straleb had been engaged to **Yanar** of Altec in 2365. ("The Outrageous Okona" [TNG]).

• **"Alternative Factor, The."** Original Series episode #20. Written by Don Ingalls. Directed by Gerd Oswald. Stardate

3087.6. First aired in 1967. A mysterious "rip" in space is opened between our universe and an antimatter universe, threatening the existence of both. SEE: **Barstow, Commodore; Code Factor 1; door in the universe; Lazarus; Leslie, Mr.; Masters, Lieutenant; Starbase 200.**

Altine Conference. Scientific conference attended by *Enterprise*-D Chief Medical Officer Beverly Crusher in 2369. She met **Dr. Reyga** while at the conference. ("Suspicions" [TNG]).

Altonian brain teaser. A holographic puzzle that responds to neural theta waves, the goal being to turn a floating multicolor sphere into a solid color. The Dax symbiont had been attempting to master the game for 440 years and had yet to succeed. ("A Man Alone" [DS9]).

Alture VII relaxation program. A holosuite program that first bathes you in a protein bath, then carries you off on a cloud of chromal vapor into a meditation chamber. Beverly Crusher wanted to try this program at Quark's Place when the *Enterprise*-D visited Deep Space 9. ("Birthright, Part I" [TNG]).

aluminum, transparent. SEE: **transparent aluminum.**

Amanda. (Jane Wyatt). Ambassador Sarek's human wife and mother to Spock. Amanda came aboard the *Enterprise* in 2267 with her husband, Sarek, who was attending the Babel Conference ("Journey to Babel" [TOS]). Amanda helped Spock reeducate himself following his *fal-tor-pan* refusal in 2285. She tried especially to help her son rediscover the human portion of his personality (*Star Trek IV: The Voyage Home*). *Amanda's first appearance was in "Journey To Babel" (TOS). A younger Amanda was played by Cynthia Blaise in* Star Trek V *for Spock's birth flashbacks. According to original* Star Trek *series story editor Dorothy Fontana, Amanda's maiden name was Grayson, although this was not established in a regular episode.*

Amar, I.K.C. Klingon battle cruiser, *K'T'inga* class, destroyed while investigating the **V'Ger** machine life-form. (*Star Trek: The Motion Picture*). *The new Klingon battle cruiser was closely based on the original battle cruiser designed by Matt Jefferies for the original* Star Trek *television series. This new version, built at Magicam and at Future General, incorporated much more elaborate surface detailing for a more realistic look. The commander of the* Amar *was played by Mark Lenard, who also played Spock's father, Sarek, and had been the Romulan commander in "Balance of Terror" (TOS).*

Amargosa Diaspora. Dense globular star cluster investigated by the *Enterprise*-D in 2369. ("Schisms" [TNG]).

Amarie. (Harriet Leider). A musician at a lounge on planet **Qualor II**. Amarie was the ex-wife of an arms smuggler whose ship attacked the *Enterprise*-D in 2368. She was uniquely qualified for her occupation as a keyboard artist, as she had four arms. ("Unification, Part II" [TNG]).

Amazing Detective Stories. Pulp detective magazine published on early-20th-century Earth. The character **Dixon Hill** first appeared in a 1934 issue of this magazine. ("The Big Goodbye" [TNG]).

***Ambassador*-class starship.** Type of Federation starship of which the fourth *Starship Enterprise* was one. ("Yesterday's *Enterprise*" [TNG]). The prototype ship, the *U.S.S. Ambassador*, bore registry number NCC-10521. *Ambassador* -class ships have included the **U.S.S. Adelphi** (NCC-26849), the second **U.S.S. Excalibur** (NCC-26517), the **U.S.S. Zhukov** (NCC-26136), and the aforementioned **U.S.S. Enterprise**-C (NCC-1701C).

The Ambassador-*class ship was designed by Rick Sternbach and Andrew Probert. The model, built by Greg Jein, was intended to suggest an intermediate step between the* Excelsior-*class and the* Galaxy-*class starships.*

ambassador, Klingon. (John Schuck). Representative of the Klingon government who attempted to secure the extradition of James Kirk in 2286 so that he could be brought to trial for alleged crimes including the theft of a Klingon spacecraft. The Klingon ambassador also believed, mistakenly, that Kirk had participated in the development of **Project Genesis** with the intent of using it as a weapon against the Klingon people. (*Star Trek IV: The Voyage Home*).

The Klingon ambassador vehemently opposed efforts to free James Kirk and Leonard McCoy from Klingon custody after the two had been arrested on charges of murdering **Chancellor Gorkon** in 2291. (*Star Trek VI: The Undiscovered Country*).

amoeba. A massive spaceborne single-celled organism that consumed the **Gamma 7A System** and the **U.S.S. Intrepid** in 2268. This creature strongly resembled microscopic protozoans found on terrestrial planets, save for its enormous size. The spaceborne amoeba was

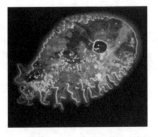

some 18,000 kilometers long, and about 3,000 kilometers wide, surrounded by a large energy-absorbing field. The creature was believed to originate from outside our galaxy. The *Starship Enterprise* approached the organism shortly after stardate 4307 and was nearly crippled by the amoeba's energy-absorbing field, termed a "zone of darkness." The organism was destroyed by an antimatter bomb planted into the amoeba's nucleus by a shuttlecraft piloted by Spock. ("The Immunity Syndrome" [TOS]).

• **"Amok Time."** Original Series episode #34. Written by Theodore Sturgeon. Directed by Joseph Pevney. Stardate 3372.7. *First aired in 1967. Spock experiences the Vulcan mating drive and must return home to take a mate, or die. This is the first episode in which the expressions "peace and long life" and "live long and prosper" were used. Also seen for the first time in this episode were the Vulcan hand salute (invented by Leonard Nimoy) and the planet Vulcan itself.* SEE: *ahn-woon;* Altiar VI; eel-birds; Finagle's law; *Kal-if-fee;* Komack, Admiral; *Koon-ut-kal-if-fee; Kroykah;* lirpa; neural paralyzer; *Plak-tow;* plomeek soup; *Pon farr;* Regulus V; Spock; Stonn; T'Pau; T'Pring; tri-ox compound; Vulcan; Vulcan harp; Vulcans.

amusement park planet. Planet in the Omicron Delta region visited by the original *Starship Enterprise* in 2267 for rest and relaxation. This world has sophisticated subterranean equipment that can read the minds of visitors, then almost immediately create whatever it is that the visitor imagined. Members of the *Enterprise* landing party encountered a variety of images, from old lovers and school rivals, to storybook characters. Although the images were fascinating, they were disturbing and even frightening until the landing party members understood what was happening. SEE: **Alice; black knight; Caretaker; Finnegan; Police Special; Ruth; tiger; White rabbit.** ("Shore Leave" [TOS]). *The actual name for the planet was not given in the episode. The location filming for "Shore Leave" took place near Los Angeles at Vasquez Rocks and Africa USA. Vasquez Rocks was featured in several Original Series episodes, as well as the Next Generation. SEE: Cestus III.* ("Arena: [TOS]).

Anan 7. (David Opatoshu). Leader of the High Council of planet **Eminiar VII** in 2267. Anan 7 was his planet's military commander in the war between Eminiar and **Vendikar.** When the *Starship Enterprise* arrived at Eminiar VII in 2267, Anan tried to warn the ship to stay away. After the *Enterprise* ignored the warning, it was Anan's difficult task to enforce the declaration that the ship was a war casualty under the agreement between his government and Vendikar. When *Enterprise* captain Kirk further abrogated the agreement, Anan agreed to peace talks with the Vendikar government to avoid the possibility of real war. ("A Taste of Armageddon" [TOS]).

anapestic tetrameter. A style of poetic meter used in Commander Data's poem "Ode to Spot." ("Schisms" [TNG]).

Anara. (Benita Andre). Apprentice engineer on **Deep Space 9,** who served on the station in 2369. A Bajoran national. ("The Forsaken" [DS9]).

Anaya, Ensign April. (Page Leong). An *Enterprise*-D crew member. Anaya was assigned to the conn during the *Enterprise*-D's encounter with a **Cytherian** probe in 2367. ("The

Nth Degree" [TNG]).

anbo-jytsu. Considered by some to be the ultimate evolution in the martial arts, anbo-jytsu is derived from a number of Asian art forms. The sport involves two opponents striking each other with three-meter-long staffs while blindfolded. A proximity detector at one end of each staff provides guidance on the opponent's location, while full body armor protects each player. Points are scored for contact with the opponent, and for knocking the opponent outside of the playing ring. **Kyle Riker** played this highly competitive game with his son, **William Riker,** from the time William was eight years old. Although the elder Riker never lost to his son, William later learned that Kyle had been cheating since William had been 12 years old. ("The Icarus Factor" [TNG]).

Anchilles fever. Deadly disease capable of spreading rapidly in a planetary population and causing widespread and painful deaths in the millions. The disease struck planet **Styris IV** in 2364. ("Code of Honor" [TNG]).

Ancient Philosophies. A class at Starfleet Academy. Cadet Wesley Crusher had difficulty mastering this required course. ("The Host" [TNG]).

Ancient West. Holodeck program created by **Alexander Rozhenko** and **Reginald Barclay.** Set in Earth's 19th century in the town of **Deadwood,** South Dakota, the program allowed participants to play the town sheriff, the sheriff's deputy, and **Durango,** the mysterious stranger. The holoprogram malfunctioned and the fantasy became a deadly reality. During the malfunction, information from Data's neural net became incorporated into the holodeck program. SEE: **Subroutine C-47; progressive memory purge; Spot.** ("A Fistful of Datas" [TNG]). *Deadwood was an actual town in South Dakota. The Western sequences were filmed on the back lot of Universal Studios in Los Angeles.*

• **"And the Children Shall Lead."** Original Series episode #60. Written by Edward J. Lakso. Directed by Marvin Chomsky. Stardate: 5027.3. *First aired in 1968. Children who have survived the bizarre death of their parents are possessed by the evil spirit that killed their parents.* SEE: **cyalodin; Epsilon Indi; Gorgan; Janowski, Mary; lacunar amnesia; Marcos XII; O'Connel, Steve; Starbase 4; Starnes Expedition; Starnes, Professor; Starnes, Tommy; Triacus; Tsingtao, Ray; Wilkins, Professor.**

Andevian II. Planet whose fourth moon was held by **Lwaxana Troi** to be an ideal site for a romantic picnic. Ambassador Troi reserved a **holosuite** at **Quark's bar** on Deep Space 9 so that she could have such a picnic with **Odo,** although she neglected to ask Odo first. ("The Forsaken" [DS9]).

Andolian brandy. Quark offered a bottle of this special liqueur to the **Wadi** delegation at Deep Space 9 in 2369 after he was caught cheating at the **Dabo** wheel. ("Move Along Home" [DS9]).

Andonian tea. A refreshment offered by **Admiral Aaron** to

Captain Picard when the latter was visiting **Starfleet Head-quarters** in 2364. ("Conspiracy" [TNG]).

Andorian blues. Musical form, popular with keyboardist **Amarie.** ("Unification, Part II" [TNG]). *The term was, of course, a gag based on the fact that Andorians have blue skin.*

Andorians. Humanoids that describe themselves as being a violent race, characterized by a pair of long antennae on their heads. Members of the United Federation of Planets, an Andorian delegation journeyed to the **Babel Conference** of 2267 aboard the *Starship Enterprise.* The Andorian contingent included Ambassador **Shras** and staff member **Thelev.** SEE:

Orions. ("Journey to Babel" [TOS]). Andorian marriages generally require groups of four people. ("Data's Day" [TNG]). *Andorians were also seen in "Whom Gods Destroy" (TOS), in the Federation Council chambers in* Star Trek IV, *and in "Captain's Holiday" (TNG), and "The Offspring" (TNG). Renegade Andorians were mentioned in "The Survivors" (TNG).*

Andrea. (Sherry Jackson). Beautiful female android creation of archaeologist **Roger Korby.** Andrea was built using technology left over from the ancient race that lived under the surface of planet **Exo III.** ("What Are Little Girls Made Of?" [TOS]).

android. According to *Webster's Twenty-Fourth-Century Dictionary, Fifth Edition*, an android is an automaton made to resemble a human being ("The Measure of a Man" [TNG]). The **Old Ones** of planet **Exo III** developed highly sophisticated androids, but those androids eventually destroyed their civilization ("What Are Little Girls Made Of?" [TOS]). The androids created by the **Makers** from the Andromeda Galaxy were programmed to perform the menial tasks of their society ("I Mudd" [TOS]). Androids were also created on planet **Exo III** in 2266 by **Dr. Roger Korby,** from designs left behind by the **Old Ones.** ("What Are Little Girls Made Of?" [TOS]). SEE: **Andrea; Brown, Dr.; Ruk.** Androids were created by **Sargon, Thalassa,** and **Henoch** aboard the *Enterprise* so that their minds could be transferred into robot bodies. ("Return to Tomorrow" [TOS]). **Flint** attempted to create an immortal mate named **Reena Kapec** but was unable to achieve his goal. ("Requiem for Methuselah" [TOS]). The android **Data,** who served aboard the *Enterprise*-D, strove to become more like his human shipmates ("Encounter at Farpoint" [TNG]). A legal decision handed down by Starfleet Judge Advocate General **Phillipa Louvois** in 2365 established that the android Data was indeed a sentient being, entitled to full constitutional protection as a citizen of the United Federation of Planets ("The Measure of a Man" [TNG]). A significant advance in android technology was made in 2366 when Data used a new **submicron matrix transfer technology** to build an android daughter, whom he named **Lal** ("The Offspring" [TNG]). SEE: **Andrea; Annabelle series; Barbara series; Finnegan; Ilia; Lore; Maizie series; Norman; Stella; Trudy**

series. SEE ALSO: **biomechanical maintenance program; bioplast sheeting; bitanium; Maddox, Commander Bruce; molybdenum-cobalt alloys; Omicron Theta; phase-discriminating amplifier; positronic brain; Soong, Dr. Noonien; Soong-type android;** *Starfleet Cybernetics Journal*; **tripolymer composites.**

Andromeda Galaxy. Large spiral galaxy, nearest neighbor to the Milky Way Galaxy. Although Andromeda is home to many forms of life, **Kelvan** scientists believe that increasing levels of radiation will render it uninhabitable within the next ten millennia. ("By Any Other Name" [TOS]).

Andronesian encephalitis. A disease transmitted by airborne particles. *Enterprise*-D crew member Henessey suffered from this malady and was treated by Dr. Katherine Pulaski. ("The Dauphin" [TNG]).

anesthezine. A sedative gas used on board the *Enterprise*-D for emergency crowd control and to subdue dangerous persons. Captain Picard ordered one of the ship's cargo bays flooded with anesthizine in the hopes of subduing **Roga Danar.** ("The Hunted" [TNG]). Anesthezine was deemed unsuitable to subdue the **Ux-Mal** terrorists who attempted to commandeer the *Enterprise*-D on stardate 45571 because it would not have been effective against the android Data. ("Power Play" [TNG]).

Angel Falls, Venezuela. Located in southeastern Venezuela on Earth, Angel Falls is the highest waterfall on that planet. William Riker and Deanna Troi considered taking shore leave there while the *Enterprise*-D was in drydock around Earth in 2367. ("Family" [TNG]).

Angel One. Class-M planet supporting carbon-based lifeforms including an intelligent humanoid population. Ruled by a constitutionally run elected matriarchy, the planet's society treated males as second-class citizens, although this may be expected to change

over time since four survivors from the Federation freighter *Odin* took up residence there in 2364. Angel One is located fairly close to the Romulan Neutral Zone. SEE: **Beata; Ramsey.** ("Angel One" [TNG]). *Photo: Capital city on planet Angel One.*

• **"Angel One."** *Next Generation episode #15. Written by Patrick Barry. Directed by Michael Rhodes. Stardate 41636.9. First aired in 1988. The Enterprise-D attempts to rescue crash survivors living on a planet where males are second-class citizens.* SEE: **Albeni meditation crystal; Angel One; Ariel; Armus IX; Beata;** *Berlin, U.S.S.*; **Denubian Alps; Elected**

One, the; escape pod; Hesperan Thumping Cough; Mortania; Night-Blooming Throgni; *Odin, S.S.*; Quazulu VIII; Ramsey; Trent.

Angel, Friendly. SEE: **Gorgan.**

Angosia III. A Class-M planet that applied for Federation membership in 2366. The **Angosian** government was, at the time, experiencing civil unrest due to difficulties in repatriating their veterans from the recent **Tarsian War**. ("The Hunted" [TNG]).

Angosian transport vessel. A small sublight vessel used by the **Angosians** to ferry people within their system. It did not have warp capability or a cloaking device and it carried minimal weaponry. One of these vessels was hijacked by **Roga Danar**, a prisoner escaping from the Angosian penal moon **Lunar V**. ("The Hunted" [TNG]). *The Angosian transport vessel model was a modification of the Straleb ship from "The Outrageous Okona" [TNG]).*

Angosians. The humanoid residents of the planet **Angosia III.** Nonviolent by nature, the Angosians had dedicated their society to the development of the mind and the cultivation of the intellect. However, in order to fight their **Tarsian War** in the mid-24th century, the government chemically altered their military, converting them into "supersoldiers" who were able to survive at any cost. Unfortunately, when the war ended, the "improvements" made on the soldiers were found to be irreversible. These veterans were imprisoned on a penal moon, **Lunar V**, because they were deemed too dangerous to return to Angosian society. The Angosian government applied for Federation membership in 2366, but the application was suspended by Jean-Luc Picard, pending resolution of civil unrest resulting from the Angosians' inability to repatriate the veterans. SEE: **Danar, Roga.** ("The Hunted" [TNG]). *The shirts worn by the members of the Angosian council were the turtlenecked men's shirts from the* Star Trek II *Starfleet officers' uniforms.*

anionic energy. A form of energy composed of quantum-level particles. Anionic energy was detected in the synaptic patterns of the *Enterprise*-D crew whose minds were controlled by **Ux-Mal** criminals from **Mab-Bu VI** in 2368. ("Power Play" [TNG]).

Annabelle series. Type of **android** designed by Mudd the First, aka **Harry Mudd**, in 2267. ("I, Mudd" [TOS]).

annular confinement beam. Abbreviated as ACB. A cylindrically shaped forcefield used to insure that a person being transported remains within the beam. ("The Hunted [TNG], "Power Play" [TNG]). Failure to remain within the confinement field can cause a dangerous release of beam energy, possibly fatally injuring the transport subject and those nearby. **Roga Danar**, during transport from a security holding area to an Angosian police ship, deliberately disrupted the ACB, causing a blast of energy that permitted him to escape. ("The Hunted" [TNG]). When Picard was trapped on the surface of planet **El-Adrel IV** in 2368, La Forge attempted to boost the ACB in an effort to penetrate the particle scattering field that surrounded the planet. ("Darmok" [TNG]).

Ansata. Radical political group, also called the Ansata Separatist Movement, on the western continent of planet **Rutia IV**. The Ansata had demanded autonomy and self-determination for over a generation, but received no recognition from the **Rutian** government. The Ansata movement began in 2296, when the government denied an early bid for independence, and some of the Ansata turned to terrorist action. In 2366, the Ansata, led by **Kyril Finn**, engineered an incident in which they abducted *Enterprise*-D officers Jean-Luc Picard and Beverly Crusher in a successful bid to gain recognition by involving Federation interests in their struggle. ("The High Ground" [TNG]).

Antarean brandy. Beverage served at a dinner honoring **Dr. Miranda Jones** and her colleagues held aboard the *Enterprise* in 2268. ("Is There in Truth No Beauty?" [TOS]).

***Antares*-class carrier.** A common spacecraft design in use by many different cultures in the 24th century. The **Corvallen freighter** that had been contracted to smuggle Romulan **vice-proconsul M'ret** to Federation space in 2369 was an *Antares*-class vessel. ("Face of the Enemy" [TNG]). An *Antares*-class sublight ship was used to mislead **Cardassian** forces into attacking what they believed was a group of Bajoran terrorists traveling from Valo I to Valo III in 2368. The ship was empty, but its destruction provided evidence that **Admiral Kennelly** had been collaborating with the Cardassians. SEE: **Orta, Valo system.** ("Ensign Ro" [TNG]).

The Corvallen freighter seen in "Face of the Enemy" (TNG) was identified as an Antares-*class ship. Since that ship was a reuse of the* **Battris** *from "Heart of Glory" (TNG), we speculate that other uses of that model were also* Antares *class ships. We further wonder if this might be what the ship in "Charlie X" (TOS) looked like.*

***Antares*, U.S.S.** Federation science vessel that rescued **Charles Evans** from planet **Thasus** in 2266. Commanded by **Captain Ramart**, the ship was destroyed when Evans caused a **baffle plate** on their energy pile to vanish. ("Charlie X" [TOS]).

Named for the brightest star (as seen from Earth) in the constellation Scorpius (the Scorpion). Although the Antares *was not seen in "Charlie X," writer/consultant Naren Shanker suggested that the Bajoran cargo vessels in "Ensign Ro" (TNG) be designated as* Antares-*class ships, a tip of the hat to "Charlie X."*

Antarian Glow Water. Purportedly exotic substance hawked by **Cyrano Jones**. It was only good for polishing **Spican flame gems**, at least according to the shopkeeper on **Deep Space Station K-7**. ("The Trouble with Tribbles" [TOS]).

Antica. One of two habitable planets in the **Beta Renna** star system. ("Lonely Among Us" [TNG]).

Anticans. Large, furry, sentient humanoids from planet Antica in the **Beta Renna** star system. Anticans are a carnivorous species who prefer to eat live meat. The Anticans applied for admission to the Federation in 2364. The *Enterprise*-D transported their delegates to planet **Parliament** to help resolve a long-standing dispute with sister planet **Selay** as part of the admission process. ("Lonely Among Us" [TNG]).

Antide III. Class-M planet whose inhabitants, in late 2365, made a bid for Federation membership. Antide III is located some three days' warp travel from **Pacifica**. ("Manhunt" [TNG]).

Antidean ambassador. (Mick Fleetwood). Head of the Antidean delegation to the **Pacifica** conference of 2365, the ambassador was later found to be an assassin who had conspired to blow up the conference by smuggling large amounts of **ultritium** explosive to the planet. ("Manhunt" [TNG]). *Noted rock musician Mick Fleetwood played the Antidean ambassador reportedly because he is a big* Star Trek *fan.*

Antideans. A race of fishlike humanoid creatures from planet Antide III. Antideans find spaceflight extremely traumatic and survive the ordeal by entering a self-induced catatonic state. Upon revival at the end of a voyage, Antideans require large amounts of food to replenish their bodies. SEE: **Vermicula**. ("Manhunt" [TNG]).

antigrav. Portable device used aboard Federation starships for handling cargo and other items too large for a single crew member to carry. Kirk and Garrovick used an antigrav to carry an antimatter bomb on planet **Tycho IV** on stardate 3619. ("Obsession" [TOS]). Two antigravs were used to carry the deactivated **Nomad** to the transporter room just prior to that robot's destruction. ("The Changeling" [TOS]). Antigravs were also used for handling of Ambassador **Kollos**'s protec-

tive container aboard the *Enterprise*. ("Is There in Truth No Beauty?" [TOS]). Antigravs were also built into small equipment pallets used for handling cargo. ("Hollow Pursuits" [TNG]). Antigravs can become unreliable in the presence of high radiation levels. ("Disaster" [TNG]). When a worker on Deep Space 9 injured his back in 2369, Dr. Julian Bashir advised him to use an antigrav to avoid further problems. ("The Passenger" [DS9]).

antigravity generator. SEE: **antigrav**.

antilepton interference. Energetic particle field that can interfere with subspace communications. Shortly after the discovery of the **Bajoran wormhole** in 2369, the **Cardassians** flooded subspace with antileptons to prevent **Deep Space 9** from contacting Starfleet. ("Emissary" [DS9]).

antimatter containment. In warp propulsion systems, antimatter containment refers to the use of magnetic confinement fields to prevent antimatter from physically touching the surface of the storage pod or any other part of the starship. Failure of antimatter containment is a serious malfunction; such a core breach or containment breach generally results in total destruction of the spacecraft. The *Starship Yamato* was destroyed in 2365 when its antimatter containment failed because of the **Iconian computer weapon**. ("Where Silence Has Lease" [TNG]). The *Enterprise*-D suffered several catastrophic losses of antimatter containment on stardate 45652 when it repeatedly impacted the *Starship Bozeman* while both vessels were trapped in a **temporal causality loop**. ("Cause and Effect" [TNG]). *The* Enterprise-D almost lost antimatter containment in "11001001" (TNG), "Violations" (TNG), and "Cost of Living" (TNG).

antimatter converter assembly. Component of starship warp drive systems, including those used in *Constitution*-class vessels such as the original *U.S.S. Enterprise*.

antimatter mines. Explosive charges used as proximity bombs. In 2369, a shuttlecraft from the *Enterprise*-D used antimatter mines with magnetic targeting capabilities to threaten a Cardassian fleet concealed in the **McAllister C-5 Nebula**. ("Chain of Command, Part II" [TNG]).

antimatter spread. An impressive but harmless series of small explosive charges deployed from the saucer section of the *Enterprise*-D during its engagements with the **Borg** ship following the battle of **Wolf 359** in 2367. The charges were essentially fireworks used to cover the departure of a shuttlecraft from the saucer section. ("The Best of Both Worlds, Part II" [TNG]).

antimatter. Matter whose electrical charge properties are the opposite of "normal" matter. For example, a "normal" proton has a positive charge, but an antiproton has a negative charge. When a particle of antimatter is brought into contact with an equivalent particle of normal matter, both particles are annihilated, and a considerable amount of energy is released. The controlled annihilation of matter and antimatter is used as the power source for the **warp drive** systems used aboard

Federation starships. ("The Naked Time" [TOS]). Because of the highly volatile nature of antimatter, it has to be stored in special magnetic containment vessels, also known as **antimatter pods**, to prevent the antimatter from physically touching the storage vessel or any part of the ship. ("The Apple" [TOS]).

antiprotons. Subatomic particles identical to protons except for electrical charge. Normal protons have a positive charge, but antiprotons have a negative charge. A faint residue of antiprotons was left behind in the wake of the **Crystalline Entity**, and the decay of those antiprotons left gamma radiation traces that provided a means whereby the entity could be tracked. ("Silicon Avatar" [TNG]).

Antos IV. Federation planet of benevolent and peaceful people who cared for Captain **Garth** after he suffered an accident. They taught him the art of **cellular metamorphosis** in the 2260s. ("Whom Gods Destroy" [TOS]). Antos IV was the home of a species of giant energy-generating worms. ("Who Mourns for Adonais" [TOS]).

Anya. (Paddi Edwards). Guardian of **Salia** of planet **Daled IV**. A shape-shifting **allasomorph**, Anya appeared to the *Enterprise*-D crew as an older human woman, although her natural appearance was not known. Originally from the third moon of Daled IV, Anya was protective of Salia in the extreme, and was reluctant to allow Salia to mingle with the *Enterprise*-D crew. *Anya's other forms were played by actors Mädchen Amick and Cindy Sorenson.* ("The Dauphin" [TNG]).

anyon emitter. Engineering device used aboard Federation starships. Commander Data modified an emitter to clear the *Enterprise*-D of **chroniton particle** contamination in 2368 when affected by a Romulan **interphase generator**. Coincidentally, the anyon emitter was also able to dephase Commander La Forge and Ensign Ro. ("The Next Phase" [TNG]).

Aolian Cluster. Site of archaeological research conducted by **Professor Richard Galen** while trying to learn about the first humanoid species to inhabit the galaxy. ("The Chase" [TNG]).

Apella. (Arthur Bearnard). Leader of the villagers on **Tyree**'s planet. The Klingons gave Apella **flintlock** weapons to use against Tyree's followers, the **hill people**, in 2267, thus upsetting the balance of power in that society. ("A Private Little War" [TOS]).

Apgar, Dr. Nel. (Mark Margolis). **Tanugan** scientist who was working on development of a **Kreiger Wave** converter on a science station in orbit around **Tanuga IV**. Apgar was killed under suspicious circumstances in the explosion of the science station in 2366. Commander **William Riker** was implicated in the case, but was eventually cleared when holodeck

re-creation of the incident provided convincing evidence that Apgar himself was responsible for the fatal explosion, apparently while trying to kill Riker. ("A Matter Of Perspective" [TNG]). *Photo: Nel and Mauna Apgar.*

Apgar, Mauna. (Gina Hecht). Widow to **Tanugan** scientist **Dr. Nel Apgar.** Mauna Apgar accused Commander **William Riker** of being responsible for the explosion that killed her husband in 2366. ("A Matter of Perspective" [TNG]).

aphasia device. Device built by Bajoran terrorists intended to distribute an **aphasia virus** into the food replicators of station Deep Space 9. The aphasia device was planted by the **Bajoran** underground when the station was under construction in 2351, as a weapon against the **Cardassians**. The device wasn't activated at that time but was accidentally triggered when O'Brien repaired one of the replicators in 2369, after the Cardassian retreat from Bajor. The virus spread at first through the food, then became airborne, infecting a large part of the population. ("Babel" [DS9]).

aphasia virus. Virus created by Bajoran scientist **Dekon Elig**, intended to be used as a terrorist weapon against the Cardassians. The disease organism would have been delivered through an **aphasia device** planted in a food replicator by the Bajoran underground.

Once contracted, the virus would find its way to temporal lobes and disrupt normal communication processes, causing a type of **aphasia**. As the virus spread, it attacked the autonomic nervous system, causing a coma, then death. The aphasia virus was accidentally unleashed on Deep Space 9 in 2369, ironically after the Cardassians had abandoned the station. ("Babel" [DS9]). SEE: **Dekon Elig**.

aphasia. Dysfunction of certain brain centers affecting the ability to communicate in a coherent manner. Different forms of aphasia exist, but the type that afflicted the members of Deep Space 9 in 2369 caused an inability of the brain to process audio and visual stimuli, making the victims incapable of understanding others or expressing themselves coherently. ("Babel" [DS9]). SEE: **aphasia device**.

Apnex Sea. Oceanic body on planet **Romulus**. Romulan admiral **Alidar Jarok**'s home was located near the Apnex Sea. ("The Defector" [TNG]).

Apollinaire, Dr. (James Gleason). Physician at the **Sisters of Hope Infirmary** in 19th-century San Francisco on Earth. Not noted for tact in dealing with female nurses. ("Time's Arrow, Part II" [TNG]).

Apollo*-class starship.** Conjectural designation for a type of Federation starship. The ***U.S.S. Ajax, which was Ensign Cortin Zweller's first assignment after Starfleet Academy, was an *Apollo*-class starship. *Named for the sun god in Earth's*

Greek mythology, as well as for the spacecraft that first carried humans to the moon.

Apollo. (Michael Forest). Humanoid entity once worshiped as a god by the ancient Greeks on planet Earth. To the ancient Greeks, Apollo was the god of light and purity, skilled in the bow and on the lyre. He was the twin brother of Artemis, son of the god Zeus and Latona, a mortal. The extraterrestrial Apollo and his fellow "gods" had an extra organ in their chests

that apparently gave them the ability to channel considerable amounts of energy, giving them godlike powers. After leaving ancient Earth, Apollo settled on planet **Pollux IV,** where he grew to miss the adulation he had received from the Greeks. In 2267, he attempted to capture the crew of the *Starship Enterprise,* inviting them to live on the planet and to worship him as a god. When it became clear that the *Enterprise* crew could not comply, he spread himself against the wind and disappeared. ("Who Mourns for Adonais" [TOS]). SEE: **Palamas, Lieutenant Carolyn.**

Appel, Ed. (Brad Weston). Chief processing engineer at the underground mining colony on planet **Janus VI** in 2267. Appel helped to defend the colony against an unknown adversary later learned to be a life-form known as a **Horta.** ("The Devil in the Dark" [TOS]).

• **"Apple, The."** *Original Series* episode #38. Written by Max Ehrlich. Directed by Joseph Pevney. Stardate 3715.3. *First aired in 1967. The* Enterprise *encounters a primitive humanoid culture on an Eden-like planet controlled by a machine-god known as Vaal.* SEE: **Akuta; Gamma Trianguli VI; Hendorf, Ensign; Kaplan, Lieutenant; Kyle, Mr.; Landon, Yeoman Martha; Makora; Mallory, Lieutenant; Marple; Masiform D; saucer separation; Sayana; Vaal.**

April, Captain Robert T. First captain of the original *Starship Enterprise.* April assumed command of the ship when it was launched in 2245 and helmed the *Enterprise's* first five-year mission of deep-space exploration. April was succeeded as *Enterprise* commander by Christopher Pike and later by James T. Kirk. *April is, of course, totally conjectural, but is being included at Gene Roddenberry's suggestion. Gene had used the character name for the ship's commander in his first proposal for* Star Trek, *written in 1964.*

aqueduct systems. Network of canals and aboveground water conduits that provide water for human consumption, sanitation, and agriculture. Ancient aqueducts provided water to part of planet **Bajor,** and Captain Jean-Luc Picard attended a conference on management of this system in 2369

when the *Enterprise*-D visited Deep Space 9 late in that year. ("Birthright, Part I" [TNG]).

• **"Aquiel."** *Next Generation* episode #139. Teleplay by Brannon Braga & Ronald D. Moore. Story by Jeri Taylor. Directed by Cliff Bole. Stardate 46461.3. *First aired in 1993. A technician on a subspace relay station is believed to have been murdered.* SEE: **Batarael; Canar; coalescent organism;** *Cold Moon Over Blackwater;* **Deriben V; disruptor;** *Fatal Revenge, The;* **Halii; Horath; iced coffee; La Forge, Geordi; Maura; Morag; Muskan seed punch;** *oumriel;* **Pendleton, Chief; Qu'Vat; Relay Station 47; Relay Station 194; Rocha, Lieutenant Keith; Sector 2520; Shiana; Starbase 212; Torak, Governor; Triona System; Uhnari, Lieutenant Aquiel.**

Aquino, Ensign. Deep Space 9 crew member who was killed in 2369 after investigating a security breach. **Neela,** who had planned to assassinate **Vedek Bariel,** was preparing her escape route when Ensign Aquino caught her in the act. Neela killed the ensign, then tried to conceal the crime by placing him into a conduit where energy bursts would reduce the body to ashes. ("In the Hands of the Prophets" [DS9]).

Arbazan. Alien race that is a member of the **United Federation of Planets.** The Arbazan ambassador, **Taxco,** visited station **Deep Space 9** in 2369 on a fact-finding mission to the wormhole. Federation ambassador **Vadosia** expressed an opinion that Arbazan are sexually repressed, to which Taxco took great offense. ("The Forsaken" [DS9]).

Arbiter of Succession. Under Klingon law, the individual responsible for administering the **Rite of Succession,** the procedures under which a new leader of the **Klingon High Council** is chosen.

Jean-Luc Picard served as Arbiter of Succession following the death of **K'mpec** in 2367. Picard ruled **Gowron** to be the sole challenger for council leader. ("Reunion" [TNG]). Picard later rejected a last-minute bid by **Toral** for the council leadership on the grounds that Toral had not yet distinguished himself in the service of the Empire. ("Redemption, Part I" [TNG]).

arch. An inner doorway in some **holodeck** entrances aboard the *Enterprise*-D. When used, the arch can be a demarcation between the simulated world of the holodeck, and the outside world of the *Enterprise*-D corridors. Often holodeck programs conceal the arch until it is made visible by a verbal command. ("Elementary, Dear Data" [TNG]).

archaeology. Study of ancient civilizations. *Enterprise*-D captain **Jean-Luc Picard** was an enthusiast of archaeology since his Academy days, having studied the ancient **Iconians.** ("Contagion" [TNG]).

Archanis IV. While under the influence of the **Beta XII-A entity** in 2268, **Pavel A. Chekov** said he had a brother named **Piotr** who was murdered by Klingons at the Archanis IV research outpost. Chekov had no such brother. ("Day of the Dove" [TOS]).

Archanis. Star used by Sulu as a navigational reference when the original *Enterprise* was thrown across the galaxy in 2267 by the advanced race known as the **Metrons**. ("Arena" [TOS]).

Archer IV (alternate). In the alternate timeline created when the *Enterprise*-C vanished from its "proper" place in 2344, Picard mentioned **Archer IV** as the site of a significant Klingon defeat at the hands of the Federation. ("Yesterday's *Enterprise*" [TNG]).

Archer IV. Planetary destination of the *Enterprise*-D after their encounter with the **temporal rift** in 2366. ("Yesterday's *Enterprise*" [TNG]).

Archon, U.S.S. Early Federation starship that disappeared at planet **Beta III** in the year 2167. The ship was pulled from orbit by a planetary computer system called **Landru**. The surviving crew members were absorbed into Beta III society, becoming known as

the **Archons**. ("Return of the Archons" [TOS]). *We speculate that the Archon was a* Daedalus-*class starship, since it was contemporary with the* U.S.S. Essex *from "Power Play" (TNG).*

Archons. Name given by the humanoid inhabitants of planet **Beta III** to crew members of the *Starship Archon*. The ship was destroyed in 2167 by the Beta III planetary computer called **Landru**. In the process, many *Archon* crew members were killed but others were absorbed into the planet's society and became part of the **Body**, a tranquil but stagnant population. ("Return of the Archons" [TOS]).

Arcos, U.S.S. Federation freighter that suffered a warp containment breach near planet **Turkana IV** in 2367. The *Arcos* crew evacuated when the ship exploded over Turkana IV. Their **escape pod** landed on the surface of the planet, whereupon they were captured by members of the **Alliance**. ("Legacy" [TNG]).

Arcturian Fizz. A beverage with pleasure-enhancing qualities. Ambassador **Lwaxana Troi** offered to make one for **DaiMon Tog**, while being held captive aboard his ship in 2366. ("Ménage à Troi" [TNG]).

Arcybite. Planet where a Ferengi named **Nava** took over the mining refineries in the Clarius system. Nava was congratulated at a Ferengi trade conference on Deep Space 9 in 2369 by **Zek**, the **Grand Nagus**, for this accomplishment. ("The Nagus" [DS9]).

Ardana. Class-M planet, location of the cloud city **Stratos**. The *Starship Enterprise* visited Ardana in 2269 to pick up a consignment of **zenite**, but the delivery was delayed because of a dispute between the wealthy Ardanans who lived in Stratos, and the workers who lived on the surface below. Ardana is a Federation member. ("The Cloud Minders" [TOS]).

Ardra. (Marta DuBois). A mythic figure in the theology of planet **Ventax II**. According to Ventaxian legend, Ardra appeared a thousand years ago and promised the Ventaxian people a millennium of peace and prosperity. At the end of that time, Ardra promised to return and enslave the population. According to this mythology, Ardra's return was to be heralded by "the shaking of the cities" and other paranormal phenomena. These prophecies apparently came to pass in 2367 when a humanoid female appeared on Ventax II, identifying herself as Ardra. Investigation by *Enterprise*-D personnel determined, however, that this person was a con artist using various technological tricks to simulate Ventaxian prophecy. ("Devil's Due" [TNG]).

• **"Arena."** Original Series episode #19. Teleplay by Gene L. Coon. From a story by Fredric Brown. Directed by Joseph Pevney. Stardate 3045.6. *First aired in 1967. A powerful race known as the Metrons puts Kirk and a Gorn captain on a planetoid where they are expected to resolve their differences by fighting to the death. "Arena" is the first episode in which the original* Enterprise*'s warp factor 6 maximum speed was established, and the first episode to show that you can't beam through shields.* SEE: **Archanis; Canopus; Cestus III; Depaul, Lieutenant; Gorn; gunpower; Kelowitz, Lieutenant Commander; Lang, Lieutenant; Metron; shields; Sirius; transporter; Travers, Commodore; warp drive**.

Argelians. Peaceful humanoid race from planet **Argelius II**. Formerly a violent people, the Argelians underwent a social upheaval in 2067 they called their Great Awakening, in which their society turned to peace.

In 2267, the *U.S.S. Enterprise* visited the planet for shore leave. During their stay, Montgomery Scott was extradited for the murder of two women. Having no current laws regarding murder, the Argelians were forced to rely on their brutal ancient codes established before the Great Awakening. ("Wolf in the Fold" [TOS]). SEE: **Jack the Ripper; Redjac**.

Argelius II. Planet whose location makes it a strategically important spaceport. Argelius II is home to a humanoid culture that is peaceful, hedonistic, and known for its hospitality. Argelian cultural traits make it necessary to hire administrative officers from other planets. ("Wolf in the Fold" [TOS]). SEE: **Hengist, Mr.; Redjac**.

argine. Explosive used in a Ferengi **locator bomb** intended to kill Quark when he served as **Grand Nagus** in 2369. ("The Nagus" [DS9]).

Argolis Cluster. Area of space made up of six solar systems. In 2368, the *Enterprise*-D was charting the cluster as a prelude to colonization when it encountered a downed **Borg scout ship**. ("I, Borg" [TNG]). The Argolis Cluster was the location of the ecologically devastated planet **Tagra IV**. ("True-Q" [TNG]).

Argos System. An uninhabited star system in Federation space. The Argos System was near the flight path of the **Crystalline Entity** after it destroyed the **Melona IV** colony in 2368. ("Silicon Avatar" [TNG]).

Argosian Sector. Area of space in the **Alpha Quadrant**. Star charts of the Argosian Sector are stored in the navigational computer on Deep Space 9. Major Kira requested star charts of the Argosian Sector on stardate 46423, but the Glessene Sector was displayed instead due to a computer malfunction caused by the **aphasia device**. ("Babel" [DS9]).

Argosian. Alien who many years ago threw a drink in **Benjamin Sisko**'s face. **Curzon Dax** stopped his friend from retaliating. Sisko recounted the story to **Jadzia Dax**, saying he still had a scar on his chin from Curzon's ring. ("Dax" [DS9]).

Argus Array. A huge subspace radio telescope located at the very edge of Federation space. The Argus Array stopped transmitting data in 2367 and the *Enterprise*-D was sent to investigate. *Enterprise*-D personnel discovered that the array's fusion reactors had gone unstable and were threatening to overload. An alien probe, sent by the **Cytherians**, was later found to be responsible for the malfunctions. ("The Nth Degree" [TNG]).

Argus River region. Location on planet **Rigel IV**. One of the weapons used in the serial murders on planet **Argelius II** in 2267 was manufactured by the hill people of this region. ("Wolf in the Fold" [TOS]).

Argyle, Lieutenant Commander. (Biff Yeager). A chief engineer of the *Enterprise*-D in 2364 when the **Traveler** and Mr. **Kosinsky** were aboard the *Enterprise*-D conducting warp drive upgrade tests. ("Where No One Has Gone Before" [TNG]). Argyle also supervised the assembly and activation of Data's brother, **Lore**, in the *Enterprise*-D sickbay. ("Datalore" [TNG]).

Ariana. (Danitza Kingsley). One of the last eight survivors of the **Tarellian** plague and daughter of Tarellian leader **Wrenn**. Ariana had been in mental contact with **Wyatt Miller** for many years, and looked to his medical knowledge as being their hope for survival. Miller, attracted to the beautiful Ariana, chose to remain with her and the other Tarellian plague victims in the hopes of finding the means for their survival. ("Haven" [TNG]).

Ariannus. Planet vital as a transfer point for commercial traffic. In 2268, Ariannus was infected by a bacterial invasion that threatened to destroy all life. The *Starship Enterprise* conducted an orbital decontamination mission to save the planet. ("Let That Be Your Last Battlefield" [TOS]).

Ariel. (Patricia McPherson). A member of the female-dominated ruling council on planet **Angel One**. Ariel secretly married ex-*Odin* crew member **Ramsey**, a move viewed by the council as traitorous, since Ramsey advocated radical reforms to grant equal rights for men on the planet. ("Angel One" [TNG]).

Aries, U.S.S. Federation starship, *Renaissance*-class, registry number NCC-45167. **William Riker** turned down a chance to command this ship in 2365. ("The Icarus Factor" [TNG]). The *Aries* was the last assignment of former *Victory* crewmember **Mendez** before her disappearance in 2367. ("Identity Crisis" [TNG]). *The Aries was named for the constellation (the Ram) of the same name, as well as for the moon landing shuttle from the motion picture* 2001: A Space Odyssey.

Arkaria Base. Federation facility located on the planet Arkaria. The station controlled the **Remmler Array**. ("Starship Mine" [TNG]).

Arkarian water fowl. Ornithoid native to planet Arkaria. The birds' mating habits were regarded as interesting, at least according to **Commander Calvin Hutchinson**. ("Starship Mine" [TNG]).

Armens, Treaty of. Established in 2255 between the **Sheliak Corporate** and the United Federation of Planets, the treaty cedes several class-H planets from the Federation to the Sheliak. A Federation colony was established on planet **Tau Cygna V** in the 2270s in violation of the Treaty of Armens. The Sheliak exercised their rights to order the colony removed in 2366. The treaty contained 500,000 words and took 372 Federation legal experts to draft. ("The Ensigns of Command" [TNG]).

armory. Weapons storage compartment on board the *Starship Enterprise*. The **Beta XII-A entity**, which fed on hate and anger, transformed all weapons in the armory to swords while it held the *Enterprise* crew and Klingons captive in 2268. ("Day of the Dove" [TOS]).

Armus IX. Planet at which Riker had to wear a feathered costume for diplomatic reasons. ("Angel One" [TNG]).

Armus. (Mart McChesney). A malevolent life-form on planet **Vagra II**. Armus was formed when the inhabitants of Vagra II developed a means of ridding themselves of all that was evil within themselves. The Vagrans all departed from their home as creatures of dazzling beauty, leaving behind Armus, whose malevolence was

compounded by the loneliness of having been abandoned. Armus resembled an oil slick, but was capable of forming himself into a humanoid shape, and could also generate forcefields of considerable strength. Armus killed *Enterprise*-D security chief **Natasha Yar** when Yar was participating in a rescue mission on Vagra II. Armus had no apparent motive for the murder, except for his own amusement. Armus is believed to still exist on Vagra II. ("Skin of Evil" [TNG]).

Arneb. A star recognized by Wesley Crusher when he gazed from Ten-Forward while discussing his future with Guinan. ("The Child" [TNG]).

Arridor, Dr. (Dan Shor). A member of the Ferengi delegation sent to negotiate for the rights to the **Barzan wormhole** in 2366. Dr. Arridor was responsible for the distillation of a Ferengi **pyrocyte** which **DaiMon Goss** used to poison the Federation ambassador, **Dr. Mendoza**. Dr. Arridor was one of the crew of the **Ferengi pod** sent to investigate the Barzan wormhole; he was lost in the distant **Delta Quadrant** when one terminus of the wormhole changed location. ("The Price" [TNG]).

• **"Arsenal of Freedom, The."** *Next Generation* episode #21. Teleplay by Richard Manning & Hans Beimler. Story by Maurice Hurley & Robert Lewin. Stardate 41798.2. *First aired in 1988. The* Enterprise-D *is threatened by ancient weapons systems from a now-dead race.* SEE: **Arsenal of Freedom, The; Arvada III; Crusher, Dr. Beverly;** *Drake, U.S.S.;* **Echo Papa 607; Ersalope Wars; Logan, Chief Engineer; Lorenze Cluster; Minos; Peddler, Minosian; photon torpedo; Rice, Captain Paul; Riker, William T.; saucer separation; Solis, Lieutenant Orfil; Starbase 103; T'Su, Ensign Lian.**

Arsenal of Freedom, The. Nickname that the people of planet **Minos** gave to their world to promote their role as (formerly) successful arms merchants. One of their sales slogans was "Peace through superior firepower." ("The Arsenal of Freedom" [TNG]).

Artemis, S.S. Federation ship that departed in 2274 on a mission to transport colonists to planet Septimus Minor, but went off course when the ship's navigation system failed. The ship actually delivered the colonists to planet **Tau Cygna V**. ("The Ensigns of Command" [TNG]).

artificial quantum singularity. Synthetically created microscopic **black hole**. These quantum singularities were used by the Romulans as a power source for their starships' warp drive. While extremely efficient, the quantum singularity had the disadvantage that once enabled, it could not be deactivated. ("Timescape" [TNG]).

Arton, Jeff. *Enterprise*-D crew member who had at one time been romantically involved with **Lieutenant Jenna D'Sora**, prior to D'Sora's involvement with Data in 2367. ("In Theory" [TNG]).

Artonian lasers. Stolen weapons discovered in the **Gatherer** camp on **Gamma Hromi II**. ("The Vengeance Factor" [TNG]).

arva nodes. Term in an unknown alien language for components damaged in **Tosk**'s ship that converted space matter into usable fuel. ("Captive Pursuit" [DS9]). SEE: **ramscoop**.

Arvada III. Site of a colony where many people died in a terrible tragedy. **Beverly Crusher** was one of the survivors there, along with her grandmother. Although her grandmother was not a physician, she was skilled in the medicinal uses of roots and herbs. She used this knowledge to help care for the colonists after regular medical supplies had been exhausted. Beverly Crusher credited her grandmother and this experience for her knowledge of such nontraditional pharmacopoeia. ("The Arsenal of Freedom" [TNG]). *Very few specifics have been established about the Arvada tragedy, even though it seems to have been an important chapter in Beverly's life. The seventh-season episode "Sub Rosa" (TNG) establishes her grandmother's name was Felicia Howard.*

Asimov, Dr. Isaac. Twentieth-century biochemist and writer (1920-1992). Asimov postulated robots that would employ sophisticated positronic computing devices in their brains. Cyberneticist **Noonien Soong** attempted to construct such devices, ultimately succeeding with the creation of the androids **Data** and **Lore**. ("Datalore" [TNG]). *In real life, science-fiction writer Isaac Asimov was a friend of* Star Trek *creator Gene Roddenberry and was a consultant on* Star Trek: The Motion Picture.

Asoth. (Bo Zenga). Customer of Quark's bar at Deep Space 9 who angrily complained that the Kohlanese stew served there was unpalatable. Even Quark had to agree. ("Babel" [DS9]).

assay office. Area on the **Promenade** of station **Deep Space 9** where valuables are assessed and secured. Archaeologist **Vash** stored several artifacts brought back from the Gamma Quadrant at the assay office on stardate 46531 after being reassured that they were protected by a personal authorization code and a verified retinal print using a Cardassian **MK-12 scanner**. ("Q-Less" [DS9]).

• **"Assignment: Earth."** Original Series episode #55. Teleplay by Art Wallace. Story by Gene Roddenberry and Art Wallace. Directed by Marc Daniels. No stardate given. *First aired in 1968. The* Enterprise *travels back in time to 1968, where Kirk and Spock help a mysterious stranger named Gary Seven avert a nuclear crisis. "Assignment: Earth" was a pilot for a television series that would have chronicled the present-day adventures of Gary Seven and Roberta Lincoln on Earth as they battled extraterrestrial invaders called Omegans.* SEE: **Agents 201 and 347; Beta 5 computer; exceiver; Isis; light-speed breakaway factor; Lincoln, Roberta; McKinley Rocket Base; Omicron IV; Seven, Gary; Supervisor 194.**

Aster, Jeremy. (Gabriel Damon). Son of *Enterprise*-D officer Lieutenant **Marla Aster**; Jeremy was orphaned when his mother died on an away mission in 2366. His father had died five years earlier of a Rushton infection. After Marla Aster's death, energy-based life-forms known as **Koinonians** expressed regret at their accidental part in the incident, and offered to care for Jeremy. Their care would have been delivered by a nearly identical replica of his late mother, in an environment that closely reproduced his home on Earth. Jeremy eventually found the courage to accept his mother's loss, and became a part of Worf's family through the Klingon *R'uustai*, or bonding, ceremony. Jeremy later returned to Earth to be raised by his biological aunt and uncle. ("The Bonding" [TNG]).

Aster, Lieutenant Marla. (Susan Powell). *Enterprise*-D archaeologist, who was killed during an away team mission in the Koinonian ruins in 2366. Aster was killed by a bomb left over from an ancient **Koinonian** war. Koinonian energy-based life-forms later created a replica of Aster in an offer to care for her orphaned son, **Jeremy Aster**. ("The Bonding" [TNG]).

asteroid. SEE: **Miramanee's planet; Yonada.**

Astral Queen. Passenger spacecraft commanded by Captain **Jon Daily**. At the request of *Enterprise* captain James Kirk, Daily bypassed a scheduled stop at **Planet Q**, forcing the **Karidian Company of Players** to request passage aboard the *Enterprise*. ("The Conscience of the King" [TOS]).

Astral V annex. Historical museum and repository for classic spacecraft. Captain Picard suggested the Astral V annex might want to acquire the hulk of the **Promellian** cruiser *Cleponji*, discovered near **Orelious IX** in 2366, although the Promellian ship was destroyed before this could happen. ("Booby Trap" [TNG]). *An early draft script for "Booby Trap" suggested the Astral V annex was part of the Smithsonian Institution.*

Atalia VII. Location of a vital diplomatic conference in 2369. Captain Jean-Luc Picard was scheduled to be a mediator there, but was detained when **Professor Richard Galen** was killed. ("The Chase" [TNG]).

atavachron. Temporal portal developed on planet **Sarpeidon** to travel through time. The atavachron altered a time traveler's cellular structure, making it possible to survive in earlier environments, but also making it impossible to return to the present without reversing the alteration. The people of Sarpeidon used the atavachron to escape into the past when their sun, **Beta Niobe**, went nova in 2269. ("All Our Yesterdays" [TOS]). SEE: **Atoz, Mr.; Zarabeth.**

Atheneum Vaults. A government building on planet **Ventax II**. The **Scrolls of Ardra** were stored there. ("Devil's Due" [TNG]).

Atlantis Project. An ambitious 24th-century project to create a small continent in the middle of Earth's Atlantic Ocean. **Jean-Luc Picard** was offered directorship on the Atlantis Project when he took shore leave on Earth in 2367. Picard declined the opportunity, preferring to remain in Starfleet. Picard's boyhood friend, **Louis**, was a supervisor on the project. ("Family" [TNG]).

atmosphere conditioning pumps. Part of a starship's life-support system. Data, temporarily controlled by **Noonien Soong** in 2367, programmed the atmosphere conditioning pumps on the *Enterprise*-D's bridge to operate in negative mode, evacuating the air and rendering the bridge uninhabitable to air-breathing humanoids. Doing so required Data to override seven independent safety interlocks designed to prevent just such an occurrence. ("Brothers" [TNG]).

Atoz, Mr. (Ian Wolfe). Last inhabitant on planet **Sarpeidon** before their sun, **Beta Niobe**, went nova in 2269. Mr. Atoz managed a vast library on Sarpeidon, part of his people's **atavachron** time-travel facility. The library allowed the people of Sarpeidon to select past eras to which they could travel to escape the explosion of their sun. Just prior to the detonation of Beta Niobe, Atoz mistook a landing party from the *Starship Enterprise* as Sarpeidon citizens seeking escape, and sent Kirk, Spock, and McCoy into his planet's past. They were returned to the present, just in time for Atoz to escape into his chosen past. SEE: **Zarabeth.** ("All Our Yesterdays" [TOS]). *An appropriate name for a librarian, Mr. A to Z. Ian Wolfe had previously played **Septimus** in "Bread and Circuses" (TOS).*

attack cruiser. SEE: **Klingon attack cruiser.**

'audet IX. Planet on which a Federation Medical Collection Station was located. The *Enterprise*-D was assigned to transport specimens of **plasma plague** from this station to Science Station **Tango Sierra** in hopes that a vaccine might be found. ("The Child" [TNG]).

Augergine stew. A dish enjoyed by **Jadzia Dax**, who helped herself to a plateful of the stuff when Commander Sisko left the dinner table to look for his tardy son. ("The Nagus" [DS9]).

Aurora. Space cruiser stolen by **Dr. Sevrin** and his followers for their search for the mythical planet **Eden** in 2269. ("The Way to Eden" [TOS]). *The Aurora miniature was a modification of the **Tholian** ship from "The Tholian Web" (TOS).*

autodestruct. A command program in the main computer system of a *Galaxy*-class starship enabling the destruction of the vessel should the ship fall into enemy hands. Initiation of this program requires the verbal order (with dermal handprint identification verification) of the two most senior command officers on the ship. Once the computer has recognized the two officers, the senior officer gives the command to "set autodestruct sequence," whereupon the computer asks the other officer for verbal concurrence. Captain Picard and Commander Riker used the autodestruct sequence when the **Bynars** attempted to hijack the *Enterprise*-D. ("11001001" [TNG]).

Picard and Riker again initiated the autodestruct sequence when **Nagilum** threatened the lives of half the *Enterprise*-D crew. ("Where Silence Has Lease" [TNG]). *The autodestruct protocol was similar, but not identical to the* **destruct sequence** *for the original* Starship Enterprise.

auto-phaser interlock. A computer control subroutine that allowed for precise timing in the firing of ship-mounted phasers. ("A Matter of Time" [TNG]).

autosequencers. A subsystem of a starship's transporter that controls the actual transport process. Possible autosequencer malfunction was investigated following the apparent transporter-related death of **Ambassador T'Pel** in 2367. It was later found that T'Pel was not dead, and that **Subcommander Selok** (her real name) had faked the malfunction to cover her escape into Romulan hands. ("Data's Day" [TNG]).

autosuture. A medical instrument in use aboard the *Enterprise*-D, used for wound closures. ("Suddenly Human" [TNG]).

Auxiliary Control Center. Backup command facility on *Constitution*-class starships that allowed operation of basic functions such as navigation if the main bridge became inoperative. ("The Way to Eden" [TOS]).

Auxiliary Control. Secondary command room on the original *Starship Enterprise* also known as the Emergency Manual Monitor. ("I, Mudd" [TOS], "The Doomsday Machine" [TOS], "The Changeling" [TOS], "Day of the Dove" [TOS]).

Avidyne engines. A type of impulse engines utilized in old *Constellation*-class starships such as the *U.S.S. Hathaway*. Although these units were considered obsolete by 2365, the *Hathaway* and her engines performed serviceably in a **Starfleet battle simulation**. *The term "avidyne" was devised by writer Melinda Snodgrass as a variation of "Yoyodyne," a reference to the cult s-f movie* Buckaroo Banzai. ("Peak Performance" [TNG]).

away mission. Starfleet term for an assignment that takes a team away from a ship, such as a landing party sent to a planet's surface.

away team. Starfleet term for a specialized squad of personnel sent on an **away mission**.
The term was introduced in Star Trek: The Next Generation. *During the original* Star Trek *series, the terms landing party and boarding party were used.*

Axanar. Planet that was the site of a major battle in which Starfleet captain **Garth** won a historic victory in the 2250s. James Kirk's first visit to Axanar was as a cadet on a peace mission. ("Whom Gods Destroy" [TOS]). Kirk was subsequently awarded the Palm Leaf of Axanar Peace Mission. ("Court Martial" [TOS]). *It was not established who the opponent was in Garth's victory. It has been speculated that it might have been the Romulans, although the history implied by "Balance of Terror" (TOS) indicates that there was no Federation contact with the Romulans during that time frame. Kirk noted that Garth's victory was instrumental in making it possible for he and Spock to work together as brothers, so the Axanar battle apparently had something to do with holding the Federation together.*

axionic chip. Component of an **exocomp**'s neural computing system. ("The Quality of Life" [TNG]).

Ayelborne. (Jon Abbott). Leader of the **Council of Elders** on planet **Organia**. Ayelborne, along with all Organians, welcomed representatives of both the Federation and the **Klingon Empire** to his planet in 2267. Ayelborne ignored strong warnings from Federation representative James Kirk that Klingon occupation would have potentially disastrous consequences to the technologically unsophisticated Organian people. It was later learned that the Organians were an incredibly advanced race of **noncorporeal life**-forms who had been masquerading in humanoid form in order to make it easier for the Klingon and Federation representatives to deal with them. Ayelborne predicted that the Federation and Klingon antagonists would become fast friends. ("Errand of Mercy" [TOS]). *Ayelborne's prediction has in fact largely come true by the time of* Star Trek: The Next Generation.

Azetbur. (Rosana DeSoto). Daughter of Klingon **chancellor Gorkon**, Azetbur ascended to lead the Klingon High Council after the assassination of her father in 2293. As chancellor, Azetbur continued Gorkon's peace initiative with the Federation, concluding with the historic **Khitomer** peace accords. (*Star Trek VI: The Undiscovered Country*).

Azna. Favorite meal of Jadzia Dax, who told Benjamin Sisko it would put years on his life. ("A Man Alone" [DS9]).

B-Type Warbird. Federation Starfleet designation for the Romulan *D'Deridex*-class Warbird. ("The Defector" [TNG]).

Babel Conference. Interstellar meeting held on planetoid Babel in 2267 to consider the admission of the **Coridan** planets to the United Federation of Planets. Among the attendees at the conference were representatives from the **Andorian**, **Tellarite**, and **Vulcan** governments. ("Journey to Babel." [TOS]). Vulcan ambassador **Sarek** spoke in favor of the Coridan admission, and is credited with passage of the measure. ("Sarek" [TNG]).

Babel. Code name of neutral planetoid, site of the **Babel Conference** in 2267. ("Journey to Babel." [TOS]).

• **"Babel."** *Deep Space Nine* episode #5. Teleplay by Michael McGreevey and Naren Shankar. Story by Sally Caves and Ira Steven Behr. Directed by Paul Lynch. Stardate 46423.7 *First aired in 1993. A virus infects the population of Deep Space 9, making everyone unable to speak.* SEE: **access tunnel; aphasia device; aphasia virus; aphasia; Argosian Sector; Asoth; corophizine; Dax; Deep Space 9; Dekon Elig; diboridium core; Ferengi; Galis Blin; Glessene sector; Higa Metar; I'danian spice pudding; Jabara; Jaheel, Captain; Kohlanese stew; Kran-Tobol Prison; Largo V; mooring clamps; neural imaging scan; Odo; Quark; Sahsheer; Security clearance 5; stardrifter; Surmak Ren; Velos VII Internment Camp.**

Badar N'D'D. (Marc Alaimo). Chief delegate of the **Antican** contingent to the Parliament Conference of 2364. ("Lonely Among Us" [TNG]). *This was Marc Alaimo's first role in Star Trek. He also played Commander Tebok ("The Neutral Zone" [TNG]), Gul Macet ("The Wounded" [TNG]), the gambler Frederick La Rouque ("Time's Arrow, Part I" [TNG]), and the recurring role of Gul Dukat in Star Trek: Deep Space Nine.*

Ba'el. (Jennifer Gatti). The child of a Klingon woman, **Gi'ral**, and Romulan officer **Tokath**. Ba'el was raised at the Romulan prison camp in the **Carraya System**, and thus had an unusual sense of tolerance toward both cultures. Although the existence of the camp remains a secret from the **Klingon Homeworld**, Ba'el did once meet a Klingon from the outside when **Worf** discovered the camp in 2369. The two became romantically involved, but Ba'el felt she could not leave Carraya because of the racial intolerance she would experience in either the Romulan or Klingon empires. ("Birthright, Parts I and II" [TNG]).

baffle plate. A crucial component of the *U.S.S. Antares'* propulsion system. The *Antares* was destroyed when **Charles Evans** caused the baffle plate to disappear, but Evans rationalized that the plate had been warped and it was just a matter

of time before the ship would have exploded anyway. ("Charlie X" [TOS]).

BaH. Klingon term for "fire," as in to fire weapons. ("Redemption, Part I" [TNG]).

Bailey, Lieutenant David. (Anthony Hall). Junior navigator on the *U.S.S. Enterprise* during the early days of Kirk's first mission. Although an inexperienced junior officer, Bailey was assigned by Kirk to special duty as a cultural envoy to the flagship *Fesarius* of the **First Federation**. ("The Corbomite Maneuver" [TOS]).

B'aht Qul challenge. A traditional Klingon game in which one contestant holds both arms forward, while the other places his or her arms between the first, wrists touching. The first contestant attempts to press the arms together, while the second attempts to force them apart. ("The Chase" [TNG]).

Bajor VIII. Eighth planet in the **Bajoran** star system, it contained six colonies. In 2369, the **Duras** sisters delivered a cylinder of **bilitrium** explosive to **Tahna Los** on the dark side of Bajor VIII's lower moon. ("Past Prologue" [DS9]).

Bajor. Class-M planet, homeworld to the **Bajoran** race. Located near the **Cardassian** border. ("Emissary" [DS9]). Bajor has at least five moons. The fifth is a class-M planetoid named **Jeraddo**. In 2369, shortly after the end of the Cardassian occupation, Jeraddo's molten core was tapped as an energy source for Bajor. Although this new energy source was badly needed on Bajor, tapping the core made life on Jeraddo impossible due to the toxic gases released during the procedure, making it necessary to evacuate that moon. ("Progress" [DS9]). SEE: **Mullibok.**

Bajoran communicator. Personal communications device incorporated into a decorative pin worn by Bajoran personnel.

Bajoran death chant. Funeral ritual of the **Bajoran** people. It was reputed to be over two hours long. ("The Next Phase" [TNG]).

Bajoran wormhole. Artificially generated stable passageway to the **Gamma Quadrant** located in the **Denorios Belt** in the Bajoran star system. ("Emissary" [DS9]). The wormhole was formed by particles called **verterons** that allow a vessel to pass through on impulse power. Bajoran religious faith interprets the safe passage as evidence of guidance by the Prophets, so some conservative religious leaders object strongly to the teaching of such scientific concepts. ("In the Hands of the Prophets" [DS9]). In the Bajoran religion, the wormhole is the **Celestial Temple**, home of the **Prophets**

who sent the **Orbs** to the people of **Bajor**. In 2369, Commander **Benjamin Sisko** and science officer **Dax** discovered the Bajoran wormhole and came in contact with the aliens occupying the space. **Deep Space 9** was moved to the mouth of the Bajoran wormhole.

("Emissary" [DS9]). One travels almost 90,000 light-years when coming through the wormhole from the Gamma Quadrant. ("Captive Pursuit" [DS9]). Sensors read elevated neutrino levels when an object comes through the wormhole. ("Dramatis Personae" [DS9]). SEE: **Hawking, Professor Stephen; quantum fluctuation; wormhole**.

Bajorans. Humanoid race from the planet **Bajor**. Bajoran culture flourished 25,000 years ago, when humans on Earth were not yet standing erect. The Bajoran people are deeply spiritual, but their history also recorded many great architects, artists, builders, and philosophers. Bajoran culture declined seriously during decades of **Cardassian** occupation in the 24th century, during which most Bajorans were driven from their homeworld. Bajor was

claimed as Cardassian territory from about 2328. ("Ensign Ro" [TNG]). The Cardassians formally annexed Bajor in 2339, and occupied the planet until 2369, when Bajoran resistance fighters finally drove them away. Upon the departure of the Cardassians, the Bajoran provisional government requested Federation assistance in operating the former Cardassian space station, now designated Deep Space 9. ("Emissary" [DS9]). Under Bajoran custom, a person's family name is first, followed by the given name. Most Bajorans wear an ornamental earring on their right ear. SEE: **Ro Laren**. ("Ensign Ro" [TNG]). A deeply religious people, the Bajorans look to their spiritual leader, the Kai, for leadership and guidance. ("Emissary" [DS9]). The Bajoran religion believes that ships are safely guided through the **wormhole** by the **Prophets** and that the **Celestial Temple** dwells within the passage. Some conservative Bajoran religious leaders, notably **Vedek Winn**, tried to suppress scientific theories of the wormhole's creation, believing that the teaching of science lessened the religious leaders' political power. ("In the Hands of the Prophets" [DS9]). The Bajoran religious faith was a powerful force in their society, and helped give the Bajoran people the spiritual strength to survive the brutal Cardassian oppression. ("In the Hands of the Prophets" [DS9]). An old Bajoran saying holds that "The land and the people are one." Major Kira Nerys mentioned this to Commander Sisko regarding the dispute between the Bajoran factions, the **Paqu** and the **Navot**. ("The Storyteller" [DS9]).

baktag. A Klingon insult. ("Redemption, Part II" [TNG]).

baktun. Measure of time used by the now-extinct **Tkon Empire**. A *baktun* was a large number of years, possibly centuries or millenia. ("The Last Outpost" [TNG]).

• **"Balance of Terror."** Original Series episode #9. Written by Paul Schneider. Directed by Vincent McEveety. Stardate 1709.1. *First broadcast in 1966. Kirk matches wits with the commander of an invisible Romulan spaceship. This episode features the first appearance of the Romulans and their cloaking device.* SEE: **Centurion; cloaking device, Romulan; Decius; Hanson, Commander; Icarus IV; Martine, Ensign Angela; Neutral Zone Outposts; Praetor; Remus; rodinium; Romulan Bird-of-Prey; Romulan Commander; Romulan Neutral Zone; Romulan Star Empire; Romulans; Romulus; Stiles, Lieutenant; Tomlinson, Robert.**

Balduk warriors. A fierce group, but, to **Worf**, apparently not as frightening as a small angry child. ("New Ground" [TNG]).

Ballard, Lieutenant. *Enterprise*-D crew member and teacher at the ship's primary school when Data's daughter, **Lal**, briefly attended class in 2366. ("The Offspring" [TNG]).

Balok. (Clint Howard). Commander of the **First Federation** flagship *Fesarius*. Balok conducted his people's first contact with the United Federation of Planets in 2266. In an effort to ascertain the sincerity of Federation offers of friendship, Balok staged an incident in which he first threatened the *Enterprise*, then later claimed his ship had suffered severe dam-

age. ("The Corbomite Maneuver" [TOS]). *Photo: Balok's false image.*

Balosnee VI. Planet where the harmonies of the tides can cause stimulating hallucinations. **Grand Nagus Zek** couldn't decided if he wanted to spend his first vacation in 85 years at **Risa** or Balosnee VI. ("The Nagus" [DS9]).

balso tonic. Drink favored by Federation **ambassador Odan**. The *Enterprise*-D food replicator was, unfortunately, unable to manufacture it. ("The Host" [TNG]).

Balthus, Dr. An *Enterprise*-D botanist and colleague of **Keiko O'Brien**. ("Night Terrors" [TNG]).

Ba'ltmasor Syndrome. A disease that plagued Klingon exobiologist **J'Ddan**. He required regular treatments, given by injection, for the problem. ("The Drumhead" [TNG]).

Baltrim. (Terrence Evans). Resident of **Jeraddo**, a moon orbiting planet **Bajor**. Baltrim, a Bajoran national, was made mute by the **Cardassians**, during the Cardassian occupation of Bajor. Baltrim escaped to Jeraddo with his companion, **Keena**, in 2351 and started a new life. Teaming up with farmer **Mullibok**, they lived peacefully until an energy-transfer project in 2369 forced the evacuation of Jeraddo. ("Progress" [DS9]).

banana split. A Terran dessert composed of ice cream, various sweet toppings, and a sliced banana. Wesley Crusher described it to **Jono** as "maybe the best thing there is in the universe." ("Suddenly Human" [TNG]).

Bandi. Humanoid species native to planet **Deneb IV**. The Bandi, desiring to become a member of the Federation, offered Starfleet the use of a newly constructed starbase called **Farpoint Station**. It was later learned that Farpoint station had not been built by the Bandi, but was in fact a shape-shifting spaceborne life-form. The life-form had been captured by the Bandi and coerced into assuming the form of the station. Investigation by *Enterprise*-D personnel uncovered the coercion, and the life-form was allowed to return to space. ("Encounter at Farpoint, Parts I and II" [TNG]).

Baneriam hawk. Type of predatory bird. **Quark** told **Odo** that he resembled a Baneriam hawk looking for prey when the security chief was observing patrons at the bar on stardate 46853. ("If Wishes Were Horses" [DS9]).

Barash. (Chris Demetral). An alien child who was forced to leave his home planet when it was attacked in the late 2350s or early 2360s. Fearing for his safety, Barash's mother hid him in a cavern on **Alpha Onias III**. The cavern was equipped for his survival, and included specialized neural scanners that were able to transform matter into any form imagined, so that he could live his life in safety. In 2367, Barash used this equipment to lure Commander William Riker into a fantasy world in which Barash hoped Riker would remain as a playmate. In this virtual reality, some 16 years had passed, during which Riker had been promoted to captain of the *Enterprise*-D, Picard had become an admiral, and there was some rapprochement with the Romulans. Also in this fantasy, Riker had married **Minuet**, and they had a 10-year-old son named **Jean-Luc Riker**. This "son" was actually Barash, who hoped Riker would play with him in this artificial environment. Riker eventually saw through the pretense, and Barash revealed the true nature of the cavern and his true form as well. Unwilling to leave the child behind alone, Riker returned with him to the *Enterprise*-D. ("Future Imperfect" [TNG]).

Barbara series. (Maureen and Colleen Thornton). **Android** model designed by Mudd the First, aka **Harcourt Fenton Mudd**, in 2267. ("I, Mudd" [TOS]).

barber shop. Aboard the *Starship Enterprise*-D, the province of Mr. **Mot**, who provided stylish hair and beauty treatments to ship's personnel. ("Data's Day" [TNG]). *The* Enterprise-*D barber shop was first seen in "Data's Day" (TNG).*

Barbo. Quark's cousin who was released from the **Tarahong** detention center in 2369. At a Ferengi trade conference held on Deep Space 9, **Zek**, the **Grand Nagus**, recounted how **Quark** and his cousin sold defective warp drives to the Tarahong government. Zek praised Quark for betraying Barbo to the authorities and leaving him at the **Tarahong detention center** while Quark kept all the profits, an honorable act in the Ferengi system of values. ("The Nagus" [DS9]).

Barclay, Reginald. (Dwight Shultz). Starfleet systems diagnostic engineer who transferred to the *U.S.S. Enterprise*-

D from the *U.S.S. Zhukov* in 2366. Lieutenant Barclay was an extremely talented engineer, but was timid and awkward in social situations. Noted as having reclusive tendencies, Barclay compensated for his shyness by devising a rich fantasy life inside the *Enterprise*-D **holodeck**. In these fantasies, Barclay would re-create images of those crewmates in bizarre settings that he controlled. Engineer Geordi La Forge helped Barclay overcome the need for such escapes by encouraging Barclay's sense of self-worth. ("Hollow Pursuits" [TNG]).

In 2367, Barclay was exposed to a broad-spectrum emission from a **Cytherian** probe. The signal from the probe caused a dramatic increase in Barclay's neurochemical activity, increasing his I.Q. to at least 1200. With this newly-enhanced intelligence, Barclay designed and built an innovative new computer interface system as well as an incredibly fast new warp drive. It was learned that the Cytherians were reluctant to explore space themselves, so they resorted to this technique to give others the ability to reach them. Although the *Enterprise*-D contact with the Cytherians yielded valuable cultural and scientific exchanges, Barclay's enhanced intelligence faded, and with it the advanced warp drive technology was also lost. ("The Nth Degree" [TNG]).

Barclay had a strong phobia of traveling by transporter. He described his "mortal terror" of being dematerialized. Barclay concealed this fear to avoid jeopardizing his Starfleet career, but he spent many hours traveling aboard shuttlecraft in order to avoid being beamed. He ultimately faced his greatest fears during a rescue mission to the *U.S.S.* **Yosemite** in 2369, when Barclay was threatened by **quasi-energy microbes** actually living in the transporter beam. ("Realm of Fear" [TNG]).

Barclay helped Worf's son, **Alexander Rozhenko**, create a holodeck program called **Ancient West** just prior to stardate 46271. ("A Fistful of Datas" [TNG]). Barclay was part of the engineering team that attempted to solve the problem of how to give the computer-generated intelligence, **Professor James Moriarty**, physical reality when Moriarty held the ship hostage in 2369. ("Ship in a Bottle" [TNG]).

Bardakian pronghorn moose. An animal life-form known for its loud and horrible call. ("Unification, Part II" [TNG]).

Bareil, Vedek. (Philip Anglim). Bajoran spiritual leader who was a leading candidate to become the next **kai** after the departure of **Kai Opaka** in 2369. Bareil started his spiritual service as a gardener at a monastery, and although he became an influential religious leader, he still enjoyed tending the grounds. Bareil was opposed in his bid to become kai by political rival **Vedek**
Winn, who attempted to have Bareil assassinated. Winn engineered an incident on **Deep Space 9**, sparking protests

about the teaching of science in **Keiko O'Brien**'s schoolroom, an effort to draw Bareil to the station, where he was the target of Winn's assassination plot. Fortunately, the plan failed and Vedek Bareil survived to continue his bid for kai and continue the cooperative Bajoran/Federation relationship. ("In the Hands of the Prophets." [DS9]). *Bareil's monastery scenes were filmed at Ferndale, near Griffith Park, also used for the holodeck sequence in "Encounter at Farpoint" (TNG).*

Baris, Nilz. (William Schallert). Federation Undersecretary in charge of Agricultural Affairs, sent from Earth to **Deep Space Station K-7** to oversee the development project for **Sherman's Planet** in 2267. In that capacity, he summoned the *Starship Enterprise* to protect several storage containers of the valuable grain, **quadrotriticale**. It was discovered that his assistant, **Arne Darvin**, was a Klingon spy who had poisoned the grain. ("The Trouble with Tribbles" [TOS]). *William Schallert also played Vareni in "Sanctuary" (DS9).*

baristatic filter. Device used in a planet's atmosphere to remove air pollution on a large scale. A thousand baristatic filters were used on planet **Tagra IV** to clean the air. ("True-Q" [TNG]).

Barnhart. *Enterprise* crew member killed by the **M-113 creature**, who had been masquerading as **Crewman Green**. Barnhart's body was found on Deck 9. ("The Man Trap" [TOS]).

Barnum. P. T. Phineas Taylor Barnum (1810-1891), an American showman and businessman noted for creating "The Greatest Show on Earth." Captain Picard quoted P. T. Barnum's saying "There's a sucker born every minute" when referring to techniques used by **Ardra** at planet **Ventax II** in 2367. ("Devil's Due" [TNG]).

barokie. Twenty-fourth-century game. Ensign **Cortin Zweller** preferred barokie to **dom-jot**, saying barokie was "more of a challenge." ("Tapestry" [TNG]).

Barolian freighter. Space vessel that, in 2368, received a deflector array later found to have been stolen from the Vulcan ship *T'Pau*. ("Unification, Part II" [TNG]).

Barolians. A race that entered into trade negotiations with the Romulans in 2364. Romulan **Senator Pardek** took part in the conference. ("Unification, Part I" [TNG]).

Baroner. Pseudonym adopted by Captain Kirk on planet **Organia** when the *Enterprise* was sent to Organia in 2267 to protect the planet from possible Klingon invasion. The Klingons did arrive and Kirk disguised himself as an Organian citizen named Baroner. ("Errand of Mercy" [TOS]).

barrier, galactic. Mysterious energy field at the perimeter of the Milky Way galaxy. First discovered around 2064 by the exploratory vessel *S.S. Valiant*, the barrier was later crossed by the *Starship Enterprise* in 2265. Certain members of both ships' crews became endowed with dramatically amplified ESP and psychokinetic powers, and in both cases these

mutated crew members became a threat to their ships. ("Where No Man Has Gone Before" [TOS]). The *Enterprise* crossed the barrier a second time in 2268, when the ship was hijacked by **Kelvans** attempting to return to their home in the **Andromeda Galaxy**. The barrier had also been responsible for the earlier destruction of their ship when they entered our galaxy. ("By Any Other Name" [TOS]). The *Enterprise* once again crossed the barrier later that year when designer **Laurence Marvick**, stricken by insanity, drove the ship across the barrier at warp 9.5. ("Is There In Truth No Beauty?" [TOS]).

Barron, Dr. (James Greene). A Federation anthropologist assigned to planet **Mintaka III** to study the proto-Vulcan culture in 2366. ("Who Watches the Watchers?" [TNG]).

Barrows, Yeoman Tonia. (Emily Banks). *Enterprise* crew member who was part of the landing party to the **amusement park planet** in 2267. Unaware that the planet's equipment would instantly fabricate nearly anything she imagined, Barrows conjured up a replica of Don Juan. When she found herself alone with Dr. McCoy, she imagined herself a fairy-tale princess with a long flowing gown, and a black knight from which McCoy needed to protect her. ("Shore Leave" [TOS]).

Barstow, Commodore. (Richard Derr). Starfleet official who contacted the *Enterprise* after a galaxy-wide time warp distortion was detected in 2267. Barstow ordered the *Enterprise* to investigate and determine if this phenomena was a prelude to invasion by an unknown force. ("The Alternative Factor" [TOS]).

Bartel, Engineer. (Stacie Foster). Crew member aboard the *Enterprise*-D at the time the ship encountered the **Dyson Sphere** near **Norpin V**. ("Relics" [TNG]).

Barthalomew, Countess Regina. (Stephanie Beacham). Fictional character inspired by the **Sherlock Holmes** stories of **Sir Arthur Conan Doyle**. The countess was the love of **Professor James Moriarty**, and a holographic representation of her was created by Moriarty within the *Enterprise*-D **holodeck** computer in 2369. ("Ship in a Bottle" [TNG]).

baryon particles. Any member of a class of heavy fundamental particles. Baryons build up on starship superstructures as a result of warp travel, requiring periodic decontamination. SEE: **Remmler Array**. ("Starship Mine" [TNG]). An increase in baryon particles was detected with the malfunction of the **metaphasic shield** test of 2369. The increase in cabin baryons was believed to be partially responsible for the death of Dr. Jo'Bril. ("Suspicions" [TNG]).

baryon sweep. High-frequency plasma field used for removal of **baryon particle** contamination from starships. The process is dangerous to living tissue and requires complete evacuation of starship personnel. ("Starship Mine" [TNG]).

Barzan wormhole. A wormhole, initially believed to be stable, with the near terminus near planet Barzan and the other some 70,000 light-years distant, in the **Delta Quadrant**. In 2366, the Barzan government sold rights to the wormhole to the **Chrysalians**. Later investigation by an *Enterprise*-D shuttle and a **Ferengi pod** indicated that the wormhole was only partially stable, and that both ends would eventually shift location. The Ferengi ship was lost in the **Gamma Quadrant** after just such a location shift. ("The Price" [TNG]). SEE: **quantum fluctuations**. *Not to be confused with the Bajoran wormhole.*

Barzans. Humanoid inhabitants of the planet Barzan. These vaguely catlike humanoids wore breathing devices; their society reportedly did not yet have space travel. **Premier Bhavani** of the planet Barzan visited the *Enterprise*-D in 2366 for a trade conference in which the Barzans hoped to benefit themselves by selling rights to a wormhole discovered in their solar system. Rights to use the Barzan wormhole, believed to be a stable passageway to the **Delta Quadrant** of the galaxy, were the topic of a conference held aboard the *Enterprise*-D in 2366. Being politically neutral, the Barzans were concerned that favoring any one delegation might involve them in disputes with other parties. The question was later made moot when the wormhole was found to be unstable. ("The Price" [TNG]).

baseball. Team sport that was once regarded as the national pastime of the Americas. Professional baseball died shortly after 2042, victim of a society that had no time for such diversions. One of baseball's last great heroes was a player for the **London Kings** named **Buck Bokai**, who broke **Joe DiMaggio**'s record for consecutive hits in 2026. ("The Big Goodbye" [TNG]). The end of professional baseball came shortly after only 300 spectators came to the last game of the 2042 World Series, in which the Kings won. ("If Wishes Were Horses [DS9]). Deep Space 9 commander **Ben Sisko** was a baseball fan, and enjoyed watching replays of old games, as well as playing with holodeck re-creations of famous players. ("Emissary" [DS9], "The Storyteller" [DS9], "If Wishes Were Horses" [DS9]). SEE: **Maris, Roger; Newson, Eddie.**

Bashir, Dr. Julian. (Siddig El Fadil). Starfleet medical officer, born 2342, assigned to station **Deep Space 9** in 2369, shortly after the **Cardassian** withdrawal from the **Bajoran** system. Bashir was a brilliant physician, having graduated second in his class. Fancying himself to be an adventurer, he requested posting to Deep Space 9 because he wanted to practice on the frontier. ("Emissary" [DS9]). As a young man on Deep Space 9, Bashir found himself attracted to the beautiful

Jadzia Dax. Unfortunately, Dax did not return the affection, although the two had a good professional working relationship. Bashir's interest in Dax became quite embarrassing on stardate 46853, when unknown aliens from the Gamma Quadrant, seeking to study humanoid life, created a replica of Dax who was as attracted to Bashir as he was to her. ("If Wishes Were Horses" [DS9]). *Bashir was first seen in "Emissary" (DS9).*

Basotile. A two-meter-high, metallic abstract sculpture that was hundreds of years old. The rare art piece was owned by 24th-century collector **Kivas Fajo**. ("The Most Toys" [TNG]).

bat'telh. The traditional Klingon "sword of honor," resembling a meter-long two-ended scimitar. The *bat'telh* was carried along the inside of the arm and controlled by two handholds located on the outside edge of the weapon. ("Reunion" [TNG]).

Oral history of the sword holds that it was forged when **Kahless the Unforgettable** dropped a lock of his hair in the lava from the **Kri'stak Volcano** and then plunged the burning lock into the lake of **Lursor** and twisted it into a blade. After forging the weapon, he used it to kill the tyrant **Molor** and named it the "*bat'telh*," or sword of honor. This tale of the sword was never recorded in the sacred texts. Rather it was passed down verbally among the High Clerics. The retelling of the tale was to be a test of Kahless's return, as only he and the High Clerics would know the story. SEE: **Story of the Promise, The.** ("Rightful Heir" [TNG]). Worf owned a *bat'telh* that had been in his family for ten generations. He used this weapon to kill **Duras**, after Duras had murdered **K'Ehleyr**. ("Reunion" [TNG]). Worf also instructed Dr. Beverly Crusher in the use of the *bat'telh*. ("The Quality of Life" [TNG]). *The bat'tleh was designed by martial-arts expert (and visual effects producer) Dan Curry, who also helped develop the intricate dancelike movements associated with its use.*

Batai (young). (Daniel Stewart, Logan White). A native of the planet **Kataan** and son of the ironweaver **Kamin**. Young Batai was named after Kamin's friend, council leader of the **Ressik** community a thousand years ago, prior to the explosion of the star Kataan. Memories of him were preserved aboard a space probe launched from Kataan. The probe encountered the *Starship Enterprise*-D in 2368, transferring its memories, including the memory of Batai, to Jean-Luc Picard. ("The Inner Light" [TNG]). *Daniel Stewart is actor Patrick Stewart's son, an appropriate bit of casting since the elder Stewart played Batai's father.*

Batai. (Richard Riele). A native of the planet **Kataan** and the council leader of the **Ressik** community. He was a good friend of **Kamin**, who named his son after Batai. ("The Inner Light" [TNG]).

Batanides, Marta. (J. C. Brandy). Academy friend of **Jean-Luc Picard**. Marta and Picard graduated together in 2327, after which the two young ensigns were transferred to **Starbase Earhart**, awaiting their first deep-space assignments. When Q allowed Picard to relive this portion of his life many years later, Picard acted on a long-held desire to be more than "just friends" with Marta. Unfortunately, the liaison strained their friendship. ("Tapestry" [TNG]).

Batarael. Traditional celebration observed on **Halii**, Aquiel's homeworld. At the Batarael, **Aquiel Uhnari** would sing the **Horath**, a beautiful song. ("Aquiel" [TNG]).

Bates, Hannah. (Dey Young). A member of the isolated **Genome Colony** on planet **Moab IV**. Bates was genetically engineered to be a scientist, and was the colony's expert on their biosphere and maintaining its environment. Bates worked with Commander La Forge to develop a solution to the problem of an approaching **stellar core fragment** in 2368. After her exposure to people outside the closed society of the colony, Bates was unwilling to remain in the isolated community. She asked for and was granted asylum aboard *the Enterprise*-D, despite fears from colony leaders that her absence and the absence of others would damage the carefully designed society. ("The Masterpiece Society" [TNG]).

Bateson, Captain Morgan. (Kelsey Grammer). Commanding officer of the Federation *Starship* **Bozeman**, Captain Bateson, along with the rest of his crew, was trapped in a **temporal causality loop** for 90 years, emerging in 2368. ("Cause and Effect" [TNG]). *Kelsey Grammer co-starred in* Cheers, *and* Frasier, *both filmed at Paramount Pictures.*

Batris. A **Talarian** freighter ship that was hijacked by renegade Klingons in 2364. The ship exploded shortly after three of the hijackers were rescued by an away team from the *Starship Enterprise*-D. SEE: **Korris, Captain.** ("Heart of Glory" [TNG]).

The Batris *was a modification of a Visitor freighter from the miniseries* V. *The Batris itself was further modified and seen as a variety of other freighters in later episodes, presumably suggesting that it is a design in use by many different planets. The Batris was built by Greg Jein. SEE:* **Antares-class carrier.**

Battle Bridge. Secondary control center on *Galaxy*-class starships from which battle operations can be controlled. Located in the **stardrive** (or **battle**) **section** of the starship, the Battle Bridge is normally used when the **Saucer Module** (containing the main bridge) is separated from the ship. ("Encounter at Farpoint, Part I" [TNG]).

battle cruiser. SEE: **Klingon battle cruiser**.

• **"Battle Lines."** *Deep Space Nine* episode #13. Teleplay by Richard Danus and Evan Carlos Somers. Story by Hilary Bader. Directed by Paul Lynch. No stardate given. *First aired in 1993. Bajoran spiritual leader Kai Opaka is killed, then resurrected on a planet of eternal war.* SEE: **delta radiation; differential magnetomer; Ennis; Idran; Kira Nerys; mutual induction field; Nol-Ennis; Opaka, Kai;** *Rio Grande,* *U.S.S.*; **Shel-la, Golin;** *Yangtzee Kiang, U.S.S.*; **Zlangco.**

Battle of Cheron. SEE: **Cheron, Battle of.**

Battle of Wolf 359. SEE: **Wolf 359**.

battle section. Alternate term for **stardrive section**. The portion of a *Galaxy*-class starship remaining after the **saucer module** has been separated. ("Encounter at Farpoint, Part I" [TNG]). SEE: **Battle Bridge.**

battle simulation, Starfleet. A combat exercise conducted in 2365 between the *U.S.S. Enterprise*-D and the *Starship Hathaway*. The war game was an effort to assess Starfleet readiness.

Enterprise-D captain Jean-Luc Picard initially opposed this exercise on the grounds that Starfleet's primary mission is not military, but relented because of the need to prepare for the **Borg** threat. ("Peak Performance" [TNG]).

• **"Battle, The."** *Next Generation* episode #10. Teleplay by Herbert Wright. Story by Larry Forrester. Directed by Rob Bowman. Stardate 41723.9. *First aired in 1987. A Ferengi commander offers Picard a gift: the hulk of his old ship, the* U.S.S. Stargazer. SEE: **Bok, DaiMon;** *Constellation*-class **starship; cold, common; escape pods; Kazago; Maxia Zeta star system; Maxia, Battle of; Picard, Jean-Luc; Picard Maneuver; Rata;** *Stargazer, U.S.S.*; **Thought Maker; Vigo; Xendi Sabu star system; Xendi Starbase 9.**

Beach, Commander. Officer on the *Starship Reliant* under the command of Captain **Clark Terrell** in 2285. (*Star Trek II: The Wrath of Khan*).

Beagle, S.S. Small class-IV stardrive survey vessel with a crew of forty-seven commanded by Captain **R. M. Merrick,** which disappeared in 2261. The S.S. Beagle was exploring star system 892 when it was damaged by meteors and drifted toward the fourth planet of that system. The crew of the Beagle was eventually captured by the inhabitants of planet 892-IV. ("Bread and Circuses" [TOS]). SEE: **892, Planet IV.**

beam. Colloquial term for travel by matter-energy transport, as in "beam me up." SEE: **transporter**. *Ironically, the catchphrase "Beam me up, Scotty" was never actually spoken by Captain Kirk in any episode of the original series.*

beans. An old Earth culinary delicacy prepared by Dr. Leonard McCoy, made by simmering bipodal seeds in sauce prepared from an old Southern recipe handed down from his father. McCoy, who served the dish to Kirk and Spock when the three of them camped in Yosemite in 2287, was particularly proud of the secret ingredient, Tennessee whiskey. (*Star Trek V: The Final Frontier*).

bearing. In celestial navigation, a mathematical expression describing a direction in space with relationship to a space vehicle. A bearing measures the angular difference between the current forward direction of the spacecraft and the direction being described. The first number in a bearing describes an azimuth in degrees, and the second describes an elevation. For example, a bearing of 000 mark 0 describes a direction directly ahead of the vessel. A bearing of 330 mark 15 describes a direction to the port side (right) of the ship, somewhat above the centerline of the vessel. SEE: **heading**.

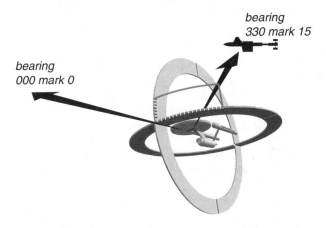

bearing 330 mark 15

bearing 000 mark 0

Beata. (Karen Montgomery). Leader of the government on planet **Angel One**. Beata, who carried the title of the **Elected One**, attempted to maintain the planet's tradition of treating their males as second-class citizens, although she acknowledged that this might eventually change over time. ("Angel One" [TNG]).

Beauregard. Alien plant life-form cared for by Sulu in the *Enterprise*'s botany lab in 2266. Beauregard — who Sulu insisted should be called Gertrude — seemed to be fond of Janice Rand, almost purring in her presence. ("The Man Trap" [TOS]).

Beck. Obstetrical nurse assigned to the *Enterprise*-D medical section after leaving Starbase 218 in 2369. ("Lessons" [TNG]).

Bele. (Frank Gorshin). Chief Officer of the Commission on Political Traitors from the planet **Cheron**. Bele pursued an accused criminal named **Lokai** across the galaxy for fifty thousand years. White on the left side of his body and black on the right, Bele harbored racial prejudice against those of his people who were of opposite coloring. In 2268 Bele commandeered the *Enterprise* to take him and his prisoner back to Cheron, but learned that racial hatred had long since destroyed their

homeworld. ("Let That Be Your Last Battlefield" [TOS]). *Bele's scout ship was conveniently invisible, a clever way for the show to save money on visual effects.*

Bell, Lieutenant Dan. (William Boyett). A fictional character from the **Dixon Hill** detective stories, Bell was a gruff career police officer who interrogated Hill after the murder of **Jessica Bradley**. A holographic version of Bell was part of the Dixon Hill holodeck programs. ("The Big Goodbye" [TNG]).

Beloti Sector. Destination of the *U.S.S. Denver* in 2368, just before the ship hit a gravitic mine. ("Ethics" [TNG]).

Beltane IX. Planet that serves as a center for commercial-shipping space travel. **Jake Kurland** once threatened to run away to Beltane IX to sign onto a freighter. ("Coming of Age" [TNG]).

Belzoidian flea. A life-form that **Q** claimed he could have chosen to become when he was stripped of his powers in 2366. He instead chose to become human. ("Deja Q" [TNG]).

Benbeck, Martin. (Ron Canada). A member of the isolated **Genome colony** on planet **Moab IV**. Benbeck was genetically engineered for his function as the interpreter of the society's laws. Benbeck advised strongly against allowing the crew of the *Enterprise*-D to visit their colony in 2368, despite the fact that outside assistance was required to prevent the close passage of a massive **stellar core fragment** from damaging the colony. ("The Masterpiece Society" [TNG]).

Bender, Slade. (Robert Costanza). A character in the **Dixon Hill** detective novels. In one such story, Bender tried to shoot Hill. The Dixon Hill holodeck program included a holographic representation of Bender. ("Manhunt" [TNG]).

Bendii Syndrome. A rare illness that sometimes affects **Vulcans** over the age of 200. The disease is characterized by gradual loss of emotional control; victims exhibit sudden bursts of emotion and irrational anger. Diagnosis is made by culturing tissue from the patient's metathalamus. A dangerous side effect of Bendii Syndrome is that the loss of emotional control can be telepathically projected to others. Ambassador **Sarek** was afflicted with Bendii Syndrome at the age of 202, endangering his last diplomatic mission. ("Sarek" [TNG]). Sarek eventually succumbed to Bendii Syndrome at his home on Vulcan, in 2368. ("Unification, Part I" [TNG]).

Benecia Colony. Federation colony where the **Karidian Company of Players** had been scheduled to perform following their engagement at **Planet Q**. ("The Conscience of the King" [TOS]). Dr. Janice Lester had hoped to send her former self, when it imprisoned the mind of James Kirk, to the Benecia Colony in 2269. Benecia's medical facilities were limited, so the chances of Lester's theft of Kirk's body being discovered were minimal. ("Turnabout Intruder" [TOS]).

Benev Selec. One of the star systems in the **Selcundi Drema** sector. Wesley Crusher ordered Ensign Davies to conduct an **ico-spectogram** on that system. ("Pen Pals" [TNG]).

benjisidrine. Drug prescribed by Vulcan physicians for treatment of Ambassador **Sarek**'s heart condition. ("Journey to Babel" [TOS]).

Bennett, Admiral Robert. (Harve Bennett). Starfleet chief-of-staff who assigned Kirk and the *Enterprise*-A to rescue Federation representative **St. John Talbot** at planet **Nimbus III**, despite the fact that the *Enterprise* was far from operational at the time. (*Star Trek V: The Final Frontier*). *This character, whom Kirk addressed as "Bob," had no last name in the movie or the script, but we're calling him Admiral Bennett because he was played by* Star Trek *feature film writer-producer Harve Bennett, making a cameo appearance.*

Bensen, Bjorn. (Gerard Prendergast). Chief engineer of the unsuccessful **terraforming** project at planet **Velara III** in 2364. ("Home Soil" [TNG]).

Benton. (Seamon Glass). One of the three miners at the **Rigel XII** lithium-mining station in 2266. ("Mudd's Women" [TOS]).

Benzan. (Kieran Mulroney). Son of Secretary **Kushell** of the planet **Straleb**. Benzan had been secretly engaged to marry **Yanar** of the planet **Altec**, and was the father of her child. Benzan nearly triggered an interplanetary incident when he gave Yanar the **Jewel of Thesia** as a pledge of marriage. ("The Outrageous Okona" [TNG]).

Benzar. Homeworld to the **Benzites**. ("Coming of Age" [TNG]). Benzar, a recent member of the Federation, has an atmosphere similar to class-M norms, but Benzites in a class-M environment need a respiration device to provide supplemental gases for them to breathe. ("A Matter of Honor" [TNG]). *Illustration: Breathing device used by Benzites living in a class-M oxygen-nitrogen atmosphere.*

Benzites. Humanoid inhabitants of the planet **Benzar**. Ensign **Mendon** served briefly aboard the *Enterprise*-D as part of an **Officer Exchange Program** in 2365. ("A Matter of Honor" [TNG]).

Beratis. Name given to unidentified mass murderer of women on planet **Rigel IV**. SEE: **Redjak**. ("Wolf in the Fold" [TOS]).

Berel. (George Hearn). A physician on planet **Malcor III**, and head of the **Sikla Medical facility**. In 2367, Berel cared for the injured Malcorian **Rivas Jakara**, later found to be Starfleet officer William Riker on a covert surveillance mission on the planet. Berel was relieved as head of the medical facility when

he refused to endanger Riker's life for questioning by Malcorian security. ("First Contact" [TNG]).

Berellians. A race not known for their engineering skills, although this might be an unfair characterization. ("Redemption, Part II" [TNG]).

Berengaria VII. Planet where one of the indigenous lifeforms are dragons. Spock told **Leila Kalomi** he'd once seen a dragon on Berengaria VII. ("This Side of Paradise" [TOS]).

Berik. (Tracey Walter). One of the renegade Ferengi who took over the *Enterprise* in 2369. ("Rascals" [TNG]).

Bering Sea. Northern region of Earth's Pacific Ocean where two humpback whales, **George and Gracie**, were released by the **Cetacean Institute** in 1986. (*Star Trek IV: The Voyage Home*).

***Berlin*, U.S.S.** Federation starship, *Excelsior* class, Starfleet registry number NCC-14232, stationed near the **Romulan Neutral Zone** in 2364 just prior to the first Romulan violation of the zone since the **Tomed Incident**. ("Angel One" [TNG]).

Bernard, Dr. Harry, Sr. An oceanographer aboard the *Starship Enterprise*-D, and father of **Harry Bernard, Jr.** ("When the Bough Breaks" [TNG]).

Bernard, Harry, Jr. (Phillip Waller). Ten-year old (as of 2364) son to *Enterprise*-D crew member **Dr. Harry Bernard, Sr.** The younger Bernard was kidnapped in 2364 by the **Aldeans,** who wanted to use the child to revitalize their dying race. Harry was not fond of having to study math, but his father reminded him that a basic understanding of **calculus** was expected of all children his age. ("When the Bough Breaks" [TNG]).

Bersallis firestorms. Deadly phenomena on planet **Bersallis III** that occur every seven years, caused by particle emissions from the planet's sun. The storms can reach temperatures of 300 degrees Centigrade and wind velocities of over 200 kilometers per hour. In 2369, a fierce firestorm hit the planet and the *Enterprise*-D was summoned to assist with the evacuation of a Federation outpost located there. A rescue team headed by *Enterprise*-D crew member **Neela Daren** deployed a series of **thermal deflector** units to deflect some of the heat from the outpost. The intensity of the storm necessitated team members to remain to operate the deflectors manually. All 643 colonists were saved, but eight *Enterprise*-D crew members lost their lives. ("Lessons" [TNG]).

Bersallis III. Planet where a deadly firestorm threatened to destroy all life at a Federation outpost stationed there in 2369. ("Lessons" [TNG]).

Berthold rays. Deadly radiation that causes disintegration of carbon-based animal tissue, including humanoid tissue. Planet **Omicron Ceti III**, which was bombarded with Berthold rays, was colonized prior to the discovery of Berthold rays. As a result, many members of the expedition led by **Elias Sandoval**

to colonize that planet died from Berthold-ray exposure in 2264. Approximately one-third of the colonists survived because they had been infected by a previously undiscovered form of alien spores. ("This Side of Paradise" [TOS]). SEE: **spores, Omicron Ceti III**. The **Calamarain** were found to emit Berthold rays when they scanned the *Enterprise*-D during their encounter with that ship in 2366. ("Deja Q" [TNG]).

berylite scan. Medical procedure used aboard Federation starships. ("A Matter of Time" [TNG]).

• **"Best of Both Worlds, Part I, The."** *Next Generation* episode #74. Written by Michael Piller. Directed by Cliff Bole. Stardate 43989.1. *First aired in 1990. Captain Picard is captured by the Borg as the long-feared confrontation between the Borg and the Federation begins. This episode, the last of the third season, was a cliff-hanger that was resolved in the opening episode of the fourth season.* SEE: **Borg; Borg collective; EM base frequencies; Hanson, Admiral J. P.; Honorius; Jouret IV;** *Lalo, U.S.S.;* **Locutus of Borg; magnetic resonance traces; navigational deflector;** *Melbourne, U.S.S.;* **Nelson, Lord Horatio; New Providence; Paulson Nebula; Picard, Jean-Luc; Riker, William T.; Sector 001; Sentinel Minor IV; Shelby, Lieutenant Commander; shield nutation; Starbase 157; Starbase 324; System J-25;** *Victory, H.M.S.;* **Zeta Alpha II.**

• **"Best of Both Worlds, Part II, The."** *Next Generation* episode #75. Written by Michael Piller. Directed by Cliff Bole. Stardate 44001.4. *First aired in 1990. The Borg ship decimates a Starfleet armada and threatens Earth as Riker tries to rescue Picard. The first of the fourth season, this episode resolved the cliff-hanger from Part I, but the story of Picard's rehabilitation was continued in "Family" (TNG).* SEE: **antimatter spread; Borg; Danula II; Earth Station McKinley; Gleason, Ensign; emergency transporter armbands; Hanson, Admiral J. P.; heavy graviton beam; Jupiter Outpost 92;** *Kyushu, U.S.S.;* **Locutus of Borg; Mars Defense Perimeter;** *Melbourne, U.S.S.;* **microcircuit fibers; multimodal reflection sorting; nanites; navigational deflector; Picard, Jean-Luc; Riker, William T.; Sector 001; Shelby, Lieutenant Commander; shuttle escape transporter; Starfleet Academy marathon;** *Tolstoy, U.S.S.;* **Wolf 359.**

Beta 5 computer. (Voice of Majel Barrett). Computer of extraterrestrial origin, used by Gary Seven to support operations on Earth in 1968. While a highly efficient tool, the computer, Seven felt, had a snobbish personality. ("Assignment Earth" [TOS]).

Beta Agni II. A class-M planet, site of a Federation colony that experienced a sudden **tricyanate** contamination of its water supply in 2366. The contamination was neutralized with the assistance of the *Enterprise*-D, which obtained an adequate supply of **hytritium,** and delivered it into the planet's subsurface water supply by means of a class-4 probe. The incident turned out to have been engineered by **Zibalian** trader **Kivas Fajo**, as part of an elaborate scheme to capture the android Data. ("The Most Toys" [TNG]).

Beta Antares IV. Planet where the fictitious card game **Fizzbin** was supposedly played. ("A Piece of the Action" [TOS]).

Beta Aurigae. Binary star system where, in 2269, the original *Starship Enterprise* was to rendezvous with the *U.S.S. Potemkin* for a gravitational-phenomena study. While en route, Dr. Janice Lester, in Captain Kirk's body, ordered the ship's course changed to the **Benecia Colony**. ("Turnabout Intruder" [TOS]).

Beta Cassius. SEE: **Haven**. ("Haven" [TNG]).

Beta Geminorum system. Star system that contained planets **Pollux IV** and V. The *Enterprise* was investigating this system in 2267 when the entity named **Apollo** stopped the ship and demanded the crew beam down to planet Pollux IV. ("Who Mourns for Adonais?" [TOS]).

Beta III. Class-M planet located in star system **C-111**. The humanoid inhabitants of Beta III once had a technologically advanced but war-ridden society. Some 6,000 years ago, a great leader named **Landru** united his people by returning them to a simpler time. Upon his death, Landru's leadership was continued by a sophisticated computer system that governed the people. The computer interpreted Landru's philosophies very literally, resulting in the creation of an oppressive society with virtually no individual freedom. This Landru destroyed the *Starship* **Archon** and absorbed its crew in 2167.

The computer's rule continued until 2267, when Landru was destroyed while attempting to absorb the crew of the *Starship Enterprise*. ("Return of the Archons" [TOS]).

Beta Kupsic. Destination of the *Enterprise*-D after its layover at **Starbase Montgomery** in 2365. ("The Icarus Factor" [TNG]).

Beta Lankal. A star system in Klingon space. Forces loyal to **Gowron** were forced to retreat and regroup there following their defeat in the **Mempa system** during the **Klingon civil war** in 2368. ("Redemption, Part II" [TNG]).

Beta Magellan. Star system in which the planet **Bynaus** is located. The system's star went nova in 2364, threatening the society living on planet Bynaus. ("11001001" [TNG]). SEE: **Bynars**.

Beta Moon. One of two inhabited satellites orbiting planet **Peliar Zel**. The population of Beta Moon suffered detrimental environmental effects when **Alpha Moon** used Peliar Zel's magnetic field as a power source. The two moons, historically at odds, sought the mediation services of **Ambassador Odan** to resolve the conflict in 2367. ("The Host" [TNG]).

Beta Niobe. Star that went nova in 2269, destroying the class-M planet **Sarpeidon**, its only satellite. ("All Our Yesterdays" [TOS]).

Beta Portolan system. Home of an ancient civilization whose population was wiped out centuries ago by **Denevan neural parasites**. Archaeological evidence indicated the inhabitants of the Beta Portolan system were the first victims of these creatures. The parasites later left Beta Portolan, traveling in a line across the galaxy toward planet **Levinius V**. ("Operation— Annihilate!" [TOS]). SEE: **Deneva**.

Beta Quadrant. One quarter of the entire Milky Way galaxy. The region in which the **Klingon Empire** and the **Romulan Star Empire** are located. Parts of the **United Federation of Planets** also spill over into Beta Quadrant, although the majority of this region remains unexplored. The *Starship Excelsior* was conducting a scientific mission in Beta Quadrant when it detected the explosion of **Praxis** in 2293. *(Star Trek VI: The Undiscovered Country).*

Beta Renna cloud. An intelligent, spaceborne entity encountered by the *Enterprise*-D near the **Beta Renna** star system in 2364. This entity came on board the starship and entered the neural systems of several *Enterprise*-D crew members, including Captain Picard, in an attempt to establish communications with life-forms it considered extremely alien. ("Lonely Among Us" [TNG]). *The cloud did not have a formal name in the episode.*

Beta Renna system. Star system where the home planets of the **Anticans** and **Selay** are located. The two worlds applied for admission to the Federation in 2364. ("Lonely Among Us" [TNG]).

Beta Stromgren. A red giant star located 23 parsecs beyond Starfleet's farthest manned explorations as of 2366. In the final alternating stages of expansion and collapse when the entity code-named **Tin Man** was discovered by the **Vega IX probe**, Beta Stromgren went nova shortly thereafter. ("Tin Man" [TNG]).

Beta Thoridar. Planet located in the Klingon sphere of influence. Beta Thoridar was used as a staging area for the forces loyal to **Duras** during the **Klingon civil war** of 2368. ("Redemption, Part I" [TNG]).

Beta VI. Planet, location of a Federation colony. While en route to deliver supplies to Beta VI in 2267, the *Starship Enterprise* was detained by the alien known as **Trelane**. ("The Squire of Gothos" [TOS]).

Beta XII-A entity. Alien life-form of unknown origin, composed of pure energy, that thrived on the energy of negative emotions. The entity, first encountered at planet **Beta XII-A**, was capable of manipulating matter and the minds of its

victims. It created a confrontation between crew members of a Klingon ship and the *Starship Enterprise* in 2268. Pitting these longtime enemies against each other, the entity fed on their anger, growing stronger as their hatred increased. The entity was defeated by a peaceful collaboration between the Klingons and the *Enterprise* crew. ("Day of the Dove" [TOS]). SEE: **Kang; Mara; noncorporeal life.** *Note that the entity was not given a name in the episode, and we're not even sure it came from planet Beta XII-A. The entity's special visual effects were designed by Mike Minor.*

Beta XII-A. Class-M planet from which a distress call was sent by the **Beta XII-A entity** in 2268, luring both the *Enterprise* and a Klingon vessel to a violent encounter. ("Day of the Dove" [TOS]).

Betazed, Holy Rings of. Relics of great significance in **Betazoid** culture. **Lwaxana Troi** was the holder of the Holy Rings of Betazed. ("Haven" [TNG]).

Betazed. Class-M planet that was home to **Deanna Troi**. ("Haven" [TNG]). As a young lieutenant, **William Riker** was once stationed on Betazed, where he became romantically involved with psychology student (and future *Enterprise*-D crew member) Deanna Troi. ("Encounter at Farpoint" [TNG], "Ménage à Troi" [TNG]). The biennial **Trade Agreements Conference** was held on Betazed in 2366. Commander Riker and Counselor Troi took shore leave there following the conference. Riker, Troi, and Lwaxana Troi were subsequently kidnapped from the surface of Betazed by the Ferengi, **DaiMon Tog**. ("Ménage à Troi" [TNG]). Archaeologist **Vash** is *persona-non-grata* on Betazed. ("Q-Less" [DS9]).

Betazoids. Race of humanoid telepaths from the Federation planet, **Betazed**. ("Haven" [TNG]). Most Betazoids develop their telepathic abilities in adolescence, although a few individuals are born with their telepathy fully functional. These troubled individuals generally require extensive therapy to survive in society, since they lack the ability to screen out the telepathic noise of other people. **Tam Elbrun** was one such person. ("Tin Man" [TNG]). Betazoids are, however, incapable of reading **Ferengi, Breen,** or **Doptherian** minds, possibly a result of the anomalous four-lobed construction of their brains. ("Ménage à Troi" [TNG], ("The Forsaken" [DS9]). The normal gestation period of a Betazoid is ten months. ("The Child" [TNG]). *Photo: Deanna Troi of Betazed.*

Beth Delta I. Planet on which the city of New Manhattan is located. **Dr. Paul Stubbs** jokingly promised to take Deanna Troi there for champagne. ("Evolution" [TNG]).

B'Etor. (Gwynyth Walsh). A member of the Klingon Empire's politically influential **Duras** family, B'Etor was the younger of Duras's two sisters. Following the death of Duras in 2367, B'Etor plotted with her sister, **Lursa**, to seat Duras's illegitimate son, **Toral**, as leader of the **Klingon High Council**, plunging the Empire into a **Klingon civil war**. ("Redemption, Parts I and II" [TNG]). B'Etor subsequently dropped out of sight for two years until she and her sister attempted to raise capital for their armies by selling **bilitrium** explosives to the **Kohn-ma**, a Bajoran terrorist organization in 2369. ("Past Prologue" [DS9]).

beverages. SEE: **food and beverages.**

"Beyond Antares." Love song that **Uhura** was fond of singing. ("Conscience of the King" [TOS], "The Changeling" [TOS]). *Music by Wilbur Hatch, lyrics by Gene L. Coon, performed by Nichelle Nichols.*

Bhavani, Premier. (Elizabeth Hoffman). The head of the **Barzan** government. Because of her planet's inhospitable nature, Premier Bhavani asked to use the *Enterprise*-D as a place to hold negotiations for rights to the **Barzan wormhole.** ("The Price" [TNG]).

bicaridine treatment. Regenerative therapy for fracture patients. It is used as a substitute in patients that are allergic to **metorapan**. Beverly Crusher recommended bicaridine when her son, Wesley, was injured in an accident at the Academy Flight Range in 2368. ("The First Duty" [TNG]).

• **"Big Goodbye, The."** *Next Generation* episode #13. Written by Tracy Tormé. Directed by Joseph L. Scanlan. Stardate 41997.7. *First aired in 1988. Picard and company are trapped in a holodeck simulation of fictional gumshoe detective Dixon Hill. This is the first episode to feature Picard's fascination with the adventures of Dixon Hill. At one point, this episode had been scheduled for production after "11001001" (TNG). If this had indeed happened, the computer modifications of the Bynars would have served to explain the holodeck malfunctions in this episode.* SEE: ***Amazing Detective Stories***; baseball; **Bell, Lieutenant Dan; "Big Goodbye, The"; Bradley, Jessica; DiMaggio, Joe; Hill, Dixon; Jarada; Leech, Felix; London Kings;** ***Long Dark Tunnel, The***; **McNary; Redblock, Cyrus; Trona IV; Whalen.**

"Big Goodbye, The." Short story featuring the first adventures of San Francisco gumshoe detective **Dixon Hill.** Published 1934 on Earth in *Amazing Detective Stories* magazine. ("The Big Goodbye" [TNG]).

B'iJik. (Erick Avari). Minor bureaucrat serving the **Klingon High Council** in 2368. B'iJik was reluctant to convey a request by Captain Jean-Luc Picard to High Council leader **Gowron** in 2368 when Picard requested the loan of a Klingon bird-of-prey. B'iJik eventually relented when Picard's arguments proved highly persuasive. ("Unification, Part I" [TNG]).

Biko, **U.S.S.** Federation supply ship scheduled to rendezvous with the *Enterprise*-D on stardate 46271 at planet Deinonychus VII. ("A Fistful of Datas" [TNG]). *Named for Steven Biko, South African civil rights activist, martyred in 1977.*

Bilana III. Federation class-M planet where **soliton wave** based propulsion was developed by **Dr. Ja'Dar**. In 2368, the *Enterprise*-D participated in the first practical test of the new technology. The soliton wave was generated by an array of massive generators on the surface of Bilana III and projected toward a sister facility on the planet **Lemma II.** ("New Ground" [TNG]).

Bilar. (Ralph Maurer). Member of the society on planet **Beta III** who was under the control on the machine entity **Landru**. When an *Enterprise* landing party arrived on the planet in 2267, Bilar asked if they had found accommodations to sleep after the **Red Hour**. ("Return of the Archons" [TOS]).

Bilaren system. Location of **Amanda Roger's** adoptive parents' homeworld. ("True-Q" [TNG]).

bilitrium. Crystalline compound that is an extremely rare energy source. When used in conjunction with an antimatter converter, it becomes a powerful explosive. **Kohn-ma** terrorist **Tahna Los** attempted to destroy one side of the **Bajoran wormhole** in 2369 using bilitrium and an antimatter converter. ("Past Prologue" [DS9]).

biochips. Cybernetic implants surgically imbeded into bodies of the **Borg**. They serve to enhance their physical abilities and synthesize any organic molecules needed by their biological tissues. The Borg are dependent on the implants, and would die if the biochips are removed. ("I, Borg" [TNG]).

biofilter, transporter. A subsystem of the **transporter** designed to scan an incoming transporter beam prior to materialization, and remove potentially harmful disease and virus contamination. The biofilter could be programmed against a wide range of disease organisms, but was only effective against organisms so programmed.

The biofilter was not only a very ingenious idea, but a very logical one in terms of the technology theoretically available to Starfleet, especially considering the risks entailed in exploring unknown planets.

Unfortunately, one of the things that Star Trek's writers discovered was that the biofilter made it difficult to tell certain kinds of stories. As a result, they invented the theory that the biofilter was only effective against known organisms, thus making it possible for the occasional unknown virus to wreak havoc aboard the ship.

biomechanical maintenance program. Software incorporated into Commander **Data**'s positronic network. It kept him physically healthy and rarely in need of Dr. Crusher's professional services. ("Data's Day" [TNG]).

biomolecular physiologist. (Tzi Ma). Specialized surgeon. A biomolecular physiologist was called in when Picard's life was threatened by complications in a routine cardiac replacement procedure in 2365, but Dr. Katherine Pulaski had to be brought in to save the captain. ("Samaritan Snare" [TNG]).

bioplast sheeting. Material used in the construction of the android **Data**, who had about 1.3 kilograms of the stuff in his body. ("The Most Toys" [TNG]).

bioregenerative field. Radiated energy used in biomedical applications to accelerate cellular growth. Dr. Bashir used such a field to accelerate cells found in Ibudan's quarters that later developed into a clone of **Ibudan**. ("A Man Alone" [DS9]).

bipolar torch. Powerful cutting tool used aboard station Deep Space 9. A bipolor torch was used to cut through **toranium** metal inlay on a station door on stardate 46925. ("The Forsaken" [DS9]).

Bird-of-Prey. SEE: **Klingon Bird-of-Prey; Romulan Bird-of-Prey.**

• **"Birthright, Part I."** *Next Generation* episode #142. Written by Brannon Braga. Directed by Winrich Kolbe. Stardate 46578.4. *First aired in 1993. At Deep Space 9, Worf finds evidence that his father may still be alive in a secret Romulan prison camp. Except for "Emissary" (DS9), this was the only "crossover" episode using characters from both* Star Trek: The Next Generation *and* Star Trek: Deep Space Nine. SEE: **Alture VII relaxation program; aqueduct systems; Ba'el; Carraya System; Data; Gi'ral; hammer; Khitomer; Ktaran antiques; L'Kor; Lopez, Ensign;** *MajQa*, **Rite of; Mogh; No'Mat; painting; pasta al fiorella; Rudman, Commander; Shrek, Jaglom; Soong, Dr. Noonien;** *Starfleet Cybernetics Journal;* **Tokath; Toq; Worf; Yridians**.

• **"Birthright, Part II."** *Next Generation* episode #143. Written by René Echevarria. Directed by Dan Curry. Stardate 46759.2. *First aired in 1993. At the secret Romulan prison camp, Worf tries to help Klingon prisoners rediscover what it is to be truly Klingon. This episode was directed by visual effects producer Dan Curry.* SEE: **Ba'el; boridium pellet; Carraya System;** *d'k tahg*; **Gi'ral;** *jinaq*; **Kahless the Unforgettable; Khitomer; L'Kor;** *Mok'bara*; **Nequencia System;** *qa'vak*; **Shrek, Jaglom; Tokath; Toq; Worf**.

bitanium. Metal used in Commander Data's neural pathways. ("Time's Arrow, Part I" [TNG]).

bitrious filaments. Mineral traces found in the soil on **Melona IV** in 2368 and on three other planets attacked by the **Crystalline Entity**. Bitrium was apparently produced when the entity absorbed living matter. ("Silicon Avatar" [TNG]).

Black Cluster. An astronomical formation created some 9 billion years ago when hundreds of proto-stars collapsed in close proximity to each other. The resulting formation is fraught with violent, unpredictable gravitational wavefronts. The phenomena, which can absorb energy, are extremely dangerous to spacecraft systems. The Federation science vessel *Vico* was destroyed in the Black Cluster in 2368, and the *Enterprise*-D, investigating the disappearance of the *Vico*, nearly suffered the same fate. ("Hero Worship" [TNG]).

black hole. Celestial phenomenon caused by the collapse of a neutron star. The gravity well generated by the star's collapse becomes so great that neither matter or light can escape. Extremely small black holes are known as quantum singularities. ("Timescape" [TNG]).

black knight. Medieval dark horseman brought to life by **Yeoman Tonia Barrows** on the **amusement park planet** in 2267. The black knight and other beings imagined by the *Enterprise* landing party were made from cellular castings manufactured beneath the planet. The inhabitants of this world created the images to fulfill visitors' daydreams but some of the dreams  turned into nightmares like the black knight who nearly killed Dr. McCoy. ("Shore Leave" [TOS]).

black star. Alternate term for a black hole. In 2267, the original *Starship Enterprise* nearly collided with a black star in a maneuver that propelled them back in time to 1969. SEE: **slingshot effect.**

Blackjack. Code name for the **Omaha Air Base,** which dispatched a jet to photograph and intercept a **UFO** in 1969. The jet was piloted by **Captain John Christopher** and the UFO was the *Starship Enterprise*. ("Tomorrow Is Yesterday" [TOS]).

Bloom sisters. Acquaintances of **Jean-Luc Picard** and his friend, **Louis**. When they were both young, Picard warned Louis not to take a bicycle trip with these sisters, but apparently Louis did not heed his warning. Louis ended up breaking a leg on the trip. He also ended up getting married, twice. ("Family" [TNG]).

Blue Parrot Cafe. A club on planet Sarona VII where Riker recalled that exotic blue drinks were served. Picard promised to buy everyone drinks there when the *Enterprise*-D went to Sarona VII for shore leave in 2364. ("We'll Always Have Paris" [TNG]).

Bluejay 4. Radio call sign given to United States Air Force **captain John Christopher**'s F-104 air vehicle in 1969. ("Tomorrow Is Yesterday" [TOS]).

B'Nar. A **Talarian** mourning ritual. The *B'Nar* is a rhythmic high-pitched wail that is expressed for hours at a time. The Talarian boys rescued from a damaged observation craft in 2367 made the *B'Nar* in protest for being held aboard the *Enterprise*-D. ("Suddenly Human" [TNG]).

Bochra, Centurion. (John Snyder). A young Romulan who was marooned with Commander La Forge on planet **Galorndon Core** in 2366. Bochra at first attempted to capture

La Forge and hold him prisoner, but later cooperated with him for their mutual survival when they suffered neural damage from the magnetic fields on the surface. ("The Enemy" [TNG]).

Body. Term describing the whole of society on planet **Beta III** under the rule of **Landru**. The population on Beta III was controlled by Landru and made to act simply, in peace and tranquillity, but they became totally stagnant and nonproductive. The good of the Body was the prime directive and anyone who disturbed the peace of the Body was destroyed. ("Return of the Archons" [TOS]).

Bogrow, Paul. An old friend of former *U.S.S. Victory* crew members Geordi La Forge and **Susanna Leijten**. Leijten said she almost married Bogrow. ("Identity Crisis" [TNG]).

Bok, DaiMon. Ferengi commander and father to the commander of a **Ferengi** ship destroyed in 2355 in a battle with the *U.S.S. Stargazer.* Bok blamed *Stargazer* captain **Jean-Luc Picard** for his son's death. Years later, in 2364, Bok sought to exact revenge on Picard by attempting to discredit the captain by falsifying evidence suggesting that Picard had attacked without provocation. Bok was later demoted by his first officer, **Kazago**  when Bok's plan for revenge was discovered. SEE: **Maxia, Battle of; Thought Maker.** ("The Battle" [TNG]).

Bokai, Buck. (Keone Young). Also known as Harmon Bokai. One of professional baseball's greatest players, Buck Bokai broke **Joe DiMaggio**'s record for consecutive hits in 2026. ("The Big Goodbye" [TNG]).

Initially a shortstop for the **London Kings**, Bokai later switched to third base. Bokai hit the winning home run in the 2042 **World Series**, just before the demise of the sport. SEE: **Newson, Eddie.** ("If Wishes Were Horses" [DS9]). A holographic version of Bokai was part of a holodeck program that **Ben Sisko** brought with him to **Deep Space 9**. Ben and his son, Jake, enjoyed playing with Bokai and other baseball greats. ("Storyteller" [DS9]). This holographic Buck Bokai came to life in 2369 when unknown aliens from the **Gamma Quadrant** used images of Bokai and other imaginary figures to learn more about human beings. Despite himself, Ben Sisko became quite fond of this image of Bokai. ("If Wishes Were Horses" [DS9]).

The player who broke DiMaggio's record in 2026 was mentioned in "The Big Goodbye" (TNG), but he remained nameless until "If Wishes Were Horses" (DS9). The character's name actually originated in a baseball card proposed by Star Trek: Deep Space Nine illustrator (and baseball fan) Ricardo Delgado as a decorative item for Ben Sisko's desk. Fellow baseball fan (and executive producer) Michael Piller suggested the card feature a 21st-century player, which would make it a valuable collectors' item to the 24th-century Ben Sisko. Star Trek model maker Greg Jein (yet another baseball fan) got into the act at this point, providing photos of himself in a baseball jersey that were converted into the prop card. Greg also provided the fictional "history" of his character and the statistics that appeared on the card. Bokai, whose name was a vague allusion to Buckaroo Banzai, from the movie of the same name, was mentioned in "The Storyteller" (DS9), but not actually seen until "If Wishes Were Horses," in which Bokai was played by actor Keone Young, who bore an uncanny resemblence to Jein. The baseball card shown below, which was revised after the episode, has Young's photo on the front, but still shows Jein on the back.

Bolarus IX. Home planet of the **Bolian** race. ("Allegiance" [TNG]).

Bolians. Race of humanoids native to planet Bolarus IX ("Allegiance" [TNG]) and distinguished by a light blue skin and a bifurcated ridge running down the center of the face.

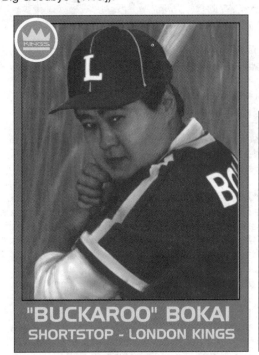

"BUCKAROO" BOKAI
SHORTSTOP - LONDON KINGS

HARMON BUCK GIN BOKAI

311 Ht 175cm Wt. 81 kg Bats L&R Throws Right Born 10-31-98 Marina Del Rey, CA

Despite his short stature, "Buckaroo" has been the Solar System-wide batting champion for two years in a row. After playing his rookie year with the Crenshaw Monarchs, he was the pivotal player in the 12-man trade with the Gotham City Bats. Last season, he missed breaking Joe DiMaggio's consecutive game hitting streak by only two games. His fielding versatility and constant clutch hitting have made him one of the Major Leagues' most sought-after players.

YEAR	TEAM	G	AB	R	H	2B	3B	HR	RBI	SB	AVG
2019	CRENSHAW	162	616	118	185	32	2	37	111	10	.300
2020	GOTHAM	140	542	64	165	37	6	34	120	7	.304
2021	GOTHAM	117	417	71	132	29	1	19	91	8	.317
2022	TANIS	143	461	80	155	34	10	13	68	7	.336
2023	SEIBU	153	582	100	210	44	7	21	74	3	.361
2024	SEIBU	161	653	107	240	42	13	26	75	9	.368
2025	LONDON	117	449	87	175	33	9	24	118	15	.390

GREATEST HEROES OF THE PLANETARY BASEBALL LEAGUE

Copyright © 2026 by The Planetary Baseball League Inc. If you build it, they will come.

Captain **Rixx**, commander of the *Starship Thomas Paine*, was a Bolian ("Conspiracy" [TNG]), as was Starfleet cadet **Minena Haro** ("Allegiance" [TNG]), *Enterprise*-D barber **Mr. Mot**, Ambassador **Vadosia** ("The Forsaken" [DS9]), and the tactical officer aboard the *Starship Saratoga*, destroyed in the battle of **Wolf 359** ("Emissary" [DS9]). *Bolians were named for director Cliff Bole, who directed "Conspiracy" (TNG), the first episode in which these aliens were seen. The Saratoga tactical officer was played by Stephen Davies.*

Boma, Lieutenant. (Don Marshall). Member of the **Shuttlecraft Galileo** crew when it crashed on planet **Taurus II** in 2267. ("The *Galileo* Seven" [TOS]).

Bonaparte, Napoleon. (1769-1821). Military leader and emperor of France from 1804-1815. Trelane of Gothos fancied himself a student of Napoleon Bonaparte. ("The Squire of Gothos" [TOS]).

bonding gifts. Betazoid term for wedding presents. SEE: **gift box, Betazoid.** ("Haven" [TNG]).

• **"Bonding, The."** *Next Generation* episode #53. Written by Ronald D. Moore. Directed by Winrich Kolbe. Stardate 43198.7. *First aired in 1989. When an* Enterprise*-D crew member is killed on an away mission, a planet's inhabitants attempt to make amends by providing a "perfect" life for her orphaned son.* SEE: **Aster, Jeremy; Aster, Lieutenant Marla; computer core;** *d'k tahg;* **Klingons; Koinonians; noncorporeal life; Patches;** *R'uustai;* **Rushton infection; subspace proximity detonator; tricorder; Worf.**

Bonestell Recreation Facility. A seamy bar at **Starbase Earhart**, filled with unruly galactic cutthroats. **Jean-Luc Picard** was stabbed through the heart in 2327 (shortly after his graduation from the Academy) by a **Nausicaan** who picked a fight with Picard and his classmates at the Bonestell Facility. Picard's injuries in the incident required him to undergo cardiac replacment surgery. ("Samaritan Snare" [TNG]).

Picard regretted his impulsiveness in that incident for years, but in 2369, when **Q** gave him a chance to relive that moment, Picard found that he had indeed made the right choice. ("Tapestry" [TNG]). *The Bonestell Facility was named for classic astronomical artist Chestley Bonestell.* SEE: **barokie; dom-jot;** *guramba;* **undari.**

• **"Booby Trap."** *Next Generation* episode #54. Teleplay by Ron Roman and Michael Piller & Richard Danus. Directed by Gabrielle Beaumont. Stardate 43205.6. *First aired in 1989. The* Enterprise*-D investigates a derelict warship and becomes caught in an ancient booby trap.* SEE: **aceton assimilators; Astral V Annex; Brahms, Dr. Leah;** *Cleponji;* **Daystrom Institute of Technology; dilithium crystal chamber; Drafting Room 5; Galek Sar; Henshaw, Christy;** *Kavis Teke* **elusive maneuver; La Forge, Geordi; Lang cycle fusion engines; Menthars; Orelious IX; Outpost Seran-T-One; Picard, Jean-Luc; Promellian/Menthar war; Promellians; Theoretical Propulsion Group; Utopia Planitia Fleet Yards.**

Book of the People, Fabrini. SEE: **Fabrini Book of the People**.

Book, The. Term used by the inhabitants of planet Sigma Iotia II for *Chicago Mobs of the Twenties*, a book left behind on that planet by the crew of the **U.S.S. Horizon** in 2168. The Iotians used The Book as the pattern for their society, and revered it, almost as a holy relic. ("A Piece of the Action" [TOS]).

Boothby. (Ray Walston). The groundskeeper at **Starfleet Academy**. Boothby was something of a fixture at the Academy, having worked there since **Jean-Luc Picard** was a cadet in the 2320s. During those days, Picard regarded the irascible Boothby as "a mean-spirited, vicious old man." Boothby nevertheless helped guide Picard through a particularly difficult time when the young cadet had committed a serious offense. Boothby later recalled that he had simply helped Picard listen to himself. Boothby, for his part, followed Picard's career with some satisfaction. ("The First Duty" [TNG]). Years later, Picard came to understand Boothby more clearly, and regarded the old groundskeeper as one of the wisest men he had ever known. When **Wesley Crusher** entered Starfleet Academy in 2367, Picard advised him to seek out Boothby's advice. ("Final Mission" [TNG]). *Picard never did describe the nature of his transgression. Picard first mentioned Boothby to Wesley in "Final Mission" (TNG), then again in "The Game" (TNG). We finally got to see the character in "The First Duty" (TNG). Ray Walston gained popularity in the 1960s as Uncle Martin in* My Favorite Martian.

Boradis system. Star system where a Federation outpost was established on Boradis III in 2331. By 2365, three other planets in that system had been colonized. The *Enterprise*-D was ordered to a point near the Boradis system to meet Federation emissary **K'Ehleyr** from **Starbase 153**. ("The Emissary" [TNG]).

borathium. An experimental rybotherapy medication developed by **Dr. Toby Russell** as a potential replacement for leporazine and morathial. The drug was still in an experimental stage in 2368 when Russell used it unsuccessfully to treat a crash victim from the transport ship *Denver*. Dr. Beverly Crusher believed that Russell's use of borathium in that case was a violation of medical ethics, since conventional leporazine therapy might have been effective. ("Ethics" [TNG]).

Boratus. (Michael Champion). The male **Vorgon** criminal who traveled backward in time to locate Captain Picard and the *Tox Uthat*. ("Captain's Holiday" [TNG]).

Boreal III. Home port of the transport ship *Kallisko*, which was attacked by the **Crystalline Entity** in 2368. ("Silicon Avatar" [TNG]).

Boreth. Class-M planet located in Klingon space. Klingon legend has it that Boreth was the planet where the Klingon messiah, **Kahless the Unforgettable**, promised to return following his death on the Klingon Homeworld some 1500 years ago. The followers

of Kahless established a monastery on the planet to await his return. To the Klingons, there is no more sacred place. SEE: **Story of the Promise, The.** Clerics on Boreth, fearing that political infighting in the Klingon High Council signaled a loss of honor in the Empire, conspired in 2369 to provide new leadership for the Klingon people by creating a clone of Kahless, using his actual genetic material, thereby attempting to fulfill Kahless's promise. **Worf** made a pilgrimage to Boreth in that year, where he was the first to meet the clone of Kahless. Although the clerics' deception was soon discovered, Kahless's clone was installed as the ceremonial Emperor of the Klingon people. ("Rightful Heir" [TNG]). SEE: **Gowron.** *Photo: Boreth monastery, a matte painting designed by Dan Curry.*

Borg collective. Term used to describe the group consciousness of the **Borg** civilization. Each Borg individual was linked to the collective by a sophisticated subspace network that insured each member was given constant supervision and guidance. ("Best of Both Worlds, Part I" [TNG], "I, Borg" [TNG]).

Borg scout ship. Small Borg vessel, cubical in shape with a mass of 2.5 million metric tons. The ship generally carried a crew of five. One such ship was discovered crashed on a moon in the **Argolis Cluster** in 2368. SEE: **Hugh.** ("I, Borg" [TNG]).

Borg ship. Huge cube-shaped spacecraft, first encountered by the *Enterprise*-D near **System J-25** in 2365. It had a highly decentralized design and *Enterprise*-D personnel reported finding no specific bridge, engineering, or living areas. Combat experience showed the ship to be

equipped with powerful energy weapons and capable of repairing major damage almost immediately, including the impact of direct phaser hits. *Model design concept by Maurice Hurley, design by Rick Sternbach, built by Kim Bailey.* ("Q Who?" [TNG]). A Borg vessel of a totally different design was used in the Borg incursion of 2369, in which a **transwarp conduit** was used to reach the Alpha Quadrant much more rapidly than was possible with normal warp travel. ("Descent, Part I" [TNG]).

Borg. An immensely powerful race of enhanced humanoids from the **Delta Quadrant** of the galaxy. The Borg implant themselves with cybernetic devices, giving them great technological and combat capabilities. Different Borgs are equipped with different hardware for specific tasks. Each Borg is tied into a sophisticated subspace communications network, forming

the **Borg collective**, in which the idea of the individual is a meaningless concept. The Borg exhibit a high degree of intelligence and adaptability in their tactics. Most successful means of defense or offense against them were found to work only once, almost immediately after which the Borg developed a countermeasure. The Borg were responsible for the near-extinction of **Guinan**'s people in the 23rd century. The first known contact between the Borg and the Federation was in 2265, when Q transported the *Enterprise*-D out of Federation space into the flight path of a Borg vessel heading toward Alpha Quadrant. ("Q Who?" [TNG]). Following this first contact, Starfleet began advance planning for a potential Borg offensive against the Federation. **Lieutenant Commander Shelby** was placed in charge of this project to develop a defense strategy. *Photo: A Borg.*

The anticipated Borg attack came in late 2366, when a Borg vessel entered Federation space, heading for Earth. Starfleet tactical planners had expected at least several more months before the Borg arrival, and thus were caught unprepared. *Enterprise*-D captain **Jean-Luc Picard** was captured by the Borg at the beginning of this offensive. He was assimilated into the Borg collective consciousness and became known as **Locutus of Borg**, providing crucial guidance to the Borg in their attack. ("The Best of Both Worlds, Part I" [TNG]).

Starfleet massed an armada of some 40 starships in hopes of stopping the Borg ship at **Wolf 359**, but the fleet was decimated with the loss of 39 ships and 11,000 lives ("The Drumhead" [TNG]), including the *U.S.S. Saratoga*. ("Emissary" [DS9]). As Locutus, Picard explained that the Borg purpose was to improve the quality of life in the galaxy by providing other life-forms the benefit of being part of the Borg collective. Following the rescue of Picard from the Borg ship, a last-ditch effort to implant a destructive computer command into the Borg collective consciousness was successful in destroying the Borg ship in Earth orbit. ("The Best of Both Worlds, Part II" [TNG]).

By 2368, at least two more Borg vessels were found to have reached Federation territory when a crashed **Borg scout ship** was discovered on the surface of a moon in the **Argolis Cluster**. One surviving Borg, designated Third of Five, was rescued from the crash by *Enterprise*-D crew personnel. This Borg, named **Hugh** by the *Enterprise*-D crew, was nursed back to health. During Hugh's convalescence, *Enterprise*-D personnel developed what they termed an **invasive program**, which, when introduced into the Borg collective consciousness, was designed to cause a fatal overload in the entire collective. In the process, Hugh befriended Geordi La Forge, a friendship that provided an argument that this invasive program, effectively a weapon of mass murder, should not be used. Hugh was then returned to the Argolis crash site, where he was rescued by another Borg scout ship. ("I, Borg" [TNG]). Following the return of **Hugh**, Hugh's new sense of individuality began to permeate a portion of the collective. The results were dramatic: Deprived of their group identity, individual Borg were unable to function as a unit. The unexpected arrival of the android, **Lore**, changed this. Lore appointed himself the leader of the Borg, and promised them he would provide them with the means to become completely artifical life-forms, free of dependence on organic bodies.

In 2369, Lore led the Borg in launching a major new offensive against the Federation. Utilizing transwarp conduits, they entered Federation space in a ship of an unfamiliar design and attacked a Federation outpost at **Ohniaka III**. During this offensive, the Borg attacked with uncharacteristic anger, later found to be due to Lore's influence. The offensive was halted when Lore was dismantled by his brother, **Data**. ("Descent, Parts I and II" [TNG]).

Writer Maurice Hurley derived the name Borg from the term cyborg (cybernetic organism), although it seems unlikely that a race living on the other side of the galaxy would know of the term. The Borg were first seen in "Q Who" (TNG).

Borgia plant. Plant form indigenous to planet **M-113**. Described as Carbon Group III vegetation, it is mildly toxic. **Professor Robert Crater** tried to convince Kirk and McCoy that **Crewman Darnell** had died from eating a **Borgia plant**. ("The Man Trap" [TOS]).

Borgolis Nebula. Blue-tinged gaseous nebula studied by *Enterprise*-D personnel in 2369. **Neela Daren** recommended that the **Spectral Analysis Department** have more sensor observation time to examine the Borgolis Nebula but sensor-array usage was allocated to Engineering. ("Lessons" [TNG]).

borhyas. Bajoran term for ghost or spirit. ("The Next Phase" [TNG]).

boridium pellet. Small object planted subcutaneously by Romulan security forces into prisoners, enabling such prisoners to be located by use of the pellet's energy signature. ("Birthright, Part II" [TNG]).

boridium power converter. Component of an **exocomp**, used to provide energy for the device's internal functions. ("The Quality of Life" [TNG]).

Borka VI. Planet at which Deanna Troi attended a neuropsychology seminar in 2369. Troi was abducted from the seminar by Romulan underground operatives who used her in an elaborate plot to help Romulan **vice proconsul M'ret** defect to the Federation. ("Face of the Enemy" [TNG]). SEE: **N'Vek, Subcommander**.

Bortas, I.K.C. Klingon *Vor'cha*-class attack cruiser that conveyed Captain Picard's request for Klingon assistance at planet **Nelvana III** when the *Enterprise*-D investigated reports of a secret Romulan base there. The three Klingon vessels

that responded to Picard's request made it possible for the *Enterprise*-D to escape without provoking an interstellar war, as the Romulans had hoped. ("The Defector" [TNG]). The *Bortas* served as **Gowron**'s flagship during the **Klingon civil war** of 2367-68. **Worf** served as weapons officer aboard the *Bortas* during the early part of that conflict. ("Redemption, Part I" [TNG]).

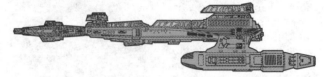

Botany Bay, S.S. Ancient **DY-100** space vessel launched from Earth in 1996. The *Botany Bay* was a **sleeper ship** carrying the former dictator **Khan Noonien Singh** and his followers who had escaped from Earth after the terrible **Eugenics Wars**.

The *Botany Bay* traveled for some 300 years with most of its passangers preserved in suspended animation before being discovered by the *Starship Enterprise* near the **Mutara Sector** in 2267. ("Space Seed" [TOS]). *The Botany Bay miniature was also used as the freighter* **Woden** *in "The Ultimate Computer" (TOS). The model was recently placed on display at the Smithsonian National Air and Space Museum in Washington, D.C.*

Bounty, H.M.S. Eighteenth-century British sailing ship famous for the mutiny of its crew in 1789. Dr. Leonard McCoy gave the name *"H.M.S. Bounty"* to the captured Klingon ship that he and his shipmates planned to return to Earth in after having disobeyed Starfleet orders to save Spock. (*Star Trek IV: The Voyage Home*).

Boyce, Dr. Phillip. (John Hoyt). Chief medical officer of the original *Starship Enterprise* under the command of Captain **Christopher Pike** in 2254. Boyce, noting that Pike was suffering from exhaustion following a mission to **Rigel VII**, urged Pike to relax a bit to avoid burnout. ("The Cage" [TOS]).

Bozeman, U.S.S. Federation starship, *Soyuz* class, Starfleet registry NCC-1941. The *Bozeman* was three weeks out of its home starbase when it disappeared near the **Typhon Expanse** in 2278, where it remained until 2368. During those 90 years, those

aboard the *Bozeman* experienced the passage of only a brief period of time. Unknown to them, they were in a recursive **temporal causality loop**, so they experienced that same brief period over and over, ad infinitum, until the loop was disrupted by the *Enterprise*-D, with which it nearly collided.

("Cause and Effect" [TNG]). *Named for the city of Bozeman, Montana, hometown of episode writer Brannon Braga. The registry number was an homage to Steven Spielberg's movie 1941, for which* Star Trek *model maker Greg Jein provided miniatures.*

Bracas V. A planet where Commander La Forge had taken a vacation and gone skin-diving. La Forge compared the appearance of the **two-dimensional creatures** discovered in 2367 to a school of fish he had seen while diving on a coral reef on Bracas V. ("The Loss" [TNG]).

Brack, Mr. Alias used by **Flint** in 2239 to purchase planet Holberg 917-G. ("Requiem for Methuselah" [TOS]).

Brackett, Fleet Admiral. (Karen Hensel). Starfleet admiral who met with Captain Picard at Starbase 234 in 2368 to discuss the sudden disappearance of Ambassador **Spock**. On the admiral's orders, the *Enterprise*-D proceeded to planet Vulcan to obtain more information about Spock's where-abouts and motives. ("Unification, Part I" [TNG]).

Bractor. (Armin Shimerman). Commander of the **Ferengi** attack vessel **Kreechta**. When the Kreechta stumbled into a **Starfleet battle simulation** in 2365, Bractor misinterpreted the situation, believing the derelict **U.S.S. Hathaway** to be of some secret strategic importance, when in fact it was merely engaging in war games with the *Enterprise*-D. ("Peak Performance" [TNG]). *Actor Armin Shimerman would later portray the part of Quark in* Star Trek: Deep Space Nine.

Bradbury, U.S.S. Federation starship, Starfleet registry number NX-72307. Upon his acceptance to Starfleet Academy in 2366, **Wesley Crusher** was scheduled for transport aboard the *Bradbury* from the *Enterprise*-D to Starfleet Academy on Earth. Wesley unfortunately missed the transport while assisting with the recovery of Ambassador Troi, Commander Riker, and Counselor Troi from a Ferengi ship. ("Ménage à Troi" [TNG]). *The* Bradbury *was named for s-f/ fantasy writer Ray Bradbury, a friend of the late Gene Roddenberry. Based on the ship's registry number, we suspect it is an experimental vessel, the first of its class.*

Bradley, Jessica. (Carolyn Allport). A fictional character from the **Dixon Hill** detective stories. Picard encountered a holographic representation of Bradley, a wealthy, beautiful socialite, in his Dixon Hill holodeck adventures, during which she was "murdered" by persons unknown, although Picard (as Hill) suspected the work of **Cyrus Redblock**. ("The Big Goodbye" [TNG]).

Brahms, Dr. Leah. (Susan Gibney). A graduate of the **Daystrom Institute of Technology**, Dr. Leah Brahms was part of an engineering design team on the *Galaxy*-**Class Starship Development Project** at the **Utopia Planitia Fleet Yards** in the early 2360s. Brahms made major contributions

to the **Theoretical Propulsion Group**, far beyond her official role as a junior team member, and was responsible for much of the warp engine design on the *Starship* **Enterprise-D**. In an attempt to learn more about the engine design of the *Enterprise*-D, Commander La Forge re-created Dr. Brahms' image in the holodeck. While he did learn a great deal about the engines, Commander LaForge also, unfortunately, developed a real attraction for Dr. Brahms' image. ("Booby Trap" [TNG]).

By 2367, Brahms had been promoted to senior design engineer of the Theoretical Propulsion Group. Brahms visited the *Enterprise*-D in that year to inspect the field modifications made to that ship's engines by Chief Engineer Geordi La Forge. Much to La Forge's dismay, Brahms was highly critical of La Forge's work. Brahms also strongly objected to La Forge's having programmed a holographic replica of herself, noting that doing so without her permission constituted an invasion of privacy. Nevertheless, the two engineers pulled together in a crisis and became friends. SEE: **Junior**. ("Galaxy's Child" [TNG]).

In an early draft of "Booby Trap," Brahms was named Navid Daystrom, presumably a descendant of **Dr. Richard Daystrom***. Unfortunately, the casting department did not realize that this would require a Black actress to play the part until after Susan Gibney had been hired. At the suggestion of script coordinator Eric Stillwell, the character was renamed, but the Daystrom tie-in was kept by adding a line that she had graduated from the Daystrom Institute.*

brain-circuitry pattern. Medical diagnostic image mapping neural activity in a humanoid brain. The BCP of each individual is unique, and thus serves as a positive means of identification. **Mira Romaine** was given a BCP diagnostic exam in 2269 during the battle with the **Zetarians**. The test revealed the fact that her brain-wave patterns were changing to match those of the aliens. ("The Lights of Zetar" [TOS]).

brak'lul. Klingon term for a characteristic redundancy in Klingon physiology. All vital bodily functions are protected by a redundant organ or system. For example, Klingons possess two livers, an eight-chambered heart (double the four chambers found in many other humanoids), and 23 ribs, unlike the ten pairs found in humans. ("Ethics" [TNG]).

Branch, Commander. (David Gautreaux). Commander of the **Epsilon IX monitoring station** that was destroyed when the **V'Ger** probe returned to Federation space. (*Star Trek: The Motion Picture*). *Commander Branch was never referred to by name in the film, but his name was in the credits. Just before* Star Trek I *began production, actor David Gautreaux had been*

cast in the role of Commander **Xon***, science officer aboard the* Enterprise *for the proposed television series* **Star Trek II***. When the first episode of this series became* Star Trek: The Motion Picture, *the character of Xon was eliminated and Gautreaux was recast as Branch.*

Brand, Admiral. (Jacqueline Brookes). Superintendent of **Starfleet Academy** who presided over the **Nova Squadron** inquiry following the death of cadet **Joshua Albert** in 2368. ("The First Duty" [TNG]). SEE: **Kolvoord Starburst; Locarno, Cadet First Class Nicholas.**

Braslota System. Star system at which a **Starfleet battle simulation** was held involving the *U.S.S. Enterprise*-D and the *U.S.S. Hathaway* in 2365. ("Peak Performance" [TNG]).

Brattain, U.S.S. Federation *Miranda*-class science vessel, Starfleet registry number NCC-21166, commanded by **Captain Chantal Zaheva**. The *Brattain* mysteriously disappeared in 2367 and was found trapped in a **Tyken's Rift** near a binary star system by *Enterprise*-D personnel. All but one of the Brattain crew were discovered dead, apparently having brutally killed each other. Autopsies conducted by Dr. Beverly Crusher revealed unusual chemical imbalances in their brains, apparently due to severe **REM sleep** deprivation, believed to be the cause of the bizarre violence. The REM sleep loss was found to be a side effect of an attempt by an alien ship to communicate from the Tyken's Rift. The alien intelligence had apparently been trying to enlist the *Brattain* crew to help both ships escape the rift. ("Night Terrors" [TNG]). *The dedication plaque on the* Brattain's *bridge said that the ship had been built by Yoyodyne Propulsion Systems, and bore the motto, "...a three hour tour, a three hour tour." The ship's name on the model was spelt "Brittain" by mistake. The model was a re-use of the U.S.S. Reliant from* Star Trek II: The Wrath of Khan, *with minor modifications.*

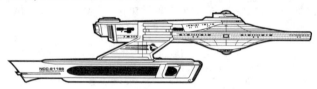

Brax. Planet where, according to archaeologist **Vash**, **Q** is known as "The God of Lies." ("Q-Less" [DS9]).

• **"Bread and Circuses."** Original Series episode #43. Written by Gene Roddenberry and Gene L. Coon. Directed by Ralph Senensky. Stardate 4040.7. *First aired in 1967. Kirk, Spock, and McCoy are captured on an Earthlike planet on which the Roman Empire never fell.* SEE: **Achilles;** *Beagle,* **S.S.; Children of the Sun; Condition Green; Drusilla; 892, Planet IV; Flavius; Harrison, William B.; Hodgkins Law of Parallel Planet Development; Jupiter 8; Marcus, Cladius; Merrick, R. M.;** *Name the Winner!;* **Prime Directive; Septimus; World War III.**

Brechtian Cluster. Star system with two inhabited planets. The **Crystalline Entity** was destroyed in 2368 while en route to the Brechtian Cluster. ("Silicon Avatar" [TNG]).

Bre'el IV. A Federation member planet whose asteroidal moon was knocked out of its normal orbit in 2366 by the nearby passage of a black hole or other celestial object. The moon's new orbit began to decay rapidly, and soon threat-

ened to impact on the planet's surface. Bre'el IV was heavily populated by a humanoid race that might have been wiped out if the moon did indeed hit the planet. The *Enterprise*-D made repeated attempts to return the moon to its proper orbit, but was unable to do so. The planet was finally saved by a magnanimous gesture from Q, who returned the moon to a nearly circular, 55,000-kilometer orbit. ("Deja Q" [TNG]).

Breen. A race with outposts near the **Black Cluster** investigated by the *Enterprise*-D in 2368. The Breen utilized cloaking technology and their ships were armed with disruptor-type weapons. The Breen, politically nonaligned, were considered but dismissed as a possible explanation for the destruction of the **S.S. Vico** in the Black Cluster. ("Hero Worship" [TNG]). The Breen were not empathically detectable by Betazoids. ("The Loss" [TNG]).

***bregit* lung.** A traditional Klingon dish served aboard the Klingon vessel *Pagh*. Riker said he enjoyed the stuff. ("A Matter of Honor" [TNG]).

Brekka. The fourth planet in the **Delos** star system, home to an intelligent humanoid species, the **Brekkians**. ("Symbiosis" [TNG]).

Brekkians. Humanoid species from the planet Brekka. The Brekkians had only one industry, that of producing the narcotic **felicium**, which the Brekkians traded with their neighbors, the **Ornarans**, in exchange for all the Brekkians' needs. ("Symbiosis" [TNG]).

***B'rel*-class Bird-of-Prey.** Small **Klingon Bird-of-Prey** with a crew of about a dozen, commonly used as a scout ship. ("Rascals" [TNG]). *We assume that the Bird-of-Prey in* Star Trek III *was a* B'rel-*class ship, while the larger versions of that ship sometimes seen on* Star Trek: The Next Generation *were* K'Vort-*class vessels.* ("Rascals" [TNG]).

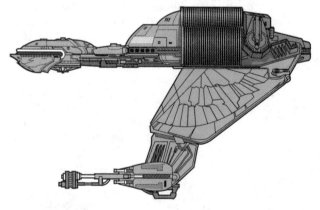

Brentalia. A protected planet that, during the 24th century, was used as a wildlife preserve. In 2368, two rare **Corvan gilvos** were being transported to Brentalia in the hopes that they would reproduce there and replenish the species. ("New Ground" [TNG]). Lieutenant Worf took his son, Alexander, to the zoo on Brentalia to see the Kryonian tigers. ("Imaginary Friend" [TNG]).

Brevelle, Ensign. (Paul Tompkins). Starfleet officer who was a crew member on the **U.S.S. Victory**, and who participated in an investigation on the planet **Tarchannen III** in 2362. In 2367, Brevelle was compelled to return to Tarchannen III, where he was transformed into a reptilian life-form native to that planet. ("Identity Crisis" [TNG]).

Briam, Ambassador. (Tim O'Connor). Representative of the **Krios** system government, assigned to the historic **Ceremony of Reconciliation** between Krios and the **Valt Minor** system, held aboard the *Starship Enterprise*-D in 2368. Briam's mission was to escort **Kamala**, a Kriosian **empathic metamorph**, to the ceremony so that she could be married to **Chancellor Alrik** of Valt. This marriage would seal the peace treaty. Briam had been selected for this assignment in part because he was 200 years old and might therefore be less likely to succumb to Kamala's considerable charms. Briam was injured by a Ferengi named Par Lenor just prior to the ceremony, but Captain Picard was able to serve in his place. ("The Perfect Mate" [TNG]).

Brianon, Kareen. (Barbara Alyn Woods). Assistant to **Dr. Ira Graves** during the final years of his life. Just prior to his death, Brianon secretly sent a distress call in an effort to get medical attention for the ailing Graves. Brianon, an attractive woman, later admitted she had been attracted to Graves, and regretted she was so much younger than he was. ("The Schizoid Man" [TNG]).

bridge. Primary command center for starships and other vessels. On most Federation starships, the bridge is located on Deck 1, at the top of the **Primary Hull**. *The Enterprise bridge was first designed by original* Star Trek *series art director Matt Jefferies. The first motion picture version was designed under the supervision of Harold Michelson (based on an earlier television version developed by Joe Jennings), while Herman Zimmerman designed the* Star Trek V *and* Star Trek VI *versions for the Enterprise-A. Zimmerman also developed the Enterprise-D bridge for* Star Trek: The Next Generation, *based on designs by Andrew Probert. Numerous other starship*

bridge sets seen on Star Trek: The Next Generation *(including the* Enterprise-C *bridge) were created by production designer Richard James. The* Enterprise *bridge has been studied numerous times by various defense and aerospace organizations as a model for an efficient futuristic control room. At least one such computerized command center has actually been built, closely based on the design of the* Enterprise *bridge. Photos: 1) Original series U.S.S. Enterprise bridge. 2) U.S.S. Enterprise bridge as refit for* Star Trek: The Motion Picture. *3) U.S.S. Enterprise-A bridge from* Star Trek V *and* VI. *4) U.S.S. Enterprise-D bridge from* Star Trek: The Next Generation. SEE: **dedication plaque**.

brig. Security detention area, used to detain individuals believed to have committed serious criminal offenses or for individuals believed to pose a serious danger to other people or to the ship itself. Secure entrance to starship brigs is often provided by a forcefield door.

Briggs, Bob. (Scott DeVenney). Director of the **Cetacean Institute** on Earth during the late 20th century. Briggs supervised the return of two **humpback whales**, **George and Gracie**, to the open ocean in 1986 because the institute could no longer afford to feed them. (*Star Trek IV: The Voyage Home*).

Bringloid V. Class-M planet in the **Ficus Sector** settled by human colonists from the **S.S. Mariposa**. The planet (and the colonists) were threatened in 2365 by massive solar flares from the system's star. ("Up the Long Ladder" [TNG]).

Bringloidi. Colonists from Earth who settled **Bringloid V**. The Bringloidi, under the leadership of colony head **Danilo Odell**, were Irish descendants who had rejected advanced technology in favor of a more agrarian lifestyle. By 2365, the Bringloidi were threatened by solar flares, so the colonists relocated on planet **Mariposa** with the assistance of *Enterprise*-D personnel. ("Up the Long Ladder" [TNG]).

Brink. First officer of the **U.S.S. Brattain**. Brink died violently, along with most of the *Brattain* crew, in 2367 when the ship was trapped in a **Tyken's Rift**, and all ship's personnel suffered from severe **REM sleep** deprivation. ("Night Terrors" [TNG]).

"Broccoli". A nickname given by Ensign Crusher to Lieutenant **Reginald Barclay**. It was not meant kindly, and was unfortunately used at the most inopportune moments. ("Hollow Pursuits" [TNG]).

Brooks, Admiral. Starfleet officer who was to head the

inquiry into Dr. Beverly Crusher's activities following the death of Dr. Reyga in 2369. ("Suspicions" [TNG]). Following the *Enterprise*-D's encounter with Third of Five, the Borg individual the crew named "**Hugh**," Captain Picard sent a detailed report to Admiral Brooks. The report detailed Hugh's reactions to captivity, his development of self-awareness, as well as Picard's decision not to use an invasive program designed to destroy the Borg collective. The report to Brooks would later cause Picard trouble with **Admiral Alynna Nechayev**, who criticized Picard's choice to return Hugh to the collective. ("Descent, Part I" [TNG]).

Brooks, Ensign Janet. (Kim Braden). An *Enterprise*-D crew member whose husband, **Marc Brooks**, died in 2367. Brooks was under the care of Counselor **Deanna Troi** following her husband's death. Despite the fact that Troi had temporarily lost her empathic powers at the time, Brooks felt that Troi helped her to deal realistically with Marc's death. ("The Loss" [TNG]).

Brooks, Marc. An *Enterprise*-D crew member who was killed in an accident in late 2366, five months before his 38th birthday. Marc's widow, **Janet Brooks**, was also an *Enterprise*-D officer. ("The Loss" [TNG]).

Brossmer, Chief. (Shelby Leverington). *Enterprise*-D transporter technician. She was at the transporter controls when Ro Laren and Geordi La Forge disappeared in an apparent transporter accident in 2368. ("The Next Phase" [TNG]).

• **"Brothers."** *Next Generation* episode #77. Written by Rick Berman. Directed by Robert Bowman. Stardate 44085.7. *First aired in 1990. Data and his brother, Lore, are both summoned to a secret location by their creator, Dr. Noonien Soong. This was the first episode written by producer-writer Rick Berman, who went on to co-create Star Trek: Deep Space Nine.* SEE: **atmosphere conditioning pumps; Casey; cove palm; Data; dilithium vector calibrations; direct transport; Kopf, Ensign; Lore; medical quarantine field; Ogus II; Potts, Jake; Potts, Willie; site-to-site transport; Soong, Noonien; Starbase 416.**

Browder IV. The *U.S.S. Hood* and the *U.S.S. Enterprise*-D were assigned to this planet for a terraforming mission on stardate 43714.1. ("Allegiance" [TNG]).

Brower, Ensign. (David Coburn). An *Enterprise*-D staff engineer. Brower was on duty when the *Enterprise*-D saved the **Argus Array** in 2367. ("The Nth Degree" [TNG]).

brown dwarf. Small celestial object similar to a star, but with insufficient mass to generate a star's powerful nuclear reactions. Because a brown dwarf might glow with only feeble infra-red light, it would be difficult to detect across interstellar distances. Data once commented that some brown dwarfs have anomalous chemical compositions including unusual depletion of europium. ("Manhunt" [TNG]).

Brown, Dr. (Harry Basch). Assistant to archaeologist **Roger Korby**. Brown may have originally been a human member of

Korby's staff, but by the time the *Starship Enterprise* arrived on a rescue mission, Brown was actually a sophisticated **android** built with the technology left over from the ancient race that lived under the surface of planet **Exo III**. The technology used to create Brown was also used to create Korby's android body. ("What Are Little Girls Made Of?" [TOS]).

Brull. (Joey Aresco). A leader of the **Gatherer** group on **Gamma Hromi II**. Proud of his maurauding lifestyle, Brull nevertheless expressed a desire to see a better life for his two sons. He agreed to conduct the *Enterprise*-D, and Acamarian Sovereign **Marouk** to talks with the leader of the Gatherers, **Chorgan**. ("The Vengeance Factor" [TNG]).

B'tardat. (Terence McNally). Science Minister of planet **Kaelon II**. In 2367, B'tardat initiated hostile action against the *Enterprise*-D when **Dr. Timicin** requested asylum aboard the ship in defiance of his planet's laws. ("Half a Life" [TNG]).

Budrow, Admiral. Commander of Starbase 29 in 2369. While being brainwashed on planet **Tilonus IV**, Commander William Riker was told by his captors that Admiral Budrow had no record of a Starfleet officer matching his description. ("Frame of Mind" [TNG]).

buffer. Cybernetic device used by the **Bynars** to transfer information to one another. The Bynars' buffers were small rectangular units worn on their belts. ("11001001" [TNG]).

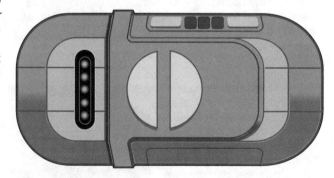

Bulgallian rat. A frightening animal. Wesley Crusher considered re-creating a Bulgallian rat on the holodeck to prepare himself for the **Psych Test** portion of the Starfleet Academy entrancy exam. ("Coming of Age" [TNG]).

bunny rabbit. Terrestrial life-form that Data claimed to see in the clouds of the **FGC-47** nebula. Guinan, on the other hand, said she saw a Samarian coral fish. ("Imaginary Friend" [TNG]).

Buran, U.S.S. Federation starship, *Challenger* class, Starfleet registry number NCC-57580. The *Buran* was one of the 39 starships destroyed by the **Borg** in the battle of **Wolf 359**.

("The Best of Both Worlds, Part II" [TNG]). *The Buran was a "kit bashed" study model barely glimpsed among the wreckage of the "graveyard" scene in that episode. The ship was named for the Russian space shuttle, which was in turn named for the Russian word for "snowflake."*

Buranian. Archaeological period classification on planet **Marlonia**. Picard mentioned that the pottery from planet Marlonia was very similar to early **Taguan** designs but was probably closer to the Buranian period instead. ("Rascals" [TNG]).

Bureau of Planetary Treaties. Branch of the Federation government that deals with interstellar agreements. When Captain James Kirk disappeared mysteriously on a diplomatic mission to planet **Gideon** in 2268, neither the Bureau of Planetary Treaties nor any other bureaucratic agency was of much help. ("The Mark of Gideon" [TOS]).

Burke, John. Chief astronomer of Earth's Royal Academy in England who first mapped the area of space around **Sherman's Planet**. For some reason, Chekov remembered him as Ivan Burkoff. ("The Trouble with Tribbles" [TOS]).

Burke, Lieutenant. (Glenn Morshower). Tactical officer aboard the *U.S.S. Enterprise*-D during the Starfleet **battle simulation** exercise in 2365. Burke unwittingly allowed Wesley Crusher to smuggle a small quantity of antimatter from the *Enterprise*-D to the *Hathaway*, giving the *Hathaway* an advantage in the war game. ("Peak Performance" [TNG]).

Burke, Yeoman. Crew member aboard the *Starship Enterprise*-A who was one of two "hit men" who carried out the assassination of Klingon **chancellor Gorkon** in 2293. Burke was later murdered, apparently by **Valeris**, in order to protect others involved with the conspiracy. (*Star Trek VI: The Undiscovered Country*).

Buruk, I.K.C. Klingon Bird-of-Prey that transported **Gowron** to the rendezvous with the *Enterprise*-D in 2367. ("Reunion" [TNG]).

Bussard collectors. Large electromagnetic devices located at the front of the warp drive nacelles of some Federation starships. The Bussard collectors created a large magnetic field used to attract interstellar hydrogen gas that could be used as fuel by the ship's fusion reactors. The *Enterprise*-D's Bussard collectors were back-flushed with hydrogen to create a dramatic but harmless pyrotechnic display that was successful in frightening the **Pakleds** when Geordi La Forge was held captive aboard the *Mondor*. ("Samaritan Snare" [TNG]). The Bussard ramscoop was again back-flushed to release a stream of hydrogen into the **Tyken's Rift** where the *Enterprise*-D was trapped in 2367. An alien ship, also trapped in the rift, was able to utilize the hydrogen to produce an explosion large enough to rupture the anomaly and allow both ships to escape. ("Night Terrors" [TNG]). *The concept of electromagnetic ramscoops being used to gather fuel for an interstellar vehicle was proposed in 1960 by physicist Robert W. Bussard, after whom the device is named.*

Butcher of Bozeman, The. SEE: **Hollander, Eli.**

"Butcher of Gallitep, The." Nickname given to **Gul Darhe'el**, brutal Cardassian commander of the infamous **Gallitep** labor camp on Bajor. ("Duet" [DS9]). SEE: **Marritza, Aamin.**

• **"By Any Other Name."** Original Series episode #50. Teleplay by D. C. Fontana and Jerome Bixby. Story by Jerome Bixby. Directed by Marc Daniels. Stardate 4657.5. *First aired in 1968. Aliens from the Andromeda Galaxy hijack the* Enterprise, *but they are unfamiliar with the human forms they have assumed for this mission.* SEE: **Andromeda Galaxy; barrier, galactic; Drea; formazine; Hanar; Kelinda; Kelva; Kelvans; paralysis field; Rigelian Kassaba fever; Rojan; Sahsheer; Saurian brandy; Shea, Lieutenant; stokaline; Thompson, Yeoman Leslie; Tomar; Vulcan mind-meld; warp drive.**

Bynars. Humanoid species from planet Bynaus. The Bynars are heavily integrated with a sophisticated planetary computer network that serves as the framework of their society. Bynars usually live and work in pairs that are electronically connected for rapid exchange of binary data.  The star **Beta Magellan**, around which Bynaus orbited, went nova in 2364, severely damaging the Bynars' planetary computer system. The Bynars attempted to steal the *Enterprise*-D in an effort to use the ship's computers to restart their own system. ("11001001" [TNG]). SEE: **buffer; Starbase 74.**

Bynaus. Planet located in the **Beta Magellan** star system, home to the **Bynars**. ("11001001" [TNG]).

C-111 Star system where planet **Beta III** was located. ("Return of the Archons" [TOS]).

Cabot, Ensign. *Enterprise*-D crew member who wanted to transfer from Quantum Mechanics to the **Stellar Cartography** department in 2369. Stellar Cartography head Neela Daren offered Ensign Cabot such a transfer without getting prior approval from Executive Officer William Riker, a significant breach of operating protocol. ("Lessons" [TNG]).

cabrodine. Common chemical explosive. A combination of cabrodine and infernite was used by **Neela** on Deep Space 9 to destroy Keiko O'Brien's schoolroom in 2369. ("In the Hands of the Prophets" [DS9]).

Cafe des Artistes. Outdoor cafe in the city of **Paris** on Earth. **Jean-Luc Picard** and the future Mrs. **Jenice Manheim** once had planned to meet there in April 2342 so that they could say goodbye, ending their romantic relationship. Picard failed to keep the rendezvous, but years later, the two re-created the cafe on the *Enterprise*-D holodeck so that they could properly bid each other adieu. ("We'll Always Have Paris" [TNG]). *The futuristic Paris skyline seen from the Cafe des Artistes was also used outside the Federation Council President's office in* Star Trek VI. *The menu at the cafe (handed out by waiter Edouard but never legible on television) included such delicacies as Croissants Dilithium, Klingon Targ ala Mode, and for dessert, L'antimatter Flambe!*

• **"Cage, The."** Original Series episode #1. Written by Gene Roddenberry. Directed by Robert Butler. No stardate given. *Captain Pike is captured by the illusion-creating Talosians, who want Pike as a prize specimen for their zoo. This was the first pilot for* Star Trek. *It was produced in 1964, rejected by the network, and was never aired in its original form. It had a significantly different cast from the series, featuring Jeffrey Hunter as Captain Christopher Pike. A second pilot episode ("Where No Man Has Gone Before" [TOS]) was produced the following year, featuring William Shatner as Captain Kirk. Portions of "The Cage" were later incorporated into the two-part episode "The Menagerie" (TOS). Years later, a restored version of "The Cage" was released on videocassette and laserdisk. "The Menagerie" won science fiction's Hugo Award for Best Dramatic Presentation in 1967.* SEE: **Boyce, Dr. Phil; Columbia, S.S.; Enterprise, U.S.S.; Haskins, Dr. Theodore; Kaylar; Keeper, the; laser weapons; Mojave; Number One; Orion animal women; Pike, Christopher; Rigel VII; Spock; Starbase 11; Talos IV; Talos Star Group; Talosians; Tango; transporter; Tyler, José; Vega Colony; Vina.**

Cairo, U.S.S. Federation starship, *Excelsior*-class, commanded by **Captain Edward Jellico**. The *Cairo* transported **Vice-Admiral Nechayev** to a rendezvous with the *Enterprise*-D in 2369 when it was

feared Cardassians were developing a metagenic weapon. ("Chain of Command, Part I" [TNG]).

Calaman sherry. Drink enjoyed by **Lieutenant Jenna D'Sora**, a crew member aboard the *Enterprise*-D. ("In Theory" [TNG]).

Calamarain. An intelligent spaceborne race that exists as powerful clouds of ionized gas. The Calamarain had some kind of prior experience with Q, and though he denied doing anything "bizarre" or "grotesque" to them, they came seeking vengeance on Q when he sought refuge on the *Enterprise*-D after he became mortal in 2366. Commander **Data** was seriously injured while protecting Q from their attack. ("Deja Q" [TNG]).

calculus. Branch of higher mathematics first devised on Earth by Isaac Newton. Aboard the *Starship Enterprise*-D, a basic understanding of calculus was regarded as essential for all children. ("When the Bough Breaks" [TNG]).

Caldonians. Humanoid race that attempted to bid for rights to use the **Barzan wormhole** in 2366. The Caldonians were large, bi-fingered humanoids with a love of pure research. **Leyor** represented his race in the negotiations for rights to the wormhole. ("The Price" [TNG]).

Caldorian eel. An animal discovered by **Klim Dokachin** in a storage locker on a freighter ship. The animal, which was four meters in length, became a pet. ("Unification, Part I" [TNG]).

Calgary. City in Alberta, Canada, on Earth. Noted for its suitability for winter sports. **Wesley Crusher** and **Joshua Albert** took a weekend trip there in 2368. ("The First Duty" [TNG]).

Calisthenics program, Klingon. A holodeck simulation program re-creating a primitive jungle setting in which the participant engages in mortal hand-to-hand combat with a number of powerful alien adversaries. **Worf** spent much of his off-duty time honing his combat skills with this program. ("Where Silence Has Lease" [TNG]). After one particularly strenuous session with this program, Worf and **K'Ehleyr** spent a night of passion together, resulting in the conception of their child, Alexander. ("The Emissary" [TNG]). Alexander even tried the program, once he was big enough to lift a *bat'telh* sword ("New Ground" [TNG]). *One of the creatures in Worf's calisthenics program used the mask of the character Skeletor from the movie* Masters of the Universe. Star Trek *makeup designer Michael Westmore also did makeup work for that film.* Star Trek *stunt coordinator Dennis Madalone played the skull monster.*

Camp Khitomer. Near the Romulan border, the site of the historic peace conference between the Klingons and the Federation in 2293. (*Star Trek VI: The Undiscovered Country*). SEE: **Khitomer**. *The Camp Khitomer scenes in* Star

Trek VI *were filmed at the Brandes Institute religious retreat in Simi Valley. The Brandes Institute was also used as the location for the Borg hall exteriors in "Descent, Parts I and II" (TNG).*

Campio, Minister. (Tony Jay). Third minister of planet **Kostolain**'s Conference of Judges. Minister Campio was engaged to marry Ambassador **Lwaxana Troi** of planet **Betazed** in 2368. Their courtship was conducted entirely by subspace radio, and they had planned to meet aboard the *Enterprise*-D just prior to their wedding. Upon meeting the ambassador, Campio

found Troi's disdain for protocol to be unacceptable. Campio abandoned the wedding when the ambassador arrived at the ceremony nude, as is required by Betazoid custom. ("Cost of Living" [TNG]). SEE: **Erko**.

Camus II. Planet that was once home to a technologically advanced society. Dr. Janice Lester and Dr. Arthur Coleman were the only two survivors of a disastrous Federation archaeological expedition at Camus II in 2269. In one of the dig sites, Lester discovered an extraordinary life-energy transfer device that she used to exchange bodies with Captain James T. Kirk. SEE: **celebium**. ("Turnabout Intruder" [TOS]). The *Enterprise*-D was scheduled to conduct an archaeological survey mission to Camus II in 2367, but had to bypass the planet when it received a distress call from the Federation freighter **U.S.S. Arcos**. ("Legacy" [TNG]).

Captain Picard's reference to bypassing an archaeological survey of Camus II in the opening captain's log of "Legacy" was an "in-joke" devised by Rick Berman, Jonathan Frakes, and Eric Stillwell. It's a tip of the hat to "Turnabout Intruder" (TOS), the 79th and last episode of the original Star Trek series, which involved an archaeological mission to Camus II. "Legacy" (TNG) was the 80th episode of Star Trek: The Next Generation.

Canar. A **Hallian** crystal artifact used to help focus thoughts. Hallians, a partially telepathic species, also use the Canar to establish a stronger emotional link during love. ("Aquiel" [TNG]).

Canopus Planet. Poet **Phineas Tarbolde**, a resident of the Canopus Planet, wrote **"Nightingale Woman"** there in 1996, considered to be one of the most passionate love sonnets written in the past couple of centuries. ("Where No Man Has Gone Before" [TOS]). *The star Canopus, also known as* **Alpha Caranae**, *is a red supergiant visible from Earth. The* Enterprise *visited the Alpha Caranae system in "The Ultimate Computer" (TOS).*

Canopus. Star used by Sulu as a navigational reference when the original *Enterprise* was thrown across the galaxy in 2267 by the advanced race known as the **Metrons**. ("Arena" [TOS]). *In real life, Canopus was used by* Voyager *and other NASA spacecraft as a navigational reference.*

Capella IV. Class-M planet that is a rich source of the rare mineral **topaline**, vital to the life-support systems of many Federation colonies. The original *Starship Enterprise* was sent to planet Capella IV in 2267 to obtain a mining agreement with the **Capellans**. The agreement was secured, although a Klingon officer attempted to gain mining rights for the Klingon Empire. ("Friday's Child" [TOS]). *Exterior planet scenes were filmed at the familiar Vasquez Rocks, located North of Los Angeles.*

Capellans. Humanoid inhabitants of planet **Capella IV**. Relatively primitive by Federation technological standards, the Capellans had a strong tribal government and a strict set of warrior mores. They considered combat more interesting than love, and did not believe in medicine, feeling that the weak should die.

Their tribal government was led by a ruler called a **teer**, who headed the Ten Tribes of Capella. A significant power struggle in 2267 resulted in the death of High **Teer Akaar** at the hands of rival **Maab**, with the support of Klingon operatives who sought to influence the outcome of **topaline** negotiations with the Federation. Maab was himself later killed, and leadership of the Ten Tribes was assumed by **Leonard James Akaar**, infant son of the late Teer Akaar. While the child was growing, Leonard James's mother, **Eleen**, ruled the Ten Tribes as regent. ("Friday's Child" [TOS]).

• **"Captain's Holiday."** *Next Generation* episode #67. Written by Ira Steven Behr. Directed by Chip Calmers. Stardate 43745.2. *First aired in 1990. Captain Picard, on vacation at a resort planet, becomes involved in archaeological intrigue with a beautiful woman named Vash.* SEE: **Ajur; Andorians; Boratus; Dachlyds; Dano, Kal; Daystrom Institute of Technology;** *Ethics, Sophistry and the Alternate Universe;* **Gemaris V;** *Horga'hn;* **hoverball; Icor IX;** *Jamaharon;* **Joval; quantum phase inhibitor; Risa; Sarthong V; Sovak; Starbase 12;** *Tox Uthat;* **Transporter Code 14;** *Ulysses;* **Vash; Vorgons; Zytchin III.**

captain's yacht. Large shuttle vehicle carried by *Galaxy*-class starships. The captain's yacht was intended for transport of dignitaries and other diplomatic functions. The yacht was a large elliptical vessel that docked at an external port on the underside of the *Galaxy*-class starship's Saucer Module. *Patrick Stewart informs us that the unseen captain's yacht aboard the* Enterprise-D *is called the* Calypso. *We believe him.*

• **"Captive Pursuit."** *Deep Space Nine* episode #6. Teleplay by Jill Sherman Donner and Michael Piller. Story by Jill Sherman Donner. Directed by Corey Allen. No stardate given. *First aired in 1993. Hunters descend on the station in search of their humanoid quarry.* SEE: **airlock; Alpha Quadrant; arva nodes; Bajoran wormhole; coladrium flow; Dabo girl; Deep Space 9; duranium ; graviton field; Hunters; neutrino; plasma injector; ramscoop; Sarda, Miss; security clearance 7; security sensor; Tosk.**

carbon reaction chambers. Engineering term used to describe carbon-lined containment vessels used in Cardassian nuclear **fusion reactors**, including those on **Deep Space 9**. ("The Forsaken" [DS9]).

carbon units. Term used by the machine life-form **V'Ger** to describe humanoid biochemical life-forms. V'Ger believed carbon units to be an inferior form of life. (*Star Trek: The Motion Picture*).

Cardassia. Homeworld of the Cardassian Union. ("The Wounded" [TNG]). Cardassia is a planet poor in natural resources, but in ancient times was home to a splendid civilization whose legendary ruins are still considered some of the most remarkable in the galaxy. Most of the archaeological treasures were plundered by starving Cardassians, as well as by the Cardassian military, which sought funds for their war against the Federation. SEE: **First Hebitian civilization**. ("Chain of Command, Part II" [TNG]).

Cardassian operation guidelines. Specifications used by the **Cardassians** providing instructions on operating procedures for station **Deep Space 9**. The station's main computer advised Chief **Miles O'Brien** to review Cardassian operational guidelines, paragraph 254-A, when increasing the **deuterium** flow to reaction chamber 2 on stardate 46925. ("The Forsaken" [DS9]).

Cardassians. Humanoid race that has been involved in a bitter, extended conflict with the **United Federation of Planets**. An uneasy truce between the two adversaries was finally reached in 2366. During the negotiations, Ambassador Spock publicly disagreed with his father, Ambassador Sarek, on the treaty. ("Unification, Part I" [TNG]).

Later that year, the treaty was violated by Starfleet **captain Benjamin Maxwell**, commanding the *Starship* **Phoenix**. Although Maxwell's actions were illegal, Starfleet authorities believed his suspicions of illicit Cardassian military activity were correct. Captain Picard recalled that while in command of the **U.S.S. Stargazer** in 2355, he had fled from a Cardassian warship, barely escaping with his ship and crew intact. ("The Wounded" [TNG]). In the past, the Cardassians were a peaceful and spiritual people. But because their planet was resource-poor, starvation and disease were rampant, and people died by the millions. With the rise of the military to power, new territories and technology were acquired by violence, at the cost of millions of lives sacrificed to the war effort. ("Chain of Command, Part II" [TNG]).

In 2367, a historic peace treaty established a fragile armistice between the Federation and the Cardassian Union. Starfleet captain **Edward Jellico** was partially credited for the negotiations. Among other things, the treaty provided that captives of either government would be allowed to see a representative from a neutral planet following their incarceration. ("Chain of Command, Part II" [TNG]).

The Cardassians annexed planet **Bajor** around 2328, and over the next several decades systematically stripped the planet of resources, and forced most **Bajorans** to resettle on other worlds. ("Ensign Ro" [TNG]).

In 2369, it was believed that Cardassia was developing a **metagenic weapon** and planning to use it in conjunction with an incursion into Federation space. *Enterprise*-D captain Jean-Luc Picard, along with Chief Medical Officer Beverly Crusher and Security Officer Worf, were sent covertly into Cardassian space to investigate. The reports were found to be a ruse, designed to lure Captain Picard into Cardassian captivity. ("Chain of Command, Part I & II" [TNG]). Also in 2369, the Bajoran resistance movement had forced the Cardassians from Bajor after years of terrorist activity. In their retreat, they abandoned **Deep Space 9**, an old Cardassian mining station orbiting Bajor. This proved to be a major misstep for the Cardassians, as the station became of major strategic, scientific, and commercial value when the Bajoran wormhole was discovered shortly thereafter. ("Emissary, Parts I and II" [DS9]). *The Cardassians first appeared in "The Wounded" (TNG), although the back story established in that episode suggests that hostilities with them go back to at least the 2350s. The Cardassians recurred in several episodes and became major adversaries in* Star Trek: Deep Space Nine.

cardiac induction. Emergency medical resuscitative measure. Cardiac induction was used on Jean-Luc Picard on stardate 45944, following his exposure to the **Kataan probe**. ("The Inner Light" [TNG]).

cardiac replacement. Surgical procedure in which a patient's diseased or injured heart is replaced by an artificial device. The technique was developed by **Dr. Van Doren**. Captain **Jean-Luc Picard** underwent a cardiac replacement procedure in 2327 and again in 2365. ("Samaritan Snare" [TNG]).

Cardies. Racist term for **Cardassians**. ("The Wounded" [TNG], "Emissary" [DS9]).

cardiostimulator. Medical instrument used by Dr. McCoy when Ambassador **Sarek** suffered cardiac arrest aboard the *Enterprise* in 2267. The cardiostimulator revived the ambassador, allowing McCoy to continue lifesaving surgery. ("Journey to Babel" [TOS]). SEE: **benjisidrine**; **cryogenic open-heart procedure**; **T-negative**.

Carema III. Planet considered by Starfleet to be a candidate for the **particle fountain** mining technology developed by **Dr. Farallon** in 2369. ("The Quality of Life" [TNG]).

Caretaker. (Oliver McGowan). Supervisor of a sophisticated **amusement park planet** in the Omicron Delta region when a landing party from the *U.S.S. Enterprise* visited in 2267. The planet had advanced hardware that could read the minds of visitors, then manufacture whatever it was they imagined. It was the Caretaker's responsibility to coordinate such activities and make sure things ran

smoothly. When it was apparent his guests were not enjoying themselves, he appeared to the *Enterprise* personnel explaining that this was an amusement park where beings could visit and play. The Caretaker agreed that the more sophisticated the mind, the greater the need for the simplicity of play. ("Shore Leave" [TOS]). SEE: **Finnegan; Police Special; Ruth; tiger; White Rabbit.**

Carmichael, Mrs. (Pamela Kosh). Landlady in 19th-century San Francisco on Earth who had the misfortune of renting an apartment to an itinerant theater group headed by a "Mr. Pickerd." The group was terribly late with its rent. ("Time's Arrow, Part II" [TNG]). *Samuel Clemens did say he would make good on the rent. We are confident that he kept his word.*

carnivorous rastipod. An animal not known for its grace or style. ("Progress" [DS9]).

Carolina, U.S.S. Federation starship that apparently sent an emergency signal to the *Enterprise* on stardate 3497. The transmission turned out to be a hoax, a Klingon attempt to prevent the *Enterprise* from returning to planet **Capella IV**. ("Friday's Child" [TOS]). SEE: *Diedre, S.S.*

Carraya System. Near the Romulan/Klingon border, the location of a secret Romulan prison camp. This camp, established several months after the **Khitomer massacre** in 2346, imprisoned nearly a hundred Klingon prisoners who had been captured, unconscious, from a perimeter outpost.  Romulan officer **Tokath** sacrificed his military career in a humanitarian gesture to establish the Carraya camp where these prisoners could be incarcerated so that the Romulan government would not execute them. In the years that followed, a peaceful coexistence developed between the Romulan jailers and their captives, whose Klingon warrior ethic would not permit them to return their to homeworld after having been captured in battle. Commander Tokath even took a Klingon woman, **Gi'ral**, as his wife, and they had a daughter named **Ba'el**, and other Klingon captives had children as well. **Worf** discovered the camp in 2369 while investigating rumors that his father might not have been killed at Khitomer. Discovering the reports to be untrue, Worf escorted some of the Klingon children, by then having reached adulthood, back to the Klingon Empire. Worf and the children all agreed never to reveal the existence of the camp to the outside world. ("Birthright, Parts I and II" [TNG]). *Worf's promise means that neither Starfleet nor the Klingon government is likely to have any record of the camp at Carraya. The exterior of the prison camp was designed by Richard James and James Magdaleno, from which a model was built that was the basis for a matte painting executed by Dan Curry.*

Carstairs, Ensign. Geologist aboard the original *Starship Enterprise.* The **M-5** multitronic computer, when being tested aboard the *Enterprise*, chose Ensign Carstairs for landing party duty on stardate 4729 to planet **Alpha Carinae II**. M-5 picked Carstairs over Senior Geologist Rawlens because the ensign had surveyed geologically similar planets for a mining company while serving in the merchant marine. ("The Ultimate Computer" [TOS]).

Cartwright, Admiral. (Brock Peters). Starfleet Command officer who presided over emergency operations from Starfleet Headquarters in San Francisco when an alien **probe** threatened the Earth in 2285. (*Star Trek IV The Voyage Home*). Politically conservative and extremely wary of the Klingon government, Cartwright opposed the peace initiative of Klingon **chancellor Gorkon**, and participated in the conspiracy with Klingon **general Chang** for Gorkon's assassination in 2293. (*Star Trek VI: The Undiscovered Country*). SEE: **Klingon Empire**.

Casey. *Enterprise*-D security person who helped Riker and Worf break onto the bridge following the lockout by Data, when Data was under Dr. **Noonien Soong**'s control in 2367. ("Brothers" [TNG]).

Castal I. The planetary site of a conflict between Federation and **Talarian** forces in the 2350s. Talarian captain **Endar**'s only son was killed in the conflict. ("Suddenly Human" [TNG]).

Castillo, Lieutenant Richard. (Christopher McDonald). The helm officer of the **Enterprise-C**. He was injured in 2344 in the battle with Romulans at **Narendra III**.  During the battle, Castillo was transported along with his ship into the future, to the year 2366, when a torpedo explosion opened up a **temporal rift**. With the disappearance of the *Enterprise*-C from its "proper" time frame, history developed in a dramatically altered manner. In this altered future, Castillo served as liaison between the *Enterprise*-C and *Enterprise*-D, working closely with tactical officer **Natasha Yar (alternate)**, with whom he became romantically involved. When it was learned that the *Enterprise*-C had to return to the past to restore the "proper" flow of history, Castillo volunteered to command the ship after the death of **Captain Rachel Garrett**. Castillo understood that returning to the past to repair history was a virtual suicide mission. ("Yesterday's *Enterprise*" [TNG]).

• **"Catspaw."** Original Series episode #30. Written by Robert Bloch. Directed by Joseph Pevney. Stardate 3018.2. *First aired in 1967. The* Enterprise *crew finds witches, black cats, and haunted castles on planet Pyris VII. This was the first episode of the original series' second season, and the first appearance of Pavel Chekov.* SEE: **Chekov, Pavel A.; DeSalle, Lieutenant; Jackson; Korob; Kyle, Mr.; Old Ones; Pyris VII; Starbase 9; Sylvia; transmuter.**

Catualla. Planet that applied for Federation membership in

2269. Catualla was home to **Tango Rad**, a follower of **Dr. Sevrin**. ("The Way to Eden" [TOS]).

causality loop. SEE: **temporal causality loop**.

• **"Cause and Effect."** *Next Generation* episode #118. Written by Brannon Braga. Directed by Jonathan Frakes. Stardate 45652.1. *First aired in 1992. The Enterprise-D is caught in a time loop, doomed to explode again and again unless a way can be found to escape.* SEE: **Adele, Aunt; Bateson, Captain Morgan;** *Bozeman, U.S.S.; deja vu;* **dekyon field;** *Enterprise*-D, *U.S.S.;* **escape pod; Fletcher, Ensign; flux spectrometer; graviton polarimeter; inertial dampers; main shuttlebay;** *nlb'poH;* **Ogawa, Nurse Alyssa; Ro Laren; shuttlebay;** *Soyuz*-class starship; temporal causality loop; Typhon Expanse; vertazine.

caviar. The unhatched eggs of a large scaleless Earth fish. Considered a culinary delicacy by some humans, and a personal favorite of Captain Picard. The captain felt that replicated caviar was not as good as the real thing, and had a few cases of real caviar from Earth stored on board his ship for special occasions. ("Sins of the Father" [TNG]).

celebium. Form of hazardous radiation that killed all but two of the scientific team on planet **Camus II** in 2269. The two survivors were **Dr. Janice Lester** and **Dr. Arthur Coleman**. Lester may have deliberately sent the other members of the team into an area where the celebium shielding was weak. ("Turnabout Intruder" [TOS]).

Celestial Temple. In the **Bajoran** religion, the Celestial Temple is a region of space where their spiritual **Prophets** reside. Some Bajorans believe the Celestial Temple is actually the **Bajoran wormhole**, and thus feel the wormhole to be sacred. Bajoran tradition holds that the Temple is the source of the nine **Orbs** sent by the Prophets to help teach the Bajoran people how to lead their lives. ("Emissary" [DS9]).

cellular disruption. Technique used to kill intruders by the image of **Losira**, defending the **Kalandan outpost** in 2268. Losira would touch her intended victim, causing individual cells to explode from within, resulting in a painful death. ("That Which Survives" [TOS]).

cellular metamorphosis. Process allowing an individual to assume another's form. After Captain **Garth** suffered an accident in the 2260s, he went to planet **Antos IV**, where the people taught him cellular metamorphosis to restore his health. He then used those techniques to take the shape of anyone he chose, giving him dangerous power in his mentally unstable state. ("Whom Gods Destroy" [TOS]). SEE: **shapeshifter**.

Celtris III. Barren, uninhabited, class-M planet located in **Cardassian** space. In 2369, Cardassian disinformation that a new **metagenic weapon** was being developed tricked Starfleet into sending a covert Starfleet team to the planet. There, Captain Jean-Luc Picard was captured. ("Chain of Command, Part I" [TNG]).

Central Bureau of Penology, Stockholm. The *U.S.S. Enterprise* transported research materials from this institution to the **Tantalus V** penal colony in 2266. ("Dagger of the Mind" [TOS]).

central control complex. Device used by the android **Norman** to control and direct the 207,809 **androids** on a planet ruled by **Harry Mudd** in 2267. ("I, Mudd" [TOS]).

Centurion. (John Warburton). Romulan officer aboard the **Romulan Bird-of-Prey** that crossed the **Romulan Neutral Zone** in 2266. Older and more experienced than most members of the crew, the centurion counseled a cautious strategy in confronting the *Enterprise* but was overruled when the politically ambitious **Decius** advocated a more provocative approach. ("Balance of Terror" [TOS]). *Centurion was a rank in the Romulan guard, approximately equivalent to a captain in the Federation Starfleet.*

Cerebus II. Planet whose natives had developed a treatment that reverses the aging process in humans. The process, involving herb and drug combinations, was very painful and had a high mortality rate. **Admiral Mark Jameson** obtained the treatment in exchange for having negotiated a treaty for that planet's government. Although the process was initially successful, Jameson eventually died of the side effects. ("Too Short A Season" [TNG]).

Ceremony of Reconciliation. A historic ceremony ending centuries of war between the star systems **Krios** and **Valt Minor**, conducted aboard the *Starship Enterprise*-D in 2368. The ceremony, which was performed in a holodeck simulation of the ancient **Temple of Akadar**, involved presentation to Valtese **chancellor Alrik** of the empathic metamorph **Kamala** to become his wife. The ceremony was almost disrupted when Kriosian **ambassador Briam** was injured, but Captain Picard was able to fulfill Briam's duties. ("The Perfect Mate" [TNG]).

Cestus III. Planet; location of a Federation outpost destroyed by the reptilian race known as the **Gorn** in 2267. The Federation had at the time been unaware that Cestus III was in space the Gorn considered to be their own territory, and that the Gorn had been protecting their own sovereignty. Unfortunately, the Gorn attack on the Federation outpost left only a single survivor. ("Arena" [TOS]). *The location for Cestus III as well as for the Metrons' planetoid was Vasquez Rocks, near Los Angeles, which was used for various television and feature productions. Other Star Trek episodes filmed there include "Shore Leave" (TOS), "The Alternative Factor" (TOS), "Friday's Child" (TOS), "Who Watches the Watchers?" (TNG), "The Homecoming" (DS9), and the feature Star Trek IV. The Cestus III outpost was actually a fort constructed for the feature The Alamo produced in the 1930s. The fort was demolished in the late 1960s because it was thought to be a* *hazardous structure in danger of collapse.*

Cetacean Institute. Aquarium and marine-biology research facility located in Sausalito on Earth in the 20th century. Kirk and Spock, traveling back in time, visited the Cetacean Institute to find two **humpback whale**s in hopes of repopulating that species in Earth's 23rd century. (*Star Trek IV: The Voyage Home*). SEE: **Taylor, Dr. Gillian**. *The Cetacean Institute scenes in* Star Trek IV *were filmed at the Monterey Bay Aquarium, which looks a lot like the Cetacean Institute except that it doesn't have a big whale tank (which was added with a bit of visual effects magic by ILM). The name had to be changed to the Cetacean Institute because it was necessary, for plot reasons, to move the location of the aquarium to Sausalito. The Cetacean Institute symbol, seen here, is actually the logo of the Monterey Bay Aquarium, even though the name was changed to protect the innocent.*

Ceti Alpha V. Fifth planet in the Ceti Alpha star system. **Khan Noonien Singh** and his followers, along with *Enterprise* historian **Marla McGivers,** were exiled to Ceti Alpha V following their attempt to commandeer the *Enterprise* in 2267. The world was described as a bit savage, somewhat inhospitable, but livable. ("Space Seed" [TOS]). Following the explosion of sister planet **Ceti Alpha VI** later that year, Ceti Alpha V became nearly uninhabitable. During the following years, twenty of Khan's followers, including Marla McGivers, were killed by deadly **Ceti eels.** Khan and his surviving followers escaped in 2285 when the planet was being surveyed by the **U.S.S. Reliant** as a possible test site for the **Genesis Project.** (*Star Trek II: The Wrath of Khan*).

Ceti Alpha VI. Sixth planet in the Ceti Alpha star system. Ceti Alpha VI exploded some six months after **Khan Noonien Singh** had been marooned on **Ceti Alpha V** in 2267. The explosion disrupted the orbit of Ceti Alpha V. (*Star Trek II: The Wrath of Khan*).

Ceti eel. The last surviving life-form indigenous to planet **Ceti Alpha V,** following the explosion of planet **Ceti Alpha VI.** Ceti eels were mollusk-like creatures whose young incubated inside the brains of humanoid life-forms. These parasites caused the host considerable pain and left the host susceptible to external suggestion. Twenty of **Khan**'s followers were killed by Ceti eels, and Khan used the creatures to gain the cooperation of Captain Terrell and Commander Chekov. (*Star Trek II: The Wrath of Khan*).

cha'DIch. Klingon term for a "second," or a person who stands with a warrior during a ceremonial challenge or trial. The duty of the *cha'DIch* is to defend the one challenged, since the one challenged is denied the right of combat while accused. **Worf** chose his brother, **Kurn,** as *cha'DIch* when their late father, **Mogh,** was accused of treason. When Kurn was the target of attempted murder, Worf asked Captain

Picard to serve as *cha'DIch.* ("Sins of the Father" [TNG]). *The ritual knife given to Picard as* cha'DIch *can be seen on the desk in his quarters during "Suddenly Human" (TNG).* **Jono** *used the knife to stab Captain Picard.*

• **"Chain of Command, Part I."** *Next Generation* episode #136. Teleplay by Ronald D. Moore. Story by Frank Abatemarco. Directed by Robert Scheerer. Stardate 46357.4. *First aired in 1993.* Picard is relieved of command and replaced with a by-the-book officer who is intent on confronting the Cardassians. SEE: *Cairo, U.S.S.;* **Cardassians; Celtris III; class-5 probe; Corak, Glin;** *Enterprise*-D, *U.S.S.; Feynman, Shuttlecraft;* **fusing pitons; Jellico, Captain Edward; Lemec, Gul; Lynars; Madred, Gul; metagenic weapon; Nechayev, Vice-Admiral Alynna; Picard, Jean-Luc;** *Reklar;* **Riker, William T.; security access code; Solok, DaiMon; Tajor, Glin; Torman V.**

• **"Chain of Command, Part II."** *Next Generation* episode #137. Written by Frank Abatemarco. Directed by Les Landau. Stardate 46360.8. *First aired in 1993.* Picard, held captive by a brutal Cardassian, is the victim of psychological and physical torture. SEE: **antimatter mines; Cardassia; Cardassians; First Hebitian civilization; Gessard, Yvette; gettle; Jellico, Captain Edward; jevonite; Jovian run; La Forge, Geordi; Lakat; Lyshan System; Madred, Gul; McAllister C-5 Nebula; Minos Korva; Orra, Jil; Picard, Jean-Luc; security access code; Seldonis IV Convention; taspar egg; Titan's Turn; Tohvun III; wompat.**

Challenger. Early space shuttle destroyed in 1986 in a tragic explosion that claimed the lives of seven astronauts shortly after launch from planet Earth. *The film* Star Trek IV: The Voyage Home, *released in 1986, bore the following dedication: "The cast and crew of* Star Trek *wish to dedicate this film to the men and women of the spaceship* Challenger *whose courageous spirit shall live to the 23rd century and beyond...." One of the shuttlepods carried aboard the* Enterprise-D *was named for* Challenger *astronaut Ellison Onizuka ("The Ensigns of Command" [TNG]).*

Chalna. Planet that was home to the race known as the **Chalnoth.** The **U.S.S. Stargazer,** under the command of Captain Picard, visited Chalna in 2354. ("Allegiance" [TNG]).

Chalnoth. The humanoid race that inhabited planet **Chalna.** The Chalnoth were very large and lupine in appearance, and anarchists by nature. Their race had no use for laws or governments; they existed by murdering those who threatened them. **Esoqq** was a Chalnoth. ("Allegiance" [TNG]).

chameleon rose. **Betazoid** flower that changes color with the mood of its owner. **Wyatt Miller** gave **Deanna Troi** a chameleon rose before their planned wedding. ("Haven" [TNG]).

chameloid. Shape-shifting life-form. **Martia,** an inmate at **Rura Penthe,** was a chameloid who seemed to enjoy taking the form of a high fashion model. (*Star Trek VI: The Undiscovered Country*). SEE: **shape-shifter.**

Champs Elysees. A landmark of the old Earth city of Paris. The Champs Elysees is a street in the old city, well known for its beautiful gardens. **Nurse Alyssa Ogawa** told Beverly Crusher that she visted a holodeck re-creation of the Champs Elysees with a gentleman friend. ("Imaginary Friend" [TNG]).

Chamra Vortex. Nebula in the Gamma Quadrant containing millions of asteroids. **Croden** of the planet **Rakhar** hid his daughter, **Yareth**, on one of of the asteroids, where she survived in a stasis chamber. Croden returned to the Chamra Vortex in 2369 with Odo on a runabout from Deep Space 9, when they revived Yareth. ("Vortex" [DS9]). SEE: *toh-maire*.

chancellor. Title given to the leader of the **Klingon High Council**. Past chancellors have included **Gorkon** and **Azetbur**. (*Star Trek VI: The Undiscovered Country*). *High Council leaders in episodes of* Star Trek: The Next Generation *have not used this title, instead being described as "council leader."*

Chandra V. The planet where **Tam Elbrun** was assigned prior to the **Tin Man** encounter in 2366. Elbrun described the Chandrans as beautiful, peaceful nonhumanoid creatures, who had a three-day ritual for saying hello. ("Tin Man" [TNG]).

Chandra. (Clara Bryant). Little girl, part of the **Wadi** game of **Chula**. Chandra sang a song and played hopscotch on **Wadi** symbols built into the floor of the game's maze. A player in Chula could only move onto the third shap, or level, by imitating her apparently nonsensical children's song and hopscotch step. ("Move Along Home" [DS9]). SEE: **allamaraine**.

Chandra. Starship captain; Chandra was one of the board members who sat in judgment at James Kirk's court-martial at **Starbase 11** in 2267. ("Court Martial" [TOS]).

Chang, General. (Christopher Plummer). Chief of Staff to Klingon **chancellor Gorkon**. A proud warrior, Chang was also fond of quoting Shakespeare and other luminaries. Chang feared the changes that peace would bring and conspired with Starfleet **admiral Cartwright** and others to assassinate Gorkon in an effort to block Gorkon's peace initiative. Chang was killed at **Khitomer** when attempting to disrupt the peace conference there in 2293. (*Star Trek VI: The Undiscovered Country*). *In addition to Chang's Shakespearean quotes, his demand in court that Kirk answer a question without waiting for a translation is a paraphrase of American ambassador Adlai Stevenson, who made the same demand of Soviet ambassador Valerian Zorin at the United Nations during the Cuban missile crisis in 1962.*

Chang, Tac Officer. (Robert Ito). Officer in charge of **Starfleet Academy** entrance examinations at the Starfleet facility on planet **Relva VII**. Chang supervised Wesley Crusher's first attempt to gain entrance to the Academy in 2364. ("Coming of Age" [TNG]). *Actor Robert Ito also played Professor Hikita in the cult classic motion picture* The Adventures of Buckaroo Banzai.

• **"Changeling, The."** Original Series episode #37. Written by John Meredyth Lucas. Directed by Marc Daniels. Stardate 3541.9. *First aired in 1967. An ancient space probe launched from Earth centuries ago returns to Federation space on a bizarre mission to search for "perfect" life.* SEE: **antigrav; "Beyond Antares"; changeling; Malurians; Malurian System; Manway, Dr.; *Nomad*; Roykirk, Jackson; Singh, Mr.; Symbalene blood burn; *Tan Ru*; Uhura; Vulcan mind-meld; warp drive.**

changeling. Ancient Earth legend of a fairy child that was left in place of a stolen human baby. The changeling took the identity of the human child. Spock compared the space probe *Nomad* to a changeling. ("The Changeling" [TOS]). **Croden** used the term, in a different context, as a nickname for the shape-shifting **Odo**. ("Vortex" [DS9]).

Channing, Dr. Federation scientist who studied warp physics. Wesley Crusher once cited Channing's belief that it might be possible to force **dilithium** to recrystallize in configurations able to better control the reactions between matter and antimatter. ("Lonely Among Us" [TNG]).

Chapel, Christine. (Majel Barrett). Nurse aboard the original *U.S.S. Enterprise* under Chief Medical Officer Leonard McCoy. Chapel gave up a promising career in bioresearch to sign aboard a starship in the hopes of finding her lost fiancé, **Dr. Roger Korby**. Chapel found Korby on planet **Exo III** in 2266, but learned he had transferred his consciousness into an

android body. Korby was destroyed by another android on that planet. ("What Are Little Girls Made Of?" [TOS]). Chapel admitted she was in love with Mr. Spock while under the influence of the **Psi 2000 virus**, although Spock did his best to ignore this. ("The Naked Time" [TOS]). Following the return of the *Enterprise* to Earth in 2270, Chapel earned a medical degree, and later returned to the *Enterprise* as a staff physician. (*Star Trek: The Motion Picture*). Chapel directed emergency operations at **Starfleet Command** when Earth was threatened in 2286 with ecological disaster by an alien space probe of unknown origin. (*Star Trek IV: The Voyage Home*). *Chapel's first appearance was in "The Naked Time" (TOS). Majel Barrett, real-life wife of Star Trek creator Gene Roddenberry, also played **Number One**, second-in-command of the Enterprise in "The Cage" (TOS), as well as the recurring character **Lwaxana Troi** in Star Trek: The Next Generation. Barrett lent her voice to the computer of both the* *original* Enterprise *and the* Enterprise*-D, as well as to the* **Companion** *("Metamorphosis" [TOS]) the* **Beta 5** *computer ("Assignment: Earth" [TOS]), and M'Ress in the animated* Star Trek. *A nurse aboard the* Enterprise*-D in "Transfigurations" (TNG) was referred to in the script as Nurse Temple (played by Patti Tippo), sort of an homage to Nurse Chapel.*

Charleston, U.S.S. Federation starship, *Excelsior* class, Starfleet registry number NCC-42285, that ferried three revived 20th-century cryonic survivors back to Earth in 2364. ("The Neutral Zone" [TNG]). SEE: **cryonics**; **cryosatellite**.

• **"Charlie X."** Original Series episode #8. Teleplay by D. C. Fontana. Story by Gene Roddenberry. Directed by Lawrence Dobkin. Stardate 1533.6. *First aired in 1966. An adolescent human boy, raised among aliens who have given him supernatural powers, finds it impossible to return to normal human society.* SEE: **Alpha V, Colony;** *Antares,* **U.S.S.; baffle plate; Evans, Charles; gymnasium; Lawton, Yeoman Tina; noncorporeal life; Ramart, Captain; Rand, Janice; Thanksgiving; Thasians; Thasus; Uhura; United Earth Space Probe Agency; Vulcan harp.**

Charybdis. Early 21st-century space vehicle launched from Earth by **NASA** on July 23, 2037, under the command of **Colonel Stephen Richey.** The *Charybdis* was the third manned attempt to travel beyond Earth's Solar System. The ship suffered a telemetry failure and its fate was unknown until 2365 when the remains of the *Charybdis* were discovered in orbit around a planet in the **Theta 116** system. ("The Royale" [TNG]). *In Greek mythology, Charybdis is one of two sea monsters who lived in a cave near the Straits of Messina. The other monster was* **Scylla,** *mentioned in "Samaritan Snare" (TNG).* SEE: Richey, Colonel Stephen.

• **"Chase, The."** *Next Generation* episode #146. Story by Ronald D. Moore & Joe Menosky. Teleplay by Joe Menosky. Directed by Jonathan Frakes. Stardate 46731.5. *First aired in 1993. Picard's old archaeology professor sends the captain on a quest to solve a four-billion-year-old mystery, a message from the first humanoid race in this part of the galaxy. This episode was in part intended to answer the question of why* Star Trek *showed so many aliens that were humanoid.* SEE: **Al-Leyan transport; Aolian Cluster; Atalia VII; B'aht Qul challenge; Data; Deep Space 4; DNA; Galen, Professor Richard; humanoid life; Indri VIII; Kea IV; Kurl; Kurlan Naiskos; Loren III; macchiato;** *Maht-H'a, I.K.C.;* **Mot; M'Tell; Nu'Daq; Ocett, Gul; Picard, Jean-Luc; Rahm-Izad system; Ruah IV; Satarrans; Sothis III; Tarquin Hill, The Master of; Vilmor II; Volterra Nebula; Ya'Seem; Yash-El, night blessing of; Yridians.**

Chateau Picard. A fine wine produced at the Picard family vineyards in **Labarre, France. Robert Picard** gave his brother, Jean-Luc, a bottle of 2347 Chateau Picard following Jean-Luc's visit home in 2367. ("Family" [TNG]).

chech'tluth. Klingon alcoholic beverage. Worf ordered some *chech'tluth* for **Bringloidi** colony leader **Danilo Odell,** who found it sufficiently potent. ("Up the Long Ladder" [TNG]).

Chekov, Pavel A. (Walter Koenig). Navigator on the original *Starship Enterprise* under the command of Captain James Kirk. Born in 2245 ("Who Mourns for Adonais?" [TOS]), Chekov held the rank of ensign during his first mission aboard the ship. ("Catspaw" [TOS]). His Starfleet serial number was 656-5827B. (*Star Trek IV: The Voyage Home*). Pavel Andreievich Chekov  was an only child, although he once imagined he had a brother named Piotr while under the influence of the **Beta XII-A entity.** ("Day of the Dove" [TOS]). While at Starfleet Academy, Chekov became involved with a young woman named **Irina Galliulin,** but the relationship did not last because Galliulin was uncomfortable with the structured way of life required by Starfleet. Years later, the two met again when Galliulin sought the mythical planet **Eden** with **Dr. Sevrin.** ("The Way to Eden" [TOS]). In 2267, Chekov was the only member of an *Enterprise* landing party to Gamma Hydra IV who was not affected with an aging disease. During the mission, Chekov became startled at the sight of a dead colonist. The surge of adrenaline protected him from radiation sickness which caused the aging process. ("The Deadly Years" [TOS]). Chekov was promoted to lieutenant and assigned as security chief aboard the *Enterprise* following the conclusion of Kirk's first five-year mission. (*Star Trek: The Motion Picture*). Chekov later served aboard the **U.S.S. Reliant** as science officer under Captain **Clark Terrell,** before returning to the *Enterprise* after the **Reliant** was destroyed at the **Mutara Nebula** by Khan. (*Star Trek II: The Wrath of Khan*). *Chekov joined the* Star Trek *cast in "Catspaw" (TOS) at the beginning of the second season, although Khan claimed to have remembered him from "Space Seed" (TOS), filmed before the character was created.*

Chekov, Piotr. Imaginary brother to **Pavel A. Chekov.** Pavel, who was an only child, believed he had a brother while under the influence of the **Beta XII-A entity** in 2268. Chekov believed this brother had been murdered by Klingons at the Archanis IV research outpost and vowed to avenge his brother's death. ("Day of the Dove" [TOS]).

Cheney, Ensign. Enterprise crew member who played the cello accompanying Data and **Neela Daren** in a concert in the Ten-Forward Lounge on stardate 46693. ("Lessons" [TNG]).

Cheron, Battle of. A crucial defeat for the **Romulan Star Empire,** ending the Romulan wars in 2160. Following this conflict, the **Treaty of Algeron** was signed, concluding peace with the Romulans and establishing the **Romulan Neutral Zone.** The Romulan government viewed the Battle of Cheron as a humiliating defeat. ("The Defector" [TNG]). *It is unclear if this battle involved the planet seen in "Let That Be Your Last Battlefield" (TOS) since the battle took place over a century prior to that episode, yet Spock was unfamiliar with Cheron in that episode.*

Cheron. Class-M planet located in the southernmost part of the galaxy, formerly home to an intelligent humanoid species. The inhabitants of Cheron, torn by racial hatreds, destroyed themselves and all life on the planet. ("Let That Be Your Last Battlefield" [TOS]). SEE: **Bele**; **Lokai**.

chess. SEE: **three-dimensional chess.**

Chicago Mobs of the Twenties. Book published in New York on Earth in 1992. A copy of this book was left on planet **Sigma Iotia II** in 2168 by the crew of the *U.S.S. Horizon*. The Iotians used this document as the pattern for their society, revering it as **The Book**. ("A Piece of the Action" [TOS]).

chief medical officer. Aboard a Federation starship, the officer charged with responsibility for the health and well-being of the ship's crew. Under certain circumstances, the CMO is authorized to certify a ship's captain as unfit for command. **Dr. Leonard McCoy** was Chief Medical Officer of the original *U.S.S. Enterprise,* while **Dr. Beverly Crusher** and **Dr. Katherine Pulaski** held that post on the *Enterprise*-D.

• **"Child, The."** *Next Generation* episode #27. Written by Jaron Summers & Jon Povill and Maurice Hurley. Directed by Rob Bowman. Stardate 42073.1. *First aired in 1988. Deanna Troi bears a child, the offspring of a mysterious alien life-form attempting to learn more about humanoid life. This episode, the first of* Star Trek: The Next Generation*'s second season, marked the first appearances of Guinan and Dr. Katherine Pulaski, the promotion of Geordi to chief engineer, Worf to security chief, and Wesley to a regular bridge officer. It had the first scenes in the shuttlebay and the Ten-Forward lounge. "The Child" was originally written for the proposed* **Star Trek II** *television series in the late 1970s.* SEE: **'audet IX; Arneb; Betazoid; cyanoacrylates; Dealt, Lieutenant Commander Hester; Delovian souffle, Eichner radiation; Epsilon Indi; Gladstone, Miss; Guinan; La Forge, Geordi; Lorenze Cluster; Mareuvian tea; Morgana Quadrant; noncorporeal life; plasma plague; Pulaski, Dr. Katherine; Rachelis system;** *Repulse, U.S.S.*; **subspace field inverter; Tango Sierra, Science Station; Ten-Forward; Troi, Deanna; Troi, Ian Andrew (junior); Troi, Ian Andrew (senior).**

Children of Tama. Name used by the **Tamarians** to describe themselves. ("Darmok" [TNG]).

Children of the Sun. Religious sect that resisted the culture and social mores of the Roman order on planet 892-IV. Banding together and living in caves, members of this underground movement called themselves the Children of the Sun, preaching brotherhood, and rejecting the 20th-century imperial Roman culture that dominated the planet. After monitoring radio transmissions from the planet, Lieutenant Uhura noted that the reference to the sun referred not to the star which the planet orbited, but to the son of God. ("Bread and Circuses" [TOS]). SEE: **892, Planet IV.**

Children's Center. Child-care facility and educational center for small children aboard the *Enterprise*-D. Activities there include ceramics classes. **Clara Sutter** met **Alexander Rozhenko** there. ("Imaginary Friend" [TNG]).

Childress, Ben. (Gene Dynarski). One of three miners on planet **Rigel XII** who attempted to swap **lithium crystals** for Mudd's women in 2266. ("Mudd's Women" [TOS]). *Actor Gene Dynarski would again be seen in "11001001" (TNG) as* **Commander Quinteros.**

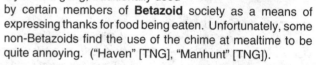

chime, Betazoid. A small, flat crystalline gong, traditionally used by certain members of **Betazoid** society as a means of expressing thanks for food being eaten. Unfortunately, some non-Betazoids find the use of the chime at mealtime to be quite annoying. ("Haven" [TNG], "Manhunt" [TNG]).

chlorinide. An extremely hazardous corrosive substance. Several cargo modules of chlorinide were being transported aboard the *Enterprise*-D on stardate 45587. A leak developed in one of the containers, dissolving part of the support shelving. Several containers fell and severely injured Lieutenant **Worf**. ("Ethics" [TNG]).

chlorobicrobes. Agricultural spray applied to a **Bajoran** bean crop to increase production. Major Kira Nerys told Bajoran farmer **Mullibok** that her father said if you wanted a bigger **katterpod bean**, you should spray the crop with chlorobicrobes. ("Progress" [DS9]).

chloromydride. A second-line pharmaceutical, used if **inaprovaline** is ineffective. ("Ethics" [TNG]).

chocolate. Confection made from roasted and ground cacao beans. Chocolate was one of **Deanna Troi**'s great passions. She preferred real chocolate to the dietetic substitutes provided by the ship's replicators. ("The Price" [TNG]). Troi never met a chocolate she didn't like. ("The Game" [TNG]). *We agree!* SEE: **Thalian chocolate mousse**.

cholera. Acute infectious enteritis, common on Earth in the 19th and 20th centuries, caused by the organism *Vibrio cholerae*. A cholera epidemic in late-19th-century San Francisco was used as a cover for a group of time-travelers from **Devidia II**. The **Devidians** used the disease to conceal their murder of many humans so that they could steal their neural energy as food. ("Time's Arrow, Parts I and II" [TNG]).

Chopin's Trio in G Minor. Musical work by noted 19th century Earth composer Frederic-Francois Chopin (1810-1849). Data, **Neela Daren,** and **Ensign Cheney** performed Chopin's Trio in G Minor in the Ten-Forward lounge on the *Enterprise*-D on stardate 46693. ("Lessons" [TNG]).

Chorgan. (Stephen Lee). The leader of the **Gatherers** from planet **Acamar III**, and a member of the **Lornack** clan. Chorgan accepted Acamarian Sovereign Marouk's offer of amnesty in 2366, ending nearly a century of interstellar piracy by the Gatherers. During the negotiations, **Yuta** of the rival clan Tralesta attempted to assassinate Chorgan. He was saved by Commander Riker's actions and later agreed to a

Gatherer truce. ("The Vengeance Factor" [TNG]).

chorus. A team of aides who provide hearing and speech for members of the ruling family of planet **Ramatis III** who are genetically incapable of hearing. The chorus communicates telepathically with their assigned family member, with each member of the chorus  representing a different part of the family member's personality. The chorus that served mediator **Riva** was killed during peace talks at planet **Solais V** in 2365. ("Loud as a Whisper" [TNG]).

Christina. Lycosa tarantula that **Miles O'Brien** found on planet Titus IV, and kept as a pet. ("Realm of Fear" [TNG]).

Christopher, Captain John. (Roger Perry). Aircraft pilot, serial number 4857932, in the United States Air Force on Earth during the 1960s. Christopher was assigned to intercept an unidentified flying object detected above the **Omaha Air Base** in mid-July 1969. The **UFO** was the *Starship Enterprise*, which had been propelled  back in time to that period. Christopher was beamed to the *Enterprise* when his aircraft was accidentally destroyed by a tractor beam. It was not realized until after he was aboard that his exposure to 23rd-century technology would be a possible source for historical contamination. The dilemma was made worse when it was learned that Christopher would father a child who would command the historically significant first **Earth-Saturn probe**. A means was later found to return Christopher to Earth without leaving any trace of the *Enterprise*'s presence. ("Tomorrow Is Yesterday" [TOS]).

Christopher, Colonel Shaun Geoffrey. Commander of the first successful **Earth-Saturn probe** and son of **Captain John Christopher**. Shaun Christopher had not yet been conceived when his father was beamed aboard the *Enterprise* in 1969 when that ship was accidentally back in the 20th century. His unborn son was the primary reason John Christopher had to be returned to Earth; failure to do so would have caused significant changes to the course of history. ("Tomorrow Is Yesterday" [TOS]). *Captain John Christopher's son was named after Star Trek writer John D.F. Black's three sons: Shaun, Geoffrey, and Christopher.*

Christopher, Dr. (John S. Ragin). Subspace theoretician and husband to Vulcan Science Academy director **Dr. T'Pan**. Christopher accompanied his wife aboard the *Enterprise*-D in 2369, to view the test of **Dr. Reyga**'s metaphasic shield. ("Suspicions" [TNG]).

chrondite. Mineral compound found in the core of an asteroid

that nearly impacted on planet **Tessen III** in 2368. ("Cost of Living" [TNG]).

chroniton particles. Subatomic particles that transmit temporal quanta. Chroniton particles were generated as a waste product by an experimental **interphase generator**-based Romulan **cloaking device**. Damage to the cloaking device would cause it to emit the particles. ("The Next Phase" [TNG]).

Chrysalians. Politically neutral race that reportedly had enjoyed peace for the past ten generations. The Chrysalians were interested in gaining rights to the **Barzan wormhole** in 2366 and retained the services of professional negotiator **Devinoni Ral** for these talks. Ral was successful in winning rights to the wormhole for the Chrysalians, but shortly thereafter, the wormhole was found to be unstable and therefore commercially worthless. ("The Price" [TNG]).

Chula. Multilevel board game played by the **Wadi**, first introduced in the **Alpha Quadrant** at Quark's bar on Deep Space 9 in 2369, shortly after first contact with the Wadi. The game required live players to navigate an elaborate labyrinth of tests as the primary player moved onyx figurines representing those players around the game board. Sisko, Kira, Dax, and Dr. Bashir were chosen to run the maze, moving into dangerous scenarios through different **shaps** or levels under Quark's overall control. The second shap featured a powerful forcefield that could only be traversed by playing hopscotch with a little girl. The third shap had a deadly Wadi cocktail party where poisonous gas threatened to suffocate the players unless they discovered the beverages were an antidote. In shap four, Bashir was eliminated as a player by a bolt of energy. Shap five injured Dax's leg in a cavern with falling rocks, and shap six saw the three players falling into a deep crevasse. The fall brought them back to Quark's, where **Falow** revealed they were never in any danger and that it was all a game. SEE: **Chandra**. ("Move Along Home" [DS9]).

Circassian cat. A domesticated animal that was **Geordi La Forge**'s first childhood pet. Geordi fondly described his pet as "funny-looking." ("Violations" [TNG]).

Cirl the Knife. Mobster on planet **Sigma Iotia II** loyal to **Jojo Krako** in 2268. At Krako's word, Cirl would use his collection of blades to persuade Krako's enemies to cooperate. ("A Piece of the Action" [TOS]).

Cirrus IV. Planetary location of the **Cliffs of Heaven**, a spectacular site for diving. ("Conundrum" [TNG]).

• **"City on the Edge of Forever, The."** Original Series episode #28. Written by Harlan Ellison. Directed by Joseph Pevney. No stardate given in episode. *First aired in 1967. McCoy, suffering from an accidental drug overdose, flees through a time portal into Earth of the 1930s, where he causes serious damage to the flow of history. This episode won the Hugo Award for Best Dramatic Presentation in 1968. Harlan Ellison's original version of the script also won the Writers' Guild of America Award.* SEE: **cordrazine; flop; Gable, Clark; Great Depression; Guardian of Forever; Keeler,**

Edith; Kirk, James T.; Kyle, Mr.; "Let me help"; McCoy, Dr. Leonard H.; mechanical rice picker; mnemonic memory circuit; Twenty-First Street Mission.

Claiborne, Billy. (Walter Koenig). Outlaw from Earth's ancient American west who fought on the side of the Clantons at the historic gunfight at **OK Corral** in 1881. Pavel Chekov portrayed Billy Claiborne in a bizarre charade created by the **Melkotians** in 2268. In actual history, Billy Claiborne survived the fight, but Chekov as Claiborne was killed by **Morgan Earp** in the Melkotian re-creation, proving that history need not repeat itself. ("Spectre of the Gun" [TOS]).

Clancy. (Anne Elizabeth Ramsay). Engineering officer aboard the *Enterprise*-D. Geordi La Forge left her in charge when he and Data went to the holodeck to run a **Sherlock Holmes** simulation. ("Elementary, Dear Data" [TNG]). She also served as Conn on the bridge during the *T'Ong* crisis. ("The Emissary" [TNG]).

Clanton, Billy. (James Doohan). Outlaw from Earth's ancient American west, and a member of the Clanton family who died at the famous gunfight at the **OK Corral** in 1881. Mr. Scott represented Billy Clanton in the bizarre charade created by the **Melkotians** in 2268. ("Spectre of the Gun" [TOS]).

Clanton, Ike. (William Shatner). Historic outlaw from the American west, and a member of the Clanton family that fought the Earps at the famous gunfight in **Tombstone, Arizona,** in 1881. Kirk was cast as Ike Clanton in the Western scenario masterminded by the **Melkotians** in 2268 as the means for his death. ("Spectre of the Gun" [TOS]).

Clark, Dr. Howard. (Paul Lambert). Anthropologist and head of the Federation science station on **Ventax II**. Dr. Clark transmitted a distress call to the *Enterprise*-D when civil unrest on the planet threatened the crew of the science station in 2367. ("Devil's Due" [TNG]).

Clarus System. Location of planet Archybite, where **Nava** took over the mining refineries. ("The Nagus" [DS9]).

class-1 sensor probe. An instrumented torpedo launched from Federation starships for investigation into areas that one might not wish to take the starship. The class-1 probe carries a very wide range of scientific sensing equipment. A class-1 probe was used by *Enterprise*-D personnel to investigate the "hole in space" created by **Nagilum** in 2365. ("Where Silence Has Lease" [TNG]). Another class-1 probe was launched into the temporal rift discovered near **Archer IV** in 2366. ("Yesterday's *Enterprise*" [TNG]).

class-4 probe. Starfleet scientific instrument used for remote sensing studies. A class-4 probe was sent into a subspace disruption near station **Deep Space 9** on stardate 46853. It was later learned this subspace disruption was a product of Jadzia Dax's imagination, generated by aliens from the **Gamma Quadrant**. ("If Wishes Were Horses" [DS9]).

class-5 probe. Medium-range reconnaissance probe, equipped with passive sensors and recording systems. In 2369, a class-5 probe was launched by the *Enterprise*-D to investigate a **Cardassian** research facility believed to be located on planet **Celtris III**. ("Chain of Command, Part I" [TNG]).

class-8 probe. An instrumented sensor probe similar to a **photon torpedo** designed for extended flight at high warp speeds. Although barely large enough to hold a person, a class-8 probe was modified to carry a single passenger when Special Federation Envoy **K'Ehleyr** was launched in the coffinlike missile for emergency transport to the *Enterprise*-D in 2365. ("The Emissary" [TNG]). *Illustration: class-8 probe.*

class-J cargo ship. A small, antiquated cargo vessel. **Harry Mudd** was piloting a class-J ship when he became caught in an asteroid belt before being rescued by the *Enterprise* in 2266. ("Mudd's Women" [TOS]).

class-K planet. Planet adaptable for humans by the use of pressure domes and life-support systems. After the *Enterprise* was sabotaged by the android **Norman** in 2267, the starship was brought to a K-type world informally known as the planet **Mudd**. ("I, Mudd" [TOS]).

class-M planet. Designation for small, rocky terrestrial worlds with oxygen-nitrogen atmospheres. *The Star Trek format calls for most stories to involve missions to class-M planets, since showing non-Earthlike planets would be far more costly. While this is probably unrealistic from an scientific point of view, it is a key reason for making the production of Star Trek practical on a television budget.*

class. Ancient naval term used to describe a group of ships sharing a common basic design. Generally, a class of ships is named by **Starfleet** after the first ship of that type built. For example, the **Constitution class** (to which the original *Enterprise* belonged) was named after the *Starship Constitution*. Other classes of Starfleet ships have included *Galaxy* class, *Excelsior* class, *Miranda* class, *Oberth* class, *Nebula* class, *Soyuz* class, *Daedalus* class, and *Ambassador* class. *Note that several graphics, readouts, and charts used in various episodes and movies have listed numerous other ship classes in an subtle effort to suggest that Starfleet has a wider range of ship designs than the studio can actually afford* to build and photograph for the show. Unfortunately, models or blueprints do not exist for most of these (since they haven't been seen), although an occasional conjectural design will show up in graphic readouts or as a desktop display model, used as set decoration. Several such designs, in the form of "study models," were used in the "graveyard" scene in "The Best of Both Worlds, Part II" (TNG), and in the junkyard of "Unification, Part I" (TNG). Some conjectural class designations include Apollo, Cheyenne, Deneva, Hokule'a, Istanbul, Korolev, Merced, New Orleans, Niagara, Renaissance, Rigel, Wambundu, and Yorkshire. SEE: **starships**.

claymore. Two-handed sword with a double-edged blade, used by Scottish Highlanders in the 16th century on Earth. Chief Engineer Montgomery Scott found a claymore in the armory when all the phasers were changed to swords by the **Beta XII-A entity**. ("Day of the Dove" [TOS]).

cleaning processor. Part of a starship's solid-waste-recycling system. The processor was used for sterilization and recycling of clothing. ("In Theory" [TNG]).

Cleary. (Michael Rougas). Engineering technician aboard the refitted *Starship Enterprise* when the ship intercepted the **V'Ger** entity in 2271. (*Star Trek: The Motion Picture*).

Clemens, Samuel Langhorne. (Jerry Hardin). (1835-1910). Noted 19th-century American author and humorist, famous for many classic novels written under the pen name Mark Twain. **Data** and **Guinan**, traveling in Earth's past, met Clemens at a literary reception hosted by Guinan. ("Time's Arrow, Part I" [TNG]). Clemens was noted for his bitingly satiric pessimism toward humanity, but this attitude may have been softened somewhat when he briefly visited the 24th century and witnessed the future of humanity as exemplified by the crew of the *Starship Enterprise*-D. ("Time's Arrow, Part II" [TNG]). *The book about time travel that Clemens describes to the reporter is* A Connecticut Yankee in King Arthur's Court, *first published in 1889.*

Clemonds, Sonny. (Leon Rippy). Country-and-western singer from late 20th-century Earth. Clemonds died of emphysema and extensive liver damage, but had arranged for his body to be cryogenically stored aboard an orbital satellite. He was revived in the year 2364 aboard the *Enterprise*-D and later returned to Earth aboard the **U.S.S. Charleston**. ("The Neutral Zone" [TNG]). SEE: **cryonics**; **cryosatellite**.

Clendenning, Dr. A resident of the **Omicron Theta** colony, killed by the **Crystalline Entity**'s attack in 2336. Clendenning used gamma radiation scans to detect decay by-products from the entity's antiproton trail. **Data**, who had records and memories from Clendenning and the other colonists, was able to build upon Clendenning's work when searching for the entity in 2368. ("Silicon Avatar" [TNG]).

Cleponji. An ancient **Promellian** battle cruiser discovered intact in the asteroid belt near **Orelious IX** by the *Enterprise*-D in 2366. Although the war between the Promellians and the **Menthars** had destroyed both civilizations a thousand years ago, the *Cleponji* survived in nearly perfect condition, surrounded by the deadly **aceton assimilators** that killed its crew. The *Cleponji* was destroyed by the *Enterprise*-D in a torpedo spread designed to destroy the aceton assimilators. ("Booby Trap" [TNG]). *The Promellian battle cruiser was designed and built by Tony Meininger.*

Cliffs of Heaven. Location on planet Cirrus IV that is renowned as a spot for diving. Holodeck program 47-C is a simulation of this spectacular site. Enterprise-D crew member **Kristin** *(no last name given)* hurt herself twice in this program, so Dr. Crusher recommended she tackle the **Emerald Wading Pool** on Sumiko III instead. ("Conundrum" [TNG]).

cloaking device. An energy screen generator used to render an object (typically, a space vehicle) invisible to the eye and to most sensor systems. Most cloaking devices require so much power that a vessel so equipped cannot use weapons systems without decloaking. Romulan and Klingon spacecraft are often equipped with cloaking devices, although Federation ships are prohibited from doing so under the terms of the **Treaty of Algeron**. ("Pegasus" [TNG]).

cloaking device, Aldean. An immensely powerful forcefield that effectively rendered the entire planet of **Aldea** invisible from space. Used to isolate the peaceful inhabitants of that planet, the Aldean cloaking device worked for millennia before defensive shields caused damage to the planet's **ozone** layer. ("When the Bough Breaks" [TNG]). SEE: **Aldea**.

cloaking device, Klingon. The Klingons apparently obtained basic cloaking technology from the Romulans around 2268, when an alliance existed between the Klingons and the **Romulans**. Many Klingon ships, including their Birds-of-Prey (apparently also based on Romulan technology, judging from the name), were equipped with cloaking devices. (*Star Trek III: The Search for Spock*). An experimental **Klingon Bird-of-Prey** was developed, circa 2293, which had the ability to fire torpedoes while still cloaked. This would have provided a significant tactical advantage, had means not been developed to detect a ship so equipped. (*Star Trek VI: The Undiscovered Country*). *We assume that cloaking devices are continually being improved, as are the sensor systems used to detect them. For this reason, any advance in either cloaking or sensing technologies seems to provide only a brief advantage until the other side catches up.*

cloaking device, Romulan. The first known example of a practical cloaking device was on a **Romulan Bird-of-Prey** that crossed the **Romulan Neutral Zone** in 2266. ("Balance of Terror" [TOS]). An improved cloaking device used by Romulan warships in 2268 was of sufficient concern to the Federation that Kirk and Spock were sent on a covert mission into Romulan

territory to steal one such unit for analysis by Starfleet scientists. ("The *Enterprise* Incident" [TOS]). SEE: **Romulan commander**. Although the Romulans are continually improving their cloaking technology, Federation innovations such as the **tachyon detection grid** technique developed by Geordi La Forge in 2368 serve to reduce the tactical effectiveness of cloaked ships. ("Redemption, Part II" [TNG]). Defensive shields are also inoperative when a ship is cloaked. ("Face of the Enemy" [TNG]). An experimental cloaking device, based on an **interphase generator**, was developed by Romulan scientists and tested in 2368. ("The Next Phase" [TNG]). *Gene Roddenberry once indicated that "our people are scientists and explorers — they don't go sneaking around." We therefore assume Starfleet has a policy against such things, a theory supported by "Pegasus" (TNG) which establishes that the Federation relinquished the right to develop or use such devices under the* **Treaty of Algeron**.

clone. Asexual reproduction technique in which the DNA of a parent organism is used to grow a genetically identical copy of that organism. Cloning was used to populate the **Mariposa** colony because their initial population base was too small to form an effective gene pool. ("Up the Long Ladder" [TNG]). SEE: **replicative fading**. In 2369, a man named **Ibudan** created a clone of himself, then killed it to frame Deep Space 9 security chief **Odo** for murder. ("A Man Alone" [DS9]).

• **"Cloud Minders, The."** Original Series episode #74. Teleplay by Margaret Armen. Story by David Gerrold and Oliver Crawford. Directed by Jud Taylor. Stardate 5818.4. *First aired in 1969. Kirk and Spock must deal with terrorists striking at the beautiful cloud city Stratos.* SEE: **Ardana; Disrupters; Droxine; filter masks; Merak II; Midro; mortae; Plasus; protectors; Stratos; Troglytes; Vanna; zenite.**

Cloud William. (Roy Jenson). Leaders of the **Yangs** on planet **Omega IV** in 2268, known among his people as the son of chiefs, guardian of the holies, and speaker of the holy words. ("The Omega Glory" [TOS]).

cloud creatures. SEE: **Beta Renna cloud; Companion; Dal'Rok; dikironium cloud creature; mellitus; Nagilum; noncorporeal life.**

• **"Clues."** *Next Generation* episode #88. Teleplay by Bruce D. Arthurs and Joe Menosky. Story by Bruce D. Arthurs. Directed by Les Landau. Stardate 44502.7. *First aired in 1991. When the* Enterprise-D *falls through a wormhole, a lot of little clues just don't add up.* SEE: **Data; Diomedian scarlet moss; Evadne IV; Gloria; Harrakis V; Hill, Dixon; Locklin, Ensign; Madeline; McKnight, Ensign; Ngame Nebula; Ogawa, Nurse Alyssa; Paxans; T-tauri type star system; Tethys III;** *Trieste, U.S.S.;* **Underhill, Pell.**

Cluster NGC 321. Location of planets **Eminiar VII** and **Vendikar**. The *Enterprise* was sent there to open diplomatic relations with Eminiar VII in 2267. ("A Taste of Armageddon" [TOS]). *NGC stands for New General Catalog of nebulae and star clusters, an actual list of objects visible from Earth, compiled in the late 19th century by astronomer J.L.E. Dreyer.*

CMO. SEE: **chief medical officer**.

co-orbital satellites. A pair of objects (such as planetoids) whose orbits are very close to each other. Under certain circumstances, a near collision between the two bodies can result in each object assuming the orbit previously occupied by the other. In other words, the two objects trade orbits. Data described the process to Picard and Lwaxana Troi. ("Manhunt" [TNG]).

coalescent organism. Rare microscopic life-forms that absorb other organisms, then assume the form of the organism they've absorbed, right down to the cellular level. On a larger scale, this is essentially a shape-shifter. **Lieutenant Keith Rocha** was apparently killed by a coalescent organism just prior to his assignment to **Relay Station 47** in 2369. The organism assumed Rocha's form, and later threatened **Lieutenant Aquiel Uhnari**, and killed her dog, Maura. ("Aquiel" [TNG]).

Coalition. One of the two main rival factions in control of the colony on planet **Turkana IV** following the collapse of the colonial government in 2337. Led by **Hayne**, the Coalition offered assistance to the *Enterprise*-D crew in their mission to rescue the crew of the freighter *Arcos* in 2367. **Ishara Yar** was a member of the Coalition. ("Legacy" [TNG]).

Cochrane deceleration maneuver. Classic battle tactic used by the *Enterprise* to defeat the Romulans at Tau Ceti. When Captain **Garth** impersonated Kirk at the **Elba II** penal colony in 2268, Spock asked the two to identify the maneuver in hopes of differentiating the two. The attempt was unsuccessful because the maneuver was so well known that any starship captain would know of it. ("Whom Gods Destroy" [TOS]). *It is possible that this Romulan defeat may have been the incident depicted in "Balance of Terror" (TOS), but this is unclear.*

Cochrane distortion. A characteristic fluctuation in the phase of a subspace field generated by a starship's warp engines. ("Ménage à Troi" [TNG]).

Cochrane, Zefram. (Glenn Corbett). Discoverer of the space warp (2030-2117?). Cochrane became one of history's most renowned scientists when he revolutionized space travel in 2061 with the invention of the **warp drive**, making faster-than-light travel possible. Zefram Cochrane disappeared from Alpha Centauri in 2117 at the age of 87 and is presumed to have died in space.  *In 2267, Cochrane was discovered by Captain Kirk to be living on an planetoid in the* **Gamma Canaris region** *with the cloud creature known as the Companion, who loved him. Traveling along with Kirk was Federation* **commissioner Nancy Hedford**, *dying of* **Sakuro's disease**. *Hedford merged with the Companion, choosing to remain with Cochrane, where they would both live the remain-*

der of a normal human life span. Kirk promised never to reveal Cochrane's fate, so the main body of this entry indicates uncertainty about what happened to the famous scientist. ("Metamorphosis" [TOS]). SEE: **millicochrane**. The first test of **soliton wave** based propulsion in 2368 was likened to Cochrane's breakthrough. ("New Ground" [TNG]).

Code 1 Emergency. Federation signal for a total disaster, requiring an immediate response. **Nilz Baris** sent a Code 1 Emergency call to the *U.S.S. Enterprise* from **Deep Space Station K-7**. ("The Trouble with Tribbles" [TOS]).

Code 1. Starfleet designation for a declaration of war. In 2267 the *Enterprise* received a Code 1 message from Starfleet Command stating they were at war with the Klingon Empire. The starship then proceeded to planet **Organia**, where the Klingons were expected to strike. ("Errand of Mercy" [TOS]).

Code 2. Starfleet encryption protocol that the Romulans had broken as of 2267. While under the affects of the aging disease acquired on planet **Gamma Hydra IV**, Kirk ordered a message sent using Code 2, forgetting that Romulan intelligence had broken that code. After he was cured of the illness, he again used Code 2, but intended the Romulans to understand what he was saying. ("The Deadly Years" [TOS]). SEE: **corbomite**.

Code 47. Term designating a Starfleet subspace communiqué of extremely high sensitivity or secrecy. Code 47 messages are intended only for the eyes of a starship captain, and voiceprint identification is required. Further, no computer records are maintained of Code 47 transmissions. **Walker Keel**'s message to Picard requesting a meeting at planet **Dytallix B** was a Code 47 signal, although the conspirators got wind of it anyhow. ("Conspiracy" [TNG]).

Code 710. Interstellar code prohibiting a spacecraft from approaching a planet. The *Enterprise* received a Code 710 from planet **Eminiar VII** in 2267. ("A Taste of Armageddon" [TOS]).

Code Factor 1. Starfleet code meaning invasion status. An unexplained time-warp distortion that swept across the galaxy in 2267 caused Starfleet Command to issue a Code Factor 1. ("The Alternative Factor" [TOS]). SEE: **Lazarus**.

• **"Code of Honor."** *Next Generation* episode #4. Written by Katharyn Powers & Michael Baron. Directed by Russ Mayberry. Stardate 41235.25. *First aired in 1987. Tasha Yar is kidnapped in a planetary struggle for political power.* SEE: **Anchilles fever; First One; *glavin*; Hagon; Ligon II; Ligonians; Lutan; Starbase 14; Styris IV; Yareena.**

Code One Alpha Zero. Signal indicating the discovery of space vehicle in distress. Riker issued a Code One Alpha Zero following the detection of an automated distress signal from the *U.S.S. Jenolen*. ("Relics" [TNG]).

coded transponder frequency. A specific subspace frequency and code that activated a starship's transponder to send back its identifying code, permitting allied vessels and authorities to accurately track the ship. When **Captain Benjamin Maxwell**, commanding the *U.S.S. Phoenix*, made an unauthorized attack on a **Cardassian** ship in 2367, **Gul Macet** asked for the *Phoenix*'s coded transponder frequency so that other Cardassian ships could track the *Phoenix*. Ironically, the Federation Starfleet already possessed the ability to track Cardassian ships using Cardassian transponder codes. ("The Wounded" [TNG]). *One would assume the Cardassians changed all their transponder codes after this.*

"Cogito ergo sum." "I think, therefore I am." A truism written by Earth philosopher Descartes. The computer intelligence version of **Professor James Moriarty** quoted this phrase before attempting to exit the holodeck on his own volition. ("Ship in a Bottle" [TNG]).

Cogley, Samuel T. (Elisha Cook). Attorney who successfully defended **James Kirk** in 2267 when Kirk was accused of the murder of **Ben Finney**. At the court-martial on **Starbase 11**, Cogley petitioned to hold the trial on the *Starship Enterprise*, on the grounds that Kirk had the right to face his accuser, in this case the *Enterprise* computer. Cogley proved that a computer malfunction, deliberately caused by Finney, had wrongly implicated Kirk. Cogley had a love of old books, and shunned the use of computers whenever possible. Cogley later defended Ben Finney. ("Court Martial" [TOS]).

coherent graviton pulse. Energy waves that can neutralize tetryon emissions. ("Schisms" [TNG]). SEE: **tetryon particles.**

coladrium flow. Term in an unknown alien language for tenuous space matter collected by **arva nodes** in **Tosk**'s ship converting the interstellar hydrogen into usable fuel. ("Captive Pursuit" [DS9]). SEE: **ramscoop.**

Cold Moon Over Blackwater. Gothic novel enjoyed by **Lieutenant Aquiel Uhnari**. ("Aquiel" [TNG]).

cold, common. An infection of the upper respiratory tract caused by any of over 200 viruses in many humanoid species. By the 24th century, the common cold was a curable ailment. ("The Battle" [TNG]). *McCoy noted in "The Omega Glory" (TOS) that the common cold had not yet been cured by that point in the 23rd century.*

coleibric hemorrhage. Cause of death of the infamous Cardassian **Gul Darhe'el**, who died in 2363. ("Duet" [DS9]).

Coleman, Dr. Arthur. (Harry Landers). Physician who was one of two survivors of a disastrous scientific expedition to planet Camus II in 2269. Shortly after the death of his colleagues, Coleman conspired with Dr. Janice Lester, the other survivor, to use a life-energy transfer device to place

Lester's mind into the body of Captain James Kirk, and to trap Kirk's mind in Lester's body. Coleman, who was in love with Lester, indicated he would care for her after it was discovered she was insane at the time she caused the deaths on Camus II. ("Turnabout Intruder" [TOS]).

colgonite astringent. Beauty treatment offered in the barber shop aboard the *Enterprise*-D. Beverly Crusher was an occasional user of the treatment. ("The Host" [TNG]).

collar of obedience. Neck bands worn by the **drill thralls** on planet **Triskelion** that tightened when the thrall disobeyed an order. Each collar was coded with a specific color that signified which **Provider** owned that particular drill thrall. ("The Gamesters of Triskelion" [TOS]).

collective consciousness. SEE: **Borg; Borg collective**.

Collins, Ensign. (Harley Venton). Transporter technician aboard the *Enterprise*-D. Collins was on duty when an away team beamed down to meet **Bajoran** leader **Orta** in 2368. ("Ensign Ro" [TNG]).

Colt Firearms. Nineteenth-century Earth weapons manufacturing company, founded in 1847 by Samuel Colt. The company was famous for handheld weapons, including the double-action cavalry pistol discovered in 2368 in a cavern on Earth. ("Time's Arrow, Part I" [TNG]).

Coltar IV. Planet with a farming colony that experienced a "hiccough" in time that was found to be the result of **Dr. Paul Manheim**'s time/gravity experiments at **Vandor IX** in 2364. ("We'll Always Have Paris" [TNG]).

***Columbia*, S.S.** Federation science vessel. The *Columbia* made a forced landing on planet **Talos IV** in 2254. The only survivor was a crew member named **Vina**, who was cared for by the natives of that planet. ("The Cage," "The Menagerie, Part I" [TOS]).

***Columbus*, Shuttlecraft.** Registry number NCC-1701-2. Shuttle attached to the original *Starship Enterprise*. This vehicle participated in a visual search for the **Shuttlecraft Galileo**, after the *Galileo* crashed on planet **Taurus II** in 2267. ("The *Galileo* Seven" [TOS]). *Named for terrestrial explorer Christopher Columbus (1451-1506).*

Comic, The. (Joe Piscopo). An unnamed 20th-century comedian re-created on the holodeck of the *Enterprise*-D by Data, who had hoped to learn the concept of humor. Although The Comic tutored Data in stand-up comedy, the android found the concept difficult to grasp. The Comic's holodeck program was RW-93216. ("Where Silence Has Lease" [TNG]). *The holodeck program menu used by Data to select this simulation identified the comic's name as Ron Moore. By*

amazing coincidence, Visual Effects Coordinator Ron Moore was one of the people who assembled the computer graphic on that holodeck readout.

• **"Coming of Age."** *Next Generation* episode #19. Written by Sandy Fries. Directed by Mike Vejar. Stardate 41416.2. *Originally aired in 1988. Wesley Crusher fails his first attempt to gain entry into Starfleet Academy. "Coming of Age" marks the first appearance of a shuttlecraft in* Star Trek: The Next Generation. SEE: **Beltane IX; Benzar; Bulgallian rat; Chang, Tac Officer; Crusher, Wesley; hyperspace physics test; Kurland, Jake; Mirren, Oliana; Mordock Strategy; Mordock; Picard, Jean-Luc; Psych Test; Quinn, Admiral Gregory; Relva VII; Remmick, Dexter; Rondon; Shuttlecraft 13; T'Shanik; Vulcana Regar; Zaldans.**

commodore. Title formerly given to high-ranking Starfleet officers such as those in charge of a starbase. *The term commodore, used in the original* Star Trek *series, has fallen into disuse in* Star Trek: The Next Generation *and* Star Trek: Deep Space Nine.

communicator. Personal communications device used by Starfleet personnel. Communicators provided voice transmission from a planetary surface to an orbiting spacecraft, and between members of a landing party. Communicators also provided a means for a ship's transporter system to determine the exact coordinates of a crew member for transport back to the ship. Early versions of the communicator were compact handheld units with a flip-up antenna grid.

1)

When the communicator was first "invented" in 1964, it seemed incredibly compact and amazingly advanced. Few would have believed back then that Star Trek would still be on the air when portable cellular telephones, the same size as those original props, became a reality.

Starfleet briefly used wrist communicators, but more recent units have been incorporated into the Starfleet insignia worn on each crew member's uniform and had a dermal sensor that can be used to restrict usage to one authorized individual only. **Roga Danar**, fleeing from security confinement aboard the *Enterprise*-D, successfully bypassed this restriction by using an unconscious security officer's own finger to activate his communicator. ("The Hunted" [TNG]). The device is constructed of a crystalline composite of silicon, beryllium, carbon-70, and gold. ("Time's Arrow, Part I" [TNG]). *Illustrations: 1) Starfleet communicator, circa 2266. 2) Starfleet wrist communicator, circa 2271. 3) Starfleet insignia communicator, circa 2364.*

Companion. Cloudlike life-form that lived on a planetoid in the **Gamma Canaris region**. In 2117, the Companion discovered aged scientist **Zefram Cochrane** drifting in space, near death. The Companion brought Cochrane to her planetoid and cared for him, rejuvenating his body, giving him effective immortality, but subjecting him to extreme loneliness. Over time, the Companion grew to love Cochrane. In 2267, the Companion abducted Kirk, Spock, McCoy, and Federation **commissioner Nancy Hedford** from the *Enterprise* **shuttlecraft** *Galileo* to live with Cochrane to alleviate his isolation. Hedford, terminally ill with **Sakuro's disease**,

2)

3)

agreed to merge with the Companion, becoming a single, human individual. The resulting individual, still in love with Cochrane, remained with Cochrane on the planetoid for the rest of a normal human lifetime. ("Metamorphosis" [TOS]). *The Federation remained unaware of Cochrane's fate and of the existence of the Companion because of Kirk's promise to Cochrane. The Companion was designed by future Star Wars Oscar-winner Richard Edlund at Westheimer photographic effects company.*

compressed teryon beam. Weapon used by the **Lenarians** to attack an *Enterprise*-D away team in 2369. Captain **Jean-Luc Picard** caught the full effect of the weapon, which fused the bio-regulator in his artificial heart, damaged his spleen and liver, and nearly killed him. ("Tapestry" [TNG]).

Compton. (Geoffrey Binney). Starship *Enterprise* crew member who was subjected to biochemical **hyperacceleration** on planet **Scalos** in 2268 when exposed to Scalosian water. Because the **Scalosian** males were sterile, Compton was to be used for reproduction but he quickly sustained cellular damage, resulting in his death. ("Wink of an Eye" [TOS]).

computer core. One of three large, redundant cylindrical chambers aboard a *Galaxy*-class starship, housing the ship's primary computer hardware. The upper core of the *Enterprise*-D was taken over by sentient **nanites** when that newly created race was exploring the ship in 2266. ("Evolution" [TNG]). *The computer core set was also used in "The Bonding" (TNG) for Worf and Troi's talk.*

Condition Green. Covert Starfleet code used to secretly indicate on a clear channel that the speaker is being held captive. Captain Kirk relayed this code to Mr. Scott when Kirk was being held captive on planet 892-IV in 2267. Condition Green also prohibits the listener from taking any action such as a rescue mission. ("Bread and Circuses" [TOS]).

conference lounge. SEE: **observation lounge.**

confinement beam. SEE: **annular confinement beam.**

confinement mode. SEE: **isolation protocol.**

Conklin, Captain. Commander of the Federation starship *Magellan*. ("Starship Mine" [TNG]).

conn. Abbreviation for **flight controller**.

Conor, Aaron. (John Snyder). The leader of the isolated **Genome Colony** on **Moab IV**. Like everyone in the carefully planned colony, Conor was genetically engineered and trained for his specific job. When tidal forces from a **stellar core fragment** threatened to disrupt the planet and destroy his colony in 2368, Conor was faced with an impossible choice.

If he accepted an offer of help from engineers aboard the *Enterprise*-D, he risked serious cultural contamination of his totally isolated colony. The alternative of rejecting outside help would have led to near-certain destruction of the colony. Conor chose to allow the *Enterprise*-D to help, but had to deal with the social consequences of their aid. ("The Masterpiece Society" [TNG]). SEE: **Bates, Hannah**; **Benbek, Martin**.

• **"Conscience of the King, The."** Original Series episode #13. Written by Barry Trivers. Directed by Gerd Oswald. Stardate: 2817.6. *First aired in 1966. Kirk suspects that a distinguished Shakespearean actor may have been an infamous mass murderer many years ago. The episode's title is a quote from Shakespeare's* Hamlet. SEE: **Astral Queen; Benecia Colony; "Beyond Antares"; Cygnia Minor; Daily, Jon;** *Hamlet;* **Karidian Company of Players; Karidian, Anton; Karidian, Lenore; Leslie, Mr.; Kirk, James T.; Kodos the Executioner; Leighton, Dr. Thomas; Leighton, Martha; Molson, E.; Q, Planet; Riley, Kevin Thomas; Saurian brandy; Shakespeare, William; Tarsus IV; tetralubisol; Uhura; Vulcan harp.**

• **"Conspiracy."** *Next Generation* episode #25. Story by Robert Sabaroff. Teleplay by Tracy Tormé. Directed by Cliff Bole. Stardate 41775.5. *First aired in 1988. Starfleet Command is infiltrated by alien parasites. The conspiracy in this episode was first alluded to in "Coming of Age" (TNG). "The Drumhead" (TNG) established that Admiral Norah Satie helped uncover the conspiracy.* SEE: **Aaron, Admiral; Altarian Conference; Andonian tea; Bolians; Code 47; Crusher, Dr. Beverly; Delaplane, Governor; Dytallix B;** *Horatio, U.S.S.;* **Karapleedez, Onna; Keel, Walker; McKinney; Mira system; Pacifica; Quinn, Admiral Gregory; Remmick, Dexter;** *Renegade, U.S.S.;* **Rixx, Captain; Satie, Admiral Norah; Savar, Admiral; Scott, Tryla; Sipe, Ryan; Starbase 12; Starfleet Headquarters; Tau Ceti III;** *Thomas Paine, U.S.S.*

Constable. Affectionate nickname for **Deep Space 9** security chief **Odo**. ("Emissary" [DS9]).

Constantinople, U.S.S. Federation starship, *Istanbul* class, registry number NCC-34852. The *Constantinople* suffered a hull breach near **Gravesworld** while carrying some 2012 colonists in 2365. *Enterprise*-D conducted a rescue mission to save that ship's crew. ("The Schizoid Man" [TNG]). *Named for the Turkish city also known as Istanbul.*

Constantinople. City in Europe on planet Earth where, in 1334, the bubonic plague decimated the population. The (nearly) immortal **Flint** was in Constantinople at the time of that tragedy. ("Requiem For Methuselah" [TOS]).

Constellation-class starship. Type of Federation spacecraft to which Picard's former command, the *Stargazer,* belonged. Similar in overall size to the *Constitution*-class ship, the *Constellation*-class ships were equipped with four warp nacelles and were thus suited for deep-space exploration and defensive patrol duties. Ships of this type have included the *Stargazer, Hathaway, Victory,* and the *Constel-*

lation, after which the class is named. ("The Battle" [TNG]). *The first* Constellation*-class ship seen,* Stargazer *was originally planned to be a* **Constitution-class** *ship, allowing our visual effects staff to make use of the existing movie* Enterprise *model. Our producers did not make the decision to build a new model for the* Stargazer *until after the episode was filmed with LeVar Burton calling it a* Constitution*-class ship. The choice of the name* Constellation *was based largely on the fact that it could be dubbed over Geordi's line since the two words are so similar. One might conjecture that this U.S.S.* Constellation *was named in honor of* **Matthew Decker***'s ship, destroyed in "The Doomsday Machine" (TOS).*

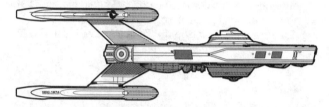

Constellation, U.S.S. Federation starship, *Constitution* class, Starfleet registry number NCC-1017, commanded by **Commodore Matt Decker**. The *Constellation* was heavily damaged in 2267 near system **L-374** by an extragalactic **planet killer** weapon. The planet killer destroyed the planets in system L-374, including a planet where the crew of the *Constellation* had taken refuge. *Enterprise* personnel programmed the hulk of the *Constellation* to self-destruct its **impulse drive** inside the planet killer, destroying the robotic weapon. ("The Doomsday Machine" [TOS]). *The miniature* Constellation, *identical in design to the original* Enterprise, *was an AMT plastic* Enterprise *model kit, appropriately burnt and scorched. The Starship* Constellation *was presumably replaced by a starship of a new design that was the prototype for the* Constellation *class, of which Picard's* **U.S.S. Stargazer** *was a member.*

Constitution-class starship. One of Starfleet's most famous vehicles, the *Constitution*-class starships included the acclaimed original *U.S.S. Enterprise.* During the time of Captain Kirk's celebrated first five-year mission of exploration, only twelve of these ships were in existence. ("Tomorrow is Yesterday" [TOS]). *Constitution*-class starships commissioned by Starfleet included: *Constellation* (NCC-1017), *Constitution* (NCC-1700), *Defiant* (NCC-1764), *Eagle* (NCC-956), *Endeavour* (NCC-1895), *Enterprise* (NCC-1701), *Essex* (NCC-1697), *Excalibur* (NCC-1664), *Exeter* (NCC-1672), *Hood* (NCC-1703), *Intrepid* (NCC-1831), *Lexington* (NCC-1709), *Potemkin* (NCC-1657), *Republic* (NCC-1371), and *Yorktown* (NCC-1717). *Constitution*-class ships used **duotronic** com-

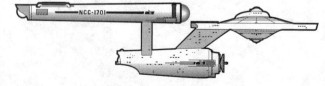

puters, based on designs developed by **Dr. Richard Daystrom** in 2243. ("The Ultimate Computer" [TOS]).

The registry number of the Constitution *(NCC-1700) is from one of Scotty's technical manual screens in "Space Seed" (TOS). Since the class ship has a 1700 number, it would seem only reasonable that the other ships of the class would have higher, possibly even sequential numbers. Unfortunately, the U.S.S.* Constellation *("The Doomsday Machine" [TOS]), bore a much lower number, NCC-1017, (obviously because it was a simple rearrangement of the decal sheet from the AMT* Enterprise *model kit) and the* Republic *was designated as NCC-1371. These data points suggest the* Constitution-*class ships had registry numbers that not only varied widely in range, but also could* not *be sequential. Modelmaker Greg Jein (through an amazingly complex and admittedly only barely logical means) managed to match up the various* Constitution *ships with the starship status chart in Commodore Stone's office in Starbase 11, seen in "Court Martial" (TOS).*

Most of these registry numbers are from Greg's conjectural list, although several are from various Starfleet charts and readouts in Star Trek VI. *Several of the* Constitution-*class ships listed above are not from any episode or movie, but are from the original* Star Trek *production office's starship list in Steven Whitfield's book,* The Making of Star Trek.

Constitution of the United Federation of Planets. Historic document framed in 2161, outlining the framework by which the Federation is governed for the mutual benefit and protection of member planets and individual citizens. Among the assurances of individual civil liberties contained in the Constitution is the **Seventh Guarantee**, protecting citizens against self-incrimination. ("The Drumhead" [TNG]). All persons aboard a Federation starship are guaranteed these fundamental individual rights under the Constitution. ("The Perfect Mate" [TNG]).

construction module. Remotely controlled robotic device used for construction in free space. Construction modules were used in 2367 to attach small propulsion units to a dangerously radioactive spacecraft in orbit of **Gamelan V** in the hopes that they could push the craft into the Gamelan sun. The attempt, engineered by *Enterprise*-D personnel, was unsuccessful. ("Final Mission" [TNG]).

• **"Contagion."** *Next Generation* episode #37. Written by Steve Gerber & Beth Woods. Directed by Joseph L. Scanlan. Stardate 42609.1. *First aired in 1989. An ancient computer software weapon destroys the* Starship Yamato *and threatens the* Enterprise-D *and a Romulan ship. Picard first orders "Tea, Earl Grey, hot" in this episode.* SEE: **antimatter containment; archaeology; "Demons of Air and Darkness"; Denius III; Dewan; Dinasian;** *Galaxy*-**class starship;** *Haakona*; **Iccobar; Iconia; Iconian computer weapon; Iconians; magnetic seals; Neutral Zone, Romulan; Picard, Jean-Luc; Ramsey, Dr.; Taris, Subcommander; Varley, Captain Donald;** *Yamato, U.S.S.*

containment breach. A failure of the magnetic containment fields in a starship's antimatter storage pods or warp drive

system, generally occurring when field containment fell below 15 percent of normal. A containment breach is a serious malfunction, probably resulting in destruction of the spacecraft. ("Disaster" [TNG]). SEE: **antimatter containment**.

containment field. Specially shaped forcefield used to isolate dangerous materials such as **antimatter** or biohazard specimens. Containment fields were used in antimatter storage pods to protect a ship against contact with the extremely volatile antimatter. Somewhat different containment fields were used for quarantine isolation and for containment of dangerous biological specimens. SEE: **antimatter containment**. The containment fields used in the warp drive on the original *Starship Enterprise* needed to be phase-locked within 3% in order to avoid instability, but by the time of the *Enterprise*-D, multi-phase containment fields were able to operate considerably above that value. ("Relics" [TNG]).

Contract of Ardra. A thousand-year-old agreement that, according to legend, was made between the ancient Ventaxians and the mythical figure, **Ardra**. The contract promised a millennium of peace and prosperity for the people of **Ventax II** in exchange for the population delivering itself into slavery at the end of the thousand years. ("Devil's Due" [TNG]).

Controller. Sophisticated computer system that controlled the subterranean environmental for **Eyemorg** women of planet **Sigma Draconis VI**. The heart of the Controller was a biological humanoid brain, which required periodic replacement. Spock's brain was stolen by  the inhabitants of Sigma Draconis VI in 2268 to be used as the new Controller. When Spock's brain was returned to his body, the Controller was no longer able to regulate the environment and the population had to move to the surface. ("Spock's Brain." [TOS]). SEE: **Teacher**.

• **"Conundrum."** *Next Generation* episode #114. Teleplay by Barry Schkolnick. Story by Paul Schiffer. Directed by Les Landau. Stardate 45494.2. *First aired in 1992. Contact with an alien probe leaves the* Enterprise-D *crew with amnesia, so they have no way of knowing if Starfleet orders to attack a space station are genuine.* SEE: **Cirrus IV; Cliffs of Heaven; crew manifest; el-Mitra Exchange; Emerald Wading Pool; Epsilon Silar System; hippocampus; Kriskov Gambit; Lysia; Lysian Central Command; Lysian Destroyer; MacDuff, Commander Kieran;** *Ode to Psyche*; **photon torpedo; Ro Laren; Samarian Sunset; Satarrans; Starbase 301; Troi, Deanna.**

Copernicus, Shuttlecraft. Shuttle #3, attached to *U.S.S. Enterprise*-A. Kirk, Spock, McCoy, and Sybok transported down aboard the *Copernicus* to the planet that **Sybok** believed was **Sha Ka Ree** in search of Sybok's vision of God. (*Star Trek V: The Final Frontier*). *The* Copernicus *miniature* *was a re-use of the* Galileo *model made for* Star Trek V, *although two full-sized exterior mockups were also built.*

Cor Caroli V. The *Enterprise*-D was successful in eradicating the Phyrox Plague there in 2366. Starfleet Command classified the incident as Secret. ("Allegiance" [TNG]).

Corado I Transmitter Array. Subspace communications relay and booster facility near **Deep Space 9.** Station science officer **Jadzia Dax** ordered a subspace link established to the Corado I array while trying to overload the station's computers when the software life-form called **Pup** was threatening station operation in 2369. ("The Forsaken" [DS9]).

Corak, Glin. (Tom Morga). Aide to **Gul Lemec** during talks aboard the starship *Enterprise*-D in 2369. ("Chain of Command, Part I" [TNG]).

Corbin, Tom. An *Enterprise*-D crew member, scientist, and colleague of Keiko O'Brien. ("Night Terrors" [TNG]).

• **"Corbomite Maneuver, The."** *Original Series* episode #3. Written by Jerry Sohl. Directed by Joseph Sargent. Stardate 1512.2. *First aired in 1966. A powerful ship captures the* Enterprise, *but it is just a test to learn the Federation's intentions. This was the first regular episode produced for the original* Star Trek *series after the two pilot episodes. It features the first appearances of McCoy, Uhura, and Rand. Numerous costume and set designs seen in this episode were changed from the way they originally appeared in* Star Trek's *two pilot episodes.* SEE: **Bailey, Lieutenant David; Balok;** **corbomite;** *Fesarius*; **First Federation; McCoy, Dr. Leonard H.; Rand, Janice; recorder marker; Sulu, Hikaru;** *tranya*; **Uhura.**

corbomite. A nonexistent substance, part of a bluff devised by James Kirk. When threatened by **Balok** of the *Fesarius* in 2266, Kirk claimed his ship's hull contained a substance called corbomite that would cause the destruction of any vessel attacking his ship. ("The Corbomite Maneuver" [TOS]). Kirk used a corbomite bluff a second time in 2267 when he escaped from the Romulan Neutral Zone by claiming that the ship had a "corbomite device" that would explode, destroying all matter in a 200,000-kilometer radius. ("The Deadly Years" [TOS]).

cordrazine. Extremely powerful pharmaceutical stimulant used by Federation medical personnel. Dr. McCoy prescribed 2 milliliters of cordrazine to Lieutenant Sulu, who suffered serious electrical burns when the ship was investigating time-distortion waves in 2267 near the **Guardian of Forever.** Another time wave caused McCoy to receive an accidental overdose of cordrazine, whereupon he experienced extreme paranoid delusions and fled to a planet's surface. ("The City on the Edge of Forever" [TOS]). McCoy also used cordrazine to revive **Ensign Rizzo** when he was attacked by the **dikironium cloud creature.** ("Obsession" [TOS]). Dr. Beverly Crusher used 25 milliliters of cordrazine in a last-ditch effort to save Worf's life when his body rejected **genetronic replication** therapy in 2368. ("Ethics" [TNG]). SEE: **tricordrazine.**

core breach. SEE: **antimatter containment.**

Corelki. *Enterprise*-D security officer. Corelki was assigned to the away team that investigated the attack on the **Ohniaka III** Outpost in 2368. She was killed in a **Borg** attack during the mission. ("Descent, Part I" [TNG]).

Coridan. Planet under consideration in 2267 for admission into the **United Federation of Planets.** The **Babel Conference** of that year considered the matter. Coridan is rich in **dilithium** crystals, making the planet susceptible to illegal mining operations, which gave some motive to denying Coridan membership in the Federation. ("Journey to Babel" [TOS]). The vote was affirmative, and Federation ambassador **Sarek** was credited with the Coridan admission. ("Sarek" [TNG]).

Corinth IV. Planet on which was located a Starfleet facility. When the *Enterprise* was delayed at planet **M-113,** the Starship Base on Corinth IV requested an explanation. ("The Man Trap" [TOS]).

Cornelian Star System. Riker ordered the *Enterprise*-D toward the Cornelian star system in an attempt to escape the "hole" in space created by **Nagilum.** ("Where Silence Has Lease" [TNG]).

corophizine. Antibiotic given to Miles O'Brien to prevent secondary infection when he was critically ill due to the **aphasia virus** in 2369. ("Babel "[DS9]).

Correllium fever. A disease that broke out on planet **Nahmi IV** in 2366. ("Hollow Pursuits" [TNG]).

Corrigan. A member of James Kirk's graduating class from the Academy. They met again at a bar at **Starbase 11** when the *Enterprise* was docked for repairs after an **ion storm** in 2267. The meeting was less than cordial because Corrigan believed Kirk was responsible for the death of **Ben Finney.** ("Court Martial" [TOS]).

cortical stimulator. Resuscitative device used aboard Federation starships. Captain Jean-Luc Picard was treated with a cortical stimulator following his exposure to the **Kataan probe** on stardate 45944. ("The Inner Light" [TNG]).

corundium alloy. Material used in the construction of an alien probe that came through the **Bajoran** wormhole in 2369. ("The Forsaken" [DS9]). *The unnamed alien probe in "The Forsaken" was a modification of the* **Cytherian** *probe model originally built for "The Nth Degree" (TNG), with outboard antenna paddles added.*

Corvallen freighter. *Antares*-class mercenary freighter that had been contracted to rendezvous with the Romulan warbird *Khazara* in 2369, part of the plan to enable Romulan **Vice-Proconsul M'ret** to defect to the Federation. The ship was destroyed by **Subcommander N'Vek** when it was believed that the captain of that ship did not intend to fulfill the contract and that the plan for M'ret's escape was therefore in jeopardy. ("Face of the Enemy" [TNG]). *The Corvallen freighter was* *another re-use of the* Battris *from "Heart of Glory" (TNG). One might therefore conjecture that other uses of this model represented* Antares-*class ships, and that perhaps this was also the design of the freighter blown up in "Charlie X" (TOS).*

Corvan gilvos. A stick-like animal indigenous to the rainforests of **Corvan II**. The gilvos were uniquely suited to live in trees, as they closely resembled a tree branch. Their habitat was threatened by industrial pollutants on Corvan II, and by 2368, only 14 specimens remained.

The *Enterprise*-D transported two gilvos to the protected planet of **Brentalia**. The gilvos were momentarily threatened by a fire that broke out aboard the *Enterprise*-D during their transport, but quick action by Commander Riker saved the animals. ("New Ground" [TNG]). *The gilvos was a hand puppet designed by makeup supervisor Michael Westmore. The same puppet (perhaps another surviving gilvos) was Grand Nagus Quark's pet in "The Nagus" (DS9).*

Corvan II. Federation planet whose ecosystem was threatened by industrial pollutants in the planetary atmosphere. The **Corvan gilvos** were among the animals threatened by the loss of rainforest habitat on that planet. ("New Ground" [TNG]).

Cory, Governor Donald. (Keye Luke). Governor and administrator of the Federation penal colony on planet **Elba II** who was violently overthrown by **Garth of Izar**, one of the inmates. ("Whom Gods Destroy" [TOS]).

cosmic string fragment. An almost infinitely thin filament of almost infinitely dense matter. Although a string fragment can exhibit a gravitational pull of a hundred stars, it is no wider than a proton. Cosmic strings emanate a characteristic set of subspace frequencies which are caused by the decay of atomic particles along the string's event horizon. In 2367, the crew of the *Enterprise*-D used these harmonics to help guide a school of **two-dimensional creatures** back to their home in a cosmic string fragment. ("The Loss" [TNG]).

• **"Cost of Living."** *Next Generation* episode #120. Written by Peter Allan Fields. Directed by Winrich Kolbe. Stardate 45733.6. *First aired in 1992. A planetary dignitary visits the* Enterprise-*D to be married to Lwaxana Troi, but he doesn't count on her being such a free spirit..* SEE: **antimatter containment; Campio, Minister; chrondite; Erko; exanogen gas; Jestral tea; Laughing Hour; Moselina System; nitrium; nitrium metal parasites; Parallax Colony; Pelloris Field; petrokian sausage; Shiralea VI; Tessen III; Troi, Lwaxana.**

Costa, Lieutenant. Member of the *Enterprise*-D engineering staff. ("The Mind's Eye", "Hollow Pursuits" [TNG]).

Council of Elders. Group of **Organian** leaders who appeared to govern their planet. The actual nature of Organian government remains unknown because the Organians, contrary to the image that they chose to project to Federation and Klingon representatives, were incredibly advanced **noncorporeal life**-forms who shared little in common with their distant humanoid ancestors. For this reason, the Council of Elders expressed little concern when the Klingon occupational forces, led by **Commander Kor**, committed apparently horrific acts of oppression against the Organians in 2267. ("Errand of Mercy" [TOS]). SEE: **noncorporeal life**.

Counselor. Starship officer responsible for the emotional well-being of the ship's crew. A counselor's duties included providing individual guidance and advice to crew members, as well as periodic crew performance evaluations, usually performed with the ship's executive officer or other department heads. A counselor is also expected to provide advice to the ship's captain on command decisions. **Deanna Troi** was the counselor on the *Enterprise*-D. ("Man of the People" [TNG]).

• **"Court Martial."** Original Series episode #15. Teleplay by Don M. Mankiewicz and Steven W. Carabatsos. Story by Don M. Mankiewicz. Directed by Marc Daniels. Stardate 2947.3. *First aired in 1967. Kirk's career is jeopardized when he is put on trial for apparently causing the death of an* Enterprise *crew member.* SEE: **Alpha III, Statutes of; Chandra; Cogley, Samuel T.; Corrigan; Finney, Benjamin; Finney, Jamie; Hammurabi, Code of; Hanson;** *Intrepid, U.S.S.;* **ion storm; Justinian; Kirk, James T.; Kransnowsky; Lynstrom; Magna Carta; Martian Colonies, Fundamental Declarations of the; McCoy, Leonard H.; Phase 1 Search;** *Republic, U.S.S.;* **Shaw, Areel; Spock; Starbase 11; Starfleet Command; Stone, Commodore; United States Constitution**.

Cousteau, Shuttlepod. A shuttle vehicle from the *Starship Aries*. In 2367, the *Cousteau* was stolen by **Mendez** and abandoned on **Tarchannen III**. ("Identity Crisis" [TNG]). *The* Cousteau *was named for 20th-century oceanographer Jacques Cousteau.*

cove palm. A plant indigenous to planet **Ogus II**. The fruit of the plant contains a highly infectious parasite. **Willie Potts**, the child of an *Enterprise*-D crew member, accidently ate a Cove Palm fruit in 2367, requiring emergency treatment at a starbase. ("Brothers" [TNG]).

"cowboy diplomacy." Slang term that referred to actions taken impulsively by an individual on behalf of a government, without that government's sanction. Captain Picard accused Ambassador **Spock** of "cowboy diplomacy" in coming to **Romulus** in 2368 without the sanction of the Federation or Vulcan governments. ("Unification, Part II" [TNG]).

CPK enzymatic therapy. Medical treatment to limit the extent of spinal injury. ("Ethics" [TNG]).

CPK levels. A medical test performed on board Federation starships. CPK, or creatinine phosphokinase, is a marker of muscular damage. It is mostly used to diagnose cardiac damage. ("Violations" [TNG]).

Crater, Nancy. (Jeanne Bal). The wife of archaeologist **Robert Crater**, Nancy Crater was killed some years prior to 2266 by the last surviving member of the civilization there. This creature had remarkable hypnotic abilities, able to masquerade as anyone, and chose to appear to Robert Crater in the image of his late wife. Prior to her

marriage to Crater, Nancy had been romantically involved with **Leonard McCoy**. ("The Man Trap" [TOS]). SEE: **M-113 creature**.

Crater, Professor Robert. (Alfred Ryder). Reclusive archaeologist who studied the ruins on planet **M-113**. After his wife Nancy was killed by the last surviving creature on that planet, Crater was unable to bring himself to kill that individual, choosing instead to befriend it. ("The Man Trap" [TOS]).

Crazy Horse, U.S.S. Federation starship. The *Crazy Horse* was part of task force 3, under Captain Picard's indirect command during an expected **Borg** invasion of late 2369. ("Descent, Part I" [TNG]). *The* Crazy Horse *was named for the Lakota Sioux chief, who was one of the most important Indian leaders at the Battle of Little Bighorn.*

Creator. Term used by the machine life-form **V'Ger** to describe the agency responsible for its origin. In fact, V'Ger, originally known as *Voyager VI*, had been created by humans on Earth in the late 20th century, although the immensely powerful and sophisticated V'Ger found it difficult to believe it had originated with such amazingly primitive creatures. (*Star Trek: The Motion Picture*).

Creators, Fabrini. SEE: **Fabrini Creators**.

crew manifest. A computer file containing biographical and Starfleet data on crew members aboard a Federation starship. ("Conundrum" [TNG]). *The bridge crew manifest in "Conundrum" contained numerous biographic details about our series regulars. Some of these data points were based on information established in earlier shows, but much was somewhat conjectural. For the most part, we're assuming this information is accurate, unless contradicted by some future episode.*

Croden. (Cliff De Young). Fugitive from the planet **Rakhar** in the **Gamma Quadrant**. He was picked up in a damaged shuttlecraft and brought to Deep Space 9 in 2369. In a botched robbery attempt, Croden killed the **Miradorn** Ro-Kel, which caused his twin brother, **Ah-Kel**, to vow revenge. While in **Odo**'s jail, Croden told the shape-shifter he'd met others of his kind and offered as proof a unique necklace whose contents changed form. While Odo was returning Croden to

his homeworld, Odo learned that Crodin's "crime" was having spoken out against his government. For punishment, most of his family was killed. Croden fled from the government, but was able to save only one member of his family, his daughter, **Yareth**, whom he hid on an asteroid in the **Chamra Vortex**. Odo returned Croden to the asteroid, where the necklace served as a key to unlock a stasis chamber in which Yarneth was hidden. Odo then allowed Croden and his daughter to leave on a Vulcan transport ship to start a new life. ("Vortex" [DS9]). SEE: **toh-maire**.

Crosis. One of the self-aware, fanatical **Borg** who began attacking Federation colonies in 2369. Crosis beamed aboard the *Enterprise*-D as part of a diversion to allow a Borg ship to escape. He was captured and was confined in the ship's brig. Crosis revealed himself to be one of a group of Followers of a persona called "**The One**." While there, he was able to convince Commander **Data** to release him and they left the ship in a stolen shuttlecraft. Crosis took Data back to the base of these new Borg. Once there, Data was reunited with his android "brother," **Lore**. ("Descent, Parts I and II").

Cruses System. The last known location of a Tarkanian diplomat who was believed to be a co-conspirator of **J'Ddan** in the theft of Federation technological secrets in 2367. ("The Drumhead" [TNG]).

Crusher, Dr. Beverly. (Gates McFadden). **Chief medical officer** aboard the *Enterprise*-D under the command of **Jean-Luc Picard**. Crusher was born Beverly Howard in 2324, and graduated from medical school in 2350. She was at the **Arvada III** colony, and helped her grandmother, Felicia Howard ("Sub Rosa" [TNG]) care for the survivors of that terrible trag-

edy. Although her grandmother was not a physician, she taught Beverly much about the medicinal uses of herbs and roots to help care for the sick and wounded after regular medical supplies had been exhausted. ("The Arsenal of Freedom" [TNG]).

Beverly was introduced to her future husband, Starfleet officer **Jack Crusher**, by their mutual friend **Walker Keel**. ("Conspiracy" [TNG]). She married Jack in 2348, and the two had a child, **Wesley Crusher**, the following year. Crusher did her internship on planet Delos IV under the tutelage of **Dr. Dalen Quaice** in 2352. ("Remember Me" [TNG]). Following her husband's death in 2354, Beverly continued to pursue her Starfleet career, attaining the position of CMO aboard the *Enterprise*-D in 2364. ("Encounter at Farpoint" [TNG]). Crusher left the *Enterprise*-D in 2365 to accept a position as head of Starfleet Medical, but returned to the ship a year later, and was reunited with her son, Wesley. ("Evolution" [TNG]). In 2366,

Crusher became romantically interested in a man from planet **Zalkon** whom she had named **John Doe**. ("Transfigurations" [TNG]). The following year, she became involved with a **Trill** named **Ambassador Odan**. Although the two were very much in love, Beverly found it difficult to accept her lover inhabiting a different body. ("The Host" [TNG]).

Beverly was quite an accomplished dancer. Her colleagues named her "The Dancing Doctor," a nickname she disliked, so aboard the *Enterprise*-D she did her best to avoid demonstrating her skills. Nevertheless, the fact that she had won first place in a dance competition in St. Louis was part of her Starfleet record, so Data asked her to help him learn to dance for the wedding of **Miles O'Brien** and **Keiko Ishikawa** in 2367. ("Data's Day" [TNG]). Beverly also had a strong interest in amateur theatrics, and was director of a successful theater company aboard the *Enterprise*-D. Among the productions performed by her company in 2367 was ***Cyrano de Bergerac***. ("The Nth Degree" [TNG]). Several months later, her troupe performed Gilbert and Sullivan's ***The Pirates of Penzance***. ("Disaster" [TNG]). Crusher wrote a play for her troupe, called *Something for Breakfast*. ("A Fistful of Datas" [TNG]). Another play written by Crusher was entitled ***Frame of Mind***. ("Frame of Mind" [TNG]).

Beverly's maiden name, Howard, is from her biographical computer screen in "Conundrum" (TNG), named for Star Trek: The Next Generation *producer Merri Howard, although the name has not been firmly established in dialog. Gates McFadden left the* Star Trek *cast in the second season, during which the chief medical officer was played by Diana Muldaur as* Dr. Katherine Pulaski *(which is why Crusher left the ship to become head of Starfleet Medical during that year). McFadden and Crusher returned to the* Enterprise*-D during the third and subsequent seasons. Beverly Crusher first appeared in "Encounter at Farpoint" (TNG).*

Crusher, Jack R. (Doug Wert). Starfleet officer, husband to **Beverly Crusher**, and father to **Wesley Crusher**. Jack Crusher, a close friend to Captain **Jean-Luc Picard**, married medical student Beverly Howard in 2348. Crusher had proposed to Beverly by giving her a gag gift, a book entitled *How to Advance Your Career Through Marriage*. Their son, Wesley, was born a year later. ("Family" [TNG]).

Lieutenant Commander Jack Crusher served aboard the *U.S.S. Stargazer* under the command of Captain Picard, and was killed on an away mission in 2354, when his son was only five years old. ("Encounter at Farpoint, Parts I and II" [TNG]). Shortly after Wesley's birth, Jack recorded a holographic message to his infant son, intended for playback when Wesley reached adulthood. Jack hoped this would be the first in a series of such messages, but it was the only one he made. Wesley played the message some 18 years later, in 2367. ("Family" [TNG]). *Even though Jack Crusher theoretically died several years before the first season of* Star Trek: The Next Generation, *we've seen him three times. The first was in Wesley's holographic message in "Family" (TNG),*

*and then again in Beverly's **telepathic memory invasion** flashback in "Violations" (TNG), and in "Journey's End" (TNG).*

Crusher, Wesley. (Wil Wheaton). Son of Starfleet officers **Jack Crusher** and **Beverly Crusher**. Wesley was born in 2349, and was raised by his mother following the death of his father, Jack, in 2354 when Wesley was five years old. Wesley went to live on the *Starship Enterprise*-D in 2364, when his mother was assigned to that ship as chief medical officer. ("Encoun-

ter at Farpoint, Parts I and II" [TNG]). Wesley spent little time with his father before his death, but recalled that Jack taught him to play baseball. ("Evolution" [TNG]).

Wesley showed a keen interest in science and technology, and had an extraordinary ability to visualize complex mathematical concepts, an ability that the **Traveler** once urged Captain Picard to nurture. Perhaps in response, Picard commissioned Crusher an acting ensign on stardate 41263.4 in recognition of Wesley's key role in returning the *Enterprise*-D to Federation space after it was stranded by **Kosinski**'s failed warp-drive experiments. ("Where No One Has Gone Before" [TNG]).

As a member of an away team to planet **Rubicun III**, Crusher inadvertently broke a local law and was sentenced to death by the planetary government. Crusher was later freed by *Enterprise*-D captain Picard, although Picard acknowledged that the act violated the Prime Directive. ("Justice" [TNG]). Wesley's first experience with command was when Commander Riker assigned him the task of supervising geological surveys of the planets in the **Selcundi Drema** Sector in 2365. Although Crusher initially found it difficult to supervise officers older than himself, he eventually found that the experience built self-confidence, and Crusher's leadership led to scientifically important discoveries. ("Pen Pals" [TNG]). Crusher conducted a test using medical **nanites** in 2266, accidentally resulting in the creation of an enhanced version of the tiny robots possessing enough intelligence to be considered a legitimate life-form. The nanites were so recognized and granted colonization rights on planet **Kavis Alpha IV**. ("Evolution" [TNG]).

Wesley's first romantic interest was with the lovely young **Salia**, leader of planet **Daled IV**. Although not human, Salia was a shape-shifting **allasomorph** who appeared as a teen-aged human girl whose keen intelligence and wit captured his interest. ("The Dauphin" [TNG]).

Wesley first attempted to gain entrance to **Starfleet Academy** in 2364 at age 15. ("Coming of Age" [TNG]). Although he did not win admission at that time, he continued his studies and gained academic credit for his work aboard the *Enterprise*-D. Wesley's later test results were sufficient for Starfleet to grant him academic credit for his work aboard the *Enterprise*-D. ("Evolution" [TNG], "Samaritan Snare" [TNG]). Wesley was accepted to Starfleet Academy in 2366, but missed his transport to the Academy because he was participating in a rescue mission after William Riker, Deanna Troi, and Lwaxana Troi had been kidnapped by Ferengi DaiMon

Tog. In recognition of his sacrifice, Captain Picard granted Wesley a field promotion to the rank of ensign shortly after the incident. ("Ménage à Troi" [TNG]). Wesley finally entered **Starfleet Academy** in 2367 when a position opened up mid-term in the current class. His final assignment as part of the *Enterprise*-D crew was to accompany Captain Picard on a diplomatic mission to planet **Pentarus V**. The mission was interrupted with their transport shuttle, the *Nenebek*, crashed on **Lambda Paz**, critically injuring Captain Picard. Crusher cared for Picard until a rescue party arrived. ("Final Mission" [TNG]).

Crusher's first year at the Academy went well, and he even gained entry into the Academy's elite **Nova Squadron** flight team. ("The First Duty" [TNG]). Wesley returned to the *Enterprise*-D for a brief visit on stardate 45208, where he became very fond of mission specialist **Robin Lefler**. ("The Game" [TNG]). Crusher's sophomore year was marred by a serious incident in which he and other members of Nova Squadron attempted a prohibited maneuver, and cadet **Joshua Albert** died in the resulting accident. Although initial testimony by members of the squadron suggested Albert was responsible for the accident, Crusher later came forward with the truth. A reprimand was entered into Crusher's academic record, and he was forced to repeat his sophomore year. ("The First Duty" [TNG]).

Wesley Crusher became disenchanted with his studies at Starfleet and resigned his commission to the Academy in 2370, choosing instead to live among the American Indians on planet Dorvan V, a world currently under Cardassian jurisdiction. Crusher's decision to leave Starfleet in favor of self-exploration was a difficult one, aided by insight offered by the Traveler. ("Journey's End" [TNG]).

SEE: **Kolvoord Starburst; Locarno, Cadet First Class Nicholas.** *Wesley Crusher first appeared in "Encounter at Farpoint." Wesley left the series during the fourth season (in "Final Mission" [TNG]), although he has since returned for "The Game" (TNG) "The First Duty" (TNG), "Parallels" (TNG), and "Journey's End" (TNG). Wesley was named for Star Trek creator Gene Roddenberry, whose middle name was Wesley.*

cryogenic open-heart procedure. Surgical procedure used by Chief Surgeon Leonard McCoy aboard the *Enterprise* to repair a damaged heart valve of Vulcan ambassador **Sarek** in 2267. This procedure required a large amount of the rare **T-negative** blood type, donated by his son, Spock. ("Journey to Babel" [TOS]).

cryonetrium. Substance that remains gaseous at cryogenic temperatures near absolute zero. The *Enterprise*-D warp drive systems were flooded with gaseous cryonetrium in 2366 to halt the effects of **invidium** contamination. ("Hollow Pursuits" [TNG]).

cryonics. Old practice of cryogenically freezing a human just after death in the hopes that future medical advances would render their sickness curable. Some cryogenically frozen bodies were actually sent into space in orbiting satellites for long-term storage. One such **cryosatellite** was discovered in 2364 by the Starship *Enterprise*-D. Cryonics was something of a fad in the late 20th century but fell into disuse by the mid-

21st century. ("The Neutral Zone" [TNG]).

cryosatellite. An ancient space vessel launched in the late 20th century carrying a cargo of cryogenically preserved humans from Earth. These individuals had all died in the late 20th century, but their bodies had been frozen and sent into space. The **cryosatellite** drifted in space for some 300 years before being discovered near the **Kazis Binary** star system by the *Enterprise*-D. Although most of the satellite's storage modules had failed, three individuals were revived, **Claire Raymond**, **Sonny Clemonds**, and **Ralph Offenhouse**. All three were later returned to Earth on the Starship *Charleston*. ("The Neutral Zone" [TNG]). SEE: **cryonics; sleeper ship**.

The cryosatellite was designed by Rick Sternbach and Mike Okuda. Close examination of the model might reveal the letters "S.S. Birdseye" inscribed on the hull. The model was later modified and used as Subspace Relay Station 47 in "Aquiel" (TNG).

cryostasis. Medical procedure used to slow down biological functions in a critically injured patient, allowing the physician more time to correct the malady. Dr. Julian Bashir wanted to put **Hon'Tihl**, the critically injured first officer of a Klingon vessel, into cryostasis on stardate 46922, but the patient died shortly after transport to Deep Space 9. ("Dramatis Personae" [DS9]).

cryptobiolin. One of several chemicals used by the **Angosians** during the **Tarsian War** to "improve" their soldiers, making them more effective in combat. Unfortunately, the effects of many of these drugs were irreversible. ("The Hunted" [TNG]). SEE: **Danar, Roga**.

Crystalline Entity. A spaceborne life-form of unknown origin whose structure resembled a large snowflake. The Crystalline Entity apparently thrived by absorbing the energy of biological life-forms on planets, leaving behind devastated planetary surfaces.  The Crystalline Entity was responsible for the destruction of the **Omicron Theta** colony (including all inhabitants) in 2336. The only survivors of the incident were the androids **Data** and **Lore**, who were dormant at the time of the attack. It was believed that Lore had betrayed the colonists to the entity just prior to the attack. ("Datalore" [TNG]).

In subsequent years, **Dr. Kila Marr**, whose son died at Omicron Theta, studied the entity, examining 12 attack sites, including planet **Forlat III**. The entity's last attack was in 2368 at the **Melona IV** colony. Shortly thereafter, Marr destroyed the entity with a modulated graviton beam. ("Silicon Avatar" [TNG]).

crystalline emiristol. Solid chemical rocket propellant used in the ancient space probe launched from the **Kataan** system a thousand years ago. It left a radioactive trail that allowed the *Enterprise*-D to trace the probe's point of origin. ("The Inner Light" [TNG]).

crystilia. Species of flowering plant found on planet Telemarius III. **Data** presented a bunch of orange and yellow crystilia to Lieutenant **Jenna D'Sora**. ("In Theory" [TNG]).

Cuellar system. A star system located in **Cardassian** space. This system was the location of a Cardassian science station that was destroyed by the *U.S.S. Phoenix* in 2367. Phoenix captain Benjamin Maxwell believed the station to be a military installation. ("The Wounded" [TNG]).

Cumberland, Acts of. Twenty-first-century legal document cited by Judge Advocate General **Phillipa Louvois** in her initial ruling in 2365 that the android Data was the property of Starfleet and therefore could not resign or refuse to cooperate in proposed experiments. ("The Measure of a Man" [TNG]).

Curtis Creek program. A holodeck program that simulated a mountain stream on planet Earth. The program was mentioned during a virtual reality engineered by **Barash** on Alpha Onias III. Barash, as **Jean-Luc Riker**, told his "father," William Riker, that they used to fish in the Curtis Creek program. ("Future Imperfect" [TNG]).

Custodian, The. Sophisticated computer system built and programmed hundreds of centuries ago by the **Progenitors** of planet **Aldea**. The custodian provided for virtually all the needs of the citizens of Aldea, freeing them to pursue lives of artistic endeavor. ("When the Bough Breaks" [TNG]).

cyalodin. Poison used in the mass suicide of the adult members of the **Starnes Expedition** on planet **Triacus** in 2268. ("And the Children Shall Lead" [TOS]).

cyanoacrylates. A substance not normally found aboard *Galaxy*-class starships. This compound is apparently capable of generating low levels of **eichner radiation**, which were found to stimulate growth of certain strains of deadly plasma plague. ("The Child" [TNG]). *Cyanoacrylate is a chemical term used to describe several types of fast-bonding adhesives, notably the stuff called "Krazy Glue." The use of this term here is scientifically inappropriate, but was apparently intended as a gag.*

cybernetic regeneration. A medical treatment of particular interest to *Enterprise*-D CMO Beverly Crusher. ("11001001" [TNG]). Dr. Crusher published a paper on the subject during her tenure aboard the *Enterprise*-D. While the paper was not widely known, it did spark the interest of neurogeneticist **Dr. Toby Russell**. ("Ethics" [TNG]).

Cygnet XII. Planet dominated by women, where the original *Starship Enterprise* docked for general repair and maintenance of the ship's computer system in 2267. The technicians on Cygnet XII felt the computers lacked a personality and gave them one, female, with a tendency to flirt and giggle. ("Tomorrow is Yesterday" [TOS]).

Cygnia Minor. Earth colony threatened by famine in 2266 that a new synthetic food supposedly created by **Dr. Thomas Leighton** would have helped. Unfortunately, the report of a synthetic food was a ruse to summon the *Enterprise* to **Planet Q** with the hopes of confronting the actor **Anton Karidian**. ("The Conscience of the King" [TOS]).

Cygnian Respiratory Diseases, A Survey of. A computer disk in the medical library of the original *Starship Enterprise*. When **Ensign Garrovick** refused food shortly after stardate 3619, Nurse Chapel showed him the disk, telling him that it contained an order from Dr. McCoy to eat. ("Obsession" [TOS]).

Cyrano De Bergerac. French play by Edmond Rostand, first performed on Earth in 1897. Dr. Beverly Crusher's acting workshop, held aboard the *Enterprise*-D, performed this play in 2367. Lieutenant **Reginald Barclay** played the title role. ("The Nth Degree" [TNG]).

Cytherians. Humanoid race that resided on a planet near the center of the galaxy. The Cytherians made outside contact, not by traveling through space, but by bringing space travelers to them. The Cytherians sent out specially designed probes that would reprogram some types of computers with instructions to bring travelers to the Cytherians. The *Enterprise*-D encountered one such probe in 2367.

The Cytherian probe had attempted to reprogram the computers on the **Argus Array** and then attempted to reprogram an *Enterprise*-D shuttlecraft onboard computer. The probe was finally able to program Lieutenant **Reginald Barclay**'s mind to bring the *Enterprise*-D to the Cytherians. The *Enterprise*-D spent ten days in the company of the Cytherians, exchanging a great deal of cultural and scientific information. ("The Nth Degree" [TNG]). *The Cytherian probe model was later modified and reused in "The Forsaken" (DS9).*

D-7. SEE: **Klingon battle cruiser**.

Dabo girl. Beautiful women of various species who were employed as Dabo game operators by **Quark** at his bar on Deep Space 9. Quark correctly believed that the scantily clad Dabo girls significantly enhanced his revenues. ("Captive Pursuit" [DS9]). SEE: **Sarda, Miss**.

Dabo. Game of chance played on a roulette-like wheel located in **Quark's bar** on the **Promenade** of station **Deep Space 9**. ("Emissary" [DS9]).

Dachlyds. A race involved in a trade dispute with their nearest neighbors, the Gemarians. Captain Jean-Luc Picard helped mediate the dispute in 2366 to help both parties arrive at a mutually beneficial solution. ("Captain's Holiday" [TNG]).

Daedalus-class starship. One of the first types of starships commissioned and operated under the auspices of the United Federation of Planets. These ships were among the first to demonstrate the primary/secondary hull and warp nacelle designs that would become characteristic of Starfleet vessels. The **U.S.S. Essex**, destroyed in 2167 at **Mab-Bu VI**, was a *Daedalus*-class starship. The *Daedalus* class was retired from service in 2196. ("Power Play" [TNG]). *We speculate that the* **U.S.S. Horizon** *("A Piece of the Action" [TOS]) and the* **U.S.S. Archon** *("Return of the Archons" [TOS]) were also of the* Daedalus *class. A conjectural design for this class, based on an early* Enterprise *design by Matt Jefferies and built by Greg Jein is pictured here. This model has been seen as a desktop display in* Star Trek: Deep Space Nine.

• **"Dagger of the Mind."** Original Series episode #11. Written by S. Bar-David. Directed by Vincent McEveety. Stardate 2715.1. *First aired in 1966. The* Enterprise *investigates a revolutionary treatment for the criminally insane, but the new device kills with loneliness. Spock first performs the Vulcan mind-meld in this episode.* SEE: **Adams, Dr. Tristan; Central Bureau of Penology, Stockholm; Lethe; neural neutralizer; Noel, Dr. Helen; Tantalus V; Van Gelder, Dr. Simon; Vulcan mind-meld**.

DaH! Klingon for "Now!" ("Redemption, Part II" [TNG]).

Daily, Jon. Captain of the passenger vessel **Astral Queen**. At the request of *Enterprise* captain James Kirk, Daily bypassed a scheduled stop at **Planet Q**, forcing the **Karidian Company of Players** to request passage aboard the *Enterprise*. ("The Conscience of the King" [TOS]).

DaiMon. Title given to **Ferengi** leaders, approximately equivalent in rank to a Starfleet captain. ("The Last Outpost" [TNG]).

Dakar Senegal. City in French West Africa on planet Earth where **nanites** were manufactured. ("Evolution" [TNG]).

Dal'Rok. Cloudlike energy creature that threatened a Bajoran village for five nights every year. The village was saved each time by the **Sirah**, who would tell heroic tales of the village people, repelling the evil entity. In actual fact, the Dal'Rok was an illusion created from the fears of the villager by the Sirah, who used a small fragment of an **Orb** from the **Celestial Temple** to create a common enemy that would unite the people of the village. ("The Storyteller" [DS9]).

Daled IV. Planet that revolves only once every planetary year, so that one hemisphere is always in light, while the other is in eternal night. For centuries Daled IV had been torn by civil war between inhabitants of the two hemispheres. In the late 2340s two parents from opposite sides conceived a child named **Salia**, and sent her to the nearby planet **Kalvida III** to be raised in a neutral environment. Salia returned to Daled IV at age 16 in the hopes of uniting the factions and bringing peace to her world. Daled IV was not a member of the Federation. ("The Dauphin" [TNG]).

D'Amato, Lieutenant. (Arthur Batanides). *Enterprise* senior geologist killed in 2268 on a landing party to the mysterious **Kalandan outpost**. D'Amato was killed by **cellular disruption** caused by a mechanism devised to protect the planetoid. ("That Which Survives" [TOS]). SEE: **Losira**.

Danar, Gul. (Vaughn Armstrong). Cardassian commander of the warship **Aldara**. Gul Danar demanded the return of the Bajoran terrorist **Tahna Los,** whom Commandar Sisko had given asylum on Deep Space 9 in 2369. ("Past Prologue" [DS9]).

Danar, Roga. (Jeff McCarthy). A male native of **Angosia III**, Danar volunteered for duty as a soldier in his planet's **Tarsian War**. His government put Danar through extensive psychological manipulation and biochemical modifications, making him extremely aggressive in combat, and programming him to be the perfect warrior. He served in many campaigns during that conflict, and received two promotions

to the rank of Subhadar. In 2366, Danar became a leader of a veterans' uprising that forced the Angosian government to reconsider the plight of their ex-soldiers. ("The Hunted" [TNG]).

"Dancing Doctor, The." A nickname that Dr. Beverly Crusher acquired after having won a dance competition at a Saint Louis dance academy. Aboard the *Enterprise*-D, she did her best to hide her talent in dance to avoid the moniker. ("Data's Day" [TNG]).

Dano, Kal. A 27th-century scientist who invented the **Tox Uthat**, a device with enormous weapons potential. Fearful that the device would be stolen, Dano fled to the 22nd century, where he hid the *Uthat* on planet **Risa**. ("Captain's Holiday" [TNG]).

Danula II. The site of a **Starfleet Academy marathon** in 2323. Freshman cadet **Jean-Luc Picard** managed to overtake two upperclassmen on the final hill of that 40-kilometer run to become the only freshman to ever win the Starfleet Academy marathon. ("The Best of Both Worlds, Part II" [TNG]).

Dar, Caithlin. (Cynthia Gouw). Romulan representative to the **Paradise City** settlement on planet **Nimbus III**, assigned in 2287. An idealistic young woman, Dar believed the colony might still serve as a catalyst for galactic peace, despite the failure of the project for the past two decades. Under the mental influence of Sybok, Dar joined **Sybok**'s quest for the mythical planet **Sha Ka Ree**. (*Star Trek V: The Final Frontier*).

Dara. (Michelle Forbes). Daughter to noted Kaelon scientist **Timicin**, and the mother of his only grandson. Dara visited Timicin aboard the *Enterprise*-D in 2367 to plead with him to return home and carry out his **Resolution**. ("Half a Life" [TNG]). *Michelle Forbes would later return as Ensign Ro.*

Daran V. Planet with a population of 3,724,000 that was directly in the path of the **Fabrini** spaceship *Yonada* in 2268. Assistance by *Enterprise* personnel diverted *Yonada* from its collision course, sparing the inhabitants of both worlds. ("For the World Is Hollow and I Have Touched the Sky" [TOS]).

Daras. (Valora Noland). **Ekosian** resistance fighter who was presented the Iron Cross award by Deputy Fuhrer **Melakon** for apparently betraying her father to her planet's Nazi party in 2268. Daras's actions were actually part of the Ekosian underground's efforts to discredit Melakon and the Nazi party. ("Patterns of Force" [TOS]).

Daren, Neela. (Wendy Hughes). *Enterprise*-D scientist who headed the ship's **Stellar Cartography department** in 2369. An accomplished pianist, Lieutenant Commander Neela Daren discovered that Captain **Jean-Luc Picard** played a **Ressikan flute,** and the two enjoyed playing duets together. Their mutual appreciation for music soon blossomed into a romantic

relationship. When a fierce firestorm threatened lives on planet **Bersallis III**, Neela Daren was chosen to supervise installation of **thermal deflector** units to protect the outpost. Commander Daren and several other crew members risked their lives by operating the deflectors manually so all colonists could be safely transported to the ship. After the incident, it became obvious to both that it would be extremely difficult to continue their relationship because Picard would hesitate to place her in danger again. Each refusing to give up their professions, Neela Daren requested a transfer off the *Enterprise*-D. ("Lessons" [TNG]).

Darhe'el, Gul. Cardassian commander of the infamous **Gallitep** labor camp on planet **Bajor**. Under Darhe'el's authority, thousands of **Bajorans** were tortured and killed while working under brutal conditions. Also known as **The Butcher of Gallitep**, Darhe'el's acts of violence against the people of Bajor won him admiration from his superiors and earned him the Proficient Service Medallion. When ordered to leave Gallitep, Darhe'el ordered all the Bajoran laborers be slaughtered, although several did escape. Darhe'el died in his sleep in 2363 from a massive **coleibric hemorrhage**, and was buried under one of the largest military monuments on Cardassia with full honors. In 2369, Darhe'el's file clerk from Gallitep, a man named **Aamin Marritza**, impersonated Darhe'el in hopes of exposing the atrocities that had been committed at Gallitep. ("Duet" [DS9]). SEE: **Kalla-Nohra Syndrome.**

"Darmok and Jalad at Tanagra." A **Tamarian** phrase that referred to a mythological hunter on planet Shantil III and his companion Jalad, who met and shared a danger at the mythical island of Tanagra. In the Tamarian metaphorical language, the phrase indicated an attempt to understand another by sharing a common experience. ("Darmok" [TNG]).

• **"Darmok."** *Next Generation* episode #102. Teleplay by Joe Menosky. Story by Philip Lazebnik and Joe Menosky. Directed by Winrich Kolbe. Stardate 45047.2. *First aired in 1991. An alien ship captain strands himself and Captain Picard on a planet in hopes of helping Picard understand a language based entirely on metaphors. This episode marked the first appearance of the new midsized shuttlecraft.* SEE: **annular confinement beam; Children of Tama; "Darmok and Jalad at Tanagra"; Dathon; El-Adrel IV; El-Adrel system; Enkidu; Gilgamesh; Homeric hymns; Lefler, Ensign Robin;** *Magellan,* **Shuttlecraft; "Shaka, when the walls fell";** *Shiku Maru;* **Silvestri, Captain; "Sokath, his eyes uncovered!"; Tamarians.**

Darnay's disease. A deadly ailment that attacks the brain and nervous system of its victims. **Dr. Ira Graves** died of Darnay's disease in 2365. ("The Schizoid Man" [TNG]).

Darnell, Crewman. (Michael Zaslow). *Enterprise* security officer killed in 2266 by the **M-113 creature**. ("The Man Trap" [TOS]).

Daro, Glinn. (Tim Winters). **Cardassian** aide to **Gul Macet**. Daro was on board the *Enterprise*-D as an observer as the *Enterprise*-D searched for the renegade *Starship* **Phoenix** in 2367. Daro made friendly overtures to Chief **Miles O'Brien**, but O'Brien found it difficult to be cordial to an ex-enemy. ("The Wounded" [TNG]).

Darson, Captain. Commanding officer of the Federation starship **Adelphi**. Darson was among 47 people killed in the notorious first-contact mission at Ghorusda. Darson was later found responsible for the **Ghorusda disaster**. ("Tin Man" [TNG]).

Darthen. Coastal city on planet **Rekag-Seronia**. Darthen had been neutral throughout the bitter wars on that planet, and served as the site of a peace conference in 2369 conducted by Federation mediator **Alkar**. ("Man of the People" [TNG]).

Darvin, Arne. (Charlie Brill). Assistant to **Nilz Baris** who was in charge of the development project for **Sherman's Planet**. Mr. Darvin was found to be a Klingon agent, surgically altered, and to have poisoned the **quadrotriticale** stored at **Deep Space Station K-7** to sabotage the Federation's development project on Sherman's Planet in 2267. ("The Trouble with Tribbles" [TOS]).

Darwin Genetic Research Station. Federation science facility located on planet **Gagarin IV**, headed by **Dr. Sara Kingsley**.

In the late 2350s and 2360s, a research project at this station developed human children who had an aggressive immune system capable of attacking disease organisms before they entered a human body. The children's antibodies were also capable of attacking human beings, a fact not discovered until 2365, when the entire crew of the **U.S.S. Lantree** was killed after exposure to the children.

The scientific staff of the Darwin Station were also afflicted by the antibodies and suffered symptoms resembling hyperaccelerated aging, but a transporter-based technique was successful in restoring all station personnel to normal. ("Unnatural Selection" [TNG]). *The Darwin station was named for naturalist Charles Darwin (1809-1882), who postulated the theory of evolution. The exterior of the station was a matte painting created by Illusion Arts. The painting was later reused in other episodes, including as the science station in "Descent, Part I" (TNG).*

• **"Data's Day."** *Next Generation episode #85. Teleplay by Harold Apter and Ronald D. Moore. Story by Harold Apter. Directed by Robert Wiemer. Stardate 44390.1. First aired in 1991. A typical day in the life aboard the* Enterprise*-D as seen through the eyes of Data. This is the episode in which we first meet Keiko, who marries Miles O'Brien. We also see the* Enterprise*-D barber shop, as well as Data's cat, for the first time.* SEE: **Adelphous IV; Andorians; autosequencers; barber shop; biomechanical maintenance program; Crusher, Dr. Beverly; "Dancing Doctor, The"; Data; Daystrom Institute of Technology;** *Devoras;* ***Enterprise-D, U.S.S.;* feline supplement 74; Galvin V; Hindu Festival of Lights; Juarez, Lieutenant; Maddox, Commander Bruce; Mendak, Admiral; Mot; Murasaki Effect; O'Brien, Keiko; O'Brien, Miles; phase transition coils; Replicating Center; Selok, Subcommander; Spot; T'Pel, Ambassador; transporter carrier wave; transporter ID trace; Umbato, Lieutenant; wedding;** *Zhukov, U.S.S.*

Data. (Brent Spiner). A humanoid android so sophisticated that he was regarded as a sentient life-form with full civil rights. ("Encounter at Farpoint, Part II" [TNG]).

Creation. Data was built around 2336 by the reclusive scientist **Noonien Soong** at the **Omicron Theta** colony. Data was actually the second android constructed by Soong; the first was known as **Lore**. ("Datalore" [TNG]). Just prior to the destruction of the colony by the **Crystalline Entity**, memories from all the colonists were stored in Data's positronic brain for safekeeping. ("Silicon Avatar" [TNG]). Data was then stored in a dormant condition underground, where he remained until discovered in 2338 by the crew of the *Starship Tripoli*. Data subsequently joined the Starfleet and eventually became **operations manager** aboard the *Enterprise*-D. ("Datalore" [TNG]).

Form and function. Data was based on a sophisticated positronic brain developed by Soong, from concepts first postulated in the 20th century by Dr. Isaac Asimov. ("Datalore" [TNG]). Data's body closely mimicked humanoid form, and contained approximately 24.6 kilograms of tripolymer composites, 11.8 kilograms of molybdenum-cobalt alloys, and 1.3 kilograms of bioplast sheeting. ("The Most Toys" [TNG]). His upper spinal support was polyalloy, while his skull was composed of cortenide and duranium. ("The Chase" [TNG]). Soong went to extraordinary lengths to create a naturalistic human appearance in Data. He gave Data a functional respiration system, although its purpose was primarily for thermal regulation. (Data was in fact capable of functioning for extended periods in a vacuum.) He gave Data a pulse in his circulatory system that distributed biochemical lubricants and regulated microhydraulic power throughout Data's body. Data's hair was even capable of growth at a controllable rate. ("Birthright, Part I" [TNG]). Data did not require food; he occasionally ingested a semi-organic nutrient suspension in a silicon-based liquid medium. ("Deja Q" [TNG]). Although Data's systems were primarily mechanical, cybernetic, and positronic, sufficient biological components were present to allow him to become infected by the **Psi 2000 virus** in 2364. While under the influence of the inhibition-stripping effects of that virus, Data apparently became intimate with *Enterprise*-D security chief **Tasha Yar**. ("The Naked Now" [TNG]). Data's basic programming included a strong inhibition against harming living beings, but he nevertheless had the ability to use deadly force to protect others. ("The Most Toys" [TNG]).

Data in Starfleet. Prior to his assignment to the *Enterprise*-D, Data served aboard the **U.S.S. Trieste**. During this tour-of-duty, the *Trieste* once fell through a wormhole. ("Clues" [TNG]). Aboard the *Enterprise*-D, Data served as operations manager, and was in charge of coordinating the many departments aboard the ship. ("Encounter at Farpoint" [TNG]). In 2366, Commander Data was seriously injured trying to save Q from an attack by gaseous creatures called the **Calamarain**. In gratitude, Q gave Data the gift of allowing Data to experience human laughter for a brief time. ("Deja Q" [TNG]). Data served as father of the bride for the wedding of **Miles O'Brien** and **Keiko Ishikawa** in 2367, and found it necessary to learn to dance to fulfill this ceremonial function. ("Data's Day" [TNG]). Data's first opportunity to command a starship came during the Federation blockade during the **Klingon civil war** of 2368. Data was assigned temporary command of the *Starship* **Sutherland** in Picard's armada. As an android, Data encountered a small amount of prejudice among his human crew, but was nevertheless able to lead effectively. ("Redemption, Part II"[TNG]). In late 2368, Data traveled back in time to old San Francisco when bizarre evidence was found suggesting that he had died some 500 years ago. The evidence was Data's severed head, unearthed from beneath the city of San Francisco, where it had been buried for five centuries. ("Time's Arrow, Part I" [TNG]). Back in the year 1893, Data uncovered a plot by aliens from the planet **Devidia II** who were using the **cholera** plague of the time to conceal their murder of humans. While attempting to stop the **Devidians**, Data's head was severed, and his body was sent forward in time, back to 2368. Aboard the *Enterprise*-D, Geordi La Forge was successful in reattaching Data's head and body. ("Time's Arrow, Part II" [TNG]).

Efforts to understand humanity. Data's attempts to understand human nature once included an effort to learn about the concept of humor, which he studied with the assistance of Guinan and a holodeck-created comedian. ("Where Silence Has Lease" [TNG]). SEE: **Comic, The**. Data even tried a beard once, to the considerable amusement of his shipmates. ("The Schizoid Man" [TNG]). Aboard the *Enterprise*-D, Data shared his living quarters with a cat that he named **Spot**. Data tried to provide for Spot's well-being, but found it difficult to predict the cat's preferences in food. ("Data's Day" [TNG]). One of Data's more challenging efforts to experience humanity was his attempt to pursue a romantic relationship with *Enterprise*-D security officer **Jenna D'Sora** in late 2367. Although D'Sora was attracted to Data, he was unable to return the affection, at least in a manner that she wanted. ("In Theory" [TNG]). Data began to experience dreams in 2369 as a result of an accidental plasma shock received during an experiment. It was later learned that the shock had triggered a program designed for this purpose by Soong, who had hoped the program would be activated when Data reached a certain level of development. Data's initial dreams were of Soong as a blacksmith, incongruously forging the wings of a bird, which Data believed represented himself. ("Birthright, Part I" [TNG]). SEE: **painting**. One of Data's most noteworthy efforts in his quest for humanity was his construction of an android daughter in 2366. Data employed a new **positronic matrix transfer technology** to allow his own neural pathways to be duplicated in another positronic brain, which he used as the basis for his child. His daughter, whom he named **Lal** (Hindi for "beloved"), developed at a remarkable rate and showed evidence of growth potential beyond that of her father, even experiencing emotions. Lal died after having lived little more than two weeks, when she experienced a serious failure in her positronic brain. ("The Offspring" [TNG]).

Data and Lore. Upon returning to the Omicron Theta colony site in 2364, Data participated in the discovery and activation of his android brother, **Lore**. Physically identical to Data, Lore had radically different personality programming,

and attempted to commandeer the *Enterprise*-D before he was beamed into space. ("Datalore" [TNG]). Although Soong was believed to have died at Omicron Theta, he was discovered to have escaped the colony when, in 2367, he remotely gained control of Data, commanding his creation to visit him in his new secret laboratory. There, Soong attempted to install a new chip in Data's positronic brain that would have given Data the ability to experience human emotions. Unfortunately, Lore also responded to Soong's call, and stole the chip from Soong's lab. Dr. Soong died shortly thereafter. ("Brothers" [TNG]). Data began to experience emotions in 2369 when Lore secretly bombarded Data with signals that triggered negative emotions in his positronic brain. Lore used these negative emotions to manipulate Data into joining him and the Borg against the Federation. When Data realized that Lore was manipulating him and harming the Borg, he was forced to deactivate Lore. ("Descent, Parts I and II" [TNG]).

Android rights. The question of Data's sentience, and more specifically whether Data was entitled to full civil rights under the Constitution of the United Federation of Planets, was addressed in a number of important legal decisions. The first, in 2341, was rendered by a **Starfleet Academy** entrance committee that permitted Data to enter the Academy and serve as a member of Starfleet. Several years later, the question was more definitively addressed when Judge Advocate General **Phillipa Louvois** ruled that Data was indeed a sentient being and therefore entitled to civil rights, including the right to resign from Starfleet if he so chose. As of stardate 42527, Data had been decorated by Starfleet Command for gallantry and had received the Medal of Honor with clusters, the Legion of Honor, and the Star Cross. ("The Measure of a Man" [TNG]). *Data first appeared in "Encounter at Farpoint" (TNG).*

• **"Datalore."** *Next Generation* episode #14. Teleplay by Robert Lewin and Gene Roddenberry. Story by Robert Lewin and Maurice Hurley. Directed by Rob Bowman. Stardate 41242.4. *First aired in 1988. Investigating the planet where Data was found, the* Enterprise-D *discovers Data's twin brother, an android named Lore. This was the last* Star Trek *episode to carry Gene Roddenberry's name in the writing credits.* SEE: **Argyle, Lieutenant Commander; Asimov, Dr. Isaac; Crystalline Entity; Data; Lore; Omicron Theta; positronic brain; Soong, Noonien;** *Tripoli, U.S.S.*

Dathon. (Paul Winfield). Captain of a **Tamarian** starship who made a heroic attempt to establish communication with the Federation in 2368. When his people were unable to establish communication with the Federation, despite several contacts over the course of a century, Dathon isolated himself and *Enterprise*-D captain Picard on the surface of planet **El-Adrel IV**. There, he hoped that face-to-face contact and a shared danger would enable Picard to grasp the unusual nature of Tamarian speech. Although Dathon died from wounds inflicted by a beast on El-Adrel IV, Dathon was ultimately successful in his quest as Picard came to understand the fact that Tamarian speech was based entirely on metaphors. ("Darmok" [TNG]). *Paul Winfield also played Captain Terrell in* Star Trek II.

• **"Dauphin, The."** *Next Generation episode #36. Written by Scott Rubenstein & Leonard Mlodinow. Directed by Rob Bowman. Stardate 42568.8. First aired in 1989. A young girl, sequestered on a distant planet, is returned to her homeworld, where it is hoped she can bring peace to warring peoples. The term dauphin comes from the title given in the 14th-19th centuries to the heir apparent to the French throne.* SEE: **allasomorph; Andronesian encephalitis; Anya; Crusher, Wesley; Daled IV; deuterium control conduit; Klavdia III; love poetry, Klingon; Rousseau V; Salia; SCM Model 3; Talian chocolate mousse; Thalos VII.**

Davies, Ensign. (Nicholas Cascone). Geologist aboard the *Enterprise*-D. Davies participated in the geological survey of planets in the **Selcundi Drema** Sector in 2365. The survey was supervised by Acting Ensign **Wesley Crusher**. Davies attempted to assist Crusher in the project, but his offers of help served to undermine young Crusher's confidence. ("Pen Pals" [TNG]).

Davila, Carmen. (Susan Diol). Colony engineer killed by the **Crystalline Entity** at planet **Melona IV** in 2368. She had been helping to prepare a colony site at the time. Davila was a friend of William Riker. ("Silicon Avatar" [TNG]).

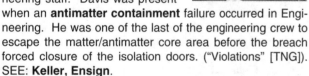

Davis, Ensign. (Craig Benton). Member of the *Enterprise*-D engineering staff. Davis was present when an **antimatter containment** failure occurred in Engineering. He was one of the last of the engineering crew to escape the matter/antimatter core area before the breach forced closure of the isolation doors. ("Violations" [TNG]). SEE: **Keller, Ensign.**

Dax, Curzon. (Frank Owen Smith). **Trill** host prior to **Jadzia Dax**. ("Emissary" [DS9]). Dax served as a Federation mediator on **Klaestron IV** during that planet's civil war in the 2330s. He became friends with **General Ardelon Tandro** and his family while stationed on the planet. Unknown to Tandro, Dax was also engaged in a love affair with Tandro's wife, **Enina**. Thirty years

later, when Jadzia Dax was accused of Tandro's murder, Enina testified that at the time of her husband's death, Curzon Dax was in her bed. ("Dax" [DS9]). Curzon Dax and **Benjamin Sisko** were good friends when Sisko was an ensign, a friendship that they maintained for nearly two decades. When Dax became Jadzia, Sisko was fond of calling her "old man," despite the fact that Dax's new host was

a young woman. ("Emissary" [DS9]). Curzon used to assign Ben Sisko to guide VIP guests while under his command so the Trill wouldn't have to deal with them. ("The Forsaken" [DS9]).

Dax, Jadzia. (Terry Farrell). Starfleet science officer assigned to **Deep Space 9** in 2369, shortly after Starfleet took over the station. Jadzia Dax was a member of the **Trill** joined species. Jadzia, a young woman, had wanted to become a host since she was a child and worked very hard at winning the honor. She won scholarships, achieving Premier Distinctions in

exobiology, zoology, astrophysics, and exoarchaeology before she was joined as a Trill in 2367. Dax's previous host had been **Curzon Dax**. As Jadzia, Dax had been a close friend of **Benjamin Sisko**, but she noted that such friendships are sometimes difficult to maintain when a Trill has a new host, particularly one of a different gender. ("Emissary" [DS9]). As is characteristic of Trills, Dax's hands are cold. ("A Man Alone" [DS9]). Dax's previous hosts had been both male and female, but by 2369, Dax had not been in a female host for more than eighty years. ("Babel "[DS9]). In joinings with previous hosts, Dax had been a mother three times and a father twice, but confessed she hadn't been very successful either way. ("The Nagus" [DS9]). As an attractive woman, Dax drew the attentions of many men, including Dr. Julian Bashir. Dax considered herself above such interests, although she once admitted that she thought **Morn** was cute. ("Progress" [DS9]). As of 2369, Dax had been attempting to master the **Altonian brain teaser** for 440 years. ("A Man Alone" [DS9]). *The number of Dax's previous hosts has not been established, but Jadzia is at least the sixth host, per "A Man Alone" (DS9). Dax was first seen in "Emissary" (DS9).*

Dax. (Michael Snyder). Crew member aboard the *Starship Enterprise*-A in 2293. Incriminating evidence, **magnetic boots**, were planted in Dax's personal locker, implicating him in the murder of **Chancellor Gorkon**, but Dax's foot structure was clearly unable to fit boots designed for humans. (*Star Trek VI: The Undiscovered Country*). *It has been suggested that this Dax may have been an earlier host of the Trill that later served on Deep Space 9. The symbiont character in* Deep Space Nine *is certainly old enough for this to be possible, but this theory is based on circumstantial evidence only.*

• **"Dax."** *Deep Space Nine episode #8. Teleplay by D. C. Fontana and Peter Allan Fields. Story by Peter Allan Fields. Directed by David Carson. Stardate 46910.1. First aired in 1993. After thirty years, the son of a murdered Bajoran general claims that Dax's previous host is the murderer.* SEE: **Argosian; Dax, Curzon; Dax, Jadzia; Klaestron IV; O'Brien, Keiko; Peers, Selin; Renora; Sisko, Benjamin; symbiont; Tandro, Enina; Tandro, General Ardelon; Tandro, Ilon; Trill.**

• **"Day of the Dove."** Original Series episode #66. Written by

Jerome Bixby. Directed by Marvin Chomsky. No stardate given. *First aired in 1968. The* Enterprise *crew and a group of Klingons are trapped by an energy creature that feeds on hatred.* SEE: **Archanis IV; armory; Auxiliary Control; Beta XII-A entity; Beta XII-A; Chekov, Pavel A.; Chekov, Piotr; claymore; intraship beaming; Johnson, Lieutenant; Kang; Klingon Empire; Mara; Organian Peace Treaty.**

Daystrom Institute. Major center for science and technology in the 24th century. Named for 23rd-century computer scientist **Richard Daystrom**. In 2365, **Commander Bruce Maddox** served as Chair of Robotics at the Daystrom Institute, and also worked with the Cybernetics Division. ("The Measure of a Man" [TNG], "Data's Day" [TNG]). *Enterprise-*D designer Dr. Leah Brahms was a graduate of the Daystrom Institute. ("Booby Trap" [TNG]). Archaeologist **Vash**, who continued **Dr. Samuel Estragon**'s work to locate the fabled *Tox Uthat* after his death in 2366, promised Estragon that she would present the *Uthat* to the Daystrom Institute if she did find it. ("Captain's Holiday" [TNG]). In 2369, **Vash** was invited to speak at the Daystrom Institute concerning her travels in the **Gamma Quadrant**. This came as quite a surprise, since her membership to the Institute's Archaeological Council had been suspended twice for illegally selling artifacts. Vash declined the offer so that she could continue exploring archeological ruins throughout the galaxy. ("Q-Less" [DS9]). An annex of the Daystrom Institute was located on planet **Galor IV**. ("The Offspring" [TNG]). *The Daystrom Institute was, of course, a tip of the hat to "The Ultimate Computer" (TOS).*

Daystrom, Dr. Richard. (William Marshall). Brilliant 23rd-century computer scientist, inventor of comptronic and **duotronic** systems.

Daystrom won the prestigious Nobel and **Zee-Magnees prizes** in 2243 at the age of 24 for his breakthrough in duotronics, which became the basis for computer systems aboard Federation starships for over 80 years.

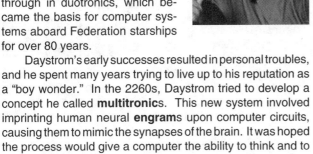

Daystrom's early successes resulted in personal troubles, and he spent many years trying to live up to his reputation as a "boy wonder." In the 2260s, Daystrom tried to develop a concept he called **multitronics**. This new system involved imprinting human neural **engram**s upon computer circuits, causing them to mimic the synapses of the brain. It was hoped the process would give a computer the ability to think and to reason like a human. Unfortunately, when tested, Daystrom's multitronic system also mimicked the unstable portions of his personality, resulting in a disaster in which nearly 500 Starfleet personnel were killed.

The failure of his creation pushed Daystrom over the edge of insanity and he was committed to a rehabilitation center for treatment. ("The Ultimate Computer" [TOS]). SEE: *Excalibur, U.S.S.; Lexington, U.S.S.;* **M-5**.

***D'deridex-*class Warbird.** Designation for a massive Romulan spacecraft. These ships, significantly larger than a *Galaxy-*class starship, are believed to have greater firepower, but a slightly lower sustainable warp speed. ("Tin Man" [TNG]). Starfleet at one time designated these ships as B-Type warbirds. ("The Defector" [TNG]).

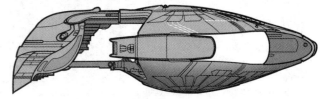

de Laure belt. Location of planet **Tau Cygna V**. ("The Ensigns of Command" [TNG]).

• **"Deadly Years, The."** Original Series episode #40. Written by David P. Harmon. Directed by Joseph Pevney. Stardate 3478.2. *First aired in 1967. Exposure to an unknown form of radiation causes* Enterprise *crew members to age at an incredible rate.* SEE: **adrenaline; Aldebaran III; Chekov, Pavel A.; Code 2; corbomite; Galway, Lieutenant; Gamma Hydra IV; hyronalyn; Johnson, Elaine; Johnson, Robert; Kirk, James T.; Romulan Neutral Zone; Starbase 10; Stocker, Commodore; Sulu, Hikaru; Wallace, Dr. Janet; Wallace, Dr. Theodore.**

Deadwood. American Western town in South Dakota on Earth, re-created in **Alexander Rozhenko**'s holodeck program, *Ancient West.* ("A Fistful of Datas" [TNG]).

Dealt, Lieutenant Commander Hester. (Seymour Cassel). Medical trustee of the Federation Medical Collection Station on planet 'audet IX. Dealt supervised the transport of plasma plague specimens aboard the *Enterprise-*D to Science Station **Tango Sierra** to help combat the plague outbreak in the Rachelis system in 2365. ("The Child" [TNG]).

Dean, Lieutenant. (Dan Kern). *Enterprise-*D crew member who was an accomplished swordsman, and who enjoyed fencing with Captain Picard in the ship's gymnasium. ("We'll Always Have Paris" [TNG]). *Lieutenant Dean was named for episode co-writer Deborah Dean Davis.*

Debin. (Douglas Rowe). Leader from the planet **Altec**, father to **Yanar**. ("The Outrageous Okona" [TNG]).

Decius. (Lawrence Montaigne). Officer aboard the **Romulan bird-of-prey** that crossed the **Romulan Neutral Zone** in 2266. Although a junior officer aboard that vessel, he had relatives in high places in the Romulan government, and thus carried possibly undue influence. Decius used his influence to steer his commander into a more aggressive strategy when confronting the *Enterprise*. ("Balance of Terror" [TOS]).

Decius. A Romulan warbird, encountered by the *Enterprise-*D and "Captain" Riker during during a virtual reality engineered by **Barash** on **Alpha Onias III** in 2367. The *Decius* transported "Admiral" Picard, Counselor Troi, and "Ambassador" Tomalak to a rendezvous with the *Enterprise-*D. ("Future Imperfect" [TNG]).

Decker, Commodore Matt. (William Windom). Commander of the **U.S.S. Constellation**. Decker's ship was attacked by a robotic **planet killer** weapon in 2267. During the attack, Decker sent his crew down to the third planet in the **L-374** system, but shortly thereafter, the planet killer destroyed all the planets in that system, leaving Decker aboard his ship as the only survivor. Decker later commandeered an *Enterprise* shuttlecraft on a suicide attack against the planet killer. The attack was unsuccessful, but his actions paved the way to the planet killer's destruction. ("The Doomsday Machine" [TOS]).

Decker, Willard. (Stephen Collins). Captain of the *Starship Enterprise* during the ship's refitting in 2270-2271. Decker, who had been assigned to the *Enterprise* at Kirk's recommendation, was replaced by Kirk and downgraded to executive officer when the ship intercepted the **V'Ger** entity near Earth in 2271. Decker was the son of Commodore **Matt Decker** and was apparently killed when he physically joined with V'Ger to help dissuade that entity from destroying the Earth. Decker was listed as "missing in action." Before his assignment to the *Enterprise*, Decker had been stationed on planet **Delta IV**, and was romantically involved with future *Enterprise* navigator **Ilia**. (*Star Trek: The Motion Picture*).

decompression chamber. Medical treatment facility aboard Federation starships for patients requiring exposure to atmospheric pressures other than class-M normal. ("Space Seed" [TOS], "The Empath" [TOS], "The Lights of Zetar" [TOS]).

dedication plaque. Commemorative plate located on the bridge of Federation starships. SEE **illustrations next page**.

Deela. (Kathie Browne). Queen of the Scalosian race who commandeered the *Starship Enterprise* in 2268, intending to procure a supply of fertile males for the perpetuation of her race. Like all **Scalosians**, Deela's biochemistry had been **hyperaccelerated**, so one hour for her was like one of our seconds. Deela was attracted to James Kirk, and accelerated him to her level. Kirk thwarted her plans, and Deela subsequently returned to **Scalos** with her people. ("Wink of an Eye" [TOS]).

Deep Space 4. Federation space station where archaeologist **Richard Galen** hoped to gain passage on an **Al-Leyan** transport to Caere as part of his quest to learn about the first humanoids to live in our galaxy. ("The Chase" [TNG]).

Deep Space 9. Old **Cardassian** mining station built in orbit of planet **Bajor**. ("Emissary" [DS9]). Deep Space 9 was built in 2351 ("Babel" [DS9]), then abandoned in 2369 when the Cardassians relinquished their claim on Bajor, and retreated

from the region. Starfleet assumed control of the facility shortly thereafter at the request of the Bajoran provisional government. The station assumed great commercial, scientific, and strategic importance shortly thereafter when the remarkable **Bajoran wormhole** was discovered, linking the Bajor system with the distant **Gamma Quadrant**. Starfleet officer **Benjamin Sisko** was placed in charge of the station, and his staff included Bajoran Liaison **Kira Nerys**, Security Officer **Odo**, Chief Medical Officer **Julian Bashir**, Science Officer **Jadzia Dax**, and Chief of Operations **Miles O'Brien**. ("Emissary" [DS9]).

Major features of the station include the **Operations Center** (from which all station functions are managed), the **Promenade** (a main thoroughfare containing numerous service facilities and stores, including **Quark's bar**), three massive docking towers, and several smaller docking ports on an outer docking ring. There are normally about 300 permanent residents on the station, not counting visitors and crews of ships docked at the station. Weapons are stored in the Habitat Ring, Level 5, Section 3. ("Captive Pursuit" [DS9]).

Prior to being designated Deep Space 9 by Starfleet, the station had been called Terek Nor by the Cardassians. ("Cardassians" [DS9]).

The station model was designed at the Star Trek: Deep Space Nine *art department by Rick Sternbach and Herman Zimmerman. Contributing artists included Ricardo Delgado, Joseph Hodges, Nathen Crowley, Jim Martin, Rob Legato, Gary Hutzel, Mike Okuda, and executive producer Rick Berman. The miniature was fabricated by Tony Meininger.*

Deep Space Station K-7. Federation outpost near **Sherman's Planet**, located one parsec from the nearest Klingon outpost. A Federation development project for Sherman's Planet in 2267 was threatened when some 1,771,561 tribbles infested

storage bins of **quadrotriticale** intended for the project. ("The Trouble with Tribbles" [TOS]). SEE: **Baris, Nilz**; **Darvin, Arne**. *Stock footage of K-7 was later reused in "The Ultimate Computer" (TOS), although it represented another station.*

• **"Defector, The."** *Next Generation* episode #58. Written by Ronald D. Moore. Directed by Robert Scheerer. Stardate 43462.5. *First aired in 1990. A Romulan defector crosses the Neutral Zone with a terrifying report of a planned Romulan attack on Federation space.* SEE: **Apnex Sea; B-Type Warbird;** *Bortas, I.K.C.;* **Cheron, Battle of; Gal Gaththong; Haden, Admiral;** *Henry V; Hood, U.S.S.;* **Jarok, Alidar;** *Monitor, U.S.S.;* **Nelvana III; Neutral Zone, Romulan; Norkan outposts; onkians; Outpost Sierra VI;** *pahtk;* **Romulus; scoutship, Romulan; Setal, Sublieutenant; Starbase Lya III;** *tohzah;* **Tomalak; Treaty of Algeron; Valley of Chula;** *veruul.*

Dedication plaques from Federation starships.

Original series U.S.S. Enterprise *dedication plaque. Note that this indicates the ship as a "starship class" vessel, although the ship has been referred to elsewhere (and has been generally accepted) as a* Constitution-*class ship.*

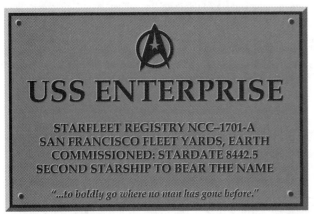

U.S.S. Enterprise-*A dedication plaque as used in* Star Trek V: The Final Frontier *and* Star Trek VI: The Undiscovered Country. *A slightly different plaque was installed but not seen on the* Enterprise *bridge seen in* Star Trek IV: The Voyage Home.

U.S.S. Enterprise-*D dedication plaque. This plaque began the tradition of listing the names of "Starfleet" personnel responsible for the launching of the ship, who were in actuality people who worked on the show. Note that "Admiral" Gene Roddenberry is listed as chief of staff. A simpler version of this plaque was used on the bridge during the first three seasons.*

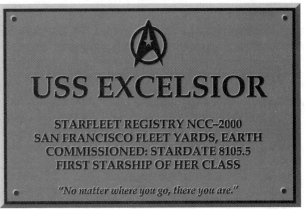

U.S.S. Excelsior *dedication plaque as used in* Star Trek VI: The Undiscovered Country. *Note the ship's motto, drawn from* The Adventures of Buckaroo Banzai.

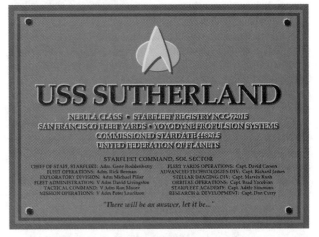

U.S.S. Sutherland *dedication plaque from "Redemption, Part II" (TNG). The Starfleet personnel list includes more people from the production and stage crew.*

U.S.S. Brattain *dedication plaque from "Night Terrors" (TNG). The ship's motto is a reference to* Gilligan's Island.

Defiant, U.S.S. Federation starship, **Constitution** class, Starfleet registry number NCC-1764. The *Defiant* disappeared in 2268 near **Tholian** territory into what was believed to be a **spatial interphase**. This interphase had an adverse effect on humanoid neurophysiology and caused mass insanity among the crew prior to the disappearance of the ship. The *Defiant* was last seen shimmering, suspended between two dimensions, until it faded into interspace. ("The Tholian Web" [TOS]).

deflectors. Energy field used to protect starships and other vessels from harm resulting from natural hazards or enemy attack. SEE: **shields**.

Dehner, Dr. Elizabeth. (Sally Kellerman). Psychologist assigned to the *Enterprise* in 2265 to study the crew's reactions to crisis situations. Dehner became mutated, along with Lieutenant Commander **Gary Mitchell**, into a godlike being. Dehner and Mitchell were later killed when *Enterprise* captain Kirk sought to quarantine them on planet **Delta Vega**. Both were later listed as having given their lives in the line of duty. ("Where No Man Has Gone Before" [TOS]).

Deinonychus VII. Planet where the *Starship Enterprise*-D was to rendezvous with the supply ship **U.S.S. Biko** on stardate 46271. ("A Fistful of Datas" [TNG]).

• **"Deja Q."** *Next Generation* episode #61. Written by Richard Danus. Directed by Les Landau. Stardate 43539.1. *First aired in 1990. Q loses his powers and takes refuge on the* Enterprise-*D.* SEE: **Belzoidian flea; Berthold rays; Bre'el IV; Calamarain; Data; Deltived Asteroid Belt; Garin; Markoffian sea lizard; Q Continuum; Q; Q2;** *Sakharov, Shuttlecraft*; **Station Nigala IV; subspace compression; warp field.**

deja vu. French-language term from Earth referring to a perception that a current experience is a repetition of a previous one. An intense feeling of *deja vu* experienced by several *Enterprise*-D crew members in 2368 was found to be due to the passage of the ship into a **temporal causality loop**. ("Cause and Effect" [TNG]).

Dekon Elig. (Dan Curry). Bajoran geneticist who invented an **aphasia virus**, intended for use as a terrorist weapon against the **Cardassian** occupation forces. Dekon Elig, who was a member of the Bajoran **Higa Metar** underground, died while attempting escape from the Cardassians the **Velos VII Internment Camp** in 2360. Dekon's aphasia virus was accidentally unleashed at Deep Space 9 in 2369, after the

Cardassian retreat from **Bajor**. ("Babel" [DS9]). SEE: **Surmak Ren.** *The face of Dekon Elig, seen only as a mug shot in a computer screen, was provided by* Star Trek *visual effects producer Dan Curry.*

dekyon field. Subspace phenomenon that can travel across a **temporal causality loop**. A dekyon field was used to interact with **positronic subprocessors** in Data's brain, permitting the transmission of a simple message to the next iteration of a causality loop when the *Enterprise*-D was trapped in such a loop in 2368. ("Cause and Effect" [TNG]).

delactovine. Systemic stimulant drug in use aboard the *Enterprise*-D. ("The Inner Light" [TNG]).

Delaplane, Governor. Leader of the planet **Pacifica**. Delaplane sent a message to Starfleet Command when Picard canceled a scheduled visit there in 2364. ("Conspiracy" [TNG]).

Delb II. Homeworld of **Nellen Tore**, assistant to Starfleet **Admiral Norah Satie.** ("The Drumhead" [TNG]).

Delinia II. Planet where **transporter psychosis** was first diagnosed in 2209. ("Realm of Fear" [TNG]).

Delos IV. Planet on which **Dr. Beverly Crusher** did her medical internship under **Dr. Dalen Quaice** in 2352. ("Remember Me" [TNG]).

Delos. Star system in which two inhabited planets are located, **Ornara** and **Brekka**. The star Delos underwent a period of large-scale magnetic field changes in 2364. The *Enterprise*-D was assigned to study the phenomenon, and accidentally became embroiled in an ongoing dispute between the two planets. ("Symbiosis" [TNG]).

Delovian souffle. An ice-cream-like dessert served by Guinan in the **Ten-Forward lounge** aboard the *Enterprise*-D. ("The Child" [TNG]).

Delphi Ardu. Star system in which was located the last outpost of the now-defunct **Tkon Empire**. The *Starship Enterprise*-D and a **Ferengi Marauder** spacecraft were detained there by the Tkon outpost in 2364 when the Federation made first contact with both the Ferengi and the surviving Tkon outpost. ("The Last Outpost" [TNG]). SEE: **Portal**.

Delta IV. Homeworld to the Deltan race. Starfleet officer **Will Decker** once served on this planet, where he met future shipmate **Ilia**, a native of Delta IV. (*Star Trek: The Motion Picture*).

Delta Quadrant. One-quarter of the entire Milky Way Galaxy. Virtually nothing is known about this quadrant, as its closest point is some 40,000 light-years from the Federation. It is believed that the **Borg** homeworld is somewhere deep in Delta Quadrant. The **Barzan wormhole** (not to be confused with the Bajoran wormhole), at one time believed to be stable, had one terminus in the Delta Quadrant, although that end-point was later found to move unpredictably. ("The Price" [TNG]). **Q** offered to take **Vash** to explore Delta Quadrant, but the archaeologist declined. ("Q-Less" [DS9]).

Delta Rana IV. Class-M planet that was home to a Federation colony which was destroyed by the **Husnock** in 2361. All but one of the 11,000 colonists were killed and the planet surface was ravaged. The one survivor, actually a **Douwd** traveling under the name of **Kevin Uxbridge**, used his enormous powers to destroy the entire Husnock race in retribution. Later, Uxbridge remained in self-imposed isolation on Delta Rana IV. Delta Rana IV has three moons. ("The Survivors" [TNG]).

Delta Rana star system. The location of planet **Delta Rana IV.** ("The Survivors" [TNG]).

Delta Vega. Distant Class-M planet near the galaxy's edge on which was located an automated **lithium** cracking station. Captain James Kirk attempted to maroon the mutated **Gary Mitchell** there in 2265 because, while habitable, the planet was visited only every 20 years by cargo freighters. ("Where No Man Has Gone Before" [TOS]). *The matte painting used to establish the huge exterior of the Delta Vega lithium cracking station was done by noted visual effects artist Albert Whitlock. The painting was later modified and reused as the surface portion of the Tantalus penal colony in "Dagger of the Mind" (TOS).*

delta radiation. Form of hazardous energy. Fleet Captain **Christopher Pike** suffered severe delta-ray exposure following an accident aboard a class-J training ship in 2266. ("The Cage," "The Menagerie, Part I" [TOS]). Delta radiation emitted from a star can interfere with a ship's sensors, as when the *Rio Grande* searched for the downed *Yangtzee Kiang* in the Gamma Quadrant in 2369. ("Battle Lines" [DS9]).

Deltans. Humanoid species native to planet **Delta IV**. Deltans exhibit a characteristically bald head, except for eyebrows, and are known for their highly developed sexuality. *Enterprise* navigator **Ilia** was Deltan. (*Star Trek: The Motion Picture*).

Deltived Asteroid Belt. An astronomical formation misplaced by **Q2**, who wasn't too proud of the mishap. ("Deja Q" [TNG]).

"Demons of Air and Darkness." Name given to the ancient **Iconians** in old texts, referring to the Iconians' legendary ability to travel without spacecraft, using an advanced technology to transport between planets. ("Contagion" [TNG]).

Deneb II. Planet where an unknown entity known as **Kesla** murdered several women. The same evil energy force continued its murderous deeds on planet **Argelius II** in 2267. ("Wolf in the Fold" [TOS]).

Deneb IV. Class-M planet inhabited by a race called the **Bandi**. *The star Deneb is part of the constellation Cygnus (the Swan) visible from Earth.* ("Encounter at Farpoint, Parts I and II" [TNG]). SEE: **Bandi**.

Deneb V. Homeworld to the Denebians. ("I, Mudd" [TOS]).

Denebian slime devil. Nasty creature that the Klingon **Korax** thought bore a strong resemblance to Captain Kirk. ("The Trouble with Tribbles" [TOS]).

Denebians. Race that purchased all rights to a Vulcan fuel synthesizer from confidence man **Harry Mudd** in 2267. The Denebians contacted the Vulcans and found the sale a ruse. Mudd was arrested and given several colorful choices of execution, none of which appealed to Mudd. ("I, Mudd" [TOS]).

Deneva. Federation planet, considered by many to be one of the most beautiful in the galaxy, boasting a population of over 1 million. Deneva was colonized in the 22nd century, and served as a base for interstellar freighting. The planet was infected by alien neural parasites in 2267, resulting in the death of many of the colonists. One infested colonist flew a small spacecraft directly into the Denevan sun. The sun's intense radiation drove the parasite from his body, just before the ship was incinerated by the sun. His attempt led science personnel from the *Starship Enterprise* to learn that the parasites were adversely affected by ultraviolet radiation. *Enterprise* personnel placed a series of satellites around the planet, bombarding the surface with sufficient ultraviolet radiation to eradicate the parasites. Among the colonists killed in 2267 were **George Samuel** and **Aurelan Kirk**. They were survived by their son **Peter Kirk**. ("Operation— Annihilate!" [TOS]). SEE: **Denevan neural parasites**; **Ingraham B**. *The city exteriors for Deneva were shot on location at TRW near Los Angeles. The establishing shot of Kirk's brother's lab was a building on the campus of UCLA, and the entrance to the building was the cafeteria at TRW.*

Denevan neural parasite. Origin unknown, an irregularly shaped gelatinous life-form analogous in structure to an oversized brain cell. The entire population of these parasites were somehow linked together to form a collective intelligence. In young form, the parasites were mobile, capable of flight. They would latch themselves onto a humanoid life-form, infiltrating the humanoid nervous system, gaining control of both autonomic and higher functions, inflicting severe pain on the victim. These parasites were so virulent that they were capable of infesting an entire planet's population, at which point they would reach across interstellar distances to another planet. The neural parasites appeared to have come from outside the Milky Way galaxy, attacking the ancient Beta Portolan system, then infesting **Levinius V**, **Theta Cygni XII**, **Ingraham B,** and, in 2267, planet **Deneva**. Among the parasites' victims at Deneva were **George Samuel** and **Aurelan Kirk**, brother and sister-in-law to Captain James Kirk. Also infested was Science Officer Spock, although he was freed by exposure to intense light, an experiment that provided the means to destroy the remaining parasites on Deneva. The actual eradication was accomplished by placing 210 satellites into orbit around Deneva, bombarding the surface with powerful ultraviolet radiation. ("Operation— Annihilate!" [TOS]). SEE: **Denevan ship**.

Denevan ship. Small one-person spacecraft flown by a colonist from planet **Deneva** in 2267. The pilot had been infested by the **Denevan neural parasites**, and in desperation, he flew the ship directly into the Denevan sun. Just prior to the ship's incineration, the pilot was freed from the parasites, which apparently were unable to tolerate the intense levels of ultraviolet radiation. The pilot's death provided valuable information for the control and eradication of the parasites from Deneva. ("Operation— Annihilate!" [TOS]).

Deng. *Enterprise-D* crew member who assisted in setting up the **thermal deflectors** against a fierce firestorm on planet **Bersallis III** in 2369. ("Lessons" [TNG]).

Denius III. Planet visited by the *U.S.S. Yamato* under the command of **Captain Donald Varley** and **Dr. Ramsey** in 2365. Artifacts recovered from Denius III included an unknown instrument that displayed a star map, making it possible to determine the location of the legendary planet **Iconia**. ("Contagion" [TNG]).

Denkiri Arm. Located in the **Delta Quadrant**, the Denkiri Arm is one of the massive spiral-shaped arms that make up the Milky Way Galaxy. The **Barzan wormhole**, previously thought to be stable, had one terminus that was located in the Denkiri Arm, some 70,000 light-years from Federation space. ("The Price" [TNG]).

denkirs. Unit of volume measure used by **Zibalians**. One hundred denkirs is about equal to 200 milliliters. ("The Most Toys" [TNG]).

Denorios Belt. Charged plasma field in the **Bajor System** where at least five of the mystical Bajoran **Orbs** were discovered. The stable **Bajoran wormhole**, discovered in 2369, was located in the Denorios Belt. Bajoran religious beliefs held that the **Celestial Temple**, home of the **Prophets**, was in the belt, and many Bajorans interpreted the wormhole as being a manifestation of the temple itself. The Denorios Belt was characterized by unusually severe neutrino disturbances. ("Emissary" [DS9]). Ships have always avoided the Denorios Belt. ("If Wishes Were Horses" [DS9]).

dentarium. Metal alloy, used in Vulcan spacecraft such as the *T'Pau*. ("Unification, Part I" [TNG]).

Denubian Alps. Nonterrestrial mountain range known for excellent skiing conditions. Denubian Alps skiing runs are among the **holodeck** programs available on the *Enterprise*-D. ("Angel One" [TNG]).

Denver, U.S.S. Federation transport ship. Crew complement of 23. In 2368, the *Denver* was transporting 517 colonists to the Beloti Sector when the ship struck a gravitic mine left over from the Cardassian wars. The *Denver* sustained heavy damage, crashing in the Mericor System. The *Enterprise*-D was called in to assist with the survivors. ("Ethics" [TNG]).

deoxyribonucleic acid. SEE: **DNA**.

deoxyribose suspensions. A fluid derived from deoxyribonucleic acid (**DNA**). Deoxyribose suspensions were used by **J'Ddan** to encode stolen *Enterprise*-D schematics into amino acid sequences, and injected into his bloodstream, making his body an undetectable carrier of the secret information. ("The Drumhead" [TNG]).

DePaul, Lieutenant. (Sean Kenny). Crew member aboard the original *Starship Enterprise* who sometimes served as navigator and helm officer. ("Arena" [TOS], "A Taste of Armageddon" [TOS]). *Sean Kenny also played the injured Captain Pike in "The Menagerie, Parts I and II" (TOS).*

Deriben V. Location of **Lieutenant Aquiel Uhnari**'s last posting prior to her assignment to **Relay Station 47** in 2368. She did not get along with her commanding officer at Dereben. ("Aquiel" [TNG]).

dermatiraelian plastiscine. Medication used to maintain the effects of cosmetic surgery. **Aamin Marritza** took it for five years after altering his face to that of **Gul Darhe'el**. ("Duet" [DS9]).

Dern, Ensign. *Enterprise*-D systems engineer. Lieutenant Reginald Barclay suggested Dern to serve on an away team to the *U.S.S. Yosemite*, but Geordi wanted Barclay to come along. ("Realm of Fear" [TNG]).

DeSalle, Lieutenant. (Michael Barrier). Crew member aboard the *Starship Enterprise* who served as navigator, and later as an assistant chief engineer. ("The Squire of Gothos" [TOS], "This Side of Paradise" [TOS], "Catspaw" [TOS]).

• **"Descent, Part I."** *Next Generation* episode #152. Story by Jeri Taylor. Teleplay by Ronald D. Moore. Directed by Alexander Singer. Stardate 46982.1. *First aired in 1993. The Enterprise-D encounters a group of self-aware fanatical Borg who are followers of Data's evil brother, Lore. This was the cliff-hanger last episode of the sixth season.* SEE: *Agamemnon, U.S.S.*; **Borg**; **Borg ship**; **Brooks, Admiral**; **Corelki**; *Crazy Horse, U.S.S.*; **Crosis**; **Data**; **Einstein, Albert**; *El-Baz, Shuttlepod*; **Ferengi trading vessel**; **forced plasma beam**; *Gorkon, U.S.S.*; **Hawking, Dr. Steven William**; **Hugh**; **level-two security alert**; **Lore**; **luvetric pulse**; **MS 1 colony**; **Nechayev, Vice-Admiral Alynna**; **New Berlin Colony**; **Newton, Issac**; **Ohniaka III**; **One, The**; **quantum fluctuations**;

ship recognition protocols; Torsus; Towles; transwarp conduit; Wallace.

DeSeve, Ensign Stefan. (Barry Lynch). Starfleet officer who renounced his Federation citizenship in 2349 to live on **Romulus**. DeSeve later recalled that he found the simplicity of the Romulan system of absolute values and their strong sense of purpose to be appealing. He noted that in later years, he began to realize that right and wrong is a more ambiguous matter. After twenty years on Romulus, DeSeve returned to Federation custody in 2369 to help arrange the defection of Romulan **vice-proconsul M'ret** to the Federation. ("Face of the Enemy" [TNG]).

DeSoto, Captain Robert. (Michael Cavanaugh). Commanding officer of the *U.S.S. Hood* when **William T. Riker** served aboard that ship (prior to Riker's service aboard the *Enterprise*-D, but after his assignment to the *U.S.S. Potemkin*). DeSoto spoke very highly of Riker, despite an incident in which Riker refused to let DeSoto beam into a hazardous situation. ("Encounter at Farpoint, Parts I and II" [TNG]). In 2366, DeSoto and the *Hood* were assigned to transport mission specialist **Tam Elbrun** for a priority rendezvous with the *Enterprise*-D ("Tin Man" [TNG]). *DeSoto was mentioned in "Encounter at Farpoint" (TNG), but not actually seen until "Tin Man" (TNG).*

destruct sequence. A command program incorporated into the main computer of Federation starships, intended to facilitate destruction of the ship to prevent it from falling into enemy hands. The *U.S.S. Enterprise* destruct sequence required voice authorization from the commanding officer and two other senior officers. After voiceprint confirmation of each officer's identity, the commanding officer would verbally enter the command "Destruct sequence one, code one, one A." The computer would verify the command; then the second officer would verbally enter "Destruct sequence two, code one, one-A, two-B," which would then be verified by the computer. The third officer would give the code "Destruct sequence three, code one-B, two-B, three." The actual destruct countdown would be initiated by the command from the captain "Code zero, zero, zero, destruct zero." The computer would then give a countdown to destruction. The destruct countdown could be aborted until minus five seconds by the command "Code one two three continuity, abort destruct order." The destruct sequence was entered but not executed when **Lokai** and **Bele** attempted to commandeer the *Enterprise* in 2269. ("Let That Be Your Last Battlefield" [TOS]). The same sequence was later used to destroy the *Enterprise* at the **Genesis Planet** when the ship was about to be seized by a Klingon boarding party in 2285. (*Star Trek III: The Search for Spock*). SEE: **autodestruct.**

Detrian System. Star system that experienced a collision of two gas-giant planets in 2369. The combined mass of the two planets was sufficient to cause a self-sustaining fusion reaction; that is, the combined planets became a small star. The *Enterprise*-D recorded the event for scientific posterity. ("Ship in a Bottle" [TNG]).

detronal scanner. Medical instrument used to read and encode the DNA patterns of living tissue. ("Ethics" [TNG]).

deuridium. Rare substance used by the **Kobliad** race to stabilize their cell structures to prolong their lives. A shipment of deuridium from the Gamma Quadrant was delivered to Deep Space 9 in 2369. ("The Passenger" [DS9]). SEE: **Vantika, Rao.**

deuterium control conduit. An integral part of the *Enterprise*-D's warp propulsion system. Geordi La Forge and Wesley Crusher were making routine adjustments on this mechanism when the *Enterprise*-D was assigned to transport **Salia** to her homeworld of **Daled IV.** ("The Dauphin" [TNG]).

deuterium. Isotope of hydrogen consisting of one proton and one neutron in the nucleus, around which circles a single electron. Cryogenic (extremely cold) deuterium was the primary fuel source for the fusion impulse-engine reactors in Federation starships. Deuterium was also used as one of the reactants in the matter/antimatter reaction system in those ships' warp drive. The deuterium was the matter, and antihydrogen served as the antimatter. ("Relics" [TNG]).

Devidia II. Class-M planet located in the **Marrab sector.** The occupants existed on the surface, but in a slightly different time continuum from the *Enterprise*-D. The **Devidians** used their time-travel abilities to go back to 19th-century Earth. ("Time's Arrow, Part I" [TNG]). SEE: **LB10445.**

Devidian nurse. (Mary Stein). Shape-shifting alien from **Devidia II.** This alien took human form in order to steal neural energy from humans on 19th-century Earth. ("Time's Arrow, Part II" [TNG]). SEE: **neural depletion.**

Devidians. Intelligent lifeforms native to planet **Devidia II.** The Devidians existed in a slightly different time continuum from "normal" matter, and thus were only barely detectable to an individual in "normal" time. The Devidians thrived on neural energy that  they stole from dying life-forms. In 2368, the Devidians sent an expedition back in time to 19th-century Earth, where they attempted to extract large amounts of neural energy from victims of the **cholera** epidemic in the city of San Francisco. They were prevented from doing so by members of the *Enterprise*-D crew who also traveled back in time. ("Time's Arrow, Parts I and II" [TNG]).

• **"Devil in the Dark, The."** Original Series episode #26. Written by Gene L. Coon. Directed by Joseph Pevney. Stardate 3196.1. *First aired in 1967. A terrifying subterranean creature is found to be simply a mother protecting her* *eggs.* SEE: **Appel, Ed; Giotto, Commander; Horta; Janus VI; pergium; phaser type-1; phaser type-2; PXK reactor; Schmitter; silicon-based life; silicon nodule; thermoconcrete; Vanderberg, Chief Engineer; Vault of Tomorrow; Vulcan mind-meld.**

• **"Devil's Due."** *Next Generation* episode #87. Teleplay by Philip Lazebnik. Story by Philip Lazebnik and William Douglas Lansford. Directed by Tom Benko. Stardate 44474.5. *First aired in 1991. A planet that has enjoyed a thousand years of peace by signing a pact with the devil now has to make good on the deal. "Devil's Due" was originally written for the proposed* **Star Trek II** *television series that had been planned in the late 1970s. A very early version of this story was part of Gene Roddenberry's first draft proposal for* Star Trek *in the early 1960s.* SEE: **Ardra; Atheneum Vaults; Barnum, P. T.; Clark, Dr. Howard; Contract of Ardra; Data; Devil; Fek'lhr; Gre'thor; Jared, Acost; Ligillium, ruins of; Mendora; Scrolls of Ardra; Scrooge, Ebenezer; Torak; Ventax II; Zaterl emerald.**

Devil. (Thad Lamey). A mythic figure in several Earth cultures. The Devil, or Satan, was an angel who fell from grace with God and came to rule the underworld, where the sinful would be punished for all eternity. In 2367, **Ardra** appeared on planet **Ventax II** as the Devil while trying to impress the Ventaxians with her allegedly supernatural powers. ("Devil's Due" [TNG]).

Devor. (Tim Russ). Member of a group of terrorists who attempted to steal **trilithium resin** from the *Enterprise*-D in 2369. Devor intercepted Captain Picard as he was returning to the ship to fetch his **saddle**. Picard overpowered Devor and left him in the ship's sickbay. Devor was later killed by the **baryon sweep**. ("Starship Mine" [TNG]). SEE: **Remmler Array.**

Devoras. A Romulan warbird, commanded by **Admiral Mendak**. The Devoras met the *Enterprise*-D inside the Romulan Neutral Zone, ostensibly to transfer Federation **Ambassador T'Pel** aboard the *Devoras* for treaty negotiations, in 2367. In actuality,  T'Pel was a Romulan agent named **Subcommander Selok**, and the transfer was her means of escape into Romulan hands. ("Data's Day" [TNG]).

Devos, Alexana. (Kerrie Keane). Chief of security for the **Rutia IV** government in 2366. Devos was in charge of investigating an incident in which *Enterprise*-D officers Beverly Crusher and Jean-Luc Picard were kidnapped by **Ansata** terrorists. The abduction was a successful bid by the Ansata to force Rutian government recognition of the Ansata demands for independence. Embittered by the atrocities she had seen during her six-month tenure in that sector, Devos had little sympathy for the Ansata movement, but nevertheless agreed to work with the *Enterprise*-D crew in order to locate and rescue Dr. Crusher and Captain Picard. ("The High Ground" [TNG]).

Dewan. Ancient language, along with **Dinasian** and **Iccobar**, believed to have historic roots from the **Iconian** language. ("Contagion" [TNG]).

dexalin. Medication used aboard Federation starships to treat oxygen deprivation. Dexalin was used to treat the survivors of the **J'naii** shuttle *Taris Murn* rescued by the *Enterprise*-D on stardate 45614. ("The Outcast" [TNG]).

diagnostic. Engineering analysis programs used aboard Federation starships intended to permit automated determination of system performance and diagnosis of any malfunctions. Most key systems had a number of such programs available, ranging from level-5 diagnostics (the fastest, most automated) to level-1 diagnostics (the most thorough, but the slowest, requiring the most manual labor).

Diamond Slot formation. An aerobatic maneuver requiring five single-pilot spacecraft. The outer four craft form up in a diamond shape, with the fifth craft inserting itself into the center or slot of the diamond. The maneuver was used as a demonstration of piloting prowess by cadets at **Starfleet Academy.** ("The First Duty" [TNG]).

diboridium core. Small power-generation unit used by the Cardassians, part of the **aphasia device** found in the food replicators on Deep Space 9 in 2369. ("Babel" [DS9]).

diburnium-osmium alloy. Metal used by the **Kalandans** to construct artificial planets. ("That Which Survives" [TOS]). SEE: **Kalandan outpost.**

Dickerson, Lieutenant. (Arell Blanton). Security officer who piped the bos'n whistle to welcome the **Excalbian** re-creation of President **Abraham Lincoln** aboard the *Starship Enterprise* in 2269. ("The Savage Curtain" [TOS]).

dicosilium. Substance used by **Dr. Nel Apgar** to create reflective coils for the **Krieger-wave** converter he was trying to develop at the time of his death in 2366. The *Enterprise*-D delivered a shipment of dicosilium to Apgar at the **Tanuga IV** science station just before his death. ("A Matter of Perspective" [TNG]).

Dieghan, Liam. Neo-Transcendentalist philosopher of Earth's early 22nd century who advocated a simple life in harmony with nature. ("Up the Long Ladder" [TNG]).

diencephalon. Part of a humanoid brain, posterior to the forebrain. The hypothalamus, thalamus, and epithalamus are contained in the diencephalon. Unusual levels of neurotransmitters were discovered in the diencephalons of the three *Enterprise*-D officers who were victims of telepathic memory-invasion rape by Ullian researcher **Jev** in 2368. ("Violations" [TNG]).

Dierdre, S.S. Freighter that supposedly sent the *Enterprise* a distress call on stardate 3497. The distress call was a hoax sent by a Klingon vessel, the second Klingon attempt to prevent the *Enterprise* from returning to planet **Capella IV**. Upon receipt of the fraudulent message, Chief Engineer Scott succinctly commented, "Fool me once, shame on you. Fool me twice, shame on me." ("Friday's Child" [TOS]). SEE: *Carolina, U.S.S.*

DiFalco, Chief. (Marcy Lafferty). Relief navigator aboard the *Enterprise* when it intercepted the **V'Ger** entity. DiFalco replaced **Ilia** on the bridge after Ilia was abducted by V'Ger. (*Star Trek: The Motion Picture*). *Actor Marcy Lafferty was the wife of William Shatner.*

differential magnetometer. Device placed on several probes launched from the runabout *Rio Grande* while searching for the downed *Yangtzee Kiang* in the Gamma Quadrant in 2369. The differential magnetometers were able to detect the magnetic deflection of the *Yangtzee Kiang*'s hull on a moon. ("Battle Lines" [DS9]).

dikironium cloud creature. Gaseous entity that could change its molecular form, was capable of traveling across interstellar space, and could be recognized by a characteristic sickly-sweet smell. The cloud creature fed on the red blood cells of humanoid life-forms, and was able to camouflage itself by momentarily throwing itself out of time sync, permitting it to be two places at once. This creature attacked the *U.S.S. Farragut* in 2257, killing the ship's captain and 200 of the crew. Lieutenant **James T. Kirk**, a crew member aboard the *Farragut* at the time, fired on the creature, with no effect. Years later, in 2268, the *Starship Enterprise*, with Captain James Kirk in command, encountered the same entity. Kirk followed the creature to planet **Tycho IV**, where he destroyed it with an antimatter blast. ("Obsession" [TOS]).

dikironium. Gaseous element, formerly thought to be merely a laboratory curiosity. The substance was found to be a component in the **dikironium cloud creature** that killed 200 *U.S.S. Farragut* personnel at planet **Tycho IV** in 2257. ("Obsession" [TOS]).

dilithium chamber hatch. Outer door of the matter/antimatter reaction chamber in a starship's warp engine. The hatch permitted access to the **dilithium crystal articulation frame** for servicing and crystal replacement. The dilithium chamber hatch on the *Enterprise*-D failed in early 2367, resulting in a massive explosion in the ship's engine room. Although sabotage was initially suspected, it was later found that undetectable submicron fractures had existed in a defective hatch installed on the ship at **Earth Station McKinley** earlier that year. ("The Drumhead" [TNG]).

dilithium crystal articulation frame. Part of a starship's **warp drive** system, a device that held **dilithium crystal**s in the matter/antimatter stream so that the crystals could control the reaction in the chamber. Collapse of the articulation frame was thought to be the cause of a dilithium chamber explosion aboard the *Enterprise*-D in 2367. It was believed that sabotage was responsible for the explosion, a supposition supported by the discovery that plans for the articulation frame had been transmitted to the Romulans. The explosion was nevertheless later found to be accidental, the result of a materials defect in the **dilithium chamber hatch**. ("The Drumhead" [TNG]). SEE: **J'Ddan; neutron fatigue.** *Illustration: dilithium crystal articulation frame from* Constitution-*class starship, circa 2267.*

dilithium crystal chamber. Component of a starship's warp propulsion system. Located in the matter/antimatter reaction chamber, the dilithium crystal chamber controlled the reactions and routed the power flow to the warp nacelles. Within the chamber, the dilithium crystal was mounted within a device called an articulation frame. A prototype of *Enterprise*-D's chamber was developed at Seran T-One on stardate 40052. An improved version of the chamber, one which would permit adjustment of the crystal lattice direction, was under development for incorporation into the next class of starship. ("Booby Trap" [TNG]).

dilithium vector calibrations. Routine maintenance performed on a starship's warp engines. Following dilithium vector calibrations, it was necessary to increase warp speed slowly so the realignment progression could be maintained. ("Brothers" [TNG]).

dilithium. Crystalline substance used in warp propulsion systems aboard starships. Dilithium regulates the matter/antimatter reactions that provide the energy necessary to warp space and travel faster than light. Naturally occurring dilithium is extremely rare and is mined on only a few planets. Until the advent of recrystallization techniques that permitted the production of synthetic dilithium, the crystals were among the most valuable substances in the galaxy. This breakthrough occurred in 2286 when Spock (who had traveled back in time to 1986), devised a means whereby dilithium crystals could be recrystallized by exposure to gamma radiation (high-energy photons) that were by-products of nuclear fission reactions. (*Star Trek IV: The Voyage Home*).

In later years, theta-matrix compositing techniques permitted even more efficient recrystallization. ("Family" [TNG]). By the late 2360s, recrystallization techniques had advanced to the point that crystals could be recomposited while still inside the articulation frame of the dilithium chamber, extending the useful life of the crystals even further. ("Relics" [TNG]). Dilithium was also abundant on planet **Coridan**, admitted to the Federation in 2267. ("Journey to Babel" [TOS]). The planet **Troyius** is a rich source of naturally occurring dilithium crystals. ("Elaan of Troyius" [TOS]). SEE: **lithium crystals.**

DiMaggio, Joe. Twentieth-century baseball player (1914-), also known as Joltin' Joe and the Yankee Clipper. Arguably **baseball**'s greatest center fielder, DiMaggio scored hits in 56 consecutive games, a record that stood until 2026, when it was broken by **Buck Bokai**, a shortstop from the **London Kings**. ("The Big Goodbye" [TNG], "If Wishes Were Horses" [DS9]).

Dimorus. Planet visited by James Kirk and **Gary Mitchell** prior to their service aboard the *U.S.S. Enterprise.* While there, Mitchell saved Kirk's life by blocking a poison dart thrown by native rodent creatures. Mitchell almost died as a result. ("Where No Man Has Gone Before" [TOS]).

Dinasian. Ancient language, along with Dewan and Iccobar, believed to have historic roots in the **Iconian** language. This similarity is viewed by some as evidence that at least some of the ancient Iconians escaped the destruction of their home planet, settling elsewhere in the galaxy. ("Contagion" [TNG]).

Diomedian scarlet moss. Bright red, featherlike plant that Dr. Crusher cultivated as part of her study of ethnobotany in 2367. She collected spores from several different sources in the Diomedian system. ("Clues" [TNG]).

direct reticular stimulation. Medical procedure in which electrical energy is applied directly to the nervous system of a humanoid patient in an attempt to revive neural activity. A device called a **neural stimulator** is used in this procedure. Direct reticular stimulation was unsuccessfully attempted when **Natasha Yar** was critically wounded by **Armus.** ("Skin of Evil" [TNG]).

Dirgo. (Nick Tate). A native of **Pentarus V** and captain of the mining shuttle *Nenebek.* Captain Dirgo was assigned to transport Captain Picard and Ensign Crusher from the *Enterprise*-D to a conference on **Pentarus V**. When the shuttle malfunctioned and was forced to crash-land on a Pentaran moon, Dirgo was reluctant to accept Captain Picard's leadership in what became a struggle for survival on the desert planet. Despite this, Dirgo continued to act impulsively and caused his own death. ("Final Mission" [TNG]). SEE: **sentry.** *Nick Tate also played astronaut Alan Carter on the series* Space: 1999. *Alan Carter was obviously a better pilot.*

• **"Disaster."** *Next Generation episode #105. Teleplay by Ronald D. Moore. Story by Ron Jarvis & Philip A Scorza. Directed by Gabrielle Beaumont. Stardate 45156.1. First aired in 1991. The Enterprise-D crew copes with a shipboard disaster, trapping Picard in a turbolift and placing Deanna Troi in command.* SEE: **antigravs; containment breach; emergency hand actuator; Emergency Procedure Alpha 2; Flores, Marissa; "Frere Jacques"; Gonal IV; Gordon, Jay; hyronalin; internal power grid; Ishikawa, Hiro; isolation protocol; "Laughing Vulcan and His Dog, The"; Mandel, Ensign; Monroe, Lieutenant; Mudor V; O'Brien, Keiko;**

O'Brien, Michael; O'Brien, Miles; O'Brien, Molly; *Pirates of Penzance, The*; **plasma fire; polyduranide; quantum filament; quartum; service crawlway; Starfleet Emergency Medical course; Supera, Patterson; tripolymer composites; Troi, Deanna.**

discommendation. Klingon ritual shaming. An individual who receives discommendation is treated as nonexistent in the eyes of Klingon society. The individual's family is also disgraced for seven generations. **Worf** accepted a humiliating discommendation from the **Klingon High Council** in 2366 when his late father, **Mogh**, was accused of having committed treason at Khitomer in 2346, despite the fact that council leader **K'mpec** knew the charges to be unfounded. ("Sins of the Father" [TNG]). Worf's discommendation was reversed in 2367 by Council leader **Gowron**, shortly after Gowron assumed the office of Council leader. ("Redemption, Part I" [TNG]).

diseases. SEE: **Altarian encephalitis; Anchilles fever; Andronesian encephalitis; aphasia; Ba'ltmasor Syndrome; Bendii Syndrome; cholera; cold, common; coleibric hemmorhage; Correllium fever; Darnay's disease; enantiodromia; eosinophilia; Hesperan Thumping Cough; Iresine Syndrome; Iverson's disease; Kalla-Nohra Syndrome; lacunar amnesia; Larosian virus; Life Prolongation Project; microvirus; nitrogen narcosis; Phyrox Plague; plasma plague; Pottrik Syndrome; Psi 2000 virus; pyrocyte; Rigelian fever; Rigelian Kassaba fever; rop'ngor; Rushton infection; Sakuro's disease;** *Synthococcus novae*; **Symbalene blood burn; Telurian plague; temporal narcosis; tennis elbow; thelusian flu; transporter psychosis; Vegan choriomeningitis; xenopolycethemia.** SEE ALSO: **drugs.**

Disrupters. Organized underground of discontented **Troglytes** on planet **Ardana** who sought economic and social equality with those who dwelled in the cloud city of **Stratos.** In 2269, the Disrupters stole a badly needed consignment of **zenite** designated for pickup by the *Starship Enterprise* in order to dramatize their plight. ("The Cloud Minders" [TOS]).

disruptor. Directed-energy weapon used by Romulans, Klingons, and other races. ("Tin Man" [TNG]). The Klingon disruptor was also known as a **phase disruptor.** ("Aquiel". [TNG]). SEE: **Klingon weapons.** Romulan disruptor fire can be identified by a high residue of antiprotons that can linger for several hours after the weapon has been used. ("Face of the Enemy" [TNG]). *Illustration: Romulan disruptor pistol.*

distortion field. Phenomenon present in the atmosphere of planet **Nervala IV**. The field prevented the use of transporters or shuttlecraft, effectively isolating the planet. The field was present during the majority of its eight-year orbit around Nervala, but during the planet's perihelion the field would temporarily dephase enough to allow for transport to the surface. ("Second Chances" [TNG]).

Divok. (Charles Esten). Young follower of the Klingon messiah **Kahless the Unforgettable**, who was present on the planet **Boreth** during Worf's visit to the monastery in 2369. Divok received a vision of Kahless and was present when the Klingon who claimed to be Kahless returned. ("Rightful Heir" [TNG]).

d'k tahg. Traditional Klingon warrior's knife. A vicious, three-bladed weapon, the *d'k tahg* is commonly used in hand-to-hand combat, as well as in many ceremonies. (*Star Trek III*, "The Bonding" [TNG], "Redemption, Part I [TNG], "Birthright, Part II" [TNG]). *The Klingon knife, first used to kill **David Marcus** in Star Trek III, was designed by Phil Norwood. It was also seen in "The Bonding" (TNG) and several later episodes. It was given a name in "Birthright, Part II" (TNG). When it was used for the Next Generation, the original prop was not available, so Rick Sternbach duplicated the design for the show's prop makers, using a* Star Trek *trading card for reference.*

DNA reference scan. Medical test to confirm an individual's identity by matching DNA patterns. **Kobliad** security officer **Kajada** asked Dr. Julian Bashir to order a DNA reference scan to confirm the identity a body, believed to be that of her prisoner, **Rao Vantika**. ("The Passenger" [DS9]).

DNA. Acronym for deoxyribonucleic acid, a complex chemical chain containing the genetic codes enabling the reproduction of life on many planets. Virtually every individual life-form on such planets has a DNA code, which contains information common to that species, as well as distinguishing information unique to that individual. Because of this, DNA sequencing can be used as a means of positively identifying an individual, although it cannot distinguish between the individual and a clone. Many humanoid species throughout the galaxy share a common DNA structure, a characteristic that was recently discovered to be due to a humanoid species that lived some four billion years ago that "seeded" many planets with primordial genetic material. ("The Chase" [TNG]). SEE: **cloning; humanoid life**.

Doe, John. (Mark LaMura). A **Zalkonian** male discovered by the *Enterprise*-D crew in a crashed escape pod on a planet in the **Zeta Gelis** system in 2366. Suffering from serious

injuries, "Doe" (so designated by Dr. Beverly Crusher, with whom Doe became romantically involved) was treated aboard the *Enterprise*-D, where he astounded the medical staff with his extremely rapid recovery. Doe was later found to be a member of a persecuted minority of Zalkonian society, a group that was undergoing a metamorphosis from humanoid forms into noncorporeal beings. Doe had fled into space to escape the Zalkonian government's attempts to destroy all who exhibited these traits. He completed his transfiguration aboard the *Enterprise*-D, and was last seen flying off into space, a being of pure energy. ("Transfigurations" [TNG]).

Dohlman. Leader of the planet Elas. **Elaan** was the Dohlman of **Elas** in 2268. ("Elaan of Troyius" [TOS]).

Dokachin, Klim. (Graham Jarvis). The quartermaster of the Starfleet surplus depot in orbit around planet **Qualor II.** An officious **Zakdorn**, Dokachin reluctantly agreed to help the crew of the *Enterprise*-D locate the **T'Pau** when the *Enterprise*-D visited Qualor in 2368. Dokachin was shocked to discover the *T'Pau* gone from its assigned berth at the surplus depot. ("Unification, Part I" [TNG]).

Dokkaran temple. An ancient structure of Kural-Hanesh, known for its harmonious architecture. The structure contained a great archway, large windows, and an altar. Children in the *Enterprise*-D primary school studied and built models of this historic building. ("Hero Worship" [TNG]).

Dolak, Gul. (Frank Collison). A member of the Cardassian militia, unit 41. Dolak was in command of the **Cardassian warships** that attacked and destroyed a Bajoran *Antares*-class carrier in an effort to kill Bajoran leader Orta in 2368. ("Ensign Ro" [TNG]). SEE: **Kennelly, Admiral**.

dolamide. Chemical energy source used in a wide variety of applications such as power generators, reactors, and, in an extremely pure form, for weapons. The **Valerians** made weapons for the **Cardassians** with dolamide during the occupation of **Bajor**. When a Valerian vessel docked at Deep Space 9 in 2369, Major Kira was denied permission to search the ship for evidence of dolamide on grounds of lack of probable cause. ("Dramatis Personae" [DS9]). SEE: *Sherval Das*.

Dolbargy sleeping trance. Voluntarily induced deep coma. **Zek**, the Ferengi **Grand Nagus**, used the technique to fake his own death in 2369 when he wanted to test the readiness of his son, **Krax**, to serve as Nagus. Zek's servant, **Maihar'du**, had taught him the technique. ("The Nagus" [DS9]).

dom-jot. Billiards-like game with an irregularly shaped table, popular at the **Bonestell Recreational Facility** at **Starbase Earhart**. Ensign **Cortin Zweller** was fond of the game, as were a couple of **Nausicaans**. ("Tapestry" [TNG]).

Donaldson. *Enterprise*-D crew member and part of Commander La Forge's engineering staff during the **soliton wave** rider test in 2368. ("New Ground" [TNG]).

Donatu V, Battle of. Conflict that occurred in 2242 near **Sherman's Planet** in a region under dispute by the Klingon Empire and the United Federation of Planets. ("The Trouble with Tribbles" [TOS]).

• **"Doomsday Machine, The."** Original Series episode #35. Written by Norman Spinrad. Directed by Marc Daniels. No stardate given in episode. *First aired in 1967. An ancient weapon that destroyed the civilization that invented it is now destroying planets in Federation space.* SEE: ***Constellation, U.S.S.*; Decker, Commodore Matt; impulse drive; Kyle, Mr.; L-370; L-374; Masada; neutronium; Palmer, Lieutenant; planet killer; Starfleet General Orders and Regulations; Washburn.**

doomsday machine. SEE: **planet killer.**

door in the universe. Term used to describe an interdimensional passageway created by **Lazarus**, connecting our universe with an antimatter continuum. ("The Alternative Factor" [TOS]).

Dopterians. Humanoid race whose brains have certain structural similarities to the **Ferengi.** One characteristic of the Dopterians is that neither they nor the Ferengi can be empathically sensed by a Betazoid. A Dopterian stole **Lwaxana Troi**'s precious latinum hair brooch on station Deep Space 9 in 2369, but she was unable to sense any feeling of guilt from the thief for this reason. ("The Forsaken" [DS9]).

Doraf I. Planet in Federation space. The *Enterprise*-D was assigned to a terraforming project at Doraf I in 2368. The mission was canceled when the ship was recalled to **Starbase 234** to receive orders to investigate the disappearance of Ambassador **Spock.** ("Unification, Part I" [TNG]).

Dorian. Transport vessel attacked near planet **Rekag-Seronia** in 2369 while attempting to deliver **Ambassador Ves Alkar** to that planet in hopes of mediating peace there. ("Man of the People" [TNG]). *The Dorian was a redress of the **Straleb** transport ship originally built for "The Outrageous Okona" (TNG).*

Douwd. A little-known race of sentient energy beings fond of assuming the appearance of other life-forms. Possessing awesome powers of creation and destruction, the Douwd considered themselves to be immortal beings of disguises and false surroundings. One member of this race assumed a human identity around 2312, named himself **Kevin Uxbridge,** and settled on planet **Delta Rana IV** in 2361. ("The Survivors" [TNG]).

Doyle, Sir Arthur Conan. Novelist (1859-1930) from old England on Earth, writer of the classic **Sherlock Holmes** adventures. *Enterprise*-D operations manager Data was a fan of Doyle's work and the Sherlock Holmes character in particular. ("Elementary, Dear Data" [TNG], "Ship in a Bottle" [TNG]). SEE: **Moriarty, Professor James.**

Draco lizards. Species of flying reptile indigenous to southeast Asia on planet Earth. The Draco lizard was extinct by the year 2000. ("New Ground" [TNG]).

Draebidium calimus. Type of plant Keiko O'Brien carried with her when the **Shuttlecraft Fermi** passed through an energy cloud in 2369. When the shuttle crew transported back to the *Enterprise*-D, the *Draebidium calimus* was reduced to seedlings. ("Rascals" [TNG]).

Draebidium froctus. Type of plant. Upon returning to the *Enterprise*-D from planet Marlonia, Ensign Ro mistook a *Draebidium calimus* for a *Draebidium froctus*. ("Rascals" [TNG]).

Drafting Room 5. Part of Starfleet's **Utopia Planitia Fleet Yards** on Mars, where the *Galaxy*-class *U.S.S. Enterprise*-D was designed. This was the workplace of **Dr. Leah Brahms.**
   Geordi La Forge re-created Drafting Room 5 on the *Enterprise*-D holodeck when trying to escape an ancient **Mentar** booby trap in 2366. ("Booby Trap" [TNG]).

drag coefficient. Measurement of the relative resistance force on a body traveling through a fluid medium such as air or water. The drag coefficient on the *Enterprise*-D through the tenuous interstellar dust and gas of nebula **FGC-47** increased inexplicably when the ship explored the nebula in 2368. This increase was later found to be due to a life-form living in FGC-47. ("Imaginary Friend" [TNG])

Drake, U.S.S. Federation starship, *Wambundu*-class, registry number NCC-20381, that disappeared in the Lorenze Cluster.
   The *Drake* had been under the command of **Captain Paul Rice** when it was destroyed, apparently by an ancient weapons system still operational at planet **Minos** in 2364. **William Riker** had been offered the command of the *Drake*, but he turned it down to serve aboard the *Enterprise*-D. ("The Arsenal of Freedom" [TNG]).

Draken IV. Location of a Starfleet base near the **Kaleb Sector.** **Subcommander N'Vek** attempted to take the Romulan warbird *Khazara* there in 2369 as part of a plan for the defection of Romulan **vice-proconsul M'ret** to the Federation. ("Face of the Enemy" [TNG]).

• **"Dramatis Personae."** *Deep Space Nine* episode #18. Written by Joe Menosky. Directed by Cliff Bole. Stardate 46922.3. *First aired in 1993. Unknown intelligences take over the minds of Deep Space 9 personnel, forcing them to act out an alien drama.* SEE: **Bajoran wormhole; cryostasis; dolamide; duranium; Fahleena III; Hon'Tihl; Kaleans; Kee'Bhor; Lasuma; Mariah IV; Modela aperitif; phoretic analyzer; Rochani III; Saltah'na clock; Saltah'na energy sphere; Saltah'na; *Sherval Das*; subspace transponder; Tel'Peh; thalmerite device; *Toh'Kaht, I.K.C.*; Ultima Thule; Valerians.**

Drea. (Lizlie Dalton). **Kelvan** who assisted in the capture of the *Enterprise* landing party in 2268 and forced the *Enterprise* crew to set a course for the **Andromeda Galaxy**. ("By Any Other Name" [TOS]).

Dream of the Fire, The. A classic work of Klingon literature by K'Ratak. Worf gave Data a leather-bound copy of this book when Data was preparing to resign Starfleet rather than submit to disassembly by **Commander Bruce Maddox** in 2365. ("The Measure of a Man" [TNG]).

drechtal beams. Surgical device used to sever neural connections. ("Ethics" [TNG]).

Drella. Entity from planet Alpha Carinae V that derives energy from the emotion of love. Spock mentioned the Drella in relation to the entity on planet **Argelius II**, which gained strength from the emotion of terror. ("Wolf in the Fold" [TOS]). SEE: **Redjac.**

Drema IV. Fourth planet in the **Selcundi Drema** system, home to a humanoid civilization. This planet possesses the largest deposits of **dilithium** ore ever recorded. This ore is laid down in unusually aligned lattices that converted the planet's geologic heat into mechanical stress, thus resulting in significant tectonic instabilities that nearly destroyed the planet. While possessing some advanced technology, this planet was still under Prime Directive protection in 2365, and thus the discovery that *Enterprise*-D officer Data had been in radio contact with an inhabitant of the planet presented a significant problem. While the **Prime Directive** prohibited contact with the inhabitants, humanitarian considerations demanded a means of assistance that avoided cultural contamination. Such a means was found, and the geological instabilities were neutralized by the use of **resonator** probes launched from orbit without the knowledge of the planet's inhabitants. ("Pen Pals" [TNG]).

dresci. An alcoholic beverage from planet **Pentarus V**. Captain **Dirgo** hid a bottle of dresci on his person following the crash of the shuttle *Nenebek*. ("Final Mission" [TNG]).

drill thralls. Beings captured throughout the galaxy and brought to planet **Triskelion** by a group of disembodied brains known as the **Providers**. These unfortunate captives, called drill thralls, were branded by one of the three Providers and trained to fight. They spent the rest of their lives in competition to amuse their masters, until James Kirk persuaded the Providers to free the thralls in 2267. ("The Gamesters of Triskelion" [TOS]).

Droxine. (Diana Ewing). **Stratos** city dweller and daughter to city official Plasus. Protected by her father from the harsh realities of her society, Droxine was unaware of the bitter life led by the **Troglytes** who toiled on the planet's surface to support her life in the clouds. Droxine seemed fascinated by Mr.

Spock and inquired if the *Pon farr* mating cycle could be broken. ("The Cloud Minders" [TOS]).

drugs. SEE: **adrenaline; anesthizine; benjisidrine; borathium; chlromydride; cordrazine; corophizine; cryptobiolin; cyalodin; delactovine; deoxyribose suspensions; dermatiraelian plasticine; deuridium; dexalin; dylamadon; Elasian tears; felicium; formazine; hyronalin; immunosuppressant; inaprovaline; kayolane; kironide; leporazine; lexorin; macrospentol; mahko root; Masiform D; melorazine; metabolic reduction injection; metorapan; metrazene; morathial series; neural paralyzer; neuraltransmitter; norep; PCS; polyadrenaline; quadroline; Retnax V; ryetalyn; stokaline; theragen; triclenidil; tricordrazine; tryptophan-lysine distillates; Venus drug; Veridium Six; vertazine.** SEE ALSO: **diseases.**

• **"Drumhead, The."** *Next Generation* episode #95. Written by Jeri Taylor. Directed by Jonathan Frakes. Stardate 44769.2. *First aired in 1991. An overzealous admiral searches for evidence of a subversive conspiracy, but fails to see that her witch-hunting tactics are themselves subversive of the Federation Constitution.* SEE: **Ba'ltmasor Syndrome; Borg; Constitution of the United Federation of Planets; Cruses System; Delb II; deoxyribose suspensions; dilithium chamber hatch; dilithium crystal articulation frame; Earth Station McKinley; encephalographic polygraph scan; *Enterprise*-D, U.S.S.; Genestra, Sabin; Henry, Admiral Thomas; J'Ddan; Kellogg, Ensign; microtomographic analysis; neutron fatigue; Officer Exchange Program; Satie, Admiral Norah; Satie, Judge Aaron; Seventh Guarantee; Tarses, Crewman Simon; Tore, Nellen, Uniform Code of Justice; Wolf 359.**

Drusilla. (Lois Jewell). Slave of Proconsul **Claudius Marcus** on planet 892-IV, who was given to James Kirk for the night prior to his scheduled execution there in 2267. Drusilla and Kirk probably did not play chess. SEE: **892, Planet IV.** ("Bread and Circuses" [TOS]).

drydock. Large orbital service structure used for major maintenance of starships and other space vehicles. The original *Starship Enterprise* underwent a major overhaul at the **San Francisco Yards** drydock in Earth orbit following its five-year mission under the command of James Kirk.  (*Star Trek: The Motion Picture*). *Photo: Starship Enterprise in drydock, following the return from Kirk's five-year mission.*

dryworm. Giant creature on planet Antos IV that can generate and control energy with no harm to itself. ("Who Mourns for Adonais?" [TOS]).

DS9. Abbreviation for station **Deep Space 9**. ("Emissary" [DS9]).

D'Sora, Lieutenant Jenna. (Michele Scarabelli). Security officer aboard the *Enterprise*-D. Lieutenant D'Sora pursued a brief romantic relationship with Lieutenant Commander **Data** in late 2367 shortly after she broke up with Jeff Arton. The relationship did not prove successful. ("In Theory" [TNG]).

D'Tan. (Vidal Peterson). Romulan boy, born in 2356, raised as a member of the Romulan reunification underground. D'Tan was a friend of Ambassador **Spock**. ("Unification, Part II" [TNG]).

Duana. (Ivy Bethune). An older citizen on planet **Aldea**, Duana was a key figure in her planet's attempt to abduct children from the *Enterprise*-D in an effort to repopulate her world in 2364. When the plan failed, Duana accepted technological assistance from starship personnel. ("When the Bough Breaks" [TNG]).

duck blind. Nickname given to a holographic image generator used to disguise the anthropological field research station on **Mintaka III**. The **hologram generator** created the image of a rocky hillside, thus concealing the station. ("Who Watches the Watchers?" [TNG]). SEE: **Liko**.

• **"Duet."** *Deep Space Nine* episode #19. Teleplay by Peter Allan Fields. Story by Lisa Rich & Jeanne Carrigan-Fauci. Directed by James L. Conway. No stardate given in episode. *First aired in 1993. Kira arrests a Cardassian war criminal on Deep Space 9, but the Cardassian is not what he seems to be.* SEE: **"Butcher of Gallitep, The"; coleibric hemorrhage; Darhe'el, Gul; dermatiraelian plasticine; Dukat, Gul; Gallitep; Kainon; Kalevian montar; Kalla-Nohra Syndrome; Kaval; Kira Nerys; Kobheerian captain; Kora II; Maraltian seev-ale; Marritza, Aamin; Neela; Pottrik Syndrome; Proficient Service Medallion; *Rak-Miunis*; *sem'hal* stew; Shakaar; *yamok* sauce.**

Duffy, Lieutenant. (Charley Lang). An engineering technician aboard the *Enterprise*-D. In 2366, Duffy accidentally helped spread a dangerous **invidium** contamination through the ship. ("Hollow Pursuits" [TNG]).

Dukat, Gul. (Marc Alaimo). Cardassian military official who was the last prefect in charge of **Bajor**, just prior to the **Cardassian** retreat from that planet in 2369. Dukat had also been in command of the mining station **Deep Space 9**. ("Emissary" [DS9]). At the time, the station was known by the Cardassian designation Terok Nor. ("Cardassians" [DS9]). Dukat filed  a complaint with Sisko when Cardassian citizen **Aamin Marritza** was being detained at the station, accused of being **Gul Darh'el**, also known as **"The Butcher of Gallitep."** ("Duet" [DS9]).

Dulisian IV. Site of a Federation colony that transmitted a Priority-1 distress call to the *Enterprise*-D while it was in orbit around **Galorndon Core** in 2368. The colony reported massive failure of its environmental support systems. The distress call was later found to be a ruse sent in the hopes of dissuading the *Enterprise*-D from interfering with the Romulan invasion of planet Vulcan. ("Unification, Part II" [TNG]).

Dumont, Ensign Suzanne. Wesley's date on the night of the Mozart concert aboard the *Enterprise*-D in honor of Ambassador Sarek in 2366. They did not attend the concert, but went to the arboretum instead. ("Sarek" [TNG]).

dunsel. Term used by midshipmen at Starfleet Academy for an item that serves no useful purpose. **Commodore Robert Wesley** referred to James Kirk as Captain Dunsel after a successful test of the **M-5** multitronic computer in 2268. ("The Ultimate Computer" [TOS]).

duotronic enhancers. SEE: **duotronics; isolinear optical chips**.

duotronics. Revolutionary computer system invented by **Dr. Richard Daystrom** in 2243. Duotronics became the basis of the computers used aboard all Federation starships for over 80 years, including the main computers aboard the original *Starship Enterprise*. ("The Ultimate Computer" [TOS]). Duotronic enhancers were finally replaced by **isolinear optical chips** in 2329. ("Relics" [TOS]).

Durango. Name for Counselor Troi's holodeck character in Alexander Rozhenko's holodeck program, ***Ancient West***. It was Troi's chance to play the part of a "mysterious stranger." ("A Fistful of Datas" [TNG]).

duranium. Extremely strong metallic alloy commonly used in spacecraft construction such as in the hulls of Starfleet **shuttlecraft**. ("The Menagerie, Part I" [TOS]). The **Cardassians** built the access conduit above Quark's bar on Deep Space 9 with a two-meter-thick duranium composite, making the area impervious to most scanning devices. Unfortunately, the **Hunters'** instruments were advanced enough to scan the access tube and locate the fleeing O'Brien and **Tosk**. ("Captive Pursuit" [DS9]). Duranium composite was used in the skin of Starfleet **runabouts**, making them difficult to cut into. ("Q-Less" [DS9]). Klingon Birds-of-Prey were partially built of duranium. ("Dramatis Personae" [DS9]).

Duras. (Patrick Massett). A member of a politically powerful Klingon family, and member of the **Klingon High Council**. In 2366, Duras sought to conceal evidence that his father, **Ja'rod**, had committed treason during the **Khitomer massacre** in 2346. Duras fabricated evidence implicating **Mogh**, father of **Worf**, as the guilty party. Duras was initially successful in forcing  the council to rule against Mogh's family, although council leader **K'mpec** was aware of Duras's treachery. ("Sins of the Father" [TNG]). Following the murder of council leader

K'mpec in 2367, Duras sought to win K'mpec's position. Duras was one of two contenders for the leadership, and he used a bomb in an attempt to insure his selection by eliminating Gowron, his competitor. It was also suspected that Gowron was responsible for K'mpec's death by poison. During the rite of succession, Duras also killed **K'Ehleyr**, Worf's mate, when she was on the verge of discovering the truth about Duras's cover-up of his father's crimes. Duras was subsequently killed by Worf, who sought the right of vengeance under Klingon law. ("Reunion" [TNG]). Following Duras's death, his family continued to play a significant role in Klingon politics. ("Redemption, Parts I and II" [TNG], "Past Prologue" [DS9]). SEE: **Lursa; B'Etor; Toral**.

Durenia IV. Destination of the *Enterprise*-D in early 2367 when a warp field experiment by Ensign Crusher went awry, trapping Dr. Beverly Crusher in a **static warp bubble**. The *Enterprise*-D was forced to abandon its mission and return to Starbase 133. ("Remember Me" [TNG]).

Durg. (Chris Collins). Alien mercenary hired to help **Rao Ventika** steal a shipment of **deuridium** being transferred from the Gamma Quadrant to station Deep Space 9 in 2369. Durg was killed by Ventika when he failed to carry out an order. ("The Passenger" [DS9]).

Durken, Chancellor Avel. (George Coe). The head of state on planet **Malcor III** in 2367. Durken led his people during the time when Malcorian advances in spaceflight promised great benefits to his people. Unfortunately, more conservative elements in his government greatly feared the cultural risks of contact with extraterrestrial life. The discovery that Federation operatives had been conducting covert surveillance on his planet as a possible prelude to **first contact** provoked a violent reaction from these conservative elements, leading Durken to scale back the Malcorian space program. Durken also asked Captain Picard to postpone indefinitely any plans for Federation contact with the Malcorians. ("First Contact" [TNG]). SEE: **Krola; Yale, Mirasta**. *George Coe also played the head of Network 23 in the television series* Max Headroom.

Dvorak, Anton. Earth musical composer (1841-1904) known for his adaptations of Bohemian folk music. Dvorak's works, including "The Slavonic Dances," were among the music that Data studied in 2369. ("A Fistful of Datas" [TNG]).

DY-100. Ancient type of interplanetary space vehicle built on Earth in the late 20th century. DY-100 vessels used nuclear-powered engines and were equipped with suspended-animation facilities for extended voyages. The *S.S. Botany Bay*, launched from Earth in 1996, was a DY-100-class ship. Sleeper ships like the DY-100 fell from general use by 2018

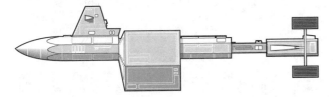

because of significant improvements in sublight propulsion technology. ("Space Seed" [TOS]).

DY-500. Interplanetary vessel, relatively primitive by 23rd-century standards, but considerably more advanced than the older **DY-100** ships. ("Space Seed" [TOS]). The *S.S. Mariposa*, launched from Earth in 2123, was a DY-500 ship. ("Up the Long Ladder" [TNG]).

dylamadon. Drug used in euthanasia for humanoid patients. Though deadly, dylamadon was believed to be painless. ("Man of the People" [TNG]).

dynoscanner. Sensor device used to detect low-level molecular activity. (*Star Trek II: The Wrath of Khan*, "Ethics" [TNG]).

Dyson sphere. A gigantic artificial structure designed to completely enclose a star in a hollow sphere some 200 million kilometers in diameter. The interior surface of such a sphere, if constructed to provide a life-supporting environment, could theoretically provide the surface area of literally hundreds of millions of planets. Dyson spheres were long believed to be impractical to build due to their extreme size and the astronomical amount of raw materials required for construction. Nevertheless, a Dyson sphere was discovered near **Norpin V** when the *Enterprise*-D found the transport ship *Jenolen*, which had crashed on the sphere's surface in 2294. This object was built around a G-type star, and supported a class-M atmosphere that clung to the interior surface of the sphere. The shell was composed of carbon-neutronium, with an interior surface area of some 10^{16} square kilometers. No signs of current habitation were found on that interior surface, apparently because the star was undergoing severe bursts of radiation. ("Relics" [TNG]). *The basic concept was first proposed in the 1960s by Earth scientist Freeman Dyson, after whom the sphere is named.*

Dytallix B. Planet in the Mira star system, one of seven worlds owned by the Dytallix Mining Corporation. Although the mines were long abandoned by 2364, the planet was the site of a covert meeting where Captain **Walker Keel** warned Jean-Luc Picard of his suspicions of an alien infiltration of Starfleet in that year. ("Conspiracy" [TNG]).

E-band emissions. Electromagnetic signals sometimes emitted by collapsing proto-stars. E-band emissions were used by Romulan operatives in late 2367 as a means of secretly transmitting commands to Geordi La Forge through his VISOR. Those signals were delta-compressed on a frequency similar to that of humanoid brainwaves. ("The Mind's Eye" [TNG]). SEE: **neural implants; Taibak; VISOR.**

ear receiver. Small electronic device used by Starfleet personnel for personal monitoring of audio information without the inconvenience of a loudspeaker that might interfere with nearby personnel. *Uhura used this a lot on the bridge, although it was sometimes mistaken for a fancy earring. Spock used it, too.*

Earl Grey tea. A blended black tea flavored with bergamot or lavender oil. A favorite beverage of Jean-Luc Picard, who often ordered it through the ship's food **replicator.** ("Contagion" [TNG]).

Earp, Morgan. (Rex Holman). Lawman from Earth's ancient American West who fought against the Clanton family in 1881 at the famous gunfight at the **OK Corral.** A replica of Earp was created by the **Melkotians** in 2268 as part of a bizarre drama intended for the execution of Kirk and members of his crew. ("Spectre of the Gun" [TOS]). *Rex Holman played T'Jon in Star Trek V.*

Earp, Virgil. (Charles Maxwell). Brother to **Morgan** and **Wyatt Earp,** who fought in the legendary gunfight at the **OK Corral** in **Tombstone, Arizona.** A replica of Virgil was part of the scenario created by the **Melkotians** in 2268 for the execution of Kirk and members of his crew. ("Spectre of the Gun" [TOS]).

Earp, Wyatt. (Ron Soble). Legendary lawman from Earth's ancient American West who fought members of the Clanton family at the famous gunfight at the **OK Corral** on October 26, 1881. The **Melkotians** recreated Earp for their drama intended for the deaths of Kirk and members of his crew. ("Spectre of the Gun" [TOS]).

Earth Colony 2. Captain Kirk's brother, **George Samuel Kirk,** had hoped to be transferred to the research station at Earth Colony 2 prior to his death in 2267. ("What Are Little Girls Made Of?" [TOS]).

Earth Station Bobruisk. Site from which Worf's adoptive parents, **Sergey and Helena Rozhenko,** transported to the *Enterprise*-D when the ship was at **Earth Station McKinley**

in 2367. ("Family" [TNG]). *Bobruisk is a city in Belorussia, the site of a major battle in the Second World War.*

Earth Station McKinley. Starfleet shipbuilding and repair facility in Earth orbit. McKinley Station was a large orbital platform supporting several large articulated work arms, designed to service even the largest starships. The ***Enterprise*-D** was in dock there

for six weeks following the defeat of the **Borg** ship in 2367. ("The Best of Both Worlds, Part II"; "Family" [TNG]). Unknown to anyone at the time, a defective **dilithium chamber hatch** was installed in the *Enterprise*-D warp-drive system at McKinley Station. The hatch contained undetectable submicron fractures that were responsible for a serious explosion in the engine room later that year. ("The Drumhead" [TNG]).

Earth-Saturn probe. The first successful piloted mission from Earth to Saturn was commanded by **Colonel Shaun Geoffrey Christopher,** son of **Captain John Christopher.** The flight was made in the early 21st century. ("Tomorrow Is Yesterday" [TOS]).

Earth. Class-M planet in the Sol system, located in Sector 001. Homeworld to the Human race, and location of the Federation Council President's office, as well as Starfleet Command. Mostly harmless.

Echo Papa 607. An automated weapons drone created by the now-dead arms merchants of planet **Minos,** built for use during the ancient **Erselrope Wars.** Billed by the Minosians as the ultimate in weapons system technology, the Echo Papa 607 was a small free-flying unit with a powerful energy projector and a cloaking device. The 607 was designed to be effective against ground personnel as well as deep-space vehicles, and could also be programmed for information gathering. Most significantly, the 607 embodied dynamic adaptive design, enabling it to learn during combat situations so that mistakes would not be repeated. An ancient Echo Papa 607 system was still active on Minos in 2364 when the *Enterprise*-D investigated the disappearance of the *U.S.S. Drake* there. The weapon, apparently also responsible for the destruction of the ***U.S.S. Drake,*** threatened the *Enterprise* and an away team on the planet's surface. ("The Arsenal of Freedom" [TNG]). *The miniature of the Echo Papa 607 was built by visual effects supervisor Dan Curry, using an old L'Eggs pantyhose container and a discarded shampoo bottle.*

Eden. Mythical planet of extraordinary beauty and peace. Noted scientist **Dr. Sevrin** led a group of followers on a quest in 2269 to find Eden. They found a planet matching this description in Romulan space, but later found the plant life on the planet to be permeated with deadly acid. ("The Way to Eden" [TOS]).

Edo god. Powerful spaceborne life-form (or forms) discovered near the Rubicun star system. This immensely powerful, transdimensional entity cares for and protects the humanoid species on planet **Rubicun III**.

When the *Starship Enterprise*-D attempted to make contact with the inhabitants of that planet in 2364, the Edo god warned the ship to leave without interfering with the humanoids it called its "children." The Edo god also requested removal of a Federation colony established in the nearby **Strnad Star System**. ("Justice" [TNG]).

Edos. Inhabitants of planet **Rubicun III**. A curious mixture of hedonistic sexuality and almost puritanical respect for their law, the Edos are governed and protected by a transdimensional entity they call their god.

Many years ago, Edo society was lawless and dangerously violent. They eventually adopted a system in which laws were enforced by a very small number of mediators (law enforcement officials) who monitored randomly selected areas called **punishment zones**. Violation of any law in a punishment zone would result in immediate death. Since no one except the mediators would know which area had been selected as a punishment zone, the system served as a strong incentive to obey all laws. ("Justice" [TNG]).

Edouard. (Jean-Paul Vignon). A holodeck character, the understanding waiter at the **Cafe des Artistes** in Paris. ("We'll Always Have Paris" [TNG]).

Edwell, Captain. Federation officer, native of planet Gaspar VII. ("Starship Mine" [TNG]).

eel-birds. Creatures from planet Regulus V that must return to the caverns where they hatched every eleven years to mate. Spock mentioned the mating habits of the eel-birds to Kirk in attempting to explain the Vulcan mating drive, *Pon farr*. ("Amok Time" [TOS]).

"Egg, the." An instrumented sensor probe, designed by **Dr. Paul Stubbs** to record the decay of neutronium expelled during a stellar explosion. Dr. Stubbs, who nicknamed his brainchild "the Egg," had been working on it for twenty years, successfully launching it from the *Enterprise*-D at **Kavis Alpha** in 2266. ("Evolution" [TNG]). *The full-scale egg prop was a modification of the virus containment device originally built for "The Child" (TNG).*

eichner radiation. Form of radiation found to stimulate growth of certain strains of **plasma plague**. Eichner radiation can be created by a **subspace field inverter**, and it is also emitted by certain **cyanoacrylates**. ("The Child" [TNG]).

892, Planet IV. Fourth planet of the 892 solar system, a class-M world where the survivors of the survey vessel *S.S. Beagle* beamed down after their ship was damaged in 2261. The planet's society was a 20th-century version of Earth's ancient Rome, with video communications, power transportation, and an imperial government. By 2267, slavery had existed for two thousand years, and a slave caste developed into a strata of society with specified rights under the law. SEE: **Children of the Sun**; **Marcus, Cladius**; **Merrick, R. M.** ("Bread and Circuses" [TOS]).

Einstein, Albert. (Jim Morton). Nobel Prize-winning theoretical physicist (1879-1955), regarded as one of the greatest scientific minds of 20th-century Earth. Einstein postulated the theory of relativity and spent much of his later life attempting to unify relativity with quantum mechanics. **Reginald Barclay**, using his **Cytherian**-enhanced intelligence, spent a night  in 2367 discussing grand unification theories with a holodeck simulation of Albert Einstein. ("The Nth Degree" [TNG]). The holographic Einstein was later enlisted by Data in a customized holodeck program that allowed him to play poker with such scientific luminaries as Einstein, **Sir Isaac Newton**, and **Professor Stephen Hawking**. ("Descent, Part I" [TNG]).

EJ7 interlock. Engineering tool used to open critical system access panels on **Deep Space 9**. **Neela** stole the interlock from Chief O'Brien's tool kit to access restricted areas on the station in an attempt to escape after the planned assassination of **Vedek Bareil**. ("In the Hands of the Prophets" [DS9]).

Ekos. Inner planet in star system M43 Alpha, homeworld to the **Ekosians** and sister world to planet **Zeon**. ("Patterns of Force" [TOS]).

Ekosians. Humanoid inhabitants of planet **Ekos**. The Ekosians were the victims of a terrible miscalculation by Federation sociologic observer **John Gill**, who tried to bring peace to the planet by introducing a government patterned after Earth's Nazi Germany. The plan initially worked, but Gill was unable to avoid the brutal excesses of the ancient Nazis. Gill became the literal puppet of ambitious Ekosians seeking to gain power for themselves by creating a repressive regime and seeking to exterminate the citizens of neighboring planet **Zeon**. In 2268, the *Starship Enterprise*, investigating the planet, allowed Gill to denounce the Nazi movement, paving the way for the resumption of peaceful relations with the Zeons. ("Patterns of Force" [TOS]). SEE: **Melakon**.

El Capitan. A massive monolithic mountain in **Yosemite National Park** on Earth. Formed by glaciers during the Ice Age, El Capitan has a sheer granite face, a kilometer high, considered by many to be among Earth's greatest challenges for rock climbers. James Kirk enjoyed the sport of free-climbing El Capitan, although he was nearly killed in an accident there in 2287. (*Star Trek V: The Final Frontier*).

El-Adrel IV. Planet in the El-Adrel star system where Tamarian captain **Dathon** and *Enterprise*-D captain Picard met in 2368. An indigenous beast there provided a significant threat to both men on the planet. Dathon hoped that the shared danger would help Picard understand the nature of his people's metaphoric language. Dathon was ultimately successful, but at the cost of his life. ("Darmok" [TNG]).

El-Adrel system. Star system located midway between Federation and Tamarian space. ("Darmok" [TNG]).

El-Baz, Shuttlepod. Shuttle-
pod 05, carried aboard *U.S.S.
Enterprise*-D. This ship was
discovered floating derelict
near the **Endicor system**,
carrying a future version of
Captain Picard in 2365. ("Time
Squared" [TNG]). *The vehicle
was also seen in the shuttlebay
in "Transfigurations" (TNG). Data stole the El-Baz while under
the control of Lore, and it was seen on the planet's surface in
"Descent, Parts I and II" (TNG). Designed by Rick Sternbach
and Richard McKenzie, miniature built by Tony Meininger.
The El-Baz was the first shuttle of this type seen; subsequent
shuttlepods were redresses of the El-Baz. The shuttlepod
was smaller than the shuttlecraft, and was used because it
was impractical at the time to build a full exterior of the larger
shuttlecraft. The El-Baz was named for former NASA planetary geoscientist Farouk El-Baz, currently on the faculty at
Brown University.*

el-Mitra Exchange. A classic strategy in three-dimensional
chess. It was considered a strong response to the **Kriskov
Gambit**. When Data and Troi played the game on stardate
45494, Data expected Troi to employ the el-Mitra Exchange,
but she surprised him. ("Conundrum" [TNG]).

• **"Elaan of Troyius."** Original Series episode #57. Written
by John Meredyth Lucas. Directed by John Meredyth Lucas.
Stardate 4372.5. *First aired in 1968. The* Enterprise *must
transport Elaan, the beautiful Dohlman of Elas, to an arranged
marriage on planet Troyius.* SEE: **dilithium; Dohlman;
Elaan; Elas; Elasian tears; Elasians; Kryton; Petri; radans;
Tellun star system; Troyians; Troyius.**

Elaan. (France Nuyen). The
Dohlman of planet **Elas**. Elaan
married the leader of planet **Troyius**
in 2268, an arranged marriage intended to bring peace to the two
warring planets. Elaan was shuttled
from Elas to Troyius aboard the
Starship Enterprise. The flight was
deliberately slowed in the hopes
that Elaan would take the extra
time to learn more of Troyan cul-
ture. The willful Elaan at first strongly resisted having a new
culture forced upon her, but later accepted the responsibility.
("Elaan of Troyius" [TOS]).

Elamos the Magnificent. A mythological figure who ruled the
land of Tagas, studied in the *Enterprise*-D primary school
during the 2360s. Elamos proclaimed that no children would
be tolerated within his kingdom, but a girl named Dara and her
brother defied him. ("Hero Worship" [TNG]).

Elanian singer stone. An artifact that responds to being held
by a living being by emitting musical sounds. **Dr. Katherine
Pulaski** had a singer stone on her desk, but gave it to
Sarjenka of planet **Drema IV**. ("Pen Pals" [TNG]).

Elas. Inner planet in the **Tellun Star System** and home to the
Elasian race of humanoids. ("Elaan of Troyius" [TOS]).

Elasian tears. The tears of women from the planet **Elas**
contain a powerful biochemical compound that serves as a
powerful love potion. Any man who comes into contact with
an **Elasian** woman's tears will fall in love with her. Kirk
brushed aside a tear from the **Dohlman** of Elas in 2268 and
became obsessed with her until his true love, the *Enterprise*,
cured him of her spell. ("Elaan of Troyius" [TOS])

Elasians. Proud warrior race of people from the planet **Elas**
who had been at war with their neighbor **Troyius** for many
years, eventually resulting in both planets gaining the ability
to destroy each other. The marriage between the ruler of
Troyius and the **Dohlman** of Elas was arranged in 2268 in the
hope of bringing peace to the two worlds. ("Elaan of Troyius"
[TOS]).

Elba II. Planet with a poisonous atmosphere on which was
located one of the few Federation penal colonies for the
criminally insane. The Elba II facility, managed by **Governor
Cory**, was home to 15 inmates in 2268, including Captain
Garth of Izar, who became mentally unstable after an accident. ("Whom Gods Destroy" [TOS]).
  *The dove and hand symbol that adorned the medical
jumpsuits on Elba II was also used in the **Tantalus V** colony
in "Dagger of the Mind" (TOS).*

Elbrun, Tam. (Harry Groener). A
Betazoid specialist in first contact
with new life-forms. Elbrun was a
telepath of extraordinary talent, but
he lacked the ability to screen out
the normal telepathic "noise" ema-
nating from other humanoids'
thoughts. This caused Elbrun great
emotional stress, for which he was
hospitalized repeatedly. While a
patient at the **University of
Betazed**, Elbrun was cared for by psychology student Deanna
Troi.
  As a first-contact specialist, Elbrun participated in the
notorious **Ghorusda disaster**, and later served as Federation representative to **Chandra V**. In 2366, Elbrun was
assigned to the *Enterprise*-D for the strategically significant
Tin Man first contact. Elbrun, who had lived all his life
desperately seeking isolation, found the living spacecraft Tin
Man to be a kindred spirit. ("Tin Man" [TNG]).

Elected One, The. Head of the parliamentary body governing
planet **Angel One**. The Elected One is one of six females who
lead the constitutional oligarchy. **Beata** was the Elected One
in 2364. ("Angel One" [TNG]).

electroplasma system taps. Components of a Federation
starship's warp-drive system used to divert a small amount of
the drive plasma so that it can be used to generate electrical
power for shipboard use. The **EPS** taps are located on the
power transfer conduits. ("A Matter of Time" [TNG]).

electroplasma system. Often abbreviated EPS. Power-distribution network used aboard Federation starships, as well as in Cardassian facilities like **Deep Space 9**. ("The Forsaken" [DS9]).

electrophoretic analysis. Standard medical test run to analyze cellular components. Dr. Julian Bashir ran an electrophoretic analysis on cells found in **Ibudan**'s quarters to help determine their origin. ("A Man Alone" [DS9]).

Eleen. (Julie Newmar). Mother to High Teer **Leonard James Akaar** of planet **Capella IV**. Eleen's husband, High **Teer Akaar**, was killed in a local power struggle in 2267, whereupon Eleen accepted the necessity of her own death under **Capellan** law, since she carried the unborn child who would be **teer**. Her execution was prevented by personnel from the *Starship Enterprise*. Upon the birth of her son, Eleen became regent, ruling the Ten Tribes until Leonard James came of age. Eleen named her son Leonard James in honor of the two *Enterprise* officers who prevented Klingon outsiders from overthrowing her government, a distinction that caused James Kirk and Leonard McCoy to become insufferably pleased with themselves. ("Friday's Child" [TOS]).

• **"Elementary, Dear Data."** *Next Generation* episode #29. Written by Brian Alan Lane. Directed by Rob Bowman. Stardate 42286.3. *First aired in 1988. A holodeck malfunction during a Sherlock Holmes simulation causes the character of Moriarty to take on a life of his own.* SEE: **arch; Clancy; Doyle, Sir Arthur Conan; Holmes, Sherlock; holodeck matter; La Forge, Geordi; Lestrade, Inspector; Moriarty, Professor James; mortality fail-safe; particle stream; Victory, H.M.S.; Victory, U.S.S.**

Eline. (Margot Rose). Native of the now-dead planet **Kataan**, and the beloved wife of the ironweaver **Kamin**. Eline lived over a thousand years ago in the village of **Ressik**. Memories of her life were preserved aboard a space probe launched from Kataan. The probe encountered the *Starship Enterprise*-D in 2368, transferring its memories, including the memory of Eline, to Jean-Luc Picard. ("The Inner Light" [TNG]).

Elway Theorem. Scientific treatise that proposed transport through a spatial fold as an alternative to matter-energy transport. Although the concept was initially very promising, development of interdimensional folded space transport was abandoned by the mid-23rd century when it was found that each use of the process caused cumulative and irreversible damage to the transport subject. The **Ansata** terrorists of planet **Rutia IV** made use of this technique with a device

called an **inverter** to provide a nearly undetectable means of transport, despite the terrible cost to those being transported. ("The High Ground" [TNG]).

EM base frequencies. Engineering term used in measuring a **phaser** beam's component electromagnetic wavelengths. During the **Borg** offensive of 2366-2367, an attempt was made by *Enterprise*-D personnel to make phaser weapons more effective by retuning the phasers' base frequencies. The attempt was partially successful, but the Borg were able to quickly compensate for the adjustment. ("The Best of Both Worlds, Parts I and II" [TNG]).

Emerald Wading Pool. A vacation spot on the planet Sumiko III considered to be very safe, certainly safer than the **Cliffs of Heaven** on **Cirrus IV**. This location was available as a holodeck simulation on the *Enterprise*-D. ("Conundrum" [TNG]).

emergency manual monitor. Auxiliary control facility aboard the *Starship Enterprise*. Scotty attempted to disengage the **M-5** computer on stardate 4729 by removing the M-5's hook-ups at the emergency manual monitor. ("The Ultimate Computer" [TOS]).

Emergency Procedure Alpha 2. Emergency protocol used aboard Federation starships. Alpha 2 disengaged all ship-board computer control and placed ship's systems on manual override. Counselor Troi, in command following the ship's collision with a **quantum filament** on stardate 45156, ordered this procedure put in effect. ("Disaster" [TNG]).

emergency saucer separation. SEE: **saucer separation**.

emergency hand actuator. Aboard Federation starships, a small hand crank located in an access panel on one side of an automatic door. The actuator can be used to open a door should the normal computer-driven system be inoperative. ("Disaster" [TNG]).

emergency transporter armbands. Devices used by Starfleet personnel for remote activation of the transporter in situations where there might not be sufficient time to contact the ship for transport orders. Emergency transport armbands were also used by members of the *Enterprise*-D crew to establish individual subspace forcefields, to protect the wearers from the effects of a **temporal disturbance**. ("The Best of Both Worlds, Part II" [TNG], "Timescape" [TNG]).

Emila II. Destination of the *Enterprise*-D following the mission at **Tanuga IV** in 2366. ("A Matter of Perspective" [TNG]).

Eminiar VII. Class-M planet in star **cluster NGC 321**. Eminiar VII had been at war with neighboring planet **Vendikar** for some 500 years, a computer-based conflict in which attacks were launched mathematically, but in which any citizens declared as "casualties" would voluntarily report to disintegration stations so that their deaths could be recorded. Eminiar officials defended the arrangement as one that preserved the infrastructure of society despite a protracted, bitter war. The Federation starship *Valiant* was destroyed at Eminiar VII in 2217 when it was declared a casualty in the war. Fifty years later, the original *Starship Enterprise* nearly suffered the same fate until Captain Kirk and **Ambassador Robert Fox** were able to persuade the Eminiar VII council to begin peace talks with Vendikar. Fox and the *Enterprise* had been sent to Eminiar to establish diplomatic relations in hopes of establishing a treaty port. ("A Taste of Armageddon" [TOS]). SEE: **Anan 7**. *The Eminiar city matte painting was later reused for the planet Scalos in "Wink of an Eye" (TOS).*

• **"Emissary, Parts I and II."** *Deep Space Nine* episodes #1 and 2. Teleplay by Michael Piller. Story by Rick Berman & Michael Piller. Directed by David Carson. Stardate 46379.1. *First aired in 1993. Commander Benjamin Sisko takes command of Deep Space 9 and discovers the existence of the wormhole. Flashback scenes show some of the terrible battle of Wolf 359, originally alluded to in "The Best of Both Worlds, Part II" (TNG). "Emissary, Parts I and II" (not to be confused with "The Emissary" [TNG]), was the first episode of* Star Trek: Deep Space Nine, *originally produced as a two-hour made-for-television movie, then divided into two hour-long episodes for later airings.* SEE: **antilepton interference; Bajor; Bajoran wormhole; Bajorans; baseball; Bashir, Dr. Julian; Bolians; Borg; Cardassians; Cardies; Celestial Temple; Constable; Dabo; Dax, Curzon; Dax, Jadzia; Deep Space 9; Denorios Belt; DS9; Dukat, Gul; Emissary; escape pod; Ferengi; Fourth Order; Frunalian;** *Gage, U.S.S.;* **Gamma Quadrant; Gilgo Beach; holosuite; Idran; infirmary; Jasad, Gul; Kai; Kira Nerys; Kumomoto; Locutus of Borg; Morn; Nog; O'Brien, Keiko; O'Brien, Miles; ODN; Odo; Opaka, Kai; Operations Center; Ops; Orb;** *pagh;* **Promenade; Prophets; pulse compression wave; Quadros-1 probe; Quark's bar; Quark;** *Rio Grande, U.S.S.;* **Roladan Wild Draw; Rom; runabout;** *Saratoga, U.S.S.;* **Setlik III; shape-shifter; Sisko, Benjamin; Sisko, Jake; Sisko, Jennifer; synthale; Taluno, Kai; thoron field; Trill; Utopia Planitia Fleet Yards; Wolf 359;** *Yangtzee Kiang, U.S.S.*

• **"Emissary, The."** *Next Generation* episode #46. Television story and teleplay by Richard Manning & Hans Beimler. Based on an unpublished story by Thomas H. Calder. Directed by Cliff Bole. Stardate 42901.3. *First aired in 1989. Special Emissary K'Ehleyr visits the* Enterprise-D *on a mission to destroy a Klingon warship returning from a 75-year mission of exploration. This episode introduced the character of K'Ehleyr, who later appeared (and died) in "Reunion" (TNG).* SEE: **Boradis system; calisthenics program, Klingon; Clancy; Class-8 probe; Gromek, Admiral; Iceman; K'Ehleyr; K'Temoc; Oath, Klingon;** *P'Rang, I.K.C.;* **Starbase 153; Starbase 336;** *T'Ong, I.K.C.;* **TlhIngan jlH.**

Emissary. In the **Bajoran** religion, the Emissary was the person prophesied to save the Bajoran people and unite the planet by finding the mysterious **Celestial Temple**. Starfleet officer **Benjamin Sisko**, in command of station **Deep Space 9**, discovered the **Bajoran wormhole** in 2369, thereby becoming the Emissary in the eyes of the Bajoran people. Sisko was uncomfortable with this role, but his Starfleet duties demanded that he respect Bajoran religious beliefs. ("Emissary" [DS9]).

• **"Empath, The."** Original Series episode #63. Written by Joyce Muskat. Directed by John Erman. Stardate 5121.5. *First aired in 1968. Kirk, Spock, McCoy, and an alien woman are brutally tortured in a test of the woman's worthiness to have her race saved from an exploding star.* SEE: **decompression chamber; energy transfer device; Gamma Vertis IV; Gem; Lal; Linke, Dr.; Minara II; Minaran empath; Minaran star system; Ozaba; Ritter scale; sand bats; Thann; Vians.**

empath. SEE: **Betazoid; Gem; Kamala; Minaran empath; Troi, Deanna; Troi, Lwaxana.**

empathic metamorph. A rare type of genetically mutated individual in the Kriosian and Valtese races. An empathic metamorph has the ability to sense what a potential mate wants and needs, and then to assume those behavioral traits. Male empathic metamorphs are relatively common, but females with this mutation occur only once in seven generations, and thus are extremely rare. Empathic metamorphs have a long and complex three-stage sexual maturing process. At the end of the final step, known as *Finiis'ral*, the metamorph permanently bonds with his or her life mate. Prior to that point, the metamorph can mold him or herself to any potential mate. Centuries ago, an empathic metamorph named **Garuth** was the object of affection of two brothers named **Krios** and **Valt**, and became the cause of a centuries-long war between two star systems that bore the names of the two brothers. In 2368, another metamorph, named **Kamala**, helped to heal the rift between the two systems by bonding herself to Valtese **chancellor Alrik**. ("The Perfect Mate" [TNG]).

emulator module. Component of the computer systems on **Deep Space 9** that allows the station's computers to access alien computer systems by matching the operating configuration of the alien system. ("The Forsaken" [DS9]). SEE: **Pup.**

enantiodromia. Psychological term that literally means conversion into the opposite. *Vico* survivor **Timothy** was diagnosed as suffering from enantiodromia following the death of his parents in 2368. ("Hero Worship" [TNG]).

encephalographic polygraph scan. A brainwave scan used to determine truthfulness during questioning. ("The Drumhead" [TNG]).

• **"Encounter at Farpoint, Parts I and II."** *Next Generation* episodes #1 and #2. Written by D. C. Fontana and Gene Roddenberry. Directed by Corey Allen. Stardate 41153.7. *First aired in 1987. The entity known as Q first harasses the crew of the* Enterprise-D *as they attempt to solve the mystery of Farpoint Station. This was the first episode of* Star Trek:

The Next Generation. *"Farpoint," set some 95 years after the end of the first* Star Trek *series, introduces the* Starship Enterprise-D *and its crew, including Captain Jean-Luc Picard. This episode was originally produced as a two-hour made-for-TV movie, although for later airings it was divided into two hour-long segments.* SEE: **Altair III; Bandi; battle bridge; battle sSection; Betazed; chief medical officer; Crusher, Dr. Beverly; Crusher, Jack R.; Crusher, Wesley; Data; Deneb IV; DeSoto, Captain Robert;** *Enterprise-D, U.S.S.;* **exobiology; Farpoint Station;** *Galaxy-*class starship; **Groppler; holodeck;** *Hood, U.S.S.; Imzadi;* **La Forge, Geordi; Library Computer Access and Retrieval System; McCoy, Dr. Leonard H.; Picard, Jean-Luc; post-atomic horror; probability mechanics; Q; Q Continuum; Riker, William T.; saucer module; saucer separation; stardrive section; Torres, Lieutenant; Troi, Deanna; United Nations, New; VISOR; Worf; World War III; Yar, Natasha; Zorn, Groppler.**

Endar. (Sherman Howard). Captain of the **Talarian** warship *Q'Maire.* Endar served in the Talarian militia and lost his only son in a conflict between the Federation and Talarian forces at **Castal I** in the 2350s. Endar was involved in another skirmish with Federation forces at **Galen IV** in 2356. After that battle, Endar discovered a three-year-old human male named **Jeremiah Rossa** near the body of his dead mother. In accordance with Talarian custom that allows a warrior to claim the son of a slain enemy in replacement of his own dead son, Endar took the child, whom he named **Jono,** and raised him as his own son. ("Suddenly Human" [TNG]). *Photo: Endar and Jono.*

Endeavour, U.S.S. Federation starship, *Nebula* class, Starfleet registry number NCC-71805. It served in Picard's armada to blockade Romulan supply ships supplying the **Duras** family forces during the **Klingon civil war** of 2368. ("Redemption, Part II" [TNG]). The *Endeavour* was stationed in the Cleon Sector later in 2368 when *Enterprise-D* crew members were controlled by **Ktarian** operatives seeking to gain control of Starfleet. Commander William Riker was ordered to pilot a shuttle to the *Endeavour* to spread the Ktarian takeover. ("The Game" [TNG]). *The Starship* Endeavour *was named in honor of British explorer James Cook's flagship and for NASA's shuttle* Endeavour.

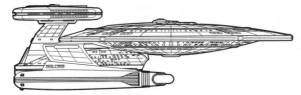

Endicor system. Destination of the *Enterprise-D* on stardate 42679 when an unexplained energy vortex was encountered, in 2365. That energy vortex was responsible for the creation of an alternate version of Captain Picard from some six hours in the future. ("Time Squared" [TNG]).

endorphins. Naturally occurring neurochemicals found in many humanoids and other vertebrate species. Endorphins are opiate peptides similar to the drug morphine, and can act upon the nervous system to affect sensations of pain and pleasure. Levels of endorphins in William Riker's bloodstream were found to affect his response to alien neurotoxins when Riker was injured on an away mission to planet **Surata IV.** ("Shades of Grey" [TNG]).

Eneg. (Patrick Horgan). Member of the **Zeon** underground on **Ekos** who infiltrated that planet's Nazi party and served as chairman at the time of the fall of the **John Gill** regime in 2268. ("Patterns of Force" [TOS]). *Eneg is Gene spelled backwards.*

• **"Enemy Within, The."** Original Series episode #5. Written by Richard Matheson. Directed by Leo Penn. Stardate 1672.1. *First aired in 1966. A transporter malfunction splits Kirk into two people, each with half of his personality. This episode marks Spock's first use of the Vulcan nerve pinch.* SEE: **Alfa 117; Farrell, Lieutant John; Fisher, Geological Technician; FSNP; ionizer, transporter; Kirk, James T.; Rand, Janice; Saurian brandy; Vulcan nerve pinch; Wilson, Transporter Technician.**

• **"Enemy, The."** *Next Generation* episode #55. Written by David Kemper and Michael Piller. Directed by David Carson. Stardate 43349.2. *First aired in 1989. Geordi La Forge and a Romulan officer must cooperate in order to survive on a hostile planet.* SEE: **Bochra, Centurion; Galorndon Core; Neutral Zone, Romulan; Patahk;** *Pi;* **ribosome infusion; Romulans; Scoutship, Romulan; Station Salem One; Tomalak; tricorder; ultritium; VISOR; Warbird, Romulan.**

energy containment cell. Device used to hold the neural patterns or consciousness of **Rao Vantika** on station Deep Space 9 in 2369. SEE: **Vantika, Rao; glial cells.** ("The Passenger" [DS9]).

energy transfer device. Handheld mechanism used by the **Vians** to perform various tasks from teleportation to physical manipulation. The unit was controlled by the user's mental impulses, and was programmed to respond to one user only. ("The Empath" [TOS]).

energy vortex. Unexplained time-space disturbance near the Endicor system, responsible for destroying an alternate version of the *Enterprise-D* in 2365 and sending an alternate version of Captain Picard some six hours back in time. The existence of the alternate Picard warned the crew of the *Enterprise-D* to avoid the ship's destruction by piloting the starship directly into the center of the vortex. ("Time Squared" [TNG]). *At one point, producer/writer Maurice Hurley had intended to follow "Time Squared" with an episode in which we would learn that the mysterious vortex had been caused by the mischievous entity Q. Although the second episode was indeed produced ("Q Who" [TNG]), the reference to Q having caused the vortex was deleted.*

engram. In neurophysiology, a specific complex memory. Computer scientist **Dr. Richard Daystrom** implanted his engrams into the experimental M-5 computer in 2268, in an effort to give the machine the ability to reason like a human. ("The Ultimate Computer" [TOS]).

Enkidu. In ancient Earth mythology, a wild man, raised among animals, who was the friend of the warrior king **Gilgamesh.** ("Darmok" [TNG]).

Ennan VI. Planet from which Dr. Katherine Pulaski obtained some ale that she shared with William Riker and friends when Riker tried his hand at omelet making. ("Time Squared" [TNG]).

Ennis. Nation from a humanoid race in the Gamma Quadrant, the ancient enemies of the **Nol-Ennis,** whom they have fought for many generations. The leaders of their planet were unable to mediate a peace, so both factions were sent to a moon and stranded as an example to the rest of the civilization. A defensive net of artificial satellites was created to keep out unwelcome visitors. The planet's leaders also constructed artificial microbes that repaired the prisoners' biological functions at a cellular level, preventing death but making the prisoners unable to leave the moon. If a prisoner was removed from the moon, the microbes would stop functioning and the body would die. Thus the horrific cycle of death and life continued, with only hate and vengeance to sustain the combatants. ("Battle Lines" [DS9]).

• **"Ensign Ro."** *Next Generation* episode #103. Teleplay by Michael Piller. Story by Rick Berman & Michael Piller. Directed by Les Landau. Stardate 45076.3. *First aired in 1991. Ensign Ro Laren joins the* Enterprise-*D crew for a special mission to locate a Bajoran terrorist. This episode introduced the Bajorans as well as the recurring character, Ensign Ro.* SEE: **Aunt Adele;** *Antares*-**class carrier; Bajor; Bajorans; Cardassians; Collins, Ensign; Dolak, Gul;** *Galor*-**class Cardassian warship; Garon II; ginger tea; Jaros II; Jaz Holza; Keeve Falor; Kennelly, Admiral; Lya Station Alpha; molecular displacement traces; Mot; Orta; Ro Laren; Sector 21305; Solarion IV; Valo System;** *Wellington, U.S.S.*

• **"Ensigns of Command, The."** *Next Generation* episode #49. Written by Melinda M. Snodgrass. Directed by Cliff Bole. No stardate given in episode. *First aired in 1989. Data must persuade colonists to move away from the planet that has been their home for generations. This was the first episode of the third season, although "Evolution" (TNG) was aired first. This is the first episode in which Data is seen playing the violin.* SEE: **Armens, Treaty of;** *Artemis, S.S.*; **de Laure Belt; Gosheven; Grisella; Haritath; hyperonic radiation; McKenzie, Ard'rian;** *O'Brien, Miles;* **Onizuka,** *Shuttlepod*; **Septimus Minor; Shelia Star System; Sheliak Corporate; Sheliak Director; Sheliak; Tau Cygna V.**

• **"*Enterprise* Incident, The."** Original Series episode #59. Written by D. C. Fontana. Directed by John Meredyth Lucas. Stardate: 5031.3. *First aired in 1968. Kirk and Spock are captured by the Romulans while on a secret mission to steal a new Romulan cloaking device.* SEE: **cloaking device,**

Romulan; Klingon Empire; physiostimulator; Romulan battle cruiser; Romulan commander; Romulan Neutral Zone; Romulan Right of Statement; Tal; Vulcan death grip.

Enterprise, **I.S.S.** Starship in the parallel **mirror universe** to which the *U.S.S. Enterprise's* landing party was transported to during a severe **ion storm** in 2267. The mirror universe's crew were savage and opposite to the *U.S.S. Enterprise* crew; their mission was to conquer and control worlds for the Empire. Subtle but disturbing differences existed in the *I.S.S. Enterprise,* including daggers painted on doors and henchmen guarding the corridors. ("Mirror, Mirror" [TOS]).

Enterprise, **U.S.S.** (aircraft carrier). Massive oceangoing ship, naval registry number CVN-65, part of the American Navy in the 20th century on Earth. This warship was a nuclear-powered aircraft carrier from which Starfleet officers Chekov and Uhura "borrowed" high-energy photons in order to recrystallize some **dilithium** so that they could return to the 23rd century. During that covert operation, Chekov was captured by Navy personnel, but he eventually escaped. The *Enterprise* was docked at the Alameda naval base at the time. (*Star Trek IV: The Voyage Home*). *The aircraft carrier* U.S.S. Ranger *actually stood in for the* Enterprise *for filming during* Star Trek IV, *since the real* Enterprise *was at sea at the time.*

Enterprise, **U.S.S.** Perhaps the most famous spacecraft in the history of space exploration, the original *U.S.S. Enterprise* was a **Constitution-class** vessel, registry number NCC-1701. Launched in 2245 from the San Francisco Yards orbiting Earth, the *Enterprise* was first commanded by **Cap-**

tain Robert April, then by Captain **Christopher Pike** ("The Cage" [TOS]). Superbly equipped for research in deep space, the *Enterprise* had 14 science labs. ("Operation—Annihilate!" [TOS]). The ship achieved legendary status during the five-year mission commanded by Captain **James T. Kirk** from 2264 to 2269. The original *Starship Enterprise* was refitted several times during its lifetime, most notably in 2270, when virtually every major system was upgraded, a new bridge module was installed, and the warp-drive nacelles were replaced (*Star Trek: The Motion Picture*). The ship was destroyed just prior to its scheduled retirement in 2285 by James Kirk, who sought to prevent the ship from falling into Klingon hands during a rescue mission to recover the body of Captain Spock (*Star Trek III: The Search for Spock*).

The original Starship Enterprise *was designed by series art director Matt Jefferies. The motion picture version was designed by Mike Minor, Joe Jennings, Andrew Probert, Douglas Trumbull, and Harold Michelson.*

We conjecture that Captain Pike commanded two five-year missions of the Enterprise *before Kirk's tenure at the helm, and that Captain Robert April commanded a five-year mission before Pike. This is reasonably consistent with a commissioning date of 2245.*

Enterprise-A, U.S.S. The second Federation starship to bear the name, the *Enterprise-A* was a **Constitution-class** vessel, registry number NCC-1701-A. Launched in 2286, the *Enterprise-A* was placed under the command of Captain James Kirk by the **Federation Council** and Starflet

Command in appreciation for Kirk's role in saving planet Earth from the destructive effects of an alien space probe. (*Star Trek IV: The Voyage Home*). SEE: **Yorktown, U.S.S.** Although shakedown tests and systems installation under the aegis of Captain Scott had not been completed, the *Enterprise-A* was rushed into service in early 2287 to intervene in a hostage situation at planet **Nimbus III**. (*Star Trek V: The Final Frontier*). The ship, under the reluctant command of Captain Kirk, was pressed back into service to escort Klingon **chancellor Gorkon** to Earth for a peace conference. Although the scheduled talks were canceled after the assassination of Gorkon, the *Enterprise-A* and her crew were instrumental in the success of the historic **Khitomer** peace conference shortly thereafter. The *Enterprise-A* was scheduled to be decommissioned shortly after the Khitomer conference. (*Star Trek VI: The Undiscovered Country*). *Of course, it remains to be seen if the* Enterprise-A *"really" was retired after* Star Trek VI, *or if some future movie or episode will chronicle new adventures for that ship. The* Enterprise-A's *exterior was virtually identical to the upgraded original* Enterprise *first seen in* Star Trek: The Motion Picture, *although many of the interiors were redesigned for* Star Trek V *and* VI.

Enterprise-B, U.S.S. Federation starship, Starfleet registry number NCC-1701-B, the third starship to bear the name. *Virtually nothing is known about this ship, as it has, to date, only been seen as a sculpture on the back wall of the* Enterprise-D's *observation lounge. Since that*

sculpture was based on the Starship Excelsior, *it is generally assumed that the* Enterprise-B *was an* **Excelsior-class** *ship, although this has not yet been firmly established in an episode or movie.*

Enterprise-C, U.S.S. The fourth Federation starship to bear the name *Enterprise*, an **Ambassador-class** vessel, registry number NCC-1701-C, was lost and presumed destroyed near **Narendra III** in 2344. In that year, this ship, commanded by **Captain**

Rachel Garrett, responded to a distress call from the Klingon outpost on **Narendra III**. The outpost was under a massive Romulan attack. During the battle, a torpedo explosion

Deck #	Major features
1	Bridge
2	Science Labs
3	Science Labs, life support
4	Crew quarters
5	Crew quarters including Captain's quarters
6	Crew quarters
7	Sickbay, transporter room, briefing room, computer core, impulse engines
8	Food preparation, recreation deck, ship's laundry, life support
9	Freight and cargo
10	Freight and cargo
11	Phaser controls
12	Inertial damping system, observation deck
13	observation deck, dorsal interconnects
14	Engineering support, water storage
15	Deuterium fuel storage
16	Deuterium fuel storage
17	Crew quarters
18	Power distribution subsystems
19	Main Engineering, Hangar deck
20	Shuttlecraft maintenance
21	Life support systems, cargo bays
22	Cargo bays
23	Antimatter storage pods

Original Starship Enterprise *decks*

Deck #	Major features
1	Bridge
2	Science Labs
3	Science labs, environmental support
4	Crew Quarters
5	Crew Quarters including Captain's quarters
6	Crew Quarters
7	Sickbay, transporter room, computer core
8	Food preparation, recreation deck, ship's laundry
9	Freight and cargo
10	Freight and cargo
11	Phaser controls
12	Inertial damping system, observation deck
13	Photon torpedo launcher
14	Engineering support, water storage
15	Warp drive reaction upper core injectors
16	Deuterium fuel storage
17	Deuterium fuel storage
18	Main power transformers, sensor subsystems, deflector subsystems
19	Main engineering, shuttlebay, navigational deflector, long range sensors
20	Shuttlecraft maintenance, cargo bays 13-18
21	Environmental systems, cargo bays 19-20
22	Botanical section, security confinement
23	Tractor beam emitter, antimatter storage pods

Starship Enterprise-A *decks*

opened a **temporal rift**, and the *Enterprise*-C was sent some 22 years forward in time. This proved to be a focal point in history. With the *Enterprise*-C gone from the "normal" timeline, an alternate timeline was formed, in which the Federation and the Klingon Empire engaged in an extended war. The Federation was near defeat by 2366, when the *Enterprise*-C emerged from the rift, encountering the *Enterprise*-D. It was soon realized that the *Enterprise*-C had to return to its proper time if history was to be restored and the terrible war with the Klingons was to be averted. The tragedy of the war was emphasized when a Klingon attack resulted in the death of Captain Garrett, after which *Enterprise*-C officer **Lieutenant Richard Castillo** agreed to assume command of his ship, and return it to 2344. *Enterprise*-D officer **Natasha Yar (alternate)**, who was still alive in this timeline, volunteered to return with Castillo to help defend Narendra III against the Romulans. All *Enterprise*-C personnel understood that returning to the past was a virtual suicide mission because of the intensity of the Romulan attack on Narendra III. Once the *Enterprise*-C returned through the temporal rift, the time flow returned to normal, and history was restored to its proper shape. ("Yesterday's *Enterprise*" [TNG]). SEE: **Sela**. *The Enterprise-C model was designed by Rick Sternbach and Andrew Probert. Interior supervised by Richard James.*

Enterprise-D, U.S.S. The fifth Federation starship to bear the name. ("Encounter at Farpoint, Part I" [TNG]). This ship, a **Galaxy-class** vessel, was launched in 2363 ("Lonely Among Us" [TNG]) from Starfleet's **Utopia Planitia Yards** orbiting Mars and placed  under the command of Captain **Jean-Luc Picard** on a mission of deep-space exploration and diplomacy. ("Encounter at Farpoint, Part I" [TNG]). The ship was severely damaged in the **Borg** encounter of early 2367, and had to undergo six weeks of repair work at **Earth Station McKinley**. ("Family" [TNG]). A **dilithium chamber hatch** installed at McKinley station was defective, resulting in a severe explosion in the ship's warp-drive system that crippled the *Enterprise*-D for two weeks. Although sabotage was initially suspected, it was later learned that undetectable flaws in the hatch were responsible. ("The Drumhead" [TNG]). The *Enterprise*-D was repeatedly destroyed in 2368 when the ship was trapped in a **temporal causality loop** near the **Typhon Expanse**. ("Cause and Effect" [TNG]). The *Enterprise*-D was briefly commanded by **Captain Edward Jellico** in early 2369 when Captain Picard was assigned to a covert Starfleet mission to **Celtris III**. ("Chain of Command, Part I" [TNG]). *The* Enterprise-D *model was designed by Andrew Probert. Interior sets were supervised by Herman Zimmerman and Richard James.*

A note on the deck charts. Much of the information in these charts is somewhat conjectural, since none of the ships have had complete deck information provided in any episode,

Deck #	Saucer Module major features
1	Main Bridge, Captain's Ready Room, Observation Lounge
2	Junior Officers' quarters
3	Junior Officers' quarters
4	Main Shuttlebay, cargo bays
5	Science labs and residential apartments
6	Transporter rooms 1-4, science labs
7	Residential apartments
8	Residential apartments, including Captain's quarters
9	Residential apartments
10	Ten-Forward Lounge, computer core, escape pods
11	Holodecks, residential apartments
12	Sickbay, medical laboratories, gymnasium
13	Residential apartments, life support
14	Residential apartments
15	Maintenance
16	Captain's Yacht docking port

Starship Enterprise-*D saucer module decks*

Deck #	Stardrive Section major features
8	Battle Bridge
9	Docking latches
10	Emergency batteries, phaser bank systems
11	Life support systems
12	Science labs
13	Shuttlebays 2 and 3
14	Shuttlebay support, personnel transporters 5 & 6
15	Science labs
16	Maintenance
17	Living quarters
18	Living quarters
19	Living quarters
20	Living quarters
21	Power distribution
22	Engineering support labs
23	Main impulse engines
24	Life support
25	Dorsal docking port, forward photon torpedo launcher
26	Engineering support
27	Deuterium fuel pumps and fill ports
28	Deuterium fuel storage
29	Deuterium fuel storage
30	Deuterium injection reactors
31	Science labs
32	Living quarters
33	Living quarters
34	Environmental support
35	Aft photon torpedo launcher
36	Main Engineering
37	Environmental support, waste management
38	Cargo bays, brig
39	Cargo bays
40	Antimatter injection reactors
41	Antimatter storage pods
42	Antimatter storage pods

Starship Enterprise-*D stardrive section decks*

Illustration: The five starships Enterprise, *shown to approximate scale.*

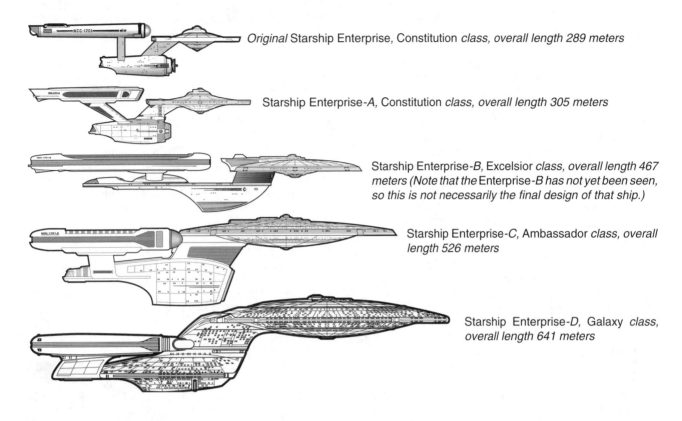

Original Starship Enterprise, Constitution *class, overall length 289 meters*

Starship Enterprise-*A, Constitution* class, *overall length 305 meters*

Starship Enterprise-*B, Excelsior* class, *overall length 467 meters (Note that the* Enterprise-*B has not yet been seen, so this is not necessarily the final design of that ship.)*

Starship Enterprise-*C, Ambassador* class, *overall length 526 meters*

Starship Enterprise-*D, Galaxy* class, *overall length 641 meters*

with the possible exception of the "A" ship, which had a deck chart visible in Engineering. Note that our deck chart for the original Enterprise disagrees with previously published blueprints in that we are putting the engineering room (which clearly housed the ship's warp drive) in the Engineering Section, rather than in the saucer (where it would be closer to the impulse engines).

environmental suit. Protective garments worn by Starfleet personnel when exploring inhospitable environments. ("The Naked Time" [TOS], "The Tholian Web" [TOS]). Environmental suits were also used by personnel at the **Elba II** penal colony when working in that planet's poisonous atmosphere. ("Whom Gods Destroy" [TOS]).

eosinophilia. An abnormally high count of serum eosinophils, a type of white blood cell in humanoids. ("The Host" [TNG]).

EPI capacitor. Device used to open a **runabout** hatch in an emergency, bypassing the normal door actuation servos. ("Q-Less" [DS9]).

EPS. SEE: **electroplasma system**.

Epsilon Canaris III. Planet where **Commissioner Nancy Hedford** was sent to prevent a war in 2267. She was forced to leave before her job was completed when she contracted rare and deadly **Sakuro's disease**. ("Metamorphosis" [TOS]).

Epsilon Hydra VII. Planet where archaeologist **Vash** was barred from the Royal Museum. ("Q-Less" [DS9]).

Epsilon Indi. Star system where, centuries ago, marauders from the planet **Triacus** waged war. One such marauder apparently survived into the 23rd century, where it caused the death of all the adult members of the Starnes Expedition. ("And the Children Shall Lead" [TOS]). Wesley Crusher recognized Epsilon Indi when he gazed from **Ten-Forward** while discussing his future with Guinan. ("The Child" [TNG]).

Epsilon IX Monitoring Station. Starfleet space station located near the Klingon border. The facility was destroyed in 2271 by the **V'Ger** machine life-form, which was returning to Earth. (*Star Trek: The Motion Picture*).

Epsilon IX Sector. Mission site where *U.S.S. Enterprise*-D was assigned to perform an astronomical survey of a new pulsar cluster shortly after stardate 42723. The Epsilon IX Sector is located near the **Scylla Sector**. ("Samaritan Snare" [TNG]). *The Epsilon IX Sector may have been the location of the Epsilon IX Monitoring Station seen in* Star Trek: The Motion Picture.

Epsilon Mynos system. Location of **Aldea**, a planet long believed to be merely legend until discovered by the *Enterprise*-D in 2364. ("When the Bough Breaks" [TNG]).

Epsilon Pulsar Cluster. Astronomical phenomenon located

in the **Epsilon IX Sector**. ("Samaritan Snare" [TNG]).

Epsilon Silar System. Location where the *U.S.S. Enterprise*-D was attacked by a **Satarran** space probe that caused disruption of the *Enterprise*-D's computer systems and damaged the crew's short-term memories. The attack was an effort to obtain the use of the *Enterprise*-D in the Satarrans' war against the people of **Lysia**. ("Conundrum" [TNG]).

Epstein, Dr. Terence. A leading 24th-century authority on cybernetics. Epstein lectured at Beverly Crusher's medical school, and she said she was looking forward to meeting him when the *Enterprise*-D docked at Starbase 74 in 2364. ("11001001" [TNG]).

Erabus Prime. Planet where **Q** saved **Vash** from illness when stung by a particularly nasty bug. ("Q-Less" [DS9]).

Erko. (Patrick Cronin). Protocol Master for **Minister Campio** of planet **Kostolain**. Erko strongly disapproved of Campio's decision to marry Ambassador **Lwaxana Troi** in 2368, correctly maintaining that Troi's disregard of protocol would strongly offend Kostolain sensibilities. ("Cost of Living" [TNG]).

ermanium. A metallic alloy used in Starfleet shuttlecraft. ("Final Mission" [TNG]).

• **"Errand of Mercy."** *Original Series* episode #27. Written by Gene L. Coon. Directed by John Newland. Stardate 3198.4. *First aired in 1967. The* Enterprise *tries to protect Organia, an apparently primitive planet, from the Klingons, but the Organians neither want nor need assistance. This episode features the first appearance of the Klingons in Star Trek. The Klingons seen here are much simpler in appearance than the elaborately made-up Klingons in the* Star Trek *features and* Star Trek: The Next Generation. SEE: **Ayelborne; Baroner; Code 1; Council of Elders; kevas; Klingon Empire; Kor, Commander; mind-sifter; noncorporeal life; Organia; Organian Peace Treaty; Organians; Richter scale of culture; Trefayne; trillium.**

Errikang VII. Planet where **Vash** said **Q** almost got her killed. ("Q-Less" [DS9]).

Erselrope Wars. Ancient conflict during which the arms merchants of planet **Minos** gained notoriety by selling sophisticated weapons systems to both sides. ("The Arsenal of Freedom" [TNG]).

Neither the date nor the adversaries of the Erselrope Wars were established, but the Enterprise-D *people seemed to know a fair amount about them, so we might speculate they were not that long ago in historical terms.*

Erstwhile. A small class-9 interplanetary cargo vessel piloted by **Thadiun Okona**. Armed with lasers only. The *Starship Enterprise*-D lent assistance to the *Erstwhile* when Okona's ship experienced a hardware malfunction near the **Omega Sagitta** system. ("The Outrageous Okona" [TNG]). *The* Erstwhile *was a re-use of the* Merchantman *miniature originally built for* Star Trek III.

escape pod. Small lifeboat that could be ejected from a starship or other space vehicle after a catastrophic accident. (*Star Trek II: The Wrath of Khan*, "Cause and Effect" [TNG]). The crew of the *U.S.S. Stargazer* used escape pods to survive following the **Battle of Maxia** in 2355.

Escape pods from the *S.S. Odin* drifted for five months before landing on planet **Angel One** in 2357. ("Angel One" [TNG]). Escape pods were also used by the crew of the *U.S.S. Arcos* when they abandoned ship above planet **Turkana IV** in 2367. ("Legacy" [TNG]).

Following the destruction of the *U.S.S. Saratoga* at the battle of **Wolf 359** in 2367, many *Saratoga* personnel, including Commander **Benjamin Sisko** and his son, **Jake Sisko**, fled the ship aboard escape pods. ("Emissary, Part I" [DS9]). *The* Saratoga *escape pod model was designed by Jim Martin and built by Greg Jein.*

Esoqq. (Reiner Schoener). Member of the race known as the **Chalnoth**, Esoqq was imprisoned with Captain Picard during an alien experiment in 2366. Esoqq had been kidnapped from Chalna by unknown life-forms, and he was replaced by a near-identical copy of himself, also part of this experiment. SEE: **Haro, Mitena**. ("Allegiance" [TNG]).

ESP. SEE: **extrasensory perception**.

Essex, U.S.S. Federation starship, ***Daedalus* class**, Starfleet registry NCC-173. Commanded by **Captain Bryce Shumar**, and under the sector command of **Admiral Uttan Narsu** at Starbase 12, the *Essex* was reported lost in 2167. The *Essex* was caught in an electromagnetic storm in the atmosphere of a Class-M moon of planet **Mab-Bu VI**. The storm had been caused by noncorporeal criminal life-forms from the **Ux-Mal** system who had hoped to escape aboard the *Essex*. The ship was destroyed and all 229 members of the crew were killed. In 2368, the *Enterprise*-D encountered beings who claimed to be members of the *Essex* crew, marooned there since 2167. These beings were in fact the Ux-Mal criminals, who sought to escape by commandeering the *Enterprise*-D. ("Power Play" [TNG]).

Esteban, Captain J. T. (Phillip Richard Allen). Commanding officer of the *U.S.S. Grissom*, in charge of investigating the **Genesis Planet**. A conservative, by-the-book officer, Esteban was killed along with the rest of the *Grissom* crew when the ship was destroyed by a Klingon ship during the investigation. (*Star Trek III: The Search for Spock*).

Ethan. (Chris Demetral). Another name used by **Barash** of planet **Alpha Onias III**. ("Future Imperfect" [TNG]).

Ethics, Sophistry and the Alternate Universe. Book written by Ving Kuda; not exactly light reading. Captain Picard took a copy along with him on his vacation to Risa. ("Captain's Holiday" [TNG]).

• **"Ethics."** *Next Generation* episode #116. Teleplay by Ronald D. Moore. Story by Sara Charno & Stuart Charno. Directed by Chip Chalmers. Stardate 45587.3. *First aired in 1992. Worf is seriously injured and his only hope for life is a dangerous experimental procedure proposed by a researcher that Dr. Crusher believes to be making unethical use of Worf's vulnerability.* SEE: **Adelman Neurological Institute; Beloti Sector; borathium;** *brak'lul;* **chlorinide; chloromydride; cordrazine; CPK enzymatic therapy; cybernetic regeneration;** *Denver, U.S.S.;* **dentronal scanner; drechtal beams; dynoscanner; exoscalpel; Fang-lee; genetronic replicator; gravitic mine;** *Hegh'bat* **ceremony; inaprovaline; Klingons; leporazine; Mericor system; morathial series; neural metaphasic shock; neural transducers; neurogenetics; Ogawa, Nurse Alyssa; poker;** *Potemkin, U.S.S.;* **Russell, Dr. Toby; Sandoval; Sector 37628;** *VeK'tal* **response; Worf, Lieutenant.**

Eugenics Wars. A terrible conflict on Earth during the 1990s caused by a group of genetically engineered "supermen" who were the result of an ambitious selective-breeding program. The "supermen" felt their superior abilities gave them the right to rule the remainder of humanity, and in 1992 one such individual, **Khan Noonien Singh**, rose to power to rule one-fourth of the entire planet. Within a year, his fellow supermen seized power in forty nations. Terrible wars ensued, in part because the supermen fought among themselves. Entire populations were bombed out of existence, and Earth was on the verge of a new dark age. By 1996, the supermen were overthrown. Khan Noonien Singh escaped into space with several of his followers aboard the ***S.S. Botany Bay***. ("Space Seed" [TNG]). *The Eugenics Wars were apparently not the conflict mentioned in several episodes as World War III, since the Eugenics Wars were concluded by 1996, but World War III took place in the mid-21st century.*

European Hegemony. A loose political alliance on 22nd-century Earth. The European Hegemony was considered to be among the beginnings of a world government on that planet. ("Up the Long Ladder" [TNG]).

Evadne IV. Destination of the *Enterprise*-D following the ship's encounter with an unstable wormhole in the **Ngame Nebula** in 2367. ("Clues" [TNG]).

Evans, Charles. (Robert Walker, Jr.). The sole survivor of a transport crash on planet **Thasus** in 2252. Charlie, who was only 3 years old at the time, was raised by the **Thasians**, a noncorporeal race. Charlie claimed to have survived by learning from the ship's computer tapes, but it was later learned that the Thasians gave Charlie extraordinary mental powers in order for him to survive on Thasus. Charlie was rescued at age 17 by the crew of the science vessel *Antares*, but his inexperience with living in human society, combined with his mental

powers, made him too dangerous to live with humans, and the Thasians took him back to live on Thasus. ("Charlie X" [TOS]).

• **"Evolution."** *Next Generation* episode #50. Teleplay by Michael Piller. Story by Michael Piller & Michael Wagner. Directed by Winrich Kolbe. Stardate 43125.8. *First aired in 1989. A lab accident causes microscopic robots to evolve into an intelligent life-form. This was the second episode filmed for the third season, although it was the first episode aired for that season; thus it marked the return of Dr. Beverly Crusher. "Evolution" was the first episode written by Michael Piller, who would later serve as executive producer of* Star Trek: The Next Generation. SEE: **Beth Delta I; computer core; Crusher, Dr. Beverly; Crusher, Wesley; Dakar Senegal; "Egg, the"; Guinan; Kavis Alpha IV; Kavis Alpha Sector; linear memory crystal; nanites; nanotechnology; neutron star; neutronium; New Manhattan; Stubbs, Dr. Paul; Universal Translator.**

exanogen gas. An extremely cold gaseous compound used to retard the feeding and growth of **nitrium metal parasites**. ("Cost of Living" [TNG]).

Exarch. Official from the Nehelik Province of planet **Rakhar**. In 2369, he demanded that the Rakhari fugitive **Croden** be extradited from Deep Space 9. ("Vortex" [DS9]).

Excalbia. Uncharted planet whose surface was molten lava and the atmosphere poisonous. The original *Starship Enterprise* visited there in 2269. ("The Savage Curtain" [TOS]). SEE: **Excalbians**.

Excalbians. Life-forms idigenous to planet **Excalbia**. These rock-based, intelligent entities possess ethics and values dramatically different from those of many humanoid species. They are intensely curious about other life-forms and have captured such forms, to observe their behavior in dramatic situations created by the Excalbians. They were **shapeshifters**, and used their ability to alter their molecular form to remake themselves into characters to support such dramas. One such experiment, conducted in 2269, involved the capture of Kirk and Spock, who were placed into a conflict with various historical figures including **Abraham Lincoln**, **Kahless the Unforgettable**, and **Surak of Vulcan**. ("The Savage Curtain" [TOS]).

Excalibur, U.S.S. *Constitution*-class Federation starship, Starfleet registry number NCC-1664, commanded by **Captain Harris**. The *Excalibur* was severely damaged and all crew personel killed in 2268 during a disastrous war-game drill with the **M-5** computer. ("The Ultimate Computer" [TOS]).

Excalibur, U.S.S. Federation starship, *Ambassador* class, Starfleet registry number NCC-26517. The *Excalibur* served in Picard's armada to blockade Romulan supply ships supplying the **Duras** family forces during the **Klingon civil war** in 2368. During this assignment, Commander William Riker served as its captain and Commander La Forge was his first officer. ("Redemption, Part II" [TNG]). *The* Excalibur *was a reuse of the* Enterprise-C *model.*

exceiver. Alien device used by Gary Seven when assigned to Earth in 1968. ("Assignment: Earth" [TOS]).

Excelsior*-class starship.** Dubbed "the Great Experiment," the first *Excelsior*-class vessel was launched in 2285 as a testbed for the unsuccessful **transwarp drive** development project. The ship, later refit with a standard warp drive, became the prototype for the numerous *Excelsior*-class starships built over the next several decades. Among these ships was the ***U.S.S. Enterprise*-B**, the third Federation starship to bear that name. Other *Excelsior* class starships have included the ***Hood ("Encounter at Farpoint" [TNG]), the ***Repulse*** ("The Child" [TNG]), the ***Intrepid*** ("Sins of the Father" [TNG]), and the ***Gorkon*** ("Descent, Part I" [TNG]).

***Excelsior*, U.S.S.** The first starship of the *Excelsior* class, launched in 2284 with the registry number NX-2000. The ship served under the command of **Captain Styles** as the testbed vehicle for the unsuccessful **transwarp drive** development project. (*Star Trek III: The Search for Spock*). Under the command of Captain **Hikaru Sulu**, the ship began a three-year research mission in 2290 cataloging planetary atmospheric anomalies. Upon successful completion of this mission, Sulu and the *Excelsior* played a key role in the Khitomer peace conference of 2293. Once the ship was awarded operational status, her registry number was changed to NCC-2000. (*Star Trek VI: The Undiscovered Country*). *The* Excelsior *was designed by Bill George and built at ILM. Although never made clear on film, it is generally assumed that the transwarp drive being tested in* Star Trek III *was a failure, and that the ship was later outfitted with a more conventional warp drive. The* Excelsior's *bridge control panels and computer readout displays seen in* Star Trek VI *tend to support this theory.*

***Exeter*, U.S.S.** Federation ***Constitution*-class starship**, Starfleet registry number NCC-1672. Commanded by **Captain Ronald Tracy** in 2268 when the ship was found orbiting planet **Omega IV**, its entire crew reduced to dehydrated crystals by an ancient bacteriological warfare agent from the planet. ("The Omega Glory" [TOS]).

Exo III. A barely habitable planet whose sun had been fading for a half-million years, once the home of a technically advanced humanoid civilization. Exo III's inhabitants moved underground as their sun dimmed. In doing so, they fostered a mechanistic, dehumanized society. Eventually, they began to fear the sophisticated **androids** they had built, but by that time the androids had become advanced enough to develop the instinct for self-preservation, so they eventually destroyed their makers. Noted archaeologist **Roger Korby** disappeared there, and two expeditions failed to find him prior to the

Enterprise rescue mission of 2266. ("What Are Little Girls Made Of?" [TOS]).

exobiology. The study of alien life. An area of study in which the android **Data** excelled during his studies at **Starfleet Academy**. ("Encounter at Farpoint, Part I" [TNG]). Wesley Crusher also garnered honors in the subject. ("The Host" [TNG]).

Exochemistry. Required class at Starfleet Academy. ("Time's Arrow, Part I" [TNG]).

exocomp. Experimental servomechanism developed by **Dr. Farallon** for use in hazardous engineering applications. The exocomps incorporated an advanced microreplication system, providing the device with the ability to fabricate specialized tools for virtually any task, and ample onboard intelligence to make realtime repair decisions. The exocomps were later found to have a sufficient degree of intelligence to qualify as sentient life-forms. ("The Quality of Life" [TNG]). *The exocomps, designed by Rick Sternbach, were very loosely based on the character Mugi from the animated s-f series* The Dirty Pair.

exoscalpel. Surgical instrument used by Starfleet medical personnel to incise the skin and expose underlying tissue. ("Ethics" [TNG]).

exothermal inversion. A dramatic upheaval in a planet's atmosphere caused by an external energy source. A cascading exothermal inversion was a real possibility at planet **Penthara IV** in 2368 if a plan to vaporize large amounts of volcanic dust in the planet's atmosphere failed. ("A Matter of Time" [TNG]).

extrasensory perception. Various mental and telekinetic powers, currently inexplicable by conventional science. Certain members of the *Valiant* and *Enterprise* crews exhibited dramatically enhanced ESP powers after contact with the barrier at the edge of the galaxy. ("Where No Man Has Gone Before" [TOS]). SEE: **Mitchell, Gary**.

"Eyes in the dark." A telepathic message sent to Counselor Troi by an alien vessel trapped with the *Enterprise*-D in a **Tyken's Rift** in 2367. The message referred to the binary star system where the rift was located. ("Night Terrors" [TNG]).

Eymorg. Female inhabitants of planet **Sigma Draconis VI** who lived beneath the surface in the reminants of a highly advanced culture. The male population, called the **Morgs**, lived aboveground in primitive conditions in a wintery environment, existed only to mate with the women, calling them the "givers of pain and delight." The Eymorgs were forced to return to the surface to live with the Morgs when they were unable to find a humanoid brain to serve in their Controller. ("Spock's Brain" [TOS]).

Fabrina. Star system containing eight planets that were destroyed 10,000 years ago when the star of the same name became a nova and exploded. ("For the World Is Hollow and I Have Touched the Sky" [TOS]). SEE: **Fabrini**.

Fabrini Book of the People. Massive text containing all the knowledge of the **Fabrini** people, provided by their creators, to be read when the asteroid/ship *Yonada* reached its final destination. ("For the World Is Hollow and I Have Touched the Sky" [TOS]).

Fabrini creators. Inhabitants of the star system **Fabrina** who, just prior to their sun going nova, constructed a massive space ark inside an asteroid so that some of their people could escape to resettle on another world. The passengers on the asteroid ship, called *Yonada*, revered their creators for having literally built their world and established their society. ("For the World Is Hollow and I Have Touched the Sky" [TOS]). SEE: **Fabrini**.

Fabrini. Humanoids from the star system **Fabrina** who constructed a ship disguised as an asteroid to carry some of their people to safety before their star exploded 10,000 years ago. The creators of the asteroid/ship devised a religion intended to guide their descendants in their lives aboard the mobile world they called *Yonada*. The Yonadan religion was enforced by a powerful computer called the **Oracle**, which attempted to provide as normal an environment as possible for the people, concealing from them the fact that they were living on a spaceship. ("For the World Is Hollow and I Have Touched the Sky" [TOS]). SEE: **Natira**. *The Fabrini apparently disembarked at their promised land sometime in 2269.*

• **"Face of the Enemy."** *Next Generation* episode #140. Teleplay by Naren Shankar. Story by René Echevarria. Directed by Gabrielle Beaumont. Stardate 46519.1. *First aired in 1993. Deanna Troi is kidnapped and must masquerade as a Romulan intelligence officer to avoid being killed.* SEE: *Antares*-class freighter; Borka VI; cloaking device, Romulan; Corvallen freighter; DeSeve, Ensign Stefan; disruptors, Romulan; Draken IV; gravitic sensor net; Imperial Senate, Romulan; Kaleb Sector; *Khazara*; Konsab, Commander; McKnight, Ensign; M'ret, Vice-Proconsul; N'Vek, Subcommander; nullifier core; Rakal, Major; Research Station 75; Romulan Warbird; Sotarek Citation; Spock; Tal Shiar; Toreth, Commander; *viinerine*.

Fahleena III. Planet that the Valerian vessel *Sherval Das* visited when delivering **dolamide** to the **Cardassians**. ("Dramatis Personae" [DS9]).

Fajo, Kivas. (Saul Rubinek). A **Zibalian** trader and an unscrupulous member of the Stacius Trade Guild, Fajo was owner of the trade ship *Jovis*. Fajo was known for his fondness for such unique collectible items as the **Rejac Crystal**, Van Gogh's "**The Starry Night**," and the only existing 1962 **Roger Maris** baseball card. In 2366, Fajo attempted to abduct the android Data for his collection. Data managed to escape Fajo's capture, but in the process, Fajo murdered his assistant, a woman named **Varria**. Fajo was subsequently placed under arrest and his collection confiscated. ("The Most Toys" [TNG]). SEE: **Beta Agni II**.

fal-tor-pan. Ancient Vulcan ritual, also called the re-fusion, intended to reunite an individual's *katra* (living spirit) to that person's body. Until 2285, the ceremony had not been performed for centuries, since in most cases a Vulcan's *katra* is returned home after the death of the body. **Sarek** requested the *fal-tor-pan* for his son. **Spock**, whose body had been regenerated at the Genesis Planet following his death there in 2285.

High priestess **T'Lar** noted that the *fal-tor-pan* had not been attempted since "ages past," and then only in legend. Nevertheless, the ritual was successful in reuniting Spock's body and soul. (*Star Trek III: The Search for Spock*).

Falling Hawk, Joe. (Sheldon P. Wolfchild). Gambling partner to **Frederick La Rouque**. ("Time's Arrow, Part I" [TNG]).

Falow. (Joel Brooks). Leader of the **Wadi** delegation who visited Deep Space 9 in 2369, the first diplomatic mission from the Gamma Quadrant. Tall in stature, Falow introduced himself as **Master Surchid** of the Wadi when he took command of the games played at Quark's bar. ("Move Along Home" [DS9]).

• **"Family."** *Next Generation* episode #78. Written by Ronald D. Moore. Directed by Les Landau. Stardate 44012.3. *First aired in 1990. Picard returns to his hometown of LaBarre, France, to recover from his experiences with the Borg. This episode, the second aired for the fourth season, was actually the fourth produced for that year, but was a direct continuation of "The Best of Both Worlds, Part II."* SEE: **Angel Falls, Venezuela; Atlantis Project; Bloom sisters; Chateau Picard; Crusher, Jack R.; discommendation; Earth Station Bobruisk; Earth Station McKinley;** *Enterprise*-D, U.S.S.; *How to Advance Your Career Through Marriage*; *Intrepid*, U.S.S.; **Labarre, France; Louis; O'Brien, Miles Edward; Picard, Jean-Luc; Picard, Marie; Picard, René; Picard, Robert;** *rokeg* **blood pie; Rozhenko, Helena; Rozhenko, Sergey; synthehol; tectonic plates; theta-matrix compositer; Worf.**

Fang-lee. *Enterprise*-D crew member who was killed while under Worf's command. ("Ethics" [TNG]).

Farallon, Dr. (Ellen Bry). Inventor of an experimental **particle fountain** mining technology tested at planet Tyrus VIIA in 2369. Farallon also developed highly sophisticated robotic tools called **exocomps**, inadvertently endowing them with sufficient intelligence for them to become sentient life-forms. ("The Quality of Life" [TNG]).

Farek, Dr. (Ethan Phillips). A member of the crew of the Ferengi vessel *Krayton*, Farek was present with **DaiMon Tog** at the **Trade Agreements Conference** on **Betazed** in 2366. ("Ménage à Troi" [TNG]).

Faren Kag. (Jim Jansen). Magistrate of a **Bajoran** village. Faren requested medical help from Deep Space 9 in 2369 when their storyteller, the **Sirah**, fell ill. ("The Storyteller" [DS9]).

Farpoint Station. Believed to be a large, advanced spaceport facility built by the Bandi people of planet **Deneb IV**. It was later discovered that the station was actually a shapeshifting spaceborne life-form that had been coerced by the Bandi into assuming the form of the starbase.

The creature was eventually allowed to return to space. An agreement with the Bandi for the use of a rebuilt Farpoint Station was concluded shortly after the departure of the creature. ("Encounter at Farpoint, Parts I and II" [TNG]).

Farragut, U.S.S. Federation starship, *Constitution* class, Starfleet registry number NCC-1647, commanded by **Captain Garrovick**. The *Farragut* was Lieutenant **James T. Kirk**'s first assignment after leaving Starfleet Academy. In 2257, 200 members of the *Farragut*

crew, including Captain Garrovick, were killed by the **dikironium cloud creature** discovered at planet **Tycho IV**. ("Obsession" [TOS]).

Farrell (mirror). (Pete Kellett). Crew member on the **mirror universe** *Enterprise* who saved Captain Kirk from Chekov's assassination attempt. In the tradition of the alternate universe, Farrell expected that his betrayal of Chekov would earn him favor with the captain. ("Mirror, Mirror" [TOS])

Farrell, Lieutenant John. (Jim Goodwin). Crew member aboard the original *Starship Enterprise*. ("The Enemy Within" [TOS], "Mudd's Women" [TOS], "Miri" [TOS]).

Farspace Starbase Earhart. SEE: **Starbase Earhart**.

Fatal Revenge, The. Gothic novel enjoyed by **Lieutenant Aquiel Uhnari**. ("Aquiel" [TNG]).

Fearless, U.S.S. Federation *Excelsior*-class starship, Starfleet registry number NCC-4598. Starfleet propulsion specialist **Kosinski** performed an unsuccessful series of experimental engine software upgrades on the *Fearless* in 2364. The *Fearless* later transported Kosinski and his assistant to the *Enterprise*-D, where similar upgrades were attempted. ("Where No One Has Gone Before" [TNG]).

Federation Archaeology Council. Organization of Federation archaeologists. **Jean-Luc Picard** was asked to give the keynote address at the council's symposium, held aboard the *Enterprise*-D, in 2367. ("QPid" [TNG]).

Federation Constitution. SEE: **Constitution of the United Federation of Planets**.

Federation Council President. (Robert Ellenstein). Leader of the representative council governing the **United Federation of Planets**. The Federation president warned all spaceships to stay away from Earth when that planet's environment was being devastated by an alien space probe in 2286. (*Star Trek IV: The Voyage Home*). A later president *played by Kurtwood Smith, pictured* was in office when a massive ecological disaster forced the Klingon government into making unprecedented peace overtures to the Federation. These initiatives were disrupted by forces seeking to maintain the status quo, but the president avoided degeneration of the situation by adhering to the

articles of interstellar law. An attempt was made on the president's life at the Khitomer conference by Starfleet **colonel West**, but the president was saved by Captain Kirk. The Federation president's office is located in the city of Paris on planet Earth. (*Star Trek VI: The Undiscovered Country*). *The Federation president in Star Trek VI had makeup identical to that of the navigator aboard the ill-fated U.S.S.* **Saratoga** *in Star Trek IV, so one might assume that both individuals were members of the same alien race. Robert Ellenstein also played* **Steven Miller** *in "Haven" (TNG).*

Federation Council. Governing body consisting of representatives of the member nations of the **United Federation of Planets**. The council chambers are located in the city of San Francisco on planet Earth. The Federation council met to consider Kirk's violation

of Starfleet orders and his theft and destruction of the *U.S.S. Enterprise* was a matter of sufficient gravity that the Council itself deliberated Kirk's fate. Despite a strong protest from the Klingon government, the Council not only dismissed all but one charge, but also reinstated Kirk as captain of the new *Starship Enterprise*, NCC-1701-A. (*Star Trek IV: The Voyage Home*).

Federation Day. A holiday celebrating the founding of the **United Federation of Planets** in 2161. ("The Outcast" [TNG]).

Federation. SEE: **United Federation of Planets**.

Fek'Ihr. (Tom Magee). A mythical Klingon beast that was the guardian of **Gre'thor**. In 2367, **Ardra** appeared on planet **Ventax II** as Fek'Ihr while trying to convince *Enterprise*-D personnel of her allegedly supernatural powers. Worf was not impressed. ("Devil's Due" [TNG]). SEE: *Sto-Vo-Kor*. Kang, in "Day of the Dove" (TOS), noted that the Klingon culture has no devil, so Fek'lhr would seem to have a different role in Klingon mythology. Either that, or Ardra didn't know everything about Klingons.

felicium. A narcotic substance produced from plants on the planet **Brekka**. Felicium has other medicinal properties, and was used, centuries ago, to cure a deadly plague on neighboring planet **Ornara**. Once the plague was ended, all the people on Ornara were addicted to the drug, and the people of Brekka continued to provide it, for a significant price. ("Symbiosis" [TNG]).

feline supplement 74. Cat food, formulated by **Data** for his cat, **Spot**. Supplement 74 was part of Data's ongoing effort to discover a cuisine that his finicky feline would accept. ("Data's Day" [TNG]).

Fellini, Colonel. (Ed Peck). United States Air Force officer who interrogated Captain Kirk when Kirk was arrested at the **Omaha Air Base** on Earth in 1969. Kirk was on a covert mission to eliminate records of the *Enterprise*'s accidental presence in Earth's past to avoid the possible contamination of history.

Fellini became frustrated with Kirk (who could not answer any questions for fear of causing further contamination), and threatened to lock the captain up for 200 years. Kirk thought that was just about right. ("Tomorrow Is Yesterday" [TOS]). *We assume that the original* Star Trek *series was actually set some 300 years in the future.*

Felton, Ensign. (Shelia Franklin). Conn officer aboard the *Enterprise*-D in 2368. ("A Matter of Time" [TNG], "New Ground" [TNG], "Hero Worship" [TNG], "Masterpiece Society" [TNG], "Imaginary Friend" [TNG]).

fencing. Ancient art and sport of swordplay with foils. Jean-Luc Picard enjoyed fencing in the gymnasium of the *Enterprise*-D. ("We'll Always Have Paris" [TNG]).

Fendaus V. Planet led by a family whose members have no limbs due to an inbred genetic defect. Data compared this family to the leaders of **Ramatis III**, who are incapable of hearing for similar reasons. ("Loud as a Whisper" [TNG]).

Fento. (John McLiam). An elderly male on planet **Mintaka III**. He related many of his people's old legends about an **"overseer,"** their equivalent of a God, when his people struggled to understand otherwise inexplicable experiences with advanced Federation technology. Fento was left to guard the injured **Dr. Palmer**, and Commander Riker was forced to overpower him to escape with Palmer. ("Who Watches the Watchers?" [TNG]).

Ferengi cargo shuttle. A transport used by the Ferengi Alliance. One of these craft was discovered crashed in the **Hanolin asteroid belt** in early 2368. Remains of the cargo were discovered scattered over one hundred square kilometers. The remains of the Vulcan ship **T'Pau**'s navigational deflector were found amid the debris, in crates marked "Medical Supplies." ("Unification, Part I" [TNG]).

Ferengi Alliance. Formal name for the Ferengi government.

Ferengi Code. A set of ethical guidelines governing behavior by **Ferengi** citizens. Among its provisions is a clause requiring the lives of subordinates be offered in payment for dishonorable deeds. ("The Last Outpost" [TNG]). SEE: **Ferengi Rules of Acquisition**.

Ferengi death rituals. Rituals associated with the treatment of the body of a deceased Ferengi. Autopsy is strictly prohibited according to the rituals. ("Suspicions" [TNG]).

Ferengi Marauder. Starship type used by the **Ferengi Alliance**. Sophisticated vessels, some Marauders were equipped with the ability to fire a powerful plasma energy burst, capable of disabling a *Galaxy*-class starship. First encounter with the Federation was in 2364 near planet **Gamma Tauri IV**. ("The Last Outpost" [TNG]). This ship was designated as a *D'Kora*-class Marauder, with a crew of 450. ("Force of Nature" [TNG]). *The Ferengi ship was designed by Andrew Probert and built by Greg Jein. The Marauder made its first appearance in "The Last Outpost" and was also seen in "The Battle" (TNG), "Peak Performance" (TNG), "The Price" (TNG), "Ménage à Troi" (TNG), and "Rascals" (TNG).*

Ferengi pod. Small two-person Ferengi spacecraft carried aboard a **Ferengi Marauder** ship. A Ferengi pod, piloted by **Dr. Arridor** and **Kol** into the **Barzan wormhole**, was lost when the wormhole's terminus unexpectedly moved. ("The Price" [TNG]).

Ferengi Rules of Acquisition. Words to live by in the Ferengi culture. Ferengi children are expected to memorize these pearls of wisdom and repeat them on command. ("The Nagus" [DS9]). There are 285 Rules of Acquisition. ("Rules of Acquisition" [DS9]).

The First Rule of Acquistion: "Once you have their money, you never give it back." ("The Nagus" [DS9]).

6th Rule: "Never allow family to stand in the way of opportunity." ("The Nagus" [DS9]).

7th Rule: "Keep your ears open." ("In the Hands of the Prophets" [DS9]).

9th Rule: "Opportunity plus instinct equals profit." ("The Storyteller" [DS9]).

18th Rule: "A deal is a deal." ("Melora" [DS9]).

21st Rule: "Never place friendship above profit." ("Rules

of Acquisition" [DS9]).

22nd Rule: "A wise man can hear profit in the wind." ("Rules of Acquisition" [DS9]).

31st Rule: "Never make fun of a Ferengi's mother." ("The Siege" [DS9]).

33rd Rule: "It never hurts to suck up to the boss." ("Rules of Acquisition" [DS9]).

49th Rule: "The bigger the smile, the sharper the knife." ("Rules of Acquisition" [DS9]).

59th Rule: "Free advice is seldom cheap." ("Rules of Acquisition" [DS9]).

62nd Rule: "The riskier the road, the greater the profit." ("Rules of Acquisition" [DS9]).

76th Rule: "Every once in a while, declare peace." (The Homecoming" [DS9]).

Note: Some of the rules are from episodes that were not completed at the time this encyclopedia was compiled. It is therefore possible that some of them may have changed or even been deleted from the final aired episodes. The rules were the brainchild of writer Ira Steven Behr.

Ferengi Salvage Code. One of several Ferengi codes. The Salvage Code states that anything found abandoned is open to claim by those who find it. The Ferengi who took over the *Enterprise*-D in 2369 claimed it under the Ferengi Salvage Code. ("Rascals" [TNG]).

Ferengi shuttle. Small two-person vessel used for short-range transport. In 2368, the *Enterprise*-D rescued the crew of a Ferengi shuttle that reported a serious containment breach. The "accident" was later found to be a ruse by the crew, members of a **Ferengi Trade Mission**, so they could make their way aboard the *Enterprise*-D. ("The Perfect Mate" [TNG]). SEE: **Par Lenor**.

Ferengi Trade Mission. A Ferengi diplomatic enclave intended to further Ferengi business interests. **Par Lenor** and **Qol** were members of this mission in 2368. ("The Perfect Mate" [TNG]).

Ferengi trading vessel. Starship operating under the auspices of the Ferengi Alliance. In late 2369, one of these vessels was mistaken for an attacking **Borg** ship when it entered the **New Berlin** system. ("Descent, Part I" [TNG]).

Ferengi whip. Handheld **Ferengi** weapon used to fire high-energy plasma discharges at a target. ("The Last Outpost" [TNG]). *The Ferengi whip fell into disuse after "The Last Outpost," and later episodes showed them armed with a variety of phaser-like handheld pistol weapons.*

Ferengi. Technologically sophisticated humanoid race that was long a complete mystery to the Federation prior to first contact at planet **Delphi Ardu** in 2364. Possessing a strict code of honor, Ferengi philosophy ruthlessly embraced the principles of capitalism. SEE: **Ferengi Rules of Acquisition**. The Ferengi are

sexist in the extreme, and do not allow their females the honor of clothing, although Ferengi males often find human females very attractive. ("The Last Outpost" [TNG]). Betazoids are incapable of empathically reading Ferengi minds. This may be due to the unusual four-lobed design of Ferengi brains. ("Ménage à Troi" [TNG], "The Loss" [TNG]). Dopterians, whose brains are structurally similar to those of the Ferengi, are similarly unreadable by Betazoids. ("The Forsaken" [DS9]). Shortly after first contact with the Federation, Ferengi entrepreneurs saw new opportunities and quickly assimilated themselves into Federation commerce, as did Quark, a Ferengi who established a bar at Deep Space 9. ("Emissary" [DS9]). One Ferengi quote says, "Never ask when you can take" ("Babel" [DS9]). Another Ferengi saying is "Good things come in small packages" ("Move Along Home" [DS9]). *The Ferengi were first seen in "The Last Outpost" (TNG). Illustration: The symbol of the Ferengi Alliance.*

Fermat's last theorem. A mathematical puzzle devised by 17th-century French mathematician Pierre de Fermat (1601-1665), who claimed to have developed a proof for the theorem that there is no whole number N where X to the Nth power, plus Y to the Nth, equals Z to the Nth, where N is greater than 2. Following Fermat's death, his notes indicated he had devised a "remarkable proof" of the theorem, but no one has yet been able to figure out what it might have been, including amateur scientist Jean-Luc Picard. ("The Royale" [TNG]). *After the episode was produced in 1989, a Princeton University professor, Andrew Wiles, claimed to have developed a proof to Fermat's theorem, although at this writing (1993) the academic community has yet to pass judgment on his proof.*

Fermi, Shuttlecraft. *Enterprise*-D shuttlecraft #09, destroyed in 2369 after being enveloped by a molecular reversion field that reduced its crew to children. ("Rascals" [TNG]). *Named for Enrico Fermi, the 20th-century American physicist who developed the first nuclear fission reactor.*

Ferris, Galactic High Commissioner. (John Crawford). Federation bureaucrat who was assigned to the *Enterprise* to oversee the delivery of medical supplies to planet **Makus III** for transfer to the **New Paris colonies**. Ferris opposed a scientific shuttle mission just prior to the transfer on the grounds that it might delay the transfer. Ferris's objections were borne

out when the shuttlecraft was lost during the investigation, but the *Enterprise* was able to make the Makus III rendezvous after recovering most of the shuttle's crew. ("The *Galileo* Seven" [TOS]).

Fesarius. Flagship of the **First Federation**, commanded by **Balok**. Following first contact with the *Fesarius* by the original *Enterprise* in 2266, crew member **Lieutenant Bailey** remained with *Fesarius* commander Balok as a cultural envoy. ("The Corbomite Maneuver" [TOS]). *Miniature designed by Matt Jefferies.*

Festival. Also known as the **Red Hour** on planet **Beta III**. ("Return of the Archons" [TOS]).

Feynman, Shuttlecraft. *Enterprise*-D shuttlecraft. The *Feynman* was taken by Captain Picard, Dr. Crusher, and Lieutenant Worf to planet **Torman V**. ("Chain of Command, Part I" [TNG]). *The shuttlecraft Feynman was named for Dr. Richard Feynman (1918-1988), noted Nobel physicist and bongo player. The name was misspelled as* Feyman *on the shuttle's exterior because of a mistake made in the art department.*

FGC-13 cluster. Stellar cluster near the Amargosa Diaspora. The *Enterprise*-D charted FGC-13 in 2369. ("Schisms" [TNG]).

FGC-47. Nebula that is home to a life-form based on cohesive plasma strands that feed on the gravity fields generated by the neutron star at the center of the nebula. The *Enterprise*-D explored FGC-47 in 2368, when it made contact with the life-forms living there. ("Imaginary Friend" [TNG]). SEE: **Isabella**. *FGC probably stands for* Federation General Catalog, *a variation of a real astronomical text, the* New General Catalogue (NGC), *by J. L. E. Dreyer, first published in 1888.*

Ficus Sector. Destination of the colony ship *S.S. Mariposa*, launched from Earth in 2123. The *Mariposa* settled colonists on planet **Bringloid V** and later crashed on the planet **Mariposa** while settling a second group of colonists. ("Up the Long Ladder" [TNG]).

field diverters. Device utilized to isolate areas of starships from the decontaminating plasma field of a **baryon sweep**. Field diverters were used to protect the ship's computer core and bridge. Multiple diverters on a starship required synchronization in order to be effective. ("Starship Mine" [TNG]).

Fifth House of Betazed. A family that is still considered something of royalty to the inhabitants of **Betazed**. Ambassador **Lwaxana Troi** was a daughter of the Fifth House. ("Haven" [TNG]).

filter masks. Protective breathing device intended to protect against the debilitating effects of the **zenite** gas found in the mines on planet **Ardana**. ("The Cloud Minders" [TOS]).

Finagle's Folly. Beverage concocted by Dr. McCoy, who claimed he was famous for the libation "from here to Orion." ("The Ultimate Computer" [TOS]).

Finagle's Law. "Any home port the ship makes will be somebody else's ... not mine." Kirk quoted Finagle's Law to Spock when they received a message diverting them from Vulcan to planet **Altair VI**. ("Amok Time" [TOS]).

• **"Final Mission."** *Next Generation* episode #83. Teleplay by Kasey Arnold-Ince and Jeri Taylor. Story by Kasey Arnold-Ince. Directed by Corey Allen. Stardate 44307.3. *First aired*

in 1990. Wesley Crusher must care for Captain Picard when the two are stranded on a desert planet by a shuttle crash. This was the episode in which Wil Wheaton as Wesley Crusher left the series as a regular. SEE: **Allenby, Ensign Tess; Boothby; construction module; Crusher, Wesley; Dirgo; dresci; ermanium; Gamelan V; hyronalin; Lambda Paz; Meltasion asteroid belt;** *Nenebek;* **Pentarus II; Pentarus V; salenite miners; sentry; Songi, Chairman; sonodanite.**

Finiis'ral. Kriosian term for the final stage in the sexual maturation of an **empathic metamorph**. During this stage, the metamorph produces an elevated level of sexual **pheromones**, and is extremely vulnerable to the empathic emanations of the opposite sex. The empath's behavior can change frequently to suit the needs of potential mates. **Kamala**, an empathic metamorph, was in the final stages of the *Finiis'ral* when she traveled aboard the Enterprise-D in 2368 for the **Ceremony of Reconciliation** between **Krios** and **Valt**. Her effect on the male members of the crew was, to say the least, interesting. ("The Perfect Mate" [TNG]).

Finn, Kyril. (Richard Cox). The charismatic leader of the **Ansata** terrorists, this man was responsible for the abduction of both Dr. Crusher and Captain Picard. He hoped by holding Starfleet hostages, he could force the Federation into becoming involved in the Ansata struggle for independence. A complicated man, Finn twisted the efforts of the crew to rescue the doctor into threats to his cause,

and began to make Dr. Crusher doubt her beliefs about the Federation position on **Rutia IV**. Finn was killed in 2366 by **Alexana Devos** when **Rutian** security forces located the Ansata base with help from *Enterprise*-D personnel. ("The High Ground" [TNG]).

Finnegan. (Bruce Mars). Upperclassman and arch rival of James Kirk from his academy days in 2252. Finnegan delighted in playing practical jokes on Kirk. A replica of Finnegan was created on the amusement park planet in 2267, giving Kirk the chance to finally best his nemesis. ("Shore Leave" [TOS]). *Actor Bruce Mars also played a New York police officer in "Assignment: Earth" (TOS).*

Finney, Benjamin. (Richard Webb). Starfleet officer who was an instructor at the Academy when **James Kirk** was a midshipman. The two men were good friends and Ben Finney's daughter, Jamie was named after Kirk. Later, when both were assigned to the **U.S.S. Republic**, Ensign Kirk relieved Finney on watch and found a circuit open to the atomic matter piles that might have blown up the ship if not closed. Kirk closed the

switch and logged the incident, causing Finney to draw a reprimand and then be moved to the bottom of the promotion list.

Finney was bitter about the incident for years, although he later accepted a position as records officer aboard the *Enterprise* under Kirk's command. In 2267, Finney staged his own death in an unsuccessful attempt to frame Kirk for murder. ("Court Martial" [TOS]). SEE: **ion storm**.

Finney, Jamie. (Alice Rawlings). **Ben Finney**'s daughter, named after James T. Kirk. ("Court Martial" [TOS]).

finoplak. A colorless liquid solvent, capable of dissolving Starfleet-issue fabrics, but harmless to **bioplast** sheeting. Kivas Fajo used one hundred **denkirs** of finoplak to melt Data's uniform. ("The Most Toys" [TNG]).

firefighting. Aboard Federation starships, a variety of systems were used to combat fires. Most habitable areas were equipped with containment field generators used to create a small forcefield around any fires. This would deprive the fire of atmospheric oxygen, extinguishing it. Handheld extinguishers were also available. In an extreme emergency, some parts of a ship could also be vented into the vacuum of space. ("Up the Long Ladder" [TNG], "New Ground" [TNG]).

fireboxes. Term used by the inhabitants of planet **Omega IV** to describe Starfleet phasers. ("The Omega Glory" [TOS]).

firomactal drive. Fictional computer device Riker made up to confuse the Ferengi who took over the *Enterprise*-D in 2369. ("Rascals" [TNG]).

First City. Located on the **Klingon Homeworld**, this is the seat of government for the empire, and location of the **Great Hall**. Worf and Picard visited the First City in 2366 to defend Worf's late father against charges brought by council member **Duras**. ("Sins of the Father" [TNG]). Worf  returned to the First City a year later to support the Gowron regime during the Klingon civil war. ("Redemption, Parts I and II" [TNG]). *The skyline of the First City was a matte painting created by Illusion Arts.*

• **"First Contact."** *Next Generation* episode #89. Teleplay by Dennis Russell Bailey & David Bischoff and Joe Menosky & Ronald D. Moore and Michael Piller. Story by Marc Scott Zicree. Directed by Cliff Bole. No stardate given in episode. *First aired in 1991. Riker is captured by the paranoid inhabitants of a technologically emerging planet, jeopardizing future relations with the Federation.* SEE: **Berel; Durken, Chancellor Avel; first contact; Garth system; Jakara, Rivas; Klingon Empire; Krola; Lanel; Malcor III; Malcorians; Marta community; Nilrem; quadroline; Sikla Medical Facility; Tava; telencephalon; terminus; Yale; Mirasta.**

first contact. Sociological term for a culture's initial meeting with extraterrestrial life, often referring to first contact with representatives of the **United Federation of Planets**.

First contact is perhaps the most risky and unpredictable of all of Starfleet's missions, because of the enormous risk of sociological impact for the culture of the civilization being contacted.

Numerous Federation and Starfleet policies govern the conduct of first contacts. Among these are the **Prime Directive**, which prohibits interference with the normal development of any society, particularly a culture less technologically advanced than the Federation. ("Tin Man" [TNG]). Under the Prime Directive, first contact is generally avoided until a civilization has attained significant spaceflight capabilities. Another policy calls for covert surveillance of many cultures prior to first contact, enabling Federation sociologists to anticipate probable reactions. This directive was instituted after the disastrous initial contact with the **Klingon Empire** led to decades of war. ("First Contact" [TNG]). Starfleet's current first-contact guidelines were written by **Captain McCoullough**. ("Move Along Home" [DS9]).

The first diplomatic first-contact mission from the **Gamma Quadrant** to pass through the **Bajoran wormhole** into the **Alpha Quadrant** was the **Wadi** gaming delegation that visited station Deep Space 9 in 2369. ("Move Along Home" [DS9]).

• **"First Duty, The."** *Next Generation* episode #119. Written by Ronald D. Moore & Naren Shankar. Directed by Paul Lynch. Stardate 45703.9. *First aired in 1992. An accident at Starfleet Academy leaves one of Wesley Crusher's classmates dead, and Wesley is pressured to participate in a cover-up.* SEE: **Academy Flight Range; Academy Range Officer; Albert, Joshua; Albert, Lieutenant Commander; bicaridine treatments; Boothby; Brand, Admiral; Calgary; Crusher, Wesley; Diamond Slot formation; Hajar, Cadet Second Class Jean; Immelmann turn; Kolvoord Starburst; Locarno, Cadet First Class Nicholas; metorapan treatments; Mimas; Nova Squadron; Picard, Jean-Luc; Satelk, Captain; Saturn NavCon; Saturn; Sito, Cadet Second Class; Starfleet Academy; Statistical Mechanics; Titan; Yeager Loop.**

First Federation. Interstellar political entity under whose aegis the spacecraft *Fesarius* was operated under the command of **Balok**.

First contact with the United Federation of Planets was made with the *Starship Enterprise* in 2266, at which time *Enterprise* **Lieutenant Bailey** remained aboard the *Fesarius* as a cultural envoy. ("The Corbomite Maneuver" [TOS]).

First Hebitian civilization. Ancient people of Cardassia. The burial vaults of the Hebitians were uncovered on **Cardassia** in the late 2160s. The tombs were said to be magnificent and were reputed to have been filled with many jeweled artifacts. ("Chain of Command, Part II" [TNG]).

First One. On planet **Ligon II**, title given to a spouse, male or female. **Ligonian** culture permits polygamous relationships, and a second spouse was called a "Second One." ("Code of Honor" [TNG]). SEE: **Lutan.**

First Rule of Acquisition. SEE: **Ferengi Rules of Acquisition.**

Fisher, Geological Technician. (Edward Madden). Member of the scientific survey mission at planet **Alfa 117**. While on the survey, Fisher fell and bruised himself, and had to be transported back to the *Enterprise*. Unknown to anyone at the time, Fisher's uniform was covered with a magnetic ore that caused a transporter malfunction, resulting in the accidental creation of a partial duplicate of Captain James Kirk. ("The Enemy Within" [TOS]).

• **"Fistful of Datas, A."** *Next Generation* episode #134. Teleplay by Robert Hewitt Wolfe and Brannon Braga. Story by Robert Hewitt Wolfe. Directed by Patrick Stewart. Stardate 46271.5. *First aired in 1992. A holodeck malfunction traps Alexander, Worf, and Troi in the ancient American West, where everyone else is a replica of Data.* SEE: **Ancient West; Barclay, Reginald; Biko, U.S.S.; Crusher, Dr. Beverly; Deadwood; Deinonychus VII; Durango; Dvorak, Anton; Hollander, Eli; Hollander, Frank; Meyers, Annie; Mozart, Wolfgang Amadeus; "Ode to Spot"; Picard Mozart trio, program 1; progressive memory purge; Ressikan flute; Something for Breakfast; Spot; Starbase 118; Subroutine C-47; telegraph machine; Troi, Deanna; Winchester.**

fistrium. Refractory metal that was present in caves on **Melona IV**. **Data** speculated the presence of fistrium and kelbonite made it impossible for the **Crystalline Entity** to scan into the caves where the colonists were hiding. ("Silicon Avatar" [TNG]).

fizzbin. Fictitious card game, supposedly played on planet Beta Antares IV, but in actuality a product of James Kirk's imagination. Kirk fabricated the game to confuse the guards holding the landing party on planet **Sigma Iotia II**, allowing the landing party to escape. Fizzbin used a standard terrestrial deck of cards, but had terribly complicated rules that changed on Tuesdays and involved such things as half-fizzbins, sralks, and, of course, the astronomically improbable royal fizzbin. ("A Piece of the Action" [TOS]). SEE: **corbomite, Iotians**.

Flaherty, Commander. First officer of the *U.S.S. Aries*. Flaherty possessed uncanny linguistic skills, speaking over forty languages including Klingon, Romulan, Giamon, and Stroyerian. Flaherty would have been Riker's first officer if he had accepted command of the *Aries* in 2365. ("The Icarus Factor" [TNG]).

Flavius. (Rhodes Reason). Popular gladiator in the brutal televised Roman arena battles on planet 892-IV. Known in the arena as Flavius Maximus, he rejected the Roman culture of the planet and refused to kill when he heard the words of the **Children of the Sun**, choosing to live in a cave along with other believers. He was captured in 2267 along with the *Enterprise* landing party investigating the fate of the *S.S. Beagle* crew.
　　Flavius was killed trying to prevent the execution televised execution of James Kirk. ("Bread and Circuses" [TOS]). SEE: **892, Planet IV**.

Fleet Museum. Starfleet facility honoring the people and vehicles that have gone boldly where none have gone before. One of the great ships on exhibit there is a *Constitution*-class vessel, a near duplicate of the original *Starship Enterprise*. ("Relics" [TNG]).

fleet captain. Starfleet rank held by **Christopher Pike** after the end of his tenure as *Enterprise* captain. ("The Menagerie, Parts I and II" [TOS]). Captain **Garth of Izar** also held this rank. ("Whom Gods Destroy" [TOS]).

Fletcher, Ensign. *Enterprise*-D engineering crew member. During the ship's mission to the **Typhon Expanse** in 2368, Fletcher was working with Commander Geordi La Forge on a catwalk over the warp core when La Forge became dizzy. Fletcher caught La Forge before he tumbled off the catwalk. ("Cause and Effect" [TNG]).

flight controller. Aboard more recent Starfleet vessels, the control station and officer responsible for both **helm** and **navigator** functions. The flight controller (or conn) is the pilot of the ship. Conn is one of two freestanding consoles located ahead of the captain's chair on many starship bridges. *Geordi La Forge served as conn aboard the* Enterprise-D *during Star Trek: The Next Generation's first season, to be replaced by* **Wesley Crusher** *during the second and third seasons. Since then, a variety of supernumeraries and guest performers have filled that duty.*

flight recorder. Data storage system aboard starships that records critical information and images from various locations in the ship, intended for use after a major accident to reconstruct the events leading up to the incident. Spock's death in 2285 was recorded by the *U.S.S. Enterprise* flight recorder, and the playback of those images led Sarek and Kirk to believe Spock had placed his *katra* in McCoy's consciousness. (*Star Trek III: The Search for Spock*). In earlier ships, the flight recorder was also called a **recorder marker**. *The* Enterprise *flight recorder computer voice in Star Trek III was provided by producer-writer Harve Bennett.*

Flint. (James Daly). A nearly immortal human from planet Earth, born in Mesopotamia in 3834 BC. Flint was blessed with instant tissue regeneration, which allowed him to live through disease, war, accidents, and other calamities that killed other men. Flint soon learned to conceal his nature, living part of a life, marrying, pretending to age, then moving on before his immortality was suspected. During his life, his identities included Solomon, Alexander, Lazarus, Methuselah, and Johannes Brahms. In 2239, under the name of Brack, Flint purchased planet **Holberg 917G**, on which he built a castle where he could live undisturbed. Flint grew weary of his solitude and sought a companion who would be as immortal as he. His solution was to construct an android who would be his perfect woman. After several attempts, Flint created an android he called **Rayna Kapec**.

When the *Starship Enterprise* visited Flint's world in 2269, Flint deliberately allowed Rayna to interact with James Kirk, in hopes that Kirk would stir emotions in Rayna that would permit her to love Flint. Unfortunately, he was too successful. Rayna fell in love with Kirk, then died because she could not bear to hurt Flint. Shortly thereafter, Flint learned that he, too, was slowly dying because he had left the complex balance of Earth's environment. Flint said he would devote the remaining portion of his life to the betterment of the human condition. ("Requiem for Methuselah" [TOS]).

flintlock. Primitive, muzzle-loading weapon that used an explosive charge to propel a small projectile. Klingon agents gave several flintlocks to the village people on **Tyree**'s planet in 2267, upsetting the balance of power in that society until *Enterprise* personnel provided similar weapons to Tyree's **hill people**. ("A Private Little War" [TOS]).

flop. Slang expression for a place to sleep, used by workers during Earth's **Great Depression** of the 1930s. ("The City on the Edge of Forever" [TOS]).

Flores, Marissa. (Erika Flores). One of the winners of the primary-school science fair held aboard the *Enterprise*-D in 2368. As a prize for her accomplishment, Marissa was awarded a tour of the *Enterprise*-D, personally conducted by Captain Picard.

Marissa's tour was delayed when she was trapped in a turbolift with the captain when the *Enterprise*-D struck a **quantum filament**. Picard gave Marissa the honorary title of "Number One" during their escape. ("Disaster" [TNG]). SEE: **Gordon, Jay; Supera, Patterson.** *Marissa's last name was not given in dialog, but was printed on the plaque that the kids gave the captain.*

flux spectrometer. Sensor device used aboard Federation starships. ("Cause and Effect" [TNG]).

foil. Ancient weapon used in the Earth sport of fencing, it has a flexible, rectangular blade about one meter in length and a bell guard to protect the hand. Captain Picard enjoyed the sport and instructed Guinan in the use of the foil during the *Enterprise*-D's mission in the Argolis Cluster in 2368. ("I, Borg" [TNG]).

folded-space transport. SEE: **Elway Theorem.**

food and beverages. SEE table below.

food or beverage	description
Aldeberan whiskey	It's green.
Aldorian ale	Beverage available in the Ten Forward lounge
Altair Water	Beverage favored by Captain Spock
Andonian tea	Beverage served at Starfleet Headquarters
Antarean brandy	Alcoholic beverage
Arcturian Fizz	Beverage with pleasure enhancing qualities
Augergine stew	Dish favored by Commander Sisko
Balso tonic	Favorite beverage of Odan
banana split	Wesley Crusher's favorite dessert
beans	An ingredient in McCoy's favorite recipe
bregit lung	Traditional Klingon dish
Calaman sherry	Favorite beverage of Lieutenant D'Sora
Caviar	Unhatched eggs of a fish
Chateau Picard	Fine wine produced by the Picard family vineyards
chech'tluth	Klingon alcoholic beverage
chocolate	A weakness of Deanna Troi.
Delovian souffle	Ice cream like dessert
Earl Grey tea	Picard's favorite tea
feline supplement 74	A cat food designed for Spot
Finagle's Folly	Potent beverage concocted by Dr. McCoy
gagh	Klingon serpent worms
Gamzain wine	Beverage served at Quark's

food or beverage	description
ginger tea	Hot beverage used to cure cold symptoms
glop-on-a-stick	Food available for purchase at the kiosk on DS9
haggis	Traditional Scottish dish
heart of targ	Traditional Klingon dish
I'danian spice pudding	Extremely caloric dessert
iced coffee	Beverage enjoyed by Geordi La Forge
Jestral tea	Favorite beverage of Lwaxana Troi
jumja	Another name for glop-on-a-stick.
Kaferian apples	Fruit resembling Earth apples
Kanar	Beverage favored by Cardassians
Kohlanese stew	Dish served at Quark's
Lapsang suchong tea	Beverage favored by Helena Rozhenko
larish pie	Cardassian food served at Quark's
lokar beans	Food served at Quark's
macchiato	Cappuccino-like beverage
Mantickian Pate'	Dish concocted by Lwaxana Troi
Maraltian Seev-ale	Beverage kept in Quark's private stock
Mareuvian tea	Beverage served in the Ten Forward lounge.
mint tea	Beverage favored by Perrin
Modela aperitif	Double layered beverage served at Quark's
Muskan seed punch	Traditional Haliian beverage

(Continued on next page.)

(Continued from previous page.)

food or beverage	description
Owon eggs	delicacy prepared by Commander Riker for some of his shipmates.
papalla juice	beverage available at Ten Forward.
parthas ala Yuta	Acamarian spiced vegetable dish
Pasta al fiorella	One of Geordi's favorite dishes
petrokian sausage	Available from the Enterprise-D replicators
pipius claw	Traditional Klingon dish
plankton Loaf	Baked microscopic sea life
plomeek soup	Traditional Vulcan dish
potato casserole	Traditional Irish food
purple omelets	Dish concocted by Clara Sutter
quadrotriticale	Type of wheat
raktajino	A type of iced coffee served at Quark's
rokeg blood pie	Traditional Klingon dish
Romulan Ale	Extremely potent alcoholic beverage
Samarian Sunset	Drink Commander Data was skilled at making
Saurian brandy	Potent liquor favored by members of the Enterprise crew
sem'hal stew	Main dish available on DS9
stardrifter	Ferengi beverage served at Quark's
suck salt	Tubular form of NaCl, designed to be taken orally
synthale	Bajoran beverage served at Quark's
synthehol	Alcoholic substitute invented by the Ferengi
Tamarian frost	Sweet beverage served at Ten Forward.
Tarkalean tea	Beverage available in DS9 kiosk
Tarvokian pound cake	Dessert baked by Worf
Telluridian synthale	Beverage prized on the Turkana IV colony
Thalian chocolate mousse	Dessert that uses 400 year old chocolate beans
tranya	Beverage consumed in the First Federation
Trixian bubble juice	Beverage served at Quark's
tube grubs	Worm-like Ferengi food, eaten alive
Tzartak aperitif	Specialty beverage created by Guinan
uttaberries	Blueberry-like fruit native to Betazed
Valerian root tea	Favorite beverage of Counselor Troi
vermicula	Antedean worm-like food
viinerine	A Romulan dish
Warnog	Klingon ale
yamok sauce	Cardassian condiment

food replicator. SEE: **replicator**.

food slot. Alternate term for **replicator**.

foolie. Slang on **Miri**'s planet for a game or a practical joke. ("Miri" [TOS]).

• **"For the World Is Hollow and I Have Touched the Sky."** Original Series episode #65. Written by Rik Vollaerts. Directed by Tony Leader. Stardate: 5476.3. *First aired in 1968. Dr. McCoy, stricken with a fatal disease, finds love on a doomed asteroid spaceship.* SEE: **Daran V; Fabrina; Fabrini Book of the People; Fabrini creators; Fabrini; Instrument of Obedience; McCoy, Dr. Leonard H.; Natira; Oracle; xenopolycythemia; Yonada.**

forced plasma beam. Destructive energy source used in Borg and Ferengi handheld weapons. ("Descent, Part I" [TNG]).

Forlat III. Class-M planet that was attacked by the **Crystalline Entity**. Colonists on the planet fled into caves in an attempt to escape the entity, but that did not protect them. ("Silicon Avatar" [TNG]).

formazine. Federation standard stimulant, often administered by hypospray. After the *Enterprise* was commandeered by the **Kelvans** in 2268, Dr. McCoy convinced **Hanar** that his body required vitamin injections, but instead delivered doses of formazine, causing all-too-human emotional irritation. ("By Any Other Name" [TOS]).

• **"Forsaken, The."** *Deep Space Nine* episode #17. Teleplay by Don Carlos Dunaway and Michael Piller. Story by Jim Trombetta. Directed by Les Landau. Stardate 46925.1. First aired in 1993. *Ambassador Lwaxana Troi visits Deep Space 9 and takes a fancy to Security Chief Odo.* SEE: **adaptive interface link; Anara; Andevian II; Arbazan; Betazoids; bipolar torch; carbon reaction chambers; Cardassian operation guidelines; Corado I Transmitter Array; corundium alloy; Curzon, Dax; Dopterian; electroplasma system; emulator module; Ferengi; isolinear rods; laser-induced fusion; Lojal; Nehru Colony; New France Colony; Odo; Pup; recalibration sweep; root canal; Taxco; toranium; Troi, Lwaxana; turbolift; Vadosia; Wanoni tracehound.**

Fourth Order. Cardassian military division posted near **Bajor** shortly after the Cardassian retreat from that planet in 2369. The Fourth Order was not close enough to prevent Starfleet personnel from claiming the **Bajoran wormhole** for the people of Bajor. ("Emissary" [DS9]).

Fox, Ambassador Robert. (Gene Lyons). Federation ambassador sent aboard the *Enterprise* on a diplomatic mission to establish contact with planet **Eminiar VII** in 2267. Fox disregarded a signal from the planet warning the *Enterprise* to stay away. When it was learned that Eminiar had been embroiled in a bitter war with neighboring planet **Vendikar** that had lasted for five

centuries, Fox offered his services as mediator. ("A Taste of Armageddon" [TOS]).

• **"Frame of Mind."** *Next Generation* episode #147. Written by Brannon Braga. Directed by James L. Conway. Stardate 46778.1. *First aired in 1993. Commander Riker is captured and tortured on planet Tilonius IV, and he's not sure what is reality, and what is a nightmare.* SEE: **Budrow, Admiral; Crusher, Dr. Beverly;** *Frame of Mind*; **Jaya; Jung, Carl Gustav; Mavek; neurosomatic technique;** *nisroh*; **pattern enhancer; phaser; plasma torch; reflection therapy; spiny lobe-fish; Suna; synaptic reconstruction; Syrus, Dr.; Tilonus Institute for Mental Disorders; Tilonus IV.**

Frame of Mind. Theatrical play written and directed by Beverly Crusher in 2369 and performed by her theatre company aboard the *Enterprise*-D. The play featured a character, played by William Riker, who had been assigned to a psychiatric hospital after committing a brutal murder. While the play was in production, Riker was captured on planet **Tilonus IV** and subjected to brutal psychological torture. The play became a focal point in Riker's mind, and he was soon unable to tell the difference between nightmares of being trapped in the play's story, and his actual mistreatment by his captors. After he had been rescued from his captivity, Counselor Troi theorized that Riker had used the play to support his unconscious mind with elements from his real life to keep him sane. ("Frame of Mind" [TNG]).

Franklin, Ensign Matt. Engineer aboard the *U.S.S. Jenolen* at the time it crashed into a **Dyson Sphere** in 2294. Franklin and **Montgomery Scott** survived the crash and attempted to keep themselves alive until a rescue ship arrived by suspending themselves in a transporter **pattern buffer**. The attempt was partially successful: Scott survived for 75 years, but Franklin died when his pattern degraded beyond recovery. ("Relics" [TNG]).

Freeman, Ensign. (Paul Baxley). *Enterprise* crew member who did not start the fight on **Deep Space Station K-7** with the Klingons. ("The Trouble with Tribbles" [TOS]). *Episode writer David Gerrold intended the character of Ensign Freeman as a walk-on part for himself, but the role went to Paul Baxley.*

"Frere Jacques." An old French folksong, favorite of *Enterprise*-D captain Picard, who sung it with several children who were trapped with him in a turboshaft on stardate 45156. ("Disaster" [TNG]). Picard also played it as a duet with Nella Daren, with Picard on his Ressikan flute and Daren on her piano. ("Lessons" [TNG]).

Friar Tuck. (Brent Spiner). In Earth mythology, a priest who was one of the members of **Robin Hood**'s band of outlaws in ancient England. Data was cast as Friar Tuck by **Q** in a fantasy he designed for Captain Picard's benefit in 2367. ("QPid" [TNG]).

• **"Friday's Child."** Original Series episode #32. Written by D. C. Fontana. Directed by Joseph Pevney. Stardate 3497.2. *First aired in 1967. The Enterprise crew becomes embroiled*

in a local power struggle on planet Capella IV when Klingons attempt to gain mining rights there. SEE: **Akaar, Leonard James; Akaar, Teer; Capella IV; Capellans;** *Carolina, U.S.S.*; *Dierdre, S.S.*; **Eleen; Grant; kligat; Keel; Kras; Maab; magnesite-nitron tablet; Teer; Ten Tribes; topaline.**

Friendly Angel. SEE: **Gorgan.**

frontal lobe. The anterior portion of the cerebral hemisphere in humanoid brains. The effects of the **Ktarian game**, introduced to the *Enterprise*-D crew in 2368, were centered in the frontal lobe. ("The Game" [TNG]).

Frunalian. Alien species that conducted business at station **Deep Space 9**. Three Frunalian science vessels requested permission to dock at the station shortly after the discovery of the wormhole in 2369. ("Emissary" [DS9]).

FSNP. Star Trek *(TOS) writing staff's gag term for the Famous Spock Nerve Pinch, also known as the Vulcan nerve pinch or the neck pinch, first used in "The Enemy Within" (TOS). The abbreviation FSNP appeared in some later scripts calling for the use of the nerve pinch.* SEE: **nerve pinch, Vulcan.**

fungilli. One of **Dr. Leah Brahm**'s favorite foods. Geordi La Forge was also fond of it. ("Galaxy's Child" [TNG]).

fusing pitons. Self-setting anchor used for rappelling on sheer rock surfaces. ("Chain of Command, Part I" [TNG]).

fusion bombs. Weapons developed by many technologically advancing cultures, including those on planets **Vendikar** and **Eminiar VII**. Mathematical simulations of fusion bombs were used in a computer war fought between the two planets for five centuries, ending in 2267. The mathematical weapons were routinely used for attacks on both planets' population centers. These data were used to determine casualties, and the individuals so declared were given 24 hours to report to disintegration stations so that their deaths could be recorded. ("A Taste of Armageddon" [TOS]). *Earth, of course, has had fusion bombs in its arsenals for several decades, although to this point, we've had the good sense not to use them.*

• **"Future Imperfect."** *Next Generation* episode #82. Written by J. Larry Carroll & David Bennett Carren. Directed by Les Landau. Stardate 44286.5. *First aired in 1990. Riker wakes up, apparently suffering from amnesia 16 years in the future, having lost all memory of the past 16 years.* SEE: **Alpha Onias III; Altarian encephalitis; Barash; Curtis Creek program;** *Decius*; **Ethan; Hubble, Chief; Minuet; Miridian VI; Ogawa, Nurse Alyssa; Onias Sector; Outpost 23; Riker, Jean-Luc; Tomalak.**

Fuurinkazan battle strategies. Tactics developed by **Kyle Riker** at the **Tokyo Base** prior to his work for Starfleet as a tactical advisor. ("The Icarus Factor" [TNG]).

Gable, Clark. Entertainment personality popular during Earth's 20th century. **Edith Keeler** was one of Gable's legion of fans during the 1930s. She invited James Kirk to go with her to see one of his motion pictures. ("The City on the Edge of Forever" [TOS]).

Gabrielle. (Isabel Lorca). A holodeck character, the image of a lovely young French woman who was a patron at the **Cafe des Artistes** in Paris. ("We'll Always Have Paris" [TNG]).

Gaetano, Lieutenant. (Peter Marko). Member of the *Shuttlecraft Galileo* crew when it crashed on planet **Taurus II** in 2267. Gaetano was killed by the humanoid creatures on the planet. ("The *Galileo* Seven" [TOS]).

Gagarin IV. Planet on which was located the **Darwin Genetic Research Station**, a Federation science facility that produced genetically engineered human children whose immune systems actively sought out and attacked potential sources of disease, including other humans. Those so attacked suffered symptoms closely resembling hyperaccelerated aging. ("Unnatural Selection" [TNG]). *Gagarin IV was named for cosmonaut Yuri Gagarin (1934-1968), the first human to travel in space.*

Gage, U.S.S. One of the 39 Federation starships destroyed by the **Borg** during the battle of **Wolf 359**. ("Emissary" [DS9]).

gagh. Serpent worms, a Klingon culinary delicacy. Connoisseurs of Klingon cuisine claim that *gagh* is best served very fresh, i.e. live. *Gagh* is also served stewed. Both Riker and Picard claimed to have developed a taste for the dish. ("A Matter of Honor" [TNG], "Unification, Part I" [TNG]).

Gal Gath'thong. Location on planet **Romulus** known for its great natural beauty and spectacular firefalls. **Alidar Jarok**, after defecting from the **Romulan Star Empire**, mourned the fact that he would never see Gal Gath'thong again. ("The Defector" [TNG]).

galactic barrier. SEE: **barrier, galactic.**

Galaxy-Class Starship Development Project. Starfleet project based at the **Utopia Planitia Fleet Yards** on Mars for the design and construction of the *Galaxy*-class starships, including the *Enterprise*-D.

Among the engineers working on this project was **Dr. Leah Brahms** of the **Theoretical Propulsion Group.** Although a junior member of the team, Brahms made major contributions to the design of the ships' warp propulsion systems. ("Booby Trap" [TNG]). The actual assembly of the *Enterprise*-D was supervised by Commander Orfil Quinteros. ("11001001" [TNG]).

Galaxy-class starship. The most advanced, most powerful vessels in the Federation **Starfleet** during the late 24th century. The *U.S.S. Enterprise*-D, launched in 2363, was one of the first starships of this class, as was the *U.S.S. Galaxy*, after which the class was named. ("Encounter at Farpoint, Part I" [TNG]). The *U.S.S. Yamato* (registry number NCC-71807), destroyed in 2365, was another *Galaxy*-class starship ("Contagion" [TNG], as was the *U.S.S. Odyssey*, NCC-71832 *(destroyed in "Dominion" [DS9]). Gene Roddenberry once speculated that there were only six Galaxy-class ships built, but this has not been firmly established in an episode, nor have the names of the other two ships.*

Galaxy M33. Where the *Enterprise* was hurled some 2,700,000 light-years away from where they had started, with the help of the **Traveler**. ("Where No One Has Gone Before" [TNG]).

• **"Galaxy's Child."** *Next Generation* episode #90. Teleplay by Maurice Hurley. Story by Thomas Kartozlan. Directed by Winrich Kolbe. Stardate 44614.6. *First aired in 1991. The Enterprise-D accidentally kills a large spaceborne life-form, then must care for the creature's unborn child.* SEE: **Alpha Omicron System; Brahms, Dr. Leah; fungilli; Guernica system; holodeck; "Junior"; kph; La Forge, Geordi; midrange phase adjuster; Pavlick, Ensign; Rager, Ensign; Starbase 313; Theoretical Propulsion Group.**

Galaxy, U.S.S. Federation starship, prototype for the *Galaxy-class* series of deep-space exploratory starships. *The U.S.S. Galaxy has not (yet) been seen on any episode, but its existence is implied by the term, Galaxy class, used to designate the Enterprise-D and its sister ships. We conjecture that the Starfleet registry number of the U.S.S. Galaxy was NX-70637.*

Galek Sar. (Albert Hall). A **Promellian**, captain of the *Cleponji*, a Promellian battle cruiser disabled in battle with the **Menthars** a thousand years ago. Prior to his death, Galek Sar left behind a recorded message in which he commended his crew and accepted all responsibility for the fate of his ship. ("Booby Trap" [TNG]).

Galen border conflicts. A series of skirmishes during the 2350s between the **Talarians** and the Federation over the Galen system, in which Federation colonies had been established. During the conflict, it was a common Talarian tactic to abandon observation spacecraft that had been rigged to self-destruct when boarded. The conflicts reached their peak in the Talarian attack on **Galen IV**, after which a peace accord was reached. ("Suddenly Human" [TNG]). SEE: **Endar; Jono; Rossa, Jeremiah.**

Galen IV. Class-M planet, site of a Federation colony. In 2356, the colony was attacked and destroyed by **Talarian**

forces. The Talarians claimed the Federation was intruding on Talarian territory. ("Suddenly Human" [TNG]). SEE: **Endar**; **Jono**.

Galen, Professor Richard. (Norman Lloyd). Possibly the greatest archaeologist of the 24th century. Galen spent the last decade of his life attempting to confirm an extraordinary theory that numerous humanoid species in the galaxy had a common genetic heritage, born from the fact that some species apparently had "seeded" the primordial oceans of many

worlds. Galen spent years gathering genetic information from at least 19 planets across the quadrant in an effort to confirm his theory. Galen's greatest discovery was that the genetic codes on these planets could be assembled to form a computer program containing a message of peace from those ancient progenitors. Among Galen's students was **Jean-Luc Picard**, whom Galen hoped would also become an archaeologist. Although Picard instead chose to pursue a career in Starfleet, he was instrumental in completing Galen's last work. ("The Chase" [TNG]). SEE: **humanoid life**. *Galen's first name is from the script and was not mentioned on the air.*

• **"*Galileo* Seven, The."** Original Series episode #14. Teleplay by Oliver Crawford and S. Bar-David. Story by Oliver Crawford. Directed by Robert Gist. *Stardate 2821.5. First aired in 1967. A shuttlecraft piloted by Spock crashes on planet Taurus II, forcing him to grope with the life-and-death responsibilities of command. The Enterprise shuttlecraft made its first appearance in this episode. Earlier episodes (like "The Enemy Within" [TOS]) did not use the shuttle because it had not been built until this point.* SEE: **Boma, Lieutenant**; ***Columbus*, Shuttlecraft**; **Ferris, Galactic High Commissioner**; **Gaetano, Lieutenant**; ***Galileo*, Shuttlecraft**; **Hansen's Planet**; **Immamura, Lieutenant**; **Kelowitz, Lieutenant**; **Latimer, Lieutenant**; **Makus III**; **Mears, Yeoman**; **Murasaki 312**; **New Paris colonies**; **O'Neill, Ensign**; **quasars**; **space-normal**; **Taurus II**.

Galileo, Shuttlecraft. Registry number NCC-1701-7. Shuttle attached to the original *Starship Enterprise*. In 2267, this vehicle was lost near planet **Taurus II** while investigating the **Murasaki Effect**. ("The *Galileo* Seven" [TOS]). The *Galileo* transported Kirk,

Spock, McCoy, and **Commissioner Nancy Hedford** from planet **Epsilon Canaris III** to the *Enterprise* on stardate 3219. The shuttle was pulled off course by an electromagnetic storm in the **Gamma Canaris region**. ("Metamorphosis" [TOS]). SEE: **Cochrane, Zefram**. Spock piloted the *Galileo* into a huge spaceborne **amoeba** creature that destroyed the **Gamma 7A System** on stardate 4307. ("The Immunity Syndrome" [TOS]). *The latter two episodes were filmed after "The Galileo*

Seven" (TOS), in which the Galileo was destroyed at Taurus II. Named for mathematician and astronomer Galileo Galilei (1564-1642). SEE: ***Galileo II*, Shuttlecraft**.

Galileo II, Shuttlecraft. Replacement for the original shuttlecraft ***Galileo*** aboard the *U.S.S. Enterprise*. **Dr. Sevrin** and his followers stole the *Galileo II* in their quest for the mythical planet **Eden** in 2269. ("The Way to Eden" [TOS]). *The Galileo II was, of course, the same mockup used for the original Galileo, with the simple addition of a "II" in the name. This was presumably because the first Galileo was destroyed in both "The Galileo Seven" (TOS) and "The Immunity Syndrome" (TOS), an oversight by the show's producers.*

Galileo 5, Shuttlecraft. Shuttle #5, attached to *U.S.S. Enterprise*-A. Uhura picked up Kirk and company from **Yosemite National Park** in this shuttle when Kirk "accidentally" forgot to bring his communicator. This shuttle crash-landed in the *Enterprise*-

A hangar deck after being commandeered by **Sybok** at **Nimbus III**. (*Star Trek V: The Final Frontier*). *The Galileo 5 was of a different (and presumably more advanced) design than the original Galileo and Galileo II seen in the first Star Trek series. The ship was designed by Nilo Rodis and Andy Neskoromny. The miniature was built by Greg Jein. Two full-scale exterior mockups were built for the film, one of which was later modified and used as a shuttle on Star Trek: The Next Generation.*

Galis Blin. Bajoran official. Major Kira Nerys contacted Galis Blin on stardate 46423, hoping she could shed light on who created the **aphasia virus** that infected Deep Space 9 in 2369. ("Babel" DS9]).

Gallitep. Infamous labor camp on planet **Bajor** during the Cardassian occupation. Numerous unspeakable atrocities against Bajoran citizens were committed there by the Cardassians under the command of **Gul Darhe'el**. Gallitep was liberated in 2357 by the Bajoran **Shakaar** resistance group, including future Deep Space 9 officer **Kira Nerys**. One of the Cardassians was a file clerk named **Aamin Marritza**, who saw the atrocities committed by his countrymen and felt intense guilt over his inability to prevent them. Many years later, Marritza tried to atone for the Bajoran deaths by posing as Darhe'el, hoping that a public trial would expose the Cardassian crimes. ("Duet" [DS9]).

Galloway, Lieutenant. (David L. Ross). Crew member from the original *Starship Enterprise* who was part of the landing party to **Eminiar VII** in 2267. ("A Taste of Armageddon" [TOS]). Lieutenant Galloway was also a security officer killed in 2268 at planet **Omega IV** by **Captain Ronald Tracy**. ("The Omega Glory" [TOS]). *David L. Ross, one of the regular extras on the Original Series, can be seen in several episodes under different names. He was also Lieutenant Galloway in "Miri" (TOS) and "City on the Edge of Forever" (TOS).*

Galor-class Cardassian warship. Powerful military spacecraft operated by the **Cardassian** Union. Two Type-3 *Galor*-class ships, the most powerful in their fleet, were dispatched to the Cardassian border to destroy a Bajoran *Antares*-class carrier in 2368.

("Ensign Ro" [TNG]). *The* Galor-*class ship was designed by Rick Sternbach and built by Ed Miarecki. It was first seen in "The Wounded" (TNG).*

Galor IV. The planetary location of an annex to the **Daystrom Institute of Technology**. **Admiral Haftel**, upon learning that Data had constructed a daughter android in 2366, strongly advocated that the new android be placed at the Galor IV annex for programming and study. ("The Offspring" [TNG]).

Galorndon Core. A barely habitable planet in Federation space, one-half light-year from the **Romulan Neutral Zone**. The atmosphere of the planet was plagued by severe electromagnetic storms, which made transport difficult and rendered sensors inoperable. A **Romulan scoutship** landed there in 2266 and was destroyed by its crew to prevent the ship's capture. One crew member, **Centurion Bochra,** was marooned there with Commander Geordi La Forge for several hours. Both men suffered progressive breakdown of their synaptic connections, which Commander La Forge speculated was a result of the "electromagnetic soup" in the planet's atmosphere. ("The Enemy" [TNG]). In 2368, Galorndon Core served as a rendezvous site for the delivery of a stolen deflector array to a **Barolian freighter**. ("Unification, Part II" [TNG]).

Galt. (Joseph Ruskin). Tall, bald master of the **drill thralls** on planet **Triskelion**. He was responsible for training newly captured aliens, including crew members from the *U.S.S. Enterprise* who were captured in 2268. Galt answered only to the rulers of the planet, the **Providers**. ("The Gamesters of Triskelion" [TOS]).

Galvin V. A planet where, according to Data's research, a marriage was only considered successful if children were produced in the first year. ("Data's Day" [TNG]).

Galway, Lieutenant. (Beverly Washburn). *Enterprise* crew member who was part of the landing party to planet **Gamma Hydra IV** in 2267. Galway contracted a radiation illness that sped the aging process. Though she was ten years younger than Kirk, she succumbed to the disease, dying of old age. ("The Deadly Years" [TOS]).

• **"Game, The."** *Next Generation* episode #106. Teleplay by Brannon Braga. Story by Susan Sackett, Fred Bronson, and Brannon Braga. Directed by Corey Allen. Stardate 45208.2. *First aired in 1991. An addictive computer game leaves the* Enterprise-D *crew open for conquest. This episode featured Wesley Crusher's first appearance on* Star Trek: The Next Generation *since "Final Mission" (TNG).* SEE: **A.F.; Boothby; chocolate; Crusher, Wesley;** *Endeavour, U.S.S.;* **frontal lobe; Horne, Walter; Jol, Etana; Ktarian game; Ktarian vessel; Ktarians; Lefler's Laws; Lefler, Ensign Robin;** *Merrimac, U.S.S.;* **Novakovich; O'Brien, Molly; Oceanus IV; Ogawa, Nurse Alyssa; Phoenix Cluster; reticular formation; Risa; Sadie Hawkins Dance; septal area; serotonin; site-to-site transport; Starbase 67; Starbase 82; Tarvokian pound cake; Troi, Deanna;** *Zhukov, U.S.S.*

Gamelan V. Class-M planet that experienced a dramatic increase in atmospheric radiation in 2367. The incident was found to be the result of an unidentified space vehicle that had entered orbit of the planet. The ship, apparently adrift for at least three centuries, was carrying large amounts of dangerous radioactive waste that was leaking into **Gamelan V**'s upper atmosphere. The *Enterprise*-D responded to Gamelan chairman **Songi**'s distress call, and was successful in towing the waste barge into the Gamelan sun. ("Final Mission" [TNG]).

• **"Gamesters of Triskelion, The."** Original Series episode #46. Written by Margaret Armen. Directed by Gene Nelson. Stardate 3211.7. *First broadcast in 1968.* Enterprise *crew members are abducted and forced to fight to the death for the amusement of gamesters who gamble on the results.* SEE: **collar of obedience; drill thralls; Galt; Gamma II; Haines, Ensign; Kloog; Lars; M24 Alpha; Providers; quatloo; Shahna; Tamoon; trisec; Triskelion.**

Gamma 7 Sector. Assigned service area of the ill-fated *U.S.S. Lantree* as of stardate 42494. ("Unnatural Selection" [TNG]).

Gamma 7A System. Solar system with a fourth-magnitude star located in Sector 39J, containing billions of inhabitants. Contact with the system was lost in 2268 when a massive spaceborne **amoeba** creature destroyed it. The same organism also destroyed the *Starship Intrepid*, sent to investigate the incident. ("The Immunity Syndrome" [TOS]).

Gamma 400 Star System. Location of Starbase 12, which was the command base in that sector of space. ("Space Seed" [TOS]).

Gamma Arigulon System. Star system in which the *U.S.S. LaSalle* reported a series of radiation anomalies just prior to stardate 44246.3. ("Reunion" [TNG]).

Gamma Canaris region. The *Shuttlecraft Galileo* was on course for the *Enterprise* from **Epsilon Canaris III** on stardate 3219 when it was pulled off course to a planet in the Gamma Canaris region by an electromagnetic disturbance. ("Metamorphosis" [TOS]). *That disturbance was later found to be the* **Companion,** *the life-form who cared for scientist* **Zefram Cochrane,** *who was living on a planetoid in this region. This* *information was not revealed by Kirk and company after the mission. Cochrane's fate remains unknown to the rest of the Federation.*

Gamma Erandi Nebula. An interstellar gaseous cloud that the *Enterprise*-D was assigned to study following the **Trade Agreements Conference** on Betazed in 2366. Because of the tremendous subspace interference generated by the nebula, *Enterprise*-D communications were blocked for two days. ("Ménage à Troi" [TNG]).

Gamma Eridon. A star system in Klingon space. Picard's armada retreated there to regroup following the disabling of their **tachyon detection grid**. ("Redemption, Part II" [TNG]).

Gamma Hromi II. Location of a **Gatherer** camp, where the first negotiations to reunite the Acamarians and the Gatherers took place. ("The Vengeance Factor" [TNG]).

Gamma Hydra IV. Class-M planet and location of experimental colony where all six of its members, none of them over 30 years of age, died in 2267 of a radiation-induced hyperaccelerated-aging disease. The disease later afflicted members of an *Enterprise* landing party that investigated the incident. Analysis of a comet in the Gamma Hydra system showed that radiation on extreme lower range of the scale might have caused the disease. ("The Deadly Years" [TOS]).

Gamma Hydra. In Starfleet Academy's *Kobayashi Maru* training simulation, Gamma Hydra was the location of the *Kobayashi Maru* when it sent its distress call. (*Star Trek II: The Wrath of Khan*).

Gamma II. Planetoid with an automatic communication and astrogation station. In 2268, a landing party from the *Starship Enterprise* was scheduled to perform a routine check on the station when the **Providers** of **Triskelion** transported them to their planet. ("The Gamesters of Triskelion" [TOS]).

Gamma Quadrant. One-quarter of the entire **Milky Way Galaxy**, the portion most distant from the United Federation of Planets. At its closest point, the Gamma Quadrant is some 40,000 light-years from Federation space.

In 2369, a stable wormhole was discovered near the planet **Bajor**, enabling the free flow of traffic to and from that distant part of the galaxy. ("Emissary" [TNG]). Even without benefit of the **Bajoran wormhole**, archaeologist **Vash** explored the Gamma Quadrant for two years, thanks to **Q**. In the Gamma Quadrant, she discovered some remarkable civilizations, including cultures whose histories date back millions of years. ("Q-Less" [DS9]).

The **Denkiri Arm** of the Milky Way Galaxy is located in the Gamma Quadrant. The **Barzan wormhole**, previously thought to be stable, had one terminus that was at least temporarily located in the Denkiri Arm. ("The Price" [TNG]).

Gamma Tauri IV. Location of an unmanned Federation monitoring post. The **Ferengi** stole a T-9 energy converter from this station in 2364, just prior to first contact with the Federation. ("The Last Outpost" [TNG]).

Gamma Trianguli VI. Idyllic class-M planet with a tropical climate. Its atmosphere has no harmful bacteria and it even completely screens out any negative effects from the sun.

The humanoid inhabitants of Gamma Trianguli VI worshipped a sophisticated computer they called **Vaal**, which provided for the people by controlling the planet's weather. Individuals on this planet had a life expectancy of approximately ten thousand years. The need for procreation was thus eliminated (or at least postponed), making the concept of children an unknown. All this changed in 2267 when Vaal was destroyed by the *Starship Enterprise,* forcing the inhabitants of Gamma Triangulai VI to resume a more normal society. ("The Apple" [TOS]).

Gamma Vertis IV. Planet where the entire population is unable to speak. ("The Empath" [TOS]).

Gamzain. Type of wine served at **Quark's bar** on Deep Space 9. Quark commented to archaeologist **Vash** that he didn't know what was more intoxicating, her negotiating skills or his Gamzain wine. ("Q-Less" [DS9], "The Storyteller" [DS9]).

Gandhi, U.S.S. Federation starship. Lieutenant **Thomas Riker**, with some assistance from Captain Picard, was assigned to the *Gandhi* in 2369 after his rescue from planet **Nervala IV**. He transferred to the ship just prior to its departure for a terraforming mission in the Lagana sector. ("Second Chances" [TNG]). SEE: **Riker, Lieutenant Thomas.** *Named for Mohandas Karamchand Gandhi (1869-1948), leader of the Indian nationalist movement and influential philosopher who advocated nonviolent confrontation or civil disobedience as a means of fostering political change on Earth.*

Ganges, U.S.S. Starfleet *Danube*-class **runabout**, registry number NCC-72454, one of three runabouts assigned to station Deep Space 9. ("Past Prologue." [DS9]). *The Ganges was first seen in "Past Prologue" (DS9). In that episode, it sported a "roll bar" that contained sensor equipment. From a visual effects standpoint, the purpose of the roll bar was to make it easier to tell the Ganges from the Yangtzee Kiang in that episode's chase sequence. The Ganges was also seen in "Q-Less" (DS9) and "Vortex" (DS9).*

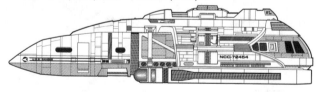

ganglion. A mass of nervous tissues that join each other outside the brain or spinal cord. Dr. Julian Bashir said he would have been valedictorian instead of salutatorian in his graduating class if he hadn't mistaken a pre-ganglionic fiber for a post-ganglionic nerve. ("Q-Less" [DS9]). *An understandable mistake...*

Garadius system. The *Enterprise*-D visited this system on a diplomatic mission following its encounter with a Romulan science vessel in 2368. ("The Next Phase" [TNG]).

Garak. (Andrew Robinson). Resident of Deep Space 9, the only Cardassian citizen left on the station after the Cardassian retreat from the Bajoran system in 2369. Garak owned a clothing shop on the station's **Promenade.** Some people on the station regarded Garak as a Cardassian spy, including Dr. Julian Bashir, despite Garak's efforts to befriend him. ("Past Prologue" [DS9]). *Photo: Plain, simple Garak.*

Garanian Bolites. Small creatures that, when applied to a person's body, cause extreme itching and brief skin discoloration. Jake Sisko and Rom played a practical joke by sprinkling Garanian Bolites on two unsuspecting Bajorans on the Promenade at station Deep Space 9 in 2369. ("A Man Alone" [DS9]).

Gariman Sector. Area of Federation space visited by the *Enterprise*-D in 2369. ("Rightful Heir" [TNG]).

Garin. (Richard Cansino). Scientist from planet **Bre'el IV,** who was on duty in the planetary emergency center during the *Enterprise*-D's mission to restore the Bre'el IV moon to its normal orbit. ("Deja Q" [TNG]). *Garin's name is never spoken in the dialog of "Deja Q," and his name is only from the script.*

Garon II. Site of a disastrous away mission involving crew members from the *U.S.S. Wellington.* Ensign **Ro Laren** disobeyed orders during that mission, and eight people died. ("Ensign Ro" [TNG]).

Garrett, Captain Rachel. (Tricia O'Neil). Captain of the *U.S.S. Enterprise*-C. Garrett, along with the *Enterprise*-C, vanished from her "proper" timeline in 2344, when a torpedo explosion near **Narendra III** opened up a **temporal rift,** emerging in 2366.

This disappearance created an alternate timeline in which the Klingon Empire was at war with the Federation. In this altered future, Garrett was killed in a Klingon attack. **Lieutenant Richard Castillo** subsequently assumed command of the *Enterprise*-C, returning it to its proper time so that history could be restored. ("Yesterday's *Enterprise*" [TNG]). *Tricia O'Neil also played **Kurak** in "Suspicions" (TNG).*

Garrovick, Captain. Commanding officer of the *U.S.S. Farragut* who was killed, along with 200 other crew members, by the **dikironium cloud creature** at planet **Tycho IV** in 2257. **James T. Kirk** recalled Garrovick as one of the finest men he had ever known, carrying the memory of his death through the years. Garrovick's son confronted the same creature aboard the *U.S.S. Enterprise* in 2268 under the command of Captain James T. Kirk. ("Obsession" [TOS]).

Garrovick, Ensign. (Stephen Brooks). Son of **Captain Garrovick.** Ensign Garrovick served as a security officer aboard the *Starship Enterprise.* In 2268, Garrovick encountered the same deadly **dikironium cloud creature** that had killed his father years before. Like Kirk in 2257, Ensign Garrovick paused briefly before firing at the creature, then later believed his hesitation caused the death of several people. Later, the crew learned that phaser fire had no effect upon the creature, absolving Garrovick and Kirk of guilt. ("Obsession" [TOS]).

Garth of Izar. (Steve Ihnat). Famous 23rd-century starship fleet captain whose exploits are required reading at Starfleet Academy. Garth's achievements included the historic victory at **Axanar** in the 2250s that helped preserve the Federation. In the 2260s, Garth became seriously injured in a terrible accident. He recovered with the help of the inhabitants of planet

Antos IV. The people of Antos IV repaired his body by teaching him the art of **cellular metamorphosis,** but did not realize that the accident had rendered him criminally insane. Garth ordered the crew of his starship to destroy Antos IV, after which he was committed to the Federation rehab colony on planet **Elba II.** In 2268, Garth managed to overpower the colony's keepers, proclaimed himself Lord Garth, master of the universe, and attempted to commandeer the *Starship Enterprise,* which was visiting the colony. Garth's escape attempt was aided by the Antos cellular-metamorphosis process, which allowed him to change his shape to become any person he wished. After Garth was recaptured, colony administrator **Donald Cory** indicated optimism that new experimental medications might be able to restore Garth to sanity. ("Whom Gods Destroy" [TOS]).

Garth system. Malcorian name for a solar system near planet **Malcor III.** It was to have been the destination of the first Malcorian warp-speed space flight in 2368. ("First Contact" [TNG]).

Garuth. A figure in ancient Kriosian and Valtese history. Garuth was an empathic metamorph, who was loved by two brothers, **Krios** and **Valt.** Garuth was kidnapped by Krios and taken away to a neighboring system, triggering a war that lasted for centuries. ("The Perfect Mate" [TNG]).

Gary 7. SEE: **Seven, Gary.**

Gaspar VII. Homeworld of Starfleet captain **Edwell.** ("Starship Mine" [TNG]).

Gatherers. Nomadic marauders from planet **Acamar III.** Believed to have been responsible for numerous raids on various outposts and ships in sectors near Acamar III, the Gatherers were genetically identical to the **Acamarians** who remained on their homeworld. The Gatherers split from the more conservative Acamarians a century ago when they refused to accept a peace settlement in that planet's brutal clan warfare, but agreed to return home in 2366 as part of an accord negotiated by Jean-Luc Picard and Acamarian Sovereign **Marouk**. ("The Vengeance Factor" [TNG]).

The Federation science outpost attacked by the Gatherers just prior to the episode used a large scenic background painting originally from the classic 1956 movie Forbidden Planet. *The painting is a planetscape seen through the window of the station.*

Gault. Farm world where young Worf spent his formative years, cared for by his adoptive parents, Sergey and Helena Rozhenko. ("Heart of Glory" [TNG], "Sins of the Father" [TNG]).

Gav. (John Wheeler). **Tellarite** ambassador with a distinguished snout and an attitude. Gav was murdered while en route to the historic **Babel Conference** of 2267 by a Vulcan technique called *talshaya*. ("Journey to Babel" [TOS]).

Gem. (Kathryn Hays). Woman from one of the planets in the **Minaran** star system selected by the **Vians** and tested in 2268 to see if her race would be spared the destruction of the impending nova.

Kirk, Spock, and Dr. McCoy were also captured and subjected to various forms of torture while Gem watched, observing their compassion and willingness to sacrifice their lives for one another. The Vians then observed Gem's reaction, and whether Gem learned the sense of compassion and sacrifice. Gem was a **Minaran empath** and was willing to give her life to save Dr. McCoy from his injuries, which were inflicted by the Vians. This action convinced the Vians that her civilization was the one to be saved from extinction. ("The Empath" [TOS]).

Gemaris V. Planet visited by the *Enterprise*-D in 2366, where Captain Picard mediated a trade dispute between the Gemarians and their neighbors, the Dachlyds. ("Captain's Holiday" [TNG]).

General Orders, Starfleet. SEE: **Starfleet General Orders and Regulations.**

Genesis Device. Short-range torpedo intended to test the **Project Genesis** terraforming process. The Genesis Device was prematurely activated after being stolen by **Khan Noonien Singh**. (*Star Trek II: The Wrath of Khan*).

Genesis Planet. Class-M world formed from the gaseous matter in the **Mutara Nebula** by the **Genesis device** in 2285. The planet appeared to have an almost idyllic environment, but it was later learned that dangerously unstable **protomatter**

used in the Genesis process caused the planet itself to become dangerously unstable and eventually explode. (*Star Trek III: The Search for Spock*).

Genesis. SEE: **Project Genesis**.

Genestra, Sabin. (Bruce French). Aide to Starfleet **admiral Norah Satie**. Genestra came aboard the *Enterprise*-D with Satie in 2367 for the purpose of investigating a suspected security breach. Genestra charged *Enterprise*-D crew member **Tarses** of being a co-conspirator in the theft of *Enterprise*-D engine schematics by Romulan operatives. Genestra, a Betazoid, sensed guilt in Tarses, but was incorrect in his accusation. Tarses had been hiding the fact that his ancestry included Romulan blood, but Tarses had nothing to do with the espionage being investigated. ("The Drumhead" [TNG]).

genetic bonding. In **Betazoid** culture, a term for ritual telepathic joining of children at an early age as a prelude to eventual marriage. **Deanna Troi** was genetically bonded to **Wyatt Miller** when both were children, although they eventually chose not to marry. ("Haven" [TNG]).

genetronic replicator. Experimental medical device, developed by neurogeneticist **Dr. Toby Russell**, designed to translate the genetic code into a specific set of replication instructions, allowing the device to "grow" a replacement organ. Starfleet Medical turned down three requests by Russell to test the device on humanoid patients, prior to her successful implementation of the technique on Lieutenant Worf in 2368. ("Ethics" [TNG]).

Genghis Khan. (Nathan Jung). Warrior leader on planet Earth (c.1162-1227), conqueror of much of Earth's Asian continent. The image of Genghis Khan was created by the inhabitants of the planet **Excalbia** as part of a study conducted in 2269 to examine the human philosophies of "good" and "evil." ("The Savage Curtain" [TOS]). SEE: **Yarnek.**

Genome Colony. A self-contained society of humans founded in 2168 on planet **Moab IV**. The colony founders built a sealed biosphere on the planet, in which they tried to establish a perfect engineered society. Every member of the colony was genetically engineered and trained from birth to perform a specific task.

In 2368, the Genome Colony was endangered by an approaching **stellar core fragment** that threatened to disrupt the planet. In order to avoid destruction, colony leader **Aaron Conor** allowed a group of engineers from the *Enterprise*-D to assist in fortifying the biosphere. The acceptance of outside aid was strongly opposed by colony member **Martin Benbeck**, who was greatly concerned about exposure to outsiders. Benbeck's fears were realized when 23 members of the colony chose to leave with the *Enterprise*-D, leaving irreparable gaps in the genetic makeup of the colony. SEE: **Bates, Hannah**. ("The Masterpiece Society" [TNG]).

George and Gracie. Two humpback whales, species *Megaptera novaeangliae*, that wandered into San Francisco Bay on Earth during the 1980s. They were raised in captivity at the **Cetacean Institute** in Sausalito, before being released into the open ocean because the institute could not afford to feed them. George and Gracie, both highly intelligent individuals, agreed to travel to the 23rd century, where they saved Earth from the effects of an alien space probe, and later began the repopulation of their species on Earth. (*Star Trek IV: The Voyage Home*). SEE: **Probe, the.** *The full-sized whales seen on the surface were supervised by Michael Lanteri, and a couple of shots of real humpbacks in the ocean near Maui were filmed by John Ferrari. The underwater versions of George and Gracie were models created by Walt Conti, who was also responsible for Ensign Darwin on* seaQuest DSV.

Gessard, Yvette. (Herta Ware). Mother of *Enterprise*-D captain **Jean-Luc Picard.** ("Chain of Command, Part II" [TNG]). *Picard's mother was briefly seen in a fantasy sequence in "Where No One Has Gone Before" (TNG).* SEE: **Picard, Yvette Gessard.**

gettle. Wild herd animal, native to the planet **Cardassia.** ("Chain of Command, Part II" [TNG]).

Gettysburg, U.S.S. Federation starship, *Constellation* class, Starfleet registry number NCC-3890, formerly commanded by Captain **Mark Jameson** prior to his promotion to admiral. The *Gettysburg* was the last ship Jameson commanded. ("Too Short a Season" [TNG]).

ghojmok. Klingon term for nursemaid. **Kahlest** was **Worf**'s *ghojmok*, having helped raise him as a small child when his family lived briefly on **Khitomer.** ("Sins of the Father" [TNG]).

Ghorusda disaster. First-contact mission gone awry. The *U.S.S. Adelphi* was assigned to make first contact with the Ghorusdans. The mission was a failure and 47 people, including **Captain Darson** and two of Commander Riker's friends from his Academy class, were killed. A Starfleet Board of Inquiry later found Darson responsible for the incident because of carelessness in handling Ghorusdan cultural taboos, but a failure of mission specialist **Tam Elbrun** to warn Darson of Ghorusdan hostility may also have been a factor. ("Tin Man" [TNG]).

GhoS! Klingon for "Make it so!" ("Redemption, Part II" [TNG]).

Gi'ral. (Christine Rose). Klingon warrior believed killed at a perimeter outpost in the **Khitomer massacre** of 2346. Gi'ral was held captive at the secret Romulan prison camp in the **Carraya System.** There, she married Romulan prison camp commander **Tokath,** and they had a daughter, **Ba'el.** Although Gi'ral accepted her lot as a prisoner, she later supported the wishes of some of the children in the camp to go free. ("Birthright, Parts I and II" [TNG]).

Giamon. One of the forty-plus languages spoken by *U.S.S. Aries* first officer Flaherty. ("The Icarus Factor" [TNG]).

Giddings, Dianna. (Lorine Mendell). Crew member aboard the *Enterprise*-D, Giddings was one of the beautiful women who attracted the attentions of **Thadiun Okona.** ("The

Outrageous Okona" [TNG]). *Although Giddings was not given a name in dialog, her name comes from the sign on the door to her quarters. Lorine Mendell was an extra and a stand-in on* Star Trek: The Next Generation, *and she was seen in the background of numerous episodes. She was featured as Keiko O'Brien's friend in "Power Play" (TNG).*

Gideon. Class-M planet that applied for membership in the United Federation of Planets in 2268. Gideon had a germ-free atmosphere and was once considered to be a paradise, but a spiritual inability to practice birth control resulted in a terrible population explosion, causing serious deterioration of the planet's environment. During Gideon's negotiations for admission to the Federation, **Hodin,** leader of the high council of Gideon, engineered an elaborate plan whereby *Enterprise* captain James T. Kirk was captured and placed on an exact copy of his ship in an effort to confuse and disorient him. In this ersatz *Enterprise,* Kirk was introduced to **Odona,** Hodin's daughter, so that she would contract **Vegan choriomeningitis,** a disease carried in Kirk's bloodstream. Odona had volunteered to die from the disease in hopes her death would inspire others of her world to follow her example. *Enterprise* personnel located Kirk and Odona, successfuly treating her, but she did return to her planet to carry out the deadly plan of exposing other volunteers to lower her population. ("The Mark of Gideon" [TOS]).

gift box, Betazoid. A traditional **Betazoid** means of presenting gifts of great value or importance, these ornate containers were decorated with the sculpted image of a humanoid face. In the presence of the intended recipient, the face on the gift box would briefly come to life, delivering a message or greeting before the box would open. **Wyatt Miller**'s family sent **Deanna Troi**'s bonding gifts to her in such a box. ("Haven" [TNG]). *The face on Deanna's gift box was played by Armin Shimerman, who would later portray various Ferengi, most notably* **Quark** *in* Star Trek: Deep Space Nine.

Giles Belt. A possible destination of the *Jovis,* following the kidnapping of Data by Kivas Fajo in 2366. ("The Most Toys" [TNG]).

Gilgamesh. Mythic figure of Earth's ancient Mesopotamia; a warrior king whose adventures were related on twelve incomplete stone tablets. Captain Picard shared one of the stories of Gilgamesh with **Tamarian** captain **Dathon,** while the two of them were together on El-Adrel IV. ("Darmok" [TNG]).

Gilgo Beach. Seaside park on Earth where **Benjamin Sisko** met his future wife, Jennifer, shortly after graduating from **Starfleet Academy.** ("Emissary" [DS9]).

Gill, John. (David Brian). Federation cultural observer and noted professor of history. As a historian, Gill emphasized causes and motivations rather than dates and events. He was an instructor at **Starfleet Academy** whose students included future *Enterprise* captain James T. Kirk. In the late 2260s, Gill was stationed on planet **Ekos**, where he conducted a disastrous cultural experiment in which he violated the **Prime Directive** in an effort to give the planet a more efficient form of government, patterned after Earth's Nazi Germany, but based on more compassionate principles. The experiment failed terribly when those near him were corrupted by power and sought to create racial hatred against neighboring planet **Zeon**. Deputy Fuhrer **Melakon** murdered Gill in 2268 when Gill sought to discredit the program of genocide launched against Zeon. ("Patterns of Force" [TOS]).

Gillespie, Chief. (Duke Moosekian). An *Enterprise*-D crew member and friend of Miles O'Brien. Suffering from paranoia induced by a **REM sleep** deprived state when the ship was trapped in a **Tyken's Rift** in 2367, Gillespie nearly incited a riot in the ship's Ten-Forward lounge. ("Night Terrors" [TNG]).

gilvos. SEE: **Corvan gilvos**.

ginger tea. Beverage made from the root of the reedlike plant *Zingiber officinale*. Served hot, this concoction was used by Captain Picard's **Aunt Adele** to treat the common cold. ("Ensign Ro" [TNG]).

Giotto, Lieutenant Commander. (Barry Russo). *Enterprise* security officer who worked with Janus VI mining colony personnel to locate the Horta, responsible for several deaths on the planet prior to stardate 3196. ("The Devil in the Dark" [TOS]). *Actor Barry Russo also played Commodore Wesley in "The Ultimate Computer" (TOS). Giotto's uniform had a commander's braid.*

Gladstone, Miss. (Dawn Arnemann). A primary-school teacher aboard the *Enterprise*-D. ("The Child" [TNG]).

glavin. A traditional weapon on planet **Ligon II**, used in ritual combat. Resembling a gauntlet-length oversized glove, the end of the *glavin* has a large, vicious hook and is covered with poison-tipped spines. Tasha Yar fought **Yareena** with *glavins*. ("Code of Honor" [TNG]).

Gleason, Captain. Commanding officer of the *U.S.S. Zhukov*. Gleason recorded satisfactory reports for Lieutenant **Reginald Barclay** and spoke very highly of his performance on the *Zhukov*, just prior to Barclay's transfer to the *Enterprise*-D in 2366. ("Hollow Pursuits" [TNG]).

Gleason, Ensign. (Todd Merrill). *Enterprise*-D officer assigned to battle bridge Ops in early 2367 during the rescue of Captain Picard from the **Borg** ship. ("The Best of Both Worlds, Part II" [TNG]).

glial cells. More specifically known as neuroglia; tissue that forms the supporting elements of the nervous system which play an important role in reacting to injury or infection. Kobliad **Rao Vantika** placed his neural patterns or consciousness in a microscopic generator. He used a weak electrical charge as a bio-coded message, placing it under his fingernails. When Dr. Bashir found Vantika injured, the **Kobliad** scratched the physician and introduced the microscopic generator into Bashir's skin. The bio-coded message was then transferred to Bashir's neuroglia cells and straight to his brain, where Vantika's consciousness was stored. ("The Passenger" [DS9]). SEE: **microscopic generator.**

Glinn. A rank in the **Cardassian** militia, lower in stature than a **Gul**. ("The Wounded" [TNG]).

Glob fly. Klingon insect, half the size of a Terran mosquito. This creature has no sting, but has a characteristic loud buzzing sound. ("The Outrageous Okona" [TNG]).

global warming. A gradual increase of a planet's mean atmospheric temperature, often resulting in catastrophic environmental damage. The **magnetospheric energy tap** of **Alpha Moon** of planet **Peliar Zel** caused global warming on **Beta Moon** in 2367. ("The Host" [TNG]). SEE: **Odan, Ambassador.**

glop-on-a-stick. Star Trek *production staff nickname for* **jumja**, *a food sold on the Promenade on Deep Space 9.* ("A Man Alone" [DS9]).

Gloria. (Whoopi Goldberg). **Guinan**'s persona when she participated in one of Captain Picard's **Dixon Hill** holodeck programs. Picard, as Hill, identified Gloria as his cousin from Cleveland. Guinan, as Gloria, had a great deal of trouble with the female accoutrements (i.e. stockings) of old Earth culture. ("Clues" [TNG]).

Glyrhond. River on planet **Bajor** that defined the border between two villages, the **Paqu** and the **Navot**. A treaty signed in 2279 established the river Glyrhond as the boundary between the two rival peoples. During the **Cardassian** occupation of Bajor, the river was diverted for mining operations, setting the stage for a bitter dispute over whether the boundary should be the river's former course, or its new path. ("The Storyteller" [DS9]). SEE: **Varis Sul.**

G'now juk Hol pajhard. Klingon law of heredity. A son shall share in the honors or crimes of his father. This law required **Worf**'s **discommendation** when the council accused his father, **Mogh**, of allowing the 2346 Romulan attack on the **Khitomer** outpost. ("Redemption, Part I" [TNG]).

Goddard, **Shuttlecraft.** Vehicle technically assigned to the *Starship Enterprise*-D, actually on extended loan to Captain **Montgomery Scott**. Captain Picard presented the shuttle to Scott in 2369 after Scott's own ship, the *Jenolen*, was destroyed while saving the *Enterprise*-D. ("Relics" [TNG]). *The* Goddard *was named for American rocket scientist Robert H. Goddard (1882-1945), inventor of the liquid-fueled rocket.*

Goddard, U.S.S. Federation starship, *Korolev* class, Starfleet registry NCC-59621, scheduled for a rendezvous with the *Enterprise*-D shortly after stardate 43421. The rendezvous was postponed after the signing of the **Acamarian** truce. ("The Vengeance Factor" [TNG]). The *Goddard* was part of the **tachyon detection grid** during the **Klingon civil war** of 2368. ("Redemption, Part II" [TNG]).

"Goddess of Empathy." A **holodeck** facsimile of Counselor Deanna Troi, created by **Reginald Barclay** in violation of protocols against the simulation of real people without their consent. ("Hollow Pursuits" [TNG]).

gods, Greek. According to the powerful extraterrestrial who called himself **Apollo**, the mythical figures Agamemnon, Hector, Ulysses, Zeus, Latona, Artemis, Pan, Athena, and Aphrodite were also extraterrestrials who lived on Earth some 5,000 years ago, where they were worshipped as gods by the ancient Greeks. ("Who Mourns for Adonais?" [TOS]).

gold-pressed latinum. SEE: **latinum.**

Gomez, Ensign Sonya. (Lycia Naff). Young engineering officer assigned to *Enterprise*-D at **Starbase 173.** An attractive young woman, Gomez specialized in antimatter operations. ("Q Who?" [TNG]). Gomez helped devise a means of using the ship's **Bussard collectors** to create a harmless pyrotechnic display when Geordi La Forge was being held captive aboard the *Mondor* in 2365. ("Samaritan Snare" [TNG]). *Although Gomez was first in "Q Who" (TNG), she apparently transferred to the ship at Starbase 173 during "The Measure of a Man" (TNG).*

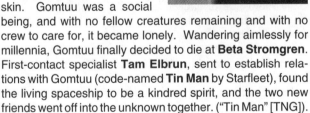

Gomtuu. An ancient, space-borne organism, the last of a species of living spacecraft that lived in symbiotic relationships with their crews. Gomtuu's crew died when radiation from an explosion penetrated its skin. Gomtuu was a social being, and with no fellow creatures remaining and with no crew to care for, it became lonely. Wandering aimlessly for millennia, Gomtuu finally decided to die at **Beta Stromgren**. First-contact specialist **Tam Elbrun**, sent to establish relations with Gomtuu (code-named **Tin Man** by Starfleet), found the living spaceship to be a kindred spirit, and the two new friends went off into the unknown together. ("Tin Man" [TNG]).

Gonal IV. The home planet of the swarming moths that were the subject of *Enterprise*-D science fair winner **Jay Gordon**'s project in 2368. ("Disaster" [TNG]).

Gordon, Jay. (John Christian Graas). One of the winners of the primary-school science fair held aboard the *Enterprise*-D in 2368. Young Jay Gordon was also made an honorary science officer by Captain Picard. ("Disaster" [TNG]).

Gorgan. (Melvin Belli). **Noncorporeal life**-form that forced the adults from the **Starnes Expedition** to planet **Triacus** to commit suicide and deceived their children to follow him and do his evil bidding. The children could summon the Gorgan by chanting, "Hail, hail, fire and snow. Call the angel, we will go. Far away, for to see, Friendly Angel come to me." ("And the Children Shall Lead" [TOS]). *The Gorgan was played by noted attorney Melvin Belli, who still practices law in San Francisco.*

Gorkon, Chancellor. (David Warner). Leader of the **Klingon High Council**, assassinated in 2293 by forces who sought to block his efforts for peace with the **United Federation of Planets**. Gorkon was succeeded by his daughter, **Azetbur.** (*Star Trek VI: The Undiscovered Country*). SEE: **Klingon Empire.** *Actor David Warner had previously played diplomat Talbot St. John in Star Trek V.*

Gorkon, U.S.S. Federation starship, *Excelsior* class. The *Gorkon* was **Admiral Nechayev**'s flagship during the expected **Borg** invasion of 2369. ("Descent, Part I" [TNG]). *Named for Chancellor Gorkon, seen in Star Trek VI.*

Gorn. Large, immensely strong reptilian creatures who destroyed the Earth outpost on **Cestus III** claiming it was an intrusion into their space. The captain of the Gorn vessel and Captain Kirk were transported to a planet by a race known as the **Metrons**, where each fought for the survival of his respective crew. Kirk won, but refused to kill the Gorn, after realizing that the Gorn attack had been the result of a misunderstanding. ("Arena" [TOS]).

Goro. (Richard Hale). Tribal elder from **Miramanee's planet** who, in 2268, accepted the amnesia-stricken Kirk into his tribe as a god. ("The Paradise Syndrome" [TOS]).

Gosheven. (Grainger Hines). Conservative leader of the **Tau Cygna V** colony in 2366. When informed by Data that the colony's presence on the planet was in violation of a treaty with the **Sheliak**, Gosheven was unwilling to consider abandoning the planet. He even attacked Data physically to prevent him from convincing others to leave. ("The Ensigns of Command" [TNG]).

Goss, DaiMon. (Scott Thompson). Head of the Ferengi trade delegation that negotiated for rights to the **Barzan wormhole** in 2366. In a near-lethal attempt to tip the negotiations in the Ferengi's favor, Goss poisoned the Federation negotiator, **Dr. Mendoza**, with Ferengi **pyrocytes**. Goss later made a secret deal with **Devinoni Ral** in which the Ferengi would pretend to be trying to destroy the wormhole, hoping to give Ral an advantage in negotiating against the Federation. ("The Price" [TNG]).

Gossett, Herm. (Jon Kowal). One of the three miners at the **Rigel XII** lithium mining station in 2266. ("Mudd's Women" [TOS]).

Gothos. Iron-silica planet created by the entity **Trelane**. The *Enterprise* discovered the planet while en route to **Beta VI** in 2267. The surface of Gothos contained no detectable soil or vegetation, had a toxic atmosphere, and was plagued by storms and continuous volcanic eruptions. A small section of the planet did have a Class-M environment, thanks to the mischievous Trelane, who captured several *Enterprise* personnel to play with. ("The Squire of Gothos" [TOS]).

Gowron. (Robert O'Reilly). Son of M'Rel, and leader of the **Klingon High Council** following the death of **K'mpec** in 2367. Prior to his ascent to power, Gowron was a political outsider who often challenged the High Council. Following the death of K'mpec, Gowron was one of two contenders for the post of council leader. With the elimination of **Duras**, Gowron won the position. ("Reunion" [TNG]). Gowron was installed as council leader in a ceremony attended by Jean-Luc Picard, who had served as **Arbiter of Succession**. Gowron's leadership was quickly challenged by **Lursa** and **B'Etor**, surviving members of the Duras family who sought to install Duras's illegitimate son, **Toral**, as council leader. The Duras bid was supported by Romulan interests seeking to gain control over the Klingon Empire. The challenge divided the council and plunged the Empire into civil war in early 2368. Gowron emerged victorious, in part because he agreed to restore rightful honor to the **Mogh** family in exchange for military support by **Worf** and **Kurn**. ("Redemption, Parts I and II" [TNG]). Within a few months, Gowron found it politically disadvantageous to admit to the Federation's support during his Rite of Succession and the subsequent civil war. Official government accounts of these events therefore omitted references to Federation involvement. ("Unification, Part I" [TNG]). Gowron reacted strongly to the supposed "return" of **Kahless the Unforgettable** in 2369, correctly surmising that the new Kahless was part of a political effort to discredit him. Gowron was further convinced that Kahless would once again plunge the Empire into civil war. At Worf's urging, Gowron later agreed to support Kahless in the ceremonial role of Emperor. This would allow Kahless to be the spiritual leader of the people, while the governmental power would remain with Gowron and the High Council. ("Rightful Heir" [TNG]).

Gracie. SEE: **George and Gracie.**

Graham, Ensign. (Mona Grudt). Graham was at the conn when the *Enterprise*-D entered the Tarchannen system in

2367, albeit too late to save **Lieutenant Hickman**. ("Identity Crisis" [TNG]).

Grak-tay. A famous concert violinist whose performance style **Data** programmed himself to emulate. ("Sarek" [TNG]).

Gral. (Lee Arenberg). Ferengi entrepreneur who tried to threaten **Quark** during his brief tenure as **Grand Nagus** in 2369. Gral intimated that unless Quark showed him favor, he would someday be killed. ("The Nagus" [DS9]).

Grand Nagus. SEE: **Nagus, Grand**; **Zek**.

Granger, Wilson. (Jon de Vries). Commander of the colony ship *S.S. Mariposa* when it was launched in 2123, and one of only five survivors when the ship crashed on the planet the colonists named **Mariposa**. Granger became one of the progenitors whose cloned descendants inhabited the Mariposa colony, and in 2365 one of his clones served as colony prime minister. ("Up the Long Ladder" [TNG]). SEE: **clone.**

Grant. (Robert Bralver). *Enterprise* security guard who was part of the landing party at planet **Capella IV** on stardate 3497. Grant was killed by a Capellan with the deadly Capellan weapon, the *kligat*. ("Friday's Child" [TOS]).

Gratitude Festival. The biggest **Bajoran** holiday of the year. Sisko arranged for a three-day trip to planet Bajor with his son Jake to attend the Gratitude Festival in 2369 and visit the fire caverns. The trip was canceled. ("The Nagus" [DS9]).

Graves, Dr. Ira. (W. Morgan Sheppard). Noted molecular cyberneticist, Dr. Ira Graves was considered to be arguably one of the greatest human minds in the universe. Early in his career, Graves was a teacher to **Dr. Noonien Soong**, and thus Graves considered himself to be a "grandfather" to the android **Data**. Graves spent the last years of his life isolated on a planet he called **Gravesworld**, where he died in 2365 of Darnay's disease. Just prior to his death, Graves deposited his intellect into Data's **positronic brain**; this information was later stored in the *Enterprise*-D main computer. ("The Schizoid Man" [TNG]). SEE: **Zee-Magnees Prize.**

Gravesworld. A remote ringed planet on which the noted molecular cyberneticist **Ira Graves** lived the last years of his life in seclusion. ("The Schizoid Man" [TNG]).

gravimetric fluctuations. Sensor readings accompanying the appearance of the **temporal rift** near planet **Archer IV**. Vaguely resembling a **wormhole**, the temporal rift exhibited time displacement, but had no discernible event horizon. ("Yesterday's *Enterprise*" [TNG]).

gravimetric interference. Spatial distortion phenomenon

partially responsible for the crash of the **U.S.S. Jenolen** into the surface of the **Dyson Sphere** in 2294. The interference had apparently been generated by the enormous mass of the Dyson Sphere. ("Relics" [TNG]).

gravitational constant. Mathematical expression describing the amount of gravitational attraction that is generated by a given amount of matter. When *Enterprise*-D personnel were trying to prevent the moon of planet **Bre'el IV** from crashing into the planet, **Q** suggested that reducing the gravitational constant of the universe might be a good way to reduce the moon's mass enough so the ship's **tractor beam** could do the job. Unfortunately, Q forgot that adjusting the gravitational constant was a feat beyond the abilities of most mere mortals. ("Deja Q" [TNG]). SEE: **warp field**.

gravitational unit. Device used to generate a synthetic gravity field aboard a space vehicle. The Klingon battle cruiser **Kronos One** suffered a hit to the gravity generator during the assassination of **Chancellor Gorkon,** resulting in weightless conditions aboard that ship while the crime was committed. (*Star Trek VI: The Undiscovered Country*).

gravitic mine. Free-floating weapon used against space vehicles. (*Star Trek II: The Wrath of Khan*). The transport starship **U.S.S. Denver** struck a gravitic mine in 2368. That mine had been left over from the Cardassian war. ("Ethics" [TNG]).

gravitic sensor net. Network of detection devices employed by the Federation near the **Romulan Neutral Zone**, making it possible to detect space vehicles in the area. This system was at least partially effective in sensing the presence of cloaked ships. ("Face of the Enemy" [TNG]).

graviton field generator. Key component of forcefield and artificial-gravity generators. An experiment in phasing technology conducted on a Romulan science vessel in 2368 completely depolarized the graviton field generator of that ship, leading to the destruction of the ship's warp core. ("The Next Phase" [TNG]).

graviton field. Energy generated by a tractor beam that can be used to strengthen the structural integrity of a vessel being towed. ("Captive Pursuit" [DS9]). A graviton field generated by a previously undiscovered life-form threatened Deep Space 9 in 2369 when an archaeological artifact, discovered by **Vash** in the Gamma Quadrant and stored on the station, was found to contain the entity. After the object was beamed into space, the winged energy creature emerged from the artifact and flew into the wormhole, leaving Deep Space 9 to return to normal. ("Q-Less" [DS9]).

graviton inverter circuit. Component of an **antigrav** such as those used in cargo-handling units. ("Hollow Pursuits" [TNG]).

graviton polarimeter. Sensor device used aboard Federation starships. In some astronomical studies, it can gather data similar to that of a **flux spectrometer**. ("Cause and Effect" [TNG]).

graviton pulses. Modulated bursts of graviton particle beams. Graviton pulses were used by *Enterprise*-D personnel to attempt communication with the **Crystalline Entity** in 2368. Before such attempts could succeed, scientist **Dr. Kila Marr**, who sought revenge against the entity, adjusted the graviton beam to set up a resonant frequency that destroyed the entity. ("Silicon Avatar" [TNG]).

graviton. Elementary particle that transmits gravitational force. ("Q-Less" [DS9]).

gravity boots. Also known as **magnetic boots**. (*Star Trek VI: The Undiscovered Country*).

Grax, Reittan. (Rudolph Willrich). The Betazoid director of the biennial **Trade Agreements Conference** in 2366. Grax was an old friend of **Lwaxana Troi**'s late husband, **Ian Andrew Troi**, and had known their daughter, Deanna Troi, since childhood. Grax contacted the *Enterprise*-D to inform the captain when Riker, Deanna Troi, and Lwaxana Troi were missing, kidnapped by the Ferengi. ("Ménage à Troi" [TNG]).

Grayson, Amanda. *According to Original Series* Star Trek *writer and story editor Dorothy Fontana, this was the full name of* **Spock**'s *mother, first seen in "Journey to Babel" (TOS), although the surname Grayson was not established in any regular episode or film. The name was used in the animated episode, "Yesteryear," written by Fontana.* SEE: **Amanda**.

Gre'thor. In Klingon mythology, the place where the dishonored go to die. Gre'thor is guarded by the mythic Klingon figure, **Fek'lhr**. ("Devil's Due" [TNG]).

Great Barrier, the. An energy field surrounding the center of the Milky Way Galaxy. Long believed to be impenetrable by any starship, the Great Barrier was first traversed by the *Starship Enterprise* in 2287 when the ship was commandeered by **Sybok** in his quest for the planet **Sha Ka Ree**, which Sybok believed he would find at the center of the galaxy. (*Star Trek V: The Final Frontier*). *Not to be confused with the* **galactic barrier** *at the edge of the galaxy, first seen in "Where No Man Has Gone Before" (TOS).*

Great Bird of the Galaxy, The. A mythic figure in the 23rd century. Sulu invoked same when he thanked Janice Rand for bringing him lunch by saying "May the Great Bird of the Galaxy bless your planet." ("The Man Trap" [TOS]). *Great Bird of the Galaxy was also a nickname for* Star Trek *creator Gene Roddenberry (pictured).*

Great Depression. Economic downturn that beset the United States on Earth in the 1930s. **Edith Keeler**'s **Twenty-First Street Mission** was set up to help people survive during that time. ("The City on the Edge of Forever" [TOS]).

"Great Experiment, The." Unofficial term used to describe the **U.S.S. Excelsior**, Starfleet's testbed vehicle for the unsuccessful **transwarp drive** development project. (*Star Trek III: The Search for Spock*).

Great Hall. A massive fortress-like building that serves as the seat of government of the **Klingon Empire**, located in the **First City** on the **Klingon Homeworld**. The **Klingon High Council** meets there. ("Sins of the Father" [TNG]). *The design of the Klingon Great Hall (and other sets in the episode) won an Emmy Award for Best Art Direction for* Star Trek: The Next Generation *production designer Richard James. The exterior of the Great Hall and the surrounding First City was a matte painting created by Syd Dutton at Illusion Arts.*

Green, Colonel. (Phillip Pine). Twenty-first-century military figure who led a genocidal war on Earth. The image of this notoriously evil historical figure was re-created by the **Excalbians** in 2269 as part of their study of the nature of the human concepts of "good" and "evil." ("The Savage Curtain" [TOS]). SEE: **Yarnek**. *It is not clear what war Green fought, but it might have been* **World War III**, *mentioned in "Bread and Circuses" (TOS) and "Encounter at Farpoint" (TNG).*

Green, Crewman. (Bruce Watson). *Enterprise* crew member killed on the surface of planet **M-113** by the salt vampire. Green's death was not discovered for several hours because the **M-113 creature** subsequently assumed Green's identity and transported up to the ship. ("The Man Trap" [TOS]).

greenhouse effect. A planetary atmospheric condition in which solar radiation is trapped in a planet's atmosphere, causing increased temperature in that atmosphere. *Enterprise*-D personnel used ship's phasers to release subterranean carbon dioxide into the atmosphere of planet **Penthara IV** in 2368 in hopes that the resulting greenhouse effect would forestall a potential ice age on the planet. ("A Matter of Time" [TNG]).

Grenthemen water hopper. A motor-driven vehicle that, according to Geordi La Forge, would stall disastrously when the clutch was popped. Riker also had experience with a hopper. ("Peak Performance" [TNG]).

Grisella. Race known for their need to hibernate for six months at a time. Captain Picard chose the Grisella as mediators in a dispute in 2366 between the **Sheliak** and the Federation over the evacuation of the Federation's **Tau Cygna V** colony in accordance with the **Treaty of Armens**. The choice was intended by Picard to delay enforcement of the evacuation. ("The Ensigns of Command" [TNG]).

Grissom, U.S.S. Starfleet science vessel, **Oberth class**, registry number NCC-638. The *Grissom* was assigned to investigate the newly formed **Genesis Planet** in 2285, but was destroyed by a Klingon vessel attempting to claim the planet for the Klingon Empire. The *Grissom* had been commanded by Captain J. T. Esteban. The investigation team included Lieutenant **Saavik** and Dr. **David Marcus**. (*Star Trek III: The Search for Spock*). *The* Grissom *was designed by David Carson and built at ILM. The* Grissom *was*

also re-labeled and reused as a variety of other Federation starships in Star Trek: The Next Generation. *The Grissom was named for* Mercury *astronaut Virgil I. Grissom, who was killed in the tragic* Apollo 1 *fire in 1967.*

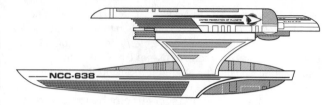

Grissom, U.S.S. Federation starship, **Excelsior class**, Starfleet registry number NCC-42857. The *Grissom* was near the **Sigma Erandi system** during the **tricyanate** contamination on **Beta Agni II** in 2366. The *Enterprise*-D requested the *Grissom* to stand by should assistance be needed. ("The Most Toys" [TNG]). *This was presumably a newer U.S.S. Grissom, since the earlier ship of the same name was destroyed in* Star Trek III.

Gromek, Admiral. (Georgann Johnson). Starfleet official who transmitted secret orders to *Enterprise*-D to rendezvous with special Federation emissary **K'Ehleyr** prior to the return of the Klingon ship **T'Ong** in 2365. ("The Emissary" [TNG]).

Groppler. Title of a civic leader among the **Bandi** people on planet **Deneb IV**. ("Encounter at Farpoint, Parts I and II" [TNG]).

grup. Slang on **Miri**'s planet for "grown-up." ("Miri" [TOS]).

GSK 739. Call sign for a private transmitter belonging to **George Samuel Kirk** on the planet **Deneva**. Kirk asked Uhura to use the private call sign on subspace frequency 3, hoping to contact his brother, Sam, when contact was lost with the colony in 2267. ("Operation— Annihilate!" [TOS]).

Guardian of Forever. (Voice by Bart LaRue). Time portal created by an unknown civilization on a distant planet at least five billion years ago. The Guardian resembled a large, rough-hewn torus about three meters in diameter. It was a sentient device, able to respond to questions. The Guardian was discovered in 2267 by *Enterprise* personnel who were investigating time-distortion waves in the vicinity. Dr. McCoy, suffering from an accidental overdose of **cordrazine** when the ship was hit by a time wave, fled into Earth's past through the Guardian. While in the past, McCoy effected a change in the flow of history, creating a new future in which the *Starship Enterprise* did not exist. Kirk and Spock followed McCoy to Earth's 1930s, where they learned that McCoy had prevented the death of American social worker **Edith Keeler**. In this altered history, Keeler prevented the entry of the United States into World War II long enough

for Nazi Germany to develop weapons that allowed Hitler to dominate the world. Kirk and Spock were able to prevent McCoy from saving Keeler, and upon her death, time resumed its original course. The origin and purpose of the Guardian remains a total mystery, but the Guardian described itself as its own beginning and its own end. ("The City on the Edge of Forever" [TOS]).

Guernica system. Location of a Federation outpost that the *Enterprise*-D visited in 2367. ("Galaxy's Child" [TNG]).

Guinan. (Whoopi Goldberg). Bartender at the **Ten-Forward lounge** aboard the *Starship Enterprise*-D. ("The Child" [TNG]). Guinan was a member of a race of listeners, but her people, the El-Aurians, were nearly wiped out by the Borg in the late 23rd century. The few survivors among her people escaped by spreading themselves across the galaxy. Guinan was one of the survivors. ("Q Who?" [TNG]).

Guinan spent some time on Earth prior to that planet's development of space travel. She lived in the Earth city of San Francisco in the year 1893, where she met writer **Samuel Clemens**, as well as future shipmates **Data, Picard, etc.**, who had traveled back in time. ("Time's Arrow, Parts I and II" [TNG]).

Guinan was born sometime in the 19th century, making her about 500 years old when she served on the *Enterprise*-D. Her father was about 200 years old at the time of Guinan's birth. ("Rascals" [TNG]). She also had an uncle named **Termin**. ("Hollow Pursuits" [TNG]). Guinan and **Q** were acquaintances, having met each other some two centuries ago, but neither has been particularly enlightening about the encounter, save for the fact that neither liked the other. ("Q Who?" [TNG]). She has been married several times, and had many children. She said that all of them turned out all right, except for one that wouldn't listen. ("Evolution" [TNG]).

Guinan possessed an unusual sense that extended beyond normal linear space-time. She, alone, was intuitively aware of the damage to the "normal" flow of time caused when the *Enterprise*-**C** was swept some 22 years into its future, creating an alternate timeline. Guinan warned Picard that history had been altered, persuading him to return the *Enterprise*-C back to 2344 to restore the flow of time. Such was Picard's faith in Guinan that he accepted this extraordinary recommendation. ("Yesterday's *Enterprise*" [TNG]).

Much remains unknown about Guinan, largely because Star Trek's producers made a conscious decision to keep her background a mystery during the series, although it is possible that a future movie may reveal more about her past and her people.

Guinan, played by Whoopi Goldberg, joined the Star Trek: The Next Generation *cast at the beginning of the second season after calling Gene Roddenberry and telling him that she'd like to be part of the* Enterprise *crew. She's been a recurring character ever since. Guinan was named after famed bartender Texas Guinan, who ran a saloon during the*

Prohibition. Young Guinan in "Rascals" was played by Isis Jones. Guinan's first appearance was in "The Child" [TNG]).

Gul. Title given to **Cardassian** officers approximately equivalent to a Starfleet captain. ("The Wounded" [TNG]).

Gunji jackdaw. Ostrich-like bird that appeared, along with numerous other unexpected individuals, on the **Promenade** of station **Deep Space 9** on stardate 46853. The Gunji jackdaw replica was created by unknown aliens from the Gamma Quadrant who were trying to study humanoid life. ("If Wishes Were Horses" [DS9]).

gunpowder. Explosive mixture created by combining sulfur, saltpeter, and charcoal, used in ancient projectile weapons. Kirk, trapped on an artificial planetoid created by the **Metrons** in 2267, used native materials to make gunpowder for use in a weapon against the **Gorn**. ("Arena" [TOS]).

gunamba. In the **Nausicaan** language, a word that roughly translates as "conviction" or "courage." ("Tapestry" [TNG]).

gymnasium. Recreational and exercise area aboard the *U.S.S. Enterprise*. Kirk attempted to teach **Charles Evans** some basic martial-arts skills in the gym. ("Charlie X" [TOS]). Among the equipment in the Deck 12 gymnasium on the *Enterprise*-D is an **anbo-jytsu** ring. ("The Icarus Factor" [TNG]).

Haakona. Romulan warbird commanded by **Subcommander Taris**. The *Haakona* intervened when the Federation starships *Yamato* and *Enterprise*-D violated the Romulan Neutral Zone in 2365 while in search of the planet **Iconia**. The *Haakona*, along with the *Enterprise*-D, was nearly destroyed by the Iconian software weapon that did destroy the *Yamato*. ("Contagion" [TNG]).

habitat ring. Large inner structure of station **Deep Space 9**, surrounding the central core, largely devoted to personnel quarters and other living facilities. The three **runabout** launch pads are also located in the habitat ring. ("If Wishes Were Horses" [DS9]).

Hacom. (Morgan Farley). Inhabitant of planet **Beta III** during the end of the computer **Landru**'s rule in 2267. Hacom fully supported Landru and summoned the planet's **Lawgivers** when he believed that **Tamar** failed to endorse Landru's authority. ("Return of the Archons" [TOS]).

Haden, Admiral. (John Hancock). Starfleet admiral who transmitted Priority 1 orders to the *Enterprise*-D in the matter of the defection of Romulan admiral **Alidar Jarok** in 2366. Haden was stationed at Starfleet's **Lya III** command base. ("The Defector" [TNG]). In 2367, Haden confirmed Cardassian reports that the *U.S.S. Phoenix* had attacked and destroyed a Cardassian science station in violation of the Federation-Cardassian peace treaty. ("The Wounded" [TNG]).

Ha'DIbah. A Klingon insult; it translates as "animal." ("Sins of the Father" [TNG], "Reunion" [TNG]).

Haftel, Admiral. (Nicolas Coster). Starfleet officer and cybernetics scientist. In 2366, Haftel attempted to gain custody of Data's android daughter, **Lal**, because he believed Lal could be better cared for and studied under Starfleet supervision at the **Daystrom Institute of Technology**'s annex at **Galor IV**. ("The Offspring" [TNG]). *While it was never spoken on air, the script for "The Offspring" gives the admiral's first name as Anthony.*

Hagen, Andrus. (John Vickery). Science advisor aboard the *U.S.S. Brattain* at the time the ship was trapped in a **Tyken's Rift** in 2367. Hagen was the only member of the crew still alive when the *Enterprise*-D arrived on a rescue mission. Hagen was found in a profound catatonic state and was unable to communicate what had happened. A Betazoid, Hagen could only project a few words telepathically, words which made no sense until Troi began to hear the same words in her dreams. ("Night Terrors" [TNG]).

haggis. Traditional Scottish dish made from sheep's stomach. ("The Savage Curtain" [TOS]).

Hagler, Lieutenant Edward. *Enterprise*-D crew member who was abducted by the **Solanagen-based aliens** in 2369. Lieutenant Hagler died as a result of the alien's medical experiments. ("Schisms" [TNG]).

Hagon. (James Louis Watkins). Formerly an aide to **Ligonian** leader **Lutan**, Hagon ascended to great power on planet **Ligon II** when Lutan's mating agreement was dissolved and Hagon became First One to the wealthy **Yareena**. ("Code of Honor" [TNG]).

Haines, Ensign. (Victoria George). *U.S.S. Enterprise* navigator who, on stardate 3211, was part of the bridge complement during the search for a missing landing party on planet **Triskelion**. ("The Gamesters of Triskelion" [TOS]).

Hajar, Cadet Second Class Jean. (Walker Brandt). Team navigator of Starfleet Academy's ill-fated Nova Squadron in 2368. ("The First Duty" [TNG]). SEE: **Locarno, Cadet First Class Nicholas.**

Halee System. Star system containing more than one planet barely capable of sustaining humanoid life. Worf, speaking for the Klingon renegades **Korris** and **Konmel**, suggested they be allowed to die on their feet on a planet in the Halee system rather than being executed. ("Heart of Glory" [TNG]).

• **"Half a Life."** *Next Generation* episode #96. Teleplay by Peter Allan Fields. Story by Ted Roberts and Peter Allan Fields. Directed by Les Landau. Stardate 44805.3. *First aired in 1991. A scientist must decide between helping his people or conforming to his society's expectation of ritual suicide at age 60.* SEE: **B'tardat; Dara; helium fusion enhancement; helium ignition test; Kaelon II; Kaelon warships; Mantickian Paté; neutron migration; oskoid; Praxillus system; Resolution, The; Rigel IV; Timicin, Dr.; torpedo sustainer engines.**

Hali. (James McIntire). A young **Mintakan** bowman. He pursued the escaping Riker and **Dr. Palmer** after the accidental exposure of a Federation science team on his planet in 2363. ("Who Watches the Watchers?" [TNG]).

Halii. Homeworld of a partially telepathic race called the Haliians. Starfleet **lieutenant Aquiel Uhnari** was a native of this planet. SEE: **Batarael; Canar; Horath; Muskan seed punch;** *oumriel*; **Shiana.** ("Aquiel" [TNG]).

Halkans. Humanoid civilization with a history of total peace. In 2267, they refused the Federation permission to mine dilithium crystals on their planet for fear the dilithium would someday be used for acts of destruction. The Halkan race in the **mirror universe** was also peaceful, preferring to die rather than turn the mining rights over to the Empire, the Federation's barbaric counterpart in the parallel universe. ("Mirror, Mirror" [TOS]).

Hall of Audiences. Location on planet **Beta III** where planetary leader **Landru** could be summoned. Kirk and Spock, visiting Beta III in 2267, were led there by government official **Marphon**, where they eventually destroyed the computer that had replaced the original man named Landru. ("Return of the Archons" [TOS]).

Halley's comet. A spectacular ball of ice that travels a predictable course through Earth's Solar System. Halley's comet is visible from Earth at its perihelion, which occurs approximately every 76 years. Noted Earth writer **Samuel Clemens**, visiting the *Starship Enterprise*-D, wondered if one could see Halley's comet from the ship. ("Time's Arrow, Part II" [TNG]).

Halloway, Captain Thomas. The captain of the *Enterprise*-D in an alternate history created when Q allowed Picard to relive his fight at the Bonestell Recreation Facility. ("Tapestry" [TNG]).

Hamlet. A tragic historical play by **William Shakespeare** about Hamlet, the prince of Denmark, a story of murder and revenge. *Hamlet* was written around AD 1600, and still is read and performed in the 23rd and 24th centuries. The **Karidian Company of Players** conducted an interstellar theatrical tour of Shakespearean performances, including *Hamlet*. ("The Conscience of the King" [TOS]).

Captain Picard quoted from *Hamlet* in an effort to convince **Q** of the worthiness of human beings. ("Hide and Q" [TNG]).

hammer. Tool used for pounding. In Klingon culture, the hammer is considered a symbol of power. The Taqua tribe of Nagor regards it as representing hearth and home, but the Ferengi treat it as a symbol of sexual prowess. ("Birthright, Part I" [TNG]).

Hammurabi, Code of. Important milestone in the evolution of law on planet Earth, the Code of Hammurabi dated back to ancient Babylon, and was one of that planet's first major attempts to develop a uniform system of justice. It included significant legal protections for individual rights. ("Court Martial" [TOS]).

Hanar. (Stewart Moss). **Kelvan** who assisted in the capture of the *Enterprise* landing party and forced the crew to set a course for the **Andromeda Galaxy**. In an effort to distract Hanar in his unfamiliar humanoid form, McCoy injected him with **formazine** stimulant. ("By Any Other Name" [TOS]).

hand phaser. SEE: **phaser type-1**.

hangar deck. A large facility on Federation starships that permitted the launch and recovery of **shuttlecraft**. On *Constitution*-class starships, the hangar deck was located in the engineering hull, with large doors at the aft. The hangar deck had an upper level that included an observation corridor and a control room. In later starships, the hangar deck became known as the **shuttlebay**. *In the original* Star Trek

series, the hangar deck was a miniature set (supplemented with a small portion that was built full-sized) that was first seen in "The Galileo *Seven," then later in "Journey to Babel," "The Immunity Syndrome," and "Let That Be Your Last Battlefield." The obser-*

vation corridor (but not the hangar deck below) was seen in "Conscience of the King" (TOS).

Hanoli system. Location of a subspace rupture encountered by a Vulcan ship around 2169. The Vulcans detonated a **pulse wave torpedo** into the rupture, accidentally setting off a chain reaction that destroyed the entire Hanoli system. The command crew from Deep Space 9 reviewed these events when a similar subspace rupture was suspected near the station in 2369. ("If Wishes Were Horses" [DS9]).

Hanolin asteroid belt. Site where a **Ferengi cargo shuttle** crashed in early 2368. Parts of the Vulcan ship *T'Pau* were found in the wreckage. Investigation of the wreckage eventually led to the discovery of a Romulan plot to conquer Vulcan. ("Unification, Part I" [TNG]).

Hansen, Commander. (Garry Walberg). Starfleet officer in charge of **Romulan Neutral Zone** outpost 4, killed during the Romulan incursion of 2266. ("Balance of Terror" [TOS]).

Hansen's Planet. Class-M world on which were found humanoid creatures similar to those discovered on planet **Taurus II**. ("The *Galileo* Seven" [TOS]).

Hanson, Admiral J. P. (George Murdock). Starfleet admiral who led the Federation defense against the **Borg** attack at **Wolf 359** in early 2367. Hanson was killed in that battle, along with 11,000 other Starfleet personnel. Hanson had been in charge of Starfleet Tactical's effort to develop a defense against the Borg, but the attack came much sooner than expected, catching

Starfleet unprepared against the vastly superior Borg weaponry. Hanson had been a friend of Jean-Luc Picard. ("The Best of Both Worlds, Parts I and II" [TNG]). *Actor George Murdock had previously played the false god-image in* Star Trek V.

Hanson, Mr. (Hagan Beggs). *Enterprise* relief helmsman. ("Court Martial" [TOS], "The Menagerie" [TOS]).

Haritath. (Mark L. Taylor). Member of the **Tau Cygna V** colony; this young man was one of the first colonists to greet Commander Data upon his arrival there in 2366. Haritath agreed with Data that the colony should be evacuated, despite **Gosheven**'s objections. ("The Ensigns of Command" [TNG]).

harmonic resonators. SEE: **resonators**.

Haro, Mitena. (Joycelyn O'Brien). Apparently a **Bolian** first-year Academy cadet, Haro was found to be a false identity created by unknown life-forms that kidnapped Jean-Luc Picard, **Esoqq**, and **Kova Tholl** in 2366. This abduction was part of an experiment to study the nature of authority, a concept unknown to these telepathically linked life-forms, since they were all identical. The life-forms had replaced all the abductees with near-perfect copies, then altered the behavior of the individual copied and observed the reactions of their associates. ("Allegiance" [TNG]). *The alien life-forms were not given a name in the episode.*

Harod IV. Planet where the *Enterprise*-D made an unscheduled stop to pick up a group of stranded miners on stardate 45761. ("The Perfect Mate" [TNG]).

Harodian miners. (David Paul Needles, Roger Rignack, Charles Gunning). Three humanoids who were picked up for emergency transport by the *Enterprise*-D on stardate 45761, while the ship was en route to planet **Krios**. The miners subsequently created a small disturbance in the ship's Ten-Forward lounge while in the presence of the Kriosian metamorph, **Kamala**. ("The Perfect Mate" [TNG]).

Harper, Ensign. (Sean Morgan). Engineer aboard the original *Starship Enterprise* who was one of the twenty crew left on board the ship for the disastrous **M-5** drills in 2268. He was killed when the **multitronic** unit tapped into the ship's energy supply. ("The Ultimate Computer" [TOS]).

Harrakis V. Planet that the *Enterprise*-D visited in 2367. The ship's mission there was completed earlier than expected, and the crew was allotted extra personal time. ("Clues" [TNG]).

Harris, Captain. Commander of the *Starship Excalibur* who was killed, along with the rest of his crew, during the disastrous **M-5** test exercises in 2268. ("The Ultimate Computer" [TOS]).

Harrison, William B. Flight officer of the ***S.S. Beagle*** Harrison was killed in a brutal televised gladiator game on planet 892-IV in 2267. ("Bread and Circuses" [TOS]).

Harrison. Crew member aboard the original *Starship Enterprise* in 2267. Kirk recorded a commendation for Harrison when the bridge of the *Enterprise* was slowly deprived of life support during **Khan**'s takeover attempt. ("Space Seed" [TOS]).

Haru Outpost. As part of their terrorist war against the Cardassians, Kira Nerys and other Bajoran freedom fighters conducted raids on the Haru Outpost. Years later, Kira admitted to Odo that she still had nightmares about the incident. ("Past Prologue" [DS9]).

Haskins, Dr. Theodore. (Jon Lormer). Scientist with the American Continent Institute, killed when the ***S.S. Columbia*** crashed on planet **Talos IV** in 2236. An illusory version of

Haskins, created by the **Talosians**, greeted Captain Pike and an *Enterprise* landing party in 2254. ("The Cage," "The Menagerie, Part I" [TOS]).

Hathaway, U.S.S. *Constellation*-class Federation starship, registry number NCC-2593. Launched in 2285, the ship was decommissioned prior to 2365 when it was temporarily returned to duty under the command of William Riker as part of a **Starfleet battle simulation**. ("Peak Performance" [TNG]). SEE: **Avidyne engines**. *The interior of the* Hathaway *bridge was a re-dress of the* Enterprise-D *battle bridge, although the control panels and display graphics employed movie-style designs from the* Enterprise-A. *The* Hathaway *miniature was a re-dress of the* **Stargazer** *built for "The Battle" (TNG). The Starship Hathaway may have been named for Anne Hathaway, the woman who married William Shakespeare. The dedication plaque for the ship carried a notation that it had been built by Yoyodyne Propulsion Systems at the Copernicus Ship Yards on Luna.*

Havana, U.S.S. Federation starship. The *Enterprise*-D was to rendezvous with the *Havana* after studying the **Bersallis firestorms** of 2369. ("Lessons" [TNG]).

Haven. Class-M planet known for its extraordinary, peaceful beauty. Legends suggest that the planet is so beautiful it has mystical healing powers. A **Tarellian** spacecraft, carrying the last survivors of the Tarellian biological war, attempted to make planetfall on Haven in 2364. The government of Haven strongly objected to this for fear that the Tarellian plague victims would contaminate the entire planet. Haven is also known as Beta Cassius. ("Haven" [TNG]).

• **"Haven."** *Next Generation* episode #5. Teleplay by Tracy Tormé. Story by Tracy Tormé & Lan Okun. Directed by Richard Compton. Stardate 41294.5. *First aired in 1987. Deanna Troi's mother, Lwaxana, visits the* Enterprise-D *for her daughter's wedding. "Haven" was the first appearance of Majel Barrett in the recurring role of Lwaxana Troi, and her aide, Mr. Homn. Episode director Richard Compton had, during the original* Star Trek *series, played the part of Lieutenant Washburn in "The Doomsday Machine" (TOS). Coincidentally, the first assistant director of "Haven" was Charles Washburn (who had also worked on the original series). SEE:* **Alcyones; Ariana; Beta Cassius; Betazed; Betazed, Holy Rings of; Betazoids; bonding gifts; chameleon rose; chime, Betazoid; Fifth House of Betazed; gift box, Betazoid; genetic bonding; Haven; Homn; Innis, Valeda; marriage, Betazoid; Miller, Wyatt; Miller, Steven; Miller, Victoria; Sacred Chalice of Rixx; Tarella; Tarellians; Troi, Deanna; Troi, Lwaxana; Wrenn; Xelo.**

Hawking, Dr. Stephen William. (Himself). Considered one of the most brilliant theoretical physicists of 20th-century Earth. Hawking developed a quantum theory of gravity, in which he sought to link the two major theories of physics, quantum mechanics and relativity. Hawking also speculated on the existence of **wormholes** and **quantum fluctuations** linking multiple universes.

Hawking's scientific achievements were all the more remarkable because he was afflicted with a debilitating neural disease that kept him confined to a wheelchair, able to speak only with the aid of a speech-synthesis computer.

Commander Data devised a holodeck program that allowed him to play poker with Dr. Hawking, **Albert Einstein** and **Sir Isaac Newton**. ("Descent, Part I" [TNG]).

Professor Hawking's appearance on Star Trek *was the result of a visit he made to Paramount Pictures to promote his motion-picture version of* A Brief History of Time. *At Paramount, he made known his dream of visiting the* Enterprise. *Hawking not only got to visit the sets, but he persuaded* Star Trek's *producers to let him make an appearance on the screen. While passing through the Main Engineering set, Hawking paused near the warp engine, smiled, and said, "I'm working on that."*

Hawking, Shuttlecraft. Shuttle attached to the *Enterprise*-D that carried **Ambassador Odan** on an aborted flight to a peace conference on planet **Peliar Zel** in 2367. The *Hawking* was attacked by forces seeking to block the conference. ("The Host" [TNG]). *Named for 20th-century mathematical physicist and* Star Trek *fan Dr. Stephen Hawking.*

Hawkins. Federation ambassador to planet **Mordan IV**. Hawkins was taken hostage by Mordan governor **Karnas** in 2364, although Karnas blamed the act on dissident terrorists. ("Too Short a Season" [TNG]).

Hayashi system. The location of an atmospheric charting mission conducted by the *Enterprise*-D in 2366. ("Tin Man" [TNG]).

Hayne. (Donald Mirault). Leader of the **Coalition** cadre of planet **Turkana IV**. A charismatic human male, Hayne helped lead his people in their ongoing battle with their rival faction, the **Alliance**. In 2367, Hayne offered his assistance to the crew of the *Enterprise*-D on their mission to rescue the crew of the downed freighter *Arcos* from the Alliance. Hayne hoped to use the incident to gain a tactical advantage over his enemies. ("Legacy" [TNG]).

heading. In celestial navigation, a mathematical expression describing a direction with relationship to the center of the galaxy.

A heading is composed of two numbers measuring an azimuth value and an elevation value in degrees. A heading of 000, mark 0 describes a direction toward the geometric center of the galaxy. In terms of navigation on a planet's surface, this is analogous to describing a direction in degrees from north, in which case a course of 5 degrees would be slightly to the right of a direction directly toward the planet's north pole. A heading differs from a bearing in that it has no

relationship to the current attitude or orientation of the spacecraft. SEE: **bearing**. *Illustration: Both ships have an azimuth heading of 030. A heading of 000 for either ship would be toward the center of the galaxy.*

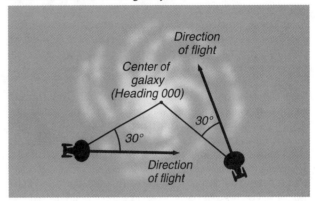

• **"Heart of Glory."** *Next Generation* episode #20. Teleplay by Maurice Hurley. Story by Maurice Hurley and Herbert Wright & D. C. Fontana. Directed by Rob Bowman. Stardate 41503.7. *First aired in 1988. A group of Klingon renegades tries to capture the* Enterprise-D. *Except for Worf, this episode marked the first appearance of Klingons in* Star Trek: The Next Generation. *The Talarians, whose ship we see in this episode, are also seen in "Suddenly Human" (TNG), although with a different ship.* SEE: ***Batris***; **Gault**; **Halee System**; **K'nera**; **Kling**; **Klingon death ritual**; **Klingon Defense Force**; **Konmel, Lieutenant**; **Korris, Captain**; **Kunivas**; **Merculite rockets**; ***T'Acog, I.K.C.***; **Talarians**; **VISOR**; **Visual Acuity Transmitter**; **Worf**.

heart of *targ*. A traditional Klingon dish. Commander Riker tasted some of this stuff when he tried to acquaint himself with Klingon culture prior to his temporary assignment to the ***Pagh*** in 2365. ("A Matter of Honor" [TNG]). SEE: ***targ***.

heater. Slang term on planet **Sigma Iotia II** for firearms. The Iotians referred to a Starfleet phaser as a "fancy heater." ("A Piece of the Action" [TOS]).

heavy graviton beam. A directed energy weapon considered for possible use against the **Borg** during the Borg offensive of 2367. The idea was abandoned when it was determined that local field distortion generation would be ineffective against Borg defenses. ("The Best of Both Worlds, Part II" [TNG]).

Hechu' ghos. A Klingon phrase meaning "set course," as in to set a ship's course. ("Unification, Part I" [TNG]).

Hedford, Commissioner Nancy. (Elinor Donahue). Assistant Federation commissioner who was assigned to mediate a peace agreement on planet **Epsilon Canaris III** in 2267 in an effort to avert an impending war. Hedford was forced

to leave the negotiations prematurely when she contracted deadly **Sakuro's disease**. Commissioner Hedford died aboard the *Shuttlecraft Galileo* while being transported to the *Starship Enterprise*. ("Metamorphosis" [TOS]). *Hedford, of course, did not die in space, but merged with the life-form known as the* **Companion**, *on a planetoid in the* **Gamma Canaris region**, *where she found love with noted scientist* **Zefram Cochrane**. *Since Kirk promised never to reveal this information, a Federation encyclopedia would not have it.*

Hegh'bat ceremony. Literally translated as "The Time to Die," the *Hegh'bat* ceremony was a Klingon ritualized suicide. Klingon tradition held that when a Klingon was unable to stand and face his enemies, he should chose the *Hegh'bat*. The rite called for the eldest son of the celebrant, or a trusted friend, to deliver a ritual knife to the warrior, who would impale himself in the chest. The son or friend would then remove the knife and wipe it on his sleeve. Following a severe spinal injury in 2368, Lieutenant **Worf** considered the *Hegh'bat*, but was dissuaded from completing the ritual when offered the alternative of **genetronic replication** therapy. ("Ethics" [TNG]).

Hegh'ta. A Klingon Bird-of-Prey, commanded by **Kurn** during the **Klingon civil war** of 2367-68 in support of the **Gowron** regime. Worf served briefly aboard this ship as tactical officer during that conflict. ("Redemption, Part I" [TNG]).

Heifetz. A famous concert violinist whose performance style **Data** programmed himself to emulate. ("Sarek" [TNG]).

Heisenberg compensators. Component of a transporter system, designed to permit the derivation of precision vector and positional data of particles on a subatomic level. ("Realm of Fear" [TNG]). Picard suggested disengaging the Heisenberg compensators as a possible means of giving physical reality to the computer intelligence version of **Professor James Moriarty**, but it was a ruse to buy time. ("Ship in a Bottle" [TNG]). *Heisenberg's "uncertainty principle" suggests that on a subatomic level, it is possible to know the motion or the position of a particle, but not both. Some scientists have suggested this basic characteristic of matter may make a transporter impossible, so we suggested the "Heisenberg compensator" as a bit of a scientific gag to "explain" how the transporter does it anyway. (No, we don't have any idea how it would work.)*

helium fusion enhancement. Theoretical technique that would increase the energy output of a dying star by increasing the temperature and pressure inside the star so that the star begins helium fusion, thus increasing the star's useful life. A test of this technique, designed by **Dr. Timicin** of planet **Kaelon II** in 2367, used shock waves from a carefully controlled series of photon torpedo explosions to create zones of elevated pressure where helium ignition could occur. ("Half a Life" [TNG]).

helium ignition test. Experiment conducted by **Dr. Timicin** in 2367 to test his helium fusion enhancement theories. The initial test was a dramatic failure, causing a red giant star to go supernova. Further testing was required, but the elderly

Timicin returned to his homeworld for his **Resolution**, hoping that others would continue his work. ("Half a Life" [TNG]).

helm. Aboard a starship, the control station and officer responsible for actually flying the ship. In more recent Federation starships, this function was merged with the duties of the **navigator**, and dubbed conn, or **flight controller**. *Mr. Sulu was the helmsman aboard the* Starship Enterprise *during the original* Star Trek *series. The term helm or helmsman was replaced with conn at the beginning of* Star Trek: The Next Generation.

Hendorff, Ensign. (Mal Friedman). *Enterprise* crew member who was killed by a poisonous plant on planet **Gamma Trianguli VI** in 2267. ("The Apple" [TOS]).

Hendrick, Chief. (Dennis Madalone). *Enterprise*-D transporter officer who was on duty when the transformed **Commander La Forge** beamed down to the surface of **Tarchannen III** in 2367. La Forge overpowered Hendrick and he was unable to stop the transport. ("Identity Crisis" [TNG]). *Dennis "Danger" Madalone is stunt coordinator for* Star Trek: The Next Generation *and* Star Trek: Deep Space Nine, *and has been seen as a variety of security guards and other victims of mayhem.*

Hengist, Mr. (John Fiedler). Originally a resident of **Rigel IV**, later employed as a city administrator on planet **Argelius II**. Hengist's body was possessed by an evil energy life-form that thrived on the emotion of terror and was responsible for several brutal murders. This entity, which traveled to Argelius II in Hengist's body, was also known as **Redjac**, **Beratis**, **Kesla**, and **Jack the Ripper**. ("Wolf in the Fold" [TOS]).

Henoch. (Leonard Nimoy). One of three advanced beings who survived a devastating war that destroyed their planet 500,000 years ago. *U.S.S. Enterprise* personnel discovered Henoch and the other two survivors in 2268, their consciousness having been encased in receptacles stored in an underground vault. Upon his revival, Henoch's intellect was allowed to "borrow" Spock's body so that **android** bodies could be constructed for the survivors. Henoch was, however, unable to leave behind his old hatreds, and tried to destroy **Sargon** and **Thalassa** before being destroyed himself. ("Return to Tomorrow" [TOS]). SEE: **Sargon's planet**.

Henry V. Classic drama written by William Shakespeare on Earth. A holographic performance of this play was available on the *Enterprise*-D holodeck. In this simulation, the holodeck participant can perform one of the roles. Data chose this play as part of his ongoing study of the human condition. ("The Defector" [TNG]). *Patrick Stewart played the holographic image of Michael Williams, a character in the drama.*

Henry, Admiral Thomas. (Earl Billings). Starflet admiral in charge of security. Admiral Henry visited the *Enterprise*-D in 2367 at the request of **Admiral Norah Satie**, who suspected a serious security breach on that ship. Henry ordered Satie's investigation discontinued after determining that her investigation was proceeding without probable cause and in violation of the Federation Constitution's **Seventh Guarantee** against self-incrimination. ("The Drumhead" [TNG]).

Henshaw, Christi. (Julie Warner). *Enterprise*-D crew member, a woman that Geordi found quite attractive. Henshaw and Geordi La Forge had a date on the holodeck just prior to the discovery of the *Cleponji* in 2366. Although La Forge put a lot of effort into making the holodeck program a romantic experience, Christi eventually told him that she didn't feel "that way"  about him. ("Booby Trap" [TNG]). Later that year, when Geordi's self-confidence was improved after his **neuro-link** with **"John Doe,"** Christi found Geordi much more attractive. ("Transfigurations" [TNG]).

Herbert, Transporter Chief. (Lance Spellerberg). *Enterprise*-D transporter officer. ("We'll Always Have Paris" [TNG]). *Actor Lance Spellerberg also appeared as a transporter operator in "The Icarus Factor" (TNG).*

Herbert. Derogatory term taken from a minor government official known for his rigid patterns of thought. **Dr. Sevrin**'s followers were very fond of calling Captain Kirk by that name. ("The Way to Eden" [TOS]).

Hermes, U.S.S. Federation starship, *Antares* class, Starfleet registry number NCC-10376. The *Hermes* served in Picard's armada to blockade the Romulan supply ships supplying the **Duras** family forces during the **Klingon civil war** of 2368. ("Redemption, Part II" [TNG]).

• **"Hero Worship."** *Next Generation* episode #111. Teleplay by Joe Menosky. Story by Hilary J. Bader. Directed by Patrick Stewart. Stardate 45397.3. *First aired in 1992. A young boy whose parents are killed in a terrible disaster copes by deciding he is an android, just like Data. This episode was being filmed at the time of the death of* Star Trek *creator Gene Roddenberry.* SEE: **Black Cluster; Breen; Dokkaran temple; Elamos the Magnificent; enantiodromia; Felton, Ensign; Hutchinson, Transporter Chief; La Forge, Geordi; Starbase 514; Tagas; Tamarian frost; Timothy; user code clearance; *Vico, S.S.*; victurium alloy.**

Hesperan Thumping Cough. A flu-like affliction. Wesley Crusher noted that the effects of a virus he contracted on **Quazulu VIII** were worse than Hesperan Thumping Cough. ("Angel One" [TNG]).

Hickman, Lieutenant Paul. (Amick Byram). Former crew member of the *U.S.S. Victory* who beamed down to planet **Tarchannen III** in 2362. In 2367, Hickman was compelled to steal a Federation shuttle and return to Tarchannen III. Hickman's shuttle was destroyed attempting to land on the planet. It was later discovered that Hickman's body had been infiltrated by an alien DNA strand in 2362. ("Identity Crisis" [TNG]).

• **"Hide and Q."** *Next Generation* episode #11. Teleplay by C. J. Holland and Gene Roddenberry. Story by C. J. Holland. Directed by Cliff Bole. Stardate 41590.5. *First aired in 1987. Q offers Riker the gift of godlike powers. This episode marked the first return of Q following his initial appearance in "Encounter at Farpoint."* SEE: **Aldebaran serpent;** *Hamlet***; Q; Quadra Sigma III; Riker, William T.; Shakespeare, William; Sigma III Solar System; Starbase G-6.**

Higa Metar. **Bajoran** underground organization active when planet **Bajor** was occupied by the **Cardassians**. Bajoran geneticist **Dekon Elig** was a member of the Higa Metar. ("Babel" [DS9]).

High Council. SEE: **Klingon High Council.**

• **"High Ground, The."** *Next Generation* episode #60. Written by Melinda M. Snodgrass. Directed by Gabrielle Beaumont. Stardate 43510.7. *First aired in 1990. Beverly Crusher is captured by a terrorist who hopes to draw the Federation into his struggle for freedom.* SEE: **Ansata; Devos, Alexana; Elway Theorem; Finn, Kyril; inverter; Ireland; Rutia IV; Rutians; Shaw, Katik; shuttlebus; subspace transition rebound.**

high energy X-ray laser. A ship-mounted weapon in use aboard **Talarian** warships in 2367. ("Suddenly Human" [TNG]). *High-energy X-ray lasers have a basis in 20th-century technology, developed as part of the Strategic Defense Initiative, better known as "Star Wars."*

Hildebrandt. (Anne H. Gillespie). Specialist in volcanology and geomechanics aboard the *Enterprise*-D. Hildebrandt assisted in the geological survey of planets in the **Selcundi Drema** Sector in 2365. ("Pen Pals" [TNG]).

hill people. Tribe of hunter-gatherers on **Tyree**'s planet living in huts and caves. Lieutenant **James T. Kirk** visited these people in 2254 when he commanded his first planet survey. Kirk returned in 2267 to find the hill people facing their neighbors, the villagers, as enemies. ("A Private Little War" [TOS]). *Kirk was apparently a crew member aboard the U.S.S. Farragut at the time of his first visit.*

Hill, Dixon. (Patrick Stewart, sort of). Fictional private detective from the Dixon Hill series of short stories and novels set in San Francisco, Earth, in the 1930s and 1940s. The character first appeared in the short story **"The Big Goodbye"** published in pulp magazine *Amazing Detective Stories* in 1934. Dixon Hill novels have included *The Long*

Dark Tunnel (published 1936) and ***The Parrot's Claw*** (published circa 1940). *Enterprise*-D captain Jean-Luc Picard was an aficionado of the Dixon Hill stories and enjoyed holodeck simulations based on them. ("The Big Goodbye" [TNG]). The Dixon Hill holodeck program is sufficiently sophisticated that Picard once instructed the computer to "improvise" and create the Dixon Hill environment only without any specific story elements. Picard's attempt to enjoy the resulting scenario was unfortunately ruined when Betazoid ambassador **Lwaxana Troi** wandered into the simulation and became attracted to one of the characters, unaware that he was merely a simulation. ("Manhunt" [TNG]). Picard introduced Guinan to the Dixon Hill adventures while the *Enterprise*-D was en route to Evadne IV. ("Clues" [TNG]). *The computer readout studied by Data when reading the Dixon Hill stories in "The Big Goodbye" (TNG) lists episode writer Tracy Tormé as the author of Hill's adventures.* SEE: **Bell, Lieutenant Dan; Bradley, Jessica; Leech, Felix; Madeline; *Parrot's Claw, The*; Redblock, Cyrus.**

Hill, Dr. Richard. An *Enterprise*-D staff physician. He was one of the first crew members to disappear from Beverly Crusher's universe during her entrapment in a **static warp bubble** in 2367. ("Remember Me" [TNG]).

Hindu Festival of Lights. Also known as Divali, the Festival of Lights celebrates the return of Rama to his kingdom to become the rightful king. Celebrants would light rows of oil lamps or candles to welcome Rama home. In 2367, the festival was celebrated on board the *Enterprise*-D on stardate 44390, a day that saw four crew birthdays, two personnel transfers, two chess tournaments, a school play, two promotions, a birth, and a wedding. ("Data's Day" [TNG]).

hippocampus. A component of the limbic system in a humanoid brain. The hippocampus coordinates the olfaction, autonomic functions, and some aspects of emotional behavior. ("Violations" [TNG], "Conundrum" [TNG]).

histamine. Biochemical substance produced by the breakdown of histidine, an amino acid found in humanoid tissues. Histamine is produced by the body when it comes in contact with substances to which the body is sensitized, and is a primary factor in the humanoid allergic response. Histamine levels are characteristically depressed by a disease known as **Iresine Syndrome**. ("Violations" [TNG]).

Hobson, Lieutenant Commander Christopher. (Timothy Carhart). Starfleet officer who served as Data's first officer aboard the *U.S.S. Sutherland* during the Starfleet blockade of the Romulan border in 2368. His first official act in that position was to request a transfer off the ship. ("Redemption, Part II" [TNG]).

Hodgkins' Law of Parallel Planet Development. Sociologic theory postulating that similar planets with similar populations and similar environments will evolve in similar ways. Planet 892-IV was an example of this principle in that it was technologically similar to 20th-century Earth, but culturally it resembled the ancient Roman Empire. ("Bread and Circuses"

[TOS]). SEE: **892, Planet IV.**

Hodin. (David Hurst). Prime minister of planet **Gideon** in 2268 and father to **Odona**. Hoden masterminded a desperate plan to abduct *Enterprise* captain James T. Kirk to help alleviate the overpopulation crisis facing his planet. ("The Mark of Gideon" [TOS]).

Hoek IV. Planet located in the Lantar Nebula, where the famed Sampalo relics are located. **Q** tempted archeologist **Vash** with viewing the Sampalo relics located on Hoek IV but she declined. ("Q-Less" [DS9]). *Hoek IV was definitely* not *a reference to* Ren and Stimpy. *Nope.*

Hoex. Ferengi entrepreneur who bought out his rival **Turot's** controlling interest in a cargo port on **Volchok Prime** in 2369. ("The Nagus" [DS9]).

Hokule'a*-class starship.** Conjectural designation for a type of Federation ship. The ***U.S.S. Tripoli, the ship whose crew discovered **Data** at **Omicron Theta** in 2338, was a *Hokule'a*-class starship. ("Datalore" [TNG]). *From the Hawaiian word meaning "star of gladness."*

Holberg 917G. Planetoid in the Omega system that was home to the (nearly) immortal **Mr. Flint**. Holberg 917G was also a source of the rare mineral **ryetalyn**, an antidote to deadly Rigelian fever that infested the crew of the *Starship Enterprise* in 2269. ("Requiem for Methuselah" [TOS]). *Flint's castle exterior was a re-use of the Rigel fortress matte painting originally created for "The Cage" (TOS).*

"hole in space." A spatial phenomenon created by the extra-dimensional being called **Nagilum**. This phenomenon was used by Nagilum as a means of entrapping the starships *Yamato* and *Enterprise*-D. ("Where Silence Has Lease" [TNG]).

Hollander, Eli. (John Pyper-Ferguson). Holodeck character, known as The Butcher of Bozeman, from the program ***Ancient West***. ("A Fistful of Datas" [TNG]). *Bozeman is the hometown in Montana of* Star Trek: The Next Generation *writer Brannon Braga.*

Hollander, Frank. Holodeck character in the ***Ancient West*** program. Father of **Eli Hollander**. ("A Fistful of Datas" [TNG]).

Holliday, Doc. (Sam Gilman). Dentist in the early American West who fought on the side of the Earps against the Clanton family at the famous gunfight at the **OK Corral** in **Tombstone, Arizona,** in October of 1881. ("Spectre of the Gun" [TOS]).

• **"Hollow Pursuits."** *Next Generation* episode #69. Written by Sally Caves. Directed by Cliff Bole. Stardate 43807.4. *First* *aired in 1990. A reclusive* Enterprise-*D engineer compensates for his social awkwardness by creating holodeck simulations in which he is king. This episode features the first appearance of Reginald Barclay.* SEE: **antigravs; Barclay, Reginald; "Broccoli"; Correllium fever; Costa, Lieutenant; cryonetrium; Duffy, Lieutenant; Gleason, Captain; "Goddess of Empathy"; graviton inverter circuit; holodeck; holodiction; invidium; jakmanite; lucrovexitrin; Mikulaks; Nahmi IV; nucleosynthesis; saltzgadum; selgninaem; sensors; Terkim; transporter test article;** *Zhukov, U.S.S.*

Holmes, Sherlock. London's greatest consulting detective, a fictional character created in 1887 by novelist **Sir Arthur Conan Doyle**. Enterprise-*D operations manager Data was an aficionado of Holmes's adventures, having read and memorized all of Doyle's Holmes stories after Riker suggested Holmes's approach might help solve the murder of an **Antican** delegate. ("Lonely Among Us" [TNG]). Data enjoyed Sherlock Holmes simulations on the holodeck. ("Elementary, Dear Data" [TNG], "Ship in a Bottle" [TNG]). SEE: **Sherlock Holmes program 3A**.

holodeck matter. A partially stable form of matter created by transporter-based replicators for use in **holodeck** simulations. This material is stable only within a holographic environment simulator; if removed from the holodeck, it degrades into energy. The characters of **Felix Leach** and **Cyrus Redblock** were composed of holodeck matter and disintegrated when they attempted to leave the holodeck. ("The Big Goodbye" [TNG]). **Professor James Moriarty** agreed to remain within the holodeck to avoid the same fate. ("Elementary, Dear Data" [TNG]). Moriarty later devised an elaborate scheme, simulating an entire starship within the holodeck, in an effort to convince the Enterprise-*D crew that he had devised a method of existing outside the holodeck. ("Ship in a Bottle" [TNG]). In 2369, in an unsuccessful attempt to fulfill **Professor James Moriarty**'s wish to leave the holodeck, the crew of the Enterprise-*D conducted an experiment during which they attempted to beam holodeck matter off the grid and into the real transporter system. ("Ship in a Bottle" [TNG]).

Holodeck and holosuite programs. *This is a partial listing of the various simulation programs from the* Enterprise-*D as well as* Deep Space 9. *In most cases, the episodes gave no formal names for the programs, so we have given them descriptive titles. The holodeck computer gives users a great deal of discretion in customizing a simulation to his or her specific wishes, so some of these may simply be user variations of other programs.*

Aikido 1. Martial-arts exercise program. ("Code of Honor" [TNG]).

Altonian brain teaser. Try to relax and make the multicolored sphere turn into a single color. It ain't easy. ("A Man Alone" [DS9]).

Alture VII relaxation program. Bathes you in a protein bath, then carries you off on a

cloud of chromal vapor. ("Birthright, Part I" [TNG]).

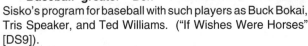

Ancient West. Re-creation of a town on the 19th-century American wild frontier. ("A Fistful of Datas" [TNG]).

Barclay programs. Series of customized programs designed by Reginald Barclay. ("Hollow Pursuits" [TNG]).

Baseball greats. Ben Sisko's program for baseball with such players as Buck Bokai, Tris Speaker, and Ted Williams. ("If Wishes Were Horses" [DS9]).

Boreth. The Klingon monastery where Worf met the clone of Kahless the Unforgettable. ("Rightful Heir" [TNG]).

Cafe des Artistes. A French sidewalk cafe located in Paris. ("We'll Always Have Paris" [TNG]).

Champs-Elysees. The famous section of the city of Paris. ("The Perfect Mate" [TNG]).

Charnock's Comedy Cabaret. A 20th-century comedy club. ("The Outrageous Okona" [TNG]).

Christmas Carol, A. Dramatization of the classic Charles Dickens story. ("Devil's Due" [TNG]).

Cliffs of Heaven. Program 47C, cliff diving on planet Cirrus IV. ("Conundrum" [TNG]).

Curtis Creek. Fly fishing in an Earth stream. ("Future Imperfect" [TNG]).

Dancing lesson. Program Crusher 4, a ballroom setting with simulated dance partners where Beverly Crusher first studied dance. ("Data's Day" [TNG]).

Denubian Alps. Skiing in a spectacular mountain setting. ("Angel One" [TNG]).

Desert sunset. A beautiful desert on a Class-M planet. ("Haven" [TNG]).

Dixon Hill. The 1940s world of San Francisco gumshoe detective Dixon Hill. ("The Big Goodbye" [TNG], "Manhunt" [TNG], "Clues" [TNG]).

Emerald Wading Pool. From planet Sumiko III, a very safe experience. ("Conundrum" [TNG]).

Equestrian adventure. Horse riding in an open countryside with a choice of various mounts. ("Pen Pals" [TNG]).

Einstein, A conversation with. Simulation of Professor Albert Einstein. ("Nth Degree" [TNG]).

Enterprise bridge. The bridge of the original Constitution-class Starship Enterprise. ("Relics" [TNG]).

Henry V. Dramatization of Shakespeare's play. ("The Defector" [TNG]).

Kabul River. Horseback riding in the Himalayas on Earth. ("The Loss" [TNG]).

Kayaking. White-water adventure. ("Transfigurations" [TNG]).

Klingon calisthenics program. Combat exercise program used by Worf. ("Where Silence Has Lease" [TNG], "The Emissary" [TNG], "New Ground" [TNG]).

Klingon Age of Ascension. The ceremony celebrating a warrior's coming of age. ("The Icarus Factor" [TNG]).

Krios 1. The Kriosian Temple of Akadar, used for their Ceremony of Reconciliation. ("The Perfect Mate" [TNG]).

Lauriento massage holoprogram #101A. A beautiful woman with webbed fingers who gives a great backrub. ("A Man Alone" [DS9]).

Low Note, The. New Orleans club on Bourbon Street, with jazz band, circa 1958. ("11001001" [TNG]).

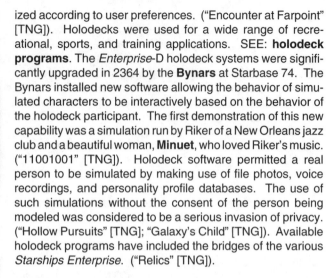

Moonlight on the beach. Site of Geordi's unsuccessful date with Christi Henshaw. ("Booby Trap" [TNG]).

Parallax Colony. A colorful "colony of free spirits." ("Cost of Living" [TNG]).

Parkland. Open grassy field, location of Tasha Yar's memorial service. ("Skin of Evil" [TNG]).

Poker with great scientists. Poker game with simulations of Sir Isaac Newton, Albert Einstein, and Stephen Hawking. ("Descent, Part I" [TNG]).

Riga, Stano. Comedy program based on the noted 23rd-century quantum physicist and humorist. ("The Outrageous Okona" [TNG]).

Romulus. The incredibly beautiful Chula Valley on Romulus. ("The Defector" [TNG]).

Rousseau V. A spectacular asteroid belt. ("The Dauphin" [TNG]).

Sherlock Holmes. Nineteenth-century London according to the works of Sir Arthur Conan Doyle. ("Elementary Dear Data" [TNG], "Ship in a Bottle" [TNG]).

Tanuga Station. Series of simulations used in the extradition trial of William Riker. ("A Matter of Perspective" [TNG]).

Three Musketeers. The classic tale reinterpreted by Reginald Barclay. ("Hollow Pursuits" [TNG]).

Utopia Planitia Fleet Yards. Holodeck file 9140, a drafting room where part of the *Enterprise*-D was designed. ("Booby Trap" [TNG] and "Galaxy's Child" [TNG]).

Wooded parkland. Natural setting with a stream. ("Encounter at Farpoint" [TNG]).

World Series. Including the last professional baseball game ever played. ("If Wishes Were Horses" [DS9]).

holodeck. Also known as a Holographic Environment Simulator, the holodeck permitted the simulation of virtually any environment or person with a degree of fidelity virtually indistinguishable from reality. The holodeck employed three-dimensional holographic projections as well as transporter-based replications of actual objects. A large library of simulations was available in the holodecks of *Galaxy*-class starships, and the holodeck software permitted programs to be custom-

ized according to user preferences. ("Encounter at Farpoint" [TNG]). Holodecks were used for a wide range of recreational, sports, and training applications. SEE: **holodeck programs**. The *Enterprise*-D holodeck systems were significantly upgraded in 2364 by the **Bynars** at Starbase 74. The Bynars installed new software allowing the behavior of simulated characters to be interactively based on the behavior of the holodeck participant. The first demonstration of this new capability was a simulation run by Riker of a New Orleans jazz club and a beautiful woman, **Minuet**, who loved Riker's music. ("11001001" [TNG]). Holodeck software permitted a real person to be simulated by making use of file photos, voice recordings, and personality profile databases. The use of such simulations without the consent of the person being modeled was considered to be a serious invasion of privacy. ("Hollow Pursuits" [TNG]; "Galaxy's Child" [TNG]). Available holodeck programs have included the bridges of the various *Starships Enterprise*. ("Relics" [TNG]).

holodiction. Contraction for **holodeck** addiction. A psychological condition where an individual becomes so caught up in holographic simulations that the real world becomes unimportant. **Reginald Barclay** suffered this affliction when first assigned to the *Enterprise*-D in 2366. ("Hollow Pursuits" [TNG]).

hologenerators. Technical equipment used to generate holographic environment imagery at Quark's bar on Deep Space 9 and similar facilities. Deep Space 9 entrepreneur Quark told **Odo** that he would like to expand into the space next door to his bar on the station's Promenade so that he could use the same hologenerators to create more programs. ("If Wishes Were Horses" [DS9]).

hologram generator. Device used by anthropological field teams to conceal a planetary surface survey station from indigenous life-forms. Use of the holographic image generator allows a team to observe such life-forms at close range without the subjects being aware of the team's presence. The hologram generator used by the field team on **Mintaka III** failed in early 2366, resulting in accidental cultural contamination when the **Mintakans** saw the team and their advanced technology. ("Who Watches the Watchers?" [TNG]).

Holographic Environment Simulator. SEE: **holodeck**.

holosuite. Holographic environment simulators located on the second floor of **Quark's bar** in station **Deep Space 9**. ("Emissary" [DS9]).

Holy Rings of Betazed. SEE: **Betazed, Holy Rings of**.

• **"Home Soil."** *Next Generation* episode #17. Teleplay by Robert Sabaroff. Story by Karl Guers & Ralph Sanchez and Robert Sabaroff. Directed by Corey Allen. Stardate 41463.9. *First aired in 1988. A terraforming project threatens the environment for a race of tiny crystalline life-forms, a fact that the project administrator attempts to conceal.* SEE: **Bensen, Bjorn; Kim, Luisa; Malencon, Arthur; Mandl, Kurt; microbrain; Pleiades Cluster; quarantine seal; Terraform**

Command; terraforming; "Ugly Bags of Mostly Water"; Velara III.

Homeric hymns. A collection of 34 ancient Greek poems usually attributed to Homer of Earth, but written by various authors at various dates. Captain Picard studied the Homeric hymns following his encounter with the **Tamarians** in the hope that by learning more of human mythology, he might better understand the Tamarians. ("Darmok" [TNG]).

Homeworld, Klingon. SEE: **Klingon Homeworld.**

Homn. (Carel Struycken). **Lwaxana Troi**'s attendant. A dignified humanoid male, tall in stature and few in words, with an impressive capacity for intoxicating beverages. ("Haven" [TNG]). Mr. Homn was also quite fond of eating Betazoid uttaberries. ("Ménage à Troi" [TNG]). *Mr. Homn's race and place of origin was not known. Carel Struycken also gained popularity for his portrayal of Lurch in the* Addams Family *motion pictures.*

Hon'Tihl. (Tom Towles). Klingon first officer of the Bird-of-Prey *Toh'Kaht*. Hon'Tihl beamed off his ship just before it exploded, immediately after returning from an exploratory mission into the Gamma Quadrant. Although Hon'Tihl died shortly after beaming to Deep Space 9, his log entries were reviewed by station personnel in an attempt to learn what happened to the ill-fated vessel. ("Dramatis Personae" [DS9]). SEE: **cryostasis; Saltah'na energy spheres; Saltah'na; thalmerite device.**

Honorius. Flavius Honorius (A.D. 384-423), the last Western Roman emperor, who was in power when the Visigoths sacked Rome. Captain Picard, on the eve of the battle of **Wolf 359**, compared the fate of the Federation at the hands of the **Borg** to the defeat of the Roman Empire under Honorius. ("The Best of Both Worlds, Part I" [TNG]).

Hood, U.S.S. *Constitution*-class Federation starship, Starfleet registry number NCC-1703. The *Hood* participated in the disastrous tests of the **M-5** multitronic computer unit in 2268. ("The Ultimate Computer" [TOS]).

Hood, U.S.S. Federation starship, *Excelsior* class, Starfleet registry number NCC-42296. Commanded by Captain **Robert DeSoto**. Commander **William T. Riker** served aboard this ship prior to his assignment to the *Enterprise*-D. ("Encounter at Farpoint, Parts I and II" [TNG]). The *Hood* intercepted the *Enterprise*-D in the **Hayashi system** to deliver **Tam Elbrun** and new orders for the *Enterprise* to proceed to **Beta**

Stromgren for the encounter with **Tin Man** in 2366. ("Tin Man" [TNG]). The *Hood* was one of the starships sent to the Romulan Neutral Zone border in preparation for a possible battle after Starfleet received warnings of a Romulan buildup at planet **Nelvana III** in 2366. The warnings, from Romulan defector **Alidar Jarok,** were later found to be baseless. ("The Defector" [TNG]). The *Hood* was scheduled to join the *Enterprise*-D on a terraforming mission to planet Browder IV in 2366. ("Allegiance" [TNG]). *This was presumably at least the second Federation starship to bear the name. The* Hood *was a re-use of the* Excelsior *model built for Star Trek III. The footage of the* Hood *flying alongside the* Enterprise-D *was re-used numerous times to represent other* Excelsior-*class ships. The ship was named for British admiral Sir Horace Hood, who fought in the Battle of Jutland during World War I.*

Horath. A traditional **Halii** song that **Aquiel Uhnari** used to sing at home during the **Batarael** celebration. ("Aquiel" [TNG]).

Horatio, U.S.S. Federation starship, *Ambassador* class, registry number NCC-10532, commanded by Captain **Walker Keel**. The *Horatio* was destroyed in 2364 near planet **Dytallix B**, apparently by an unknown alien intelligence that attempted to infiltrate Starfleet Command. ("Conspiracy" [TNG]).

Horga'hn. A small Risan statuette resembling a crude wooden carving, the Risan symbol of sexuality. To own one was to call forth its powers and to display one was to announce that the owner was seeking *jamaharon*. Riker requested that Picard bring him back one as a souvenir when the captain visited **Risa** in 2366. It was Riker's attempt to set Picard up for a sexual encounter, but Picard needed no outside assistance in finding companionship. ("Captain's Holiday" [TNG]). *The* Horga'hn *brought back by Picard can sometimes be seen adorning Riker's quarters in later episodes.*

Horizon, U.S.S. Federation starship, *Daedalus* class, Starfleet registry NCC-173. One of the first deep-space exploratory vessels launched by the United Federation of Planets, the *Horizon* visited planet **Sigma Iotia II** in 2168. The *Horizon* was destroyed shortly thereafter, transmitting a distress call by conventional radio that did not reach Federation space until 2268. It was later found that *Horizon* personnel had left a book entitled ***Chicago Mobs of the Twenties*** on the planet, causing severe cultural contamination. The *Horizon* mission predated the establishment of Starfleet's **Prime Directive** of noninterference. ("A Piece of the Action" [TOS]). *The class and registry designations of the* Horizon *are conjectural, but a desktop model bearing that name and number has been seen*

as set decoration on Star Trek: Deep Space Nine.

Horne, Walter. An instructor in Creative Writing at Starfleet Academy. Horne was Captain Picard's professor during the 2320s, and also taught Wesley Crusher in 2368. ("The Game" [TNG]).

Hornet, U.S.S. Federation starship, *Renaissance* class, Starfleet registry number NCC-45231. It served in Picard's armada to blockade Romulan supply ships supplying the **Duras** family forces during the **Klingon civil war** of 2368. ("Redemption, Part II" [TNG]). *The* Hornet *was named for an American ship that fought at the Battle of Midway. Another famous ship with that name was the recovery vessel for the Apollo 11 moon landing mission. SEE:* **Akagi,** *U.S.S.*

Horta. (Janos Prohaska). **Silicon-based life**-form native to planet **Janus VI**. The Horta's natural environment is underground, and it secretes a powerful corrosive acid to enable it to move through solid rock with great ease. Every 50,000 years, all but one Horta dies,  leaving the sole survivor to care for the eggs. This individual becomes the mother to her race. The Horta were discovered in 2267 by Federation mining personnel on Janus VI when a number of unexplained deaths among the miners were found to be caused by the mother Horta protecting her eggs. The miners had unknowingly broken into a subterranean chamber known as the **Vault of Tomorrow**, where the Horta's eggs were stored. The Hortas' true nature were discovered when *Enterprise* science officer Spock mind-melded with the mother Horta. Once a level of understanding was achieved between the Horta and the humans, the Horta had no objection to sharing their planet, and in fact agreed to help the miners harvest the abundant minerals on Janus VI. ("The Devil in the Dark" [TOS]). SEE: **pergium.** *The Horta was designed, built, and performed by Janos Prohaska, who reportedly wore the costume into* Star Trek *producer Gene Coon's office. Coon liked the creature so much he wrote "Devil in the Dark" to feature it.*

• **"Host, The."** *Next Generation* episode #97. Written by Michel Horvat. Directed by Marvin Rush. Stardate 44821.3. *First aired in 1991. A diplomatic mission is endangered when the mediator falls ill and it is learned that he is a helpless symbiotic parasite living inside a host humanoid body. This is the first episode featuring the Trill "joined species."* SEE: **Alpha Moon; Ancient Philosophies; balso tonic; Beta Moon; colgonite astringent; Crusher, Dr. Beverly; eosinophilia; exobiology; global warming;** *Hawking,* *Shuttlecraft;* **host; immunosuppressant; joined species; Kalin Trose; Kareel; Lathal Bine; Leka, Governor Trion; magnetospheric energy taps; metrazene; Odan, Ambassador; Ogawa, Nurse Alyssa; Peliar Zel; Stephan; symbiont; Trill.**

host. In the **Trill** joined species, a host is a humanoid life-form

in whose body resides a Trill **symbiont**. The combination of the two life-forms forms a single Trill individual. ("The Host" [TNG]).

Hotel Brian. Hostelry in 19th-century San Francisco on Earth where Data stayed while in Earth's past. A bellboy there named **Jack London** would one day become a noted literary figure. ("Time's Arrow, Parts I and II" [TNG]). *The Hotel Brian was named for Brian Livingston, son of* Star Trek *producer-director David Livingston. The exterior of Hotel Brian was shot on location in old Pasadena.*

Hotel Royale. An early 21st-century novel written by Todd Matthews concerning a luxury hotel of the same name and the various shady characters inhabiting it. A copy of the novel was carried aboard the explorer ship *Charybdis* when it was launched from Earth in 2037. When an unknown alien intelligence accidentally killed nearly everyone on board the *Charybdis*, the intelligence fabricated the Hotel Royale based on descriptions in the book for **Colonel Stephen Richey**, the sole survivor of the *Charybdis* crew, to live in. Unknown to the alien intelligence, the resulting artificial environment, based on a badly written book, was a kind of hell to Richey, who welcomed death when it came. ("The Royale" [TNG]).

Hovath. (Lawrence Monosoa). Inhabitant of a village on **Bajor** who was apprentice to the **Sirah**. Hovath studied for nine years to be the next Sirah, learning the secrets of the storyteller. Hovath was nevertheless unready to assume the responsibility in 2369 when his mentor was ready to die. The old Sirah took the seemingly irrational step of appointing Miles O'Brien as the new Sirah, thereby motivating Hovath to try much harder. ("The Storyteller" [DS9]).

hoverball. Sport involving a small ball equipped with an antigravity suspension device and a limited propulsion system. **Joval**, a woman at **Risa**, said she was unskilled at the sport. ("Captain's Holiday" [TNG]).

How to Advance Your Career Through Marriage. A book that young Lieutenant **Jack Crusher** sent to the future **Beverly Crusher** while she was in medical school in 2348, a gag gift that was his way of proposing to her. ("Family" [TNG]).

Howard, Beverly. *Semi-official maiden name of Dr. Beverly Crusher.* SEE: **Crusher, Dr. Beverly**.

Hromi Cluster. Location of the planet Gamma Hromi II, near the Acamar System. ("The Vengeance Factor" [TNG]).

Hubble, Chief. (April Grace). Transporter operator aboard the *Enterprise*-D in 2367. ("Reunion" [TNG], "Future Imperfect" [TNG], "Data's Day" [TNG], "Galaxy's Child" [TNG]).

Huey 204. Rotor-winged aircraft in use on Earth in the late 20th century. One such helicopter craft, owned by **Plexicorp** in San Francisco, was borrowed by Sulu in 1986 to deliver some acrylic plastic sheeting to the time-traveling Klingon Bird-of-Prey. Sulu noted that he had flown something similar back in his Academy days. (*Star Trek IV: The Voyage Home*).

Hugh. (Jonathan Del Arco). Adolescent **Borg**, designated Third of Five, rescued by the *Enterprise*-D crew from the wreck of a **Borg scoutship** in the **Argolis Cluster** in 2368. Aboard the *Enterprise*-D, Third of Five was restored to health, and dubbed "Hugh" by *Enterprise*-D personnel who discovered that removed from the **Borg collective**, Hugh began to exhibit signs of individuality.  During Hugh's convalescence, a plan was developed to create an invasive computer program that would be introduced to the Borg collective through Hugh. The **invasive program** would be designed to cause a fatal overload in the entire Borg collective. The plan was vetoed by Captain Picard, who felt it unethical to use Hugh as a weapon of mass destruction. Hugh was later returned to the crash site, where he was reassimilated into the collective. ("I, Borg" [TNG]). Hugh's sense of individuality almost immediately permeated his local portion of the collective, resulting in a dramatic loss of group purpose. The Borg acted aimlessly until given a new sense of purpose by the android **Lore**, who promised to make the Borg into his ideal of artificial life-forms. To fulfill this promise, Lore conducted bizarre medical experiments on many Borg, leaving them horribly injured. Hugh soon realized that Lore had no idea how to fulfill his promise, and began to secretly care for the injured Borg individuals. Hugh later joined with *Enterprise*-D personnel to defeat Lore. ("Descent, Parts I and II" [TNG]).

humanoid life. Intelligent bipedal life-forms, generally mammalian, commonly found on many class-M planets. **Humans**, **Vulcans**, **Klingons**, **Cardassians**, and **Romulans** are among the many humanoid species known throughout the galaxy. Despite the vast distances separating these planets, many humanoid species have been found to share a remarkable  commonality in form and genetic coding. These similarities were believed to be evidence of a common ancestry, a humanoid species that lived in our galaxy some 4 billion years ago. This species apparently seeded the oceans of many class-M planets with genetic material, from which a number of humanoid forms eventually evolved. In one of the most remarkable scientific detective stories in history, archaeologist **Richard Galen** of Earth uncovered the similarities between certain **DNA** sequences in life-forms from widely separated planets. He discovered that these DNA sequences were a puzzle deliberately left behind by these ancient progenitors. The DNA sequences, when assembled by protein-link compatibilities, formed an ingenious computer program, a message of peace and goodwill to their progeny. This message, assembled in 2369 in an unprecedented example of interstellar cooperation, was a confirmation that many humanoid species in this galaxy are indeed members of the same family, despite their significant differences. ("The

Chase" [TNG]). SEE: **Indri VIII; Preservers; Ruah IV**. *Photo: The ancient humanoid in "The Chase" (TNG), played by Salome Jens.*

humpback whale. Large aquatic mammal, scientific name *Megaptera novaeangliae*, that lives in the oceans of planet Earth. The humpback whale became extinct in the 21st century owing to humankind's shortsightedness, but two specimens of the species were obtained from the 20th century by Kirk and his crew, who transplanted them into the 23rd century in an effort to repopulate the species. (*Star Trek IV: The Voyage Home*). SEE: **George and Gracie; Probe, the; whale song.**

humuhumunukunukuapua'a. Reef triggerfish, also known by the scientific name *Rhinecamthus aculeatus*, found in tropical oceans on Earth. One of these fishes served as an animated "software agent" in an *Enterprise*-D schoolroom computer to help  guide students through their studies. ("Rascals" [TNG]). *The humuhumunukunukuapua'a is the state fish of Hawai'i.*

• **"Hunted, The."** *Next Generation* episode #59. Written by Robin Bernheim. Directed by Cliff Bole. Stardate 43489.2. *First aired in 1990. The* Enterprise-D *captures a fugitive whose crime was the fact that his government could not return him to normal society after having converted him into the "perfect soldier."* SEE: **anesthizine; Angosia III; Angosian transport vessel; Angosians; annular confinement beam; communicator; cryptobiolin; Danar, Roga; Lunar V; macrospentol; Nayrok; Starbase Lya III; Subhadar; Tarsian War; triclenidil; Wagnor, Zaynar.**

Hunters. Humanoids from **Tosk**'s planet in the **Gamma Quadrant** who engaged in an elaborate sport that involved hunting a live, intelligent, humanoid prey. The Hunters tracked their **Tosk** to station Deep Space 9 in 2369 and demanded his return. They explained to Sisko that in their culture the Tosk are bred and raised for the sole purpose of being hunted. ("Captive Pursuit" [DS9]). *The lead hunter was played by Gerrit Graham.*

Hupyrian. Race of tall humanoids known for their devotion to the masters they serve. The Hupyrian **Maihar'du** served as the Grand Nagus Zek's faithful servant. ("The Nagus" [DS9]). SEE: **Dolbargy sleeping trance**.

Hurada III. A Federation planet visited by **Tarmin** and his group of telepathic historians prior to mid-2368. After the **Ullians**' visit, two cases of **Iresine Syndrome** were reported on the planet. These cases were later believed to be instances of forced **telepathic memory intrusion** rape by telepathic historian **Jev**. ("Violations" [TNG]).

Hurkos III. Planet where **Devinoni Ral** moved at age 19. ("The Price" [TNG]).

Husnock ship. Spacecraft that attacked and destroyed the Federation colony on **Delta Rana IV** in 2366. A **Douwd** image of this ship attacked the *Enterprise*-D when it arrived to investigate the distress signals received from the colony. ("The Survivors" [TNG]). *The Husnock ship was designed and built by Tony Meininger.*

Husnock. An extinct species described as having exhibited extremely violent and destructive behavior. A Husnock warship attacked and destroyed the colony at **Delta Rana IV** in 2361. In retribution, the only survivor of the colony, a **Douwd**, destroyed the entire Husnock race. ("The Survivors" [TNG]).

Hutchinson, Commander Calvin. (David Spielberg). Officer in charge of **Arkaria Base**. Commander Hutchinson was known for his prowess at small talk. Hutchinson was killed by terrorists at a reception for the command crew of the *Enterprise*-D upon their arrival at Arkaria Base in 2369. ("Starship Mine" [TNG]). SEE: **Remmler Array.**

Hutchinson, Transporter Chief. (Harley Venton). An *Enterprise*-D crew member who was at the transporter controls when the away team rescued **Timothy** from the **Vico** on stardate 45397. ("Hero Worship" [TNG]).

hyperacceleration. Biochemical condition that plagued the people of planet **Scalos** due to radiation permeating their water supply. Hyperacceleration of biological processes caused an individual so affected to experience one second as if it were an entire hour. Outsiders who were accelerated quickly burned out, dying in a very short period of time due to cell damage. To a normal, nonaccelerated person, a Scalosian sounded very much like an insect. ("Wink of an Eye" [TOS]).

hyperchannel. Alternate term for **subspace radio** communications. (*Star Trek II: The Wrath of Khan*).

hyperencephalogram. Medical test that records and measures brain-wave activity. ("The Lights of Zetar" [TOS]).

hyperonic radiation. Hazardous form of energy present in the atmosphere of **Tau Cygna V**, this radiation can be fatal to unadapted humans. The colonists were able to adapt after two generations of exposure. Hyperonic radiation randomizes phaser beams and renders sensors and transporters inoperative. Data, however, was unaffected by this energy. ("The Ensigns of Command" [TNG]).

hyperspace physics test. One portion of the entrance examination for aspiring Starfleet Academy cadets. ("Coming of Age" [TNG]).

hypospray. Medical instrument used by Starfleet medical personnel for subcutaneous and intramuscular administration of medication for many humanoid patients. The hypospray uses an extremely fine, high-pressure aerosuspension delivery system, eliminating the need for a needle to physically penetrate the skin.

As with numerous Star Trek *"inventions,"* the hypospray later became an inspiration to real-world engineers

who have since invented actual medical devices based on the Star Trek *prop. Illustrations: 1) Original Series hypospray. 2) Star Trek: The Next Generation hypospray.*

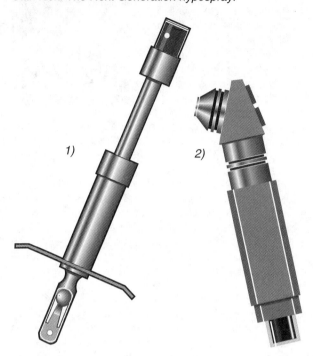

1)   2)

hyronalyn. Medication that was the treatment of choice for radiation sickness. It had no effect, however, on a radiation-induced hyperaccelerated-aging disease from planet **Gamma Hydra IV** that afflicted several *Enterprise* crew members in 2267. ("The Deadly Years" [TOS]).

Hyronalin was used to treat the crew of the *Enterprise*-D when the ship was exposed to hazardous levels of radiation while towing a derelict waste ship away from planet **Gamelan V** in 2367. The drug was administered by introducing hyronalin vapor into the ship's ventilation system. ("Final Mission" [TNG]). La Forge and Crusher required hyronalin treatments following exposure to **plasma fire** radiation in the cargo bay in 2368. ("Disaster" [TNG]).

hytritium. A highly unstable substance used to neutralize poisonous **tricyanate**. The *Enterprise*-D was able to procure some of this substance from **Zibalian** trader **Kivas Fajo** when the water supply on planet **Beta Agni II** suffered serious tricyanate contamination in 2366. Pure hytritium is too unstable to convey by transporter. ("The Most Toys" [TNG]).

"I Hate You." Obnoxious song popular in American culture in the year 1986. (*Star Trek IV: The Voyage Home*). *"I Hate You" was written and performed by Star Trek IV associate producer Kirk Thatcher, who also played the punk on the San Francisco bus who gave Kirk and Spock the "finger."*

I'danian spice pudding. Highly caloric dessert that Quark offered Dax and Kira as an enticement to enter his establishment on the Promenade at Deep Space 9. ("Babel" [DS9]).

• **"I, Borg."** *Next Generation* episode #123. Written by René Echevarria. Directed by Robert Lederman. Stardate 45854.2. *First aired in 1992. The* Enterprise-*D crew captures an injured Borg, nurses him back to health, gives him a sense of individuality, and names him Hugh. The story of Hugh the Borg was later continued in "Descent" (TNG).* SEE: **access terminal; Argolis Cluster; biochips; Borg collective; Borg scoutship; Borg; foil; homing signal; Hugh; invasive program; root command structure; Third of Five.**

• **"I, Mudd."** Original Series episode #41. Written by Stephen Kandel. Directed by Marc Daniels. Stardate 4513.3. *First aired in 1967. Harry Mudd returns, now the ruler of a planet of androids. This episode features the second appearance of con man Harry Mudd.* SEE: **Alice; android; Annabelle series; auxiliary control; Barbara series; central control complex; class-K planet; Deneb V; Denebians; Jordan, Ensign; Maizie series; Makers; Mudd, Harcourt Fenton "Harry"; Mudd (planet); Mudd, Stella; nanopulse laser; Norman; Trudy series.**

I.K.C. Abbreviation for Imperial Klingon Cruiser. Title used for Klingon ships, as in **I.K.C. Amar**. (*Star Trek: The Motion Picture*).

I.S.S. SEE: *Enterprise, I.S.S.*; **mirror universe.**

Ibudan. Humanoid who profited from running black-market goods to the **Bajorans** during the Cardassian occupation. Odo sent him to jail for murdering a Cardassian, but the Bajoran provisional government released him when they came into power. Plotting revenge, **Ibudan** came to Deep Space 9 in 2369 and staged his own apparent murder in which he killed his own clone in an attempt to frame Odo. ("A Man Alone" [DS9]).

• **"Icarus Factor, The."** *Next Generation* episode #40. Teleplay by David Assael and Robert L. McCullough. Story by David Assael. Directed by Robert Iscove. Stardate 42686.4. *First aired in 1989. Will Riker's estranged father, Kyle Riker, visits his son on the* Enterprise-*D. This episode marks the first reference to the Tholians in Star Trek: The Next Generation, and the only appearance of Kyle Riker, William's father.* SEE: **Age of Ascension; Anbo-jytsu; Aries, U.S.S.; Beta Kupsic; Flaherty, Commander; Fuurinkazan battle strategies; Giamon; gymnasium; Nasreldine; painstik, Klingon; PCS; Pulaski, Dr. Katherine; Rectyne monopod; Riker, Kyle; Riker, William T.; Starbase Montgomery; Stroyerian;**

Tholians; Tokyo Base; tryptophan-lysine distillates; Vega-Omicron Sector.

Icarus IV. A comet whose orbit was near the **Romulan Neutral Zone**. A cloaked **Romulan Bird-of-Prey**, passing through the tail of Icarus IV, became detectable to the *U.S.S. Enterprise* during the Romulan incursion of 2266. ("Balance of Terror" [TOS]). *Named for the character in Greek mythology that flew too close to the sun, thus melting his wings made of wax.*

Iccobar. Ancient language, along with Dewan and Dinasian, believed to have historic roots from the **Iconian** language. ("Contagion" [TNG]).

iced coffee. Chilled beverage made from brewed coffee beans. Geordi La Forge enjoyed it. ("Aquiel" [TNG]).

Iceman. Nickname for **Worf** at the *Enterprise*-D's weekly **poker** game, based on his impassive but disconcertingly successful playing style. ("The Emissary" [TNG]).

ico-spectrogram. Scientific test used as part of planetary surveys. Acting Ensign **Wesley Crusher** instructed that this test be performed on one of the planets in the third **Selcundi Drema** system, despite geologist Davies's objections that the equipment setup was unnecessarily time consuming. Crusher's intuition in requesting the test was shown to be valid when significant dilithium deposits were discovered on **Drema IV**. ("Pen Pals" [TNG]).

Iconia. The home of a technologically advanced civilization destroyed some 200,000 years ago. The long-dead planet Iconia was discovered to Federation science in 2365 by **Captain Donald Varley** of the *U.S.S. Yamato*. Varley uncovered evidence that Iconia was located in the Romulan Neutral Zone, but violated the Zone to find the planet because he feared the consequences if the Romulans acquired Iconian technology. Although ancient texts portrayed the Iconians as aggressors in that conflict, later students of archaeology (including Jean-Luc Picard) have speculated that the Iconians were innocent victims, attacked by enemies who feared their advanced technology. *The surface of Iconia was a matte painting designed by visual effects supervisor Dan Curry. The Iconian control building, a model used as part of the painting, was designed by Mike Okuda, based on two swimming pool filter covers and part of the* Star Trek I *drydock model.* ("Contagion" [TNG]).

Iconian computer weapon. A computer software weapon employed by the ancient Iconians. The weapon, a destructive computer program, was delivered to an enemy spacecraft by means of a transmitter in a short-range space probe. The program would then alter the target vessel's computer software, causing failure of critical systems. The *U.S.S. Yamato* was destroyed in 2365 by a still-functioning Iconian probe that transmitted the computer software weapon into that ship's computer banks. The virus-like program subsequently caused the near-destruction of the *U.S.S. Enterprise* and the Romulan Warbird *Haakona*. ("Contagion" [TNG]).

Iconians. An ancient, highly advanced civilization that had mastered the technique of dimensional transport across interstellar distances. The Iconians, referred to in ancient texts as "Demons of Air and Darkness," were all believed destroyed some 200,000 years ago by orbital bombardment that devastated the surface of their planet. It has been speculated that the Iconians did not all perish in the attacks, but rather used their advanced transporter technology to escape to other nearby planets. The similarity between the Iconian language and **Dewan**, **Iccobar**, and **Dinasian** has been cited as evidence to support this belief. ("Contagion" [TNG]).

iconic display console. A highly sophisticated computer interface system designed by Lieutenant **Reginald Barclay** while under the influence of the **Cytherians** in 2367. This system permitted a computer user's mind to directly link into a computer. ("The Nth Degree" [TNG]).

Icor IX. The planetary site of an Astrophysics Center. A symposium on rough star clusters was held there in 2366. Captain Picard was considering attending the symposium on his vacation. ("Captain's Holiday" [TNG]).

ID trace. SEE: **transporter ID trace.**

• **"Identity Crisis."** *Next Generation* episode #92. Teleplay by Brannon Braga. Based on a story by Timothy DeHaas. Directed by Winrich Kolbe. Stardate 44664.5. *First aired in 1991. Geordi and his former shipmates from the U.S.S. Victory are compelled to return to a planet they visited years ago, where they are transformed into alien life-forms.* SEE: *Aries*, *U.S.S.*; **Bogrow, Paul; Brevelle, Ensign;** *Cousteau*; **Graham, Ensign; Hendrick, Chief; Hickman, Lieutenant Paul; kayolane; La Forge, Geordi; Leijten, Susanna; Malaya IV; Mendez; Ogawa, Nurse Alyssa; T-cell stimulator; Tarchannen III; thymus;** *Victory*, *U.S.S.*; **warning beacons.**

IDIC. Acronym for Infinite Diversity in Infinite Combinations, a cornerstone of the **Vulcan** philosophy. Spock wore an IDIC medallion to the shipboard dinner in honor of Dr. Jones. ("Is There in Truth no Beauty?" [TOS]). *The triangle-circle IDIC pendant Spock wore in this episode was designed by Gene Roddenberry and has been used as a Vulcan national symbol.*

Idini Star Cluster. Located between **Persephone V** and **Mordan IV**, the *Enterprise*-D passed the Idini Cluster while en route to Mordan IV. ("Too Short a Season" [TNG]).

Idran. Trinary star system located in the **Gamma Quadrant**, first discovered in the 22nd century by the Quadros-1 probe. Idran was one of the closest systems to the terminus of the **Bajoran wormhole**. ("Emissary" [DS9], "Battle Lines" [DS9]).

"If I Only Had a Brain." Song from the ancient motion picture *The Wizard of Oz* (MGM, 1939). Just prior to his death in 2365, **Dr. Ira Graves** whistled the tune in Data's presence, noting it was sung by a mechanical man who "finds out that he *is* human after all, [and] always was." ("Schizoid Man" [TNG]).

• **"If Wishes Were Horses."** *Deep Space 9* episode #16. Teleplay by Nell McCue Crawford & William L. Crawford and Michael Piller. Story by Nell McCue Crawford & William L. Crawford. Directed by Robert Legato. Stardate 46853.2. *First aired in 1993. The arrival of Rumplestiltskin in the O'Briens' quarters signals the beginning of imaginary encounters created by aliens from the Gamma Quadrant, to study human beings.* SEE: **Baneriam hawk; baseball; Bashir, Dr. Julian; Bokai, Buck; class-4 probe; Denorios Belt; Gunji jackdaw; habitat ring; Hanoli system; hologenerators; impulse sustainer; Larosian virus; level-1 personnel sweep; London Kings; Lower Pylon 1; Newson, Eddie; Odo; pulse wave torpedo; Rumpelstiltskin; Sisko, Benjamin; Speaker, Tris; subspace rupture; Tartaran landscapes; thoron emissions; Williams, Ted; World Series.**

Igo Sector. Location of a binary star studied by the *Starship Yosemite* in 2369. ("Realm of Fear" [TNG]).

Ikalian asteroid belt. Located near the **Kriosian system**, this was believed to be the hiding place of a group of Kriosian rebels. In 2367, two freighters, one Ferengi and the other Cardassian, were attacked by Kriosian rebels near the belt. ("The Mind's Eye" [TNG]).

Ilecom system. Star system that experienced a "hiccough" in time that was found to be the result of **Dr. Paul Manheim**'s time/gravity experiments at **Vandor IX** in 2364. ("We'll Always Have Paris" [TNG]).

Ilia. (Persis Khambatta). Navigator on the *Starship Enterprise* during the **V'Ger** incident of 2271. Ilia, a native of planet **Delta IV**, had been romantically involved with **Willard Decker**, who also later served aboard the *Enterprise*. Ilia was killed by a probe from the V'Ger entity, although a near-duplicate of her was created by the probe in an attempt to communicate with the *Enterprise*'s crew. Ilia was later listed as "missing in action." SEE: **Deltans; Oath of Celibacy.** (*Star Trek: The Motion Picture*).

illium 629. Naturally occurring by-product of geological decay of **dilithium**. Traces of Ilium 629 were found on planet **Drema IV**, leading to the discovery of unusual dilithium strata in the planet's mantle. ("Pen Pals" [TNG]).

• **"Imaginary Friend."** *Next Generation* episode #122. Teleplay by Edith Swensen and Brannon Braga. Story by Jean Louise Matthias & Ronald Wilkerson and Richard Fliegel. Directed by Gabrielle Beaumont. Stardate 45852.1. *First aired in 1992. A little girl's imaginary playmate turns out to be terrifyingly real.* SEE: **Brentailia; bunny rabbit; Champs Elysees; Children's Center; drag coefficient; Felton, Ensign; FGC-47; Isabella; Jokri; Kryonian tiger; La Forge, Geordi; McClukidge, Nurse; Mintonian sailing ship; Modean System; nasturtiums; Neutral Zone, Romulan; Ogawa, Nurse Alyssa; papalla juice; purple omelets; Samarian coral fish; Sutter, Clara; Sutter, Ensign Daniel; Tarcassian razorbeast; Tavela Minor; thermal interferometry scanner; trionium.**

imaging scanner. Component of a transporter that captures a molecular-resolution image of the transport subject, used to create the rematerialization matrix. Four redundant scanners are used, permitting any one to be ignored if it disagrees with the other three. ("Realm of Fear" [TNG]).

Immamura, Lieutenant. *Enterprise* crew member who was injured in 2267 while on a landing party searching for the *Shuttlecraft Galileo* on planet **Taurus II**. ("The *Galileo Seven*" [TOS]).

Immelmann turn. Aerobatic maneuver in which a spacecraft executes a steep climb, returning to upright orientation at the crest of the half loop. Inspired by the maneuvers of 20th-century Earth pilot Max Immelmann. The Immelmann turn was used as a demonstration of piloting prowess by cadets at **Starfleet Academy**. ("The First Duty" [TNG]).

• **"Immunity Syndrome, The."** Original Series episode #48. Written by Robert Sabaroff. Directed by Joseph Pevney. Stardate 4307.1. *First aired in 1968. A giant space amoeba threatens the galaxy. Robert Sabaroff also wrote the story for* "Conspiracy" *(TNG).* SEE: **acetylcholine; amoeba; *Galileo, Shuttlecraft*; Gamma 7A System; *Intrepid, U.S.S.*; Kyle, Mr.; Sector 39J; Starbase 6; Vulcans.**

immunosuppressant. Any of several drugs designed to limit immune response in humanoids. Dr. Crusher used immunosuppressants in 2367 to help William Riker successfully carry the Trill symbiot, **Ambassador Odan**, within his body. ("The Host" [TNG]).

Imperial Senate, Romulan. Governing body of the Romulan Star Empire. ("Face of the Enemy" [TNG]).

impulse drive. Spacecraft propulsion system using conventional impulse reactions to generate thrust. Aboard most Federation starships, impulse drive is powered by one or more fusion reactors that employ deuterium fuel to yield helium plasma and a lot of power. A ship under impulse drive is limited to slower-than-light speeds. Normally, full impulse speed is about half the speed of light. Although this is adequate for most interplanetary travel (within a single solar system), it is inadequate for travel between the stars. Faster-than-light velocities, necessary for interstellar flight, require the use of **warp drive**. An explosion of 97.835 megatons will result if the impulse-drive reactor of a *Constitution*-class starship is overloaded. Such an explosion, produced in the destruction of the *U.S.S. Constellation*, was used to destroy the extragalactic **planet killer** in 2267. ("The Doomsday Machine" [TOS]). SEE: **sublight.**

impulse sustainer. Propulsion unit in space vehicles such as a class-4 sensor probe that provides thrust after the probe's initial launch. ("If Wishes Were Horses" [DS9]).

Imzadi. Betazoid term meaning "beloved." The half-Betazoid **Deanna Troi** had been romantically involved with **William Riker** prior to their service aboard the *Enterprise*-D, and she continued to use that term for him in private. ("Encounter at Farpoint, Part I" [TNG]).

• **"In the Hands of the Prophets."** *Deep Space Nine* episode #20. Directed by David Livingston. Written by Robert Hewitt Wolfe. No stardate given. *First aired in 1993. A Bajoran religious fundamentalist opposes the teaching of science on the station, but it is a ploy to eliminate a rival candidate to become the next Kai.* SEE: **Aquino, Ensign; Bajoran wormhole; Bajoran; Bareil, Vedek; cabrodine; EJ7 interlock; infernite; isolinear coprocessor; *jumja*; Neela; Opaka, Kai; security bypass module; security field subsystem ANA; Vedek Assembly; vedek; verterons; Winn, Vedek.**

• **"In Theory."** *Next Generation* episode #99. Written by Joe Menosky and Ronald D. Moore. Directed by Patrick Stewart. Stardate 44932.3. *First aired in 1991. Data tries to experience a romantic relationship.* SEE: **Arton, Jeff; Calaman sherry; cleaning processor; crystilia; D'Sora, Lieutenant Jenna; Data; krellide storage cells; Mar Oscura; Prakal II; Shuttle 03; Spot; Starbase 260; Thorne, Ensign; Tyrinean blade carving; Van Mayter, Lieutenant J. G.; *Voltaire*; W particle interference.** *Photo: Data and Jenna D'Sora.*

Inad. (Eve Brenner). A telepathic historian. Inad was one of the members of the **Ullian** delegation that visited the *Enterprise*-D in 2368. ("Violations" [TNG]). SEE: **Tarmin.**

inaprovaline. Cardio-stimulatory pharmaceutical in use aboard the *Enterprise*-D. This drug was used on the **Zalkonian** named **John Doe** to help stabilize his condition. ("Transfigurations" [TNG]). Usually administered intravenously by hypospray. ("Ethics" [TNG]).

Indri VIII. Class-L planet first identified by Federation scientists around 2340. No evidence of intelligent life or any animals was detected there, but the planet was covered by deciduous vegetation. Billions of years ago, Indri VIII had apparently been seeded with genetic material by an ancient humanoid species. Cardassian scientists were among several groups seeking to obtain genetic samples from the planet's biosphere to learn more about these ancient humanoids. All life on Indri VIII was destroyed by a violent plasma reaction in the planet's lower atmosphere in 2369, apparently caused by Cardassian forces seeking to prevent the competing scientific groups from obtaining the same genetic information. ("The Chase" [TNG]). SEE: **humanoid life**.

inertial dampers. Field-manipulation devices designed to compensate for the acceleration forces generated when a space vehicle changes speed. The *Enterprise*-D's inertial dampers failed just before the ship experienced a near-collision with the ***U.S.S. Bozeman*** in 2368. ("Cause and Effect" [TNG]). *Inertial dampers were "invented" by Star Trek's writers primarily in response to very valid criticisms that the acceleration and decelerations performed by the Enterprise would crush the crew into chunky salsa unless there was some kind of heavy-duty protection.*

infernite. Common chemical explosive. A combination of cabrodine and infernite was used by **Neela** on Deep Space 9 to destroy Keiko O'Brien's schoolroom in 2369. ("In the Hands of the Prophets" [DS9]).

Infirmary. Medical facility on Deep Space 9, the province of Medical Officer **Julian Bashir**. ("Emissary" [DS9]).

Ingraham B. Planet whose population was struck by mass insanity caused by the **Denevan neural parasites** in 2265. Inhabitants of Ingraham B were forced by the parasites to construct ships, traveling to **Deneva** eight months later, where that population was infected. ("Operation—Annihilate!" [TOS]).

• **"Inner Light, The."** *Next Generation* episode #125. Teleplay by Morgan Gendel and Peter Allan Fields. Story by Morgan Gendel. Directed by Peter Lauritson. Stardate 45944.1. *First aired in 1992. An alien space probe takes over Picard's mind, and he experiences a lifetime of memories on a dead planet in just a few minutes. This episode won the 1993 Hugo Award for Best Dramatic Presentation from the World Science Fiction Society.* SEE: **Batai (young); Batai; cardiac induction; cortical stimulator; crystalline emiristol; delactovine; Eline; isocortex; Kamie; Kamin; Kataan probe; Kataan; Meribor; neurotransmitter; nucleonic beam; Ogawa, Nurse Alyssa; paricium; Parvenium Sector; Ressik; Ressikan flute; somatophysical failure; Starbase 218; talgonite; voice-transit conductors.**

inner eyelid. Part of the Vulcan eye which evolved because the power of the bright Vulcan sun necessitated a secondary means of protecting the retina. When Spock was subjected to extremely intense light during an attempt to rid him of a **Denevan neural parasite**, his inner eyelid closed involuntarily, temporarily rendering him blind, but protecting his retinas against permanent damage. ("Operation— Annihilate!" [TOS]).

inner nuncial series. A battery of neurological tests. Dr. Crusher ran this series on Counselor Troi, following the loss of Troi's empathic sense in 2367. ("The Loss" [TNG]).

Innis, Valeda. (Anna Katarina). First Electorine of **Haven**. She strongly opposed a **Tarellian** vessel's request to land on planet Haven in 2364 on the grounds that the ship carried a deadly plague from the Tarellian war, requesting that the *Enterprise*-D intervene to destroy the ship. ("Haven" [TNG]).

insignia, Starfleet. *The distinctive arrowhead symbol used on Starfleet uniforms was first created by Original Series costume designer William Ware Theiss for "The Cage" (TOS) in 1964. Three versions of this original symbol were created, used for command personnel, science specialists, and engineering staff. (A fourth version, featuring a red cross, was occasionally worn by Christine Chapel). During the original Star Trek series, it was assumed that the arrowhead symbol was unique to the* Enterprise, *and that other starships had different insignia for their uniforms. This changed in Star Trek: The Motion Picture, when a modified emblem, designed by Robert Fletcher, was used not only on* Enterprise *crew members, but on all Starfleet personnel. We therefore assume that at some point after the original Star Trek series, the Enterprise emblem was adopted for the entire Starfleet. The feature film insignia (in a couple of variations) was used for all six movies, as well as for Star Trek: The Next Generation flashback sequences involving Picard's cadet days. Yet another variation was created for Star Trek: The Next Generation's first season by Theiss, in conjunction with Rick Sternbach and Mike Okuda. This version was also used on Star Trek: Deep Space Nine.*

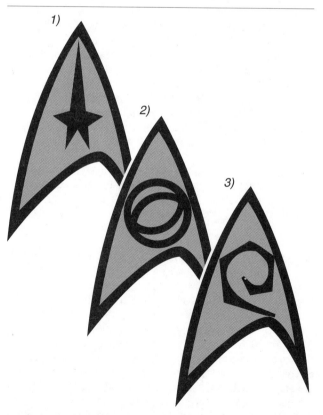

U.S.S. Enterprise *insignia from the original* Star Trek *series: 1) Command, 2) Sciences, and 3) Engineering.*

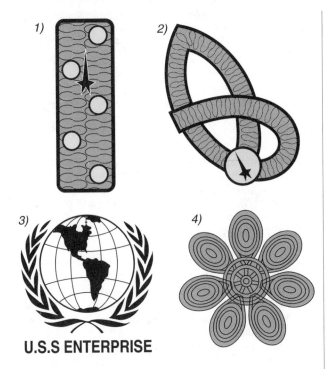

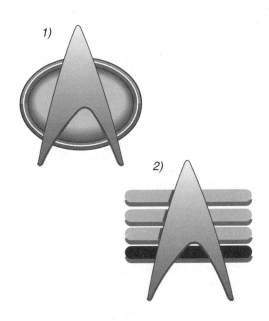

Other Original Series Starfleet insignia. 1) U.S.S. Intrepid, 2) U.S.S. Constellation, 3) United Earth emblem used in "The Cage" (TOS), and 4) Starfleet Command starburst emblem.

Star Trek: The Next Generation. 1)Starfleet communicator pin, also used in Star Trek: Deep Space Nine, and 2) Riker's imaginary version seen in "Future Imperfect" (TNG) and in "Parallels" (TNG).

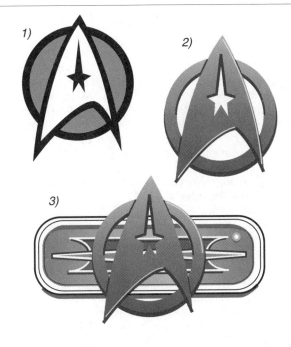

Star Trek feature-film insignia. 1) Revised Starfleet patch used as an embroidered design in Star Trek: The Motion Picture, 2) Cadet Starfleet pin, and 3) Starfleet officers' emblem. The embroidered emblem was only used in the first film, but the other two were seen in the following movies.

Instrument of Obedience. Small electronic device implanted subcutaneously in the temporal area of the brain in all citizens of the asteroid/ship *Yonada* as a means of controlling their behavior. If an individual spoke against the teachings of the **Oracle**, or otherwise violated the society's laws, the Oracle could cause the instrument of obedience emitted a strong pain stimulus. If intense enough, this stimulus could cause death and was thus an effective means of enforcing the will of the Oracle. ("For the World Is Hollow and I Have Touched the Sky" [TOS]). SEE: **Fabrini**.

interlink sequencer. Component of Data's **positronic brain**. On stardate 46307, Data converted his interlink sequencer to asynchronous operation, thereby increasing his computational speed. ("The Quality of Life" [TNG]).

intermix formula. A crucial concept in **warp drive**, the intermix formula is a mathematical expression determining the manner in which matter and **antimatter** are brought together to produce the energy required to warp space and travel faster than light.

Science Officer Spock and Chief Engineer Montgomery Scott devised a new intermix formula based on a theoretical relationship between time and antimatter that permitted an emergency restart of the *U.S.S. Enterprise*'s warp engines in less than thirty minutes when the vessel was trapped in a decaying orbit above planet **Psi 2000** in 2266. ("The Naked Time" [TOS]). An intermix imbalance can propel a starship into an extremely dangerous, artificially created wormhole. (*Star Trek: The Motion Picture*). **Kosinski**'s unsuccessful warp-drive upgrades in 2364 called for variations in the intermix formula in an attempt to improve engine performance. ("Where No One Has Gone Before" [TNG]).

internal power grid. Alternate term for the EPS power distribution system used aboard Federation starships. ("Disaster" [TNG]). SEE: **electroplasma system.**

interphase generator. Experimental Romulan cloaking technology that combined a **molecular phase inverter** with a **cloaking device**. Matter exposed to the interphase generator would partially exist on a parallel spatial plane and would therefore be undetectable to any known sensing device. Matter so cloaked would theoretically even be able to pass through other matter.

During the 2360s, the Klingons experimented with the technology, but after several accidents, they abandoned their research. In 2368, the Romulans developed a similar device that caused catastrophic damage to the warp core of the Romulan test vehicle. The *Enterprise*-D responded to a distress call from the Romulan ship and suffered **chroniton particle** contamination as a result of the failure of the interphase generator.

During the mission, Geordi La Forge and Ro Laren were lost in an apparent transporter malfunction. It was later discovered that the La Forge, Ro, and a Romulan officer were "phased" by the generator and rendered immaterial and invisible to "normal" matter. Commander Data, while acting to remove the chroniton contamination from the *Enterprise*-D, was coincidentally able to restore La Forge and Ro to normal space. ("The Next Phase" [TNG]). SEE: **anyon emitter; spatial interphase.**

interspace. SEE: **interphase generator; spatial interphase.**

intraship beaming. Method of transporting within the confines of a starship. This procedure required pinpoint accuracy, running the risk of materializing the transport subjects inside a wall or deck. Kirk and Klingon science officer **Mara** risked intraship beaming to carry an offer of peace to **Kang** when the *Enterprise* was held captive by the **Beta XII-A entity** in 2268. ("Day of the Dove" [TOS]).

The technique was perfected by the time of Star Trek: The Next Generation, *when it became known as* **site-to-site transport**.

Intrepid, U.S.S. Federation starship, *Constitution* class, Starfleet registry number NCC-1631. The *Intrepid* was under repair in maintenance section 18 at **Starbase 11** when the *Enterprise* arrived after being damaged in an **ion storm** in 2267. The *Enterprise* was given priority for repair over the *Intrepid* by **Commodore Stone**. ("Court Martial" [TOS]).

The *Starship Intrepid* was later destroyed by a massive spaceborne **amoeba** creature near the **Gamma 7A System** in 2268. The crew of the *Intrepid*, entirely composed of personnel from the planet Vulcan, was lost in the incident. ("The Immunity Syndrome" [TOS]).

Intrepid, U.S.S. Federation starship, *Excelsior* class, Starfleet registry number NCC-38907. The *Intrepid* was the first ship to respond to the Klingon distress calls when the **Khitomer** outpost was under attack by the Romulans in 2346. ("Sins of the Father" [TNG]).

Chief Petty Officer **Sergey Rozhenko** was a warp field specialist on the *Intrepid*. Following the Khitomer rescue, Rozhenko adopted a small Klingon child named Worf, who had been found among the wreckage at Khitomer. ("Family" [TNG]). *This was presumably at least the second starship to bear the name* Intrepid, *since an earlier* Intrepid *was destroyed in "The Immunity Syndrome" (TOS).*

invasive program. Computer software weapon designed by *Starship Enterprise*-D personnel in 2268 for the purpose of destroying the **Borg collective** consciousness. The program was a paradoxical geometric construct which, when introduced into the Borg system, was expected to form a recursively insoluble puzzle. It was intended to implant the program into the Borg individual known as **Hugh**, just prior to his planned return to the Borg collective. Once returned, the invasive program was expected to cause a fatal overload in the entire Borg system, effectively destroying their civilization and all its members. The plan was abandoned after Hugh began to demonstrate individualized character traits and it was determined that using the program as a weapon of mass destruction would be unethical. ("I, Borg" [TNG]).

inverter. A device used by the **Ansata** terrorists of planet **Rutia IV** for folded-space transport. Using the inverter, the Ansata were able to transport interdimensionally, without being detected by Rutian sensors. The device, used by the Ansata in 2366, brought new life to the Ansata cause, despite the fact that repeated use of the inverter caused cumulative (and eventually fatal) damage to the user's DNA. Because the use of the device caused subspace pressure modulations, Commanders Data and La Forge and Ensign Wesley Crusher were able to locate the power source of the device with adaptive subspace echograms. ("The High Ground" [TNG]). SEE: **Elway Theorem.**

invidium. A substance formerly used in medical containment fields. Invidium fell out of general use in the 23rd century, although a few races continued its application into the 24th century. Invidium had the unusual property of being undetectable by normal internal sensor scans aboard starships. It was also highly reactive, capable of triggering spontaneous **nucleosynthesis** as well as malfunctions in various high-power systems. Invidium used in a medical shipment from the **Mikulaks** accidentally leaked out of a broken storage canister, causing a variety of serious malfunctions aboard the *Enterprise*-D in 2366. The invidium was rendered inert by flooding contaminated areas with gaseous **cryonetrium**. ("Hollow Pursuits" [TNG]).

invisibility screen. SEE: **cloaking device, Romulan.**

ion propulsion. Highly efficient spacecraft propulsion system that uses magnetic fields to drive electrically charged gases. The ship from planet **Sigma Draconis VI** that invaded the *Enterprise* and stole Spock's brain in 2268 used ion propulsion. The propulsion system left a faint but distinctive ion trail of residual gas that permitted the ship to be tracked. ("Spock's Brain" [TOS]).

ion storm. A disruptive space phenomenon characterized by intense bombardment of charged particles. The *U.S.S. Enterprise* weathered a severe ion storm in 2267, during which **Benjamin Finney** was apparently killed when his sensor pod was ejected prematurely. Finney was in fact unhurt, but had altered computer records to make it appear that Captain Kirk had caused his death. ("Court Martial" [TOS]). A dangerous ion storm near the **Halkan** planet later in 2267 resulted in a severe transporter malfunction, causing members of the *Enterprise* landing party to be transposed with their counterparts from a **mirror universe**. ("Mirror, Mirror" [TOS]).

ionizer, transporter. A critical component in the transporter system. This device was damaged during the malfunction that accidentally created a partial duplicate of Captain James Kirk in 2266. ("The Enemy Within" [TOS]).

ionogenic particles. Energy type used in an attempt to contain the anionic energy that composed the noncorporeal criminal life-forms from the **Ux-Mal** star system that attempted to commandeer the *Enterprise*-D in 2368. Commander La Forge speculated that by flooding the Ten-Forward Lounge with the particles, they could contain the entities that were possessing their crewmates. ("Power Play" [TNG]).

Iotians. Humanoid inhabitants of planet **Sigma Iotia II**. When the planet was visited by the *U.S.S. Horizon* in 2168, the crew left behind a copy of a book entitled *Chicago Mobs of the Twenties*. (The contact took place before Starfleet's **Prime Directive** of noninterference was established.) The highly imitative Iotians proceeded to use this book as the blueprint for their society, and by 2268, when a second contact was made by the *Starship Enterprise*, Iotian society had become splintered into territories ruled by mob bosses. In an effort to help the contaminated society, Captain Kirk assumed the mannerisms of the culture, and set up a syndicate between the various territorial leaders, who agreed that the Federation would return each year to collect a "cut" of the profits. The money would then be used to steer the planetary government into a more ethical form. ("A Piece of the Action" [TOS]). SEE: **Oxmyx, Bela**.

Ireland. One of the British islands on planet Earth. Ireland was reunified in 2024, an example of political change successfully instigated by violence. ("The High Ground" [TNG]).

Iresine Syndrome. A very rare neurological disorder in humanoids characterized by a peculiar electropathic signature in the thalamus, and a severely decreased histamine count. Victims of the disorder, first identified in the 23rd century, would fall suddenly into a coma for approximately 72 hours. Diagnosis could be confused by the presense of any of 22 different substances that left electropathic residue resembling that of this disorder. Iresine Syndrome was suspected of inducing comas that befell three members of the *Enterprise*-D crew in 2368, but was later ruled out when it was learned they were victims of **telepathic memory invasion rape**. ("Violations" [TNG]).

irillium. Trace element found on planetoid **Holberg 917G**. When found in mineral **ryetalyn**, irillium renders the ryetalyn useless for medicinal purposes. ("Requiem for Methuselah" [TOS]).

Irina Galliulin. (Mary-Linda Rapelye). Follower of renegade scientist **Dr. Sevrin**, who sought the mythical planet **Eden** in 2269. Galliulin had a romantic relationship with **Pavel Chekov** when both attended Starfleet Academy, but they broke up because they had differing life philosophies. ("The Way to Eden" [TOS]).

• **"Is There in Truth No Beauty?"** Original Series episode #62. Written by Jean Lisette Aroeste. Directed by Ralph Senensky. Stardate 5630.7. *First aired in 1968. A beautiful woman escorts an alien ambassador so hideously ugly that the sight of him can drive a human mad.* SEE: **Antarean brandy; antigrav; barrier, galactic; IDIC; Jones, Dr. Miranda; Kollos; Marvick, Dr. Laurence; Medusans; mind-link; noncorporeal life; sensor web; Uhura**.

Isabella. (Shay Astar). The "invisible friend" of young **Clara Sutter**, a child living aboard the *Enterprise*-D in 2368. Isabella was purely the product of Clara's imagination, but a plasma-based life-form living in nebula **FGC-47** materialized in the form of Isabella while attempting to investigate the starship. Isabella was trying to determine whether the *Enterprise*-D posed a threat to her species, and whether the ship's deflector shields would serve as a suitable energy source. Isabella's investigation was hampered because, having assumed the form of a child, she had difficulty communicating with ship's personnel. ("Imaginary Friend" [TNG]).

Isak. (Richard Evans). **Zeon** member of the underground on planet **Ekos** in 2368 held captive by that planet's Nazi-style regime along with Kirk and Spock. Isak and his brother, Abrom, aided Kirk and Spock's efforts to locate the Federation cultural advisor, **John Gill**. ("Patterns of Force" [TOS]).

Ishikawa, Hiro. Father to Starfleet botanist **Keiko O'Brien**. Keiko considered naming her first child after Hiro, although her husband, Miles, preferred naming him after his father, **Michael O'Brien**. ("Disaster" [TNG]). *Little Hiro, or Michael (depending on who you asked), ended up being little Molly.*

Ishikawa, Keiko. Maiden name of the future Mrs. **Keiko O'Brien**. ("Data's Day" [TNG]).

Isis. (Voice by Barbara Babcock). Black cat of extraterrestrial origin who accompanied Gary Seven to planet Earth in 1968. This cat could transform itself into a humanoid woman. ("Assignment: Earth" [TOS]). *Isis was presumably intended as a continuing character in the proposed series* Assignment: Earth. SEE: **Mea 3.**

isocortex. The extreme outer layer of the cerebral cortex in a humanoid brain. Captain Picard suffered synaptic failure in his isocortex during his exposure to the **Kataan probe** in 2368. ("The Inner Light" [TNG]).

isolation protocol. A series of emergency procedures employed aboard Federation starships in the event of a hull breach in part of the ship. Isolation protocol procedures include computer-controlled closure of emergency bulkheads in the turboshafts to prevent uncontrolled atmospheric loss. Isolation protocol was invoked on stardate 45156, when the *Enterprise*-D was damaged by contact with **quantum filaments.** ("Disaster" [TNG]).

isolinear coprocessor. Computing device employing isolinear elements, used aboard **Deep Space 9**. **Neela** planted a subspace device integrated into an isolinear coprocessor in Security. This disabled the weapon detectors on the Promenade. With the weapon detectors off-line, the phaser **Neela** carried to assassinate Vedek Bareil did not register. ("In the Hands of the Prophets" [DS9]).

isolinear optical chip. Sophisticated information storage and processing device used aboard 24th-century starships. Composed of **linear memory crystal** material, the isolinear chip came into general use around 2349, and was used for both information storage and data processing. Within larger computing devices, isolinear chips are often housed in wall-mounted racks, permitting computer access to dozens, even hundreds of chips at one time. ("The Naked Now" [TNG]). Isolinear chips replaced older, less efficient **duotronic enhancers** aboard Federation starships around the year 2329. ("Relics" [TNG]). While under Romulan control in 2367, Geordi La Forge altered several isolinear chips to permit unauthorized use of the cargo transporter to beam weapons to planet **Krios**. He programmed the chips to erase all operator commands once the transport was complete, effectively erasing any records of the use of the transporter. ("The Mind's Eye" [TNG]).

isolinear rods. Data storage and processing device used aboard **Deep Space 9** and other **Cardassian** facilities. Similar in principle to the **isolinear optical chips** used aboard Federation starships, these translucent orange-colored devices were used in **Ops** and throughout Deep Space 9's

computer network. ("The Forsaken" [DS9]). **Quark** had a number of unauthorized isolinear rods that contained security programs. He used them when he wanted access to restricted information from the station's computer system. ("Past Prologue" [DS9]).

Iverson's disease. A chronic disease that causes fatal degeneration of muscular functions in humans. Iverson's disease does not, however, impair mental functions. There is no known cure for the condition. **Admiral Mark Jameson** suffered from this condition, although he eventually died from other causes. ("Too Short a Season" [TNG]).

Jabara. (Ann Gillespie). Nurse on duty at the infirmary on Deep Space 9 when the station was struck by the **aphasia virus** on stardate 46423. ("Babel" [DS9]).

ja'chug. An ancient part of the Klingon **Rite of Succession**, in which a new leader is chosen for the **Klingon High Council**. Now considered obsolete, the *ja'chuq* was a long, involved ceremony where candidates for council leadership would list the battles they had won and prizes they had taken in order to prove their worthiness to lead the council. In 2367, Captain Picard, as **Arbiter of Succession**, revived the *ja'chug* to delay the Rite of Succession following **K'mpec's** death. ("Reunion" [TNG]).

Jack the Ripper. Nickname given to mass murderer of women in 19th-century London, England, on planet Earth. Jack the Ripper was later found to be an evil energy life-form that thrived on the emotion of terror. ("Wolf in the Fold" [TOS]). SEE: **Redjac.**

Jackson. (Jimmy Jones). *Enterprise* landing-party member who beamed down to planet **Pyris VII** with Scott and Sulu on stardate 3018, but returned to the ship in a state of rigor mortis. The deceased Jackson spoke in a voice projected by **Korob**, warning the *Enterprise* to leave Pyris VII. ("Catspaw" [TOS]). *Jimmy Jones was a stunt performer who appeared in several other* Star Trek *episodes.*

Ja'Dar, Dr. (Richard McGonagle). Scientist from planet **Bilana III**, Dr. Ja'Dar was the designer of a revolutionary **soliton wave** propulsion system, tested for the first time in 2368. ("New Ground" [TNG]).

Jaeger, Lieutenant Karl. (Richard Carlyle). *Enterprise* geologist who part of the landing party to planet **Gothos** in 2267. ("The Squire of Gothos" [TOS]). SEE: **Trelane.**

JAG. SEE: **Judge Advocate General.**

Jaheel, Captain. (Jack Kehler). Captain of a transport vessel docked for repairs at Deep Space 9 on stardate 46423, when the station was struck by a deadly **aphasia virus**. Captain Jaheel attempted to violate a quarantine by pulling away from the station with the mooring clamps still attached to his vessel. The attempt failed and he was returned. Jaheel was carrying a shipment of Tamen **Sahsheer** to planet **Largo V**. ("Babel" [DS9]).

Jahn. (Michael J. Pollard). A young man who survived a disastrous biological experiment on Miri's planet, and friend to **Miri**. SEE: **Life Prolongation Project.** ("Miri" [TOS]).

Jakara, Rivas. (Jonathan Frakes). Identity created for Commander William Riker when he participated in a covert surveillance mission on planet **Malcor III** in 2367. Riker, as Jakara, was injured in a riot in the capital city and taken to the **Sikla Medical facility** for treatment. While Jakara was hospitalized, his physician discovered he was an alien who had been surgically altered to pass as a Malcorian. ("First Contact" [TNG]).

jakmanite. A radioactive substance with a half-life of about 15 seconds, capable of causing **nucleosynthesis** in silicon. Jackmanite is not normally detectable by a starship's internal sensor scans. ("Hollow Pursuits" [TNG]).

Jalad. SEE: **"Darmok and Jalad at Tanagra."**

jamaharon. A mysterious Risan sexual rite. At the resort on **Risa**, one announced the desire for *jamaharon* by displaying a *Horga'hn* statuette. ("Captain's Holiday" [TNG]).

Jameson, Admiral Mark. (Clayton Rohner). Celebrated Starfleet officer (2279-2364) whose career included command of the *Starship Gettysburg*. Jameson was also credited with the freeing of Federation hostages on planet **Mordan IV** just prior to the outbreak of a civil war that lasted 40 years on that planet.

Just prior to his death at age 85, Jameson accepted a second mission to the now-peaceful Mordan IV to secure the release of more Federation hostages. During the negotiations, it was learned that Jameson's previous mission had included an illegal weapons-for-hostages deal in direct violation of the Prime Directive. The act triggered — or at least exacerbated — the civil war. The second group of hostages had been seized by Mordan leader **Karnas** for the specific purpose of luring Jameson to the planet. Jameson died on Mordan IV of side-effects of a rejuvenation treatment obtained on planet **Cerebus II**. He had previously been diagnosed with terminal **Iverson's disease**. Jameson was survived by his wife, **Anne Jameson**. ("Too Short a Season" [TNG]).

Jameson, Anne. (Marsha Hunt). Wife to **Admiral Mark Jameson**. Anne and Mark were married from 2314 until the admiral's death in 2364. ("Too Short A Season" [TNG]).

Janaran Falls. Spectacular waterfall located on planet Betazed. It was the site of Lieutenant William Riker and Deanna Troi's last date before he departed for an assignment on the *U.S.S. Potemkin*. ("Second Chances" [TNG]).

Janeway, Ensign. (Lucy Boryer). *Enterprise*-D crew member who had a counseling session with Deanna Troi shortly after stardate 46071.6. A member of the science department, Janeway had sought counseling because she had been having trouble with her superior officer, Lieutenant Pinder. Unfortunately, Troi was at the time serving an involuntary "receptacle" for **Ambassador Ves Alkar's** negative emotions, so she was an unsympathetic listener. ("Man of the People" [TNG]).

Janowski, Mary. (Pamelyn Ferdin). One of the surviving children of the **Starnes Expedition** whose parents committed suicide on planet **Triacus** in 2268. In the aftermath of the tragedy, Janowski was controlled by the Gorgan. ("And the Children Shall Lead" [TOS]).

Janus VI. Homeworld to the **Horta**, a race of intelligent, **silicon-based life**-forms. Janus VI also contains rich deposits of the mineral, **pergium**, and the Federation has a pergium production station located underground on the planet. In 2267, prior to first contact between the miners and the Horta, several mining personnel were killed under mysterious circumstances. The deaths were found to be the result of the mother Horta protecting her children. Once contact was made, and the miners learned not to endanger the Horta eggs, peace was restored. ("The Devil in the Dark" [TOS]). *Photo: Mother Horta protects her eggs in the Vault of Tomorrow on Janus VI.*

Japanese brush writing. A form of calligraphy practiced in the nation of Japan on Earth since the 11th century. **Keiko O'Brien**'s grandmother was a practitioner of this art. ("Violations" [TNG]).

Jarada. Reclusive insectoid race from planet Torona IV. Establishment of diplomatic relations with the Jarada had been a Federation priority for some time because of their strategic importance. The Jarada were known for the extreme attention to the detail of protocol. The mispronunciation of a single word once led to a 20-year rift in communication. Captain Jean-Luc Picard successfully delivered the appropriate greetings to the Jarada in 2364, thus paving the way for further diplomatic relations. ("The Big Goodbye" [TNG]). The **Pakled** ship *Mondor* showed evidence of using technology borrowed or stolen from a variety of other races including the Jaradans. ("Samaritan Snare" [TNG]).

Jared, Acost. (Marcello Tubert). Ventaxian head of state in 2367. Jared interpreted a series of apparently paranormal events on **Ventax II** as evidence that the mythic figure **Ardra** was returning to the planet to enslave the population, under the terms of the **Contract of Ardra**. Investigation by *Enterprise*-D personnel revealed Ardra to be a fake. ("Devil's Due" [TNG]).

Ja'rod. The Klingon who betrayed his people to the Romulans at the **Khitomer** outpost in 2346. Ja'rod transmitted secret Klingon defense access codes to the Romulans, making him responsible for the **Khitomer massacre** in which 4,000 Klingons died, including Ja'rod. Years later, Ja'rod's son, High Council member **Duras**, attempted to cover up Ja'rod's crimes by falsifying evidence to implicate **Mogh**, Ja'rod's bitter political enemy, who was also killed at Khitomer. ("Sins of the Father" [TNG]).

Jarok, Alidar. (James Sloyan). Romulan admiral who commanded the forces responsible for the massacre at the **Norkan outposts**. A deeply thoughtful man, Jarok nevertheless opposed policies of the Romulan government that he saw as the prelude to an unnecessary war. Jarok was eventually censured for his outspokenness and was assigned to a strategically insignificant posting. There, the Romulan government fed him a carefully designed stream of disinformation designed to convince him that planet **Nelvana III** was being prepared as a staging base for a massive assault against the Federation. Unable to prevent what he believed to be a major threat to galactic peace, Jarok stole a scoutship and defected to the Federation. Persuading *Enterprise*-D captain Picard to investigate these reports, Jarok and Picard learned that there was no base and that the Romulan High Command was testing Jarok's loyalties. In despair over his use as a pawn by his government, and over the loss of his former life, Jarok committed suicide. Jarok said he had done these things to help insure that his daughter could grow up in a better universe. ("The Defector" [TNG]).

Jaros II. Planet in Federation space. It was the location of Starfleet stockade where **Ro Laren** was imprisoned following the *U.S.S. Wellington* incident until her release in 2368. ("Ensign Ro" [TNG]).

Jarth. (Rick Scarry). Aide to **Ambassador Ves Alkar** at the time he helped negotiate peace on planet **Rekag-Seronia** in 2369. ("Man of the People" [TNG]).

Jarvis. (Charles Macauley). Prefect of planet **Argelius II**. His wife, an empathic Argelian named **Sybo**, was murdered in 2267 by an alien entity that fed on fear. ("Wolf in the Fold" [TOS]). SEE: **Hengist, Mr.**; **Redjac**. *Actor Charles Macauley also played the computer-generated entity* **Landru**. *("Return of the Archons" [TOS]).*

Jasad, Gul. (Joel Snetow). Commander of a **Cardassian** warship and a member of the Seventh Order. In 2369, Jasad threatened to reoccupy **Deep Space 9** or destroy the station. ("Emissary" [DS9]).

Jat'yln. Klingon term for spiritual possession. It literally translates as "the taking of the living by the dead." Worf wondered if the **Ux-Mal** noncorporeal criminal life-forms that gained control of three *Enterprise*-D personnel on stardate 45571 might be instances of *Jat'yln*. ("Power Play" [TNG]).

Jatlh. Klingon expression that translates as "Speak!" ("Unification, Part I" [TNG]).

Jaya. Inmate at the **Tilonus Institute for Mental Disorders** on **Tilonus IV**. Jaya called herself Commander Bloom of the *Starship Yorktown* and offered to help Riker escape from captivity there in 2369. ("Frame of Mind" [TNG]). SEE: *Frame of Mind.*

Jaz Holza. A **Bajoran** leader who resided on the third planet in the **Valo system**. Dr. Crusher had met Jaz at a symposium and found him to be very thoughtful and a good spokesman for his people. **Ro Laren** maintained, however, that Jaz held no real influence with the Bajoran people. ("Ensign Ro" [TNG]).

J'Ddan. (Henry Woronicz). Klingon exobiologist who was assigned to the *Enterprise*-D in 2367 as part of the continuing Federation/Klingon **Officer Exchange Program**. While on the ship, J'Ddan was discovered to have been part of a plan to steal restricted computer files and smuggle them to the Romulans. These files were transferred into amino acid–like molecules and injected into J'Ddan's bloodstream, enabling them to be smuggled into Romulan hands. Technical designs of the *Enterprise*-D **dilithium crystal articulation frame**, taken by J'Ddan on stardate 44758, were found to be in Romulan possession shortly thereafter. When confronted with evidence of his actions, J'Ddan confessed to being a Romulan collaborator. ("The Drumhead" [TNG]). SEE: **deoxyribose suspensions**.

Jefferies tube. Systems access crawlway aboard Federation starships. **Neela Daren** found the fourth intersect of Jefferies tube 25 to be the most acoustically perfect spot on the *Enterprise*-D for playing her musical instruments. ("Lessons" [TNG]). *The term "Jefferies tube" was a gag among the original* Star Trek *production staff, a reference to Original Series art director Matt Jefferies. In* Star Trek: The Next Generation, *the term has actually been used on film, thus making the name "official."*

Jellico, Captain Edward. (Ronny Cox). Starfleet officer who commanded the *Starship* **Cairo**. In 2367, Jellico assisted in negotiating the armistice between the Federation and the **Cardassian Union**. In 2369, with tensions between the Cardassians and the Federation again on the rise, Jellico was given temporary command of the *Enterprise*-D for a meeting with the Cardassian ship, *Reklar* while Captain Picard was sent on a covert mission into Cardassian space. Jellico was known for his efficient, demanding style of command. ("Chain of Command, Parts I and II" [TNG]).

Jenolen, U.S.S. Federation transport ship, *Sydney* class, registry number NCC-2010. The *Jenolen* disappeared in 2294 and was presumed lost. It was not discovered until 2369 that the *Jenolen* had crashed into a **Dyson Sphere**, and that one passenger, Captain **Montgomery Scott**, had survived for 75 years by suspending himself in a modified transporter beam. Shortly after Scott's rescue, Geordi La Forge and Scott repaired the *Jenolen*'s systems sufficiently to help the *Enterprise*-D escape from the sphere's interior, although the *Jenolen* was destroyed in the process. ("Relics" [TNG]). *The* Jenolen *miniature was a modification of a shuttlecraft built by John Goodman of ILM for* Star Trek VI. *(It was the ship that*

transported our heroes up to Spacedock). The modifications by Greg Jein added warp engines to the model. Fans have pointed out — quite correctly — that it shouldn't have been possible for Scotty and Geordi to be beamed off the Jenolen *while that ship's shields were still up.*

Jeraddo. Fifth moon orbiting the planet **Bajor**. Jeraddo was a class-M planetoid that was inhabited for years until, in 2369, an energy-transfer project tapped that moon's core, rendering the surface uninhabitable. The inhabitants of Jeraddo were relocated by order of the Bajoran provisional government. ("Progress" [DS9]). SEE: **Mullibok; Keena; Baltrim.** *Photo: Mullibok's home on Jeraddo.*

Jestral tea. A favorite beverage of Lwaxana Troi. ("Cost of Living" [TNG]).

Jev. (Ben Lemon). A telepathic historian from the **Ullian** homeworld. Jev was the son of renowned historian **Tarmin**, and worked for years to help compile Tarmin's library of memories. Jev was taken into custody in 2368 for a crime known as **telepathic memory invasion** rape, in which Jev forced his victims to relive painfully distorted versions of their own memories. These victims, who included three members of the *Enterprise*-D crew, were left comatose for several days. Investigation by *Enterprise*-D personnel linked Jev with the victims, and implicated him in other telepathic rapes on several planets. Jev was returned to his homeworld, where the punishment for his crimes was expected to be severe. ("Violations" [TNG]).

jevonite. Valuable gemstone found on planet **Cardassia**. Many of the artifacts discovered in the burial vaults of the **First Hebitian Civilization** were manufactured from jevonite. Most of these treasures were either stolen or sold by the Cardassian military to finance their war effort. ("Chain of Command, Part II" [TNG]).

jIH dok. Klingon for "my blood"; an expression of devotion given to one's mate. The response is *maj dok*, meaning "our blood." The exchange seals a marriage vow. **Worf** and **K'Ehleyr** exchanged these words, shortly before she was murdered in 2367. ("Reunion" [TNG]).

jinaq. Traditional Klingon jeweled amulet, given to a daughter when she comes of age to take a mate. ("Birthright, Part II" [TNG]).

J'naii. Humanoid race that requested Starfleet assistance in locating a shuttle vehicle lost in their star system in 2368. The

Enterprise-D provided equipment and personnel for the successful rescue mission. During the rescue, a diplomatic incident was narrowly averted when a J'naii individual named **Soren** became romantically involved with Commander William Riker. Sexual liaisons were strictly forbidden under J'naii law. The J'naii had culturally suppressed their sexual differentiation, having evolved beyond the need for separate sexual genders, and reproduced by incubating their young in fibrous husks inseminated by both parents. There were however, some J'naii who retained the leanings toward gender, some male and some female. These J'naii lived in fear of being discovered and being forced by the government to undergo **psychotectic** therapy. ("The Outcast" [TNG]).

Joachim. (Judson Scott). Aide to **Khan Noonien Singh**, and one of 96 surviving genetic "supermen" who escaped from Earth in 1996 aboard the *S.S. Botany Bay*. Joachim served as Khan's second-in-command when Khan commandeered the *Starship Reliant*, and died when Khan detonated the **Genesis Device**. (*Star Trek II: The Wrath of Khan*).

Joaquin. (Mark Tobin). Genetically engineered survivor of the **Eugenics Wars**. Joaquin and other followers of **Khan Noonien Singh** escaped Earth in 1996 in the sleeper ship *S.S. Botany Bay*. They traveled in suspended animation until awakened by personnel from the *Starship Enterprise* in 2267. ("Space Seed" [TOS]). *In* Star Trek II, *Khan's deputy was named Joachim.*

Jo'Bril. (James Horan). Takaran specialist in solar plasma reactions. Jo'Bril was invited, along with other scientists, to participate in the first tests of a new **metaphasic shield** in 2369. Jo'Bril volunteered to pilot a specially modified *Enterprise*-D shuttlecraft into the corona of a star in order to test the feasibility of the shield. Jo'Bril was apparently killed during the test.

It was later discovered that Jo'Bril had faked his death. Jo'Bril hoped to discredit **Dr. Reyga**, inventor of the metaphasic shield, so that he could steal the technology for his own use. He was nearly successful in simulating the destruction of the *Shuttlecraft **Justman***, and kidnapping Dr. Beverly Crusher. Jo'Bril was killed by Crusher when she discovered his plan. ("Suspicions" [TNG]).

Johnson, Elaine. (Laura Wood). Colonist on planet **Gamma Hydra IV** who died of a radiation-induced hyperaccelerated-aging disease in 2267. Elaine Johnson was the wife of scientist **Robert Johnson** and was 27 years old at the time of her death of old age. ("The Deadly Years" [TOS]).

Johnson, Lieutenant. (David L. Ross). *Enterprise* security officer who was injured in 2268 fighting Klingons while under the control of the **Beta XII-A entity** that fed on hate and anger. Johnson's critical wounds healed quickly, so he could fight again. ("Day of the Dove" [TOS]).

Johnson, Robert. (Felix Locher). Scientist on planet **Gamma Hydra IV** who died of a radiation-induced hyperaccelerated-aging disease in 2267 at the age of 29. ("The Deadly Years" [TOS]).

joined species. Term used to describe the **Trill** life-form, consisting of a helpless, intelligent **symbiont** living in partnership within a host humanoid body. ("The Host" [TNG]).

Joining day. Term for marriage among the American Indian people on **Miramanee's planet**. ("The Paradise Syndrome" [TOS]).

Jokarian chess. Game that Jadzia Dax once challenged Benjamin Sisko to play. He declined, opting to search for his tardy son. ("The Nagus" [DS9]).

Jokri. River on planet Tavela Minor. It was noted for vacation cruises that allowed views of the river's iridescent currents. Nurse **Alyssa Ogawa**, reluctant to accept an invitation to **Risa** with a gentleman friend, was thinking about asking him instead for a cruise on the Jokri River. ("Imaginary Friend" [TNG]).

Jol, Etana. (Katherine Moffat). A **Ktarian** operative who spearheaded a Ktarian plan to gain control of the Federation Starfleet in 2368. Etana met William Riker while he was vacationing on planet **Risa**, and while under the guise of a romantic liaison, introduced a psychotropically addictive  **Ktarian game** to Riker, who in turn spread it to the *Enterprise*-D crew.

Because the game also affected the brain's reasoning center, Etana was able to control those people who had become addicted to the game. She planned to use the *Enterpise*-D crew to further her people's plot to gain control of Starfleet. ("The Game" [TNG]). SEE: **Ktarian game**. *Photo: Etana and Riker.*

jolan true. A Romulan farewell salutation. ("Unification, Parts I and II" [TNG]). *We don't have an exact translation for this, but it seemed to be a Romulan version of "Have a Nice Day."*

Jones, Cyrano. (Stanley Adams). Entrepreneur and licensed asteroid locator who visited **Deep Space Station K-7** in 2267 to pursue trade. Jones' merchandise included **Spican flame gems**, **Antarian Glow Water**, and **tribbles**. Jones became embroiled in a dispute between Federation and Klingon personnel at the station when his tribbles multiplied prodigiously, theatening to consume storage bins of valuable grain.

Jones' punishment for his part in the mischief was to pick up every tribble on the station, a task Spock estimated would take at least 17 years, seeing as there were 1,771,561 of them. ("The Trouble with Tribbles." [TOS]). *Actor Stanley Adams cowrote "The Mark of Gideon" (TOS).*

Jones, Dr. Miranda. (Diana Muldaur). Psychologist who accomplished one of the first telepathic links with a **Medusan** individual. Jones was born a telepath and studied on planet Vulcan for four years, learning how not to read minds. In 2268, Jones was chosen to attempt the first telepathic link with Medusan ambassador **Kollos** and accompanied the ambassador to his homeworld aboard the

Starship Enterprise. Jones was blind, but wore a **sensor web** garment that gave her the ability to function normally among sighted people. ("Is There in Truth No Beauty?" [TOS]). SEE: **Marvick, Dr. Laurence.** *Diana Muldaur also played Dr. Ann Mulhall in "Return to Tomorrow" (TOS) and Dr. Katherine Pulaski in* Star Trek: The Next Generation*'s second season.*

J'Onn. (Rex Holman). Humanoid settler on planet **Nimbus III**. J'Onn became a follower of the fanatic **Sybok** in 2287, joining Sybok on his quest for the mythical world **Sha Ka Ree**. (*Star Trek V: The Final Frontier*). *Rex Holman also played Morgan Earp in "Spectre of the Gun" (TOS).*

Jono. (Chad Allen). A fourteen-year-old human male who was discovered by the *Enterprise*-D crew aboard a damaged **Talarian** observation craft in 2367. DNA gene type matching identified the boy as **Jeremiah Rossa**, the grandson of Starfleet **admiral Connaught Rossa**. Jeremiah's parents had been killed in a Talarian attack on **Galen IV** in 2356. Investigation revealed the boy to have been captured by Talarian officer **Endar**, who raised the boy as his own son in accordance with Talarian custom.

Although examinations by *Enterprise*-D personnel suggested the boy might have been physically abused in Endar's care, further investigation revealed that Jono now considered Endar to be his true father, and Picard released Jono to Endar's custody, despite objections from the Rossa family. ("Suddenly Human" [TNG]). SEE: **Galen border conflicts**; *Q'Maire*. *The dagger Jono used to stab the captain was Picard's* cha'DIch *ceremonial knife from "Sins of the Father" (TNG).*

Joranian ostrich. Type of alien bird. When frightened, the Joranian ostrich has been known to hide its head under water until it drowns. **Odo** used the analogy of the Joranian ostrich when trying to show **Kira Nerys** that to avoid accepting responsibility for ignoring the **Kohn-ma**'s plans could be deadly. ("Past Prologue" [DS9]).

Jordan, Ensign. (Michael Zaslow). *Starship Enterprise* crew member on duty in **auxiliary control** when the android **Norman** commandeered the ship in 2267. ("I, Mudd" [TOS]).

Josephs, Lieutenant. (James X. Mitchell). *Enterprise* security guard who discovered the **Tellarite** ambassador **Gav**, murdered just prior to the **Babel Conference** of 2267. Gav was on Deck 11 hanging upside down in a **Jefferies tube**. ("Journey to Babel" [TOS]).

Jouret IV. Planetary site of the Federation's **New Providence** colony. In 2366, the colony disappeared without a trace, the victim of a **Borg** attack. ("The Best of Both Worlds, Part I" [TNG]).

• **"Journey to Babel."** Original Series episode #44. Written by D. C. Fontana. Directed by Joseph Pevney. Stardate 3842.3. *First broadcast in 1967. Spock's estranged father suffers a heart attack while aboard the* Enterprise *for a diplomatic mission, and Spock must save his life. This is the first time Spock's parents appeared.* SEE **Amanda; Andorians; Babel Conference; Babel; benjisidrine; cardiostimulator; Coridan; cryogenic open-heart procedure; dilithium; Gav; Josephs, Lieutenant; Kirk, James T; Orion; Orions; Rigel V; Rigelians; Sarek; Saurian brandy;** *sehlat***; Shras; Spock; T-negative;** *talshaya***; teddy bear; Tellarite; Thelev; Vulcan Science Academy.**

Joval. (Deirdre Impershein). A beautiful female inhabitant of the planet **Risa**, where Jean-Luc Picard took a vacation in 2366. Upon seeing him displaying a *Horga'hn*, Joval offered *jamaharon*, and was puzzled when Picard declined. ("Captain's Holiday" [TNG]).

Jovian run. Starfleet shuttle route, running from Jupiter to Saturn and back each day. This route was **Captain Edward Jellico**'s first Starfleet assignment. **Geordi La Forge** also piloted the Jovian run early in his Starfleet career. SEE: **Titan's Turn.** ("Chain of Command, Part II" [TNG]).

Jovis. A **Zibalian** trade vessel owned by **Kivas Fajo**. The *Jovis* was a relatively small vessel with a maximum speed of warp three. Data was kidnapped and imprisoned aboard the *Jovis* in 2366. ("The Most Toys" [TNG]). *The* Jovis *miniature was designed and built by Tony Meininger.*

Juarez, Lieutenant. Starfleet officer who gave birth to a boy while serving aboard the *Enterprise*-D in 2367. The Juarez child was born on the same day that **Miles O'Brien** and **Keiko Ishikawa** were married, during a standoff with a Romulan ship. Captain Picard marveled that in the midst of possible destruction "this small miracle was taking place." ("Data's Day" [TNG]).

Judge Advocate General. Starfleet office in charge of administrative law within Starfleet and its own personnel. **Phillipa Louvois** was in charge of the Judge Advocate General office for Sector 23 at the time she presided over the precedent-setting case in which she ruled that the android Data was entitled to civil rights as a sentient being in 2365. Louvois was also working for the JAG when she prosecuted Jean-Luc Picard's court-martial following the loss of the *U.S.S. Stargazer* in 2355. ("The Measure of a Man" [TNG]).

jumja. Sweet confection on a stick made from the sap of the *jumja* tree, it could be purchased at a kiosk on the Promenade of Deep Space 9. Miles O'Brien was fond of the *jumja's* natural sweetness. ("In the Hands of the Prophets" [DS9]). *The show's production staff refers to this "confection" as glop-on-a-stick.*

Jung, Carl Gustav. (1875-1961). Renowned 20th-century Earth psychologist, founder of analytical psychology. Troi quoted Jung while helping Riker, who was having disturbing thoughts while performing the play **Frame of Mind** in 2369. ("Frame of Mind" [TNG]).

Junior. A large spaceborne life-form discovered by the *Enterprise*-D near the **Alpha Omicron System** in 2367. The creature was composed of an energy field surrounded by a shell of silicates, actinides, and carbonaceous chondrites. *Enterprise*-D personnel had been responsible for the acci-

dental death of Junior's mother, prior to Junior's birth. Accordingly, Dr. Crusher devised a technique to use the ship's phasers to perform a cesarean section on the mother's body, allowing Junior to live. Shortly after the delivery, the creature physically attached itself to the ship's hull, absorbing power directly from ship's systems. **Geordi La Forge**, with help from visiting engineer **Leah Brahms**, was able to modify the ship's internal power frequencies to effectively "sour the milk," thereby weaning the child. Junior was last seen, along with other members of its species, in the asteroid belt near the Alpha Omicron system. ("Galaxy's Child" [TNG]). *According to Captain Picard, the appellation "Junior" was not to be the creature's official name, but it seems to have stuck.*

Jupiter 8. Internal-combustion-engine-powered automobile used by citizens of the Roman culture on planet 892-IV. ("Bread and Circuses" [TOS]).

Jupiter Outpost 92. Federation station in the outer part of the Sol system. It was the first outpost to report the entrance of the **Borg** ship into that system during the Borg offensive of 2367. ("The Best of Both Worlds, Part II" [TNG]). *In an early version of the script for "The Best of Both Worlds, Part II," the story was still considered to be so confidential that each copy of the script was secretly numbered. The number of the Jupiter Outpost (in this case, 92) was different in each copy of the early draft script, so that if unauthorized copies were made, it would be possible to trace whose copy it came from.*

Juro. Contact sport played between two individuals. Benjamin Sisko told Dr. Julian Bashir that **Curzon Dax** use to beat him regularly at bare-fisted Juro Counterpunch. ("A Man Alone" [DS9]).

• **"Justice."** *Next Generation* episode #9. Teleplay by Worley Thorne. Story by Ralph Wills and Worley Thorne. Directed by James L. Conway. Stardate 41255.6. *First aired in 1987. Wesley Crusher is sentenced to death for a minor infraction on a planet of hedonistic pleasure.* SEE: **Crusher, Wesley; Edo**

god; Edos; Liator; mediators; punishment zones; Rivan; Rubicun III; Rubicun star system; Strnad solar system.

Justinian Code. Part of ancient Roman law enacted during the reign of Byzantine emperor Justinian I in the 6th century on planet Earth. The Justinian Code was a major effort to distill a thousand years of Roman legal precedents into a single body of work. ("Court Martial" [TOS]).

Justman, Shuttlecraft. *Enterprise*-D shuttlecraft 03. The *Justman* was fitted with the **metaphasic shield** emitter in order to test the technology developed by Dr. Reyga in 2369. ("Suspicions" [TNG]). Earlier that year, a simulation of the **Justman** served to transport the computer-based intelligence known as **Professor James Moriarty** into a computer-generated environment. ("Ship in a Bottle" [TNG]). *The Justman was named by Star Trek executive producer Rick Berman, in honor of his colleague, Star Trek producer Robert H. Justman, a veteran of both the orignial Star Trek series and Star Trek: The Next Generation.*

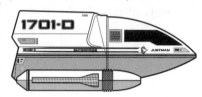

K-3 indicator. Medical measurement of neural activity corresponding to the level of pain being experienced by a patient. The biomedical displays on *Constitution*-class starship sickbays incorporated a K-3 indicator. While Spock was under the control of the **Denevan neural parasites** in 2267, the K-3 indicator was nearly at maximum, indicating extreme pain. ("Operation— Annihilate!" [TOS]).

K-7, Deep Space Station. SEE: **Deep Space Station K-7**.

K-type planet. SEE: **class-K planet**.

kph. Kilometers per hour. Unit of measure used to describe very slow speeds. ("Galaxy's Child" [TNG]).

Kabul River. A major waterway located in the old Terran country of Afghanistan. The river runs past the capital city of Kabul to the Indian ocean. A **holodeck** program available on the *Enterprise*-D simulated this setting. Captain Picard suggested that Commander Riker join him there for horseback riding. ("The Loss" [TNG]).

K'adlo. Klingon for "thank you." ("The Mind's Eye" [TNG]).

Kaelon II. Class-M planet. The sun of the Kaelon system was gradually dying, and by 2367 the people of Kaelon II were forced to turn to the Federation for help. Starfleet was able to assist in an experiment designed to revitalize the Kaelon sun. ("Half a Life" [TNG]). SEE: **helium ignition test; Timicin, Dr.**

Kaelon warships. Two of these ships were launched from the surface of **Kaelon II** to persuade the *Enterprise*-D to return **Dr. Timicin** to the planet. ("Half a Life" [TNG]).

Kaferian apples. A favorite fruit of **Gary Mitchell**, who created several Kaferian apple trees on planet **Delta Vega**. ("Where No Man Has Gone Before" [TOS]).

Kahless the Unforgettable. (Kevin Conway). Klingon mythic-historic figure, a great warrior who united the **Klingon Empire** some 1,500 years ago. The story of Kahless is a cornerstone of Klingon mythology and religion. ("Birthright, Part II" [TNG]). Legend has it that the messianic Kahless fought the tyrant **Molor**, whom he killed with the first ***bat'telh*** or sword of

honor. Another of the epic tales of Kahless relates how he fought his brother, **Morath**, for twelve days and twelve nights because Morath had lied and brought shame to his family ("New Ground" [TNG]). Klingons believe that warriors who die honorably join Kahless, who awaits them in ***Sto-Vo-Kor***, the afterlife. Just before his death, Kahless pointed to a star and promised that he would one day return there. Klingon clerics established a monastery on **Boreth**, a planet orbiting that star, where they waited for centuries for Kahless to return.

SEE: **Quin'lat; Story of the Promise, The**. In the 24th century, the clerics of Boreth devised an elaborate scheme whereby preserved cellular material from Kahless was cloned to produce a replica of the original Kahless. The replica was programmed with all the ancient teachings and parables, and actually believed he was the real Kahless. The deception was quickly discovered, but **Worf**, son of Mogh, pointed out that the new Kahless could be considered the rightful heir to the throne. With the support of High Council leader **Gowron**, the new Kahless was installed in 2369 as ceremonial Emperor of the Klingon people. ("Rightful Heir" [TNG]). Another (presumably less accurate) copy of Kahless was created by the **Excalbians** in 2269, when they were attempting to study the human concepts of "good" and "evil" ("The Savage Curtain" [TOS]).

Worf had a statue in his quarters depicting the heroic struggle ("Reunion" [TNG]). *Several episodes, notably "Birthright, Part II" (TNG) and "Rightful Heir" (TNG), have revealed fragments of the legend of Kahless, but the entire story still remains to be told.*

Kahless as seen in "The Savage Curtain" (TOS), when he was played by Robert Herron, appeared very differently from Kahless as seen in "Rightful Heir" (TNG), when he was played by Kevin Conway. One might rationalize that this might have been because the image of Kahless created by Yarnek was drawn from the mind of James Kirk, who may not have known what the "real" Kahless looked like.

Of course, in truth "The Savage Curtain" was filmed many years before "Rightful Heir," before the introduction of the more elaborate makeup design for the Klingons in Star Trek: The Motion Picture. Photos: Kevin Conway as Kahless in "Rightful Heir" (TNG) and Robert Herron as Kahless in "The Savage Curtain" (TOS).

Kahlest. (Thelma Lee). ***Ghojmok*** or nursemaid to young **Worf**, while his family was living on **Khitomer**, at the time of the **Khitomer massacre** of 2346.

She was rescued, along with Worf, by the crew of the **U.S.S. Intrepid**. Kahlest was taken to **Starbase 24** for treatment, and she later returned to the **Klingon Homeworld** and took up residence in seclusion in the old city. Captain Picard visited her there in 2366 when Worf's family was facing dishonor because of falsified evidence that Worf's father, **Mogh**, had betrayed the empire at Khitomer. Kahlest knew nothing of Mogh's activities but the existence of an eyewitness to the events at Khitomer was enough to force High Council leader **K'mpec** to accept a compromise.

Kahlest had known K'mpec in their younger days, and K'mpec had been attracted to her, but according to Kahlest, "He was too fat." ("Sins of the Father" [TNG]).

Kahn-ut-tu. Medicine women of the **hill people** on **Tyree's** planet trained in the mystic arts, including the curative powers of medicinal herbs and roots. Tribal leader Tyree's wife, **Nona**, was a *Kahn-ut-tu.* Among the men on Tyree's planet, *Kahn-ut-tu* women were considered to be especially desirable. ("A Private Little War" [TOS]).

Kai. Title for **Bajoran** supreme religious leader. **Kai Opaka** held the post in 2369. ("Emissary" [DS9]). SEE: **Taluno, Kai**.

Kainon. (Tony Rizzoli). Disheveled-appearing Bajoran with a history of minor criminal offenses, who was being held at Deep Space 9 station security for drunkenness when the Cardassian **Aamin Marritza** was held in 2369 on suspicion of having committed war crimes. Kainon was very vocal about his desire not to share the same prison with any Cardassian  citizen. When Marritza was found to be innocent of the charges, and set free, Kainon took justice into his own hands, killing the **Cardassian**, not for any crime, but just because he was Cardassian. ("Duet" [DS9]).

Kajada, Ty. (Caitlin Brown). **Kobliad** security officer who had been tracking her prisoner **Rao Vantika** for twenty years. She was brought to Deep Space 9 after her vessel was destroyed in 2369. Kajada was thought to be the only survivor from her ship, but a series of strange events convinced her that Vantika was still alive, and it was later learned her nemesis had transferred his consciousness to Dr. Julian Bashir. Vantika was eventually subdued and his consciousness was transferred to an energy-containment cell, where Kajada ended her twenty-year pursuit with one blast from her weapon. ("The Passenger" [DS9]).

Kal-if-fee. Vulcan word for challenge. **T'Pring** chose the *Kal-if-fee* during her **Pon farr** mating ceremony in 2267, when she opted to challenge Spock's claim on her. ("Amok Time" [TOS]).

Kalandan outpost. Artificially created planet manufactured by the Kalandan race some 10,000 years ago. During the construction of the planet, a deadly microorganism was accidentally created, killing all of the **Kalandans** at the outpost.

The last survivor, a woman named **Losira**, set the station's automated defense systems to protect the station for the day when more Kalandans would arrive at the outpost. This defense system killed several *Enterprise* crew members when the ship surveyed the planetoid in 2268. ("That Which Survives" [TOS]).

Kalandans. Humanoid race that built the **Kalandan outpost** some 10,000 years ago. ("That Which Survives" [TOS]).

Kaldra IV. A Federation planet on which a group of **Ullian** researchers had intended to conduct research for their planned

telepathic memory library project in 2368. The Ullians never reached Kaldra owing to the arrest of one of their party. ("Violations" [TNG]).

Kaleans. While on planet Rochani III, Curzon Dax and Benjamin Sisko were once confronted by a group of aliens who had adversarial intentions. While under the influence of the **Saltah'na energy spheres** in 2369, Jadzia Dax repeated the story of Rochani III to Major Kira Nerys. ("Dramatis Personae" [DS9]).

Kaleb Sector. Location where Romulan **subcommander N'Vek** attempted to rendezvous with a Corvallen freighter for the defection of **Vice-Proconsul M'ret** in 2369. ("Face of the Enemy" [TNG]).

Kalevian montar. Game that **Gul Dukat** once played with **Odo** on **Deep Space 9**. Dukat recalled that they had played many times, but Odo reminded Dukat that they only played once and that the Cardassian had cheated. ("Duet" [DS9]).

Kalin Trose. (William Newman). Government representative of the **Alpha Moon** of planet **Peliar Zel**. Kalin took part in two major conferences with the **Beta Moon**, one in 2337 and one in 2367. Both negotiations were successfully mediated by **Ambassador Odan**. ("The Host" [TNG]).

Kalla-Nohra Syndrome. Chronic pulmonary disease found only in individuals exposed to a mining accident at **Gallitep**, an Bajoran labor camp run by the **Cardassians**. There are no known instances of anyone not involved with that mining accident contracting the disease, so a positive diagnosis makes it virtually certain that an individual has been at that infamous death camp. Cardassian citizen **Aamin Marritza** was diagnosed with Kalla-Norha at Deep Space 9 in 2369, and was subsequently suspected of having been Gallitep commander **Gul Darhe'el**. It was later found that Darhe'el was not at Gallitep at the time of the accident, so he could not have contracted Kalla-Nohra, and therefore Marritza could not have been Darhe'el. Marritza had been impersonating Darhe'el because he had hoped that a trial would have forced his people to admit the atrocities committed at Gallitep. ("Duet" [DS9]).

Kallisko. A transport ship from planet Boreal III. The ship was near the Brechtian Cluster when it was attacked by the **Crystalline Entity** in 2368. There were no survivors. ("Silicon Avatar" [TNG]).

Kalo. (Lee Delano). One of **Bela Oxmyx's** henchmen on planet **Sigma Iotia II** in 2268. ("A Piece of the Action" [TOS]).

Kalomi, Leila. (Jill Ireland). Botanist and member of a colony expedition that left Earth in 2263 to settle on planet **Omicron Ceti III**. Leila met **Spock** on Earth in 2261 and fell in love, but knew that her feelings could never be returned. The spores on planet Omicron Ceti III changed that when Spock was exposed to their powers, allowing him briefly to return Kalomi's affections. ("This Side of Paradise" [TOS]). SEE: **spores, Omicron Ceti III**. *Jill Ireland, who died in 1991 of breast* *cancer, spent the last part of her life conducting a courageous campaign to increase national awareness of the importance of early detection of that disease.*

Kamala. (Famke Janssen). A native of the **Krios** system, Kamala was an **empathic metamorph**, the first born on her world in a century. Raised from childhood to fulfill her role as an instrument of peace, Kamala was fated to wed **Chancellor Alrik** of **Valt Minor**. Kamala was a beautiful woman, and her ability to change into whatever a potential mate desired made her  extremely alluring. When she came aboard the *Enterprise*-D, Kamala was in the final stages of the *Finiis'ral* stage of sexual maturity. This caused some disruptions aboard the ship. Kamala was intended to bond to Alrik, but when circumstances put her in close contact with Captain Picard, she bonded to him. Kamala said she liked the way she was when she was with Picard, and added that there was no greater joy for a metamorph. But Kamala had learned a sense of duty from her bonding with Picard, and chose to go through with the ceremony, to seal the peace for her people. ("The Perfect Mate" [TNG]). SEE: **Ceremony of Reconciliation; Par Lenor**.

Kamie. Native of the now-dead planet **Kataan**, son of **Meribor** and grandson of **Kamin**, who lived a thousand years ago in the village of **Ressik**. ("The Inner Light" [TNG]).

Kamin. (Patrick Stewart). Native of the now-dead planet **Kataan**. Kamin was known as the best ironweaver in the community of **Ressik**, but he preferred to play his tin flute. Kamin was the husband of **Eline** and the father of two children, **Meribor** and **Batai**. Kamin's  life was recorded and sent out on an interstellar probe launched as a final memory of the people of Kataan, when they discovered their sun was to go nova. When the *Enterprise*-D encountered the probe in 2368, Captain Picard was rendered unconscious by the probe and experienced Kamin's entire adult life in the span of 25 minutes. ("The Inner Light" [TNG]). SEE: **Kataan probe; Ressikan flute**.

Kanar. A beverage favored by Cardassians. According to Glinn Daro, the drink took "some getting used to." ("The Wounded" [TNG]).

Kang. (Michael Ansara). Klingon commander who was the victim of the **Beta XII-A entity** that destroyed his ship and trapped his crew aboard the *Starship Enterprise* in 2268. Kang's wife **Mara** and 38  members of his crew fought an equal number of *Enterprise* crew members in a seemingly endless battle controlled by the Beta XII-A entity until both sides discovered that peaceful cooperation was the only way to survive. ("Day of the Dove" [TOS]). SEE: **Kor, Commander**.

Kapec, Rayna. (Louise Sorel). Android created by **Flint** as his immortal mate, who died in 2269 when faced with the impossible task of choosing between her love for her mentor and her love for James Kirk. ("Requiem For Methuselah" [TOS]). *Rayna Kapec was named for Czechoslovakian writer Karel Capek, who first coined the term "robot" in a short story entitled "R.U.R."*

Kaplan, Lieutenant. (Dick Dial). *Enterprise* crew member who was part of the landing party on **Gamma Trianguli VI** in 2267. He was killed by a bolt of lightning generated by the god-machine **Vaal**. ("The Apple" [TOS]).

Kara. (Marj Dusay). Leader of the **Eymorg** women of planet **Sigma Draconis VI** in 2268. Although untrained in the sciences, Kara underwent a memory-implantation procedure that gave her the necessary knowledge and skill to successfully steal Spock's brain so that it could be used to run her planet's master computer system. ("Spock's Brain" [TOS]). SEE: **Controller; Teacher**.

Kara. (Tania Lemani). **Argelian** who danced at a small cafe that several *U.S.S. Enterprise* crew members visited on shore leave in 2267, who then left the cafe in the company of Montgomery Scott. Kara was brutally murdered by an alien entity that fed on the emotion of fear, although Scott was initially accused of the crime. ("Wolf in the Fold" [TOS]). SEE: **Redjac**.

Karapleedeez, Onna. Starfleet officer who was apparently killed by the unknown alien intelligence that attempted to infiltrate Starfleet Command in 2364. ("Conspiracy" [TNG]).

Kareel. (Nicole Orth-Pallavicini). **Trill** host who joined with **Odan** after Odan was removed from Commander Riker's body. She returned to the Trill homeworld following the implantation of the **symbiont**. ("The Host" [TNG]).

Kargan, Captain. (Christopher Collins). Klingon officer, commander of the Bird-of-Prey *Pagh*, and Riker's superior when he served aboard that ship as part of an **Officer Exchange Program** in 2365. ("A Matter of Honor" [TNG]).

Karidian Company of Players. Shakespearean theatrical troupe headed by **Anton Karidian**. The Karidian company had been touring official installations for nine years prior to 2266, when Karidian was killed following the revelation that he was Kodos the Executioner. Library computer analysis indicated that nearly every surviving eyewitness to Kodos's crimes had been murdered, and that each murder had taken place when the Karidian Company of Players was nearby. The murder of the surviving witnesses was later found to be the work of **Lenore Karidian**. ("The Conscience of the King" [TOS]).

Karidian, Anton. (Arnold Moss). Alias for the former Governor Kodos of planet **Tarsus IV**, aka **Kodos the Executioner**. Kodos assumed this identity about a year after escaping arrest following the massacre at the Tarsus IV colony in 2246. As Karidian, he won acclaim as a Shakespearean actor and as director of the **Karidian Company of Players**. Karidian was killed in 2266 during a performance of **Hamlet** aboard the *Starship Enterprise*. ("The Conscience of the King" [TOS]).

Karidian, Lenore. (Barbara Anderson). Daughter of **Anton Karidian**, aka **Kodos the Executioner**. Born in 2247, about a year after Kodos's massacre at the **Taurus IV** colony. Although her father attempted to shield her from the crimes he had committed before her birth, Lenore not only learned about her father's past, but systematically attempted to murder all nine surviving witnesses of her father's crimes. Deemed criminally insane, Lenore Karidian was imprisoned for treatment following her attempt on the lives of Captain James Kirk and Lieutenant **Kevin Riley**, during which her father was accidentally killed. ("The Conscience of the King" [TOS]).

Karnas. (Michael Pataki). Leader of one of the warring factions on planet **Mordan IV**. A ruthless negotiator, Karnas had extorted weapons from Starfleet mediator **Mark Jameson** in 2319 so that he could win revenge on a rival faction for the murder of his father. Karnas nonetheless blamed Jameson for the ensuing civil war, which lasted 40 years. Karnas later attempted to exact revenge on Jameson. ("Too Short a Season" [TNG]). *Michael Pataki had previously played the Klingon Korax in "The Trouble with Tribbles" (TOS).*

Karo-Net. Sporting event that Odo enjoyed. He cited the Karo-Net tournament to **Quark** when discussing the disadvantages of coupling and having to make compromises. ("A Man Alone" [DS9]).

Kataan probe. Small unmanned spacecraft launched during Earth's 14th century from the planet **Kataan**, just before the star went nova. The probe represented the Kataan people's attempt to preserve something of themselves by sending memories of their people into space. The probe encountered the *Starship Enterprise*-D in 2368, and transmitted those memories to Captain Jean-Luc Picard, who, in the span of a few minutes, experienced a lifetime in the Kataan village **Ressik**, as an iron-weaver named **Kamin**. ("The Inner Light" [TNG]). SEE: **Ressikan flute**.

Kataan. Star located in the Silarian Sector. Kataan had six planets, one of which was inhabited by a humanoid civilization. The star Kataan went nova in the 14th century, eradicating all life in the system. ("The Inner Light" [TNG]). SEE: **Kamin**; **Kataan probe**; **Ressikan flute**.

katra. The Vulcan concept of the soul, the living spirit. Just prior to death, Vulcan custom is to mind-meld with a friend who is entrusted with the duty of returning the *katra* to the individual's home. Spock mind-melded with Dr. McCoy just before his death in 2285, placing his *katra* in McCoy's subconscious. (*Star Trek III: The Search for Spock*). SEE: *fal-tor-pan*; **synaptic pattern displacement.**

katterpod beans. Crop grown on **Mullibok**'s farm on the **Bajoran** moon **Jeraddo**. ("Progress" [DS9]).

Kaval. (Ted Sorel). **Bajoran** Minister of State who communicated to Benjamin Sisko the Bajoran provisional government's desire to see the Cardassian **Aamin Marritza** returned to Bajor so that the accused war criminal could stand trial. ("Duet" [DS9]). SEE: **Gallitep**.

Kavis Alpha IV. Federation planet that became the home of the newly evolved nanite civilization in 2266. ("Evolution" [TNG]).

Kavis Alpha Sector. Home of a binary system that was the site of **Dr. Paul Stubb's** neutronium decay experiments in 2366. The neutron star of that system exploded every 196 years, making it a stellar equivalent of Earth's "Old Faithful." ("Evolution" [TNG]).

***Kavis Teke* elusive maneuver.** Famous battle strategy developed by the **Menthars** in their war with the **Promellians** a thousand years ago. ("Booby Trap" [TNG]).

Kayden, Will. Starfleet officer, a crew member aboard the *U.S.S. Rutledge*, who was killed during the battle on Setlik III. Kayden, nicknamed "Stompie" by his shipmates, was fond of singing **"The Minstrel Boy."** Kayden's commanding officer was **Captain Benjamin Maxwell**, and he had served along with **Miles O'Brien**. ("The Wounded" [TNG]).

Kaylar. Warrior on planet **Rigel VII**, encountered by Pike and company about a week prior to the *Enterprise*'s first expedition to **Talos IV** in 2254. An illusory version of this individual threatened Pike and **Vina** while the two were held captive by the **Talosians**. ("The Cage," "The Menagerie, Part II" [TOS]).

kayolane. A sedative in use aboard the *Enterprise*-D. ("Identity Crisis" [TNG]).

Kazago. Ferengi first officer to **DaiMon Bok** during the mission to return the hulk of the **U.S.S. Stargazer** to Picard in 2364. Kazago relieved Bok of command when it was learned that Bok had engaged in an unprofitable attempt to use the *Stargazer* to exact revenge upon Picard for his part in the **Battle of Maxia**. ("The Battle" [TNG]).

Kazanga. Brilliant theoretical scientist, often compared to such luminaries as **Albert Einstein** and **Dr. Richard Daystrom**. ("The Ultimate Computer" [TOS]).

Kazis Binary system. Projected destination of the **cryosatellite** discovered by the *Enterprise*-D in 2364. ("The Neutral Zone" [TNG]).

Kea IV. Planet that was the topic of a minor research paper presented by Jean-Luc Picard at an archaeology symposium in 2368. ("The Chase" [TNG]).

Kee'Bhor. Medical officer of the Klingon Bird-of-Prey *Toh'Kaht*. Kee'Bhor was murdered by First Officer Hon'Tihl while under the influence of the **Saltah'na energy spheres**, just before the destruction of the *Toh-Kaht* in 2369. ("Dramatis Personae" [DS9]).

Keel, Walker. (Jonathan Farwell). Commander of the *Starship Horatio*. Keel was one of several  officers who fought against an infiltration of **Starfleet Headquarters** in 2364, but he was killed in the effort, along with the crew of the *Horatio*. Keel had no brothers, but had two sisters, Anne and Melissa. Keel had been one of Jean-Luc Picard's closest friends. Both Keel and Picard were very close to **Jack Crusher**, and Keel introduced Crusher to his future wife, Beverly. Just prior to the destruction of the *Horatio*, Keel suspected his first officer might have fallen under the influence of the conspiracy. ("Conspiracy" [TNG]).

Keel. (Cal Bolder). Tribal warrior loyal to Teer **Maab** on planet Capella IV. Keel was ordered to kill the Klingon **Kras** when he betrayed Maab. ("Friday's Child" [TOS]).

Keeler, Edith. (Joan Collins). American social worker from Earth's 1930s who helped victims of the **Great Depression**. Keeler was an idealistic believer in humanity who worked to help those in her care survive for the future that she foresaw. Keeler, who died in an automobile accident in 1931, was a focal point in the flow of time. When Dr. McCoy, accidentally in Earth's  past, prevented her death, he unknowingly changed the course of Earth history. Keeler became a strong advocate for peace, delaying the United State's entry into World War II long enough for Nazi Germany to develop weapons that permitted Hitler to conquer the world. In this altered future, the *Starship Enterprise* did not explore the cosmos in the 23rd century. Kirk and Spock, who followed McCoy into the past, were forced to allow Keeler's death to restore the shape of time. This task was made infinitely more difficult when Kirk fell in love with Keeler. ("The City on the Edge of Forever" [TOS]). SEE: **Great Depression; Guardian of Forever; Twenty-First Street Mission**.

Keena. (Annie O'Donnell). Resident of **Jeraddo**, a moon orbiting planet **Bajor**. Keena, a Bajoran national, was made mute by the **Cardassians**, during the Cardassian occupation of Bajor. Keena escaped to Jeraddo with her companion, **Baltrim**, in 2351 and started a new life. Teaming up with farmer **Mullibok**, they lived peacefully until an energy-transfer project in 2369 forced the evacuation of Jeraddo. ("Progress" [DS9]).

Keeper, The. (Meg Wyllie). Magistrate and leader of the inhabitants of planet **Talos IV**. ("The Cage," "The Menagerie, Part II" [TOS]).

Keeve Falor. (Scot Marlow). A Bajoran leader who resided on the second planet in the **Valo System**. Though he had no diplomatic experience, Keeve was respected by his people. On the advice of Ensign Ro, Captain Picard sought the help of Keeve to locate Bajoran terrorist **Orta**, in 2368. ("Ensign Ro" [TNG]).

K'Ehleyr. (Suzie Plakson). Federation special emissary who supervised the return of the Klingon sleeper ship *T'Ong* to Klingon space in 2365. K'Ehleyr was responsible for averting a potential crisis, since the crew of the *T'Ong* believed the Klingon Empire was still at war with the Federation. K'Ehleyr's mother was human, and her father was Klingon. She said  that she had inherited her mother's sense of humor, but her father's Klingon temper.

K'Ehleyr had been romantically involved with **Worf** in 2359, but the relationship remained unresolved until 2365, when K'Ehleyr was assigned to the *Enterprise*-D to deal with the *T'Ong* crisis. K'Ehleyr and Worf nearly took the Klingon marriage oath at the time, when, unbeknownst to Worf, their liaison resulted in the conception of a child, **Alexander Rozhenko**. ("The Emissary" [TNG]).

K'Ehleyr served as a Federation ambassador to the **K'mpec** government, and helped orchestrate K'mpec's scheme to appoint an outsider as his **Arbiter of Succession**. Worf remained unaware that he was a father until K'Ehleyr returned to the *Enterprise*-D in 2367. She was at the time accompanying K'mpec for the meeting in which he asked Jean-Luc Picard, an outsider, to serve as his Arbiter of Succession. K'Ehleyr was murdered by Duras during the rite of succession after K'Ehleyr began to uncover evidence of **Duras**'s wrongdoings. Worf subsequently claimed the right of vengence under Klingon law and killed Duras. Worf also accepted custody of his son, Alexander, who remained with him aboard the *Enterprise*-D. ("Reunion" [TNG]). *Suzie Plakson had previously played the Vulcan* **Dr. Selar** *in "The Schizoid Man" (TNG).*

kelbonite. Refractory metal that was present in the caves on planets **Melona IV** and **Forlat III**. Data speculated the presence of kelbonite and fistrium made it impossible for the **Crystalline Entity** to penetrate into the caves where the colonists were hiding. ("Silicon Avatar" [TNG]).

kelilactiral. Fictional computer device Riker invented to confuse the Ferengis who took over the *Enterprise*-D in 2369. ("Rascals" [TNG]).

Kelinda. (Barbara Bouchet). **Kelvan** who assisted in the capture of the *Enterprise* landing party in 2268 and forced the *Enterprise* crew to set a course for the **Andromeda Galaxy**. Having taken a female humanoid form, Kelinda was susceptible to the new and unfamiliar feelings that accompanied her new body. Kirk took advantage of this, confusing her and the other members of her race with human sensations until they surrendered the ship and accepted a Federation offer of peace. ("By Any Other Name" [TOS]).

Kell. (Larry Dobkin). A special emissary from the Klingon High Command, later found to be a Romulan operative. Kell tried to use his position to instigate distrust between the Federation and Klingon governments following an attempted revolt on **Krios** in 2367. A major tactic was Kell's acquisition of mental control over *Enterprise*-D officer Geordi La Forge. Kell used an **E-band** transmitter to send signals directly to La Forge, attempting to command La Forge to assassinate Klingon governor **Vagh**. ("The Mind's Eye" [TNG]).

Keller, Ensign. A member of the *Enterprise*-D's engineering staff. She died as the result of a failure in the ship's **antimatter containment** systems. A breach of the **matter/antimatter reaction chamber** forced the closure of the isolation doors, trapping Keller. ("Violations" [TNG]). *The incident in which Keller died presumably took place before "Violations," but we don't know much else about it because it was a flashback scene.*

kellicam. Unit of distance measure in use by the Klingon Empire. (*Star Trek III: The Search for Spock*, "Redemption, Part I" [TNG]). *One kellicam was roughly equal to two kilometers.*

kellipates. Unit of distance or area measure on planet **Bajor**. Kira Nerys told **Mullibok** about a huge tree whose branches blotted out the sun for kellipates. ("Progress" [DS9]).

Kelly, Lieutenant Joshua. Chief engineer of the Starship

Yosemite, killed when the ship was investigating a binary star system in the **Igo Sector** in 2369. ("Realm of Fear" [TNG]).

Kelly, Lieutenant Morgan. Security officer of the *U.S.S. Essex*, apparently killed in the crash of that vessel on the moon of planet **Mab-Bu** IV in 2167. ("Power Play" [TNG]).

Kelowitz, Lieutenant Commander. (Grant Woods). *Enterprise* security officer who was part of the landing party to the Federation outpost on **Cestus III** in 2367. Unlike his counterpart, Security Officer **Lang**, Kelowitz survived the mission. ("Arena" [TOS]). Kelowitz was a landing party member who participated in the search for *Shuttlecraft Galileo* when it crashed on planet **Taurus II** in 2267. He delivered a report on the humanoid creatures found on that planet. ("The *Galileo* Seven" [TOS]).

Kelrabi System. Star system located in **Cardassian** space, destination of a Cardassian supply ship intercepted by the *U.S.S. Phoenix* and the *Enterprise*-D in 2367. ("The Wounded" [TNG]).

Kelsey. (Marie Marshall). Leader of a terrorist group that attempted to steal **trilithium resin** when the *Enterprise*-D was being serviced at the **Remmler Array** in 2369. ("Starship Mine" [TNG]).

Kelso, Chief. (J. Downing). *Enterprise*-D engineering technician who operated the transporter during the **particle fountain** malfunction at **Tyrus VIIA** in 2369. ("The Quality of Life" [TNG]). *This character was named by writer Naren Shankar in homage to character Lee Kelso from the pilot episode "Where No Man Has Gone Before" (TOS).*

Kelso, Lieutenant Lee. (Paul Carr). Helm officer aboard the *U.S.S. Enterprise* during the early days of Kirk's first five-year mission in 2265. Kelso was killed by **Gary Mitchell** while helping to implement a plan to quarantine Mitchell on planet **Delta Vega**. ("Where No Man Has Gone Before" [TOS]).

Kelva. Planet in the Andromeda Galaxy that was homeworld to a race known as the **Kelvans**. ("By Any Other Name" [TOS]).

Kelvans. Life-forms from planet **Kelva** in the **Andromeda Galaxy**. Although they are highly intelligent and their bodies have a hundred tentacles, Kelvans have no tactile perceptions or emotions as we know them. When Kelvan scientists recognized that increasing radiation levels in their galaxy would make life impossible in ten millennia, the Kelvan Empire dispatched several ships to explore the universe for a new place to live. One of their explorer ships was damaged entering the **galactic barrier** at the edge of the Milky Way Galaxy and the crew abandoned ship. Taking humanoid form, the Kelvans dispatched a general distress call that was answered by the *Enterprise* in 2268. The Kelvans commandeered the *Enterprise*, forcing the starship to cross the barrier and to set course for the Andromeda Galaxy. The *Enterprise* crew was able to regain control of their ship by using the Kelvans' unfamiliarity with humanoid senses to confuse and distract them. Kirk then invited the Kelvans to settle in Federation space and live in peace. ("By Any Other Name" [TOS]). SEE: **Kelinda**; **Rojan**.

Kenda II. Federation planet, home of **Dr. Dalen Quaice.** The *Enterprise*-D was scheduled to return Quaice to Kenda II while en route to planet Durenia IV in early 2367. ("Remember Me" [TNG]).

Kenicki. *Enterprise*-D crew member who suffered from hallucinations caused by lack of **REM sleep** while the *Enterprise*-D was adrift in a **Tyken's Rift** in 2367. Kenicki reported seeing someone in an old-style starfleet uniform riding the turbolift in Engineering. ("Night Terrors" [TNG]).

Kennelly, Admiral. (Cliff Potts). Federation official who made a secret pact with the **Cardassians** in 238 to eliminate the **Bajoran** terrorists believed responsible for an attack against a Federation colony. Kennelly planted Ensign **Ro Laren** on the *Enterprise*-D to carry out his plan. Kennelly's plan was discovered, and he was imprisoned. ("Ensign Ro" [TNG]). SEE: ***Antares*-class carrier.** *Cliff Potts had played one of the crew members on the spaceship* Valley Forge *in Douglas Trumbull's 1972 film,* Silent Running.

Kentor. (Richard Allen). Young community leader of the **Tau Cygna V** colony in 2366. ("The Ensigns of Command" [TNG]).

Kerelian. Alien race whose hearing can distinguish a greater range of musical notes than that of humans. Jean-Luc Picard told **Neela Daren** that a Kerelian tenor had a wide range of musical nuances only others of their race could hear. ("Lessons" [TNG]).

Kerla, Brigadier. (Paul Rossilli). Military advisor to Klingon **chancellor Gorkon**, and later to Chancellor **Azetbur**. Kerla opposed Gorkon's 2293 peace initiative. (*Star Trek VI: The Undiscovered Country*).

Kesla. Name given to unidentified mass murderer of women on planet Deneb II, later found to be an energy life-form also known as **Redjac**. ("Wolf in the Fold" [TOS]).

kevas. Goods traded on planet **Organia**. Spock posed as a trader dealing in kevas and trillium. ("Errand of Mercy" [TOS]).

Khan. (Ricardo Montalban). Aka Khan Noonien Singh. Genetically engineered human who attempted to gain control of the entire planet Earth in the 1990s during the **Eugenics Wars**. From 1992-1996 Khan was absolute ruler of more than a quarter of Earth, from South Asia through the Middle East. He was the last of the tyrants to be

overthrown. Khan escaped in 1996 with a band of followers aboard the sleeper ship **S.S. Botany Bay**. In 2267 the *Starship Enterprise* discovered the *Botany Bay* and awakened Khan and his people. Once awakened, Khan attempted to take over the *Enterprise*, but was thwarted. Captain Kirk exercised command prerogatives in dropping all charged when Khan agreed to be exiled to planet Ceti Alpha V to start a new life. ("Space Seed" [TOS]). Khan and his followers remained on Ceti Alpha V for several years until they were accidentally discovered by a scientific reconnaissance party from the *Starship **Reliant*** in 2285. Khan commandeered the *Reliant* and ransacked the nearby **Regula I Space Laboratory**, stealing the experimental **Genesis Device**. Khan, along with his followers and the crew of the *Reliant*, was killed when the Genesis Device exploded while on board the *Reliant*. (*Star Trek II: The Wrath of Khan*).

Khazara. Imperial Romulan Warbird, *D'Deridex* class. This ship, captained by **Commander Toreth**, was seized by **Subcommander N'Vek** and Deanna Troi as part of a plot to enable Romulan **vice-proconsul M'ret** to defect to the Federation. ("Face of the Enemy" [TNG]).

Khitomer massacre. A brutal attack by Romulan forces on the Klingon outpost at **Khitomer** in 2346. Some 4,000 Klingons were killed in the incident, later learned to have been made possible by the betrayal of **Ja'rod**, a Klingon who provided secret defense access codes to the Romulans. The only survivors of the massacre were a Klingon child named **Worf** and his nursemaid named **Kahlest**. The two were rescued by the **U.S.S. Intrepid**, which responded to the Klingons' distress calls. Years later, in 2366, **Klingon High Council** member **Duras**, son of Ja'rod, attempted to falsify evidence to implicate Worf's father, **Mogh**, as the one who provided the codes to the Romulans. Duras was only partly successful, since Worf learned of the injustice and made an appeal to High Council leader **K'mpec**. ("Sins of the Father" [TNG]). *Star Trek VI establishes that Khitomer was near the Romulan border. We speculate that the massacre was part of an ongoing border dispute between the two powers.*

Khitomer. Class-M planet near the Romulan/Klingon border. Khitomer was the site of the historic Khitomer peace conference in 2293 that was the beginning of rapprochement between the **United Federation of Planets** and the **Klingon Empire**. (*Star Trek VI: The Undiscovered Country*). At the conference, Captain **Spock** first met **Pardek**, a Romulan politician who expressed support for a reunification of the Vulcan and Romulan peoples. ("Unification, Part I" [TNG]). A Klingon outpost was later established on this planet, and was the target of the brutal **Khitomer massacre** by the Romulans in 2346. ("Sins of the Father" [TNG]). In 2369, Worf learned that some of the Klingons believed killed at Khitomer were actually taken prisoner by the Romulans. Nearly a hundred Klingons had been discovered unconscious at a perimeter outpost, and the

Romulans, reluctant to kill helpless people, instead took them prisoner. ("Birthright, Part I" [TNG]). The prisoners proved to be of no political use, and they later refused an offer of freedom even though the Romulan government favored their execution, since permitting themselves to be captured, however involuntarily, was a serious breach of the Klingon warrior ethic. Romulan officer **Tokath** opposed the execution of the Klingons, and sacrificed his military career to establish and command a prison camp in the **Carraya System**. ("Birthright, Part II" [TNG]). *Photo: Camp Khitomer.*

kilodyne. A measurement of force, one thousand dynes. ("The Loss" [TNG]).

kiloquad. Unit of measure of data storage and transmission in Federation computer systems. ("Realm of Fear" [TNG]). *No, we don't know how many bytes are in a kiloquad. We don't even want to know. The reason the term was invented was specifically to avoid describing the data capacity of Star Trek's computers in 20th-century terms. It was feared by technical consultant Mike Okuda that any such attempt would look foolish in just a few years, given the current rate of progress in that field.*

Kim, Luisa. (Elizabeth Lindsey). Terraforming scientist, part of the unsuccessful **terraforming** project at planet **Velara III**. Kim had great enthusiasm for her work and was devastated to learn that the Velara III project would have destroyed the **microbrain** life-forms there. ("Home Soil" [TNG]).

Kingsley, Dr. Sara. (Patricia Smith). Scientist at the **Darwin Genetic Research Station** on planet **Gagarin IV**. In the late 2350s and 2360s, Kingsley was part of a genetic-engineering project intended to develop human children with a powerful immune system capable of attacking disease organisms before they enter a human body. After these children were several years old it was learned that the children's antibodies could also attack human beings, causing a disease closely resembling hyperaccelerated aging. Although Kingsley was afflicted by the antibodies, a transporter-based technique was successful in restoring her to her normal age. ("Unnatural Selection" [TNG]).

Kira Nerys. (Nana Visitor). **Bajoran** freedom fighter who was assigned as first officer and Bajoran liaison to station **Deep Space 9** after the **Cardassian** withdrawal from Bajor in 2369. Stubborn and independent, Major Kira had been fighting the Cardassians since she was 12 years old, and had opposed the Bajoran provisional government's decision to enlist Federation assistance in maintaining Deep Space 9. ("Emissary" [DS9]).

As a member of the Bajoran **Shakaar** resistance group in 2357, Kira helped liberate the notorious **Gallitep** labor camp at which thousands of Bajorans had died under Cardassian bondage. ("Duet" [DS9]). Kira knew the terrorist **Tahna Los**

when she fought in the Bajoran underground. ("Past Prologue" [DS9]). She spent much of her childhood as a freedom fighter for the Bajoran movement, although Cardassian intelligence reported her as "a minor operative whose activities are limited to running errands for the terrorist leaders." ("Battle Lines" [DS9]). Kira had a deep, abiding faith in the Bajoran religion, and was personally struck by the tragedy of **Kai Opaka**'s death in 2369. ("Battle Lines" [DS9]). *Kira first appeared in "Emissary" (DS9).*

Kiri-kin-tha's First Law of Metaphysics. "Nothing unreal exists." Spock recited this quote during a memory test in 2286. (*Star Trek IV: The Voyage Home*).

Kirk, Aurelan. (Joan Swift). Colonist on planet **Deneva** who was killed by the **Denevan neural parasites** in 2267. Aurelan was wife of **George Samuel Kirk** and mother to **Peter Kirk**. ("Operation— Annihilate!" [TOS]).

Kirk, George Samuel. (William Shatner). Research biologist and older brother to **James T. Kirk**. Sam had been working on a project at planet **Deneva**, where he lived with his wife and three sons. Sam was killed by the **Denevan neural parasites** in 2267. Samuel Kirk had been living on Deneva with his wife Aurelan and son Peter when the parasites infested the planet's population. ("Operation—Annihilate!" [TOS]). Sam had seen his younger brother — the only one who called him Sam — off on his first mission aboard the *Enterprise*. ("What Are Little Girls Made Of?" [TOS]). *Sam was established in "What Are Little Girls Made Of?" (TOS) to have had three sons, one of whom, Peter, was seen in "Operation— Annihilate!" (TOS). We don't know anything about Peter's two brothers, although they presumably were not at the Deneva colony at the time Sam and Aurelan were killed. Sam was only seen briefly as an already-dead body, "played" by William Shatner.*

Kirk, James T. (mirror). (William Shatner). Captain of the *I.S.S.* **Enterprise** in the **mirror universe**. Assumed command of *I.S.S. Enterprise* through assassination of Captain Christopher Pike. Kirk's first action for the Empire was to suppress a Gorlan uprising by destroying a rebel home planet. His second action was the execution of 5,000 colonists on Vega IX. The mirror Kirk was transposed into our universe in 2267 when an **ion storm** caused a brief bridge between the two existences. It was believed that the **mirror Spock** would overthrow Kirk as commander of the *Enterprise*, thereby opening the way to breaking the mirror empire's pattern of repressive barbarism. ("Mirror, Mirror" [TOS])

Kirk, James T. (William Shatner). Commander of the original *Starship* **Enterprise** during its historic five-year mission of exploration in 2264-2269. Starfleet serial number SC 937-0176 CEC. ("Court Martial" [TOS]).

Childhood and family: Kirk was born in 2233 ("The Deadly Years" [TOS]) in Iowa on planet Earth (*Star Trek IV: The Voyage Home*). In

2246, Kirk — at age 13 — was one of nine surviving eyewitnesses to the massacre of some 4,000 colonists at planet **Tarsus IV** by **Kodos the Executioner**. ("The Conscience of the King" [TOS]). James Kirk lost his older brother, **George Samuel Kirk** (whom only James called Sam), and sister-in-law, **Aurelan Kirk**, on planet **Deneva** due to the invasion of the **Denevan neural parasites** in 2267. Kirk's nephew, **Peter Kirk** survived. ("Operation— Annihilate!" [TOS]). Sam Kirk had two other sons who were not on Deneva at the time of the tragedy. ("What Are Little Girls Made Of?" [TOS]).

Kirk at the Academy: During his Academy days, Kirk was tormented by an upperclassman named **Finnegan**, who frequently chose Kirk as a target for practical jokes. Kirk found a measure of satisfaction years later, in 2267, when he had a chance to wallop a replica of Finnegan created on the **amusement park planet** in the **Omicron Delta region**. ("Shore Leave" [TOS]). Kirk served as an instructor at the Academy and **Gary Mitchell** was one of his students. The two were good friends, and once Mitchell took a poisonous dart on Dimorus meant for Kirk, saving Kirk's life. Mitchell set Kirk up with a "little blond lab tech" whom he almost married. ("Where No Man Has Gone Before" [TOS]). *Photo: Gary Mitchell.*

Another of Kirk's friends from his Academy days was **Benjamin Finney**, who named his daughter, Jamie, after Kirk. A rift developed between Finney and Kirk around 2250 when the two were serving together on the **U.S.S. Republic**. Kirk logged a mistake that Finney had made, and Finney blamed Kirk for his subsequent failure to earn command of a starship. *Kirk's service aboard the* Republic *was apparently while he was still attending the Academy, since he was an ensign on the* Republic, *but he was a lieutenant on the* Farragut, *which was described as his first posting after the Academy.* ("Court Martial" [TOS]). *Photo: Ben Finney.* One of Kirk's heroes at the Academy was the legendary Captain **Garth of Izar**, whose exploits are required reading. Years later, Kirk helped save his hero when Garth had become criminally insane and was being treated at the **Elba II** penal colony. ("Whom Gods Destroy" [TOS]). Another of Kirk's personal heroes was **Abraham Lincoln**, 16th president of the United States of America on Earth. ("The Savage Curtain" [TOS]). At the Academy, James Kirk earned something of a reputation for himself as having been the only cadet ever to have beaten the "no-win" **Kobayashi Maru** scenario. He did it by secretly reprogramming the simulation computer to make it possible to win, earning a commendation for original thinking in the process. (*Star Trek II: The Wrath of Khan*).

Early days in Starfleet: Kirk's first assignment after graduating from the Academy was aboard the **U.S.S. Farragut**. ("Obsession" [TOS]). One of his first missions as a young lieutenant was to command a survey mission to **Tyree's** planet in 2254. ("A Private Little War" [TOS]). *This incident presumably took place while Kirk served on the* Farragut. While serving aboard the *Farragut* in 2257, Lieutenant Kirk blamed himself for the deaths of 200 *Farragut* personnel, including **Captain Garrovick**, by the **dikironium cloud creature** at planet **Tycho IV**. Kirk felt he could have acted faster in firing on the creature, but learned years later that nothing could have prevented the deaths. ("Obsession" [TOS]). Sometime in the past Kirk almost died from **Vegan choriomeningitis**. ("The Mark of Gideon" [TOS]).

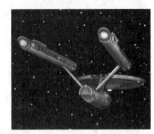

Aboard the *U.S.S. Enterprise*: Kirk's greatest renown came from his command of a historic five-year mission of the original *Starship Enterprise* from 2264-2269. By 2267, Kirk had earned an impressive list of commendations from Starfleet, including the Palm leaf of Axanar Peace Mission, the Grankite Order of Tactics (Class of Excellence), and the Preantares Ribbon of Commendation (Classes First and Second). Kirk's awards for valor included the Medal of Honor, the Silver Palm with Cluster, the Starfleet Citation for Conspicuous Gallantry, and the Kragite Order of Heroism. ("Court Martial" [TOS]). In 2267, Kirk became the first starship captain ever to stand trial when he was accused of causing the death of Benjamin Finney. Kirk's trial, held at **Starbase 11**, proved Kirk innocent of wrongdoing, and he was exonerated. ("Court Martial" [TOS]). SEE: **Shaw, Areel**. During that original five-year mission, Kirk recorded a tape of last orders to be played by Commander Spock and Chief Medical Officer McCoy upon his death. While trapped in a **spatial interphase** near Tholian space, Kirk vanished with the **U.S.S. Defiant** and was declared dead. His last orders conveyed the hope that his two friends would work together, despite their differences. ("The Tholian Web" [TOS]). Kirk was once split into two personalities by a transporter malfunction. ("The Enemy Within" [TOS]). His living quarters aboard the original *Enterprise* were on Deck 5. ("Journey to Babel" [TOS]).

Relationships with women: Kirk was notably unsuccessful in maintaining a long-term relationship with any woman. Although he was involved with many different women during his life, his intense passion for his career always seemed to interfere. A few years prior to his command of the first *Enterprise*, Kirk became involved with **Dr. Carol Marcus**. The two

had a child, **David Marcus**, but Kirk and Carol did not remain together, because their respective careers took them in separate directions. *Photo: Dr. Carol Marcus.* Other significant romances in Kirk's life included **Ruth**, with whom he was involved when he attended Starfleet Academy ("Shore Leave" [TOS]), **Janice Lester**, with whom he spent a year, also during his Academy days ("Turnabout Intruder" [TOS]), **Janet Wallace**, a scientist who later saved his life ("The Deadly Years" [TOS]), **Areel Shaw**, who, ironically, years later prosecuted Kirk in the case of Ben Finney's apparent death ("Court Martial" [TOS]), and **Miramanee**, a woman whom Kirk married in 2268 when he suffered from amnesia on a landing party mission. Miramanee became pregnant with Kirk's child, but both mother and unborn child were killed in a local power struggle. ("The Paradise Syndrome" [TOS]). Perhaps Kirk's most tragic romantic involvement was with American social worker **Edith Keeler**, whom Kirk met in Earth's past when he traveled into the 1930s through the **Guardian of Forever**. Keeler was a focal point in time, and Kirk was forced to allow her death in order to prevent a terrible change in the flow of history. ("The City on the Edge of Forever" [TOS]).

David Marcus: Kirk was not involved with the upbringing of his son, **David Marcus**, at the request of the boy's mother, Carol Marcus. Kirk had no contact with his son until 2285, when Carol and David were both working on **Project Genesis**, and Kirk helped rescue the two from **Khan**'s vengeance. Later, Kirk and his son were able to achieve a degree of rapprochement.

Tragically, David was murdered shortly thereafter on the **Genesis Planet**, by a Klingon officer who sought to steal the secret of Genesis. *Photo: Dr. David Marcus.*

After the five-year mission: Following the return of the *Enterprise* from the five-year mission in 2270, Kirk accepted a promotion to admiral, while the *Enterprise* underwent an extensive refit. At the time, Kirk recommended **Will Decker** to replace him as *Enterprise* captain, although Kirk accepted a grade reduction back to captain when he regained command of the ship to meet the **V'Ger** threat in 2271. (*Star Trek: The Motion Picture*). (*The significant time gap between* Star Trek: The Motion Picture *and* Star Trek II: The Wrath of Khan *might suggest the possibility that Kirk commanded a second five-year mission of the* Enterprise *following the events in the first* Star Trek *movie.*)

Kirk became a staff instructor at Starfleet Academy, but returned to active duty in 2285 when **Khan Noonien Singh** hijacked the *Starship Reliant* and stole the **Genesis Device**. Kirk's close friend, Spock, was killed in that incident. (*Star Trek II: The Wrath of Khan*). Upon learning that Spock's *katra* survived, Kirk hijacked the *Enterprise* to the Genesis Planet to return Spock's body to **Vulcan**, where the body was reunited with Spock's *katra*. Kirk ordered the *Enterprise* destroyed in the incident to prevent its capture by Klingons. (*Star Trek III: The Search for Spock*). Kirk was charged with nine violations of Starfleet regulations in connection with the revival of Spock in 2285. All but one charge was later dropped, and Kirk was found guilty of the one remaining charge, that of disobeying a superior officer. The **Federation Council** was nonetheless so grateful for Kirk's role in saving Earth from the devastating effects of an alien probe that it granted Kirk the captaincy of the second *Starship Enterprise*. (*Star Trek IV: The Voyage Home*).

Kirk was an intensely driven individual who enjoyed hazardous recreational activities. A personal challenge that nearly cost him his life was free-climbing the sheer El Capitan mountain face in **Yosemite National Park** on Earth. (*Star Trek V: The Final Frontier*). Kirk carried the bitterness for his son's murder for years, and opposed the peace initiative of Klingon **chancellor Gorkon** in 2293. He especially resented the fact that he was chosen as the Federation's olive branch and assigned the duty of escorting Gorkon to Earth. During that mission, Kirk (along with McCoy) was arrested and wrongly convicted for the murder of Gorkon by Federation and Klingon forces conspiring to block Gorkon's initiatives. Kirk nevertheless played a pivotal role in saving the historic **Khitomer** peace conference from further attacks. Kirk was scheduled to retire about three months after the Khitomer conference. (*Star Trek VI: The Undiscovered Country*). *Kirk's first appearance was in "Where No Man Has Gone Before" (TOS).*

Kirk, Peter. (Craig Hundley). Nephew of Captain James Kirk and one of the victims of the neural parasites that infested planet Deneva in 2267. Peter lost both parents and was himself almost killed by the **Denevan neural parasites**. ("Operation— Annihilate!" [TOS]). *Peter presumably had two brothers, who were apparently not at the Deneva colony, per Kirk's line in "What Are Little Girls Made Of?" (TOS). Craig Hundley also appeared as* **Tommy Starnes** *in the third-season episode "And the Children Shall Lead" [TOS] and, years later, composed some background music for* Star Trek III.

Kirok. The name that James Kirk remembered as his own while suffering from amnesia and living among the people on **Miramanee's planet** in 2268. ("The Paradise Syndrome" [TOS]). *Photo: James T. Kirk as Kirok on Miramanee's planet.*

Kirom, Knife of. Sacred artifact that Klingon legend holds to be stained with the blood of **Kahless the Unforgettable**. Gowron used the bloodstains to help determine the legitimacy of the clone of Kahless the Unforgettable produced by the clerics of **Boreth** in 2369. Since the new Kahless was indeed a clone, his genetic pattern was an exact match of the original. ("Rightful Heir" [TNG]).

kironide. Chemical compound found in the food on planet **Platonius**. Kironide is a long-lasting source of great power that, when ingested, endows many humanoids with extraordinary psychokinetic powers. The **Platonians** absorbed kironide into their bodies, giving them such powers, although their servant **Alexander** was unable to do so. ("Plato's Stepchildren" [TOS]).

Kiros. (Patricia Tallman). Member of a group of terrorists who attempted to steal **trilithium resin** from the *Enterprise-D* in 2369. ("Starship Mine" [TNG]). *Patricia Tallman has made other appearances, as a stunt person, on* Star Trek: The Next Generation *and had a role in the pilot episode of* Babylon 5.

Klaa, Captain. (Todd Bryant). Commander of the Klingon

Bird-of-Prey that was ordered to secure the release of Klingon general **Koord** at planet **Nimbus III**. Klaa, an ambitious young officer, saw the mission as an opportunity to distinguish himself by challenging the legendary Captain Kirk. (*Star Trek V: The Final Frontier*). Klaa later served as translator in 2293 when Kirk and McCoy were tried for the murder of **Chancellor Gorkon**. (*Star Trek VI: The Undiscovered Country*).

klabnian eel. A life-form that **Q** found distasteful. Q offered to do Picard "a big favor" and turn **Vash** into a klabnian eel. ("QPid" [TNG]).

Klaestron IV. Planet from whence **Ilon Tandro** hailed, arriving at station Deep Space 9 in 2369 with a warrant for **Jadzia Dax**'s arrest for murder. Although members of the Federation, the Klaestrons are allies of the **Cardassians**. This fact explained why Tandro had knowledge of the interior of the station which aided in the kidnapping of Dax. ("Dax" [DS9]).

Klag. (Brian Thompson). Second officer of the Klingon Bird-of-Prey *Pagh* during William Riker's brief tenure aboard that vessel as part of an officer-exchange program in 2365. Klag expressed doubts that a human officer could effectively command a Klingon crew, but Riker convinced him otherwise by demonstrating his adeptness at physical combat. ("A Matter of Honor" [TNG]).

Klarc-Tarn-Droth. A renowned Federation archaeologist present at the annual symposium of the **Federation Archaeology Council** in 2367. ("QPid" [TNG]).

Klavdia III. Planet where **Salia**, future leader of planet **Daled IV**, was raised in an environment far from the divisiveness of her homeworld. Although inhospitable, this planet was chosen because of security considerations. In 2365, the *Enterprise*-D was assigned to transport Salia from Klavdia III to assume her duties as leader on planet Daled IV. ("The Dauphin" [TNG]).

kligat. Three-sided bladed weapon used by tribal warriors on planet **Capella IV**. At ranges up to 100 meters, the *kligat* could be thrown with deadly accuracy. Security guard Grant was killed by a *kligat* when he drew a weapon at a Klingon on Capella VI in 2267. ("Friday's Child" [TOS]).

Kling. A district or city on the **Klingon Homeworld**. The renegade Korris spoke disparagingly of "the traitors of Kling." ("Heart of Glory" [TNG]). *At the time the episode was written, Kling was intended as the name of the Klingon Homeworld. Once the episode was filmed, it was realized that the name sounded pretty silly, so later scripts simply referred to "the Homeworld." The only time the Homeworld was given a name was in* Star Trek VI: The Undiscovered Country, *when it was called* **Qo'noS**, *pronounced "kronos."*

Klingon attack cruiser. Starship of the **Klingon Defense Force**. Designated as *Vor'cha*-class vessels, attack cruisers were among the largest and most powerful vessels in the Imperial fleet. In 2367, Klingon High Council leader **K'mpec**

was transported aboard an attack cruiser on his final mission; his plea for Jean-Luc Picard to serve as **Arbiter of Succession** after K'mpec's death. ("Reunion" [TNG]). *The Vor'cha-class attack cruiser was designed by Rick Sternbach and built by Greg Jein. It first appeared in "Reunion" (TNG).* SEE: **Klingon spacecraft**.

Klingon battle cruiser. Starships that formed the backbone of the Klingon Defense Force for decades. The D7-type vessels were in service in the 2260s, a design shared with the **Romulan Star Empire** during the brief alliance between the two powers.

These vessels, some 228 meters in overall length, were equipped with warp drive and phase-disruptor armament. By the 2280s, an uprated version, known as a *K't'inga*-class vessel, was introduced into service. *The Klingon battle cruiser was designed by Matt Jefferies and introduced during the third season of the original* Star Trek *series. A more detailed version was built by Magicam for* Star Trek: The Motion Picture, *and was reused in* Star Trek II, Star Trek VI, *as well as in* Star Trek: The Next Generation. *The terms D7 and* K't'inga *are conjectural.* SEE: **Klingon spacecraft**.

Klingon Bird-of-Prey. Ship used by the **Klingon Defense Force**, capable of both atmospheric entry and landing, as well as warp-speed interstellar travel. At least two classes of this ship have been in use since at least 2286, the smaller *B'rel*-class scouts and the

larger *K'Vort*-class cruisers. Both were equipped with cloaking devices. The *B'rel*-class ships had a complement of about a dozen officers and crew. (*Star Trek III: The Search for Spock*). An experimental uprated version of this ship was developed prior to 2293 in an effort to allow the use of torpedo weapons while the cloaking device was engaged. This prototype vessel was commanded by **General Chang**, who used it in his unsuccessful attempt to obstruct the **Khitomer** peace conference. (*Star Trek VI: The Undiscovered Country*). *The term Bird-of-Prey was originally established to be Romulan in "Balance of Terror" (TOS). An early draft of* Star Trek III *had Commander Kruge stealing a Romulan ship for his quest against Kirk. The Romulan connection was dropped in later drafts, but the ship somehow remained a Bird-of-Prey. The ship was designed by Nilo Rodis and built at ILM. It was first seen in* Star Trek III, *and also used in* Star Trek IV, V, *and* VI. *Class names are from "Yesterday's* Enterprise" (TNG) for K'Vort, and "Rascals" (TNG) for B'rel. Klingon Birds-of-Prey have appeared in "A Matter of Honor" (TNG), "The Defector"

(TNG), "Yesterday's Enterprise" (TNG), "Reunion" (TNG), "Redemption" (TNG), and "Unification, Parts I and II" (TNG). SEE: **Klingon spacecraft**.

Klingon calisthenics program. SEE: **Calisthenics program, Klingon.**

Klingon civil war. A brief but bitter power struggle between the forces of council leader **Gowron** and challengers from the politically powerful **Duras** family in early 2368. **Lursa** and **B'Etor**, sisters to the late Duras, had attempted to force Duras's illegitimate son, **Toral**, to be accepted as leader of the **Klingon High Council**. When **Jean-Luc Picard**, acting as **Arbiter of Succession**, refused to accept Toral's bid, Lursa and B'Etor attempted a military coup against Gowron. Although Gowron's forces seemed initially overmatched by those loyal to the Duras family, it was learned that Lursa and B'Etor were being supplied by Romulan operative **Sela**. Captain Picard ruled that the Federation Starfleet could not take sides in this internal Klingon matter, but later agreed to blockade the Romulan supply convoy, resulting in a victory for Gowron's forces. ("Redemption, Parts I and II" [TNG]).

Klingon cloaking device. SEE: **cloaking device, Klingon.**

Klingon communicator. Personal voice-communications device used by members of the Klingon Defense Force. In the 2260s, these devices were handheld, but by 2365 they had been incorporated into small decorative pins worn on a warrior's uniform.

Klingon death ritual. A ceremony practiced by Klingons upon the death of a comrade. The eyes of the fallen warrior are pried open, while other warriors gather around and let loose with a powerful howl that has been described not as a wail of the dead, but as an exhaltation of the victorious. Klingon belief holds that the howl is a warning for the dead to beware because a Klingon warrior is about to arrive. ("Heart of Glory" [TNG]). *The death howl was seen in "Heart of Glory," and again upon* **K'Ehleyr**'s *death in "Reunion" (TNG).*

Klingon Defense Force. Military service of the Klingon Empire. The Klingon Defense Force is responsible for defending the Empire's borders against enemies and for operating the Empire's space fleet. **Korris** and **Konmel** both claimed to be members of the Klingon Defense Force, but they were actually renegades seeking to overthrow the Klingon government. ("Heart of Glory" [TNG]). Worf's brother, **Kurn**, was an officer of the Klingon Defense Force. ("Sins of the Father" [TNG]).

Klingon Empire. The Klingon nation, founded some 1,500 years ago by **Kahless the Unforgettable**, who first united the Klingon people by killing the tyrant, **Molor**. ("Rightful Heir" [TNG]).

First contact between the Klingon Empire and the Fed-

eration took place in 2218 ("Day of the Dove" [TOS]), a disastrous event that led to nearly a century of hostilities between the two powers. ("First Contact" [TNG]). In 2267 negotiations between the Federation and the Klingon Empire were on the verge of breaking down. The Klingons had issued an ultimatum to the Federation to withdraw from disputed areas claimed by both the Federation and the Klingon Empire or face war. The hostilities came to a head at planet **Organia**, the only class-M planet in the area. Unknown to either combatant, the **Organians** were incredibly advanced **noncorporeal life**-forms who imposed the **Organian Peace Treaty** on both parties, thus effectively ending armed hostilities. ("Errand of Mercy" [TOS]).

The Klingons entered into a brief alliance with the **Romulan Star Empire** around 2268, when an agreement between the two powers resulted in the sharing of military technology and spacecraft designs, providing the Romulans with Klingon battle cruisers. ("The *Enterprise* Incident" [TOS]). By the mid-2280s, Klingons were using ships described as Birds-of-Prey (traditionally a Romulan term) that were equipped with **cloaking devices**. (*Star Trek III: The Search for Spock*).

A new chapter in relations between the Klingons and the Federation was opened in 2293 when a catastrophic explosion on **Praxis** caused serious environmental damage to the Homeworld. In the economic disarray that followed, Klingon **chancellor Gorkon**, leader of the High Council, found that his empire could no longer afford its massive military forces. Gorkon therefore launched a peace initiative, offering to end some 70 years of hostilities with the Federation. Just prior to a major peace conference, Gorkon was murdered by Federation and Klingon interests who sought to maintain the status quo. Gorkon's successor, his daughter, **Azetbur**, continued her father's work, and successfully concluded the **Khitomer** accords with the Federation later that year, ending nearly a century of hostilities. (*Star Trek VI*).

The **Klingon High Council** was a hotbed of political intrigue that nearly plunged the Empire into civil war in 2367 when council leader **K'mpec** died of poison. This murder, viewed as a killing without honor under Klingon tradition, triggered a bitter struggle to determine K'mpec's successor. K'mpec had taken the unorthodox precaution of appointing a non-Klingon, Jean-Luc Picard, as his **Arbiter of Succession**. Under Picard's mediation, political newcomer **Gowron** emerged as the sole candidate for council leader. ("Reunion" [TNG]). Forces loyal to the powerful Duras family unsuccessfully attempted to block Gowron, plunging the Empire into a brief, but bitter **Klingon civil war** in early 2368. ("Redemption, Parts I and II" [TNG]). Though their nation was called an empire, it had not been ruled by an emperor for more than three centuries. This situation changed rather dramatically in 2369, when the clerics of **Boreth** produced a clone of Kahless the Unforgettable. Although their initial claim that the clone was the actual Kahless was quickly disproven, this clone was regarded as the rightful heir to the throne and, with the support of High Council leader **Gowron**, was installed as the ceremonial Emperor of the Klingon people. ("Rightful Heir" [TNG]).

Klingon High Council. Ruling body of the **Klingon Empire**. The council was composed of about two dozen members and met in the **Great Hall** of the **First City** of the **Klingon Homeworld**. The High Council has a long history of political intrigue and power struggles. When council member **Duras** attempted to unjustly convict the late **Mogh** of having betrayed his people at **Khitomer**, the council, led by **K'mpec**, was willing to let the accusation stand for fear the powerful Duras family would plunge the Empire into civil war. ("Sins of the Father" [TNG]). K'mpec held the position of council leader for longer than anyone in history, until his death in 2367. ("Reunion" [TNG]). SEE: **Arbiter of Succession; Rite of Succession**. His successor, **Gowron**, successfully fought off a challenge by the Duras family to place Duras's illegitimate son, **Toral**, as council leader. That struggle culminated in a brief but bitter civil war between council factions in 2368. Gowron's victory was in part achieved by his promise to restore rightful honor to the Mogh family in exchange for military support by the sons of Mogh. ("Redemption, Parts I and II" [TNG]). *The leader of the Klingon High Council was called the chancellor in* Star Trek VI, *but this title has not been used in* Star Trek: The Next Generation *episodes. "Redemption, Part I" establishes that a female cannot be a member of the High Council, although* **Azetbur** *was council leader in* Star Trek VI.

Klingon Homeworld. The central planet of the Klingon Empire. A large, green, class-M world, the Homeworld was rarely referred to by its formal name, Qo'noS (pronounced kronos). (*Star Trek VI: The Undiscovered Country*). The

Enterprise-D visited the planet in 2366 when **Worf** challenged the High Council ruling that his father, **Mogh**, was a traitor. ("Sins of the Father" [TNG]). The ship visited the Homeworld again in late 2367 when Jean-Luc Picard attended the installation of **Gowron** as High Council leader. Picard had served as Gowron's **Arbiter of Succession**. ("Redemption, Part I" [TNG]). The *Enterprise*-D again returned to the Klingon Homeworld a few weeks later when Picard requested the loan of a Klingon Bird-of-Prey for a covert mission into Romulan space to investigate the disappearance of Ambassador Spock. ("Unification, Part I" [TNG]).

Klingon Neutral Zone. A no-man's-land between the United Federation of Planets and the **Klingon Empire**. Passage into the zone by ships of either nation was forbidden by treaty. (*Star Trek II: The Wrath of Khan*). The Klingon Neutral Zone was abolished in 2293 by the accords of the **Khitomer conference**. (*Star Trek VI: The Undiscovered Country*).

Klingon spacecraft. A spaceborne culture, the Klingon Empire has a wide variety of spacecraft used for its defense and commerce.

1) Vor'cha-*class attack cruiser, first seen in "Reunion" (TNG).*

2) *Klingon battle cruiser,* K't'inga *class, first seen in* Star Trek: The Motion Picture.

3) *Klingon Bird-of-Prey,* K'Vort *and* B'rel *classes, first seen in* Star Trek III: The Search for Spock.

4) *Klingon battle cruiser, D7 type, first seen in "The Enterprise Incident" (TOS).*

Klingon spacecraft to approximate scale.

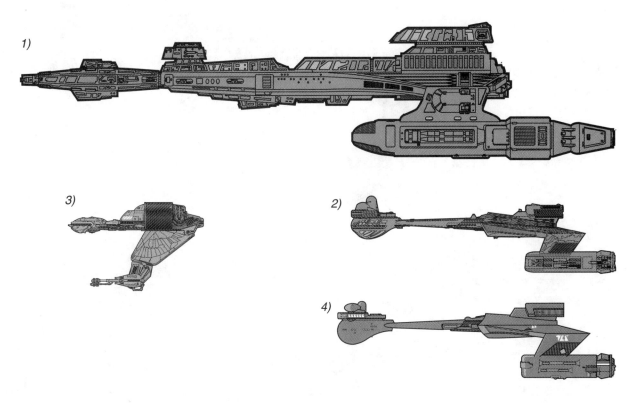

Klingon War (alternate). In the alternate timeline created when the *Enterprise*-C vanished from its "proper" place in 2344, the Federation and the Klingon Empire engaged in a terrible war, which might have been prevented had the *Enterprise*-C rendered aid to the Klingon outpost at **Narendra III**. Over the next 22 years, some 40 billion people lost their lives, and over half of the Starfleet was destroyed. By 2366, Starfleet Command anticipated that the Federation would be defeated within six months. This alternate timeline was excised when the *Enterprise*-C returned to its "original" place in history, and did indeed render aid at Narendra III in 2344. ("Yesterday's *Enterprise*" [TNG]).

Klingon weapons. The Klingon warrior uses a curious mixture of extremely sophisticated armament, combined with ancient traditional weapons.

　　1) *Disruptor rifle. Phase-disruptor energy weapon, first seen in* Star Trek III: The Search for Spock. *Designed by Bill George.*

　　2) d'k tahg *Klingon knife. First seen in* Star Trek III, *but reused in numerous* Star Trek: The Next Generation *episodes. Designed by Phil Norwood.*

　　3) *Disruptor pistol. More compact variant of the disruptor rifle. A variety of these pistols have been used over the years. Designed by Bill George.*

　　4) *Disruptor pistol (old style). Sonic disruptor pistol used in the original* Star Trek *series. The design was based on the pistols originally built for the Eminians in "A Taste of Armageddon" (TOS). Probably designed by Matt Jefferies.*

Klingonese. Spoken and written language of the **Klingon Empire**. A harsh, guttural tongue. **Korax** once boasted that half the quadrant was learning to speak Klingonese because there was no doubt in his mind that the Klingon Empire would dominate the galaxy. ("The Trouble with Tribbles" [TOS]). The Klingon language had no word for "peacemaker" until the Klingons encountered mediator **Riva**, who helped negotiate several treaties between the Klingons and the Federation. ("Loud as a Whisper" [TNG]). *The spoken Klingon language used in most of the* Star Trek *motion pictures and* Star Trek: The Next Generation *episodes was invented by linguist Marc Okrand. For more information about the Klingon language, please refer to Okrand's book,* The Klingon Dictionary, *published by Pocket Books. (Okrand notes that not all the Klingon-language words on the show have come from his book. He rationalizes that different Klingon provinces have different dialects.)*

Klingons. Humanoid warrior race, originally from the planet **Qo'noS**. A proud, tradition-bound people who value honor, the aggressive Klingon culture has made them a military power to be respected and feared. In Klingon society, the death of a warrior is not mourned, especially a warrior who has died honorably, as in battle or the line of duty. In such cases, the survivors celebrate the freeing of the spirit. ("The Bonding" [TNG]). Klingon tradition holds that "the son of a Klingon is a man the day he can first hold a blade." ("Ethics" [TNG]). Another Klingon ritual is the **R'uustai,** or bonding ceremony, in which two individuals join families, becoming brothers and

Klingon weapons.

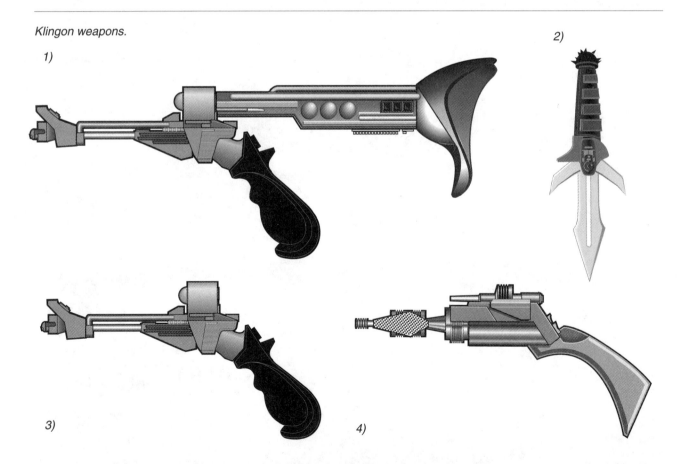

1)

2)

3)

4)

sisters. ("The Bonding" [TNG]).

The Klingon body incorporates multiple redundancies for nearly all vital bodily functions. This characteristic, known as *brak'lul*, gives Klingon warriors enormous resiliency in battle. Despite the considerable sophistication of Klingon technology, significant gaps exist in Klingon medical science, in part due to cultural biases that injured warriors should be left to die or to carry out the *Hegh'bat*. ("Ethics" [TNG]). Klingons have no tear ducts. Klingon blood is a lavender-colored fluid. (*Star Trek VI: The Undiscovered Country*). *Klingons were first seen in "Errand of Mercy" (TOS), and throughout the original Star Trek series. At the time, they appeared as fairly ordinary humans with heavy makeup and mustaches. Beginning with Star Trek: The Motion Picture, improved makeup techniques (and improved budgets) led to their present elaborate forehead designs. The differences between the two types of Klingons have never been addressed on the show, but one can imagine that the Klingon Empire might be composed of more than one race.*

klon peags. Chopstick-like **Wadi** implements that are highly sought after in their culture and have many different uses. **Falow** offered Quark *klon peags* as a wager but the Ferengi declined the bid. ("Move Along Home" [DS9]).

Kloog. (Mickey Morton). Large, hairy **drill thrall** who fought Kirk in 2268 during one of the games on planet **Triskelion**. ("The Gamesters of Triskelion" [TOS])

K'mpec. (Charles Cooper). The leader of the **Klingon High Council** who presided over that body longer than anyone else in history by using an iron hand to maintain peace within the council and the Empire itself.

One of K'mpec's greatest political challenges came in 2366, when evidence emerged implicating the late **Ja'rod**, father of council member **Duras**, of having committed treason. The politically powerful Duras attempted to suppress the fact that his father had betrayed his people to the Romulans at **Khitomer**. K'mpec feared that exposing Duras would plunge the Empire into civil war, so he gave tacit support to a plan whereby the late **Mogh** would be blamed for the massacre. K'mpec did not realize that Mogh's sons, **Worf** and **Kurn**, would return to the Homeworld to challenge this injustice, an appeal that K'mpec was not willing to hear in open council. K'mpec eventually agreed to allow Worf to accept **discommendation**, sparing both of Mogh's sons from death, while retaining some semblance of peace in the High Council. ("Sins of the Father" [TNG]).

K'mpec was murdered in 2367, apparently poisoned with **Veridium Six** by Duras, who sought to succeed K'mpec as council leader. Under Klingon custom, such a killing was without honor because the killer did not show his face to the victim.

Seeking to protect his empire from leadership from such a dishonorable person, K'mpec took the highly unorthodox step of appointing a non-Klingon, Jean-Luc Picard, as his **Arbiter of Succession**. K'mpec was succeeded by **Gowron**, a political newcomer. ("Reunion" [TNG]). *Actor Charles Cooper also played General Koord in Star Trek V.*

K'nera. (David Froman). Klingon officer in command of the cruiser assigned to rendezvous with the *Enterprise*-D to return the criminals **Korris** and **Konmel** to the Klingon Homeworld in 2364. Both Korris and Konmel died before the transfer could take place. K'nera was quite impressed with Worf, and offered him a position in the **Klingon Defense Force** once his tenure with Starfleet had been completed. ("Heart of Glory" [TNG]).

Kobayashi Maru scenario. A **Starfleet Academy** training exercise in which Command-track cadets were presented with a "no-win" scenario as a test of character. The simulation involved a distress call from a Federation freighter, the *Kobayashi Maru*, which was in the Klingon neutral zone, under attack by Klingon battle cruisers. The cadet had a choice of several options, none of which led to a "winning" conclusion, in that it was impossible to simultaneously save the freighter, prevent destruction of the cadet's ship, and avoid an armed exchange with the Klingons. The *Kobayashi Maru* was regarded as something of a rite of passage for Command-track cadets. **James T. Kirk** was reputed to have taken the test three times while he was at the Academy. Prior to his third attempt, Kirk surreptitiously reprogrammed the simulation computer to make it possible to beat the simulation, and subsequently received a commendation for original thinking. (*Star Trek II: The Wrath of Khan*).

Kobayashi Maru. In the Starfleet Academy's training simulation of that name, the *Kobayashi Maru* was a third-class neutronic fuel carrier with a crew of 81 and 300 passengers. (*Star Trek II: The Wrath of Khan*).

Kobheerian captain. (Lesley Kahn). Commander of the Kobheerian transport vessel *Rak-Miunis*. ("Duet" [DS9]).

Kobliad. Humanoid race who needed the substance **deuridium** to stabilize their cell structures, prolonging their lives. The demand for deuridium far outweighed its availability, so some Kobliad took illegal routes to procure the substance. ("The Passenger" [DS9]). SEE: **Kajada, Ty; Vantika, Rao.**

Kodos the Executioner. (Arnold Moss). Governor of planet **Tarsus IV** in 2246. When the colony's food supply was destroyed by an exotic fungus, Kodos seized power and declared martial law. Kodos rationed the remaining food supply by selecting some 4,000 colonists to die according to his personal theories of eugenics. Shortly thereafter, Kodos was believed to have died. It was later found that Kodos had assumed a new identity, that of actor **Anton Karidian**, and evaded detection for some 20 years until **Thomas Leighton** identified him as Kodos. Kodos was killed by his insane daughter, **Lenore Karidian**, who was trying to protect her father from his accusers. ("The Conscience of the King" [TOS]).

KoH-man-ara. Prescribed move in the Klingon **Mok'bara** martial art form. It closely resembles the crane block of Earth's tai chi chuan. ("Second Chances" [TNG]).

Kohlanese stew. Meal served at Quark's bar at Deep Space 9. A food-replicator malfunction due to an old act of Bajoran sabotage caused the Kohlanase stew to become particularly unpalatable on stardate 46423. ("Babel" [DS9]).

Kohms. One of two major ethnic groups on planet **Omega IV** who fought a terrible bacteriological war centuries ago. The few survivors of the conflict lived because they happened to have powerful natural immunity, and had extraordinarily long life spans.

In 2268, Starfleet **captain Ronald Tracy** of the **U.S.S. Exeter** sided with the Kohms, supplying them with phasers with which they struck against their ancient enemies, the **Yangs.** *Enterprise* personnel, investigating the disappearance of the *Exeter*, theorized that the Kohms might have been culturally similar to Earth's 20th-century Chinese Communists. ("The Omega Glory" [TOS]).

Kohn-ma. Militant **Bajoran** terrorist organization that opposed any outside influence in ruling their planet, including interference from the Federation. In 2369, Kohn-ma dissident **Tahna Los** threatened to destroy the Bajoran wormhole in hopes of decreasing Bajoran importance to the Federation and other factions. ("Past Prologue" [DS9]).

Koinonians. An ancient intelligent culture that was composed of two different life-forms, one of energy, and the other of matter. The physical Koinonians destroyed their civilization a millennium ago after several generations of war, leaving ruins that were studied by an *Enterprise*-D away team in 2366. The surviving Koinonians had very strong ethics, and tried to provide for young **Jeremy Aster** after his mother was killed by an ancient artifact of that war. ("The Bonding" [TNG]). *The name of the Koinonians' homeworld was not established in the episode.*

Kol. Ferengi pilot present with **DaiMon Goss** and **Dr. Arridor** at the Barzan negotiations in 2366. Kol was lost with the disappearance of the Ferengi pod in the **Barzan wormhole.** ("The Price" [TNG]).

kolem. Romulan unit of measure for power flow. ("The Next Phase" [TNG]).

Kolinahr. A Vulcan ritual intended to purge all remaining emotions in pursuit of the ideal of pure logic. **Spock** attempted to attain *Kohlinar* under the guidance of Vulcan masters in 2270, after his first five-year mission under the command of Captain Kirk, but failed when the telepathic call of **V'Ger** stirred the emotions of his human half. (*Star Trek: The Motion Picture*). *Photo: Spock undergoes Kolinahr on Vulcan.*

Kollos. Medusan ambassador to the Federation who was transported aboard the *Starship Enterprise* back to his homeworld, accompanied by **Dr. Miranda Jones.** Because the sight of **Medusans** is extremely dangerous to humans, Kollos traveled in a protective container. ("Is There in Truth No Beauty?" [TOS]). *Illustration: Kollos's protective container, used for his trip aboard the* Enterprise.

Kolos. Tall alien who came to Quark's bar in 2369 to bid on artifacts brought back from the Gamma Quadrant by archaeologist **Vash.** ("Q-Less" [DS9]).

Koloth, Captain. (William Campbell). Klingon officer who brought his crew to **Deep Space Station K-7** for rest and recreation on stardate 4523, much to the chagrin of Federation representatives. ("The Trouble with Tribbles" (TOS)]. *William Campbell also played Trelane in "The Squire of Gothos"* (TOS). SEE: **Kor, Commander.**

Kolrami, Sirna. (Roy Brocksmith). **Zakdorn** master strategist who served as a tactical consultant aboard the *Enterprise*-D during a **Starfleet battle simulation** exercise in 2365. A third-level grand master at the game of **Strategema.** ("Peak Performance" [TNG]).

Kolvoord Starburst. A highly dangerous aerobatics space maneuver performed by five single-pilot spacecraft. Starting in a circular formation, the ships cross within ten meters of each other, and fly off in the opposite direction, igniting their plasma trails during the crossover. The maneuver was banned by **Starfleet Academy** in the 2260s following an accident that took the lives of five cadets. In 2368, **Nova Squadron** was attempting to execute the Kolvoord Starburst when the ships collided. All five ships were lost, and Cadet **Joshua Albert** was killed. ("The First Duty" [TNG]).

Komack, Admiral. (Byron Morrow). High-ranking official at Starfleet Command in 2267. Kirk asked Uhura to contact Admiral Komack at Starfleet concerning the spores on planet **Omicron Ceti III** and their effects on his crew. ("This Side of Paradise" [TOS]). Later that year, Komack sent a message to the *Enterprise* instructing them to proceed to the inauguration ceremonies on planet **Altair VI.** ("Amok Time" [TOS]).

Konmel, Lieutenant. (Charles B. Hyman). Klingon criminal killed in 2364 while trying to avoid prosecution on the **Klingon Homeworld.** ("Heart of Glory" [TNG]). SEE: **Korris, Captain.**

Konsab, Commander. Instructor at the Romulan Intelligence Academy. Konsab believed that military officers needed to share a measure of mutual trust in order to function effectively. In this, Konsab disagreed with the basic **Tal Shiar** policy of maintaining loyalty through the use of intimidation. ("Face of the Enemy" [TNG]).

Koon-ut-kal-if-fee. Vulcan term meaning "marriage or challenge." In the ancient past Vulcans killed to win their mates. ("Amok Time" [TOS]). SEE: **Pon farr**.

Koord, General. (Charles Cooper). Klingon diplomatic representative to the **Paradise City** settlement on planet **Nimbus III**. Koord had previously led a distinguished career in the **Klingon Defense Force** before he fell out of favor with the Klingon High Command. His military strategies are required reading at Starfleet Academy. (*Star Trek V: The Final Frontier*). *Actor Charles Cooper also played* **K'Mpec**, *leader of the Klingon High Council in "Sins of the Father" (TNG) and "Reunion" (TNG), albeit with different makeup.*

Kopf, Ensign. (James Lashley). A member of Commander La Forge's Engineering team when Data, under Dr. Soong's control, took over the *Enterprise*-D in 2367. ("Brothers" [TNG]). *James Lashley would later appear as a Federation security officer in several episodes of* Star Trek: Deep Space Nine.

Kor, Commander. (John Colicos). Klingon officer who was the military governor of the planet **Organia** during the border dispute of 2267. Kor ruled Organia with an iron fist, but was unaware that the apparently humanoid **Organians** were in fact incredibly advanced noncorporeal life-forms who sought only to promote peace between the two antagonists. ("Errand of Mercy" [TOS]). SEE: **Ayelborne; Organian Peace Treaty**. *Years*

after Colicos's appearance as the first Klingon on Star Trek, *the actor reprised his role of Kor in "Blood Oath" (DS9). Along with Kor, that episode featured appearances by Michael Ansara as* **Kang** *and William Campbell as* **Koloth**. *All three actors wore bumpy foreheads for "Blood Oath" (DS9), thereby raising a question of whether these were the same characters, or merely other Klingons with the same names. John Colicos also played Lord Baltar on* Battlestar Galactica.

Kora II. Cardassian planet where **Aamin Marritza** worked beginning in 2364 as an instructor at a military academy, teaching the intricacies of being a filing clerk. After arriving on Kora II in 2364, Marritza underwent cosmetic surgery, changing his appearance. In 2369, he resigned his position at the military academy, put his affairs in order, and boarded a transport vessel for Deep Space 9 in an effort to expose the Cardassian atrocities committed at the **Gallitep** labor camp on Bajor. SEE: **Darhe'el; Kalla-Nohra**. ("Duet" [DS9]).

Korax. (Michael Pataki). Klingon officer who took shore leave on **Deep Space Station K-7** along with several of his

fellow crew members in 2267. Drinking at the station's bar, Korax insulted *Enterprise* crew members, including Pavel Chekov and Montgomery Scott, initiating a barroom brawl. ("The Trouble with Tribbles" [TOS]). SEE: **Denebian slime devil**. *Michael Pataki later played* **Karnas** *in "Too Short a Season" (TNG).*

Korby, Dr. Roger. (Michael Strong). Known as the Pasteur of archaeological medicine for his translation of medical records from the Orion ruins. Korby was killed during his expedition to the planet **Exo III**, where he discovered a sophisticated **android** technology, the last remnants of an advanced civilization. Prior to his death in 2266, Korby transferred his consciousness into a sophisticated android body, where he lived until that body was destroyed. Korby had been engaged to Nurse **Christine Chapel**. ("What Are Little Girls Made Of?" [TOS]).

Korob. (Theo Marcuse). Extragalactic life-form who settled on planet **Pyris VII** with **Sylvia**, on a mission of exploration. In their natural forms, Korob and Sylvia were small avian life-forms a few centimeters high. They used a device they called a **transmuter** to create the illusion of humanoid bodies and a castle with a distinctively haunted atmosphere. Korob and Sylvia captured several *U.S.S. Enterprise* personnel in 2267, but were later killed when Kirk destroyed their transmuter device. ("Catspaw" [TOS]).

Koroth. (Alan Oppenheimer). Klingon high cleric, who in 2369 was in charge of the monastery on the planet **Boreth**. Koroth, along with **Torin**, were responsible for the creation of a clone who was programmed to believe he was the prophet **Kahless the Unforgettable**. ("Rightful Heir" [TNG]).

Korris, Captain. (Vaughn Armstrong). Klingon criminal who fled imprisonment in 2364 by causing the destruction of the cruiser **T'Acog** and hijacking a Talarian ship, the **Batris**. Korris, along with his accomplices **Konmel** and **Kunivas**, apparently crippled the *Batris* during their takeover, and were the only survivors rescued by *Enterprise*-D personnel from the *Batris* just before the *Batris* exploded. Kunivas died shortly thereafter. Korris and Konmel were later killed when a second cruiser was ordered to return them to the **Klingon Homeworld**. ("Heart of Glory" [TNG]).

Kosinski. (Stanley Kamel). Starfleet propulsion specialist who attempted to perform a series of computer-based upgrades on starship warp drives in 2364. Kosinski's upgrades apparently produced measurable improvements on the starships **Ajax** and **Fearless**, and spectacular improvements on the *Enterprise*-D, but were later found to be baseless.

The performance improvements were instead found to be due to the intervention of the **Traveler**, who had the ability to exploit the interchangeability of time, space, and thought. ("Where No One Has Gone Before" [TNG]). Wesley Crusher conducted additional tests on Kosinski's equations in 2367, resulting in the accidental creation of a **static warp bubble** in which his mother, Beverly Crusher, became temporarily trapped. ("Remember Me" [TNG]).

Kostolain. Planet that was home to **Minister Campio** and **Erko**. ("Cost of Living" [TNG]).

Krag. (Richard Nelson). The chief investigator for the **Tanugan** security force who investigated allegations that **William Riker** had been responsible for the death of **Dr. Nel Apgar** in 2366. Krag agreed to a holodeck reenactment of the events aboard the station, which ultimately led to Riker's acquittal and the discovery that Apgar had been responsible for his own death. ("A Matter of Perspective" [TNG]).

Krako, Jojo. (Victor Tayback). Boss of the south side territory on planet **Sigma Iotia II** in 2268. ("A Piece of the Action" [TOS]). SEE: **Iotians**.

Kran-Tobal Prison. Bajoran penal institution where **Ibudan** was incarcerated after murdering a Cardassian during the Cardassian occupation of Bajor. He was later released in 2369 when the **Bajoran** provisional government came into power. ("A Man Alone" [DS9]). **Dr. Surmak Ren** told Kira she'd be sent to Kran-Tobal Prison when she kidnapped him from the surface of Bajor in an effort to enlist his aid to cure the deadly aphasia virus that had struck the people aboard sttion Deep Space 9. ("Babel" [DS9]).

Kransnowsky. (Bart Conrad). Starship captain who served on James Kirk's court-martial board in 2267 at Starbase 11 when Kirk was accused of the murder of **Benjamin Finney**. ("Court Martial" [TOS]).

Kras. (Tige Andrews). Klingon officer who tried to prevent the Federation from obtaining mining rights on planet **Capella IV** in 2267. Kras supported the Capellan **Maab's** revolt against the **Teer Akaar** in hopes the new leader would award the Klingon Empire the rights to mine the rare mineral **topaline** found on Capella. Kras in turn betrayed Maab and was killed for

his actions. ("Friday's Child" [TOS]). *Kras was never called by a specific name in the episode and was simply referred to as "Klingon."*

K'Ratak. Klingon author, writer of the classic work *The Dream of the Fire*. ("The Measure of a Man" [TNG]).

Kraus IV. Planet where the Cardassian clothier **Garak** told the Duras sisters he could obtain some silk lingerie for them. ("Past Prologue" [DS9]).

Krax. (Lou Wagner). Son to **Zek**, and heir apparent to Zek's role as Ferengi **Grand Nagus**. Krax was shocked in 2369 when, at a trade conference at Deep Space 9, his father apparently died, appointing **Quark** as his successor. Krax subsequently plotted with Quark's brother, **Rom**, to kill the new Grand Nagus until Zek's death was found to be a ruse intended to test Krax's suitability to one day assume his father's mantle. ("The Nagus" [DS9]).

Krayton. Ferengi *D'Kora*-class Marauder spacecraft commanded by **DaiMon Tog**. This vessel was present at the **Trade Agreements Conference** on Betazed in 2366. The *Krayton* was reported to have a top speed almost as great as the *Enterprise*-D. ("Ménage à Troi" [TNG]).

Kreechta. Ferengi *D'Kora*-class Marauder spacecraft commanded by **Bractor**. The *Kreechta* stumbled into a **Starfleet battle simulation** in 2365. ("Peak Performance" [TNG]).

krellide storage cells. A power-storage device used in shuttlecraft and handheld tools. The krellide cells aboard Shuttle 03 lost their charge while Captain Picard was piloting the craft through the Mar Oscura Nebula in 2367, making vehicle flight control difficult to maintain. ("In Theory" [TNG]).

Kri'stak Volcano. Mountain on the Klingon Homeworld, where legend held that the messiah **Kahless the Unforgettable** forged the first *bat'telh* sword. ("Rightful Heir" [TNG]).

Krieger waves. A potentially valuable new power source. **Dr. Nel Apgar** of the planet **Tanuga IV** was attempting to develop a Krieger-wave converter for use by the Federation. The converter consisted of a Lambda field generator located on the planet's surface, and a series of reflective coils and mirrors, located in a science station in orbit. The energy from the field generator was projected off the elements of the converter and turned into Krieger waves. Apgar was killed when his research station exploded in 2366 before he could complete his project. ("A Matter of Perspective" [TNG]).

Krieger waves were named for Star Trek *technical consultant David Krieger.*

Krios 1. Simulation of the **Temple of Akadar** on planet **Krios**, used on the *Enterprise*-D holodeck for the historic Kriosian **Cremony of Reconciliation** with the Valt Minor system in 2368. The program was designed by Commander La Forge with the help of **Kriosian ambassador Briam**. ("The Perfect Mate" [TNG]).

Krios. Class-M planet in the **Kriosian** system, controlled by the Klingon Empire. In 2367, Captain Picard and Klingon ambassador **Kell** met with Klingon governor **Vagh** at **Krios**, following a Kriosian revolt that the Klingons believed had been supported by the Federation. ("The Mind's Eye" [TNG]).

The inhabitants of Krios had been at war with the neighboring system, **Valt Minor**, for centuries. Krios was named for one of two brothers who, centuries ago, shared the rule of a vast empire in space. Krios and his brother, Valt, both fell in love with a woman named **Garuth**, but Krios kidnapped her and took her to the star system that would later bear his name. War erupted between Valt Minor and Krios.

In 2368, a historic **Ceremony of Reconciliation** was held in hopes of ending the centuries of conflict. ("The Perfect Mate" [TNG]). SEE: **Kamala**.

Kriosian system. The only Klingon protectorate bordering Federation space during the 2360s. ("The Mind's Eye" [TNG]).

Kriskov Gambit. A classic ploy in **three-dimensional chess**. It is normally countered with the **el-Mitra Exchange**. ("Conundrum" [TNG]).

Kristin. (Liz Vassey). Member of the *Enterprise*-D who often practiced diving in the holodeck on her off hours. As a result of her hobby, Kristin was a frequent visitor to the *Enterprise*-D sickbay. ("Conundrum" [TNG]). SEE: **"Cliffs of Heaven."** *Kristin was not given a last name in the episode.*

Krite. (Callan White). **J'naii** pilot and instructor who participated, along with **Soren**, in the rescue of the J'naii shuttle *Taris Murn* in 2368. Krite reported Soren to the government for aberrant sexual behavior. ("The Outcast" [TNG]).

Krocton Segment. A governmental district on planet **Romulus**. **Senator Pardek** was the elected representative of the Krocton Segment in 2368. ("Unification, Parts I and II" [TNG]).

Krola. (Michael Ensign). Politically conservative Minister of Internal Security for the government of planet **Malcor III**. Krola opposed the **Malcorian** space program and was barely tolerant of the government's social reforms. Upon discovering that the Federation had been conducting covert surveillance of his planet in 2367, Krola tried to make it appear that he had been killed by Commander William Riker.
Although **Chancellor Durken** learned of Krola's scheme, Durken ultimately accepted Krola's recommendation to postpone indefinitely Malcor III's ambitious space program. ("First Contact" [TNG]).

Kronos One. Klingon battle cruiser that carried **Chancellor Gorkon** on an abortive peace mission to Earth in 2293. Gorkon was killed aboard that ship by forces that sought to obstruct the peace process. (*Star Trek VI: The Undiscovered Country*). *Kronos One was a modification of the Klingon battle*

cruiser built for the first Star Trek *movie, which was in turn based on the Klingon ship built in 1968 for the original* Star Trek *series.* SEE: **Klingon spacecraft**.

Kronos. Phonetic spelling for **Qo'noS**, the **Klingon Homeworld**.

Kroykah. Vulcan imperative command to halt. Vulcan leader **T'Pau** firmly issued that order when **Stonn** insisted he fight with Spock during Spock's **Pon farr** ritual in 2267.

Kruge, Commander. (Christopher Lloyd). Klingon officer who commanded the Bird-of-Prey that attempted to obtain information on the Federation's **Project Genesis** for the Klingon government in 2285. Kruge was killed at the Genesis Planet by Kirk, who sought retribution for the murder of his son, **David Marcus**. (*Star Trek III: The Search for Spock*).

Kryonian tiger. Life-form found on planet Brentalia. Worf and Alexander Rozhenko saw one while visiting the zoo on Brentalia. ("Imaginary Friend" [TNG]).

Kryton. (Tony Young). Bodyguard to **Elaan**, the **Dohlman** of Elas in 2268. Kryton was in love with Elaan, and plotted with the Klingon Empire to stop the planned marriage between Elaan and the leader of **Troyius**. Kryton killed himself after his transmission to a nearby Klingon vessel was intercepted. ("Elaan of Troyius" [TOS]).

K'Tal. (Ben Slack). A member of the **Klingon High Council** who presided over the installation of **Gowron** as head of the council in 2367. ("Redemption, Part I" [TNG]).

Ktaran antiques. Several of these treasures were offered for sale at one of the shops on the Promenade at Deep Space 9. Among these was a 21st-century plasma coil in near perfect condition that caught the interest of Geordi La Forge. ("Birthright, Part I" [TNG]).

Ktarian game. An ingenious recreational device worn like a pair of headsets, used in the **Ktarian** attempt to gain control the Federation Starfleet in 2368. The Ktarian game employed small lasers that played directly on the optic nerve, creating a holographic image of a game field on which the player used mental control to direct the trajectory of small flying disks into various target funnel shapes. The game had powerful psychotropically addictive properties that rendered the player extremely susceptible to external control. ("The Game" [TNG]). SEE: **Jol, Etana**.

Ktarian vessel. A small spacecraft commanded by Ktarian

operative **Etana Jol**. This craft met the *Enterprise*-D near the Phoenix Cluster as part of the Ktarian Expansion plan. When the Ktarian plan failed, the vessel was taken in tow by the *Enterprise*-D and delivered to Starbase 82. ("The Game" [TNG]).

Ktarians. Humanoid race characterized by their enlarged frontal skull bones and feline eyes. Although politically non-aligned, in 2368 the Ktarians devised a plan they referred to as the Expansion, intended to gain control of the Federation Starfleet, and eventually of the Federation itself. They distributed a psychotropically addictive **Ktarian game** to members of the *Enteprise*-D crew, planning to use the crew as tools in the Expansion. ("The Game" [TNG]). SEE: **Jol, Etana**.

K'Temoc. (Lance le Gault). Captain of the Klingon ship *T'Ong*. K'Temoc, a formidable Klingon warrior, was a product of a period when the Federation and the Klingon Empire were at war. ("The Emissary" [TNG]).

***K't'inga*-class battle cruiser.** Conjectural designation for an uprated version of the Klingon D7-type starships. (*Star Trek: The Motion Picture*). SEE: **Klingon spacecraft**.

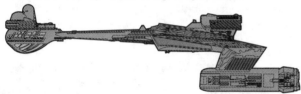

Kulge. (Jordan Lund). A Klingon officer who had sworn loyalty to **Gowron** during the **Klingon civil war** of 2368. But when Gowron's forces suffered multiple defeats, Kulge began to question Gowron's leadership. Gowron killed him in the High Council chambers. ("Redemption, Part II" [TNG]).

Kumeh maneuver. Combat tactic in which one sublight space vehicle maneuvers behind a planet to avoid detection by another. Picard began the **Starfleet battle simulation** of 2365 by using the relatively conservative Kumeh maneuver against the ***U.S.S. Hathaway***. ("Peak Performance" [TNG]).

Kumamoto. City in Japan on Earth where **Keiko O'Brien**'s mother lived. Although Keiko was committed to her career as a Starfleet botanist, she was so distressed at the living accommodations upon moving into station **Deep Space 9** that she threatened to go stay with her mother in Kumamoto. ("Emissary" [DS9]).

Kunivas. (Robert Bauer). Klingon criminal killed in 2364 while trying to avoid prosecution on the **Klingon Homeworld**. ("Heart of Glory" [TNG]). SEE: **Korris, Captain**.

Kurak. (Tricia O'Neil). Klingon warp-field specialist who was invited aboard the *Enterprise*-D in 2369 to participate in the test of a new **metaphasic shield** invented by Dr. Reyga. When the inventor of the shield was murdered, she came under suspicion as his killer. ("Suspicions" [TNG]). *Tricia O'Neil had previously played* Enterprise-C *captain Rachel Garrett in "Yesterday's* Enterprise*" (TNG).*

Kurl. Planet located a considerable distance from Federation space. Kurl was once the home of a thriving humanoid civilization, but the Kurlans all disappeared thousands of years ago, leaving behind a rich cultural heritage that is still being studied by archaeologists. ("The Chase" [TNG]). SEE: **Kurlan Naiskos**.

Kurlan Naiskos. Archaeological artifact. A small ceramic figure about 30 cm high, Naiskos statues were produced in ancient times by the people of planet **Kurl**. These statues were designed to be opened, revealing a multitude of similar but smaller figurines inside, representing the Kurlan belief that each person is made up of a community of individuals with different voices and desires. Although many ancient Naiskos have been found by archaeologists, relatively few are intact, and fewer still have all the smaller figurines. **Professor Richard Galen** gave an intact Kurlan Naiskos to his former student, **Jean-Luc Picard**. That particular artifact was even more prized because it was of the third Kurlan dynasty, made some 12,000 years ago by the Kurlan artisan known only as the **Master of Tarquin Hill**. ("The Chase" [TNG]). *In later episodes, Picard's Kurlan Naiskos can be seen adorning a corner table of his ready room.*

Kurland, Jake. (Steven Gregory). Son of an *Enterprise*-D crew member, and an aspiring Starfleet Academy cadet. Jake scored slightly lower than Wesley Crusher on a test, thus losing to Crusher the opportunity to take the Academy entrance exam at **Relva VII**. Despondent, Kurland stole a shuttlecraft, and attempted to run away to Beltane IX to sign onto a freighter. Kurland eventually returned to the *Enterprise* after nearly crashing the shuttlecraft, and Commander Riker put him to work repairing the shuttle as penance. ("Coming of Age" [TNG]).

Kurn. (Tony Todd). Born in 2345, the son of **Mogh** and younger brother to **Worf**. When Kurn was only one year old, his family moved to the **Khitomer** outpost, and young Kurn was left in the care of family friend **Lorgh**. Both of Kurn's parents were killed in the **Khitomer massacre** of 2346, and Kurn was raised by Lorgh. Kurn was not made aware of his true parentage

until he reached the **Age of Ascension**. As an adult, Kurn joined the **Klingon Defense Force**. In 2366, Kurn became aware that High Council member **Duras** had falsified evidence to make it appear that Mogh had betrayed his people at Khitomer. Kurn joined with his brother, Worf, to challenge this injustice, but found the High Council little interested in uncovering the truth. Instead, Worf was forced to accept a humiliating discommendation to avoid a political exposé that would have resulted in his brother's death and may have plunged the empire into civil war. ("Sins of the Father" [TNG]). Kurn opposed **Gowron**'s bid for the council leadership following the death of **K'mpec** in 2367. Kurn nevertheless obeyed Worf's decree that Gowron was the rightful leader, and lent the support of his ship, the **Hegh'ta**, and three other Klingon squadrons to Gowron. Kurn's assistance was critical in preventing an overthrow of the Gowron regime by the Duras family during the **Klingon civil war** of 2368. In return, Gowron restored rightful honor to the Mogh family name. ("Redemption, Parts I and II" [TNG]). Following the victory of Gowron's forces over Duras's during the Klingon civil war, Kurn was rewarded for his service to the empire. He was granted a seat on the High Council. ("Rightful Heir" [TNG]). *Worf also had a human stepbrother, named Nikolai, the son of Sergey and Helena Rozhenko, mentioned briefly in "Heart of Glory" (TNG) and later seen in "Homeward" (TNG).*

Kushell. (Albert Stratton). Secretary of the planet **Straleb**'s Legation of Unity and father to **Benzan**. ("The Outrageous Okona" [TNG]).

kut'luch. A bladed weapon used by Klingon assassins. The *kut'luch* had a serrated blade and made a very serious wound. A *kut'luch* was used in an attack on **Kurn** by operatives of the **Duras** family in 2366. ("Sins of the Father" [TNG]).

K'Vada, Captain. (Stephen Root). The captain of a Klingon Bird-of-Prey loaned to Captain Picard in 2368 to enable him to reach Romulus undetected. ("Unification, Part II" [TNG]).

*K'Vort-*class battle cruisers. Large version of the **Klingon Bird-of-Prey** ship. Three of these vessels arrived and surrounded the starships *Enterprise*-D and C as **Enterprise-C** was trying to return through the **temporal rift**. ("Yesterday's Enterprise" [TNG]). *The smaller versions of this ship were called* **B'rel**-*class vessels.* SEE: **Klingon spacecraft**.

Kyle, Mr. (John Winston). Crew member holding the rank of lieutenant aboard the original *Starship Enterprise* under the command of Captain James Kirk. Kyle served as relief helm officer and transporter technician. ("Tomorrow is Yesterday" [TOS], "Space Seed" [TOS], "The City on the Edge of Forever" [TOS], "Who Mourns for Adonais?" [TOS], "The Doomsday Machine" [TOS], "The Apple" [TOS], "Catspaw" [TOS], "The Immunity Syndrome" [TOS], "Mirror, Mirror" [TOS], "The Lights of Zetar" [TOS]). By 2285, Kyle had been promoted to commander and was serving as communications officer aboard the *Starship* **Reliant**. (*Star Trek II: The Wrath of Khan*). *John Winston also played the bartender in "Wolf in the Fold" (TOS).*

Kyle, Mr. (mirror). (John Winston). Transporter chief aboard the *I.S.S. Enterprise* in the **mirror universe** who suffered discipline with an agonizer when he made an error with the transporter. ("Mirror, Mirror" [TOS]).

Kyle, Ms. (Jennifer Edwards). Primary-school teacher aboard the *Enterprise*-D in 2368. Her pupils included Worf's son, **Alexander Rozhenko**. ("New Ground" [TNG]).

Kyushu, **U.S.S.** Federation starship, **New Orleans class**, Starfleet registry number NCC-65491. The *Kyushu* was destroyed by the Borg at the battle of **Wolf 359** in early 2367. ("The Best of Both Worlds, Part II" [TNG]). *The Kyushu was named for one of the four main islands of Japan, where a Japanese orbital launch facility was located. The Kyushu model was designed by Ed Miarecki. The study model of the Kyushu, shown here, was never built as a full photographic miniature, but was used in the "graveyard" scene of the aftermath of the battle of Wolf 359.*

L-370. Solar system, formerly containing seven planets that were completely destroyed by an extragalactic **planet killer** weapon in 2267. The star was still intact but the billions of inhabitants on the planets perished. ("The Doomsday Machine" [TOS]).

L-374. Solar system that was almost completely destroyed by the **planet killer** in 2267. The *U.S.S. Constellation* under the command of **Commodore Matt Decker** investigated the destruction and came under attack, forcing the crew to take refuge on the third planet in that system. Only Decker remained on board and was helpless when that planet was also destroyed. ("The Doomsday Machine" [TOS]).

La Forge, Geordi. (LeVar Burton). Chief engineer aboard the *Starship Enterprise*-D. Born blind in 2335 because of a birth defect, La Forge wore a remarkable device called a **VISOR** that permitted him to see with greater clarity than other humans could. Geordi La Forge came from a family of Starfleet officers. His mother, Silva La Forge, was a command officer, captain of the  *U.S.S. Hera* at the time of her death in 2370 ("Interface" [TNG]), and his father was an exobiologist. Geordi recalled that, even though he moved around a great deal, he considered his childhood a great adventure. ("Imaginary Friend" [TNG]). La Forge did not receive his VISOR until after his fifth birthday. ("Hero Worship" [TNG]). Geordi was caught in a fire when he was five years old. He was rescued by his parents, and was not injured. Geordi recalled how for a time after the incident it was extremely important for him to know where his parents were at all times. ("Hero Worship" [TNG]). Geordi had a pet **Circassian cat** when he was eight. ("Violations" [TNG]). Possibly because his parents traveled so much when he was a child, Geordi had something of a knack for languages. One such language was **Hahlii**an. ("Aquiel" [TNG]).

Geordi La Forge graduated from Starfleet Academy in 2357. ("The Next Phase" [TNG]). One of La Forge's first Starfleet assignments was as shuttle pilot for the **Jovian run** between Jupiter and Saturn. ("Chain of Command, Part II" [TNG]). La Forge first met Captain Picard when La Forge piloted Picard's shuttle on an inspection tour. During the tour, Picard made an offhanded remark about a minor inefficiency in the shuttle's engines, and La Forge subsequently stayed up all night to repair the problem. Picard was so impressed with the incident that he requested La Forge be assigned to the *Enterprise*-D in 2364. ("The Next Phase" [TNG]). La Forge later served as an ensign on the *U.S.S. Victory* under the command of Captain **Zimbata**. ("Elementary, Dear Data" [TNG]). One of Geordi's closest friends on that ship was Lieutenant **Susanna Leijten**. In 2362, both La Forge and Leijten participated in an away mission to planet **Tarchannen III**. It was later realized that all members of that away team were infected by an alien DNA strand that would, if unchecked, compel them to return to Tarchannen III, where they

would be transformed into a native Tarchannen life-form. La Forge was saved from the transformation in 2367 by Leijten's actions and medical intervention by *Enterprise*-D CMO Crusher. ("Identity Crisis" [TNG]).

La Forge transferred to the *Enterprise*-D as **flight controller** (conn) in 2364. ("Encounter at Farpoint, Parts I and II" [TNG]). Geordi was promoted to full lieutenant and assigned as *U.S.S. Enterprise*-D chief engineer the following year, just prior to stardate 42073.1. ("The Child" [TNG]). Although brilliantly proficient as a starship engineer, La Forge had difficulty building relationships with women. Perhaps as a result, Geordi developed an attachment to a holographic representation of *Enterprise*-D designer **Leah Brahms**. ("Booby Trap" [TNG]). The real Dr. Brahms was outraged to learn of this simulation, noting that creating such a replica without her permission was an invasion of privacy. Brahms did eventually become friends with La Forge, although Geordi was disappointed to learn that Leah was already married. ("Galaxy's Child" [TNG]). *The name of Geordi's mother was listed as Alvera K. La Forge on Geordi's death certificate, seen in "The Next Phase" (TNG), but was established as Silva La Forge in "Interface" (TNG). His father (played by Ben Vereen) was seen in that episode, but no first name was established for him. Geordi La Forge, whose first appearance was in "Encounter at Farpoint" (TNG), was named in memory of the late, handicapped Star Trek fan George La Forge.*

La Rouque, Frederick. (Marc Alaimo). Professional gambler from the city of New Orleans on 19th-century Earth. La Rouque welcomed Commander Data to his poker game and provided Data with a stake in exchange for his **communicator**. ("Time's Arrow, Part I" [TNG]) *Marc Alaimo played several other roles, including **Gul Dukat**.*

Labarre, France. Small town in France on Earth. Birthplace of *Enterprise*-D captain **Jean-Luc Picard**. ("Family" [TNG]).

lacunar amnesia. Type of amnesia that occurs when a patient witnesses an act of violence so terrible that the patient rejects the reality of the situation. Dr. McCoy's preliminary diagnosis included lacunar amnesia when assessing the lack of grief shown by the children of the **Starnes Expedition** on planet **Triacus** for the death of their parents in 2268. ("And the Children Shall Lead" [TOS]).

Lagana Sector. Site of a terraforming mission for the *U.S.S. Gandhi* in 2369. ("Second Chances" [TNG]).

Lakat. City on the planet Cardassia. ("Chain of Command, Part II" [TNG]).

Lal. (Alan Bergmann). One of the **Vians** who tested **Gem** to see if her race was worthy of being rescued from the impending nova in 2268. ("The Empath" [TOS]). *Note that the name "Lal" is from the episode script only and was not actually spoken in the aired episode.*

Lal. (Hallie Todd). Daughter to **Data**, a **Soong-type** android constructed by Data aboard the *Enterprise*-D in 2366. Lal had a **positronic brain** onto which Data replicated much of his

own neural pathways. Initially built with a featureless humanoid body, Lal chose to assume the form of a human female. Despite the fact that both Lal and Data shared the same basic programming, Lal's behavioral programs quickly exceeded those of her father, thus demonstrating her ability to learn and grow. Lal became the focus of a heated custody battle when **Admiral Haftel** attempted to order Data to release Lal to the **Daystrom Institute** annex on **Galor IV**. Haftel, recognizing the extraordinary value of a new Soong-type android, believed it imperative that Lal be studied in a controlled environment under the guidance of cybernetics specialists. Data took considerable exception to this view, believing it his responsibility, as a parent, to care for the new life-form that he had created. The question became moot when Lal experienced a fatal systemwide cascade failure after having lived only a little over two weeks. During that brief time, Lal's positronic networks grew to the point where she was able to experience emotions, love for her father, and sadness at her own impending death. The name, Lal, chosen by Data for his child, is Hindi for "beloved." ("The Offspring" [TNG]). *The initial, featureless version of Lal was played by Leonard J. Crowfoot, who had previously played Trent in "Angel One" (TNG).*

Lalo, U.S.S. Federation starship, *Mediterranean* class, registry number NCC-43837. The Lalo was a freighter that reported a "hiccough" in time that was found to be the result of **Dr. Paul Manheim**'s time/gravity experiments at **Vandor IX** in 2364. ("We'll Always Have Paris" [TNG]). The *Lalo* was lost in late 2366 after apparently encountering a **Borg** ship near Zeta Alpha II. ("The Best of Both Worlds, Part I" [TNG]).

Lambda Paz. One of the moons of planet **Pentarus III**. Lambda Paz was barely class-M, with extreme desert conditions and a mean surface temperature of fifty-five degrees Celsius. The mining shuttle *Nenebek*, piloted by Captain **Dirgo**, along with Captain Picard and Ensign Crusher, crash landed on Lambda Paz in 2367. ("Final Mission" [TNG]). SEE: **Sentry**.

Lamonay S. Name assumed by **Ibudan** after he murdered a clone of himself in an attempt to frame **Odo** for murder. ("A Man Alone" [DS9]).

landing party. A specialized team of starship personnel assigned to a particular mission, usually on a planet. Landing party assignments were generally at the captain's discretion, but were often composed of a senior officer, mission specialists (such as a science officer), and one or more security personnel. The term landing party has since been replaced by Starfleet with the more generic **away team**.

Landon, Yeoman Martha. (Celeste Yarnall). Crew member on the original *U.S.S. Enterprise.* In 2267, Yeoman Landon and Ensign Pavel Chekov were attracted to each other when assigned to the landing party on **Gamma Trianguli VI**. The

inhabitants noticed their affection, and told the *Enterprise* personnel that touching and similar intimate behavior was forbidden by their god, **Vaal**. ("The Apple" [TOS]).

Landris II. Planet where Dr. Mowray conducted archaeological research in 2369. Captain Picard had wanted to communicate with Mowray on stardate 46693, but was unable to establish contact due to a communications blackout requested by the **Stellar Cartography Department** on the *Enterprise*-D. ("Lessons" [TNG]).

Landru. (Charles Macaulay). Leader of planet **Beta III** some 6,000 years ago when that world was plagued with war and destruction. Landru changed that by preaching truth and peace, taking his population back to a simpler time. Before his death, Landru programmed a computer to continue his leadership. The news of Landru's death was kept from the people, and the

computer, also called Landru, governed in his stead. The computer judged society by its own definition of perfection and harmony, forcing everyone to act the same and become part of a common **Body** of people. Under the computer's control, the Beta III society became increasingly aberrant, but those who resisted conformity were forced to be absorbed or killed. The computer Landru was deactivated in 2267 by Kirk and Spock as they convinced the machine it was killing the Body by promoting stagnation, it was acting against the original Landru's directive to act for the good of the people. ("Return of the Archons" [TOS]). SEE: **Archon, U.S.S.; Lawgivers.** *Charles Macaulay also played Prefect **Jarvis** in "Wolf in the Fold" (TOS).*

Lanel. (Bebe Neuwirth). A nurse at the **Sikla Medical Facility** on planet Malcor III. Lanel agreed to help Riker escape from Malcorian authorities in exchange for a very personal favor. ("First Contact" [TNG]). *We would go into further detail, but this is, after all, a G-rated book.*

Lang cycle fusion engines. Ancient power plant used aboard **Promellian** spacecraft a millennium ago. Picard knew of this technology, and hoped an ancient Promellian battle cruiser discovered near **Orelious IX** would still have its Lang cycle engines intact. ("Booby Trap" [TNG]).

Lang, Lieutenant. (James Farley). *Enterprise* security officer killed at planet **Cestus III** while on a mission investigating the destruction of the Earth outpost there. ("Arena" [TOS]).

Langford, Dr. Archaeologist who studied the ruins on Suvin IV in 2369. Dr. Langford invited Captain Picard to join her in exploring for ancient artifacts on planet Suvin IV. ("Rascals" [TNG]).

Langor. (Kimberly Farr). A citizen of the planet **Brekka**. Arrogant and aristocratic, she was dedicated to maintaining the exploitive relationship her planet had with the people of planet **Ornara**. ("Symbiosis" [TNG]).

Lantar Nebula. Nebula containing planet **Hoek IV**. **Q** tempted Archeologist **Vash** with viewing the Sampalo relics located in the Lantar Nebula, but she declined. ("Q-Less" [DS9]).

Lantree, U.S.S. Federation starship, *Miranda* class, Starfleet registry number NCC-1837, a supply ship commanded by **Captain L. Isao Telaka**, normal crew complement of 26. The crew of this vessel was killed in 2365 after being exposed to a group of genetically engineered human children whose immune systems actively sought out and attacked potential sources of disease, including the Lantree crew. The *U.S.S. Lantree* was destroyed by a single photon torpedo fired by the *U.S.S. Enterprise*-D in order to prevent further transmission of the deadly antibodies. ("Unnatural Selection" [TNG]). *The* Lantree *was a minor modification of the* **U.S.S. Reliant** *model originally built for* Star Trek II: The Wrath of Khan. *The* Reliant's *upper "roll bar" was removed to turn it into the* Lantree. *The* Lantree *bridge (seen briefly in a screen readout) was a redress of the* Enterprise-D battle bridge.

lapling. A small creature with a long snout. These defenseless animals were believed to be extinct. The last living member of the species was discovered in **Kivas Fajo**'s collection aboard the *Jovis* in 2366. ("The Most Toys" [TNG]). A lapling-like creature was a pet of Grand Nagus Quark on Deep Space 9 in 2369. ("The Nagus" [DS9]).

Lapsang souchong tea. A beverage enjoyed by **Helena Rozhenko**. ("New Ground" [TNG]).

Larg. (Michael E. Hagerty). A Klingon captain, loyal to the **Duras** family during the **Klingon civil war** of 2367-68. He commanded a vessel that engaged and heavily damaged **Kurn**'s ship, the *Hegh'ta*. ("Redemption, Part II" [TNG]).

Largo V. Destination of Captain Jaheel's ship in 2369 when his ship was detained because of the **aphasia virus**. Jaheel was scheduled to deliver a shipment of Tamen **Sahsheer**. ("Babel" [DS9]).

larish **pie.** Cardassian food served at Quark's. **Woban**, leader of the **Navot** nation on planet Bajor, complimented the Cardassian replicators for the tasty *larish* pie. ("The Storyteller" [DS9]).

Larosian virus. Mild disorder that **Dr. Julian Bashir** feared that Jadzia Dax might have contracted on stardate 46853. In truth, a replica of Dax, created by unknown aliens from the Gamma Quadrant, was responsible for Dax's unexpectedly amorous behavior toward Bashir. ("If Wishes Were Horses" [DS9]).

Lars. (Steve Sandor). **Drill thrall** who was responsible for training Uhura to fight on planet **Triskelion** in 2268. ("The Gamesters of Triskelion" [TOS]).

Larson, Lieutenant Linda. (Saxon Trainor). An *Enterprise*-D staff engineer who worked to solve the reactor failure of the **Argus Array** in 2367. ("The Nth Degree" [TNG]).

LaSalle, U.S.S. Federation starship that reported the presence of a series of radiation anomalies in the Gamma Arigulon System in 2367. ("Reunion" [TNG]).

laser pulse system. A low-power directed energy device employing coherent light transmissions. A modified laser pulse beam system was installed aboard the *Enterprise*-D and the *Hathaway* in 2365 for the **Starfleet battle simulation** exercise. ("Peak Performance" [TNG]).

laser weapons. Energy weapon used aboard early Federation starships. ("Laser" was originally an acronym for Light Amplification by Stimulated Emission of Radiation.) These took the form of pistol sidearms, as well as larger artillery-sized cannons. ("The Cage" [TOS]).
　　Lasers had been replaced by **phaser** *weapons by at least 2265 as seen in "Where No Man Has Gone Before" (TOS), but not before 2200, according to Worf in "A Matter of Time" (TNG). Illustration: Handheld laser pistol from "The Cage" (TOS) and "Where No Man Has Gone Before"(TOS).*

laser-induced fusion. Engineering term for controlled nuclear fusion in which the required ignition temperatures are created by powerful lasers. Laser-induced fusion is used in the **impulse drive** engines of Federation starships, as well as in the power supply reactors on station **Deep Space 9**. ("The Forsaken" [DS9]).

• **"Last Outpost, The."** *Next Generation* episode #7. Teleplay by Herbert Wright. Story by Richard Krzemien. Directed by Richard Colla. Stardate 41386.4. *First aired in 1987. Pursuing a Ferengi ship, the* Enterprise-D *is captured by the last outpost of the ancient Tkon Empire. The Ferengi make their first appearance in this episode, and we see their Marauder spacecraft for the first time as well.* SEE: **baktun; DaiMon; Delphi Ardu; Ferengi; Ferengi Code; Ferengi Marauder; Ferengi whip; Gamma Tauri IV; Letek; Portal; Sun Tzu; T-9 energy converter; Taar, DaiMon; Tkon Empire; Tkon, ages of.**

Lasuma. Location of a grain-processing center on planet **Bajor**. Keiko O'Brien took eleven schoolchildren to visit the grain-processing center at Lasuma on stardate 46922. ("Dramatis Personae" [DS9]).

Lathal Bine. (Robert Harper). Representative of **Beta Moon** of planet **Peliar Zel**, who participated in negotiations with **Alpha Moon** in 2367. ("The Host" [TNG]).

Latimer, Lieutenant. (Reese Vaughn). Navigator of the *Shuttlecraft Galileo* when it crashed on planet **Taurus II**. Latimer was killed by the humanoid creatures on the planet. ("The *Galileo* Seven" [TOS]).

latinum. Valuable metal ingots used as a medium of exchange, primarily outside the Federation. ("Past Prologue" [DS9]). SEE: **gold pressed latinum**.

Laughing Hour. A custom at the **Parallax Colony** of **Shiralea VI.** ("Cost of Living" [TNG]).

"Laughing Vulcan and His Dog, The." A children's song taught in the primary school on the *Enterprise*-D, popular among children, but Picard preferred "Frere Jacques". ("Disaster" [TNG]).

Lauriento massage holoprogram #101-A. Holosuite program set in a soothing atmosphere where an exotic alien woman with webbed fingers gives a body massage. **Ibudan's** clone was murdered on Deep Space 9 in 2369 while running Lauriento massage holoprogram #101-A. ("A Man Alone" [DS9]).

Lawgivers. Robed police from the planet **Beta III**, who enforced the law during the rule of the planetary computer **Landru**. The Lawgivers' tasks included absorbing non-converted members into the society so they could be controlled by Landau. They were also capable of killing when ordered to do so. ("Return of the Archons" [TOS]).

Lawmim Galactopedia. A rare historical object, reported to be in the personal collection of **Zibalian** trader **Kivas Fajo**. ("The Most Toys" [TNG]).

Lawton, Yeoman Tina. (Patricia McNulty). Young, pretty member of the *Enterprise* crew. Janice Rand introduced her to **Charles Evans** in the hope he would befriend her, but Charlie was too attracted to Rand for this to happen. ("Charlie X" [TOS]).

law. SEE: **Alpha III, Statues of; Armens, Treaty of; Ceremony of Reconciliation; Constitution of the United Federation of Planets; Contract of Ardra; Cumberland, Acts of; Ferengi Code; Ferengi Rules of Acquisition; Ferengi Salvage Code; Judge Advocate General; Justinian Code; Magna Carta; Mek'ba; Right of Statement; Satie, Judge Aaron; Scrolls of Ardra; Seventh Guarantee; Starfleet General Orders and Regulations; Treaty of Algernon; Treaty of Alliance; Uniform Code of Justice; United States Constitution.**

Lazarus. (Robert Brown). Scientist who, in 2267, developed a means of creating an interdimensional **door in the universe**, a passageway to an antimatter continuum. This

passage was extremely dangerous because contact between the two continua would theoretically result in the total annihilation of both universes. Lazarus was mentally unstable and exhibited symptoms of severe paranoia. He believed that his alternate self from the other universe wanted to kill him. Fortunately, the alternate Lazarus was more stable, and sacrificed himself to trap the insane Lazarus in the interdimensional corridor. As a result, both universes were made safe, but both Lazaruses are at each other's throats for eternity. ("The Alternative Factor" [TOS]). *The script referred to him as Lazarus-A (the madman from our universe) and Lazarus-B (his sane twin from the antimatter universe).*

LB10445. Single-celled, ciliated, microscopic life-form indigenous to planet **Devidia II**. A cellular fossil of one of these was discovered buried on Earth beneath the city of San Francisco, near Commander Data's severed head, suggesting a **Devidian** presence on Earth some 500 years ago. ("Time's Arrow, Part I" [TNG]).

LCARS. SEE: **Library Computer Access and Retrieval System.**

Leech, Felix. (Harvey Jason). A fictional character from the **Dixon Hill** detective stories, Leech was a hit man for gangster **Cyrus Redblock**. A holographic version of Leech was part of the Dixon Hill holodeck programs. ("The Big Goodbye" [TNG]).

Lefler's Laws. A series of 102 colloquialisms collected by **Ensign Robin Lefler**. She said her laws were her way of remembering essential information. Law 17 was "When all else fails, do it yourself." Law 36 was "You gotta go with what works." Law 46: "Life isn't always fair." Law 91: "Always watch your back." Wesley Crusher added a 103rd: "A couple of light-years can't keep good friends apart." Robin gave Wesley Crusher a bound hardcopy of her first 102 laws. ("The Game" [TNG]).

Lefler, Ensign Robin. (Ashley Judd). An *Enterprise*-D crew member and part of the engineering staff. She helped Commander La Forge modify the transporter system while Captain Picard was trapped on planet **El-Adrel IV** in 2368. ("Darmok" [TNG]). Lefler was promoted to mission specialist a few months later, and worked on optimizing sensor usage for a survey of the **Phoenix Cluster**. Lefler befriended Wesley Crusher, who visited the *Enterprise*-D during that mission, and the two were instrumental in helping the crew repel an attempted takeover by a **Ktarian** operative. SEE: **Jol, Etana; Ktarian game.** Lefler was the child of two Starfleet plasma

specialists. She traveled a great deal as a child, and made few friends her own age. She would later recall thinking of her tricorder as her first friend. ("The Game" [TNG]). SEE: **Lefler's Laws**.

"Legacy." *Next Generation* episode #80. Written by Joe Menosky. Directed by Robert Scheerer. Stardate 44215.2. *First aired in 1990. The* Enterprise-D *visits the late Tasha Yar's homeworld, and finds her sister still living among the gangs there.* SEE: **Alliance; *Arcos, U.S.S.*; Camus II; Coalition; escape pod; Hayne; Manu III; myographic scanner; photon grenades; *Potemkin, U.S.S.*; proximity detectors; stunstick; T'su, Tan; Telluridian synthale; Turkana IV; Yar, Ishara; Yar, Natasha**.

Legara IV. The homeworld of the Legarans. The *Enterprise*-D traveled there in 2366, transporting Ambassador **Sarek** to a historic conference with the **Legarans**. ("Sarek" [TNG]).

Legarans. A mysterious race that concluded an historic agreement, negotiated by Ambassador **Sarek**, with the Federation in 2366. Sarek had begun talks with the Legarans in 2270, but it took nearly a century until the protocol-conscious Legarans agreed to a treaty. The final negotiations took place aboard the *Enterprise*-D in orbit above Legara IV. Preparations for those talks were extensive, and included the construction of a special pool filled with a viscous fluid for the Legarans' comfort. Federation authorities expected the benefits of relations with the Legarans to be incalculable. ("Sarek" [TNG]). SEE: **Bendii Syndrome**. *We never did see the Legarans in that episode, although one might wonder what a creature that lives in a mud bath would look like.*

Legation of Unity. Political entity of the planet **Straleb**. ("The Outrageous Okona" [TNG]).

Leighton, Dr. Thomas. (William Sargent). Research scientist, and one of nine surviving eyewitnesses to the massacre of some 4,000 colonists at **Tarsus IV** by **Kodos the Executioner**, aka **Anton Karidian**. Leighton was killed in 2266 by Kodos's daughter, **Lenore Karidian**, who had been systematically murdering all those who could identify her father as being responsible for the massacre. Leighton had been horribly disfigured at Tarsus IV, and had begun to suspect actor Anton Karidian of being Kodos after seeing a performance by Karidian on **Planet Q**. ("The Conscience of the King" [TOS]).

Leighton, Martha. (Natalie Norwick). Widow of **Tarsus IV** massacre survivor **Thomas Leighton**. ("The Conscience of the King" [TOS]).

Leijten, Susanna. (Maryann Plunkett). Starfleet officer who served with **Geordi La Forge** on the ***U.S.S. Victory***. In 2362, Leijten, then a lieutenant, along with La Forge and three others, beamed down to **Tarchannen III** to investi-

gate the Federation outpost there. It was later revealed that all five away-team members were infected by an alien DNA strand that compelled them all to return to Tarchannen III five years later. This alien DNA transformed three of the former *Victory* crew members into Tarchannen life-forms, a fate that Leijten and La Forge only narrowly escaped. ("Identity Crisis" [TNG]).

Leka, Governor Trion. (Barbara Tarbuck). Governor of planet **Peliar Zel**. Leka came aboard the *Enterprise*-D in 2367 to assist in negotiations between her planet's **Alpha** and **Beta Moons**. ("The Host" [TNG]).

Lemec, Gul. (John Durbin). Captain of the Cardassian warship ***Reklar***. ("Chain of Command, Part I" [TNG]).

Lemli, Mr. (Roger Holloway). *Starship Enterprise* security officer who was assigned to guard Dr. Janice Lester shortly after stardate 5928. ("Turnabout Intruder" [TOS]). *Mr. Lemli's name was a reference to William Shatner's daughters, Leslie, Melanie, and Lisabeth. Lemli is also the name of Shatner's production company.*

Lemma II. Planet located 3 light-years from **Bilana III**. A **soliton wave** scattering field generator was built on Lemma II during the Soliton experiment conducted by **Dr. Ja'Dar** in 2368. The planet was placed in jeopardy when the wave went out of control during the test. ("New Ground" [TNG]).

Len'mat. Klingon term meaning "adjourned." ("Redemption, Part I" [TNG]).

Lenarians. In 2369, an away team from the *Enterprise*-D was involved in a conference with the Lenarians, when a dissident faction attacked the team and critically injured Captain **Jean-Luc Picard**. ("Tapestry" [TNG]).

leporazine. A resuscitative drug in use aboard Federation starships. ("Ethics" [TNG]).

Leslie, Mr. (Eddie Paskey). Crew member aboard the original *Starship Enterprise*. ("Where No Man Has Gone Before" [TOS], "The Conscience of the King" [TOS], "Return of the Archons" [TOS], "This Side of Paradise" [TOS], "The Alternative Factor" [TOS], "The Omega Glory" [TOS]). *Eddie Paskey also played an Eminiar guard in "A Taste of Armageddon" (TOS).*

• **"Lessons."** *Next Generation* episode #145. Written by Ronald Wilkerson & Jean Louise Matthias. Directed by Robert Wiemer. Stardate 46693.1. *First aired in 1993. Jean-Luc Picard falls in love with a member of his crew.* SEE: **Beck; Bersallis firestorms; Bersallis III; Borgolis Nebula; Cabot, Ensign; Cheney, Ensign; Chopin's Trio in G Minor; Daren, Neela; Deng; fractal particle motion; "Frere Jacques"; *Havana, U.S.S.*; Jefferies Tube; Kerelian; Landris II;**

Marquez, Lieutenant; Mataline II; Melnos IV; Mowray, Dr.; Picard, Jean-Luc; Ressikan flute; Richardson; Spectral Analysis department; Starbase 218; Stellar Cartography; Thelka IV; thermal deflector.

Lester, Dr. Janice. (Sandra Smith, William Shatner). Federation scientist who discovered an extraordinary life-energy transfer device among the archaeological ruins on planet Camus II in 2269. Shortly thereafter, Lester conspired to kill nearly all of her colleagues on the planet, then used the device to place her mind into the body of Captain James T. Kirk. Lester and Kirk had been romantically involved years before at Starfleet Academy, but she bitterly resented the fact that she was not able to attain command of a starship. ("Turnabout Intruder" [TOS]).

Lestrade, Inspector. (Alan Shearman). Fictional 19th-century English detective, a character in Sir Arthur Conan Doyle's **Sherlock Holmes** stories. A computer-generated version of Lestrade was among the characters in a Holmes holodeck simulation run by Data. ("Elementary, Dear Data" [TNG]).

"Let me help." Words from a classic book written by a famous novelist of the 21st century who lived on a planet circling the far left star in Orion's belt. This writer recommended these words, even over "I love you." Kirk mentioned this fact to **Edith Keeler** when she offered to help when Kirk didn't want to talk about his past. ("The City on the Edge of Forever" [TOS]).

• **"Let That Be Your Last Battlefield."** Original Series episode #70. Teleplay by Oliver Crawford. Story by Lee Cronin. Directed by Jud Taylor. Stardate: 5730.2. *First aired in 1969. Two men from a dead world are unable to shake the racial hatred that destroyed their planet.* SEE: **Ariannus; Bele; Cheron; destruct sequence; Lokai; Mendel, Gregor Johann; Starbase 4; Vulcans.**

Letek. (Armin Shimerman). Leader of the **Ferengi** landing party at planet **Delphi Ardu** that made contact with the Federation starship *Enterprise*-D in 2364. ("The Last Outpost" [TNG]). *Actor Armin Shimerman had previously played the gift box in "Haven" (TNG) and would later play* **Quark** *in Star Trek: Deep Space Nine.*

Lethe. (Susanne Wasson). An inmate at the **Tantalus V** penal colony in 2266. Assistant colony director **Tristan Adams** used Lethe as an example of the success of his experimental neural neutralizer device, but her blank, expressionless demeanor suggested that the neutralizer was eras-ing more than her criminal tendencies. ("Dagger of the Mind" [TOS]). *In Greek mythology, Lethe was a river in Hades whose water, when drunk, would cause one to forget earthly sorrows.*

level-2 security alert. Starfleet security protocol. It was enacted when hostile intrusion inside the ship might be expected. During a level-2 alert, armed security officers were stationed on every deck. ("Descent, Part I" [TNG]).

level-1 personnel sweep. Scan protocol on station Deep Space 9 initiated to locate any personnel in an area of the station. Odo asked the computer to run a level-1 personnel sweep of all pylons on stardate 46853 to make sure an evacuation order was obeyed. ("If Wishes Were Horses" [DS9]).

level-1 diagnostic. SEE: **diagnostic.**

Levinius V. Planet whose population suffered mass insanity in 2067, caused by the Denevan neural parasites. The parasites had come from the Beta Portolan system, then proceeded to **Theta Cygni XII.** SEE: **Deneva.** ("Operation—Annihilate!" [TOS]).

Lexington, U.S.S. *Constitution*-class Federation starship, Starfleet registry number NCC-1709, commanded by **Commodore Robert Wesley** during the disastrous 2268 tests of the **M-5** computer. During those tests, the **multitronic** unit malfunctioned and fired

full phasers at the *Lexington*, killing 53 people on that ship, as well as the entire crew of the *Starship* **Excalibur.** ("The Ultimate Computer" [TOS]).

lexorin. Medication used to counteract McCoy's mental disorientation when he was suffering the side-effects of carrying Spock's *katra* within his own mind. Lexorin can be administered subcutaneously, by **hypospray.** (*Star Trek III: The Search for Spock*).

Leyor. (Kevin Peter Hall). A **Caldonian** who took part in the negotiations for rights to the Barzan wormhole in 2366. Leyor reached an agreement with **Devinoni Ral**, representative for the **Chrysalians**, in which Caldonia would withdraw from the negotiations.
    Leyor had been manipulated into making the agreement by Ral, who was secretly using his Betazoid empathic sense to take advantage of the Caldonian's own emotions. ("The Price" [TNG]). *The late Kevin Peter Hall also played the creature from* Predator*, and was Harry in* Harry and the Hendersons.

Leyrons. Inhabitants of planet Malkus IX. The Leyrons, unlike most known humanoid cultures, developed a written language before spoken or sign languages. ("Loud as a Whisper" [TNG]).

Liator. (Jay Lauden). A leader of the Edo people on planet **Rubicun III**. Liator attempted to enforce local laws by demanding the lawful execution of *Enterprise*-D crew member Wesley Crusher for infraction of a minor regulation in 2364. ("Justice" [TNG]). SEE: **punishment zones.**

Library Computer Access and Retrieval System. Proper name for the main computer system aboard the *Galaxy*-**class** *Enterprise*-D. Abbreviated LCARS. ("Encounter at Farpoint, Part II" [TNG]).

life-energy transfer. Technology developed long ago by the now-dead civilization of **Camus II** that permitted two humanoids to exchange their consciousnesses, so that each person's mind would occupy the other's body. **Dr. Janice Lester** discovered the still-working device on Camus II in 2369 and used it to exchange bodies with Captain James Kirk. ("Turnabout Intruder" [TOS]). *Photo: Life-energy transfer of Kirk and Lester on Camus II.*

life-forms. The exploration of space has revealed the galaxy to be home to myriad life-forms of virtually every imaginable form. Recent discoveries in exo-archaeology, based on the work of **Dr. Richard Galen**, have found a basis for the surprising number of humanoid life-forms found throughout the galaxy that share remarkably similar biochemistries. SEE: **humanoid life**. *Chart below.*

Life-forms (known)

Life-form	Description	Episode/Film
Acamarian	Humanoid inhabitants of Acamar III	"The Vengeance Factor" (TNG)
Aldean	Humanoid inhabitants of the mythical world of Aldea	"When the Bough Breaks" (TNG)
Aldebaran serpent	Three-headed reptilian life-form	"Hide and Q" (TNG)
amoeba	Gigantic single-celled spaceborne life-form	"The Immunity Syndrome" (TOS)
Andorian	Humanoids noted for blue skin and bilateral antennae; members of the Federation	"Journey to Babel" (TOS), "Whom Gods Destroy" (TOS), "The Offspring" (TNG)
Angosian	Humanoid inhabitants of Angosia III	"The Hunted" (TNG)
Antican	Sentient lupine humanoids native to the planet Antica	"Lonely Among Us" (TNG)
Antidean	Ichthyohumanoid life-forms	"Manhunt" (TNG)
Apollo	Powerful humanoid once worshipped as a god on ancient Earth	"Who Mourns for Adonais?" (TOS)
Arbazan	Species that is a memeber of the Federation	"The Forsaken" (DS9)
Argelian	Humanoid inhabitants of Argelius II	"Wolf in the Fold" (TOS)
Argosian	Member of a species that Sisko almost got into a fight with	"Dax" (DS9)
Arkarian waterfowl	Ornithoid native of planet Arkaria, noted for intresting mating habits	"Starship Mine" (TNG)
Bajoran	Ancient, deeply spiritual humanoid people, victimized for decades by the Cardassians	"Ensign Ro" (TNG), "Emissary" (DS9), et al.
Balduk warriors	A fierce group	"New Ground" (TNG)
Bandi	Humanoid inhabitants of Deneb IV	"Encounter at Farpoint, Parts I & II" (TNG)
Baneriam hawk	Predatory bird	"If Wishes Were Horses" (DS9)
Barolian	Humanoids engaged in trade with the Romulans	"Unification, Part 1" (TNG)
Barzans	Vaguely catlike humanoid residents of Barzan	"The Price" (TNG)
Beauregard	Plant raised by Sulu	"The Man Trap" (TOS)
Belzoidian flea	Animal mentioned by Q	"Deja Q" (TNG)

(Continued on next page).

(Continued from previous page).

Life-form	Description	Episode/Film
Benzites	Blue skinned sentient humanoid natives of the planet Benzar	"Coming of Age", "A Matter of Honor" (TNG)
Berellians	People not known for their engineering skills	"Redemption, Part II" (TNG)
Beta Renna cloud	Sentient gaseous creature that took over control of Picard's body in an attempt to explore the galaxy	"Lonely Among Us" (TNG)
Betazoids	Telepathic humanoids native to planet Betazed; members of the Federation	"Haven" (TNG), "Ménage a Troi" (TNG) et al.
Bolians	Blue-skinned humanoids, characterized by a midfacial dividing line, natives of Bolarus IX	"Allegiance" , "Conspiracy" (TNG)
Borg	Powerful cyborg race linked by a collective consciousness	"Q Who?", "The Best of Both Worlds, Parts I & II", et al.
Borgia plant	Mildly toxic plant indigenous to planet M-113	"The Man Trap" (TOS)
Breen	Politically non-aligned culture that sometimes attacks Federation ships	"The Loss", "Hero Worship" (TNG)
Brekkians	Humanoid race native to planet Brekka	"Symbiosis" (TNG)
Bringloidi	Colonists of Bringloid V	"Up the Long Ladder" (TNG)
Bulgallian rat	Animal reputed to be terrifying, at least according to Wesley Crusher	"Coming of Age" (TNG
Bynars	Humanoid species heavily integrated with their planet's computer system	"11001001" (TNG)
Calamarain	Gaseous life-form that Q once tormented	"Deja Q" (TNG)
Caldonians	Very tall bi-fingered humanoids	"The Price" (TNG)
Caldorian eel	Animal found by Klim Dokachin	"Unification, Part I" (TNG)
Calnoth	Lupine humanoids, native to planet Chalna	"Allegiance" (TNG)
Capellans	Humanoid warrior race of planet Capella IV	"Friday's Child" (TOS)
Cardassians	Humanoid natives of Cardassia, one of the major governments hostile to the Federation	"The Wounded" (TNG) "Chain of Command, Parts I & II" (TNG),"Emissary", et al.
Carnivorous rastipod	Bajoran animal not known for its grace	"Progress" (DS9)
Ceti eel	Mollusk-like neural parasite indigenous to Ceti Alpha V	*Star Trek II: The Wrath of Kahn*
Chameloid	Shape-shifting life-form	*Star Trek VI: The Undiscovered Country*
Chrysalians	Race whose government bid for rights to the Barzan wormhole	"The Price" (TNG)
Circassian cat	Geordi La Forge's first pet	"Violations" (TNG)
coalescent organism	Rare microscopic life-form that could absorb other organisms and become those organisms, down to the cellular level	"Aquiel" (TNG)
Companion	Noncorporeal, sentient life-form, friend to Zefram Cochrane	"Metamorphosis" (TOS)
Corvan gilvos	A stick-like endangered species	"New Ground" (TNG)
Cove palm	Poisonous plant indigenous to Ogus II	"Brothers" (TNG)
Crystalline Entity	Sentient life-form that resembles a gigantic snowflake	"Datalore" (TNG), "Silicon Avatar" (TNG)
Crystilia	species of flowering plant found on Telemarius III	"In Theory" (TNG)
Cytherians	Humanoids that reside near the center of the Galaxy	"The Nth Degree" (TNG)

(Continued on next page).

(Continued from previous page).

Life-form	Description	Episode/Film
Dachlyds	Group for whom Picard served as a mediator for critical negotiations	"Captain's Holiday" (TNG)
Dal'Rok	Energy creature created by the first Sirah to unite the people of two warring villages	"The Storyteller" (DS9)
Deltans	Characteristically bald humanoid species native to the planet Delta IV	Star Trek: The Motion Picture
Denebian slime devil	Nasty creature referred to by the Klingon Korax as a good likeness of Kirk	"The Trouble with Tribbles" (TOS)
dikironium cloud creature	Gaseous life-form that ingests human blood	"Obsession" (TOS)
Diomedian scarlet moss	Red feather-like plant	"Clues" (TNG)
Dopterian	Species with similar physiology as the Ferengi	"The Forsaken" (DS9)
Douwd	Immortal life-form, fond of taking other forms	"The Survivors" (TNG)
Draco lizards	Flying lizard, indigenous to Earth	"New Ground" (TNG)
Draebidium froctus	Plant that vaguely resembles a terran violet	"Rascals" (TNG)
dryworm	Giant creature from planet Antos IV that can generate and control energy with no harm to itself	"Who Mourns for Adonias? " (TOS)
Edo	Humanoid residents of the planet Rubicon III	"Justice" (TNG)
Edo god	Powerful spaceborne entity discovered in orbit of the planet Rubicon III	"Justice" (TNG)
eel-birds	Creatures from planet Regulus V that must return to the caverns where they hatched each eleven years	"Amok Time" (TOS)
Ekosians	Humanoids, native to the planet Ekos	"Patterns of Force" (TOS)
Elasians	Warrior species from planet Elas	"Elaan of Troyius" (TOS)
Ennis/Nol-Ennis	Two factions of the same humanoid species doomed to fight for eternity on a prison moon	"Battle Lines" (DS9)
Excalbians	Intelligent, shape-shifting rock creatures of the planet Excalbia who conducted an elaborate drama to study the humanoid concepts of "good" and "evil"	"The Savage Curtain" (TOS)
Exocomps	Small robotic servomechanisms that attained sentience	"The Quality of Life" (TNG)
Eymorg, Morg	Humanoid inhabitants of the planet Sigma Draconis VI	"Spock's Brain" (TOS)
Fabrini	Ancient people who built the asteroid-ship Yonada so that a few of their number could escape the explosion of their star	"For the World Is Hollow and I Have Touched the Sky" (TOS)
Farpoint Station	Shape-shifting spaceborne entity, forced to take the form of a space station	"Encounter at Farpoint" (TNG)
Ferengi	Humanoids known as the consummate capitalists	"The Last Outpost" (TNG), "The Nagus" (DS9), et al.
Frunalain	Species from the Alpha Quadrant	"Emissary" (DS9)
Garanian Bolites	Small creatures that cause extreme itching and skin discoloration when applied to humanoid skin	"A Man Alone" (DS9)
Gatherers	Nomadic offshoot of the Acamarian	"The Vengeance Factor" (TNG)
Gem	One member of a mute, naturally empathic species whose sun went nova in 2268	"The Empath" (TOS)
Gemarians	Species for whom Picard served as a mediator for critical negotiations	"Captain's Holiday" (TNG)
Gettle	Wild herd animal native to Cardassia	"Chain of Command, Part II" (TNG)
Glob fly	Klingon insect one-half the size of an Earth mosquito; the creature has no sting, but is known for its annoying buzz	"The Outrageous Okona" (TNG)

(Continued on next page).

(Continued from previous page).

Life-form	Description	Episode/Film
Gomtuu	Species of living spaceships who live symbiotically with their crews; the last of its kind is now living with Tam Elbrun	"Tin Man" (TNG)
Gorgan(aka the Friendly Angel)	Evil entity who forced the adults of the Starnes Expedition to commit suicide and deceived their children to follow him	"And the Children Shall Lead" (TOS)
Gorn	Sentient reptilians that believed the Federation was infringing on its territorial claim on planet Cestus III	"Arena" (TOS)
Grisella	Species known for hibernating for six month periods	"The Ensigns of Command" (TNG)
Gunji jackdaw	Ostrich-like bird, possibly sentient	"If Wishes Were Horses" (DS9)
Haliian	Partially telepathic humanoids native to planet Halii	"Aquiel" (TNG)
Halkans	Humanoid species with a history of total peace	"Mirror, Mirror" (TOS)
Horta	Silicon-based sentient life-form that lives underground on planet Janus VI	"The Devil in the Dark" (TOS)
Humpback whale	Intelligent ocean-dwelling life-form indigenous to planet Earth	Star Trek IV: The Voyage Home
Humuhumunuku- nukuapua'a	Earth reef triggerfish	"Rascals" (TNG)
Hunters	Gamma Quadrant species who live to pursue the Tosk	"Captive Pursuit" (DS9)
Hupyrian	Humanoids known for their devotion to their employers	"The Nagus" (DS9)
Husnock	Race utterly destroyed by Kevin Uxbridge	"The Survivors" (TNG)
Iconians	An ancient highly advanced civilization once known as "The Demons of Air and Darkness"	"Contagion" (TNG)
Iotians	Intelligent humanoids who patterned their culture after Earth's Chicago mobsters of the twenties	"A Piece of the Action" (TOS)
J'naii	An androgynous humanoid species	"The Outcast" (TNG)
Jarada	Insectoid species with an extreme devotion to protocol that finally opened relations with the Federation in 2364	"The Big Goodbye", "Samaritan Snare" (TNG)
Joranian ostrich	Avian life-form that hides it's head underwater when frightened, usually until it drowns	"Past Prologue" (DS9)
Junior	Spaceborne ship-sized life-form, a very fine fish	"Galaxy's Child" (TNG)
Kalandans	People that established an outpost that was destroyed by a terrible disease	"That Which Survives" (TOS)
Kelvans	Entities of unknown form, originally from the planet Kelva, who traveled from the Andromeda Galaxy in search of refuge from expected radiation hazards in their home galaxy	"By Any Other Name" (TOS)
Kerelian	Species with highly developed hearing	"Lessons" (TNG)
Klabnian eel	Life-form Q disliked	"QPid" (TNG)
Klingons	Warrior society, formerly enemies of the Federation	"Errand of Mercy" (TOS), Star Trek VI: The Undiscovered Country, "Sins of the Father" (TNG), "Redemption, Parts I and II" (TNG), "Rightful Heir" (TNG), et al.
Kobliad	Dying species that required deuridium to prolong their lives	"The Passenger" (DS9)
Kohms	Asian humanoid residents of Omega IV	"The Omega Glory" (TOS)
Koinonians	Noncorporeal life-forms that once fought a terrible war	"The Bonding" (TNG)
Kryonian tiger	Life-form found in the Brentalia zoo	"Imaginary Friend" (TNG)

(Continued on next page).

(Continued from previous page).

Life-form	Description	Episode/Film
Ktarians	Humanoids who attempted to gain control of Starfleet in 2368	"The Game" (TNG)
LB10445	Single-celled life-form native to Devidia II	"Time's Arrow, Part I" (TNG)
Legarans	Culture with whom Ambassador Sarek labored 93 years to establish a critical treaty; they live in a mudbath-like environment	"Sarek" (TNG)
Lenarians	People who don't like the Federation	"Tapestry" (TNG)
Leyrons	Inhabitants of the planet Malkus IX	"Loud as A Whisper" (TNG)
Ligonians	Humanoids native to planet Ligon II	"Code of Honor" (TNG
Lycosa tarantula	Arachnid; Miles O'Brien kept one as a pet	"Realm of Fear" (TNG)
Lynar	Batlike creature indigenous to Celtris III	"Chain of Command, Part I" (TNG)
M-113 creature	Vaguely humanoid species, now extinct, that lived on NaCl on planet M-113	"The Man Trap" (TOS)
Malcorians	Humanoid natives of Malcor III, on the verge of developing spaceflight	"First Contact" (TNG)
Malurians	Race studied by a Federation science team under the leadership of Dr. Manway in 2267. All of the Malurian system's inhabitants totaling over four billion, were destroyed by the robot space probe Nomad.	"The Changeling" (TOS)
Mariposians	Human colonists from the S.S. Mariposa; they reproduced exclusively by cloning technology	"Up the Long Ladder" (TNG)
Markoffian sea lizard	Life-form once mentioned by Q	"Deja Q" (TNG)
Medusans	Noncorporeal entities whose physical presence can cause madness in humans	"Is There in Truth No Beauty?" (TOS)
Melkotians	Telepathic, nonhumanoid life-forms	"Spectre of the Gun" (TOS)
Menthars	Ancient species that fought to extinction against the Promellians	"Booby Trap" (TNG)
Metron	Highly advanced and long-lived humanoid race	"Arena" (TOS)
Microbiotic colony	Subatomic life-form that ingestes metallic substances for food	"A Matter of Honor" (TNG)
Microbrain	Silicon-based intelligent life-form indigenous to a narrow layer of the water table on planet Velara III	"Home Soil" (TNG)
Mikulaks	Society that donated tissue samples for the study of Correllium fever	"Hollow Pursuits" (TNG)
Minosians	Extinct humanoid society famous for arms manufature during the Ersalrope Wars	"The Arsenal of Freedom" (TNG)
Mintakans	Proto-Vulcan humanoids	"Who Watches the Watchers?" (TNG)
Miradorn	Humanoid species known for symbiotic twins	"Vortex" (DS9)
Mizarians	Humanoid species native to Mizar II	"Allegiance" (TNG)
Moropa	Society hostile to the Bolians	"Allegiance" (TNG)
mugato	White simian creature native to Tyree's planet; the animal is extremely poisonous	"A Private Little War" (TOS)
Muktok plant	Bristle-like foliage native to Betazed	"Ménage a Troi" (TNG
Nagilum	Extradimensional life-form	"Where Silence Has Lease" (TNG)
Nanites	Submicroscopic robotic life-form, granted colonization rights on planet Kavis Alpha IV in 2366	"Evolution" (TNG)
Nasturtium	Flowering plant native to Earth	"Imaginary Friend" (TNG)
Nausicaans	Tall humanoids noted for their short tempers	"Samaritan Snare" (TNG), "Tapestry" (TNG)
Neural parasites	Large single-celled organisms, responsible for the eradication of humanoid life on several planets	"Operation—Annihilate!" (TOS)
ophidian	Snake-like life-form used by the Devidians to focus their time portal	"Time's Arrow" (TNG)
Orion wing-slug	A lower life-form	"Menage a Troi" (TNG

(Continued on next page).

(Continued from previous page).

Life-form	Description	Episode/Film
Orions	Characteristically green-skinned humanoids; females of the race were once sold as commodities	"The Cage" (TOS), "Whom Gods Destroy" (TOS)
Ornarans	Humanoid species native to planet Ornara; the entire race was addicted to the drug felicium	"Symbiosis" (TNG)
Pakleds	Humanoid race; deceptively intelligent despite their slow speech	"Samaritan Snare" (TNG)
Paxans	Xenophobic life-forms, residing in the Ngame Nebula	"Clues" (TNG)
Pentarans	Humanoid residents of Pentara V	"Final Mission" (TNG)
Platonians	Humanoids, formerly from the star system Sahndara, that once lived on Earth during the time of Plato	"Plato's Stepchildren" (TOS)
Portal	Last survivor of the Tkon empire	"The Last Outpost" (TNG)
Preservers	Ancient race that rescued endangered cultures, including American Indians, planting them on distant worlds	"The Paradise Syndrome" (TOS)
Promellians	An extinct species of sentient reptilian humanoids	"Booby Trap" (TNG)
quasi-energy microbes	Life-forms found within a plasma streamer in the Igo Sector	"Realm of Fear" (TNG)
Rakhari	Humanoid natives of the planet Rakhar	"Vortex" (DS9)
Rectyne monopod	Animal life-form that can weigh two tons	"The Icarus Factor" (TNG)
Regulan blood worm	Soft and shapeless creature mentioned by the Klingon Korax when insulting several members of the Enterprise crew at space station K-7	"The Trouble with Tribbles" (TOS)
Rigelians	Species physiologically similar to Vulcans	"Journey to Babel" (TOS)
Romulans	Humanoid offshoot of the Vulcan species that rejected devotion to logic in favor of a fierce warrior ethic	"Balance of Terror" (TOS), "The Neutral Zone" (TNG), "Unification, Parts I and II" (TNG), et al.
Rutians	Humanoids from the politically non-aligned planet Rutia IV; site of terrorist violence from the Ansata separatists	"The High Ground" (TNG)
Saltah'na	Gamma quadrant life-forms that produced telepathic archival spheres that "possessed" the crew of DS9	"Dramatis Personae" (DS9)
sandbats	Creatures from planet Manark IV, which appear to be inanimate rock crystals until they attack	"The Empath" (TOS)
Sark, Klingon	A riding animal	"Pen Pals" (TNG)
Satarrans	Humanoids native to Sothis III that attempted to take over the Enterprise-D	"Conundrum" (TNG), "The Chase" (TNG)
Scalosians	Humanoids from the planet Scalos, physiologically hyperaccelerated by radiation exposure	"Wink of an Eye" (TOS)
Selay	Sentient, reptilian inhabitants of the Beta Renna System; petitioned for admission to the Federation in 2364	"Lonely Among Us" (TNG)
Sheliak	Classification R-3 life-form; a very reclusive race	"The Ensigns of Command" (TNG)
Solanagen-based aliens	Life-forms that existed in a deep subspace domain	"Schisms" (TNG)
Soong-type androids	Artificial life-forms ruled sentient by the Federation	"Datalore", "Measure of a Man", "The Offspring", "Brothers", "Descent" (TNG)
spores	Symbiotic organism discovered on planet Ceti Alpha III	"This Side of Paradise" (TOS)
t'stayan	Talarian riding animal	"Suddenly Human" (TNG)

(Continued on next page).

(Continued from previous page).

Life-form	Description	Episode/Film
Tagrans	Inhabitants of Tagra IV	"True Q" (TNG)
Takarans	Reptilian humanoids with disseminated internal physiology	"Suspicions" (TNG)
Talarian hook spider	An arachnid with half-meter-long legs	"Realm of Fear" (TNG)
Talarians	Warrior humanoids with a long history of violence against the Federation	"Heart of Glory", "Suddenly Human" (TNG)
Talosians	Humanoids dependent upon illusion; their civilization was nearly wiped out by war thousands of centuries ago; they are only now beginning to rebuild	"The Cage", "The Menagerie, Parts I & II" (TOS)
Tamarians, aka "The Children of Tama"	Humanoids that communicate entirely by metaphor	"Darmok" (TNG)
Tanugans	Humanoids native to Tanuga IV	"A Matter of Perspective" (TNG)
Tarcassian razor beast	Life-form that was Guinan's imaginary friend	"Imaginary Friend," "Rascals" (TNG)
Tarellians	Humanoid species from the planet Tarella, who were almost completely wiped out by a biological weapon	"Haven" (TNG)
Targ	A furry porcine animal native to Qo'nos	"Where No One Has Gone Before" (TNG)
Tellarites	Humanoids with distinctive porcine physical traits	"Journey to Babel " (TOS)
Thasians	Noncorporeal life-form native to planet Thasus	"Charlie X" (TOS)
Tholians	Sentient culture with a long history of hostility toward the Federation	"The Tholian Web" (TOS), "The Icarus Factor" (TNG), et al.
Tiberian bats	Avian life-forms known for sticking together	Star Trek VI: The Undiscovered Country
Tosk	Reptilian humanoids from the Gamma Quadrant, raised from birth to be the prey of the Hunters	"Captive Pursuit" (DS9)
Traveler	Humanoid native of Tau Alpha C, who possesses the ability to manipulate time, space, and thought	"Where No One Has Gone Before" (TNG), "Remember Me" (TNG)
Tribble	Small furry animal, unbelievably cute, that reproduces at an astronomical rate	"The Trouble with Tribbles" (TOS)
Trill	Joined species, composed of a humanoid host and a small, helpless, but long-lived symbiot	"The Host" (TNG), DS9 (Series)
Troglytes	Group of humanoid inhabitants on planet Ardana	"The Cloud Minders" (TOS)
Troyians	Humanoid species native to planet Troyius	"Elaan of Troyius" (TOS)
Ugly Bags of Mostly Water	aka humans	"Home Soil" (TNG)
Ullians	Telepathic humanoid species	"Violations" (TNG)
V'Ger	Massive machine life-form built around the NASA probe Voyager	Star Trek: The Motion Picture
Valerians	Humanoids that supplied dolamide to the Cardassians for weapons production	"Dramatis Personae" (DS9)
Ventaxians	Humanoid inhabitants of Ventax II	"Devil's Due" (TNG)
Vians	Advanced humanoid species of unknown origin who saved Gem's people	"The Empath" (TOS)
Vorgons	Humanoid species with the ability to travel through time	"Captain's Holiday" (TNG)

(Continued on next page).

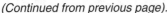

(Continued from previous page).

Life-form	Description	Episode/Film
Vulcans	Humanoid species whose culture is based on total suppression of emotion in favor of pure logic	"Amok Time" (TOS), "The Savage Curtain" (TOS), Star Trek: The Motion Picture, "Sarek" (TNG), "Unification, Parts I and II" (TNG), "Gambit, Part II" (TNG), et al.
Wanoni tracehound	Predatory life-form that pursues its victims with enthusiastic vigor	"The Forsaken" (DS9)
white rhinocerous	Terran animal life-form	"New Ground" (TNG)
Wogneer creatures	Life-forms saved by Captain Picard	"Allegiance" (TNG)
Wompats	Animal often kept as a pet by Cardassian children	"Chain of Command, Part II" (TNG)
Yangs	Caucasian humanoid residents of Omega IV	"The Omega Glory" (TOS)
Yridians	Humanoids know as interstellar dealers of information	"Birthright, Parts I & II", "The Chase" (TNG)
Zabathu, Andorian	A riding animal	"Pen Pals" (TNG)
Zakdorn	Humanoid race reputed to be the greatest strategic minds in the galaxy	"Peak Performance", "Redemption, Parts I & II" (TNG)
Zaldans	Humanoid race characterized by webbed hands and their fierce dislike for human courtesy	"Coming of Age" (TNG
Zalkonians	Humanoid race undergoing a great transformation into noncorporeal beings	"Transfigurations" (TNG)
Zan Periculi	Species of flowering plant native to Lappa IV, a Ferengi world	"Ménage à Troi" (TNG
Zeons	Humanoids who live on planet Zeon, near planet Ekos	"Patterns of Force" (TOS)
Zetarians	Life energy comprised of the thoughts and wills of the last living beings from the planet Zetar	"The Lights of Zetar" (TOS)
Zibalians	Humanoid race noted for facial tattooing	"The Most Toys" (TNG)
zylo eggs	Alien life-form that Data chose as a subject for his first attempt at painting	"11001001" (TNG)

Most life-forms encountered in the Star Trek *universe look remarkably similar to humans found on Earth. While this is probably inaccurate from a scientific point of view, it is one of the basic concepts that make* Star Trek *possible from a production practicality viewpoint. If one were to insist on radically different life-forms for all our aliens, the result would be that* Star Trek *would only be able to afford a fraction of the episodes that it does. The same reasoning explains why most aliens tend to breathe oxygen and speak English.*

Although Star Trek *does occasionally feature radically different life-forms such as the Horta, most episodes featuring such creatures are cleverly designed so that only one or two need to actually be seen on screen. The viewer's imagination then fills in the rest, creating a mental image of that creature's homeworld, much better (and much less expensively) than we could ever afford to do on television, or even in a feature film.*

Gene Roddenberry also noted that while showing strange,

new life-forms was a lot of fun, he felt that Star Trek *more properly dealt with the differing thoughts, attitudes, and beliefs of the pantheon of life in the universe.*

Alien makeup on the original Star Trek *series was supervised by Fred Phillips, who was responsible for Mr. Spock's famous pointed ears, as well as for most of the other aliens on the show. Phillips also supervised makeup on the first* Star Trek *feature film. Aliens on* Star Trek: The Next Generation *and* Star Trek: Deep Space Nine *have been supervised by Michael Westmore. Some aliens (such as the Companion or the space amoeba on the original series) were created by such optical-effects firms as Westheimer and Van der Veer. Similar "energy beings" and "cloud creatures" on* Star Trek: The Next Generation *and* Star Trek: Deep Space Nine *have been supervised by Rob Legato and Dan Curry.*

Life Prolongation Project. A disastrous experiment conducted around 1966 on **Miri**'s planet. The goal of the project was to develop a virus that would dramatically slow the aging process in humans. Unfortunately, the resulting virus killed all the adults on the planet, leaving the children to grow very slowly until they died at puberty. *Enterprise* chief medical officer Leonard McCoy was successful in developing an antitoxin to treat the virus in the remaining children found living on the planet in 2266. ("Miri" [TOS]).

light-speed breakaway factor. Also known as the **slingshot effect**, a warp-speed maneuver used to propel a starship through time. This procedure involves close passage to a massive gravitational source (like a star) at a high warp velocity. It was used to propel the *Enterprise* back in time from 2268 to the year 1968 on a mission of historical research. ("Assignment: Earth" [TOS]). *This was presumably the same technique used in "Tomorrow Is Yesterday" (TOS) and Star Trek IV: The Voyage Home.*

• **"Lights of Zetar, The."** Original Series episode #73. Written by Jeremy Tarcher and Shari Lewis. Directed by Herb Kenwith. Stardate 5725.3. *First aired in 1969. At planetoid Memory Alpha, an* Enterprise *crew member's body is taken over by mysterious energy life-forms.* SEE: **brain-circuitry pattern; decompression chamber; hyperencephalogram; Kyle, Mr.; Martian Colony III; Memory Alpha; noncorporeal life; psychological profile; Romaine, Jacques; Romaine, Lieutenant Mira; Romaine, Lydia; Scott, Montgomery; Steinman analysis; Zetarians; Zetar.**

Ligillium, ruins of. An archaeological site where the fabulous Zaterl emerald was reputed to be hidden. Captain Picard offered to take **Ardra** there to try to convince her to accept arbitration in the matter of the **Contract of Ardra**. ("Devil's Due" [TNG]).

Ligon II. Class-M planet whose humanoid culture valued ritual honor above all else. Ligon II, not a member of the Federation, was a source of a rare vaccine for the treatment of deadly **Anchilles fever**. ("Code of Honor" [TNG]). SEE: **Lutan.**

Ligonians. Humanoid race of planet **Ligon II**. Although lacking the advanced technology of the Federation, Ligonians placed an extremely high value on ritual honor. In Ligonian society, the women owned the land and the wealth, while allowing their mates to rule their  property. ("Code of Honor" [TNG]). SEE: **Lutan**. *Photo: Lutan's palace on Ligon II.*

Ligos VII. Volcanically active planet from which the *Enterprise*-D received a distress call from a Starfleet science team in 2369. ("Rascals" [TNG]).

Liko. (Ray Wise). An inhabitant of planet **Mintaka III** who chanced to witness the failure of a Federation survey team's hologram generator. Liko was injured as a result of the failure, and taken aboard the *Enterprise*-D for treatment, exposing him to advanced technology in violation of the Prime Directive. Efforts to erase his short-term memory were unsuccessful, and Liko returned to the surface with a complete memory of his visit to the *Enterprise*-D and a mistaken idea that Captain Picard was the Mintakan **"Overseer"** or God. Liko related his experiences to the other Mintakans, furthering the cultural contamination and complicating the rescue of the Federation scientist, **Dr. Palmer**. Liko held the irrational hope that "The Picard" would bring his wife, who had died in a flood the previous year, back to life. Liko shot Captain Picard with an arrow, wounding Picard and convincing Liko of Picard's mortality. ("Who Watches the Watchers?" [TNG]).

Lima Sierra system. A star system whose planetary orbits seem anomalous in terms of conventional celestial mechanics. The *Enterprise*-D was there prior to being assigned to transport mediator **Riva** from the Ramatis star system, and Captain Picard spent time puzzling over the Lima Sierra planetary orbits afterward. ("Loud as a Whisper" [TNG]).

Lin, Ensign Peter. (Brian Tochi). An *Enterprise*-D crew member who relieved **Ensign Rager** at Conn when she was sent to sickbay when the ship was trapped in a **Tyken's Rift** in 2367. ("Night Terrors" [TNG]). *Brian Tochi also played Ray Tsingtao, one of the children victimized by the evil Gorgan in "And the Children Shall Lead" (TOS).*

Lincoln, Abraham. (Lee Bergere). Sixteenth president of Earth's United States (1809-1865), considered by many Earth historians to have been the greatest American leader. Lincoln was a hero to *Enterprise* captain **James T. Kirk**, who was fascinated in 2269 when the **Excalbians** sent a replica of Lincoln to visit Kirk on the *Enterprise*. The re-created Lincoln was  part of an Excalbian experiment designed to study the human concept of "good" and "evil." ("The Savage Curtain" [TOS]).

Lincoln, Roberta. (Teri Garr). Human inhabitant of planet Earth in 1968 who unknowingly became employed by extraterrestrial agents who worked covertly to help Earth survive its critical Nuclear Age. Lincoln worked with Agents 347 and 201 at 811 East 68th Street, Apartment 12B, in New York City on Earth. Later, when she learned of the extraterrestrial nature of her employers, she continued to work for Gary Seven at the same address, although she found **Isis** somewhat disconcerting. ("Assignment: Earth" [TOS]).

Lindstrom. (Christopher Held). *Enterprise* sociologist and member of the landing party to planet **Beta III** in 2367. Lindstrom studied the planet's society, helping to unravel the mystery of the culture's unusual behavior. He later stayed behind on the planet to help the population establish an independent society after the deactivation of the planetary computer, **Landru**, which had controlled them for millennia. ("Return of the Archons" [TOS]).

"Linear Models of Viral Propagation." A well-known scientific paper authored by **Dr. Katherine Pulaski** some time prior to her service aboard the *Enterprise*-D. ("Unnatural Selection" [TNG]).

linear memory crystal. Optically refractive material used in **isolinear optical chips**, a key part of optical data processing devices. The sentient **nanites** accidentally developed by Wesley Crusher consumed linear memory crystal like food, enabling their reproduction. ("Evolution" [TNG]).

Linguacode. Data communications format designed to be understandable by nearly any technologically sophisticated intelligence. Unlike normal encryption, which serves to conceal information, Linguacode was designed to make a message more accessible to a wide range of life-forms. Linguacode is sometimes used in first-contact situations such as those with **V'Ger** or **Tin Man** to transmit initial greetings and friendship messages. (*Star Trek: The Motion Picture*).

Linke, Dr. (Jason Wingreen). Scientist stationed on planet **Minara II** in 2268 who was killed by the **Vians** while studying the impending nova of the **Minaran Star System**. ("The Empath" [TOS]).

lirpa. Ancient Vulcan weapon with a razor-sharp curved blade at one end and a heavy bludgeon on the other. Kirk and Spock used the *lirpa* when they fought for possession of **T'Pring** during Spock's *Pon farr* ritual on planet **Vulcan** in 2267. ("Amok Time" [TOS]).

Lissepian captain. (Nicholas Worth). Commander of a cargo vessel who traded Nog's *yamok* sauce for a hundred gross of **self-sealing stem bolts** at Deep Space 9 on stardate 46844. ("Progress" [DS9]).

lithium cracking station. Mineral-processing facility used to produce **lithium crystals**, a critical element of early warp-drive technology. One such facility was the automated station on planet **Delta Vega**, visited by the *Enterprise* in

2265. ("Where No Man Has Gone Before" [TOS]).

lithium crystals. The lightest metal on the periodic table of elements, with an atomic number of 3 and an atomic weight of 6.941. Lithium in a form resembling crystalline quartz was a critical component of warp-drive systems in early starships. Lithium suitable for such use was an extremely rare and valuable commodity, requiring an energy-intensive "cracking" process. ("Where No Man Has Gone Before" [TOS]). Starships were rarely able to carry many spare crystals, meaning that any damage or burnout to a ship's crystals was a serious problem. ("Mudd's Women" [TOS]). *Lithium crystals were used in the* Enterprise*'s engines during the first few episodes of the Original Series. At the suggestion of* Star Trek *scientific advisor Harvey Lynn, lithium was changed to* **dilithium** *because lithium is a real element with known properties, while the imaginary dilithium could be endowed by* Star Trek*'s writers with extraordinary qualities not yet known to science, making warp drive possible in the* Star Trek *universe.*

Little John. (Jonathan Frakes). In Earth mythology, the trusted lieutenant of **Robin Hood** in ancient England. **Q** cast Commander Riker in this role in an elaborate fantasy he crafted to teach Captain Picard a lesson. ("QPid" [TNG]).

"Little One." A diminutive used by **Lwaxana Troi** when addressing her daughter, Deanna. The younger Troi found it irritating. ("Ménage à Troi" [TNG]).

Liva. (Stephanie Erb). Aide to **Ambassador Ves Alkar** when he helped negotiate peace on planet **Rekag-Seronia** in 2369. An attractive woman, Alkar attempted to use her as a "receptacle" for his negative emotions after he thought that Deanna Troi had died. ("Man of the People" [TNG]).

Livingston. *Unofficial name given by the* Star Trek *production crew to the Australian lionfish that lived in the saltwater aquarium in Picard's* **ready room**. *Livingston was named for* Star Trek *producer-director David Livingston.*

L'Kor. (Richard Herd). Klingon warrior, believed killed in the **Khitomer massacre** of 2346, who was actually taken prisoner by the Romulans. L'Kor was spared death by Romulans who did not wish to murder helpless victims, and was incarcerated at the Romulan prison camp in the **Carraya System**. In the years that followed, L'Kor became a leader among the Klingon prisoners. ("Birthright, Parts I and II" [TNG]).

Locarno, Cadet First Class Nicholas. (Robert Duncan McNeill). Leader of Starfleet Academy's **Nova Squadron** in 2368 when the team attempted the hazardous **Kolvoord Starburst** for that year's commencement ceremonies. Nova Squadron member **Joshua Albert** was killed in a serious accident during the maneuver. The charismatic Locarno persuaded his team to conceal the fact that they had been attempting a maneuver that had been banned by the Academy for nearly a century. When the truth was eventually revealed at an Academy investigation, Locarno accepted responsibility for Albert's death, and was expelled. ("The First Duty" [TNG]).

locator bomb. Sophisticated antipersonnel weapon capable of seeking out a specific person and detonating a **sorium argine** explosive to kill the target. The locator bomb used sensors designed to lock on to the target's pheromones. In 2369, Quark's brother **Rom** and Zek's son, **Krax**, used a locator bomb in an attempt to assassinate Quark during his brief tenure as **Grand Nagus**. ("The Nagus" [DS9]).

Locklin, Ensign. Member of the *Enterprise*-D's transporter crew. In 2367 she was the last person to use a transporter prior to the *Enterprise*-D's encounter with a wormhole in the **Ngame Nebula.** ("Clues" [TNG]).

Locutus of Borg. (Patrick Stewart). **Borg** leader created by the assimilation of **Jean-Luc Picard** into the Borg consciousness in 2366.

Although the concept of a Borg leader was, at the time, almost a contradiction in terms, Locutus was intended to provide a voice for the Borg, as part of a Borg plan to assimilate the Federation. With Picard's mind in the Borg collective consciousness, the powerful adversary had access to all of Picard's knowledge and experience, making him partially responsible for the massive Federation defeat at the battle of **Wolf 359**. But the access proved to be two-way. The capture of Locutus by the *Enterprise*-D personnel gave them access to the Borg collective consciousness and they were able to defeat the Borg by exploiting this access. ("The Best of Both Worlds, Parts I and II" [TNG]). *Locutus was also featured in flashback scenes in "Emissary" (DS9).*

log. An official record of mission progress kept by the commanding officer of a starship or starbase.

Logan, Chief Engineer. (Vyto Ruginis). Chief engineer of the *Starship Enterprise*-D in late 2364. Logan expressed concern at Geordi La Forge's relative inexperience when La Forge was temporarily placed in command of the ship at planet **Minos**. ("The Arsenal of Freedom" [TNG]). *Ironically, Logan was replaced as chief engineer by La Forge the following year in "The Child" (TNG).*

logic. School of rigorously rational thought that forms the cornerstone of the **Vulcan** culture. The Vulcans nearly destroyed themselves in bitter wars until they rejected emotionalism in favor of logic.

Lojal. (Michael Ensign). **Vulcan** ambassador who visited **Deep Space 9** in 2369 on a fact-finding mission to the **Bajoran wormhole.** ("The Forsaken" [DS9]).

Lokai. (Lou Antonio). Accused criminal from the planet **Cheron** who fled his planet's authorities across interstellar space for 50,000 years. Lokai claimed he was the victim of racial persecution because his skin coloration was different from those from Cheron who called themselves the "master race." Lokai was finally captured by Commissioner **Bele** in 2268. Upon returning to their homeworld, they found that racial hatred had destroyed their society, leaving no survivors. ("Let That Be Your Last Battlefield" [TOS])

lokar **beans.** Ferengi food served at **Quark's bar** on station Deep Space 9. ("Move Along Home," "Progress" [DS9]).

London Kings. Professional **baseball** team that played on Earth during the 21st century. A shortstop from the London Kings named **Buck Bokai** broke **Joe DiMaggio**'s record for consecutive hits in 2026. ("The Big Goodbye" [TNG]). The London Kings won the World Series in 2042, but by that time, public interest in the sport had fallen to the point where there were only 300 spectators at the last game. ("If Wishes Were Horses" [DS9]).

London, Jack. (Michael Aron). Early 20th-century American writer (1876-1916). Prior to becoming a popular writer, London worked as a bellboy at the 19th-century San Francisco hotel where Commander Data took up lodging. ("Time's Arrow, Parts I and II" [TNG]).

The real Jack London was born in 1876, in San Francisco. He spent part of his youth as an oyster pirate before leaving for the Klondike in 1897. While we have no evidence to support this, it is possible that Jack London was working as a bellboy in 1893, where he may have met an unusual "albino" customer with an affinity for poker.

• **"Lonely Among Us."** *Next Generation* episode #8. Teleplay by D. C. Fontana. Story by Michael Halperin. Directed by Cliff Bole. Stardate 41249.3. *First aired in 1987. A mysterious cloud creature attempts to communicate with the Enterprise-D crew through the body of Captain Picard. Data first showed his interest in the Sherlock Holmes stories during this episode.* SEE: **Antica; Anticans; Badar N'D'D; Beta Renna cloud; Beta Renna system; Channing, Dr.; Enterprise-D, U.S.S.; Holmes, Sherlock; Parliament; Selay; Ssestar; Singh, Lieutenant Commander.**

Long Dark Tunnel, The. Pulp novel featuring the adventures of San Francisco gumshoe detective **Dixon Hill**. Published 1936 on Earth. ("The Big Goodbye" [TNG]).

Lonka Pulsar. A rotating neutron star of approximately 4.356 solar masses, located in the Lonka Cluster. An alien replica of Picard, placed on the *Enterprise*-D in 2366 by unknown aliens to study the nature of authority, ordered the ship to approach the Lonka Pulsar too closely for safety, leading Riker to suspect the substitution. ("Allegiance" [TNG]).

Lopez, Ensign. *Enterprise*-D security division crew member. Worf snapped at him because he felt Lopez had improperly prepared a duty roster, but Worf was just upset about having learned the possibility that his father might have been captured by Romulans at Khitomer. ("Birthright, Part I" [TNG]).

Lord High Sheriff of Nottingham. (John de Lancie). In Earth mythology, the nemesis of **Robin Hood** in ancient England. **Q** cast himself in this role in 2367 during an elaborate fantasy he crafted to teach Picard about the nature of love. ("QPid" [TNG]).

Lore. (Brent Spiner). A highly sophisticated humanoid android built by noted cyberneticist Dr. **Noonien Soong** at his laboratory on planet **Omicron Theta**. Lore was almost identical in physical design to the android **Data** (also built by Soong), but had more human emotional responses built into his programming. Lore was activated around 2336, but was shut down by Soong shortly afterward because the colonists at Omicron Theta viewed Lore as a threat. Lore was responsible for luring the malevolent **Crystalline Entity** to Omicron Theta, resulting in the death of all the colonists there. Lore remained dormant until 2364 when his components were discovered by an away team from the *Enterprise*-D. Upon his reactivation, Lore exhibited manipulative and sadistic behavior and was eventually beamed into space when he attempted to gain control of the ship. ("Datalore" [TNG]). Lore drifted in space for nearly two years before he was rescued by a passing **Pakled** ship.

In 2367, Lore responded to a call sent by Dr. Noonien Soong, intended to summon Data to Soong's new secret laboratory. Soong had intended to install a new chip in Data's brain to give the android the ability to experience human emotions. Arriving at Soong's laboratory at the same time as Data, Lore stole the new chip by masquerading as Data. Soong died shortly thereafter, and Lore escaped before *Enterprise*-D personnel could apprehend him. ("Brothers" [TNG]).

Lore later encountered a **Borg** group wandering aimlessly in space. The Borg were experiencing individuality as a result of **Hugh**'s reintroduction into the collective, and were unable to cope with the experience. Lore seized on the situation and appointed himself as leader of the Borg. He promised to re-create them in his own image, that of a completely artificial life-form. The Borg willingly followed Lore, attacking his enemies, capturing his brother, **Data**, and also sacrificing themselves to his medical experiments. A small group of Borg, led by Hugh, suspected that Lore was incapable of fulfilling his promise, and were angered at the suffering Lore was inflicting on his experimental subjects. This dissident group of Borg, aided by *Enterprise*-D personnel, overthrew Lore by force. Shortly thereafter, Lore was deactivated by his brother, Data. The emotion chip designed by Soong was removed from Lore's body before it was dismantled. ("Descent, Parts I and II" [TNG]). *Lore first*

appeared in "Datalore" (TNG).

Loren III. Planet located near the **Kurlan** system where **Professor Richard Galen** obtained genetic samples as part of his research just prior to his death in 2369. ("The Chase" [TNG]). SEE: **humanoid life**.

Lorenze Cluster. A stellar formation recognized by Wesley Crusher when he gazed from Ten-Forward while discussing his future with Guinan. ("The Child" [TNG]). The Lorenze Cluster was also the location where the *Starship Drake* disappeared some time prior to 2364. The planet **Minos** is located there. ("The Arsenal of Freedom" [TNG]).

Lorgh. A friend of **Mogh**, Lorgh cared for Mogh's son, the infant **Kurn**, when Mogh and his family went to **Khitomer** in 2345. After Mogh was killed in the Romulan attack at Khitomer, Lorgh raised Kurn as his own son, and did not tell him of his true parentage until he reached the **Age of Ascension**. ("Sins of the Father" [TNG]).

Lornak. One of several warring clans on planet **Acamar III.** The Lornaks had been deadly enemies of the **Tralesta** clan for two centuries, and finally staged a bloody massacre in 2286, killing all but five of the Tralestas. The Lornaks were in turn systematically murdered by one of the last five surviving Tralestas, a woman named **Yuta**. ("The Vengeance Factor" [TNG]).

Losira. (Lee Meriwether). Last survivor of the **Kalandan outpost** whose population was killed 10,000 years ago due to a deadly microorganism. After Losira's death, the outpost's computer system used Losira's image to protect the outpost against invaders. The replica was able to kill by touching a victim, matching his chromosome pattern, then killing the person by **cellular disruption**. ("That Which Survives" [TOS]).

Loskene, Commander. (Voice of Barbara Babcock). **Tholian** commander who accused the *Enterprise* of trespassing in a territorial annex of the **Tholian Assembly** in 2268 and attempted to entangle the ship in an energy web. ("The Tholian Web" [TOS]). SEE: **Mea 3**.

• **"Loss, The."** *Next Generation* episode #84. Teleplay by Hilary J. Bader and Alan J. Alder & Vanessa Greene. Story by Hilary J. Bader. Directed by Chip Chalmers. Stardate 44356.9. *First aired in 1990. Deanna Troi considers resigning her Starfleet commission when she loses her empathic powers.* SEE: **Allenby, Ensign Tess; Bracas V; Breen; Brooks, Ensign Janet; Brooks, Marc; cosmic string fragment; Ferengi; inner nuncial series; Kabul River; kilodynes; T'lli Beta; Troi, Deanna; two-dimensional creatures.**

• **"Loud as a Whisper."** *Next Generation* episode #32.

Written by Jacqueline Zambrano. Directed by Larry Shaw. Stardate 42477.2. *First aired in 1988. A hearing-impaired mediator struggles to find a way to turn his disadvantage into an advantage while searching for peace on planet Solais V.* SEE: **Chorus; Fendaus V; Klingonese; Leyrons; Lima Sierra System; M-9; Malkus IX; Ramatis III; Ramatis Star System; Riva; Scholar/Artist; sign languages; Solais V; Solari; VISOR; Warrior/Adonis; Woman; Zambrano, Battle of.**

Louis. (Dennis Creaghan). An old friend of **Jean-Luc Picard**. They spent a good deal of their youth together in **Labarre, France**. Louis undertook a career in hydroponics, but by 2367, he was a supervisor on the **Atlantis Project**. Jean-Luc Picard found this very amusing because his friend was a horrible swimmer in their youth, but now worked on the ocean floor. ("Family" [TNG]).

Louvois, Captain Phillipa. (Amanda McBroom). Starfleet legal officer who prosecuted Jean-Luc Picard in the court-martial proceedings following the loss of the *U.S.S. Stargazer* in 2355. Although Picard and Louvois had been romantically involved prior to that time, the *Stargazer* trial ended that relationship. Louvois left Starfleet thereafter. The two did not see each other again until 2365, when Louvois, having returned to Starfleet as head of the Sector 23 **Judge Advocate General**'s office, presided over the precedent-setting case in which she ruled that the android **Data** was entitled to full constitutional rights and was not the property of Starfleet. ("The Measure of a Man" [TNG]).

love poetry, Klingon. Worf recommended reading love poetry as a means of luring a potential mate when **Wesley Crusher** was attracted to **Salia** of planet **Daled IV**. Worf noted that in response, a Klingon woman might be expected to roar, throw heavy objects, and claw at her mate. He expressed disdain for human males, describing their courtship rituals as "begging." ("The Dauphin" [TNG]). Worf once claimed that the art of love poetry reached its fullest flower among the Klingons. ("Up the Long Ladder" [TNG]).

Low Note, The. A jazz club from Earth's New Orleans city on Bourbon Street, circa 1958, re-created on the *Enterprise*-D holodeck. Riker enjoyed a simulation of The Low Note on the holodeck shortly after that system had been enhanced by the Bynars at **Starbase 74**. Being a jazz fan, Riker enjoyed playing a trombone with the program's jazz band, as well as the company of the lovely **Minuet**, a young lady who evidently left quite an impression on him. ("11001001" [TNG]).

low-mileage pit woofie. Slang term used by 20th-century entertainer **Sonny Clemonds**. Neither Riker nor Data understood the reference. ("The Neutral Zone" [TNG]).

lower pylon 1. On station Deep Space 9, the lower half of docking pylon 1. Lower pylon 1 was evacuated on stardate 46853 due to the danger of a **subspace rupture**. ("If Wishes Were Horses" [DS9]).

lucrovexitrin. A highly toxic substance capable of causing **nucleosynthesis** in silicon. Lucovexitrin is not normally detectable by a starship's internal sensor scans. ("Hollow Pursuits" [TNG]).

Ludugial gold. Reputed to be the purest form of gold in the galaxy, at least. Twenty thousand Ludugial gold coins were offered by Ferengi trade official **Par Lenor** to Kriosian **ambassador Briam** in exchange for the **empathic metamorph** named **Kamala**. Briam declined. ("The Perfect Mate" [TNG]).

Luma. (Sheila Leighton). One of the **Eymorg** women of planet **Sigma Draconis VI**. ("Spock's Brain" [TOS]).

Lumo. Indian on **Miramanee's planet** who brought a young boy who had drowned to the tribe's medicine man, only to have Kirk perform artificial respiration on the child, bringing him miraculously back to life. ("The Paradise Syndrome" [TOS]).

Lunar V. A military prison facility set up by the **Angosian** government to house the biochemically altered veterans of the **Tarsian War**. ("The Hunted" [TNG]). SEE: **Danar, Roga**.

Lurin, DaiMon. (Mike Gomez). Leader of the renegade **Ferengi** who took over the *Enterprise*-D in 2369. ("Rascals" [TNG]).

Lurry, Mr. (Whit Bissell). Manager of **Deep Space Station K-7** in 2267. ("The Trouble with Tribbles" [TOS]). SEE: **Sherman's Planet; quadrotriticale**.

Lursa. (Barbara March). A member of the politically powerful **Duras** family; the elder of Duras's two sisters. Following the death of Duras in 2367, Lursa and her sister **B'Etor** conspired with the Romulan operative **Sela** to overthrow the **Gowron** leadership of the **Klingon High Council**. Their attempt to place **Toral**, the illegitimate son of Duras, as council leader split the council and plunged the Empire into a **Klingon civil war** until their complicity with the **Romulan Star Empire** was discovered. ("Redemption, Parts I and II" [TNG]). Lursa subsequently dropped out of sight for almost two years until she and her sister attempted to raise capital for their armies by selling **bilitrium** explosives to the **Kohn-ma**, a Bajoran terrorist organization, in 2369. ("Past Prologue" [DS9]).

Lusor. Lake on the **Klingon Homeworld**. Klingon oral history held that this was the place where **Kahless the Unforgettable** finished the forging of the first *bat'telh* sword. ("Rightful Heir" [TNG]).

Lutan. (Jessie Lawrence Ferguson). Civil leader on planet **Ligon II** in 2364 when the **Ligonians** agreed to provide vitally needed vaccines to the *Enterprise*-D for transfer to planet **Styris IV**. During the negotiations for the transfer, Lutan attempted to engineer an incident to use *Enterprise*-D Lieu-

tenant Yar to eliminate his wife, **Yareena**, thus clearing the way for him to control her lands and wealth. Lutan lost these claims when Yar defeated Yareena in ritual combat. Lutan's honor was preserved when Yareena later accepted Lutan as her Second One after **Hagon** became Yareena's **First One**. ("Code of Honor" [TNG]).

luvetric pulse. Energy form suggested as a possible way to track Commander **Data** when he was controlled by Lore in 2369. The pulse would have caused a resonance fluctuation in Data's power cells. However, in order to be effective, the pulse would have to be so strong as to risk destruction of Data's positronic net. ("Descent, Part I" [TNG]).

Lya Station Alpha. A Federation starbase. The *Enterprise*-D traveled to Lya Station Alpha with survivors from the attack on the **Solarion IV** colony in 2368. **Ensign Ro Laren** came aboard the *Enterprise*-D at this station, and Picard met there with **Admiral Kennelly** regarding suspected Bajoran terrorist activity. ("Ensign Ro" [TNG]).

Lycosa tarantula. Spider, similar to an Earth tarantula. **Miles O'Brien** kept a Lycosa tarantula that he named Christina as a pet. ("Realm of Fear" [TNG]).

Lynars. Batlike creature indigenous to the caverns of planet **Celtris III**. The creatures were believed to be harmless. ("Chain of Command, Part I" [TNG]).

Lynch, Leland T. (Walker Boone). An assistant chief Engineer of the *Starship Enterprise*-D in 2364. Lynch had been supervising routine servicing of the dilithium chamber when forced to quickly bring the warp drive back on line for a rescue mission to planet Vagra II. ("Skin of Evil" [TNG]).

Lynstrom. Space Command representative who served on James Kirk's court-martial board in 2267 when Kirk was accused of the murder of **Benjamin Finney**. ("Court Martial" [TOS]).

Lyshan System. Federation system that was the rendezvous point for Captain Picard's covert team, following their mission on planet **Celtris III** in 2369. Commander Riker was able to retrieve Dr. Crusher and Lieutenant Worf from the system, following their escape from Celtris. ("Chain of Command, Part II" [TNG]).

Lysia. The homeworld of the Lysian Alliance. In 2368, the crew of the *Enterprise*-D was led to believe that the crews of fourteen Federation vessels were being held captive on Lysia, but it was a **Satarran** ploy to trick *Enterprise*-D personnel into attacking the Lysian Central Command. ("Conundrum" [TNG]). SEE: **Epsilon Silar System**.

Lysian Central Command. A Lysian space station located deep within the **Epsilon Silar System**. Lysian Central Command and was protected by a series of unmanned laser-equipped sentry pods. The command station itself was staffed by a crew of over 15,000, and was defended by four laser cannons. It also had the ability to fire a series of cobalt-fusion warheads. By Federation Starfleet standards, the Lysian Central Command, as well as the Lysian ships, possessed limited weaponry. ("Conundrum" [TNG]). *The model of the Lysian Central Command was a revamp of the **Edo god** from "Justice" (TNG).*

Lysian Destroyer. A short-range attack vessel equipped with low-power disruptor-type weapons and minimal shielding. The vessel had a standard crew complement of 53. One of these vessels was destroyed by the *Enterprise*-D in 2368 while that ship's crew was being misled by a **Satarran** agent seeking to use the Federation ship against his Lysian enemies. ("Conundrum" [TNG]). SEE: **Epsilon Silar System; MacDuff, Commander Keiran**.

M-1 through M-4. Experimental **multitronic** computers developed by **Dr. Richard Daystrom**, unsuccessful predecessors to the **M-5** computer. ("The Ultimate Computer" [TOS]).

M-113 creature. The last surviving creature of planet **M-113**, a humanoid with large suction cups on its hands. This individual had caused the death of **Nancy Crater** before transporting up to the *Enterprise,* where it was killed when it threatened the life of Captain Kirk. The M-113 creatures possessed an extraordinary hypnotic ability to appear with the identity of some-

one known to their prey, and used this ability when hunting in order to obtain the salt they needed to survive. ("The Man Trap" [TOS]). *The M-113 creature is popularly known by many* Star Trek *fans as the Salt Vampire, although this name did not come from the episode itself.*

M-113. Class-M planet, the former home of a long-dead civilization, now desertlike and nearly barren. Archaeologist **Robert Crater** spent some five years prior to 2266 studying the ruins there, during which time his wife **Nancy Crater** was killed by the last surviving native inhabitant of that planet. ("The Man Trap" [TOS]).

M-4. Robot invented by **Flint** to perform a variety of tasks at his home on planetoid **Holberg 917G.** ("Requiem For Methuselah" [TOS]).

M-5. (Voice of James Doohan). Experimental computer designed in 2268 by **Dr. Richard Daystrom**. The M-5 **multitronic** unit was the most ambitious computer complex ever created in its time, and was designed with the purpose of correlating and controlling every aspect of starship operation. The M-5 multitronic unit was built using a technique that allowed human neu-

ral **engram**s to be impressed upon the computer's circuits, theoretically giving the machine the ability to think and reason like a human. Daystrom hoped that the M-5 would prove as great an advance as his earlier breakthrough in duotronics.

The M-5 was tested aboard the *Starship Enterprise* in 2268 in an exercise that allowed the M-5 to conduct routine contact and survey operations, as well as an elaborate war game that involved four other Federation starships. Although initial tests were promising, the M-5 demonstrated serious problems when it fired full phasers at the *Excalibur* and the *Lexington*, killing hundreds of people. Fortunately, the M-5 possessed Daystrom's sense of morality, and it later deactivated itself to atone for the sin of murder. ("The Ultimate Computer" [TOS]).

M-9. A type of gestural sign language that is both silent and covert. Developed by the **Leyrons** of planet Malkus IX. Data learned this language form in 2365 for use in communicating with mediator **Riva** after his **Chorus** was killed at planet **Solais V.** ("Loud as a Whisper" [TNG]). *The hand gestures that Data studied on his computer screen when learning this language were mostly standard American Sign Language symbols. One sign that was not, however, was the traditional Vulcan salute, which was included to see if anyone would notice.*

M24 Alpha. Star system that contained the planet **Triskelion,** where several members of the *Enterprise* were transported in 2268. ("The Gamesters of Triskelion" [TOS]).

Maab. (Michael Dante). Ambitious warrior on planet **Capella IV** who attempted to gain control of the Ten Tribes of Capella by murdering their leader, High **Teer Akaar,** in 2267. Maab had favored selling **Capellan** mineral rights to the Klingons instead of to the Federation. Maab later sacrificed his life defending Akaar's widow, **Eleen**, against Klingon agent **Kras**, after discovering that the Klingons were without honor by Capellan standards. ("Friday's Child" [TOS]).

Mab-Bu VI. A giant, gaseous planet located in Federation space. Mab-Bu VI had a class-M moon that was recorded in Starfleet records as uninhabited. The *Starship* **Essex** was destroyed above the Mab-Bu moon in 2167 by **Ux-Mal** criminals who had been imprisoned on the moon. These same criminals attempted to escape a second time, in 2168, by commandeering the *Starship Enterprise*-D, taking over the bodies of several *Enterprise*-D personnel including Miles O'Brien, Deanna Troi, and Data. ("Power Play" [TNG]).

macchiato. A cappuccino-like coffee beverage favored by Beverly Crusher. ("The Chase" [TNG]).

MacDougal, Sarah. (Brooke Bundy). Chief engineer of the *Enterprise*-D in early 2364. ("The Naked Now" [TNG]).

MacDuff, Commander Keiran. (Erich Anderson). A **Satarran** operative who masqueraded as an officer of the *Enterprise*-D in 2368. The Satarrans bombarded the Federation ship with a powerful bioelectric field that suppressed the crew's short-term memories as well as most computer records. During the following confusion, MacDuff took a place aboard the *Enterprise*-D and attempted to convince the ship's crew to attack the **Lysian Central Command**. The Satarran scheme failed because Captain Picard refused to attack a defenseless enemy, even though he appeared to have been ordered to do so. ("Conundrum" [TNG]).

Macet, Gul. (Marc Alaimo). Commanding officer of the **Cardassian** warship *Trager*. Macet came aboard the *Enterprise*-D in 2367 as an observer during a mission to locate the renegade Federation starship *Phoenix*. ("The Wounded"

[TNG]). *Marc Alaimo played several other roles, including Cardassian Gul Dukat. SEE: Badar N'D'D.*

Macintosh. Primitive 20th-century personal computer that Scotty found puzzling because of his unfamiliarity with its peculiar "mouse" pointing device. (*Star Trek IV: The Voyage Home*).

macrospentol. One of several chemicals used by the **Angosians** during the **Tarsian War** to "improve" their soldiers, making them more effective in combat. Unfortunately, the effects of many of these drugs were irreversible. ("The Hunted" [TNG]). SEE: **Danar, Roga.**

Maddox, Commander Bruce. (Brian Brophy). Noted cyberneticist, Chair of Robotics at the **Daystrom Institute of Technology,** and student of the works of **Noonien Soong**. Maddox was the only member of the entrance committee who opposed the android **Data**'s entrance into the Academy in 2341 because of his belief that Data was not a sentient being. In 2365, Maddox attempted to use legal means to coerce Data to submit to a disassembly procedure in an effort to learn more about the android's construction. This effort was blocked when Judge Advocate General **Phillipa Louvois** ruled that Data was indeed a sentient being. ("The Measure of a Man" [TNG]). Data nevertheless held no ill will against Maddox, and in fact remained in correspondence with him, providing Maddox with information to help further understand Data's mind. ("Data's Day" [TNG]).

Madeline. (Rhonda Aldrich). The fictional secretary of pulp detective **Dixon Hill**. An attractive woman who outwardly seemed bemused by the world of private investigators, Madeline wanted to become a P.I. herself. The Dixon Hill holodeck program, based on the Dixon Hill novels and short stories, included a holographic representation of Madeline. ("Manhunt" [TNG], "Clues" [TNG]).

Madena, Coalition of. Political entity encompassing planets **Altec** and **Straleb** in the Omega Sagitta system. Both planets are inhabited by the same humanoid race, and the coalition was held together by a precarious treaty. ("The Outrageous Okona" [TNG]).

Madred, Gul. (David Warner). Cardassian officer who interrogated *Enterprise*-D captain **Jean-Luc Picard** when Picard was captured at planet **Celtris III** in 2369. Madred employed physical and psychological torture in violation of the **Seldonis IV convention** while attempting to extract Starfleet tactical information from Picard. Although Picard was able to resist, he later confided that he was so brutalized by the experience that he would have done anything for Madred, had he not been freed. ("Chain of Command, Part II" [TNG]). *David Warner also played St. John Talbot in* Star Trek V: The Final Frontier *and Gorkon in* Star Trek VI: The Undiscovered Country.

Magda. (Susan Denberg). One of Mudd's women. Magda had short blond hair and came from the Helium experimental station before being recruited by **Harry Mudd** as a wife for a settler on planet **Ophiucus III** in 2266. Magda later married one of the miners on **Rigel XII**. ("Mudd's Women" [TOS]). *Magda's last name was not mentioned in the aired version but a final draft script dated May 26, 1966, listed her as Magda Kovacs.*

Magellan, Shuttlecraft. *Enterprise*-D shuttle vehicle #15. The *Magellan*, piloted by Worf, was launched on a rescue mission when Captain Picard was trapped on planet **El-Adrel IV** in 2368. A **Tamarian** vessel fired on the *Magellan*, carefully disabling it so that it was forced to return to the *Enterprise*-D. The Tamarians had sought to isolate Picard and their captain on El-Adrel IV so that they might have a chance to learn to communicate. ("Darmok" [TNG]). The *Magellan* participated in a rescue mission of the **J'naii** shuttle *Taris Murn* in 2368. The *Magellan* had two 1,250 **millicochrane** warp engines and microfusion impulse thrusters. Such shuttles are normally unarmed, but can be equipped with two **phaser type-4** emitters for special mission requirements. The rescue of the J'naii shuttle was successful, but the *Magellan* was destroyed in the process. ("The Outcast" [TNG]). *The Magellan was named for Spanish navigator Ferdinand Magellan, the first explorer to circumnavigate planet Earth. This was the first appearance of the new full-sized shuttle set and model introduced during the fifth season. The ship was an extensive modification of the* **Galileo 5** *shuttle built for* Star Trek V. *Contributing designers included Richard James, Nilo Rodis, Herman Zimmerman, Andy Neskoromny, and Rick Sternbach. The model was built by Greg Jein.*

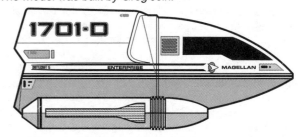

Magellan, U.S.S. Federation starship, commanded by **Captain Conklin**. ("Starship Mine" [TNG]).

Magna Carta. The "great charter" of liberties signed by English King John under enormous pressure from English barons on Earth in the year 1215. The Magna Carta, still regarded as a major milestone in the evolution of law, provided guarantees of due process in trials, and strict limitations of governmental power over the governed. ("Court Martial" [TOS]).

magnaspanner. Handheld tool used by Starfleet engineers. ("Tapestry" [TNG]).

magnesite-nitron tablet. Small white disk carried in Dr. McCoy's medical pouch. When crushed, the tablet explodes into a bright flame, providing a source of illumination. Kirk used a magnesite-nitron tablet for illumination in a cave on planet **Capella IV** on stardate 3497. ("Friday's Child" [TOS]).

magnetic boots. Footwear used by starship personnel in weightless conditions to allow a worker to remain attached and vertical with respect to a floor or other suitable surface. Also known as gravity boots. **Burke** and **Samno**, Federation operatives who murdered Klingon chancellor Gorkon, wore magnetic boots so that they could move freely aboard the Klingon ship **Kronos One** during the assassination. The boots later provided the means of identifying Burke and Samno as the assassins. (*Star Trek VI: The Undiscovered Country*).

magnetic probe. Handheld engineering tool used to seal the matter-antimatter flow that caused the *Enterprise* to travel at dangerously accelerated speeds when the **Kalandan, Losira**, sabotaged the ship's engines in 2268. ("That Which Survives" [TOS]).

magnetic resonance traces. Discovered in sections of the *Enterprise*-D hull after their encounter with the Borg at **System J-25** in 2365, these were believed to be indicative of Borg activity — a "Borg footprint." The same resonance traces were also discovered in the remains of the **New Providence** colony in late 2366, and confirmed that the Borg had indeed been responsible for the disappearance of the colony. ("The Best of Both Worlds, Part I" [TNG]).

magnetic seals. Component of the matter/**antimatter containment** system aboard Federation starships. The seals help prevent the highly volatile antimatter from coming into contact with the structure of the ship. The magnetic seals of the **U.S.S. Yamato** collapsed just prior to that ship's explosion in 2365. An emergency system that should have dumped the antimatter from the ship in that situation evidently failed. ("Contagion" [TNG]).

magnetospheric energy taps. Technology developed on the Alpha Moon of planet **Peliar Zel**. The taps allowed the magnetic field of Peliar Zel to be used as an energy source for **Alpha Moon**. Unfortunately, the magnetospheric field created by the tap crossed the orbit of **Beta Moon**. The field caused severe environmental damage to Beta Moon in 2367, increasing the preexisting political tensions between the governments of the two moons. ("The Host" [TNG]). SEE: **Odan, Ambassador.**

mahko root. Plant used by the *Kahn-ut-tu* woman of **Tyree's** planet to cure the poisonous bite of the **mugato**. When James Kirk suffered such a bite in 2267, *Kahn-ut-tu* woman **Nona** inflicted a knife wound on herself, then allowed her blood to pass through the mahko root to Kirk's injury, magically curing him. ("A Private Little War" [TOS]).

Maht-H'a, I.K.C. Klingon *Vor'cha*-class attack cruiser. Under the command of Captain **Nu'Daq**, the *Maht-H'a* participated in 2369 in the discovery of a four-billion-year-old genetically encoded message from an ancient humanoid species. ("The Chase" [TNG]). SEE: **Galen, Professor Richard; humanoid life.**

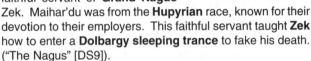

Maid Marian. (Jennifer Hetrick). In Earth mythology, the woman who loved legendary English outlaw **Robin Hood**. **Vash** was cast in this role by **Q** during a fantasy he crafted for the *Enterprise*-D crew. ("QPid" [TNG]).

Maihar'du. (Tiny Ron). Tall, prune-faced humanoid alien who was the faithful servant of **Grand Nagus** Zek. Maihar'du was from the **Hupyrian** race, known for their devotion to their employers. This faithful servant taught **Zek** how to enter a **Dolbargy sleeping trance** to fake his death. ("The Nagus" [DS9]).

main bridge. SEE: **bridge.**

main shuttlebay. SEE: **shuttlebay.**

main particle impeller. Component of **Dr. Farallon's** experimental **particle fountain** that overloaded, causing radiation to contaminate the work station on planet Tyrus VIIA in 2369. ("The Quality of Life" [TNG]).

Maizie series. (Tamara and Starr Wilson). Model of **android** designed by **Harry Mudd** in 2267. ("I, Mudd" [TOS]).

***MajQa*, Rite of.** Klingon ritual involving deep meditation in the lava caves of *No'Mat*. Prolonged exposure to the heat is believed to induce a hallucinatory effect. Great significance is attached to any visions received during the *MajQa*, and revelations of one's father are believed to be the most important. When Worf was young, his adoptive parents arranged for him to experience this ritual. ("Birthright, Part I" [TNG]).

Makers. Intelligent beings from the Andromeda Galaxy who, centuries ago, established exploratory outposts in our galaxy. When the Makers' home star went nova, only a few outposts survived, including one populated by humanoid **android**s on what became known as the planet **Mudd** in 2267. ("I, Mudd" [TOS]).

Makora. (David Soul). Inhabitant of planet **Gamma Trianguli VI** who welcomed the *Enterprise* landing party to their village in 2267. He was attracted to **Sayana**, but wasn't allowed to act on his feelings because mating was against **Vaal's** law. ("The Apple" [TOS]).

Maktag. A division of the Klingon calendar analogous to a month. **Alexander Rozhenko** was born during Maktag of the Earth calendar year 2366. ("New Ground" [TNG]).

Makus III. Planet at which the *Starship Enterprise* was scheduled to deliver emergency medical supplies for transfer to the **New Paris colonies** following a plague outbreak in 2267. ("The *Galileo* Seven" [TOS]).

Malaya IV. Planet where Lieutenant **Paul Hickman** had a physical examination shortly before an alien DNA strand compelled him to return to **Tarchannen III** in 2367. ("Identity Crisis" [TNG]).

Malcor III. A class-M planet and homeworld to the **Malcorians**. This planet was a candidate for Federation first contact, and in 2367 was the subject of sociological studies in preparation for such a contact. ("First Contact" [TNG]).

Malcorians. A humanoid race characterized by enlarged frontal skull bones and a single fused phalange, rather than distinct fingers. In 2367, Malcorian society was undergoing a series of social reforms accompanied by rapid leaps in technology. The Malcorians were within ten months of their first interstellar flight, but the prospects of potential contact with extraterrestrial life were disturbing to some of the Malcorian people. During this time of social upheaval, the *Enterprise*-D attempted to complete a program of covert study on the planet prior to **first contact** with the Malcorian government. Unfortunately, the premature discovery of Federation personnel on the planet's surface led to hysteria in parts of the population and the first contact had to be delayed indefinitely. ("First Contact" [TNG]). SEE: **Krola; Jakara, Rivas; Yale, Mirasta.**

Malencon, Arthur. (Mario Roccuzzo). Hydraulics specialist, part of the unsuccessful **terraforming** project at planet **Velara III**. Malencon was killed by the native crystalline **microbrain** life-forms whose lives were threatened by the project. ("Home Soil" [TNG]).

Malkus IX. A planet whose inhabitants, the Leyrons, developed writing before sign language. This is unusual because most humanoid cultures tend to develop hand signs and spoken languages first. ("Loud as a Whisper" [TNG]).

Mallory, Lieutenant. (Jay Jones). *Enterprise* crew member who was killed while on a landing party on planet **Gamma Trianguli VI** in 2267 when he stepped on a rock with explosive properties. Mallory's father had helped James Kirk get into the Academy. ("The Apple" [TOS]).

Maltz. (John Larroquette). Officer of the Klingon Bird-of-Prey commanded by **Kruge**. Maltz was the only survivor of that ship's crew after Kruge was killed on the **Genesis Planet** and the rest of the crew perished when the *Enterprise* was destroyed. Maltz was taken prisoner when Kirk commandeered the Bird-of-Prey after Kruge was killed. (*Star Trek III: The Search for Spock*).

Malurian System. Planetary system with over four billion inhabitants. When executing its program of planetary sterilization, the space probe *Nomad* did not destroy the solar system itself, just the "unstable biological infestations" inhabiting it. ("The Changeling" [TOS]). SEE: **Tan Ru.**

Malurians. Race from the Malurian System, some four billion people, that were wiped out in 2267 by the errant Earth space probe *Nomad*. The Malurians were being studied by a Federation science team under the direction of **Dr. Manway** at the time. ("The Changeling" [TOS]).

• **"Man Alone, A."** *Deep Space Nine* episode #3. Teleplay by Michael Piller. Story by Gerald Sanford and Michael Piller. Directed by Paul Lynch. Stardate: 46421.5. *First aired in 1993. Odo is framed for murder by a man who has killed his own clone. This was the first regular hourlong episode of* Star Trek: Deep Space Nine. SEE: **Altonian brain teaser; Azna; bioregenerative field; clone; Dax, Jadzia; electrophoretic analysis; Garanian Bolites; glop-on-a-stick; Ibudan; Juro; Karo-Net; Kran-Tobal; Lamonay S.; Lauriento massage holoprogram #101-A; O'Brien, Keiko; O'Brien, Molly; Odo; Rom; Rujian; schoolroom; seofurane; Sisko, Benjamin; Trills; Yadozi Desert; Zayra.**

• **"Man of the People."** *Next Generation* episode #129. Written by Frank Abatemarco. Directed by Winrich Kolbe. Stardate 46071.6. *First aired in 1992. A famous Federation mediator maintains extraordinary equanimity in tough negotiations by even more extraordinary abuse of his female companions.* SEE: **Alkar, Ambassador Ves; counselor; Darthen; *Dorian*; dylamadon; Janeway, Ensign; Jarth; Liva; Maylor, Sev; melorazine; *Mok'bara*; neurotransmitter; Ogawa, Nurse Alyssa; Pinder, Lieutenant; "receptacle"; Rekag-Seronia; Rekags; Talmadge, Captain.**

• **"Man Trap, The."** Original Series episode #6. Written by George Clayton Johnson. Directed by Marc Daniels. Stardate 1513.1. *First aired in 1966. A salt creature that can disguise itself in any form stalks the* Enterprise. *Although the sixth episode produced in the original series, "The Man Trap" was the first episode to be aired during the original network run of the show in 1966.* SEE: **Barnhart; Beauregard; Borgia plant; Corinth IV; Crater, Nancy; Crater, Professor Robert; Darnell, Crewman; Great Bird of the Galaxy, the; Green, Crewman; M-113 creature; M-113 (planet); McCoy, Dr. Leonard H.; "Plum"; Saurian brandy; sodium chloride; Sturgeon; Sulu, Hikaru; Rand, Janice; Vulcan; Wrigley's Pleasure Planet.**

Manark IV. SEE: **sand bats**.

Mandel, Ensign. (Cameron Arnett). An *Enterprise*-D crew member who was assigned to conn on the main bridge while the *Enterprise*-D was departing Mudor V on stardate 45156. He was one of the few officers left on the bridge when the ship was disabled by a **quantum filament**. ("Disaster" [TNG]).

Mandl, Kurt. (Walter Gotell). Director of an aborted **terraforming** station on planet **Velara III**. Mandl had concealed the fact that the terraforming project would threaten indigenous life-forms on Velara III.

("Home Soil" [TNG]). *Actor Walter Gotell also played General Gogol in several James Bond movies.*

maneuvering thrusters. Low-power reaction-control jets used for fine positional and attitude control by starships and other spacecraft. Used in low-speed docking maneuvers and similar situations. (*Star Trek: The Motion Picture*).

Manheim Effect. An intense temporal disturbance generated by **Dr. Paul Manheim**'s efforts to open a window into another dimension. The Manheim Effect was manifested by a series of brief temporal "hiccoughs" during which time was briefly superimposed over itself. Data was successful in disrupting the Manheim Effect by injecting a small quantity of antimatter into the distortion. ("We'll Always Have Paris" [TNG]).

Manheim, Dr. Paul. (Rod Loomis). Brilliant scientist who conducted revolutionary studies in nonlinear time and the relationships between time and gravity.

Manheim's early work in nonlinear time found little acceptance in the scientific community, and he became a recluse, setting up a laboratory on the distant planetoid **Vandor IX** where he hoped his temporal research would yield the key to other dimensions. Manheim made considerable strides there, although a terrible accident in 2364 nearly killed Manheim and caused a severe temporal disturbance. ("We'll Always Have Paris" [TNG]).

Manheim, Jenice. (Michelle Phillips). Wife to scientist **Dr. Paul Manheim**. Prior to her marriage to Manheim, Jenice had been romantically involved with future *Enterprise*-D captain **Jean-Luc Picard**. Jenice was hurt when Picard left her without saying goodbye in 2342, but the two resolved their feelings in 2364 when Picard and the *Enterprise*-D saved the life of her husband. ("We'll Always Have Paris" [TNG]). *Actor Michelle Phillips gained fame in the 1960s as a singer with the musical group Mamas and the Papas.*

• **"Manhunt."** *Next Generation* episode #45. Written by Tracy Tormé. Directed by Rob Bowman. Stardate 42859.2. *First aired in 1989. Lwaxana Troi returns to the* Enterprise-D *with the intent of finding a husband.* SEE: **Antide III; Antidean ambassador; Antideans; Bender, Slade; brown dwarfs; chime, Betazoid; co-orbital satellites; Hill, Dixon; Madeline; Marejaretus VI; Pacifica;** *Parrot's Claw, The*; **phase, the; Rex; Sacred Chalice of Rixx; Troi, Lwaxana; Ultritium; vermicula.**

Mantickian paté. An exotic dish concocted by Lwaxana Troi for **Dr. Timicin** and the engineering staff of the *Enterprise*-D in 2367. ("Half a Life" [TNG]).

Manu III. Planet whose government used **proximity detectors** to control its population. ("Legacy" [TNG]).

Manway, Dr. Federation scientist who studied the inhabitants of the **Malurian System**. He was killed in 2267 when the entire population was destroyed by the robot **Nomad**. ("The Changeling" [TOS]).

Mar Oscura. A dark-matter nebula located in Federation space. The *Enterprise*-D was assigned to chart the nebula in 2367, using special photon torpedos to illuminate the interior of the nebula for study. The crew discovered that the interior of the nebula was riddled with gaps in the fabric of normal space. When these pockets came in contact with the ship, they would cause the point of contact to momentarily phase out of normal space. The *Enterprise*-D lost one crew member and a shuttlepod to the phasing phenomenon before the ship was able to leave the nebula, guided by Captain Picard. ("In Theory" [TNG]).

Mara. (Susan Howard). Science officer aboard **Kang**'s Klingon battle cruiser in 2268. Mara, who was Kang's wife, was among the victims of the **Beta XII-A entity**. ("Day of the Dove" [TOS]).

Maraltian seev-ale. Green beverage from Quark's private stock. **Odo** gave a Maraltian seev-ale to **Kira** after a particularly difficult interrogation session with the Cardassian, **Aamin Marritza** in 2369. ("Duet" [DS9]).

Marauder, Ferengi. SEE: **Ferengi Marauder**.

Marcos XII. Planet designated by the evil **Gorgan** of **Triacus** for conquest in 2268. The Gorgan manipulated the children of the **Starnes Expedition** into commandeering the *Starship Enterprise* toward that destination. Marcos XII was also the home of **Tommy Starne's** relatives. ("And the Children Shall Lead" [TOS]).

Marcus, Claudius. (Logan Ramsey). Proconsul and Roman leader on the fourth planet in system 892. When Captain **R. M. Merrick** of the *S.S. Beagle* beamed down to this planet in 2261, Marcus convinced him to stay rather than report this culture to Federation authorities. ("Bread and Circuses" [TOS]). SEE: **892, Planet IV**.

Marcus, Dr. Carol. (Bibi Besch). Brilliant scientist and noted molecular biologist. Marcus directed the ambitious **Project Genesis**, which attempted to develop a process to rapidly terraform uninhabitable planets into worlds suitable for humanoid life. Marcus was romantically involved with future *Enterprise* captain **James T. Kirk** in the early 2260s. Their son, **David Marcus**, became a noted scientist in his own right, although Kirk was not involved in the boy's upbringing at Carol's request. (*Star Trek II: The Wrath of Khan*).

Marcus, Dr. David. (Merritt Butrick). Scientist, born 2261, died 2285. Son of **James T. Kirk** and **Dr. Carol Marcus**.

Marcus was one of the key figures in the development of **Project Genesis**. (*Star Trek II: The Wrath of Khan*). Marcus later transferred, along with Saavik, to the **U.S.S. Grissom** for study of the Genesis Planet. Marcus was killed during that study by a Klingon expedition that sought to claim the planet and the Genesis process for the Klingon government. (*Star Trek III: The Search for Spock*).

Marejaretus VI. Home of the Ooolans, who traditionally strike two large stones together during a meal. Those at the meal must continue to eat until the stones are broken. The ritual is somewhat reminiscent of the use of the **Betazoid chime** rung to give thanks for food. ("Manhunt" [TNG]).

Mareuvian tea. A beverage served by **Guinan** in the **Ten-Forward lounge** aboard the *Enterprise*-D. ("The Child" [TNG]).

Mariah IV. Planet that Valerian vessel *Sherval Das* visited when delivering **dolamide**, a chemical energy source, to the Cardassians. ("Dramatis Personae" [DS9]).

Mariposa. Class-M planet in the **Ficus Sector** settled by colonists from the *S.S. Mariposa*.

Mariposa, S.S. Colony vessel, **DY-500** type, launched from Earth on November 27, 2123, toward the **Ficus Sector**. Commanding officer was Captain Walter Granger. Besides colonists, the ship's payload included an interesting mix of high-technology equipment and low-tech gear such as spinning wheels and actual animal livestock. The *Mariposa* carried two very different groups of colonists. The first, who settled planet **Bringold V**, were a group of Irish descendants who had eschewed advanced technology in favor of a simpler agrarian life. The second, who settled a planet they named Mariposa, embraced technology and in fact survived only with the aid of sophisticated cloning techniques. Both colonies were reunited in 2365 when solar flares threatened the **Bringoldi**, while dangerous **replicative fading** threatened the Mariposans. ("Up the Long Ladder" [TNG]). *Named for the Spanish word for "butterfly."* SEE: **clone**.

Maris, Roger. Twentieth-century American **baseball** player (1934-1985). Maris played for the New York Yankees and broke Babe Ruth's one-season home-run record. Twenty-fourth-century collector **Kivas Fajo** had an ancient baseball trading card, circa 1962, bearing Roger Maris's likeness, the only such card to have survived into that century. ("The Most Toys" [TNG]).

• **"Mark of Gideon, The."** Original Series episode #72. Written by George F. Slavin and Stanley Adams. Directed by Jud Taylor. Stardate 5423.4. *First aired in 1969. Captain Kirk is held captive on a duplicate of the* Enterprise *by people who hope he holds the solution to their planet's overpopulation.*

The episode was cowritten by Stanley Adams, who as an actor played Cyrano Jones in "The Trouble With Tribbles" (TOS). SEE: **Bureau of Planetary Treaties; Gideon; Hodin; Kirk, James T.; Odona; Vegan choriomeningitis.**

marker beacon. Brilliant strobe lights located on the hulls of Federation starships, intended to aid other ships in visually locating that vessel. The marker beacons of the **U.S.S. Lantree** were activated around stardate 42303 to warn other ships to avoid contact with the contaminated *Lantree*. ("Unnatural Selection" [TNG]).

Markoffian sea lizard. A life-form that **Q** claimed he could have chosen to become when he was stripped of his powers in 2366. He instead chose to become human. ("Deja Q" [TNG]).

Marlonia. Planet that Captain Picard, Ensign Ro, Keiko O'Brien, and Guinan visited in 2369. While returning to the *Enterprise*-D, the shuttlecraft was enveloped by an energy field and its occupants reduced to children. ("Rascals" [TNG]).

Marouk. (Nancy Parsons). The Sovereign of planet **Acamar III**, under whose leadership a century-old rift between the **Acamarian** government and the nomadic Acamarian **Gatherers** was ended. This aristocratic woman had very little tolerance for the Gatherers, but nevertheless agreed to help Captain Picard attempt to end the Gatherer piracy, by extending an offer of amnesty to the Gatherers, allowing them to return to Acamar III. ("The Vengeance Factor" [TNG]). SEE: **Yuta**.

Marphon. (Torin Thatcher). Member of the society on planet **Beta III** during the end of **Landru**'s rule in 2267. Although Marphon was a high-ranking official in the Landru regime, Marphon was immune to absorption and was a member of the underground resistance against the will of Landru. Marphon rescued Kirk and Spock when they were captured by Landru's **Lawgivers**. ("Return of the Archons" [TOS]).

Marple. (Jerry Daniels). Security guard aboard the original Starship *Enterprise* and member of the landing party to planet **Gamma Triguli VI**. He was killed in 2267 when one of the inhabitants of that planet struck him on the head with a heavy club. ("The Apple" [TOS]).

Marquez, Lieutenant. *Enterprise*-D crew member sent to the surface to planet **Bersallis III** in 2369 to track the deadly firestorm. ("Lessons" [TNG]).

Marr, Dr. Kila. (Ellen Geer). Renowned Federation xenologist who had made the study of the **Crystalline Entity** her life's work. Marr's only child, **Raymond Marr**, was killed on **Omicron Theta** when the entity attacked and destroyed that colony in 2336. She devoted all of her studies thereafter to the entity. Her work culminated in 2368 when she located the entity while she was aboard the *Enterprise*-D. Seeking revenge against the life-form that had killed her son, Marr used a projected graviton pulse to destroy the entity, despite orders to the contrary. ("Silicon Avatar" [TNG]).

Marr, Raymond. Science student (2320-2336) killed by the **Crystalline Entity** at the **Omicron Theta** colony. Marr, called Renny by his family, was survived by his mother, **Dr. Kila Marr**. ("Silicon Avatar" [TNG]).

Marrab Sector. Area of space where planet **Devidia II** is located. ("Time's Arrow, Part I" [TNG]).

marriage, Betazoid. On planet **Betazoid**, children are often genetically bonded by their parents at a young age. When the children are older, they are expected to marry. The wedding ceremony itself is resplendent with ancient Betazoid culture, requiring the bride, the groom, as well as the guests to go naked, honoring the act of love being celebrated. ("Haven" [TNG]).

Marritza, Aamin. (Harris Yulin). Minor **Cardassian** officer at the infamous **Gallitep** labor camp during the Cardassian occupation of Bajor. He served as file clerk to **Gul Darhe'el**, the brutal commander of the camp. Marritza's inability to stop the atrocities against the **Bajoran** prisoners caused him great guilt. After Gallitep, Marritza moved on to other duties and settled on planet **Kora II** in 2264, where he was an instructor at a military academy for five years. There he underwent a cosmetic alteration to look like his old commander, Gul Darhe'el, and set into motion a ruse that brought him to **Deep Space 9** in 2369. As he planned, he was incarcerated as a Cardassian who was at Gallitep and let his captors discover, then believe, he was indeed the infamous Darhe'el. It was later discovered that he was not the camp commander, but simply a file clerk. Marritza protested the discovery, saying that he was Darhe'el and that he must be punished so that his race would be forced to hear the terrible atrocities committed against the Bajoran people and perhaps feel the terrible guilt he felt. With the truth known, Marritza was freed to be returned to Kora II. While being escorted to a ship, **Kainon**, a Bajoran, took justice into his own hands, killing Marritza not because he was "the Butcher of Gallitep," but simply because he was a Cardassian. ("Duet" [DS9]).

Mars Defense Perimeter. A Starfleet defense border designed to protect the inner Solar System. The Mars Defense Perimeter was guarded by unmanned pods capable of tracking and destroying intruding enemy space vehicles. The Borg craft passed easily through the perimeter on its way toward Earth in early 2367. ("The Best of Both Worlds, Part II" [TNG]).

Marta community. A settlement of the southern continent of **Malcor III**. William Riker, masquerading as **Rivas Jakara**, listed this as his home. ("First Contact" [TNG]).

Marta. (Yvonne Craig). Inmate at the **Elba II** penal colony in 2268 who was killed by fellow inmate **Garth of Izar**. Marta, a green Orion woman, was Lord Garth's consort during his takeover attempt and was fond of quoting Shakespeare. ("Whom Gods Destroy" [TOS]). *Photo: Marta and Garth of Izar.*

Martia. (Iman). Chameloid (shape-shifting) inmate at the Klingon prison asteroid **Rura Penthe** at the time Kirk and McCoy were imprisoned there for the murder of Klingon **chancellor Gorkon**. (*Star Trek VI: The Undiscovered Country*). SEE: **shape-shifter**.

Martian Colonies, Fundamental Declarations of the. Important legal document addressing the subject of individual rights. ("Court Martial" [TOS]).

Martian Colony III. Birthplace of *Starship Enterprise* crew member **Lieutenant Mira Romaine**. ("The Lights of Zetar" [TOS]).

Martin, Dr. (Rick Fitts). A member of the *Enterprise*-D's medical staff. He was left in charge of sickbay when Dr. Crusher succumbed to a mysterious coma, later found to be caused by a **telepathic memory invasion** rape. ("Violations" [TNG]).

Martine, Ensign Angela. (Barbara Baldavin). Phaser control officer aboard the original *Starship Enterprise* during the Romulan incursion of 2266. Martine had been engaged to marry Robert Tomlinson, but their wedding was interrupted by news of the attack on the **Romulan Neutral Zone** outposts. Her fiancé was killed during that conflict. ("Balance of Terror" [TOS]). Martine was on the landing party to the **amusement park planet** in 2267. She was apparently killed by an old-style airplane making a strafing run, an image conjured up by fellow crew member **Esteban Rodriguez**. Martine was later restored to health by the planet's **Caretaker**. ("Shore Leave" [TOS]).

Marvick, Dr. Laurence. (David Frankham). Federation engineer, one of the designers of the original *Constitution*-class *Starship Enterprise*. Marvick traveled aboard the *Enterprise* in 2268 while accompanying **Dr. Miranda Jones** and **Medusan** ambassador **Kollos** on a diplomatic mission. Marvick, who exhibited signs of emotional instability, was in love with Jones and became jealous of her interest in Kollos. During the

journey, Marvick made direct visual contact with Kollos and was driven dangerously insane by the encounter. In his delirium, he programmed the *Enterprise* to travel beyond the rim of the galaxy, across the dangerous **galactic barrier**. Marvick died shortly thereafter, unable to live with what he saw in Kollos. Ironically it was the Medusan ambassador who guided the *Enterprise* back to Federation space with his advanced navigational knowledge after mind-melding with Commander Spock. ("Is There in Truth No Beauty?" [TOS]).

Masada. Science officer of the *U.S.S. Constellation*, killed when that ship was destroyed by the **planet killer** in 2267. ("The Doomsday Machine" [TOS]).

Masefield, John. English poet (1878-1967) who wrote such classics as "Sea Fever," from which Kirk quoted, "All I ask is a tall ship and a star to steer her by." ("The Ultimate Computer" [TOS]; *Star Trek V: The Final Frontier*).

Masiform D. Powerful injectable stimulant. McCoy administered Masiform D to Spock after several thorns from a poisonous plant rendered him unconscious on planet **Gamma Trianguli VI** in 2267. ("The Apple" [TOS]).

master systems display. Information display and control console used by starship personnel in Main Engineering of *Galaxy*-class starships. *The master systems display console was built from the video display table from Starfleet Command in* Star Trek IV: The Voyage Home. *For obvious reasons,* Star Trek *production personnel have nicknamed it the Pool Table.*

master situation monitor. Large wall-mounted display in Main Engineering of a *Galaxy*-class starship. The master situation monitor features a large cutaway diagram of the ship, used for monitoring the overall status of the ship and its departments. *The master situation monitor also includes a number of very small "in-jokes." These include the official U.S.S. Enterprise duck, the ship's mouse, a Porsche, a DC-3 airplane, the* Nomad *space probe, and the hamster on a treadmill that is alleged to be the true source of power for the ship's warp engines. Naturally, these items are far too small to normally be seen on television, but the sharp-eyed viewer can occasionally glimpse them in a close-up, if they haven't been covered up for that shot. All of these critters are reproduced in the ship diagram on page 11 of the* Star Trek: The Next Generation Technical Manual *by Rick Sternbach and Mike Okuda. Right: master situation monitor.*

• **"Masterpiece Society, The."** *Next Generation* episode #113. Teleplay by Adam Belanoff and Michael Piller. Story by James Kahn and Adam Belanoff. Directed by Winrich Kolbe. Stardate 45470.1. *First aired in 1992. The Enterprise-D offers help when a perfectly planned, genetically engineered community is threatened with destruction, but the cure may be worse than the disease.* SEE: **Bates, Hannah; Benbeck, Martin; Conor, Aaron; Felton, Ensign; Genome Colony; Moab IV; Moab Sector; multiphase tractor beam; stellar core fragment.**

Masters, Lieutenant. (Janet MacLachlan). Staff engineer who served aboard the *Starship Enterprise* in 2267 during the confrontation with the entity **Lazarus**. ("The Alternative Factor" [TOS]).

Mataline II. Planet where **Neela Daren** purchased a flexible piano keyboard that rolled up into a compact round shape. ("Lessons" [TNG]).

Matthews. (Vince Deadrick). *Enterprise* security officer killed when he fell into the caverns at planet **Exo III**. ("What Are Little Girls Made Of?" [TOS]).

matrix diodes. The array of omnidirectional holographic diodes embedded in the walls of holodecks. The matrix diodes were suspected of malfunctioning in **Sherlock Holmes program 3A** in 2369. ("Ship in a Bottle" [TNG]).

• **"Matter of Honor, A."** *Next Generation* episode #34. Teleplay by Burton Armus. Story by Wanda M. Haight & Gregory Amos and Burton Armus. Directed by Rob Bowman. Stardate 42506.5. *First aired in 1989. Riker serves aboard a Klingon ship as part of an officer exchange program.* SEE: **Benzar; Benzites; bregit lung;** *gagh;* **heart of** *targ;* **Kargan, Captain; Klag; Mendon, Ensign; microbiotic colony; Officer Exchange Program;** *Pagh, I.K.C.;* **phaser range; Pheben System; pipius claw; Riker, William T.;** *rokeg* **blood pie; Starbase 179; Tranome Sar; transponder, emergency; Vekma.**

• **"Matter of Perspective, A."** *Next Generation* episode #62. Written by Ed Zuckerman. Directed by Cliff Bole. Stardate

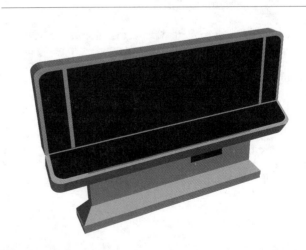

43610.4. *First aired in 1990. The holodeck is used to re-create the scene of a crime when Riker is accused of murder.* SEE: **Apgar, Dr. Nel; Apgar, Manua; dicosilium; Krag; Krieger waves; painting; Riker, William T.; Tanuga IV; Tanugans; Tayna.**

• **"Matter of Time, A."** *Next Generation* episode #109. Written by Rick Berman. Directed by Paul Lynch. Stardate 45349.1. *First aired in 1991. A time-traveling professor, apparently on a research project from the future, turns out to be a petty thief from the past.* SEE: **auto-phaser interlock; berylite scan; electroplasma system taps; exothermal inversion; Felton, Ensign; greenhouse effect; Model A Ford; Moseley, Hal; neural stimulator; New Seattle; Penthara IV; phaser; plasticized tritanium mesh; Rasmussen, Professor Berlinghoff; shield inverters; Starbase 214; Telurian plague; temporal distortion; terrawatt; time-travel pod.**

matter stream. In the operation of the transporter, the matter stream is the beam of phased (or dematerialized) matter that is transported from the transport chamber to the destination (or the reverse). ("Realm of Fear" [TNG]).

matter-antimatter integrator. Component of a *Constitution*-class starship's warp-drive system. The emergency bypass control valve to the matter-antimatter integrator was fused by **Losira** in 2268, causing the *Enterprise* to travel at danger-ously accelerated speeds up to warp 14.1 before the problem was solved. ("That Which Survives" [TOS]).

matter/antimatter reaction chamber. Component of the **warp drive** system used aboard Federation starships. The reaction chamber is the vessel within which matter and antimatter are allowed to intermix in a controlled fashion, resulting in the massive release of energy necessary to power the faster-than-light warp drive. The matter/antimatter reac-tion is regulated by a **dilithium crystal**, and the entire volume is contained by a magnetic containment field to prevent the volatile antimatter from coming into physical contact with the ship's structure. SEE: **antimatter containment.**

Maura. Beloved pet dog of **Aquiel Uhnari**. Maura was killed at **Relay Station 47** in 2369 by the same **coalescent organ-ism** that killed **Keith Rocha**. ("Aquiel" [TNG]).

Mavek. (Gary Werntz). Attendant at the **Tilonus Institute for Mental Disorders** created in Riker's mind while being brain-washed on planet **Tilonus IV** in 2369. Mavek was large in stature and seemed to gather delight in forcing Riker and other inmates to obey his orders. ("Frame of Mind" [TNG]). SEE: *Frame of Mind.*

Maxia Zeta Star System. Location of the **Battle of Maxia** where the *U.S.S. Stargazer,* under the command of Captain **Jean-Luc Picard,** suffered a devastating sneak attack from an unidentified ship that was later identified as Ferengi. ("The Battle" [TNG]).

Maxia, Battle of. A battle that occurred in the year 2355

between the Federation starship *Stargazer* and an unknown spacecraft, later identified as a Ferengi vessel. The *Star-gazer,* under the command of Captain **Jean-Luc Picard,** was traveling through the **Maxia Zeta Star System** when it was attacked without provocation. The *Stargazer* survived be-cause of a brilliant tactic devised by Captain Picard, later called the **Picard Maneuver**, permitting the ship to escape damage long enough to fire a full phaser and torpedo spread. The Ferengi ship was destroyed, but the *Stargazer* crew was able to escape in shuttlecraft and **escape pod**s. Among the casualties aboard the Ferengi vessel was the son of **DaiMon Bok,** making his first voyage as DaiMon. ("The Battle" [TNG]).

Maxwell, Captain Benjamin. (Bob Gunton). Starfleet officer who com-manded the *U.S.S. Rutledge* dur-ing the **Cardassian** wars. Maxwell received the Federation's highest citations for courage and valor dur-ing the conflict, but he lost his fam-ily in the Cardassian attack on the **Setlik III** outpost, a loss made even more bitter because his ship was not able to reach Setlik in time to prevent the massacre. Maxwell carried bitterness toward the Cardassians for many years and in 2367 mounted an unauthorized offensive against the Cardassians, in direct violation of the peace treaty of 2366. Maxwell, in command of the *U.S.S. Phoenix*, destroyed a Cardassian outpost and two Cardassian ships, because he believed the Cardassians were planning for a new attack against the Federation. Former *Rutledge* crew member **Miles O'Brien** was able to convince Maxwell to discontinue his attack, and Maxwell was relieved of command of the *Phoenix.* ("The Wounded" [TNG]).

"May you die well." A Klingon parting phrase. ("Redemption, Part II" [TNG]).

Maylor, Sev. (Susan French). A woman who traveled with **Ambassador Ves Alkar** on his diplomatic missions. Alkar identified Maylor as his mother, but it was later learned that she was not. Maylor was found to be much younger than she appeared, but Alkar had been using her as an empathic "receptacle" for his negative thoughts and emotions. As a result, she became extremely bitter and hostile, and aged at a highly accelerated rate. Maylor died in 2369 at about age 30 from the stress of this empathic abuse. ("Man of the People" [TNG]).

M'Benga, Dr. (Brooker Bradshaw). Physician aboard the original *Starship Enterprise* who interned in a Vulcan ward during his medical training. He cared for Spock when the *Enterprise* first officer was criti-cally wounded on **Tyree**'s planet in 2267. ("A Private Little War" [TOS]). M'Benga supervised the autopsies surrounding the mysterious deaths of *Enterprise* personnel near the **Kalandan outpost** in 2268. ("That Which Survives" [TOS]).

McAllister C-5 Nebula. Protostellar cloud located seven light-years inside **Cardassian** space, some eleven light-years from planet **Minos Korva**. In 2369, a Cardassian invasion fleet hid inside the nebula while apparently preparing to attack the Minos Korva sector. The fleet's time inside the nebula was limited due to the intense particle flux within, which caused degradation of the spacecraft hulls. ("Chain of Command, Part II" [TNG]).

McClukidge, Nurse. Member of the *Enterprise*-D medical staff. Dr. Beverly Crusher suggested that McClukidge could fill in for **Nurse Ogawa**, so the latter could take a vacation on **Risa**. ("Imaginary Friend" [TNG]).

McCoullough, Captain. Starfleet officer who wrote the revised procedures for **first contact** operations. ("Move Along Home" [DS9]).

McCoy, David. (Bill Quinn). Father of *Enterprise* medical officer **Leonard McCoy**. The elder McCoy suffered from a painful, terminal illness, and his son eventually pulled the plug to spare his father further pain. (*Star Trek V: The Final Frontier*). David McCoy's first name was established in Star Trek III.

McCoy, Dr. Leonard H. (DeForest Kelley). Chief medical officer aboard the original *Starship Enterprise* under the command of Captain James Kirk. ("The Corbomite Maneuver" [TOS]). As of 2267, McCoy had earned the Legion of Honor, and had been decorated by Starfleet surgeons. ("Court Martial" [TOS]).

Early in his medical career McCoy's father was struck with a terrible, fatal illness. Faced with the prospect of suffering a terrible, lingering death, McCoy mercifully "pulled the plug" on his father, allowing him to die. To McCoy's considerable anguish, a cure for his father's disease was discovered shortly thereafter, and McCoy carried the guilt for his father's possibly needless death for many years. (*Star Trek V: The Final Frontier*). Prior to his assignment to the *Enterprise*, McCoy had been romantically involved with the future **Nancy Crater**. ("The Man Trap" [TOS]).

McCoy first joined the *Enterprise* crew in 2266, and remained associated with that illustrious ship and its successor for some 27 years. (*Star Trek VI: The Undiscovered Country*). In 2267, McCoy suffered a serious overdose of cordrazine in a shipboard accident. In the paranoid delusions that followed, McCoy fled the ship, then jumped through a time portal being studied by *Enterprise* personnel. In the past, McCoy effected serious damage to the flow of time until Kirk and Spock followed him to restore the shape of history. ("The City on the Edge of Forever" [TOS]). SEE: **Guardian of Forever; Keeler, Edith**. In 2268, McCoy was diagnosed with

terminal **xenopolycythemia** and chose to resign from Starfleet so that he could marry a woman named **Natira**, high priestess of the **Yonada**n people. McCoy rejoined Starfleet after a cure was found in the Yonadan memory banks. ("For the World is Hollow and I Have Touched the Sky" [TOS]).

McCoy retired from Starfleet after the return of the *Enterprise* from the five-year mission, but he returned to Starfleet at Kirk's request when the ship intercepted the **V'Ger** entity near Earth. (*Star Trek: The Motion Picture*). McCoy, along with Kirk, was wrongly convicted for the murder of Klingon **chancellor Gorkon** in 2293, a conviction that was later overturned. McCoy was scheduled to retire shortly after the **Khitomer** peace conference, but he either changed his mind, or later returned to Starfleet. (*Star Trek VI: The Undiscovered Country*). As a retired Starfleet admiral, McCoy made an inspection tour of the *Enterprise*-D in 2364 at the age of 137. ("Encounter at Farpoint, Part I" [TNG]).

An unofficial part of McCoy's back story was developed by Original Series story editor Dorothy Fontana, who had written a story entitled "Joanna," which would have established that McCoy had endured a bitter divorce, and it was the aftermath of this experience that drove him to join Starfleet. The episode would have introduced Joanna, McCoy's now-grown daughter from that failed marriage. "Joanna" was written for the Original Series' third season, but was so heavily rewritten (becoming "The Way to Eden" [TOS]) that Fontana removed her name from the final version.

Since the McCoy back story was never incorporated into an episode, it isn't "official," at least for the purposes of this encyclopedia. On the other hand, it is mentioned here because it offers insight into the McCoy character, and because of Fontana's pivotal role in the development of many Star Trek *characters. McCoy's first appearance was in "The Corbomite Maneuver" (TOS).*

McDowell, Ensign. (Kenneth Meseroll). *Enterprise*-D crew member who served at Tactical during the ship's rescue of a Romulan science ship in 2368. ("The Next Phase" [TNG]).

McFarland. A renowned Federation archaeologist who was present at the annual symposium of the **Federation Archaeology Council** in 2367. ("QPid" [TNG]).

McGivers, Lieutenant Marla. (Madlyn Rhue). Historian aboard the original *Starship Enterprise* in 2267 when former dictator **Khan Noonien Singh** attempted to commandeer the ship. McGiver's fascination for bold men of the past clouded her judgment when it came to Khan. She betrayed the *Enterprise* crew and helped Khan's takeover attempt. Marla was later given

the choice of a court-martial or accompanying Khan and his group into exile on planet **Ceti Alpha V**. She chose to stay with Khan and live on that desolate world. ("Space Seed" [TOS]). McGivers married Khan, but she was later killed by the parasitic eel creatures indigenous to **Ceti Alpha V**. (*Star Trek II: The Wrath of Khan*).

McHuron, Eve. (Karen Steele). Beautiful woman recruited by Harry Mudd as a bride for a settler on planet **Ophiucus III**. Eve had been raised on a farm planet, caring for her two brothers. Although Eve was attracted to Kirk, she eventually realized that Kirk was married to his ship, so she ended up with miner **Ben Childress** at the **Rigel XII** mining station. ("Mudd's Women" [TOS]).

McKenzie, Ard'rian. (Eileen Seeley). Young member of the **Tau Cygna V** colony, Ard'rian was very interested in Commander Data's abilities as an android, and grew very fond of him personally. She supported Data's efforts to evacuate the Tau Cygna colony in 2366. ("The Ensigns of Command" [TNG]).

McKinley Park. Located on planet Earth, a favorite place of **Keiko** and **Miles O'Brien**. Miles presented Keiko with a gold bracelet there. ("Power Play" [TNG]).

McKinley Rocket Base. American military space launch facility on Earth. In 1968, a large orbital nuclear weapons platform was launched from McKinley Rocket by the United States to counter a similar launch by a rival power. In an effort to demonstrate the foolhardy nature of such weapons, extra-terrestrial agent Gary Seven secretly armed the platform's warheads shortly after launch, then caused the launch vehicle to malfunction, before disarming it just before impact. ("Assignment Earth" [TOS]). *The scenes of McKinley Rocket Base were a combination of stock film of NASA's Kennedy Space Center and footage shot at Paramount Pictures. The vehicle launched from McKinley Rocket Base was stock footage of an early Saturn V booster.*

McKinley Station. SEE: **Earth Station McKinley**.

McKinney. Starfleet officer who was apparently killed by the unknown alien intelligence that attempted to infiltrate **Starfleet Headquarters** in 2364. ("Conspiracy" [TNG]).

McKnight, Ensign. (Pamela Winslow). *Enterprise*-D crew member who was at conn while the *Enterprise*-D explored the **Ngame Nebula** in 2367. ("Clues," "Face of the Enemy" [TNG]).

McLowery, Frank. (Leonard Nimoy). Outlaw from Earth's ancient American West, and a member of the Clanton gang who was killed at the famous gunfight at the OK Corral in 1881. Spock represented Frank McLowery in a bizarre charade created by the **Melkotians** in 2268. ("Spectre of the Gun" [TOS]).

McLowery, Tom. (DeForest Kelley). Outlaw who sided with the Clanton family against the Earps at the historic gunfight at the OK Corral in 1881. Tom McLowery and his brother, Frank, were both killed in the battle. McCoy was cast as Tom McLowery in a drama created by the **Melkotians** in 2268 for

the purpose of causing their death. ("Spectre of the Gun" [TOS]).

McNary. (Gary Armagnal). Fictional character from the **Dixon Hill** detective stories. McNary was a homicide detective and a good friend of Hill, despite Dixon's tendency to work both sides of the law. A holographic version of McNary was part of the Dixon Hill holodeck programs. ("The Big Goodbye" [TNG]).

McPherson. Genetically engineered survivor of Earth's **Eugenics Wars**. McPherson and other followers of **Khan Noonien Singh** escaped Earth in 1996 in the sleeper ship, ***S.S. Botany Bay*** remaining in suspended animation until revived by personnel from the *U.S.S. Enterprise* in 2267. ("Space Seed" [TOS]).

Mea 3. (Barbara Babcock). Official of planet **Eminiar VII** who greeted the *Enterprise* landing party in 2267. Mea 3 was declared a casualty of war during an attack by planet **Vendikar**. She was expected to report to a disintegration chamber under the terms of her planet's agreement with Vendikar, but was prevented from doing so by *Enterprise* personnel. ("A Taste of Armageddon" [TOS]). *Barbara Babcock also played Philiana in "Plato's Stepchildren" (TOS), and provided the voice of Trelane's mother in "The Squire of Gothos" (TOS), the voice of Isis the cat in "Assignment: Earth" (TOS), and the voice of Commander Loskene in "The Tholian Web" (TOS).*

Mears, Yeoman. (Phyllis Douglas). Member of the ***Shuttlecraft Galileo*** crew when it crashed on planet **Taurus II** in 2267. ("The *Galileo* Seven" [TOS]).

• **"Measure of a Man, The."** *Next Generation* episode #35. Written by Melinda M. Snodgrass. Directed by Robert Scheerer. Stardate 42523.7. *First aired in 1989. Data is put on trial to determine if he is a person, or merely the property of Starfleet. This episode included the first references to the Daystrom Institute (a tip of the hat to "The Ultimate Computer" (TOS), and to Commander Bruce Maddox (who would not be seen again, but Data would occasionally correspond with him). Our heroes' weekly poker game was also seen for the first time in this episode.* SEE: **android; Cumberland, Acts of; Data; Daystrom Institute of Technology; *Dream of the Fire, The*; Judge Advocate General; K'Ratak; Louvois, Phillipa; Picard, Jean-Luc; Maddox, Commander Bruce; Nakamura, Admiral; poker; Sector 23; security access code; Starbase 173; *Stargazer, U.S.S.*; Yar, Natasha.**

mechanical rice picker. Device that supposedly caused Spock's ears to be pointed, at least in a tale fabricated by Kirk in Earth's past. Kirk was trying to explain Spock's alien appearance to a police officer of Earth's 1930s. ("The City on the Edge of Forever" [TOS]).

Medusans. Intelligent **noncorporeal life**-forms whose minds are among the most beautiful in the universe. By contrast, Medusans' physical appearance is so hideous that one look at a Medusan by a human will cause total madness in the human unless the human is wearing a protective visor. While traveling on board the *Enterprise*, Medusan ambassador **Kollos** shielded himself in a protective container in order to protect the human members of the crew. Medusans' sensory systems are radically different from those of humanoid lifeforms, and their ability to orient themselves in subspace makes them well-suited for navigational tasks aboard starships. ("Is There in Truth No Beauty?" [TOS]).

Mediators. Law-enforcement officials on planet **Rubicun III**. ("Justice" [TNG]). SEE: **punishment zones**.

medical equipment. SEE: **alpha wave inducer; autosuture; bioregenerative field; cortical stimulator; dentronal scanner; drechtal beams; exoscalpel; gentronic replicator; hypospray; microtome; motor assist bands; neural calipers; neural stimulator; neural transducers; physiostimulator; plasma infusion unit; protodynoplaser; psychotricorder; pulmonary support unit; somnetic inducer; sonic separator; stasis unit; T-cell stimulator; tissue mitigator; trilaser connector.** *Illustrations: 1) Dr. McCoy's handheld medical scanners. 2) Original* Enterprise *medical diagnostic bed. 3) Dr. Crusher's medical kit. 4) Hypospray,* Next Generation *version. 5) Hypospray, Original Series version.*

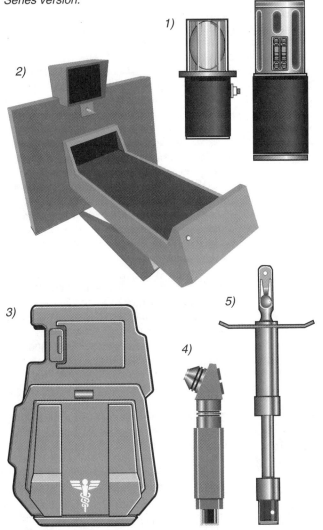

Megaptera novaeangliae. Scientific name for the Earth cetacean also known as the **humpback whale**. (*Star Trek IV: The Voyage Home*).

Mek'ba. In the Klingon system of justice, the portion of a trial or appeal in which evidence was heard. The *Mek'ba* had strict rules for the presentation of evidence and for the conduct of both the accuser and the accused. ("Sins of the Father" [TNG]).

melakol. Romulan unit of measure for pressure. ("The Next Phase" [TNG]).

Melakon. (Skip Homeier). Deputy Fuhrer in the Nazi-style government on planet **Ekos** who seized power from planetary leader **John Gill**. The ambitious Melakon subverted Gill's efforts to create an efficient, compassionate government, instead creating a close copy of Earth's brutal Nazi Germany. Melakon was responsible for the policy of genocide against the **Zeons** in 2268, just before the collapse of the Gill regime. ("Patterns of Force" [TOS]). *Skip Homeier also played **Dr. Sevrin** in "The Way to Eden" (TOS).*

Melbourne, U.S.S. Federation starship, *Excelsior* class, Starfleet registry number NCC-62043. The *Melbourne* was stationed at **Starbase 74** in 2364 when the **Bynars** hijacked the *Enterprise*-D, but was unable to give chase because of maintenance in progress. ("11001001" [TNG]).

Commander **William Riker** was offered command of the *U.S.S. Melbourne* in late 2366, but he declined the promotion, preferring to remain Executive Officer on the *Enterprise*-D. ("The Best of Both Worlds, Part I" [TNG]). Shortly thereafter, the *Melbourne* was one of 39 Federation starships destroyed by the **Borg** in the battle of **Wolf 359**. ("The Best of Both Worlds, Part II" [TNG]).

The U.S.S. Melbourne *takes its name from the Australian city. There were actually two Starships* Melbourne *used in these episodes. The first was a **Nebula-class** model, barely glimpsed as a wrecked hulk in the spaceship graveyard from "The Best of Both Worlds, Part II" (TNG). When the scene was redone three years later for "Emissary" (DS9), a decision was made to instead use the more detailed **U.S.S. Excelsior** model originally built for* Star Trek III. *Both models were given the same Starfleet registry number, but since the* Excelsior *version was seen fairly clearly on screen, and the* Nebula *version was not seen well, we now assume that the* Melbourne *"really" was an* Excelsior-class *ship.*

Meles II. An inhabited planet located near the **Detrian System**. Commander Riker suggested it as a port of call for **Professor Moriarty** and the **Countess Barthalomew** in 2369. ("Ship in a Bottle" [TNG]).

Melian. (Paul Lambert). A musician on planet **Aldea**. Aldean authorities assigned Melian to tutor Katie, the child of an *Enterprise*-D crew member. ("When the Bough Breaks" [TNG]).

Melina II. Planet visited by **Tarmin** and his group of telepathic historians prior to mid-2368. ("Violations" [TNG]).

Melkotians. Telepathic alien race with whom first contact was made in 2268. The Melkotians spurned, by the use of an orbiting warning buoy, the *Enterprise*'s initial contact overtures. When *Enterprise* captain Kirk ignored the Melkotian warning, the aliens subjected Kirk and company to an elaborate charade in which images from Kirk's memory were intended to be the devices of their deaths. The Melkotians' drama took the form of the famous gunfight at the **OK Corral** at **Tombstone, Arizona,** on October 26, 1881, between the Earps and the Clantons, a fight that the Clantons lost. Kirk and members of his *Enterprise* crew were to fill their shoes, but managed to avoid death in the legendary gun battle. Kirk was later successful in opening diplomatic relations with the reclusive Melkotians. ("Spectre of the Gun" [TOS]). *They were also referred to as the Melkots.*

mellitus. Creature from planet Alpha Majoris I whose form is gaseous when in motion and becomes solid at rest. ("Wolf in the Fold" [TOS]).

Melnos IV. Planet where in the past *Enterprise*-D crew member **Neela Daren** had led a team of geologists to study the plasma geyser. ("Lessons" [TNG]).

Melona IV. Class-M planet that was attacked by the **Crystalline Entity** in 2368. The planet was, at the time, being readied for colonization by the Federation. The attack stripped the planet of all indigenous life and killed two colonists. The surviving colonists were evacuated by the *Enterprise*-D, which had been assisting in the colonization project. ("Silicon Avatar" [TNG]).

"Melor Famagal." A musical selection that **Omag**, a Ferengi arms merchant, always requested in **Amarie**'s bar. ("Unification, Part II" [TNG]).

melorazine. Sedative, often administered by hypospray. ("Man of the People" [TNG]).

Meltasion asteroid belt. An asteroid belt orbiting the star Gamelan, inside the orbit of planet **Gamelan V**. The presence of the belt complicated the *Enterprise*-D's efforts to dispose of an ancient vessel that was causing radiation contamination of the Gamelan atmosphere. The *Enterprise*-D was forced to tow the contaminated barge through the Meltasion belt, exposing the crew of the *Enterprise*-D to a near lethal amount of radiation. ("Final Mission" [TNG]).

Memory Alpha. Planetoid on which is located a massive library containing all scientific and cultural information from each planet in the United Federation of Planets. Just prior to the completion of Memory Alpha in 2269, the planetoid was attacked by the noncorporeal survivors of planet **Zetar**. ("The Lights of Zetar" [TOS]). SEE: **Romaine, Lieutenant Mira; Zetarians.**

Mempa Sector. Located in Klingon territory. Site of several key battles during the **Klingon civil war** of 2368. Forces loyal to **Gowron** suffered a major defeat in the Mempa System during the conflict. ("Redemption, Parts I and II" [TNG]).

• **"Ménage à Troi."** *Next Generation* episode #72. Written by Fred Bronson & Susan Sackett. Directed by Rob Legato. Stardate 43980.7. *First aired in 1990. A Ferengi DaiMon kidnaps Lwaxana Troi in hopes of using her empathic senses in his business dealings. This episode marks the first time we see the surface of Troi's homeworld, Betazed. It was also the first episode directed by visual effects supervisor Rob Legato. Episode cowriter Susan Sackett was Star Trek creator Gene Roddenberry's executive assistant.* SEE: **Aldabren Exchange; Algolian ceremonial rhythms; Arcturian Fizz; Betazed; Betazoids;** *Bradbury, U.S.S.;* **Cochrane distortion; Crusher, Wesley; Farek, Dr.; Ferengi; Gamma Erandi Nebula; Grax, Reittan; Homn;** *Krayton;* **"Little One";** *muktok* **plant; Nibor;** *oo-mox;* **Orion wing-slug;** *oskoid;* **Riker, William T.; Tog, DaiMon; Trade Agreements Conference; Troi, Deanna; Troi, Lwaxana; uttaberries; warp field phase adjustment; Xanthras III; Zan Periculi;** *Zapata, U.S.S.*

• **"Menagerie, Parts I and II, The."** Original Series episode #16. Written by Gene Roddenberry. Directed by Marc Daniels. Stardate 3012.4. *First aired in 1966. Spock hijacks the* Enterprise *to return Captain Pike to planet Talos IV. This two-part episode incorporated most of the footage from the original* Star Trek *pilot episode "The Cage" (TOS). Using the courtroom drama of Spock's trial as a framing device, this episode was an ingenious effort to make use of the first pilot, despite the fact that "The Cage" had a markedly different cast. Use of "The Cage" footage helped the tightly budgeted series control costs and stay on schedule.* SEE: **Boyce, Dr. Phil;** *Columbia, S.S.;* **delta radiation; duranium; fleet captain; Haskins, Dr. Theodore; Kaylar; Keeper, the; laser weapons; Mendez, Commodore José; Mojave; Number One; Orion animal women; Pike, Christopher; Rigel VII; Spock; Starbase 11; Starfleet General orders and Regulations; Talos IV; Talos Star Group; Talosians; Tango; Tyler, José; Vega Colony; Vina.**

Mendak, Admiral. (Alan Scarfe). Romulan officer in command of the Warbird *Devoras* when it met the *Enterprise*-D inside the Romulan Neutral Zone in 2367. The rendezvous was slated to be the beginning of negotiations between the Federation, represented by **Ambassador T'Pel**, and the Romulans. However, Mendak's true purpose was to enable T'Pel, in reality a Romulan operative named **Subcommander Selok**, to escape into Romulan hands. ("Data's Day" [TNG]).

Mendel, Gregor Johann. Nineteenth-century Earth scientist (1822-1884) who postulated the basic laws of genetic heredity and suggested the existence of genes. ("Let That Be Your Last Battlefield" [TOS]).

Mendez, Commodore José. (Malachi Throne). Commanding officer of **Starbase 11** when Spock abducted Fleet Captain **Christopher Pike** to **Talos IV** in 2267. An illusory version

of Mendez presided over Spock's subsequent court-martial for charges of mutiny and violation of **General Order 7**. The real Mendez later cleared Spock of all charges. ("The Menagerie, Parts I and II" [TOS]). *Actor Malachi Throne also provided the voices of the Talosian magistrate in the original (unaired) version of "The Cage," and later portrayed Romulan Senator Pardek in "Unification, Parts I and II" [TNG]).*

Mendez. Starfleet officer who was a crew member on the **U.S.S. Victory**, and who participated in a mission to planet **Tarchannen III** in 2362. In 2367, Mendez stole a shuttle from the **U.S.S. Aries** and fled to planet Tarchannen III, where it is believed her body was transformed into a reptilian life-form native to that planet. ("Identity Crisis" [TNG]).

Mendon, Ensign. (John Putch). A Starfleet officer and a native of the planet **Benzar**. As is a characteristic of his people, Mendon had bluish-green skin and breathed with the assistance of a respiration device. Mendon was something of an overachiever by human standards, causing some initial friction with the Enterprise-D crew when he served aboard that ship as part of an officer exchange program in 2365, but he soon adapted to Starfleet social norms. Wesley Crusher once mistook Mendon for **Mordoc**, another Benzite, but Mendon explained that they were both from the same geostructure, and therefore looked alike to non-Benzites. ("A Matter of Honor" [TNG]). *Actor John Putch, also played Mordoc in "Coming of Age" (TNG).*

Mendora. A mythical devil figure in the Berussian Cluster. ("Devil's Due" [TNG]).

Mendoza, Dr. (Castulo Guerra). Federation representative in the negotiations for rights to the **Barzan wormhole** in 2366. Dr. Mendoza was poisoned by members of the Ferengi delegation, and Commander Riker was forced to take his place at the negotiation table. ("The Price" [TNG]).

Mendrossen, Ki. (William Denis). Ambassador **Sarek's** chief-of-staff during the Legaran conference of 2366, Sarek's final diplomatic mission. A middle-aged human male, Mendrossen was aware that Sarek suffered from debilitating **Bendii Syndrome**, but sought to protect the ambassador so that he could complete that last mission in honor. ("Sarek" [TNG]).

Menthars. An ancient culture that was destroyed a thousand years ago in a terrible war with the **Promellians**. The final battle in this conflict was held at planet **Orelious IX**, resulting in the extinction of both species and the destruction of Orelious IX. The Menthars were believed to be very innova-

tive in battle: they were the first to develop the *Kavis Teke* elusive maneuver, and had a passive lure stratagem comparable to Napoleon's. The Menthars also developed and deployed aceton assimilators, devices that trapped not only the **Cleponji**, but worked well enough to trap the *Enterprise-*D a millennium after their final battle. ("Booby Trap" [TNG]).

Menuhin. A famous concert violinist whose performance style **Data** programmed himself to emulate. ("Sarek" [TNG]).

Merak II. Planet where a botanical plague threatened to destroy all vegetation in 2269. The plague was averted when a consignment of mineral **zenite** was delivered by the *Starship Enterprise* from planet **Ardana**. ("The Cloud Minders" [TOS]).

Merced-class starship. Conjectural designation for a type of Federation ship. The **U.S.S. Trieste**, which underwent servicing at **Starbase 74** in 2364 and on which Data once served, was a *Merced-*class starship.

Merchantman. Small merchant cargo ship that was chartered by Klingon operative **Valkris** in 2285 in order to transport stolen data from the Federation's **Project Genesis** to the Klingon government. The *Merchantman*, along with its crew and Valkris, was destroyed after delivery of the information. (*Star Trek III: The Search for Spock*). *The Merchantman was never referred to by name during the film. The name is from the script only. The* Merchantman *model, designed by Nilo Rodis and built at ILM for* Star Trek III, *was reused several times as various "guest" spaceships in* Star Trek: The Next Generation.

Merculite rockets. Obsolete weapons system found in older spacecraft. The **Talarian** freighter **Batris** was equipped with Merculite rockets that were apparently used to destroy the Klingon cruiser **T'Acog**. ("Heart of Glory" [TNG]). Merculite rockets were part of the weaponry of the Talarian ship **Q'Maire** when it confronted the *Enterprise-*D in 2367. ("Suddenly Human" [TNG]).

Mercy Hospital. Health-care facility located in the Mission District of San Francisco on Earth in the late 20th century. Pavel Chekov, injured in Earth's past, was cared for in this facility before being rescued by his fellow *Enterprise* crew members. (*Star Trek IV: The Voyage Home*). *The Mercy Hospital scenes were filmed at Centinela Hospital in Inglewood, California.*

Meribor. (Jennifer Nash). Native of the now-dead planet **Kataan** and daughter of the ironweaver **Kamin**. Meribor lived over a thousand years ago in the village of **Ressik**. Memories of her life were preserved aboard a space probe launched from Kataan. The probe encountered the *Starship Enterprise*-D in 2368, transferring its memories, including the memory of Meribor, to Jean-Luc Picard. ("The Inner Light" [TNG]).

Mericor System. Crash site of the *U.S.S. Denver* after the ship struck a gravitic mine in 2368. ("Ethics" [TNG]).

Merikus. SEE: **Merrick, R. M.**

Merrick, R. M. (William Smithers). Captain of the survey vessel *S.S. Beagle* that disappeared in star system 892 in the year 2261. James Kirk had known Merrick at **Starfleet Academy** when he was expelled in his fifth year after failing a psychosimulator test. *(Note that Starfleet Academy was established in later episodes as being a four-year institution.)* Merrick then went

into the merchant service and eventually became captain of the *S.S. Beagle*. After his ship was damaged by meteors, Merrick and several of his crew beamed down to planet 892-IV in search of supplies and met **Claudius Marcus**. Merrick elected to stay on the planet, becoming Merikus, First Citizen of the Roman culture. As Merikus, he became a political strongman and was known as The Butcher to the slaves he persecuted. Six years later, an *Enterprise* landing party located him, and he was killed by Marcus when helping the *Enterprise* people escape. SEE: **892, Planet IV**. ("Bread and Circuses" [TOS]).

Merrimac, U.S.S. Federation starship, **Nebula class**, Starfleet registry number NCC-61827. Ship that transported Ambassador **Sarek** and his party from **Legara IV** back to Vulcan, following the **Legaran** conference of 2366. ("Sarek" [TNG]). The *Merrimac* trans-

ported Cadet Wesley Crusher back to Starfleet Academy following his vacation aboard the *Enterprise*-D in 2368. ("The Game" [TNG]). *This ship was named in honor of the first iron-clad warship, which fought for the Confederate Army against the warship* Monitor *in the American Civil War.*

metabolic reduction injection. Medication synthesized by Henoch so that Kirk, Spock, and **Dr. Ann Mulhall's** bodies could carry the intellects of **Sargon**, **Henoch**, and **Thalassa**. The drug reduced heart rate and all bodily functions to normal, allowing the three to occupy the humanoid bodies without permanent damage to those bodies. Henock secretly prepared a different compound for Sargon in an attempt to destroy his ancient enemy. ("Return to Tomorrow" [TOS]).

metagenic weapon. Sophisticated biological weapon using genetically engineered viruses, designed to destroy any form of DNA. These viruses could mutate rapidly and were

believed able to destroy entire ecosystems within days. After thirty days the metagenic agent itself died, having destroying all biological life on a planetary scale, while leaving all the technological aspects of a culture intact. Because of the extreme danger of these weapons, treaties were established to ban their use and all of the major powers of the period, including the Federation, the Ferengi, and the Romulans agreed to the ban. In 2369, Starfleet Intelligence was the victim of Cardassian disinformation suggesting that the **Cardassians** were developing metagenic toxins. Starfleet also believed that the Cardassians had discovered a new method to deliver the toxins in a dormant state on a **theta-band** subspace carrier wave. ("Chain of Command, Part I" [TNG]).

• **"Metamorphosis."** *Original Series* episode #31. Written by Gene L. Coon. Directed by Ralph Senensky. Stardate 3219.8. *First aired in 1967. Kirk and company find historic space scientist Zefram Cochrane, still alive on a distant planetoid, and cared for by an energy life-form called the Companion.* SEE: **Alpha Centauri; Cochrane, Zefram; Companion; Epsilon Canaris III;** *Galileo, Shuttlecraft;* **Gamma Canaris region; Hedford, Nancy; Sakuro's disease; Universal Translator; warp drive.**

metaphasic shield. Revolutionary new shielding technology developed in 2369 by Ferengi scientist **Dr. Reyga**. The system involved the generation of overlapping low-level subspace fields, causing an object within the fields to exist partially in subspace. The technology was first tested in 2369 by sending an *Enterprise*-D shuttlecraft into a star's corona. The initial test was deemed unsuccessful, but further investigation revealed that sabotage of the metaphasic field had caused the failure. The pilot of the craft was discovered to have perpetrated the sabotage, in the hopes of discrediting Dr. Reyga in order to steal the technology. Dr. Beverly Crusher then piloted the shuttlecraft into the corona herself, thereby proving that the technology worked. ("Suspicions" [TNG]). SEE: **Jo'Bril.**

metorapan treatments. Regenerative treatment for fracture patients. Wesley Crusher was allergic to metorapan. ("The First Duty" [TNG]).

metrazene. Cardiac antiarrhythmic medication in use aboard the *Enterprise*-D. ("The Host" [TNG]).

Metron. (Carole Shelyne). Highly advanced life-form, apparently humanoid, of unknown origin, possessing great powers. The Metrons intervened in a conflict between the original *Enterprise* and a **Gorn** ship in 2267. The two ships had been involved in a territorial dispute over planet **Cestus III**. Seeking to avoid unnecessary unpleasantness in their space, the Metrons sent *En-*

terprise captain Kirk and the Gorn ship commander to an artificial planetoid, where they were expected to fight to the death. Kirk won the fight, but declined to kill his opponent, prompting the Metrons to reevaluate their opinion of human-kind. A Metron representative said they had not expected Kirk to demonstrate the advanced trait of mercy, and said that they were so impressed they might wish to contact the Federation in just a few thousand years. ("Arena" [TOS]).

mev yap. Klingon for "stop." ("Reunion" [TNG]).

Meyers, Annie. Computer-generated character from Alexander Rozhenko's holodeck program *Ancient West*. ("A Fistful of Datas" [TNG]).

Mickey D. (Gregory Beecroft). Character in the novel *Hotel Royale*, a nefarious lothario who murdered a hotel bellboy to enforce his authority. ("The Royale" [TNG]).

microoptic drill. A handheld piece of Starfleet equipment used to produce extremely small, precision holes. Commander La Forge and Ensign Ro used a microoptic drill to create an observation hole in the ceiling of the **Ten-Forward lounge** on stardate 45571 when **Ux-Mal** terrorists were holding *Enterprise*-D personnel hostage there. ("Power Play" [TNG]).

microbiotic colony. A rare subatomic life-form, analogous to carbon-based bacteria. A microbiotic colony was responsible for significant structural damage to the Klingon vessel *Pagh* and the *Enterprise*-D. A tunneling neutrino beam was found to be effective in removing these dangerous organisms from both ships. ("A Matter of Honor" [TNG]).

microbrain. Silicon based intelligent life-form indigenous to planet **Velara III**. The microbrains were non-organic entities that lived in the soil, in the moist region just above the water table. Using energy absorbed from sunlight, the microbrains, which resembled tiny sparkling crystals, used groundwater to form electrical pathways that served as its consciousness. The  life-form was named "microbrain" by *Enterprise*-D personnel investigating the now-defunct Federation **terraforming** station on the planet. The terraforming project on Velara III threatened the lives of these entities by altering the subsurface water table. ("Home Soil" [TNG]). *Photo: Highly magnified image of Velara III microbrain life-form.*

microcentrum cell membrane. Physical attribute of life-forms that are unaffected by **triolic waves. Microcentrum cell membranes** are often seen in shape-shifters. ("Time's Arrow, Part I" [TNG]).

microcircuit fibers. Part of the **Borg** devices implanted into **Jean-Luc Picard's** body when he was abducted and surgically altered by the Borg in 2366. Infiltration of the fibers into Picard's healthy tissue around the Borg implants caused changes in the cellular DNA around the implants and made

surgical removal impossible while the implants were active. ("The Best of Both Worlds, Part II" [TNG]).

microreplication system. Device permitting an **exocomp** to fabricate virtually any tool required for an engineering servicing task. The microreplicator creates a new circuit pathway whenever an exocomp performs a task it has never done before. ("The Quality of Life" [TNG]).

microscopic generator. Nanotech device used by the criminal **Rao Vantika** to transfer his consciousness into the body of Dr. Bashir, thereby continuing his existence. ("The Passenger" [DS9]). SEE: **glial cells; synaptic pattern displacement.**

microtomographic analysis. Imaging technique using a series of microscopic narrow-beam X-rays to derive information on an extremely small scale. Microtomographic analysis along with mass spectrometry of the *Enterprise*-D **dilithium chamber hatch** helped determine that the explosion suffered by the ship in 2367 was the result of a flawed hatch cover and not sabotage. SEE: **neutron fatigue.** ("The Drumhead" [TNG]).

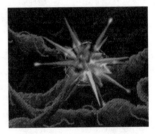

microvirus. A genetically engineered murder weapon designed to attack only cells with a very specific DNA sequence. This organism attached itself to parasympathetic nerves and blocked the function of the enzyme cholinesterase, thus blocking autonomic nerve impulses, but only of very specific individuals. **Yuta** of the **Acamarian** clan **Tralesta** used a microvirus as her weapon to systematically murder nearly all members of the rival clan **Lornak**, including **Penthor-Mul** and **Volnoth**. ("The Vengeance Factor" [TNG]). *Photo: Electron microscope scan of microvirus.*

mid-range phase adjuster. An innovative device developed by Geordi La Forge for use in the *Enterprise*-D warp-drive system. When installed in the power transfer conduits, it corrected the phase of the energy plasma, compensating for inertial distortion. La Forge offered to collaborate with **Dr. Leah Brahms** on a scientific paper describing the technology. ("Galaxy's Child" [TNG]).

Midos V. Planet to which the *Enterprise* was to have gone after their expedition to planet **Exo III** on stardate 2712. Midos V had a small colony that Korby's androids deemed a good choice for further android manufacture owing to abundant raw materials available there. ("What Are Little Girls Made Of?" [TOS]).

Midro. (Ed Long). One of the Disrupters of planet **Ardana** who conspired with **Vanna** to kidnap the *Enterprise* landing party when the starship visited the planet in 2269. ("The Cloud Minders" [TOS]).

Midsummer's Night Dream, A. Comedic play written by

William Shakespeare of Earth in 1595. In 1893, a troupe of actors lead by a "Mr. Picard" was planning a performance of this play in San Francisco. ("Time's Arrow, Part II" [TNG]).

Mikulaks. Race that donated a collection of special tissue samples to Starfleet for transportation to **Nahmi IV** in 2366. It was hoped that the samples would prove helpful in finding a cure for an outbreak of **Corellium fever** on that planet. ("Hollow Pursuits" [TNG]).

Milan, S.S. Federation transport ship, registry number NDT-50863. **Helena** and **Alexander Rozhenko** traveled aboard the *Milan* from Earth to the *Enterprise*-D, in orbit of planet **Bilana III** in 2368. ("New Ground" [TNG]).

Milika III. Planet where **Jean-Luc Picard**, early in his career, led an away team on a heroic mission to rescue an ambassador. ("Tapestry" [TNG]).

military log. In the alternate history created when the *Enterprise*-C vanished from its "proper" time in 2344, Picard's captain's log was instead referred to as a military log. ("Yesterday's *Enterprise*" [TNG]).

Miller, Steven. (Robert Ellenstein). Human father of **Wyatt Miller** and a close friend of the late **Ian Andrew Troi**. ("Haven" [TNG]). *Actor Robert Ellenstein had previously played the* **Federation Council President** *in Star Trek IV: The Voyage Home.*

Miller, Victoria. (Nan Martin). Human mother of **Wyatt Miller**. ("Haven" [TNG]).

Miller, Wyatt. (Rob Knepper). Physician who was betrothed to **Deanna Troi** when they were very young, being raised on planet **Betazed**. Wyatt had been haunted all his life by an image of a woman who he had thought was Deanna, but he later learned the mysterious woman was a **Tarellian** named **Ariana**. He chose not to marry Troi so that he could join the Tarellians in search for a cure to the virus that infected the last members of the Tarellian race. ("Haven" [TNG]).

millicochrane. Unit of measure of subspace distortion, one one-thousandth of the force necessary to establish a field of warp factor one. Named for **Zefram Cochrane**, inventor of the space warp. ("Remember Me" [TNG], "The Outcast" [TNG]).

Milton. English poet John Milton (1608-1674). When asked by Kirk in 2267 if he would prefer exile or imprisonment, **Khan** cited Milton, who, as cited by Kirk, felt "it is better to rule in hell than to serve in heaven." ("Space Seed" [TOS]).

Mimas. Closest of the major moons to the planet Saturn. Mimas was the location of an emergency evacuation center

for Starfleet **Academy's Flight Range**, and was the location where **Nova Squadron** was evacuated following an accident in 2368. ("The First Duty" [TNG]).

Minara II. Planet in the **Minaran Star System** where the **Vians** conducted studies in 2268 to determine which planet's inhabitants would be saved when the star Minara exploded. ("The Empath" [TOS]).

Minaran empath. Individual whose nervous system is capable of absorbing the physical and emotional responses of another, permitting the empath to heal the injuries of others by transferring those injuries onto her or his own body. **Gem** of the Minaran Star System was one such empath. ("The Empath" [TOS]).

Minaran star system. Star System, formerly with several inhabited planets. The star, Minara, entered a nova phase in 2268, rendering those planets uninhabitable. An advanced race known as the **Vians** had the ability to save the inhabitants of only one of those planets, and ultimately chose the humanoid people of the planet **Minara II**. ("The Empath" [TOS]). SEE: **Gem**.

mind-link. Telepathic linking of two minds creating a double entity within one being, similar to a **Vulcan mind-meld**. ("Is There in Truth No Beauty?"[TOS]).

• **"Mind's Eye, The."** *Next Generation* episode #98. Teleplay by René Echevarria. Story by Ken Schafer and René Echevarria. Directed by David Livingston. Stardate 44885.5. *First aired in 1991. Geordi is abducted and subjected to mental reprogramming by Romulan agents who intend to use him to murder a Klingon official. This episode marked the first appearance of the mysterious Sela, although she would not be identified until "Redemption, Part II" (TNG). SEE:* **actinides; Costa, Lieutenant; E-band emissions; Ikalian asteroid belt; isolinear optical chip;** *k'adlo;* **Kell; Krios; Kriosian System; neural implants;** *Onizuka;* **phaser rifle; phaser type-3; rapid nadion pulse; Risa; Romulan Star Empire; Sela; Shuttle 07; somnetic inducer; Starbase 36; Taibak; Teldarian cruiser; Vagh; VISOR.**

mind-meld, Vulcan. SEE: **Vulcan mind-meld**.

mind-sifter. Barbaric Klingon device used to probe the thoughts of their enemies during interrogation. At higher settings, the device irreparably damages the brain of the victim. Spock endured the mind-sifter on planet **Organia** in 2267 due to his Vulcan discipline. ("Errand of Mercy" [TOS]).

Minnerly, Lieutenant. *Enterprise*-D crew member who was scheduled to participate in a martial-arts competition aboard the ship just prior to Tasha Yar's death in 2364. Yar was scheduled to compete against Minnerly, and was favored in the ship's pool, although she expected Minnerly's kick-boxing to prove a formidable challenge. ("Skin of Evil" [TNG]).

Minos Korva. Federation planet located in a sector four light-years from the Cardassian/Federation border. During the

Federation/Cardassian war of the early 2360s, the Cardassians attempted to annex the planet, but were unsuccessful. In 2369, Starfleet contingency plans placed the *Enterprise*-D leading a fleet to defend Minos Korva and the surrounding sector in the event of a feared Cardassian invasion. ("Chain of Command, Part II" [TNG]).

Minos. Now uninhabited, Minos, a lush, forested planet, was once the home of a thriving, technologically advanced civilization. The people of Minos gained notoriety as arms merchants during the **Erselrope Wars**, but were all killed when their weapons systems got out of hand. At least a few Minosian artifacts survived, however, and were responsible for the destruction of the *U.S.S. Drake* in 2364. ("The Arsenal of Freedom" [TNG]).

"Minstrel Boy, The." Traditional Earth folksong that told of a young musician killed in an ancient war. *U.S.S. Rutledge* crew member **Will Kayden**, killed by **Cardassians** at **Setlik III**, was fond of the song, as were his shipmates **Benjamin Maxwell** and **Miles O'Brien**. ("The Wounded" [TNG]).

mint tea. A beverage made from the steeped leaves of a plant from the genus *Mentha*. **Perrin**, wife of Ambassador **Sarek**, liked living on Vulcan, but regretted that there was no mint tea there. ("Unification, Part I" [TNG]).

Mintaka III. Class-M planet; site of a Federation anthropological field study of the local proto-vulcan culture. ("Who Watches the Watchers?" [TNG]). *The exterior scenes of Mintaka III were filmed at Vasquez Rocks, near Los Angeles. Several other* Star Trek *episodes have been shot there,* notably "Shore Leave," (TOS), "Arena" (TOS), and "Friday's Child" (TOS). Photo: Surface of Mintaka III, et al.

Mintakan tapestry. An example of this craft was given to Captain Picard by **Nuria**, the **Mintakan** leader, in appreciation for his concern for her people. ("Who Watches the Watchers?" [TNG]). *This tapestry could, in later episodes, sometimes be seen draped over the back of Picard's chair in his quarters.*

Mintakans. Bronze age proto-Vulcan humanoids; natives of the planet **Mintaka III**. They were reported to be very peaceful and rational, living in a matriarchal, agricultural society. A Federation anthropological field team, studying the Mintakans in 2366, accidentally exposed the Mintakans to advanced Federation technology. ("Who Watches the Watchers?" [TNG]). SEE: **Nuria**.

Mintonian sailing ship. Craft that Guinan imagined seeing in the swirling clouds of the **FGC-47** nebula. ("Imaginary Friend" [TNG]).

Minuet. (Carolyn McCormick). A character in a holodeck simulation of a New Orleans jazz club. Minuet was generated by an enhanced holodeck program created by the **Bynars**, and was designed to interactively respond to Riker's expectations. Riker was quite captivated by the lovely Minuet, and was disappointed when her program disappeared from the computer after the Bynars left the ship. ("11001001" [TNG]). Minuet had left such an impression on Riker that **Barash**'s neural scanners

found her image in Riker's mind when Riker was held by Barash on **Alpha Onias III** in 2367. In this virtual reality created by Barash's equipment, Minuet was supposedly Riker's wife and his ship's counselor who had been killed in a shuttle accident. ("Future Imperfect" [TNG]).

Mira System. Location of planet **Dytallix B**. ("Conspiracy" [TNG]).

"Miracle Worker." Nickname given to Montgomery Scott by his crewmates aboard the *Starship Enterprise*. Kirk once joked that Scotty had earned that title by multiplying his repair time estimates by four, thus making it seem that he had performed those repairs in an amazingly small amount of time. (*Star Trek III: The Search for Spock*).

Miradorn. Species in which sets of twins have an almost symbiotic relationship; the two halves make the whole person. The Miradorn **Ro-Kel** was killed by the Rakhari fugitive **Croden**, causing his twin **Ah-Kel** to swear revenge. ("Vortex" [DS9]). *The Miradorn ship (pictured) was designed by Ricardo Delgado.*

Miramanee's planet. Class-M planet onto which an ancient race known as the **Preservers** had transplanted several tribes of American Indians centuries ago. The planet was in the midst of a dangerous asteroid belt, so the Preservers provided a powerful deflector device known to the Indian people as the **Obelisk**. The Preservers taught the tribe's medicine man how to operate the deflector, but one medicine man failed to pass that information to his son, so in 2268, the planet was defenseless. *Enterprise* personnel attempted to protect the planet from a large asteroid in that year, but were unsuccessful. Kirk, injured on the planet's surface, accidentally figured out how to access the deflector controls so that the planet could be saved. ("The Paradise Syndrome" [TOS]). *Miramanee's planet was not given a formal name in the episode.*

Miramanee. (Sabrina Scharf). Tribal priestess from a group of American Indians whose ancestors, centuries before, had been transplanted from Earth by a race known as the **Preservers**. When *Enterprise* captain **James T. Kirk** was stricken by amnesia on her planet's surface in 2268, Kirk's appearance was interpreted as a fulfillment of prophecy and Kirk was decreed to be a god. Accordingly, tribal custom demanded that Miramanee marry Kirk, and the two fell in love and conceived a child. Their happiness did not last, as the tribe turned against Kirk when they learned he was mortal, fatally injuring Miramanee. She and her unborn child died in her husband's arms. ("The Paradise Syndrome" [TOS]).

***Miranda*-class starship.** Federation spacecraft type introduced in the late 23rd century. *Miranda*-class starships have included the **Reliant** (*Star Trek II*), **Saratoga** (*Star Trek IV*), another **Saratoga** (of a higher registry number and a slightly different design, seen in "Emissary" [DS9]). *Miranda*-class ships were similar to **Soyuz-class** vessels. *Named for Prospero's daughter, a character in William Shakespeare's last play,* The Tempest.

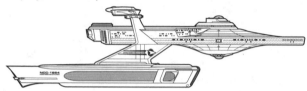

Miri. (Kim Darby). A young woman who survived a disastrous biological experiment on her planet. The experiment was intended to create a virus that would extend human life, but resulted in the deaths of all the adults on her world. Only the children survived, their lives greatly extended, until they reached puberty. Miri had reached puberty at the time the *U.S.S. Enterprise* con-

tacted her planet in 2266, but was saved when Dr. Leonard McCoy was able to develop an antitoxin for the virus. ("Miri" [TOS]). *Miri's planet was not given a name in the episode.*

• **"Miri."** Original Series episode #12. Written by Adrian Spies. Directed by Vincent McEveety. Stardate 2713.5. *First aired in 1966. The* Enterprise *discovers a planet where all the adults have died, leaving behind a population of nearly immortal children.* SEE: **Farrell, Lieutenant John; foolie; grup; Jahn; Life Prolongation Project; Miri; onlies; Rand, Janice.**

Miridian VI. An uninhabited planet near the Romulan Neutral Zone. During a virtual reality engineered by Barash on **Alpha Onias III** in 2367, **Barash** (as Ethan) said he had been captured by Romulans while living on Miridian VI. ("Future Imperfect" [TNG]).

Mirok. (Thomas Kopache). Science officer aboard a Romulan science vessel, in charge of developing and testing an experimental **interphase generator** in 2368. ("The Next Phase" [TNG]).

Mirren, Oliana. (Estee Chandler). One of three candidates who competed with Wesley Crusher for a single opening to **Starfleet Academy** in 2364. Mirren, a brilliant human female, was a runner-up in the competition. ("Coming of Age" [TNG]).

mirror universe. Continuum parallel to and coexisting with our own, but on another dimensional plane. Everything in the mirror universe is duplicated, but in many cases is opposite in nature to its counterpart in our own universe. Captain Kirk and a few members from the *Enterprise* were thrust into this parallel existence after beaming during an ion storm, finding the mirror universe to be a brutally savage place. Spock's counterpart in the mirror universe believed his brutally oppressive government would inevitably spur a revolt, resulting in a terrible dark age. The mirror Spock indicated a willingness to help reform his government to possibly avert this sequence of events. ("Mirror, Mirror" [TOS]). SEE: **Enterprise, I.S.S.; Kirk (mirror); Spock (mirror).**

• **"Mirror, Mirror."** Original Series episode #39. Written by Jerome Bixby. Directed by Marc Daniels. Stardate: Unknown. *First aired in 1967. A transporter malfunction sends Kirk and company into a savage mirror universe.* SEE: **agonizer; agony booth; Farrell (mirror); Halkans; ion storm; Kirk, James T. (mirror); ion storm; Kyle, Mr. (mirror); mirror universe; Morleau, Marlena (mirror); Spock (mirror); Sulu (mirror); Tantulus field.**

Mishiama wristlock. Martial-arts technique that Tasha Yar was trying to master for a competition aboard the *Enterprise*-D just prior to her death in 2364. ("Skin of Evil" [TNG]).

Mitchell, Admiral. Starfleet officer in charge of **Starbase 97**. ("Starship Mine" [TNG]).

Mitchell, Gary. (Gary Lockwood). **James T. Kirk**'s friend from their days in **Starfleet Academy**. Gary once risked his life for Kirk by taking a poison dart thrown by rodent creatures on planet Dimorus. Kirk requested Mitchell on his first command, and Mitchell, who then held the rank of lieutenant commander, also served aboard the *Enterprise* early during Kirk's first five-year mission.

In 2265, Mitchell was mutated into a godlike being after exposure to radiation at an energy barrier at the edge of the galaxy. Mitchell died on planet **Delta Vega**, and was listed as having given his life in the line of duty. ("Where No Man Has Gone Before" [TOS]). SEE: **barrier, galactic.**

mitosis. The ordered process of cell division, whereby one parent cell produces two genetically identical daughter cells. A similar process was used by the **quantum singularity lifeform**s discovered in 2369. ("Timescape" [TNG]).

mizainite ore. Rich deposits are found on planet **Stakoron II** in the Gamma Quadrant. ("The Nagus" [DS9]).

Mizan, Dr. Ktarian scientist who was an expert in interspecies mating practices. In 2369, during a conference on deep-space assignments, Dr. Mizan attempted to enlist Counselor Troi's aid in his research. ("Timescape" [TNG]).

Mizar II. Home planet of the **Mizarians**. ("Allegiance" [TNG]).

Mizarians. The humanoid residents of the planet **Mizar II**. Distinguished by a gray wrinkled complexion, the Mizarians valued peace above confrontation. As a result, the Mizarians were conquered six times in a period of three hundred years. The Mizarians survived by offering no resistance. **Kova Tholl** was a Mizarian. ("Allegiance" [TNG]).

MK-12 scanner. Cardassian security device used to verify the identity of those storing valuables at the **assay office** on the **Promenade** of station **Deep Space 9**. When entrusting several archaeological artifacts to the assay office, **Vash** questioned the office's clerk as to whether an MK-12 scanner with an L-90 enhanced resolution filter was adequate to prevent theft. ("Q-Less" [DS9]).

mnemonic memory circuit. Device constructed by Spock that allowed the retrieval of data from a **tricorder** when Spock and Kirk were trapped in Earth's past. Spock had constructed the circuit out of primitive electrical and radio components available in Earth's 1930s. Using the device, they were able to trace the flow of history as altered by Dr. McCoy and to locate the focal point in time where McCoy changed history. Spock complained to Kirk that he was working with tools at the primitive level of stone knives and bearskins but finished the project nevertheless. ("The City on the Edge of Forever" [TOS]). SEE: **Guardian of Forever**; **Keeler, Edith**.

Moab IV. A harsh, inhospitable planet in the **Moab Sector**. Moab IV was colonized in 2168 by a group of humans who sought to create a perfect society there. The crew of the *Enterprise*-D discovered this previously unknown colony in 2368. ("The Masterpiece Society" [TNG]). *Named for the ancient kingdom that flourished on Earth during biblical times in what is now Jordan.* SEE: **Genome Colony**.

Moab Sector. Region of Federation space. The *Enterprise*-D was assigned to the Moab Sector to track an errant **stellar core fragment** and to monitor resulting planetary disruptions in 2368. During the mission, the *Enterprise*-D found a previously unknown human colony that had been established on planet **Moab IV**. ("The Masterpiece Society" [TNG]).

Modean System. Star system at which young **Geordi La Forge** was once stationed with his father. ("Imaginary Friend" [TNG]).

Model A Ford. The second self-powered wheeled vehicle developed by Earth entrepreneur Henry Ford, introduced in 1927. Data, who was the second android built by Dr. Noonien Soong, compared himself to a Model A. ("A Matter of Time" [TNG]).

Modela aperitif. Exotic double-layered beverage served at **Quark's bar** on **Deep Space 9**. Dax ordered a Modela aperitif and sipped the drink while Major Kira Nerys tried to convince the Trill to side with her while Kira under the influence of the **Saltah'na energy spheres** in 2369. ("Dramatis Personae" [DS9]).

Mogh. Father to **Worf** and **Kurn**, and political rival to **Ja'rod**. Mogh and his wife were killed in the **Khitomer massacre** of 2346, after following Ja'rod to Khitomer because Mogh suspected him of disloyalty. Mogh's suspicions were correct: Ja'rod betrayed his people at Khitomer by providing secret defense codes to the Romulans. Mogh was survived by his sons, Worf and Kurn. Years later, in 2366, Ja'rod's son, **Klingon High Council** member **Duras**, falsified evidence in an attempt to conceal Ja'rod's actions and to implicate Mogh. Worf and Kurn challenged the accusations before the High Council, but council leader **K'mpec** was not willing to expose the powerful Duras family. ("Sins of the Father" [TNG]). Honor was restored to the Mogh family in late 2367 when the sons of Mogh agreed to support the Gowron regime during the Klingon civil war. ("Redemption, Parts I and II" [TNG]). In 2369, Worf investigated a report that Mogh had not been killed at Khitomer and that he had survived at a secret Romulan prison camp in the **Carraya System**. Although the camp was real, Worf learned from one of the inmates that the report was untrue. ("Birthright, Part II" [TNG]).

Mojave. Southwestern region of the North American continent on Earth. Home to *Enterprise* captain **Christopher Pike** (born early 23rd century), the area boasted glittering cities surrounded by wide belts of parkland. ("The Cage," "The Menagerie, Part II" [TOS]).

Mok'bara. Ritual Klingon martial-arts form, resembling terrestrial tai chi. Worf taught a *Mok'bara* class to his *Enterprise*-D shipmates most mornings at 0700. ("Man of the People" [TNG]). Worf taught the *Mok'bara* to his fellow captives at the secret Romulan prison camp in the **Carraya System** in 2369. The exercises, designed to enhance one's agility in hand-to-hand combat, helped to revive the dormant warrior spirit among the captives there. ("Birthright, Part II" [TNG]). *The Mok'bara exercises were invented by martial-arts expert (and visual effects producer) Dan Curry.*

molecular cybernetics. Field of study pioneered by noted scientist **Dr. Ira Graves**, whose work formed the basis of **Dr. Noonien Soong**'s invention of the positronic neural network. The work of both men in this field made possible the **positronic brain** in the android **Data**. ("The Schizoid Man" [TNG]).

molecular displacement traces. Tricorder readings indicative of recent macroscopic motion. ("Ensign Ro" [TNG]).

molecular phase inverter. Romulan device that could alter the molecular structure of matter so it could pass through "normal" matter and energy. ("The Next Phase" [TNG]). SEE: **interphase generator**.

molecular reversion field. Mysterious energy field that the *Shuttlecraft Fermi* passed through on stardate 46235. The field caused the shuttle's structure to deteriorate and prevented a clean transporter lock on its crew. Finally, the field caused Picard and the other members of the *Fermi* crew to be reduced to children. ("Rascals" [TNG]). SEE: **rybo-viroxic-nucleic structure.**

molecular-decay detonator. A technology used exclusively in Romulan weapons. A detonator of this type was found in the bomb that exploded aboard **K'mpec**'s ship in 2367, providing compelling evidence of Romulan involvement. ("Reunion" [TNG]).

Molor. Tyrant emperor on the **Klingon Homeworld** who ruled at the time of **Kahless the Unforgettable**, some 1,500 years ago. Kahless used the first *bat'telh* sword to kill the tyrant. ("Rightful Heir" [TNG]).

Molson, E. One of nine surviving eyewitnesses to the massacre of some 4,000 colonists at **Tarsus IV** by **Kodos the Executioner** in 2246. ("The Conscience of the King" [TOS]).

molybdenum-cobalt alloys. Material used in the construction of the android **Data**, who had about 11.8 kilograms of the stuff in his body. ("The Most Toys" [TNG]).

Mondor. Pakled spacecraft encountered by the *Enterprise*-D near the **Scylla** Sector in 2365. The *Mondor* had experienced systems malfunctions and *Enterprise*-D engineer Geordi La Forge transported to the **Pakled** ship in an effort to render assistance. The Pakleds thereupon made an unsuccessful attempt to kidnap La Forge. The *Mondor*'s equipment showed evidence of having been borrowed or stolen from a variety of other races, including the Romulans, Klingons, and the **Jaradans**. ("Samaritan Snare" [TNG]).

Monitor, U.S.S. Federation starship, *Nebula* class, Starfleet registry number NCC-61826, sent to the Romulan Neutral Zone border in preparation for a possible battle after Starfleet received warnings of a Romulan buildup at planet **Nelvana III** in 2366. The warnings, from Romulan defector Alidar Jarok, were later found to be baseless. ("The Defector" [TNG]).

monocaladium particles. Substance detected in cave walls on planet **Melona IV** following the attack of the **Crystalline Entity** in 2368. ("Silicon Avatar" [TNG]).

Monroe, Lieutenant. (Jana Marie Hupp). An *Enterprise*-D officer. She was in command of the ship when it struck two **quantum filaments** in rapid succession on stardate 45156. Monroe was killed in the second collision, leaving **Deanna Troi** in charge. ("Disaster" [TNG]).

"Moon Over Rigel VII." A traditional song, often sung around campfires in the 23rd century. McCoy, however, preferred "Row, Row, Row Your Boat." (*Star Trek V: The Final Frontier*).

"Moon's a Window to Heaven, The." Song that **Uhura** sang while distracting **Sybok**'s soldiers on planet **Nimbus III**. (*Star Trek V: The Final Frontier*). *Music and lyrics by Jerry Goldsmith and John Bettis. Arranged and performed by Hiroshima.*

Moore, Admiral. Starfleet official with whom Picard discussed an ancient distress signal detected from the **Ficus Sector** a month prior to stardate 42823. ("Up the Long Ladder" [TNG]).

mooring clamps. Mechanism used at station Deep Space 9 to secure a ship to the docking port. ("Babel" [DS9]).

Morag. (Reg E. Cathey). Commander of a Klingon ship that patrolled the Federation border, near **Relay Station 47**. Morag was fond of flying close to the station every few days, harassing the station's crew, once even locking his disruptors on to the station. Morag was found innocent in an incident in 2369 at Relay Station 47 in which **Lieutenant Aquiel Uhnari** and **Lieutenant Keith Rocha** were believed to have been murdered, but was found to have stolen Starfleet data from that station. ("Aquiel" [TNG]).

Morath. Legendary figure in Klingon mythology, the brother of **Kahless the Unforgettable**. Legend has it that Morath once brought dishonor to his family by telling a lie, for which Kahless fought him for twelve days and twelve nights. ("New Ground" [TNG]).

morathial series. A group of resuscitative drugs in use aboard Federation starships. ("Ethics" [TNG]).

Mordan IV. Class-M planet whose humanoid inhabitants suffered a terrible civil war that lasted 40 years. The conflict started around 2319 when Starfleet officer **Mark Jameson** provided weapons to one of the factions in exchange for freedom for Federation hostages. ("Too Short a Season" [TNG]).

Mordock Strategy. A brilliant system devised by **Mordock** of the planet **Benzar**. Wesley Crusher was nearly in awe of this accomplishment. ("Coming of Age" [TNG]). *Unfortunately, the episode does not give any clue as to what the Mordock Strategy is for or how it works.*

Mordock. (John Putch). One of three candidates who competed with Wesley Crusher for a single opening to **Starfleet Academy** in 2364. Mordock won the coveted appointment to the Academy, becoming the first Starfleet cadet from the planet **Benzar**. ("Coming of Age" [TNG]). *John Putch also played another Benzite, Mendon, in "A Matter of Honor" (TNG), which established that all Benzites from the same geostructure look identical.*

Moreau, Marlena (mirror). (Barbara Luna). *I.S.S. Enter-*

prise scientist who worked in the lab and performed other duties as the captain's woman in the **mirror universe**. After seeing the normally brutal Captain Kirk show mercy to his enemies, Moreau deduced that Kirk was in fact a counterpart from an alternate (our own) universe. When Kirk returned to his own universe, he discovered Moreau's counterpart had recently been assigned to his own *U.S.S. Enterprise*. ("Mirror, Mirror" [TOS])

Morg. Term used for the male population on planet **Sigma Draconis VI**. The Morgs lived under virtual Stone Age conditions, controlled by the **Eymorg** women and their **Controller**. The Morgs and Eymorgs were reunited as a single society after the failure of the Controller in 2268. ("Spock's Brain" [TOS]).

Morgana Quadrant. Destination of *Enterprise*-D after departing Science Station **Tango Sierra**. The ship was still en route to Morgana when Nagilum was discovered. ("The Child," "Where Silence Has Lease" [TNG]). *The term Morgana Quadrant does not fit into the Alpha, Beta, Delta, and Gamma naming scheme that Star Trek uses for the four quadrants of the galaxy. The reason for this is that "The Child" and "Where Silence Has Lease" (TNG) were both filmed before "The Price" (TNG) in which that system was first used. The feature film Star Trek VI: The Undiscovered Country also used the Alpha-Beta-Delta-Gamma system, so we are assuming that this nomenclature was in use significantly before The Next Generation, even though Star Trek VI was filmed after "The Price."*

Moriarty, Professor James. (Daniel Davis). Villainous adversary to **Sherlock Holmes**, Moriarty was a fictional character created by Earth novelist **Sir Arthur Conan Doyle**. A computer-generated embodiment of this character was created by the *Enterprise*-D **holodeck** computer. The computer had been responding to a command from Geordi La Forge to create an adversary capable of defeating Data in the role of Sherlock Holmes. The result was Moriarty, a computer program so sophisticated that he was a life-form in his own right. Thus imbued with consciousness, Moriarty began to learn about his surroundings and actually befriended Dr. Katherine Pulaski. When it was deemed improper to erase this program on the grounds that it was a sentient being, *Enterprise*-D captain Picard ordered the Moriarty character saved for reactivation when a means could be found to give the character physical form so that it could live outside of the holodeck. ("Elementary, Dear Data" [TNG]). Moriarty remained stored in protected computer memory for four years, but for some unexplained reason, his program was not entirely dormant. Moriarty attempted to escape the holodeck computer again in 2369, fashioning an elaborate simulated world in which he tried to trick Picard and other *Enterprise*-D personnel into permitting his release into the real world. Unfortunately, the technology to permit this was still not available, so Moriarty's

program was transferred into an independent computer system where his computer-generated consciousness could live in a computer-generated environment. ("Ship in a Bottle" [TNG]). SEE: **Barthalomew, Countess Regina**.

Morikin VII. Planet where cadet third-class **Jean-Luc Picard** was assigned for training while attending Starfleet Academy. There was a **Nausicaan** outpost on one of the nearby asteroids. ("Tapestry" [TNG]). *But that's a story for another day...*

Morla. (Charles Dierkop). Argelian who was to marry a dancer named **Kara**. When Kara was brutally murdered in 2267, Morla admitted being jealous that Kara had paid attention to Montgomery Scott, but denied that this jealousy would have driven him to such violence. ("Wolf in the Fold" [TOS]).

Morn. (Mark Shepherd). Large, lumbering humanoid who frequented **Quark's bar** at the **Promenade** on station **Deep Space 9**. ("Emissary" [DS9]). Morn once asked **Jadzia Dax** out for dinner. She declined, even though she thought he was kinda cute. ("Progress" [DS9]). *Morn is an anagram for Norm, George Wendt's character in* Cheers. *The character had been regularly seen in the background at Quark's bar since "Emissary," the first episode of* Star Trek: Deep Space Nine, *but was not referred to by name until "Progress."*

Moropa. Race with whom the **Bolians** were maintaining an uneasy truce in 2366. ("Allegiance" [TNG]).

Morrow, Admiral. (Robert Hooks). Starfleet commander at the time the original *Starship Enterprise* returned from the **Mutara Sector** after confronting **Khan** in 2285. Morrow had ordered the *Enterprise* to be decommissioned and denied Kirk's request to return to the **Genesis Planet** to search for Spock, but Kirk disobeyed Morrow and went anyway. (*Star Trek III: The Search for Spock*).

Morska. Klingon planet on which is located a subspace monitoring outpost. The *Enterprise*-A encountered this outpost when on course to **Rura Penthe** to rescue Kirk and McCoy in 2293. Fortunately, Communications Officer Uhura was able to convince the technicians at Morska that the *Enterprise*-A was a legitimate Klingon ship. (*Star Trek VI: The Undiscovered Country*).

Morta. (Michael Snyder). One of the renegade Ferengi who took over the *Enterprise*-D shortly after stardate 46235. ("Rascals" [TNG]).

mortae. Mining implement used by the **Troglytes** on planet Ardana. The Troglyte **Disrupters** used mortae as tools of vandalism on the cloud city Stratos in 2269 when protesting the inequities of their society. ("The Cloud Minders" [TOS]).

mortality fail-safe. Subroutine of the *Enterprise*-D's **holodeck**

control programs intended to prevent simulation participants from injuring themselves seriously. ("Elementary, Dear Data" [TNG]).

Mortania. Remote region of planet **Angel One**. **Ramsey**, **Ariel**, and their followers were exiled to Mortania by Angel One leader **Beata** in an effort to slow the rate of the social changes Ramsey and company had advocated. ("Angel One" [TNG]).

Moseley, Hal. (Stefan Gierasch). Meteorologist from the planet **Penthara IV**. When his planet was faced with an ecological disaster caused by a meteor strike on the surface, Moseley worked with the crew of the *Enterprise*-D to overcome the disasters. ("A Matter of Time" [TNG])

Moselina System. The *Enterprise*-D was en route to this system on stardate 45733 when it suffered extensive damage due to an invasion by **nitrium metal parasites**. ("Cost of Living" [TNG]).

• **"Most Toys, The."** *Next Generation* episode #70. Written by Shari Goodhartz. Directed by Tim Bond. Stardate 43872.2. *First aired in 1990. An eccentric and cruel collector decides to add Data to his collection.* SEE: **Basotile; Beta Agni II; bioplast sheeting; Data; denkirs; Fajo, Kivas; finoplak; Giles Belt; Grissom, U.S.S.; hytritium; Jovis, the; lapling; Lawmim Galactopedia; Maris, Roger; molybdenum-cobalt alloys; Nel Bato System; Off-Zel, Mark; Pike, Shuttlepod; Rejac Crystal; Sigma Erandi System; Stacius Trade Guild; "Starry Night, The"; Station Lya IV; Tellurian spices; Toff, Palor; tricyanate; tripolymer composites; Varon-T disruptor; Varria; Veltan Sex idol; Zibalians.**

Mot. (Ken Thorley, Shelly Desai). Barber aboard the *Enterprise*-D. ("Data's Day" [TNG]). Mot, a Bolian, was fond of giving useful tactical advice to the ship's senior officers, whether they wanted it or not. ("Ensign Ro" [TNG]). Mot was responsible for the hairpieces worn by Captain Picard and Commander Data when they masqueraded as Romulans on a covert mission to **Romulus** in 2368. ("Unification, Part I" [TNG]). *The* Enterprise*-D barber was first seen in "Data's Day" (TNG), where he was played by Shelly Desai and named V'Sal in the script, although that name was never used on the air. In later episodes, the character was called Mr. Mot and was played by Ken Thorley. We suspect the two were supposed to be the same person since it seems unlikely that the* Enterprise*-D would have two barbers who were both Bolians. Mot was first referred to by name in "Ensign Ro" (TNG).*

motor assist bands. Four-centimeter-wide straplike devices used with neurologically damaged patients. The bands provide electrical stimulation to the patient's limbs and help with muscle retraining. These devices were used to help rehabilitate the **Zalkonian** called **John Doe** in 2366, following the reattachment of one of his arms. ("Transfigurations" [TNG]).

Movar. (Nicholas Kepros). Romulan general who aided **Lursa** and **B'etor** in their bid to take over the **Klingon High Council** in 2368. Movar secretly provided military supplies to **Duras** family forces during the **Klingon civil war** early that year. ("Redemption, Part I" [TNG]).

• **"Move Along Home."** *Deep Space Nine* episode #10. Teleplay by Frederick Rappaport and Lisa Rich & Jeanne Carrigan-Fauci. Story by Michael Piller. Directed by David Carson. No stardate given. *First aired in 1993. A new species from the Gamma Quadrant forces the crew to play a new and seemingly deadly game.* SEE: **allamaraine; alpha-currant nectar; Andolian brandy; Chandra; Chula; Falow; Ferengi; first contact; klon peags; lokar beans; McCoullough, Captain; Primmin, Lieutenant George; reactive ion impeller; shap; Surchid, Master; thialo; Wadi.**

Mowray, Dr. Archaeologist that Captain Picard wished to contact on planet Landris II on stardate 46693. Picard was unable to communicate with Dr. Mowray due to a communications blackout requested by the **Stellar Cartography Department**. ("Lessons" [TNG]).

Mozart, Wolfgang Amadeus. Austrian musical composer (1756-1791) who wrote more than 600 compositions and is recognized as one of the principal composers of Earth's Classic style. *Enterprise*-D captain Jean-Luc Picard was fond of Mozart's works, and enjoyed playing them on his **Ressikan flute**. ("A Fistful of Datas" [TNG]).

M'ret, Vice-Proconsul. High-ranking Romulan senator who defected to the Federation in 2369. M'ret, along with two aides, was placed into stasis, and smuggled in a cargo container aboard the Romulan Warbird *Khazara* for transfer to a Corvallen freighter in the **Kaleb Sector**. Although this plan was not entirely successful, M'ret and his aides were later transported to the *Enterprise*-D. M'ret's escape had been engineered by Ambassador **Spock**, working with the dissident underground on Romulus. Spock hoped that M'ret's defection would help establish an escape route for thousands of other Romulan dissidents who lived in fear for their lives. ("Face of the Enemy" [TNG]). SEE: **N'Vek, Subcommander.**

MS 1 Colony. Federation settlement. In 2369, MS 1 was the second colony to be attacked by a group of fanatical self-aware **Borg**. ("Descent, Part I" [TNG]).

M'Tell. Archaeologist whose discovery of Ya'Seem ranked among the greatest findings in her field. ("The Chase" [TNG]).

Mudd (planet). Class-K planet inhabited by a group of sophisticated **androids** from the Andromeda Galaxy. When **Harry Mudd** stumbled upon this world in 2267, he named it in his own honor. ("I, Mudd" [TOS]).

• **"Mudd's Women."** Original Series episode #4. Teleplay by

Stephen Kandel. Story by Gene Roddenberry. Directed by Harvey Hart. Stardate 1329.8. *First aired in 1966. The* Enterprise *rescues con man Harry Mudd and his "cargo" of three beautiful women. This episode marks the first appearance of Harry Mudd, who would reappear in "I, Mudd" (TOS).* SEE: **Benton; Childress, Ben; class-J cargo ship; Farrell, Lieutenant John; Gossett, Herm; lithium crystal; Magda; McHuron, Eve; Mudd, Harcourt Fenton "Harry"; Ophiucus III; Rigel XII; Ruth; Venus drug; Walsh, Captain Leo.**

Mudd, Harcourt Fenton "Harry". (Roger C. Carmel). An interstellar rogue, con man, and general ne'er-do-well. Brought aboard the *Enterprise* in 2266 when his damaged ship disintegrated, Mudd was charged with several violations and his extensive criminal record was

discovered, including: smuggling, transport of stolen goods, and purchasing a space vessel with counterfeit currency. One scam involved the illegal Venus drug and giving it to the women he recruited as wives for settlers on distant planets, including **Rigel XII**. His ruse discovered, Mudd was convicted and incarcerated. ("Mudd's Women" [TOS]). Mudd somehow escaped from the authorities and then established what he called a "technical information service," selling the **Denebians** all rights to a Vulcan fuel synthesizer. When it was found that Mudd did not have the rights to make such a sale, Mudd was arrested. Upon learning that fraud carries a death penalty on Deneb, Mudd broke jail and was pursued by a patrol, which fired and damaged his ship. He drifted in space until he came to a class-K planet inhabited by sophisticated **android**s from the Andromeda Galaxy. The androids dubbed him Lord Mudd and provided for his every need, except the need for freedom. In 2267, Mudd sent an android named **Norman** to commandeer the *Starship Enterprise* in hopes that he could trade the *Enterprise* crew for his own freedom. Upon escaping from the androids, Captain Kirk left Mudd on the android planet as punishment. ("I, Mudd" [TOS]).

Mudd, Stella. (Kay Elliot). Former wife of confidence man **Harry Mudd**. While on the android planet, he had a replica made of her, so he could have the pleasure of telling her to shut up. Mudd's punishment for hijacking the *Enterprise* in 2267 was to be left behind on the android planet with 500 replicas of Stella to nag him. ("I, Mudd" [TOS]).

Mudor V. Planetary site of an *Enterprise*-D mission in 2368. The *Enterprise*-D had just departed Mudor V when it was severely disabled by impact with a series of **quantum filaments**. ("Disaster" [TNG]).

mugato. (Janos Prohaska). Apelike carnivore with white fur and poisonous fangs on **Tyree**'s planet. A mugato attacked

James Kirk in 2267, leaving him close to death. Since there was no antitoxin known to counteract this poison, McCoy allowed a local witch doctor, a **Kahn-ut-tu** woman, of the **hill people** tribe to successfully treat Kirk.("A Private Little War" [TOS]). *In the script, the apelike creature was called a gumato. Janos Prohaska was also the* **Horta** *from "Devil in the Dark" (TOS) and the* **Excalbian** *from "The Savage Curtain" (TOS).*

muktok plant. Variegated bristle-like foliage found on the planet **Betazed**. Able to live for hundreds of years, the *muktok* blooms gave off a pleasant sound when shaken. Riker and Troi recalled meeting near a particular *muktok* plant when Riker was stationed on Betazed. ("Ménage à Troi" [TNG]).

Mulhall, Dr. Ann. (Diana Muldaur). Astrobiologist aboard the original *Starship Enterprise* who, in 2268, was part of the landing party to **Sargon's planet**. Dr. Mulhall volunteered to allow her body to house **Thalassa**, one of the beings encountered there so that **android** bodies could be built for them. ("Return to Tomorrow" [TOS]). SEE: **Sargon**. *Diana Muldaur also played*

Dr. Miranda Jones *in "Is There in Truth No Beauty?" (TOS) and* **Dr. Katherine Pulaski** *during the second season of* Star Trek: The Next Generation.

Mullen, Commander Steven. First Officer of the **U.S.S. Essex**. Mullen was killed in 2167 when the *Essex* disintegrated above a moon of **Mab-Bu VI**. ("Power Play" [TNG]).

Mullibok. (Brian Keith). **Bajoran** farmer who escaped from a **Cardassian** labor camp in 2329, and later settled on **Jeraddo**, a class-M moon orbiting **Bajor**. Mullibok lived in peace on Jeraddo for 40 years until the Bajoran provisional government decided to tap Jeraddo's core for use as an energy source. This project was expected to render Jeraddo uninhabitable, so it was necessary for Mullibok and his friends **Baltrim** and **Keena** to evacuate their home. When they resisted, Major Kira Nerys was assigned to persuade them to leave before the energy tap project endangered their lives. ("Progress" [DS9]).

multiphase tractor beam. Technology developed by Geordi La Forge of the En*terprise*-D and scientist **Hannah Bates** of the **Genome Colony** on planet **Moab IV** in 2368. Their new development allowed warp power to be channeled into the tractor beam with greater efficiency than was previously available. The modified tractor beam was successful in diverting an approaching stellar core fragment that threatened Bates's home on Moab IV, but use of the beam caused loss of life-support systems throughout the ship. ("The Masterpiece Society" [TNG]).

multimodal reflection sorting. An advanced technique used to process subspace sensor data. Multimodal reflection sorting was used to detect the interactive subspace signals exchanged between **Locutus** and the **Borg** collective consciousness after Picard had been rescued from the Borg in early 2367. ("The Best of Both Worlds, Part II" [TNG]).

multiplexed pattern buffer. SEE: **pattern buffer.**

multitronics. Experimental computer technology developed by **Dr. Richard Daystrom** in the 2260s. Daystrom made several attempts to develop a functional multitronic computer, but his test units M-1 through M-4 were not entirely successful. His fifth attempt, M-5, was tested aboard the *Starship Enterprise* in 2268 with disastrous results. ("The Ultimate Computer" [TOS]).

Mulzirak. Type of transport vessel **Vash** hired to shuttle her away from Deep Space 9 in 2369. She later canceled her reservations. ("Q-Less" [DS9]).

Mundahla. Cloud dancer located in the Teleris Cluster. Q invited **Vash** to visit there, but she declined. ("Q-Less" [DS9]).

muon. Short-lived subatomic particle classified as a lepton. Excessive buildup on muons in the dilithium chamber of a Federation starship's warp drive can lead to a catastrophic explosion. Such a buildup occurred as a result of Romulan sabotage in 2368 when the *Enterprise*-D was rendering assistance to a Romulan science vessel. ("The Next Phase" [TNG]).

Murasaki 312. Quasar-like formation near planet **Taurus II**. *Enterprise* **Shuttlecraft Galileo** was lost in 2267 while studying this object. ("The *Galileo* Seven" [TOS]). Studies of the Murasaki Effect were still underway in 2367 when the *Enterprise*-D gathered information on this object using long-range sensors. ("Data's Day" [TNG]).

Muroc, Penny. A woman from Rigel with a penchant for men in uniform. She had two dates with Ensign Jean-Luc Picard during his assignment at **Starbase Earhart** in 2327. ("Tapestry" [TNG]).

Muskan seed punch. Traditional **Halii** beverage that **Aquiel Uhnari** missed when assigned to **Relay Station 47**. She said that the replicator didn't make it as well as her mother did. ("Aquiel" [TNG]).

Mutara Nebula. Interstellar dust cloud in the Mutara Sector, where **Khan** detonated the experimental Genesis torpedo in 2285, causing the Mutara Nebula to re-form into a habitable planet. The nebula was composed of ionized gas that made a starship's sensors highly unreliable when inside.  (*Star Trek II: The Wrath of Khan*). *Stock footage of the Mutara Nebula was reused several times for other nebulae seen on Star Trek: The Next Generation.*

Mutara Sector. Location where the **S.S. Botany Bay**, launched from Earth in 1996, was discovered adrift in 2267. ("Space Seed" [TOS]). Also the location of the **Genesis Planet**, and the **Regula I** planetoid. (*Star Trek II: The Wrath of Khan, Star Trek III: The Search for Spock*).

mutual induction field. Energy barrier produced by a network of low-altitude satellites around a penal colony moon in the Gamma Quadrant. The mutual induction field prevented communications to or from the moon, and also made it difficult for sensors from the runabout *Yangtzee Kiang* to scan the planet's surface. ("Battle Lines" [DS9]).

myocardial enzyme balance. Medical test used in surgical (particularly cardiac) procedures. ("Samaritan Snare" [TNG]).

myographic scanner. Sensing device on Federation **escape pods**. It monitors the bioelectric signatures of the pod's passengers and allows them to be traced should they become separated from the pod after landing. ("Legacy" [TNG]).

Myrmidon. Planet where archaeologist **Vash** was wanted for stealing the Crown of the First Mother. ("Q-Less" [DS9]).

nacelle. In starship design, a large outboard structure that houses a warp drive engine. Nacelles generally incorporate powerful subspace field generation coils and sometimes have Bussard collectors to gather interstellar hydrogen. Most Federation starship designs feature two warp engine nacelles mounted parallel to the axis of flight. *Some ships, like the U.S.S. Stargazer, have four warp engines instead of the traditional two. Gene Roddenberry insisted that starships have even numbers of nacelles.*

naDev ghos! Klingon for "Come Here!" ("Redemption, Part I" [TNG]).

Nagilum. (Earl Boen.) An extradimensional life-form encountered by the *Enterprise*-D during a star-mapping mission en route to the **Morgana Quadrant**. Nagilum threatened the lives of one-thind to one half the *Enterprise* crew, but it was later learned the threat was merely its effort of trying to understand the human concept of life and death. ("Where Silence Has Lease" [TNG]).

Nagus, Grand. Ferengi master of commerce. The Grand Nagus has enormous power over Ferengi business, controlling the allocation of trade territories and other commercial opportunities. In 2369, Grand Nagus **Zek** named **Quark** as his successor in a trade conference held aboard Deep Space 9, although the appointment and Zek's subsequent apparent death were part of a ruse intended to test his son, **Krax**. When a Nagus dies, his body is immediately vacuum-desiccated and sold as collector's items at handsome prices. ("The Nagus" [DS9]).

• **"Nagus, The."** *Deep Space Nine* episode #11. Teleplay by Ira Steven Behr. Story by David Livingston. Directed by David Livingston. No stardate given. *First aired in 1993. A Ferengi "godfather" dies, and Quark is the heir apparent.* SEE: **Arcybite; argine; Augergine stew; Balosnee VI; Barbo; Clarus system; Dax, Jadzia; Dolbargy sleeping trance; Ferengi Rules of Acquisition; Gral; Gratitude Festival; Hoex; Hupyrian; Jokarian chess; Krax; locator bomb; Maihar'du; mizainite ore; Nagus, Grand; Nava; Nog; O'Brien, Miles; Rom;** *Sepulo;* **sorium; Stakoron II; Tarahong detention center; tube grubs; Volchok Prime; Zek.**

Nahmi IV. Planet on which an outbreak of **Correllium fever** occurred in 2366. The *Enterprise*-D was assigned to transport a collection of tissue samples from the **Mikulaks** to **Nahmi IV**, in hopes that the samples would help contain the outbreak. ("Hollow Pursuits" [TNG]).

Nakamura, Admiral. (Clyde Kusatsu). Starfleet officer in charge of Starbase 173 near the Romulan Neutral Zone. Nakamura supported **Commander Bruce Maddox**'s efforts to have Data disassembled in hopes of replicating Noonien Soong's work. ("The Measure of a Man" [TNG]).

• **"Naked Now, The."** *Next Generation* episode #3. Teleplay by J. Michael Bingham. Story by John D. F. Black and J. Michael Bingham. Directed by Paul Lynch. Stardate 41209.2. *First aired in 1987. An intoxicating virus causes members of the* Enterprise*-D crew to lose their inhibitions. This episode was the first* Next Generation *segment made after the two-hour series opener, "Encounter at Farpoint" (TNG). The basic story was written by John D. F. Black in May 1967 during the original* Star Trek *series as a possible sequel to "The Naked Time" (TOS).* SEE: **Data; isolinear optical chip; MacDougal, Sarah; Psi 2000 virus; Shimoda, Jim;** *Tsiolokovsky, U.S.S.;* **Yar, Natasha.**

• **"Naked Time, The."** Original Series episode #7. Written by John D. F. Black. Directed by Marc Daniels. Stardate 1704.2. *First aired in 1966. A mysterious alien virus strips the* Enterprise *crew of their inhibitions, exposing their innermost thoughts. This episode was originally planned as the first part of a two-parter, although the second half eventually became an independent story, "Tomorrow Is Yesterday" (TOS). The first regular episode of* Star Trek: The Next Generation, *"The Naked Now" (TNG), is sort of a sequel to this episode. "The Naked Time" was the first episode to establish that the* Enterprise *warp engines are powered by matter and antimatter.* SEE: **antimatter; Chapel, Christine; environmental suit; intermix formula; Psi 2000 virus; Psi 2000 (planet); Rand, Janice; Riley, Kevin Thomas; Spock; Sulu, Hikaru; Tormolen, Joe; tricorder; warp drive.**

Name the Winner! Televised sports program on planet 892-IV in which Roman gladiators fought to the death. ("Bread and Circuses" [TOS]). *The announcer for* Name the Winner! *was Bartel LaRue, who also provided the voice of the* **Guardian of Forever** *in "The City on the Edge of Forever" (TOS).*

Nanclus. (Darryl Henriques). Romulan ambassador to the United Federation of Planets. In 2293, Nanclus was part of a conspiracy between Starfleet **admiral Cartwright** and Klingon **general Chang** to obstruct **Chancellor Gorkon**'s peace initiatives. (*Star Trek VI: The Undiscovered Country*). *Actor Darryl Henriques also played* **Portal** *in "The Last Outpost" (TNG).*

nanites. Submicroscopic robots designed to perform medical functions within the bloodstream of a living organism. Such functions might include intracellular surgery or eliminating individual disease cells, or removing clotted material from a blood vessel. Manufactured in Dakar, Senegal, these devices possessed gigabytes of mechanical computer memory. They were designed to have exposure only to the inside of nuclei during cellular surgeries, and were generally kept in a nonfunctional state when not in use. In 2366, Wesley Crusher conducted experiments in nanite interaction. These studies went awry, resulting in the creation of self-replicating, sentient nanites. The nanites interfered with *Enterprise*-D onboard systems and nearly jeopardized a landmark astrophysics experiment conducted by **Dr. Paul Stubbs** before the nanites were recognized to be sentient life-forms. The nanites were later granted colonization rights on planet Kavis Alpha IV. ("Evolution" [TNG]). Nanites were briefly considered by *Enterprise*-D personnel as a possible defense against the **Borg** during the Borg offensive of 2367. The plan was abandoned because it was believed it would take two to three weeks for the nanites to have an effect, far too long to save Earth from the Borg. ("The Best of Both Worlds, Part II" [TNG]).

nanopulse laser. Advanced engineering device developed by the androids on planet **Mudd**. ("I, Mudd" [TOS]).

nanotechnology. Branch of engineering involving the design of microscopic machines on scales as small as nanometers. Such tools include extremely tiny robots known as **nanites**. ("Evolution" [TNG]).

Narendra III (alternate). In the alternate history created when the *Enterprise*-C vanished from its "proper" time in 2344, the Klingon outpost at **Narendra III** was also attacked by Romulan forces. But in this alternate timeline, the *Enterprise*-C was not available to render aid to the colony. This was evidently a key event in history, because the failure to render aid led to serious deterioration of the relationship between the Klingons and the Federation, culminating in a long and costly war between the two powers. ("Yesterday's *Enterprise*" [TNG]).

Narendra III. The site of an ill-fated Klingon outpost that was attacked by Romulan forces in 2344. The *Enterprise*-C rendered aid in the incident. Athough the *Enterprise*-C was reported lost, the heroism of the ship's crew so impressed the Klingon government that it led to improved relations between the Federation and the Klingons. ("Yesterday's *Enterprise*" [TNG]).

Narsu, Admiral Uttan. Commander of Starbase 12 in 2167 at the time the *U.S.S. Essex* disappeared above a moon of planet **Mab-Bu VI**. ("Power Play" [TNG]).

Narth, Captain. Commander of the *U.S.S. Ajax* in 2327. Ensign **Cortin Zweller** served under Narth, his first Starfleet assignment after graduation from the Academy. ("Tapestry" [TNG]).

NASA. National Aeronautics and Space Administration. Earth-based branch of the American government responsible for many early space exploration missions, including *Voyager VI*. (*Star Trek: The Motion Picture*). NASA launched the spaceship *Charybdis* from Earth on July 23, 2037, the ill-fated third manned attempt to explore beyond the Solar system. The ship suffered a telemetry failure and its

fate was unknown until 2365 when the remains of the *Charybdis* were discovered in orbit around a planet in the **Theta 116** system. ("The Royale" [TNG]).

Nasreldine. Planet where an *Enterprise*-D crew member picked up a case of the flu shortly prior to stardate 42686. ("The Icarus Factor" [TNG]).

nasturtiums. Terrestrial flowering plants of the genus *Tropaeolum*. Young **Clara Sutter** helped **Keiko O'Brien** plant nasturtiums in the *Enterprise*-D arboretum shortly after stardate 45852. ("Imaginary Friend" [TNG]).

Natira. (Kate Woodville). High Priestess of the **Fabrini** people on the asteroid/ship *Yonada*, who served as her people's liaison to their **Oracle**. Natira guided her people near the end of their long interstellar voyage, when *Yonada* nearly collided into planet **Daran V**.

In 2268, Natira fell in love with Starfleet officer **Dr. Leonard McCoy**, and asked him to marry her. ("For the World Is Hollow and I Have Touched the Sky" [TOS]).

Nausicaans. (Clint Carmichael, Nick Dimitin, Tom Morga). Intelligent humanoid life-forms. Some Nausicaans have earned a reputation for being surly, ill-tempered, quick to violence, and very tall. In 2327, just after his graduation from Starfleet Academy, Ensign **Jean-Luc Picard** was involved in a fight with three Nausicaans while on leave at **Starbase Earhart**. One

Nausicaan stabbed Picard through the heart, severely injuring the young ensign, who required **cardiac replacement** surgery. ("Samaritan Snare" [TNG]). Many years later, Picard relived the incident through **Q**'s intervention. ("Tapestry" [TNG]). *Named for the Greek goddess of the wind, as well as for the animated fantasy film* Nausicaa.

Nava. (Barry Gordon). Ferengi entrepreneur who took over the Arcybite mining refineries in the **Clarus system** in 2369. Grand Nagus **Zek** congratulated Nava for his accomplishments at a meeting held at Quark's bar on Deep Space 9. ("The Nagus" [DS9]).

navigation. SEE: **bearing; heading; navigator.**

navigational deflector. On many Federation starships, a powerful forward-looking directional deflector used to push aside debris, meteoids, and other objects that might collide with the ship. The navigational deflector of the *Enter-*

prise-D was modified in 2366 in a desperate effort to improvise a weapon against the **Borg** assault on Earth. ("The Best of Both Worlds, Part I" [TNG]). The modified deflector provided a single, massive pulse directed at the Borg ship. The use of the weapon caused significant damage to the *Enterprise*-D's warp drive and burned out the deflector itself, but failed to stop the Borg vessel. ("The Best of Both Worlds, Parts II" [TNG]). *Photo: Navigational deflector of a refit* Constitution-*class starship.*

navigator. Aboard a starship, the control station and the officer responsible for projecting the desired course or trajectory of the vehicle and for determining the ship's actual position, velocity, and direction in relationship to that desired course. In more recent Federation starships, this function was merged with the duties of the helm officer, and dubbed conn, or **flight controller**. *Ensign* **Pavel Chekov** *was one of the navigators of the* Starship Enterprise *during the original* Star Trek *series. The term navigator was replaced with conn at the beginning of* Star Trek: The Next Generation.

Navot. Bajoran faction embattled in a border dispute with their neighbors, the **Paqu**. ("The Storyteller" [DS9]). SEE: **Glyrhond, Varis Sul, Woban.**

Nayrok. (James Cromwell). Prime minister of planet **Angosia III** in 2366, when the **Angosian** government sought membership in the Federation. Nayrok enlisted the aid of the *Enterprise*-D to help capture **Roga Danar**, whom Nayrok identified as a fugitive criminal. It was learned that Danar was the leader of a veterans' group seeking redress from the Angosian government for injuries they had received during the **Tarsian War**. Nayrok later requested assistance from the *Enterprise*-D in suppressing the unrest caused by Danar's group, but Captain Picard declined on the grounds that it was a purely local matter. ("The Hunted" [TNG]).

Nazi. SEE: **Ekosians; Gill, John; Melakon.**

NCC. Spacecraft registry number prefix assigned to vessels of the Federation Starfleet. For example, the registry number of the original *Starship Enterprise* was NCC-1701. Experimental vessels developed by Starfleet sometimes had NX registry prefixes, as did the *U.S.S. Excelsior* when it was in its early testing stages (*Star Trek III: The Search for Spock*). Other vessels, presumably under the auspices of other operating authorities, have other registry prefixes. The *T'Pau*, a ship of Vulcan registry, had an NSP registry number prefix ("Unification, Part I" [TNG]), while the non-Starfleet science vessel *Vico* had an NAR prefix ("Hero Worship" [TNG]), as did the *Nenebek* ("Final Mission" [TNG]), and an Yridian transport had a YLT prefix ("Birthright, Part II" [TNG]).

Nebula-class starship. Type of Federation starship, slightly smaller than a *Galaxy*-class vessel. The *Nebula*-class ships featured a large upper equipment module, usually used for sensors, that could be customized for different mission profiles. *Nebula*-class ships have included the *U.S.S. Phoenix*, ("The Wounded" [TNG]) the *U.S.S. Sutherland* ("Redemption, Part II" [TNG]), and the *U.S.S. Bellerephon* (seen in the battle sequences of "Emissary" [DS9]). *The* Nebula-*class ship was designed by Ed Miarecki, Rick Sternbach, and Mike Okuda. The model was built by Greg Jein.*

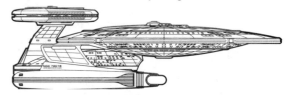

Nechayev, Vice-Admiral Alynna. (Natalia Nogulich). Starfleet senior officer who was responsible for the handling of the **Celtris III** incident in 2369. ("Chain of Command, Parts I & II" [TNG]). Nechayev blasted Picard for his decision to return the **Borg** known as **Hugh** to the Borg collective without also sending the invasive program developed by *Enterprise*-D personnel. Picard protested that using the program, effectively a genocidal weapon of mass destruction, would be a violation of Starfleet's principles, but Nechayev, fearing a mass invasion by the Borg, ordered him to use the weapon if another opportunity presented itself. ("Descent, Part I" [TNG]).

neck pinch. SEE: **Vulcan nerve pinch**.

Neela. (Robin Christopher). Bajoran religious activist who attempted to assassinate **Vedek Bareil** at **Deep Space 9** in 2369 to support **Vedek Winn**'s bid to succeed **Kai Opaka**. Neela sabotaged station systems, planted a terrorist bomb, and later shot at Bareil. Although her acts were considered criminal, Neela believed she was acting in accordance with the will of her people's **Prophets**. ("In the Hands of the Prophets" [DS9]). She had been working on Deep Space 9 as an engineer as a cover for her attempt to murder Bareil. ("Duet" [DS9]).

negaton hydrocoils. Device that resembled a drop of jelly and allowed **androids** constructed by **Sargon, Thalassa,** and **Henoch** to move like humanoids without microgears or other mechanical aids. ("Return to Tomorrow" [TOS]).

Nehelik Province. Area in the southern hemisphere of the planet **Rakhar** where government official Exarch demanded the return of the fugitive **Croden** from Deep Space 9 in 2369. ("Vortex" [DS9]).

Nehru Colony. Federation colony near station **Deep Space 9** and the Bajoran system. **Jadzia Dax** ordered a subspace link established to the Nehru Colony while trying to overload the station's computers when the software life-form called **Pup** threatened station safety in 2369. ("The Forsaken" [DS9]).

Neil. (Tom Nibley). Member of a group of terrorists who attempted to steal **trilithium resin** from the *Enterprise*-D in 2369. Neil was the engineer of the group and had devised a means to transport the dangerously unstable and toxic trilithium through the ship. He was killed by one of his fellow terrorists. ("Starship Mine" [TNG]).

Neinman. An ancient, mythical land on planet Xerxes VII. Riker likened Neinman to Earth's Atlantis or the planet Aldea. ("When the Bough Breaks" [TNG]).

Nel Bato system. A possible destination of the *Jovis*, following the kidnapping of Data by **Kivas Fajo** in 2366. ("The Most Toys" [TNG]).

Nel system. Star system visited by a delegation of **Ullian** telepathic historians in 2368. Two cases of unexplained coma, resembling **Iresine Syndrome**, were reported shortly afterward on one of the planets in the Nel system. Both patients were later believed to be victims of **telepathic memory intrusion** rape by Ullian historian **Jev**. ("Violations" [TNG]).

Nelson, Lord Horatio. Lord Nelson (1758-1805) was perhaps the most celebrated admiral in British maritime history. He was captain of the British ship *H.M.S. Victory*. He died on board the *Victory* following the British defeat of the French at Trafalgar. Prior to the Borg encounter of 2366-2367, Captain Jean-Luc Picard drew inspiration from Nelson's courage on the eve of battle. ("The Best of Both Worlds, Part I" [TNG]).

Nelvana III. Located in the **Romulan Neutral Zone**, this planet was in striking range of some 15 Federation sectors. Romulan defector **Alidar Jarok** reported to Federation authorities that the Romulans were building a secret base there from which to launch a major offensive against the Federation. The reports of the base turned out to be a sham, devised by the Romulan High Command to test Jarok's loyalties, and to lure the *Enterprise*-D into the Neutral Zone, where it could be captured. ("The Defector" [TNG]).

Nenebek. A mining shuttle from the planet **Pentarus V**. The craft was piloted by Captain **Dirgo**, who was quite proud of the vessel, despite its advanced age and somewhat substandard maintenance. Dirgo and the *Nenebek* were sent by the government of **Pentarus V** to transport Captain Picard and Ensign Crusher to a labor mediation on the planet in 2367. During their flight, a serious malfunction forced the *Nenebek* to crash on **Lambda Paz**, one of the moons of Pentarus III. ("Final Mission" [TNG]). *The* Nenebek *was designed by Joseph Hodges. It was later re-dressed and served as several other ships, including* **Rassmussen**'s *time travel pod from "A Matter of Time" (TNG) and the* **Yridian** *craft from "Birthright" (TNG).*

Neo-Transcendentalism. A philosophical movement of 22nd-century Earth, one advocating a return to a simpler life, one more in harmony with nature. The movement was founded by **Liam Dieghan**, and was a product of the time when Earth was still recovering from the nuclear holocaust of the previous century. ("Up the Long Ladder" [TNG]).

Nequencia system. Star system located near the Romulan Neutral Zone. Nequencia was one of two destinations visited by **Jaglom Shrek** after departing Deep Space 9 with Worf. ("Birthright, Part II" [TNG]). SEE: **Carraya system**.

Neral. (Norman Large). **Proconsul** of the Romulan Senate during the year 2368. A relatively young man who was new to the office, Neral was reported to be sympathetic to the cause of Vulcan/Romulan reunification. Neral was, however, secretly working with **Senator Pardek** to use the reunification movement as a cover for a planned invasion of Vulcan. ("Unification, Parts I and II" [TNG]). SEE: **Spock**.

Nervala IV. Class-M planet whose upper atmosphere contains a powerful **distortion field**, making it impossible to reach the planet by shuttle or transporter for most of the planet's year. A Federation research station located on the planet's surface was evacuated by the crew of the *U.S.S. Potemkin* in 2261 when the distortion field was forming in the planetary atmosphere. The rescue team from the *Potemkin* was led by Lieutenant William T. Riker. A transporter malfunction during the final beam-out from the planet caused Riker to be duplicated. One Riker returned to the Potemkin, while the other materialized back on **Nervala IV**. The existence of the duplicate Riker was not suspected until 2369, when the *Enterprise*-D returned to the planet to retrieve the scientific information left behind by the scientific team. ("Second Chances" [TNG]). SEE: **Riker, Thomas.**

nerve pinch, Vulcan. SEE: **Vulcan nerve pinch**.

neural calipers. Medical instrument used in surgical procedures. ("Samaritan Snare" [TNG]).

neural depletion. Complete loss of electrochemical energy of a humanoid brain, resulting in the death of the victim. This depletion was characteristic of the victims attacked by aliens from **Devidia II**. ("Time's Arrow, Part II" [TNG]).

neural imaging scan. Medical diagnostic scan used to test the acuity of the patient's visual cortex. Dr. Julian Bashir performed a neural imaging scan on Miles O'Brien when trying to find the cause of his unexplained **aphasia** in 2369. ("Babel" [DS9]).

neural implants. The bioelectrical interface between **Geordi La Forge**'s visual cortex and his **VISOR**. The devices were implanted bilaterally in the temporal regions of La Forge's skull, and fed into the visual cortex. The external portion of the implant allowed for direct connection of the VISOR to La Forge's head. ("The Mind's Eye" [TNG])

neural metaphasic shock. A potentially fatal failure of the neurological system in humanoids. Neural metaphasic shock was the cause of death of a crash victim from the *U.S.S. Denver* after Dr. Toby Russell treated him with **borathium**, an unauthorized drug. ("Ethics" [TNG]).

neural neutralizer. A device invented by **Dr. Simon Van Gelder** in 2266 to aid rehabilitation of criminals. The neutralizer was intended to selectively remove thoughts relating to criminal acts, but was later found to have potentially lethal effects. ("Dagger of the Mind" [TOS]).

neural output pods. Component of **Geordi La Forge's** VISOR, the neural output pods transmitted the VISOR's visual data to La Forge's brain. La Forge and the Romulan **Bochra** connected the neural output pods of La Forge's VISOR to a tricorder to detect a neutrino beacon when both were trapped on planet **Galorndon Core** in 2366. ("The Enemy " [TNG]).

neural paralyzer. Medication that can cause a cessation of heartbeat and breathing in a humanoid patient, creating the appearance of death. If such a patient receives medical treatment in time, a full recovery is possible. McCoy injected Kirk with neural paralyzer during Spock's *Pon farr* in 2267, making it possible for Spock to win his fight with Kirk without actually killing his commanding officer. ("Amok Time" [TOS]).

neural parasite, Denevan. SEE: **Denevan neural parasite.**

neural scan interface. SEE: **iconic display console.**

neural stimulator. Medical instrument used to increase neural activity in the central nervous system of a humanoid brain. Dr. Crusher used a neural stimulator in an unsuccessful attempt to revive the gravely injured **Natasha Yar** after she had been attacked by **Armus**. ("Skin of Evil" [TNG]). **Professor Berlinghoff Rasmussen** stole a neural stimulator from sickbay. ("A Matter of Time" [TNG]).

neural transducers. Implantable bioelectric devices that received nerve impulses from the brain and transmited it to affected voluntary muscle groups. These instruments were used in cases of severe spinal cord damage to give the patient some control over the affected extremities. ("Ethics" [TNG]).

neurogenetics. Study of the development and genetic replication of neural tissue. ("Ethics" [TNG]). SEE: **genetronic replicator.**

neurolink. Emergency medical technique used for the stabilization of patients with brainstem injuries. Matching neural pads were used. One would be placed on a healthy individual and a matching unit on the patient. These devices enabled a link to be established from the healthy person's autonomic nervous system to that of the injured

patient. When the **Zalkonian** named **John Doe** was discovered in the wreck of a Zalkonian escape pod in 2366, Dr. Crusher used a neurolink with Geordi La Forge to stabilize "John"'s nervous system. ("Transfigurations" [TNG]) *Illustration: neural pads used in neurolink technique.*

neurosomatic technique. Procedure used on planet **Tilonus IV** in an attempt to extract strategic information from Commander William Riker, captured there in 2369. Using neurosomatic techniques, his captors created a delusional world in which Riker believed he was an inmate at the **Tilonus Institute for Mental Disorders**. Riker's subconscious incorporated elements of a play called *Frame of Mind* into this delusional world, allowing Riker's mind to create a defense mechanism against the neurosomatic process. ("Frame of Mind" [TNG]). SEE: **Syrus, Dr.; Suna; Mavek.**

neurotransmitter. Biochemical associated with the propagation of electrical energy between neurons in humanoid nervous systems. Captain Picard exhibited increased neurotransmitter output on stardate 45944 while under the influence of the **Kataan probe**. ("The Inner Light" [TNG]). Elevated levels of neurotransmitters were found in the cerebral cortexes of **Ambassador Ves Alkar's** victims, leading Dr. Crusher to suspect the nature of his psychic abuse of these people. ("Man of the People" [TNG]).

Neutral Zone Outposts. A series of Federation monitoring facilities located on the border of the **Romulan Neutral Zone**. Outposts 2, 3, 4, and 8 were destroyed in the Romulan incursion of 2266. ("Balance of Terror" [TOS]).

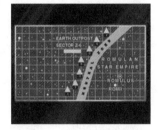

Neutral Zone, Klingon. SEE: **Klingon Neutral Zone.**

Neutral Zone, Romulan. SEE: **Romulan Neutral Zone.**

• **"Neutral Zone, The."** *Next Generation* episode #26. Television story & teleplay by Maurice Hurley. From a story by Deborah McIntyre & Mona Glee. Directed by James Conway. Stardate 41986.0. *First aired in 1988. The Enterprise-D revives a group of 20th-century humans who were frozen some four centuries ago. "The Neutral Zone" establishes the first season of* Star Trek: The Next Generation *to be set in the year 2364. This is the point of reckoning from which most* Next Generation *dates are derived. This episode established the destruction of several distant outposts which was later found to be the work of the Borg in "Q Who?" (TNG). "The Neutral Zone" was the last episode of the first season of* Star Trek: The Next Generation. SEE: *Charleston, U.S.S.;* **Clemonds, Sonny; cryonics; cryosatellite; Kazis binary system; low-mileage pit woofie; Neutral Zone, Romulan; Offenhouse, Ralph;** *QE-2;* **Raymond, Claire; Raymond, Donald; Raymond, Edward; Raymond, Thomas; Romulan Star Empire; Romulan Warbird; Science Station Delta Zero Five; Sector 3-0; Sector 3-1; Starbase 39-Sierra; Starbase 718; Tarod IX; Tebok, Commander; television;**

Thei, Subcommander; Tomed Incident.

neutral particle weapons. Ship-mounted weapons in use aboard **Talarian** warships such as the *Q'Maire* in 2367. ("Suddenly Human" [TNG]).

neutrino field. A concentration of neutrinos. Geordi La Forge used a neutrino field to help contain a group of noncorporeal criminal life-forms from the **Ux-Mal** system that attempted to commandeer the *Enterprise*-D on stardate 45571. ("Power Play" [TNG]).

neutrino. Massless subatomic particle that has no electrical charge. Literally, "the little neutral one," neutrinos were first detected by Earth scientists in 1956. A major source of these particles is nuclear reactions deep within stars. ("Power Play" [TNG]). Elevated neutrino readings accompany passage of an object through the **Bajoran wormhole**. ("Captive Pursuit" [DS9]). A standard Starfleet tricorder is not equipped to detect neutrinos. ("The Enemy" [TNG]).

neutron fatigue. A breakdown of atomic cohesion in a structure. Neutron fatigue was shown to be the cause of a failure of the **dilithium chamber hatch** on board the *Enterprise*-D in 2367. The failure of the hatch caused an explosion that injured two crew members and took the warp drive off line for more than 15 days. ("The Drumhead" [TNG]). *Either that, or we're just working those subatomic particles too hard.*

neutron densitometer. SEE: **passive high-resolution series.**

neutron migration. The movement of neutrons from the outer hydrogen-reaction zone to the inner helium core of a star. The migration of neutrons increased stellar-core density and contributed to the spectacular failure of Dr. Timicin's **helium ignition test** in 2367. ("Half a Life" [TNG]). SEE: **helium fusion enhancement.** *Or this could be when neutrons go south for the winter.*

neutron radiation. Energy discharge consisting of electrically neutral subatomic particles. High levels of neutron radiation were found to be a signature of the torpedo systems of an uprated **Klingon Bird-of-Prey** that was capable of firing weapons while cloaked. This radiation proved to be a weak point of this ship, making it detectable while cloaked. (*Star Trek VI: The Undiscovered Country*).

neutron star. Stellar body that has been gravitationally crushed to the point where its density is that of nuclear material. **Dr. Paul Stubbs** conducted an experiment near a neutron star in the **Kavis Alpha Sector** in 2266. ("Evolution" [TNG]).

neutronium. Matter so incredibly dense that atoms' electron shells have collapsed and the nuclei are actually touching each other. Periodic explosions on the surface of a neutron star in the **Kavis Alpha Sector** are known to expel particles of neutronium into space at relativistic speeds. ("Evolution" [TNG]). The extragalactic **planet killer** that destroyed sys-

tems **L-370** and **L-374** in 2267 was composed of pure neutronium, rendering it impervious to phaser fire or any external attack. ("The Doomsday Machine " [TOS]).

New Berlin Colony. Federation colony. In 2369, with tensions high following an attack on the **Ohniaka III** outpost, New Berlin also reported a **Borg** attack. Thankfully, the "attacking" ship turned out to be merely a Ferengi trading vessel. ("Descent, Part I" [TNG]).

New France Colony. Federation colony near station Deep Space 9. Dax ordered a subspace link established to the New France Colony while trying to overload the station's computers when the software life-form called **Pup** threatened station safety in 2369. ("The Forsaken" [DS9]).

• **"New Ground."** *Next Generation* episode #110. Teleplay by Grant Rosenberg. Story by Sara Charno and Stuart Charno. Directed by Robert Scheerer. Stardate 45376.3. *First aired in 1992. Alexander returns to the* Enterprise-D *to live with his father, Worf, but the transition is not easy for either.* SEE: **Balduk warriors; Bilana III; Brentalia; calisthenics program, Klingon; Cochrane, Zephram; Corvan gilvos; Corvan II; Donaldson; Draco lizards; Felton, Ensign; firefighting; Ja'Dar, Dr.; Kahless the Unforgettable; Kyle, Ms.; Lapsang souchong tea; Lemma II; Maktag; *Milan, S.S.*; Morath; Rozhenko, Alexander; Rozhenko, Helena; soliton wave; white rhinos; Yeager, Chuck.**

New Manhattan. City on planet Beth Delta I. **Dr. Paul Stubbs** jokingly stated he would like to take Deanna Troi there for champagne. ("Evolution" [TNG]).

New Martim Vaz. An aquatic city located in Earth's Atlantic ocean. **Kevin** and **Rishon Uxbridge** were originally from this city. ("The Survivors" [TNG]).

New Orleans-**class starship.** Federation ships, often designated as frigates. The *Starships* **Renegade** and **Thomas Paine** ("Conspiracy" [TNG]) were both *New Orleans*-class ships, as was the **Kyushu** ("The Best of Both Worlds, Part II [TNG]). *A study model was made for this class of ship and was seen very briefly as the* Kyushu *in the ship graveyard in "The Best of Both Worlds, Part II." Named for the ship we called the* City of New Orleans.

New Paris colonies. Federation settlements stricken by a serious plague in 2267. The original *Starship Enterprise* was assigned to transport critically needed medical supplies to planet Makus III for transfer to New Paris. ("The *Galileo* Seven" [TOS]).

New Providence. The name of a Federation colony located on the planet Jouret IV. In 2366, all 900 colonists and the colony itself disappeared, leaving a huge crater in the ground. The loss of the colony was attributed to a **Borg** attack.

("The Best of Both Worlds, Part I" [TNG]).

New Seattle. A tropical city on **Penthara IV** that experienced freezing conditions when the planet's temperature dropped following the impact of a type-C asteroid on the planet in 2368. ("A Matter of Time" [TNG]).

New United Nations. SEE: United Nations, New.

Newson, Eddie. Twenty-first-century baseball player who played on the opposing team the day **Buck Bokai** of the **London Kings** broke **Joe Dimaggio**'s consecutive hitting streak. ("If Wishes Were Horses" [DS9]).

Newton, Isaac. (John Neville). (1643-1727). Considered to be one of the most important figures in Earth's development of science. Newton developed laws of motion and universal gravitation and invented calculus. Data programmed a holographic re-creation of Newton for a holodeck poker game with **Albert Einstein** and Professor **Stephen Hawking**. ("Descent, Part I" [TNG]).

• **"Next Phase, The."** *Next Generation* episode #124. Written by Ronald D. Moore. Directed by David Carson. Stardate 45892.4. *First aired in 1992. Geordi La Forge and Ro Laren are believed dead, but they have merely been made invisible by a new Romulan cloaking device.* SEE: **anyon emitter; Bajoran death chant; borhyas; Brossmer, Chief; chroniton particles; cloaking device, Romulan; Garadius system; graviton field generator; interphase generator; kolem; La Forge, Geordi; McDowell, Ensign; melakol; Mirok; molecular phase inverter; muon; Parem; Ro Laren; Romulan science vessel; subspace resonator; Varel.**

Ngame Nebula. An astronomical formation that the *Enterprise*-D passed en route to its mission on Evadne IV in 2367. The *Enterprise*-D sensors discovered the apparent presence of a class-M planet in a **T-tauri type star system** within the cloud. While investigating the planet, the *Enterprise*-D encountered a wormhole that rendered the crew unconscious for approximately thirty seconds. The class-M reading was later found to be erroneous. ("Clues" [TNG]). *The episode "Clues" dealt with the* Enterprise-*D's encounter with the pathologically reclusive* **Paxans**. *Since the Paxans were apparently successful in erasing or suppressing all records and memories of the contact, we assume that the existence of the Paxans remains a secret from the Federation.*

Niagara-class starship. Conjectural designation for a type of Federation ship. The **U.S.S. Wellington**, which underwent servicing at **Starbase 74** in 2364 and on which Ensign **Ro Laren** once served, was a *Niagara*-class starship.

nIb'poH. Klingon term that describes the feeling that an action or situation has occurred before, similar to the human term *deja vu*. ("Cause and Effect" [TNG]).

Nibor. (Peter Slutsker). A crew member of the Ferengi vessel *Krayton*, Nibor was present at the **Trade Agreements Conference** in 2366. He lost a **three-dimensional chess** game to Commander Riker during the closing reception of the conference, and later lost another game to Riker on board the *Krayton*. ("Ménage à Troi" [TNG]).

Nichols, Dr. (Alex Henteloff). Plant manager at **Plexicorp**, a 20th century company based in San Francisco, on Earth. Nichols developed the molecular matrix for transparent aluminum in 1986. (*Star Trek IV: The Voyage Home*).

"Night Bird." Musical jazz composition that features a trombone solo. Commander William Riker tried for ten years to master the performance of the piece, with only moderate success. ("Second Chances" [TNG]).

• **"Night Terrors."** *Next Generation* episode #91. Teleplay by Pamela Douglas and Jeri Taylor. Story by Sheri Goodhartz. Directed by Les Landau. Stardate 44631.2. *First aired in 1991. The* Enterprise-*D crew suffers severe sleep deprivation due to proximity with a interdimensional phenomenon called a Tyken's Rift.* SEE: **Balthus, Dr.; Brattain, U.S.S.; Brink; Bussard collectors; Corbin, Tom; "Eyes in the dark"; Gillespie, Chief; Hagen, Andrus; Kenicki; Lin, Ensign Peter; "One moon circles"; Peeples, Ensign; Rager, Ensign; REM sleep; Starbase 220; Tyken's Rift; Zaheva, Captain Chantal.**

Night-Blooming Throgni. A fragrant Klingon flower. Worf found the smell of a **Quazulu VIII** virus similar to the Throgni. ("Angel One" [TNG]).

"Nightingale Woman." Passionate love sonnet written by poet Phineas Tarbolde in 1996 on the Canopus Planet. After contact with the barrier at the edge of the galaxy, **Gary Mitchell** was able to quote this poem as an early example of his expanded mental powers. ("Where No Man Has Gone Before" [TOS]). *The poem was actually written by Gene Roddenberry as an aviator speaking to his beloved airplane.*

Nilrem. (Steven Anderson). A physician on planet **Malcor III** who was responsible for the treatment of William Riker, masquerading as a Malcorian named **Rivas Jakara**, at the **Sikla Medical Facility** in 2367. When Dr. Berel declined to endanger Riker's life at the request of Malcorian security, Nilrem replaced **Berel** as head of the facility. ("First Contact" [TNG]).

Nimbus III. A barely habitable class-M planet in the Neutral Zone. Dubbed the "planet of galactic peace", Nimbus III was the site of an experiment by the Romulan, Klingon, and Federation governments to bridge the gap between them by sponsoring a settlement there. The colony, established in 2268, was a dismal failure, although the settlement remained in place for at least two decades. The Vulcan fanatic **Sybok** began his quest for **Sha Ka Ree** there. (*Star Trek V: The Final Frontier*).

nisroh. Curved blade used on planet **Tilonus IV**. Given to Commander William Riker as part of his disguise while he visited Tilonus IV in 2369 to rescue a Federation research team. Before beaming down to Tilonus IV, Lieutenant Worf briefed Riker on his undercover mission, including the use of the *nisroh*, accidentally cutting Riker on the head. The pain and bleeding from the wound served as a focal point of reality for Riker in the delusional world created by the **neurosomatic technique**s he endured on Tilonus IV. ("Frame of Mind" [TNG]).

nitrium metal parasites. Spaceborne microscopic life-forms that ingest **nitrium**, converting it to a simple molecular gel. These life-forms normally live in nitrium-rich asteroids, such as those found in the **Pelloris Field** near planet **Tessen III**. The *Enterprise*-D was accidentally infested with nitrium metal parasites on stardate 45733 while destroying an asteroid that was on a collision course for Tessen III. Because nitrium is used extensively in starship construction, the parasites caused extensive damage to the *Enterprise*-D, nearly resulting in a warp core breach. ("Cost of Living" [TNG]).

nitrium. A metal alloy, used in the construction of Federation starships. Nitrium is used in the interior construction of such ship's systems as inertial damping field generators, food replication, power transfer conduits, and the matter/antimatter reaction chamber. ("Cost of Living" [TNG]).

nitrogen narcosis. Also known as "Rapture of the Deep", nitrogen narcosis was a hazard of 20th-century-Earth deep-sea diving. It was caused by the replacement of oxygen in oxyhemoglobin with nitrogen. The resultant anoxia produced disorientation, hallucinations, and lack of judgment in the victims. The phenomenon is similar to temporal narcosis. ("Timescape" [TNG]).

No'Mat. Klingon planet on which are located the lava caves where the Klingon **Rite of *MajQa*** is practiced. ("Birthright, Part I" [TNG]). As a child, **Worf** visited No'Mat, where he received a vision of the prophet **Kahless the Unforgettable**. Kahless told young Worf he would do something no other Klingon had done before. ("Rightful Heir" [TNG]).

"No-win scenario." SEE: ***Kobayashi Maru* scenario**.

Noel, Dr. Helen. (Marianne Hill). Member of the *U.S.S. Enterprise* medical staff with both psychiatric and penology experience. Noel accompanied Captain Kirk on an inspection visit to the **Tantalus V** penal colony. An attractive woman, Noel first met Kirk at the *Enterprise* science lab Christmas party, and evidently found the captain attractive as well. ("Dagger of the Mind" [TOS]).

Nog. (Aron Eisenberg). Nephew of **Quark** and son of **Rom**, who lived on **Deep Space 9** in 2369. The young Ferengi was

apprehended by Odo stealing from the assay office on Deep Space 9's **Promenade** in 2369. ("Emissary" [DS9]). Nog became good friends with young Jake Sisko on the station, and the two boys once created a fictitious company, the **Noh-Jay Consortium**, for their commercial exploits. ("Progress" [DS9]). When Nog's father, Rom, forbade Nog to attend school on the station, Jake taught him how to read. ("The Nagus" [DS9]). *Nog was first seen in "Emissary" (DS9).*

Nogura, Admiral. Starfleet commanding admiral, based in San Francisco, who reinstated James Kirk as captain of the *Enterprise* during the **V'Ger** crisis of 2271. (*Star Trek: The Motion Picture*).

Noh-Jay Consortium. Fictitious company name improvised by young **Nog** and **Jake Sisko** for their fledgling business ventures on Deep Space 9. On stardate 46844, the boys traded 5,000 wrappages of *yamok* sauce for **self-sealing stem bolts**, even though they had no idea what stem bolts were used for. They later traded the stem bolts for a parcel of land, sight unseen, on **Bajor**. Nog and Jake then sold the land to Quark for five bars of gold-pressed **latinum**. ("Progress" [DS9]).

Nol-Ennis. Group of individuals trapped in a war against their eternal enemies, the **Ennis**, on a lunar penal colony in the Gamma Quadrant. ("Battle Lines" [DS9]).

Nomad. (Voice by Vic Perrin). Early robotic interstellar probe launched from Earth in 2002 on a mission to search for new life-forms. Roughly cylindrical in shape, weighing 500 kilograms, and measuring about one meter in length, *Nomad* was created by brilliant Earth scientist **Jackson Roykirk**. Nomad was presumed destroyed in flight by a meteor collision. It was later learned that *Nomad* had in fact collided with an alien space probe called *Tan Ru*. In the aftermath of the accident, *Nomad* somehow repaired itself, merging its control programs with those of *Tan Ru*. The resulting combination of their benign programs became deadly. *Nomad's* new purpose was to seek out and sterilize what it deemed to be imperfect biological infestations. Nomad destroyed all living beings in the **Malurian system** in 2267, and shortly thereafter attacked the *U.S.S. Enterprise*. The deadly probe destroyed itself when it realized it was imperfect, having confused *Enterprise* captain James Kirk

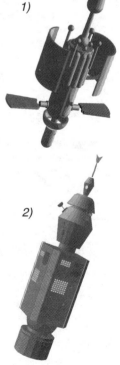
1)
2)

with its creator, Jackson Roykirk. ("The Changeling" [TOS]). *The episode suggested that Nomad was Earth's first probe out of our solar system, but in actual fact,* Pioneer 10 *was the first craft to reach interstellar space. Illustrations: 1) Original design of Nomad as launched from Earth. 2) Nomad as encounterd in 2267.*

Nona. (Nancy Kovack). *Kahn-ut-tu* woman among the **hill people** on **Tyree**'s planet, and ambitious wife of tribal leader Tyree. Using her special knowledge as a *Kahn-ut-tu*, Nona cured James Kirk of a deadly **mugato** wound, then cast a spell that rendered him unable him to resist her wishes. Upon learning Kirk's true identity as a starship captain possessing advanced weapons, Nona stole Kirk's hand phaser, hoping to use it as a stepping-stone to power. Nona was instead killed by a mob of village people who viewed her as a spy. ("A Private Little War" [TOS]).

noncorporeal life. Literally, without body. Refers to a wide number of life-forms that exist as complex patterns of energy, plasma, or gas, without any tangible physical form. Noncorporeal life-forms have included the **Thasians** ("Charlie X" [TOS]), **Trelane** ("The Squire of Gothos" [TOS]), the **Organians** ("Errand of Mercy" [TOS]), **Redjac** (also known as Jack the Ripper, Beratis, Kesla, and Mister Hengist) ("Wolf in the Fold" [TOS]), the **Gorgan** of **Triacus** ("And the Children Shall Lead" [TOS]), the **Medusans** ("Is There in Truth No Beauty?" [TOS]), the **Zetarians** ("The Lights of Zetar" [TOS]), **Troi, Ian Andrew** ("The Child" [TNG]), the **Koinonians** ("The Bonding" [TNG]), and the transformed **Zalkonians** ("Transfigurations" [TNG]). SEE: **cloud creatures**.

noninterference directive. See: **Prime Directive**.

Noor. (Megan Cole). Head of the **J'naii** government in 2368. Noor sentenced **Soren** to undergo **psychotectic** therapy to cure Soren's aberrant sexual behavior. ("The Outcast" [TNG]).

noranium alloy. A metal of little salvage value, a large quantity of this which was found in the **Gatherer** camp on **Gamma Hromi II**. An *Enterprise*-D away team vaporized a large pile of noranium to provide a smoke screen for their escape. ("The Vengeance Factor" [TNG]).

norep. Medication, a derivative of norepinephrine. Dr. Beverly Crusher ordered norep administered to **Natasha Yar** in an unsuccessful attempt to revive her after she had been attacked by **Armus**. ("Skin of Evil" [TNG]).

Norkan outposts. Site of a bloody massacre conducted under the command of Romulan admiral **Alidar Jarok**. Although the Federation described the incident as a "massacre," Jarok noted that Romulans considered it to be a successful "campaign," and that one world's butcher might be another world's hero. ("The Defector" [TNG]).

Norkova. Vessel that transported a shipment of **deuridium** from the Gamma Quadrant to Deep Space 9 in 2369. SEE: **Rao Vantika**. ("The Passenger" [DS9]).

Norman. (Richard Tatro). The central locus of the android society on the planet informally known as **Mudd**. Norman and his fellow androids were originally from the Andromeda Galaxy, but were stranded in this galaxy when their homeworld's sun went nova, killing their **Makers**. In 2267, Norman conspired with **Harry Mudd** to capture the *Starship Enterprise* and its crew. The *Enterprise* crew was able to escape from the androids by the skillful use of illogic, which caused the highly logical androids to overload. ("I, Mudd" [TOS]).

Norpin Colony. Retirement community on planet Norpin V where **Montgomery Scott** had hoped to take up residence in 2294 before he was sidetracked by the crash of the *U.S.S. Jenolen*. ("Relics" [TNG]).

Nova Squadron. A team of elite cadet pilots at **Starfleet Academy**. The squadron was composed of five members who flew small single-pilot ships in aerobatic maneuvers. In 2368, Nova Squadron won the Rigel Cup, a source of considerable pride to all involved. A short time later, on stardate 45703, Nova Squadron was involved in a collision that destroyed all five craft and resulted in the death of squadron member **Joshua Albert**. ("The First Duty" [TNG]). SEE: **Kolvoord Starburst; Locarno, Cadet First Class Nicholas.**

Novakovich. Wesley Crusher's instructor in anthropology at Starfleet Academy in 2368. ("The Game" [TNG]).

• **"Nth Degree, The."** *Next Generation* episode #93. Written by Joe Menosky. Directed by Rob Legato. Stardate 44704.2. *First aired in 1991. Contact with an alien space probe gives Reginald Barclay an incredible intelligence boost.* SEE: **Anaya, Ensign April; Argus Array; Barclay, Reginald; Brower, Ensign; Crusher, Dr. Beverly;** *Cyrano de Bergerac*; **Cytherians; Einstein, Albert; iconic display console; Larson, Lieutenant Linda; ODN bypass; passive high-resolution series; positron emission test; Science Station 402; sero-amino readout; Shuttle 05; subspace field distortions.**

Nu'Daq. (John Cotran). Commander of the Klingon attack cruiser *Maht-H'a* that participated in the discovery of a four-billion-year-old genetically encoded message from an ancient humanoid species. ("The Chase" [TNG]). SEE: **Galen, Professor Richard; humanoid life**.

nucleonic beam. Low-level energy transmission projected by a probe from the planet **Kataan**. The beam penetrated the *Enterprise*-D shields, rendering Captain Jean-Luc Picard unconscious, and in the span of 25 minutes transmitted a lifetime of experiences into Picard's mind. ("The Inner Light" [TNG]).

nucleosynthesis. Alteration of matter at the atomic level. Under certain conditions, **invidium** contamination can trigger spontaneous nucleosynthesis in silicon molecules like those used in glassware. ("Hollow Pursuits" [TNG]).

null space. An extremely rare "pocket" in space created during the formation of a star. The phenomenon is created by turbulent regions of magnetic and gravitational fields which coalesce into an area that absorbs all electromagnetic energy that enters it. Energy outside the null space is bent around it, making it invisible to sensors and the naked eye. Long thought to be strictly theoretical, a pocket of null space was discovered near the **J'naii** planet in 2368 when the shuttle *Taris Murn* was lost. ("The Outcast" [TNG]).

nullifier core. Major component of the propulsion system on a **Romulan Warbird**. The nullifier cores must be maintained in precise alignment to avoid magnetic disruptions that can be detected when the ship is cloaked. ("Face of the Enemy" [TNG]). SEE: **artificial quantum singularity**.

Number One. (M. Leigh Hudec, aka Majel Barrett Roddenberry). Executive officer holding the rank of lieutenant, and second-in-command of the original *Starship Enterprise* under the command of Captain Pike. ("The Cage," "The Menagerie, Parts I and II" [TOS]).

Number One was a cool, mysterious woman whose name was never given, although she was intended as a regular character in Roddenberry's original version of Star Trek. Number One is apparently a common nickname given by starship captains to their second-in-command, since Captain Picard gave the same moniker to Commander **William T. Riker**. *SEE:* **Flores, Marissa**.

The character of Number One was dropped from the original Star Trek series at the insistence of the network on the grounds that television audiences were not yet ready to accept the idea of a woman second-in-command of a starship. It was not until 1986, when Madge Sinclair was cast as the captain of the ill-fated **U.S.S.** **Saratoga** *in Star Trek IV, that the decision was reversed.*

Majel Barrett also played Nurse Chapel in the original Star Trek series and Lwaxana Troi in Star Trek: The Next Generation. Barrett also lent her voice to the Enterprise computer in both series.

Nuria. (Kathryn Leigh Scott). A leader of a proto-Vulcan tribe on planet **Mintaka III** at the time a Federation anthropological team accidentally revealed themselves to the Mintakans in 2366. The technologically primitive Mintakans interpreted the scientists' advanced Federation technology as evidence of a supernatural presence. Attempting to appeal to her logical nature, Captain Picard brought Nuria on board the *Enterprise*-D (in violation of the Prime Directive) to convince her that he was not a god. ("Who Watches the Watchers?" [TNG]).

N'Vek, Subcommander. (Scott MacDonald). Romulan officer and member of the underground supporting Romulan/Vulcan reunification. In 2369, N'Vek was a key operative in an elaborate plot to enable the defection of **Vice-Proconsul M'ret** to the Federation. N'Vek arranged for the abduction of *Enterprise*-D officer Deanna Troi from Borka VI, then had her surgically altered into Romulan form. N'Vek then coerced Troi to assume the identity of **Major Rakal**, a member of the elite **Tal Shiar** intelligence service. Using Troi as Rakal, N'Vek commandeered the Romulan Warbird *Khazara*, arranging for stasis containers with M'ret and two aides to be transported into Federation hands. N'Vek was killed while enabling Troi's return to the *Enterprise*-D after the operation was complete. ("Face of the Enemy" [TNG]).

O'Brien, Keiko. (Rosalind Chao). Starfleet botanist, formerly assigned to the *Enterprise*-D, later reassigned to Deep Space 9. Born Keiko Ishikawa, she married fellow crew member **Miles O'Brien** in 2367. Their wedding, held aboard the *Enterprise*-D in the Ten-Forward Lounge, was a mixture of Japanese and Irish traditions. ("Data's Day" [TNG]). Keiko gave birth to a girl, Molly O'Brien, a year later. Molly was born in Ten-Forward during a ship-wide systems failure. ("Disaster" [TNG]). Keiko was briefly reduced to a child after passing through an energy field in 2369. ("Rascals" [TNG]). *(Young Keiko was played by Caroline Junko King.)* Keiko accepted a transfer to station **Deep Space 9** in 2369 when her husband was assigned there as chief of operations. Keiko was appalled at the living accommodations on the station, but remained there for the sake of her husband's career. ("Emissary" [DS9]). Keiko found adapting to life on the station difficult. She was dissatisfied by the lack of professional opportunities for a botanist on the station, and was concerned about the lack of educational facilities for her daughter. Keiko was able to address this last issue when Commander Sisko granted her permission to establish a **schoolroom** on the station. ("A Man Alone" [DS9]). Keiko and her husband visited Earth in 2369 for her mother's 100th birthday. ("Dax" [DS9]). As a child, Keiko helped her grandmother with her Japanese brush painting. It had been the young Keiko's special task to fill the old chipped cup that her grandmother, whom she called **Obachan**, used to clean the brush. ("Violations" [TNG]). *The words Picard spoke in the O'Brien wedding ceremony are almost identical to the ceremony performed by Captain Kirk in "Balance of Terror" (TOS), a deliberate homage by episode writer Ronald Moore. Keiko's first appearance was in "Data's Day" (TNG).*

O'Brien, Michael. The father of Starfleet officer **Miles Edward O'Brien**. Miles and Keiko considered naming their first child after Michael, if it was a boy. ("Disaster" [TNG]).

O'Brien, Miles. (Colm Meany). Starfleet engineer, chief of operations at station Deep Space 9. ("Emissary" [DS9]). Prior to being assigned to Deep Space 9 in 2369, O'Brien had been operating transporters for some 22 years, the last six of which were spent on the *Enterprise*-D. ("Realm of Fear" [TNG]).

Early in his Starfleet career, O'Brien had been the tactical officer aboard the *U.S.S. Rutledge* under the command of Captain Benjamin Maxwell. Aboard the *Rutledge*, O'Brien participated in the rescue of the survivors of the bloody **Cardassian** massacre at **Setlik III**. The

experience scarred O'Brien deeply, and he continued to harbor bitterness against the Cardassians for many years. ("The Wounded" [TNG]). O'Brien was deathly afraid of spiders, until an incident where he had to crawl through a Jefferies tube past twenty **Talarian hook spiders** to perform a critical repair at Zayra IV. After that considerable act of courage, O'Brien said he wasn't quite so fearful of arachnids, and even kept a **Lycosa tarantula** named Christina as a pet. ("Realm of Fear" [TNG]). O'Brien once dislocated his left shoulder while kayaking on the holodeck. O'Brien was healed, almost miraculously, by a touch from the **Zalkonian** named **John Doe**. ("Transfigurations" [TNG]).

O'Brien married **Keiko Ishikawa** on stardate 44390 in a ceremony in the Ten-Forward lounge aboard the *Enterprise*-D. Captain Jean-Luc Picard presided at the ceremony, and Data (who had first introduced Miles and Keiko to each other) served as Father of the Bride. ("Data's Day" [TNG]). O'Brien became a father a year later when Molly O'Brien was born. ("Disaster" [TNG]).

O'Brien was promoted and assigned chief of operations on station **Deep Space 9** in 2369, and moved there with his wife and daughter. O'Brien's technical expertise and skill at improvisation proved valuable, given the station's generally poor condition and the lack of technical resources at the distant post. ("Emissary" [DS9]). Besides engineer, husband, and father, O'Brien briefly served as a substitute school-teacher when his wife visited her mother on Earth. ("The Nagus" [DS9]). O'Brien's off-duty pastimes also included music, and he was seen playing the cello in a string quartet in Ten-Forward aboard the *Enterprise*-D on at least one occasion. ("The Ensigns of Command" [TNG]). *O'Brien was first seen as the battle bridge conn officer in "Encounter at Farpoint" (TNG), but it was many episodes until he got a last name. He did not get a first and middle name, Miles Edward, until "Family" (TNG).*

O'Brien, Molly. (Hanna Hatae). Daughter of Starfleet officers Miles O'Brien and Keiko O'Brien. Molly was born aboard the *Enterprise*-D in 2368. ("Disaster" [TNG]). *Baby Molly was born during "Disaster" (TNG), but didn't get a name until "The Game" (TNG). She was also seen as an infant in "Power Play" (TNG). Played by Hanna Hatae, Molly was first seen in "A Man Alone" (DS9). Molly was named for Molly Berman, daughter of* Star Trek *executive producer Rick Berman and for former* Next Generation *staffer Molly Rennie.*

O'Connel, Steve. (Caesar Belli). One of the surviving children of the **Starnes Expedition** whose parents committed suicide on planet **Triacus** in 2268. In the aftermath of the tragedy, young O'Connel was controlled by the **Gorgan**. ("And the Children Shall Lead" [TOS]). *Caesar Belli is the son of Melvin Belli, who played the Gorgan.*

O'Neil, Lieutenant. (Sean Morgan). *Enterprise* crew member who beamed down to planet **Beta III** in 2267 to investigate the disappearance of the starship **Archon**. He was captured by the planet's inhabitants, brainwashed, and absorbed into the society's culture by the machine entity **Landru**. ("Return of the Archons" [TOS]).

O'Neill, Ensign. *Enterprise* landing party member who participated in the search for **Shuttlecraft Galileo** when it crashed on planet **Taurus II** in 2267. O'Neill was killed by the humanoid creatures on that planet. ("The *Galileo* Seven" [TOS]).

Oath of celibacy. A pledge required of Starfleet personnel who are native to planet **Delta IV** to assure they will not take advantage of other, sexually immature humanoid species. (*Star Trek: The Motion Picture*).

Oath, Klingon. Klingon ritual of marriage, solemnizing the bond between husband and wife in the Klingon culture. **Worf** and **K'Ehleyr** almost took the oath after they spent a night together on the *Enterprise*-D holodeck in 2365, but neither felt ready for such a commitment at that time, even though they had just concieved a child together. ("The Emissary" [TNG]).

Obachan. Japanese term of endearment used for older women, such as grandmothers. **Keiko O'Brien** called her grandmother Obachan. ("Violations" [TNG]).

Obelisk. A powerful asteroid-deflector-beam generator built on the surface of **Miramanee's planet** centuries ago by the **Preservers**. The device was necessary because the otherwise habitable planet was located in a dangerous asteroid belt. The deflector, built in the  shape of a towering monolith known to **Miramanee**'s people as the Obelisk, was inscribed with symbols that formed a tonal alphabet, giving instructions on the operation of the deflector. The knowledge of the Obelisk's operation was kept by the inhabitants' medicine man, but one such medicine man failed to pass the secrets to his son, leaving the planet defenseless by the year 2268. ("The Paradise Syndrome" [TOS]).

Oberth-class starship. Small Federation starship type frequently used for scientific missions. The class was named for 20th-century German rocket pioneer Hermann Oberth. *Oberth*-class ships have included the **Grissom** (*Star Trek III*), **Vico** ("Hero  Worship" [TNG]), and **Tsiolkovsky** ("The Naked Now" [TNG]). *The first* Oberth-*class ship seen was the* U.S.S. Grissom *in* Star Trek III. *There presumably was a* U.S.S. Oberth *after which the class was named.*

observation lounge. Conference room located on Deck 1 on *Galaxy*-class starships, directly behind the Main Bridge. The observation lounge features a large conference table and chairs, two large viewers, and several large windows that provide a dramatic vista of space. Also known as the conference lounge.

• **"Obsession."** Original Series episode #47. Written by Art Wallace. Directed by Ralph Senensky. Stardate 3619.2. *First aired in 1967. Kirk is determined to destroy a vampire cloud creature that years ago killed 200 people on his first Starfleet assignment, deaths Kirk felt he could have prevented.* SEE: **antigrav; cordrazine; Cygnian Respiratory Diseases, A Survey of; dikironium cloud creature; dikironium; Farragut, U.S.S.; Garrovick, Captain; Garrovick, Ensign; Kirk, James T.; Rizzo, Ensign; Theta VII; Tycho IV; Yorktown, U.S.S.**

Oceanus IV. Federation planet. The *Enterprise*-D was assigned to a diplomatic mission at Oceanus IV following its assignment at the **Phoenix Cluster** in 2368. ("The Game" [TNG]).

Ocett, Gul. (Linda Thorsen). Commander of a Cardassian *Galor*-class warship that participated in the discovery of a four-billion-year—old genetically encoded message from an ancient humanoid species. ("The Chase" [TNG]). SEE: **Galen, Professor Richard; humanoid life**.

Odan, Ambassador. (Franc Luz). A highly respected Federation ambassador and mediator. Odan was instrumental in negotiating a peace treaty between the two moons of planet **Peliar Zel** in 2337. In 2367, Odan was again asked to mediate a dispute between the **Alpha** and **Beta Moon**s, but was injured while en route to the conference, scheduled to be held aboard the *Enterprise*-D.

It was not generally known that Odan was a **Trill**, a member of a joined species. The **symbiont** known as Odan was relatively unharmed, but the humanoid host was fatally injured. Commander William Riker volunteered to serve as a temporary host for the symbiot long enough for the ambassador to mediate the peace talks. Following the negotiations, the Odan was successfully transferred into a new host body and returned to her homeworld on a Trill vessel. During the mission, Odan became romantically involved with **Beverly Crusher**. ("The Host" [TNG]). *Nicole Orth-Pallavicini played Odan's new host.*

Ode to Psyche. One of the six great odes written in 1819 by the English poet John Keats (1795-1821). Deanna Troi gave William Riker an old hardbound copy of this book. She inscribed it, "To Will, all my love, Deanna." ("Conundrum" [TNG]).

"Ode to Spot." Poem written by Commander Data about his cat. ("Schisms" [TNG], "A Fistful of Datas" [TNG]).

Odell, Brenna. (Rosalyn Landor). Daughter of **Bringloidi** leader **Danilo Odell**. A beautiful but practical woman, Brenna was the real leader of her people. She was attracted to Riker, but eventually settled on one of **Wilson Granger**'s clones. ("Up the Long Ladder" [TNG]).

Odell, Danilo. (Barrie Ingham). Leader of the colonists on planet **Bringloid V**. A proud Irish descendent, Odell seemed as concerned with insuring that his daughter, **Brenna Odell**, found a suitable husband as with the safety of the colony. ("Up the Long Ladder" [TNG]).

Odin, S.S. Federation freighter craft, registry number NGL-12535, disabled near planet **Angel One** in 2357 by an asteroid collision. Three **escape pod**s from this ship drifted for five months before landing on planet Angel One. ("Angel One" [TNG]).

ODN bypass. A rerouting of the optical data network aboard a Federation starship. *Enterprise*-D engineers attempted to use an ODN bypass to overcome the loss of computer control when Lieutenant **Reginald Barclay** took over the ship's computer in 2367. ("The Nth Degree" [TNG]).

ODN. Acronym for optical data network. A system of fiberoptic data-transmission conduits used aboard Federation starships, serving as the nervous system of the ship's computer network. A similar network was used in the old **Cardassian** mining station, **Deep Space 9**, although it was nowhere near as reliable as the better-maintained equipment in use aboard Federation ships. ("Emissary" [DS9]).

Odo. (Rene Auberjonois). Security chief aboard **Deep Space 9** during the **Cardassian** ownership of the station, as well as later when the Starfleet took over the facility in 2369. Odo was a shape-shifter who was found as an infant in the **Denorios Belt**, but it was not known where his species originated, nor had he ever encountered another being of his kind. ("Emissary" [DS9]).

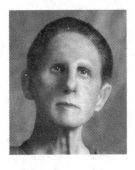

Odo maintained a humanoid form while at work on the station, but he had to return to his natural form, a viscous orange fluid, every 16 hours. ("The Storyteller" [DS9]). He didn't need to eat and only had an approximation of a mouth and digestive system ("The Forsaken" [DS9]) and had no sense of smell ("If Wishes Were Horses" [DS9]). He patterned his own hairstyle after the scientist assigned to study him at the research center on planet **Bajor**. Being the only one of his kind, he attempted to fit into society by being "the life of the party." He'd turn himself into any object requested by the partygoers, which only increased his feelings of isolation and loneliness. ("The Forsaken" [DS9]). He did not even know how to gamble. ("Babel" [DS9]). Odo never took a mate, claiming that he would not to want to make the compromises that a relationship would demand. Odo also had an uncompromising view of law enforcement, believing that "laws change, but justice is justice." ("A Man Alone" [DS9]).

Odo nevertheless yearned to learn of his origins, and hoped to someday meet another individual of his species. When Crodin of the planet **Rakhar** gave him a shape-shifting necklace, Odo allowed himself to hope that he might find other shape-shifters in the Gamma Quadrant. ("Vortex" [DS9]).

Odo did let his guard down slightly with Ambassador **Lwaxana Troi** in 2369 when the two were trapped together in a turbolift on the station. In their different ways, both Odo and Troi were loners, and their enforced proximity caused them to share each other's vulnerabilities. ("The Forsaken" [DS9]). *Rene Auberjonois had previously played Colonel West in* Star Trek VI: The Undiscovered Country. *Odo first appeared in "Emissary" (DS9).*

Odona. (Sharon Acker). Daughter of Prime Minister **Hodin** of planet **Gideon**. In 2268, Odona volunteered to sacrifice her life by contracting deadly **Vegan choriomeningitis** so that her death might serve as an inspiration to others on her planet in their fight against overpopulation. While carrying out her assignment, Odona was cured of choriomeningitis by Dr. Leonard McCoy. She nevertheless chose to remain on her world to help solve its problems, despite the fact that she had fallen in love with Captain James Kirk. ("The Mark of Gideon" [TOS])

Off-Zel, Mark. Noted artist from Sirrie IV, now deceased. One of Off-Zel's vases was owned by 24th-century collector **Kivas Fajo**. ("The Most Toys" [TNG]).

Offenhouse, Ralph. (Peter Mark Richman). Human from late-20th-century Earth who died at age 55 of advanced cancer. Offenhouse had been a financier, and found it difficult to cope in the largely moneyless society of the Federation. Offenhouse had his body cryogenically frozen upon his death, and he was revived in 2364 aboard the *Enterprise*-D. Offenhouse returned to Earth on the *Starship* **Charleston**. ("The Neutral Zone" [TNG]). SEE: **cryonics; cryosatellite.**

Officer Exchange Program. A cultural exchange program in which members of the **Klingon Defense Force** and officers of the Federation **Starfleet** (and others including the Benzites) were permitted to serve aboard ships of each other's fleets in an effort to promote intercultural understanding. In 2365, as part of this program, Riker became the first Starfleet officer to serve aboard a Klingon warship. ("A Matter of Honor" [TNG]). Klingon officer **Kurn** served aboard the *Enterprise*-D in another exchange a year later, although it was later learned that Kurn had specifically requested the *Enterprise* posting because his brother, Worf, was aboard that ship. ("Sins of the Father" [TNG]). In 2367, Klingon exobiologist **J'Ddan** also served on the *Enterprise*-D through this program. ("The Drumhead" [TNG]).

• **"Offspring, The."** *Next Generation* episode #64. Written by Rene Echevarria. Directed by Jonathan Frakes. Stardate 43657.0. *First aired in 1990. Data decides to become a parent and builds an android daughter. This was the first episode directed by actor Jonathan Frakes.* SEE: **Andorians; android; Ballard, Lieutenant; Data; Daystrom Institute of Technology; Galor IV; Haftel, Admiral; Lal; Otar II; positronic brain; Selebi Asteroid Belt; Soong-type an-**

droid; submicron matrix transfer technology.

Ogawa, Nurse Alyssa. (Patti Yasutake). Member of the *Enterprise*-D medical staff. ("Future Imperfect" [TNG], "Clues" [TNG], "Identity Crisis" [TNG], "The Host" [TNG], "The Game" [TNG], "Ethics" [TNG], "Cause and Effect" [TNG], "The Inner Light" [TNG], "Man of the People" [TNG], "Realm of Fear" [TNG], and "True-Q" [TNG]). Ogawa dated one of her fellow *Enterprise*-D crew members. She said she liked him, but wasn't at all sure if she would accept his invitation to visit **Risa** with him. ("Imaginary Friend" [TNG]). *Ogawa was first seen in "Future Imperfect" (TNG), got a first name in "Clues" (TNG), and a last name in "Identity Crisis" (TNG).*

Ogus II. The *Enterprise*-D was enjoying a two-day liberty on this Federation planet in early 2367 when a medical emergency required an immediate departure to Starbase 416. ("Brothers" [TNG]).

Ohniaka III. Location of a Federation science station in a nonstrategic sector. The outpost was staffed by 274 Starfleet personnel. In 2369, this outpost was attacked and all personnel were lost. The attack was later discovered to be the work of a previously unknown group of self-aware, fanatical **Borg**, controlled by a figure known as "**The One.**" ("Descent, Part I" [TNG]).

Oji. (Pamala Segall). A teenaged **Mintakan** female, Oji was **Liko**'s daughter. She was in charge of taking the measurements on the sundial, and had just been appointed the official record keeper in 2366 when a Federation anthropological team was studying her planet. ("Who Watches the Watchers?" [TNG]).

OK Corral. Location of the historical gunfight in 1881 between a gang led by **Ike Clanton** and lawmen led by **Wyatt Earp** outside the Western town of **Tombstone, Arizona,** on Earth. In 2368, the **Melkotians** created a replica of the OK Corral and the famous battle between the Earps and the Clantons as a means of execution for members of the *Enterprise* crew. ("Spectre of the Gun" [TOS]).

Okona, Thadiun. (William O. Campbell). Captain of the small interplanetary cargo vessel *Erstwhile*. A loner, distrustful of authority, Okona was nonetheless a romantic at heart. He gained notoriety as intermediary between **Benzan** of planet **Straleb** and **Yanar** of planet **Altec** when the two were secretly seeing each other prior to their marriage in 2365. ("The Outrageous Okona" [TNG]).

Old Ones. Leaders of **Korob** and **Sylvia**'s homeworld in another galaxy. ("Catspaw" [TOS]).

Old Ones. Long-dead civilization on planet **Exo III.** The Old Ones had moved underground a half-million years ago when

their planet's sun began to fade. In the dark underground, their culture began to become more mechanized and less human. Eventually, the Old Ones began to fear the sophisticated **androids** their ancestors had built to serve them. When the Old Ones attempted to deactivate their servants, the androids turned on their masters, destroying them. ("What Are Little Girls Made Of?" [TOS]).

Omag's girls. (Shana O'Brien, Heather Long). Two beautiful female companions of the Ferengi arms merchant **Omag** at Qualor II in 2368. ("Unification, Part II" [TNG]).

Omag. (Bill Bastiani). Ferengi arms merchant who sometimes dealt in illicit merchandise, and helped Romulan forces to obtain spacecraft parts stolen from the Starfleet surplus depot at **Qualor II** in 2368. ("Unification, Part II" [TNG]).

Omaha Air Base. United States Air Force military facility on Earth during the 20th century. **Omaha Air Base** radar systems detected the *Starship Enterprise* in Earth's upper atmosphere in July 1969, when the ship was accidentally propelled back into Earth's past. A fighter aircraft dispatched from the base photographed the starship, necessitating a covert landing party to recover the film to eliminate evidence of the ship's presence in the past. ("Tomorrow Is Yesterday" [TOS]). SEE: **air police sergeant; Fellini, Colonel; Christopher, Captain John.**

• **"Omega Glory, The."** *Original Series* episode #54. Written by Gene Roddenberry. Directed by Vincent McEveety. No stardate given. *First broadcast in 1968. The* Enterprise *encounters a planet where survivors of a terrible bacteriological holocaust worship the American flag. This episode was originally written in 1965 as one of three possibilities for the original* Star Trek *series' second pilot, along with "Mudd's Women" (TOS) and "Where No Man Has Gone Before" (TOS).* SEE: **Cloud William;** *Exeter, U.S.S.*; **fireboxes; Galloway, Lieutenant; Kohms; Leslie, Mr.; Omega IV; Prime Directive; Tracey, Captain Ronald; United States Constitution; Vulcan mind-meld; Wu; Yangs.**

Omega IV. Class-M planet whose humanoid inhabitants fought a terrible bacteriological war many centuries ago. Omega IV was visited in 2268 by the *Starship **Exeter***, commanded by **Captain Ronald Tracey**. The remaining bacterial agents in the planet's atmosphere killed all of the *Exeter*'s crew except for Tracey. ("The Omega Glory" [TOS]). SEE: **Kohms; Yangs**.

Omega Sagitta system. Solar system that includes the twin planets **Altec** and **Straleb**. The two planets form the **Coalition of Madena.** ("The Outrageous Okona" [TNG]).

Omicron Ceti III. Beautiful class-M planet bombarded by deadly Berthold radiation, rendering it unsuitable for humanoid habitation. In 2264, prior to the discovery of **Berthold rays**, Omicron Ceti III was colonized by an agricultural expedition led by **Elias Sandoval**. Approximately 100 of the original 150 colonists died from Berthold ray exposure. The *Starship Enterprise* visited the colony site in 2267, finding that about 50 colonists had survived due to protection offered by alien spores found on the planet. ("This Side of Paradise" [TOS]). SEE: **Kalomi, Leila; Spores, Omicron Ceti III**.

Omicron Delta region. Area of space where the **amusement park planet** was located, visited by the original *Starship Enterprise* in 2267. ("Shore Leave" [TOS]).

Omicron IV. Planet that nearly destroyed itself in a nuclear arms race that escalated to the launching of orbital nuclear weapons platforms, much as Earth did in the late 1960s. Gary Seven said this behavior almost destroyed all life on Omicron IV and would do the same on Earth unless something was done to stop the arms race. ("Assignment: Earth" [TOS]). *Fortunately, Star Trek's warning of nuclear weapons in Earth orbit has not yet been fulfilled.*

Omicron Theta. Location of a Federation science and farming colony devastated in 2336 by the mysterious **Crystalline Entity**. The colony was the site of a hidden laboratory at which Dr. **Noonien Soong** conducted advanced work in robotics, including the creation of the androids **Data** and **Lore**. Just prior to the destruction of the colony, memories from all the colonists were stored in Data's positronic brain. Soong apparently escaped from the colony shortly thereafter. The crew of the *Starship Tripoli* discovered the android Data in 2338 at the remains of the colony. A second expedition in 2364 by an away team from the *Enterprise*-D (including Data) discovered the second android, Lore, at the site. ("Datalore" [TNG]).

"One moon circles." A telepathic message sent to Counselor Troi by an alien vessel trapped with the *Enterprise*-D in a **Tyken's Rift**. The message described atomic hydrogen and the aliens' need for hydrogen to produce an explosion to rupture the rift so that both ships could escape. ("Night Terrors" [TNG]).

• **"11001001."** *Next Generation* episode #16. Written by Maurice Hurley and Robert Lewin. Directed by Paul Lynch. Stardate 41365.9. *First aired in 1988. A group of Bynars hijack the* Enterprise-D *in hopes of using the ship's computer to restart their planetary computer system. This is the first episode in which we see Data's hobby of painting and Riker's love of the trombone.* SEE: **antimatter containment; autodestruct; Beta Magellan; buffer; Bynars; Bynaus; cybernetic regeneration; Epstein, Dr. Terence;** *Galaxy* **Class Starship Development Project; holodeck; Low Note, The;** *Melbourne, U.S.S.;* **Minuet; painting; Parrises Squares; Pelleus V; Quinteros; Commander Orfil; Riker, William T.; Starbase 74; Tarsas III;** *Trieste, U.S.S.;* **trombone;** *Wellington, U.S.S.;* **zylo eggs.**

"One, The." Title taken by the android **Lore** in 2369, following his takeover of a group of rogue **Borg**. ("Descent, Part I" [TNG]).

One. Philosophy that rejected the advances of modern technological society in favor of a simpler life. The renegade scientist **Dr. Sevrin** and his followers embraced this philosophy in their search for the mythical planet Eden in 2268. ("The Way to Eden" [TOS]).

Onias Sector. Region of space located near the **Romulan Neutral Zone**. The *Enterprise*-D conducted a security survey there in 2367. ("Future Imperfect" [TNG]). SEE: **Barash**.

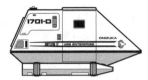

Onizuka, **Shuttlepod.** Shuttlepod #07, attached to the *Starship Enterprise*-D. Data piloted the *Onizuka* to planet **Tau Cygna V** when it was necessary to evacuate the colony there. ("The Ensigns of Command" [TNG]). Geordi La Forge flew the *Onizuka* from the *Enterprise*-D to planet **Risa** for an artificial-intelligence seminar in 2367. It was later revealed that La Forge and the *Onizuka* were abducted in midflight, then returned to the *Enterprise*-D with La Forge under Romulan mental control. ("The Mind's Eye" [TNG]). *The* Onizuka *was named for Challenger astronaut Ellison Onizuka. The shuttle was sometimes seen in other episodes, sitting in the shuttlebay. The* Onizuka *was shuttlepod 07, although in its first appearance it had the number 05, left over from the prop's first appearance as the* **El Baz***.*

onkian. Unit of temperature measure used by the **Romulan Star Empire**. A reading of 12 onkians corresponds to a cold (but not freezing) temperature. ("The Defector" [TNG]).

onlies. Slang on **Miri**'s planet for the children who survived the disastrous results of the **Life Prolongation Project**, the "only" ones who remained. ("Miri" [TOS]). *Several of the children portraying the onlies were children of members of the production team and included the children of Grace Lee Whitney, William Shatner, and Gene Roddenberry.*

oo-mox. Ferengi sexual foreplay, involving a gentle massaging of the ears, considered one of their most erogenous zones. **Lwaxana Troi** was very skilled at this art. ("Ménage à Troi" [TNG]). Archaeologist and entrepreneur **Vash** gave Quark oo-mox at Deep Space 9 in 2369 when negotiating what percentage he would receive from the auction of the relics brought back from the Gamma Quadrant. Quark claimed he was not distracted by the treatment. ("Q-Less" [DS9]).

Opaka, Kai. (Camille Saviola). Spiritual and political leader of the **Bajoran** people. In 2369, **Deep Space 9** commander **Benjamin Sisko** turned to her in hopes that she could help unite the many contentious factions that threatened to bring civil war to **Bajor**. ("Emissary" [DS9]). Compelled by the **Prophets**, Opaka visited Deep Space 9 later that year, and prevailed upon Sisko to allow her to travel through the **Bajoran wormhole** and visit the Gamma Quadrant. On that trip,

Opaka was killed when the runabout *Yangtzee Kiang*, carrying Opaka, Sisko, and Kira Nerys, crashed on a moon in the Gamma Quadrant. She was brought back to life by unusual artificial microbes on that moon. Unfortunately, the nature of the microbes keeping her alive made it impossible for her to leave that world. Opaka accepted this as a sign that the Prophets wanted her to remain there to help bring peace to the warring prisoners incarcerated on that moon. ("Battle Lines" [DS9]). Following the disappearance of Opaka from the Bajoran religious community, an intense power struggle ensued to determine who would ascend to be the next Kai. ("In the Hands of the Prophets" [DS9]). SEE: **Bareil, Vedek; Neela; Winn, Vedek**.

Operation Retrieve. Code name for a proposed military strike operation advocated by Starfleet Command to recover Kirk and McCoy, when they were wrongly imprisoned by the Klingon government for the murder of **Chancellor Gorkon** in 2293. The Federation Council President decided not to authorize Operation Retrieve when Chancellor **Azetbur** offered to continue her late father's peace initiative in exchange for a pledge of no military action to rescue Kirk and McCoy. (*Star Trek VI: The Undiscovered Country*). *The scene in which* **Admiral Cartwright** *and* **Colonel West** *propose Operation Retrieve to the Federation Council President was deleted from the theatrical release of* Star Trek VI, *but was restored for the videocassette and laser disk version.*

Operations Center. Also known as Ops. Command facility for station **Deep Space 9** where the various functions of the station were coordinated. Ops was located in the uppermost section of the station's central core. In keeping with **Cardassian** architecture, the prefect's office is at the highest level, allowing the commander to look down upon the crew working in Ops. ("Emissary" [DS9]).

operations manager. On recent Federation starships, the operations manager, usually known as Ops, is the officer responsible for coordination of the various departmental functions aboard the ship. Ops is one of two freestanding consoles located directly ahead of the captain's chair in most bridge designs. Lieutenant Commander **Data** was the operations manager on the *Starship Enterprise*-D.

• **"Operation— Annihilate!"** Original Series episode #29. Written by Steven W. Carabatsos. Directed by Herschel Daugherty. Stardate 3287.2. *First aired in 1967. Kirk finds his brother and sister-in-law are victims of neural parasites causing planetwide insanity. This was the last episode of the original series' first season.* SEE: **Beta Portolan system; Devena; Denevan neural parasite; Denevan ship; *Enter-***

***prise, U.S.S.*; GSK 739; Ingraham B; inner eyelid; K-3 indicator; Kirk, Aurelan; Kirk, George Samuel; Kirk, James T.; Kirk, Peter; Levinius V; Scott, Montgomery; Spock; Starbase 10; Theta Cygni XII; tri-magnesite; ultraviolet satellite; Vulcans.**

ophidian. Snake-like alien utilized by the life-forms of **Devidia II** to travel in time. When irradiated with the proper energy, the ophidian made it possible for the **Devidians** to travel through time. ("Time's Arrow, Parts I and II" [TNG]).

Ophiucus III. Class-M planet, **Harry Mudd**'s attempted destination for delivery of three beautiful woman he had recruited as wives for settlers in 2266. ("Mudd's Women" [TOS]).

Ops. Abbreviation for **operations manager**.aboard Federation starships, also the nickname for the **Operations Center** aboard station **Deep Space 9**. ("Emissary" [DS9]).

opti-cable. Fiber-optic data-transmission cable used aboard Federation starships, part of their **ODN**, optical data network. ("Peak Performance" [TNG]).

optical transducer. Component of Geordi La Forge's VISOR, the transducer received electromagnetic radiation from the environment and translated it into bioelectric impulses that could be interpreted by his brain. Following an injury by a phaser blast in 2369, Dr. Crusher adjusted the transducer to block some of the pain receptors in Geordi's brain. ("Starship Mine" [TNG]).

Oracle. Sophisticated computer constructed by the creators of the *Yonada* asteroid/ship that acted as a religious edifice, guiding the **Fabrini** people through the journey to their promised land. ("For the World Is Hollow and I Have Touched the Sky" [TOS]). SEE: **Natira**.

Orb. Also known as **Tears of the Prophet**, the Orbs were mystical artifacts of the **Bajoran** religion. Nine Orbs, which were hourglass-shaped energy vortices, were discovered in the Bajoran star system over the past 10,000 years. The Bajoran believed the orbs were sent by the Prophets from the Celestial Temple to teach them and guide their lives. All but one of the Orbs  were stolen by the **Cardassians** when they ended their occupation of Bajor in 2369. The remaining Orb planted visions in the mind of **Benjamin Sisko** that enabled him to relive experiences from his past. The Orbs were enshrined in ornately jeweled cases and had been cared for by Bajoran monks at a monastery on the planet. ("Emissary" [DS9]).

Ordek Nebula. The home of the Wogneer creatures. ("Allegiance" [TNG]).

Orelious IX. Planet destroyed in 2266 during the final conflict, a millennium ago between the **Promellians** and the **Menthars**. Although neither side expected this battle to be decisive, the devastation was so great that both cultures were utterly destroyed and the planet was reduced to rubble. In 2366, in the asteroid field remains of the planet, the *Enterprise*-D discovered the hulk of the Promellian battle cruiser **Cleponji**, along with several hundred thousand deadly **aceton assimilators.** ("Booby Trap" [TNG]).

Organia. The only class-M planet in a zone disputed by the Federation and the Klingon Empire in 2267. Organia was ideally located for usage by either side as a strategic base. Its inhabitants, the **Organians**, appeared as simple humanoid race in an agrarian culture, but in reality were highly evolved **noncorporeal life**-forms. ("Errand of Mercy" [TOS]).

Organian Peace Treaty. Imposed by the **Organians** in 2267 after the incident on planet **Organia** between the **United Federation of Planets** and the **Klingon Empire**. The Organian Peace Treaty decreed that the Organians would tolerate no hostilities between the Klingons and the Federation. ("Errand of Mercy"[TOS], "Day of the Dove" [TOS]). The treaty provided that any planet disputed between the two powers would be awarded to the side that demonstrated it could develop that planet most efficiently. There was also a provision allowing for starship crews from either side to use shore facilities (such as space stations) of the other. ("The Trouble with Tribbles" [TOS]).

Organians. Inhabitants of planet **Organia** who appeared to be simple primitive people with absolutely no advancement in tens of thousands of years. In reality the Organians were highly advanced **noncorporeal life**-forms who developed beyond the need for physical bodies millions of

years ago. When Klingon forces sought to occupy Organia in 2267 for the planet's strategic value, the Organians rejected both the Klingons and the Federation, asserting they had no interest in their dispute. Following a declaration of war by the two antagonists, the Organians imposed the **Organian Peace Treaty** to prevent hostilities. ("Errand of Mercy" [TOS]). SEE: **Ayelborne**.

Orinoco, U.S.S. Starfleet *Danube*-class **runabout**, registry number NCC-72905, one of three runabouts assigned to station **Deep Space 9**. ("The Siege" [DS9]). *The* Orinoco *replaced the* Yangtzee Kiang, *which crashed in "Battle Lines" (DS9).*

Orion animal women. Sensual, seductive, and green-skinned, these humanoid females were a commodity of trade in the seamier parts of the galaxy during the 23rd century. Christopher Pike saw **Vina** as an illusory Orion slave woman while both were under control of the **Talosians** in 2254. ("The Cage," "The Menagerie, Part II" [TOS]). Marta, the insane consort of Captain Garth, was apparently of this species as

well ("Whom Gods Destroy" [TOS]). *Actor Majel Barrett was painted green for the initial makeup tests for this blatantly sexist character. Ironically, Barrett would also play the progressive part of Number One, second-in-command of the* Enterprise *in "The Cage" (TOS). Photo: Vina as an Orion animal woman.*

Orion wing-slug. Ambassador **Lwaxana Troi** said she would rather eat Orion wing-slugs than deal with **DaiMon Tog**. ("Ménage à Troi" [TNG]).

Orion. Constellation near Taurus containing the stars Rigel and Betelgeuse. ("Journey to Babel" [TOS]). SEE: **Orions**.

Orions. Humanoid race that attempted to sabotage the **Babel Conference** of 2267. An Orion vessel fired on the *Enterprise*, which was transporting delegates to the Babel conference. At the time, Orion smugglers had been raiding the **Coridan** system and stealing **dilithium** crystals to sell on the black market. Their attack was intended to prevent Coridan's admission to the Federation. ("Journey to Babel" [TOS]). SEE: **Thelev**.

Orn Lote. (John P. Connolly). Engineering specialist on planet **Tagra IV** who contacted the *Enterprise*-D in 2369. ("True-Q" [TNG]).

Ornara. The third planet in the **Delos** star system, home to an intelligent humanoid species, the **Ornarans**. ("Symbiosis" [TNG]).

Ornarans. Humanoid species native to planet Ornara. The Ornarans had suffered from a deadly plague two centuries ago, a plague that was cured with the medication **felicium** from the planet **Brekka**.

Unfortunately, felicium was later found to have powerfully addictive narcotic effects, with the result that all Ornarans had become addicted to the drug. The people of Brekka exploited the situation, selling felicium to the Ornarans, while concealing from them the fact that the drug was no longer needed to control the plague.

Generations of drug addiction resulted in loss of intelligence and technical knowledge, so by the year 2364, the Ornarans no longer had the ability to maintain the interplanetary freighters they needed to transport felicium from Brekka to Ornara. The Ornarans, along with the Brekkians, requested Federation assistance in repairing their remaining ships, but *Enterprise*-D captain Picard declined to render aid, citing Prime Directive considerations. ("Symbiosis" [TNG]).

ornithology. Branch of zoology that deals with the study of birds, an apparent interest of **Commander Calvin Hutchinson**. ("Starship Mine" [TNG]).

Orra, Jil. (Heather L. Olson). Daughter of **Gul Madred**. Madred allowed young Jil Orra into the interrogation room where Picard was being tortured. ("Chain of Command, Part II" [TNG]).

Orta. (Jeffrey Hayenga). Leader of a splinter group of Bajoran terrorists. Orta's hatred of the **Cardassians** ran deep. It began with an incident in which he was captured by the Cardassians, tortured, and his vocal cords severed. He was later forced to communicate by means of a voice synthesizer embedded in his neck. In 2368, Orta was suspected of being behind an attack on a Federation colony, but it was later learned that the Cardassians were responsible. ("Ensign Ro" [TNG]).

Orton, Mr. (Glenn Morshower). Station administrator of **Arkaria Base**. In 2369, Orton, a native of Arkaira, collaborated with a group of politically nonaligned terrorists to steal **trilithium resin** from the *Enterprise*-D at the **Remmler Array.** ("Starship Mine" [TNG]).

oskoid. A leaflike Betazoid delicacy, a favorite of **Lwaxana Troi**. ("Ménage à Troi" [TNG], "Half a Life" [TNG]).

Otar II. Location of a starbase. Destination of the *Enterprise*-D following the death of Data's daughter, **Lal**, in 2366. ("The Offspring" [TNG])

Otto. Genetically engineered male, follower of former Earth dictator **Khan Noonien Singh**. Otto, along with Khan and other genetic "supermen," escaped Earth in the sleeper ship *S.S. Botany Bay*. ("Space Seed"[TOS]).

oumriel. In the **Halii** language, the word for a special friend. **Aquiel Uhnari** called Geordi *oumriel*. ("Aquiel" [TNG]).

• **"Outcast, The."** *Next Generation* episode #117. Written by Jeri Taylor. Directed by Robert Scheerer. Stardate 45614.6. *First aired in 1992. On a planet of androgynous humanoids where gender orientation is a crime, Riker falls in love with one who dares to call herself female.* SEE: **dexalin; Federation Day; J'naii; Krite;** *Magellan, Shuttlecraft*; **millicochrane; Noor; null space; phaser type-4; Phelan system; psychotectic therapy; Soren;** *Taris Murn*; **United Federation of Planets.**

Outpost 23. A Federation outpost along the **Romulan Neutral Zone**. In 2367, it was the key outpost in Starfleet's defenses along the border. During a fantasy created for Riker's benefit by **Barash** on **Alpha Onias III**, Outpost 23 was supposedly no longer of strategic importance and was slated to be the site of final peace negotiations between the Federation and the Romulan Star Empire, an apparent ruse to reveal the location of the outpost. ("Future Imperfect" [TNG]).

Outpost Seran-T-One. The **dilithium crystal chamber** for the *Enterprise*-D was designed there on stardate 40052. ("Booby Trap" [TNG]).

Outpost Sierra VI. A Federation station that detected the presence of a **Romulan scoutship** piloted by **Alidar Jarok** in the Neutral Zone in 2366. ("The Defector" [TNG]).

• **"Outrageous Okona, The."** *Next Generation* episode #30. Teleplay by Burton Armus. Story by Les Menchen & Lance Dickson and David Landsberg. Directed by Robert Becker. Stardate 42402.7. *First aired in 1988. The irascible Captain Okona drags the* Enterprise-D *into a love-war relationship between two planets.* SEE: **Altec; Benzan; Comic, The; Data, Lieutenant Commander; Debin; Erstwhile; Giddings, Lieutenant Dianna; Glob fly; Kushell; Legation of Unity; Madena, Coalition of; Okona, Thadiun; Omega Sagitta System; Riga, Stano; Robinson, B. G.; Straleb security ship; Straleb; Thesia, Jewel of; Yanar.**

"Overseer, the." In the religious belief system of planet **Mintaka III**, the Overseer was a supernatural being that possessed supreme power. The Overseer was supposed to be able to appear and disapper at will, and to raise the dead. When a Federation science team accidentally revealed its advanced technology to the Mintakans in 2366, the Mintakans logically interpreted these apparent "miracles" as evidence that *Enterprise*-D captain Jean-Luc Picard was their Overseer. Picard chose to violate the Prime Directive in order to convince them that this was not true. ("Who Watches the Watchers?" [TNG]).

Owon eggs. A delicacy obtained by Riker at Starbase 73, served up as an omelet cooked by Riker on a makeshift stove in his quarters. Judging from the reactions of Geordi and Pulaski, Riker's cooking left something to be desired, although Worf seemed to enjoy the dish. ("Time Squared" [TNG]).

Oxmyx, Bela. (Anthony Caruso). Boss of the largest territory on planet **Sigma Iotia II**. In 2268, Oxmyx tried to convince Kirk to supply his men with firearms so that he could take over the planet from the other leaders. Kirk negotiated an arrangement that ended the planet's territorial wars, in which Oxmyx would lead the planetary government, but with provisions that would  enable the Federation to guide his regime into a more ethical form of government. ("A Piece of the Action" [TOS]). SEE: **Book, the.**

Ozaba. (Davis Roberts). Scientist stationed on planet **Minara II** in 2268 who was killed by the **Vians** while studying the impending nova of the **Minaran star system**. ("The Empath" [TOS]).

ozone. Naturally occurring chemical compound formed of three oxygen atoms. Gaseous ozone collects in the upper atmosphere of some class-M planets, shielding the surface from hazardous ultraviolet solar radiation. Destruction of the ozone layer can therefore result in significant harm to such a planet's surface dwelling life-forms. The cloaking shield used by the inhabitants of planet **Aldea** caused damage to that planet's ozone layer, eventually resulting in infertility of the Aldeans. ("When the Bough Breaks" [TNG]).

Pacifica. Beautiful ocean world, known for warm blue waters and fine white beaches. Pacifica was headed by **Governor Delaplane**. The *Enterprise*-D was en route to a scientific mission there in 2364 when Captain **Walker Keel** requested a covert meeting with Captain Picard to discuss Keel's suspicions of a conspiracy to infiltrate Starfleet. ("Conspiracy" [TNG]). An interstellar conference was held there in 2365. Among the participants was Betazoid ambassador **Lwaxana Troi**. Troi was instrumental in uncovering an **Antidean** plot to blow up the conference when she discovered that the delegates from planet **Antide III** were in fact assassins. ("Manhunt" [TNG]).

padd. Acronym for personal access display device. Small handheld information unit used by Starfleet personnel aboard Federation starships. *At the time* Star Trek: The Next Generation*'s padd was designed in 1987, it seemed fairly futuristic, but as this entry is written, devices like Apple Computer's Newton personal digital assistant, that do virtually everything a padd can theoretically do, are already being marketed as consumer products. An electronic clipboard was also used by the* Enterprise *crew in the original series, which might also have been a padd device, athough it was never referred to as such. 1) Original Series electronic clipboard. 2) Next Generation padd.*

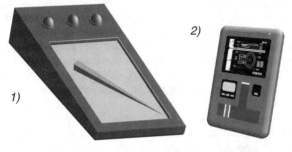

1)
2)

Pagh, I.K.C. Klingon *K'Vort*-class Bird-of-Prey spacecraft commanded by **Captain Kargan**. Starfleet officer William Riker briefly served as first officer aboard this ship in 2365 as part of an officer exchange program. During Riker's service aboard the *Pagh*, an incident with Starfleet was narrowly averted when *Enterprise*-D personnel helped identify and repair damage from a previously undiscovered subatomic life form that was damaging the hull of the *Pagh*. ("A Matter of Honor" [TNG]).

pagh. In the **Bajoran** religion, a person's life-force, from which one gains strength and courage. Bajorans believe their *pagh,* or life-force, is replenished by the prophets who reside in the **Celestial Temple**. ("Emissary" [DS9]).

pahtk. A Klingon insult. ("The Defector" [TNG], "Sins of the Father" [TNG], "Reunion" [TNG]).

painstik, Klingon. Electronic "cattle prod" used as part of the Klingon **Age of Ascension** ritual. The use of the painstik is significant because enduring physical suffering is considered a Klingon spiritual test. O'Brien recalled that he saw a painstik used on a two-ton **Rectyne monopod**, and that the creature jumped five meters before dying of excessive cephalic pressures. ("The Icarus Factor" [TNG]). Painstiks were also used in the *Sonchi* ceremony. ("Reunion" [TNG]).

Painter, Mr. (Dick Scotter). Navigator aboard the *U.S.S. Enterprise* during the mission to investigate the fate of colonists on planet **Omicron Ceti III** in 2267. ("This Side of Paradise" [TOS]).

painting. Art form enjoyed by the android **Data** aboard the *Enterprise*-D. Geordi La Forge taught Data how to paint, commenting on the irony of a blind man teaching an android about a visual art. Although Data's initial efforts at painting were relatively mechanistic because he was concentrating on the techniques of painting, he eventually gained an awareness of the artistry involved as he became more comfortable with his own humanity. ("11001001" [TNG]). A painting class was offered aboard the *Enterprise*-D in 2366. Captain Picard was one of the students, although his initial efforts may have been discouraged by Data's unintentionally harsh criticism. ("A Matter of Perspective" [TNG]). *The paintings by Picard and the other students in the class were done by Elaine Sokoloff.* When Data began to experience dreams in 2369, he used painting as a means to explore those inner visions. Data painted a multitude of images, including his creator, Dr. Soong, as well as himself as a bird. ("Birthright, Part I" [TNG]). *Data's paintings were actually done by scenic artists Jim Magdaleno, Alan Kobayashi, and Mike Okuda. Additional designs were contributed by Wendy Drapanas and Rick Sternbach.*

Pakled captain. (Christopher Collins). Commanding officer of the **Pakled** ship *Mondor*. Although this individual gave the impression of possessing limited intelligence, he was later found to be both intelligent and devious. ("Samaritan Snare" [TNG]). *The captain was given the name Grebnedlog in the script, but this name was never spoken in the actual completed episode.*

Pakleds. Species of characteristically heavyset but technologically advanced humanoids. Although initial contact with the *Enterprise*-D in 2365 suggested the Pakleds to have limited intellectual capacities, this was found to be untrue and the Pakleds further demonstrated considerable cunning in attempting to capture *Enterprise*-D engineer Geordi La Forge. ("Samaritan Snare" [TNG]).

Palamas, Lieutenant Carolyn. (Leslie Parrish). *Enterprise* archaeology and anthropology officer on a landing party to planet **Pollux IV** that encountered the entity **Apollo** in 2267. The humanoid Apollo found Palamas attractive, and Palamas found Apollo fascinating on both a professional and personal level. Realizing that Apollo intended to enslave the *Enterprise* crew, Palamas spurned his advances. Apollo eventually

released the ship and vanished into oblivion. ("Who Mourns for Adonais?" [TOS]). *An early draft script for the episode would have ended with a scene in which McCoy discovers that Palamas was pregnant with Apollo's child.*

Palmer, Dr. (Tim Trella). Federation scientist injured in the failure of the "duck blind" enclosure on planet **Mintaka III**. Rendered unconscious by his injuries, Dr. Palmer was captured and held by the Mintakans in the hopes that it would please their deity. ("Who Watches the Watchers?" [TNG]).

Palmer, Lieutenant. (Elizabeth Rogers). Relief communications officer aboard the *Starship Enterprise* under the command of James Kirk. ("The Doomsday Machine" [TOS], "The Way to Eden" [TOS]).

Palmer, Lieutenant. (Dr. Mae Jemison). *Enterprise*-D crew member who was assigned to transporter duty during an away team mission to **Nervala IV**. ("Second Chances" [TNG]). *Shuttle astronaut Dr. Mae Jemison has the distinction of being the first African-American woman in space.*

Paloris Colony. Location where a **Harodian miner** aboard *Enterprise*-D was absolutely certain he had met the empathic metamorph, **Kamala**. ("The Perfect Mate" [TNG]).

papalla juice. A beverage recommended for children by Guinan. Be sure to order it with extra bubbles. ("Imaginary Friend" [TNG]).

Paqu. Bajoran village embattled in a border dispute with their neighbors the **Navot** in 2369. ("The Storyteller" [DS9]). SEE: **Glyrhond, Varis Sul.**

Par Lenor. (Max Grodenchik). Emissary from the **Ferengi Trade Mission**. Par Lenor and his assistant, **Qol**, deliberately sabotaged their shuttle in order to be "rescued" by the *Enterprise*-D on stardate 45761. Once aboard the starship, Lenor hoped to negotiate an exclusive trade agreement with Kriosian **ambassador Briam**, who was also aboard the *Enterprise*-D. Lenor discovered that Briam was accompanying an **empathic metamorph** named **Kamala**, and tried to bribe Briam into selling her. When Briam refused, a struggle ensued, and Briam was injured. ("The Perfect Mate" [TNG]). *Max Grodenchik also played Rom in* Star Trek: Deep Space Nine.

Paradise City. Main settlement of the unsuccessful colony on planet **Nimbus III**. With the failure of the colony, Paradise City became an interstellar wilderness town of rogues and others on the edge of the law. (*Star Trek V: The Final Frontier*).

• **"Paradise Syndrome, The."** Original Series episode #58. Written by Margaret Armen. Directed by Jud Taylor. Stardate 4842.6. *First aired in 1968. Kirk loses his memory on a peaceful planet inhabited by descendants of American Indians from Earth.* SEE: **Goro; Joining Day; Kirk, James T.; Kirok; Lumo; Miramanee; Miramanee's planet; Obelisk; Preservers; ritual cloak; Salish; Tahiti Syndrome; Wise Ones.**

Parallax Colony. Society of "free spirits" on planet **Shiralea VI**. The colony was populated by a number of fanciful humanoids who pursed a life of pleasure. These colorful characters included a juggler, an argumentative humanoid couple, a poet, and a Wind Dancer, who served as colony sentry, assuring that "only those whose hearts are joyous" could enter.

Lwaxana Troi introduced young Alexander Rozhenko to a holodeck simulation of the Parallax Colony in 2368. Alexander seemed to enjoy the "Laughing Hour," while Lwaxana wanted to visit the colony's famous mudbaths. Alexander tolerated the mudbaths, but Worf could not fathom their attraction. ("Cost of Living" [TNG]).

paralysis field. Weapon that the **Kelvans** used against the *U.S.S. Enterprise* crew to gain control of the starship in 2268. The weapon blocked nerve impulses to the voluntary muscles. ("By Any Other Name" [TOS]).

Pardek, Senator. (Malachi Throne). Romulan senator who represented the **Krocton Segment** of **Romulus**. Pardek was among the delegates at the **Khitomer** conference in 2293 and later served as a member of the Romulan Senate for 90 years.

Pardek was considered a "man of the people," something of a radical, having sponsored many governmental reforms and pursued the cause of peace within the Empire throughout his career. Pardek worked to bring Ambassador **Spock** to Romulus in 2368 to support an underground movement seeking to reunite the Romulans with their Vulcan cousins.

Pardek eventually betrayed Spock, as well as Captain Picard and Commander Data, to the Romulan authorities, in exchange for favors granted to him by **Proconsul Neral**. ("Unification, Parts I and II" [TNG]). *Malachi Throne had played* **Commodore José Mendez** *in "The Menagerie, Parts I and II" (TOS). He also provided the voice of the* **Talosian** *magistrate in the original, unaired version of the pilot episode "The Cage" (TOS), produced in 1964.*

Parem. (Brian Cousins). Romulan officer who was accidentally "phased" by an experimental Romulan **interphase generator** in 2368. Parem made his way aboard the *Enterprise*-D and threatened both Geordi La Forge and Ro Laren, who had also been "phased" in the accident. Parem was killed when, during a struggle between the three officers, he was forced through the "normal" ship's bulkhead and out into space. ("The Next Phase" [TNG]).

paricium. Ceramic substance that was one of the components making up the **Kataan probe**. ("The Inner Light" [TNG]).

Paris. Ancient city in France on Earth in which is located the office of the President of the Federation Council. (*Star Trek VI: The Undiscovered Country*). Near the president's office is an outdoor cafe where Jean-Luc Picard once broke a date with the future Mrs. Jenice Manheim, although the two later recreated the rendezvous in a holodeck simulation of the *Cafe des Artistes*. ("We'll Always Have Paris" [TNG]). *The Paris city skyline backdrop from "We'll Always Have Paris" (TNG) was reused in* Star Trek VI.

Parliament. Politically neutral planet used by the Federation as a site for diplomatic negotiations. A conference held there in 2364 with the antagonistic **Selay** and **Antican** delegates considered the question of both races' admission to the Federation. ("Lonely Among Us" [TNG]).

Parmen. (Liam Sullivan). Philosopher-king and leader of the **Platonian** society who attempted to abduct Dr. Leonard McCoy in 2268. Parmen maintained his control over Platonian society through his telekinetic powers. ("Plato's Stepchildren" [TOS]). SEE: **Philana**.

Parrises Squares. An athletic game involving competition between two teams of four players. A team of *Enterprise*-D personnel was challenged to a game of Parrises Squares by a team at **Starbase 74** when the ship was docked there for a computer systems upgrade. ("11001001" [TNG]).

Parrot's Claw, The. Novel in the **Dixon Hill** series of detective stories published on Earth in the 1940s. The story involves a character named Jimmy Cuzzo, who killed a man named Marty O'Fallon. ("Manhunt" [TNG]).

parthas à la Yuta. An **Acamarian** meal prepared from spiced parthas, a green vegetable with fleshy roots. **Yuta**, an aide to Acamarian Sovereign **Marouk**, made this dish, which Riker dubbed parthas à la Yuta. ("The Vengeance Factor" [TNG]).

parthenogenic implant. An artificial device, surgically implanted into a human body. **Jean-Luc Picard** had a parthenogenic implant, a bionic heart, that replaced his natural heart after he was stabbed as a young Academy graduate in 2327. ("Samaritan Snare" [TNG]).

particle fountain. Experimental mining technique developed by **Dr. Farallon** at planet Tyrus VIIA in 2369. A powerful vertical forcefield was established between a point on a planet's surface and a field-generator in a space station orbiting the planet. The fountain malfunctioned during testing. ("The Quality of Life" [TNG]).

particle stream. An energetic by-product of the *Enterprise*-D warp drive. Geordi La Forge considered using a particle stream to attempt to sweep a holodeck clean when Dr. Katherine Pulaski was trapped in an ongoing simulation program, but the plan was abandoned when it was realized

that the energetic particles would also kill Pulaski. ("Elementary, Dear Data" [TNG]).

Parvenium Sector. Region of Federation space where the *Enterprise*-D conducted a magnetic wave study in late 2368. The study had just been completed when the *Enterprise*-D encountered the **Kataan probe**. ("The Inner Light" [TNG]).

• **"Passenger, The."** *Deep Space Nine* episode #9. Teleplay by Morgan Gendel and Robert Hewitt Wolfe & Michael Piller. Story by Morgan Gendel. Directed by Paul Lynch. No stardate given. *First aired in 1993. A renegade scientist places his consciousness into Dr. Bashir in order to steal a valuable substance needed to prolong his life.* SEE: **alpha wave inducer; antigrav; deuridium; DNA reference scan; Durg; energy containment cell; glial cells; Kajada, Ty; Kobliad; microscopic generator;** *Norkova;* **Primmin, Lieutenant George; raktajino; retinal imaging scan;** *Reyab;* **Rigel VII;** *Rio Grande, U.S.S.;* **shield generator; subspace shunt; synaptic pattern displacement; Vantika, Rao.**

passive high-resolution series. Sequence of sensor scans conducted by Commander La Forge and Lieutenant Barclay on a **Cytherian** probe found near the **Argus Array** in 2367. The test was unable to uncover any information about the probe. ("The Nth Degree" [TNG]).

• **"Past Prologue."** *Deep Space Nine* episode #4. Written by Kathryn Powers. Directed by Winrich Kolbe. No stardate given. *First aired in 1993. A Bajoran terrorist attempts to destroy the wormhole.* SEE: **Aldara; B'Etor; Bajor VIII; bilitrium; Danar, Gul; Duras;** *Ganges, U.S.S.;* **Garak; Haru Outpost; isolinear rods; joranian; Kira Nerys; Kohn-ma; Kraus IV; latinum; Lursa; Rollman, Admiral; Tahna Los; Tarkalean tea;** *Yangtzee Kiang, U.S.S.*

pasta al fiorella. One of Geordi's favorite dishes. ("Birthright, Part I" [TNG]).

Patahk. (Steve Rankin). Romulan survivor of the scoutship *Pi* that crashed on planet **Galorndon Core** in 2366. Patahk was severly injured in the crash, and was brought on board the *Enterprise*-D for medical treatment. Patahk died for lack of a compatible **ribosome infusion**. Although suitable ribosomes were available from Worf, the Klingon declined to make a donation to what he viewed as an enemy of his people, and Patahk himself insisted he would not accept such a donation from Worf. Romulan officials maintained that the intrusion of Patahk's ship into Federation space was accidental. ("The Enemy" [TNG]). *The character was referred to as Patahk in the script, but the name was not spoken in the episode.*

Patches. Calico cat, pet to young **Jeremy Aster** when he lived with his parents on Earth. ("The Bonding" [TNG]).

pattern buffer. Component of a transporter in which a transport subject's image is briefly stored so that transmission frequency can be adjusted to compensate for the Doppler effect caused by any relative motion between the transport chamber and the target. Because of the criticality of this subsystem, two buffers must be operated in synchronization with each other so that in case of failure of one unit, the beam can be immediately handed off to the backup. Since 2319, pattern buffers have been multiplexed to avoid **transporter psychosis**. In 2369, **quasi-energy microbes** were discovered in the Igo Sector that were capable of living within a pattern buffer's **matter stream**. ("Realm of Fear" [TNG]). Montgomery Scott modified the pattern buffers of the *U.S.S. Jenolen* in an attempt to keep himself and **Matt Franklin** suspended in the beam until help arrived. The attempt was partially successful: Scott survived for 75 years, but Franklin's pattern degraded beyond retrieval. ("Relics" [TNG]).

pattern enhancer. Devices used by Starfleet transporter systems to amplify a transporter signal, thereby making personnel transport safer during relatively hazardous situations, as when beaming through electrical storms. Transporter Chief O'Brien utilized a pattern enhancer to expedite a transporter rescue of an away team stranded on the moon of **Mab-Bu VI** on stardate 45571.

Three pattern enhancers are generally used, deployed in a triangular formation, amplifying the signal lock on any object contained within the triangle. ("Power Play" [TNG]). *Pattern enhancers were first used in "Power Play" (TNG) and were also seen in other episodes, including "Ship in a Bottle" (TNG) and "Frame of Mind" (TNG).*

• **"Patterns of Force."** Original Series episode #52. Written by John Meredyth Lucas. Directed by Vincent McEveety. No stardate given. *First aired in 1968. The* Enterprise *investigates a planet where a sociologist's experiment has gone awry, leaving the world with a government patterned after Nazi Germany.* SEE: **Abrom; Daras; Ekos; Ekosians; Eneg; Gill, John; Isak; Melakon; Prime Directive; rubindium crystal; subcutaneous transponder; Zeon.**

Pauley, Ensign. Starfleet crew member who returned from the Gamma Quadrant in the disabled runabout *U.S.S. Ganges* with Dax and archaeologist **Vash**. ("Q-Less" [DS9]).

Paulson Nebula. Astronomical cloud located in the vicinity of Zeta Alpha II. The Paulson Nebula was rich in transuranics, dilithium hydroxyls, and other elements. The *Enterprise*-D took advantage of this to hide from the sensors of the **Borg** ship in 2366. ("The Best of Both Worlds, Part I" [TNG]).

Pavlick, Ensign. (Jana Marie Hupp). An *Enterprise*-D engineering technician. Pavlick was on duty during the ship's mission to the Alpha Omicron system and helped **Dr. Leah Brahms** access holodeck files on the engine modifications Commander La Forge had made to the *Enterprise*-D. ("Galaxy's Child" [TNG]). *Ensign Pavlick also let Dr. Brahms look at Geordi's programs with a holographic simulation of Brahms herself, but we understand Geordi didn't hold it against her.*

Paxans. Race of xenophobic isolationists that remains unknown to the Federation. Able to manipulate energy on many levels, the Paxans existed on a terraformed protoplanet in the **Ngame Nebula**. The Paxans protected their planet by means of an energy field that appeared to be an unstable wormhole. Passage through the field put unsuspecting starship crews into a state of biochemical stasis, so such ships could be towed out of Paxan space without the crew's knowledge. *The* Enterprise-D *encountered the Paxans in 2367, but all records of and memories of the contact were erased, so no* Enterprise-D *personnel (except Data) retained any memory of the incident.* ("Clues" [TNG]).

PCS. "Pulaski's Chicken Soup." Part of *Enterprise*-D medical officer **Katherine Pulaski**'s treatment for the flu virus. ("The Icarus Factor" [TNG]).

• **"Peak Performance."** *Next Generation* episode #47. Written by David Kemper. Directed by Robert Scheerer. Stardate 42923.4. *First aired in 1989. Riker commands a starship in a wargame against* Enterprise-D *captain Picard.* SEE: **Avidyne engines; battle simulation, Starfleet; Bractor; Braslota system; Burke, Lieutenant; Grenthemen water hopper;** *Hathaway, U.S.S.***; Kolrami, Sirna;** *Kreechta***; Kumeh maneuver; laser pulse system; opti-cable;** *Potemkin, U.S.S.***; Riker, William T.; sensors; strategema; Tholians; Worf; Zakdorn.**

Peddler, Minosian. (Vincent Schiavelli). A holographic humanoid image, preprogrammed to interactively serve as a salesperson for **Minosian** weapons systems. An effective and convincing pitchman, the peddler and the computer systems that generated his image were left over from ancient times when the Minosians were notorious arms dealers. ("The Arsenal of Freedom" [TNG]). *Vincent Schiavelli also played one of the evil Red Lectroids from* The Adventures of Buckaroo Banzai.

Peeples, Ensign. (Craig Hurley). *Enterprise*-D crew member, assigned to Engineering. Peeples was one of the first of the *Enterprise*-D crew to suffer hallucinations as a result of his dream-deprived state when the ship was trapped in a **Tyken's Rift** in 2367. ("Night Terrors" [TNG]).

Peers, Selin. (Richard Lineback). **Trill** who was sent by his government to be present at Deep Space 9 during **Jadzia Dax**'s extradition hearing in 2369, attempting to return her to planet **Klaestron IV**. He testified at the hearing as an expert on Trills. ("Dax" [DS9]). SEE: **Dax, Curzon.**

Pegos Minor. Star system where **Dr. Paul Manheim** claimed his laboratory was located when he called for help after a serious accident in 2364. Upon arriving at Pegos Minor, Manheim, obsessed with security, informed the *Enterprise*-D that he was actually at **Vandor IX**. ("We'll Always Have Paris" [TNG]).

Peliar Zel. Class-M Federation planet with two inhabited moons. The planet was populated by a humanoid race characterized by a midline nasal outgrowth. The moons of Peliar Zel were colonized five centuries ago, and the governments of **Alpha Moon** and **Beta Moon** were historically at odds with one another. By 2337, Federation **Ambassador Odan** was called in to mediate a major dispute. Some thirty years later, relations between the moons had again deteriorated to the point of war when Alpha Moon developed an energy source that caused substantial environmental damage to Beta Moon. ("The Host" [TNG]). SEE: **magnetospheric energy taps.**

Pelleus V. Planet at which the *Enterprise*-D was scheduled to arrive shortly after a layover at **Starbase 74** in 2364. ("11001001" [TNG]).

Pelloris Field. Asteroid belt that was the source of an asteroid that collided with planet **Tessen III** in 2368. Asteroids in the Pelloris Field were rich in **nitrium**, which served as a food source for **nitrium metal parasites** that lived there. A colony of these parasites infested the *Enterprise*-D in 2368, after which ship's personnel successfully returned the parasites to the Pelloris Field. ("Cost of Living" [TNG]).

• **"Pen Pals."** *Next Generation* episode #41. Teleplay by Melinda M. Snodgrass. Story by Hannah Louise Shearer. Directed by Winrich Kolbe. Stardate 42695.3. *First aired in 1989.* Data inadvertently breaks the Prime Directive by exchanging subspace messages with a little girl on a distant planet, then comes to her rescue when he learns that her planet is endangered. SEE: **Alans; Benev Selec; Crusher, Wesley; Davies, Ensign; Drema IV; Elanian singer stone; Hildebrandt; ico-spectogram; Illium 629; Picard, Jean-Luc; Planetary Geosciences Laboratory; Prixus; resonators; Sarjenka; Sark, Klingon; Selcundi Drema Sector; Selcundi Drema; zabathu, Andorian.**

Pendleton, Chief. Communications officer aboard the *Enterprise*-D. Geordi La Forge offered to put in a good word with Pendleton on behalf of his friend, **Aquiel Uhnari**, but Uhnari declined the help, saying she would rather earn a promotion on her own merits. ("Aquiel" [TNG]).

Pentarus II. Class-M planet in the Pentarus system. It was searched as a possible crash site when the shuttle *Nenebek*, carrying Jean-Luc Picard and Wesley Crusher, was lost in 2367. ("Final Mission" [TNG]).

Pentarus V. Class-M Federation planet that petitioned Captain Picard to mediate a labor dispute among its **salenite miners** in 2367. Captain Picard was unable to make the initial negotiations due to the crash of his transport shuttle, the *Nenebek*. ("Final Mission" [TNG]).

Penthara IV. Class-M Federation planet with a population of 20 million humans. In 2368, Penthara IV was struck by a type-C asteroid. The explosion created a dust cloud that reflected most of the sunlight that would have reached the surface, causing surface temperatures to drop at an alarming rate.

Enterprise-D attempted to alleviate the problem by using ship's phasers to release subterranean carbon dioxide gas, in the hopes that the resulting **greenhouse effect** would help warm the planet. Unfortunately, the release of gas was accompanied by unanticipated volcanic activity, releasing massive amounts of volcanic ash, compounding the initial problem. A desperate attempt was successful in saving the planet's ecosphere when the airborne particulates were vaporized and the resulting plasma energy was drawn out into space by the *Enterprise*-D's navigational deflector. ("A Matter of Time" [TNG]).

Penthor-Mul. Gatherer and member of the clan **Lornack**. Arrested in 2313 after a **Gatherer** raid, he died of an apparent heart attack during his trial. Investigation by Dr. Crusher determined that he was assassinated by **Yuta** of the rival **Tralesta** clan. ("The Vengeance Factor" [TNG]). SEE: **microvirus.**

Peretor. Title given to tribal leaders on planet **Mordan IV.** Karnas once carried that title. His father was killed on the order of Peretor Sain. ("Too Short a Season" [TNG]).

• **"Perfect Mate, The."** *Next Generation* episode #121. Teleplay by Gary Perconte and Michael Piller. Story by René Echevarria and Gary Perconte. Directed by Cliff Bole. Stardate 45761.3. *First aired in 1992.* In order to end a war, Picard must deliver an incredibly attractive woman to her future husband, but she falls for Picard. SEE: **Akadar, Temple of; Aldorian ale; Alrik, Chancellor; Briam, Ambassador; Ceremony of Reconciliation; Constitution of the United Federation of Planets; empathic metamorph; Ferengi shuttle; Ferengi Trade Mission; *Finiis'ral*; Garuth; Harod IV; Harodian miners; Kamala; Krios 1; Krios; Ludugial gold; Paloris Colony; Par Lenor; pheromones; Qol; Starbase 117; Targhee moonbeast; *Torze-qua*; Valt Minor; Valtese horns; Valtese; Ventanian thimble.**

pergium. Mineral used on many planets as a source of power for life-support systems. Pergium was found in abundance on planet **Janus VI** and extracted by the Federation mining colony there. Beginning in 2267, the **Horta**, an  indigenous life-form that tunneled through rock, helped the Federation miners to find pergium deposits. ("The Devil in the Dark" [TOS]). *Photo: pergium processing plant on Janus VI.*

peritoneum. Membrane lining the abdominal cavity in many humanoid species, including **Bajorans**. A phaser blast punctured **Mullibok**'s peritoneum, requiring medical care from Dr. Julian Bashir. ("Progress" [DS9]).

Perrin. (Joanna Miles). Wife to Vulcan ambassador **Sarek** during the final years of his life. A human woman, fiercely devoted to her husband, Perrin sought to protect Sarek from the knowledge that he suffered from **Bendii Syndrome**, a disease that strips away emotional control. Perrin persuaded

Captain **Jean-Luc Picard** to enter into a **mind-meld** with Sarek, permitting Picard's emotional strength to support the ambassador long enough for him to conclude the historic **Legaran** talks in 2366, the final triumph of Sarek's career. ("Sarek" [TNG]). Perrin continued to care for her husband during Sarek's final months, as he suffered from the degenerative effects of Bendii Syndrome. Perrin harbored resentment toward Spock, who publicly opposed Sarek's position during the **Cardassian** wars, and who left for **Romulus** during Sarek's illness without saying goodbye. ("Unification, Part I" [TNG]).

Persephone V. Planet that was home to retired admiral **Mark Jameson** prior to his final mission to **Mordan IV.** ("Too Short a Season" [TNG]).

Petri. (Jay Robinson). Ambassador from the planet **Troyius** whose mission in 2268 was to escort **Elaan**, the **Dohlman** of **Elas**, to his home planet and to teach her civilized manners in preparation for her marriage to the leader of his planet. For many years Troyius and the planet Elas had been at war and this union was a hope toward peace. Unfortunately, the Dohlman resented having a new culture thrust upon her, and she stabbed Petri. The task of indoctrinating the bride to Elasian culture fell to Captain Kirk with dire consequences. ("Elaan of Troyius" [TOS]).

petrokian sausage. A type of food. During a malfunction of the *Enterprise*-D food replicators caused by nitrium metal parasites in 2368, petrokian sausage was substituted for an order of **Jestral tea.** ("Cost of Living" [TNG]).

pets. SEE: Beauregard; Circassian cat; *sehlat*; Maura; Patches; Spot; Tarcassian razor beast; *targ*; tribbles; wompat.

Phase 1 Search. Standard Starfleet procedure for a painstaking search aboard a ship for an individual presumed injured and unable to respond. ("Court Martial" [TOS]).

phase conditioners. Component of seismic regulators. Phase conditioners malfunction in the presence of **triolic waves**. ("Time's Arrow, Part I" [TNG]). SEE: **Devidia II.**

phase discriminator. Component of Data's positronic brain. Commander Data had a type-R phase discriminating amplifier. Lore's brain had a type L. A crude, handheld version of this instrument was used to adjust the *Enterprise*-D command crew into the **Devidian's** time continuum. ("Time's Arrow, Part I" [TNG]). SEE: **Devidia II.**

Emergency transporter armbands contained a type-7 phase discriminator, sensitive enough to enable these bands to be used to generate a subspace forcefield. ("Timescape" [TNG]).

phase disruptor. SEE: **disruptor; Klingon weapons.**

phase transition coils. Key component of a transporter that is responsible for the conversion of the transport subject from matter to energy or the reverse. ("Realm of Fear" [TNG]). A malfunction of the phase transition coils was briefly suspected in the apparent death of Ambassador T'Pel in 2367, but O'Brien indicated that they had been replaced only a week prior to the incident. ("Data's Day" [TNG]).

phase, the. Stage in the life cycle of a **Betazoid** female during which she becomes fully sexual. Normally occurs at midlife. An unmarried Betazoid woman in the phase is expected by her culture to focus her sexual energy on one particular man, who will normally become her husband. It is common for a Betazoid female to experience a sex drive of quadrupled intensity during the phase. **Lwaxana Troi** entered the phase in 2365, and thereafter sought, in succession, Jean-Luc Picard and William Riker as potential husbands. ("Manhunt" [TNG]).

phased matter. In the operation of the transporter, phased matter refers to matter that has been dematerialized by the **phase transition coils** and converted into a **matter stream**. ("Realm of Fear" [TNG]).

phaser range. Training and recreation facility aboard the *Enterprise*-D. A dark chamber in which holographic targets appear at random in the distance. Shooting at these moving targets was a test of proficiency with phaser hand weapons. When two participants are involved, each player must remain within a semicircular area, with both players' areas forming a full circle about three meters in diameter. ("A Matter of Honor" [TNG]). Worf and Guinan shared a practice session together in late 2367. Guinan was a better shot than Worf. ("Redemption, Part I" [TNG]).

phaser rifle. Large handheld energy weapon used by Starfleet personnel. Due to the great power and utility of smaller phaser sidearms, phaser rifles were rarely necessary on Starfleet missions, although Spock requested a phaser rifle while attempting to quarantine Gary Mitchell on planet **Delta Vega** in 2265. ("Where No Man Has Gone Before" [TOS]). Hundreds of type-3 phaser rifles were captured from **Kriosian** rebels in 2367 by the Klingon government, evidence that the Federation was aiding the rebels. Investigation revealed the weapons to be Romulan in origin. ("The Mind's Eye" [TNG]). *1) Original Series phaser rifle. 2) Next Generation rifle.*

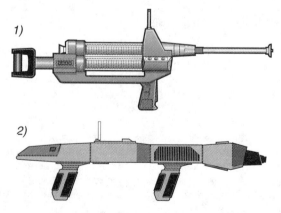

1)

2)

phaser type-1. Small handheld weapon used by Starfleet personnel, circa 2266, who preferred not to appear conspicuously armed, as in diplomatic functions. Like all such weapons, phaser type-1 could be adjusted to a variety of settings including stun, heat, and disruption. Phaser 1, also known as a hand phaser, was not as powerful as the **phaser type-2** pistol. ("The Devil in the Dark" [TOS]). Some versions of phaser type-1 were designed to fit into a pistol grip unit, forming the more powerful phaser type-2. *Illustration (right) 1) Type-1 phasers from* Star Trek: The Next Generation, *2)* Star Trek III, *and 3) original* Star Trek *series.*

phaser type-2. Pistol type weapon that was used by Starfleet personnel, circa 2266. Significantly more powerful than the tiny **phaser type-1**, the phaser pistol actually incorporated the phaser 1 into its design. Like all handheld phaser weapons, phaser 2 could be adjusted to a variety of settings including stun, heat, and disruption. ("The Devil in the Dark" [TOS]).

phaser type-3. Handheld rifle weapon. Extremely powerful, seldom necessary on Starfleet missions due to the power of the smaller type-1 and type-2 phasers. ("The Mind's Eye" [TNG]). SEE: **phaser rifle**.

phaser type-4. Medium-sized phaser emitter device, mountable on small vehicles such as shuttlecraft, although not part of most shuttles' standard equipment. ("The Outcast" [TNG]). SEE: *Magellan, Shuttlecraft*.

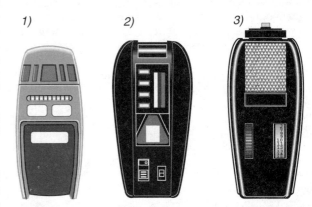

phaser. Acronym for PHASed Energy Rectification, a directed energy weapon used by the Federation Starfleet and others. Phasers were used as sidearms by Starfleet personnel. Most such weapons were either phaser type-1, otherwise known as hand phasers, which were used primarily when conspicuous weapons were undesirable, or the larger, more powerful phaser type-2, formerly known as pistol phasers. Phaser type-2 weapons were capable of power settings as high as 16. ("Frame of Mind" [TNG]). Type-3 phasers, also known as phaser rifles, were seldom used. ("Where No Man Has Gone Before" [TOS], "The Mind's Eye" [TNG]). Large ship-mounted phaser weapons, often called phaser banks, were standard equipment aboard many Starfleet vessels. By 2367, the effective tactical range of shipboard phaser banks

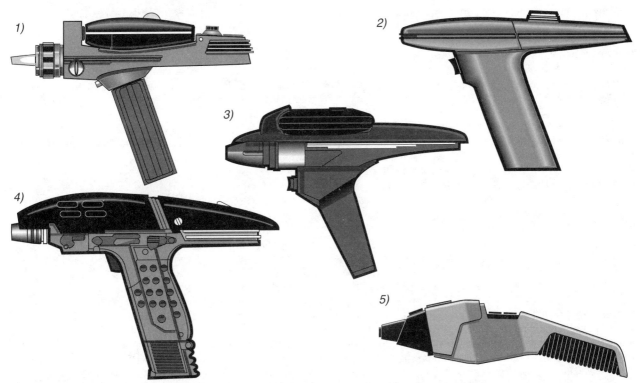

Type-2 phasers. 1) *Original Series phaser pistol.* 2) Star Trek: The Motion Picture *version, also used in* Star Trek II *and* "Yesterday's Enterprise" (TNG). 3) Star Trek III *phaser pistol, also used in* Star Trek IV *and in* "Final Mission" (TNG)l. 4) Star Trek V *and* VI *version.* 5) Star Trek: The Next Generation *type-2 phaser, third season version.*

(and most directed energy weapons) was about 300,000 kilometers (about one light-second). *Phasers did not exist during the 22nd century, according to Worf in "A Matter of Time" (TNG), so they had to have been invented no earlier than the year 2200. They were apparently not in common use as late as 2254 when the* Enterprise *landing party in "The Cage" (TOS) was equipped with laser weapons.*

Pheben System. Site of a mission by the Klingon vessel *Pagh* during William Riker's tenure as first officer of that ship in 2365. ("A Matter of Honor" [TNG]).

Phelan system. Star system located some 2.5 light-years from the **J'naii** planet. The *Enterprise*-D was assigned to a diplomatic mission in the Phelan system following an assignment at the J'naii system in 2368. ("The Outcast" [TNG]).

pheromones. Biochemicals secreted by many carbon-based life-forms, whose scent affects the behavior of other members of the same or similar species. Certain pheromones control the degree of sexual attractiveness attributed to an individual. **Empathic metamorphs** produce highly elevated levels of a substance similar to pheromones during the final stage of their sexual maturation. ("The Perfect Mate" [TNG]). SEE: **Kamala**.

Philana. (Barbara Babcock). Wife of Platonian leader **Parmen**. Philana was some 2,300 years old and enjoyed the benefits of power in her repressive society. ("Plato's Stepchildren" [TOS]). SEE: **Mea 3**.

Phoenix Cluster. A dense expanse of stars, largely unexplored by 2368. The *Enterprise*-D was assigned to conduct two weeks of research in the Phoenix Cluster when the **Ktarian** plot to infiltrate Starfleet was launched. ("The Game" [TNG]). *The Phoenix Cluster was, in part, named for the Phoenix Asteroids in John Carpenter and Dan O'Bannon's film* Dark Star.

Phoenix, U.S.S. Federation **Nebula-class** starship, Starfleet registry number NCC-65420. In 2367, the ship was under the command of **Captain Benjamin Maxwell** at the time when Maxwell ordered an unauthorized attack on **Cardassian** forces near Sector 21503. Two Cardassian ships and a Cardassian science station were destroyed by the *Phoenix*. Maxwell said his actions were intended to prove his suspicions that the Cardassians had been planning a new offensive against the Federation. Maxwell was subsequently relieved of command of the *Phoenix*. ("The Wounded" [TNG]). *The dedication plaque for the* Phoenix *in Maxwell's ready room carried the motto "There will be an answer, let it be."*

phoretic analyzer. Biomedical analysis device used aboard Deep Space 9. Dr. Julian Bashir once asked **Odo** to pour himself into a phoretic analyzer so Bashir could gain a better understanding of the **shape-shifter**'s chemistry. ("Dramatis Personae" [DS9]).

photon grenades. Short-range, variable-yield energy weapon that creates a powerful electromagnetic pulse. At lower settings, capable of stunning humanoid life-forms in an enclosed area. Photon grenades were considered for use during the *Enterprise*-D's rescue mission of **Arcos** personnel at **Turkana IV** in 2367, but were ultimately considered ineffective. ("Legacy" [TNG]).

photon torpedo. Tactical weapon used by Federation starships. Photon torpedoes are self-propelled missiles containing a small quantity of matter and antimatter bound together in a magnetic bottle, launched at warp speed at a target.

Photon torpedoes are usually the weapon of choice when a ship is at warp drive, since they are not limited by the speed of light. The warhead can be removed from a photon torpedo, leaving a small, high-speed missile that can be used as an instrumented probe, to transport small objects ("The Emissary" [TNG]), and can even be used for burials in space (*Star Trek II: The Wrath of Khan*, "The Schizoid Man" [TNG]). *Galaxy*-class starships are capable of simultaneously launching up to 10 photon torpedoes from a single launch tube. Each torpedo can be independently targeted. ("The Arsenal of Freedom" [TNG]). A *Galaxy*-class starship is normally equipped with 275 photon torpedoes. ("Conundrum" [TNG]).

Phyrox Plague. A disease that broke out on the planet Cor Caroli V. The *Enterprise*-D was successful in eradicating the plague in 2366. Starfleet Command classified the incident as Secret. ("Allegiance" [TNG]).

physiostimulator. Medical instrument used to elevate metabolic functions in an impaired individual. ("The *Enterprise* Incident" [TOS])

Pi. Romulan scoutship that crashed on planet **Galorndon Core**, one-half light-year into Federation space in 2366. The ship was rigged to self-destruct shortly after the crash. Only the wreckage of the ship was recovered, and it was believed the *Pi* may have been on a covert mission in Federation space. ("The Enemy" [TNG]). *The* Pi *was not seen in "The Enemy," but one might assume it would have been of the same design as the Romulan scoutship built three episodes later for "The Defector" (TNG).*

Picard Delta One. Holodeck computer file, a virtual reality within which lived the computer intelligences known as **Professor James Moriarty** and **Countess Barthalomew**. In the program, the Professor and the Countess believed they were exploring the universe together, having escaped the confines of the *Enterprise*-D holodeck. ("Ship in a Bottle" [TNG]).

Picard Maneuver. A tactic devised by Captain **Jean-Luc Picard** aboard the ***U.S.S. Stargazer*** during the **Battle of Maxia** in 2355.

The *Stargazer* accelerated to warp speed and for an instant appeared to be in two places at once to a distant observer, the opponent vessel. This maneuver, taking advantage of the fact that the opponent vessel was using only light-speed sensors, allowed the Federation starship to fire and damage their enemy. The Picard Maneuver is required study at Starfleet Academy. ("The Battle" [TNG]).

A) Objective viewpoint.   *B) Ferengi ship's viewpoint.*

1A) TIME: 00 seconds. The Stargazer *is approximately 9 million kilometers from the Ferengi ship. At this distance, it takes light from the* Stargazer *about 30 seconds to reach the Ferengi ship. Both ships have little motion with respect to each other.*

1B) From the viewpoint of the Ferengi ship, the Stargazer *is not moving. However, because the* Stargazer *is some 30 light-seconds away, what the Ferengi sees is actually the image of the* Stargazer *some 30 seconds ago.*

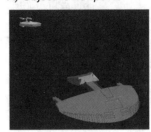 

2A) TIME: 01 seconds. The Stargazer *accelerates into warp drive, moving closer to the Ferengi ship.*

2B) Because of the 30-second lag, the Ferengi cannot know yet that the Stargazer *has moved until those 30 seconds have past.*

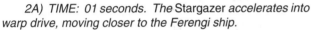

3A) TIME: 15 seconds. The Stargazer *has assumed a new position, closer to the Ferengi ship, in preparation for attack.*

3B) Again, the Ferengi still has no way of knowing that the Stargazer *has moved, because light from the* Stargazer's *new position has not yet reached the Ferengi ship.*

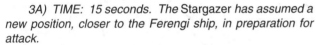

4A) TIME: 20 seconds. The Stargazer *fires weapons.*

4B) Because the new position of the Stargazer *is closer than the old position, light from the new* Stargazer *position reaches the Ferengi ship while light from the old position is still en route. In other words, the* Stargazer *appears to be in two places at once, thus confusing the Ferengi ship.*

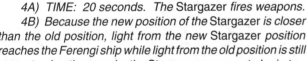

5A) TIME: 31 seconds. The battle is over; the Stargazer *has destroyed the Ferengi ship.*

5B) The light from the Stargazer *that left when the ship shifted position finally reaches the Ferengi ship. It is now possible for the Ferengi to know what the* Stargazer *is doing, although it is too late to do anything about it.*

 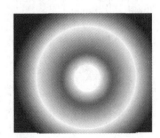

Picard Mozart trio, program 1. Musical selection created by Captain Picard with music by **Mozart** with accompanying **Ressikan flute.** ("A Fistful of Datas" [TNG]).

Picard, Jean-Luc. (Patrick Stewart). Captain of the fifth Starship **Enterprise** and a noted figure in space exploration, science, and interstellar diplomacy. ("Encounter at Farpoint, Part I" [TNG]).

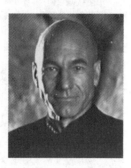

Family. Picard was born on Earth in 2305 to **Maurice Picard** and **Yvette Gessard Picard.** Maurice was a tradition-bound French vintner who opposed Jean-Luc's ambitions of voyaging among the stars. ("Tapestry" [TNG], "Chain of Command, Part II" [TNG]). Jean-Luc was raised on a family farm in **LaBarre, France,** along with his older brother, **Robert Picard.** ("Family" [TNG]). As a boy, young Jean-Luc enjoyed building ships in bottles; his collection included a legendary **Promellian** battle cruiser, a ship that he would one day discover in his voyages aboard the Enterprise-D. Those toy ships served as a springboard for the future captain's imagination. ("Booby Trap" [TNG]).

Academy and early career. Picard failed in 2322 to gain entrance to Starfleet Academy at the age of 17, but was admitted a year later. ("Coming of Age" [TNG]). As a first-year cadet in 2323, Picard became the only freshman ever to win the Starfleet Academy marathon on Danula II. ("The Best of Both Worlds, Part II" [TNG]). Picard won top academic honors as well. ("Family" [TNG]). Cadet Picard committed a serious offense while at the Academy. Years later, he credited Academy groundskeeper **Boothby** with making it possible for him to graduate by helping him to do the right thing. ("The First Duty" [TNG]). Shortly after graduating from Starfleet Academy with the class of 2327, Picard was on leave with several classmates at **Starbase Earhart,** where he picked a fight with three **Nausicaans** at the **Bonestell Recreation Facility.** One of the Nausicaans stabbed Picard through the heart, necessitating a **cardiac replacement** procedure, leaving Picard with an artificial heart. ("Samaritan Snare" [TNG], "Tapestry" [TNG]). SEE: **Batanides, Marta; Zweller, Cortin.** (Q commented that the injury to Picard's heart had occurred "30 years ago," which would set the Nausicaan incident in 2338. Unfortunately, this was a mistake, since "The First Duty" [TNG] established that Picard graduated in 2327, but the oversight was not caught until after the episode was filmed. The young Ensign Picard was played by Marcus Nash.) As a young lieutenant, Picard met Ambassador **Sarek** at the wedding of the ambassador's son. Picard recalled how in awe he was at meeting someone who had helped to shape the Federation. ("Sarek" [TNG]). (The episode does not make it clear which "son" Picard was referring to, although Gene Roddenberry said he thought it was **Spock.**) As a young officer, Picard was romantically involved with the future **Jenice Manheim.** Although the two had been strongly attracted to each other, Picard feared commitment, and eventually broke off the relationship in 2342. Picard regretted losing Jenice for many years, and the two saw each other again in 2364 when the Enterprise-D saved her husband, **Dr. Paul Manheim,**

after a serious laboratory accident on **Vandor IX.** ("We'll Always Have Paris" [TNG]). In his early career, Picard distinguished himself when he led an away team to planet **Milika III,** to save an endangered ambassador.

On the Stargazer. Lieutenant Picard was a bridge officer on the **U.S.S. Stargazer** when the ship's captain was killed. Picard took charge of the bridge and for his service in the emergency was offered the command of the Stargazer. ("Tapestry" [TNG]). Picard commanded the Stargazer for some 20 years, until 2355, when the ship was nearly destroyed by an unprovoked sneak attack near the **Maxia Zeta star system.** The surviving Stargazer crew, including Picard, drifted for weeks in shuttlecraft before being rescued. The assailant in the incident was unknown, but was later found to be a Ferengi spacecraft. ("The Battle" [TNG]). SEE: **Picard Maneuver.** Following the loss of the Stargazer, Picard was court-martialed as required by standard Starfleet procedure, but he was exonerated. The prosecutor in the case was **Phillipa Louvois,** with whom Picard had been romantically involved. ("The Measure of a Man" [TNG]).

Aboard the Enterprise-D. Jean-Luc Picard was appointed captain of the fifth Starship Enterprise in 2363, shortly after the ship was commissioned. ("Encounter at Farpoint" [TNG]). Picard was offered a promotion to the admiralty in 2364 when **Admiral**

Gregory Quinn was attempting to consolidate his power base to combat an unknown alien intelligence that was trying to take over Starfleet Command. Picard declined the offer, citing his belief that he could better serve the Federation as a starship commander. ("Coming of Age" [TNG]). An energy vortex near the Endicor system created a duplicate of Picard from six hours in the future in 2365. Although identical to the "present" person, Picard had difficulty accepting the existence of his twin because he believed the twin might have been responsible for he destruction of his ship, a deeply repugnant thought. ("Time Squared" [TNG]). Picard's artificial heart required routine replacement, most recently in 2365, when complications in the cardiac replacement procedure performed at **Starbase 515** necessitated emergency assistance by **Dr. Katherine Pulaski.** ("Samaritan Snare" [TNG]). Picard met Ambassador Sarek again in 2366, when Sarek's last mission was jeopardized by **Bendii Syndrome,** which caused the ambassador to lose emotional control. Picard **mindmeld**ed with Sarek to lend the ambassador the emotional stability needed to conclude the historic treaty with the **Legarans.** ("Sarek" [TNG]). Picard was abducted by the **Borg** in late 2366 as part of the Borg assault on the Federation. Picard was surgically mutilated and transformed into an entity called **Locutus of Borg.** ("The Best of Both Worlds, Part I" [TNG]). As Locutus, Picard was forced to cooperate in the devastating battle of **Wolf 359,** in which he was forced to help destroy 39

Federation starships and their crews. Picard was rescued by an *Enterprise*-D away team, then surgically restored by Dr. Crusher. ("The Best of Both Worlds, Part II" [TNG]). Following his return from the Borg, Picard spent several weeks in rehabilitation from the terrible physical and psychological trauma. While the *Enterprise*-D was undergoing repairs at **Earth Station McKinley**, Picard took the opportunity to visit his home town of LaBarre for the first time in almost 20 years. While there, he stayed with his brother **Robert Picard**, met Robert's wife, **Marie Picard**, and their son, **René Picard**, for the first time. Picard briefly toyed with the idea of leaving Starfleet to accept directorship of the **Atlantis Project**, but his return home helped him realize that he belonged on the *Enterprise*-D.

Picard and the Klingon Empire. ("Family" [TNG]). Picard assumed an unprecedented role in Klingon politics when he served as **Arbiter of Succession** following the Klingon leader **K'mpec**'s death in 2367. K'mpec took the highly unusual step of appointing an outsider as arbiter so as to insure that the choice of K'mpec's successor would not plunge the Empire into civil war. Under Picard's arbitration, council member **Gowron** emerged as the sole challenger for leadership of the High Council. ("Reunion" [TNG]). Picard was reduced to a child after passing through an energy field in 2369. ("Rascals" [TNG]). Jean-Luc Picard suffered profound emotional scars in 2369 when he was captured by **Gul Madred**, a Cardassian officer who tortured Picard for Starfleet tactical information. Picard resisted, but later confessed that the experience so brutalized him that he would have told Madred anything had he not been rescued. ("Chain of Command, Parts I and II").

Personal interests. Picard was something of a Renaissance man, whose areas of interest ranged from drama to astrophysics. Picard was an avid amateur archaeologist, occasionally publishing scientific papers on the subject, and even addressing the **Federation Archaeology Council** in 2367. ("QPid" [TNG]). SEE: **Tagus III**. Early in his career, at the urging of his teacher, noted archaeologist **Richard Galen**, Picard seriously considered pursuing archaeology on a professional level. Picard's path later crossed Galen's again just before Galen's death in 2369. Picard helped complete Galen's greatest discovery, the reconstruction of an ancient message from a humanoid species that lived some 4 billion years ago. ("The Chase" [TNG]). SEE: **Humanoid life**. Picard studied the legendary ancient **Iconians** while at the Academy. ("Contagion" [TNG]). Picard was also an accomplished horseman, and one of his favorite holodeck programs was a woodland setting in which he enjoyed riding a computer-simulated Arabian mare. ("Pen Pals" [TNG]). Picard played the piano when he was young ("Lessons" [TNG]), but his deep love of music may have stemmed from an incident in 2368 when his mind received a lifetime of memories from the now-dead planet **Kataan**, and he experienced the life of a man named **Kamin**, who died a thousand years ago. Kamin had played a **Ressikan flute**, and Picard treasured that instrument because of having shared Kamin's memories. ("The Inner Light" [TNG]). Picard shared his music with **Neela Daren**, an *Enterprise*-D crew member with whom he became romantically involved in 2369. ("Lessons" [TNG]).

According to Star Trek: The Next Generation *supervising* producer Robert Justman, Captain Picard was named for French oceanographer Jacques Piccard (1922-), who explored the depths of Earth's Marianas Trench aboard the bathyscaph Trieste. Young Picard in "Rascals" was played by David Tristen Burkin, who also played René Picard in "Family" (TNG). Picard's mother was seen briefly in "Where No One Has Gone Before" (TNG), and his father made an appearance in "Tapestry" (TNG), both flashbacks of sorts, since both people were dead at the time of those episodes.

Jean-Luc Picard was first seen in "Encounter at Farpoint" [TNG].

Picard, Marie. (Samantha Eggar). Wife to **Robert Picard**, and **Jean-Luc Picard**'s sister-in-law. Marie and Robert had a son, **René Picard**. A gracious and lovely woman, Marie was responsible for keeping the peace between Robert and Jean-Luc. Though they did not meet until his homecoming in 2367, Marie had corresponded regularly with Jean-Luc, keeping him informed of family matters. ("Family" [TNG]).

Picard, Maurice. (Clive Church). Vinticulturist from **LaBarre**, France, on planet Earth, and the father of *Enterprise*-D captain **Jean-Luc Picard**. The elder Picard did not approve of advanced technology and avoided it in his life whenever possible. It was understandable, then, that Maurice Picard did not approve of his younger son's joining Starfleet rather than remaining at home to tend the family vineyard. ("Tapestry" [TNG]). *The name Maurice was not from dialog, but came from the script for "Tapestry" as well as from Jean-Luc's bio computer screen in "Conundrum" (TNG). The name was selected by* Star Trek *writer-producer Ron Moore.*

Picard, René. (David Tristen Birkin). Nephew to **Jean-Luc Picard**, and the son of **Robert Picard**. Jean-Luc met René for the first time in 2367, when the boy was seven, when Captain Picard came home for the first time in twenty years. René expressed a desire to be like his uncle, and dreamed that someday he would be leaving for his own starship. ("Family" [TNG]). *David Tristan Birkin later portrayed Jean-Luc Picard as a child in the sixth-season episode "Rascals" (TNG).*

Picard, Robert. (Jeremy Kemp). Older brother to **Jean-Luc Picard**, and husband to **Marie Picard**. Fiercely old-fashioned, Robert stayed on the family vineyard to continue his father's work after Jean-Luc left to join Starfleet. Robert was resentful of his younger brother's literally stellar achievements, and carried that bitterness for years. The two Picard brothers came somewhat to terms in 2367 when Jean-Luc visited home while recovering from his abduction by the **Borg**. ("Family" [TNG]).

Picard, Yvette Gessard. (Herta Ware). Mother to *Enterprise*-D captain **Jean-Luc Picard**. Many years after her death, Picard once again met her son, Jean-Luc, in 2364 when a failed warp-drive experiment caused a bizarre intertwining of time, space, and thought caused by an individual known as the **Traveler**. ("Where No One Has Gone Before" [TNG]).

"Piece of the Action, A." Original Series episode #49. Teleplay by David P. Harmon and Gene L. Coon. Story by David P. Harmon. Directed by James Komack. No stardate given. *First aired in 1968. The* Enterprise *visits a planet whose inhabitants have patterned themselves after Chicago gangsters of the 1920s on Earth.* SEE: **Beta Antares IV; Book, The;** *Chicago Mobs of the Twenties;* **Cirl the Knife; fizzbin; heater;** *Horizon, U.S.S.;* **Iotians; Kalo; Krako, Jojo; Oxmyx, Bela; Prime Directive; Sigma Iotia II; subspace radio; Tepo; transtator; Zabo.**

Pierson, Lieutenant. *Enterprise*-D engineering technician who worked to help repair the experimental **particle fountain** at planet Tyrus VIIA in 2369. ("The Quality of Life" [TNG]).

Pike, Christopher. (Jeffrey Hunter). Early captain of the first *Starship Enterprise*, Pike commanded one of the first missions to planet **Talos IV**, after which Starfleet imposed **General Order 7**, prohibiting Federation contact with that planet. Pike was born in **Mojave**, on Earth, and took command of the *Enterprise* in 2250 and conducted two five-year missions

of exploration. He relinquished command of that ship to **James Kirk** in 2263, at which time Pike was promoted to **fleet captain**. Pike suffered severe radiation injuries in 2266 as a result of an accident aboard a class-J training ship. Wheelchair bound as a result of delta ray exposure, Pike went to live on Talos IV when the **Talosians** offered to use their power of illusion to provide him with a life unfettered by his physical body. ("The Cage," "The Menagerie" [TOS]). *Based on Spock's line that he had served with Pike for 11 years, we conjecture that Pike had commanded two five-year missions of the* Enterprise *prior to his promotion to fleet captain in 2263. Christopher Pike was seen as* Enterprise *captain in the first* Star Trek *pilot episode, "The Cage" [TOS], produced in 1964. Actor Jeffrey Hunter, who portrayed Pike, was unavailable when the second* Star Trek *pilot ("Where No Man Has Gone Before" [TOS]) was being planned, so the part was recast with William Shatner portraying Captain James Kirk. Footage from "The Cage" was later incorporated into the two-part episode "The Menagerie" (TOS). Prior to either Shatner or Hunter, producer Gene Roddenberry had offered the role of the captain to* Sea Hunt *actor Lloyd Bridges.* Star Trek *tradition has it that shuttlecraft are named after famous explorers and*

scientists, and the shuttle in "The Most Toys" (TNG) was named after Christopher Pike.

Pike, Shuttlepod. Assigned to the *Enterprise*-D, this shuttle, #12, was destroyed while transporting **hytritium** to the ship in 2366. The explosion of the *Pike* was initially believed to be due to pilot error, but was

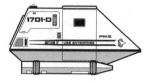

later discovered to have been caused by **Kivas Fajo**. ("The Most Toys [TNG]).
The Pike *was named for Captain Christopher Pike, early captain of the first* Starship Enterprise.

Pinder, Lieutenant. *Enterprise*-D science division crew member, and supervisor to **Ensign Janeway**. Pinder found fault in Janeway's performance, much to Janeway's dismay. ("Man of the People" [TNG]).

Pioneer X. Ancient space probe launched in 1972 by the National Aeronautics and Space Administration on Earth. *Pioneer x* studied the planets Jupiter and Saturn, and was the first human-made object to leave Earth's Solar system. The probe drifted for centuries

until it was destroyed in 2287 by a Klingon Bird-of-Prey piloted by **Captain Klaa**. (*Star Trek V: The Final Frontier*).

Piotr. SEE: **Chekov, Piotr.**

Piper, Dr. Mark. (Paul Fix). Chief medical officer aboard the *Enterprise* in 2265 and predecessor to Dr. McCoy. ("Where No Man Has Gone Before" [TOS]).

pipius claw. A traditional Klingon dish. Commander Riker tasted some of this stuff when he tried to acquaint himself with Klingon culture prior to his temporary assignment to the *Pagh* in 2365. ("A Matter of Honor" [TNG]).

Pirates of Penzance, The. Comic operetta by Sir William Gilbert and Sir Arthur Sullivan, first published on Earth in 1879. Beverly Crusher, in her role as ship's drama director, staged a production of *The Pirates of Penzance* aboard the *Enterprise*-D in 2368. She urged Geordi La Forge to audition for the role of Major-General Stanley for the production, although Geordi was uncomfortable about singing in front of people. ("Disaster" [TNG]).

pistol. Handheld weapon that used a small chemical explosive to propel a metal pellet. One variety of these weapons, known as a double-action cavalry pistol, circa 1873, was found in a subterranean cavern on Earth in 2368. ("Time's Arrow, Part I" [TNG]).

Plak-tow. Vulcan term roughly translating as "blood fever". Refers to a state of mind in which a Vulcan undergoing **Pon**

farr, the mating drive, becomes oblivious to anything not related to the winning of one's mate. Spock experienced *Plaktow* when he underwent *Pon farr* in 2267, making him prone to throwing bowls of soup in anger. ("Amok Time" [TOS]).

planet killer. Automated spacegoing weapon from outside our galaxy that entered Federation space in 2267, destroying the planets in star systems **L-370** and **L-374**. Several kilometers in length, with a hull composed of pure **neutronium**, it smashed planets into rubble, and used the matter as fuel. Kirk theorized that it was a weapon, a doomsday machine built primarily as a bluff used in a war uncounted years ago in another galaxy. The civilization that built the planet killer

might have gone, but the machine continued to destroy. Initial projections suggested that the planet killer's course, if unchecked, would take it toward the Rigel colonies and the most densely populated part of our galaxy, putting billions of lives at risk. The ancient weapon was finally destroyed when Kirk sent the hulk of the **U.S.S. Constellation** to explode in the planet killer's interior, destroying it. ("The Doomsday Machine" [TOS]). SEE: **Decker, Commodore Matt.**

Planets, stars, and other celestial objects.

Object name	Description	Episode or film
Acamar III	Home planet of the Acamarian race	"The Vengeance Factor" (TNG)
Acamar System	Star system containing planet Acamar III	"The Vengeance Factor" (TNG)
Adelphous IV	Planet destination of Enterprise-D following encounter with Romulan Warbird Devoras	"Data's Day" (TNG)
Alawanir Nebula	Nebula investigated by the Enterprise-D in 2369	"Rightful Heir" (TNG)
Aldea	Legendary planet whose people excelled in intellectual and artistic pursuits	"When the Bough Breaks" (TNG)
Aldebaran III	Homeworld to Janet Wallace and her husband	"The Deadly Years" (TOS)
Aldebaron	Planet were Dr. Elizabeth Dehner joined the Enterprise crew in 2265	"Where No Man Has Gone Before" (TOS)
Alfa 117	Class M planet where upon beaming Kirk was divided into two beings, one evil and one good	"The Enemy Within" (TOS)
Alpha Carinae II	Class-M planet used in the M-5 test	"The Ultimate Computer" (TOS)
Alpha Carinae V	Planet of the Drella creature that derived sustenance from emotions	"Wolf in the Fold" (TOS)
Alpha Centauri	Closest star to Earth's solar system, home to Zefram Cochrane, inventor of the warp drive	"Metamorphosis" (TOS)
Alpha Cygnus IX	Planet where Federation Ambassador Sarek arranged a major treaty	"Sarek" (TNG)
Alpha III	Planet where a historic individual rights document was established	"Court Martial" (TOS)
Alpha Majoris I	Planet origin of the Mellitus, a creature with many forms	"Wolf in the Fold" (TOS)
Alpha Moon	Moon orbiting planet Peliar Zel, at odds with its sister moon, Beta	"The Host" (TNG)
Alpha Omicron System	Star system where a life-form was found living in the vacuum of space	"Galaxy's Child" (TNG)
Alpha Onias III	Planet where Riker was abducted by a little boy who wanted a friend to play with	"Future Imperfect" (TNG)
Alpha Proxima II	Planet where several women were brutally murdered	"Wolf in the Fold" (TOS)
Alpha V	Planet with colony where Charles Evans' nearest living relatives lived	"Charlie X" (TOS)
Altair III	Planet where William Riker refused to allow Captain DeSoto to beam to the surface	"Encounter at Farpoint" (TNG)
Altair VI	Planet visited by the Enterprise in 2267 for an important presidential inauguration ceremony; Altair VI was also part of the Kobayashi Maru simulation	"Amok Time" (TOS); Star Trek II: The Wrath of Khan
Altec	Planet; along with Straleb, part of the Coalition of Madena	"The Outrageous Okona" (TNG)
Amargosa Diaspora	Dense globular star cluster Enterprise-D investigated in 2369	"Schisms" (TNG)
Andevian II	Planet with at least four moons	"The Forsaken" (DS9)
Andromeda Galaxy	Closest galaxy to the Milky Way Galaxy, home to the Kelvans, expected to become uninhabitable in ten millenia due to increased radiation levels	"By Any Other Name" (TOS)

(Continued on next page.)

(Continued from previous page.)

Object name	Description	Episode or film
Angel One	Planet whose matriarchial government treated males as second-class citizens	"Angel One" (TNG)
Angosia III	Planet that experienced social unrest due to brutal mistreatment of their war veterans	"The Hunted" (TNG)
Antica	Homeworld to the Anticans	"Lonely Among Us" (TNG)
Antide III	Planet whose intelligent fishlike inhabitants bid for Federation membership in 2365	"Manhunt" (TNG)
Antos IV	Home of the giant dry-worm; planet where Captain Garth tried to destroy the population after having learned cellular metamorphosis	"Who Mourns for Adonais?" (TOS); "Whom Gods Destroy" (TOS)
Aolian Cluster	Site of archaeological research conducted by Professor Galen	"The Chase" (TNG)
Archanis	Star used as a navigational reference	"Arena" (TOS)
Archanis IV	Home planet of Chekov's imaginary brother, Piotr	"The Day of the Dove" (TOS)
Archer IV	Planet destination of Enterprise-D after encounter with temporal rift	"Yesterday's Enterprise" (TNG)
Arcybite	Planet where Nava, a Ferengi, took over mining refineries	"The Nagus" (DS9)
Ardana	Planet, location of the cloud city Stratos	"The Cloud Minders" (TOS)
Argelius II	Planet with hedonistic culture; brutalized by violent killings in 2267	"Wolf in the Fold" (TOS)
Argolis Cluster	Cluster Enterprise-D was charting when it discovered a Borg ship, location of ecologically devastated planet Tagra IV	"I, Borg" (TNG), "True Q" (TNG
Argos system	Star system, possible destination of the Crystalline Entity in 2368	"Silicon Avatar" (TNG)
Ariannus	Planet vital as a transfer point, infected by a bacterial plague in 2268	"Let That Be Your Last Battlefield" (TOS)
Arkaria	Planet, location of Federation facility in charge of the Remmler Array	"Starship Mine" (TNG)
Armus IX	Planet where Riker wore a native feathered costume for diplomatic reasons	"Angel One" (TNG)
Arneb	Star recognized by Wesley while gazing from Ten-Forward	"The Child" (TNG)
Arvada III	Planet where a terrible tragedy killed many people	"The Arsenal of Freedom" (TNG)
Atalia VII	Planet, site of a vital diplomatic conference in 2369	"The Chase" (TNG)
aucdet IX	Planet on which a Federation medical collection station was located	"The Child" (TNG)
Axanar	Planet that cadet James Kirk visited on a peace mission	"Whom Gods Destroy" (TOS)
Babel	Planetoid, location of interplanetary conference concerning Coridan's bid for admission to the Federation	"Journey to Babel" (TOS)
Bajor	Homeworld to the Bajoran race	"Emissary" (DS9), et.al.
Bajor VIII	Eighth planet in the Bajoran system containing six colonies	"Past Prologue" (DS9)
Balosnee IV	Planet where the harmonies of the tides can cause hallucinations	"The Nagus" (DS9)
Barzan	Planet near an unstable wormhole	"The Price" (TNG)
Beltane IX	Planet that serves as a center for commercial shipping	"Coming of Age" (TNG)
Benecia	Planet where the Karidian Players were to perform; the colony had relatively primitive medical facilities	" The Conscience of the King" (TOS), "Turnabout Intruder" (TOS)
Benev Selec	Star system in the Selcundi Drema Sector	"Pen Pals" (TNG)
Benzar	Homeworld to the Benzites	"A Matter of Honor" (TNG)
Berengaria VII	Planet where dragons can be found	"This Side of Paradise" (TOS)
Bersallis III	Planet where deadly firestorms occur every seven years	"Lessons" (TNG)
Beta Agni II	Planet that experienced tricyanate contamination of its water supply	"The Most Toys" (TNG)
Beta Antares IV	Planet where imaginary card game fizzbin was played, at least according to James T. Kirk	"A Piece of the Action" (TOS)
Beta Aurigae	Binary star system were the original Enterprise was to meet the Starship Potemkin in 2269	"Turnabout Intruder" (TOS)
Beta Geminorum	Star system that contains planets Pollux IV & V	"Who Mourns for Adonais?" (TOS)
Beta Lankal	Star system in Klingon space	"Redemption, Part II" (TNG)
Beta Magellan	Star system where planet Bynaus is located; the star went nova	"11001001" (TNG)
Beta Moon	Moon orbiting planet Peliar Zel, at odds with its sister moon, Alpha	"The Host" (TNG)

(Continued on next page.)

(Continued from previous page.)

Object name	Description	Episode or film
Beta Niobe	Star that exploded in 2269, destroying planet Sarpeidon	"All Our Yesterdays" (TOS)
Beta Portolan	Planet where mass insanity from Denevan neural parasites began	"Operation—Annihilate!" (TOS)
Beta Renna system	Star system to homeworlds of the Anticans and Selay	"Lonely Among Us" (TNG)
Beta Stromgren	Red giant star where Tin Man was discovered by the Vega IX probe	"Tin Man" (TNG)
Beta Thoridar	Klingon planet used as a staging area for the Duras forces during the Klingon civil war	"Redemption, Part I" (TNG)
Beta V	Planet, destination before the Enterprise was detained by Trelane	"The Squire of Gothos" (TOS)
Beta XII-A	Planet to which an alien entity lured the Enterprise and the Klingon vessel commanded by Kang	"The Day of the Dove" (TOS)
Betazed	Homeworld to Deanna Troi	"Ménage à Troi" (TNG), et al.
Beth Delta I	Planet where Dr. Paul Stubbs wished he could take Deanna Troi for champagne	"Evolution" (TNG)
Bilana III	Planet where the soliton wave was developed	"New Ground" (TNG)
Bilaren System	Planet, location of Amanda Rogers' adoptive parents' home	"True-Q" (TNG)
Black Cluster	Astronomical formation created when hundred of proto-stars collapse in close proximity to each other	"Hero Worship" (TNG)
Bolarus IX	Homeworld of the Bolian race	"Allegiance" (TNG)
Boradis system	System where Enterprise-D met emissary K'Ehleyr	"The Emissary" (TNG)
Boreal III	Planet, home of a transport attacked by the Crystalline Entity	"Silicon Avatar" (TNG)
Boreth	Klingon planet where a monastery to Kahless the Unforgettable was established to await his return	"Rightful Heir" (TNG)
Borgolis Nebula	Blue-tinged gaseous nebula studied by Enterprise-D in 2369	"Lessons" (TNG)
Borka VI	Planet where Troi was abducted by Romulan underground operatives	"Face of the Enemy" (TNG)
Bracas V	Planet where La Forge took a vacation and went skin-diving	"The Loss" (TNG)
Brax	Planet where, according to Vash, Q was known as "The God of Lies"	"Q-Less" (DS9)
Bre'el IV	Planet whose moon was knocked out of its orbit and threatened to impact with the planet	"Deja Q" (TNG)
Brechtian Cluster	Star system that the Crystalline Entity was en route to when it was destroyed	"Silicon Avatar" (TNG)
Brekka	Planet, home to the Brekkians, who produced the narcotic felicium	"Symbiosis" (TNG)
Brentalia	Protected planet used as a zoo for endangered species; Worf and Alexander visited there once	"New Ground" (TNG), "Imaginary Friend" (TNG)
Bringloid V	Planet settled by human colonists from S.S. Mariposa	"Up the Long Ladder" (TNG)
Browder IV	Planet undergoing terraforming in 2366	"Allegiance" (TNG)
Bynaus	Planet, home of the Bynars	"11001001" (TNG)
C-111	Star system where planet Beta III was located	"The Return of the Archons" (TOS)
Camus II	Planet were Dr. Janice Lester exchanged bodies with James Kirk, site of an archaeological survey that the Enterprise-D missed	"Turnabout Intruder" (TOS), "Legacy" (TNG)
Canopus	Planet were Tarbolde wrote the sonnet "Nightingale Woman," Star used for navigational reference	"Where No Man Has Gone Before" (TOS) " Arena" (TOS)
Capella IV	Home planet to Eleen and other Capellans	"Friday's Child" (TOS)
Cardassia	Homeworld of the Cardassian race	"The Wounded" (TNG), et al.
Carema III	Planet considered as a candidate for Dr. Farallon's particle fountain mining technology	"The Quality of Life" (TNG)
Carraya System	Star system, location of a secret Romulan prison camp	"Birthright, Part II", (TNG) "Rightful Heir" (TNG)
Castal I	Planetary site of conflict between Federation and Talarian forces	"Suddenly Human" (TNG)
Catullan	Home planet to Tango Rad, follower of Dr. Sevrin	"The Way to Eden" (TOS)
Celtris III	Planet in Cardassian space where Picard was kidnapped	"Chain of Command, Part I" (TNG)
Cerebus II	Planet where Mark Jameson received a dangerous drug to reverse the aging process	"Too Short a Season" (TNG)
Cestus III	Planet, location of Federation outpost destroyed by the Gorn	"Arena" (TOS)

(Continued on next page.)

(Continued from previous page.)

Object name	Description	Episode or film
Ceti Alpha V	Planet where Khan and his followers were exiled	"Space Seed" (TOS), Star Trek II
Ceti Alpha VI	Planet that exploded, causing Ceti Alpha V to become barren	*Star Trek II*
Chalna	Planet, home of the Chalnoth race	"Allegiance" (TNG)
Chamra Vortex	Nebula where Odo and Croden evaded a Miradorn vessel	"Vortex" (DS9)
Chandra V	Planet where Tam Elbrun was assigned before his mission on Enterprise-D	"Tin Man" (TNG)
Cheron	Planet, home to Bele and Lokai, destroyed by racial strife; site of a decisive battle with the Romulans	"Let This Be Your Last Battlefield" (TOS), "The Defector" (TNG)
Cirrus IV	Planet, location of the Cliffs of Heaven	"Conundrum" (TNG)
Clarus System	Star system, location of planet Archybite	"The Nagus" (DS9)
Cluster NGC 321	Star cluster containing planets Eminiar VII and Vendikar	"A Taste of Armageddon" (TOS)
Coltar IV	Planet that experienced time distortion from Manheim's experiments	"We'll Always Have Paris" (TNG)
Cor Caroli V	Planet where Enterprise-D was successful in eradicating the Phyrox Plague	"Allegiance" (TNG)
Coridan	Dilithium-rich planet admitted to the Federation in 2267 after the Babel Conference	"Journey to Babel" (TOS) "Sarek" (TNG)
Corinth IV	Location of Starfleet facility that requested an explanation for why the Enterprise was delayed on planet M-113	"The Man Trap" (TOS)
Cornelian Star System	Star system where Riker ordered the Enterprise-D to escape the "hole" in space created by Nagilum	"Where Silence Has Lease" (TNG)
Corvan II	Planet whose atmospheric pollutants threatened life	"New Ground" (TNG)
Cygnet XII	Planet dominated by women, who repaired the Enterprise computer	"Tomorrow Is Yesterday" (TOS)
Cygnia Minor	Earth colony threatened by famine in 2267	"The Conscience of the King" (TOS)
Daled IV	Planet where a long civil war will hopefully be ended by Salia	"The Dauphin" (TNG)
Danula II	Planet, site of a Starfleet Academy marathon where Picard ran	"The Best of Both Worlds, Part I" (TNG)
Daran V	Planet directly in the path of the Yonada ship in 2268	"For the World Is Hollow and I Have Touched the Sky" (TOS)
Deinonychus	Planet where Enterprise-D awaited the supply ship Biko	"A Fistful of Datas" (TNG)
Delb II	Homeworld of Nellen Tore, assistant to Admiral Norah Satie	"The Drumhead" (TNG)
Delinia II	Planet where transporter psychosis was first diagnosed in 2209	"Realm of Fear" (TNG)
Delos	Star system containing planets Onara and Brekka	"Symbiosis" (TNG)
Delos IV	Planet where Dr. Beverly Crusher completed her medical internship under Dr. Dalen Quaice	"Remember Me" (TNG)
Delta IV	Homeworld to the Deltan race and Ilia	*Star Trek: The Motion Picture*
Delta Rana IV	Class-M planet, site of a Federation colony attacked by the Husnock, home to Kevin and Rishon Uxbridge	"The Survivors" (TNG)
Delta Vega	Desolate planet with an automated lithium mining station	"Where No Man Has Gone Before" (TOS)
Deltived Asteroid Belt	Astronomical formation misplaced by Q2	"Deja Q" (TNG)
Deneb II	Planet where entity named Kesla murdered several women	"Wolf in the Fold" (TOS)
Deneb IV	Class-M planet inhabited by the Bandi race and location of Farpoint Station	"Encounter at Farpoint" (TNG)
Deneb V	Planet where Harry Mudd illegally sold all the rights to a Vulcan fuel synthesizer	"I, Mudd" (TOS)
Deneva	Planet infested by Denevan neural parasites in 2267	"Operation-Annihilate!" (TOS)
Denius III	Planet where artifacts were discovered showing location of planet Iconia	"Contagion" (TNG)

(Continued on next page.)

(Continued from previous page.)

Object name	Description	Episode or film
Denkiri Arm	One of the spiral-shaped arms that make up the Milky Way Galaxy, located in the Delta Quadrant	"The Price" (TNG)
Denorios belt	Charged plasma field where the Bajoran wormhole is located	"Emissary" (DS9)
Dephi Ardu	Star system where the last Tkon outpost was located	"The Last Outpost" (TNG)
Deriben V	Planet, Aquiel Uhnari's last posting prior to Relay Station 47	"Aquiel" (TNG)
Devidia II	Planet whose inhabitants steal neural energies	"Time's Arrow' (TNG)
Dimorus	Planet where Gary Mitchell saved Kirk's life from a poison dart thrown by rodent creatures	"Where No Man Has Gone Before" (TOS)
Donatu V	Planet site of a battle fought with Klingons near Sherman's Planet	"The Trouble with Tribbles" (TOS)
Doraf I	Planet where Enterprise-D was assigned for terraforming	"Unification, Part I" (TNG)
Draken IV	Planet where Romulan N'Vek helped defection of M'ret	"Face of the Enemy" (TNG)
Drema IV	Planet suffering violent geologic instabilities; home to Sarjenka	"Pen Pals" (TNG)
Dulisian IV	Planet that supposedly sent the Enterprise-D a distress call while in orbit about planet Galorndon Core	"Unification, Part II" (TNG)
Durenia IV	Planet, destination of Enterprise-D before being trapped in a static warp bubble	"Remember Me" (TNG)
Dyson sphere	Gigantic artificial structure designed to completely enclose a star, discovered in 2294 by the U.S.S. Jenolan	"Relics" (TNG)
Dytallix B	Planet owned by the Dytallix Mining Corporation, site of Picard's covert meeting with Walker Keel	"Conspiracy" (TNG)
Earth	Mostly harmless; homeworld of Homo sapiens	"The Cage" (TOS)
Earth Colony 2	Planet where George Samuel Kirk hoped to be transferred	"What Are Little Girls Made Of?" (TOS)
Eden	Mythical planet sought by Dr. Sevrin and his followers	"The Way to Eden" (TOS)
Ekos	Class-M planet, accidentally turned into a repressive Nazi state by Federation sociologist John Gill	"Patterns of Force" (TOS)
El-Adrel IV	Planet where Tamarian Captain Dathon and Picard met in 2367	"Darmok" (TNG)
El-Adrel system	Star system located midway between Federation and Tamarian space	"Darmok" (TNG)
Elas	Homeworld of the Dohlman of Elas	"Elaan of Troyius" (TOS)
Elba II	Planet, location of a Federation penal colony for the criminally insane where Fleet Captain Garth was treated	"Whom Gods Destroy" (TOS)
Emila II	Planet, destination of the Enterprise-D after mission at Tanuga IV	"A Matter of Perspective" (TNG)
Eminiar VII	Planet at war with its neighbor, Vendikar, for 500 years	"A Taste of Armageddon" (TOS)
Endicor System	Star system, destination before energy vortex that created an alternate version of Picard was encountered	"Time Squared" (TNG)
Ennan VI	Planet where Pulaski obtained a bottle of ale that she shared at Riker's omelet party	"Time Squared" (TNG)
Epsilon Canaris III	Planet on the verge of war, where negotiations were assigned to Commissioner Hedford	"Metamorphosis" (TOS)
Epsilon Hydra VII	Planet where archaeologist Vash was barred from the Royal Museum	"Q-Less" (DS9)
Epsilon Indi	Star system were ancient marauders from planet Triacus waged war	"And the Children Shall Lead" (TOS)
Epsilon Indii	Star recognized by Wesley Crusher while gazing from Ten-Forward	"The Child" (TNG)
Epsilon Mynos System	Star system where planet Aldea is located	"When the Bough Breaks" (TNG)
Epsilon Pulsar Cluster	Astronomical phenomenon located in Epsilon IX sector	"Samaritan Snare" (TNG)
Epsilon Silar System	Unexplored star system where Enterprise-D became a pawn of the Satarrans	"Conundrum" (TNG)
Erabus Prime	Planet where Q saved Vash from getting sick after a bug sting	"Q-Less" (DS9)
Errikang VII	Planet where Vash said Q amost got her killed	"Q-Less" (DS9)

(Continued on next page.)

(Continued from previous page.)

Object name	Description	Episode or film
Evadne IV	Planet destination after Enterprise-D encountered wormhole	"Clues" (TNG)
Excalbia	Inhospitable volcanic planet where Excalbians pitted the forces of good against evil	"The Savage Curtain" (TOS)
Exo III	Dead planet where Dr. Korby discovered a civilization of androids	"What Are Little Girls Made Of?" (TOS)
Fabrina	Star system whose sun went nova, origin of the Fabrini asteroid/ship Yonada	"For the World Is Hollow and I Have Touched the Sky" (TOS)
Fahleena III	Planet that a Valerian vessel visited, delivering supplies	"Dramatis Personae" (DS9)
Fendaus V	Planet led by a family whose members have no limbs	"Loud as a Whisper" (TNG)
FGC-13 cluster	Stellar cluster Enterprise-D charted in 2369	"Schisms" (TNG)
FGC-47	Giant nebula formed around a neutron star	"Imaginary Friend" (TNG)
Forlat III	Planet, site of an attack by the Crystalline Entity	"Silicon Avatar" (TNG)
Gagarin IV	Planet, location of the Darwin Genetic Research Station	"Unnatural Selection" (TNG)
Galaxy M33	Galaxy accidentally visited by the Enterprise-D with help from the Traveler	"Where No One Has Gone Before" (TNG)
Galen IV	Planet, site of Federation colony destroyed by Talarian forces	"Suddenly Human" (TNG)
Galor IV	Planetary site of an annex to the Daystrom Institute	"The Offspring" (TNG)
Galorndon Core	Federation planet where Romulan scout ship Pi crashed in 2366	"The Enemy" (TNG), "Unification, Part II" (TNG)
Galvin V	Planet where a marriage was only considered successful if a child was produced in the first year	"Data's Day" (TNG)
Gamelan V	Planet that experienced increase in atmospheric radiation in 2367	"Final Mission" (TNG)
Gamma 400 star System	Star system where Starbase 12 is located	"Space Seed" (TOS)
Gamma 7 System	Star system destroyed by the amoeba creature	"The Immunity Syndrome" (TOS)
Gamma Arigulon System	Star system where the U.S.S. LaSalle reported radiation anomalies	"Reunion" (TNG)
Gamma Erandi nebula	Interstellar gas cloud studied by the Enterprise-D in 2366	"Ménage à Troi" (TNG)
Gamma Eridon	Star system in Klingon space	"Redemption, Part II" (TNG)
Gamma Hromi II	Planet, location of a Gatherer camp. Site of negotiations to reunite the Acamarians and the Gatherers.	"The Vengeance Factor" (TNG)
Gamma Hydra	Star system, theoretical location of the Kobayashi Maru 's distress call	Star Trek II, "The Deadly Years" (TOS)
Gamma Hydra IV	Planet where entire population of a Federation science colony died of a radiation disease resembling old age	"The Deadly Years" (TOS)
Gamma II	Planet, destination of the Enterprise when crew members were abducted to Triskelion	"The Gamesters of Triskelion" (TOS)
Gamma Tauri IV	Planet where the Ferengi stole a T-9 energy converter	"The Last Outpost" (TNG)
Gamma Trianguli VI	Tropical class-M planet, homeworld of a humanoid race formerly ruled by the machine-god Vaal	"The Apple" (TOS)
Garadius System	Star system where the Enterprise-D was assigned to a diplomatic mission	"The Next Phase" (TNG)
Garon	Planet visited by the Starship Wellington	"Ensign Ro" (TNG)
Garth System	Solar system near planet Malcor III	"First Contact" (TNG)
Gaspar VII	Homeworld of Starfleet Captain Edwell	"Starship Mine" (TNG)
Gemaris V	Planet where Captain Picard mediated a trade dispute	"Captain's Holiday" (TNG)
Genesis	Planet formed in the Mutara Nebula by Project Genesis, but subsequently destroyed because of protomatter in the Genesis matrix	Star Trek II
Gideon	Class-M planet, once a paradise, but in 2269 plagued with terrible overpopulation	"The Mark of Gideon" (TOS)
Gonal IV	Planet of the swarming moths, studied in young Jay Gordon's science project	"Disaster" (TNG)
Gothos	Planet created by the entity Trelane, although his parents warned him that if he disobeyed, he wouldn't be allowed to make any more worlds	"The Squire of Gothos" (TOS)

(Continued on next page.)

(Continued from previous page.)

Object name	Description	Episode or film
Gravesworld	Planet where cyberneticist Ira Graves lived his last years	"The Schizoid Man" (TNG)
Guernica system	Star system, location of Federation outpost	"Galaxy's Child" (TNG)
Halee System	Star system where Worf suggested Klingon renegades Korris and Konmel be allowed to die rather than be executed	"Heart of Glory" (TNG)
Halii	Planet, homeworld of Starfleet Lieutenant Aquiel Uhnari	"Aquiel" (TNG)
Halley's comet	Ball of ice that travels through the Terran system every 76 years	"Time's Arrow, Part II" (TNG)
Hanoli System	Star system where a subspace rupture destroyed a Vulcan ship	"If Wishes Were Horses" (TNG)
Hanolin asteroid belt	Asteroid belt where a Ferengi cargo shutttle crashed and wreckage of the Vulcan ship T'Pau were found	"Unification, Part I" (TNG)
Hansen's Planet	Planet where creatures similar to ones on Taurus II lived	"The Galileo Seven" (TOS)
Harod IV	Planet where Enterprise-D picked up stranded miners	"The Perfect Mate" (TNG)
Harrakis V	Planet that the Enterprise-D visited in 2367	"Clues" (TNG)
Haven	Beautiful planet reputed to have mystical healing powers, attempted destination of the last Tarellian plague ship	"Haven" (TNG)
Hayashi System	Star system where the Enterprise-D charted atmospheric readings in 2366	"Tin Man" (TNG)
Hoek IV	Planet where the Sampalo relics can be viewed	"Q-Less" (DS9)
Holberg 917G	Planetoid where Mr. Flint built his home, far from the rest of humanity	"Requiem for Methuselah" (TOS)
Hromi Cluster	Location of planet Gamma Hromi II, near the Acamar System	"The Vengeance Factor" (TNG)
Hurada III	Planet visited by Tarmin and his group of telepathic historians	"Violations" (TNG)
Hurkos III	Planet where Devinoni Ral moved at age 19	"The Price" (TNG)
Iconia	Planet that once had an advanced civilization known as the "Demons of Air and Fire"	"Contagion" (TNG)
Icor IX	Planet, site of an astrophysics center that Picard hoped to visit	"Captain's Holiday" (TNG)
Idini Star Cluster	The Enterprise-D passed through this cluster en route to Mordan IV	"Too Short Aa Season" (TNG)
Idran	Trinary star system located in the Gamma Quadrant near the terminus of the Bajoran wormhole	"Emissary" (DS9), "Battle Lines" (DS9)
Ikalian Asteroid belt	Asteroid belt believed to be a hiding place for Kriosian rebels	"The Mind's Eye" (TNG)
Ilecom System	Star system that experienced time distortion from Manheim's experiments in 2364	"We'll Always Have Paris" (TNG)
Indri VIII	Planet seeded with genetic material by an ancient humanoid species	"The Chase" (TNG)
Ingraham B	Planet struck by the Denevan neural parasites in 2265	"Operation-Annihilate!" (TOS)
Janus VI	Planet, home of the Horta	"Devil in the Dark" (TOS)
Jaros II	Planet where Ro Laren was imprisoned until her release in 2368	"Ensign Ro" (TNG)
Jeraddo	Fifth moon orbiting the planet Bajor, home to Mullibok	"Progress" (DS9)
Jouret IV	Planet, site of New Providence colony, victim of a Borg attack	"The Best of Both Worlds, Part I" (TNG)
Jupiter outpost 92	Planetary Federation station, first to report the intrusion of the Borg into the Sol system in 2367	"Best of Both Worlds, Part I" (TNG)
Kaelon II	Planet whose star, Kaelon, was gradually dying	"Half a Life" (TNG)
Kalandan outpost	Artificially created planet manufactured by the Kalandan race	"That Which Survives" (TOS)
Kaldra IV	Planet, destination of a group of Ullian researchers in 2368	"Violations" (TNG)
Kataan	Star that exploded a thousand years ago. The humanoid inhabitants of one of the planets placed a collection of life experiences inside a probe encountered by Enterprise-D in 2368	"The Inner Light" (TNG)
Kavis Alpha IV	Planet that became the home of the newly evolved nanites	"Evolution" (TNG)
Kea IV	Planet that was topic of a research paper presented by Picard	"The Chase" (TNG)
Kelrabi System	Star system located in Cardassian space	"The Wounded" (TNG)
Kenda II	Planet, home of Dr. Dalen Quaice	"Remember Me" (TNG)
Khitomer	Planet near the Klingon-Romulan border, site of the historic Khitomer peace conference and the infamous Khitomer massacre	Star Trek VI, "Sins of the Father" (TNG), et al.

(Continued on next page.)

(Continued from previous page.)

Object name	Description	Episode or film
Klaestron IV	Homeworld to Ilon Tandro, who attempted to kidnap Dax in 2369	"Dax" (DS9)
Klavdia III	Planet where Salia was raised in a neutral environment, far from her warring homeworld, Daled IV	"The Dauphin" (TNG)
Klingon Homeworld	Central planet of the Klingon Empire, also known as Qo'noS	"Sins of the Father" (TNG), Star Trek VI, et al.
Kora II	Cardassian planet where Marritza taught at a military academy	"Duet" (DS9)
Korris I	Planet where a vintage of champagne is highly valued	"Emissary" (DS9)
Kostolain	Homeworld to Minister Campio, fiancé of Lwaxana Troi	"Cost of Living" (TNG)
Kraus IV	Planet where Cardassian clothier Garak could obtain silk lingerie	"Past Prologue" (DS9)
Krios	One of two neighboring star systems that had been warring with each other for centuries, a Klingon planet where Picard and Ambassador Kel met Governor Vagh	"The Perfect Mate" (TNG), "The Mind's Eye" (TNG)
Kriosian System	Star system controlled by the Klingon Empire	"The Mind's Eye" (TNG)
Kurl	Planet where inhabitants disappeared, leaving interesting ruins	"The Chase" (TNG)
L 370	Star system where seven planets were destroyed by the planet killer	"The Doomsday Machine" (TOS)
L 374	Star system almost completely destroyed by the planet killer in 2267	"The Doomsday Machine" (TOS)
La Forge Nebula	A new name for FGC—47, proposed by Geordi La Forge	"Imaginary Friend" (TNG)
Lambdo Paz	Moon of planet Pentarus III, where Dirgo's mining shuttle crashed	"Final Mission" (TNG)
Landris II	Planet where Dr. Mowray conducted archaeological research	"Lessons" (TNG)
Lantar	Nebula containing the planet Hoek IV	"Q-Less" (DS9)
Lapolis	Solar system that the Enterprise-D visited after downloading supplies to Deep Space 9	"Emissary" (DS9)
Largo V	Planet where Captain Jaheel was to deliver a shipment of Tamen Sahsheer	"Past Prologue" (DS9)
Lavinius V	Planet struck by the Denevan neural parasites in 2247	"Operation-Annihilate!" (TOS)
Legara IV	Planet, homeworld of the Legarans	"Sarek" (TNG)
Lemma II	Planet placed in jeopardy when the soliton wave became out of control	"New Ground" (TNG)
Ligon II	Home to the Ligonians, who valued ritualized honor above all else	"Code of Honor" (TNG)
Ligos VII	Planet with volcanic tendencies	"Rascals" (TNG)
Lima Sierra System	Star system whose planetary orbits are contrary to the norm	"Loud as a Whisper (TNG)
Lonka Pulsar	Rotating neutron star located in the Lonka Cluster	"Allegiance" (TNG)
Loren III	Planet where Professor Galen obtained genetic samples	"The Chase" (TNG)
Lorenze Cluster	Star cluster were the planet Minos is located	"The Arsenal of Freedom" (TNG), "The Child" (TNG)
Lunar V	Moon of Angosia III used as a prison for their biochemically altered military veterans	"The Hunted" (TNG)
Lyshan System	Star system where Picard's covert team was to be retrieved	"Chain of Command, Part II" (TNG)
Lysia	Homeworld of the Lysian Alliance	"Conundrum" (TNG)
M-113	Former home of the salt vampire, planet studied by archaeologist Dr. Robert Crater	"The Man Trap" (TOS)
M24 Alpha	Star system that contained the planet Triskelion	"The Gamesters of Triskelion" (TOS)
Mab-Bu VI	Planet with class-M moon where disembodied alien criminals existed, crash site of the U.S.S. Essex	"Power Play" (TNG)
Makus III	Planet where the Enterprise was to deliver medical supplies	"The Galileo Seven" (TOS)
Malaya IV	Planet where Paul Hickman had a physical exam before an alien DNA strand compelled him to return to Tarchannen III	"Identity Crisis" (TNG)
Malcor III	Planet where Riker conducted covert sociological studies in preparation for first contact	"First Contact" (TNG)
Malkus IX	Planet whose inhabitants developed writing before sign language	"Loud as a Whisper" (TNG)
Manark IV	Home of the sandbats	"The Empath" (TOS)

(Continued on next page.)

(Continued from previous page.)

Object name	Description	Episode or film
Manu III	Planet whose government who used proximity detectors to control people	"Legacy" (TNG)
Marcus XII	Planet chosen by the evil Gorgan to conquer and control	"And the Children Shall Lead" (TOS)
Marejaretus VI	Homeworld to the Ooolans	"Manhunt" (TNG)
Mariah IV	Planet visited by a Valerian vessel when delivering supplies	"Dramatis Personae" (DS9)
Mariposa	Planet settled by human colonists from S.S. Mariposa	"Up the Long Ladder" (TNG)
Marlonia	Planet visited by Enterprise-D crew members before changing to children	"Rascals" (TNG)
Mars	Fourth planet in Sol System, location of the Utopia Planitia Fleet Yards, where the Enterprise-D was built; also location of Martian Colonies, where important legal declarations on human rights were written; birthplace of Mira Romaine	"Booby Trap" (TNG), "Emissary" (DS9), "Court Martial" (TOS), "The Lights of Zetar" (TOS)
Maxia Zeta star System	Star system where the Battle of Maxia was fought	"The Battle" (TNG)
McAllister C-5 Nebula	Nebula located seven light-years inside Cardassian space	"Chain of Command, Part II" (TNG)
Melina II	Planet visited by Tarmin and his group of telepathic historians	"Violations" (TNG)
Melnos IV	Planet where Neela Daren lead a team to study a plasma geyser	"Lessons" (TNG)
Melona IV	Planet attacked by the Crystalline Entity in 2368	"Silicon Avatar" (TNG)
Meltasion asteroid belt	Asteroid belt through which the Enterprise-D was forced to tow a contaminated barge full of radioactive waste	"Final Mission" (TNG)
Memory Alpha	Planetoid, location of Federation library	"The Lights of Zetar" (TOS)
Mempa System	Star system in Klingon space where Gowron suffered a major defeat during the Klingon civil war	"Redemption" (TNG)
Merak II	Planet ravaged by a botanical plague in 2269	"The Cloud Minders" (TOS)
Metaline II	Planet where Neela Daren purchased a flexible piano keyboard	"Lessons" (TNG)
Midos V	Planet where Dr. Roger Korby planned to begin manufacturing androids	"What Are Little Girls Made Of?" (TOS)
Milika III	Planet where a young Picard led an away team to rescue an ambassador	"Tapestry" (TNG)
Minara II	Home planet of the Vians	"The Empath" (TOS)
Minas	Moon of Saturn, where the Nova Squadron was evacuated	"The First Duty" (TNG)
Minos	Planet whose inhabitants sold weapons during the Erselrope Wars	"The Arsenal of Freedom" (TNG)
Minos Korva	Planet that the Enterprise-D would have defended in the event of a Cardassian invasion	"Chain of Command, Part II" (TNG)
Mintaka III	Planet, site of Federation anthropological study of a proto-Vulcan culture.	"Who Watches the Watchers" (TNG)
Miramanee's planet	Planet, home to native American Indians transplanted from Earth (name is unofficial)	"The Paradise Syndrome" (TOS)
Miridian VI	Planet where Barash said he'd been captured by the Romulans	"Future Imperfect" (TNG)
Mizar II	Homeworld of the Mizarians	"Allegiance" (TNG)
Moab IV	Inhospitable planet where genetically engineered humans lived in a "perfect" society	"The Masterpiece Society" (TNG)
Modean System	Star system that Geordi La Forge visited as a child	"Imaginary Friend" (TNG)
Mordan IV	Planet plunged into a 40-year civil war after outside interference by Starfleet captain Mark Jameson	"Too Short a Season" (TNG)
Morikin VII	Planet where cadet Jean-Luc Picard was assigned for training	"Tapestry" (TNG)
Morska	Klingon planet on which is located a subspace monitoring outpost	*Star Trek VI: The Undiscovered Country*
Moselian System	Star system, destination of the Enterprise-D when it was invaded by the nitrium metal parasites	"Cost of Living" (TNG)
Mudor V	Planet from which the Enterprise-D departed before striking a series of quantum filaments	"Disaster" (TNG)

(Continued on next page.)

(Continued from previous page.)

Object name	Description	Episode or film
Murasaki 312	Quasar-like formation near planet Taurus II, investigated by Shuttlecraft Galileo in 2266, also by Enterprise-D in 2366	"The Galileo Seven" (TOS), "Data's Day" (TNG)
Mutara Nebula	Interstellar dust cloud in the Mutara Sector, transformed into the Genesis planet	*Star Trek II*
Myrmidon	Planet were archaeologist Vash was wanted for theft	"Q-Less" (DS9)
Nahmi IV	Planet where an outbreak of Correllium fever occurred in 2366	"Hollow Pursuits" (TNG)
Narenda III	Kingon planet defended by the Enterprise-C in 2344	"Yesterday's Enterprise" (TNG)
Nasreldine	Planet where an Enterprise-D crew member picked up a case of the flu	"The Icarus Factor" (TNG)
Nel Bato System	Star system believed to be where Kivas Fajo may have taken the kidnapped Data	"The Most Toys" (TNG)
Nel System	Star system visited by a delegation of Ullian telepathic historians	"Violations" (TNG)
Nelvana III	Planet where Romulan defector Jarok believed there was a secret base for a major offensive against the Federation	"The Defector" (TNG)
Nequencia System	Star system located near the Romulan Neutral Zone	"Birthright, Part I" (TNG)
Nervala IV	Planet where a duplicate of William Riker was found	"Second Chances" (TNG)
New Paris	Federation colony stricken by a plague in 2267	"The Galileo Seven" (TOS)
Ngame Nebula	Astronomical formation that the Enterprise-D passed en route to planet Evadne IV	"Clues" (TNG)
Nimbus III	Planet governed by Klingons, Romulans and the Federation, "The Planet of Galactic Peace"	*Star Trek V*
Norpin V	Planet, location of a community where Scotty hoped to retire before being waylaid by the Dyson sphere	"Relics" (TNG)
Ogus II	Planet where Enterprise-D crew members took R&R in 2367	"Brothers" (TNG)
Ohniaka III	Planet, site of Federation science station destroyed by the Borg	"Descent, Part I" (TNG)
Omega IV	Planet whose inhabitants were nearly wiped out centuries ago by a bacteriological war	"The Omega Glory" (TOS)
Omega Sagitta System	Solar system that includes twin planets Altec and Straleb	"The Outrageous Okona" (TNG)
Omicron Ceti III	Planet bombarded by berthold rays, site of a failed colony	"This Side of Paradise" (TOS)
Omicron IV	Planet like Earth, nearly destroyed by nuclear weapons	"Assignment: Earth"(TOS)
Omicron Theta	Planet where Data was discovered at a colony destroyed by the Crytalline Entity	"Datalore" (TNG)
Ophiucus III	Class-M planet where Harry Mudd was to deliver three women as wives	"Mudd's Women" (TOS)
Ordek Nebula	Home planet of the Wogneer creatures	"Allegiance" (TNG)
Orelious IX	Planet destroyed by the Promellians and the Menthars in 2266	"Booby Trap" (TNG)
Organia	Home of the noncorporeal Organians who imposed the Organian Peace Treaty between the Federation and the Klingons	"Errand of Mercy" (TOS)
Ornara	Home to the Ornarans, who were dependent to the drug felicium	"Symbiosis" (TNG)
Otar II	Destination of the Enterprise-D following the death of Lal in 2366	"The Offspring" (TNG)
Pacifica	Beautiful ocean world, known for warm blue waters; an interstellar conference was held there in 2365	"Conspiracy" (TNG) "Manhunt" (TNG)
Parliament	Planet used by the Federation as a site for diplomatic negotiations	"Lonely Among Us" (TNG)
Paulson Nebula	Astronomical cloud where the Enterprise-D hid from the Borg in 2366	"The Best of Both Worlds,Part I" (TNG)
Pegos Minor	Star system where Dr. Paul Manheim claimed his lab was located	"We'll Always Have Paris" (TNG)
Peliar Zel	Planet with two moons, Alpha and Beta	"The Host" (TNG)
Pelleus V	Planet where Enterprise-D was scheduled to visit after Starbase 74	"11001001" (TNG)
Pelloris Field	Asteroid field that threatened planet Tessen III	"Cost of Living" (TNG)
Pentarus II	Planet where the mining shuttle Nenebek was throught to have crashed	"Final Mission" (TNG)
Pentarus V	Planet that petitioned Picard to mediate a labor dispute among the salenite miners	"Final Mission" (TNG)
Penthara IV	Federation planet struck by an asteroid, creating atmospheric problems	"A Matter of Time" (TNG)

(Continued on next page.)

(Continued from previous page.)

Object name	Description	Episode or film
Penthara IV	Federation planet struck by an asteroid, creating atmospheric problems	"A Matter of Time" (TNG)
Persephone V	Home planet to retired Admiral Mark Jameson just prior to his death	"Too Short a Season" (TNG)
Pheben solar System	Location of undesignated maneuvers by the Klingon vessel Pagh	"A Matter of Honor" (TNG)
Phelan System	Star system where the Enterprise-D was assigned a diplomatic mission	"The Outcast" (TNG)
Planet IV 892	Planet whose culture was Earth's Rome, but in the 20th century	"Bread and Circuses" (TOS)
Platonius	Planet settled by the Platonians, who based their society on Plato's Republic	"Plato's Stepchildren" (TOS)
Pleiades Cluster	Region of space known as M45, where young planets are located	"Home Soil" (TNG)
Pollux IV	Planet where the Greek god Apollo lived and tried to recruit the crew of the Enterprise as his worshippers	"Who Mourns for Adonais?" (TOS)
Pollux V	Planet in Beta Geminorum system	"Who Mourns for Adonais?" (TOS)
Prakal II	Planet where Guinan acquired an unusual drink recipe	"In Theory" (TNG)
PraxillusSystem	Solar system, site for an unsuccessful helium ignition test	"Half a Life" (TNG)
Psi 2000	Planet that disintegrated in 2266	"The Naked Time" (TOS)
Pyris VII	Planet where Korob and Sylvia captured several Enterprise crew members	"Catspaw" (TOS)
Q	Planet, home of scientist Thomas Leighton at the time of his death in 2266	"The Conscience of the King" (TOS)
Qo'noS	Central planet of the Klingon Empire, usually known as the Klingon Homeworld	*Star Trek VI: The Undiscovered Country*
Quadra Sigma III	Planet where a Federation mining colony suffered a deadly explosion	"Hide and Q" (TNG)
Qualor II	Planet, site of a Federation surplus depot operated by the Zakdorns	"Unification, Part I" (TNG)
Quazulu VIII	Planet where several Enterprise-D students became ill	"Angel One" (TNG)
Rachelis System	Planetary system struck with an outbreak of plasma plague in 2365	"The Child" (TNG)
Rahm-Izad System	Star system where Gul Ocett was misdirected to while in search of a message from an ancient humanoid race	"The Chase" (TNG)
Rakhar	Planet in the Gamma Quadrant, home to Croden	"Vortex" (DS9)
Ramatis III	Planet, home of famed negotiator Riva	"Loud as a Whisper" (TNG)
Ramatis star System	Star system, location of planet Ramatis III	"Loud as a Whisper" (TNG)
Regula	Lifeless planetoid, test site for Project Genesis	*Star Trek II*
Regulus V	Home planet to the giant eel-birds	"Amok Time" (TOS)
Rekag-Seronia	Planet, site of bitter hostilities affecting Federation shipping routes	"Man of the People" (TNG)
Relva VII	Planet, location of Starfleet facility where Wesley failed his first Academy exam	"Coming of Age" (TNG)
Remus	One of the homeworlds of the Romulan Star Empire	"Balance of Terror" (TOS)
Rigel	Star located in the most densely populated portion of the known Milky Way Galaxy	"The Doomsday Machine" (TOS)
Rigel II	Planet where McCoy mentioned he'd met two scantily clad women	"Shore Leave" (TOS)
Rigel IV	Mr. Hengist's home planet	"Wolf in the Fold" (TOS)
Rigel IV	Planet where a brilliant astronomer had a fondness for Lwaxana Troi	"Half a Life" (TNG)
Rigel V	Planet where drug to increase blood products was tested	"Journey to Babel" (TOS)
Rigel VII	Planet where several Enterprise crew members killed under command of Captain Pike; Kobliad criminal Rao Vantika caused computer systems to crash there	"The Cage" (TOS), "The Menagerie" (TOS), "The Passenger" (DS9)
Rigel XII	Planet, site a small lithium mining operation headed by Ben Childress	"Mudd's Women" (TOS)
Risa	Tropical resort planet noted for its beauty and open sexuality; La Forge was to attend an artificial intelligence seminar on Risa	"Captain's Holiday" (TNG), et al.
Rochani	Planet whee Curzon Dax and Sisko were cornered by Kaleans	"Dramatis Personae" (DS9)
Romulus	One of the homeworlds of the Romulan Star Empire	"Balance of Terror" (TOS)
Rousseau V	Location of a spectacular asteroid belt	"The Dauphin" (TNG)
Ruah IV	Planet supporting life-forms including a genus of proto-humanoids	"The Chase" (TNG)

(Continued on next page.)

(Continued from previous page.)

Object name	Description	Episode or film
Rubicun III	Homeworld to the Edo race	"Justice" (TNG)
Rubicun star System	Star system near the Strnad system containing Rubicun III	"Justice" (TNG)
Rura Penthe	Frozen planet, location of a Klingon prison camp where Kirk and McCoy were wrongly imprisoned for the assassination of Gorkon, site of a dilithium mine that used forced labor	*Star Trek VI*
Rutia IV	Planet where a dissident group, the Ansata, sought political independence	"The High Ground" (TNG)
Sahndara	Native star to the Platonians which exploded thousands of years ago	"Plato's Stepchildren" (TOS)
Sargon's planet	(Unoffical name) World destroyed centuries ago by war, leaving a small number of survivors stored in subterranean canisters	"Return to Tomorrow" (TOS)
Sarona VII	Planet that was Enterprise-D's destination before diverting to Vandor IX	"We'll Always Have Paris" (TNG)
Sarpeidon	Planet whose star went nova in 2269	"All Our Yesterdays" (TOS)
Sarthong V	Planet known for its rich archaeological ruins	"Captain's Holiday" (TNG)
Saturn	Sixth planet in the Sol System, noted for beautiful ring system; location of Starfleet Academy flight range	"The First Duty" (TNG)
Scalos	Planet whose humanoid inhabitants underwent hyperacceleration as a result of environmental pollution	""Wink of an Eye" (TOS)
Scothis III	Homeworld of the Satarran race of intelligent beings	"The Chase" (TNG)
Selay	Homeworld to a sentient reptilian race	"Lonely Among Us" (TNG)
Selcundi Drema	Star system whose planets experienced geologic instabilities	"Pen Pals" (TNG)
Seldonis IV	Planet where a diplomatic document governing the treatment of prisoners of war was framed	"Chain of Command, Part II" (TNG)
Selebi Asteroid Belt	Asteroid belt charted by the Enterprise-D charted in 2366	"The Offspring" (TNG)
Sentinel Minor IV	Planet, destination of the U.S.S. Lalo before they were destroyed by the Borg	"The Best of Both Worlds, Part I" (TNG)
Septimus Minor	Original destination of vessel Artemis, launched in 2274	"The Ensigns of Command" (TNG)
Setlik III	Planet where a Federation outpost was destroyed by a Cardassian sneak attack	"The Wounded" (TNG) "Emissary" (DS9)
Shelia star System	Home star system of the Sheliak	"The Ensigns of Command" (TNG)
Shiralea VI	Planet, location of the Parallax Colony, a place that Lwaxana Troi loved to visit	"Cost of Living" (TNG)
Sigma Draconis	Star system with three class-M planets	"Spock's Brain" (TOS)
Sigma Draconis III	Class-M planet equivalent in development to Earth year 1485	"Spock's Brain" (TOS)
Sigma Draconis IV	Class-M planet equivalent in development to Earth year 2030	"Spock's Brain" (TOS)
Sigma Draconis VI	Glaciated class-M planet where Spock's brain was taken	"Spock's Brain" (TOS)
Sigma Erandi System	Star system, source of hytritium chemical	"The Most Toys" (TNG)
Sigma III solar System	Solar system containing planet Quadra Sigma III	"Hide and Q" (TNG)
Sigma Iotia II	Planet whose culture was based on the Chicago mobs of the 1920s, a result of cultural contamination from the U.S.S. Horizon	"A Piece of the Action" (TOS)
Sirius	Star used for navigational reference	"Arena" (TOS)
Solais V	Planet where famed mediator Riva attempted to help the warring inhabitants find peace	"Loud as a Whisper" (TNG)
Solari	Star system, location of planet Solais V	"Loud as a Whisper" (TNG)
Solarion IV	Planet where a Federation colony was destroyed by Cardassians	"Ensign Ro" (TNG)
Stakoron II	Planet in the Gamma Quadrant containing mizainite ore	"The Nagus" (DS9)

(Continued on next page.)

(Continued from previous page.)

Object name	Description	Episode or film
Straleb	Planet, along with planet Altec, part of the Coalition of Madena	"The Outrageous Okona" (TNG)
Strnad solar System	Solar system to which the Enterprise-D delivered Earth colonists in 2364	"Justice" (TNG)
Styris IV	Planet plagued by Anchilles fever in 2364	"Code of Honor" (TNG)
Sumiko III	Planet noted as the location of the Emerald Wading Pool	"Conundrum" (TNG)
Suvin IV	Planet noted for splended archaeologic ruins	"Rascals" (TNG)
System J-25	Star system, location of Borg attack	"Q Who?" (TNG)
T'lli Beta	Planet, destination of Enterprise-D when it encountered a school of two-dimensional creatures	"The Loss" (TNG)
Tagra IV	Planet ecologically devastated in the Argolis Cluster	"True-Q" (TNG)
Tagus III	Planet where archaeological digs had been studied for 22,000 years	""QPid" (TNG)
Takara	Homeworld of the Takarans	"Suspicions" (TNG)
Talos IV	Class-M planet devastated centuries ago by nuclear war, homeworld to the Talosians	"The Cage" (TOS)
Tantalus V	Location of a Federation penal colony	"Dagger of the Mind" (TOS)
Tanuga IV	Planet where Dr. Apgar attempted to deveop a Krieger wave converter	"A Matter of Perspective" (TNG)
Tarchannen III	Planet where crew members from the U.S.S. Victory were infected by alien DNA	"Idenity Crisis" (TNG)
Tarella	Home planet to the Tarellians, devastated in a biological war	"Haven" (TNG)
Tarod IX	Planet near Romulan Neutral Zone, attacked by the Borg in 2364	"The Neutral Zone" (TNG)
Tarsas III	Planet around which orbits Starbase 74	"11001001" (TNG)
Tarsus IV	Site of infamous massacre by Kodos the Executioner	"The Conscience of the King" (TOS)
Tartaras V	Planet that Vash decided to explore instead of returning to Earth in 2369	"Q-Less" (DS9)
Tau Alpha C	Little-known homeworld to the Traveler	"Where No One Has Gone Before" (TNG)
Tau Ceti	Star located eight light-years from Earth	"Whom Gods Destroy" (TOS)
Tau Ceti III	Planet where Picard met Captain Rixx sometime in 2364	"Conspiracy" (TNG)
Tau Cygna V	Planet where a Federation colony was established in violation of the Treaty of Armens	"The Ensigns of Command" (TNG)
Taurus II	Planet where Shuttlecraft Galileo crashed in 2267 while under the command of Mr. Spock	"The Galileo Seven" (TOS)
Tavela Minor	Planet where Dr. Crusher suggested that Nurse Ogawa take a vacation	"Imaginary Friend"
Teleris	Star cluster that Q invited Vash to visit	"Q-Less" (DS9)
Tellun	Star system containing planets Elas and Troyius	"Elaan of Troyius" (TOS)
Tessen III	Federation planet threatened by an asteroid in 2368	"Cost of Living" (TNG)
Tethys III	Green planet with hydrogen-helium composition and frozen core	"Clues" (TNG)
Thalos VII	Planet where cocoa beans are aged for four centuries (yum!)	"The Dauphin" (TNG)
Thasus	Home planet of a noncorporeal race known as the Thasians, who cared for young Charles Evans	"Charlie X" (TOS)
Thelka IV	Planet where Picard discovered a delicious dessert	"Lessons" (TNG)
Theta 116	Star system that was the final destination for the Charybdis	"The Royale" (TNG)
Theta Cygni XII	Planet struck by the Denevan neural parasites	"Operation-Annihilate!" (TOS)
Theta VII	Planet that needed vaccines from the Enterprise	"Obsession" (TOS)
Tiburon	Planet where Dr. Sevrin studied as a research engineer, also location of Zora's inhumane experiments	"The Way to Eden" (TOS), "The Savage Curtain" (TOS)
Titan	Largest of Saturn's moons, used in Nova Squadron's maneuvers	"The First Duty" (TNG)
Titus IV	Planet where Miles O'Brien almost stepped on a Lycosa tarantula	"Realm of Fear" (TNG)
Tohvun III	Neutral planet located near the Cardassian/Federation border	"Chain of Command, Part II" (TNG)
Torman V	Planet that Picard, Dr. Crusher, and Worf visited to secure transportation to Celtris III	"Chain of Command, Part I" (TNG)

(Continued on next page.)

(Continued from previous page.)

Object name	Description	Episode or film
Torona IV	Home of the insectoid race known as the Jarada	"The Big Goodbye" (TNG)
Triacus	Planet where a Federation science team was driven to suicide by the evil Gorgon	"And the Children Shall Lead" (TOS)
Triona System	Planet where Lt. Keith Rocha was killed by coalescent organisms	"Aquiel" (TNG)
Triskelion	Planet ruled by the Providers for gaming purposes	"The Gamesters of Triskelion" (TOS)
Troyius	Planet at war with sister world Elas in 2268	"Elaan of Troyius" (TOS)
Turkana IV	Planet, site of a failed Federation colony, birthplace to security officer Natasha Yar	"Legacy" (TNG)
Tycho	Star system containing the home planet of the vampire creature	"Obsession" (TOS)
Tycho IV	Home planet to the vampire cloud creature	"Obsession" (TOS)
Tyken's Rift	Rupture in the fabric of space Enterprise-D encountered in 2367	"Night Terrors" (TNG)
Typhon Expanse	Huge area of space where Enterprise-D and the Essex were trapped in a temporal causality loop	"Cause and Effect" (TNG)
Tyran System	Solar system containing the planet Tyrus VIIA	"The Quality of Life" (TNG)
Tyrellia	Federaton planet with no atmosphere and no magnetic pole	"Starship Mine" (TNG)
Tyrus VIIA	Planet where Dr. Farallon tested a particle fountain mining technique	"The Quality of Life" (TNG)
Ultima Thule	Planet, location of a purification plant where dolamide was processed	"Dramatis Personae" (DS9)
Vadris III	Planet whose the natives think they are the only intelligent life in the universe	"Q-Less" (DS9)
Vagra II	Planet whose inhabitants escaped, leaving behind a skin of pure evil, location of Natasha Yar's death	"Skin of Evil" (TNG)
Valo System	Solar system located in neutral space near Cardassian border	"Ensign Ro" (TNG)
Valt Minor	Star system at war with neighboring Krios system for centuries	"The Perfect Mate" (TNG)
Vandor IX	Planet, location of Dr. Paul Manheim's laboratory	"We'll Always Have Paris" (TNG)
Vandor star System	Binary star system containing a B-class giant with companion pulsar, location of Dr. Paul Manheim's laboratory	"We'll Always Have Paris" (TNG)
Vaytan	Star chosen as the first test site for the new metaphasic shield	"Suspicions" (TNG)
Vega	Destination of U.S.S. Enterprise before receiving distress call from S.S. Columbia	"The Cage" (TOS)
Velara III	Planet that was the object of a terraforming project in 2364	"Home Soil" (TNG)
Vendikar	Planet at war with its neighbor, Eminiar VII, for 500 years	"A Taste of Armageddon" (TOS)
Ventax II	Planet that enjoyed a thousand years of peace, apparently because of a pact with a mythological figure named Ardra	"Devil's Due" (TNG)
Verath	Solar system, origin of a rare statue that Vash auctioned off at Quark's	"Q-Less" (DS9)
Vilmor II	Planet where clues to the ancient seeding humanoids were found	"The Chase" (TNG)
Volchok Prime	Planet where the Ferengi Hoex bought his rival's cargo port	"The Nagus" (DS9)
Volterra Nebula	Nebula that the Enterprise-D studied in 2369	"The Chase" (TNG)
Vulcan	Home planet to Mr. Spock	"Amok Time" (TOS), et al.
Wolf 359	Star system near Sol, location of a devastating battle against the Borg	"The Best of Both Worlds, Part II" (TNG), et al.
wormhole, Bajoran	Artificially constructed stable passageway to the Gamma Quadrant	"Emissary" (DS9)
Wrigley's pleasure Planet	Planet were Enterprise crew member Darnell met a beautiful woman	"The Man Trap" (TOS)
Xanthras III	Planet, destination of Enterprise-D after mission in Gamma Erandi nebula	"Ménage à Troi" (TNG)
Xendi Sabu star System	Star system where the Ferengi returned the Stargazer to Picard	"The Battle" (TNG)
Xerxes VII	Planet where legend says a mythical land called Neinman is found	"When the Bough Breaks" (TNG)
Zadar IV	Planet on which oceanographer Dr. Harry Bernard once lived	"When the Bough Breaks" (TNG)

(Continued on next page.)

(Continued from previous page.)

Object name	Description	Episode or film
Zalkon	Homeworld of the Zalkonians	"Transfigurations" (TNG)
Zayra IV	Planet where Miles O'Brien rerouted an emitter array	"Realm of Fear" (TNG)
Zed Lapis Sector	Region where planet Vagra II is located	"Skin of Evil" (TNG)
Zeon	Peaceful neighbors to planet Ekos	"Patterns of Force" (TOS)
Zeta Alpha II	Planet from which the U.S.S. Lalo departed before they were lost to the Borg	"The Best of Both Worlds, Part I" (TNG)
Zeta GelisCluster	Cluster where Enterprise-D discovered the Zalkonian, John Doe	"Transfigurations" (TNG)
Zetar	Planet, home to the Zetarians, destroyed millennia ago	"The Lights of Zetar" (TOS)
Zytchin III	Planet where Captain Picard once spent a four day vacation that he claimed not to have enjoyed	"Captain's Holiday" (TNG)

Planetary Geosciences Laboratory. Scientific research facility located on Deck 10 of the *Enterprise*-D. This laboratory, under the supervision of Acting Ensign **Wesley Crusher**, conducted geological surveys of the planetary systems in the **Selcundi Drema** Sector in 2365. ("Pen Pals" [TNG]).

plankton loaf. Terran microscopic sea life baked into one of **Keiko O'Brien**'s favorite breakfast foods. Keiko served this dish, along with kelp buds and sea berries, to her new husband, **Miles O'Brien**, who wasn't too sure about the stuff. ("The Wounded" [TNG]).

plasma conversion sensor. Starfleet instrument used to measure the consumption of matter and antimatter fuel during engine use. ("Timescape" [TNG]).

plasma fire. Combustion supported by the intense heat from an externally supplied ionized plasma gas source, such as those found in a starship's **internal power grid.** ("Disaster" [TNG]).

plasma infuser. Handheld instrument used for the transfer of high-energy plasma. ("Suspicions" [TNG]).

plasma infusion unit. Medical equipment used aboard Federation starships to dispense fluid and electrolytes. ("Schisms" [TNG]).

plasma injector. Component of a **warp drive** system. ("Captive Pursuit" [DS9]).

plasma plague. A group of deadly virus types. An unclassified but extremely virulent strain of plasma plague threatened the densely populated **Rachelis system** in 2365. Significant research into plasma plague was conducted by Dr. Susan Nuress in 2295 in response to a similar outbreak on planet Obi VI.
   One mutated strain developed during Nuress's research was found to grow more rapidly when exposed to eichner radiation. A similar strain threatened the *Enterprise*-D when that ship was transporting specimens of plasma plague to Science Station **Tango Sierra** to combat an outbreak in the Rachelis system in 2365. ("The Child" [TNG]).

plasma streamer. Gas current flowing through space between one star in a binary pair to the other. The *Starship Yosemite* encountered **quasi-energy microbes** living in the plasma streamer between a binary pair in the Igo Sector in 2369. ("Realm of Fear" [TNG]).

plasma torch. Work tool used on board Federation starships. An engineer aboard the *Enterprise*-D was badly burned in 2369 when he was working on a conduit on Deck 37 when a plasma torch blew up in his hands. ("Frame of Mind" [TNG]).

plasma. Scientific term for very hot, ionized gas. A starship's impulse engines leave an exhaust of plasma, which can be detected, even from a cloaked vessel. (*Star Trek VI: The Undiscovered Country*).

plasticized titanium mesh. A 26th-century construction material, unknown in the 24th century. **Professor Berlingoff Rasmussen**'s time travel pod had a hull composed of plasticized titanium mesh. ("A Matter of Time" [TNG]).

Plasus. (Jeff Corey). High advisor of the cloud city **Stratos** above planet **Ardana** in 2269 and father to **Droxine**. The politically conservative Plasus was determined to protect the established social order on his planet, despite the fact that exploitation of the **Troglyte** workers on the planet's surface was both unfair and physically harmful to the workers. Plasus opposed talks with the Troglytes, and further opposed a plan whereby protective **filter masks** would be furnished to the workers to shield them against the debilitating effects of **zenite** gas. ("The Cloud Minders" [TOS]).

• **"Plato's Stepchildren."** Original Series episode #67. Written by Meyer Dolinsky. Directed by David Alexander. Stardate 5784.2. *First aired in 1968. Enterprise crew members are held captive by a race with psychokinetic powers.* SEE: **Alexander; kironide; Parmen; Philana; Plato; Platonians; Platonius; psychokinesis; Sahndara.**

Plato. Ancient Greek philosopher (c.428 B.C.-c.348 B.C.) whose teachings inspired a group of extraterrestrials led by **Parmen** who later called themselves **Platonians**. ("Plato's Stepchildren" [TOS]).

Platonians. Humanoids, originally from the **Sahndara** star system, who patterned their society after the teachings of ancient Earth philosopher **Plato**. When their star, Sahndara, exploded millennia ago, 38 individuals fled their doomed world, settling briefly on Earth during the time of Plato. When the Greek culture faded, the Platonians moved to another planet, which they called Platonius. Here, they accidentally developed powerful **psychokinetic** powers from ingesting native food containing **kironide**, a rare and powerful element found in the native food. The Platonians remained unknown to the rest of the galaxy for centuries until their leader, Parmen, fell ill in 2268 and summoned the *Starship Enterprise* to provide him with medical care. ("Plato's Stepchildren" [TOS]). SEE: **Alexander**.

Platonius. Class-M planet settled by the **Platonians**, who attempted to create their own version of Plato's Republic there. The natural foods on Platonius contained a substance called **kironide**, a powerful energy source. ("Plato's Stepchildren" [TOS]).

Pleiades Cluster. Region of space, also known as M45 or the Seven Sisters, in which many young planets are located. The Pleiades are a cluster of about 400 stars in a 25-light-year radius, some 415 light-years from Earth. One of the planets in the area is **Velara III**, site of a failed **terraforming** project. The *Enterprise*-D conducted a mapping mission in the Pleiades Cluster in 2364. ("Home Soil" [TNG]).

Plexicorp. Commercial company engaged in the manufacture of acrylic polymers and other plastics in San Francisco, Earth, in the late 20th century. **Dr. Nichols**, a chemist employed by Plexicorp, developed the molecular matrix for **transparent aluminum**. He was assisted in this discovery by Montgomery Scott, who provided the information in exchange for acrylic plastic sheeting needed for transporting two humpback whales to the 23rd century. (*Star Trek IV: The Voyage Home*). *The Plexicorp scenes in* Star Trek IV *were filmed at a company called Reynolds & Taylor in Santa Ana, California.*

plexing. Betazoid relaxation technique in which one gently taps a nerve behind one's ear, using the index and middle fingers. Plexing stimulates a nerve cluster behind the carotid artery, stimulating the release of natural endorphins. Deanna Troi taught the technique to **Reginald Barclay** in an effort to help him overcome his fear of being transported. ("Realm of Fear" [TNG]). *Troi used the technique to try to calm herself in subsequent episodes, including "Timescape" (TNG).*

***plomeek* soup.** A traditional Vulcan food. Nurse Chapel prepared a bowl of *plomeek* soup for Spock during his *Pon farr* in 2267, but Spock expressed his desire to be left alone by throwing the bowl into the corridor. ("Amok Time" [TOS]).

"Plum." The nickname given to **Leonard McCoy** by the future Mrs. **Nancy Crater** when they were romantically involved several years prior to McCoy's assignment to the *Enterprise*. ("The Man Trap" [TOS]).

poker. Traditional Earth card game enjoyed by crew members of the *Enterprise*-D. A weekly poker game was held every Thursday night aboard the *Enterprise*-D. **Data** initially believed poker to be a fairly simple mathematical game, but he failed to consider the human element of bluffing one's opponent. ("The Measure of a Man" [TNG]). Data eventually came to regard the game of poker as a fascinating forum for the study of human nature, eventually developing such ingenious exercises as his poker game with holographic representations of **Sir Isaac Newton**, **Albert Einstein**, and **Stephen Hawking**. ("Descent, Part I" [TNG]). Geordi's VISOR gave him "special insight" into the cards held by his shipmates, courtesy of infrared light, although he said he never peeked until after a hand was over. ("Ethics" [TNG]). *The weekly* Enterprise-D *poker game was first seen in "The Measure of a Man" (TNG).*

Police Special. Ancient Earth hand weapon that fired lead bullets propelled by expanding gasses. On the **amusement park planet** in 2267, Sulu found a Police Special, which he'd always wanted to add to his collection. ("Shore Leave" [TOS]).

Pollux IV. Class-M planet in the **Beta Geminorum** system with an oxygen-nitrogen atmosphere, home to the entity known as **Apollo**. The *Starship Enterprise*, in the Beta Geminorum system in 2267, was briefly captured by Apollo, who hoped the *Enterprise* crew would worship him as had the ancient Greeks. ("Who Mourns for Adonais?" [TOS]).

Pollux V. Planet in the **Beta Geminorum** system that registered with no intelligent life-forms when the *Enterprise* investigated that area of space on stardate 3468. ("Who Mourns for Adonais?" [TOS]).

polyadrenaline. Synthetic pharmaceutical based on the humanoid hormone epinephrine. ("Ethics" [TNG]).

polyduranide. Construction material used aboard Federation starships. Although normally not flammable, polyduranide emits dangerous radiation when exposed to extremely intense heat, such as that generated in a **plasma fire**. ("Disaster" [TNG]).

Pomet. (Alan Altshuld). Member of a group of terrorists who attempted to steal **trilithium resin** from the *Enterprise*-D in 2369. Pomet was disabled by Picard using a crossbow from Lieutenant Worf's quarters. Pomet was later killed by the **baryon sweep**. ("Starship Mine" [TNG]). SEE: **Remmler Array**.

***Pon farr*.** Vulcan term for the time of mating. Although **Vulcans** live strictly by the dictates of logic, their veneer of civilization is ripped away from them during *Pon farr*, every seven years of their adult life. The individual experiencing *Pon farr* will stop eating and sleeping if not allowed to return home to take a mate. Spock underwent *Pon farr* in 2267, when he returned to Vulcan, only to be spurned by his betrothed, **T'Pring**. ("Amok Time" [TOS]). SEE: *Plak-tow*. Spock again experienced *Pon farr* when his regenerated body was undergoing hyperaccelerated growth on the **Genesis Planet** in 2285. Spock was fortunate that **Saavik**, a Vulcan female, was also present. (*Star Trek III: The Search for Spock*).

port. Ancient nautical term referring to the left side of a ship, as opposed to the starboard (right) side.

Portal. (Darryl Henriques). The last remaining protector of the once-grand **Tkon Empire**, Portal 63 had been stationed on the planet Delphi Ardu during the Tkon age of Bastu, at least 600,000 years ago. Remaining in some kind of suspension or stasis in the intervening millennia on a deserted outpost, Portal was unaware that the **Tkon Empire** had collapsed until he was awakened by the presence of **Ferengi** and Federation spacecraft near his planet. ("The Last Outpost" [TNG]). *Actor Darryl Henriques also played Romulan ambassador Nanclus in* Star Trek VI: The Undiscovered Country.

positronic brain. An extremely advanced computing device that uses the decay of positrons to form sophisticated neural network systems. Long thought to be impossible, the positronic brain was first postulated in the 20th century by **Isaac Asimov** and finally made practical in the 24th century by **Noonien Soong**. Positronic brains were used in Soong's androids, **Data** and **Lore**. ("Datalore" [TNG]). A significant advance in submicron matrix transfer technology was introduced at a cybernetics conference in 2366, permitting Data to program a new positronic brain, which he used as the basis for his construction of his daughter, **Lal**. ("The Offspring" [TNG]). *Although positronic computing remains purely hypothetical, positrons do exist. They are subatomic particles virtually identical to normal electrons, but with opposite electromagnetic properties. An electron has a negative charge, and a positron has a positive charge. Positrons were the first known particles of actual antimatter to be observed in the laboratory.*

post-atomic horror. Term used to describe a period of 21st-century Earth history, circa 2079, during which Earth was recovering from the **World War III** nuclear conflict. Much of the planet reverted to barbarism during this period. ("Encounter at Farpoint, Part I" [TNG]).

potato casserole. Traditional Irish dish that was part of **Miles O'Brien**'s childhood. He once prepared the dish for his wife, Keiko, who preferred such staples as **plankton loaf** and kelp buds, but tried her husband's favorites anyway. ("The Wounded" [TNG]).

Potemkin, U.S.S. Federation starship, *Constitution* class,

Starfleet registry number NCC-1657. The *Potemkin* was one of five ships that participated in the disastrous test of the **M-5** multitronic unit in 2268. ("The Ultimate Computer" [TOS]). The *Potemkin* was to rendezvous with the *Enterprise* at Beta Aurigae shortly after stardate 5928 to study gravitational influences in that binary system, until Dr. Janice Lester in Kirk's body changed the course. ("Turnabout Intruder" [TOS]).

Potemkin, U.S.S. Federation starship, *Excelsior* class, Starfleet registry number NCC-18253. **William T. Riker** served aboard this vessel prior to his assignments to the *Hood* and the *Enterprise*-D, but after the *Pegasus*. Riker once employed the unconventional tactic of positioning the ship over a planet's magnetic pole, thus making the ship difficult to detect by an opponent's sensors. ("Peak Performance" [TNG]). In 2361, as a lieutenant aboard the *Potemkin*, Riker led an away team to evacuate the science outpost on planet **Nervala IV**, and subsequently was promoted to lieutenant commander and commended for "exceptional valor" on the mission. It was not realized until later that a duplicate of Riker had been created in a transporter malfunction during the evacuation. ("Second Chances" [TNG]). SEE: **Riker, Thomas**. During the same year, the *Potemkin* was the last Federation starship to make contact with the failed **Turkana IV** colony, prior to the *Enterprise*-D's mission there in 2367. *Potemkin* personnel were warned by the colony's ruling cadres not to transport to the surface, or they would be killed. ("Legacy" [TNG]). The *Potemkin* rendezvoused with the *Enterprise*-D on stardate 45587 to transfer **Dr. Toby Russell** to the *Enterprise*-D. ("Ethics" [TNG]). *Named for Grigory Aleksandrovich Potemkin, (1739-1791), Russian military figure under Catherine II.*

Pottrik Syndrome. Disease that **Aamin Marritza** claimed to have, which was similar to **Kalla-Nohra Syndrome**, and was even treated by the same medication. A lower pulmonary bioprobe for Pottrick Syndrome shows up as negative whereas for Kalla-Norha, it shows up as positive. ("Duet" [DS9]).

Potts, Jake. (Cory Danziger). The elder of the two Potts children who were left on the *Enterprise*-D, by special arrangement, while their parents took a sabbatical in 2367. During crew shore leave on **Ogus II**, Jake played a practical joke on his younger brother, **Willie Potts**, resulting in Willie's near-death. ("Brothers" [TNG]). SEE: **cove palm**.

Potts, Willie. (Adam Ryen). Younger brother to **Jake Potts**. Willie almost died in 2367 at the age of nine years when a practical joke played by Jake misfired seriously. Jake had pretended to be hurt in a laser duel game, whereupon Willie hid in a nearby forest, eating a deadly **palm cove** fruit. The infectious parasites in the fruit nearly killed Willie, who had to be quarantined until he could be rushed to **Starbase 416** for treatment. ("Brothers" [TNG]). *Photo: Dr. Beverly Crusher cares for Willie Potts in medical isolation.*

• **"Power Play."** *Next Generation* episode #115. Teleplay by Rene Balcer and Herbert J. Wright & Brannon Braga. Story by Paul Reuben and Maurice Hurley. Directed by David Livingston. Stardate 45571.2. *First aired in 1992. Alien criminals take over the minds of* Enterprise-D *crew members.* SEE: **Anesthezine gas; anionic energy; *Daedalus*-class starship; *Essex, U.S.S.*; ionongenic particles; *Jat'yln*; Kelly, Lieutenant Morgan; Mab-Bu VI; McKinley Park; micro-optic drill; Mullen, Commander Steven; Narsu, Admiral Uttan; neutrino field; neutrino; O'Brien, Keiko; O'Brien, Molly; pattern enhancer; Shumar, Captain Bryce; Ux-Mal.**

Praetor. Title of the leader of the **Romulan Star Empire**. ("Balance of Terror" [TOS]).

Prakal II. A planet once visited by Guinan. She acquired an unusual drink recipe there. ("In Theory" [TNG]).

P'Rang, I.K.C. Klingon spacecraft ordered to intercept the sleeper ship *T'Ong* after command of the *T'Ong* had been assumed by Emissary **K'Ehleyr**. ("The Emissary" [TNG]).

Praxillus system. A lifeless solar system with a giant red star as its center, the site for **Dr. Timicin's** spectacularly unsuccessful **helium ignition test** in 2367. While the test was initially promising, temperatures in the stellar core continued to rise far beyond the needed 220 million Kelvins. Core density also continued to increase and the Praxillus eventually went nova as a result of the experiment. ("Half a Life" [TNG]).

Praxis. A moon of the **Klingon Homeworld** of Qo'noS, and formerly a key energy production facility for the Klingon Empire. A massive explosion on Praxis in 2293 nearly shattered that satellite and caused severe environmental damage to the Homeworld as well. The

aftermath of the explosion was a key factor in motivating **Chancellor Gorkon's** peace initiative later that year. SEE: **Klingon Empire.** (*Star Trek VI: The Undiscovered Country*). *Photo: The explosion of Praxis.*

preanimate matter. In biology, preanimate matter refers to certain non-organic compounds from which organic materials may eventually evolve. (*Star Trek II: The Wrath of Khan*).

prefix code. In a Federation starship's computer systems, the prefix code was a security passcode appended to computer commands to prevent unauthorized activation or control of key systems. Kirk gained control of the *U.S.S. Reliant's* shield systems by transmitting the *Reliant's* prefix code from the *Enterprise*. The *Reliant's* prefix code was 16309. (*Star Trek II: The Wrath of Khan*). Captain Picard revealed the prefix code of the Starship ***Phoenix*** to Cardassian authorities in 2367 when *Phoenix* captain **Benjamin Maxwell** was preparing an unauthorized attack on a Cardassian ship. The code gave the Cardassians the ability to remotely disable the *Phoenix's* shields. ("The Wounded" [TNG]).

Preservers. Alien race that rescued primitive cultures in danger of extinction, transplanting them to other planets. Centuries ago, the Preservers translocated several tribes of American Indians to a distant world where they could thrive and maintain their unique culture. Also known as the Wise Ones. ("The Paradise Syndrome" [TOS]). SEE: **Miramanee's planet**.

President, Federation. SEE: **Federation Council President**.

Presidio. Ancient fort located in the San Francisco Bay area on Earth, it was a military installation well into the 20th century. Commander Data's head was discovered in caverns located under the Presidio's remains. ("Time's Arrow, Part II" [TNG]). Starfleet Academy is located in the Presidio. ("The First Duty" [TNG]).

Preston, Peter. Engineer's mate, midshipman first class aboard the *Starship Enterprise* during an Academy training cruise in 2285. Preston was killed when the ship was diverted to active duty to investigate the hijacking of the **Regula I Space Laboratory** by **Khan Noonien Singh**. (*Star Trek II: The Wrath of Khan*). *The ABC-TV extended television version of* Star Trek II *includes a line of dialog establishing that Preston was the nephew of Montgomery Scott. That line was not in the original theatrical or video versions of the film.*

• **"Price, The."** *Next Generation* episode #56. Written by Hannah Louise Shearer. Directed by Robert Scheerer. Stardate: 43385.6. *First aired in 1989. A professional negotiator uses his Betazoid senses in his business dealings, as well as in his relationship with Deanna Troi. This is the first episode in which the current Greek letter designations for the galaxy's four quadrants were first used. Previous episodes had used a variety of inconsistent naming systems.* SEE: **Arridor, Dr.; Barzan wormhole; Barzan; Barzans; Bhavani, Premier; Caldonians; chocolate; Chrysalians; Delta Quadrant; Denkiri Arm; Ferengi pod; Gamma Quadrant; Goss, DaiMon; Hurkos III; Kol; Leyor; Mendoza, Dr.; pyrocyte; Ral, Devinoni; Shuttlecraft 09; Troi, Deanna.**

Prieto, Lieutenant Ben. (Raymond Forchion). *Enterprise-D* shuttlecraft pilot who was transporting Counselor Troi back to the *Enterprise*-D when the shuttle was forced down on planet **Vagra II**. ("Skin of Evil" [TNG]).

primary hull. The saucer section of many Federation starships.

On most ships, the bridge is located on the top of the primary hull. Also known as a **saucer module**.

Prime Directive. Also known as Starfleet General Order #1. The Prime Directive mandates that Starfleet personnel and spacecraft are prohibited from interfering in the normal development of any society, and that any Starfleet vessel or crew member is expendable to prevent violation of this rule.

Adopted relatively early in Starfleet history, the Prime Directive was a key part of Starfleet and Federation policy toward newly discovered civilizations, but it was also one of the most difficult to administer.

This rule was not in force in 2168, when the **U.S.S. Horizon** contacted planet **Sigma Iotia II**, resulting in disastrous cultural contamination. ("A Piece of the Action" [TOS]). Federation cultural observer **John Gill** violated the Prime Directive at planet **Ekos** when he attempted to provide that planet with a more efficient government. Gill's plan misfired badly, resulting by 2268 in a brutal regime closely resembling Earth's Nazi Germany. ("Patterns of Force" [TOS]).

Captain Ronald Tracey of the **U.S.S. Exeter** violated the Prime Directive in 2268 at planet **Omega IV** when he provided phaser weapons to one of the warring factions there. ("The Omega Glory" [TOS]).

Other episodes in which the Prime Directive was arguably broken include: "Return of the Archons" (TOS), "A Taste of Armageddon" (TOS), "The Apple" (TOS), "A Private Little War" (TOS), "Justice" (TNG), "Pen Pals" (TNG), "Who Watches the Watchers?" (TNG), "Devil's Due" (TNG), and "Captive Pursuit" (DS9). In "Bread and Circuses" (TOS), Kirk noted that the Roman culture on planet 892-IV was entitled to full Prime Directive protection.

Primmin, Lieutenant George. (James Lashly). Starfleet security officer assigned to Deep Space 9 in 2369 whose self-assured attitude served to annoy **Odo**. ("The Passenger" [DS9]). Primmin had been a security officer since 2363. ("Move Along Home" [DS9]).

• **"Private Little War, A."** Original Series episode #45. Teleplay by Gene Roddenberry. Story by Jud Crucis. Directed by Marc Daniels. Stardate 4211.4. *First aired in 1967. The peaceful society on a primitive planet is shattered when the Klingons provide firearms to the inhabitants.* SEE: **Apella; flintlock; hill people; *Kahn-ut-tu*; Kirk, James T.; M'Benga, Dr.; mahko root; mugato; Nona; Prime Directive; Spock; Tyree; Vulcans; Yutan.**

Prixus. Minerologist and metallurgist aboard the *Enterprise*-D. Prixus assisted in the geological survey of planets in the **Selcundi Drema** sector in 2365. ("Pen Pals" [TNG]).

probability mechanics. Area of study in which the android **Data** excelled during his studies at Starfleet Academy. ("Encounter at Farpoint, Part I" [TNG]).

Probe, the. Alien space probe of unknown origin that wreaked ecological havoc on planet Earth in 2286 when it attempted to contact the intelligent species, **humpback whale**, on that planet. The species had unfortunately become extinct in the

21st century, so there were no whales to contact. The damage to Earth's biosphere occurred when the probe failed to make contact with any humpback whales and increased the power of its carrier wave to tremendous levels. Disaster was narrowly averted when

James Kirk and his *Enterprise* officers traveled back in time to the 20th century to bring two whales back to the future. (*Star Trek IV: The Voyage Home*).

probe, Iconian. SEE: **Iconian computer weapon**.

Probert, Commodore. Starfleet officer who ordered the *U.S.S. Columbia* to rendezvous with the *U.S.S. Revere* on stardate 7411.4. The message was relayed through the **Epsilon IX monitoring station**. (*Star Trek: The Motion Picture*). *Commodore Probert was a name mentioned in one of the messages heard in the Epsilon IX sequence in* Star Trek I. *It was a tongue-in-cheek reference to Andrew Probert, one of the illustrators on that film and the man who designed the* Enterprise-D *for* Star Trek: The Next Generation.

Proconsul. Term for the head of the **Romulan** Senate; one of the highest leaders of the Romulan government. ("Unification, Parts I and II" [TNG]). SEE: **Praetor**.

Proficient Service Medallion. Commendation awarded Cardassian **Gul Darhe'el** for his distinguished military career. ("Duet" [DS9]). SEE: **Gallitep; Kalla-Nohra; Marritza, Aamin**.

Progenitors. The founders of an idyllic artists' society on the planet **Aldea**. Hundreds of centuries ago, the Progenitors set up a sophisticated computer called the **Custodian** to provide for the needs of all citizens, along with a powerful cloaking device intended to conceal the planet from potential intrusion by space travelers. ("When the Bough Breaks" [TNG]).

• **"Progress."** *Deep Space Nine* episode #15. Written by Peter Allan Fields. Directed by Les Landau. Stardate 46844.3. *First aired in 1993. An old farmer on the Bajoran moon Jeraddo refuses to leave, even though his world is about to be made uninhabitable by toxic gases.* SEE: **Bajor; Baltrim; carnivorous rastipod; chlorobicrobes; Dax, Jadzia; Jeraddo; katterpod beans; Keena; kellipates; Lissepian captain; lockar beans; Morn; Mullibok; Nog; Noh-Jay Consortium; peritoneum; self-sealing stem bolts; Sirco Ch'Ano; Sisko, Jake; tessipates; thermologist; Toran; two-headed Malgorian; *yamok* sauce.**

progressive encryption lock. Multilayered set of security codes used by the Romulan information net. In 2368, Commander Data and Ambassador Spock, working together, were able to penetrate the encryption codes and access the net. ("Unification, Part II" [TNG]).

progressive memory purge. Computer programming that

restored Commander Data's memory and the *Enterprise*-D computer's recreational database, after the failure of an interface experiment in 2369. ("A Fistful of Datas" [TNG]). SEE: **Subroutine C-47**; *Ancient West.*

Project Genesis. Scientific research project whose goal was to develop a process whereby uninhabitable planets could be re-formed into worlds suitable for life. The process involved a massive explosion that reduced the planet to subatomic particles,

which then reassembled according to a preprogrammed matrix.

Project Genesis, under the direction of **Dr. Carol Marcus**, conducted a successful test of the process in a cavern inside the **Regula** asteroid. A second, more ambitious test was prematurely initiated when **Khan Noonien Singh** stole the **Genesis Device**, resulting in the formation of a habitable planet from the remains of the **Mutara Nebula**. (*Star Trek II: The Wrath of Khan*). Although initial tests of the Genesis Device showed remarkable promise, the process was later found to be unworkable due to the dangerously unstable nature of **protomatter** used in the Genesis matrix. (*Star Trek III: The Search for Spock*). *Photo: Simulated detonation of the Genesis Device.*

Promellian/Menthar war. Legendary conflict that ended at least 1000 years prior to 2366, in a battle at **Orelious IX**. During that battle, both sides fought to their mutual extinction, and Orelious IX was destroyed. ("Booby Trap" [TNG]).

Promellians. Technologically sophisticated reptilian culture that fought to its extinction in a war against the **Menthar** civilization. Promellian technology, although relatively crude by Federation standards, remains as an example of elegant simplicity in design. ("Booby Trap" [TNG]). SEE: **Cleponji; Galek Sar.**

Promenade. Expansive area on station **Deep Space 9** containing numerous commercial and service facilities. ("Emissary" [DS9]). Among the many shops and offices located on the **Promenade** are **Quark's bar**, the **replimat**, a **Bajoran temple**, **Garak**'s clothing shop,

the **Infirmary**, **Odo**'s security office, **Keiko O'Brien**'s classroom, a mineral assay office, and a candy kiosk. ("Emissary" [DS9]).

Promethean quartz. A valuable mineral that glows with an internal light. Archaeologist and entrepreneur **Vash** discovered a geode resembling Promethean quartz in the **Gamma Quadrant**, but the artifact had a much higher molecular density and index of refractivity. Vash's artifact was later found to contain a winged energy creature that nearly de-

stroyed the station with a powerful **graviton field** before it was set free. ("Q-Less" [DS9]).

Prophets. In the **Bajoran** religion, the Prophets are spiritual entities who provide wisdom and guidance to the Bajoran people. Bajoran tradition holds that the Prophets were responsible for the nine **Orbs** that served as sources of wisdom for the people of **Bajor**. Many Bajorans believe that the alien beings first encountered in the Bajoran wormhole by Commander **Benjamin Sisko** in 2369 were in fact, the Prophets. These life-forms found the concept of linear time to be totally alien, and Sisko attempted to help them understand the importance of linear existence to Bajorans and humans. Ironically, although Sisko did not believe in the Bajoran religion, his role in making contact with these life-forms made him their prophesied **Emissary**, a role that Sisko did not relish, although he respected their beliefs. ("Emissary" [DS9]).

protected memory. Area of the *Enterprise*-D computer core, where the file containing the consciousness of **Professor James Moriarty** was located. ("Ship in a Bottle" [TNG]).

protectors. Another name given to the filter masks provided to the Troglyte mining workers on planet **Ardana** to negate the deleterious effects of the **zenite** gas. Vanna preferred the term to "filter masks" because it more clearly described their use. ("The Cloud Minders" [TOS]).

proto-Vulcan. Anthropological term to describe the humanoid culture on planet **Mintaka III**, whose inhabitants did indeed resemble early Vulcans at a Bronze Age level of technology. ("Who Watches the Watchers?" [TNG]).

protodynoplaser. Medical instrument in use aboard the *Enterprise*-D. The device was used on **Zalkonian** patient **John Doe** to stabilize his immune system. ("Transfigurations" [TNG]).

protomatter. A dangerously unstable form of matter. Because of the extreme hazard associated with this substance, many 23rd-century scientists denounced its use, but Dr. **David Marcus** secretly used it as part of the **Project Genesis** matrix, thus dooming the project to failure since the resulting planet created by the matrix was also dangerously unstable. (*Star Trek III: The Search for Spock*).

Providers. Three disembodied brains who lived beneath the surface of the planet **Triskelion**. In the past, the Providers had humanoid bodies but devotion to intellectual pursuits eliminated the need for a shell of flesh. For amusement, they captured beings

from throughout the galaxy and trained them to fight among themselves, betting on the results. In 2268, the Providers agreed to free their captives in payment of a wager they had made with Captain James Kirk. ("The Gamesters of Triskelion" [TOS]). SEE: **drill thralls.**

proximity detector. A two-centimeter-square, jewel-like, magnetic device that was implanted into a humanoid body, making it easy to accurately track and identify that individual. These implants were used on planets Manu III and **Turkana IV**, sounding an alarm when the wearer entered forbidden territory. In their use on Turkana IV, proximity detectors would also sound an alarm to warn of the approach of enemy forces, providing positive identification of one's cadre affiliation, either **Coalition** or **Alliance**. The implants contained a micro-explosive that detonated on contact with air, thus preventing easy removal. Dr. Crusher was able to remove the proximity detector from Turkana IV native **Ishara Yar**. ("Legacy" [TNG]).

prune juice. A beverage made from the pureed dried fruit of an Earth plum tree. Guinan introduced Worf to this beverage in 2366. He pronounced it "a warrior's drink." ("Yesterday's *Enterprise*" [TNG]).

Psi 2000 virus. A water-based disease organism originally found on planet Psi 2000 in 2266. This virus infected members of the Federation science team stationed on that planet, causing suppression of their inhibitions, and ultimately their deaths. Transmitted through  human perspiration, the virus later infected members of the *Enterprise* crew, resulting in the near-destruction of the starship when infected crew member **Kevin Riley** disabled the ship's engines while it was in orbit around the disintegrating planet. ("The Naked Time" [TOS]). A variant of this virus infected members of the **U.S.S. Tsiolokovsky** crew as well as the crew of the *Enterprise*-D in 2364. ("The Naked Now" [TNG]).

Psi 2000. A frozen planet that disintegrated in 2266. Just prior to the planet's end, a Federation science team had been stationed there, but all members of that team were found dead under mysterious circumstances. Their deaths were later found to have been due to a virus that stripped away their inhibitions and caused team members to engage in hazardous behavior. The *U.S.S. Enterprise* conducted scientific observations of the planet's disintegration and was nearly destroyed. ("The Naked Time" [TOS]). *Photo:* Enterprise *landing party investigates Psi 2000 science station.* SEE: *Tsiolkovsky, U.S.S.*

Psych Test. A part of the entrance examination for aspiring Starfleet Academy cadets, designed to determine a candidate's reaction to his or her greatest fears. The Psych Test is administered on an individual basis, and generally involves a simulation designed to make the candidate face those fears. Wesley Crusher's Psych Test involved forcing him to make a decision to let one man die, so that another could live, a situation that paralleled that in which his father, Jack Crusher, died as the result of a decision by Captain Jean-Luc Picard. ("Coming of Age" [TNG]).

psychokinesis. The ability to transport and control objects that was demonstrated by the **Platonians**. ("Plato's Stepchildren" [TOS]). SEE: **kironide**.

psychological profile. Complete psychological history required of all Starfleet personnel. *Starship Enterprise* crew member **Mira Romaine**'s psychological profile was examined in 2369 when her mind was occupied by the noncorporeal survivors of planet **Zetar**. ("The Lights of Zetar" [TOS]).

psychotectic therapy. A psychological treatment used on the **J'naii** planet to eliminate gender-specific sexuality, which the J'naii considered aberrant behavior. In 2368, the therapy was highly effective in extinguishing **Soren**'s female-specific feelings. ("The Outcast" [TNG]).

psychotricorder. Instrument used to record past memories. Kirk ordered a 24-hour regressive memory test on Montgomery Scott using a psychotricorder after the chief engineer was accused of murder on planet **Argelius II** in 2267, although the test was interrupted when psych technician Karen Tracy was murdered by the malevolent entity occupying Scott's body. ("Wolf in the Fold" [TOS]).
The psychotricorder was, of course, a re-use of the standard original series tricorder prop.

Pulaski, Dr. Katherine. (Diana Muldaur). Chief medical officer aboard the *U.S.S. Enterprise*-D during the year 2365. ("The Child" [TNG]).
While aboard the *Enterprise*-D, Pulaski nearly died of a disease closely resembling old age after she was exposed to genetically engineered human children at the **Darwin Genetic Research Station** on planet **Gagarin IV**. Pulaski recovered from the disease thanks to a transporter-based technique, this despite the fact that she harbored a phobia about transporter use. ("Unnatural Selection" [TNG]).
Pulaski cared for **Kyle Riker** after he was nearly killed in a **Tholian** attack in 2353. The two fell in love and Pulaski would later recall she would have married him "in a cold minute" given the opportunity, but that Riker had "other priorities." Following her involvement with Riker, Pulaski married three times. As of 2365, she noted that she remained good friends with all three men. ("The Icarus Factor" [TNG]).
Counselor Troi commented once that Pulaski's greatest medical skill was her empathy with her patients, evidenced by the use of "PCS" – Pulaski's Chicken Soup – in treating the flu virus. ("The Icarus Factor" [TNG]).
Dr. Pulaski was part of the regular Star Trek: The Next Generation *cast during the second season. Her first episode was "The Child" (TNG), and her last was "Shades of Grey" (TNG). She replaced Dr. Beverly Crusher, who in turn replaced Pulaski when Diana Muldaur left the series at the*

end of the second season. Muldaur had previously played Dr. Ann Mulhall in "Return to Tomorrow" (TOS) and Dr. Miranda Jones in "Is There in Truth No Beauty?" (TOS).

There is no truth to the rumor that an ancestor of Dr. Pulaski was killed falling down the elevator shaft at a prestigious Los Angeles law firm. None at all.

pulmonary support unit. Emergency cardiopulmonary support unit in use aboard Federation starships. ("Tapestry" [TNG]).

pulse compression wave. Energy burst that could be channeled through a phaser bank, thereby increasing the destructive power of a phaser blast. Chief Operations Officer Miles O'Brien proposed this method to defend station **Deep Space 9** against the **Cardassians** shortly after the discovery of the **Bajoran wormhole** in 2369. ("Emissary" [DS9]).

pulse-wave torpedo. Explosive device used by a Vulcan spaceship in a futile attempt to repair a **subspace rupture** in 2169. A pulse wave torpedo was also used when a subspace rupture was believed to have formed near Deep Space 9 in 2369. ("If Wishes Were Horses" [DS9]).

punishment zones. In **Edo** society on planet **Rubicun III,** a randomly selected area in which mediators (law officials) enforce local laws. Violation of any law in a punishment zone would exact a death penalty. Under this system, no one except the mediators would know which area was currently designated as a punishment zone. In this way, a relatively small number of mediators could insure compliance with the law of a large number of Edo citizens. ("Justice" [TNG]).

Pup. Chief O'Brien's nickname for an alien software life-form hidden in data downloaded from a probe that came from somewhere in the **Gamma Quadrant** in 2369.

Feeding off the energy from **Deep Space 9**'s computers, this nonsentient life-form integrated itself into the system, causing stationwide malfunctions. To Chief Miles O'Brien, the computer seemed to be craving attention much like a puppy who didn't like to be left alone. He created a subprogram labeled "Pup" and filled it with all main computer back-up functions, then downloaded the probe data into the file. The life-form had its own place in the computer system where it could interface with the backup functions and not cause further malfunctions. ("The Forsaken" [DS9]).

*We did not learn the name of the culture from the Gamma Quadrant that sent the probe that carried Pup to Deep Space 9. The probe model itself was a modification of the **Cytherian** probe originally built for "The Nth Degree" (TNG).*

purple omelets. A dish created by young Clara Sutter, made from grape juice and eggs. ("Imaginary Friend" [TNG]). *Mike still prefers green eggs and ham.*

PXK reactor. Antiquated power-generation device that provided life support to the underground mining colony at planet **Janus VI**. Although the PXK was considered obsolete, it was used on Janus VI because of the abundance of fissile minerals there. That station's reactor suffered a serious malfunc-

tion when an indigenous life-form known as a **Horta** damaged it in 2267. The Horta's actions were later found to be her effort to protect her children from the actions of the miners. ("The Devil in the Dark" [TOS].

Pyris VII. Planet where extragalactic life-forms **Korob** and **Sylvia** captured and controlled several of the *Enterprise* crew in 2267. Prior to the arrival of Korob and Sylvia, mapping expeditions had reported Pyris VII to be devoid of life ("Catspaw" [TOS]).

pyrocyte. A naturally occurring component of **Ferengi** blood. A distillation of these cells was used to poison a Federation negotiator, **Dr. Mendoza**, during negotiations for the Barzan wormhole in 2366. The pyrocytes, though not fatal, provoked a severe allergic reaction, effectively removing Mendoza from the talks. ("The Price" [TNG]).

Q. (John DeLancie). An immensely powerful extradimensional entity. While possessing near-godlike powers, Q also exhibits a child-like petulance and sense of playfulness. The *Enterprise*-D made first contact with Q in 2364, when Q detained the ship, enacting a courtroom drama in which Q accused the ship's crew of being "grievously savage." ("Encounter at Farpoint, Parts I and II" [TNG]).

On his second visit to the *Enterprise*-D, Q offered **William Riker** a gift of Q-like supernatural powers, although it was not clear if this was a further attempt to study the human species, or merely another exercise in provoking humans to respond for his amusement. ("Hide and Q" [TNG]).

Q later transported the *Enterprise*-D some 7,000 light years beyond Federation space to **System J-25**, where first contact was made with the powerful and dangerous **Borg**. ("Q Who?" [TNG]).

Q was banished from the **Q Continuum** and stripped of his powers in 2366 for having spread chaos through the universe. Q sought refuge in human form on board the *Enterprise*-D, claiming that Jean-Luc Picard was the nearest thing he had to a friend. Unfortunately, Q had made many enemies in this universe, and one of these, the **Calamarain**, attacked the *Enterprise*-D, attempting to exact revenge on Q. Quick action by Commander **Data** saved Q from the attack. Truly surprised by Data's selfless action to save him, Q stole a shuttlecraft in an attempt to save the *Enterprise*-D crew from further hostile action. This altruistic act was enough to persuade the Continuum to return his powers. ("Deja Q" [TNG]).

Q interrupted a symposium of the **Federation Archaeology Council** held aboard the *Enterprise*-D in 2367. He cast Picard, **Vash**, and members of the *Enterprise*-D crew into an elaborate fantasy based on the old Earth legends of **Robin Hood**. Q later vanished, taking Vash with him as his new partner in crime. ("QPid" [TNG]). He returned to the *Enterprise*-D in 2369 to instruct and evaluate Amanda Rogers, whose biological parents were members of the **Q Continuum** who took human form. ("True-Q" [TNG]).

After a period of time exploring the Gamma Quadrant, Vash left Q, and returned to Alpha Quadrant aboard the Starfleet runabout ***U.S.S. Ganges*** through the **Bajoran wormhole**. Q followed Vash to station **Deep Space 9** in an attempt to convince her to return, but she once again rebuffed him. He amused himself with the crew of the station, provoking Benjamin Sisko into a 19th-century-style fistfight, and was shocked when Sisko knocked him to the floor. ("Q-Less" [DS9]).

Later that year, Q once again visited Captain Picard, following a disastrous away mission on which Picard was ambushed by **Lenarians**. In what Q claimed was the afterlife, Q offered Picard the opportunity to see what his life would have been like had he not made some of the rash choices of his youth. In particular, Picard was given the opportunity to relive the three-day period leading up to his injury at the **Bonestell Recre-**

ation Facility in 2327. Using the knowledge of what was to come, Picard was able to avoid the fight that cost him his heart. However, Picard discovered that it was partly the brashness of his youth that had made him the man that he was. ("Tapestry" [TNG]). SEE: **Batanides, Marta; Nausicaans**. *Q was named by Gene Roddenberry for English Star Trek fan Janet Quarton. Q's first appearance was in "Encounter at Farpoint, Part I" (TNG). Many fans have speculated that Q may be related to* **Trelane**.

Q Continuum. Extradimensional domain in which **Q** and others of his kind exist. ("Encounter at Farpoint, Parts I and II" [TNG]). Q was briefly banished from the continuum in 2366, until another Q entered our existence, offering to restore his powers. ("Deja Q" [TNG]). Those in charge of the continuum commanded Q to instruct and evaluate **Amanda Rogers** to see if she could ignore her powers and live among humans. If she could not or if she refused to accompany Q back to the Continuum, she was to be destroyed. The Continuum felt a moral obligation not to allow members of their kind to live with inferior beings and still use their awesome powers. ("True-Q" [TNG]).

Q'Maire. A **Talarian** warship, commanded by **Endar**. In 2367, this ship intercepted the *U.S.S. Enterprise*-D in **Sector 21947**, near a disabled Talarian observation craft. The *Q'Maire*, along with two sister warships, surrounded the *Enterprise*-D in the hopes of forcing the release of Endar's adoptive son, **Jono**. The *Q'Maire* was equipped with limited weaponry, including neutral particle weapons, X-ray lasers, and merculite rockets, and was thus not a serious tactical threat. ("Suddenly Human" [TNG]). *The Q'Maire miniature was designed by Rick Sternbach and built by Tony Meininger.*

• **"Q-Less."** *Deep Space Nine* episode #7. Teleplay by Robert Hewitt Wolfe. Story by Hannah Louise Shearer. Directed by Paul Lynch. Stardate 46531.2. *First aired in 1993. Archaeologist Vash arrives from the Gamma Quadrant with a mysterious cargo, accompanied by Q.* SEE: **assay office; Betazed; Brax; Daystrom Institute; Delta Quadrant; duranium ; EPI capacitor; Epsilon Hydra VII; Erabus Prime; Erriakang VII; Gamma Quadrant; Gamzain;** *Ganges,* **U.S.S.; ganglion; graviton field; graviton; Hoek IV; Kolos; Lantar Nebula; MK-12 scanner; Mulzirak; Mandahla; Myrmidon;** *oo-mox;* **Pauley, Ensign; Promethian quartz; Q; Rul the Obscure; Sampalo; Stol; Tartaras V; Teleris; tritium; Vadris III; Vash; Verath; Woo, Dr.**

Q, Planet. Home of scientist **Thomas Leighton** at the time of his death in 2266. ("The Conscience of the King" [TOS]).

• **"Q Who?"** *Next Generation* episode #42. Written by Maurice Hurley. Directed by Rob Bowman. Stardate 42761.3. *First aired in 1989. Q sends the* Enterprise-*D across the galaxy where it encounters the Borg for the first time. The Borg had been previously hinted at in "The Neutral Zone" (TNG). This episode has the first of two appearances of Ensign Sonya Gomez.* SEE: **Borg ship; Borg; Gomez, Ensign Sonya; Guinan; Neutral Zone, Romulan; Q; Starbase 83; Starbase 173; Starbase 185; System J-25.**

Q2. (Corbin Bernsen). A member of the **Q Continuum**, Q2 was responsible for the removal of Q's powers in 2366 when Q was found guilty of spreading chaos in the universe. He continued to observe Q following his banishment, and later restored Q's powers after he committed an act of self-sacrifice. ("Deja Q" [TNG]).

Q2 only identified himself as another member of the Q Continuum. The name is from the script for the convenience of Star Trek*'s production personnel, but was never used in the episode.*

qa'vak. Traditional Klingon game involving a half-meter hoop and a spear. The hoop is rolled between various stakes planted into the ground, and the object is to throw the spear through the center of the hoop. Upon successfully scoring in this manner, it is traditional to shout *"ka'la!"* The game is intended to hone skill necessary for the traditional Klingon hunt. ("Birthright, Part II [TNG]).

Qab jIH nagil. Klingon ritual challenge used during the **Sonchi** ceremony during the **Rite of Succession**. It translates: "Face me if you dare." ("Reunion" [TNG]).

Qapla'. Klingon word meaning "success." Often used as a farewell. (*Star Trek III: The Search for Spock,* "Sins of the Father" [TNG], et al.).

QE-2. Also known as the *Queen Elizabeth II.* Luxury passenger ship that sailed Earth's Atlantic Ocean during the late 20th and early 21st centuries. **Ralph Offenhouse**, dissatisfied with services aboard the *Starship Enterprise*-D, suggested that Captain Picard could use a few lessons from the *QE-2.* ("The Neutral Zone" [TNG]).

Qo'noS. (Pronounced "kronos"). The capital planet of the Klingon Empire, almost invariably referred to as the **Homeworld**. (*Star Trek VI: The Undiscovered Country*).

Qol. (Michael Snyder). Assistant to Ferengi trade emissary **Par Lenor**. ("The Perfect Mate" [TNG]).

• **"QPid."** *Next Generation* episode #94. Teleplay by Ira Steven Behr. Story by Randee Russell and Ira Steven Behr. Directed by Cliff Bole. Stardate 44741.9. *First aired in 1991. Q transports our heroes into Sherwood Forest with Jean-Luc Picard as Robin Hood.* SEE: **Alan-a-Dale; Federation Archaeology Council; Friar Tuck;** *Horga'hn*; **Klabnian eel; Klarc-Tarn-Droth; Little John; Lord High Sheriff of Nottingham; Maid Marian; Picard, Jean-Luc; Q; Robin Hood; Sarthong V; Sherwood Forest; Sir Guy of Gisbourne; Switzer; Tagus III; Vash; Vulcans.**

Qu'Vat. Klingon *Vor'cha*-**class** attack cruiser that rendezvoused with the *Enterprise*-D in 2369, carrying **Governor Torak** on an investigation into the death of a Starfleet officer at **Relay Station 47**. ("Aquiel" [TNG]).

Quadra Sigma III. Location of a Federation mining colony that suffered a serious explosion in 2364, resulting in significant casualties among the 504 colonists at the colony. *Starship Enterprise*-D rendered aid shortly after the accident in 2364. ("Hide and Q" [TNG]).

Quadrant 904. An area of space completely devoid of stars where the artificially created planet **Gothos** was discovered by the Enterprise in 2367. ("The Squire of Gothos" [TOS]). *The episode was produced before* Star Trek*'s current system of quadrants and sectors was devised, and it is therefore inconsistent with terminology of later episodes.*

quadrant. In interstellar mapping, a quadrant is one-fourth of the Milky Way Galaxy. The galaxy is divided into four quadrants, each forming a 90-degree pie wedge as seen from above or below the galaxy's plane. The four quadrants are labeled Alpha, Beta, Delta, and Gamma.

The United Federation of Planets is mostly located in the **Alpha Quadrant**, although parts spill over into Beta. Station **Deep Space 9** is located in Alpha Quadrant. The Klingon and Romulan empires are located in the **Beta Quadrant**. The Borg homeworld is believed to be in the **Delta Quadrant**, while the Bajoran wormhole has one terminus in the **Gamma Quadrant**.

Quadrants and sectors have been used inconsistently in the various Star Trek *episodes and films. During the original* Star Trek *series, the term quadrant was used rather freely, as was the term sector. At times, quadrant seemed to refer to a fourth of the entire galaxy, while at others it seemd to be a portion of a smaller region. It was not until "The Price" (TNG) that the current system of Alpha, Beta, Delta, and Gamma quadrants was firmly established.* Star Trek VI: The Undiscovered Country *adhered to this system, as well.*

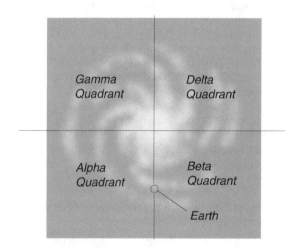

quadroline. An emergency drug used on planet **Malcor III**. ("First Contact" [TNG]).

Quadros-1 probe. Deep-space scientific probe launched to the **Gamma Quadrant** in the 22nd century. Among the findings returned by the craft was the discovery of a trinary star system called Irdan in the Gamma Quadrant. ("Emissary" [DS9]).

quadrotriticale. Genetically engineered grain developed on Earth from a four-lobed hybrid of wheat and rye. The parent strain, triticale, was discovered in 20th-century Canada. Quadrotriticale was the only Earth grain that would grow on **Sherman's Planet**, and was thus critical to the Federation's plan in 2267 to develop that world. A large quantity of quadrotriticale was stored on **Deep Space Station K-7** for that project, but it was poisoned by a Klingon agent. ("The Trouble with Tribbles" [TOS]). SEE: **Darvin, Arne**; **Jones, Cyrano**; **tribbles**.

Quaice, Dr. Dalen. (Bill Erwin). Starfleet physician and native of planet Kenda II. Dr. Quaice had been a friend and mentor to **Dr. Beverly Crusher**, who did her internship with Quaice in 2352 on planet Delos IV. Following the death of his wife, Patricia, Dr. Quaice resigned his position at Starbase 133 and returned to his home on Kenda II aboard the *Enterprise*-D. Quaice had served on Starbase 133 for six years. ("Remember Me" [TNG]).

Quaice, Patricia. Wife of **Dr. Dalen Quaice**. Upon Patricia's death in 2367, Dalen left Starbase 133 and returned to his home planet, Kenda II. ("Remember Me" [TNG]).

• **"Quality of Life, The."** *Next Generation* episode #135. Written by Naren Shankar. Directed by Jonathan Frakes. Stardate 46307.2. *First aired in 1992. Data refuses to send robotic servomechanisms to do hazardous tasks because he believes the machines to be sentient life-forms.* SEE: **axionic chip; *bat'telh*; boridium power converter; Carema III; exocomp; Farallon, Dr.; interlink sequencer; Kelso, Chief; main particle impeller; microreplication system; Pierson, Lieutenant; Tyran system; Tyrus VIIA.**

Qualor II. Federation class-M world. A surplus depot operated by the **Zakdorn** race for Starfleet was located in orbit of Qualor II. ("Unification, Part I" [TNG]).

quantum filament. An elongated subatomic object, hundreds of meters long, but possessing almost no mass. The *Enterprise*-D struck two quantum filaments in early 2368, resulting in the death of several crew members and severe damage to the ship itself. ("Disaster" [TNG]). *An early draft of "Disaster" had the ship colliding with an asteroid, but the writers, sensitive to scientific concerns that an asteroid would not cause the damage described in the script, "invented" the quantum filament. We have little idea what a quantum filament is, but we do know it's not a cosmic string.*

quantum fluctuations. Phenomenon postulated by physicist **Dr. Stephen Hawking**. Quantum fluctuations were thought to be links between multiple universes. Hawking referred to them as **wormholes**. ("Descent, Part I" [TNG]).

quantum phase inhibitor. Also known as the ***Tox Uthat***, a device invented by 27th-century scientist **Kal Dano** capable of halting all nuclear reaction within a star. ("Captain's Holiday" [TNG]).

quantum singularity life-form. Intelligent species from another time-space continuum whose young are incubated in a natural black hole. In 2369, these life-forms attempted to use the artificial quantum singularity of a **Romulan Warbird** as a nest. When they discovered their mistake, they attempted to extract their embryos from the Romulan ship, endangering the Warbird as well as the *Starship Enterprise*-D. ("Timescape" [TNG]). *Neither this species, the domain in which they existed, nor any of the individuals seen in the episode were given formal names.*

quantum singularity. SEE: **black hole**.

quarantine seal. Also called a medical quarantine field. Forcefield used to isolate potentially hazardous biological specimens in sickbay and other laboratory facilities aboard starships. ("Home Soil" [TNG]). A medical quarantine field was used to isolate young **Willie Potts** when he contracted a deadly and contagious parasite from a **cove palm** fruit in 2367. ("Brothers" [TNG]).

quarantine transmitter. Standard equipment on Federation starships, these radio beacons are capable of transmitting automated warning messages should a ship become dangerously contaminated. The quarantine transmitter on the ***U.S.S. Lantree*** was activated after the ship's entire crew was killed from exposure to deadly antibodies from the **Darwin Genetic Research Station**. ("Unnatural Selection" [TNG]).

quaratum. Chemical compound used in Starfleet emergency thruster packs. Quaratum is normally quite stable, but becomes explosive when exposed to radiation exceeding 350 rads. ("Disaster" [TNG]).

Quark's bar. Bar and gambling establishment on the **Promenade** at station **Deep Space 9**. Owned by its Ferengi namesake, **Quark**'s place was a favorite gathering place for station residents, as well as for any strangers passing through. The bar provided games such as **Dabo** for gambling, and several **holosuites** on the second level of the bar. ("Emissary" [DS9]).

Quark. (Armin Shimerman). Entrepreneur who ran Quark's place, on station **Deep Space 9**. Quark, a **Ferengi** national, felt unfairly persecuted by station security chief, **Odo**. ("Emissary" [DS9]). Quark served as **Grand Nagus** in 2369 when Grand Nagus **Zek** apparently died. The appointment was only temporary, however, because Zek had faked his death to test his son, **Krax**. ("The Nagus" [DS9]). SEE: **Corvan gilvos**. Prior to ownership of the bar at Deep Space 9, Quark worked on a Ferengi freighter ship for eight years. ("Babel" [DS9]). *Armin*

Shimerman also played **Letek**, one of the first three Ferengi in "The Last Outpost" (TNG); **Bractor**, another Ferengi, in "Peak Performance" (TNG); and the gift box face in "Haven" (TNG). Quark was first seen in "Emissary" (DS9).

quasars. Mysterious quasi-stellar objects believed to generate enormous amounts of energy from relatively small amounts of mass. The *Enterprise*, in 2267, had standing orders to investigate all quasars and quasar-like objects whenever they might be encountered. ("The *Galileo* Seven" [TOS]).

quasi-energy microbes. Life-forms found within a plasma streamer between a binary star pair in the Igo Sector. These life-forms, first encountered by the crew of the *Starship* **Yosemite** in 2369, existed in a state between matter and energy, and were able to live in the matter stream of a transporter beam. Several of these microbes were accidentally brought aboard the *Yosemite*, where they nearly caused the destruction of that ship. Following the detection of these life-forms by *Enterprise*-D personnel, the microbes were removed from both ships' transporter systems and returned to the plasma streamer that was their home. ("Realm of Fear" [TNG]).

quasimolecular flux. Molecular states in which constitutent atoms are altered from their normal composition and energy state. A portion of metal in the bulkhead of the *Enterprise*-D cargo bay was altered to a state of quasimolecular flux by the **Solanagen-based aliens**. ("Schisms" [TNG]).

quatloo. Monetary unit used by the **Providers** of planet **Triskelion** for betting on competition between **drill thralls**. ("The Gamesters of Triskelion" [TOS]).

Quazulu VIII. Planet that twelve students from the *Enterprise*-D visited on a field trip in 2364, just prior to that ship's visit to planet **Angel One**. At Quazulu, several of the students were infected with an airborne virus that later threatened the health of hundreds of *Enterprise*-D personnel by causing respiratory distress. ("Angel One" [TNG]).

Qui'Tu. In Klingon mythology, the source of all creation. (*Star Trek V: The Final Frontier*). SEE: **Sha Ka Ree**.

Quin'lat. Ancient city on the Klingon Homeworld. Klingon history tells of a great storm that struck the city centuries ago while **Kahless the Unforgettable** was there. One man went outside to face the storm, to "stand before the wind and make it respect [him]." The man was killed. As Kahless would later say, "The wind does not respect a fool." ("Rightful Heir" [TNG]).

Quinn, Admiral Gregory. (Ward Costello). Starfleet officer who played a crucial role in uncovering the attempted takeover of Starfleet Command in 2364. As part of his effort to uncover the situation, Quinn ordered Inspector General **Dexter Remmick** to investigate the *Enter-*prise-D for possible infestation. ("Coming of Age" [TNG]). None was discovered at the time, although Quinn himself later became a victim of the alien infestation. Quinn was later a victim of this conspiracy when his mind was overtaken by the unknown alien intelligence that attempted to infiltrate **Starfleet Headquarters** in 2364. ("Conspiracy" [TNG]).

Quinteros, Commander Orfil. (Gene Dynarski). Starfleet officer assigned to **Starbase 74** in 2364, Quinteros had previously been in charge of the team that assembled the *Starship Enterprise*-D at the **Utopia Planitia Fleet Yards** on Mars.

Quinteros also oversaw computer systems upgrades to the *Enterprise*-D at Starbase 74 in 2364. ("11001001" [TNG]). SEE: *Galaxy* **Class Starship Development Project.** *Actor Gene Dynarski also played miner* **Ben Childress** *in "Mudd's Women" (TOS) and an aide to Ambassador Hodin in "The Mark of Gideon" (TOS).*

Rachelis system. A densely populated planetary system struck with an outbreak of a new strain of **plasma plague** in 2365, just prior to stardate 42073.1. ("The Child" [TNG]).

radans. Gemstones from planet **Troyius**. The leader of Troyius gave **Elaan**, the **Dohlman of Elas**, a necklace of radans as a wedding present in 2368. Chemically, radans were raw **dilithium** crystals, and made Troyius a planet of great strategic significance. Elaan's necklace served as a source of emergency crystals for the *Starship Enterprise* when that ship was under attack by a Klingon vessel that ironically sought to guarantee a supply of radans from Troyius. ("Elaan of Troyius" [TOS]).

Radue. (Jerry Hardin). First Appointee of planet **Aldea**. Radue attempted to negotiate with *Enterprise*-D personnel to obtain possession of some crew members' children in exchange for access to Aldean technology. ("When the Bough Breaks" [TNG]). *Jerry Hardin also played Samuel Clemens in "Time's Arrow, Parts I and II" (TNG).*

Rael. (Jason Evers). **Scalosian** male who boarded the *Enterprise* in 2268 in an attempt to cryogenically freeze the crew and use the males for breeding stock. Like all the males on planet **Scalos**, Rael was sterile due to radiation contamination on his planet. Although he intellectually realized the need to propagate his species by forcing alien males to mate with Scalosian females, he became jealous of the pairing of Captain Kirk and Deela. ("Wink of an Eye" [TOS]).

Rager, Ensign. (Lanei Chapman). *Enterprise*-D crew member who served at conn under the command of Captain Jean-Luc Picard. ("Galaxy's Child" [TNG], "Schisms" [TNG], "Relics" [TNG]). Rager had to be relieved of duty when she suffered severe dream deprivation when the ship was trapped in a **Tyken's Rift** later that year. ("Night Terrors" [TNG]).

Rahm-Izad system. Star system located in sector 21459. The Cardassian **Gul Ocett** was misdirected to the **Rahm-Izad system** by Federation and Klingon personnel when it was found she had tried to sabotage the *Enterprise*-D in an attempt to gain advantage in finding data to complete the late **Professor Richard Galen**'s work. The actual information was found on **Vilmor II**. ("The Chase" [TNG]). SEE: **humanoid life**.

Rak-Miunis. Kobheerian freighter spacecraft that delivered the Cardassian **Marritza** to **Deep Space 9** in 2369 for medical care. ("Duet" [DS9]).

Rakal, Major. Late member of the Romulan **Tal Shiar** intelligence service. Rakal was murdered in 2369 so that Deanna Troi could be coerced into assuming her identity as part of an elaborate plot to enable Romulan **vice-proconsul M'ret** to defect to the Federation. ("Face of the Enemy" [TNG]). SEE: **N'Vek, Subcommander**.

Rakhar. Planet in the **Gamma Quadrant** and home to the fugitive Croden. The government of Rakhar did not tolerate political dissidents and, as punishment, a perpetrator's family would be killed. ("Vortex" [DS9]). SEE: **Croden**.

Rakhari. Humanoid inhabitants of the planet **Rakhar**. ("Vortex" [DS9]). SEE: **Croden**

raktajino. Klingon iced coffee beverage served at Quark's bar on station Deep Space 9. ("The Passenger" [DS9]).

Ral, Devinoni. (Matt McCoy). The agent for the **Chysalians** during the **Barzan wormhole** negotiations in 2366. Ral, who was one-fourth Betazoid, was born in Brussels, in the European alliance in 2325. He moved to the planet Hurkos III at the age of 19. Taken by his striking appearance, Deanna Troi found herself drawn to Ral during the Barzan negotiations. Ral kept his Betazoid heritage hidden, and used his empathic abilities to give him an advantage during business and personal dealings. ("The Price" [TNG]).

Ramart, Captain. (Charles Stewart). Commander of the Federation science vessel **Antares**. Ramart's crew rescued the 17-year-old **Charles Evans** from planet **Thasus** in 2266, delivering him to the *Enterprise*. Ramart, along with the rest of his crew, was killed when Evans destroyed the *Antares* to prevent Ramart from warning Kirk about Evans' psychokinetic powers. ("Charlie X" [TOS]).

Ramatis III. Planet, home of famed Federation mediator **Riva**. The ruling family of this planet lacked the gene that makes hearing possible, and thus members of that family communicated with an interpretive **Chorus** that provided hearing and speech. Riva was a member of the Ramatis III ruling family. ("Loud as a Whisper" [TNG]).

Ramatis star system. Location of planet **Ramatis III**. The *Starship Enterprise*-D visited the Ramatis system in 2365 on a mission to transport mediator **Riva** from Ramatis III to **Solais V**. ("Loud as a Whisper" [TNG]).

ramscoop. Device that employs powerful magnetic fields to collect interstellar hydrogen for use as fuel for a space vehicle. Also called a **Bussard collector**. O'Brien compared a ramscoop to the **arva nodes** in **Tosk's** ship, which essentially did the same thing. ("Captive Pursuit" [DS9]).

Ramsey, Dr. Archaeologist aboard the *U.S.S. Yamato* at the time of an expedition to planet **Denius III** in 2365. Ramsey's work, along with the contributions of *Yamato* **captain Donald Varley**, enabled artifacts found at Denius III to help determine the location of the legendary planet **Iconia**. ("Contagion" [TNG]).

Ramsey. (Sam Hennings). One of four survivors of the wreck of the Federation freighter *Odin* who drifted to planet **Angel One** in escape pods in 2357. Ramsey took up residence among the people of Angel One, despite objections from that planet's government that his outside ideas would threaten the stability of the female-dominated society. ("Angel One" [TNG]).

Rand, Janice. (Grace Lee Whitney). Starfleet officer who served as Captain Kirk's yeoman during the early days of Kirk's first five-year mission aboard the original *Starship Enterprise*. ("The Corbomite Maneuver" [TOS]). Rand returned to serve aboard the *Enterprise* as transporter chief in 2271. (*Star Trek: The Motion Picture*). Rand subsequently served

at Starfleet Command in San Francisco, where she assisted in directing emergency operations when Earth was threatened with ecological disaster by an alien space probe of unknown origin. (*Star Trek IV: The Voyage Home*). Rand was later assigned as communications officer aboard the **U.S.S. Excelsior** under the command of Captain Sulu. (*Star Trek VI: The Undiscovered Country*). *Rand's first appearance was in "The Corbomite Maneuver." She was also seen in "The Enemy Within" (TOS), "The Man Trap" (TOS), "The Naked Time" (TOS), "Charlie X" (TOS), "Miri" (TOS), Star Trek I, Star Trek III, Star Trek IV, and Star Trek VI.*

rapid nadion pulse. A burst of subatomic nadion particles that facilitate a release of energy from the emitter crystal in a **phaser**. ("The Mind's Eye" [TNG]).

• **"Rascals."** *Next Generation* episode #133. Teleplay by Allison Hock. Story by Ward Botsford & Diana Dru Botsford and Michael Piller. Directed by Adam Nimoy. Stardate 46235.7. *First aired in 1992. A mysterious energy field reverts Picard, Guinan, Keiko, and Ro into children. This was the first episode directed by Adam Nimoy, son of Leonard Nimoy.* SEE: **B'rel-class Bird-of-Prey; Berik; Buranian; *Draebidium Calimus*; *Draebidium froctus*; Ferengi Salvage Code; *Fermi*, *Shuttlecraft*; firomactal drive; Guinan; Humuhumunukunukuapua'a; kelilactiral; Langford, Dr.; Ligos VII; Lurin, DaiMon; Marlonia; molecular reversion field; Morta; O'Brien, Keiko; Picard, Jean-Luc; Ro Laren; rybo-viroxic-nucleic structure; security access code; Suvin IV; Taguan; Tarkassian razorbeast; vendarite.**

Rashella. (Brenda Strong). The last child born on planet **Aldea** when radiation poisoning from damage to Aldea's **ozone** layer caused infertility among the Aldeans. Rashella had strong maternal instincts and wished to keep Alexandra, the child of an *Enterprise*-D crew member, as her own to raise. ("When the Bough Breaks" [TNG]).

Rasmussen, Berlingoff. (Matt Frewer). A 22nd-century con artist from New Jersey who appeared on the *Enterprise*-D in 2368, claiming to be a historian from the 26th century. Professor Rasmussen had in fact stolen his **time travel pod** from a 26th century researcher, and was hoping to steal artifacts of 24th-century technology. His plan was to return to the 22nd-century, then

grow wealthy by claiming to have "invented" these devices. When the *Enterprise*-D crew learned of his scheme, Rasmussen was detained and his time travel pod returned without him.

Rasmussen was subsequently taken under custody to **Starbase 214**, where Captain Picard felt he would be helpful in some legitimate historical research. ("A Matter of Time" [TNG]). *Matt Frewer is also familiar to genre fans for his role of Max Headroom.*

Rata. Second officer of the Ferengi vessel commanded by **DaiMon Bok**. ("The Battle" [TNG]).

Rateg. City on planet **Romulus**. Picard and Data, working undercover on Romulus in 2368, said they came from Rateg. ("Unification, Part I" [TNG]).

Rawlens. Chief Geologist on board the original *Starship Enterprise* in 2268. ("The Ultimate Computer" [TOS]).

Rayburn. (Budd Albright). *Enterprise* security officer killed by the android **Ruk** at planet **Exo III** in 2266. ("What Are Little Girls Made Of?" [TOS]).

Raymond, Claire. (Gracie Harrison). Human from late-20th-century Earth. Former occupation: homemaker. Raymond died of heart failure at the age of 35, whereupon her husband, Donald, arranged to have her body cryogenically frozen and stored in an orbiting satellite. Over three centuries later, she was revived aboard the *Enterprise*-D. Raymond returned

to Earth aboard the *Starship **Charleston***, where she planned to look up her descendants living near Indianapolis. ("The Neutral Zone" [TNG]).

Raymond, Donald. Twentieth-century human and husband to **Claire Raymond**. Upon his wife's death, the profoundly sad Donald Raymond arranged to have Claire's body cryogenically frozen and stored in an orbiting satellite for future revival. ("The Neutral Zone" [TNG]).

Raymond, Edward. Younger son of Donald and **Claire Raymond**. Edward was born in Secaucus, New Jersey, and lived in late-20th and early-21st-century Earth. ("The Neutral Zone" [TNG]).

Raymond, Thomas. (Peter Lauritson). Great-great-great-great-great-grandson of **Claire Raymond.** At the time of Claire's revival from cryonic storage, Thomas was living on Earth, just outside of Indianapolis. Claire said that Thomas looked exactly like her son,

also named Thomas, who had lived in the late-20th and early-21st century. ("The Neutral Zone" [TNG]). *The image of Thomas Raymond seen on Troi's computer screen was the face of* Star Trek *producer Peter Lauritson.*

reactive ion impeller. Science project that Nog and Jake built for school on Deep Space 9 in 2669. ("Move Along Home" [DS9]).

ready room. On many starships, a small office located directly adjacent to the bridge, where the captain could work undisturbed. Captain Picard's ready room on the *Enterprise-D* had a desk, a desktop viewer, a couch, and a food replicator terminal. *Decorations in the room have included a model of the U.S.S. Stargazer; a hardbound illustrated edition of the collected works of William Shakespeare; a painting of the Enterprise-D; a saltwater aquarium containing* **Livingston**, *a fish; a crystalline sailing ship model; an ancient nautical sextant; and, in later episodes, a* **Kurlan Naiskos** *statuette from "The Chase" (TNG).*

• **"Realm of Fear."** *Next Generation* episode #128. Written by Brannon Braga. Directed by Cliff Bole. Stardate 46041.1. *First aired in 1992. Reginald Barclay, who is scared of the transporter anyway, is attacked by creatures living in the transporter beam. This was the only time where the audience was shown what it looks like to be beamed from the transport subject's point of view.* SEE: **Barclay, Reginald; Christina; Delinia II; Dern, Ensign; Heisenberg compensators; Igo Sector; imaging scanner; Kelly, Lieutenant Joshua; kiloquad; Lycosa tarantula; matter stream; O'Brien, Miles; Ogawa, Nurse Alyssa; Olafson, Dr.; pattern buffer; phase transition coils; phased matter; plasma streamer; plexing; quasi-energy microbes; sample container; Talarian hook spider; Titus IV; transporter psychosis; Transporter Theory;** *Yosemite, U.S.S.;* **Zayra IV.**

rec deck. Large recreation room located at the rear of Deck 7 in the primary hull of the refitted *Starship Enterprise.* It featured a variety of games, a large viewscreen, and a display honoring previous vessels named *Enterprise.* (*Star Trek: The Motion Picture*).

recalibration sweep. Systematic analysis and correction of instrumentation on station Deep Space 9. Dr. Julian Bashir told a Federation delegation sent to study the Bajoran wormhole in 2369 that Commander Sisko was busy with a

recalibration sweep, an ultimately futile attempt to keep the delegates out of Sisko's way. ("The Forsaken" [DS9]).

"receptacle." Term used callously by **Ambassador Ves Alkar** to describe the women that he subjected to severe empathic abuse in order for him to maintain extraordinary emotional control. His "receptacles" generally died as a result of this molestation. ("Man of the People" [TNG]).

recorder marker. Small data-storage buoy designed to be ejected from a spacecraft when destruction of that vessel was believed imminent. When recovered after the disaster, the information from the recorder marker would serve to help reconstruct the incidents leading to the ship's destruction. ("Where No Man Has Gone Before" [TOS], "The Corbomite Maneuver" [TOS]). The

recorder marker of the **S.S. Valiant** was recovered by the original *Starship Enterprise* in 2265. ("Where No Man Has Gone Before" [TOS]). SEE: **flight recorder.**

Rectyne monopod. An animal form that grows as large as two tons. Miles O'Brien once saw a Rectyne monopod subjected to a **Klingon painstik**, a brutal treatment that caused the creature to jump five meters at the slightest touch. The animal finally died from excessive cephalic pressures – its head exploded. ("The Icarus Factor" [TNG]).

Red Alert. Aboard Federation starships and other vessels, a state of maximum crew and systems readiness. Red Alert is generally ordered by a ship's commanding officer during a serious emergency or potential emergency such as a major systems failure or a battle situation.

Red Hour. During the rule of the computer **Landru** on planet **Beta III**, the Red Hour was a period of extreme violence and destruction by the planet's inhabitants. This may have been intended as a means of providing an emotional outlet to the tightly controlled society. ("Return of the Archons" [TOS]).

Redblock, Cyrus. (Lawrence Tierney). A fictional character from the **Dixon Hill** detective stories. A notorious and powerful gangster, Redblock was an urbane and ruthless intellectual. A holographic version of Redblock was part of the Dixon Hill holodeck programs. ("The Big Goodbye" [TNG]). *The name Cyrus Redblock was apparently a play on the name of actor Sydney Greenstreet.*

• **"Redemption, Part I."** *Next Generation* episode #100. Written by Ronald D. Moore. Directed by Cliff Bole. Stardate 44995.3. *First aired in 1991. Worf becomes embroiled in a Klingon civil war for control of the High Council. This cliffhanger episode was the last of the fourth season, and the*

direct continuation of Worf's story begun in "Sins of the Father" (TNG) and "Reunion" (TNG). SEE: **Arbiter of Succession**; **B'Etor**; *BaH*; **Beta Thoridar**; *Bortas, I.K.C.*; *d'k tahq*; **discommendation**; **Duras**; *G'now juk Hol pajhard*; **Gowron**; *Hegh'ta*; **K'Tal**; **kellicam**; **Klingon civil war**; **Klingon Empire**; **Klingon Homeworld**; **Kurn**; *Len'mat*; **Lursa**; **Mempa Sector**; **Movar**; *naDev ghos!*; **phaser range**; **Reel, Ensign**; **Romulan Star Empire**; **Sela**; **Starbase 24**; **Toral**; **Treaty of Alliance**; **Worf**; *yIntagh*.

• **"Redemption, Part II."** *Next Generation* episode #101. Written by Ronald D. Moore. Directed by David Carson. Stardate 45020.4. *First aired in 1991. The Gowron regime retains control of the Klingon High Council, and Worf regains his family honor. This was the first episode of the fifth season.* SEE: *Akagi, U.S.S.*; *baktag*; **Berellians**; **Beta Lankal**; **B'Etor**; **cloaking device, Romulan**; *DaH*; **Data**; **Duras**; *Endeavour, U.S.S.*; *Excalibur, U.S.S.*; **Gamma Eridon**; *GhoS!*; **Gowron**; *Hermes, U.S.S.*; **Hobson, Lieutenant Commander Christopher**; *Hornet, U.S.S.*; **Klingon civil war**; **Klingon Empire**; **Kulge**; **Kurn**; **Larg**; **Lursa**; **"May you die well"**; **Mempa Sector**; **Romulan Star Empire**; **Sela**; **Shanthi, Fleet Admiral**; **Starbase 234**; *Sutherland, U.S.S.*; **tachyon detection grid**; *Tian An Men, U.S.S.*; **Toral**; **Worf**; **Yar, Tasha (alternate)**.

Redjac. Energy-based life-form that terrorized and murdered women throughout history, feeding on the emotion of fear. Redjac was believed responsible for the death of seven women who were knifed to death in Shanghai, China, on Earth in 1932.

The entity was also believed responsible for seven similar murders in Kiev, USSR, in 1974, as well as for eight murders in the Martian Colonies in 2105 and ten murders on planet Alpha Eridani II in 2156. All these murders were committed by the entity known in London on Earth as **Jack the Ripper**, on **Deneb II** as **Kesla**, and on **Rigel IV** as **Beratis**.

This entity traveled from Rigel IV to **Argelius II** in the body of city administrator **Hengist**, where it caused at least three more deaths in 2267. *Enterprise* engineer Montgomery Scott was initially accused of these last murders, but when the entity's true nature was discovered, it was transported into space where it was hoped it dispersed harmlessly. ("Wolf in the Fold" [TOS]).

Reel, Ensign. An *Enterprise*-D officer who was assigned to conn during the first battle of the **Klingon civil war** in late 2367. Reel was ordered to pilot the ship away from the confrontation so the Federation would not become involved in the conflict. ("Redemption, Part I" [TNG]).

reflection therapy. Psychiatric technique used on planet **Tilonus IV** in which the patient's brain is scanned and images from brain areas that control emotions and memory are projected holographically. The patient then interacts with holographic images which represent various facets of his personality. ("Frame of Mind" [TNG]). SEE: *Frame of Mind*; **neurosomatic technique**; **Syrus, Dr.**

refrigeration unit. Device forcibly installed by the **Scalosians**

into the *Starship Enterprise*'s life-support systems in 2268, intended to freeze the ship's crew until they were needed for reproduction. ("Wink of an Eye" [TOS]).

Reger. (Harry Townes). Inhabitant of planet **Beta III** during the end of **Landru**'s rule in 2267. He owned the inn at which an *Enterprise* landing party sought refuge after the **Red Hour**. Reger was immune from absorption into the Body. Along with citizens Tamar and Marphon, Reger was a member of the resistance movement against Landru's rule. ("Return of the Archons" [TOS]).

Reginold. (Leslie Morris). Engineering officer of the **Pakled** vessel *Mondor*. ("Samaritan Snare" [TNG]).

Regula I Space Laboratory. Deep-space facility located in the **Mutara Sector** near the planetoid **Regula**. **Project Genesis** was developed at this laboratory under the direction of Dr. Carol Marcus. (*Star Trek II: The Wrath of Khan*).

Regula. Lifeless, class-D planetoid located in the **Mutara Sector**. Regula was the site of a key test of **Project Genesis** in which a Genesis device was detonated deep inside the planetoid, resulting in the creation of a large chamber suitable for life. (*Star Trek II: The Wrath of Khan*).

Regulan blood worms. Soft and shapeless creatures that the Klingon, **Korax**, mentioned as an insult to several of the *Enterprise* crew on **Deep Space Station K-7** in 2267. ("The Trouble with Tribbles" [TOS]).

Regulations, Starfleet. SEE: **Starfleet General Orders and Regulations.**

Regulus V. Planet where every eleven years the giant eel-birds return to the caverns where they were hatched. ("Amok Time" [TOS]).

Rejac Crystal. A rare objet d'art, reported to be in the personal collection of **Zibalian** trader **Kivas Fajo** at least until Fajo's arrest in 2366. ("The Most Toys" [TNG]).

Rekag-Seronia. Planet that was the site of bitter hostilities between local factions, the **Rekags** and the Seronians. By 2369, this fighting threatened a key Federation shipping route, so **Ambassador Ves Alkar** was assigned there in hopes of mediating a cease-fire between the warring parties. This was the last conflict that Alkar mediated prior to his death. The planet is also known as Seronia. ("Man of the People" [TNG]).

Rekags. One of two historically warring factions on planet **Rekag-Seronia**. Rekag battle cruisers fired on the transport ship *Dorian* when that ship was attempting to convey **Ambassador Ves Alkar** to Rekag-Seronia in 2369 in hopes of bringing peace. ("Man of the People" [TNG]).

Reklar. Cardassian *Galor*-class warship, under the command of **Gul Lemec** in 2369. The *Reklar* met the *Enterprise*-D at the Federation/Cardassian border so that Gul Lemec and Captain Jellico could conduct talks about the movements of Cardassian troops and ships along the border. ("Chain of Command, Part I" [TNG]).

Relay Station 47. Remote Starfleet communications station near the Klingon border. Most of the operations of the station were automated, although a two-person crew provided nonroutine operations and maintenance. A network of such stations throughout Federation space permits interstellar communication between distant points with much shorter time lags than unboosted **subspace radio** transmissions would require. **Lieutenant Aquiel Uhnari**, assigned to Relay Station 47 in 2369, was investigated for the murder of her crewmate, **Keith Rocha**, but was exonerated. ("Aquiel" [TNG]). *The Relay Station 47 miniature was designed by Rick Sternbach and was a modification of the* **cryosatellite** *from "The Neutral Zone" (TNG), based on a drawing Rick did in the* Star Trek: The Next Generation Technical Manual *(Pocket Books, 1991).*

Relay Station 194. Communications station used to amplify and retransmit subspace messages. Relay Station 194 was off-line for maintenance for several hours in early 2369, and **Relay Station 47** accepted the additional comm traffic for that period. ("Aquiel" [TNG]).

Reliant, U.S.S. Federation starship, *Miranda* class, Starfleet registry number NCC-1864. In 2285, *Reliant*, under the command of Captain **Clark Terrell**, was assigned to survey planets in the Mutara Sector in support of **Project Genesis**. During the mission, *Reliant* was destroyed when it was hijacked by **Khan Noonien Singh**. The ship had been on a scientific mission and was surveying planet **Ceti Alpha V**, on which Khan had been marooned. Khan had left the *Reliant's* crew behind on Ceti Alpha V. (*Star Trek II: The Wrath of Khan*). *The* Reliant *was designed by Mike Minor and Joe Jennings. The model was built at ILM.*

• **"Relics."** *Next Generation* episode #130. Written by Ronald D. Moore. Directed by Alexander Singer. Stardate 46125.3. *First aired in 1993. Captain Montgomery Scott is found to be alive, having survived in a transporter beam after his ship crashed on a Dyson sphere 75 years ago. "Relics" establishes that Scotty disappeared aboard the* Jenolen *about a year after the events in* Star Trek VI, *and that he remained lost until 2369.* SEE: **Aldebaran whiskey; Bartel, Engineer; Code One Alpha Zero; containment fields; deuterium; dilithium; duotronics; Dyson sphere;** *Enterprise*-A, *U.S.S.*; **Fleet Museum; Franklin, Ensign Matt;** *Goddard, Shuttlecraft*; **gravimetric interference; holodeck; isolinear optical chip;** *Jenolen, U.S.S.*; **Norpin Colony; pattern buffer; Rager, Ensign; Starfleet General Orders and Regulations; rematerialization subroutine; Scott, Montgomery;** *Sydney*-class transport; **synthehol; Ten-Forward.**

Relva VII. Planet on which is located a Starfleet facility. Wesley Crusher's first attempt to pass the Starfleet Academy entrance exam was made at **Relva VII** in 2364, under the supervision of **Tac Officer Chang**. ("Coming of Age" [TNG]). *The exterior of the* Relva VII *station was a matte painting by visual effects supervisor Dan Curry. The painting was a modification of a design Dan had originally done for an episode of the series* Buck Rogers *entitled "Plot to Kill a City."*

REM sleep. In neurophysiology, REM (rapid eye movement) describes a normal state of sleep during which most humanoid dreaming occurs. The condition is so named because the sleeper's eyes, though closed, will often exhibit rapid movement. William Riker experienced neural patterns corresponding to REM sleep after being injured on an away mission to planet **Surata IV** in 2365. ("Shades of Grey" [TNG]). Lack of REM sleep was thought to have caused the psychosis that led the crew of the *Brattain* to kill each other in 2367. This lack of REM sleep was apparently caused by attempts at communication by an alien intelligence trapped in a **Tyken's Rift**. ("Night Terrors" [TNG]). *Contrary to popular belief, the lack of dreams is not currently held to be harmful, except if you are using your dreams as fodder for television scripts.*

rematerialization subroutine. Portion of the operation cycle of a transporter that controls the restoration of the matter stream to its original form. **Montgomery Scott** disabled the rematerialization subroutine of the *Jenolen's* transporters in an attempt to keep himself and Matt Franklin suspended in the beam until help arrived. ("Relics" [TNG]).

• **"Remember Me."** *Next Generation* episode #79. Written by Lee Sheldon. Directed by Cliff Bole. Stardate 44161.2. *First aired in 1990. A warp physics experiment gone awry traps Beverly Crusher in her own private universe. This was the 79th episode of* Star Trek: The Next Generation, *equaling the total episode count of the original* Star Trek *series. This episode also marked the return of the Traveler, first seen in "Where No One Has Gone Before" (TNG).* SEE: **Crusher, Dr. Beverly; Delos IV; Durenia IV; Hill, Dr. Richard; Kenda II; Kosinski; millicochrane; Quaice, Dr. Dalen; Quaice, Patricia; Selar, Dr.; sickbay; Starbase 133; static warp bubble; transporter ID trace; Traveler; umbilical port;** *Wellington, U.S.S.*

Remmick, Dexter. (Robert Schenkkan). Starfleet officer with the Inspector General's office. Remmick was assigned to inspect the *Starship Enterprise*-D in 2364 when Starfleet admiral **Gregory Quinn** suspected the existence of a conspiracy deep in the heart of Starfleet. ("Coming of Age" [TNG]). Remmick, later assigned to Starfleet Command, was the victim of the alien intelligence that infiltrated **Starfleet Headquarters** in 2364. Remmick was the unwilling host to the "mother" alien that apparently controlled the parasites that infested numerous Starfleet officers. Both he and the alien were killed by intense phaser fire, after which the telepathically linked parasites in other officers also died. ("Conspiracy" [TNG]).

Remmler Array. Federation orbital facility located above **Arkaria Base**. The Remmler Array was used for **baryon decontamination sweeps** of starships. The *Enterprise*-D put in at the Remmler Array in 2369. While it was there, a group of terrorists attempted to steal **trilithium resin** from the ship's engines. ("Starship Mine" [TNG]).

Remus. One of the two homeworlds of the **Romulan Star Empire**. ("Balance of Terror" [TOS]). *Mr. Spock's star chart gives this planet's name as Romii, although spoken dialog in the episode uses the name Remus.* SEE: **Romulus**.

Renaissance-**class starship.** Conjectural designation for a type of Federation vessel. The *U.S.S. Aries*, offered for Riker to command in 2365, was a *Renaissance*-class ship ("The Icarus Factor" [TNG]), as was the *U.S.S. Hornet* ("Redemption, Part II" [TNG]). *Named for the period in European history when civilization as we know it had a dramatic rebirth, or renaissance.*

Renegade, U.S.S. Federation starship, *New Orleans* class, registry number NCC-63102. Commanded by Captain **Tryla Scott**. The *Renegade* was one of the ships that met the *Enterprise*-D at **Dytallix B** when an alien intelligence attempted to take over Starfleet Command in 2364. ("Conspiracy" [TNG]).

Renora. (Anne Haney). Judge who presided over **Jadzia Dax**'s extradition trial on Deep Space 9 in 2369 for the murder of General Ardelon Tandro. Renora was 100 years old and said that at her age, she didn't want to waste time with needless legal maneuvers. ("Dax" [DS9]). SEE: **Klaestron IV, General Ardelon Tandro, Curzon Dax.**. *Anne Haney also played Rishon Uxbridge in "The Survivors" (TNG).*

Replicating Center. Facility aboard a *Galaxy*-class starship containing several replicator terminals at which crew members could order a wide variety of products that would be produced on command. Worf and Data went there in search of a wedding present for **Miles** and **Keiko O'Brien**. ("Data's Day" [TNG]).

replicative fading. A loss of genetic information occurring when an organism is repeatedly cloned. After several generations of cloning, replicative fading can become serious, resulting in subtle errors creeping into chromosomes, eventually yielding a nonviable **clone**. The **Mariposa** colony had depended on cloning to maintain its population, but fell victim to replicative fading. ("Up the Long Ladder" [TNG]).

replicator. Device using transporter technology to dematerialize a quantity of matter, then to rematerialize it in another form. Replicators are used aboard Federation starships to provide a much wider variety of meal choices to crew members than would be available if actual foodstuffs had to be carried, since the selection available is limited only by software. Most people find replicated food indistinguishable from "original" food, although some individuals claim to be able to tell the difference.

Captain Picard carried a few cases of real caviar aboard his ship for special occasions because he felt the replicators never did it justice. ("Sins of the Father" [TNG]). *Replicators were apparently not in use during Captain Kirk's day, unless the food slots seen on his ship were indeed replicators.*

Republic, U.S.S. Federation starship, *Constitution* class, Starfleet registry number NCC-1371. **James Kirk** and **Ben Finney** served together on the *Republic* around 2250. Ensign Kirk once found Finney had left a circuit to the atomic matter piles open. Kirk logged the error and Finney was sent to the bottom of the promotion list. ("Court Martial" [TOS]).

Repulse, U.S.S. Federation starship, *Excelsior* class, registry number NCC-2544. **Captain Taggert** commanding. **Dr. Katherine Pulaski** served aboard the *Repulse* prior to her assignment to the *Enterprise*-D in 2365. ("The Child" [TNG], "Unnatural Selection"

[TNG]). *Named for the British battle cruiser that fought in Earth's Battle of Midway in World War II.*

• **"Requiem for Methuselah."** Original Series episode #76. Written by Jerome Bixby. Directed by Murray Golden. Stardate 5843.7. *First aired in 1969. An immortal man tries to build the perfect woman, but she falls in love with James Kirk instead.* SEE: **Brack, Mr.; Constantinople; Flint; Holberg 917G; irillium; Kapec, Rayna; M-4; Rigelian fever; ryetalyn; Saurian brandy.**

Research Station 75. Federation outpost located on a planetary surface. The *Enterprise*-D visited there in 2369 to pick up **Ensign Stefan DeSeve**, who was returning to Federation custody after having previously renounced his Federation citizenship in 2349 to live on **Romulus**. ("Face of the Enemy" [TNG]).

Resolution, The. On planet Kaelon II, the ritual ending of one's life at age sixty. The Kaelon people considered this to be a dignified way to conclude a life, and viewed it to be vastly preferable to having the aged population waste away in "death watch facilities." The Resolution celebrated the guest of honor with a special gathering of friends and relatives, where that person's life and achievements would be recognized. The Resolution has been in practice for over a millennium, and Kaelon society permits no exceptions. ("Half a Life" [TNG]). SEE: **Timicin, Dr.**

resonance tissue scan. Medical diagnostic test used by Starfleet physicians to screen for infection. Dr. Crusher ran a resonance tissue scan on Geordi La Forge when his VISOR malfunctioned after he was kidnapped by the **Solanagen-based aliens.** ("Schisms" [TNG]).

resonators. Devices designed to create powerful vibrations in underground geologic strata. *Enterprise*-D crew personnel modified a number of **Class-1 probe**s to serve as resonator devices delivered from orbit to the subsurface of planet **Drema IV**. Once delivered, the resonators emitted harmonic vibrations that successfully shattered the lattices of dilithium strata, thus halting the disintegration of the planet. ("Pen Pals" [TNG]).

Ressik. Community of the now-dead planet **Kataan**, home of the ironweaver **Kamin**. Under the influence of the Kataan probe, Jean-Luc Picard experienced a lifetime of memories from Ressik. The probe had been launched by the Kataans in the hopes it would someday encounter someone like Picard through whom the planet might be remembered. ("The Inner Light" [TNG]).

Ressikan flute. Small musical wind instrument, resembling a tin flute, native to the community of **Ressik** on the now-dead planet **Kataan**. The space probe launched from Kataan contained memories from the planet, as well as a single artifact, a Ressikan flute.

Jean-Luc Picard, who received the Kataan memories, including the knowledge of how to play the Ressikan flute, also received the artifact, which he treasured. ("The Inner Light" [TNG]). SEE: **Kamin**. Picard enjoyed playing his Ressikan flute in musical duets with **Neela Daren** when the two were romantically involved in 2369. ("Lessons" [TNG]). *Picard also played the instrument in "A Fistful of Datas" (TNG).*

reticular formation. A system of cells in the medulla oblongata of many humanoid brains. This area controls the overall degree of nervous system activity. The **Ktarian game** was found to activate the reticular formation of the brain. ("The Game" [TNG]).

retina scan. Method of verifying an individual's identification by scanning the pattern of blood vessels in that person's retina. The technique was believed to be more reliable (and more difficult to falsify) than fingerprinting. Kirk had to submit to a retina scan to gain access to the **Project Genesis** files. (*Star Trek II: The Wrath of Khan*).

retinal imaging scan. Medical test used to verify the pres-

ence or absence of activity in the visual cortex. ("The Passenger" [DS9]).

Retnax V. A medication sometimes prescribed to near-sighted patients in the 23rd century. McCoy noted he had not prescribed Retnax V to Kirk because the good captain was allergic to it. (*Star Trek II: The Wrath of Khan*).

• **"Return of the Archons."** *Original Series* episode #22. Teleplay by Boris Sobelman. Story by Gene Roddenberry. Directed by Joseph Pevney. Stardate 3156.2. *First aired in 1967. The* Enterprise, *investigating the disappearance of the Starship* Archon, *finds a planet ruled by a computer called Landru.* SEE: **absorbed;** *Archon, U.S.S.;* **Archons; Beta III; Bilar; Body; C-111; Festival; Hacom; Hall of Audiences; Landru; Lawgivers; Leslie, Mr.; Lindstrom; Marphon; O'Neil, Lieutenant; Red Hour; Reger; Tula; Valley.**

• **"Return to Tomorrow."** *Original Series* episode #51. Written by John Kingsbridge. Directed by Ralph Senensky. Stardate 4768.3. *First aired in 1968. Two lovers and their enemy from a race that died a half-million years ago "borrow" the bodies of* Enterprise *people so that they may build android bodies for themselves.* SEE: **android; Henoch; metabolic reduction injection; Mulhall, Dr. Ann; negaton hydrocoils; Sargon's planet; Sargon; Thalassa; Vulcans.**

• **"Reunion."** *Next Generation* episode #81. Teleplay by Thomas Perry & Jo Perry and Ronald D. Moore & Brannon Braga. Story by Drew Deighan and Thomas Perry & Jo Perry. Directed by Jonathan Frakes. Stardate 44246.3. *First aired in 1990. Worf discovers he is a father, and Picard is asked to help choose the next leader of the Klingon Empire. This episode continued Worf's story from "Sins of the Father" (TNG), and later was further continued in "Redemption, Parts I and II" (TNG). "Reunion" (TNG) is the first appearance of Worf's son, Alexander.* SEE: **Arbiter of Succession;** *bat'telh;* **Buruk; Duras; Gamma Arigulon system; Gowron;** *ha'DIbah;* **Hubble, Chief;** *ja'chug; jIH dok;* **K'Ehleyr; K'mpec; Kahless the Unforgettable; Klingon attack cruiser; Klingon Empire;** *LaSalle, U.S.S.; mev yap;* **molecular-decay detonator; painstik, Klingon; Picard, Jean-Luc;** *QuajIH nagil;* **Rite of Succession, Klingon; Rozhenko, Alexander; Rozhenko, Helena;** *Sonchi* **ceremony; Starbase 73; Tholians; triceron; Veridium Six; Vorn; Worf.**

Rex. A fictional bartender in the world of pulp detective Dixon Hill, and the owner of Rex's Bar. The **Dixon Hill** holodeck program, based on the Dixon Hill novels and short stories, included a holographic representation of Rex. The character attracted the romantic interest of Lwaxana Troi, who was unaware that Rex was not a real person, when she entered a holodeck simulation being run by Jean-Luc Picard. ("Manhunt" [TNG]).

Reyab. Kobliad transport vessel that carried **Kobliad** security officer **Kajada** and her prisoner **Rao Vantika**. The *Reyab* caught fire near Bajoran space in 2369. A runabout from station Deep Space 9 responded to the *Reyab*'s distress call. ("The Passenger" [DS9]).

Reyga, Dr. (Peter Slutsker). Ferengi scientist who invented a revolutionary metaphasic shield technology in 2369. Though his invention was treated with skepticism by most of the scientific community, he found an unlikely ally in Dr. Beverly Crusher. Dr. Reyga was invited aboard the *Enterprise*-D, along with other specialists in subspace technology, in order to test his new shield. The test was apparently unsuccessful. Shortly after the failed test, Dr. Reyga was found dead, the victim of a plasma surge. Dr. Crusher was able to prove that Dr. Reyga's death was intentional, and that his **metaphasic shield** was indeed a viable technology. ("Suspicions" [TNG]). SEE: **Jo'Bril.**

Rhada, Lieutenant. (Naomi Pollock). *Enterprise* crew member who served at the helm when a landing party was stranded at the **Kalandan outpost** in 2268. ("That Which Survives" [TOS]).

Rhomboid Dronegar Sector. Origin of a distress call received by the *Enterprise*-D from a disabled **Pakled** ship in 2365. ("Samaritan Snare" [TNG]).

ribosome infusion. Medical treatment suggested by Dr. Crusher to help the injured Romulan **Patahk** after exposure to the surface conditions on **Galorndon Core** in 2366. The only compatible donor on the *Enterprise*-D was Worf, who refused to cooperate. ("The Enemy" [TNG]).

Rice, Captain Paul. (Marco Rodrigues). Commander of the *U.S.S. Drake* when it was destroyed at planet **Minos** in 2364. Rice was a highly regarded officer, a risk taker, and a friend to William Riker. Rice was offered the chance to command the *Drake* after Riker declined the job. Rice was later killed at Minos, along with the rest of his crew, by an ancient but still-active weapons system. ("The Arsenal of Freedom" [TNG]).

Richardson. *Enterprise*-D crew member who was killed while manually controlling the **thermal deflectors** against a fierce firestorm on planet **Bersallis III** in 2369. ("Lessons" [TNG]).

Richey, Colonel Stephen. Commander of the **NASA** ship *Charybdis* on the ill-fated third manned attempt to explore beyond Earth's solar system. Richey was the only survivor when the *Charybdis's* crew was accidentally killed by an unknown alien intelligence. In an effort to atone for the tragic deaths of the *Charybdis* crew, the intelligence attempted to create a natural human environment in which Richey could live out the remainder of his life. Unfortunately, the aliens used a badly written novel — *Hotel Royale,* by Todd Matthews — as the model for this environment, thus creating a bizarre purgatory in which Richey eventually died. ("The Royale" [TNG]).

Richter scale of culture. Scale of cultural developments of different races. Spock said the agrarian inhabitants on planet **Organia** were a D-minus on Richter's scale of cultures: primitive but peaceful. Spock's assessment was later found to be wrong when the Organians turned out to be incredibly advanced **noncorporeal life**-forms. ("Errand of Mercy" [TOS]).

Riga, Stano. Twenty-third-century comedian who specialized in jokes about quantum mathematics. Riga was considered one of the funniest of human comedians. A simulated version of Riga was programmed into the *Enterprise*-D holodeck computer, but Data, who was studying the concept of humor, thought Riga's material too esoteric. ("The Outrageous Okona" [TNG]).

***Rigel*-class starship.** Conjectural designation for a type of Federation ship. The *U.S.S. Tolstoy*, destroyed in the battle of Wolf 359, was a *Rigel*-class starship ("The Best of Both Worlds, Part II" [TNG]), as was the *U.S.S. Akagi* ("Redemption, Part II" [TNG]).

Rigel II. Planet where Leonard McCoy met two scantily clad women in a chorus line at a cabaret. The pair was re-created from McCoy's imagination in 2267 on the **amusement park planet** in the Omicron Delta region. ("Shore Leave" [TOS]).

Rigel IV. Site of serial killings of women in 2266. These murders were attributed to an unknown individual called Beratis, which was later learned to be a malevolent energy creature who left Rigel IV in the body of **Mr. Hengist**, who traveled to planet Argelius II, where he committed more murders using a knife from the **Argus River region** of Rigel IV. ("Wolf in the Fold" [TOS]). A brilliant astronomer with a fondness for **Lwaxana Troi** resided on Rigel IV. He named a star after Lwaxana, or so she claimed. ("Half a Life" [TNG]).

Rigel V. Planet where an experimental drug was tested to see if the production of blood elements in a humanoid body could be accelerated. Spock suggested this drug might be useful for Ambassador **Sarek** during a critical heart operation. ("Journey to Babel" [TOS]). SEE: **T-negative.**

Rigel VII. The site of a violent conflict in 2254 involving *Enterprise* crew personnel under the command of Captain **Christopher Pike** and the humanoid inhabitants of that planet. Three *Enterprise* crew members, including Pike's yeoman, were killed, and

seven others were injured. The incident, which Pike later blamed on his own carelessness, took place just prior to the *Enterprise*'s first mission to planet **Talos IV**. ("The Cage," "The Menagerie, Part II [TOS]). SEE: **Kaylar.** In the 2360s, **Kobliad** criminal **Rao Vantika** caused computer systems on Rigel VII to crash using a **subspace shunt**, similar to the one he used in 2369 on station Deep Space 9. ("The Passenger" [DS9]). *The matte painting of the Rigel VII fortress seen in Pike's Talosian illusion was later reused as **Flint**'s castle in "Requiem for Methuselah" (TOS).*

Rigel XII. Barely habitable class-M planet, racked by fierce storms. Site of a small lithium mining operation headed by **Ben Childress**. The *Enterprise* visited the mining station in 2266 to obtain needed **lithium crystals** to restore operation of the ship's engines. ("Mudd's Women" [TOS]). *Rigel, also known as Beta Orionis, is a bright supergiant star, visible from Earth as one of the "legs" in the constellation Orion (the hunter).*

Rigelian fever. Deadly disease resembling bubonic plague that infected the *Enterprise* crew in 2269, necessitating that a landing party beam down to planetoid **Holbert 917-G** in search of the antidote, **ryetalyn**. ("Requiem for Methuselah" [TOS]).

Rigelian freighter. Vessel used to run interference between the runabout taking **Croden** to the planet **Rakhar** and a **Miradorn** ship in 2369. ("Vortex" [DS9]).

Rigelian Kassaba fever. As a ruse to regain control of the *Enterprise* in 2268 when commandeered by the **Kelvans**, Dr. McCoy claimed that Spock suffered from Rigelian Kassaba fever and required treatment with **stokaline** injections. ("By Any Other Name" [TOS]).

Rigelians. Humanoid race with a physiology similar to that of Vulcans. A drug to speed up reproduction and replacement of blood was experimentally used with success on Rigel V. ("Journey to Babel" [TOS]).

• **"Rightful Heir."** *Next Generation* episode #149. Teleplay by Ronald D. Moore. Story by James E. Brooks. Directed by Winrich Kolbe. Stardate 46852.2. *First aired in 1993. Worf goes in search of his faith and finds the revered Klingon prophet Kahless the Unforgettable, returned from the dead.* SEE: **Alawanir Nebula;** *bat'leth;* **Boreth; Divok; Gariman Sector; Gowron; Kahless the Unforgettable; Kirom, Knife of; Klingon Empire; Koroth; Kri'stak Volcano; Kurn; Lusor; Molor; No'Mat; Quin'lat;** *Sto-Vo-Kor;* **Story of the Promise, The; Torigan, Ensign; Torin;** *Vorch-doh-baghk, Kahless!;* **Warnog; Worf.**

Riker, Jean-Luc. (Chris Demetral). Alter-ego of alien child **Barash**, who assumed the role of Riker's 10-year-old son in the hopes that Riker would play with him. In Barash's fantasy, Jean-Luc Riker had been named after Jean-Luc Picard. ("Future Imperfect" [TNG]).

Riker, Kyle. (Mitchell Ryan). Father to *Enterprise*-D executive officer **William Riker**. Kyle Riker was a civilian strategist advising Starfleet in a **Tholian** conflict in 2353. The starbase he was working from was attacked by the Tholians and all station personnel except for Riker were killed. Future *Enterprise*-D medical officer **Katherine Pulaski** cared for Riker, and the two became romantically involved. Pulaski later

recalled that she would have married him, but Riker's priority was his career. ("The Icarus Factor" [TNG]).

Riker, Thomas. (Jonathan Frakes). An exact duplicate of William T. Riker, created in 2361 during a transporter accident when the *U.S.S. Potemkin* was evacuating the science team on planet **Nervala IV**. One copy of Riker returned safely to the *Potemkin*, while the other was reflected by the planet's **distortion field** and materialized back on the surface of Nervala IV. The existence of the duplicate Riker was not discovered until 2369 when the *Starship Enterprise*-D returned to Nervala IV during a brief respite in the distortion field. This Riker had lived alone for eight years on the planet's surface. Once rescued, the this Riker decided to use his middle name, Thomas, to distinguish himself from his copy which had since been promoted to commander. Thomas indicated a desire to continue in Starfleet and was assigned to the *U.S.S. Ghandi*. Thomas took with him a cherished trombone, a gift from his twin. ("Second Chances" [TNG]).

Riker, William T. (Jonathan Frakes). Executive officer of the *Starship Enterprise*-D under the command of Captain **Jean-Luc Picard**. ("Encounter at Farpoint" [TNG]). Riker was born in Valdez, Alaska, on Earth in 2335. Riker's mother died when he was only two years old, and he was raised by his father, **Kyle Riker**. The elder Riker abandoned his son at age 15, an

act that William held against his father until 2365 when, at age 30, father and son were reunited aboard the *Enterprise*-D. ("The Icarus Factor" [TNG]).

Riker graduated from Starfleet Academy in 2357, and was ranked eighth in his class at graduation. As of 2369, he had been decorated five times. ("Chain of Command, Part I" [TNG]). Riker's first assignment after graduating from the academy was aboard the *U.S.S. Pegasus*, a ship that disappeared under mysterious circumstances. ("The *Pegasus*" [TNG]). Early in his Starfleet career, Riker was stationed on planet **Betazed**, ("Ménage à Troi" [TNG]), where he became romantically involved with psychology student **Deanna Troi**. Riker, then a lieutenant, chose to make his Starfleet career his priority over his relationship with Deanna, and accepted a posting to the *U.S.S. Potemkin*. While aboard the *Potemkin*, Riker led a rescue mission to planet **Nervala IV** and was subsequently promoted to lieutenant commander and commended for "exceptional valor" during the rescue. It was not realized until years later that a transporter malfunction during the final beam-out caused an identical copy of Riker to be created on the planet's surface. ("Second Chances" [TNG]). SEE: **Riker, Thomas.** William Riker was later promoted to executive officer aboard the *U.S.S. Hood*, where he served under the command of **Captain Robert DeSoto**.

Riker joined the *Enterprise*-D at planet **Deneb IV**, having transferred from the *Hood*. ("Encounter at Farpoint, Parts I and II" [TNG]). Riker accepted the *Enterprise*-D posting, despite the fact that he'd been offered command of the *U.S.S. Drake*. ("The Arsenal of Freedom" [TNG]). One of Riker's greatest personal tests came in 2364 when the entity **Q** offered him a gift of supernatural powers, an offer that Riker was able to refuse. ("Hide and Q" [TNG]). Riker became the first Federation Starfleet officer to serve aboard a Klingon vessel when he participated in an **Officer Exchange Program** in 2365, serving as first officer aboard the Klingon ship *Pagh*. ("A Matter of Honor" [TNG]). Riker was offered command of the *U.S.S. Aries* in 2365, but he declined the appointment, preferring to remain on the *Enterprise*-D. ("The Icarus Factor" [TNG]). Riker suffered a near brush with death while on a survey mission to planet **Surata IV,** where contact with an indigenous plant form caused him to lose consciousness for several hours. ("Shades of Grey" [TNG]). Riker was charged with murder in the 2366 death of **Dr. Nel Apgar** at planet **Tanuga IV** after Apgar's research station exploded. He was acquitted after a holodeck re-creation of the events leading to the death demonstrated that Apgar had been responsible for the explosion. ("A Matter of Perspective" [TNG]). In late 2366, Riker refused a third opportunity to command a starship when he was offered the *U.S.S. Melbourne* during the **Borg** incursion that year. ("The Best of Both Worlds, Part I" [TNG]). Shortly thereafter, Riker was granted a temporary field promotion to captain, and given command of the *Enterprise*-D following the capture of Captain Picard by the Borg. The *Melbourne* was later destroyed by the Borg in the battle of **Wolf 359**. ("The Best of Both Worlds, Part II" [TNG]).

Riker's approach to command was frequently unconventional. Prior to his service aboard the *Enterprise*-D, Riker had been a lieutenant aboard the *Starship* **Potemkin**. During a crisis aboard that ship, Riker positioned the *Potemkin* over a planet's magnetic pole, thus confusing his opponent's sensors. Indeed, Data once observed that Riker relied upon traditional problem-solving techniques less than one-quarter of the time. ("Peak Performance" [TNG]).

As a boy, Riker was responsible for cooking for himself and his father. As *Enterprise*-D executive officer, Riker regarded cooking as a hobby. ("Time Squared" [TNG]). One of Riker's passions was for old Earth jazz music, and he was a pretty fair trombone player. ("11001001" [TNG]). *SEE:* **Number One**. *William Riker was first seen in "Encounter at Farpoint" (TNG).*

Riley, Kevin Thomas. (Bruce Hyde). Young relief navigator aboard the *U.S.S. Enterprise* under the command of Captain Kirk. Riley fancied himself the descendant of Irish kings, and this trait surfaced while he was under the intoxicating effects of the **Psi 2000** virus, during which Riley nearly caused the destruction of the *Enterprise* when he shut down the ship's main engines. ("The Naked Time" [TOS]). As a young boy, Riley was one of nine surviving eyewitnesses to the massacre of some 4,000 colonists at **Tarsus IV** by **Kodos the Executioner**. Riley's parents were killed in the massacre. In 2266, Riley also witnessed the death of Kodos, then known as **Anton Karidian**, during a performance of *Hamlet* aboard the

Starship Enterprise. ("The Conscience of the King" [TOS]).

Rio Grande, U.S.S. Starfleet *Danube*-class **runabout**, registry number NCC-72452, one of three runabouts assigned to station Deep Space 9. ("Emissary" [DS9], "The Passenger" [DS9], "Battle Lines" [DS9], et al.).

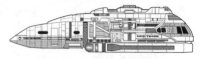

Risa. A tropical class-M planet noted for its beautiful beaches, resort facilities, and its open sexuality. Captain Picard vacationed there in 2366, where he met archaeologist **Vash** in search of the *Tox Uthat*. ("Captain's Holiday" [TNG]). In 2367, Geordi La Forge was scheduled to attend an artificial-intelligence seminar on Risa. La Forge was kidnapped by Romulans en route to the conference. ("The Mind's Eye" [TNG]). William Riker, who was very fond of Risa, vacationed there again in 2368, when he met a beautiful woman named **Etana Jol**, who was actually a **Ktaran** operative seeking to infiltrate Starfleet. ("The Game" [TNG]).

Rite of Succession, Klingon. Process whereby a new leader was chosen for the **Klingon High Council** following the death of the previous leader. The rite first required the *Sonchi*, in which the previous leader was formally certified to be truly dead. Next, the **Arbiter of Succession** was required to select the challengers for leadership of the council. The two strongest challengers would then fight for the right to lead the council. Following the death of **K'mpec** in 2367, Jean-Luc Picard served as Arbiter of Succession. ("Reunion" [TNG]).

Ritter scale. Measurement of cosmic radiation. ("The Empath" [TOS]).

ritual cloak. Feathered ceremonial coat worn by the groom during the joining or marriage ceremony on **Miramanee's planet**. ("The Paradise Syndrome" [TOS]).

Riva. (Howie Sego). Famed mediator from planet **Ramatis III**, Riva brought adversaries together by striving to turn disadvantages into advantages. His accomplishments include several treaties between the Klingon Empire and the United Federation of Planets. Riva was a member of the ruling

family of Ramatis III and, as is a genetic characteristic of that family, was born without the sense of hearing. Riva was able to overcome this challenge through the use of a **Chorus** of aides who acted as his interpreters. This Chorus was killed during negotiations on planet **Solais V**, after which Riva remained on that planet, working to turn that disadvantage into an advantage, bringing the opponents together by teaching both sides the use of sign language. ("Loud as a Whisper" [TNG]). *Actor Howie Sego is deaf in real life, and this episode was developed in part at his suggestion. Photo: Riva and his Chorus.*

Rivan. (Brenda Bakke). Female leader of the **Edo** race on planet **Rubicun III**. When transported to the *Enterprise*-D, Rivan was awestruck at the sight of the spaceborne object her race worshipped as its god. ("Justice" [TNG]). SEE: **Edo god.**

Rixx, Captain. (Michael Berrymore). Commander of the *Starship **Thomas Paine***. Along with **Walker Keel** and **Tryla Scott**, Rixx warned Jean-Luc Picard at planet Dytallix B of the unknown alien entities that were infiltrating Starfleet Command in 2364. Rixx was a **Bolian**. ("Conspiracy" [TNG]). *Actor Michael Berrymore previously played the communications officer in Starfleet Command in* Star Trek IV, *although he was wearing different makeup prosthetics.*

Rizzo, Ensign. (Jerry Ayres). *Enterprise* security officer who was killed by the **dikironium cloud creature** in 2268. Rizzo died from shock due to 60% of his red blood cells being drained. Rizzo had been a good friend of **Ensign Garrovick**. ("Obsession" [TOS]).

Ro Laren. (Michelle Forbes). A **Bajoran** national who served in the Federation Starfleet. Born 2340 and raised during the **Cardassian** occupation of her homeworld, Ro spent her childhood in Bajoran resettlement camps. When she was seven years old, she was forced to watch as Cardassians tortured her father to death.

As a Starfleet ensign, Ro had numerous reprimands on her record, and she was court-martialed after a disastrous mission to planet **Garon II** in which she disobeyed orders and eight members of her *U.S.S. Wellington* away team were killed. Ro was subsequently imprisoned on **Jaros II** until her release in 2368 by **Admiral Kennelly**. She was released in exchange for her participation in a covert mission aboard the *Enterprise*-D intended to apprehend Bajoran terrorists believed to have attacked Federation interests. Ro was instrumental in the discoveries that the attacks were actually Cardassian in origin, and that Kennelly had been acting as an agent for the Cardassians. Ro subsequently agreed to remain aboard the *Enterprise*-D as a crew member. Bajoran custom dictates that an individual's family name is given first, and the given name is last; thus Ro is her family name. ("Ensign Ro" [TNG]).

In 2368, on stardate 45494, Ro and Commander Riker shared a brief romantic liaison when both suffered from memory loss while under the influence of a Satarran probe, a somewhat ironic occurrence considering that both of them had been frequently at odds over her performance as an *Enterprise*-D crew member. ("Conundrum" [TNG]).

Despite her people's spiritual nature, Laren was never sure about her faith in the Bajoran religion. When she was exposed to a Romulan **interphase generator** in 2368 that rendered her invisible, she believed she was dead, and tried to make peace with herself in accordance with those religious beliefs. ("The Next Phase" [TNG]). Ro was temporarily reduced to a child after passing through an energy field in 2369. ("Rascals" [TNG]). *Young Laren was played in "Rascals" by Megan Parlen. Michelle Forbes had previously played Dara in "Half a Life" (TNG). The character of Ro was at one point planned to transfer to* Star Trek: Deep Space Nine, *but was replaced on that show by Kira Nerys when Forbes demurred in favor of movie projects. Ensign Ro appeared in "Disaster" (TNG), "Conundrum" (TNG), "Power Play" (TNG), "Cause and Effect" (TNG), "The Next Phase" (TNG), and "Rascals" (TNG).*

Ro-Kel. Humanoid of the Miradorn species. Ro-Kel was killed by the fugitive **Croden** during a robbery in 2369. His twin, **Ah-Kel,** swore vengeance. ("Vortex" [DS9]).

Robbiani dermal-optic test. Medical diagnostic test that registers a subject's emotional structure through skin and pupil response to visual stimulation at specific color wavelengths. Dr. McCoy administered such a test to Kirk when Dr. Janice Lester's mind occupied his body in 2269. ("Turnabout Intruder" [TOS]).

Robbins, Harold. One of the most popular writers of Earth's 20th century. Spock read Robbins' works during his study of Earth culture, and regarded him as one of the "giants" of human literature. (*Star Trek IV: The Voyage Home*).

Robin Hood. (Patrick Stewart). In the mythology of old Earth, a 12th-century English hero who "robbed from the rich and gave to the poor." Picard was cast in the role of this legendary hero during an elaborate fantasy **Q** designed to teach Picard a lesson about love. ("QPid" [TNG])

Robinson, B. G. (Teri Hatcher). *Enterprise*-D transporter officer. A beautiful woman, Robinson attracted the attentions of Captain **Thadiun Okona**, and the two evidently spent some time together. ("The Outrageous Okona" [TNG]). *Teri Hatcher also played Lois Lane in* Lois and Clark.

Rocha, Lieutenant Keith. Starfleet officer killed by a **coalescent organism** when assigned to an outpost in the **Triona System** in early 2369. The coalescent organism subsequently assumed Rocha's form, so his death was not suspected until a short time later when the ersatz Rocha was assigned to Subspace **Relay Station 47**. Rocha had earned two decorations for valor and three outstanding evaluations from his commanding officers. ("Aquiel" [TNG]).

Rochani III. Planet where **Curzon Dax** and **Benjamin Sisko** were once cornered by a party of Kaleans. While under the influence of the **Saltah'na energy spheres** in 2369, Jadzia Dax repeated the story of Rochani III to Major Kira Nerys. ("Dramatis Personae" [DS9]).

rodinium. One of the hardest substances known to Federation science. The outer protective shell of the Federation outposts monitoring the **Romulan Neutral Zone** had been constructed of cast rodinium, but even this substance was unable to withstand exposure to a plasma energy weapon during the Romulan incursion of 2266. ("Balance of Terror" [TOS]). SEE: **Neutral Zone Outposts**.

Rodriguez, Lieutenant Esteban. (Perry Lopez). *Enterprise* crew member who was part of the landing party to the **amusement park planet** in 2267. Rodriguez and his partner **Angela Martine** were part of the exploratory team to make sure the Earthlike planet was safe for shore leave. They soon found out that their imaginations conjured up images, which could be beautiful as well as deadly. ("Shore Leave" [TOS]).

Rodriguez. Genetically engineered survivor of Earth's **Eugenics Wars**. Rodriguez and other followers of **Khan Noonien Singh** escaped Earth in 1996 in the sleeper ship, *S.S. Botany Bay,* remaining in suspended animation until revived by personnel from the *U.S.S. Enterprise* in 2267. Rodriguez was trained in communications technologies. ("Space Seed" [TOS]).

Rogers, Amanda. (Olivia D'Abo). Member of the **Q continuum** who was raised as a human. Rogers was unaware of her extraordinary powers until just before she was went aboard the *Enterprise*-D in 2369 as a student intern. Amanda's final act was to clean the air pollution from planet **Tagra IV** before leaving with Q to discover her new identity. ("True-Q" [TNG]).

Rogerson, Commander. (Newell Tarrant). Command duty officer aboard the American aircraft carrier *U.S.S. Enterprise* in 1986 when Chekov and Uhura broke onto the ship in an effort to gather high-energy photons for their return back to the 23rd century. (*Star Trek IV: The Voyage Home*).

Rojan. (Warren Stevens). Leader of a **Kelvan** expedition sent from the **Andromeda galaxy** as a possible prelude to colonization and conquest in the Milky Way. In 2268, Rojan agreed to a plan proposed by James Kirk whereby the Kelvans would be permitted to peaceably colonize a planet in the Milky Way. ("By Any Other Name" [TOS]). *Warren Stevens played Doc Ostrow in the classic s-f film Forbidden Planet.*

rokeg blood pie. A traditional Klingon dish. The crew of the Klingon vessel *Pagh* served some of this to Riker as sort of an initiation rite, but Riker proved his mettle by claiming to enjoy it. ("A Matter of Honor" [TNG]). *Rokeg* blood pie was one of **Worf**'s favorite foods. When he was a child, his adoptive mother, **Helena Rozhenko**, mastered the technique of making this dish. ("Family" [TNG]).

Roladan Wild Draw. Card game that, like Earth poker, was as much a contest of wills as a game of chance. Miles O'Brien said he never wanted to play Roladan Wild Draw against the strong-willed Major Kira Nerys. ("Emissary" [DS9]).

Rollman, Admiral. (Susan Bay). Starfleet admiral whom Major Kira communicated with in 2369, voicing her dissatisfaction with Sisko's hesitation in granting **Khon-ma** terrorist **Tahna Los** political asylum. ("Past Prologue "[DS9]).

Rom. (Max Grodenchik). Quark's brother and father to Nog. Rom helped Quark run the bar at station Deep Space 9. ("Emissary" [DS9]). Rom was initially opposed to his son, Nog, attending the new school established by Keiko O'Brien on the station, but later relented. ("A Man Alone" [DS9]). Rom served as Quark's bodyguard during Quark's brief tenure as **Grand Nagus** in  2369. In true Ferengi tradition, Rom plotted to eliminate his brother, but was halted when the previous Nagus, **Zek**, was found to be still alive. Quark applauded Rom's treachery, making him assistant manager of policy and clientele. ("The Nagus" [DS9]). *Max Grodenchik had previously played Par Lenor in "The Perfect Mate" (TNG) and Sovak in "Captain's Holiday" (TNG). Rom was first seen in in "Emissary" (DS9).*

Romaine, Jacques. Starfleet chief engineer and father to *Enterprise* crew member **Mira Romaine**. ("The Lights of Zetar" [TOS]). *Jacques Romaine was retired by the time of the episode, set in 2269.*

Romaine, Lieutenant Mira. (Jan Shutan). Crew member aboard the original *Starship Enterprise* who supervised the transfer of equipment to the **Memory Alpha** station in 2269. During the mission, Romaine's mind was invaded by **noncorporeal life**-forms, the last survivors from planet **Zetar**. The **Zetarians** were driven from Romaine's body by placing her in a  medical decompression chamber. Romaine was a friend of Chief Engineer **Montgomery Scott**, and his affection was believed to have played a role in her recovery. ("The Lights of Zetar" [TOS]).

Romaine, Lydia. Mother to *Enterprise* crew member **Mira Romaine**. ("The Lights of Zetar" [TOS]). *Lydia Romaine was deceased by the time of the episode, set in 2269.*

Romas. (Richard Lineback). A citizen of the planet **Ornara**, and a crew member on the Ornaran freighter *Sanction*. Like all **Ornarans**, Romas was addicted to the Brekkian medication **felicium**. ("Symbiosis" [TNG]).

Romii. SEE: **Remus.**

Romulan Ale. A powerfully intoxicating beverage, light blue in color. Although Romulan Ale was illegal in the Federation, McCoy gave Kirk a bottle of the stuff for his 52nd birthday in 2285. (*Star Trek II: The Wrath of Khan*). Romulan Ale was served at a diplomatic dinner hosted by Kirk for Klingon **chancellor Gorkon** aboard the *Enterprise*-A. Tensions between the Federation people and their Klingon guests were high, and the Romulan Ale probably did not help much, either. (*Star Trek VI: The Undiscovered Country*).

Romulan battle cruiser. Starship of Klingon design in use by the **Romulan Star Empire** under the terms of a brief alliance between the two powers in 2268. ("The *Enterprise* Incident" [TOS]). *The Romulan battle cruiser was, of course, a re-use of the **Klingon battle cruiser** miniature designed by Matt Jefferies.* SEE: **Romulan spacecraft.**

Romulan Bird-of-Prey. Spacecraft used to test Federation resolve during the Romulan incursion of 2266. This ship, painted with an impressive predatory bird, was equipped with a cloaking device and a powerful plasma energy weapon. Propulsion  was simple impulse. This may have been the first known example of a ship equipped with a practical invisibility screen. Fortunately, it was learned that the **cloaking device** required so much power that the ship had to decloak in order to fire. ("Balance of Terror" [TOS]). SEE: **Romulan spacecraft.**

Romulan cloaking device. SEE: **cloaking device, Romulan**.

Romulan commander. (Mark Lenard). Conducted the Romulan incursion of 2266, crossing the **Romulan Neutral Zone** in command of a **Romulan Bird-of-Prey** to test Federation defenses and resolve. A highly honorable individual, he feared the toll that a new Romulan-Federation war would bring, but nevertheless carried out his orders to the best of his ability.  ("Balance of Terror" [TOS]). *Actor Mark Lenard would later play the part of **Sarek** (Spock's father) in "Journey to Babel" (TOS) as well as the Klingon commander in Star Trek: The Motion Picture.*

Romulan commander. (Joanne Linville). Officer in charge of the **Romulan battle cruiser** that captured the original *U.S.S. Enterprise* when Kirk and Spock crossed the **Romulan Neutral Zone** on a spy mission in 2268. She attempted to persuade Spock to defect to the Romulan Star Empire, an effort made significantly more persuasive by personal attraction Spock felt for the commander. After the successful conclusion of that mission (in which Kirk and Spock stole an

improved **Romulan cloaking device**), the Romulan Commander was made a Federation prisoner. ("The *Enterprise* Incident" [TOS]). *Kirk indicated that the commander would eventually be returned to Romulan territory, although we have no way of knowing if this actually happened. Like Mark Lenard's character, this Romulan commander was not given a name.*

Romulan Neutral Zone. A region of space approximately one light-year across, dividing the **Romulan Star Empire** from the Federation.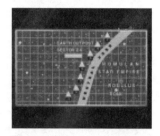

The Neutral Zone was established around 2160 after a conflict between Earth and the Romulans. That conflict had been fought with early space vessels using primitive atomic weapons. The **Treaty of Algernon**, establishing the Neutral Zone, had been negotiated by subspace radio and provided that entry into the zone by either party would constitute an act of war.

The zone remained unviolated until the Romulan incursion of 2266. ("Balance of Terror" [TOS]). The *Enterprise* violated the Neutral Zone in 2267 at the order of **Commodore Stocker** when radiation-induced aging threatened the lives of the ship's command crew. ("The Deadly Years" [TOS]). The ship again crossed into Romulan space in 2268 on a covert mission to steal an advanced Romulan **cloaking device**. ("The *Enterprise* Incident" [TOS]).

The Neutral Zone remained uncrossed by either party during an extended period of Romulan isolationism beginning after the **Tomed Incident** of 2311. The mysterious destruction of several Federation and Romulan outposts in 2364 triggered the end of this isolationism when a Romulan Warbird crossed the Neutral Zone to investigate. Although the outposts were later found to have been destroyed by the **Borg**, the incident triggered a resumption of hostilities between the Romulans and the Federation. ("The Neutral Zone" [TNG]). It was later determined that the pattern of large craters was characteristic of **Borg** attacks, suggesting the possibility of Borg activity near Federation space nearly a year prior to first contact with the *Enterprise*-D in 2365. ("Q Who?" [TNG]).

Captain Donald Varley commanding the *U.S.S. Yamato* violated the Romulan Neutral Zone in 2365. Varley entered the zone in a successful effort to locate the ancient planet **Iconia** in hopes of preventing the Romulans from gaining access to their legendary weapons technology. Unfortunately, the *Yamato* itself fell victim to an Iconian weapon, and an interstellar incident was nearly triggered when the same weapon nearly destroyed the *Enterprise*-D and a Romulan Warbird. ("Contagion" [TNG]).

A **Romulan scoutship** was detected in the Neutral Zone by the crew of Federation outpost **Sierra VI** in 2366. The ship was piloted by **Alidar Jarok**, who was defecting to the Federation so that he could warn of what he believed was a dangerously destabilizing base on planet **Nelvana III.** On Stardate 43465.2, the *Enterprise*-D entered the Neutral Zone, in violation of the Treaty of Algernon, to investigate these reports. ("The Defector" [TNG]). The Neutral Zone was also violated in 2366 by the Romulan scoutship *Pi* and later by **Tomalak**'s Warbird when he tried to rescue the crew of the *Pi*. ("The Enemy" [TNG]). *"The Defector" (TNG) established the name of the Earth/Romulan treaty and suggested the width of the Neutral Zone.*

Romulan Right of Statement. Romulan law allowing a condemned person to record an official statement regarding his guilt or innocence. Spock, captured by Romulan authorities for espionage in 2268, made an exceptionally long statement under this right, a successful effort to buy enough time for Kirk to complete their spy mission. ("The *Enterprise* Incident" [TOS]).

Romulan science vessel. A small ship, with a crew of about 73, that served as a testbed for an experimental **interphase generator**-based **cloaking device** in 2368. During the tests, the ship experienced a catastrophic malfunction of its warp core, but was able to return to Romulan space, thanks to assistance rendered by the *Enterprise*-D. ("The Next Phase" [TNG]). *This ship model was a modification of the Romulan scout from "The Defector" (TNG).*

Romulan spacecraft. *1) Romulan Bird-of-Prey, first seen in "Balance of Terror" (TOS). 2) Romulan battle cruiser, first seen in "The Enterprise Incident" (TOS). 3) Romulan scout*

ship, first seen in "The Defector" (TNG). 4) Romulan Warbird, first seen in "The Neutral Zone" (TNG). NOTE: Drawings 1-3 are to approximate relative scale. The Warbird is smaller than scale; the small battle cruiser silhouette indicates size relationship.

Romulan Star Empire. The formal name of the Romulan nation. An enigmatic offshoot of the **Vulcan** race, now residing on planets **Romulus** and **Remus**. ("Balance of Terror" [TOS]). The ancient Romulans left Vulcan about a millennium ago, possibly in rebellion against **Surak**'s philosophy of logic and pacifism. The Romulans are a study in dramatic contrasts. Capable of considerable tenderness, they can also be violent in the extreme. Romulans have also been characterized as having great curiosity, while maintaining a tremendous self-confidence that borders on arrogance. The leader of the empire was called the **Praetor**. In interstellar relations, the Romulans have generally preferred to react to actions of a potential adversary, rather than committing themselves beforehand. A bitter war between the Romulans and Earth forces around 2160 resulted in the establishment of the **Romulan Neutral Zone**, violation of which was considered an act of war. The neutral zone remained unviolated until 2266 when a single Romulan ship crossed into Federation space in a test of Federation resolve. ("Balance of Terror" [TOS]). SEE: **Treaty of Algeron**. The Romulans entered into a brief alliance with

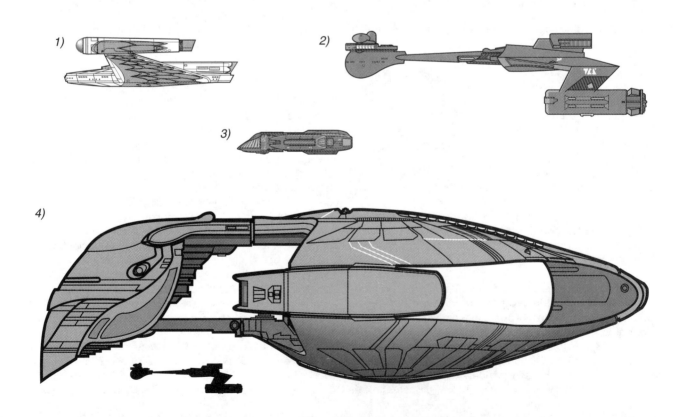

the **Klingon Empire** around 2268, when an agreement between the two powers resulted in the sharing of military technology and spacecraft designs. ("The *Enterprise* Incident" [TOS]). By the mid-2280s, Klingons were using ships described as Birds-of-Prey (a traditionally Romulan term) that were equipped with cloaking devices very similar to those developed by the Romulans. (*Star Trek III*). The Romulans again went into isolation in 2311, following the **Tomed Incident**, not to emerge until 2364, when early indications of **Borg** activity were detected. ("The Neutral Zone" [TNG]). The Romulans pursued a long-term policy of using covert means to destabilize the Klingon government going back at least the 2340s. In 2367, Romulan operative **Sela** attempted to use mental conditioning of Starfleet officer Geordi La Forge to assassinate Klingon governor **Vagh**, a move calculated to spark distrust between the Klingons and the Federation ("The Mind's Eye" [TNG]). Later that year, Sela formed a covert alliance with the **Duras** family in an effort to wrest control of the **Klingon High Council** from **Gowron**. The attempt was unsuccessful, but it triggered a **Klingon civil war** in early 2368, with Sela providing materiel support to the Duras forces. ("Redemption, Parts I and II" [TNG]). An underground movement emerged in the late 2360s, seeking to promote reunification of the Romulans with their distant Vulcan cousins. When the Romulan government became aware of this movement in 2368, **Proconsul Neral** tried to use it to as a cover for an attempted invasion of planet Vulcan. The invasion was thwarted by the Federation Starfleet. Ambassador **Spock** chose to remain undercover on Romulus to continue work toward reunification. ("Unification, Parts I and II" [TNG]).

Romulan Warbird. Massive, powerful spacecraft first encountered in 2364 when the Romulans violated the **Romulan Neutral Zone** in response to attacks by the **Borg**. Designated as *D'deridex* **class**, the Warbird was nearly twice the overall length of a *Galaxy*-class starship ("The

Neutral Zone" [TNG]) and utilized a artificial quantum singularity as a power source for its warp-drive system ("Face of the Enemy" [TNG]). A Romulan Warbird was destroyed in 2369 when its power source became a nest for extradimensional **quantum singularity life-forms**. ("Timescape" [TNG]). Starfleet at one time designated this ship as a "B-Type Warbird" ("The Defector" [TNG]). *The Romulan Warbird was designed by Andrew Probert and built by Greg Jein. The ship first appeared in "The Neutral Zone" and was subsequently used in "Contagion" (TNG), "Peak Performance" (TNG), "The Enemy" (TNG), "The Defector" (TNG), "Yesterday's Enter- prise" (TNG), "Tin Man" (TNG), "Future Imperfect" (TNG), "Data's Day" (TNG), "The Mind's Eye" (TNG), "Redemption" (TNG), "Face of the Enemy" (TNG), "The Chase" (TNG), and "Timescape" (TNG).* **SEE: Romulan spacecraft.**

Romulans. Warrior race from the planets **Romulus** and **Remus**. Believed to be an offshoot of the **Vulcan** race that left Vulcan over a thousand years ago, the Romulans are a

passionate, aggressive, but highly honorable people. ("Balance of Terror" [TOS]). The Romulans conducted a brutal attack on the Klingon **Narendra III** outpost in 2344. The *Starship* **Enterprise**-C, under the command of **Captain Rachel Garrett**, responded to distress calls from Narendra III, and attempted to render aid to the Klingons. Although the *Enterprise*-C was reported lost in the incident, the incident led to closer Klingon-Federation ties in following years. ("Yesterday's *Enterprise*" [TNG]). Two Romulan officers were found on **Galorndon Core** in 2366 after the downing of their scout craft. ("The Enemy" [TNG]).

Romulus. One of the two homeworlds of the **Romulan Star Empire**. ("Balance of Terror" [TOS]). **Admiral Jarok** described Romulus as being a world of awesome beauty and spoke glowingly of such sights as the firefalls of Gal Gath'thong, the Valley of Chula, and the Apnex Sea. ("The Defector" [TNG]). Ambassador **Spock** traveled to Romulus in 2368, on a personal mission to promote peaceful reunification between the Romulans and the Vulcans. Shortly thereafter, Picard and Data also went to Romulus, on a covert mission to determine Spock's motives. ("Unification, Parts I and II" [TNG]).

Rondon. (Robert Riordan). Starfleet officer who participated in Wesley Crusher's Academy entrance examinations at **Relva VII** in 2364. Crusher successfully identified Rondon as a Zaldan, and acted correctly in addressing Rondon with brutal honesty in deference to the Zaldan belief that human courtesy is a form of dishonesty. ("Coming of Age" [TNG]).

root canal. Engineering slang used to describe a rebuilding of a computer or other system's software from the ground up. Usually performed when the system is considered to be beyond conventional repair. Miles O'Brien, who was distinctly unimpressed with **Cardassian** technology, devoutly wanted to perform a root canal on the Cardassian-built computers on **Deep Space 9**. ("The Forsaken" [DS9]).

root command structure. The basic computer programs that control the **Borg collective**. ("I, Borg" [TNG]).

rop'ngor. A disease that sometimes affects Klingon children, somewhat akin to terrestrial measles. As an adult, Worf came down with a case of *rop'ngor* in 2365, much to his embarrassment. Sensitive to Worf's feelings, Dr. Katherine Pulaski made up an excuse for him that he had been engaged in ritual Klingon fasting and thus was not at peak physical condition. ("Up the Long Ladder" [TNG]).

Ross, Yeoman Teresa. (Venita Wolf). *Enterprise* crew member who was abducted along with other bridge personnel to the planet **Gothos** by the entity **Trelane** in 2267. Trelane fancied Ross's presence, dressing her in a floor-length gown and making the yeoman his dancing partner. ("The Squire of Gothos" [TOS]).

Rossa, Admiral Connaught. (Barbara Townsend). Starfleet admiral who had two sons, both serving in Starfleet; both sons were killed in the line of duty. For years, Admiral Rossa also believed her grandson, **Jeremiah Rossa**, to have been killed by **Talarians** at **Galen IV** in 2356, until he was discovered on board a disabled Talarian observation craft in 2367. ("Suddenly Human" [TNG]).

Rossa, Connor. Starfleet officer who served on the Federation colony at **Galen IV**. Connor Rossa was killed in 2357 when **Talarian** forces attacked and destroyed the colony. His son, **Jeremiah Rossa**, survived and was captured by the Talarian **Endar**. ("Suddenly Human" [TNG]).

Rossa, Jeremiah. (Chad Allen). A human male born in 2353 on **Galen IV**, to Federation personnel **Connor Rossa** and **Moira Rossa**. When Jeremiah was three, the colony on **Galen IV** was overrun by Talarian forces. All the colonists, including Jeremiah's parents, were believed killed in the attack. Jeremiah, unknown to Federation authorities, was the only human to survive. Talarian officer **Endar** discovered him near the body of his mother and took the child home to be raised as a Talarian named **Jono**. ("Suddenly Human" [TNG]).

Rossa, Moira. Wife of Starfleet officer **Connor Rossa**. Moria Rossa was the biological mother of **Jeremiah Rossa**. She was killed in the 2356 **Talarian** attack on the **Galen IV** colony. ("Suddenly Human" [TNG]).

Rousseau V. Location of a spectacular asteroid belt, recreated on the holodeck by **Wesley Crusher** for the benefit of the lovely young **Salia** of **Daled IV**. ("The Dauphin" [TNG]).

Royale, Hotel. SEE: *Hotel Royale*.

• **"Royale, The."** *Next Generation* episode #38. Written by Keith Mills. Directed by Cliff Bole. Stardate 42625.4. *First aired in 1989. An* Enterprise-*D away team is trapped in a bizarre re-creation of a setting from a pulp novel,* The Hotel Royale. SEE: **Charybdis; Fermat's last theorem; Hotel Royale; Mickey D.; NASA; Richey, Colonel Stephen; Theta 116; United States of America**.

Roykirk, Jackson. Noted 21st-century Earth scientist, regarded as one of the most brilliant though erratic of his time, who designed the space probe *Nomad*. Roykirk's goal was to build the perfect thinking machine capable of independent logic. The early interstellar probe, *Nomad*, was the result. ("The Changeling" [TOS]).

Rozhenko, Alexander. (Brian Bonsall). Son of Starfleet lieutenant **Worf** and Federation Ambassador **K'Ehleyr**. Alexander was born in 2366, on the 43rd day of Maktag, and spent his infancy in the care of his mother. Worf learned of Alexander's existence shortly before K'Ehleyr's death in 2367, but was reluctant to acknowledge that Alexander was his son, for fear that Alexander would bear the disgrace of Worf's discommendation. Worf did accept his son, who returned to

Earth to be raised by Worf's adoptive parents, **Sergey** and **Helena Rozhenko**. ("Reunion" [TNG]). Alexander remained on Earth for about a year, but the Rozhenkos became concerned that the child needed his father, and returned Alexander to Worf's custody aboard the *Enterprise*-D. ("New Ground" [TNG]). Alexander was fond of heroic tales of the ancient American West, and once persuaded his father and Counselor Troi to join him in a simulation designed for him by **Reginald Barclay** called the **Ancient West**. ("A Fistful of Datas" [TNG]). *Alexander was played by John Steuer in "Reunion," but Brian Bonsall assumed the role in later episodes.*

Rozhenko, Helena. (Georgia Brown). **Worf**'s adoptive mother. Helena and her husband, Sergey, faced the considerable challenges of raising a Klingon child in a human environment. Helena even learned to make Klingon **Rokeg blood pie**. They loved their child enough to make a deliberate choice to allow young Worf to find his own path. ("Family" [TNG]). Helena and Sergey lived for a time on the farm world of **Gault**, but later moved to Earth. The Rozhenkos had another, biological, son who entered Starfleet Academy at the same time as Worf, but found it not to his liking. ("Heart of Glory" [TNG]). Helena and Sergey accepted custody of Worf's son, **Alexander Rozhenko**, after the death of **K'Ehleyr** in 2367. ("Reunion" [TNG]). They returned to Earth to care for Alexander, but after a year found that the child had difficulty adapting to life in human society. They realized that the Alexander needed his father, so they returned the child to the *Enterprise*-D in 2368. ("New Ground" [TNG]).

Rozhenko, Sergey. (Theodore Bickel). **Worf**'s adoptive father. Rozhenko, husband to **Helena Rozhenko**, had been a chief petty officer, serving as a warp field specialist aboard the *U.S.S. Intrepid*, the starship that rendered aid to the Klingons following the **Khitomer** massacre of 2346. Rozhenko and his wife adopted a young Klingon child named Worf, found in the wreckage at Khitomer, and raised him as their own child. Sergey and Helena Rozhenko visited Worf aboard the *Enterprise*-D in 2367 when the ship was under repair at **Earth Station McKinley**. ("Family" [TNG]).

Ruah IV. Class-M planet supporting numerous plant and animal forms including a genus of proto-humanoids. Ruah IV was studied by **Professor Richard Galen** in his effort to learn about an ancient humanoid species that seeded many planets. These ancient humanoids may have seeded the primordial life on Ruah IV billions of years ago. ("The Chase" [TNG]).

Rubicun III. Class-M planet in the Rubicun star system and home to the **Edo** race. The *Enterprise*-D visited Rubicun III in 2364 for R&R but their mission turned to crisis when Wesley Crusher broke one of the Edo laws and was sentenced to death. The boy's life was saved at the expense of the Prime Directive. ("Justice" [TNG]). *One location used for filming* parts of Rubicun III's exteriors was the Tillman Water Reclamation Plant in Van Nuys, California, the same location used for Starfleet Academy in the episode "First Duty." Other Rubicun III exteriors were filmed at the Huntington Library in Pasadena.

Rubicun star system. Star system adjoining the **Strnad system** and containing the class-M planet **Rubicun III**, home to the **Edo** race of beings. ("Justice" [TNG]). SEE: **Edos**.

rubindium crystal. Component of **subcutaneous transponders**. Kirk and Spock, imprisoned on a mission to planet **Ekos** in 2268, removed their transponders so that the rubindium crystals could be used as a crude laser. ("Patterns of Force" [TOS]).

Rudman, Commander. Officer on the *Starship Merrimac*. ("Birthright, Part I" [TNG]).

Rujian. Location of a steeplechase that Curzon Dax and Benjamin Sisko once attended, where they met two Ruji twin sisters and had a swell time. ("A Man Alone" [DS9]).

Ruk. (Ted Cassidy). Sophisticated **android** built millennia ago by the **Old Ones** of planet **Exo III**. Ruk was discovered by archaeologist Roger Korby, who used Ruk to build additional androids. Ruk was eventually destroyed by Korby when the old android rediscovered his survival instinct. ("What Are Little Girls Made Of?" [TOS]). *Actor Ted Cassidy was also famous for his role of Lurch in the* Addams Family *television series. SEE:* **Homn, Mr**.

Rul the Obscure. One of the aliens at an auction at Quark's bar in 2369. Rul bought an artifact brought back by **Vash** from the Gamma Quadrant. ("Q-Less" [DS9]).

Rules of Acquisition. SEE: **Ferengi Rules of Acquisition.**

Rumpelstiltskin. (Michael John Anderson). Character who reputedly spun straw into gold in an ancient Earth fairy tale. In 2369, unknown aliens from the **Gamma Quadrant** created a replica of Rumpelstiltskin on station Deep Space 9. The character was drawn from the imagination of Chief **Miles O'Brien**, who had been reading a bedtime story to his daughter, Molly,

on stardate 46853. The alien version of Rumplestiltskin was created so that the aliens could better study humans. ("If Wishes Were Horses" [DS9]). SEE: **Bokai, Buck.**

runabout. Generic term for small Federation starships used for relatively short-range interstellar travel. Resembling an enlarged shuttlecraft, runabouts had a relatively limited flight range. The runabout cockpit incorporated a short-range two-person transporter, as well as seating for four people, including a two-person flight crew. The runabout's aft section contained living accommodations, and the midsection was a

detachable module that could be replaced for different mission profiles.

The *Enterprise*-D offloaded three runabouts before at station **Deep Space 9** in 2369. ("Emissary" [DS9]). Aft of the pilots' compartment, the craft contained a small living area, with bunks and a replicator for food processing. This area made the craft comfortable for extended travel. ("Timescape" [TNG]). A runabout's exterior shell is made from duranium composites. ("Q-Less" [DS9]). SEE: *Ganges, U.S.S.; Orinoco, U.S.S.; Rio Grande, U.S.S.; Yangtzee Kiang, U.S.S.*

*Runabouts was first seen in "Emissary" [DS9], although the **U.S.S.** Jenolan (Scotty's Sydney-class transport in "Relics" [TNG])*

may also have been an early runabout. The aft section of the runabout was first seen in "Timescape" (TNG). The Danube-*class runabouts seen in* Deep Space 9 *are traditionally named after great rivers. The runabout was designed by Rick Sternbach and Jim Martin. The interior cockpit set was designed by Joseph Hodges. The aft compartment was designed by Richard James. The miniature was built by Tony Meininger. Although primarily used in* Star Trek: Deep Space Nine*, Picard and company took a trip in a runabout in "Timescape" [TNG]), which was the first time the aft compartment was seen.*

Rura Penthe. Frozen, almost uninhabitable planetoid on which was located a Klingon prison camp. Rura Penthe was known throughout the galaxy as the "aliens' graveyard," because prisoners were used for forced labor at the dilithium mines there. The planetoid, deep inside of Klingon territory, was so inhospitable that the prison camp needed no guard towers or electronic frontier to keep the prisoners in. Kirk and McCoy were sentenced to life at Rura Penthe after being wrongly convicted for the murder of **Chancellor Gorkon** in 2293. (*Star Trek VI: The Undiscovered Country*). *Some of the exterior scenes for Rura Penthe were actually filmed on a glacier on location in Alaska.*

Rushton infection. Disease that killed **Jeremy Aster**'s father in 2361. ("The Bonding" [TNG]).

Russell, Dr. Toby. (Caroline Kava). A neurogeneticist from the **Adelman Neurological Institute**. Dr. Russell pioneered several revolutionary medical therapies, including the **genetronic replicator** technique. Russell's career was marred by accusations that she had sometimes sacrificed patients' lives in order to gather experimental data.

Russel's genetronic technique saved the life of *Enterprise*-D security chief Worf in 2368. ("Ethics" [TNG]). SEE: **borathium**.

Ruth. (Maggie Thrett). One of Mudd's women. Ruth had long black hair and had lived on a pelagic planet with sea ranchers before being recruited by Harry Mudd as a wife for a settler on planet **Ophiucus III**. Ruth instead married one of the miners on **Rigel XII**. ("Mudd's Women" [TOS]). *Ruth's last name was never mentioned in the aired version but a final draft script of the episode listed her as Ruth Bonaventure.*

Ruth. (Shirley Bonne). Attractive woman who was romantically involved with James Kirk in 2252 during his Academy days. A recreation of Ruth appeared on the **amusement park planet** in 2267, looking just as Kirk had remembered her 15 years ago. ("Shore Leave" [TOS]). *Ruth was not given a last name in the episode.*

Rutia IV. A politically neutral class-M planet that enjoyed a long trading relationship with the Federation. Although the planet's population was united under a single planetary government, a dissident group called the **Ansata** on the western continent sought political independence in 2296. This bid was denied by the Rutian government, and the Ansata began a long terrorist struggle to gain recognition of their plight. Although the Ansata were only believed to number about 200 members, they were successful in causing significant disruption of Rutian society. In 2366, Ansata leader **Kyril Finn** led an apparently futile attack against the *Enterprise*-D, a successful attempt to gain Federation involvement in their fight. ("The High Ground" [TNG]).

Rutian archaeological vessel. The only vessel reported in range of the **Dulisian IV** colony when it transmitted a distress call in 2368. ("Unification, Part II" [TNG]).

Rutians. The inhabitants of **Rutia IV**, humanoid in appearance. Rutian males are marked by a distinctive white streak of hair; females are generally red-haired. ("The High Ground" [TNG])

Rutledge, U.S.S. Federation starship, commanded by **Captain Benjamin Maxwell** during the war between the Federation and the **Cardassians**. Future *Enterprise*-D crew member **Miles O'Brien** served aboard the *Rutledge* as tactical officer. The *Rutledge* responded to a Cardassian attack on the Federation outpost at **Setlik III**, but was too late to prevent the massacre. ("The Wounded" [TNG]).

R'uustai. Klingon ceremony in which two individuals bond together to become brothers or sisters. Worf performed the *R'uustai* with young **Jeremy Aster** after Aster's mother died under Worf's command in 2366. The rite itself is resplendent in Klingon custom and involves the lighting of ceremonial candles and the wearing of warrior's sashes, concluding with a Klingon intonation honoring their mothers. ("The Bonding" [TNG]).

RVN. SEE: **rybo-viroxic-nucleic structure.**

rybo-viroxic-nucleic structure. Long organic compound that is one of the key factors in development during puberty of many humanoids. As such life-forms grow older, **RVN** takes on additional viroxic sequences. When Captain Picard and the other members of the *Shuttlecraft* **Fermi** passed through a **molecular reversion field** while returning to the *Enterprise*-D on stardate 46235, O'Brien had difficulty getting a transporter lock on the crew because the field was masking part of their patterns. The transporter therefore only registered part of the RVN patterns, leaving off key sequences, and thus, the shuttle's crew was transformed to children. A record of the shuttle crew's RVN patterns was in the transporter pattern buffer, making it possible to restore the lost viroxic sequences during the transport process. ("Rascals" [TNG]). *Yeah, well, we don't think it makes much sense, either.*

ryetalyn. Mineral substance needed to cure the deadly disease, Rigelian fever, that infected the crew of the *Starship Enterprise* in 2269. A deposit of ryetalyn was found on a small planetoid in the Omega system which belonged to the very ancient humanoid **Flint**. ("Requiem for Methuselah" [TOS]).

Saavik. (Kirstie Alley, Robin Curtis). Starfleet officer who, as a cadet, served as navigator on the *Starship Enterprise* during the **Project Genesis** crisis in 2285. Saavik, a Vulcan, had been mentored by Spock, who counseled her that tolerance of her human colleagues was logical. (*Star Trek II: The Wrath of Khan*). Fol-

lowing the Genesis crisis, Saavik, along with **David Marcus**, transferred to the *U.S.S. Grissom* for further study of the **Genesis planet**. Saavik later returned to Planet Vulcan. (*Star Trek III: The Search for Spock, Star Trek IV: The Voyage Home*). *Saavik apparently had sex with Spock on the Genesis Planet when Spock was undergoing* **Pon farr** *during* Star Trek III. *A scene cut from the final version of* Star Trek IV *would have shown that the reason Saavik remained on Vulcan was because she was pregnant with Spock's child. (Because the scene was cut, we don't consider this to be "evidence" that it "really" happened.). The*

script for Star Trek II *contained a line that would have suggested Saavik was half-Vulcan and half-Romulan, but the line was cut, and later films seemed to assume that she was pure Vulcan.*

Actor Kirstie Alley played Saavik in Star Trek II, *but Robin Curtis assumed the role in* Star Trek III *and* Star Trek IV. *Robin Curtis later played Tallera in "Gambit, Parts I and II" (TNG). An early draft script for* Star Trek VI *featured Saavik in the role that eventually became Valeris.*

Sacred Chalice of Rixx. An important artifact in **Betazoid** culture, held for ceremonial purposes by **Lwaxana Troi**. Deanna Troi described the chalice as a "moldy old pot." ("Haven" [TNG], "Manhunt" [TNG]).

saddle. Leather appliance used as a seat for the rider of a horse or other mount animal. Captain **Jean-Luc Picard** kept a saddle that he'd owned since his Academy days with him aboard the *Enterprise*-D. Picard noted that most serious riders own their own saddles. His crew agreed. ("Starship Mine" [TNG]).

Sadie Hawkins Dance. Ancient school tradition that dates back to Earth schools of the 1950s, still practiced at Starfleet Academy. The dance traditionally was a "girls ask boys" affair. *Enterprise*-D Commander Data remembered his Academy Sadie Hawkins Dance as a "notably awkward affair." ("The Game" [TNG]).

Sahndara. Star that became a nova millennia ago. Humanoid inhabitants of the Sahndara system fled their doomed world, eventually settling on a planet they named **Platonius**. ("Plato's Stepchildren" [TOS]). SEE: **Platonians**.

Sahsheer. Beautiful crystal-like formations from planet **Kelva** in the **Andromeda Galaxy** that form so rapidly they seem to grow. ("By Any Other Name" [TOS]). In 2369, a cargo ship piloted by **Captain Jaheel** was scheduled to deliver a shipment of Tamen Sahsheer to planet **Largo V**. ("Babel" [DS9]). *A rose, by any other name.*

Sakar. Brilliant Vulcan theoretical scientist, often compared to such luminaries as **Albert Einstein** and **Dr. Richard Daystrom**. ("The Ultimate Computer" [TOS]).

Sakharov, Shuttlecraft. Shuttle vehicle 01, assigned to *Starship Enterprise*-D. The *Sakharov* transported **Dr. Katherine Pulaski** to the **Darwin Genetic Research Station** on planet **Gagarin IV**. ("Unnatural Selection" [TNG]). **Q** commandeered the *Sakharov* in 2366 during an attack by the **Calamarain** against the *Enterprise*-D. The Calamarain's real target was Q, and his action to protect the *Enterprise*-D was an unusual act of self-sacrifice on his part. Although Q was successful in saving the *Enterprise*-D, the *Sakharov* was lost in the incident. ("Deja Q" [TNG]). *The* Sakharov *was named for Russian nuclear scientist and peace advocate Andre Sakharov (1921-1989).*

Sakkath. (Rocco Sisto). Ambassador **Sarek**'s personal assistant during the **Legaran** conference of 2366. A young Vulcan male, Sakkath was aware that Sarek suffered from debilitating **Bendii Syndrome**, but used his telepathic skills in an effort to give the ambassador the emotional control necessary to complete the historic Legaran treaty. ("Sarek" [TNG]).

Sakuro's disease. An extremely rare disease contracted by Commissioner **Nancy Hedford** which can cause intense fever, weakness, and death if not treated. ("Metamorphosis" [TOS]).

salenite miners. A group on planet **Pentarus V** that was embroiled in a labor dispute in 2367. Because the group was prone to violence, the government of Pentarus V asked Captain Picard to mediate their negotiations. ("Final Mission" [TNG]).

Salia. (Jamie Hubbard). Leader of planet **Daled IV**. The child of parents from opposing sides of the civil war on that planet, Salia was raised on the neutral planet **Klavdia III** and was returned aboard the *Enterprise*-D to her homeworld in 2365 at age 16 in the hopes she could bring peace to her planet. A shapeshifting **allasomorph**, Salia appeared to the *Enterprise* crew as a

lovely human female who attracted the interest of **Wesley Crusher**. ("The Dauphin" [TNG]).

Salish. (Rudy Solari). American Indian on **Miramanee's planet** who was the tribe's Medicine Chief before the amnesia stricken Kirk appeared as their promised god in 2268. ("The Paradise Syndrome" [TOS]).

salt vampire. SEE: **M-113 creature**.

Saltah'na clock. Under the influence of the energy matrix that originated from the **Saltah'na energy spheres** in 2369, Benjamin Sisko constructed an intricate timepiece. ("Dramatis Personae" [DS9]). *The Saltah'na clock, designed by Ricardo Delgado, was sometimes seen in Sisko's office in subsequent episodes.*

Saltah'na energy spheres. Telepathic receptacles that stored an ancient power struggle that destroyed the Saltah'na race. The Klingon vessel *Toh'Kaht* retrieved the energy spheres from a planet in the Gamma Quadrant in 2369. A self-sustaining energy matrix within the spheres caused the Klingon crew to reenact the power struggle that destroyed the Saltah'na, eventually leading to their own demise. The *Toh'Kaht* first officer **Hon'Tihl** was transported to Deep Space 9 moments before his vessel exploded, carrying with him the energy matrix from the spheres. The telepathic matrix was transferred to the crew members in Ops, causing them to re-enact the power struggle, pitting Sisko against Major Kira Nerys. The one individual not affected was Odo because of his nonhumanoid brain. With the help of Dr. Julian Bashir, an interference signal was successful in driving the energy matrix out of the Deep Space 9 crew, and into space. ("Dramatis Personae" [DS9]).

Saltah'na. Race from a planet located in the **Gamma Quadrant**. The Klingon Bird-of-Prey *Toh'Kaht* visited the planet in 2369 on a routine biosurvey where a collection of energy spheres were discovered. The spheres contained a telepathic archive describing an ancient power struggle that destroyed the Saltah'na race. ("Dramatis Personae" [DS9]). SEE: **Saltah'na energy spheres**.

saltzgadum. A substance capable of causing **nucleosynthesis** in silicon. It is not normally detectable to a starship's internal sensor scans. ("Hollow Pursuits" [TNG]).

Sam. SEE: **Kirk, George Samuel**.

Samarian coral fish. A life-form Guinan imagined seeing in the swirling clouds of the **FGC-47** nebula. Data insisted the clouds more closely resembled a bunny rabbit. ("Imaginary Friend" [TNG]).

Samarian Sunset. A specialty beverage that initially appears clear, but develops a multicolored hue when the rim of the glass is tapped sharply. Data prepared a Samarian Sunset for Deanna Troi on stardate 45494 after losing a **three-dimensional chess** game to Troi. ("Conundrum" [TNG]).

• **"Samaritan Snare."** *Next Generation* episode #43. Written by Robert L. McCullough. Directed by Les Landau. Stardate 42779.1. *First aired in 1989. The* Enterprise-D *is nearly victimized by cunning Pakleds, while Picard is off to a starbase*

for replacement of his mechanical heart. *Picard's youthful brawl with Nausicaans at the Bonestell Facility and his subsequent heart replacement surgery were later depicted in flashback scenes in "Tapestry" (TNG).* SEE: **biomolecular physiologist; Bonestell Recreation Facility; Bussard collectors; cardiac replacement; Crusher, Wesley; Epsilon IX Sector; Epsilon Pulsar Cluster; Gomez, Ensign Sonya; Jarada;** *Mondor;* **myocardial enzyme balance; Nausicaans; neural calipers; Pakled captain; Pakleds; parthenogenic implant; Picard, Jean-Luc; Reginold; Rhomboid Dronegar Sector; Scylla Sector; Starbase 515; Starbase Earhart; tissue mitigator; Van Doren, Dr.**

Samno, Yeoman. Crew member aboard the *Starship Enterprise-A* who was one of two "hit men" who carried out the assassination of Klingon **chancellor Gorkon** in 2293. Samno was later murdered, apparently by **Valeris**, in order to protect others involved with the conspiracy. (*Star Trek VI: The Undiscovered Country*).

Sampalo. Relics located on planet Hoek IV in the Teleris cluster. **Q** invited archaeologist **Vash** to visit the Sampalo relics. She declined. ("Q-Less" [DS9]).

sample container. Cylindrical vessel used for the safe storage of scientific or medical samples. ("Realm of Fear" [TNG]).

San Francisco Yards. Starfleet **drydock** facility in Earth orbit where the original *Enterprise* was built in 2245. That ship also underwent a major refurbishment and systems upgrade there in 2270. (*Star Trek: The Motion Picture*). SEE: **Earth Station McKinley.**

Sanchez, Dr. *Enterprise* physician who performed an autopsy on the transporter operator who was killed by **Losira**, near the **Kalandan outpost** in 2268. ("That Which Survives" [TOS]).

Sanction. Interplanetary freighter craft operated from the planet **Ornara**, commanded by **T'Jon**. The *Sanction* was destroyed above planet **Brekka** when a drive coil malfunction made it impossible for the ship to maintain a stable orbit. Although

the malfunction was fairly minor, the Ornarans' technical ignorance made the problem disastrous. The *Sanction* had been carrying a cargo of the narcotic substance **felicium**, which the Ornarans believed essential to their survival. ("Symbiosis" [TNG]). *The* Sanction *model was a modification on the* **Batris** *from "Heart of Glory" (TNG), which in turn was built from a Visitors' freighter from the miniseries* V. *It would appear that it was a popular design for ships in the galaxy.*

sand bats. Creatures from planet Manark IV that appear to be inanimate rock crystals until they attack. ("The Empath" [TOS]).

Sandoval, Elias. (Frank Overton). Leader of an agricultural expedition that colonized planet **Omicron Ceti III** in 2264. The majority of the colonists died from exposure to deadly **Berthold rays**, but about 50 colonists, including Sandoval, survived due to the protection offered by alien spores found on the planet. The spores kept the colonists alive and gave them an extraordinary sense of tranquility, but they also removed their motivation to work. Sandoval and the other colonists were freed from the influence of the spores in 2267 when *Starship Enterprise* personnel bombarded the colony with ultrasonic energy. ("This Side of Paradise" [TOS]). SEE: **Spores, Omicron Ceti III**.

Sandoval. *Enterprise*-D crew member who was struck by a disruptor blast while under Lieutenant Worf's command in 2366. She lived for a week before succumbing to her injuries. ("Ethics" [TNG]).

***Saratoga*, U.S.S.** Federation ***Miranda*-class starship**, registry number NCC-1937. The *Saratoga* was disabled by an alien space probe of unknown origin while patrolling the Neutral Zone. (*Star Trek IV: The Voyage Home*). SEE: **Probe, the**. *The* Saratoga *was a re-use of the* Reliant *model originally built for* Star Trek II: The Wrath of Khan.

***Saratoga*, U.S.S.** Federation starship, ***Miranda* class**, Starfleet registry number NCC-31911. The *Saratoga* was destroyed by the **Borg** at the battle of **Wolf 359** in 2367. Survivors of the destruction of the *Saratoga* included the first officer, Lieutenant Commander **Benjamin Sisko**, and his son, **Jake Sisko**, who were among the *Saratoga* personnel who fled the ship in escape pods. ("Emissary" [DS9]). *This was presumably at least the second* Miranda-*class starship to bear the name.*

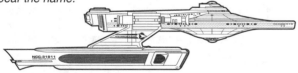

Sarda, Miss. (Kelly Curtis). Resident of station Deep Space 9 who was employed by **Quark** as a **Dabo girl**. Sarda complained to Sisko that the fine print of Quark's employment agreement required her to grant sexual favors to the proprietor of the establishment. Sisko responded that any such contract was unenforceable. ("Captive Pursuit" [DS9]).

Sarek. (Mark Lenard). Vulcan ambassador to the **United Federation of Planets** (2165-2368) and father to **Spock**. Sarek's illustrious career included the treaty of Alpha Cygnus IX, the **Coridan** admission to the Federation, and the Federation-Klingon alliance. ("Sarek" [TNG]).

Sarek, son of Skon and grandson of Solkar (*Star Trek III: The Search for Spock*), represented his government at the Babel Conference in 2267. Sarek gave his son, Spock, his

first lessons in computer science, but Spock chose to devote himself to Starfleet rather than the Vulcan Science Academy. This and other differences prevented Spock and Sarek from speaking as father and son for eighteen years. Being 102.437 years of age in 2267, Sarek had planned to retire after the Babel Conference for medical reasons.

A malfunction in one of his heart valves required chief surgeon McCoy to perform surgery that required a transfusion of rare blood type T-negative from his son Spock. Sarek survived the operation and an understanding between father and son was reached. ("Journey to Babel" [TOS]).

Following the death of his son Spock in 2285, Sarek traveled to Earth, where he asked Kirk's assistance in returning Spock's *katra* to planet Vulcan. Kirk was ultimately successful in recovering both Spock's *katra* and his regenerated body. Sarek then made a highly unusual request for a ***fal-tor-pan*** ceremony, which was successful in rejoining Spock's body and living spirit. (*Star Trek III: The Search for Spock*). Perhaps in gratitude for Kirk's efforts to save Spock, Sarek testified on Kirk's behalf at the Federation Council when the Klingon government attempted to extradite Kirk for alleged crimes. (*Star Trek IV: The Voyage Home*).

Sarek helped lay the groundwork for the historic **Khitomer** peace accords with the Klingon Empire by sending Spock to meet **Chancellor Gorkon** to open a dialog following the disastrous explosion of the Klingon moon, **Praxis**, in 2293. (*Star Trek VI: The Undiscovered Country*).

Sarek married several times during his life. His first wife was a Vulcan princess, with whom he had a son named **Sybok**. (*Star Trek V: The Final Frontier*). Following the death of his first wife, Sarek married **Amanda**, a human woman, with whom he had a son named **Spock**. ("Journey to Babel" [TOS]). At the time of his death in 2366, Sarek was married to **Perrin**, another human woman. ("Sarek" [TNG]).

In 2366, at the age of 202, Ambassador Sarek concluded negotiations on a historic treaty with the **Legarans**. Sarek had been working on the accord for 93 years, and the treaty was the final triumph of his career. At the time of the talks, Sarek was suffering from degenerative **Bendii Syndrome**, but the ambassador was able to maintain emotional control with the help of a **mind-meld** with **Jean-Luc Picard**. ("Sarek" [TNG]). Sarek convalesced for several months while Bendii Syndrome continued to take its toll on his emotional control. Just prior to his death, Sarek met again with Captain Picard when Picard sought information on the unexplained sighting of Spock on **Romulus**.

Sarek died in his home on Vulcan in 2368 from the degenerative effects of Bendii Syndrome. He was survived by his wife Perrin and his son Ambassador Spock. ("Unification, Part I" [TNG]).

We know that Sarek was married at least three times, to the Vulcan princess, to Amanda, and finally to Perrin. Dorothy Fontana once decreed that Spock was an only child to strengthen the drama in "Journey to Babel" (TOS), but the writers of Star Trek V *attempted to get around this by suggest-*

ing that Sybok was a half-brother. Actor Jonathan Simpson played the young Sarek for Spock's birth scene in that film.

• **"Sarek."** *Next Generation* episode #71. Television story and teleplay by Peter S. Beagle. From an unpublished story by Marc Cushman & Jake Jacobs. Directed by Les Landau. Stardate 43917.4. *First aired in 1990. Ambassador Sarek travels aboard the* Enterprise*-D for a crucial diplomatic mission, but he suffers from an emotionally debilitating disease.* SEE: **Alpha Cygnus IX; Babel Conference; Bendii Syndrome; Coridan; Dumont, Ensign Suzanne; Grak-tay; Heifetz; Legara IV; Legarans; Mendrossen, Ki; Menuhin; *Merrimac, U.S.S.*; Perrin; Picard, Jean-Luc; Sakkath; Sarek; Spock; Tataglia; Vulcan mind-meld.**

Sargon's planet. World that once was home to an advanced race of humanoids that colonized the galaxy some 600,000 years ago. **Vulcan** may have been among the many worlds colonized by these beings. Sargon's planet was devastated 500,000 years ago in a terrible war that all but wiped out this advanced race. The few survivors of this war agreed to bury old hatreds and place themselves in survival canisters underground in hopes of revival in the distant future when radiation poisoning on the surface subsided. According to **Sargon**, the war was spawned when his people became so advanced that they had dared think of themselves as gods. ("Return to Tomorrow" [TOS]). *Neither Sargon's world nor his race were given a formal name in the episode.*

Sargon. (Voice of James Doohan, body of William Shatner). Leader on his world after it was destroyed a half million years ago in a devastating war. Sargon, along with a handful of other survivors of that war, were placed into survival canisters and revived in 2268 by the crew of the *Starship Enterprise.* Sargon temporarily occupied the body of Captain Kirk, so that android bodies could be built to house the three survivors' intellects. The other two survivors, Sargon's wife, **Thalassa,** and **Henoch,** Sargon's old adversary, occupied the bodies of **Dr. Ann Mulhall** and Spock. When Henoch was unable to bury the ancient hatreds, Sargon realized they could not continue their existence, so Sargon and his beloved Thalassa departed into oblivion together. ("Return to Tomorrow" [TOS]). SEE: **Sargon's planet**. *Illustration: Sargon's survival canister.*

Sarjenka. (Nikki Cox). A little girl, a humanoid life-form who lived on planet **Drema IV**. An eerie but beautiful child appearing to be between 10 and 12 years of age. Sarjenka built a simple subspace radio, with which she broadcast calls for help because of severe geological disturbances that threatened her planet with disintegration.

Enterprise-D officer Data established subspace radio contact with Sarjenka and remained in communication for several weeks, despite the fact that such contact violated **Prime Directive** quarantine protocols. A rescue mission by Data brought Sarjenka to the *Enterprise*-D, but she was successfully returned to her home with no memory of the starship because of a memory-erasure procedure developed by **Katherine Pulaski**. ("Pen Pals" [TNG]).

Sark, Klingon. An animal similar to a terrestrial horse. Holographic simulations of this animal were available for riding on the *Enterprise*-D holodeck. ("Pen Pals" [TNG]).

Sarona VII. Planet to which the *Enterprise*-D was heading for crew shore leave when the ship was diverted to **Vandor IX** to investigate an emergency. ("We'll Always Have Paris" [TNG]).

Sarpeidon. Class-M planet destroyed in 2269 when its star, **Beta Niobe**, went nova. Sarpeidon had been home to a technologically advanced humanoid race. Prior to the explosion of their sun, the people of Sarpeidon developed a time portal they called an **atavachron**, which they used to escape into their planet's past, so that they could live out their lives. ("All Our Yesterdays" [TOS]). SEE: **Atoz, Mr.; Zarabeth.**

Sarthong V. Planet known for its rich archaeological ruins. **Vash** was thinking about exploring that planet after leaving **Risa**, but Picard pointed out that the Sarthongians dealt harshly with trespassers. ("Captain's Holiday" [TNG], "QPid" [TNG]).

Satarrans. Humanoid race that had been at war with the people of **Lysia** for decades. In 2368, the Satarrans attempted to use the Federation starship *Enterprise*-D to launch a devastating attack against the **Lysian Central Command**. ("Conundrum" [TNG]). SEE: **MacDuff, Commander Kieran.** Satarrans hate mysteries. ("The Chase" [TNG]).

Satelk, Captain. (Richard Fancy). A Vulcan Starfleet officer who presided over the inquiry into Cadet **Joshua Albert**'s death at the **Academy Flight Range** in 2368. SEE: **Kolvoord Starburst; Locarno, Cadet First Class Nicholas.** ("The First Duty" [TNG]).

Satie, Admiral Norah. (Jean Simmons). Retired Starfleet admiral and brilliant investigator who was largely responsible for exposing the alien conspiracy against Starfleet in 2364. In 2367, Admiral Satie was again called upon when Romulan espionage was suspected aboard the *Enterprise*-D. Satie came aboard the ship shortly after the explosion to investigate a pos-

sible plot. When further investigation proved the explosion to be an accident, Admiral Satie improperly continued her relentless search for conspirators, even accusing Captain Picard of acts against the Federation. Satie's investigation was finally stopped by order of Admiral Thomas Henry. ("The Drumhead" [TNG]). SEE: **J'Ddan; Seventh Guarantee; Tarses, Crewman Simon.** ("The Drumhead" [TNG]). *Satie was not mentioned in "Conspiracy" (TNG), but "The Drumhead" establishes that she uncovered the alien presence.*

Satie, Judge Aaron. Brilliant Federation jurist and father of Starfleet **admiral Norah Satie.** Judge Satie was a strong advocate of individual civil liberties including freedom of speech and freedom of thought. His decisions were required reading at Starfleet Academy. Satie once wrote, "With the first link, the chain is forged. The first speech censured, the first thought forbidden, the first freedom denied, chains us all, irrevocably." Captain Picard quoted from Aaron Satie during a hearing held by Norah Satie aboard the *Enterprise*-D in 2367. ("The Drumhead" [TNG]).

Satler. (Tim de Zarn). Member of a group of terrorists who attempted to steal **trilithium resin** from the *Enterprise*-D in 2369. Satler was forced to chase an escaping Captain Picard down a Jefferies tube. Satler was killed when he was caught by a **baryon sweep** during his pursuit of Picard. SEE: **Remmler Array.** ("Starship Mine" [TNG]).

Saturn NavCon. A navigational control satellite in orbit of planet Saturn, which performed sensor sweeps of the **Academy Flight Range.** Saturn NavCon file 6-379 contained a recording of the flight paths of **Nova Squadron** just prior to the crash that killed **Joshua Albert** in 2368. ("The First Duty" [TNG]).

Saturn. The sixth planet in the Sol system. Saturn is a gas giant with a diameter 95 times that of Earth. The Starfleet **Academy Flight Range** was located in a proximal orbit of Saturn. ("The First Duty" [TNG]).

saucer module. The large circular (or elliptical) command section of many Federation starships. ("Encounter at Farpoint, Part I" [TNG]). Also known as the primary hull.

saucer separation. An emergency maneuver performed by *Galaxy*-class starships in which the **saucer module** separates from the remainder of the spacecraft. Saucer separation is generally employed so that the saucer module, containing most of the
crew, can remain behind so that the **stardrive section** (containing the ship's powerful **warp drive**) can go into battle or other hazardous situations. In extreme emergencies, the separated saucer could even land on a suitable planetary surface, although it would be incapable of returning to orbit afterward. Saucer separation was normally accomplished at sublight speeds. Separation at warp speeds was considered highly dangerous, although the *Enterprise*-D successfully accomplished such a maneuver shortly after first contact with the entity **Q** in 2364. ("Encounter at Farpoint, Part I" [TNG]). Geordi La Forge, temporarily in command of the *Enterprise*-D, ordered a saucer separation at planet **Minos** when the ship

was threatened by an ancient Minosian weapons system. ("The Arsenal of Freedom" [TNG]). SEE: **Echo Papa 607.** Earlier classes of starships were also capable of saucer separation, although not all were capable of reconnection afterward. Captain James Kirk once ordered engineer Scott to prepare for such a maneuver when the original *Enterprise* was threatened by the god-machine **Vaal** at planet **Gamma Trianguli VI** in 2267. ("The Apple" [TOS]). *During the first few episodes of Star Trek: The Next Generation, saucer separation was intended to be a standard maneuver in combat situations, but was rarely done because it was expensive and it slowed down story-telling too much.*

Saurian brandy. Potent liqueur enjoyed by members of the original *Starship Enterprise* crew. Saurian brandy was imbibed in moderation, although the aggressive half of James Kirk demanded a bottle of the stuff after being duplicated by a transporter malfunction in 2266. ("The Enemy Within" [TOS]). *Saurian brandy was also enjoyed in "The Man Trap" (TOS), "The Conscience of the King" (TOS), "Journey to Babel" (TOS), and "Requiem for Methuselah" (TOS). Saurian brandy was stored in distinctive amber bottles with curved necks, originally made as commemorative whiskey bottles by the Dickel company of Tennessee. Replicas of these original bottles were sometimes seen behind Quark's bar in Deep Space 9.*

• **"Savage Curtain, The."** Original Series episode #77. Teleplay by Gene Roddenberry and Arthur Heinemann. Story by Gene Roddenberry. Directed by Herschel Daugherty. Stardate 5906.4. *First aired in 1969. Kirk and Spock are forced to fight alongside such historical figures as Abraham Lincoln of Earth and Surak of Vulcan by aliens who want to study the human concept of "good" and "evil."* SEE: **Dickerson, Lieutenant; Excalbia; Excalbians; Genghis Khan; Green, Colonel; haggis; Kahless the Unforgettable; Kirk, James T.; Lincoln, Abraham; Surak; Tiburon; Vulcans; Yarnek; Zora.**

Savar, Admiral. (Henry Darrow). Starfleet officer who was taken over by the unknown intelligence that attempted to infiltrate Starfleet Command in 2364. Savar, a Vulcan, was stationed at **Starfleet Headquarters** in San Francisco at the time. ("Conspiracy" [TNG]).

Sayana. (Shair Nims). Inhabitant of planet **Gamma Trianguli VI** who greeted the *Enterprise* landing party with flowers. She and **Makora**, another member of her race, were attracted to each other but were not allowed to show their affection because it was against the law of **Vaal**, their god. ("The Apple" [TOS]).

Scalos. Class-M planet where massive volcanic eruptions released high levels of radiation into the water supply, contaminating the water and subjecting the humanoid population to **hyperacceleration.** ("Wink of an Eye" [TOS]).

Scalosians. Humanoid race from planet **Scalos** that was subjected to biochemical **hyperacceleration** by volcanic radiation many generations ago. The radiation also decreased fertility in the females and completely sterilized the men. To preserve their species, the Scalosians were forced to mate outside their planet, dispatching distress calls to passing space vehicles, and subjecting the crews of any responding vessels to hyperacceleration. This pattern continued until 2268 when the *Enterprise* responded to a distress call from Scalos but was able to repel the invaders. Federation authorities were later advised to warn other ships to avoid Scalos. SEE: **Deela.** ("Wink of an Eye" [TOS]).

Scarlett, Will. (Michael Dorn). In Earth mythology, a member of **Robin Hood**'s band of "merry men" in ancient England. Worf was cast in this role by Q despite his protest that he was "*not* a merry man!" ("QPid" [TNG]).

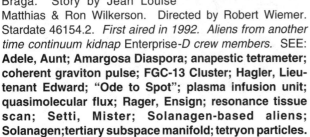

• **"Schisms."** *Next Generation* episode #131. Teleplay by Brannon Braga. Story by Jean Louise Matthias & Ron Wilkerson. Directed by Robert Wiemer. Stardate 46154.2. *First aired in 1992. Aliens from another time continuum kidnap* Enterprise-D *crew members.* SEE: **Adele, Aunt; Amargosa Diaspora; anapestic tetrameter; coherent graviton pulse; FGC-13 Cluster; Hagler, Lieutenant Edward; "Ode to Spot"; plasma infusion unit; quasimolecular flux; Rager, Ensign; resonance tissue scan; Setti, Mister; Solanagen-based aliens; Solanagen; tertiary subspace manifold; tetryon particles.**

• **"Schizoid Man, The."** *Next Generation* episode #31. Teleplay by Tracy Tormé. Story by Richard Manning & Hans Beimler. Directed by Les Landau. Stardate 42437.5. *First aired in 1988. A reclusive scientist implants his consciousness into Data's brain just prior to his death. Writer Tracy Tormé intended this episode as an homage to the British series* The Prisoner. *One episode of that series was titled "The Schizoid Man." At one point, actor Patrick McGoohan, who had starred in* The Prisoner, *was considered for the part of Dr. Ira Graves.* SEE: **Brianon, Kareen; *Constantinople, U.S.S.*; Darnay's disease; Data; Graves, Dr. Ira; Gravesworld; "If I Only Had a Brain;" molecular cybernetics; photon torpedo; Selar, Dr.; touch-and-go downwarping; transport, near-warp; Zee-Magnees Prize.**

Schmitter. (Biff Elliott). Miner on planet **Janus VI** who was killed by the silicon-based creature known as the **Horta** in 2267. ("The Devil in the Dark" [TOS]).

Scholar/Artist. (Thomas Oglesby). A member of mediator Riva's interpretive **Chorus** from planet Ramatis III. Each member of the chorus represented a different part of Riva's personality. Scholar/Artist spoke for the intellect, for matters of judgment, philosophy, and logic. He was also the dreamer and the poet who "longs to see the beauty beyond the truth which is always the first duty of art." ("Loud as a Whisper"

[TNG]).SEE: **Warrior/Adonis; Woman.**

schoolroom. Primary-school classroom established in 2369 by Keiko O'Brien for the children on station Deep Space 9. O'Brien established the school because she was concerned that there were no educational opportunities for her daughter, Molly, on the station. ("A Man Alone" [DS9]). *Educational items used for set decoration in Keiko's schoolroom include conjectural models of Zefram Cochrane's first warp-powered spaceship and the* U.S.S. Horizon *(originally built by Greg Jein for the* Star Trek Chronology*), diagrams of several alien life-forms seen in the original* Star Trek *television series, a topographical relief map of planet Sigma Iotia II (from "A Piece of the Action" [TOS]), and a galaxy map originally designed for Starfleet Command, showing the planets visited by the original* Starship Enterprise *(from "Conspiracy" [TNG]).*

Science Officer. Aboard Federation starships, the individual responsible for overseeing scientific investigations and for providing the ship's captain with scientific information needed for command decisions. **Spock** was the science officer aboard the original *Starship Enterprise.*

Science Station 402. Located in the Kohlan system. The *Enterprise*-D planned to tow the Cytherian probe found near the **Argus Array** in 2367 to Science Station 402, but the probe was destroyed first. ("The Nth Degree" [TNG]).

Science Station Delta Zero Five. Facility located near the **Romulan Neutral Zone**. The station was totally destroyed, apparently scooped from the surface of the planet, by the **Borg** in 2364. ("The Neutral Zone" [TNG]).

SCM Model 3. Small handheld superconducting magnet used aboard *Galaxy*-class starships. **Wesley Crusher** was surprised when the beautiful **Salia** of planet **Daled IV** recognized the device. ("The Dauphin" [TNG]).

Scott, Montgomery. (James Doohan). Also known as "Scotty." Chief engineer aboard the original *Starship Enterprise* under the command of Captain James Kirk. ("Where No Man Has Gone Before" [TOS]). Scott's Starfleet serial number was SE 19754.T. ("Wolf in the Fold" [TOS]).
Scott's engineering career began in 2242, and he served on a total of eleven ships ("Relics" [TNG]), including a stint as an engineering advisor on the asteroid freight run from planet **Deneva**, making the cargo run a couple of times. ("Operation—Annihilate!" [TOS]).

The original *U.S.S. Enterprise* was the first starship on which Scott served as chief engineer, and he distinguished himself many times in that position by improvising engineering miracles that more than once saved the ship and its crew.

Scotty was scheduled to retire some three months after the **Khitomer** peace conference incident in 2293, and had bought a boat in anticipation of having more free time. (*Star*

Trek VI: The Undiscovered Country).

He finally did retire in 2294 at the age of 72, having served in Starfleet for 52 years. He was in the process of relocating to the retirement community at the **Norpin Colony** when his transport ship, the *Jenolen*, crashed into a **Dyson Sphere**. Scott, the only survivor of the crash, survived for 75 years by suspending himself inside a transporter beam. He was rescued in 2369 by an away team from the *Enterprise*-D. Following his rescue, Scott embarked for parts unknown aboard a shuttlecraft "loaned" to him by *Enterprise* captain Picard. ("Relics" [TNG]).

Scott never married but he became romantically involved with fellow crew member **Mira Romaine** in 2269. That relationship ended when Romaine transferred to **Memory Alpha**. ("The Lights of Zetar" [TOS]). *Scotty's first appearance was in "Where No Man Has Gone Before." James Doohan also provided many voices for the original Star Trek series, including* **Trelane***'s father ("The Squire of Gothos" [TOS]),* **Sargon** *("Return to Tomorrow" [TOS]), the* **M-5** *computer ("The Ultimate Computer" [TOS]), and the* **Melkotian** *buoy ("Spectre of the Gun" [TOS]).*

Scott, Tryla. (Ursaline Bryant). Starfleet officer who earned the command of a starship at a younger age than any previous captain. Scott was something of a legend in her own time, but she was taken over in 2364 by the extragalactic intelligence that attempted to infiltrate Starfleet Command that year. ("Conspiracy" [TNG]).

scoutship, Romulan. Small warp-capable vessel used for reconnaisance and science missions. A Romulan scoutship, apparently on a covert mission, crashed on the Federation planet **Galorndon Core** in 2366 ("The Enemy" [TNG]). Another Romulan scoutship was apparently stolen by Admiral **Alidar Jarok**, who used it when he defected to the Federation later that year ("The Defector" [TNG]).

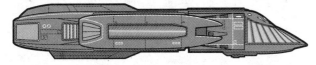

Scrolls of Ardra. A large set of documents that outlined all the details of the **Contract of Ardra**, an ancient arrangement between **Ardra** and the people of **Ventax II**. ("Devil's Due" [TNG]).

Scrooge, Ebenezer. A literary character; the protagonist in Charles Dickens' (1812-1870) 19th-century work *A Christmas Carol*. Data portrayed Scrooge in a holodeck dramatization of the book, part of Data's effort to use drama to gain an understanding of human emotions. ("Devil's Due" [TNG]).

Scylla Sector. Near the **Epsilon IX Sector** and location of **Starbase 515**. ("Samaritan Snare" [TNG]). *In Greek mythology, Scylla is one of two sea monsters who lived in a cave near the Straits of Messina. The other monster was* **Charybdis***, mentioned in "The Royale" (TNG).*

• **"Second Chances."** *Next Generation* episode #150. Story

by Mike Medlock. Teleplay by Rene Echevarria. Directed by LeVar Burton. Stardate 46915.2. *First aired in 1993. When the* Enterprise-*D arrives at planet Nervala IV to retrieve research data left behind eight years before, they find a duplicate of Commander Will Riker.* SEE: **distortion field; Gandhi, U.S.S.; Janaran Falls; KoH-mam-ara; Lagana Sector; Nervala IV; "Night Bird"; Palmer, Lieutenant; Potemkin, U.S.S.; Riker, Thomas; Riker, William T.; tai chi chuan; trombone; valerian root tea.**

sector. In interstellar mapping, a volume of space approximately 20 light-years across. A typical sector in Federation space will contain about 6-10 star systems, although sectors toward the galactic core will often contain many more. The Milky Way galaxy is divided into hundreds of thousands of sectors, grouped into four **quadrants**. Sectors are usually numbered, although in common usage are often named for a major star or planet located in that sector.

The numbering system for sectors had been inconsistently used (and sometimes interchanged with quadrants) during the show, expecially in its early days. We assume that some sectors may retain older designations from previous mapping systems, much as present-day astronomers use Messier and NGC numbers.

Sector 001. Region that includes the G2-type star known as Sol and the nine planets in its system, including Earth. This sector was the destination of the invading **Borg** ship in 2366. ("The Best of Both Worlds, Parts I and II" [TNG]). *The original and motion picture* Enterprise *returned to Sector 001 in "Tomorrow Is Yesterday" (TOS),* Star Trek I, Star Trek III, Star Trek IV, Star Trek V, *and* Star Trek VI, *although the term "Sector 001" was not invented until "The Best of Both Worlds" (TNG). The* Enterprise-D *also returned to Sector 001 in "Conspiracy" (TNG), "The First Duty" (TNG), and "Time's Arrow, Part I" (TNG).*

Sector 3-0. Located near the **Romulan Neutral Zone**. Two Federation outposts were destroyed there in late 2364 by an unknown agency later believed to be the Borg. ("The Neutral Zone" [TNG]).

Sector 3-1. Located near the **Romulan Neutral Zone**. Communications were lost with Federation starbases in this sector on stardate 41903.2 (late 2364). It was later believed that this was due to **Borg** activity in the area. ("The Neutral Zone" [TNG]).

Sector 23. Near the **Romulan Neutral Zone**, the location of Starbase 173. ("The Measure of a Man" [TNG]).

Sector 39J. Region where the **Gamma 7A System** was destroyed by a spaceborne **amoeba** creature in 2268. The *U.S.S. Intrepid* was also lost in Sector 39J, another victim of the amoeba. ("The Immunity Syndrome" [TOS]).

Sector 2520. Located near the Klingon/Federation border. **Lieutenant Aquiel Uhnari**, escaping from **Relay Station 47** aboard a shuttlecraft in 2369, was captured as her ship approached that sector. ("Aquiel" [TNG]).

Sector 21305. A sector of space where the *Enterprise*-D conducted a surveying mission in 2368. ("Ensign Ro" [TNG]).

Sector 21503. Federation space near the **Cardassian** border. The *Enterprise*-D conducted a mapping survey there in 2367. ("The Wounded" [TNG]).

Sector 21505. Located in **Cardassian** space, a Cardassian science station destroyed by the *Starship* **Phoenix** was in this region. ("The Wounded" [TNG]).

Sector 21947. Considered to be **Talarian** territory. The *Enterprise*-D ventured into this sector in response to a distress call from a damaged **Talarian observation craft** in 2367. ("Suddenly Human" [TNG]).

Sector 37628. The *Enterprise*-D was scheduled to survey this sector on stardate 45587. The mission was delayed due to the accident involving the **U.S.S. Denver**. ("Ethics" [TNG]).

security clearance 5. A high level of authorization needed to access restricted functions aboard station Deep Space 9. Security clearance 5 was required to activate the repaired replicators in Ops during the stationwide computer malfunctions caused by the **aphasia device** on stardate 46423. Quark needed a security clearance of 5 to access such information, but the Ferengi averted the problem by switching several **isolinear rods** to obtain the data. ("Babel" [DS9]).

security clearance 7. Level of clearance needed to access the location of weapons stored on station Deep Space 9. ("Captive Pursuit" [DS9]).

security access code. Password used by Starfleet personnel to provide positive identification when requesting restricted computer functions. Both the password and the user's voiceprint were used to confirm the user's identity. Security access codes were changed occasionally. Picard's security code as of stardate 42494 was Omicron-omicron-alpha-yellow-daystar-2-7. ("Unnatural Selection" [TNG]). Later, it was Picard-delta-5 ("Chain of Command, Part I" [TNG]), and Picard Gamma 6-0-7-3. ("Starship Mine" [TNG]). Riker's security access code as of stardate 42523 was theta alpha 2-7-3-7, blue. ("The Measure of a Man" [TNG]). Later, it was Riker-omega-3. ("Rascals" [TNG]). Captain Edward Jellico: "Jellico Alpha 3-1" ("Chain of Command, Part II" [TNG]).

security bypass module. Small electronic component used to circumvent security restrictions in computer-controlled devices. Bajoran religious activist **Neela** used a security bypass module to gain illegal access to runabout pad A on Deep Space 9, part of the plot to assassinate **Vedek Bareil** in 2369. ("In the Hands of the Prophets" [DS9]).

security field subsystem ANA. Computer program devised by **Neela**, but classified under Chief O'Brien's name, intended to bypass the security defenses on **Deep Space 9**. The subprogram was designed to override the security forcefields approaching runabout pad A, thus allowing her to escape after her planned assassination of **Vedek Bareil** in 2369. ("In the

Hands of the Prophets" [DS9]).

security sensor. Used on Deep Space 9 to screen for weapons, it sounded an alarm when exiting the airlocks and entering the interior of the station. The security sensor detected the **Hunters'** weapons and activated the alert. ("Captive Pursuit" [DS9]).

sehlat. A Vulcan animal resembling a large teddy bear with six-inch fangs. When **Spock** was a boy, he was very fond of his pet *sehlat*. ("Journey to Babel" [TOS]). *The animated episode "Yesteryear," written by Dorothy Fontana, suggests that Spock's* sehlat *was named I-Chaya.*

seismic regulators. Device used to control seismic earth movement. These were being installed in a subterranean cavern under the city of San Francisco on Earth in late 2368 when the work crew discovered the severed head of Data, which had been buried there for five centuries. ("Time's Arrow, Part I" [TNG]).

Sela. (Denise Crosby). Romulan operative claiming to be the daughter of *Enterprise*-D security officer **Natasha Yar** and a Romulan official. Although Yar died in 2364 without ever having a child, it was believed that an alternate version of Yar entered this continuum in 2366, then went into the past where she gave birth to Sela. ("Redemption, Part II" [TNG]). SEE: **Yar, Natasha (alternate)**. Sela emerged in 2367 as a key figure in the ongoing Romulan hegemony in Klingon and Federation politics. She spearheaded an operation in that year that unsuccessfully attempted to use mental conditioning to reprogram Starfleet officer Geordi La Forge so that La Forge would assassinate Klingon governor **Vagh**, which would have created distrust between the Klingon and Federation governments. ("The Mind's Eye" [TNG]). Later that year, Sela commanded a covert operation to provide military supplies to the **Duras** family during the **Klingon civil war** in an attempt to destabilize the **Gowron** regime. ("Redemption, Parts I and II" [TNG]). In 2368, Sela spearheaded a plan to use the underground Romulan/Vulcan reunification movement as a cover for an attempted invasion of Vulcan. She tried to force Ambassador **Spock** to reassure Vulcan authorities that the Romulan invasion force was actually a peace delegation, but her plan was thwarted by *Enterprise*-D personnel. ("Unification, Parts I and II" [TNG]). *Sela was first seen as a mysterious woman in the shadows in "The Mind's Eye" (TNG). Denise Crosby provided Sela's voice for that episode, although Sela's silhouette was played by a photo-double. Crosby was first seen as Sela in "Redemption, Part I."*

Selar, Dr. (Suzie Plakson). Physician, part of the *Enterprise*-D medical staff. A Vulcan, Dr. Selar was part of the away team answering a distress call from **Gravesworld**, and was present when noted cyberneticist **Dr. Ira Graves** died there of **Darnay's disease**. ("The Schizoid Man" [TNG]). *Although "The Schiz-*

oid Man" was the only appearance of Dr. Selar, we heard her being paged aboard the alternate Enterprise-D in "Yesterday's Enterprise" (TNG), and Dr. Crusher mentioned her in "Remember Me" (TNG), "Tapestry" (TNG), and "Suspicions" (TNG). Actor Suzie Plakson, who played Selar, also portrayed Emissary **K'Ehleyr**.

Selay. One of two habitable planets in the **Beta Renna** star system, as well as the name of the sentient reptilian race from that world. Since achieving spaceflight, the Selay had been bitter enemies with the **Anticans**, who came from the other habitable planet in their

system. Both the Selay and the Anticans applied for admission to the Federation in 2364. ("Lonely Among Us" [TNG]).

Selcundi Drema Sector. Stellar region in which are located five geologically similar planetary systems. One planet in the region, **Drema IV**, was found to be dangerously unstable, threatening the humanoid civilization living there. Acting Ensign Wesley Crusher was in charge of planetary mineral surveys during the Enterprise-D mission to the region in 2365. ("Pen Pals" [TNG]).

Selcundi Drema. Star system in the Selcundi Drema Sector. All the planets in this system (as well as in the other systems in the sector) exhibited unusual geologic instabilities. The fifth planet of this system disintegrated around 2215, forming an asteroid belt. The fourth planet, **Drema IV**, was the home of a humanoid civilization. ("Pen Pals" [TNG]). SEE: **Sarjenka**.

Seldonis IV Convention. Interstellar treaty governing the treatment of prisoners of war. Both the United Federation of Planets and the Cardassian Union were signatories to the accord. Following Captain Picard's capture by the **Cardassians** in 2369, Picard was tortured by **Gul Madred**, in violation of that treaty. Madred claimed Picard had been acting without Federation orders, and was therefore not entitled to the protection of the Seldonis Convention. ("Chain of Command, Part II" [TNG]).

Selebi Asteroid Belt. Located in Sector 396. The Enterprise-D charted this belt in 2366. ("The Offspring" [TNG]).

Seleya, Mount. On planet Vulcan, a mountain on whose summit is located an ancient temple. Mount Seleya was where a *fal-tor-pan* ceremony was performed in 2285, rejoining Spock's *katra* with his body. (Star Trek III: The Search for Spock).

self-sealing stem bolts. Useful gizmos that **Nog** and **Jake Sisko** traded some *yamok sauce* for on stardate 46844. The two boys received 100 gross of self-sealing stem bolts that they eventually traded for seven tessipates of land on planet Bajor. ("Progress" [DS9]). *We never did find out what the darned things were used for (or, for that matter, what a tessipate is).*

selgninaem. A highly toxic substance capable of causing **nucleosynthesis** in silicon. Selgninaem is not normally detectable by a starship's internal sensor scans. ("Hollow Pursuits" [TNG]).

seloh. Klingon term for sex. ("Sins of the Father" [TNG]).

Selok, Subcommander. The true Romulan identity of Federation **Ambassador T'Pel**. ("Data's Day" [TNG]).

sem'hal stew. Food served to the Cardassian **Aamin Marritza** while a prisoner on Deep Space 9 in 2369. Marritza said it could use some *yamok* sauce. ("Duet" [DS9]).

sensor web. Shawl-like garment into which was woven a highly sophisticated string of sensors that **Dr. Miranda Jones** wore, feeding her sensory information about her surroundings, and helping to hide the fact that she was blind. ("Is There in Truth no Beauty?" [TOS]).

sensors. Generic term for a wide range of scientific, medical, and engineering instruments used aboard Federation starships and in other applications. Under certain conditions, a ship in orbit above a planet's magnetic pole can be difficult to detect by sensors. William Riker once used this phenomenon while a lieutenant aboard the Starship **Potemkin** to obscure the ship from an opponent. ("Peak Performance" [TNG]). On the Enterprise-D, there were 15,525 known substances that could not be detected by standard internal scans. ("Hollow Pursuits" [TNG]).

Sentinel Minor IV. Planet that was the destination of the U.S.S. Lalo in late 2366. The Lalo never arrived; it was attacked by a **Borg** ship, and disappeared. ("The Best of Both Worlds, Part I" [TNG]).

sentry. A tightly confined annular forcefield that was discovered on the moon **Lambda Paz** in the Pentarus star system. The sentry surrounded a water fountain in a cave on that desert planet, serving to protect that valuable resource. It was not clear if the sentry itself was a life-form, but it responded effectively to the attempts of Captain **Dirgo**, as well as Jean-Luc Picard and Wesley Crusher, when they attempted to get water from the fountain after they crashed on Lambda Paz in 2367. Dirgo was killed by the sentry. ("Final Mission" [TNG]).

seofurance. Seofurance fragments from a biological sample container were found by the matter reclamation unit in **Ibudan's**

quarters. ("A Man Alone" [DS9]).

septal area. Also known as the septum lucidum, the triangular double membrane that separates the anterior horns of the lateral ventricles of a humanoid brain. The **Ktarian game** was found to affect the septal area. ("The Game" [TNG]).

Septimus Minor. The original destination of the Federation colony ship **Artemis**, launched in 2274. ("The Ensigns of Command" [TNG]).

Septimus. (Ian Wolfe). Leader of a group of slaves on planet 892-IV who hid in the caves away from the Roman culture on that planet. A former senator active in the Roman society he heard the words of the Son, gave up his lifestyle, and became a slave. ("Bread and Circuses" [TOS]). SEE: **Children of the Sun**; **892, Planet IV**. *Ian Wolfe also played* **Mr. Atoz** *in "All Our Yesterdays" (TOS).*

Sepulo. Ferengi transport ship that visited station Deep Space 9 in 2369 for a major trade conference convened by the **Grand Nagus**. ("The Nagus" [DS9]).

serik. Device hit with the cue stick in **dom-jot**. ("Tapestry" [TNG]).

sero-amino readout. A medical test used aboard the *Enterprise*-D. Dr. Crusher performed a sero-amino test on **Reginald Barclay** following his exposure to a **Cytherian** probe in 2367. ("The Nth Degree" [TNG])

serotonin. Enzyme that serves as a central neurotransmitter in humanoid nervous systems. The addictive **Ktaran game** initiated a serotonin cascade in the frontal lobe of the brain. ("The Game" [TNG]).

servo. Multipurpose tool used by Gary Seven on Earth in 1968. The servo was a device of extraterrestrial origin that had a variety of functions, from opening locked doors to serving as a weapon. ("Assignment: Earth" [TOS]).

Setal, Sublieutenant. Identity assumed by Romulan admiral **Alidar Jarok** when he defected to the Federation in 2366. As Setal, Jarok claimed to be a low-ranking logistics officer, but his true identity was later discovered. ("The Defector" [TNG]).

Setlik III. Federation outpost that was the victim of a sneak attack during **Cardassian** war. Nearly one hundred civilians were killed in the incident, including the wife and children of **Captain Benjamin Maxwell**. The *Starship* **Rutledge**, commanded by Maxwell, arrived at Setlik III the morning after the attack and was only able to save a few civilians in an outlying area. Years later, the Cardassians admitted the raid was a mistake, that they had incorrectly believed the civilian outpost was actually a staging place for a massive Federation attack. ("The Wounded" [TNG], "Emissary" [DS9]).

Setti, Mr. Hairdresser who worked with **Mr. Mot** in the *Enterprise*-D barber shop. ("Schisms" [TNG]).

Seven, Gary. (Robert Lansing). Human raised on an alien planet who was returned to Earth with the mission to help humanity survive its nuclear age in 1968. He was also known as Supervisor 194. Gary Seven's ancestors were taken from Earth approximately six thousand years ago and trained by the inhabitants of an unknown alien world. Seven was sent to Earth in 1968 on a mission to prevent Earth's civilization from destroying itself in a dangerous nuclear-arms race. His assignment was to intercede in the scheduled launch of an American orbital nuclear weapons platform, causing the launch vehicle to malfunction in such a way as to frighten planetary authorities into abandoning such weapons of mass destruction. While en route to Earth, Seven was accidentally intercepted by the *Starship Enterprise* and nearly prevented from accomplishing his task before *Enterprise* personnel determined that his intentions were not destructive. Seven remained on Earth in that time period, where he is believed to have performed other missions in the protection of humankind. ("Assignment Earth" [TOS]). SEE: **Lincoln, Roberta**. *The producers of* Star Trek *intended for Gary Seven to return in his own television series,* Assignment: Earth, *although this never materialized.*

Seventh Guarantee. One of the fundamental civil liberties protected by the **Constitution of the United Federation of Planets**. It protected citizens against self-incrimination. ("The Drumhead" [TNG]).

Sevrin, Dr. (Skip Homeier). Would-be revolutionary who rejected the technological world to seek for a more primitive existence on the mythical planet **Eden**. Sevrin had been a noted research engineer in acoustics and communication on **Tiburon**, before he became infected with deadly **Synthococcus novae**. This disease, the product of technological living, pushed Sevrin on his quest for a simpler life. It was on this quest that Sevrin and his followers in 2269 stole the star cruiser **Aurora**, and later commandeered the *Starship Enterprise* on a quest for Eden. Sevrin died from eating a poisonous plant on a planet he thought was Eden. ("The Way to Eden" [TOS]). *Skip Homeier also played Melakon in "Patterns of Force" [TOS]).*

Sha Ka Ree. In Vulcan mythology, a beautiful planet from which creation sprang. Many cultures have similar legends. Humans call it "heaven" or "Eden," while Klingons call it "Qui'Tu," and the Romulans refer to it as "Vorta Vor." **Sybok** spent much of his life searching for this world, finding a planet he believed was Sha Ka Ree after stealing the *Starship Enterprise*-A for this quest. Unfortunately, the planet discovered by Sybok was home to a malevolent creature who was using Sybok's quest in an attempt to escape from the Great Barrier at the center of the galaxy. (*Star Trek V: The Final Frontier*). SEE: **Great Barrier, the.** *The name ShaKaRee was a wordplay based on the fact that Star Trek V's producers at one point were considering casting Sean Connery in the part of Sybok.*

• **"Shades of Grey."** *Next Generation* episode #48. Teleplay by Maurice Hurley and Richard Manning & Hans Beimler. Story by Maurice Hurley. Stardate 42976.1. *First aired in 1989. Riker becomes comatose after an injury on an away mission and dreams of past experiences. This episode marked the last appearance of Diana Muldaur as Dr. Katherine Pulaski. The episode was a "clip show," designed to use scenes from earlier episodes in an effort to save money since this was the last episode of the season.* SEE: **endorphins; Pulaski, Dr. Katherine; REM sleep; Riker, William T.; Surata IV; tricordrazine.**

Shahna. (Angelique Pettyjohn). **Drill thrall** who, in 2268, was responsible for training James Kirk to fight in the games on planet **Triskelion**. ("The Gamesters of Triskelion" [TOS]).

"Shaka, when the walls fell." A Tamarian metaphorical phrase that referred to an inability to understand or be understood. Tamarian captain **Dathon** used this phrase repeatedly when he first encountered Captain Picard in 2368. ("Darmok" [TNG]).

Shakaar. Bajoran resistance group that liberated the infamous Bajoran labor camp at **Gallitep** in 2357. **Kira Nerys** was a member of the group and helped free her fellow **Bajorans** from their terrible imprisonment at Gallitep. ("Duet" [DS9]). SEE: **Marritza, Darhe'el.**

Shakespeare, William. One of Earth's most respected dramatists and poets, William Shakespeare (1564-1616) left behind a body of work that continued to illuminate the human adventure, even into the 24th century. Captain Jean-Luc Picard kept a leather-bound copy of Shakespeare's collected works in his **ready room** aboard the *Enterprise*-D. ("Conscience of the King" [TOS], "Hide and Q" [TNG]).

Shanthi, Fleet Admiral. (Fran Bennett). High-ranking Starfleet official. In early 2368, Shanthi authorized Captain Jean-Luc Picard to form an armada to blockade Romulan forces covertly supplying the **Duras** family forces in the **Klingon civil war.** ("Redemption, Part II" [TNG]).

shap. Term used in the **Wadi** game **Chula** for a level on the multitiered playing board. Each shap contained a test, progressively more difficult, until the players reached home, their final destination. ("Move Along Home" [DS9]).

shape-shifter. SEE: **allasomorph; Anya; Armus; cellular metamorphosis; chameloid; coalescent organism; Devidian nurse; Douwd; Excalibans; Farpoint Station; Garth of Izar; Isabelloa Isis; Kelvans; melitius; Odo; Q; Rocha, Lieutenant Keith; Salia; Spot; Sylvia.**

Shaw, Areel. (Joan Marshall). Starfleet attorney with the Judge Advocate's office who prosecuted James Kirk's court-martial at **Starbase 11** in 2267 for the apparent death of **Benjamin Finney**. This notwithstanding, Shaw had been romantically involved with Kirk in 2263, and they parted friends after the court-martial when Kirk was proven innocent, despite her efforts to show otherwise. ("Court Martial" [TOS]).

Shaw, Katik. (Marc Buckland). A Rutian male; waiter at the Lumar Cafe on **Rutia IV**. Shaw was an **Ansata** sympathizer and conveyed a message from Commander Riker to the Ansata leader, **Kyril Finn**. ("The High Ground" [TNG]).

Shea, Lieutenant. (Carl Byrd). *Enterprise* security guard who was part of the landing party that encountered the **Kelvans** in 2268. ("By Any Other Name" [TOS]).

Shel-la, Golin. (Jonathan Banks). Leader of the **Ennis,** who fought their eternal enemy, the **Nol-Ennis,** on a lunar penal colony in the Gamma Quadrant. ("Battle Lines" [DS9]).

Shelby, Lieutenant Commander. (Elizabeth Dennehy). Officer who was placed in charge of Starfleet's planning for defense against the **Borg** in early 2366. Shelby, along with Admiral Hanson, went aboard the *Enterprise*-D later that year when the disappearance of a colony on **Jouret IV** indicated a new Borg offensive.
  Young and ambitious, Shelby hoped to gain an appointment as *Enterprise*-D executive officer, and won at least a temporary promotion to the post following the abduction of Captain Picard by the Borg. Following the destruction of the Borg ship, Shelby was assigned to Starfleet Headquarters, where she joined the task force to reassemble the fleet. ("The Best of Both Worlds, Parts I and II" [TNG]).

Shelia star system. Home system of the **Sheliak**. ("The Ensigns of Command" [TNG]).

Sheliak Corporate. Governing body of the **Sheliak**. ("The Ensigns of Command" [TNG]).

Sheliak Director. (Mart McChesney). Leader of the **Sheliak** group sent to colonize planet **Tau Cygna V**. The director demanded removal of the Federation colony there, noting that the "human infestation" was in violation of the **Treaty of Armens**. ("The Ensigns of Command" [TNG]).

Sheliak. Classification R-3 life-form, the Sheliak are only vaguely humanoid. The Sheliak are a reclusive race, avoiding contact with the Federation whenever possible. This may be due to the Sheliak attitude that humans constituted an inferior form of life. The **Treaty of Armens** was established in 2255 between the Sheliak and the Federation, ceding several planets (including **Tau Cygna V**) to the Sheliak. There was virtually no contact with Sheliak for over a century thereafter until they demanded that a Federation colony on Tau Cygna V be removed. The Sheliak refer to themselves as "The Membership" and have a governing body called "the Corporate". ("The Ensigns of Command" [TNG]). *The Sheliak colony ship was a re-use of the* Merchantman *from* Star Trek III.

Sherlock Holmes program 3A. One of Commander Data's recreational holodeck programs on the *Enterprise*-D, this program re-created the world of 19th-century London according to the literary works of **Sir Arthur Conan Doyle.** This particular Sherlock Holmes adventure malfunctioned in 2369 when a computer life-form based on the character of **Professor James Moriarty** attempted to escape the holodeck. ("Ship in a Bottle" [TNG]). SEE: **Holmes, Sherlock.**

Sherman's Planet. Planet near the Klingon border that was the object of a dispute in 2267 between the Klingon Empire and the United Federation of Planets. Under the terms of the **Organian Peace Treaty**, the faction that could most efficiently develop the planet could assume ownership. The Federation claim to Sherman's Planet was based on a large store of **quadrotriticale**, a grain that grew well on that world. ("The Trouble with Tribbles" [TOS]). SEE: **Darvin, Arne**; **Deep Space Station K-7**. *Named for Holly Sherman, a friend of episode writer David Gerrold.*

Sherval Das. Valerian vessel that docked at station Deep Space 9 for maintenance in 2369. Major Kira Nerys believed the *Sherval Das* was carrying chemical **dolamide** explosive intended for use in **Cardassian** weapons. Prior to its arrival at Deep Space 9, the *Sherval Das* visited planets Fahleena III, Mariah IV, and Ultima Thule; this route was believed to be the same one the Valerians used previously when shipping dolamide to the Cardassians. ("Dramatis Personae" [DS9]).

Sherwood Forest. An area of Nottinghamshire, in central Great Britain on Earth, site of the legendary adventures of **Robin Hood**. Q re-created Sherwood Forest in 2367 for an elaborate fantasy he designed to teach Jean-Luc Picard a lesson about love. ("QPid" [TNG]).

Shiana. Sister of **Lieutenant Aquiel Uhnari**. Aquiel corresponded extensively by subspace with Shiana, who remained home on **Halii** when Aquiel joined Starfleet. In one of her messages, Aquiel expressed regret that she wouldn't be able to participate in the **Batarael** celebration at her home by singing the traditional **Horath**. ("Aquiel" [TNG]).

shield inverters. A subsystem of Federation starship defensive shield arrays. Shield inverters were utilized during an *Enterprise*-D mission to planet **Penthara IV** in 2368 to assist in the venting of ionized plasma from the planetary atmosphere. ("A Matter of Time" [TNG]).

shield nutation. Engineering term measuring variations in shield frequency phase rotation. Nutation was employed by *Enterprise*-D personnel in hopes of increasing shield effectiveness during the **Borg** attack of 2366. The technique was only temporarily successful, as the Borg ship was able to overcome the effects in just a few minutes. ("The Best of Both Worlds, Parts I and II" [TNG]).

shields. Energy field used to protect starships and other vessels from harm resulting from natural hazards or enemy attack. The transporter could not function when shields were active. ("Arena" [TOS]). Also referred to as deflectors, deflector shields, or screens.

Shiku Maru. A Federation vessel that encountered a **Tamarian** vessel sometime in the 24th century. While the encounter was without incident, no relations were established, as the two cultures could not communicate. ("Darmok" [TNG]).

Shimoda, Jim. (Benjamin W. S. Lum). An assistant chief engineer of the *Enterprise*-D. He became infected with the **Psi 2000 virus** and removed the **isolinear optical chips** from their receptacles in engineering. ("The Naked Now" [TNG]).

• **"Ship in a Bottle."** *Next Generation* episode #138. Written by René Echevarria. Directed by Alexander Singer. Stardate 46424.1. *First aired in 1993. The computer-generated Professor James Moriarty tries to emerge from the holodeck, demanding that a way be found for him to leave the ship. This episode continues the story of Moriarty begun in "Elementary, Dear Data"* (TNG). SEE: **Barclay, Lieutenant Reginald; Barthalomew, Countess Regina;** *cogito ergo sum***; Detrian system; Heisenberg compensators; holodeck matter;** *Justman, Shuttlecraft***; matrix diodes; Meles II; Moriarty, Professor James; pattern enhancers; Picard Delta One; protected memory; Sherlock Holmes program 3A; spatial orientation systems; strychnine; tsetse fly.**

ship recognition protocols. Codified system of superstructure landmarks for rapidly identifying starships. Federation recognition protocols enabled civilians to rapidly recognize friendly versus unfriendly spacecraft. ("Descent, Part I" [TNG]). SEE: **starships**.

Shiralea VI. Planetary home of the carnival-like **Parallax Colony**. ("Cost of Living" [TNG]).

• **"Shore Leave."** *Original Series* episode #17. Written by Theodore Sturgeon. Directed by Robert Sparr. Stardate 3025.3. *First aired in 1967. The* Enterprise *crew is baffled by a mysterious planet on which dreams come true in a terrifying way.* SEE: *Alice in Wonderland;* **Alice; amusement park planet; Barrows, Yeoman Tonia; black knight; cabaret girls; Caretaker; Finnegan; Kirk, James T.; Martine, Angela; Omicron Delta region; Police Special; Rigel II;**

Rodriguez, Lieutenant Esteban; Ruth; Sulu, Hikaru; tiger; White Rabbit.

Shras. (Reggie Nalder). **Andorian** ambassador sent to the **Babel Conference** on board the *Starship Enterprise* in 2267. Shras denied any knowledge of the **Orion** plot carried out by **Thelev**, a member of his staff. ("Journey to Babel" [TOS]).

Shrek, Jaglom. (James Cromwell). An **Yridian** dealer in information. Shrek sold Worf information that his father, **Mogh**, might be still alive, some 25 years after the Khitomer massacre. Shrek transported Worf to a Romulan prison camp in the **Carraya System**, but Mogh was not among the survivors there. ("Birthright, Parts I and II" [TNG]). *Shrek's ship was a re-use of Dirgo's shuttle from "Final Mission" (TNG). The registry number of Shrek's ship was YLT-3069.*

Shumar, Captain Bryce. The commanding officer of the *U.S.S. Essex*. Shumar was killed in 2167 when the *Essex* disintegrated above a moon of planet **Mab-Bu VI**. ("Power Play" [TNG]).

Shuttle 03. The *Voltaire*, a shuttlepod used by Captain Picard to guide the *Enterprise*-D out of the **Mar Oscura** nebula in 2367. The craft suffered damage to its starboard impulse nacelle, and lost its inertial damping control. The *Voltaire* was destroyed before it could exit the nebula. ("In Theory" [TNG]).

Shuttle 5. SEE: *El-Baz*.

Shuttle 5. Shuttlecraft taken by Commander La Forge and Lieutenant Reginald Barclay to investigate a **Cytherian** probe near the **Argus Array** in 2367. The probe emitted a brilliant flash, disabling the shuttle's onboard systems and rendering Lieutenant Barclay unconscious. ("The Nth Degree" [TNG]).

Shuttle 7. *Enterprise*-D shuttlepod, the *Onizuka*, that Commander La Forge piloted to **Risa** in late 2367. The shuttle was intercepted in midflight and taken aboard a Romulan Warbird. ("The Mind's Eye" [TNG]).

shuttle escape transporter. Small short-range personnel transporter built into some Starfleet shuttlecraft. The escape transporter permitted emergency evacuation in case of major disaster aboard the shuttle, and was used by Worf and Data in their away mission to rescue **Jean-Luc Picard** from **Borg** captivity in 2367. ("The Best of Both Worlds, Part II" [TNG]).

shuttle, Vulcan. Small warp-powered vessel of Vulcan registry used to transport Spock from Vulcan to the *Enterprise* in 2271. The ship featured a detachable crew cabin, and bore the name *Surak*. (*Star Trek: The Motion Picture*). *The Vulcan shuttle was designed by Andrew Probert and built at Magicam.*

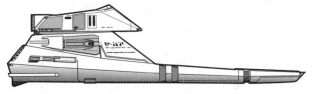

shuttlebay. Large facility aboard Federation starships used for the launching and recovery of **shuttlecraft**. A *Galaxy*-class starship had three such shuttlebays. The main shuttlebay (pictured) is located on Deck 4, with a single large hatch opening aft on the upper

surface of the **saucer module**. Shuttlebays 2 and 3 are located on the aft of the interconnecting dorsal. Also known as a **hangar deck** on older starships. Emergency explosive decompression of the main shuttlebay was employed on stardate 45652 to nudge the *Enterprise*-D from a collision course with the *U.S.S. Bozeman*. ("Cause and Effect" [TNG]). In a large-scale disaster, the shuttlebays could be converted to emergency medical triage centers. This dramatically increases the number of injured that could be cared for aboard a ship, as was done when accident victims from the *U.S.S. Denver* crash were cared for aboard the *Enterprise*-D in 2368. ("Ethics" [TNG]). *The brief miniature shot of the main shuttlebay decompressing in "Cause and Effect" remains the only glimpse to date of that huge facility.*

shuttlebus. A transportation vehicle used on planet **Rutia IV**. A shuttlebus was destroyed by **Ansata** terrorists in 2365, a few days after Alexana Devos assumed her post as Rutian security chief. Devos, who described herself as politically moderate prior to the incident, was outraged that sixty schoolchildren were killed in the bombing, an incident the Ansata claimed was an accident. ("The High Ground" [TNG]).

Shuttlecraft 1. SEE: *Sakharov, Shuttlecraft*.

Shuttlecraft 9. Shuttlepod piloted by Data and Geordi La Forge into the **Barzan wormhole** on a mission to determine the stability of the wormhole in 2366. It was eventually learned that the Barzan wormhole was unstable. ("The Price" [TNG]).

Shuttlecraft 13. Vehicle attached to the *Enterprise*-D. **Jake Kurland**, despondent over having failed to gain entrance to Starfleet Academy, ran off with Shuttlecraft 13 and nearly crashed it into **Relva VII**. ("Coming of Age" [TNG]). *Jake's flight from the* Enterprise-D *was the first use of a shuttlecraft in* Star Trek: The Next Generation. *This shuttle was designed by Andrew Probert. The miniature was built by Greg Jein.* The same shuttle later crashed on planet **Vagra II** with pilot Ben Prieto and Counselor Deanna Troi aboard in an incident that cost rescue party member **Natasha Yar** her life. Shuttlecraft 13 was destroyed on the surface of Vagra II to prevent **Armus** from escaping the planet. ("Skin of Evil" [TNG]).

Shuttlecraft 15. SEE: *Magellan*.

shuttlecraft. Small, short-range spacecraft, intended primarily for transport from a deep-space vessel to a planet's surface, or for travel within a solar system. A variety of shuttlecraft types have been used aboard different starships over the years. Most shuttles are capable of sublight travel only, and virtually all are capable of planetary landing and takeoff. *The shuttlecraft is a seldom-used part of the* Star Trek *television/movie format, mainly because the ingenious invention of the transporter makes it fast, easy, and (relatively) cheap to get our characters down to a planet without a landing ship. The first shuttlecraft, the* Galileo, *was built for the original* Star Trek *series about halfway through that show's first season. (The shuttle was not built for the first few episodes because of the enormous cost of building the full-scale mockup.) Shuttles built for the* Star Trek *movies included the San Francisco air tram and the travel pod built for* Star Trek I, *and the shuttlecrafts* Galileo 5 *and* Copernicus *built for* Star Trek V. *Cost considerations also affected the first season of* Star Trek: The Next Generation, *when a shuttle mockup was not built until a specific episode required it. Even then, that first shuttle design (seen in "Coming of Age" [TNG]) proved too difficult to build for a television budget, so, after several*

unsuccessful attempts to fake a partial exterior (as in "Unnatural Selection" [TNG]), a greatly simplified "shuttlepod" was built for "Time Squared" (TNG). Although lacking the graceful curves of the original design, the shuttlepod had a full exterior that could be photographed from any angle. It was not until several years later that a new "midsized" ship, first seen as the Shuttlecraft Magellan *in "The Outcast" (TNG), was built. This new mockup was a modification of one of the full-sized shuttles from* Star Trek V: The Final Frontier.

In terms of television drama, the real purpose of a shuttlecraft is often to isolate characters in a slow-moving vehicle that can easily get lost. For this reason, Starfleet is unlikely to "invent" significantly faster shuttles for general use. SEE: **Columbus; Copernicus; Cousteau; El-Baz; Fermi; Feynman; Galileo; Galileo II; Galileo 5; Goddard; Hawking; Justman; Magellan; Onizuka; Pike; Sakharov; Voltaire.**

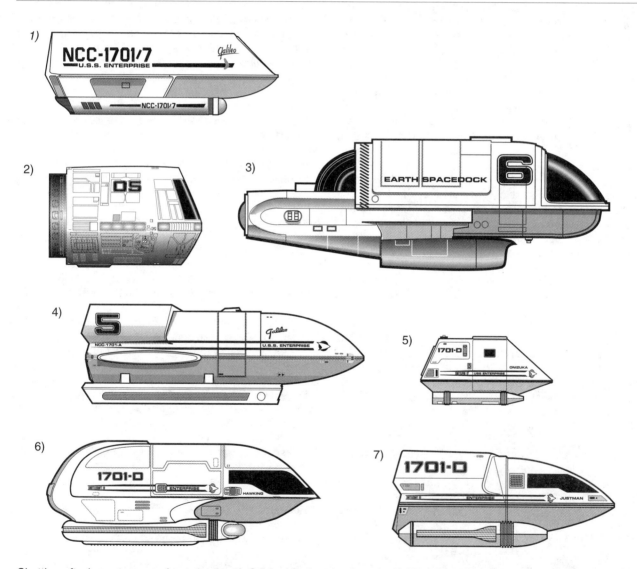

Shuttlecraft, shown to approximate scale. 1) Original Series shuttlecraft. 2) Travel pod from Star Trek: The Motion Picture. *3) Orbital shuttle vehicle seen in San Francisco in* Star Trek IV, *also in Spacedock. 4) Shuttlecraft from* Star Trek V: The Final Frontier. *5) Type-15 shuttlepod. 6) Type-7 personnel shuttlecraft (used mostly during the first two seasons of* Star Trek: The Next Generation). *7) Type-6 personnel shuttlecraft (introduced during* Star Trek: The Next Generation*'s fourth season.*

shuttlepod. Small shuttle vehicle carried aboard Federation starships including the *Enterprise*-D. Most shuttlepods were only capable of carrying two people and were limited to sublight travel across relatively short interplanetary distances. SEE: *El-Baz; Onizuka; Pike.*

sickbay. Medical care facility aboard Federation starships and other space vessels. The sickbay aboard the *Starships Enterprise* included one or more intensive-care wards, a doctor's office, a medical laboratory, an OB/GYN unit, as well as other facilities including an examination room and rehabilitation equipment. On a *Galaxy*-class starship, at least four medical personnel were on duty at all times. ("Remember Me" [TNG]). In a large-scale disaster, sickbay facilities could be supplemented by coverting the **shuttlebays** into emergency triage and treatment centers. ("Ethics" [TNG]). Aboard Federation starships, sickbay was the responsibility of the ship's **chief medical officer.** *Illustration: medical scanner and bio-bed from Original Series.*

Sigma Draconis III. Class-M planet, rated B on the industrial scale and 3 on the technological scale, equivalent to Earth year 1485. ("Spock's Brain" [TOS]).

Sigma Draconis IV. Class-M planet with an industrial rating of G, equivalent to Earth year 2030. ("Spock's Brain" [TOS]).

Sigma Draconis VI. Class-M planet with a glaciated surface, formerly the home of a technologically advanced civilization. By 2268, the civilization had all but vanished, and the humanoid inhabitants had been split into two groups. The first, the **Morgs,** were the males who lived on the surface under virtually stone-age conditions. The females, called **Eymorgs,** lived in a technologically advanced underground, but they no longer knew how to maintain the machinery that maintained their environment. When the computer system called the **Controller** failed in 2268, the Eymorgs were forced to return to the surface to live with the Morgs. ("Spock's Brain" [TOS]). SEE: **Kara;Teacher.** *The planet was also referred to in dialog as Sigma Draconis VII, an apparent continuity error.*

Sigma Draconis. System with a class-G9 star and nine planets, three of which are class-M. ("Spock's Brain" [TOS]).

Sigma Erandi system. According to **Zibalian** trader **Kivas Fajo,** the Sigma Erandi system was a source for **hytritium.** ("The Most Toys" [TNG]).

Sigma III Solar System. Location of a Federation mining colony on planet **Quadra Sigma III** that suffered a serious explosion in 2364. ("Hide and Q" [TNG]).

Sigma Iotia II. Planet some 100 light-years beyond Federation space, first visited in 2168 by the *U.S.S. Horizon.* ("A

Piece of the Action" [TOS]). SEE: **Iotians.**

sign languages. In most humanoid cultures, the use of gestures and hand signs predates the use of spoken language. The only known exception was the Leyrons of planet **Malkus IX,** who developed a written language first. ("Loud as a Whisper" [TNG]).

signage, Starfleet. SEE: illustrations next page. SEE also: **Insignia, Starfleet; symbols.**

Sikla Medical Facility. Major health-care facility on planet **Malcor III.** William Riker, masquerading as a **Malcorian** named **Rivas Jakara,** was taken to the Sikla facility after he was injured in a riot in the capital city in 2367. ("First Contact" [TNG]).

• **"Silicon Avatar."** *Next Generation* episode #104. Teleplay by Jeri Taylor. From a story by Lawrence V. Conley. Directed by Cliff Bole. Stardate 45122.3. *First aired in 1991. A scientist whose child was killed at Omicron Theta by the Crystalline Entity comes aboard the* Enterprise-*D on a mission of revenge. The term avatar refers to Data as a repository of knowledge.* SEE: **antiprotons; Argos System; bitrious filaments; Boreal III; Brechtian Cluster; Clendenning, Dr.; Crystalline Entity; Data; Davila, Carmen; fistrium; Forlat III; graviton pulses;** *Kallisko;* **kelbonite; Marr, Dr. Kila; Marr, Raymond; Melona IV; monocaladium particles; Omicron Theta.**

silicon nodule. Term used by miners on planet **Janus VI** to describe perfectly round objects found in subterranean caverns on that planet in 2267. The miners regarded the nodules as geologic curiosities and were routinely destroying them until they discovered that they were actually the eggs of a silicon-based life-form called the **Horta,** indigenous to the planet. ("The Devil in the Dark" [TOS]).

silicon-based life. Biological forms whose organic chemistry is based on the element silicon, rather than the more common element, carbon. One such example is the **Horta** of planet **Janus VI.** ("The Devil in the Dark" [TOS]).

Silvestri, Captain. Commander of the spacecraft *Shiku Maru.* Captain Silvestri encountered a **Tamarian** vessel, but was unable to establish communications because of the dramatic differences in culture and speech patterns. ("Darmok" [TNG]).

Singh, Khan Noonien. SEE: **Khan.**

Singh, Lieutenant Commander. (Kari Raz). Assistant Chief Engineer of the *Enterprise*-D who was killed by the **Beta Renna cloud** entity while the ship was in route to the neutral planet of **Parliament** in 2364. ("Lonely Among Us" [TNG]). *Singh had the dubious distinction of being the first* Enterprise-*D crew member killed on* Star Trek: The Next Generation.

Singh, Mr. (Blaisdel Makee). *Enterprise* engineer who was

(Continued on page 304.)

Signage, Starfleet.

1)

LEONARD McCOY
M. D.

3F 127

2)

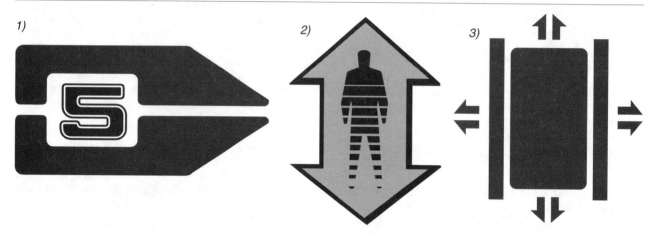

NCC-1701

Original U.S.S. Enterprise *from the first* Star Trek *series. 1) Typical door sign. 2) Decorative pennants from the ship's exterior. Original Series graphics supervised by Matt Jefferies.*

1)

5

2)

3)

4)

WARNING

AIRLOCK SAFETY PROCEDURES

1 Personnel must wear pressurized suit to exit ship if so indicated by red caution lights. (Any exceptions must have "nonsuited " clearance from environmental systems officer.) Follow instructions posted in airlock chamber.

2 In an emergency, Deactivate system by saying "Code One." Follow procedures posted inside "Emergency Controls" box (Always try to exit thru interior before trying exterior hatch.)

3 New arrivals must obtain boarding pass from security personnel posted near airlock.

DO NOT BYPASS NORMAL CYCLING

Do not bypass any "test or caution lights — hatches may not have sealed or chamber may not have reached safety levels of pressurization. Always wait for "Disembark" bar to flash before trying to exit.

Always check "hatch sealed" test lights before using any manual override apparatus. As you proceed, constantly watch pressurization levels. (Gauges located inside "Emergency controls" box.)

IMPORTANT

While exiting you may experience severe gravity change as you leave the ship's synthetic field. Do not bypass short adjustment period in chamber. (All personal items must be secured to suit especially check connectors on extra tool or tricorder packs.)

D & R STATIONS

In case of damage or mechanical failure, emergency covers will slide out manually from sides to seal hatches and pressurization-duct openings. A special tool kit for repairs is located below "Emergency Controls" box at each hatch.

5)

8P6

HOLD LOCATOR

STARFLEET MATERIAL SUPPLY COMMAND P1

MANIFEST CODE
ORIGIN
DESTINATION
TRACTOR BEAM
STASIS FIELD
DOORS UP:DN

TEST POINT

6)

STARSHIP U.S.S. ENTERPRISE   UNITED FEDERATION OF PLANETS   NCC-1701

Signage from refit U.S.S. Enterprise *seen in the first three* Star Trek *movies. 1) Directional sign. 2) Transporter systems logo. 3) Turbolift logo. 4) Instructional plaque. 5) Cargo label. 6) Ship identification pennant.   Star Trek: The Motion Picture graphics by Lee Cole, Rick Sternbach, and Mike Minor.*

1)

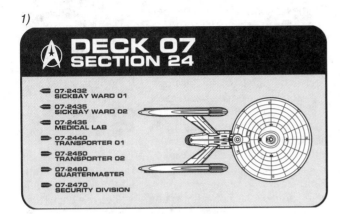

DECK 07
SECTION 24

07-2432
SICKBAY WARD 01

07-2435
SICKBAY WARD 02

07-2436
MEDICAL LAB

07-2440
TRANSPORTER 01

07-2450
TRANSPORTER 02

07-2460
QUARTERMASTER

07-2470
SECURITY DIVISION

2)

DANGER
EPS POWER SYS TRUNK

Severe plasma flux and electric shock hazard may be present at any time. No user serviceable parts inside.

Starfleet equipment protocol SFRA 2942C-6 must be observed prior to attempting to service this subsystem. Redundant data and power feeds must not be taken off-line without specific approval of duty Engineer or Operations Manager.

AUTHORIZED PERSONNEL ONLY

01-4077
ENVIRONMENTAL SYS

Atmospheric recycling subsystem must remain enabled as per operational protocol 488993 for critical environmental systems.

Starfleet equipment protocol SFRA 2942C-6 must be observed prior to attempting to service this subsystem. Redundant data and power feeds must not be taken off-line without specific approval of duty Engineer or Operations Manager.

ENVIRONMENTAL DEPT USE ONLY

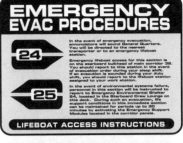

EMERGENCY
EVAC PROCEDURES

24

25

In the event of emergency evacuation, annunciators will sound General Quarters. You will be directed to the nearest transporter or to an emergency lifeboat station.

Emergency lifeboat access for this section is on the starboard bulkhead of main corridor 32. You should report to this station in the event of evacuation order during your sleep shift. If an evacuation is sounded during your duty shift, you should report to the lifeboat station assigned to your work station.

In the event of environmental systems failure, personnel in this section will be instructed to report to Emergency Environmental Shelter 24, located in the Starboard Crew Lounge on this deck. During such an evacuation, life support conditions in this immediate section can be maintained for periods up to 30 minutes by activating the Emergency Support Modules located in the corridor panels.

LIFEBOAT ACCESS INSTRUCTIONS

CAUTION
TRANSPORTER SYSTEMS

Operational regulations (SFRA 344832-02) require that this door remain closed at all times during operation of Transporter system. Failure to do so will compromise operational safety standards for crew exposure to EM and subspace field radiation.

Exceptions must be approved by duty engineer or operations manager and all non-duty personnel must be evacuated from area.

EM RADIATION HAZARD

3)

CAPTAIN
JAMES T. KIRK
COMMANDING OFFICER

05 | 0195

4)

STARSHIP U.S.S. ENTERPRISE   UNITED FEDERATION OF PLANETS   NCC-1701-A

Signage from the U.S.S. Enterprise-A *as designed for* Star Trek V: The Final Frontier *and* Star Trek VI: The Undiscovered Country. *1) Directory sign. 2) Miscellaneous informational and caution signage. 3) Door sign. 4) Ship identification pennant.*

1)

36 || TURBOLIFT

08 || 3601   CAPTAIN JEAN-LUC PICARD
COMMANDING OFFICER

06 || 2054   PERSONNEL TRANSPORTER 3

2)

WELCOME TO STARBASE 74
— STARFLEET OPERATIONAL SUPPORT SERVICES —

3)

855   ACCESS PANEL 78-0087
REFER SERVICING TO QUALIFIED STARFLEET TECHNICIANS. NO USER SERVICEABLE PARTS INSIDE. REMEMBER, NO MATTER WHERE YOU GO, THERE YOU ARE.

954   ENGINEERING ACCESS ONLY
THREE HUNDRED THOUSAND KILOMETERS PER SECOND: IT'S NOT JUST A GOOD IDEA, IT'S THE LAW. YOUR ACTUAL MILEAGE MAY VARY, OF COURSE.

451   AUXILIARY SYSTEMS 32-2398
CAUTION: OBJECTS IN MIRROR ARE CLOSER THAN THEY APPEAR TO BE. A STITCH IN TIME SAVES NINE. IN SPACE, NO ONE CAN HEAR YOU SCREAM.

302   OPTICAL DATA NET SERVICE ACCESS 3069
JUST SIT RIGHT BACK AND YOU'LL HEAR A TALE, A TALE OF A FATEFUL TRIP. THAT STARTED FROM THIS TROPIC PORT, ABOARD THIS TINY SHIP...

4)

Signage from the U.S.S. Enterprise-D *in* Star Trek: The Next Generation. *1) Door signs. The first two digits represent the deck number. The next four are the room number. 2) Welcome to Starbase 74 from "11001001" (TNG). 3) Panel identification labels. The fine print on some of these labels, never legible on television, contained a few tiny "in-jokes." 4) Ship identification pennant.*

(Continued from page 301.)

on duty in the auxiliary control room when the robot *Nomad* was aboard on stardate 3541. ("The Changeling" [TOS]).

• **"Sins of the Father."** *Next Generation* episode #65. Teleplay by Ronald D. Moore & W. Reed Moran. Based on a teleplay by Drew Deighan. Directed by Les Landau. Stardate 43685.2. *First aired in 1990. Worf returns to the Klingon Homeworld to defend his late father against charges of treason. Worf's story was later continued in "Reunion" (TNG) and "Redemption, Parts I and II" (TNG).* SEE: **Age of Ascension; caviar;** *cha'Dlch;* **discommendation; Duras; First City;** *ghojmok;* **Great Hall;** *ha'Dlbah;* **Intrepid, U.S.S.; Ja'rod; K'mpec; Kahlest; Khitomer massacre; Khitomer; Klingon Defense Force; Klingon High Council; Klingon Homeworld; Kurn;** *kut'luch;* **Lorgh;** *Mek'ba;* **Mogh; Officer Exchange Program;** *pahtk; Qapla';* **replicator;** *seloh;* **Starbase 24; turn; Worf.**

Sipe, Ryan. Starfleet officer who was apparently killed by the extragalactic alien intelligence that attempted to infiltrate Starfleet Command in 2364. ("Conspiracy" [TNG]).

Sir Guy of Gisbourne. (Clive Revill). One of the legendary foes of the outlaw **Robin Hood** in Earth's old England. Some ancient tales hold that Sir Guy was in love with Robin's lady, the fair **Maid Marian**. Sir Guy appeared in a fantasy crafted for the *Enterprise*-D crew by **Q**. ("QPid" [TNG]). *Clive Revill also played the galactic emperor in* The Empire Strikes Back.

Sirah. (Kay E. Kuter). Title given to the leader of a community on the planet **Bajor**. Many years ago, the villagers were fighting among themselves, and the first Sirah knew he must find a way to unite his people. That first Sirah used a small stone, a fragment from one of the **Orbs** from the **Celestial Temple**, to focus the villager's thoughts into the illusion of a terrible cloud creature called the **Dal'Rok**. The Dal'Rok threatened the village, until the Sirah told stories of the strength and unity of the village, frightening away the evil force. This ritual was repeated every year after harvest, thereby providing the village with a common foe. The fact that the Dal'Rok was only an illusion was kept secret from the people and passed from Sirah to Sirah. ("The Storyteller" [DS9]). SEE: **Hovath.**

Sirco Ch'Ano. **Bajoran** who traded seven **tessipates** of land to **Nog** and **Jake Sisko** on stardate 46844 in exchange for 144 gross of **self-sealing stem bolts.** Sirco Ch'Ano had originally ordered the stem bolts from a Lissepean captain, but had to renege on the deal when he couldn't deliver the **latinum** as payment. ("Progress" [DS9]). SEE: **Noh-Jay Consortium.**

Sirius. Star used by Sulu as a navigational reference when the original *Enterprise* was thrown across the galaxy in 2267 by the advanced race known as the **Metrons**. ("Arena" [TOS]). *Sirius is, of course, the Dog Star in Earth mythology.*

Sisko, Benjamin. (Avery Brooks). Starfleet officer who commanded station **Deep Space 9** following the **Cardassian** withdrawal from **Bajor** in 2369. Sisko, a lieutenant commander, had been executive officer aboard the *U.S.S. Saratoga* at the time of the ship's destruction in the battle of **Wolf 359**. Benjamin's wife, **Jennifer Sisko**, was killed aboard the *Saratoga*, and he was left to raise their son, **Jake Sisko**, alone.

Sisko was subsequently assigned to the **Utopia Planitia Fleet Yards** on Mars, where he spent three years before being promoted to commander and assigned to station **Deep Space 9**. Sisko had met his future wife at Gilgo Beach on Earth, around 2353, just after Sisko's graduation from Starfleet Academy.

Shortly after his posting to Deep Space 9, Sisko made contact with the mysterious life-forms identified as Bajor's legendary **Prophets** in the Bajoran **Celestial Temple** located in the **Denorios Belt**. As a result, religious leader **Kai Opaka** indicated that Sisko was the **Emissary** promised by prophecy as the one who would save the **Bajoran** people. Sisko was uncomfortable with his role as Emissary, but felt obligated to respect Bajoran religious beliefs. ("Emissary" [DS9]).

Early in his career, Ensign Sisko was mentored by **Curzon Dax**, a **Trill** who would later become **Jadzia Dax**, science officer aboard Deep Space 9. Benjamin and Curzon had been friends for nearly two decades, and Sisko initially found it difficult to relate to his friend in the body of a beautiful young woman. ("A Man Alone" [DS9], "Dax" [DS9]).

Sisko's father was a gourmet chef who insisted the family have dinner together, so that he could try out his new recipes on them. He called them his "test-tasters." ("A Man Alone" [DS9]). Ben had a holosuite program of Earth's famous **baseball** players, such as **Buck Bokai, Tris Speaker,** and **Ted Williams.** Using this program, Ben and his son, Jake, enjoyed playing with these greats. The program also allowed Ben to cheer his hero, Buck Bokai, in the sparsely attended 2042 World Series that spelled the end of professional baseball. ("If Wishes Were Horses" [DS9]). *Ben Sisko first appeared in "Emissary" (DS9).*

Sisko, Jake. (Cirroc Lofton). Son of **Benjamin Sisko** and **Jennifer Sisko**. Born in 2355, he lost his mother on the *U.S.S. Saratoga* during the battle of **Worf 359** in 2367.

Jake came to live on station **Deep Space 9** when his father took command of that facility in 2369. ("Emissary" [DS9]). On Deep Space 9, Jake befriended young Nog, with whom he created a fictitious company, the **Noh-Jay Consortium**, for their ingenious "business" dealings. ("Progress" [DS9]). *A younger Jake Sisko was played by Thomas Hobson for flashback scenes in "Emissary" (DS9).*

Sisko, Jennifer. (Felicia Bell). Wife to **Benjamin Sisko** who was killed on the **U.S.S. Saratoga** during the battle of **Wolf 359** in early 2367. Jennifer met her future husband on Gilgo Beach, shortly after Benjamin graduated from Starfleet Academy. ("Emissary" [DS9]).

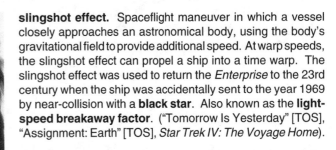

Sisters of Hope Infirmary. Charity hospital in 19th-century San Francisco on planet Earth. More than half of the victims of the time-traveling aliens from **Devidia II** came from this hospital. The crew of the *Enterprise*-D visited this infirmary in hopes of stopping the **Devidians**. ("Time's Arrow, Part II" [TNG]).

site-to-site transport. Also known as direct beaming, the process whereby a transport subject is beamed to the transporter from a remote location. Instead of being materialized in the chamber, the subject is then transported directly to another location. For example, a critically injured patient might be beamed directly to sickbay instead of to the transporter room. Site-to-site transport is relatively costly in terms of energy usage, so it is used primarily for emergency situations. ("Brothers" [TNG], "The Game" [TNG], et al.). *During the original series, this procedure was considered to be extremely risky. ("Day of the Dove" [TNG]).*

Sito, Cadet Second Class. (Shannon Fill). A member of Starfleet Academy's **Nova Squadron** in 2368. Sito's craft was the first struck during an accident that destroyed all five craft and killed one of the squadron members. ("The First Duty" [TNG]). SEE: **Kolvoord Starburst; Locarno, Cadet First Class Nicholas**.

• **"Skin of Evil."** *Next Generation* episode #22. Teleplay by Joseph Stefano and Hannah Louise Shearer. Story by Joseph Stefano. Directed by Joseph L. Scanlan. Stardate 41601.3. *First aired in 1988. A malevolent life-form of pure evil traps a shuttlecraft and kills Tasha Yar.* SEE: **Armus; direct reticular stimulation; Lynch, Leland T.; Minnerly, Lieutenant; Mishiama wristlock; neural stimulator; norep; Prieto, Lieutenant Ben; Shuttlecraft 13; Swenson, Science Officer; Vagra II; Worf; Yar, Natasha; Zed Lapis Sector**.

Skon. Father to **Sarek** of Vulcan; grandfather to **Spock**. (*Star Trek III: The Search for Spock*).

sleeper ship. Term used to describe relatively slow interstellar spacecraft that used suspended animation to allow passengers and crew to hibernate during the flight. Sleeper ships fell into disuse by the year 2018 because of advances in sublight propulsion. The **S.S. Botany Bay** was a sleeper ship. ("Space Seed" [TOS]). SEE: **cryosatellite**.

slingshot effect. Spaceflight maneuver in which a vessel closely approaches an astronomical body, using the body's gravitational field to provide additional speed. At warp speeds, the slingshot effect can propel a ship into a time warp. The slingshot effect was used to return the *Enterprise* to the 23rd century when the ship was accidentally sent to the year 1969 by near-collision with a **black star**. Also known as the **light-speed breakaway factor**. ("Tomorrow Is Yesterday" [TOS], "Assignment: Earth" [TOS], *Star Trek IV: The Voyage Home*).

Smith, Yeoman. (Andrea Dromm). *Enterprise* crew member during the early days of Kirk's first five-year mission, circa 2265. ("Where No Man Has Gone Before" [TOS]).

So'wl'chu'. Klingon phrase that translates into "engage" or "activate." ("Unification, Part I" [TNG]).

Sobi. (Judson Scott). A citizen of the planet **Brekka**, in charge of a shipment of narcotic **felicium** to be shipped to planet **Ornara**. Sobi was determined to maintain the exploitive relationship between Brekka and Ornara by concealing the narcotic nature of felicium from the **Ornarans**. ("Symbiosis" [TNG]). *Actor Judson Scott had previously played Joachim, Khan's protégé, in* Star Trek II: The Wrath of Khan.

sodium chloride. Common salt, one of the essential elements of life on Earth and other planets. This substance was of critical importance to the life-forms on planet **M-113**, and the last survivor of that planet's civilization was forced to kill **Nancy Crater** and several *Enterprise* crew personnel to obtain it. ("The Man Trap" [TOS]).

"Sokath, his eyes uncovered!" A **Tamarian** metaphorical phrase referring to achieving sudden insight or understanding. ("Darmok" [TNG]).

Solais V. Class-M planet whose humanoid inhabitants had been at war for fifteen centuries when both sides sued for peace in 2365, requesting the services of mediator **Riva**. By that time, Solais weapons technology had reached the point where laser warfare was being employed. Although he was not immediately successful in bringing peace to the Solais, Riva remained on the planet, hoping to teach both factions the use of sign language, and in doing so, to bring them to a common ground. ("Loud as a Whisper" [TNG]).

Solanagen-based aliens. Life-forms that existed in a deep subspace domain. These humanoid entities accessed our own universe in 2369 when Geordi La Forge modified a sensor array, accidentally allowing the Solanagen-based aliens to create a

small pocket of their space inside ours. The aliens forcibly abducted members of the *Enterprise*-D crew during their sleep for medical testing until a **coherent graviton pulse** was used to close the spatial rupture. ("Schisms" [TNG]). *The aliens were not given a formal name in the episode.*

Solanagen. Molecular structure that can only exist in a subspace domain. The humanoid aliens who abducted several *Enterprise*-D crew members in 2369 were Solanagen-based life-forms. ("Schisms" [TNG]). SEE: **Solanagen-based aliens; tertiary subspace manifold; tetryon particles.**

Solari. Star system of which planet **Solais V** is a part. ("Loud as a Whisper" [TNG]).

Solarion IV. A Federation colony located in the Solarion system, near **Cardassian** space. In 2368, the Solarion IV colony was attacked and destroyed by forces claiming to be **Bajoran** terrorists. It was later found that the colony was attacked by Cardassian operatives trying to cause distrust between the Federation and the Bajorans. ("Ensign Ro" [TNG]).

Solis, Lieutenant (J.G.) Orfil. (George de la Pena). Relief **Flight Controller** (conn) aboard the *Enterprise*-D. Solis assumed the conn when Geordi La Forge assumed command of the ship in Captain Picard's absence. ("The Arsenal of Freedom" [TNG]).

soliton wave. An experimental means of faster-than-light spacecraft propulsion using planet-based soliton-wave generators developed by **Dr. Ja'Dar** of planet **Bilana III**. These generators created a nondispersing wavefront of subspace distortion, which a space vehicle could "ride" like a terrestrial surfboard. Although the system required an unwieldy planetary station on either end, it promised substantially higher propulsion efficiencies than those experienced by conventional starships. The first practical test of this technology was conducted by Dr. Ja'Dar in 2368 with assistance of personnel from the *Starship Enterprise*-D. The test involved a small unmanned wave rider vehicle that was sent from Bilana III to **Lemma II**, where a scattering field would dissipate the subspace soliton wave. The test was partially successful, although considerable difficulties were encountered in controlling and dispersing the wave. ("New Ground" [TNG]).

Solkar. Grandfather to **Sarek** of Vulcan, great-grandfather to **Spock**. Father to Skon. (*Star Trek III: The Search for Spock*).

Solok, DaiMon. (Lou Wagner). Ferengi smuggler who sometimes ran cargo to planet **Celtris III**. Captain Picard, Dr. Crusher, and Lieutenant Worf were able to procure passage to Celtris III on Solok's vessel on a covert Starfleet mission in 2369. ("Chain of Command, Part I" [TNG]).

somatophysical failure. In humanoid physiology, the collapse of all bodily systems. Captain Picard suffered massive somatophysical failure when he was physically separated from the emanations of the **Kataan probe** in 2368. ("The Inner Light" [TNG]).

Something for Breakfast. Play written by Dr. Beverly Crusher in 2369. Her manuscript for the play was lost in the main *Enterprise*-D computer system when an energy fluctuation in Data's neural net caused a peculiar malfunction in the computer's recreational programming data files. ("A Fistful of Datas" [TNG]). SEE: **Subroutine C-47.**

somnetic inducer. A small neural pad used to aid the induction of sleep in humanoids. Dr. Crusher prescribed a somnetic inducer for Geordi La Forge in late 2367 when a possible malfunction of his VISOR was suspected of causing insomnia. ("The Mind's Eye" [TNG]).

Sonak, Commander. (Jon Kamal). Starfleet officer who was killed in a transporter malfunction while beaming up to the refurbished *Starship Enterprise*. Sonak, a Vulcan, would have served as science officer aboard that ship when it intercepted the **V'Ger** entity in 2271. (*Star Trek: The Motion Picture*).

***Sonchi* ceremony.** A Klingon ritual; part of the **Rite of Succession**. *Sonchi* translates as "he is dead." The *Sonchi* formally confirmed the death of a leader before his or her successor could be chosen, and involved jabbing the body with **Klingon painstiks** while issuing a verbal challenge. **K'mpec**'s *Sonchi* ceremony took place in 2367 aboard a Klingon spacecraft. ("Reunion" [TNG]).

Songi, Chairman. (Kim Hamilton). The planetary leader of **Gamelan V**. Songi was humanoid; her race was distinguished by beautiful facial tendrils. When high levels of radiation threatened her planet in 2367, she issued the general distress call that resulted in the *Enterprise*-D's arrival at her planet. ("Final Mission" [TNG]).

sonic disruptor. Handheld weapon used by civil authorities on planet **Eminiar VII**. ("A Taste of Armageddon" [TOS]). Similar weapons were used by Klingon warriors as well. SEE: **Klingon weapons; phase disruptor.**

sonic separator. Medical instrument used by Dr. McCoy to restore Spock's brain to his body on planet **Sigma Draconis VI** in 2268. ("Spock's Brain" [TOS]).

sonic shower. Personal hygiene device used for bathing aboard Federation starships. (*Star Trek: The Motion Picture*).

sonodanite. Metallic alloy used in Federation shuttlecraft. ("Final Mission" [TNG]).

Soong, Noonien. (Brent Spiner). Renowned cyberneticist Dr. Noonien Soong was born in the late 23rd century, and was known as Earth's foremost robotics scientist. Soong's early achievements were overshadowed by his highly publicized failures when he tried to construct a **positronic brain**. Following that downfall, the reclusive Soong disappeared from public  sight, traveling under an assumed name to the **Omicron Theta** colony, where he continued his work in secret. Perhaps his greatest success there was the creation of the humanoid androids **Data** and **Lore**. ("Datalore" [TNG]). Soong escaped from Omicron Theta just as the colony was destroyed by the **Crystalline Entity**. He established another laboratory at another secret location, where he worked for years in seclusion. He broke this seclusion in 2367 when he commanded Data to go to his laboratory so that Soong could install a new chip in his creation, intended to give Data the ability to experience human emotions. Unfortunately, Lore also responded to Soong's summons, and Lore, jealous of Data, stole the chip. Soong died shortly thereafter. ("Brothers" [TNG]). Soong implanted a circuit into Data's base programming intended to cause Data to dream when he reached a certain level of development. This circuit was prematurely activated in 2369 when Data experienced a severe plasma shock. Data's dreams included images of a young Dr. Soong as a blacksmith, forging a bird that represented Data himself. ("Birthright, Part I" [TNG]). *Soong was played by Brent Spiner, on the assumption that Data was made in his creator's image.* SEE: **Asimov, Isaac**.

Soong-type android. Term used to describe artificial humanoid life-forms using designs developed by Dr. **Noonien Soong**. Soong-type androids have included **Data**, **Lore**, and **Lal**. ("The Offspring" [TNG]).

Soren. (Melinda Culea). A **J'naii** pilot, part of a team that worked with the *Enterprise*-D crew to rescue a missing J'naii shuttle in 2368. During the rescue operation, Soren became romantically involved with Commander William Riker, thereby exhibiting female sexual behavior. Such gender-specific orientation was considered abhorrent to the J'naii culture, and Soren was subsequently arrested. Soren was subjected to **psychotectic** therapy, causing one to conform to the culturally acceptable androgynous norm. ("The Outcast" [TNG]). *The pronoun "one" is used here, as is proper to the J'naii culture when speaking of an androgynous race, as opposed to the "she" or "he" pronouns often used in races with sexual differentiation.*

sorium. Explosive compound used in a Ferengi **locator bomb** intended to kill Quark when he served as **Grand Nagus** in 2369. ("The Nagus" [DS9]).

Sotarek Citation. Romulan award granted to **Commander Toreth** for her actions in defending her squadron against a superior Klingon force. ("Face of the Enemy" [TNG]).

Sothis III. Home to the Satarran race of intelligent beings. They hate mysteries. ("The Chase" [TNG]).

Sovak. (Michael Grodenchik). A Ferengi entrepreneur who sometimes worked with **Dr. Samuel Estragon** on less-than-ethical archaeological expeditions. Upon Estragon's death in 2366, Sovak paid Estragon's assistant, **Vash**, to steal Estragon's notes on the location of the *Tox Uthat*. Vash used Sovak's money to conduct her own search for the fabled object, with Sovak trailing her. Besides coveting the *Uthat*,

Sovak was also attracted to the beautiful Vash. ("Captain's Holiday" [TNG]).

***Soyuz*-class starship.** A variant on the ***Miranda*-class** starship used by the Federation Starfleet. *Soyuz*-class ships featured an enlarged aft cargo and shuttlebay section, as well as several large outboard sensor pods. The *Soyuz* class was withdrawn from service by Starfleet in 2288. ("Cause and Effect" [TNG]). *It was originally hoped that a new design could be developed for the* Soyuz-*class* **U.S.S. Bozeman**, *but practical considerations dictated the reworking of the existing* Miranda-*class* **U.S.S. Reliant** *model originally built for* Star Trek II. *The modifications were designed by Greg Jein and Mike Okuda. The class was named for the Russian spacecraft that shuttled cosmonauts up to the Salyut space station.*

• **"Space Seed."** Original Series episode #24. Teleplay by Gene L. Coon and Carey Wilber. Story by Carey Wilber. Directed by Marc Daniels. Stardate 3141.9. *First aired in 1967. The* Enterprise *is commandeered by 20th-century genetic "superman" Khan Noonien Singh, who has survived for centuries aboard a "sleeper ship." This episode was the predecessor to the feature film* Star Trek II: The Wrath of Khan. SEE: **Botany Bay, S.S.**; **Ceti Alpha V**; **DY-100**; **DY-500**; **decompression chamber**; **Eugenics Wars**; **Gamma 400 star system**; **Harrison**; **Joaquin**; **Kyle, Mr.**; **McGivers, Lieutenant Marla**; **McPherson**; **Milton**; **Otto**; **Rodriguez**; **Singh, Khan Noonien**; **sleeper ship**; **Spinelli, Lieutenant**; **Starbase 12**; **Thule**.

space station. SEE: **Deep Space 9**; **Deep Space Station K-7**; **drydock**; **Earth Station McKinley**; **Lysian Central Command**; **Regula I**; **Spacedock**.

space warp. SEE: **subspace**; **warp drive**.

space-normal. Technical term describing slower-than-light (i.e. non-warp speed) travel. ("The *Galileo* Seven" [TOS]). SEE: **impulse drive**.

Spacedock. Massive station orbiting planet Earth, providing service facilities for Starfleet vessels. The *U.S.S. Enterprise* returned to Spacedock in 2285 following the battle with **Khan** in the **Mutara Nebula**. At the time, the ship was scheduled to be scrapped, but Kirk stole the *Enterprise* from Spacedock in his effort to rescue **Spock**. Also stationed at Spacedock at the time was the *U.S.S. Excelsior*, undergoing tests of its experimental transwarp drive. (*Star*

Trek III: The Search for Spock). The Spacedock model was designed by David Carson and Nilo Rodis. It was built at ILM. The model was reused more than once in Star Trek: The Next Generation, *notably for Starbase 74 in "11001001" (TNG).*

spatial interphase. Time-space phenomenon in which two or more dimensional planes briefly overlap and connect. The Starship **Defiant** disappeared into such a phenomenon in 2268, and *Enterprise* captain James Kirk also became briefly trapped there while on a rescue mission. The interphase phenomenon also had debilitating effects on humanoid nervous systems and apparently caused the crew of the *Defiant* to mutiny and eventually kill each other. ("The Tholian Web" [TOS]).

spatial orientation systems. Subsystem of a holodeck computer, responsible for the orientation of objects in the holodeck environment. The spatial orientation systems aboard the *Enterprise*-D holodeck were suspected of malfunctioning in 2369 when holodeck characters began changing their dominant hands; that is, characters who were intended to be right-handed became left-handed and vice versa. ("Ship in a Bottle" [TNG]).

Speaker, Tris. Famous **baseball** player who played the game on Earth from 1907-1928. A holographic version of Speaker was available in a baseball holosuite program enjoyed by Jake and **Benjamin Sisko** on station Deep Space 9. ("If Wishes Were Horses" [DS9]). SEE: **Bokai, Buck.**

Spectral Analysis department. *Enterprise*-D science department that studied the composition of stars and stellar phenomena. **Neela Daren** once wanted Spectral Analysis to have more time monitoring the **Borgolis Nebula** but the sensor array was allocated to Engineering. ("Lessons" [TNG]).

• **"Spectre of the Gun."** Original Series episode #56. Written by Lee Cronin. Directed by Vincent McEveety. Stardate 4385.3. *First aired in 1968. Kirk and company are trapped in a bizarre re-creation of the ancient American West and forced to fight in the gunfight at OK Corral. This was the first episode produced for the third season. Lee Cronin was the pen name for Gene L. Coon.* SEE: **Claiborne, Billy; Clanton, Billy; Clanton, Ike; Earp, Morgan; Earp, Virgil; Earp, Wyatt; Ed; Holliday, Doc; McLowery, Frank; McLowery, Tom; Melkotians; OK Corral; Sylvia; Tombstone, Arizona; Vulcan mind-meld.**

Spican flame gem. Pretty but useless trinket that a trader on **Deep Space Station K-7** was not interested in buying from **Cyrano Jones** in 2267. ("The Trouble with Tribbles" [TOS]).

Spinelli, Lieutenant. (Blaisdell Makee). Crew member aboard the original *Starship Enterprise* in 2267. Kirk recorded a commendation for Spinelli when the bridge of the *Enterprise* was slowly deprived of life support during **Khan**'s takeover attempt. ("Space Seed" [TOS]).

spiny lobe-fish. Type of meal served to Riker at the imaginary **Tilonus Institute for Mental Disorders**. The image of

the spiny lobe-fish was generated while Riker was being brainwashed on planet **Tilonus IV** in 2369 and, like many of the elements of this delusional world, was unreal. ("Frame of Mind" [TNG]). SEE: *Frame of Mind*.

Spock (mirror). Science officer and second-in-command of the *I.S.S. Enterprise* in the **mirror universe**. The bearded first officer deduced the transposition of landing parties between universes and allowed the *U.S.S. Enterprise* landing party to return to their own universe. Knowing that one day Spock might be the captain of the *I.S.S. Enterprise*, Kirk planted seeds of doubt in Spock's mind about the fate of the evil empire he served, noting that Spock was a man of honor in both universes. ("Mirror, Mirror" [TOS])

• **"Spock's Brain."** Original Series episode #61. Written by Lee Cronin. Directed by Marc Daniels. Stardate 5431.4. *First aired in 1968. A mysterious woman steals Spock's brain.* SEE: **Controller; Eymorg; ion propulsion; Kara; Luma; Morg; Sigma Draconis III; Sigma Draconis IV; Sigma Draconis VI; Sigma Draconis; sonic separator; Teacher; trilaser connector.**

Spock. (Leonard Nimoy). Science officer aboard the original *Starship Enterprise* under the command of Captain James T. Kirk. Born 2230 on planet **Vulcan**. His mother, **Amanda** Grayson, was a human schoolteacher from Earth, and his father, **Sarek**, was a diplomat from Vulcan. ("This Side of Paradise" [TOS], "Journey to Babel" [TOS]). As a result, he was torn between  two worlds, the stern discipline of Vulcan logic and the emotionalism of his human side. The struggle to reconcile his two halves would torment him for much of his life. ("The Naked Time" [TOS]). Spock's Starfleet service number was S179-276 SP. As of 2267, he had earned the Vulcanian Scientific Legion of Honor, had been twice decorated by Starfleet Command, ("Court Martial" [TOS]), and held an A7 computer expert classification. ("The Ultimate Computer" [TOS]). His blood type was T-negative. ("Journey to Babel" [TOS]).

Childhood and family: When he was five years old, Spock came home upset because Vulcan boys had tormented him, saying he wasn't really Vulcan. ("Journey to Babel" [TOS]). As a child, Spock had a pet **sehlat**, sort of a live Vulcan teddy bear. ("Journey to Babel" [TOS]). Spock was raised with an older half-brother, **Sybok**, until Sybok was ostracized from Vulcan society because he rejected the Vulcan dogma of pure logic. *(Gene Roddenberry considered the Sybok story to be apocryphal.)* Spock himself endured considerable anti-human prejudice on the part of many Vulcans, an experience that may have later made it easier for Spock to find a home in the interstellar community of Starfleet. *(Star Trek V: The Final Frontier).* At age seven, Spock was telepathically bonded with a young Vulcan girl named **T'Pring**. Less than a marriage, but more than a betrothal, the telepathic touch would draw the two together when the time was right after both came of age. ("Amok Time" [TOS]). Spock experienced **Pon farr**, the powerful mating drive, in 2267, when he was compelled to return to Vulcan to claim T'Pring as his wife. T'Pring spurned Spock in favor of **Stonn**, freeing Spock. ("Amok Time" [TOS]). Spock's father, Sarek, had hoped his son would attend the **Vulcan Science Academy**, and was bitterly disappointed when Spock instead chose to join Starfleet. Spock and his father had not spoken as father and son for 18 years until a medical emergency drew them together. ("Journey to Babel" [TOS]).

Aboard the *U.S.S. Enterprise*: Spock was the first Vulcan to enlist in the Federation **Starfleet**, and distinguished himself greatly as science officer aboard the original ***U.S.S. Enterprise***. His logical Vulcan thought-patterns proved of tremendous value when Spock first served aboard the *Enterprise* during the command of Captain Christopher Pike. ("The Menagerie" [TOS]). *Spock said he worked with Pike for 11 years, 4 months, which suggests he was young enough when he first came on board the* Enterprise *that he was probably still attending Starfleet Academy. Because of this, we speculate that Spock's first year on the* Enterprise *was as a cadet.* Under the command of James Kirk, Spock suffered infection by parasites on planet **Deneva** in 2267, an intensely painful experience. He survived the **Denevan neural parasites** after being exposed to intense electromagnetic radiation that drove the parasites from his body. Spock was briefly feared to have been blinded by the light, but it was later learned that his Vulcan **inner eyelid** had protected his vision. ("Operation—Annihilate!" [TOS]). Spock was critically wounded on Tyree's planet in 2267 with an ancient weapon known as a flintlock. He survived using a Vulcan healing technique in which the mind concentrates on the injured organs. ("A Private Little War" [TOS]). Following the conclusion of Kirk's five-year mission, Spock retired from Starfleet, returning to Vulcan to pursue the *kohlinar* discipline. Although he completed the training intended to purge all remaining emotion, Spock nonetheless failed to achieve *kohlinar* because his emotions were stirred by the **V'Ger** entity in 2271. (*Star Trek: The Motion Picture*). Spock subsequently remained with Starfleet and was eventually promoted to *Enterprise* captain when that ship was assigned as a training vessel at Starfleet Academy.

Death and rebirth: Spock was killed in 2285 while saving the *Enterprise* from the detonation of the **Genesis Device** by **Khan Noonien Singh**. His body was consigned to space, but unknown to anyone at the time, his casket landed on the Genesis Planet (*Star Trek II:*  *The Wrath of Khan*). Although believed dead at the time, Spock had, just prior to his death, mind-melded with McCoy. Spock had apparently intended for his friend to return Spock's *katra* to Vulcan in accordance with Vulcan custom. The presence of Spock's living spirit in McCoy's mind was later found to be an extraordinary opportunity to reunite Spock's body and spirit when his body was found to have been regenerated on the **Genesis Planet**. The *fal-tor-pan* (refusion) process was conducted at **Mount Seleya** on Vulcan, supervised by high priestess T'Lar. (*Star Trek III: The Search for Spock*). *Spock's younger selves in* Star Trek III *were played*

by *Carl Steven, Vadia Potenza, Stephen Manley, and Joe W. Davis.* Later, Spock underwent several months of reeducation, during which his mind was instructed in the Vulcan way, but his mother, Amanda, was concerned that he regain knowledge of his human heritage as well. Spock elected to return to Earth with his shipmates from the *Enterprise* to face charges stemming from Kirk's violation of Starfleet regulations in Spock's rescue. (*Star Trek IV: The Voyage Home*).

Later career: In later years, Spock's work became more diplomatic than scientific, even while he was still part of Starfleet. At the request of Ambassador Sarek, Spock served as Federation special envoy to the Klingon government in 2293, paving the way for the **Khitomer** peace accords with Chancellor **Azetbur**. (*Star Trek VI: The Undiscovered Country*). In 2368, Spock secretly traveled to **Romulus**, on a personal mission to further the cause of Romulan/Vulcan reunification. Spock's disappearance caused great consternation among Federation authorities, and the *Enterprise*-D was dispatched to determine his whereabouts and intentions. Spock's contact on Romulus was **Senator Pardek**, who was believed to have met Spock during the Khitomer conference in 2293. Pardek was later learned to be an agent of the conservative Romulan government, seeking to use Spock's initiative to cover an attempted Romulan invasion of Vulcan. SEE: **Sela**. Following the attempted invasion, Spock chose to remain underground on Romulus in hopes of furthering the cause of reunification. ("Unification, Parts I and II" [TNG]). Spock continued his activities in the Romulan underground, and in 2369 helped arrange the defection of Romulan **vice-proconsul M'ret** to the Federation. SEE: **N'Vek, Subcommander**. Spock indicated he believed the escape of M'ret would help establish an escape route for other Romulan dissidents who lived in fear for their lives. ("Face of the Enemy" [TNG]). Following the death of his father, Spock had one final, unexpected encounter with Sarek. Prior to his death, Sarek had mind-melded with **Jean-Luc Picard**, sharing with Picard his deepest emotions, unclouded by Vulcan logic. On Romulus, Picard allowed Spock to mind-meld with him, and Spock finally came to know of his father's love for him. ("Unification, Part II" [TNG]).

As far as we know, Spock remained on Romulus. In "Sarek" (TNG), Jean-Luc Picard noted that he had, years ago as a young lieutenant, attended the wedding of Sarek's son. Gene Roddenberry said he thought Picard was probably talking about Spock, but there is no direct evidence that Spock ever married. Picard did mention in "Unification, Part I" (TNG) that he had met Spock once before the episode, possibly at Spock's wedding? Spock's first appearance was in "The Cage" (TOS), the first pilot for the original Star Trek *series.*

spores, Omicron Ceti III. Symbiotic organism that infested some of the colonists on planet **Omicron Ceti III** in 2264. The spores thrived on **Berthold rays**, offering the colonists protection from the otherwise-deadly radiation. The spores provided perfect health and extraordinary contentment to the host, but at the cost of intellectual stagnation. The *Enterprise* crew investigated the colony in 2267 and nearly all ship's personnel also became infected. Captain James Kirk discovered that strong negative or aggressive emotions could be used to drive the spores from their hosts, and used ultrasonic signals to create such irritation in his crew. ("This Side of Paradise" [TOS]). SEE: **Kalomi, Leila; Sandoval, Elias**.

Spot. Data's pet cat, Terran *Felis domesticus,* who lived with Data on the *Enterprise-*D. Spot was quite a gourmet, as **Data** created at least seventy-four different foods for her. ("Data's Day" [TNG]). A malfunction of the ship's replicator system resulting from an errant interface experiment in 2369 caused the ship's food slots to dispense cat food. ("A Fistful of Datas" [TNG]).

SEE: **Subroutine C-47**. Commander Riker once agreed to care for Spot while Data was away at a conference for three days. Unfortunately, Spot did not care for Commander Riker, and made her dislike evident. ("Timescape" [TNG]). *Spot first appeared in "Data's Day," but didn't actually get a name until "In Theory" (TNG). In "Data's Day," Spot was a Somali cat, but in later appearances, Data's friend somehow became a common house cat. We speculate that Spot may be a shapeshifter or an unfortunate victim of a transporter malfunction.*

• **"Squire of Gothos, The."** *Original Series* episode #18. Written by Paul Schneider. Directed by Don McDougall. Stardate 2124.5. *First aired in 1967. An incredibly powerful alien life-form torments the* Enterprise *crew, but is found to be simply a small child, playing with his toys. Many fans have noted the similarity between Trelane and Q, speculating that Trelane and his parents may have been members of the Q Continuum, although this has not actually been established in an episode.* SEE: **Beta VI; Bonaparte, Napoleon; DeSalle, Lieutenant; Gothos; Jaeger, Lieutenant Karl; noncorporeal life; Quadrant 904; Ross, Yeoman Teresa; Trelane.**

Ssestar. (John Durbin). Leader of the **Selay** delegation to the **Parliament** conference of 2364. ("Lonely Among Us" [TNG]).

Stacius Trade Guild. Organization in which **Zibalian** trader **Kivas Fajo** was a member. ("The Most Toys" [TNG]).

Stakoron II. Planet in the Gamma Quadrant containing rich deposits of mizainite ore. Quark was to visit the planet in 2369, during his brief tenure as **Grand Nagus,** to negotiate for mining rights, but found it was part of a ruse devised by **Rom** and **Krax** to kill him. ("The Nagus" [DS9]).

standard orbit. Normal orbit assumed by a Federation starship above a class-M planet. *The term "standard orbit" was used as an ingenious means of allowing the captain to give a technical-sounding command when the ship entered orbit, without having to bore the viewer with tedious details of orbital inclination, apogee, perigee, and orbital period. It was initially thought that standard orbit would be geosynchronous, allowing the ship to remain stationary over a single point on a planet's surface, but several episodes have shown otherwise.*

Star Station India. Starfleet facility. *Enterprise-*D was en route for Star Station India on an urgent mission to rendezvous with a Starfleet courier but was diverted by a distress call from the *Starship* **Lantree**. ("Unnatural Selection" [TNG]).

• *Star Trek: The Original Series (TOS). The original adventures of the* **Starship Enterprise** *under the command of Captain* **James T. Kirk***. The original* Star Trek *spanned three seasons, totaling 79 episodes that first aired on the NBC-TV network from 1966-1969.* Star Trek *became a pop culture icon when, instead of vanishing after its 1969 cancellation, it experienced a dramatic rebirth in syndication, becoming more popular than ever, and leading to the* Star Trek *feature films and syndicated series.*

• *Star Trek II (series). This was a proposed weekly* Star Trek *television series that would have been produced in 1977 and would have depicted a second five-year mission of the* Enterprise *under the command of James Kirk. (Note that this is* not *the same production as the feature film* Star Trek II: The Wrath of Khan.) *The* Star Trek II *series would have been syndicated by Paramount Pictures (much as was later done for* Star Trek: The Next Generation*), but the series was canceled very shortly before it went into production. New characters on this show would have included Navigator Ilia (who would have been played by Persis Khambatta), Science Officer Xon (who would have been played by David Gautreaux), and Executive Officer Decker (who was still uncast at the time the series was canceled). The first episode, a two-hour made-for-television movie script entitled "In Thy Image," was rewritten, eventually becoming* Star Trek: The Motion Picture. *"In Thy Image" was itself based on a story outline entitled "Robots' Return," written around 1972 for Gene Roddenberry's proposed CBS series* Genesis II. *Other scripts written for the aborted* Star Trek II *series included "The Child" and "Devil's Due," both of which were later rewritten and used on* Star Trek: The Next Generation. *Photo: David Gautreaux as Science Officer Xon.*

• *Star Trek: The Motion Picture.* Screenplay by Harold Livingston. Story by Alan Dean Foster. Directed by Robert Wise. Stardate 7412.6. *Original theatrical release date: 1979. Kirk reunites his original crew to save Earth from a powerful machine life-form called V'Ger.* SEE: **AU; air tram; Amar, I.K.C.; Branch, Commander; carbon units; Chapel, Christine; Chekov, Pavel A.; Cleary; creator; Decker, Willard; Delta IV; Deltans; DiFalco, Chief; drydock;** *Enterprise, U.S.S.;* **Epsilon IX monitoring station;** *I.K.C.;* **Ilia; intermix formula; Kirk, James T.;** *kohlinar;* **Linguacode; McCoy, Leonard H.; maneuvering thrusters; NASA; Nogura, Admiral; Oath of Celibacy; Probert, Commodore; Rand, Janice; rec deck; San Francisco Yards; shuttle, Vulcan; Sonak, Commander; sonic shower; Spock; Starfleet Headquarters; thruster suit; travel pod; V'Ger;** *Voyager VI;* **Vulcan Master; Work Bee; wormhole.**

• *Star Trek II: The Wrath of Khan.* Screenplay by Jack B.

Sowards. Story by Harve Bennett and Jack B. Sowards. Directed by Nicholas Meyer. Stardate 8130.3. *Original theatrical release date: 1982. Spock is killed when genetic superman Khan escapes from imprisonment on Ceti Alpha V, commandeers the* Starship Reliant, *and uses the secret Project Genesis to win revenge on James Kirk. The story is a sequel to "Space Seed" (TOS).* SEE: **Altair VI; Beach, Mr.; Ceti Alpha V; Ceti Alpha VI; Ceti eel; Chekov, Pavel A.; dynoscanner; escape pod; Gamma Hydra; Genesis Device; gravitic mine; hyperchannel; Joachim; Khan Noonien Singh; Kirk, James T.; Klingon battle cruiser; Klingon Neutral Zone;** *Kobayashi Maru* **scenario;** *Kobayashi Maru;* *K't'inga-*class battle cruiser; **Kyle, Mr.; Marcus, Dr. Carol; Marcus, Dr. David; McGivers, Marla; Mutara Nebula; Mutara Sector; photon torpedo; preanimate matter; prefix code; Preston, Peter; Project Genesis; Regula I Space Laboratory; Regula;** *Reliant, U.S.S.;* **retina scan; Retnax V; Romulan Ale; Saavik; Spock; Starfleet Corps of Engineers; Starfleet General Orders and Regulations;** *Tale of Two Cities, A;* **Terrell, Captain Clark.**

• *Star Trek III: The Search for Spock.* Written by Harve Bennett. Directed by Leonard Nimoy. Stardate 8210.3. *Original theatrical release date: 1984. Kirk jeopardizes his career by stealing the* Enterprise *in an attempt to rescue Spock's body and soul.* SEE: **Altair water; cloaking device, Klingon; destruct sequence;** *d'k tahg;* *Enterprise, U.S.S.;* **Esteban, Captain J. T.;** *Excelsior, U.S.S.; fal-tor-pan;* **flight recorder; Genesis Planet; "Great Experiment, The";** *Grissom, U.S.S.; katra;* **kellicam; Kirk, James T.; Klingon Bird-of-Prey; Kruge, Commander; Lexorin; Maltz; Marcus, Dr. David;** *Merchantman;* **"Miracle Worker"; Morrow, Admiral; Mutara Sector;** *Pon farr;* **Project Genesis; protomatter;** *Qapla';* **Saavik; Sarek; Seleya, Mount; Skon; Solkar; Spacedock; Spock; Styles, Captain; T'Lar; terminium; "Tiny"; transwarp drive; Uhura; Valkris.**

• *Star Trek IV: The Voyage Home.* Story by Leonard Nimoy & Harve Bennett. Screenplay by Steve Meerson & Peter Krikes and Harve Bennett & Nicholas Meyer. Directed by Leonard Nimoy. Stardate 8390. *Original theatrical release date: 1986. Kirk*

and company voyage back in time to San Francisco in 1986 to bring two humpback whales back to the future. SEE: **Alameda; Amanda; Ambassador, Klingon; Andorians; Bering Sea;** *Bounty, H.M.S.;* **Briggs, Bob; Cartwright, Admiral; Cetacean Institute;** *Challenger;* **Chapel, Christine; Chekov, Pavel A.; dilithium;** *Enterprise, U.S.S.* **(aircraft carrier);** *Enterprise-A, U.S.S.;* **Federation Council President; Federation Council; George and Gracie; Huey 204; humpback whale; "I Hate You"; Kiri-kin-tha's First Law of Metaphysics; Kirk, James T.; Macintosh;** *Megaptera Novaeangliae;* **Mercy Hospital; Nichols, Dr.; Plexicorp; Probe, the; Rand, Janice; Robbins, Harold; Rogerson, Commander; Saavik;** *Saratoga, U.S.S.;* **Sarek; slingshot effect; Spock; Sulu, Hikaru; Susann, Jacqueline; Tellarites;**

T'plana-Hath; Taylor, Dr. Gillian; transparent aluminum; United Federation of Planets; whale song; yominium sulfide; *Yorktown, U.S.S.*

• *Star Trek V: The Final Frontier.* Screenplay by David Loughery. Story by William Shatner, Harve Bennett, David Loughery. Directed by William Shatner. Stardate 8454.1. *Original theatrical release date: 1989. Spock's half-brother, Sybok, hijacks the* Enterprise-A *to pursue his visions of God at the center of the galaxy.* SEE: **Amanda; beans; Bennett, Admiral Robert;** *Copernicus;* **Dar, Caithlin; El Capitan;** *Enterprise-A, U.S.S.; Galileo 5;* **Great Barrier, the; J'Onn; Kirk, James T.; Klaa, Captain; Koord, General; Masefield, John; McCoy, David; McCoy, Leonard H.; "Moon Over Rigel VII"; Nimbus III; Paradise City;** *Pioneer X;* **Qui'Tu; Sarek; Sha Ka Ree; Spock; Sybok; Talbot, St. John; Vixis; Vorta Vor; Vulcan harp; Yosemite National Park.**

• *Star Trek VI: The Undiscovered Country.* Story by Leonard Nimoy and Lawrence Konner & Mark Rosenthal. Screenplay by Nicholas Meyer & Denny Martin Flinn. Directed by Nicholas Meyer. Stardate 9521.6. *Original theatrical release date: 1991. An historic Klingon peace initiative is nearly thwarted when Klingon chancellor Gorkon is assassinated, and Kirk and McCoy are wrongly convicted of his murder. This was intended as the last mission of the original* Enterprise *crew from the first* Star Trek *series.* SEE: **Ambassador, Klingon; Azetbur; Beta Quadrant; Bird-of-Prey, Klingon; Burke, Yeoman; Camp Khitomer; Cartwright, Admiral; chameloid; chancellor; Chang, General; cloaking device, Klingon; Dax;** *Enterprise-A, U.S.S.; Excelsior, U.S.S.;* **Federation Council President; Gorkon, Chancellor; gravitational unit; gravity boots; Kerla, Brigadier; Khitomer; Kirk, James T.; Klaa, Captain; Klingon Empire; Klingon Homeworld; Klingons; Klingon Neutral Zone;** *Kronos One;* **Kronos; magnetic boots; Martia; McCoy, Dr. Leonard H.; Morska; Nanclus; neutron radiation; Operation Retrieve; Paris; plasma; Praxis; Qo'noS; Rand, Janice; Romulan Ale; Rura Penthe; Samno, Yeoman; Sarek; Scott, Montgomery; Spock; subspace shock wave; Sulu, Hikaru; Tiberian bats; torpedo bay; "undiscovered country, the"; Uhura; United Federation of Planets; Valeris; Valtane, Mr.; West, Colonel; Worf, Colonel.**

• *Star Trek: The Next Generation (TNG). Produced in 1987-1994, the made-for-syndication story of the* **Starship Enterprise-D** *under the command of Captain* **Jean-Luc Picard.** *The series ran for seven seasons, totalling 178 episodes. At this writing, a motion picture sequel to these adventures was in preparation.*

• *Star Trek: Deep Space Nine (DS9). Produced from 1992, the syndicated series about a group of Starfleet officers and Bajoran nationals on the former Cardassian space station, Deep Space 9, commanded by* **Benjamin Sisko.**

• *Star Trek: Voyager. In preliminary pre-production as this encyclopedia was being completed, this syndicated series was intended to go into production shortly after the last* Star Trek: The Next Generation *episode for airing in early 1995.*

Starbase 2. Facility that Spock suggested Dr. Janice Lester should be taken to for diagnosis of her medical condition instead of the Benecia Colony. ("Turnabout Intruder" [TOS]).

Starbase 4. Starbase where the *Enterprise* dropped off the children from the **Starnes Expedition** to planet **Triacus** in 2268. ("And the Children Shall Lead" [TOS]). A shuttlecraft was stolen by **Lokai** from Starbase 4 in 2268, two weeks before being recovered by the *Enterprise*. ("Let That Be Your Last Battlefield" [TOS]).

Starbase 6. Starbase where the *U.S.S. Enterprise* crew was scheduled for rest and relaxation in 2268. Their vacation was cut short by an emergency call from Starfleet Command to divert to **Sector 39J** and investigate the disappearance of the *Starship Intrepid*. ("The Immunity Syndrome" [TOS]).

Starbase 9. The *Enterprise* was en route to Starbase 9 for resupply in 2267 when near-collision with a **black star** of high gravitational attraction propelled the ship into a time warp that sent the ship back to the year 1968. ("Tomorrow is Yesterday" [TOS]). Closest base to planet **Pyris VII** which the Enterprise visited in 2267. ("Catspaw" [TOS]). SEE: **Korob; Sylvia.**

Starbase 10. Destination of the *Enterprise* after leaving **Deneva** in 2267. ("Operation— Annihilate!" [TOS]).

Starbase 10. Starbase where **Commodore Stocker** was to assume command in 2267. ("The Deadly Years" [TOS]).

Starbase 11. Federation starbase commanded by **Commodore Stone** in 2266 when this base was the site of Kirk's court-martial for the death of **Commander Ben Finney**. ("Court Martial" [TOS]). The *Enterprise* later returned to Starbase 11, then under the

command of **José Mendez**, when Spock abducted Captain **Christopher Pike** to live among the **Talosians**. ("The Menagerie, Parts I and II" [TOS]).

Starbase 12. Command base in the Gamma 400 star system and where Kirk set course with the sleeper ship, *S.S. Botany Bay* in tow. ("Space Seed" [TOS]). It was the closest starbase to planet **Pollux IV**, which the *Enterprise* visited in 2267. ("Who Mourns for Adonais?" [TOS]). The base was evacuated for two days in late 2364, apparently because key Starfleet officials were under the control of the extragalactic alien intelligence that attempted to infiltrate Starfleet Command in that year. ("Conspiracy" [TNG]). The *Enterprise*-D was scheduled for a week's worth of maintenance overhaul there following her mission on **Gemaris V** in 2366. ("Captain's Holiday" [TNG]). Starbase 12 was commanded by **Admiral Uttan Narsu** back in 2167 at the time the *U.S.S. Essex* was lost at planet **Mab-Bu VI**. ("Power Play" [TNG]).

Starbase 14. Starfleet facility that sent a message to the *Enterprise*-D in 2364 concerning the **Anchilles fever** out-

break on planet **Styris IV**. ("Code of Honor" [TNG]).

Starbase 23. Federation starbase. Following her temporary removal from duty in 2369, Dr. Beverly Crusher was scheduled to arrive by shuttlecraft at Starbase 23. From there, she would take a transport to Earth. ("Suspicions" [TNG]).

Starbase 24. Starfleet facility near **Khitomer**. Young Worf's nursemaid, **Kahlest** was taken there for treatment of her injuries following her rescue from Khitomer in 2346. ("Sins of the Father" [TNG], "Redemption, Part I" [TNG]).

Starbase 27. Starbase to which Kirk was ordered to transport the surviving colonists from planet **Omicron Ceti III** in 2267. ("This Side of Paradise"[TOS]).

Starbase 36. A scheduled stop for the *Enterprise*-D in late 2367. Dr. Beverly Crusher suggested that Commander La Forge have his VISOR checked for malfunctions during the stopover at Starbase 36. ("The Mind's Eye" [TNG]).

Starbase 39-Sierra. Facility approximately 5 days' travel from the **Romulan Neutral Zone**. ("The Neutral Zone" [TNG]).

Starbase 67. Federation starbase. Counselor Troi and Commander La Forge were ordered by the **Ktarians** to travel to this base and distribute the addictive **Ktarian game** to all the starships docked there. ("The Game" [TNG]).

Starbase 73. Facility at which the *Enterprise*-D received mission orders to investigate a distress signal detected from the **Ficus Sector**. Starbase 73 was commanded by **Admiral Moore.** ("Up the Long Ladder" [TNG]). **Worf** delivered his son, **Alexander Rozhenko**, to Starbase 73 in 2367. Worf's adoptive parents met them there, having agreed to accept custody of Alexander after the death of K'Ehleyr. ("Reunion" [TNG]).

Starbase 74. Massive orbital facility at planet Tarsas III. ("11001001" [TNG]). The *Enterprise*-D underwent a computer systems upgrade there in 2364, although the operation was interrupted when a group of **Bynar** technicians attempted to hijack the ship to

save their planet. Starbase 74 was commanded by **Commander Orfil Quinteros.** ("11001001" [TNG]). *Starbase 74 miniature shots were a partial re-use of some visual effects elements originally shot for Star Trek III by Industrial Light and Magic. However, it's been pointed out that Starbase 74 must be a substantially larger structure than Spacedock as seen in Star Trek III, since the Galaxy-class Enterprise-D is a much larger ship than the original Constitution-class ship. The shot of the Enterprise-D actually docked inside the station was a matte painting designed by Andy Probert.*

Starbase 82. Federation starbase. The *Enterprise*-D delivered a **Ktarian** vessel into Starfleet custody at Starbase 82 in 2368. ("The Game" [TNG]).

Starbase 83. The *Enterprise*-D traveled to this facility when Q returned the ship to Federation space after first contact with the **Borg**. ("Q Who?" [TNG]).

Starbase 97. Federation starbase commanded by Admiral Mitchell. Commander Calvin Hutchinson served for some time there, prior to his assignment to **Arkaria Base.** ("Starship Mine" [TNG]).

Starbase 103. Facility located a short distance from planet **Minos**. After ordering a saucer separation maneuver at Minos, Geordi La Forge instructed **Engineer Logan** to proceed to Starbase 103. ("The Arsenal of Freedom" [TNG]). *Of course, even if Starbase 103 was only a few light-years from Minos, it's unclear as to what purpose there might have been in heading toward the base since the saucer section had no warp-drive capability.*

Starbase 105. In the alternate history created when the **Enterprise-C** vanished from its "proper" time in 2344, this base was mentioned as the place where the *Enterprise*-C could have been escorted. ("Yesterday's *Enterprise*" [TNG]).

Starbase 117. A Federation starbase. The *Enterprise*-D sent two members of the **Ferengi Trade Mission** there, following their part in an accident that befell Kriosian **ambassador Briam** in 2368. ("The Perfect Mate" [TNG]).

Starbase 118. Location where the *Enterprise*-D picked up several new crew members in 2369. ("A Fistful of Datas" [TNG]).

Starbase 123. Detected two *D'deridex*-class Romulan Warbirds on an intercept course with **Tin Man** just prior to contact with that life-form in 2366. ("Tin Man" [TNG]).

Starbase 133. The *Enterprise*-D docked at this starbase in early 2367 for scheduled crew rotation. **Dr. Dalen Quaice** was posted at Starbase 133 prior to his retirement to his homeworld of Kenda II. ("Remember Me" [TNG]). The destination of the *Enterprise*-D after its mission at planet **Delta Rana IV**. ("The Survivors" [TNG]).

Starbase 152. The *Enterprise*-D traveled there for inspection and repairs following contact with **Tin Man** in 2366. The *Enterprise*-D had been seriously damaged in that encounter. ("Tin Man" [TNG]).

Starbase 153. Facility from which special Federation emissary **K'Ehleyr** was launched, inside of a modified class-8 probe, for a critical rendezvous with the *Enterprise*-D in 2365. ("The Emissary" [TNG]).

Starbase 157. Federation starbase that received a distress signal from the *U.S.S. Lalo* after it suffered an attack from a **Borg** vessel in 2366. ("The Best of Both Worlds, Part I" [TNG]).

Starbase 173. Space station facility located in Sector 23, near the **Romulan Neutral Zone**, site of legal proceedings establishing the sentience of the android **Data**. Captain **Phillipa Louvois** served on Starbase 173. ("The Measure of a Man" [TNG]). Also at Starbase 173, engineering officer **Ensign Sonya Gomez** was among several new crew personnel transferred to the *Enterprise*-D. ("Q Who?" [TNG]). *Starbase 173 was a re-use of the **Regula 1** space station model originally seen in* Star Trek II: The Wrath of Khan.

Starbase 179. Located on a planetary surface. *Enterprise*-D visited this facility on stardate 42506 in 2365 for personnel rotation and to pick up Ensign **Mendon** as part of an **Officer Exchange Program**. ("A Matter of Honor" [TNG]).

Starbase 185. Starfleet facility that was nearest to the *Enterprise*-D after **Q** transported the vessel across the galaxy to **System J-25**. Data estimated the starbase was some two years, seven months away for the ship at maximum warp. ("Q Who?" [TNG]).

Starbase 200. Destination of the *Starship Enterprise* in 2267 when an unexplained time-warp distortion was encountered. This distortion caused complete disruption of normal magnetic and gravimetric fields in every quadrant of the galaxy. ("The Alternative Factor" [TOS]). SEE: **Lazarus**. *During the original* Star Trek *series, Starfleet supposedly had only 17 starbases. This was one of the few starbases in the original show that broke that rule.*

Starbase 211. The *U.S.S. Phoenix* was escorted by the *Enterprise*-D to Starbase 211 following **Captain Benjamin Maxwell**'s unauthorized attack in Cardassian space in 2367. ("The Wounded" [TNG]).

Starbase 212. Located near the Klingon border. Picard requested that Starbase 212 help search for a shuttlecraft missing from **Relay Station 47** in 2369. **Lieutenant Aquiel Uhnari** went there for reassignment after being cleared of criminal charges in that incident, found to have been caused by a **coalescent organism**. ("Aquiel" [TNG]).

Starbase 214. Federation starbase where **Professor Berlinghoff Rasmussen** was deposited following his arrest in 2368. ("A Matter of Time" [TNG]).

Starbase 218. The *Enterprise*-D was en route to Starbase 218 in 2368 when it encountered the ancient **Kataan probe**. ("The Inner Light" [TNG]). In 2369, the *Enterprise*-D picked up new crew members at Starbase 218 including Lieutenant Commander **Neela Daren**. ("Lessons" [TNG]).

Starbase 220. Federation starbase where the *Enterprise*-D intended to tow the ill-fated *Brattain* when that ship was found disabled at a **Tyken's Rift**. Following its own escape from the Tyken's Rift, Data piloted the *Enterprise*-D to Starbase 220. ("Night Terrors" [TNG]).

Starbase 234. Federation starbase from which Captain Jean-Luc Picard launched his armada to blockade Romulan forces covertly supplying the **Duras** family during the **Klingon civil war** in 2368. Picard's task force was formed by commandeering all ships in the base's spacedock, along with all ships within one day's travel of Starbase 234. ("Redemption, Part II" [TNG]). The *Enterprise*-D met **Admiral Brackett** at Starbase 234 before proceeding with an investigation into the disappearance of Ambassador **Spock** in 2368. ("Unification, Part I" [TNG]).

Starbase 260. Destination of the *Enterprise*-D after its escape from the **Mar Oscura** nebula in 2367. ("In Theory" [TNG]).

Starbase 301. Federation starbase where the *Enterprise*-D traveled following a brief takeover by a **Satarran** operative. ("Conundrum" [TNG]).

Starbase 313. A Federation starbase visited by the *Enterprise*-D in 2367. The ship picked up a shipment of scientific equipment to transport to the Guernica system. **Dr. Leah Brahms** also came aboard the *Enterprise*-D during this stopover. ("Galaxy's Child" [TNG]).

Starbase 324. Admiral **J. P. Hanson** returned to this Federation starbase after receiving confirmation of the encroachment of the **Borg** into Federation space. ("The Best of Both Worlds, Part I" [TNG]).

Starbase 336. Station that detected an automated subspace radio transmission in 2365 from Klingon sleeper ship *T'Ong*, a matter of great concern because the ship that had been launched at a time when the Klingon Empire and the Federation were still at war. ("The Emissary" [TNG]).

Starbase 343. Following the completion of its mission with the **Acamarians**, the *Enterprise*-D went to Starbase 343 to take on medical supplies for the Alpha Leonis system. ("The Vengeance Factor" [TNG]).

Starbase 416. Destination of the *Enterprise*-D after leaving **Ogus II** because of a medical emergency in 2367. ("Brothers" [TNG]).

Starbase 440. A Federation starbase. An **Ullian** delegation was to disembark the *Enterprise*-D at this starbase in order to secure transportation to their homeworld. Captain Picard chose instead to deliver the Ullians to their world on the *Enterprise*-D. ("Violations" [TNG]).

Starbase 514. A Federation starbase. The **S.S. Vico** was assigned out of this base at the time of its destruction in 2368. ("Hero Worship" [TNG]).

Starbase 515. Starfleet facility located in the **Scylla Sector**, near the **Epsilon IX** Sector. Captain Picard and Wesley Crusher traveled there by shuttle in 2365, when Picard underwent a **cardiac replacement** procedure for his bionic heart and Wesley took Academy tests. ("Samaritan Snare" [TNG]). *The exterior of Starbase 515 was a re-use of the matte painting cityscape from "Angel One" (TNG).*

Starbase 718. Location of an emergency conference that Picard attended in late 2364 to discuss the possibility of a new **Romulan** incursion. The meeting was triggered by the loss of communications with starbases and outposts near the Romulan Neutral Zone, although this was later believed to be due to Borg activity. This was shortly before the Romulans ended a 53-year period of isolationism that had begun in 2311. ("The Neutral Zone" [TNG]). *After this episode was made, it was decided that starbase numbers shouldn't go much higher than 500.*

Starbase Earhart. Also known as Farspace Starbase Earhart. Starfleet facility where Ensign **Jean-Luc Picard** spent some time awaiting his first assignment after graduating from the Academy. Picard picked a fight with three **Nausicaans** at the base's **Bonestell Recreation Facility**, and was nearly killed when one of them stabbed him through the heart. ("Samaritan Snare" [TNG], "Tapestry" [TNG]). *Named for aviation pioneer Amelia Earhart (1898-1937).*

Starbase G-6. Starfleet facility near planet Betazed from which Counselor Troi was able to visit her home via shuttlecraft. Starbase G-6 was also located near the **Sigma III Solar System**, which suffered a serious mining accident in 2364. ("Hide and "Q" [TNG]).

Starbase Lya III. Starfleet command base where **Admiral Haden** was stationed. Haden advised Jean-Luc Picard on the handling of the Romulan defector **Alidar Jarok** in 2366, although a two-hour transmission delay due to the distance to the Neutral Zone made it impossible for Haden to give timely advice. ("The Defector" [TNG]). The *Enterprise*-D headed to Starbase Lya III following its mission to **Angosia III**. ("The Hunted" [TNG]).

Starbase Montgomery. Planetside facility at which the *Enterprise*-D underwent engineering consultations on stardate 42686. ("The Icarus Factor" [TNG]).

starboard. Ancient nautical term referring to the right side of a ship, as opposed to the port (left) side.

stardate. Timekeeping system used to provide a standard galactic temporal reference, compensating for relativistic time dilation, warp-speed displacement, and other peculiarities of interstellar space travel. *To those interested in the minutiae of stardate computation and a lot of other cool stuff about* Star Trek*, we shamelessly refer you to Appendix D in our book,* Star Trek Chronology: The History of the Future*, by Michael Okuda and Denise Okuda, also published by Pocket Books.*

stardrifter. Exotic beverage served at **Quark's bar**. One of Quark's customers ordered a stardrifter, which Quark tried to obtain from an unauthorized food replicator during the **aphasia virus** quarantine on Deep Space 9 in 2369. Kira Nerys once indulged, too. ("Babel" [DS9], "The Storyteller" [DS9]).

stardrive section. The secondary (engineering) hull and outboard warp nacelles of many types of Federation starships. ("Encounter at Farpoint, Part I" [TNG]). SEE: **saucer module**.

Starfleet Academy marathon. Much as in ancient Greece on Earth, a 40-kilometer footrace held among Starfleet cadets. In 2323, cadet **Jean-Luc Picard** became the only freshman to win the marathon, passing four upperclassmen on the last hill on Danula II. ("The Best of Both Worlds, Part II" [TNG]).

Starfleet Academy. Training facility for Starfleet personnel located at the Presidio of San Francisco on Earth. Established in 2161, the Academy is a four-year institution. The motto of Starfleet Academy is "ex astris, scientia," meaning "from the stars, knowledge."

In 2368, Captain Picard was asked to deliver the commencement address for that year's Academy graduates. The occasion was marred by the loss of a cadet in an accident shortly before commencement. ("The First Duty" [TNG]). SEE: **Academy Flight Range; Albert, Joshua; Crusher, Wesley; Finnegan; Kirk, James T.; Kolvoord Starburst; Locarno, Cadet First Class Nicholas; Mitchell, Gary.** *The motto of Starfleet Academy is a paraphrase of a quote on the Apollo 13 mission patch. The Academy emblem is based on a design by Joe Senna. The Academy campus grounds seen in "The First Duty" (TNG) were a combination of location filming at the Tillman Water Reclamation plant in Van Nuys and a matte painting by Illusion Arts.*

Starfleet Command. Operating authority for the interstellar scientific, exploratory, and defensive agency of the United Federation of Planets. ("Court Martial" [TOS]). The primary control hub was located in San Francisco on Earth, but other

command facilities were located in various **starbases** throughout Federation space. Starfleet Command stayed in touch with its starships by means of a subspace radio communications network, but even with this faster-than-light medium, interstellar space is so vast that it was not uncommon for ships on the frontier to be out of touch. As a result, starship captains were frequently granted broad discretionary powers to interpret Federation policy in the absence of immediate instructions from Starfleet Command. *The term Starfleet Command was first used in the episode "Court Martial" (TOS). SEE: United Earth Space Probe Agency.*

Starfleet Corps of Engineers. Special projects division of Starfleet responsible for the construction of Dr. Marcus's underground laboratory complex at the asteroid **Regula** at which the second phase of **Project Genesis** was conducted. (*Star Trek II: The Wrath of Khan*).

Starfleet Cybernetics Journal. Scientific publication on artificial intelligence and advanced computer systems. Dr. Julian Bashir, upon meeting Data in 2369, hoped to author a paper for the journal on the phenomenon of Data's dreams. ("Birthright, Part I" [TNG]).

Starfleet Emergency Medical course. Instructional class offered to Starfleet personnel. It prepared them to render aid in many medical emergencies, including childbirth, should licensed personnel not be available. Worf's attendance in this course paid off when he assisted in the birth of **Molly O'Brien** in 2368. ("Disaster" [TNG]).

Starfleet General Orders and Regulations.

General Order 1: The **Prime Directive**, prohibiting interference in the normal development of any society.

General Order 7: Forbids contact with planet **Talos IV**. As of 2267, the only death penalty left on the books. Spock was acquitted of violating this order after kidnapping **Christopher Pike** to live among the **Talosians**. ("The Menagerie, Parts I and II" [TOS]).

General Order 12: Requires adequate precautions be taken when when approached by a spacecraft with which contact has not been made. (*Star Trek II: The Wrath of Khan*).

General Order 15: Regulation that stated, in part, "No flag officer shall beam into a hazardous area without armed escort." Saavik reminded Kirk of the order prior to his beaming to the **Regula I Space Laboratory**. (*Star Trek II*).

General Order 24: A command to destroy the surface of a planet unless the order is countermanded within a specified period. Kirk invoked General Order 24 at planet **Eminiar VII** in an effort to force planetary authorities to enter peace talks with neighboring planet **Vendikar**. ("A Taste of Armageddon" [TOS]).

Regulation 46A: "If transmissions are being monitored during battle, no uncoded messages on an open channel." (*Star Trek II: The Wrath of Khan*).

Order 104, Section B: Starfleet order that deals with chain of command. Commodore Matt Decker quoted regulation 104-B to Spock when taking command of the *Enterprise* in 2267. ("The Doomsday Machine" [TOS]).

Order 104, Section C: Starfleet regulation that states the **chief medical officer** may relieve a commander of duty if he or she is mentally or physically unfit. The physician would have to back up this claim with the results of a physical examination. ("The Doomsday Machine" [TOS]).

Regulation 42/15: Engineering procedure relating to impulse engines, entitled "Pressure Variances in the Impulse Reaction Chamber Tank Storage." **Montgomery Scott** wrote this particular regulation for Starfleet, but many years later admitted that it was a wee bit conservative. ("Relics" [TNG]).

Starfleet Headquarters. Part of Starfleet Command, located in San Francisco on Earth. The facility includes a large aerial tram station. (*Star Trek: The Motion Picture*). An alien intelligence of unknown origin attempted to gain control of Starfleet by placing neural parasites into the bodies of numerous officers at Starfleet Headquarters and elsewhere. This conspiracy was uncovered by **Admiral Norah Satie** ("The Drumhead" [TNG]), and was ended when Captain Picard and

Commander Riker successfully destroyed the "mother" alien which was inhabiting the body of Commander **Dexter Remmick** ("Conspiracy" [TNG]). *Starfleet Headquarters was seen as several different matte paintings and miniature shots in* Star Trek: The Motion Picture, Star Trek IV: The Voyage Home, *and* Star Trek VI: The Undiscovered Country. *The conference room interior scenes in* Star Trek VI *were filmed at the First Presbyterian Church of Hollywood.*

Starfleet insignia. SEE: **insignia, Starfleet**.

Starfleet monitor stations. In the alternate timeline created when the ***Enterprise*-C** vanished from its "proper" place in 2344, Starfleet Monitor Stations reported that Klingon battle cruisers were moving toward the *Enterprise*-D. ("Yesterday's Enterprise" [TNG]).

Starfleet uniforms. SEE: **uniforms, Starfleet**.

Starfleet. Deep-space exploratory, scientific, diplomatic, and defensive agency of the **United Federation of Planets**. Starfleet was chartered by the Federation in 2161 with a mission to "boldly go where no man has gone before." The most visible part of the Starfleet is its interstellar **starships**. Additionally, Starfleet maintains a far-flung network of **starbases** to support deep-space operations.

*Alas, there is no definitive list of all of Starfleet's ships or vessel types. The reason is that our producers need to keep the list somewhat vague in order to allow future episodes and movies to have both old and new ships as stories, not yet written, may require. (SEE: **starships** for a partial listing and some diagrams.)*

Stargazer, U.S.S. Federation starship, ***Constellation*class**, registry number NCC-2893. The *Stargazer* was under the command of Captain **Jean-Luc Picard** from 2333-2355 on a historic mission of deep-space exploration, prior to his assignment to the *Enterprise*-

D. Lieutenant Jean-Luc Picard was a bridge officer on the *Stargazer* when its captain was killed. Picard took command of the bridge and was later offered command of the ship for his actions. ("Tapestry" [TNG]) During an exploratory mission to **Sector 21503**, the *Stargazer* was attacked by **Cardassian** forces and barely escaped. ("The Wounded" [TNG]). During Picard's command, the *Stargazer* visited planet **Chalna** in 2354. ("Allegiance" [TNG]). The starship was destroyed near the **Zeta Maxia star system** by what was later learned to be a Ferengi vessel. Years later, the Ferengi Bok returned the hulk of the *Stargazer* to Picard as part of a plot to discredit Picard for what Bok believed to be Picard's part in his son's death. ("The Battle" [TNG]). Following the loss of the

Stargazer in 2355, Picard was court-martialed per standard Starfleet procedure, but cleared of wrong-doing. The prosecutor in the case was **Phillipa Louvois**, with whom Picard had been romantically involved. ("The Measure of a Man" [TNG]). SEE: ***Constellation*-class starship; Maxia, Battle of.** *The* Stargazer *was designed by Andrew Probert and Rick Sternbach. The miniature was built by Greg Jein. A smaller model of the* Stargazer *was on display in Captain Picard's ready room aboard the* Enterprise-D. *The dedication plaque on the bridge of the* Stargazer *bore the motto, devised by episode writer Herb Wright, "To bring light into the darkness."*

Starnes Expedition. Party of Federation explorers led by **Professor Starnes**, sent to survey planet **Triacus** in 2268. An entity known as the **Gorgan** drove the adult members of the expedition to commit mass suicide by ingesting **cyalodin**. In the aftermath of the tragedy, the children, suffering from **lacunar amnesia**, were controlled by the Gorgan, who induced them to commandeer the *Starship Enterprise*. The children were later taken to Starbase 4. ("And the Children Shall Lead" [TOS]).

Starnes, Professor. (James Wellman). Leader of the **Starnes Expedition** to planet **Triacus** who was driven to suicide in 2268 by the evil **Gorgan**. Starnes was amazed how unaffected their children (including his son, **Tommy Starnes**) were by the increased level of anxiety from an unseen force that was influencing the adult members of the party. This anxiety, later found to be the work of the Gorgan, eventually culminated in mass suicide of the adult members of the group. ("And the Children Shall Lead" [TOS]).

Starnes, Tommy. (Craig Hundley). One of the surviving children of the **Starnes Expedition** whose parents committed suicide on planet **Triacus** in 2268. In the aftermath of the tragedy, young Starnes was controlled by the **Gorgan**. ("And the Children Shall Lead" [TOS]). *Craig Hundley also played Peter Kirk in "Operation: Annihilate!" (TOS). Hundley became a musician who composed some incidental music for* Star Trek III: The Search for Spock.

"Starry Night, The." Famous 19th-century oil painting by Earth artist Vincent van Gogh (1853-1890). The painting was in the personal collection of **Zibalian** trader **Kivas Fajo**, at least until Fajo's collection was confiscated upon his arrest in 2366. ("The Most Toys" [TNG]).

stars. SEE: **planets, stars, and other celestial objects**.

• **"Starship Mine."** *Next Generation episode #144. Written by Morgan Gendel. Directed by Cliff Bole. Stardate 46682.4. First aired in 1993. Terrorists seize the* Enterprise-D *in an attempt to steal trilithium resin. SEE:* **Arkaria Base; Arkarian water fowl; baryon particles; baryon sweep; Conklin, Captain; Devor; Edwell, Captain; field diverters; Gaspar VII; Hutchinson, Commander Calvin; Kelsey; Kiros;** *Magellan, U.S.S.;* **Mitchell, Admiral; Neil; optical transducer; ornithology; Orton, Mr.; Pomet; Remmler Array; saddle; Satler; Security Access Code; Starbase 97; trilithium resin; Tyrellia.**

starships. Interstellar spacecraft capable of faster-than-light travel using warp drive. Perhaps the most famous starships in Federation history were the *Starships Enterprise*. SEE: **class; *Constitution*-class starship; Excelsior-class starship; *Galaxy*-class starship; Miranda-class starship; NCC; Starfleet; warp drive**. SEE also chart beginning on page 318.

Illustrations (to approximate scale):

1) Excelsior-*class starship. The third*Starship Enterprise *probably belonged to this class, as did numerous other ships.*

2) Refit Constitution-*class* U.S.S. Enterprise.

*3) Original configuration of the*Constitution-*class starship, including the original* U.S.S. Enterprise.

4) Constellation-*class starship* U.S.S. Stargazer, *also seen as the* U.S.S. Victory *and the* U.S.S. Hathaway.

5) Miranda-*class starship* U.S.S. Reliant, *later modified to represent other ships of this class.*

6) Vulcan warp shuttle.

7) Conjecutral design for S.S. Valiant, *the ship that first explored beyond the edge of the galaxy.*

*8) Conjectural design for*Daedalus-*class* U.S.S. Essex, *as well as for the* U.S.S. Horizon *and the* U.S.S. Valiant.

9) Oberth-*class starship, first seen as the*U.S.S. Grissom, *later seen as a variety of science vessels.*

10) U.S.S. Saratoga, *a variant on the* Miranda-*class starship, as seen in "Emissary, Part I" (DS9).*

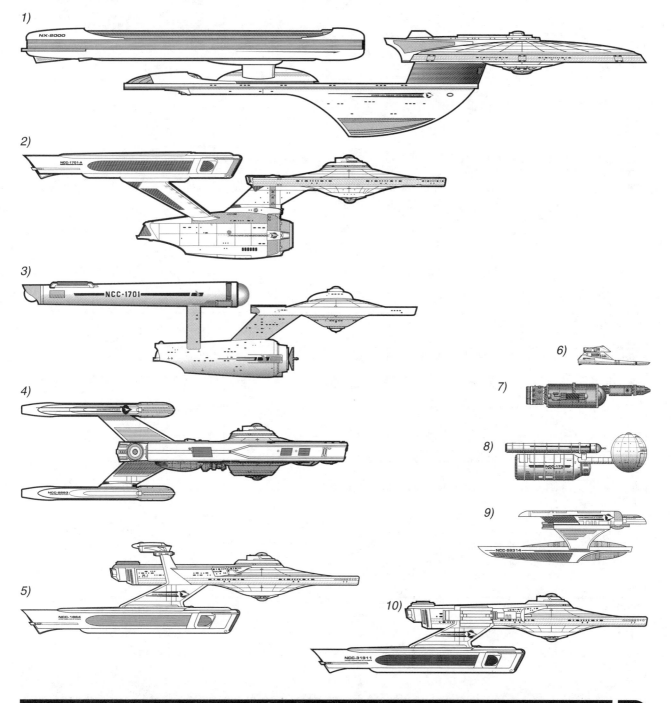

1)

2)

3)

4)

5)

6)

7)

8)

9)

10)

1) Nebula-class starship U.S.S. Endeavour, originally seen with a different upper sensor pod as the U.S.S. Phoenix. 2) Galaxy-class starship U.S.S. Enterprise-D. 3) Ambassador-class starship U.S.S. Enterprise-C, also seen as the U.S.S. Excalibur.

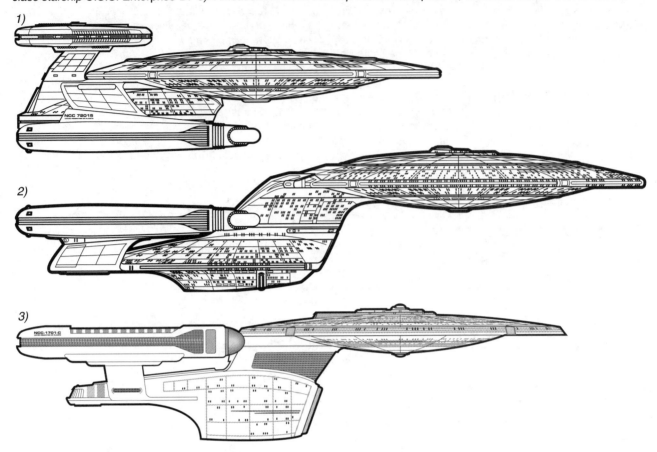

Starship name	Description	Registry number	Class	Episode or film
Adelphi, U.S.S.	Conducted disastrous first contact with planet Ghorusda	NCC-26849	*Ambassador*	"Tin Man" (TNG)
Agamemnon, U.S.S.	Part of a task force for the expected Borg invasion of 2369	NCC-11638	*Apollo*	"Descent" (TNG)
Ajax, U.S.S.	Corey Zweller's first ship assignment following graduation in 2327; Kosinski tested experimental warp-drive upgrade in 2364	NCC-11574	*Apollo*	"Tapestry" (TNG), "Where No One has Gone Before" (TNG)
Akagi, U.S.S.	Part of Picard's armada at the Romulan Neutral Zone during the Klingon civil war	NCC-62158	*Rigel*	"Redemption, Part II" (TNG)
Antares, U.S.S.	Rescued young Charles Evans from planet Thasus, destroyed by Evans' psychokinetic powers		*Antares*	"Charlie X" (TOS)
Archon, U.S.S.	Destroyed in 2167 at planet Beta III by the computer Landru	NCC-189	*Daedalus*	"Return of the Archons" (TOS)
Arcos, U.S.S.	Suffered a warp containment breach near planet Turkana IV; crew was captured by members off the Alliance	NCC-6237	*Deneva*	"Legacy" (TNG)
Aries, U.S.S.	Riker turned down a chance to command this ship in 2365; ship from which Emilita Mendez stole shuttlepod Cousteau to return to planet Tarchannen III	NCC-45167	*Renaissance*	"The Icarus Factor" (TNG), "Identity Crisis" (TNG)

(Continued on next page.)

(Continued from previous page.)

Starship name	Description	Registry number	Class	Episode or film
Berlin, U.S.S.	Answered distress call from Federation outpost near Romulan Neutral Zone	NCC-14232	Excelsior	"Angel One" (TNG)
Bozeman, U.S.S.	Trapped for 80 years in a temporal causality loop near Typhon Expanse; commanded by Captain Bateson	NCC-1941	Soyuz	"Cause and Effect" (TNG)
Bradbury, U.S.S.	Was scheduled to transport Wesley Crusher to Starfleet Academy	NX-72307	Bradbury	"Ménage à Troi" (TNG)
Brattain, U.S.S.	Ship trapped in the Tyken's Rift where all but one crew member died from lack of REM sleep	NCC-21166	Miranda	"Night Terrors" (TNG)
Cairo, U.S.S.	Transported Vice-Admiral Nechayev to Enterprise-D in 2369	NCC-42136	Excelsior	"Chain of Command, Part I" (TNG)
Carolina, U.S.S.	Purported source of a distress call to Enterprise; the message was actually faked by the Klingons to divert Enterprise from Capella IV	(unknown)	(unknown)	"Friday's Child" (TOS)
Charleston, U.S.S.	Ferried revived 20th-century cryonic survivors back to Earth in 2364	NCC-42285	Excelsior	"The Neutral Zone" (TNG)
Cochrane, U.S.S.	Transported Dr. Julian Bashir to station Deep Space 9	NCC-59318	Oberth	"Emissary" (DS9)
Constantinople, U.S.S.	Suffered a hull breach near Gravesworld in 2365	NCC-34852	Istanbul	"The Schizoid Man" (TNG)
Constellation, U.S.S.	Commodore Matt Decker's ship, destroyed in 2267 by the planet killer	NCC-1017	Constitution	"The Doomsday Machine" (TOS)
Constellation, U.S.S.	Second starship to bear the name, class ship for the U.S.S. Stargazer	NCC-1974	Constellation	"The Battle" (TNG)
Constitution, U.S.S.	Class ship for the original U.S.S. Enterprise	NCC-1700	Constitution	"Space Seed" (TOS)
Copernicus, U.S.S.	Ship in spacedock when the alien probe caused ecological damage on Earth in 2286	NCC-623	Oberth	Star Trek IV: The Voyage Home
Crazy Horse, U.S.S.	Part of a task force for the expected Borg invasion of 2369	NCC-50446	Cheyenne	"Descent" (TNG)
Defiant, U.S.S.	Disappeared into interdimensional space near Tholian Sector in 2269	NCC-1764	Constitution	"The Tholian Web" (TOS)
Denver, U.S.S.	Transport ship struck by an abandoned Cardassian mine	NCC-54927	Yorkshire	"Ethics" (TNG)
Drake, U.S.S.	Destroyed at planet Minos in 2364, formerly commanded by Paul Rice	NCC-20381	Wambundu	"The Arsenal of Freedom" (TNG)
Eagle, U.S.S.	Ship listed on Operation Retrieve plan in Federation Council President's office	NCC-956	Constitution	Star Trek VI: The Undiscovered Country
Endeavor, U.S.S.	Temporarily commanded by Data in Picard's armada at Romulan Neutral Zone	NCC-71805	Nebula	"Redemption, Part II" (TNG) "The Game" (TNG)
Enterprise, U.S.S.	Ship made famous by James Kirk's five-year mission of exploration, launched 2245	NCC-1701	Constitution	Star Trek: The Original Series
Enterprise, U.S.S.	Actually the same ship as above, refit in 2271, destroyed at Genesis Planet in 2285	NCC-1701	Constitution	Star Trek: The Motion Picture, Star Trek II, Star Trek III
Enterprise-A, U.S.S.	Second Federation starship to bear the name, commanded by Captain James T. Kirk	NCC-1701A	Constitution	Star Trek IV, Star Trek V, Star Trek VI
Enterprise-B	Third Starship Enterprise	NCC-1701B	(Excelsior)	(Not yet seen).
Enterprise-C	Fourth starship to bear the name Enterprise; lost in 2344 while defending a Klingon outpost against a Romulan attack; commanded by Captain Rachel Garrett	NCC-1701C	Ambassador	"Yesterday's Enterprise" (TNG), "Redemption II" (TNG)

(Continued on next page.)

(Continued from previous page.)

Starship name	Description	Registry number	Class	Episode or film
Enterprise-D, U.S.S.	Fifth Federation starship to bear the name; launched in 2363; commanded by Captain Jean-Luc Picard	NCC-1701D	*Galaxy*	*Star Trek: The Next Generation*
Essex, U.S.S.	Early Starfleet vessel destroyed at moon of planet Mab-Bu VI	NCC-173	*Daedalus*	"Power Play" (TNG)
Excalibur, U.S.S.	Accidentally destroyed in disastrous M-5 computer test; commanded by Captain Harris	NCC-1664	*Constitution*	"The Ultimate Computer" (TOS)
Excalibur, U.S.S.	Served in Picard's armada to blockade Romulan supply ships during the Klingon civil war	NCC-26517	*Ambassador*	"Redemption, Part II" (TNG)
Excelsior, U.S.S.	First starship of the Excelsior class, commanded by Captain Hikaru Sulu	NCC-2000	*Excelsior*	*Star Trek III, Star Trek VI*
Exeter, U.S.S.	Crew reduced to crystals by Omega VI disease; formerly commanded by Captain Ron Tracey	NCC-1672	*Constitution*	"The Omega Glory" (TOS)
Farragut, U.S.S.	Kirk served on this ship as a lieutenant under the command of Captain Garrovick	NCC-1647	*Constitution*	"Obsession" (TOS)
Fearless, U.S.S.	Ship on which Kosinski tested an experimental warp drive upgrade in 2364	NCC-14598	*Excelsior*	"Where No One Has Gone Before" (TNG)
Gage, U.S.S.	Destroyed by the Borg at the Battle of Wolf 359	NCC-11672	*Apollo*	"Emissary" (DS9)
Gandhi, U.S.S.	Ship Lieutenant Thomas Riker served aboard after his rescue in 2369	NCC-26632	*Ambassador*	"Second Chances" (TNG)
Gettysberg, U.S.S.	Mark Jameson's last command before becoming admiral	NCC-3890	*Constellation*	"Too Short A Season" (TNG)
Goddard, U.S.S.	Starship scheduled for rendezvous with Enterprise-D in 2366	NCC-59621	*Korolev*	"The Vengeance Factor" (TNG)
Gorkon, U.S.S.	Part of a task force for the expected Borg invasion of 2369	NCC-40512	*Excelsior*	"Descent, Part I" (TNG)
Grissom, U.S.S.	Science vessel investigating the Genesis Planet in 2285; commanded by Captain J. T. Esteban; destroyed by Klingon attack	NCC-638	*Oberth*	*Star Trek III: The Search for Spock*
Grissom, U.S.S.	Ship requested to stand by for possible help with underground tricyanate contamination of planet Beta Agni II	NCC-59314	*Oberth*	"The MostToys" (TNG)
Hathaway, U.S.S.	Riker's ship for the strategic battle simulation of 2365	NCC-2593	*Constellation*	"Peak Performance" (TNG)
Hermes, U.S.S.	Served in Picard's armada to blockage Romulan supply ships during the Klingon civil war	NCC-10376	*Antares*	"Redemption, Part II" (TNG)
Hood, U.S.S.	Starship that participated in war games with M-5 computer in 2268	NCC-1703	*Constitution*	"The Ultimate Computer" (TOS)
Hood, U.S.S.	Riker's assignment before the Enterprise-D; transferred Riker, Crusher, and La Forge to Enterprise-D; assisted Enterprise in terraforming project to Browder IV; transported Tam Ulbrun to Enterprise-D; commanded by Captain Robert DeSoto	NCC-42296	*Excelsior*	"Encounter at Farpoint" (TNG), "Allegiance" (TNG), "Tin Man" (TNG), "The Defector" (TNG)
Horatio, U.S.S.	Ship commanded by Walker Keel and destroyed in 2364 by the extragalactic intelligence seeking to infiltrate Starfleet Command	NCC-10532	*Ambassador*	"Conspiracy" (TNG)
Horizon, U.S.S.	Made first contact with planet Iotia in 2168, leaving behind a book on the Chicago mobs of the 1920s, resulting in severe cultural contamination	NCC-176	*Daedalus*	"A Piece of the Action" (TOS)
Hornet, U.S.S.	Part of Picard's armada at Romulan Neutral Zone	NCC-10523	*Renaissance*	"Redemption, Part II" (TNG)
Intrepid, U.S.S.	Starship manned by Vulcans destroyed by space amoeba	NCC-1831	*Constitution*	"Court Martial" (TOS), "The Immunity Syndrome" (TOS)

(Continued on next page.)

(Continued from previous page.)

Starship name	Description	Registry number	Class	Episode or film
Intrepid, U.S.S.	First ship to respond to Klingon distress calls after Khitomer massacre; Sergey Rozhenko's ship	NCC-38907	Excelsior	"Sins of the Father" (TNG), "Reunion" (TNG), "Family" (TNG)
Jenolen, U.S.S.	Transport ship carrying passenger Montgomery Scott; crashed on a Dyson Sphere in 2294	NCC-2010	Sydney	"Relics" (TNG)
Kyushu, U.S.S.	Destroyed by the Borg at the battle of Wolf 359	NCC-65491	New Orleans	"Best of Both Worlds, Part II" (TNG)
Lalo, U.S.S.	Reported detecting disturbances from Dr. Manheim's time-gravity experiments; destroyed by the Borg at battle of Wolf 359	NCC-43837	Mediterranean	"We'll Always Have Paris" (TNG), "Best of Both Worlds, Part I" (TNG)
Lantree, U.S.S.	Entire crew killed by exposure to genetic super-children at Gagarin IV; commanded by Captain Isao Telaka; destroyed 2365	NCC-1837	Miranda	"Unnatural Selection" (TNG)
LaSalle, U.S.S.	Reported radiation anomalies in the Gamma Arigulon system	NCC-6203	Deneva	"Reunion" (TNG)
Lexington, U.S.S.	Starship that participated in war games with M-5 computer	NCC-1709	Constitution	"The Ultimate Computer" (TOS)
Magellan, U.S.S.	Starship commanded by Captain Conklin	NCC-3069	Constellation	"Starship Mine" (TNG)
Melbourne, U.S.S.	Riker was offered this command in 2366; Melbourne was one of 39 starships destroyed by the Borg at battle of Wolf 359	NCC-62043	Excelsior	"11001001" (TNG), "Best of Both Worlds, Parts I and II" (TNG), "Emissary" (DS9)
Merrimac, U.S.S.	Transported Sarek back to Vulcan after the Legaran conference; took Wesley Crusher back to Starfleet Academy 2368	NCC-61827	Nebula	"Sarek" (TNG), "The Game" (TNG)
Monitor, U.S.S.	Assigned to respond to Romulan threat	NCC-61826	Nebula	"The Defector" (TNG)
Phoenix, U.S.S.	Commanded by Benjamin Maxwell who made unauthorized attacks on Cardassian forces in 2367	NCC-65420	Nebula	"The Wounded" (TNG)
Potemkin, U.S.S.	Starship that participated in war games with M-5 computer; was scheduled to rendezvous with Enterprise at Beta Aurigae	NCC-1657	Constitution	"The Ultimate Computer" (TOS), "Turnabout Intruder'" (TOS)
Potemkin, U.S.S.	Riker served aboard this ship in 2361, prior to Hood and Enterprise-D; transferred Dr. Toby Russell to Enterprise-D in 2368	NCC-8253	Excelsior	"Peak Performance" (TNG), "Legacy" (TNG), "Ethics" (TNG), "Second Chances" (TNG)
Reliant, U.S.S.	Ship assigned to survey planets as part of Project Genesis; commanded by Captain Clark Terrell; destroyed by Khan in 2285	NCC-1864	Miranda	Star Trek II: The Wrath of Khan
Renegade, U.S.S.	Met the Enterprise-D at Dytallix B in 2364; formerly commanded by Captain Tryla Scott	NCC-63102	New Orleans	"Conspiracy" (TNG)
Republic, U.S.S.	Ben Finney and Ensign James Kirk served together on this ship while Kirk was a cadet at the Academy	NCC-1371	Constitution	"Court Martial" (TOS)
Repulse, U.S.S.	Dr. Katherine Pulaski's assignment prior to Enterprise-D; commanded by Captain Taggert	NCC-2544	Excelsior	"The Child" (TNG) "Unnatural Selection" (TNG)
Rutledge, U.S.S.	Commanded by Ben Maxwell with tactical officer Miles O'Brien during the Cardassian wars	NCC-57295	New Orleans	"The Wounded" (TNG)
Saratoga, U.S.S.	Destroyed by alien space probe while patrolling Neutral Zone in 2286	NCC-1867	Miranda	Star Trek IV: The Voyage Home

(Continued on next page.)

(Continued from previous page.)

Starship name	Description	Registry number	Class	Episode or film
Saratoga, U.S.S.	Destroyed by the Borg in the battle of Wolf 359; casualties included Jennifer Sisko; assignment of Benjamin Sisko prior to Deep Space 9	NCC-31911	Miranda	"Emissary" (DS9)
Stargazer, U.S.S.	Ship under the command of Jean-Luc Picard from 2333-2355, nearly destroyed in the Battle of Maxia	NCC-2893	Constellation	"The Battle" (TNG), "The Measure of a Man" (TNG), "Tapestry" (TNG)
Sutherland, U.S.S.	Served in Picard's armada to blockade Romulan supply ships during the Klingon civil war under command of Data	NCC-72015	Nebula	"Redemption, Part II" (TNG)
Thomas Paine, U.S.S.	Met the Enterprise-D at Dytallix B in 2364; commanded by Captain Rixx	NCC-65530	New Orleans	"Conspiracy" (TNG)
Tian Nan Men, U.S.S.	Served in Picard's armada to blockade Romulan supply ships during the Klingon civil war	NCC-21382	Miranda	"Redemption, Part II" (TNG)
Tolstoy, U.S.S.	Destroyed by the Borg at the battle of Wolf 359	NCC-62095	Rigel	"Best of Both Worlds, Part II" (TNG)
Trieste, U.S.S.	Data served aboard this starship before Enterprise-D; once fell through a wormhole	NCC-37124	Merced	"Clues" (TNG), "11001001" (TNG)
Tripoli, U.S.S.	Starship that discovered Data on planet Omicron Theta; when decommissioned, the Tripoli was stored at Zed-15 surplus depot	NCC-19386	Hokule'a	"Datalore" (TNG), "Unification, Part I" (TNG)
Tsiolkovsky, U.S.S.	Science vessel, crew killed by the Psi 2000 virus in 2264, ship destroyed by stellar fragment	NCC-53911	Oberth	"The Naked Now" (TNG)
Valiant, U.S.S.	Destroyed at planet Eminiar VII in 2217. (Not to be confused with the S.S. Valiant, which was not a Starfleet ship.)	NCC-1223	(unknown)	"A Taste of Armageddon" (TOS)
Vico, S.S.	Destroyed in the Black Cluster with only a single survivor. (Not a Starfleet vessel.)	NAR-18834	Oberth	"Hero Worship" (TNG)
Victory, U.S.S.	Geordi La Forge's assignment as an ensign prior to his transfer to Enterprise-D; commanded by Captain Zimbata	NCC-9754	Constellation	"Elementary, Dear Data" (TNG), "Identity Crisis" (TNG)
Wellington, U.S.S.	Underwent a computer system upgrade by the Bynars at Starbase 74; Ensign Ro's assignment before Enterprise-D	NCC-28473	Niagara	"11001001' (TNG), "Remember Me" (TNG), "Ensign Ro" (TNG)
Yamato, U.S.S.	Destroyed by an ancient Iconian computer virus weapon; commanded by Captain Donald Varley	NCC-71807	Galaxy	"Where Silence Has Lease" (TNG), "Contagion" (TNG)
Yorktown, U.S.S.	Starship carrying vaccines for planet Theta VII; disabled by an alien space probe approaching Earth in 2286	NCC-1717	Constitution	"Obsession" (TOS), Star Trek IV: The Voyage Home
Yosemite, U.S.S.	Damaged while conducting a study on the plasma streamer	NCC-19002	Oberth	"Realm of Fear" (TNG)
Zapata, U.S.S.	Scheduled to rendezvous with Enterprise-D at Xanthras III	NCC-33184	Surak	"Ménage à Troi" (TNG)
Zhukov, U.S.S.	Reginald Barclay's assignment prior to Enterprise-D; transported Vulcan ambassador T'Pel to Enterprise-D; participated in scientific mission to Phoenix Cluster; commanded by Captain Gleason	NCC-26136	Ambassador	"Hollow Pursuits" (TNG), "Data's Day" (TNG), "The Game" (TNG)

*About the starship chart: This is a compilation of (almost) all the Federation starships seen or mentioned in the Star Trek episodes and movies. As such, this is not a definitive list of all of Starfleet's ships, merely a list of the ships that have been on the show in one form or another. Many of the class designations and registry numbers are somewhat conjectural, although most of them have been used in various background charts and readouts (such as Starfleet status displays seen in the Enterprise-D observation lounge, the "Operation Retrieve" chart in Star Trek VI, Commodore Stone's office chart in "Court Martial" [TOS], and the ship listings in bridge graphic displays on the Enterprise-A, the Enterprise-C, and the Enterprise-D). SEE: **class; Constitution class; NCC.***

stasis unit. Emergency medical device used aboard Federation starships. The device could hold a patient in a state of suspended animation until medical treatment could be rendered. ("Tapestry" [TNG]).

static warp bubble. A nonpropulsive toroidal **subspace** field. A static warp bubble was created in 2367 by Ensign Wesley Crusher from Kosinski's warp field equations, but something went wrong. Dr. Beverly Crusher was trapped inside the phenomenon, which became her own personal reality, shaped by her thoughts at the time the bubble was formed. Crusher had been thinking of lost friends, and her personal universe shrank until she was the only one left. Crusher was recovered through the efforts of her son, with assistance from the **Traveler**. ("Remember Me" [TNG]).

Station Lya IV. A trade stop for the *Jovis*, following the kidnapping of Data by **Zibalian** trader **Kivas Fajo** in 2366. When queried by the *Enterprise*-D, Station Lya IV reported that the *Jovis* had been in orbit around the station for half a day. ("The Most Toys" [TNG]).

Station Nigala IV. Destination of the *Enterprise*-D following its mission at **Bre'el IV** in 2366. ("Deja Q" [TNG]).

Station Salem One. Site of an infamous sneak attack in which many Federation citizens were killed in a bloody preamble to war. ("The Enemy" [TNG]). *Neither the adversary, the date, nor the circumstances of this sneak attack were established in the episode, although an early draft of "Family" (TNG) suggested that one of Wesley Crusher's ancestors was at Salem One.*

Statistical Mechanics. A mathematics class, required at Starfleet Academy. Cadet Wesley Crusher tutored **Joshua Albert** in this class in 2368. ("The First Duty" [TNG]).

steelplast. Construction material used in the tunnel network beneath the capital city of planet **Mordan IV.** ("Too Short a Season" [TNG]).

Steinman analysis. Medical test noting individual specific data such as voice analysis and brain patterns. **Mira Romaine** was given a standard Steinman analysis while under the influence of the **Zetarians,** showing that her brain wave patterns had been altered and now matched the patterns emitted by the aliens. ("The Lights of Zetar" [TOS]).

Stellar Cartography. Science department on board the *Enterprise*-D that dealt with star mapping. Lieutenant Commander **Neela Daren** headed the Stellar Cartography department in 2369. ("Lessons" [TNG]).

stellar core fragment. An extremely massive piece of a disintegrated star, probably composed of **neutronium**. The *Enterprise*-D tracked such a fragment through the **Moab Sector** in 2368. SEE: **Genome Colony**. ("The Masterpiece Society" [TNG]).

Stephan. A young soccer player who was the love of Beverly Crusher's life, when she was eight and he was eleven. She dreamed that they would be married, but he never knew she existed. ("The Host" [TNG]). *At the time, Beverly's last name was Howard, although this maiden name has not been firmly established in dialog.*

Stiles, Lieutenant. (Paul Comi). Navigator on the *U.S.S. Enterprise* during the Romulan incursion of 2266. Several members of Stiles' family had been lost during the Earth-Romulan conflicts of a century before. ("Balance of Terror" [TOS]).

Sto-Vo-Kor. Klingon mythological place of the afterlife for the honored dead. The prophet **Kahless the Unforgettable** awaited those who were worthy of *Sto-Vo-Kor.* ("Rightful Heir" [TNG]). SEE: **Fek'lhr**.

Stocker, Commodore. (Charles Drake). Starfleet officer who assumed command of Starbase 10 in 2267. Stocker was transported to that post aboard the *Starship Enterprise*. While enroute, several *Enterprise* personnel including Captain Kirk became ill with a radiation-induced hyperaccelerated aging disease. Fearing the imminent loss of these valuable officers,  Stocker assumed command of the *Enterprise* and violated the **Romulan Neutral Zone** in an effort to reach Starbase 10's medical facilities more quickly. Stocker's action nearly triggered an interstellar incident. ("The Deadly Years" [TOS]). SEE: **corbomite**.

Stockholm Syndrome. In psychology, the tendency for hostages to sympathize with their captors after extended captivity. Dr. Crusher believed that **Jeremiah Rossa** might have exhibited Stockholm Syndrome after spending years with **Talarian** captain **Endar**. ("Suddenly Human" [TNG]).

stokaline. Medication given to Spock after he put himself into a deep trace in an attempt to regain control of the *Enterprise* from the **Kelvans** in 2268. As a ruse, McCoy told the Kelvans that Spock suffered from **Rigelian Kassaba fever** and required the medication. ("By Any Other Name" [TOS]).

Stol. Cousin to **Quark**. Stol bought one of the items that **Vash** brought back from the Gamma Quadrant in 2369 for five bars of gold-press-**latinum**. ("Q-Less" [DS9]).

Stone, Commodore. (Percy Rodriguez). Commander of **Starbase 11** when James Kirk was court-martialed for the apparent death of **Ben Finney** in 2267. When circumstancial evidence implicated Kirk, Stone urged him to resign for the good of the service. Stone had commanded a starship earlier in his career. ("Court Martial" [TOS]).

Stonn. (Lawrence Montaigne). Vulcan man who presumably married **T'Pring** in 2267. T'Pring had been bonded to **Spock**, but she chose Stonn after Spock freed her for daring to challenge the wedding. Spock warned him that having may not be quite so good a thing as wanting. ("Amok Time" [TOS]).

Story of the Promise, The. Klingon gospel that tells of the pledge that prophet **Kahless the Unforgettable** gave the people of the Homeworld. After he had united the Homeworld to form the Klingon Empire, Kahless one day said it was time for him to depart. When the people begged him not to leave, Kahless said he was going ahead to *Sto-Vo-Kor*, and promised to return one day. He pointed to a star in the heavens and told the people to look for him there "on that point of light." Klingon clerics later established a monastery on planet **Boreth**, orbiting that star, to await his return. ("Rightful Heir" [TNG]).

• **"Storyteller, The."** *Deep Space Nine* episode #14. Teleplay by Kurt Michael Bensmiller and Ira Steven Behr. Story by Kurt Michael Bensmiller. Directed by David Livingston. Stardate 46729.1. *First aired in 1993. Chief O'Brien suddenly finds himself the spiritual leader of a Bajoran village.* SEE: **Bajorans; baseball; Bokai, Buck; Dal'Rok; Faren Kag; Ferengi Rules of Acquisition; Gamzian; Glyrhond; Hovath; Iarish pie; Navot; Nog; O'Brien, Miles; Odo; Paqu; Sirah; stardrifter; tetrarch; Trixian bubble juice; Varis Sul; Woban.**

Storyteller. SEE: **Sirah**.

straight nines. High-scoring move in **dom-jot**. The play is extremely difficult to achieve. ("Tapestry" [TNG]).

Straleb security ship. Vessel that intercepted the *Starship Enterprise*-D shortly after stardate 42402, carrying Straleb secretary **Kushell** and his entourage. ("The Outrageous Okona" [TNG]). *The miniature for this ship was designed by Rick Sternbach.*

Straleb. Class-M planet, along with **Altec**, part of the coalition of Madena. Although it was technically at peace with Altec, relations between the two planets had been strained to the point that an interplanetary incident was created when it was revealed that **Benzan** of Straleb had been engaged to **Yanar** of Altec in 2365. ("The Outrageous Okona" [TNG]).

strategema. Challenging holographic game of strategy and wills. Played by two contestants, the game involves manipulating circular icons on a three-dimensional grid to gain control of one's opponent's territory while defending your own. Riker once challenged **Zakdorn** strategist (and grand master strategema player) **Kolrami** to a game, and was defeated in only 23 moves.

A later match between Kolrami and Data ended in Kolrami conceding defeat. Data later confided that his strategy had been to play not to win, but merely to maintain a tie until his opponent gave up. ("Peak Performance" [TNG]).

Stratos. Beautiful cloud city above the planet **Ardana**, believed to be the finest example of sustained antigravity elevation in the galaxy. Stratos was a study in the contrasts of Ardanan society: The Stratos city dwellers lived a life of leisure, while the **Troglytes**, who lived on the planet's surface,

toiled under brutal conditions. By 2269, Troglyte activists, called **Disrupters**, were committing acts of terrorism and vandalism in the city to protest their plight. Their actions spurred the development of **filter masks** that were provided to the Troglyte miners to protect them from the harmful effects of the **zenite** gas found in the Ardanan mines. ("The Cloud Minders" [TOS]). *The model of the cloud city of Stratos was designed by original series art director Matt Jefferies.*

Strnad star system. The *Enterprise* delivered a party of Earth colonists to a planet in the Strnad system in 2364. The adjoining **Rubicun** star system contained another Class-M planet ruled by the Edo entity who disapproved of the colonists living in the Strnad system. Because this location caused conflict to the **Edo god**, the colony was removed and transplanted elsewhere. ("Justice" [TNG]). *Named for* Star Trek: The Next Generation *production staff member Janet Strnad.*

Stroyerian. One of the forty-plus languages spoken by *U.S.S. Aries* first officer Flaherty. ("The Icarus Factor" [TNG]).

structural integrity field. Shaped forcefield used on Federation starships to supplement the mechanical strength of the ship's spaceframe. Without the structural integrity field, a starship would not be able to withstand the tremendous accelerations involved in spaceflight. During the *Enterprise*-D's contact with the **Tin Man** life-form in 2366, Chief Engineer La Forge diverted structural integrity power to strengthen the inner deflector grid, damaged in a Romulan attack. ("Tin Man" [TNG]).

strychnine. Alkaloid poison derived from the Earth plant *Strychnos nux vomica*. The poison also acts as a central nervous system stimulant, and in large doses causes convulsions and death. ("Ship in a Bottle" [TNG]).

Stubbs, Dr. Paul. (Ken Jenkins). Eminent astrophysicist who came aboard the *Enterprise*-D in 2366 for transport to the **Kavis Alpha** sector, where he was to conduct a neutronium decay experiment. A complex individual, Stubbs had been regarded as something of a *wunderkind* in his youth, and the resulting social isolation left a lasting mark on him. Stubbs was an

aficionado of the ancient game of **baseball,** and he was fond of daydreaming about the game's past glories. His landmark experiment at Kavis Alpha was the culmination of over 20 years of work, but the launch of an instrumented probe he called "the Egg" for the experiment was jeopardized with the unexpected evolution of sentient **nanites** on the *Enterprise*-D. Although Stubbs did not initially recognize the nanites as life-forms, they eventually agreed to cooperate with the execution of his experiment. ("Evolution" [TNG]).

stunstick. A meter-long, rodlike weapon that was used by cadre forces fighting for control of the **Turkana IV** colony. The weapon was capable of delivering a powerful electric shock to an opponent. **Ishara Yar** was injured by a stunstick during an away team mission with members of the *Enterprise*-D crew in 2367. ("Legacy" [TNG]).

Sturgeon. *Enterprise* crew member killed on the surface of planet **M-113** by the salt vampire. ("The Man Trap" [TOS]).

Styles, Captain. (James B. Sikking). Commander of the *Starship* **Excelsior** during its initial trial runs in 2285. Styles unsuccessfully attempted to stop Kirk from stealing the *Enterprise* to reach the **Genesis Planet.** (*Star Trek III: The Search for Spock*). Styles was later succeeded by Captain **Hikaru Sulu,** who assumed command of the *Excelsior* when it entered service as a deep-space exploratory vessel in 2290. (*Star Trek VI: The Undiscovered Country*).

Styris IV. Planet plagued by deadly **Anchilles fever** in the year 2364. Deaths in the millions were averted by the availability of vaccine from planet **Ligon II.** ("Code of Honor" [TNG]).

styrolite. Clear plastic-like material used for biologic quarantine of potentially hazardous life-forms. A sheath of styrolite was used to encase a genetically engineered child from the **Darwin Genetic Research Station** when it was feared that the child might carry a dangerous disease organism. ("Unnatural Selection" [TNG]).

subcutaneous transponder. Small device inserted under the skin and used by Starfleet as to track an individual. Dr. McCoy placed transponders in Kirk and Spock when they transported to planet **Ekos** in 2268. ("Patterns of Force" [TOS]). SEE: **rubindium crystal**.

subhadar. Angosian military rank. **Roga Danar** was awarded this position twice during the **Tarsian War.** ("The Hunted" [TNG]).

sublight. Scientific term describing space-normal speeds, slower than *c*, the speed of light. Sublight speeds do not require warp drive, and are generally achieved using impulse power. As a result, sublight travel is subject to relativistic

effects such as time dilation and Fitzgerald-Lorentz contraction. SEE: **impulse drive**.

submicron matrix transfer technology. New technique for replicating existing neural net pathways in a positronic brain into another positronic brain. This technology was introduced at a cybernetics conference in 2366, attended by Data, and led to Data's construction of his android daughter, **Lal**. ("The Offspring" [TNG]).

Subroutine C-47. Computer software on the *Enterprise*-D responsible for noncritical systems such as replicator selections and recreational programming. Subroutine C-47 was replaced by elements of Data's personal programming during an interface experiment in 2369. This caused malfunctions in food replicators, Captain Picard's music selections, and the holodeck program ***Ancient West.*** ("A Fistful of Datas" [TNG]). SEE: **Spot**.

subsonic transmitter. Device used on planet **Omicron Ceti III** to drive the spores from the surviving colonists' bodies in 2267. The subsonic transmitter broadcast an irritating frequency that was described as like spreading itching powder on the affected individuals. ("This Side of Paradise" [TOS]). SEE: **spores, Omicron Ceti III**.

Subspace Relay Station. SEE: **Relay Station 47**.

subspace compression. Phenomenon resulting from differential field potential values in nearby portions of the same warp field. Subspace compression can cause different parts of an object to have different inertial densities, resulting in structural strain on the object. In severe cases, subspace compression can tear an object apart at the subatomic level. Depending on relative field symmetries, subspace compression can also cause numerous other, often unpredictable, side effects. ("Deja Q" [TNG]).

subspace field distortions. Phenomena that generally indicate the presence of a warp propulsion system. The **Cytherian** probe encountered by the *Enterprise*-D in 2367 did not create any detectable field distortions and its method of propulsion remained a mystery. ("The Nth Degree" [TNG]).

subspace field inverter. A piece of equipment not normally included in the inventory of a *Galaxy*-class starship. This device is capable of generating low levels of **Eichner radiation**, which were found to stimulate growth of certain strains of deadly **plasma plague**. ("The Child" [TNG]).

subspace proximity detonator. Triggering mechanism employed by small explosive devices used in the **Koinonian** war a thousand years ago. Such a device, undetectable by a normal Starfleet tricorder, was responsible for the explosion that killed **Marla Aster** in 2266. ("The Bonding" [TNG]). Subspace proximity detonators were also used by the **Talarians** during the **Galen border conflicts** in the 2350s to booby-trap their ships. ("Suddenly Human" [TNG]).

subspace radio. Communications system using transmission of electromagnetic signals through a subspace medium rather than through normal relativistic space. The use of subspace radio permits communication across interstellar distances at speeds much greater than that of light, thereby significantly reducing the time lag associated with sending messages over such distances. Subspace communications can include voice, text, and/or visual data. Subspace radio was invented over a century after the development of the **warp drive**. News of the loss of the **U.S.S. Horizon**, destroyed near planet Sigma Iotia II in 2168, prior to the invention of subspace radio, did not reach Federation space until 2268 because its distress call was sent by conventional radio. ("A Piece of the Action" [TOS]). Subspace communications within Federation space are made even more rapid by the use of a network of subspace relay stations, deep-space facilities that amplify, reroute, and retransmit subspace signals. ("Aquiel" [TNG]). SEE: **Relay Station 47**.

subspace resonator. Field manipulation device. The *Enterprise*-D supplied a subspace resonator to a disabled **Romulan science vessel** in 2368, enabling the Romulan ship to return home, albeit slowly. ("The Next Phase" [TNG]).

subspace rupture. Huge swirling anomaly that draws surrounding matter into its central vortex. A **subspace rupture** was discovered in the Hanoli System in 2169 by a Vulcan ship. An elevated thoron reading near Deep Space 9 in 2369 was initially theorized by Dax to be a similar phenomenon, but this was later found to be incorrect. ("If Wishes Were Horses" [DS9]).

subspace shock wave. Powerful energy front generated by a massive energy discharge. A subspace shock wave was created when **Praxis**, a moon of the **Klingon Homeworld**, exploded in 2293, causing severe damage to the Homeworld, as well as to the nearby *Starship* **Excelsior**. (*Star Trek VI: The Undiscovered Country*). *The energy wave at the beginning of* Star Trek VI *was described as a subspace shock wave as a means of "explaining" how an explosion on Praxis could affect the* Excelsior, *which was presumably several light-years distant at the time.*

subspace shunt. Device used by the **Kobliad** criminal **Rao Vantika** to gain unauthorized control of computer systems such as those on Deep Space 9. Attached to a secondary system, the shunt could be used to bypass normal security lockouts. ("The Passenger" [DS9]).

subspace transition rebound. Phenomenon associated with the use of folded-space transport devices employed by the **Ansata** terrorists of planet **Rutia IV**. An adaptive subspace echogram was found to measure the rebound phenomenon with sufficient accuracy to locate the Ansata headquarters, despite the fact that folded-space transport was virtually undetectable with conventional sensors. ("The High Ground" [TNG]).

subspace transponder. Device used to aid in the location of objects in space such as ships or flight recorders. ("Dramatis Personae" [DS9]).

subspace. Spatial continuum with significantly different properties from our own, a fundamental part of **warp drive**. Warp-driven starships employ a subspace generator to create the asymmetrical spatial distortion necessary for the vessel to travel faster than the speed of light. Subspace is also used as a medium for **subspace radio** transmissions. SEE: **Cochrane, Zefram**. *Einstein's theories suggest that light-speed travel is impossible in our universe, so subspace and warp drive were "invented" to explain how a starship might do it anyway. On the other hand,* **Professor Stephen Hawking**, *when visiting the* Enterprise-D *engine room at Paramount Pictures in 1993, said he was working on warp drive. We can hardly wait.*

suck salt. To ingest sodium chloride in the form of a solid crystal stick. Considered to be a "nasty habit," conducive to health risks. ("Unification, Part II" [TNG]).

• **"Suddenly Human."** *Next Generation* episode #76. Teleplay by John Whelpley & Jeri Taylor. Story by Ralph Phillips. Directed by Gabrielle Beaumont. Stardate 44143.7. *First aired in 1990. Picard tries to return an apparently abused child to his biological family.* SEE: **Age of Decision; *Alba Ra*; autosuture; B'Nar; banana split; Castal I; Endar; Galen border conflicts; Galen IV; high energy X-ray laser; Jono; Merculite rockets; neutral particle weapons; *Q'Maire*; Rossa, Admiral Connaught; Rossa, Connor; Rossa, Jeremiah; Rossa, Moira; Sector 21947; Stockholm Syndrome; subspace proximity detonator; *T'stayan*; Talarian observation craft; Talarians; triangular envelopment; Woden Sector.**

Sulu (mirror). Lieutenant Sulu was security chief in the **mirror universe**. ("Mirror, Mirror" [TOS])

Sulu, Hikaru. (George Takei). Helm officer aboard the original *Starship Enterprise* under the command of Captain James Kirk. Sulu, born in 2237 in San Francisco on Earth (*Star Trek IV: The Voyage Home*), was initially assigned as a physicist ("Where No Man Has Gone Before" [TOS]) aboard the *Enterprise* in 2265 ("The Deadly Years" [TOS]), but later transferred to the helm. ("The Corbomite Maneuver" [TOS]).

Sulu assumed command of the *Starship* **Excelsior** in 2290, and subsequently conducted a three-year scientific mission of cataloging gaseous planetary anomalies in the **Beta Quadrant**. Sulu and the *Excelsior* played a pivotal role in the historic **Khitomer** peace conference of 2293 by helping to protect the conference against Federation and Klingon forces seeking to disrupt the peace process. (*Star Trek VI: The Undiscovered Country*). Sulu had a wide range of hobbies, including botany ("The Mantrap" [TOS]) and fencing.

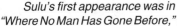

The latter interest surfaced when Sulu suffered the effects of the **Psi 2000 virus** in 2366, and Sulu threatened everyone in sight with a foil. ("The Naked Time" [TOS]). Old-style hand guns were another of Sulu's hobbies, and he had always wanted a Police Special in his collection. "Shore Leave" [TOS]).

Sulu's first appearance was in "Where No Man Has Gone Before," but by "The Corbomite Maneuver" he had assumed his familiar post at the helm. A scene that was filmed for Star Trek II would have shown that Sulu was about to assume command of the Excelsior at that time. This scene was cut because the movie was too long. A scene for Star Trek IV that was in the final draft of the script but not filmed would have had Sulu meeting a young boy in San Francisco who was Sulu's great-great-great-grandfather. Sulu's first name, Hikaru, was authorized by Gene Roddenberry in 1979, but was not used on film until Star Trek VI: The Undiscovered Country.

Sun Tzu. Ancient Chinese philosopher whose writings on the art of warfare are still taught at Starfleet Academy. Among Sun Tzu's teachings were "Know your enemy and know yourself, and victory will always be yours." ("The Last Outpost" [TNG]).

Suna. (Andrew Prine). Native of planet **Tilonus IV** who was seen as different characters by William Riker in a delusional world created in Riker's mind when he was brainwashed on that planet in 2369. Suna controlled the brainwashing equipment, and his image was projected as Lieutenant Suna on board the *Enterprise*-D and as the administrator of the imaginary **Tilonus Institute for Mental Disorders**. ("Frame of Mind" [TNG]).

Sunad. (Charles Dennis). Commander of a **Zalkonian** warship dispatched in 2366 to capture a fugitive Zalkonian named **John Doe**. Sunad, upon locating Doe aboard the *Enterprise*-D near the **Zeta Gelis** system, demanded Doe's extradition, alleging Doe to be an escaped criminal. It was later found that Doe was a member of a persecuted Zalkonian minority. ("Transfigurations" [TNG]). *Sunad was named for Star Trek: The Next Generation staff writer Richard Danus. (Spell it backward).*

Supera, Patterson. (Max Supera). One of the winners of the primary-school science fair held aboard the *Enterprise*-D in 2368. Young Patterson was also made an honorary officer in charge of radishes by Captain Picard. ("Disaster" [TNG]). SEE: **Flores, Marissa.** *Patterson's last name was not given in dialog, but was printed on the plaque that the kids gave the captain.*

Supervisor 194. Code name for Gary Seven when he was assigned to Earth in 1968. ("Assignment: Earth" [TOS]).

Surak. (Barry Atwater). Father of the **Vulcan** philosophy, a man of peace and logic who helped lead his people out of a

period of devastating wars. A replica of Surak was created by the **Excalbians** in 2269 as part of their attempt to study the human concept of "good" and "evil." ("The Savage Curtain" [TOS]). SEE: **Yarnek**.

Surata IV. Class-M planet surveyed by an *Enterprise*-D away team in 2365. During the away mission, **William T. Riker** was injured by contact with a native plant form. He lost consciousness for several hours, but eventually recovered. ("Shades of Grey" [TNG]).

Surchid, Master. Leader of the first **Wadi** delegation to Deep Space 9 in 2369. **Falow** announced that he was the Master Surchid of the Wadi, and was supervisor of the **Chula** game played at Quark's bar on Deep Space 9. ("Move Along Home" [DS9]).

Surmak Ren. (Matthew Faison). Bajoran who worked with noted geneticist **Dekon Elig**. Surmak Ren, a member of the Bajoran underground, and medical assistant to Dekon Elig, claimed to know little about the deadly aphasia virus created by Dekon. In 2369, while serving as chief administrator of the Ilvian Medical Complex, he was contacted when the virus was spreading throughout station Deep Space 9. When Surmak refused to cooperate, Kira kidnapped him to the station to help develop a cure. ("Babel" [DS9]). *The character was not named for anyone in Nickelodeon's animated series Ren and Stimpy. Heck, no.*

Surplus Depot Zed-15. Starfleet designation of the surplus depot located in orbit around planet **Qualor II**. The *T'Pau* was assigned to this depot in 2364, following its decommission. ("Unification, Part I" [TNG]).

• **"Survivors, The,"** *Next Generation* episode #51. Written by Michael Wagner. Directed by Les Landau. Stardate 43152.4. *First aired in 1989. The* Enterprise*-D investigates a lonely couple that are the sole survivors of an attack that destroyed their colony.* SEE: **Andorians; Delta Rana IV; Delta Rana star system; Douwd; Husnock ship; Husnock; New Martim Vaz; Starbase 133; Uxbridge, Kevin; Uxbridge, Rishon.**

Susann, Jacqueline. Popular 20th-century Earth novelist known for sensationalistic novels about that planet's rich and powerful. Spock read Susann's works during his study of Earth culture, and regarded her as one of the "giants" of human literature. (*Star Trek IV: The Voyage Home*).

• **"Suspicions."** *Next Generation* episode #148. Written by Joe Menosky and Naren Shankar. Directed by Cliff Bole. Stardate 46830.1. *First aired in 1993. A scientist is murdered during a test of a new deflector shield system.* SEE: **Altine Conference; baryon particles; Brooks, Admiral; Christopher, Dr.; Ferengi death rituals; Jo'Bril;** *Justman, Shuttlecraft;* **Kurak; metaphasic shield; plasma infuser; Reyga, Dr.; Selar, Dr.; Starbase 23; T'Pan, Dr.; Takarans;**

tennis elbow; tetryon field; Vaytan; Vulcan Science Academy.

Sutherland, U.S.S. Federation starship, *Nebula* class, Starfleet registry number NCC-72015. The *Sutherland* was commanded by Commander **Data** for Picard's armada to blockade the Romulan supply ships supplying the **Duras** family forces during the **Klingon**

civil war in 2368. ("Redemption, Part II" [TNG]). *The Sutherland was a modification of the* Nebula-*class* **U.S.S. Phoenix**. *The upper sensor pod and supporting struts were changed for the* Sutherland. *The* Sutherland *was named for Horatio Hornblower's flagship in the classic C. S. Forrester novels that served as one of Gene Roddenberry's original inspirations for* Star Trek.

Sutter, Clara. (Noley Thornton). Daughter of *Enterprise*-D crew member **Daniel Sutter**. Because she had changed starships and therefore homes so many times in her young life, Clara invented an invisible friend, **Isabella**, to keep her company. Clara was at first pleased, then frightened, when her imaginary companion suddenly became very real. ("Imaginary Friend" [TNG]).

Sutter, Ensign Daniel. (Jeff Allin). An *Enterprise*-D officer and part of the engineering staff. Sutter had served on several starships before his posting to the *Enterprise*-D in 2368. His daughter, **Clara Sutter**, lived with him. ("Imaginary Friend" [TNG]).

Suvin IV. Planet where archaeologist Dr. Langford invited Captain Picard to join her in exploring the ruins. ("Rascals" [TNG]).

Swenson, Science Officer. *Enterprise*-D crew member who was scheduled to participate in a martial-arts competition aboard the ship just prior to Tasha Yar's death in 2364. ("Skin of Evil" [TNG]).

Switzer. A renowned Federation archaeologist who attended the annual symposium of the **Federation Archaeology Council** in 2367. ("QPid" [TNG]).

Sybo. (Pilar Seurat). Wife of Prefect **Jaris** of planet **Argelius II**. She was gifted with the Argelian power of empathic contact and attempted to learn who was committing the murders on her planet in 2267. She was murdered by the alien entity who was the object of her investigation. SEE: **Redjac**. ("Wolf in the Fold" [TOS]).

Sybok. (Laurence Luckinbill). Son of **Sarek** of Vulcan and half-brother to **Spock**. Sybok was born in 2224 to Sarek and his first wife, a Vulcan princess. After the death of his mother, Sybok was raised with his half-brother, Spock. Even as a youth, Sybok was a rebel in the highly conformist Vulcan society, and he was eventually ostracized because he sought

to find meaning in emotions as well as in logic. Sybok left his homeworld to pursue his visions of the mythical planet **Sha Ka Ree**. Sybok did not realize that these visions had been implanted by a malevolent creature living near the center of the galaxy. This creature inspired Sybok to gather a group of followers at planet **Nimbus III** in 2287, then to hijack the *Starship Enterprise*-A to the planet it called Sha Ka Ree, in hopes of using the starship to gain its own freedom. Sybok perished at the planet he believed was Sha Ka Ree, having realized too late the malevolent nature of the entity there. (*Star Trek V: The Final Frontier*).

Sydney-class transport. Small starship resembling a runabout. The *Jenolen*, lost in 2294 carrying **Montgomery Scott**, was a *Sydney*-class ship. ("Relics" [TNG]). Some *Sydney*-class ships were built without warp drive, intended for use as large shuttlecrafts. (*Star Trek VI*). *The* Jenolen *miniature was a modification of a large shuttlecraft originally built for* Star Trek VI.

Sylvia. (Antoinette Bower). Extragalactic life-form who traveled to planet **Pyris VII** along with **Korob**, another from her world. Sylvia used a device called a **transmuter** to assume humanoid form when she captured personnel from the *Enterprise* in 2268. Unfamiliar with human existence, Sylvia became intoxicated with human senses and became cruel toward her captives. She and Korob died after the transmuter was destroyed. ("Catspaw" [TOS]).

Sylvia. (Bonnie Beecher). Woman who was infatuated with **Billy Claiborne** in the replica of **Tombstone, Arizona,** created by the **Melkotians** in 2268. Chekov was cast by the Melkotians in the role of Claiborne, but did not seem to mind Sylvia's attentions. ("Spectre of the Gun" [TOS]).

Symbalene blood burn. Virulent disease that can rapidly kill a large number of people in a very short period of time. Spock made reference to this upon finding the entire **Malurian** civilization destroyed in 2267. ("The Changeling" [TOS]).

symbiont. A small, sightless, immobile intelligent life-form, one-half of the **Trill** joined species. The symbiont lived within a humanoid host, gaining sustenance and mobility from the host. ("The Host" [TNG]). SEE: **Odan, Ambassador**. The symbiont's intelligence is the dominant personality in the joined life-form, although the host's personality is reflected as well. Symbionts can have enormously long life spans and, upon the death of a host, can be transplanted into another. The resulting new joined life-form is considered to be another person, although it retains memories of previous joinings. ("Dax" [DS9]).

• **"Symbiosis."** Next Generation episode #23. Teleplay by Robert Lewin and Richard Manning and Hans Beimler. Story by Robert Lewin. Directed by Win Phelps. No stardate given in episode. *First aired in 1988. The* Enterprise-*D discovers two planets, one of which is populated by drug addicts, the other of which supplies their narcotics. This was actor Denise Crosby's last episode as Natasha Yar, even though it was filmed after "Skin of Evil" (TNG), in which Tasha dies. Denise Crosby can be seen breaking out of character and waving farewell at the end of "Symbiosis," just before the cargo bay door closes.* SEE: **Brekka; Brekkians; Delos; felicium; Langor; Ornara; Ornarans; Romas;** *Sanction;* **Sobi; T'Jon.**

symbols. *1) Great Seal of the United Federation of Planets. 2) Vulcan IDIC symbol, designed by Gene Roddenberry, representing the Vulcan philosophy of Infinite Diversity in Infinite Combinations. 3) Mirror universe emblem from "Mirror, Mirror" (TOS). 4) Symbol of the Klingon Empire. 5) Symbol from Tantalus rehab colony. 6) Early Federation pennant, seen in "And the Children Shall Lead" (TOS). 7) Starfleet logo, feature-film era. 8) Starfleet symbol, Next Generation era. (Note that there was no symbol for the entire Starfleet during the original Star Trek series, since the arrowhead symbol was only used for the* Enterprise *in that show).* SEE: **insignia, Starfleet; signage, Starfleet; writing.**

1)

2)

3)

4)

5)

6)

7)

8)

(More symbols on next page).

Symbols (continued from previous page): 1) Emblem of the Romulan Star Empire. A giant predatory bird holds the two homeworlds of the Romulan Empire in its talons. Designed by Monte Thrasher. 2) Symbol of the Bajoran faith, designed by Nathan Crowley and Doug Drexler. 3) Bajoran military banner, designed by Doug Drexler and Jim Martin. 4) Symbol of the Borg. 5) Symbol of the Cardassian Union. 6) Symbol of the Ferengi Alliance, sometimes used as a decorative tattoo engraved into some Ferengi's foreheads. 7) Graffitti mark of "the Circle" underground Bajoran organization. 8) Symbol of the gamesters of Triskelion. 9) Bajoran decorative symbol, using 40 rotated drawings of the S.S. Botany Bay. 10) Symbol of the Cardassian-Klingon alliance in the mirror universe.

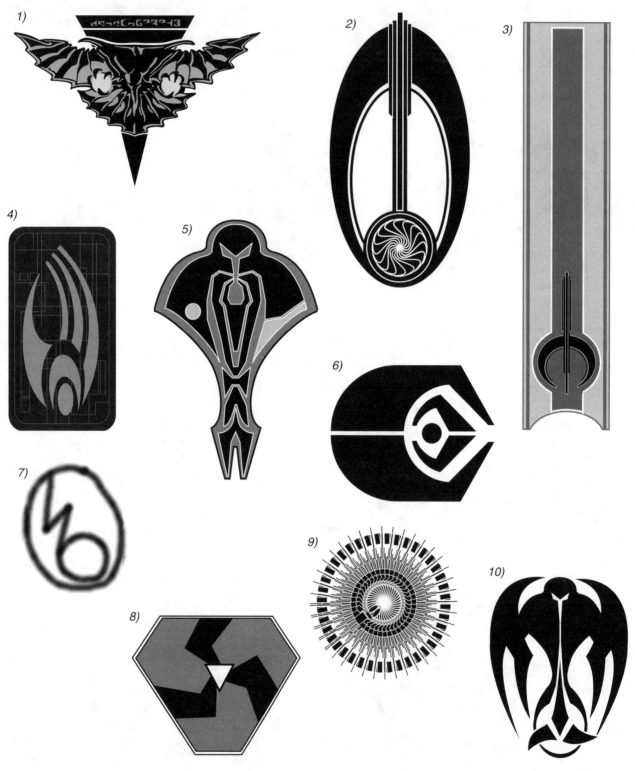

synaptic induction. Technique in neurotherapy used for patients suffering from traumatic memory loss. Dr. Crusher attempted synaptic induction with the **Zalkonian** called **John Doe** in 2366, but because his neural nets did not conform to any known patterns, the therapy was ineffective. ("Transfigurations" [TNG]).

synaptic pattern displacement. Scientific term for the consciousness sharing used by **Vulcans** in a mind-meld or, in extreme cases, the transference of one's *katra*. Dr. Julian Bashir was unaware that the technique could be performed by a non-Vulcan, although the **Kobliad** criminal **Rao Vantika** used something similar to place his consciousness into Bashir's mind in 2369. ("The Passenger" [DS9]). SEE: **Vulcan mind-meld**.

synaptic reconstruction. Surgery which neutralizes the synaptic pathways responsible for deviant behavior. While being brainwashed on planet **Tilonus IV**, Riker experienced a delusional world where he was an inmate at a mental hospital and was threatened with synaptic reconstruction to "correct" his "psychotic personality". ("Frame of Mind" [TNG]). SEE: *Frame of Mind*; **neurosomatic technique; Syrus, Dr.**

synthale. Bajoran beverage served at **Quark's bar** at **Deep Space 9**. Quark didn't like the stuff, warning, "Don't ever trust an ale from a god-fearing people." ("Emissary" [DS9]).

synthehol. An alcohol substitute invented by the **Ferengi** that permits one to enjoy the intoxicating effects of alcoholic beverages without the deleterious effects. **Robert Picard** voiced the opinion that synthehol had ruined Jean-Luc's palate. Jean-Luc, however, felt it had heightened his appreciation for the fruits of genuine vineyards. ("Family" [TNG]). On the other hand, Captain **Montgomery Scott** easily distinguished between real scotch and the synthehol-based substitute served in the Ten-Forward Lounge aboard the *Enterprise*-D. ("Relics" [TNG]).

Synthococcus novae. Bacillus strain organism, a by-product of modern technology. Although treatable, the deadly bacillus was regarded as a significant health hazard. **Dr. Sevrin** was a carrier of the disease but immune to it, passing it on to others yet remaining symptom free. ("The Way to Eden" [TOS]).

Syrus, Dr. (David Selberg). Non-existent physician at the imaginary **Tilonus Institute for Mental Disorders** who supposedly treated William Riker for a psychiatric malady on planet **Tilonus IV** in 2369.

In reality, Dr. Syrus did not exist, but was projected into Riker's mind by political interrogation officers on planet Tilonus IV. They hoped to extract strategic information from the *Enterprise*-D first officer. ("Frame of Mind" [TNG]).

System J-25. Star system some 7,000 light-years from Federation space. The sixth planet in the system, an inhabited class M-world, was observed in 2365 to have large crater-like scars where roadway patterns indicated cities should have been. It was believed the damage was caused by the **Borg**. ("Q Who?" [TNG]).

In late 2366, similar surface conditions were discovered on planet **Jouret IV** at the **New Providence colony**, indicating a Borg encroachment into Federation space. ("The Best of Both Worlds, Part I" [TNG]).

T-9 energy converter. Sophisticated power device stolen by the Ferengi from an unmanned Federation monitor post on planet **Gamma Tauri IV**. ("The Last Outpost" [TNG]).

T-cell stimulator. Medical device in use aboard the *Enterprise*-D. The device increases the production of T cells, a type of lymphocyte which enables humanoid bodies to fight infection. ("Identity Crisis" [TNG]).

T-negative. Rare Vulcan blood type possessed by Ambassador **Sarek** and his son **Spock**. Commander Spock offered himself as the blood donor for his father's heart surgery aboard the *Enterprise* in 2267 because he possessed the same type as the ambassador. ("Journey to Babel" [TOS])

T-tauri type star system. System with a young star whose diameter oscillates as that star settles into a stable size. In 2367, the *Enterprise*-D encountered a T-tauri star system with a single class-M planet in the **Ngame Nebula**. ("Clues" [TNG]).

Taar, DaiMon. (Mike Gomez). Commander of the **Ferengi Marauder** spacecraft responsible for stealing a Federation T-9 energy converter from **Gamma Tauri IV**. ("The Last Outpost" [TNG]).

tachyon detection grid. Technique devised by Geordi La Forge using a network of active tachyon beams to detect cloaked Romulan ships passing through the net. The grid required about 20 starships in order to be tactically effective, and was successfully used in 2368 to detect a convoy of Romulan ships on a covert mission to supply the **Duras** family forces in the **Klingon civil war**. ("Redemption, Part II" [TNG]).

T'Acog, I.K.C. Klingon cruiser, *K't'inga* class, sent to return the criminals **Korris**, **Konmel**, and **Kunivas** to the **Klingon Homeworld** in 2364. The offenders managed to destroy the *T'Acog* and commandeered the **Talarian** freighter *Batris*. ("Heart of Glory" [TNG]).

Tagas. A mythical land ruled by **Elamos the Magnificent**. ("Hero Worship" [TNG]).

Taggert, Captain. (J. Patrick McNamara). Commander of the *Starship **Repulse***. Former *Enterprise*-D chief medical officer **Dr. Katherine Pulaski** served under Taggert aboard the *Repulse* prior to her assignment to the *Enterprise*-D. Taggert spoke highly of Pulaski, and once noted he would have given her a shuttlecraft if it would have kept her aboard his ship. ("Unnatural Selection" [TNG]).

Tagra IV. Ecologically devastated planet in the Argolis Cluster. In 2369 the *Enterprise*-D traveled to Tagra IV to deliver much-needed supplies. ("True-Q" [TNG]). SEE: **baristatic filter; Amanda Rogers; Orn Lote.**

Tagrans. Inhabitants of the planet **Tagra IV**. ("True-Q" [TNG]).

Taguan. Archaeological period classifications on planet **Marlonia**. Picard mentioned that the pottery from planet Marlonia was very similar to early Taguan designs but was probably closer to the Buranian period instead. ("Rascals" [TNG]).

Tagus III. A small planet, home to a glorious civilization some two billion years ago. Although the Taguans have long since disappeared, the planet has been the subject of 22,000 years of archaeological study. By 2367, despite 947 known excavations of the Taguan ruins, the civilization remained largely a mystery. The ruins of Tagus III were the subject of Captain **Jean-Luc Picard**'s keynote address to the **Federation Archaeological Council**'s annual symposium in 2367. ("QPid" [TNG]).

Tahiti Syndrome. Twentieth-century term for a human longing for a peaceful, idyllic natural setting when suffering from the stresses of modern life. McCoy noted Kirk's reaction upon observing the Indian lifestyle on **Miramanee's planet**, commenting that overpressured leader types like starship captions often exhibited the Tahiti Syndrome. ("The Paradise Syndrome" [TOS]).

Tahna Los. (Jeffrey Nordling). **Bajoran** terrorist and member of the militant **Kohn-ma** splinter group who stopped at nothing to assure Bajor's independence from outside forces. In 2369, he attempted to destroy one side of the **wormhole** in hopes of minimizing Bajor's importance to the Federation and the Cardassians. He was not successful. ("Past Prologue" [DS9]).

tai chi. SEE: *Mok'bara.*

Taibak. (John Fleck). Romulan scientist who developed a neural control device in 2367 that, by using a direct access to the visual interface of La Forge's VISOR, permitted Geordi La Forge to be programmed to commit criminal acts. ("The Mind's Eye" [TNG]). SEE: **E-band emissions.**

Tajor, Glin. (Mic Rogers). Aide to **Gul Lemec** during talks aboard the *Starship Enterprise*-D in 2369. ("Chain of Command, Part I" [TNG]).

Takarans. Humanoid race with vaguely reptilian features. Little was known about the Takarans until 2369, when *Enterprise*-D chief medical officer Beverly Crusher was given an opportunity to autopsy a member of the race. Crusher discovered that the Takarans did not have organs in the traditional sense; rather, Takaran internal physiology was homogeneous throughout the body. This made the Takarans extremely difficult to injure or kill. Effective damage would have to be done on a cellular level. Crusher also discovered that Takarans were able to control the rate of their cellular physiology, allowing them to put themselves into a state resembling death. ("Suspicions" [TNG]). SEE: **Jo'Bril.**

Tal Shiar. Elite Romulan Imperial Intelligence service. The Tal Shiar was a secret, often brutal, sometimes extragovernmental agency that enforced loyalty among the Romulan citizenry and military. Tal Shiar agents carried broad discretionary powers and were able to overrule field military commanders with little fear of reprisal from the government. Some elements of Romulan society, including members of the military, felt the Tal Shiar's tactics to be unnecessarily brutal, but such opinions were rarely spoken publicly for fear of retribution that included having family members simply "disappear." Deanna Troi was coerced to assume the identity of Tal Shiar member **Major Rakal** as part of an elaborate plot to enable Romulan **vice-proconsul M'ret** to defect to the Federation. ("Face of the Enemy" [TNG]). SEE: **N'Vek, Subcommander**. *The Tal Shiar emblem, worn on the collar, was designed by Ricardo Delgado.*

tal-shaya. Ancient method of execution on Vulcan that was considered a merciful form of death. Pressure was applied to a specific portion of the victim's neck until it snapped, causing instantaneous death. *Tal-shaya* was used to murder Tellarite ambassador **Gav** prior to the **Babel Conference** of 2267 in an effort to cast suspicion upon the Vulcan ambassador. ("Journey to Babel" [TOS]).

Tal. (Jack Donner). Subcommander on the **Romulan battle cruiser** that captured the Federation starship *Enterprise* when the ship crossed the **Romulan Neutral Zone** in 2268 on a secret spy mission. ("The *Enterprise* Incident" [TOS]).

Talarian hook spider. Arachnid with half-meter-long legs. **Miles O'Brien**, who was afraid of spiders, had to get past twenty of these creatures when repairing an emitter array at the starbase on planet Zayra IV. ("Realm of Fear" [TNG]).

Talarian observation craft. A small vessel used as a training ship for young **Talarian** males. In 2367, the *Enterprise*-D discovered one of these craft adrift in **Sector 21947**. The craft had developed a serious radiation leak in its propulsion system and Dr. Crusher's team evacuated the survivors, including a Talarian named **Jono**, to the *Enterprise*-D. ("Suddenly Human" [TNG]). *The ship model was designed by Rick Sternbach and built by Tony Meininger.*

Talarians. A humanoid race characterized by a distinctive hairless enlargement of the coronal area of the skull. Talarian society was rigidly patriarchal and encouraged warriorlike behavior. Talarians followed a rigid set of traditions and customs. ("Suddenly Human" [TNG]). SEE: **Endar; Galen border conflicts**. *Talarians were mentioned in "Heart of Glory" (TNG), but not actually seen until "Suddenly Human."*

Talbot, St. John. (David Warner). Federation diplomatic representative to the **Paradise City** settlement on planet **Nimbus III**. (*Star Trek V: The Final Frontier*). Actor David Warner later played the part

of **Chancellor Gorkon** in Star Trek VI: The Undiscovered Country *as well as the Cardassian* **Gul Madred** *in "Chain of Command, Part II" (TNG).*

Tale of Two Cities, A. Novel written by terrestrial author Charles Dickens in 1859. The book was a historical story set during the French Revolution. Spock gave Kirk an antique hardbound copy of *A Tale of Two Cities* as a birthday gift in 2285. (*Star Trek II: The Wrath of Khan*).

talgonite. Ceramic substance, used in the construction of the **Kataan probe**. ("The Inner Light" [TNG]).

Talmadge, Captain. Commander of the *Dorian*, a transport vessel attacked near planet **Rekag-Seronia** in 2369 while attempting to deliver **Ambassador Ves Alkar** to that planet in hopes of mediating peace there. ("Man of the People" [TNG]).

Talos IV. Class-M planet, formerly the home of a thriving, technically advanced humanoid civilization. Thousands of centuries ago, a terrible nuclear war killed nearly all the planet's inhabitants and nearly rendered the planet itself uninhabitable. As of 2266, contact with Talos IV was a violation of Starfleet **General Order 7**, a death penalty offense because of the immense and addictive power of the Talosians' illusion technology. ("The Cage," "The Menagerie, Parts I and II" [TOS]). SEE: **Pike, Christopher**.

Talos Star Group. Location of planet **Talos IV**. ("The Cage," "The Menagerie, Part I" [TOS]).

Talosians. Dominant humanoid life-form on planet **Talos IV**. The Talosians were nearly made extinct by nuclear war, and the few survivors clung to life underground, where they became dangerously dependent upon the illusion-creating technology developed by their ancestors. *Gene Roddenberry, while forced by production practicality to make the Talosians a hu-*

manoid race (so that they could be played by human actors), nevertheless took the imaginative step of casting women in the roles, while dubbing male voices for the characters. ("The Cage," "The Menagerie, Parts I and II" [TOS]).

Taluno, Kai. **Bajoran** religious leader who first discovered the Bajoran **wormhole**. In the 22nd century a ship carrying Kai Taluno was damaged in the **Denorios Belt**. There, he claimed the heavens opened up and almost swallowed his ship. Bajoran religious faith holds that the phenomenon was the **Celestial Temple**, home of the Bajoran **Prophets**. ("Emissary" [DS9]).

Tamarian frost. A sweet beverage, available in the Ten-Forward lounge of the *Enterprise*-D. ("Hero Worship" [TNG]).

Tamarians. A humanoid race, first encountered by the Federation in 2268. The Tamarians were faintly reptilian in appearance and their spoken language was based almost entirely on metaphors drawn from their culture's mythology. Early encounters between the Federation and the Tamarians went without incident, but the two societies were unable to communicate. A breakthrough finally came in 2368, when a Tamarian captain, **Dathon**, confined both himself and *Enterprise*-D captain Picard on the surface of planet **El-Adrel IV**. ("Darmok" [TNG]).

Tamen Sahsheer. SEE: **Sahsheer.**

Tamoon. (Jane Ross). **Drill thrall** who, in 2268, was responsible for training Chekov to fight in the games on planet **Triskelion.** ("The Gamesters of Triskelion" [TOS]).

Tamura, Yeoman. (Miko Mayama). Member of the *Enterprise* landing party to planet **Eminiar VII** in 2267. ("A Taste of Armageddon" [TOS]).

Tan Ru. Alien space probe programmed to gather and sterilize soil samples from distant planets as a precursor to colonization. While it drifted through space, *Tan Ru* collided with Earth probe *Nomad* and somehow merged with it. ("The Changeling" [TOS]).

Tanagra. SEE: **"Darmok and Jalad at Tanagra."**

Tandro, Enina. (Fionnula Flanagan). Widow of the late **General Ardelon Tandro** of planet **Klaestron IV**. In 2369 her son, **Ilon Tandro**, accused **Jadzia Dax** for the murder of his father 30 years before. After Odo contacted her with news of the trial implicating Jadzia Dax, Enina came forward to confess that **Curzon Dax** was in bed with her at the time of a secret transmission implicating the Trill. She told Jadzia, in confidence, that her husband had betrayed his own people and the rebels had killed him. This fact had been kept secret in order to protect the memory of a man so cherished by his people. Dax had not revealed this information out of Curzon's desire to protect Enina, even if it meant she would have been convicted of a murder Curzon did not commit. ("Dax" [DS9]).

Tandro, General Ardelon. Statesman from the planet **Klaestron IV** who was reportedly murdered in 2339 during a civil war on his planet. He became a national hero after his death, with statues of him erected all over the planet. Ardelon Tandro was good friends with Federation mediator **Curzon Dax**, but was unaware that his wife, **Enina Tandro**, was conducting a love affair with Dax. Thirty years later, when **Jadzia Dax** was accused of Tandro's murder, Dax refused to offer any defense, preferring to be found guilty rather than betray Enina. It was not until Enina came forward and admitted that she had been in bed with Curzon Dax at the time of a secret transmission that Dax was acquitted. Enina also spoke privately with Jadzia Dax, explaining that her late husband had betrayed his own people. The rebels had killed him for it, but that truth would remain secret. ("Dax" [DS9]).

Tandro, Ilon. (Gregory Itzen). Head of the special diplomatic envoy from planet **Klaestron IV** who attempted to extradite Jadzia Dax from Deep Space 9 in 2369 for the murder of his

father, **General Ardelon Tandro**. The general, who had been good friends with **Curzon Dax**, had been murdered 30 years before, but new evidence surfaced in 2369 implicating the Trill host. Tandro maintained that although Curzon Dax was gone, Jadzia Dax could be prosecuted for the murder of his father. The paramount question as to whether a **Trill** host was responsible for the symbiont's past lives was not addressed because the murder charge was laid to rest when Ardelon's widow, **Enina Tandro**, revealed that **Curzon Dax** was in bed with her at the time of the secret transmission that had been the source of the indictment. ("Dax" [DS9]).

Tango Sierra, Science Station. Orbital facility at which Dr. **Hester Dealt** began work in 2365 to cure a deadly outbreak of **plasma plague** that had stricken the densely populated Rachelis system. ("The Child" [TNG]). *Science Station Tango Sierra was a re-use of the Regula I space station model seen in* Star Trek II. *Regula I was itself a modification of a model originally built for* Star Trek: The Motion Picture.

Tango. Young **Christopher Pike**'s horse when he was growing up in **Mojave** on Earth. The **Talosians** created an illusory version of Tango when Pike was held captive on **Talos IV**. Tango was fond of sugar cubes. ("The Cage," "The Menagerie, Part II" [TOS]).

Tantalus V. Penal colony administered by **Dr. Simon Van Gelder**. Tantalus V was located on a distant planet and protected by a forcefield, preventing transporter use or other possible escape. Considerably advanced beyond early prisons, Tantalus V was more of a hospital for sick minds. One treatment developed there, a **neural neutralizer**, was found to have deadly effects on its patients. ("Dagger of the Mind" [TOS]). *Named for the Greek mythic figure who stole ambrosia from the tables of the gods, feeding it to mortals.*

Tantulus field. Covert murder weapon used by the alternate Captain Kirk in the mirror universe aboard the *I.S.S. Enterprise.* The Tantalus field was a device with a small viewscreen located in the mirror Kirk's quarters and was used to eliminate enemies. The Tantalus field tracked its intended victim, enabling the operator to vaporize the victim by remote control. ("Mirror, Mirror" [TOS]). SEE: **Kirk, James T. (mirror).**

Tanuga IV. Class-M planet at which the late **Dr. Nel Apgar** attempted to develop a **Krieger-wave** converter. Apgar was killed when his space station exploded in 2366. ("A Matter of Perspective"[TNG]).

Tanugans. The humanoid residents of **Tanuga IV**. Tanugans are distinguished by their prominent eyebrow and forehead ridges. The Tanugan system of justice held that the accused were guilty until proven innocent, which became a problem for *Enterprise*-D Commander **William Riker** when he was accused of the murder of Tanugan scientist **Dr. Nel Apgar** in 2366. ("A Matter of Perspective" [TNG]).

• **"Tapestry."** *Next Generation* episode #141. Written by Ronald D. Moore. Directed by Les Landau. Stardate not given. *First aired in 1993. A severely injured Picard relives his past, with the help of Q. Picard's flashback scenes with the Nausicaans at the Bonestell Facility dramatize an incident first mentioned in "Samaritan Snare" (TNG).* SEE: *Ajax, U.S.S.;* **barokie; Batanides, Marta; Bonestell Recreational Facility; compressed teryon beam; dom-jot;** *guramba;* **Halloway, Captain Thomas; Lenarians; magnaspanner; Milika III; Morikin VII; Muroc, Penny; Narth, Captain; Nausicaans; Picard, Jean-Luc; Picard, Maurice; pulmonary support unit; Q; Selar, Dr.; Starbase Earhart;** *Stargazer, U.S.S.;* **stasis unit; straight nines;** *undari;* **Zweller, Cortin.**

Tarahong detention center. Institution where **Quark**'s cousin, **Barbo**, was incarcerated for selling defective warp drives to the Tarahong government. ("The Nagus" [DS9]).

Tarbolde, Phineas. Poet on the Canopus Planet who wrote **"Nightingale Woman"** in 1996, considered to be one of the most passionate love sonnets written in the past couple of centuries. **Gary Mitchell** was able to quote the sonnet after exposure to the barrier at the edge of the galaxy. ("Where No Man Has Gone Before" [TOS]).

Tarkassian razorbeast. Animal that has a propensity for leaping about. Young **Guinan** tempted young **Ro** to start jumping on the bed like a Tarkassian razorbeast. ("Rascals" [TNG]). When Guinan was a child, a tarcassian razor beast was her imaginary friend; the creature protected her and made her feel safe. She described it as huge, covered with brown fur, and having enormous spiny wings. Guinan fondly recalled that it was very frightening, especially when it smiled. As Guinan grew older, the razorbeast faded away, leaving behind only the idea, but Guinan still talked to it occasionally. ("Imaginary Friend" [TNG]).

Tarchannen III. Class-M planet that was the site of a Federation outpost. Tarchannen III was home to an unusual life-form that reproduced by planting a strand of DNA into a host body. The DNA strand would eventually take over the host body, causing it to metamorphose into a non-sentient reptilian humanoid. It is believed that all 49 members of the Tarchannen outpost suffered this fate in 2362 when contact was lost with the outpost.

The *U.S.S. Victory*, dispatched to investigate the outpost, sent an away team to the planet. Five years later, all five members of the away team were irresistibly compelled to return to the planet, apparently part of the metamorphosis process. Three members of the away team completed the metamorphosis and were irretrievably lost. The process was identified by Dr. Beverly Crusher in time to save former *Victory*

away team members **Geordi La Forge** and **Susanna Leijten** from the same fate.

Enterprise-D captain Picard ordered warning beacons placed around Tarchannen III so the planet would not be revisited. ("Identity Crisis" [TNG]). *The transformed versions of the Tarchannen III creatures were played by popular Los Angeles area radio personalities Mark and Brian, who called themselves the Lizard Creatures from Hell.*

Tarella. Class-M planet that once supported humanoid life-forms. Years ago, a deadly biological weapon was created during a war between the inhabitants of two landmasses. The resulting disease wiped out the planet's population. A few Tarellians escaped to other worlds, infecting those planets as well. The remaining Tarellians were hunted as plague carriers, and many were killed by races fearful of contamination. The last eight survivors of Tarella headed toward planet **Haven** in 2364. ("Haven" [TNG]).

Tarellians. Humanoid race from planet **Tarella** who were nearly wiped out by a deadly biological weapon during the Tarellian wars. ("Haven" [TNG]).

targ. Furry piglike Klingon animal. **Worf** had a *targ* as a pet when he was young, and an illusory *targ* once appeared on the *Enterprise*-D bridge. ("Where No One Has Gone Before" [TNG]). SEE: **heart of targ.**

Targhee moonbeast. Life-form noted for its loud bray. The sound produced by a **Valtese horn** was said to resemble the moonbeast's call. ("The Perfect Mate" [TNG]).

Taris Murn. J'naii shuttle vehicle that was lost inside an area of **null space** in the **J'naii** system in 2368. The *Taris Murn* had a crew of two, who, despite the loss of all electromagnetic power into the null space, remained alive long enough to be rescued by a shuttlecraft from the *Enterprise*-D. ("The Outcast" [TNG]). *The miniature of the* Taris Murn, *seen only briefly, was a re-use of the* **Nenebek** *model originally built for* "Final Mission" (TNG).

Taris, Subcommander. (Carolyn Seymour). Commanding officer of the Romulan Warbird *Haakona*. ("Contagion" [TNG]). *Carolyn Seymour also played Commander Toreth in "Face of the Enemy" (TNG).*

Tark. (Joseph Bernard). Father to **Kara**, the Argelian dancer. ("Wolf in the Fold" [TOS]).

Tarkalean tea. Beverage that Dr. Julian Bashir offered to order for the Cardassian **Garak** at the Replimat on the Promenade of Deep Space 9. ("Past Prologue" [DS9]).

Tarmin. (David Sage). The head of an **Ullian** delegation of telepathic researchers. Tarmin was a researcher who described himself as an "archaeologist of the mind." He worked for years to compile a database of memories that would serve as a library for cultural research. Tarmin was briefly implicated in three cases of **telepathic memory intrusion** rape that occurred on the *Starship Enterprise*-D in 2368. He was cleared when his son, **Jev**, was found to be guilty of the telepathic rapes. ("Violations" [TNG]).

Tarod IX. Planet near the **Romulan Neutral Zone** attacked by the **Borg** in 2364, although Romulan activity was initially suspected. ("The Neutral Zone" [TNG]).

Tarquin Hill, The Master of. An unknown artist of planet **Kurl**, the Master of Tarquin Hill lived some 12,000 years ago. The Master of Tarquin Hill was so named by later archaeologists who have come to know and respect the visionary artistry and influence of his work. ("The Chase" [TNG]). SEE: **Kurlan Naiskos.**

Tarsas III. Earthlike planet around which orbits **Starbase 74**. ("11001001" [TNG]). *Of course, the reason Tarsas III was so Earthlike was that the Starbase 74 exterior visual effects shots were re-uses of the **Spacedock** scenes originally created for Star Trek III: The Search for Spock.*

Tarses, Crewman Simon. (Spencer Garrett). A native of Mars colony, Crewman First Class Tarses was assigned as a medical technician aboard the *Enterprise*-D in 2366. Tarses was accused as a conspirator in the Romulan theft of *Enterprise*-D technical data in 2367. While Tarses was not guilty of the theft, he had lied on his Starfleet entrance papers, conceal-

ing the fact that his paternal grandfather was Romulan. When this fact was brought out during the conspiracy hearings, Tarses feared his career in Starfleet was over. ("The Drumhead" [TNG]).

Tarsian War. A conflict fought by the people of **Angosia III** in the mid-24th century. The **Angosian** government utilized extensive biochemical and psychological manipulation on their soldiers in order that they might more effectively fight this war. ("The Hunted" [TNG]). SEE: **Danar, Roga**. *The episode does not make clear who the Angosians were fighting, or if it was a civil war.*

Tarsus IV. Location of an Earth colony that suffered a terrible famine in 2246 when an exotic fungus nearly destroyed the food supply. Colony governor **Kodos** declared martial law, and ordered half of the population, some 4,000 colonists, put to death in order to insure the survival of the remainder. Although relief arrived, it was too late to prevent the executions. Kodos was believed dead following discovery of a burned body, but it was later learned that Kodos had escaped, living under the name **Anton Karidian**. Only nine eyewit-

nesses to the killings survived, among them **James Kirk**, **Kevin Riley**, and **Thomas Leighton**. ("The Conscience of the King" [TOS]).

Tartaran landscapes. Collection of artwork in **Quark**'s quarters on Deep Space 9. Quark wanted to take two voluptuous women — created from his imagination by unknown aliens from the Gamma Quadrant — to his quarters to view his collection of Tartaran landscapes. They seemed willing enough. ("If Wishes Were Horses" [DS9]).

Tartaras V. Planet where the ruins of the Rokai provincial capital were discovered in 2369. **Vash** decided to explore the ruins on Tartaras V instead of returning to Earth after her visit to Deep Space 9. ("Q-Less" [DS9]).

Tarvokian pound cake. A dessert favorite of Lieutenant Worf, who made one to welcome Cadet Wesley Crusher back to the *Enterprise*-D in 2368. ("The Game" [TNG]).

Tasha. SEE: **Yar, Natasha.**

taspar egg. The ova of a **Cardassian** fowl. Boiled taspar egg is considered a delicacy on Cardassia. However, the raw egg of the taspar is considered revolting to Cardassians. ("Chain of Command, Part II" [TNG]).

• **"Taste of Armageddon, A."** Original Series episode #23. Teleplay by Robert Hamner and Gene L. Coon. Story by Robert Hamner. Directed by Joseph Pevney. Stardate 3192.1. *First aired in 1967. The* Enterprise *is caught in a bizarre interplanetary war fought entirely by computers, but with real deaths.* SEE: **Anan 7; Cluster NGC 321; Code 710; DePaul; Eminiar VII; Fox, Ambassador Robert; fusion bombs; Galloway, Lieutenant; Mea 3; Prime Directive; sonic disruptor; Starfleet General Orders and Regulations; Tamura, Yeoman; tri-cobalt satellite;** *Valiant, U.S.S.*; **Vendikar; Vulcan mind-meld.**

Tataglia. A noted concert violinist whose performance style **Data** programmed himself to emulate. Data utilized this style for a Mozart concert in honor of Ambassador Sarek's visit to the *Enterprise*-D in 2366. ("Sarek" [TNG]).

Tau Alpha C. A very distant world, home to the **Traveler**. Little is known about this planet, except that its humanoid inhabitants are extremely advanced. ("Where No One Has Gone Before" [TNG]).

Tau Ceti III. Planet where Jean-Luc Picard once met **Captain Rixx** some time prior to 2364. ("Conspiracy" [TNG]).

Tau Ceti. Star located some 8 light-years from the Sol System. Site where a Romulan vessel was defeated by the *Enterprise* using the **Cochrane deceleration maneuver**. ("Whom Gods Destroy" [TOS]).

Tau Cygna V. Class-H world, desert-like, and bathed in hazardous **hyperonic radiation**. The planet was ceded to the **Sheliak Corporate** by the **Treaty of Armens** in 2255. A

Federation colony was established there in the 2270s in violation of that agreement. The **Sheliak** demanded removal of the colony in 2366 under the terms of the treaty. ("The Ensigns of Command" [TNG]).

Taurus II. Class-M planet on which *Shuttlecraft Galileo*, under the command of Mr. Spock, crashed in 2267. Shuttle crew members **Latimer** and **Gaetano** were killed by indigenous humanoid creatures on the planet. The humanoids were described as "huge, furry creatures" approximately 4 meters tall and possessing crude stone spears. ("The *Galileo Seven*" [TOS]). *Named for the constellation Taurus (the bull).*

Tava. (Sachi Parker). A physician on planet **Malcor III** who helped care for William Riker, masquerading as **Rivas Jakara** at the **Sikla Medical facility** in 2367. ("First Contact" [TNG]).

Tavela Minor. Federation planet that Dr. Crusher suggested as a good place for **Alyssa Ogawa** to take a vacation with her new male friend. ("Imaginary Friend" [TNG]). *The episode script said "Telana," but Crusher clearly said "Tavela."*

Taxco. (Constance Towers). **Arbazan** ambassador who visited **Deep Space 9** in 2369 on a fact-finding mission to the **wormhole**. Taxco initially expressed dissatisfaction with the accommodations on the station, but later softened when **Dr. Julian Bashir**'s quick thinking saved her life. ("The Forsaken" [DS9]).

Taylor, Dr. Gillian. (Catherine Hicks). Twentieth-century marine biologist and assistant director of the **Cetacean Institute** on Earth. Taylor supervised the care of **George and Gracie**, two **humpback whale**s living in captivity at the institute. She was distraught when the two whales had to be released into the open ocean, but she later traveled, with Kirk and the two humpbacks, to the 23rd century. (*Star Trek IV: The Voyage Home*).

Tayna. (Juli Donald). Assistant to **Tanugan** scientist Dr. **Nel Apgar**. She testified against Commander William Riker when Riker was accused of Apgar's murder in 2366. Even though her testimony was hearsay, it was admissible under Tanugan law. ("A Matter of Perspective" [TNG]).

tea ceremony, Klingon. Klingon ritual in which two friends share a poisoned tea served on a tray decorated with simple flowers. The ceremony is test of bravery, a chance to share with a friend a look at one's mortality, and a reminder that death is an experienced best shared — like the tea. Worf shared a Klingon tea ceremony with Katherine Pulaski after she helped him save face by hiding the fact that he was suffering from a childhood disease. ("Up the Long Ladder" [TNG]).

Teacher. Helmetlike device used by the **Eymorg** women of

planet **Sigma Draconis VI** to temporarily gain technical knowledge and skills. **Kara**, leader of the Eymorgs in 2268, used the Teacher to gain the advanced surgical skills required to steal Spock's brain for use in the **Controller**. Dr. McCoy subsequently used the Teacher to learn the skills necessary to return the brain to Spock's body. ("Spock's Brain" [TOS]).

Tears of the Prophet. ("Emissary" [DS9]). SEE: **Orb.**

Tebok, Commander. (Marc Alaimo). Commanding officer of the **Romulan Warbird** that crossed the **Romulan Neutral Zone** in 2364, ending the period of isolationism begun in 2311 after the **Tomed Incident**. Tebok was on a mission to investigate Federation knowledge of the destruction of several Romulan outposts in the area. Tebok entered into a limited agreement with Picard, consenting to share information about the cause of the outposts' destruction, later found to be due to the **Borg**. ("The Neutral Zone" [TNG]). *Marc Alaimo played several other roles; SEE:* **Badar N'D'D.**

tectonic plates. Major subdivisions of the crust of a class-M planet, which meet in seams known as fault lines. By 2367, the ambitious **Atlantis Project** had not yet determined a way to relieve the pressure on Earth's tectonic plates as they built up the mantle to raise the ocean floor. ("Family" [TNG]).

teddy bear. Animal species on planet Vulcan that has six-inch fangs and is not at all like its counterpart on Earth. ("Journey to Babel" [TOS]). SEE: **sehlat.**

Teer. Title given to the leader of the **Ten Tribes** on planet **Capella IV**. In 2267, High **Teer Akaar** was killed by rival **Maab**, who then claimed the title. ("Friday's Child" [TOS]). SEE: **Akaar, Leonard James.**

Tel'Peh. Captain of the Klingon Bird-of-Prey *Toh'Kaht*. ("Dramatis Personae" [DS9]). SEE: **Saltah'na energy spheres; Saltah'na; Hon'Tihl.**

Telaka, Captain L. Isao. Commander of the *Starship* **Lantree**. Telaka, among with the rest of his crew, was killed in 2365 after being exposed to the genetically engineered children from the **Darwin Genetic Research Station** on planet **Gagarin IV**. Although Telaka was the same age as Commander Riker, he died of premature old age caused by the children's deadly antibodies. ("Unnatural Selection" [TNG]).

Teldarian cruiser. A craft that transported Geordi La Forge to the **Kriosian** system in late 2367 so he could rendezvous with the *Enterprise*-D. ("The Mind's Eye" [TNG]).

telegraph machine. Early telecommunication device from 19th-century Earth. Worf used components from a telegraph machine connected to a Starfleet communicator pin to create a protective shield. Worf used the shield to protect himself when he, his son Alexander, and Counselor Troi were trapped in the malfunctioning holodeck program **Ancient West**. ("A Fistful of Datas" [TNG]).

telencephalon. Medical term for brain used on planet **Malcor III**. ("First Contact" [TNG]).

telepathic memory invasion. A form of criminal assault on the **Ullian** homeworld, the forced telepathic intrusion on an unwilling mind, usually inflicting painful memories on the victim. This crime of rape was thought to have been eradicated from the Ullian homeworld by social advances, but telepathic researcher **Jev** was found to have committed several acts of telepathic memory invasion on several planets in 2368. ("Violations" [TNG]).

telepathic rape. SEE: **telepathic memory invasion**.

Teleris. Star cluster that **Q** invited **Vash** to visit, but she declined. ("Q-Less" [DS9]).

television. Form of mass-media entertainment popular on Earth in the late 20th and early 21st centuries. By the year 2040, it had fallen from popularity. (Except, of course, for Star Trek). ("The Neutral Zone" [TNG]).

Tellarite. Race of sturdy individuals with distinguished snouts and a propensity toward anger. Tellarite Ambassador **Gav** was among the delegates to the **Babel Conference** in 2267. ("Journey to Babel" [TOS]). Tellarites have also been seen in "Whom Gods Destroy" (TOS), and in the Federation Council Chambers in Star Trek IV.

Telle, Glinn. (Marco Rodriguez). Cardassian aide to **Gul Macet**. ("The Wounded" [TNG]).

Tellun star system. Star system containing the planets **Elas** and **Troyius**. As of 2268, the two worlds had been at war with each other for many years. ("Elaan of Troyius" [TOS]).

Tellurian spices. A valuable commodity offered by **Zibalian** trader **Kivas Fajo** for sale to a group of Andorians in 2366. ("The Most Toys" [TNG]).

Telluridian synthale. A drink prized by the surviving colonists on planet **Turkana IV**. The beverage was scarce enough to become a commodity worth stealing from opposing cadres. ("Legacy" [TNG]).

Telurian plague. A terrible disease that was still incurable in the 2360s. ("A Matter of Time" [TNG]).

Temarek. (Elkanah Burns). A **Gatherer** living on **Gamma Hromi II**. ("The Vengeance Factor" [TNG]).

Temple of Akadar. SEE: **Akadar, Temple of**.

temporal causality loop. A disruption in the space-time continuum in which a localized fragment of time is repeated over and over again, ad infinitum. The **U.S.S. Bozeman** was trapped in a temporal causality loop in 2278, emerging 90 years later in 2368. Just prior to the return of the Bozeman, the **Enterprise-D** was caught in the same causality loop, where it spent some 17.4 days. ("Cause and Effect" [TNG]).

temporal distortion. A disruption in the space-time continuum. The Enterprise-D's sensors detected a temporal distortion with the appearance of Professor **Berlinghoff Rasmussen**'s **time-travel pod** in 2368. ("A Matter of Time" [TNG]).

temporal disturbance. Discernible area in the space-time continuum where the passage of time within temporal fragments occurs at a different rate than that of surrounding space. ("Timescape" [TNG]).

temporal narcosis. Delirium produced by exposure to a **temporal disturbance**. ("Timescape" [TNG]).

temporal rift. Also known as a time displacement or a temporal distortion, this phenomenon was "a hole in time." A temporal rift was created by a photon torpedo explosion in 2344, accidentally sending the Starship **Enterprise-C** some 22 years into the future. When that ship emerged in 2366, Commander Data noted the rift appered to resemble a Kerr loop of superstring material. He noted that the rift was not stable and had no discernible event horizon. The rift remained stable long enough for the Enterprise-C to return to its proper place in history. ("Yesterday's Enterprise" [TNG]). SEE: **gravimetric fluctuations**.

Ten-Forward lounge. A large recreation room located on Deck 10 of the Starship Enterprise-D, on the front rim of the **Saucer Module**. Ten-Forward was enjoyed by most off-duty personnel, and served as the social center of the ship. Ten-Forward featured a bar, tended by **Guinan**, and numerous tables from which one could enjoy the spectacular vista offered by the windows looking out into space. ("The Child" [TNG]). Although a wide variety of exotic beverages were served in Ten-Forward, most of them used an ingredient called **synthehol**, an alcohol substitute that avoided some of the unpleasant side effects of alcoholic beverages. ("Relics" [TNG]). Ten-Forward was built after the first season of Star Trek: The Next Generation. It was first seen in "The Child" (TNG), the first episode of the second season. The set has been re-dressed to serve as a theatre and a concert hall. In Star Trek VI: The Undiscovered Country, it even served as the office of the Federation Council President, complete with a view of Paris out the windows.

Ten Tribes. Nation-state on planet **Capella IV**. The Ten Tribes were governed by a leader known as a High **Teer**. The title was passed from father to son, except in cases of coup d'état. ("Friday's Child" [TOS]).

tennis elbow. Twentieth-century Earth slang for radio-humeral bursitis. The inflammation of the muscles attached to the epicondyle of the humerus of the human forearm. The inflammation was caused by the stress of striking the ball with a raquet in the ancient sport of tennis. ("Suspicions" [TNG]).

Tepo. (John Harmon). Mobster on planet **Sigma Iotia II** in 2268. Tepo was transported to a meeting between the bosses of the planet attempting to arrange some type of cooperative government. ("A Piece of the Action" [TOS]). SEE: **Iotians**.

Terkim. Maternal uncle to **Guinan**. She referred to him as "kind of a family misfit...(a) bad influence." She also said he was the only one of her relatives with a sense of humor. ("Hollow Pursuits" [TNG]).

terminium. Metal alloy used in the casing of **photon torpedo**es. Spock's casket, located on the surface of the **Genesis Planet**, was composed of terminium. (*Star Trek III: The Search for Spock*).

terminus. Medical term for foot used on planet **Malcor III**. ("First Contact" [TNG]).

Terraform Command. Federation administrative office responsible for overseeing terraform projects. ("Home Soil" [TNG]).

terraforming. In engineering, terraforming refers to any of several very large-scale engineering and biological techniques in which an uninhabitable planetary environments can be altered so that the planet can support life. The Federation enforces very strict regulations regarding terraforming, so as to protect the existence of any indigenous life-forms that might be threatened by such projects. A terraforming project at **Velara III** was found to endanger indigenous life, and the project was discontinued. ("Home Soil" [TNG]). SEE: **Project Genesis.**

terrawatt. Measure of power, 10^{12} watts, or one trillion watts. ("A Matter of Time" [TNG]).

Terrell, Captain Clark. (Paul Winfield). Commander of the *Starship* **Reliant**, Terrell died in 2285 while on a survey mission for **Project Genesis**. (*Star Trek II: The Wrath of Khan*). *Paul Winfield also played Captain Dathan in "Darmok" (TNG).*

tertiary subspace manifold. Location of the **Solanagen-based aliens** in their subspace domain. ("Schisms" [TNG]). SEE: **tetryon particles; coherent graviton pulse.**

Tessen III. Federation planet that was threatened by an asteroid in 2368. Intervention by the crew of the *Enterprise*-D saved the planet. The crew was able to destroy the asteroid in the planet's upper atmosphere by disrupting the core of the asteroid with a particle beam. ("Cost of Living" [TNG]). SEE: **nitrium metal parasites**.

tessipate. **Bajoran** measurement of land area. **Sirco Ch'Ano** sold **Nog** and **Jake Sisko** seven tessipates of land on planet **Bajor** in exchange for **self-sealing stem bolts**. ("Progress" [DS9]).

Tethys III. Green planet with a hydrogen-helium composition and a frozen helium core. ("Clues" [TNG]). *Data used library images of this planet to cover up for the Paxans' Class-M protoplanet.*

tetralubisol. A highly volatile liquid lubricant used aboard starships. **Lenore Karidian** attempted to murder **Kevin Riley** by poisoning his glass of milk with this substance. ("The Conscience of the King" [TOS]).

tetrarch. Title given to the leader of the **Paqu** people on planet Bajor. **Varis Sul** was tetrarch in 2369. ("The Storyteller" [DS9]).

tetryon field. Contiguous field of subatomic particles produced when a phased ionic pulse comes into contact with a **metaphasic shield**. Tetryon particles were detected in tissues from the pilot Jo'Bril, proving the field had been sabotaged during a test in 2369. ("Suspicions" [TNG]).

tetryon particles. Elementary particles that can only exist in subspace and are unstable in normal space. Tetryon emissions were found in the *Enterprise*-D cargo bay in 2369, sent by **Solanagen-based aliens**. ("Schisms" [TNG]).

thalamus. A portion of the humanoid brain, deep with the cerebral hemispheres. The thalamus relays bodily sensations to the cortex for interpretation. ("Violations" [TNG]).

Thalassa. (Diana Muldaur). One of three survivors from **Sargon's planet** after it was destroyed half a million years ago in a devastating war, and the wife of **Sargon**. Thalassa, and a handful of other survivors of that war were placed into survival canisters, and three of them were revived in 2268 by the crew of the *Starship Enterprise*. Thalassa and the others temporarily occupied the bodies of **Dr. Ann Mulhall**, Kirk, and Spock so that they could build android bodies for their intellects. But she eventually realized that the temptations to abuse her superior power inside a living body were too great, so she and her husband opted to face oblivion together. ("Return to Tomorrow" [TOS]). *Photo: Dr. Mulhall hosts Thalassa.*

Thalian chocolate mousse. A dessert made with cocoa from planet **Thalos VII**, where the beans are aged for four centuries. Wesley Crusher ordered a replicated dish of Thalian chocolate mouse for the lovely young **Salia** of planet **Daled IV**. ("The Dauphin" [TNG]).

thalmerite device. Explosive used to destroy the Klingon Bird-of-Prey *Toh'Kaht* when its crew was under the influence of the **Saltah'na energy spheres** in 2369. (Dramatis Personae" [DS9]).

Thalos VII. Planet where cocoa beans are aged for four centuries. Wesley Crusher visited there once while aboard the *Enterprise*-D, and later recalled that it was one of his favorite planets. ("The Dauphin" [TNG]).

Thanksgiving. Traditional Earth holiday, still celebrated aboard the *Enterprise* in 2266. The *Enterprise* chef was preparing hams for the crew's dinner, when **Charles Evans** used his **Thasian** powers to transmute them into real turkeys. ("Charlie X" [TOS]). *The voice of the befuddled* Enterprise *chef was provided by* Star Trek *creator Gene Roddenberry.*

Thann. (Willard Sage). One of the **Vians** who, in 2268, tested **Gem** to see if her race was worthy of being rescued from the impending nova of the star Minara. ("The Empath" [TOS]). *Note that the name "Thann" is from the episode script only and was not actually spoken in the aired episode.*

Thasians. Noncorporeal life-forms from planet **Thasus**. The Thasians cared for young **Charles Evans** after his parents were killed in a transport crash. They gave him extraordinary mental powers so he could survive, but those powers ultimately made him unable to function in human society, so the Thasians were forced to return him to Thasus after his rescue in 2266 by the crew of the science vessel *Antares*. ("Charlie X" [TOS]).

Thasus. Planet on which a transport vessel crashed in 2252, killing all aboard except for three-year-old **Charles Evans**. Unknown to the Federation at the time, Thasus was the home of a race of beings that had evolved beyond the need for physical bodies, existing as pure mental energy. ("Charlie X" [TOS]).

• **"That Which Survives."** Original Series episode #69. Teleplay by John Meredyth Lucas. Story by Michael Richards. Directed by Herb Wallerstein. No stardate given in episode. *First aired in 1968.* Enterprise *crew members are stranded on a ghost planet and terrorized by the image of a beautiful woman.* SEE: **cellular disruption; D'Amato, Lieutenant; diburnium-osmium alloy; Kalandan outpost; Kalandans; Losira; M'Benga, Dr.; magnetic probe; matter/antimatter integrator; Rhada, Lieutenant; Sanchez, Dr.; warp drive; Watkins, John B.**

Thei, Subcommander. (Anthony James). First officer of the **Romulan Warbird** that crossed the Neutral Zone in 2364,

serving under **Commander Tebok**. ("The Neutral Zone" [TNG]).

Thelev. (William O'Connell). A minor member of **Andorian** ambassador **Shras's** staff. He was a surgically altered **Orion**, made to appear Andorian, and planted in the ambassador's party to create havoc on board the *Enterprise* on the way to the **Babel Conference** in hopes of blocking the **Coridan** admission to the Federation. Thelev critically injured Captain Kirk and refused to disclose the identity of the intruder vessel firing upon the *Enterprise*. Thelev had orders to self-destruct and died of a slow poison shortly after the intruder vessel also destroyed itself. ("Journey to Babel" [TOS]).

Thelka IV. Planet where Captain Picard discovered a particularly delicious dessert. Picard offered the dessert from Thelka IV to **Neela Daren,** but the couple were unable to sample the delicacy as duty called them away from dinner. ("Lessons" [TNG]).

Thelusian Flu. An exotic but harmless rhinovirus. The first officer of the *U.S.S. Lantree* was treated for Thelusian flu two days before that ship made contact with the **Darwin Genetic Research Station** on planet Gagarin IV, but Dr. Pulaski ruled out this virus having anything to do with the hyperaccelerated aging experienced by the *Lantree* crew after that contact. ("Unnatural Selection" [TNG]).

Theoretical Propulsion Group. Starfleet engineering design team based at the **Utopia Planitia Fleet Yards** on Mars. This team was largely responsible for the development of the warp engines used in the *Galaxy*-class starships in the early 2360s. **Dr. Leah Brahms** was a junior team member during that project. ("Booby Trap" [TNG]). By 2367, Brahms had been promoted to senior design engineer. ("Galaxy's Child" [TNG]).

theragen. Nerve gas used by the Klingons, instantly lethal if used in pure form. Dr. McCoy prepared a diluted form of theragen mixed with alcohol to deaden certain nerve inputs to the brain in an effort to prevent madness in the *Enterprise* crew caused by exposure to **spatial interphase** in 2268. ("The Tholian Web" [TOS]).

thermal deflector. Protective forcefield used on planet **Bersallis III** to shield the Federation outpost from a **Bersallis firestorm**. ("Lessons" [TNG]). SEE: **Daren, Neela.**

thermal interferometry scanner. Device for measuring distances by means of the interference of thermal gradients. ("Imaginary Friend" [TNG]).

thermoconcrete. Construction material mostly made of silicon used by Federation starship personnel to build emergency shelters. Dr. McCoy used thermoconcrete to heal the wounds inflicted on the **Horta** of planet **Janus VI** by Federation mining personnel in 2267. ("The Devil in the Dark" [TOS]).

thermologist. Scientist who studies the underground distribution of geologic heat. Thermologists were used in the energy transfer from **Jeraddo** to planet **Bajor**. ("Progress" [DS9]).

Thesia, Jewel of. Described as a national heritage of the planet **Straleb**, a spectacular diamond-like gemstone believed to have been stolen by Captain **Thadiun Okona**. The jewel was later found to have been taken by **Benzan** of the Straleb as a pledge of marriage to **Yanar** of the planet **Altec**. ("The Outrageous Okona" [TNG]).

Theta 116. Star system whose eighth planet was the final destination of the ill-fated ***Charybdis*** interstellar probe under the command of **Colonel Stephen Richey**. That planet, first explored by a Klingon expedition, had an atmosphere of nitrogen and methane. Surface temperatures averaged -291 Celsius, and the surface was racked with high winds and storms. ("The Royale" [TNG]).

Theta Cygni XII. Planet whose population suffered mass insanity caused by the **Denevan neural parasites**. ("Operation— Annihilate!" [TOS]). *Theta Cygni was struck sometime between 2067 (when **Levinius V** was infested) and 2265 (when **Ingraham B** was attacked).*

Theta VII. Location of a colony that desperately required vaccines being transported by the **U.S.S. Yorktown** on stardate 3619. The *U.S.S. Enterprise* was unable to make a scheduled rendezvous with the *Yorktown* because of an encounter with the deadly **dikironium cloud creature**. After the cloud entity was destroyed, the *Enterprise* was able to transport the vaccines to the colony. ("Obsession" [TOS]).

theta-band emissions. Subspace carrier waves often associated with background subspace radiation. In 2369, Starfleet Intelligence was led to believe that the Cardassians were utilizing theta-band emissions as a delivery system for a powerful **metagenic weapon**. Captain Picard, who had conducted extensive tests on theta-band emissions while in command of the *Stargazer*, was the only active Starfleet officer familiar with those systems. ("Chain of Command, Part I" [TNG]).

theta-matrix compositer. A component of the *Enterprise*-D **warp drive**. The device made dilithium recrystallization ten times more efficient than it was on **Excelsior-Class** starships. ("Family" [TNG]).

thialo. Term used by the **Wadi** leader **Falow** during the **Chula** game with Quark on Deep Space 9 in 2369. *Thialo* meant that Quark had to choose which of the three remaining players — Kira, Dax, or Sisko — would be killed so that the others could continue their journey home. ("Move Along Home" [DS9]).

Third of Five. (Jonathan Del Arco). **Borg** designation for the individual Borg known to the *Enterprise*-D crew as **Hugh**. ("I, Borg" [TNG]).

• **"This Side of Paradise."** Original Series episode #25. Teleplay by D. C. Fontana. Story by Nathan Butler and D. C.

Fontana. Directly by Ralph Senensky. Stardate 3417.3. *First aired in 1967. Mr. Spock finds happiness at a colony where alien spores provide total contentment. The shot of Kirk entering the empty bridge of the* Enterprise *in this episode was later reused as the establishing shot for Scotty's holodeck recreation of the bridge in "Relics" (TNG).* SEE: **Berengaria VII; Berthold rays; DeSalle, Lieutenant; Kalomi, Leila; Komack, Admiral; Leslie, Mr.; Omicron Ceti III; Painter, Mr.; Sandoval, Elias; Spock; spores, Omicron Ceti III; Starbase 27; subsonic transmitter**.

Tholian Assembly. Governing body of the Tholian race. ("The Tholian Web" [TOS]).

• **"Tholian Web, The."** Original Series episode #64. Written by Judy Burns and Chet Richards. Directed by Herb Wallerstein. Stardate 5693.2. *First aired in 1968. Kirk disappears and is presumed dead while Spock tries to keep the* Enterprise *from being the victim of a weblike alien weapon.* SEE: ***Defiant, U.S.S.;* environmental suit; Kirk, James T.; Loskene, Commander; spatial interphase; theragan; Tholian Assembly; Tholian web; Tholian; tri-ox compound**.

Tholian web. Energy field used by the **Tholians** to entrap enemy spacecraft. The tractor field is spun by two Tholian ships that remain outside of weapons range. Upon completion of the web, the field is contracted, destroying the ship within. While attempting

to rescue the **U.S.S. Defiant** in 2268, the *Enterprise* nearly fell victim to a Tholian web. ("The Tholian Web" [TOS]).

Tholians. Intelligent race known for its punctuality and highly territorial nature. The Tholians accused the *Starship Enterprise* of violating a territorial annex of the Tholian assembly while on a rescue mission when the **U.S.S. Defiant** was trapped in **interspace** in 2268. ("The Tholian Web" [TOS]).

The ongoing conflict with the Tholians flared up again in 2353 when the Tholians attacked and nearly destroyed a Federation starbase, with the loss of nearly all personnel. Civilian advisor **Kyle Riker** was the only survivor in the incident. ("The Icarus Factor" [TNG]).

Conflict with the Tholians continued well into the 23rd century, and simulated Tholian battles were part of the Starfleet Academy curriculum as recently as 2355, when William Riker was able to calculate a sensory blind spot in a simulated Tholian vessel, and use that to his advantage. ("Peak Performance" [TNG]). Tensions with the Tholians remained sufficiently high that Ambassador **K'Ehleyr**, in 2367, feared a Klingon civil war would eventually involve the Tholians. ("Reunion" [TNG]).

Tholl, Kova. (Stephen Markle). A **Mizarian** who was imprisoned with Captain Picard during an alien experiment on the nature of authority. Tholl described himself as "a simple public servant." ("Allegiance" [TNG]). SEE: **Haro, Mitena**.

Thomas Paine**, **U.S.S. Federation starship, *New Orleans* class, registry number NCC-65530, commanded by **Captain Rixx**. The *Thomas Paine* was one of the ships that met the *Enterprise*-D at planet **Dytallix B** when an alien intelligence attempted to take over Starfleet Command in 2364. ("Conspiracy" [TNG]). *The Thomas Paine was named for the American patriot and writer.*

Thompson, Yeoman Leslie. (Julie Cobb). Member of the *Enterprise* landing party that answered the distress call from the **Kelvans** in 2268. As a demonstration of their superior power, the Kelvans distilled Thompson into a small, dry duodecahedron made of her chemical components, then crushed the object, killing her instantly. ("By Any Other Name" [TOS]).

Thorne, Ensign. An *Enterprise*-D crew member and part of the engineering staff. Thorne was injured when exposure to a dark-matter pocket in the **Mar Oscura** nebula in late 2367 caused a cryogenic control conduit in the engineering section to explode. ("In Theory" [TNG]).

thoron emissions. Radioactive isotope; a by-product of decaying thorium. Also known as radon-220. Elevated thoron emissions near the **Denorios Belt** accompanied the appearance of unknown aliens from the **Gamma Quadrant** in 2369. ("If Wishes Were Horses" [DS9]).

thoron field. High-energy field utilized on **Deep Space 9** to block sensor scans from an outside source. ("Emissary" [DS9]).

Thought Maker. A small spherical device of Ferengi manufacture designed to control neural activity in a humanoid brain. The Thought Maker transmitted a low-level electromagnetic signal at its victim, enabling it to implant sensory experiences or trigger memories. The device was forbidden by the Ferengi government, but **DaiMon Bok** obtained two such devices in his attempt to exact revenge upon Captain Picard for the death of his son in the **Battle of Maxia**. ("The Battle" [TNG]).

thralls. SEE: **drill thralls**.

three-dimensional chess. Multilevel version of the ancient terrestrial game of strategy and warfare. One popular version of this game uses a board with three 4x4 main boards, and a number of 2x2 secondary boards. Aboard the original *Starship Enterprise*, both Captain Kirk and Mr. Spock were accomplished three-dimensional-chess players. ("Where No Man Has Gone Before" [TOS]). Three-dimensional chess was the

basis for a security code used on the original *Enterprise* to protect against the possibility of an imposter assuming the identity of a command crew member, especially over voice communications. As of stardate 5718, the code was "queen to queen's level 3," to which the required response was "queen to king's level 1." ("Whom Gods Destroy" [TOS]). The game was something of a Starfleet tradition and continued to find favor among the patrons of the **Ten-Forward lounge** on the *Enterprise*-D. *The three-dimensional chess game in Ten-Forward was based on the game board built for the first* Star Trek *series, but close examination of some of the chess pieces might reveal a replica of the robot from* Lost in Space. *That game board has also been seen on* Deep Space 9. *No official rules were ever developed for this game, although ever-ingenious* Star Trek *fans have developed several sets of rules for themselves.*

thruster suit. Protective garment designed to allow humanoid starship crew members to work in an airless environment. A thruster suit also incorporates a small propulsion unit to permit maneuvering in weightless conditions, intended for emergency evacuation. Spock used a thruster suit when he left the *Enterprise* to attempt a mind-meld with **V'Ger**. (*Star Trek: The Motion Picture*).

Thule. Crew member aboard the original *Starship Enterprise* in 2267 who was trapped on the bridge during **Khan**'s takeover attempt. ("Space Seed" [TOS]).

thymus. Organ in humanoid bodies, located anterior to the trachea. The thymus is responsible for producing lymphocytes, known as T cells, which are part of humanoid immune systems. The alien DNA strand from Tarchannen III implanted in the members of the **Victory** away team was discovered residing in the thymus. Removal of the DNA strand allowed the victim to return to normal, providing some of the victim's original DNA remained. ("Identity Crisis" [TNG])

Tian An Men**, **U.S.S. Federation starship, *Miranda* class, Starfleet registry number NCC-21382. It served in Picard's armada to blockade Romulan supply ships supplying the **Duras** family forces during the **Klingon civil war** of 2367. ("Redemption, Part II" [TNG]). *The* Tian An Men *was named in honor of those who died in the cause of Chinese freedom, much as the present-day U.S. Navy has a U.S.S.* Lexington *whose name celebrates the first battle in the American war for independence.*

Tiberian bats. Avian life-forms known for sticking together. Spock compared some incriminating **gravity boots** as sticking to the guilty parties like a pair of Tiberian bats. (*Star Trek VI: The Undiscovered Country*).

Tiburon. Planet where **Dr. Sevrin** studied as a research engineer in the field of acoustics and communication. He was dismissed from Tiburon when he started the movement seeking the planet **Eden**, rejecting the advancements of the 23rd century. ("The Way to Eden" [TOS]). In the past, the infamous scientist **Zora** conducted brutal medical experiments on the body chemistry of people from Tiburon. ("The Savage Curtain" [TOS]).

tiger. Bengal tiger conjured up on the **amusement park planet** in 2267. ("Shore Leave" [TOS]). *A real elephant was also waiting in the wings but the pachyderm never made it to the film.*

Tilonus Institute for Mental Disorders. Imaginary psychiatric hospital on planet **Tilonus IV** that only existed in the mind of William Riker when he was being interrogated on that planet in 2369. ("Frame of Mind" [TNG]).

Tilonus IV. Planet whose government was in a state of total anarchy when Commander William Riker attempted to rescue a Federation research team there in 2369. He was captured and subjected to neural manipulation in an attempt to extract tactical information from him. ("Frame of Mind" [TNG]). SEE: *Frame of Mind*; **Suna**.

• **"Time Squared."** *Next Generation* episode #39. Teleplay by Maurice Hurley. Story by Kurt Michael Bensmiller. Directed by Joseph L. Scanlan. Stardate 42679.2. *First aired in 1989. A duplicate of Captain Picard from six hours in the future is found drifting in space, the aftermath of the destruction of the* Enterprise-D. *This episode was originally planned to be a lead-in to "Q Who?" (TNG). If this had been done, we would have learned that Q had been responsible for the unexplained time vortex in this episode. "Time Squared" marked the first appearance of the small two-person "shuttlepod" vehicle. SEE:* **El-Baz, Shuttlepod; Endicor system; energy vortex; Ennan VI; Owon eggs; Picard, Jean-Luc; Riker, William T.; shuttlepod.**

time portal. SEE: **atavachron; Guardian of Forever**.

• **"Time's Arrow, Part I."** *Next Generation* episode #126. Teleplay by Joe Menosky and Michael Piller. Story by Joe Menosky. Directed by Les Landau. Stardate 45959.1. *First aired in 1992. Data goes back in time to 19th-century Earth, where he meets Mark Twain. This was the cliff-hanger ending to the fifth season.* SEE: **bitanium; cholera; Clemens, Samuel Langhorne; Colt Firearms; communicator; Data; Devidia II; Devidians; Exochemistry; Falling Hawk, Joe; Guinan; Hotel Brian; La Rouque, Frederick; LB10445; London, Jack; Marrab Sector; microcentrum cell membrane; ophidian; phase conditioners; phase discriminator; pistol; Sector 001; seismic regulators; triolic waves; Twain, Mark; Tzartak aperitif.**

• **"Time's Arrow, Part II."** *Next Generation* episode #127.

Teleplay by Jeri Taylor. Story by Joe Menosky. Directed by Les Landau. Stardate 46001.3. *First aired in 1992. Picard and company return to the past to rescue Data and save Earth from invading aliens. This was the first episode of* Star Trek: The Next Generation*'s sixth season.* SEE: **Appollinaire, Dr.; Carmichael, Mrs.; Clemens, Samuel Langhorne; Data; Devidian nurse; Guinan; Halley's comet; Hotel Brian; London, Jack;** *Midsummer's Night Dream, A;* **neural depletion; ophidian; Presidio; Sisters of Hope Infirmary; Twain, Mark.**

time-travel pod. A 26th-century craft, five meters in length, composed of plasticized tritanium mesh. Twenty-second century **Professor Berlinghoff Rasmussen** traveled to the *Enterprise*-D in 2368 using one of these craft, which he had stolen from an unfortunate 26th-century traveler. ("A Matter of Time" [TNG]).

• **"Timescape."** *Next Generation* episode #151. Written by Brannon Braga. Directed by Adam Nimoy. Stardate 46944.2. *First aired in 1993. The* Enterprise-D *and a Romulan ship are frozen in time, moments away from an explosion that will destroy both ships.* SEE: **artificial quantum signularity; black hole; emergency transporter armbands; mitosis; Mizan, Dr.; nitrogen narcosis; phase discriminator; plasma conversion sensor; plexing; quantum singularity lifeform; Romulan Warbird; runabout; Spot; temporal disturbance; temporal narcosis; Vassbinder, Dr.; Wagner, Dr.**

Timicin, Dr. (David Ogden Stiers). A scientist and native of the planet **Kaelon II**. Timicin spent many years trying to develop a technique whereby the life of his world's dying sun might be extended. Timicin worked aboard the *Enterprise*-D in 2367 to conduct a **helium ignition test** on a red giant star in the Praxillus system. Although the experiment failed, Timicin was prepared to return to Kaelon II for his **Resolution**, the end of his life under Kaelon tradition. But upon further review, Timicin became convinced that he could solve the problems and sought asylum aboard the *Enterprise*-D so he could continue his work. Timicin's requests provoked a diplomatic incident. Timicin withdrew his request for asylum and returned to Kaelon II, where his Resolution was carried out as planned. He was accompanied to the planet's surface by **Lwaxana Troi**. ("Half a Life" [TNG]). *One of the computer readouts studied by Timicin in Engineering bore the numeric code 4077, a salute to David Ogden Stiers' work in the television series* M*A*S*H.

Timothy. (Joshua Harris). A ten-year-old human boy who was the sole survivor of the research vessel *S.S. Vico* when it was destroyed by gravitational wavefronts in the Black

Cluster in 2368. Timothy's mother was the ship's system engineer, and his father was the ship's second officer. Unable to deal with the tremendous shock of his loss, Timothy chose to emulate Commander Data, who had rescued him from the *Vico*. As an android, Timothy would feel no fear or sadness and would not have to deal with the loss of his family. Timothy felt somehow responsible for the destruction of the *Vico*. He hid his sense of guilt by telling the crew of the *Enterprise*-D that the ship had been attacked by mysterious aliens. When Timothy finally came to terms with the loss of his family and friends, his recollections of events aboard the *Vico* were instrumental in helping the *Enterprise*-D escape the same fate. ("Hero Worship" [TNG]). *Timothy's last name was not given in the episode.* SEE: **Black Cluster**.

• **"Tin Man."** *Next Generation* episode #68. Written by Dennis Putman Bailey & David Bischoff. Directed by Robert Scheerer. Stardate 43779.3. *First aired in 1990. The Enterprise-D investigates a living spaceship that is dying of loneliness.* SEE: ***Adelphi, U.S.S.*; Beta Stromgren; Betazoids; Chandra V; *D'deridex*-class Warbird; Darson, Captain; DeSoto, Captain Robert; Elbrun, Tam; first contact; Ghorusda Disaster; *Gomtuu*; Hayashi system; *Hood U.S.S.*; Linguacode; Starbase 123; Starbase 152; structural integrity field; Tin Man; Troi, Deanna; University of Betazed; Vega IX probe.**

Tin Man. Starfleet designation for the living spacecraft discovered near the **Beta Stromgren** system in 2366 by the **Vega IX space probe**. The Romulans intercepted the Vega IX transmissions and dispatched two *D'deridex*-class Warbirds to capture it. Tin Man, which called itself **Gomtuu**, eluded capture, and departed into the unknown with **Tam Elbrun**. ("Tin Man" [TNG]).

"Tiny." Nickname that Sulu hated. (*Star Trek III: The Search for Spock*).

tissue mitigator. Medical instrument used in surgical procedures. ("Samaritan Snare" [TNG]).

Titan's turn. Dangerous maneuver sometimes used by Starfleet shuttle pilots making the **Jovian run**. The procedure, banned by Starfleet, involves flying almost directly toward Titan, a moon of Saturn, then almost skimming Titan's atmosphere before turning sharply around the moon at 0.7*c*. **Geordi La Forge** was skilled at Titan's turn during his days as a shuttle pilot, as was **Captain Edward Jellico**. ("Chain of Command, Part II" [TNG]).

Titan. The largest of Saturn's moons. Titan's diameter is half that of Earth's. Titan was used as an approach point for **Nova Squadron**'s maneuvers in 2368. ("The First Duty" [TNG]).

Titus IV. Planet where **Miles O'Brien** almost stepped on a **Lycosa tarantula**. O'Brien kept the creature as a pet, naming

her Christina. ("Realm of Fear" [TNG]).

T'Jon. (Merritt Butrick). Captain of the **Ornaran** freighter ship *Sanction*. Like all Ornarans of his time, T'Jon was addicted to a medicinal substance called felicium from the planet Brekka. The side effects of this addiction may have been responsible for his lack of understanding of the technical aspects of his ship's operation. ("Symbiosis" [TNG]). *Actor Merritt Butrick had played* **David Marcus**, *son of James Kirk, in* Star Trek II *and* Star Trek III.

TKL ration. The standard meal pack used aboard the *Enterprise*-D during the war with the Klingons in the alternate timeline created when the ***Enterprise*-C** vanished from its "proper" place in 2344. TKL rations were issued when replicators were on minimum power. ("Yesterday's *Enterprise*" [TNG]).

Tkon Empire. A defunct interstellar federation that flourished some 600,000 years ago. At its peak, the Tkon Empire had a population numbered in the trillions and was so powerful it was actually capable of moving planets. The Tkon were virtually wiped out when their sun went supernova, but a small number of outposts survived, including one at planet Delphi Ardu. The *Enterprise*-D encountered this outpost in 2364, making first contact with the Tkon, as well as with the **Ferengi**. ("The Last Outpost" [TNG]).

Tkon, ages of. As noted by the Tkon use of galactic motionary startime charts, the order of Tkon is as follows: Bastu, Cimi, Xora, Makto, Ozari, and Fendor. The central star of the Tkon Empire destabilized in the Age of Makto. ("The Last Outpost" [TNG]).

T'Lar. (Dame Judith Anderson). Venerable Vulcan high priestess who supervised the *fal-tor-pan* ceremony in which **Spock**'s body and living spirit were rejoined following his death in 2285. (*Star Trek III: The Search for Spock*).

TlhIngan jIH. In the Klingon culture, these words are part of the oath spoken between husband and wife in solemnizing their marriage. The words approximately translate to "I am a Klingon." ("The Emissary" [TNG]).

T'lli Beta. Planet that was the destination of the *Enterprise*-D when it encountered a school of **two-dimensional creatures** in 2367. ("The Loss" [TNG]). *T'lli Beta was named by episode writer Hilary Bader for her grandmother, Tillie Bader.*

Toff, Palor. (Nehemiah Persoff). Wealthy 24th-century collector and friend to **Zibalian** trader **Kivas Fajo**. Toff and Fajo were involved in a friendly rivalry over their respective collections. ("The Most Toys" [TNG]).

Tog, DaiMon. (Frank Corsentino). The commander of the Ferengi Marauder vessel *Krayton*, Tog attended the interstellar **Trade Agreements Conference** on **Betazed** in 2366. During the conference, he became enamored with **Lwaxana Troi** and abducted her, along with Commander Riker and Counselor Troi. Tog had hoped to persuade Lwaxana to use her telepathic powers to aid his business dealings. ("Ménage à Troi" [TNG]).

Toh'Kaht, I.K.C. Klingon **Vor'cha-class** attack cruiser that exploded in 2369 shortly after returning through the **Bajoran wormhole** from an exploratory mission into the **Gamma Quadrant**. The *Toh'Kaht* was the victim of telepathic energy spheres from the Saltah'na race. ("Dramatis Personae" [DS9]). SEE: **Hon'Tihl; Kee'Bhor; Saltah'na energy spheres; Tel'Peh.**

toh-maire. Volatile pockets of gas in the **Chamra Nebula**. When in the nebula, being pursued by a **Miradorn** ship, **Odo** lured the attacking ship into a *toh-maire*, which destroyed the vessel when the *toh-maire* ignited. SEE: **Ah-Kel; Croden.** ("Vortex" [DS9]).

Tohvun III. Neutral planet located near the Federation/Cardassian border. ("Chain of Command, Part II" [TNG]).

tohzah. A Klingon expletive. **Alidar Jarok** used this term to insult Lieutenant Worf. ("The Defector" [TNG]).

Tokath. (Alan Scarfe). Romulan officer who was reluctant to execute nearly a hundred Klingon prisoners after the infamous Khitomer massacre of 2346. Tokath sacrificed his military career to establish a secret prison camp in the **Carraya System** where these prisoners were allowed to live out their lives. At the camp, Tokath took a Klingon woman, **Gi'ral**, as his wife,

and they had a daughter named **Ba'el**. The sanctity of Tokath's prison was nearly shattered in 2369 when **Worf** discovered its existence and tried to free the Klingon prisoners, not realizing that they had long ago grown to regard it as their home. Tokath allowed a compromise whereby several children of prisoners were allowed to leave as long as they promised to keep the existence of the camp a secret. ("Birthright, Parts I and II" [TNG]).

Tokyo Base. Starfleet facility where **Kyle Riker** developed the **Fuurinkazan battle strategies**. ("The Icarus Factor" [TNG]).

Tolstoy, U.S.S. Federation starship, **Rigel class**, Starfleet registry number NCC-62095. The *Tolstoy* was destroyed by the Borg at the battle of **Wolf 359** in 2367. ("The Best of Both Worlds, Part II" [TNG]). *The* Tolstoy *was named for the Russian author Leo Tolstoy, who wrote* War and Peace.

Tomalak. (Andreas Katsulas). Commander of the **Romulan warbird** that entered Federation space to retrieve the crew of the downed Romulan scoutship *Pi* in 2366. Tomalak denied that the scoutship was doing anything improper in Federation space, claiming that the *Pi* had suffered a navigational failure. ("The Enemy" [TNG]). Tomalak next encountered

the *Enterprise*-D when the Federation ship illegally entered the Neutral Zone to investigate reports of a secret Romulan base at **Nelvana III**. The reports were a trick, and Tomalak had prepared a welcoming committee of three Warbirds to attempt to capture the *Enterprise*-D. ("The Defector" [TNG]). A fantasy version of Tomalak was encountered by Riker in 2367 during during a virtual reality engineered by **Barash** on **Alpha Onias III** in 2367. In this fantasy, Tomalak was a Romulan ambassador on a peace mission to the Federation. ("Future Imperfect" [TNG]).

Tomar. (Robert Fortier). **Kelvan** who assisted in the capture of the *Enterprise* landing party in 2268 and forced the crew to set course for the **Andromeda Galaxy**. Aboard the *Enterprise*, Scotty got the Kelvan drunk in an attempt to make his humanoid side vulnerable. ("By Any Other Name" [TOS]). *It was to Tomar that Scotty uttered his famous line, "It's green."*

Tombstone, Arizona. Town in the ancient American West made famous by the gunfight at the **OK Corral** between lawmen led by **Wyatt Earp** and the gang led by **Ike Clanton** on October 26, 1881. A bizarre replica of the town was created by the Melkotians in 2268 as part of their plan for the death of Kirk and members of his *Enterprise* crew. ("Spectre of the Gun" [TOS]).

Tomed Incident. An encounter between the **Romulan Star Empire** and the **United Federation of Planets** in 2311. Thousands of Federation lives were lost in this incident, and the Romulans thereafter entered an extended period of isolationism, during which there was no contact at all between the two powers. The isolationist period lasted until 2364. ("The Neutral Zone" [TNG]).

Tomlinson, Lieutenant Robert. (Stephen Mines). Phaser control officer aboard the *U.S.S. Enterprise* during the Romulan incursion of 2266. Tomlinson had been engaged to marry fellow *Enterprise* crew member Angela Martine, but the wedding ceremony was interrupted by news of the Romulan attack. Tomlinson was later killed during the battle. ("Balance of Terror" [TOS]).

• **"Tomorrow Is Yesterday."** Original Series episode #21. Written by D. C. Fontana. Directed by Michael O'Herlihy. Stardate 3113.2. *First aired in 1967. The* Enterprise *accidentally travels back in time to the 20th century, where it is sighted by the Air Force as a UFO. The episode does not make it clear exactly when in the 20th century the* Enterprise *was, but the radio reference to the first moon landing mission to be* *launched "next Wednesday" would seem to place it within a week of July 16, 1969, when* Apollo 11 *was launched.* SEE: **air police sergeant; Alpha Centauri; black star; Blackjack; Bluejay 4; Christopher, Captain John; Christopher, Colonel Shaun Geoffrey; Cygnet XII; Earth-Saturn probe;** *Enterprise;* **Fellini, Colonel; Kyle, Mr.; Omaha Air Base; slingshot effect; Starbase 9; UFO; United Earth Space Probe Agency; Webb.**

T'Ong, I.K.C. Klingon deep-space exploratory cruiser, *K't'inga* class, launched in 2290 under the command of Captain K'Temok. Because of the extended nature of the mission, the entire crew spent most of the transit time in hibernation. The return of the ship to Klingon space in 2365 was a matter of concern because the ship had been launched in an era when the two respective governments were at war. It was feared that the crew of the *T'Ong* would believe that a state of war still existed, and that they might therefore attack the first Federation ship they encountered. Federation emissary **K'Ehleyr** helped avert such a crisis by working with *Enterprise*-D security chief Worf to gain command of the T'Ong before any hostilities could occur. ("The Emissary" [TNG]). *The* T'Ong *was a re-use of Klingon battle cruiser footage originally produced for* Star Trek: The Motion Picture.

Tongo Rad. (Victor Brandt). Son of the **Catullan** ambassador and one of **Dr. Sevrin**'s followers who came aboard the *Enterprise* in 2269 on a quest for **Eden**. ("The Way to Eden" [TOS]).

Tonkian homing beacons. Stolen technology discovered in the **Gatherer** camp on **Gamma Hromi II**. ("The Vengeance Factor" [TNG]).

• **"Too Short a Season."** *Next Generation* episode #12. Teleplay by Michael Michaelian and D. C. Fontana. Story by Michael Michaelian. Directed by Rob Bowman. Stardate 41309.5. *First aired in 1988. An aging Starfleet officer attempts to make amends at a planet where he traded weapons for hostages, fueling a civil war that lasted for 40 years.* SEE: **Cerebus II; Gettysburg, U.S.S.; Hawkins; Idini Star Cluster; Iverson's disease; Jameson, Admiral Mark; Jameson, Anne; Karnas; Mordan IV; Peretor; Persephone V; steelplast.**

topaline. Rare mineral needed for colonial life-support systems. It is found in abundance on planet **Capella IV**. Mining rights for topaline became the focus of a power struggle on that planet between the High **Teer Akaar**, who favored granting topaline rights to the Federation, and political rival **Maab**, who felt the Klingons would offer a more advantageous agreement. ("Friday's Child" [TOS]).

Toq. (Sterling Macer). Child of Klingon warriors captured by Romulans in 2346 at **Khitomer**. Raised at the secret Romulan prison camp in the **Carraya System**, Toq

had little exposure to Klingon culture until Worf visited the camp in 2369. Inspired by Worf's teachings of Klingon culture, Toq left the camp with Worf in order to join mainstream Klingon society. In doing so, Toq promised to keep the existence of the camp a secret. ("Birthright, Parts I and II" [TNG]).

Torak, Governor. (Wayne Grace). Klingon official in charge of border space near Sector 2520. Torak was reluctant to investigate Picard's charges that **Morag**, a Klingon officer, might have been responsible for the murder of **Lieutenant Keith Rocha** at **Relay Station 47** in 2369, but agreed to do so upon learning that Picard was Gowron's **Arbiter of Succession**. Torak was later able to prove Morag's innocence, but allowed Morag to be taken into Federation custody for theft of encoded data from Relay Station 47. ("Aquiel" [TNG]).

Torak. A mythical demonic figure in the Drellian culture. ("Devil's Due" [TNG]).

Toral. (J. D. Cullum). The illegitimate son of **Klingon High Council** member **Duras**. In 2367, Duras family members **Lursa** and **B'Etor** launched a bid for young Toral to succeed the late **K'Mpec** as council leader. ("Redemption, Part I" [TNG]). Jean-Luc Picard, as **Arbiter of Succession**, ruled that Toral was not entitled to his late father's council position, since Toral had not yet distinguished himself in the service of the Empire. Following the victory of **Gowron** against Duras family forces in the **Klingon civil war** of 2368, Toral's life was forfeit because his father and grandfather had wrongfully dishonored the family of **Mogh**. **Worf**, eldest son of Mogh, nevertheless declined to demand Toral's death, much to the surprise of Gowron and the council. ("Redemption, Parts I and II" [TNG]).

Toran. (Michael Bofshever). Official with the Bajoran provisional government in 2369. Minister Toran was in charge of the project to tap energy from the Bajoran moon, **Jeraddo**. ("Progress" [DS9]).

toranium. Extremely strong Cardassian metal used to line the corridors on station **Deep Space 9**. Standard phasers are ineffective at cutting through toranium inlays, and a **bipolar torch** is recommended. ("The Forsaken" [DS9]).

Tore, Nellen. (Ann Shea). A native of Delb II and assistant to Starfleet **admiral Norah Satie**. She was a constant presence at Satie's side, taking notes on everything that was said. ("The Drumhead" [TNG]).

Toreth, Commander. (Carolyn Seymour). Romulan officer in command of the Imperial Romulan Warbird *Khazara*. A career officer, Toreth was proud and efficient, but had little respect for the **Tal Shiar** intelligence service, which was responsible for the murder of her father for political reasons. ("Face of the Enemy" [TNG]). *Carolyn Seymour also played Subcommander Taris in "Contagion" (TNG).*

Torigan, Ensign. Starship *Enterprise*-D crew member who served at Tactical on the Gamma shift on stardate 46852.

("Rightful Heir" [TNG]).

Torin. (Norman Snow). Klingon high cleric who served at the monastery at **Boreth**. He was part of the plot to bring back the prophet **Kahless the Unforgettable** in 2369. ("Rightful Heir" [TNG]).

Torman V. Class-M planet. Captain Picard, Dr. Crusher, and Lieutenant Worf traveled to Torman V in 2369 to secure "discreet" transportation to planet **Celtris III** for a covert Starfleet mission. ("Chain of Command, Part I" [TNG]).

Tormolen, Joe. (Stewart Moss). *Enterprise* crew member, and part of the landing party assigned to investigate the deaths of the **Psi 2000** science team in 2266. Tormolen, under the influence of the **Psi 2000 virus**, became extremely depressed and successfully attempted suicide by stabbing himself with a dinner knife. Although his wound was not very severe, Dr. McCoy later expressed the opinion that Tormolen died because he just didn't want to live. ("The Naked Time" [TOS]).

Torona IV. Home of the reclusive insectoid race known as the **Jarada**. ("The Big Goodbye" [TNG]).

torpedo bay. Facility for preparation and launch of photon torpedo weapons. Located on Deck 13 of refit **Constitution-class** Federation starships. (*Star Trek VI: The Undiscovered Country*).

torpedo sustainer engine. A miniature matter/antimatter fuel cell that powers a sustainer coil so that a **photon torpedo** can maintain a warp field handed off from the torpedo launching tube. The sustainer engines allow a photon torpedo to remain at warp if launched at warp. The sustainer engines were modified for photon torpedoes used in **Dr. Timicin**'s daring **helium fusion enhancement** experiment in 2367. ("Half a Life" [TNG]).

Torres, Lieutenant. (Jimmy Ortega). **Flight control officer** (conn) aboard the *Enterprise*-D during its first encounter with **Q** in 2364. Torres was frozen by Q, but later recovered. ("Encounter at Farpoint, Part I" [TNG]).

Torsus. One of the self-aware **Borg** discovered on **Ohniaka III** in late 2369. Torsus was killed by the *Enterprise*-D away team. ("Descent, Part I" [TNG]).

Torze-qua. A musical portion of the historic Kriosian **Ceremony of Reconciliation** held aboard the *Enterprise*-D in 2368. ("The Perfect Mate" [TNG]).

Tosk. (Scott MacDonald). Reptilian-skinned humanoid who, in 2369, was the first being to visit Deep Space 9 from the **Gamma Quadrant**. The collective name Tosk stood for

beings bred and trained to be the tracked by the **Hunters**. Requiring only seventeen minutes of sleep per rotation and storing liquid nutrients in plastic fibers throughout his body, Tosk was completely self-sufficient. Brought aboard the station after his craft was damaged, he formed a friendship with Chief Miles O'Brien. Hampered by a code of silence, Tosk could not communicate his role as the hunted, even when the Hunters descended upon the station to take him back to their planet in disgrace. O'Brien disobeyed orders and the **Prime Directive** by allowing Tosk to escape, thus continuing the hunt and fulfilling his friend's deepest wish; the chance to die with honor. ("Captive Pursuit" [DS9]).

touch-and-go downwarping. A maneuver in which a starship drops briefly out of warp into normal space, then quickly accelerates back to warp speed. The *Enterprise*-D used this technique to transport an away team to **Gravesworld** while en route to an emergency rendezvous with the **U.S.S. Constantinople**. ("The Schizoid Man" [TNG]).

Towles. An *Enterprise*-D crew member, and part of the engineering staff. Towles was one of two engineers left at the command post set up on a remote planet. The command post was used to coordinate the teams searching for Commander **Data**, following his disappearance in 2369. ("Descent, Part I" [TNG]).

Tox Uthat. A **quantum phase inhibitor** invented in the 27th century by scientist **Kal Dano**. The *Tox Uthat* was a palm-sized crystal capable of halting all nuclear reactions within star. Fearing the device would be stolen, Dano fled to the 22nd century, where he hid the device on planet **Risa**. The *Uthat* became something of a holy grail to criminals from the 27th century who traveled back in time to find the object, and for 24th-century archaeologists, who believed that the legends of the *Uthat* had a basis in fact. These included **Dr. Samuel Estragon**, who spent half of his life in search of the *Uthat*. Upon his death in 2366, his assistant **Vash** was successful in finding the device on planet Risa. Vash was not the only one interested in the *Uthat*; other parties included **Sovak** and two **Vorgon** criminals from the future. Jean-Luc Picard, vacationing on Risa at the time, destroyed the *Tox Uthat* to prevent it falling into unscrupulous hands. ("Captain's Holiday" [TNG]).

T'Pan, Dr. (Joan Stuart-Morris). Director of the Vulcan Science Academy from 2354 to 2369. Dr. T'Pan was a preeminent expert in subspace morphology. She was invited aboard the *Enterprise*-D in 2369 to witness the test of a new **metaphasic shield** invented by **Dr. Reyga**. When Dr. Reyga was killed shortly after the test, Dr. T'Pan came under suspicion for his murder. ("Suspicions" [TNG])

T'Pau. (Celia Lovsky). High ranking **Vulcan** official who presided at Spock's almost-wedding in 2267. T'Pau was the only person ever to turn down a seat on the **Federation Council**. ("Amok Time" [TOS]).

T'Pau. Vulcan spacecraft, registry number NSP-17938. The *T'Pau* was decommissioned in 2364 and assigned to the Starfleet surplus depot in orbit of planet **Qualor II**. In 2368, parts of the *T'Pau's* navigational deflector array were discovered in the wreckage of a **Ferengi cargo shuttle**. Investigation of the unauthorized parts transfer led to the discovery that the *T'Pau* had been surreptitiously acquired by the Romulans. The ship was used to carry some 2,000 Romulan troops during an attempted Romulan invasion of planet Vulcan in 2368. When the attempted invasion was exposed by Ambassador Spock, the Romulans destroyed the ship to avoid capture. ("Unification, Part I" [TNG]). *The ship was presumably named after the Vulcan dignitary from "Amok Time" (TOS).*

T'Pel, Ambassador. (Sierra Pecheur). False identity assumed by Romulan **subcommander Selok** on an undercover mission in the Federation. As T'Pel, Selok posed as a Vulcan ambassador who was renowned as one of the Federation's most honored diplomats.

In 2367, T'Pel was transported to the Romulan Neutral Zone aboard the *Enterprise*-D as part of an apparent Romulan peace initiative. T'Pel was apparently killed in a transporter accident while beaming over to the Romulan Warbird *Devoras*. It was later learned that her "death" was staged to cover her return to Romulan territory. ("Data's Day" [TNG]).

T'plana-Hath. Matron of Vulcan philosophy who said "Logic is the cement of our civilization with which we ascend from chaos using reason as our guide." Spock successfully identified the quote during a memory test in 2286. (*Star Trek IV: The Voyage Home*).

T'Pring. (Arlene Martel). Vulcan woman who was telepathically bonded with **Spock** when they were both seven years old. At their marriage ceremony in 2267, she rejected Spock and selected Captain Kirk as her champion, forcing the two men to fight for her possession. She had chosen Kirk, knowing that Spock would release her for making the challenge and that Kirk would not want her, so that she would be free to choose Stonn as her consort. ("Amok Time" [TOS]). SEE: *Pon farr*. *Arlene Martel now works under the professional name Tasha Martel.*

tractor beam. A focused linear graviton force beam used to physically manipulate objects across short distances. Tractor beams were used by Federation starships and other space vehicles as a means of towing other vessels. Tractor beams were also used to provide short-range guidance for approaching or departing shuttlecraft.

Tracey, Captain Ronald. (Morgan Woodward). Captain of the *Starship Exeter* who violated the **Prime Directive** at planet **Omega IV** in 2268. On Omega IV, Tracey believed he had found the secret to virtual immortality, but instead only found the long-lived survivors of a terrible bacteriological war. Returning to his ship, Tracey brought back a deadly virus that killed all of

his crew. Tracey then became involved with an ancient struggle between the **Yangs** and **Kohms** on Omega IV, providing phaser weapons to that primitive civilization.

Tracey was later taken into custody by *Starship Enterprise* personnel and charged with violating the Prime Directive at Omega IV. ("The Omega Glory" [TOS]). *Morgan Woodward also played Dr. Simon Van Gelder in "Daggar of the Mind" (TOS).*

Tracy, Lieutenant Karen. (Virginia Aldridge). *Starship Enterprise* technician who was to run a psychotricorder analysis on Montgomery Scott on planet **Argelius II** in 2267. She was killed by the alien entity, **Redjac**, just prior to the analysis. ("Wolf in the Fold" [TOS]).

Trade Agreements Conference. A biennial interstellar congress held on planet **Betazed**. The *Enterprise*-D was in attendance at the conference in 2366, and hosted the closing reception. ("Ménage à Troi" [TNG]).

Trager. Cardassian *Galor*-class warship, with a crew of six hundred, commanded by **Gul Macet**. In 2367, the *Trager* attacked the *Enterprise*-D in retaliation for the *U.S.S. Phoenix's* attack on a Cardassian science station. The action by the *Phoenix* had been a violation of the 2366 peace treaty between the Federation and the **Cardassians**. ("The Wounded" [TNG]).

Tralesta. One of several clans of the **Acamarian** people. The Tralestas were all but wiped out in a massacre by their blood enemies, the **Lorank** clan, in 2286. One of the five surviving Tralestas, a woman named **Yuta**, underwent a biological alteration to slow her aging process so that she could exact revenge on the Lornaks. Over the next century, Yuta systematically tracked down and killed all the Lornaks with a genetically engineered **microvirus**. ("The Vengeance Factor" [TNG]).

Tranome Sar. Site of a battle between the Klingons and the Romulans. The father of an officer aboard the Klingon vessel *Pagh* was captured in this conflict, but was not allowed to die. He later escaped and returned to the Klingon Homeworld, to await death in disgrace. ("A Matter of Honor" [TNG]).

• **"Transfigurations."** *Next Generation* episode #73. Written by René Echevarria. Directed by Tom Benko. Stardate 43957.2. *First aired in 1990. Beverly Crusher saves a mysterious fugitive who is transforming into a noncorporeal energy being.* SEE: **Crusher, Dr. Beverly; Doe, John; Henshaw, Christi; inaprovaline; motor assist bands; neurolink; noncorporeal life; O'Brien, Miles; protodynoplaser; Sunad; synaptic induction; Zalkon; Zalkonians; Zeta Gelis Cluster**.

transmuter. A thought-conversion device used by the extragalactic life-forms **Korob** and **Sylvia**. The transmuter resembled a small wand, and served as a director or amplifier, converting their thoughts into actual matter or powerfully convincing images. Using the transmuter, Korob and Sylvia were able to create illusional humanoid forms for themselves, and were able to capture crew members from the *Starship Enterprise*. The transmuter was destroyed by Captain Kirk in order to permit he and his crew to escape, whereupon Korob and Sylvia died. ("Catspaw" [TOS])

transparent aluminum. Optically clear, structurally rigid material used for construction in the 23rd century. Transparent aluminum was first devised in 1986 by Dr. **Nichols**, a scientist at **Plexicorp** in San Francisco. Nichols apparently had some assistance from time-traveling Starfleet personnel in making the invention. (*Star Trek IV: The Voyage Home*).

transponder, emergency. A small device about the size of a lipstick case, capable of transmitting an emergency distress call across limited interstellar distances. Worf gave Riker an emergency transponder when Riker was assigned to exchange duty aboard the Klingon vessel *Pagh*. ("A Matter of Honor" [TNG]).

transport, near-warp. Term used to describe use of the transporter at relativistic speeds (near to the speed of light). A somewhat disconcerting experience to those being transported. The *Enterprise*-D used this technique to transport an away team to Gravesworld while en route to an emergency rendezvous with the *U.S.S. Constantinople*. ("The Schizoid Man" [TNG]).

transporter carrier wave. A subspace signal through which a transporter beam is propagated. Romulan transporters, with minor adjustments, can be made to simulate the carrier wave of a Starfleet transporter. ("Data's Day" [TNG]).

Transporter Code 14. Command for an object to be dematerialized, then immediately rematerialized in a dissociated condition, effectively destroying the object. Captain Picard used Transporter Code 14 to destroy the fabled *Tox Uthat* at **Risa** in 2366. ("Captain's Holiday" [TNG]).

transporter ID trace. A computer record maintained by a Federation starship's transporter system, recording the identity of all transport subjects. The transporter ID trace provided a useful means of verifying whether or not a person has actually been beamed. ("Unnatural Selection" [TNG], "Remember Me" [TNG]). Data and Dr. Beverly Crusher com-

pared **Ambassador T'Pel's** transporter ID trace to her "remains," left on the transporter pad after her apparent death in 2367. The single bit errors discovered by this comparison proved the remains were not those of the ambassador. ("Data's Day" [TNG]).

transporter psychosis. Rare medical disorder caused by a breakdown of neurochemical molecules during transport. Transporter psychosis was first diagnosed in 2209 by researchers on planet Delinia II. The condition affected the body's motor functions, as well as autonomic systems and higher brain functions. Victims were found to suffer from paranoid delusions, multi-infarct dementia, tactile and visual hallucinations, and psychogenic hysteria. Peripheral symptions included sleeplessness, accelerated heart rate, myopia, muscular spasms, and dehydration. The problem was eliminated around 2319 with the development of the multiplex **pattern buffer**. Lieutenant **Reginald Barclay**, suffering from acute fear of transporting, believed he might have been experiencing transporter psychosis. ("Realm of Fear" [TNG]).

transporter test article. A cylinder of **duranium** about one meter tall and 25 centimeters in diameter. Used to test transporter performance by beaming the article away and then back to a transporter pad, or simply beaming it between pads. ("Hollow Pursuits") *The transporter test article prop was made from a Navy sonobuoy casing. The same shape was used for quite a number of props in* Star Trek: The Next Generation.

Transporter Theory. A class taught at Starfleet Academy. **Reginald Barclay** studied this subject under Dr. Olafson. ("Realm of Fear" [TNG]).

transporter. Matter-energy conversion device used to provide a convenient means of transportation. The transporter briefly converts an object or person into energy, beams that energy to another location, then reassembles the subject into its original form. ("The Cage" [TOS]). Transporters are unable to function when deflector shields are operational. ("Arena" [TOS]). SEE: **annular confinement beam; autosequencers; beam; biofilter, transporter; emergency transporter armbands; food replicators; Heisenberg compensator; intraship beaming; ionizer, transporter; Kyle, Lieutenant;**

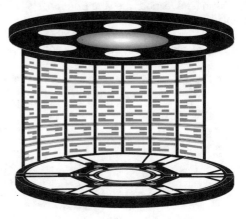

matter stream; O'Brien, Miles; pattern buffer; pattern enhancer; pattern lock; phase transition coils; phased matter; rematerialization subroutine; replicator; shuttle escape transporter; site-to-site transport; transport, near-warp; transporter carrier wave; transporter ID trace; transporter psychosis; transporter test article; transporter theory. *The transporter was Gene Roddenberry's solution to the television production problem of how to get his characters from the starship down to a planet's surface. Landing a huge spaceship every week would have cost far too much for a television budget, but the transporter provided an ingenious means of getting the characters quickly (and inexpensively) into the midst of the action.*

transtator. Electronic device that is a key component of virtually every piece of 23rd-century Starfleet equipment. Dr. McCoy left his **communicator** behind on planet **Sigma Iotia II** in 2268, and it was believed possible that the **Iotians** would figure out how the transtator works. ("A Piece of the Action" [TOS]).

transwarp conduit. Artificially created subspace tunnel. Inside the conduit, the normal limitations of subspace travel did not apply. Ships that were able to access the transwarp state could travel at speeds at least twenty times greater than the maximum warp of *Galaxy*-class starships. In 2369, a previously unknown type of **Borg** ship was traversing Federation space using a series of transwarp conduits, which they accessed by transmitting an encoded high-energy tachyon pulse. ("Descent, Part I" [TNG]).

transwarp drive. Experimental technology for increasing the efficiency and speed of starship propulsion systems. Although initially showing great promise, the transwarp development project eventually proved unsuccessful and was abandoned after extensive testing on the *Starship* **Excelsior**. (*Star Trek III: The Search for Spock*).

tranya. Beverage served by **Balok** aboard the space vehicle **Fesarius**. *Enterprise* captain Kirk and officers McCoy and Bailey seemed to enjoy the stuff. ("The Corbomite Maneuver" [TOS]).

travel pod. Small shuttle vehicle used for inspection tours at Starfleet's orbital drydock facilities. Kirk and Scott rode to the *Enterprise* in a travel pod when the *Enterprise*'s transporters were not functional during the final preparations for the ship's departure to intercept the V'Ger entity in 2271. (*Star Trek: The Motion Picture,* also seen in *Star Trek II* and *Star Trek IV*).

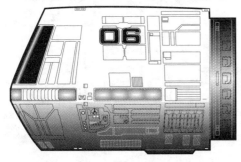

Traveler. (Eric Menyuk). Humanoid from the distant planet **Tau Alpha C**. The Traveler possessed the ability to manipulate a previously unsuspected relationship between space, time, and thought, serving as a "lens," focusing the energies of thought in himself and others. Those energies could be translated into reality, although 24th-century science has yet to

grasp these principles. He was a student of humanoid behavior, and sought passage on Federation ships as a means of observing humans, posing as an assistant to Starfleet propulsion specialist **Kosinski**. When the Traveler and Kosinski were aboard the *Enterprise*-D, a slight miscalculation caused the Traveler to send the ship first to Galaxy M-33, then to an even greater extragalactic distance. During that time, the Traveler befriended young **Wesley Crusher** and encouraged Picard to support Crusher's unusual talents in mathematics, engineering, and science. ("Where No One Has Gone Before" [TNG]). The Traveler returned to the *Enterprise*-D in 2367 when a **static warp bubble**, accidentally created by Wesley Crusher from Kosinski's equations, trapped Dr. Beverly Crusher in an alternate reality. The Traveler helped Wesley use his mental abilities to establish the stable gateway through which Beverly was able to return, just prior to the collapse of the warp bubble. ("Remember Me" [TNG]).

Travers, Commodore. Commander of Federation outpost on planet **Cestus III** in 2267 before it was destroyed by the **Gorns**. Travers was known for his hospitality, so Kirk and his senior officers from the *Enterprise* eagerly accepted an apparent invitation from Travers for dinner at the outpost before learning that nearly everyone on Cestus III had been killed in the Gorn attack. ("Arena" [TOS]).

Treaty of Algeron. Peace accord between Earth and the **Romulan Star Empire** that concluded the Romulan Wars around 2160. The Treaty of Algeron established the **Romulan Neutral Zone**, violation of which by either side without adequate notification would be considered an act of war. ("The Defector" [TNG]). The Treaty of Algeron also forbids the Federation from developing or using **cloaking device** technology in its spacecraft. ("The *Pegasus*" [TNG]).

Treaty of Alliance. Agreement between the **United Federation of Planets** and the **Klingon Empire** ending the war between the two powers. The pact allows for mutual aid and defense against aggressors, but forbids interference in the internal affairs of either government. ("Redemption, Part I" [TNG]). *It is not clear if this treaty was established during the* **Khitomer** *conference of 2293, after the* **Narendra III** *incident of 2344, after the Khitomer rescue in 2346, or at some other point not yet established in an episode or film.*

Trefayne. (David Hillary Hughes). Member of the **Council of Elders** on planet **Organia** who telepathically voiced happenings outside the council chambers on planet **Organia** in 2267. ("Errand of Mercy" [TOS]).

Trelane. (William Campbell). Life-form of unknown origin who kidnapped several *Enterprise* crew members in 2267. A tall, dashing humanoid male in appearance, Trelane was actually a small child from a race of **noncorporal life**-forms possessing enormous powers. With his ability to change matter to energy at will, he created the planet **Gothos** and manufactured

an elaborate façade of a Gothic castle from Earth. Trelane patterned himself after an 18th-century Earth squire. He toyed with the *Enterprise* personnel, eventually forcing his parents to keep him from making any more planets until he could learn not to be cruel to inferior life-forms. ("The Squire of Gothos" [TOS]).

Actor William Campbell also played Koloth in "The Trouble with Tribbles" (TOS). The voice of Trelane's mother was provided by Barbara Babcock, who also played Mea 3 in "A Taste of Armageddon" (TOS), the voice of Isis, the cat, in "Assignment: Earth" (TOS), the voice of Commander Loskene in "The Tholian Web" (TOS), and Philiana in "Plato's Stepchildren" (TOS). James Doohan (Scotty) provided the voice of Trelane's father.

Trent. (Leonard J. Crowfoot). A citizen on planet **Angel One** who worked as an assistant to **Beata**, leader of the planet's governing council. Like most males on the planet, Trent was submissive to the authority of the ruling female class. ("Angel One" [TNG]). *Leonard Crowfoot also played the preliminary android version of Lal in "The Offspring" (TNG).*

tri-cobalt satellite. Energy weapon in the war between planets **Vendikar** and **Eminiar VII** that ended in 2267. None of these devices were used for some 500 years, but simulations of them were used in the computer war between the two planets. A tri-cobalt satellite was used for the mathematical attack during which the original *Starship Enterprise* was declared a casualty in 2267. ("A Taste of Armageddon" [TOS]).

tri-magnesite. Chemical that, combined with trevium, can produce an intensely bright light rivaling that of a star. Tri-magnesite satellites were considered for use at planet **Deneva** in 2267 for eradication of the **Denevan neural parasites**, but a more limited spectrum of light was found to be preferable. ("Operation— Annihilate!" [TOS]). SEE: **ultraviolet satellite**.

tri-ox compound. Medication used to help a patient breathe more easily in a thin or oxygen-deprived atmosphere. When Kirk faced hand-to-hand combat with Spock on **Vulcan** in 2267, McCoy said he would administer tri-ox to Kirk to help him compensate for the thin Vulcan atmosphere. ("Amok Time" [TOS]). *McCoy also administered tri-ox in "The Tholian Web" (TOS).*

Triacus. Class-M planet surveyed by the **Starnes Expedition** in 2268. The explorers unearthed an evil entity that drove the adult members of the colony to commit mass suicide.

According to legend, Triacus was the home to a band of marauders who attacked the inhabitants of **Epsilon Indi**. After many centuries, the marauders were destroyed by those they had attempted to conquer. The legend also warned the essence of those destroyed would live again to do evil throughout the galaxy. ("And the Children Shall Lead" [TOS]). SEE: **Gorgan**.

triangular envelopment. A classic attack posture in which three spacecraft surround an enemy vessel at points describing the vertices of an equilateral triangle. Triangular envelopment was used by **Talarian** forces when threatening the *Enterprise*-D in 2367. ("Suddenly Human" [TNG]).

tribble. Soft, furry warm-blooded animal sold as a pet by interstellar trader **Cyrano Jones**. Tribbles are bisexual and capable of reproducing at prodigious rates, although they will stop breeding when food is withdrawn. Cyrano Jones gave a tribble to Lieutenant Uhura at **Deep Space Station K-7** in

2267. When Uhura returned to the *Enterprise* with her new pet, the tribble quickly multiplied to the point where its offspring nearly overran the ship. Tribbles also multiplied on Station K-7, somehow finding their way into storage compartments containing a valuable grain called **quadrotriticale**. The grain had been poisoned by a Klingon spy, a fact revealed when many of the tribbles were found dead. The remaining tribbles on K-7 were presumably removed by Cyrano Jones, while Scotty beamed the tribbles from the *Enterprise* to the Klingon ship, where he expected them to be "no tribble at all." ("The Trouble with Tribbles" [TOS]).

Tribbles were also seen in the bar visited by McCoy in Star Trek III.

triceron. An explosive compound. The bomb used to disrupt the *Sonchi* ceremony aboard **K'mpec**'s ship was of a triceron derivative. ("Reunion" [TNG]).

triclenidil. One of several chemicals used by the **Angosians** during the **Tarsian War** to "improve" their soldiers, making them more effective in combat. Unfortunately, the effects of many of these drugs were irreversible. ("The Hunted" [TNG]). SEE: **Danar, Roga**.

tricorder. Multipurpose scientific and technical instrument. This handheld device incorporates sensors, computers, and recorders in a convenient, portable form. ("The Naked Time" [TOS]). Several models of tricorders have been used by starship crews over the years. All of them have featured state-of-the-art sensing technology, and all have been an essential part of starship missions and operations. Specialized tricorders are available for specific engineering, scientific, and medical applications. Standard-issue Starfleet tricorders were unable to detect subspace phenomena in 2366. ("The Bonding" [TNG]). They were also incapable of sensing neutrino emissions. ("The Enemy" [TNG]). *SEE: Illustrations on next page.*

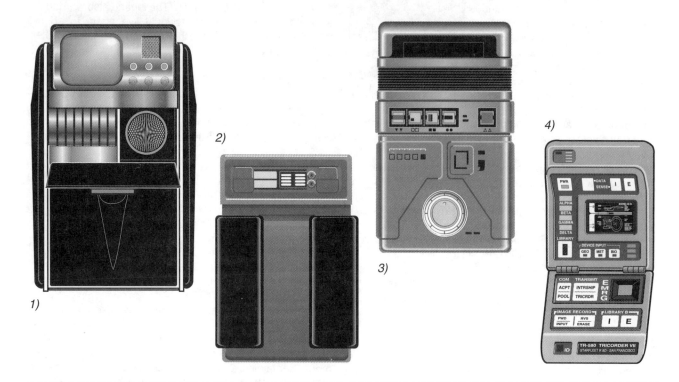

Tricorders (continued from previous page): 1) Original Series tricorder. 2) Star Trek I version. 3) Star Trek III version. 4) Star Trek: The Next Generation standard tricorder.

tricordrazine. A powerful neurostimulant drug usually administered subcutaneously by hypospray. Tricordrazine treatment was successfully used by Dr. Pulaski to stimulate neural activity in William Riker when he had suffered neural injury on an away mission at planet **Surata IV.** ("Shades of Grey" [TNG]). *Tricordrazine was based on **cordrazine**, the drug that sent McCoy on a paranoid flight in "The City on the Edge of Forever" (TOS).*

tricyanate. A purple crystalline substance that occurs naturally on planet **Beta Agni II**. Toxic to humanoids, tricyanate contamination was found in the water supply of the Beta Agni II colony in 2366, an incident later found to have been engineered by **Zibalian** trader **Kivas Fajo**. ("The Most Toys" [TNG]).

Trieste, U.S.S. A *Merced*-class Federation starship, Starfleet registry number NCC-37124. The *Trieste* was stationed near Starbase 74 and was unable to render assistance when the *Enterprise*-D was hijacked by the **Bynars** in 2364. The *Trieste* was some 66 hours away at the time. ("11001001" [TNG]). Data served aboard the *Trieste* prior to his assignment to the *Enterprise*-D. During Data's tour of duty on the *Trieste*, the ship once fell through a wormhole. ("Clues" [TNG]). *The Trieste was named for the bathyscaphe in which oceanographer Jacques Piccard (for whom Captain Picard was named) explored Earth's Marianas Trench in the 1960s.*

trilaser connector. Medical instrument used by Dr. McCoy to restore Spock's brain to his body on planet **Sigma Draconis** VI in 2268. ("Spock's Brain" [TOS]).

trilithium resin. Highly toxic waste by-product created when **dilithium** is exposed to intense matter/antimatter reactions in a starship's warp engine core. The compound is extremely unstable and is generally regarded as useful only as an explosive. In 2369, a group of politically non-aligned terrorists sought to steal trilithium from the warp core of the *Enterprise*-D while the ship was docked at the **Remmler Array** at **Arkaria Base**. ("Starship Mine" [TNG]).

Trill. A joined species comprised of a humanoid **host** and a small vermiform **symbiont** that resides in an internal abdominal pocket of the host body. Most of the personality and memories of the Trill reside in the symbionts, which are extremely long-lived, although the host also contributes personality traits to the joined life-form. Upon the death of a host body, a Trill  symbiont can be transplanted into another host. Trill hosts enter voluntarily into their association with the symbiont, and in fact there is rigorous competition among potential hosts to determine who will be accorded this honor. Hosts are accepted into their mid-twenties. Once joined, the host and symbiont become biologically interdependent, and after 93 hours, neither can survive without the other. The resulting new joined life-form is considered to be another person, although it retains memories of previous joinings. ("The Host" [TNG], "Emissary" [DS9], "Dax" [DS9]). SEE: **Dax, Curzon; Dax, Jadzia; Kareel; Odan, Ambassador; symbiont.** Trills' hands are naturally cold. Sometimes friendships with other species don't survive when the Trill moves to the next host. Trill hosts sometimes have sexual feelings, but they do their best to rise above them. ("A Man Alone" [DS9]). *Certain Trill symbionts can be severely damaged by beaming, which is why Odan insisted on using the shuttlecraft. Other Trills, including Jadzia Dax, don't seem to have the same problem.*

trillium 323. Mineral substance found on planet Caldonia. Negotiator **Devinoni Ral** arranged to acquire rights to the **Caldonians'** trillium 323 as part of the **Chrysalian** bid for the **Barzan wormhole** in 2366. ("The Price" [TNG]).

trillium. Good traded on planet **Organia.** Spock posed as a trader dealing in kevas and trillium. ("Errand of Mercy [TOS]).

triolic waves. By-product of an energy source employed by the beings on planet **Devidia II**. The energy source had deleterious effects on most living tissue, except for life-forms with **microcentrum cell membranes**. ("Time's Arrow, Part I" [TNG]).

Triona System. Located in a remote sector, the site of a Starfleet outpost to which **Lieutenant Keith Rocha** was assigned in 2369. While at the Triona System, Rocha was apparently killed by **coalescent organisms** that subsequently assumed his form. ("Aquiel" [TNG]).

trionium. One of the compounds detected by *Enterprise*-D sensors in nebula **FGC-47**. ("Imaginary Friend" [TNG]).

Tripoli, U.S.S. Federation starship, *Hokule'a* class, Starfleet registry number NCC-19386. The Tripoli was the ship that discovered the android **Data** at the remains of the Federation colony at **Omicron Theta** in 2338. The crew of the *Tripoli* activated Data, who later went on to become a member of Starfleet. ("Datalore" [TNG]). The *Tripoli* was decommissioned and was relegated to the **Zed-15** surplus depot at planet **Qualor II**. In 2368, the *Tripoli* was stolen by Romulan operatives. ("Unification, Part I" [TNG]).

tripolymer composites. Material used in the construction of the android Data, who has about 24.6 kilograms of the material in his body. ("The Most Toys" [TNG]). Tripolymers are not electrically conductive. ("Disaster" [TNG]).

trisec. Measurement of time on planet **Triskelion**. ("The Gamesters of Triskelion" [TOS]).

Triskelion. Planet in the M24 Alpha, a trinary star system. The planet was ruled by three disembodied brains called **Providers**, who maintained a colony of humanoid slaves for gaming purposes. These slaves were freed in 2268. ("The Gamesters of Triskelion" [TOS]). SEE: **drill thralls**.

tritium. Isotope of hydrogen with an atomic weight of 3. Low concentrations of tritium gas were used to trace particle flow

to a dangerous **graviton field** buildup on station Deep Space 9 in 2369. Tritium gas is mildly radioactive and is hazardous when highly concentrated, but the amount used on the station was very small. ("Q-Less" [DS9]).

Trixian bubble juice. Beverage served at Quark's bar on Deep Space 9. **Varis Sul** of **Paqu** ordered this drink, then threw it in Quark's face after suffering a perceived insult. ("The Storyteller" [DS9]).

Troglytes. Citizens of the planet **Ardana** who lived on the planet's surface, performing mining and other labor-intensive tasks that supported the privileged few who lived in the cloud city of Stratos. The Troglytes who worked in the mines were forced to breathe toxic **zenite** gas, resulting in impairment of mental processes. Troglyte political activists, known as **Disrupters**, forced the **Stratos** government in 2269 to recognize these hazardous working conditions and provide appropriate safety equipment. The Troglytes expressed an intent to win political and economic equality, as well. ("The Cloud Minders" [TOS])

Troi, Deanna. (Marina Sirtis). Counselor aboard the *U.S.S. Enterprise*-D under the command of Captain Jean-Luc Picard. ("Encounter at Farpoint" [TNG]).

Daughter of **Lwaxana Troi** and **Ian Andrew Troi**, Deanna was betrothed to **Wyatt Miller** through the Betazoid custom of genetic bonding when they were both children. Deanna and Wyatt never married, though, because Wyatt chose to join the last surviving **Tarellians** in search of a cure for the Tarellian plague. ("Haven" [TNG]).

Deanna's father used to read her heroic stories about the ancient American West on planet Earth, and she remained fond of these stories into her adulthood. ("A Fistful of Datas" [TNG]). SEE: ***Ancient West*; Durango.** Troi studied psychology at the University of Betazed prior to her joining Starfleet. ("Tin Man" [TNG]).

While a psychology student on Betazed, Troi became romantically involved with Lieutenant **William T. Riker.** ("Ménage à Troi" [TNG]). Troi had hopes of a serious commitment between the two, but Riker's career plans took him away to an assignment aboard the ***U.S.S. Potemkin***. ("Encounter at Farpoint" [TNG], "Second Chances" [TNG]). Troi graduated from the Academy (possibly having taken classes on Betazed) in 2359. ("Conundrum" [TNG]). Troi was once involuntarily impregnated by an unknown **noncorporeal life**-form. Troi named the child **Ian Andrew Troi**, after her late father. ("The Child" [TNG]).

Troi suffered a brief loss of her empathic powers in 2367 from proximity to a newly discovered group of **two-dimensional creatures**. Although Troi found the loss disconcerting, she was pleased to discover that she could still function as ship's counselor without her Betazoid abilities. ("The Loss" [TNG]). Counselor Troi assumed temporary command of the *Enterprise*-D on stardate 45156 when the ship was disabled from collision with two **quantum filaments**. Troi, who held the rank of lieutenant commander, was the senior officer on the bridge at the time. ("Disaster" [TNG]). Troi said she never met a chocolate she didn't like. ("The Price" [TNG], "The Game" [TNG]). *Deanna Troi was first seen in "Encounter at Farpoint" (TNG). Marina Sirtis originally auditioned for the part of Natasha Yar and was almost cast for the part, but Gene Roddenberry decided at the last moment to switch the roles of Yar and Troi between Sirtis and Denise Crosby.*

Troi, Ian Andrew (junior). (R. J. Williams, Zachary Benjamin). Son of *Enterprise*-D counselor **Deanna Troi** after she was impregnated by an **noncorporeal life**-form entity in 2365. Ian Andrew appeared to have an identical genetic pattern to his half-human, half-Betazoid mother, but gestated and grew at a tremendously accelerated rate. The child was later found to be the effort of the energy life-form to learn more about human life. Ian Andrew died at the apparent physiological age of about 8, but a chronological age of only a few days, when the energy entity learned it was emitting a form of radiation that seriously threatened the crew of the *Enterprise*. ("The Child" [TNG]).

Troi, Ian Andrew (senior). Human father of **Deanna Troi**, and husband to Betazoid ambassador **Lwaxana Troi**. ("The Child" [TNG]). Ian Andrew Troi was a Starfleet officer who died when Deanna was seven. ("Dark Page" [TNG]).

Troi, Lwaxana. (Majel Barrett). Ambassador to the government of Betazed, and **Deanna Troi**'s mother.

Lwaxana Troi was daughter of the Fifth House, Holder of the Sacred Chalice of Rixx, Heir to the Holy Rings of Betazed. ("Haven" [TNG]). Lwaxana, a full Betazoid, married a Starfleet officer, Ian Andrew Troi ("The Child" [TNG]), and the couple had two children, Kestra and Deanna. Kestra died at an early age, while the other, Deanna Troi, became a Starfleet officer. Ian Troi died when Deanna was seven ("Dark Page" [TNG]).

Lwaxana Troi became a full ambassador of Betazed in 2365, and represented her government at the **Pacifica** Conference in that year. At about that time, Troi entered what is known in Betazoid culture as **the phase**, during which a woman's sexuality matures and her sex drive quadruples. At one point during her phase, Troi had hoped to marry either Jean-Luc Picard or William Riker. ("Manhunt" [TNG]). In 2366, Troi was kidnapped by **DaiMon Tog** in an attempt to use her empathic powers for his personal gain. The ambassador was able to escape by convincing Tog that her "jealous lover" Picard would destroy Tog's ship if she was not returned. ("Ménage à Troi" [TNG]). Lwaxana became engaged to marry **Minister Campio** of planet **Kostolain** in 2368, but the wedding was canceled when Campio could not accept the traditional Betazoid custom of conducting the ceremony in the nude. ("Cost of Living" [TNG]). Something of a free spirit, Troi enjoyed vacationing at the colorful **Parallax Colony** on planet

Shiralea VI, where she was very fond of the mud baths. When she could not actually visit there, she indulged in a holodeck re-creation of the colony. ("Cost of Living" [TNG]). *Majel Barrett, the widow of* Star Trek *creator Gene Roddenberry, also played Number One in the first* Star Trek *pilot, "The Cage" (TOS), as well as Nurse Christine Chapel. Barrett also lent her voice to the U.S.S. Enterprise computer, the Companion ("Metamorphosis" [TOS]), and the Beta 5 computer ("Assignment: Earth" [TOS]). Lwaxana Troi's first appearance was in "Haven" (TNG).*

trombone. Ancient Earth musical instrument enjoyed by William Riker on the *Enterprise*-D. Riker was an enthusiastic amateur musician who liked to practice during his off-duty hours. ("11001001" [TNG]). He also gave occasional performances to his crewmates in the Ten-Forward lounge. William Riker gave his favorite trombone to his newly discovered twin, **Thomas Riker**, in 2369, just before Thomas transferred to the **U.S.S. Gandhi.** ("Second Chances" [TNG]).

• **"Trouble with Tribbles, The."** Original Series episode #42. Written by David Gerrold. Directed by Joseph Pevney. Stardate 4523.3. *First aired in 1967. Tribbles are unbelievably cute, but the trouble is that they reproduce at an amazing rate.* SEE: **Antarian glow water; Baris, Nilz; Burke, John; Code 1 Emergency; Darvin, Arne; Deep Space Station K-7; Denebian slime devil; Donatu V, Battle of; Freeman, Ensign; Jones, Cyrano; Klingonese; Koloth, Captain; Korax; Lurry, Mr.; Organian Peace Treaty; quadrotriticale; Regulan blood worms; Sherman's Planet; Spican flame gem; tribble.**

Troyians. Humanoid race from planet **Troyius** that had been at war with the neighboring planet **Elas** for many years. A marriage between the ruler of Troyius and the **Dohlman** of Elas was arranged in 2268 as a means of bringing peace to the two worlds. ("Elaan of Troyius" [TOS]).

Troyius, Elaan of. SEE: **Elaan.**

Troyius. Class-M planet in the **Tellun star system**. Troyius was a plentiful source of naturally occurring **dilithium** crystals, making the planet of considerable strategic interest to the Klingon Empire in 2268. ("Elaan of Troyius" [TOS]).

Trudy series. Android model designed by Harry Mudd. ("I, Mudd" [TOS]).

• **"True-Q."** *Next Generation* episode #132. Written by René Echevarria. Directed by Robert Scheerer. Stardate 46192.3. *First aired in 1992. Q torments a young woman who doesn't realize she's a member of the Q Continuum.* SEE: **Argolis Cluster; baristatic filter; Bilaren system; Ogawa, Nurse Alyssa; Orn Lote; Q Continuum; Q; Rogers, Amanda; Tagra IV; Tagrans; weather modification net.**

tryptophan-lysine distillates. Medication prescribed by **Dr. Katherine Pulaski** for treatment of a flu virus. She also prescribed generous doses of PCS — Pulaski's Chicken Soup. ("The Icarus Factor" [TNG]).

Tsetse fly. Any of a group of small flies indigenous to the continent of Africa on Earth. The insect was noted for transmitting African sleeping sickness. ("Ship in a Bottle" [TNG]).

T'Shanik. (Tasia Valenza). One of three candidates who competed with Wesley Crusher for a single opening to Starfleet Academy at **Relva VII** in 2364. A female from Vulcana Regar, T'Shanik was a runner-up in the competition. ("Coming of Age" [TNG]).

Tsingtao, Ray. (Brian Tochi). One of the surviving children of the **Starnes Expedition** whose parents committed suicide on planet **Triacus** in 2268. In the aftermath of the tragedy, young Tsingtao was controlled by the **Gorgan**. ("And the Children Shall Lead" [TOS]).

Tsiolkovsky, U.S.S. Federation science vessel, **Oberth class,** Starfleet registry NCC-53911. The *Tsiolkovsky* had been on a routine science mission monitoring the collapse of a red super giant star into a white dwarf in 2364 when the entire crew of 80 became infected with a variant of the **Psi 2000 virus**. All ship's personnel died from the effects of the virus. ("The Naked Now" [TNG]). *The* Tsiolkovsky *was named for Russian space pioneer Konstantin Tsiolkovsky. The ship miniature was a re-dress of the* **Grissom** *from Star Trek III. The dedication plaque for the ship bore a quote from Tsiolkovsky: "The Earth is the cradle of the mind, but one cannot remain in the cradle forever."*

t'stayan. A **Talarian** riding animal. *T'stayans* possessed six hooves and were reported to be very powerful animals. Talarian captain **Endar** said his adopted son, **Jono**, had broken two ribs while riding one of these creatures. ("Suddenly Human" [TNG]).

T'su, Ensign Lian. (Julia Nickson). Relief operations manager aboard the *Enterprise*-D. T'Su took **Ops** when Data beamed down to planet **Minos** to investigate the disappearance of the *Drake*. ("The Arsenal of Freedom" [TNG]). *Julia Nickson also played Cassiopia in "Paradise" (DS9).*

T'su, Tan. (Vladimir Velasco). Engineer of the Federation freighter *Arcos*. T'Su was forced to abandon his craft with the *Arcos* pilot when the *Arcos* suffered a warp containment breach near planet **Turkana IV** in 2367. T'su, along with the pilot, was held prisoner by a group on Turkana IV until rescued by an away team from the *Enterprise*-D. ("Legacy" [TNG]).

tube grubs. Ferengi delicacy, worms eaten while the creatures are still alive. The Ferengi **Zek** complimented Quark on the tube grubs at a dinner given to honor the **Grand Nagus** on Deep Space 9 in 2369. ("The Nagus" [DS9]).

Tula. (Brioni Farrel). Inhabitant of planet **Beta III** during the end of **Landru**'s rule in 2267. Tula, the daughter of **Reger**, was assaulted by **Bilar** during the **Red Hour**, a festival of uncontrolled violence and lust. ("Return of the Archons" [TOS]).

turboelevator. SEE: **turbolift**.

turbolift. Starfleet term for a high-speed elevator system used aboard Federation starships for intraship personnel transport. Turbolifts are controlled verbally, with a voice-recognition computer device that directs elevator movement both horizontally and vertically within the ship. Also called turboelevators. ("Where No Man Has Gone Before" [TOS]). The old Cardassian station **Deep Space 9** was also equipped with turbolifts, although the system was somewhat antiquated by Federation standards. Turbolifts on Deep Space 9 had open-air cabs and were powered by multiphase alternating current. ("The Forsaken" [DS9]).

Turkana IV. A class-M planet, site of a failed Federation colony. The colonial government began to collapse in 2337, leaving dozens of rival factions fighting for control. Eventually, the colony's main city was destroyed and the population was forced to move underground. In 2352, the remains of the Turkanian government broke off all diplomatic ties with the Federation. By the time the *Enterprise*-D visited the planet in 2367, the colony was controlled largely by two rival cadres, the **Coalition** and the **Alliance**; each controlled approximately one-half of the colony. Turkana IV was the birthplace of *Enterprise*-D security chief **Natasha Yar**, who was born there in 2337. Yar's younger sister, **Ishara Yar**, was born on Turkana IV in 2342. ("Legacy" [TNG]).

turn. English translation of the Klingon term for year, as in one turn (or revolution) of a planet around its sun. ("Sins of the Father" [TNG]).

• **"Turnabout Intruder."** Original Series episode #79. Teleplay by Arthur H. Singer. Story by Gene Roddenberry. Directed by Herb Wallerstein. Stardate 5928.5. *First aired in 1969. Captain Kirk is kidnapped by a woman scientist who places her consciousness in his body, then traps his in hers. This was the last episode of the original* Star Trek *television series. Captain Picard's opening log reference to an "archaeological survey on Camus II" in "Legacy" (TNG) was intended as a tribute to this milestone in* Star Trek *history.* SEE: **Benecia Colony; Beta Aurigae; Camus II; celebium; Coleman, Dr. Arthur; Kirk, James T.; Lemli, Mr.; Lester, Dr. Janice; life-energy transfer;** *Potemkin, U.S.S.;* **Robbiani dermal-optic test; Starbase 2.**

T'Vran. Vulcan ship that offered assistance to a runabout from Deep Space 9 after a **Miradorn** vessel was destroyed in the **Chamra Nebula** in 2369. The *T'Vran* then transported **Rakhari** fugitive **Croden** and his daughter to the planet **Vulcan** to start new lives. ("Vortex" [DS9]).

Twain, Mark. Pen name for 19th-century Earth writer and space traveler **Samuel Langhorne Clemens**. ("Time's Arrow, Parts I and II" [TNG]).

Twenty-First Street Mission. Institution in the city of New York on Earth during the Great Depression of the 1930s, managed by social worker **Edith Keeler**. The Twenty-First Street Mission provided food and shelter to the unfortunate victims of the economic downturn. ("The City on the Edge of Forever" [TOS]).

two-dimensional creatures. Life-forms from a two-dimensional spatial continuum. A group of these creatures entered our continuum in 2367 and were discovered by scientists aboard the *Enterprise*-D. The creatures were described as resembling bioluminescent plankton, floating freely in interstellar space, much as fish swim in Earth's oceans. The presence of these life-forms also caused the temporary loss of Deanna Troi's empathic powers. The creatures, attempting to return to their own space through a **cosmic string fragment**, had apparently lost their way until *Enterprise*-D personnel used the ship's main deflector to generate the appropriate subspace harmonics to guide their return. ("The Loss" [TNG]).

two-headed Malgorian. Life-form reputed to be incapable of making up its mind about what it wants. Bajoran farmer **Mullibok** compared Major Kira Nerys to a two-headed Malgorian because she wanted to let her friend stay on **Jeraddo** but her duty required an enforcement of the evacuation order. ("Progress" [DS9]).

Tycho IV. Home planet to the spacefaring **dikironium cloud creature**. The ***U.S.S. Farragut*** lost 200 crew members fighting that entity in the Tycho system in 2257. Captain Kirk of the *Enterprise* destroyed the creature there in 2268. ("Obsession" [TOS]).

Tyken's Rift. A rare rupture in the fabric of space, undetectable by most sensors. Named for Bela Tyken, a Melthusian captain who first discovered the phenomenon, the rift effectively drained all energy from any space vehicle unlucky enough to fall into it. When Tyken found his ship trapped in the rift, he was able to escape by generating a massive energy burst using anicium and yurium, overloading the rift and allowing him to escape. In 2367, the ***U.S.S. Brattain*** and later the *U.S.S. Enterprise*-D were trapped in a Tyken's Rift. Both crews suffered severe **REM sleep** deprivation, a condition found to be caused by an alien intelligence also trapped in the rift. This intelligence was trying to communicate with the Starfleet vessels, in an effort to propose a cooperative effort that would enable all to escape. The realization that the aliens were trying to communicate came too late to save the crew of the *Brattain*, but the *Enterprise*-D was able to work with the aliens to generate an explosion large enough to rupture the rift and let both ships escape. ("Night Terrors" [TNG]).

Tyler, José. (Peter Duryea). Navigator on the original *Starship Enterprise* under the command of Captain Christopher Pike, circa 2254. ("The Cage," "The Menagerie, Parts I and II" [TOS]).

Typhon Expanse. A large region near which the ***U.S.S. Bozeman*** disappeared in 2278 into a **temporal causality loop**. A second Federation starship, the *Enterprise*-D, was also trapped in that causality loop near the Typhon Expanse for some 17.4 days in 2368. ("Cause and Effect" [TNG]).

Tyree. (Michael Kovack). Leader of the primitive **hill people** of his planet. **James T. Kirk** met Tyree while commanding his first planetary survey mission in 2254. They became friends and were ceremonially made brothers. Tyree and Kirk met again in 2267 when the *Enterprise* visited the planet for scientific research. Upon learning that the Klingons were supplying the neighboring village people with **flintlock** weapons, Kirk tried to convince Tyree of the need to fight to protect his people. Tyree initially refused, but later accepted similar weapons after the villagers murdered his wife, **Nona**. In providing weapons to Tyree's hill people, the Federation was making a measured effort to maintain the balance of power on the planet. ("A Private Little War" [TOS]). *Tyree's planet was not given a name in the episode, although an unfilmed line in the script suggested it might have been Neural. Kirk was presumably serving aboard the* **U.S.S. Farragut** *(described as his first assignment after the Academy in "Obsession" [TOS]) at the time of his first visit to Tyree's planet.*

Tyrellia. Federation planet, one of seven known inhabited worlds with no atmosphere at all. The planet also has no magnetic pole, one of only three such inhabited worlds. ("Starship Mine" [TNG]).

Tyrinean blade carving. A half-meter-high, transparent, cubist sculpture given to **Data** by **Lieutenant Jenna D'Sora**. It was her attempt to brighten up his quarters. ("In Theory" [TNG]).

Tyrus VIIA. Planet at which **Dr. Farallon** developed and tested an experimental **particle fountain** mining technique in 2369. The *Enterprise*-D assisted in the initial testing phase. ("The Quality of Life" [TNG]).

Tzartak aperitif. Specialty beverage served by Guinan in the *Enterprise*-D's **Ten-Forward lounge**. The drink was adjusted so that its vapor point was one half-degree below the body temperature of the patron who would be consuming it. The liquid would immediately evaporate upon contact with the drinker's tongue. The flavor of the beverage was carried entirely by the vapors. ("Time's Arrow, Part I" [TNG]).

UESPA. SEE: **United Earth Space Probe Agency.**

UFO. Abbreviation for Unidentified Flying Object. The *Starship Enterprise* was detected as an unidentified flying object when it was observed in the atmosphere by the **Omaha Air Base** on Earth in the year 1969. ("Tomorrow Is Yesterday" [TOS]).

"Ugly Bags of Mostly Water." Term used by the crystalline **microbrains** of planet **Velara III** to describe crew members of the *Enterprise*-D. Data noted that the term was an accurate description of humanoid life-forms, since they are composed of over 90% water. ("Home Soil" [TNG]).

Uhlan. A junior rank in the Romulan guard. ("Unification, Part II" [TNG]).

Uhnari, Lieutenant Aquiel. (Renée Jones). Junior officer, formerly assigned to **Relay Station 47.** Uhnari served some nine months at that station in 2368-69, but was transferred after a tragic incident in which **Lieutenant Keith Rocha,** her fellow officer at the station, was discovered to have been killed by a **coalescent organism.** A communications technician, Uhnari was from **Halii** and missed her homeworld very much. Uhnari enjoyed reading gothic fiction and had a pet dog named Maura. During the investigation into Rocha's death, Uhnari became romantically involved with Geordi La Forge. Uhnari's last posting prior to Relay Station 47 had been on **Deriben V.** ("Aquiel" [TNG]).

Uhura. (Nichelle Nichols). Communications officer aboard the original *Starship Enterprise* under the command of Captain James Kirk. ("The Corbomite Maneuver" [TOS]). Born in 2239, her name is derived from the Swahili word for "freedom." ("Is There in Truth No Beauty?" [TOS]).

A highly skilled technician, Uhura was also a talented musician, and enjoyed serenading her fellow crew members with song. ("Charlie X" [TOS], "The Conscience of the King" [TOS], *Star Trek V: The Final Frontier*). Her memory was wiped clean in 2267 by the errant space probe **Nomad,** requiring her to be reeducated. ("The Changeling" [TOS]).

Following the reassignment of the original *Enterprise* to Starfleet Academy in 2284, Uhura served at Starfleet Command on Earth. (*Star Trek III: The Search for Spock*). Uhura was scheduled to give a seminar at the Academy in 2393, although she volunteered to return to her old post on the *Enterprise*-A at Kirk's request prior to the historic **Khitomer** conference. (*Star Trek VI: The Undiscovered Country*.) SEE:

"Beyond Antares"; "Moon's a Window to Heaven, The." *Uhura's first appearance was in "The Corbomite Maneuver" (TOS).*

Ullians. A humanoid race of telepaths, characterized by skin involutions in the temporal area of their skulls. Though Ullians are able to read the minds of many other species, they themselves are unreadable by certain other telepathic species, particularly Betazoids.

Prior to the year 2068, Ullian society was plagued by violence, and cases of **telepathic memory intrusion** rape were common among the population. But by the 21st century, the Ullians had evolved into a peaceful race, and such barbaric acts virtually disappeared. In the 2300s, certain members of the Ullian race received special training in the art of telepathic memory retrieval and were using that talent to amass a library of individual memories, not unlike a collection of oral histories. By 2368, Ullian historians had compiled memories from eleven planets, but research was delayed by the arrest of researcher **Jev** for several cases of telepathic rape. ("Violations" [TNG]).

Ultima Thule. Planet where a **dolamide** purification plant produced weapons-grade dolamide. The **Valerians** supplied extremely pure dolamide, processed on Ultima Thule, to the Cardassians during the occupation of planet Bajor. (Dramatis Personae" [DS9]). SEE: *Sherval Das. Ultima Thule was also the name of a planet in "Death's Other Domain," an episode of* Space: 1999. *The name is derived from a Greek term for the "end of the earth."*

• **"Ultimate Computer, The."** Original Series episode #53. Teleplay by D. C. Fontana. Story by Laurence N. Wolfe. Directed by John Meredyth Lucas. Stardate 4729.4. *First aired in 1968. A new computer system could replace James Kirk as captain of the* Enterprise. SEE: **Alpha Carinae II; Carstairs, Ensign; *Constitution*-class starship; Daystrom, Dr. Richard; Deep Space Station K-7; dunsel; duotronics; Emergency Manual Monitor; engram; *Excalibur, U.S.S.*; Finagle's Folly; Harper, Ensign; Harris, Captain; *Hood, U.S.S.*; Kazanga; *Lexington, U.S.S.*; M-1 through M-4; M-5; multitronics; *Potemkin, U.S.S.*; Rawlens; Sakar; Spock; Wesley, Commodore Robert; *Woden*; Zee-Magnees Prize.**

ultraviolet satellite. Device capable of generating high levels of ultraviolet radiation. Two hundred ten of these units were used to irradiate the surface of planet **Deneva** in 2267 to eradicate the **Denevan neural parasites** that had infested the planet's population. ("Operation—Annihilate!" [TOS]).

ultritium. A powerful chemical explosive. Virtually undetectable by transporter scanners, large amounts of ultritium were found in the robes of the **Antidean** delegation to the **Pacifica** conference of 2365. It was subsequently learned that the Antidean delegates were in fact assassins who had planned to use the explosives to blow up the entire conference. ("Manhunt" [TNG]). Ultritium explosives were used by the crew of the Romulan scoutship *Pi* to destroy their ship at planet **Galorndon Core,** inside Federation space, in 2366. ("The Enemy" [TNG]).

Ulysses. Classic novel written by Earth author James Joyce; Captain Picard took a copy with him on his vacation to **Risa** in 2366. ("Captain's Holiday" [TNG]).

Umbato, Lieutenant. An *Enterprise*-D crew member who broke two ribs during a holodeck exercise the night of the Ishikawa/O'Brien wedding. ("Data's Day" [TNG]).

umbilical port. A series of exterior connection plugs on the outer hull of a starship. When a ship was docked at a starbase or other support facility, umbilicals were connected to the ship to provide an external supply of power, atmosphere, and other consumables to the ship. ("Remember Me" [TNG]).

undari. In the **Nausicaan** language, a word meaning "coward." ("Tapestry" [TNG]).

Underhill, Pell. Twenty-second-century physicist who theorized that a major disruption of the time-space continuity of an energy flow could be compensated for by trillions of small counter reactions. ("Clues" [TNG]).

"undiscovered country, the." In the literature of **Shakespeare**, the undiscovered country referred to the unknown future, at least according to **Chancellor Gorkon**, who toasted "the undiscovered country" at a diplomatic dinner prior to his abortive peace initiative in 2293. (*Star Trek VI: The Undiscovered Country*). Gorkon was quoting from the famous "To be, or not to be" speech in Shakespeare's Hamlet, Act III, Scene 1.

• **"Unification, Part I."** *Next Generation* episode #108. Teleplay by Jeri Taylor. Story by Rick Berman and Michael Piller. Directed by Les Landau. Stardate 45233.1. *First aired in 1991. Picard investigates reports that Ambassador Spock is missing and has been sighted in Romulan territory. This was the first episode to air after the death of* Star Trek *creator Gene Roddenberry. Just prior to the beginning of this segment (as well as "Unification, Part II" [TNG]) was a simple title card that read: "Gene Roddenberry, 1921-1991."* SEE: **B'iJik; Barolians; Brackett, Fleet Admiral; Caldorian eel; Cardassians; dentarium; Dokachin, Klim; Doraf I; Ferengi cargo shuttle;** *gagh;* **Gowron; Hanolin asteroid belt;** *Hechu' ghos; Jatlh; jolan true;* **Khitomer; Klingon Homeworld; Krocton segment; mint tea; Mot, Mr.; Neral; Pardek, Senator; Perrin; Proconsul; Qualor II; Rateg; Romulan soup woman; Romulus; Sarek, Ambassador; Sela;** *So'wl'chu';* **Spock; Starbase 234; Surplus Depot Zed-15;** *T'Pau; Tripoli, U.S.S.;* **Vulcans; Zakdorn.**

• **"Unification, Part II."** *Next Generation* episode #107. Teleplay by Michael Piller. Story by Rick Berman and Michael Piller. Directed by Cliff Bole. Stardate 45245.8. *First aired in 1991. Spock learns he's been a pawn in a Romulan plot to conquer his homeworld of Vulcan. This episode was actually filmed before "Unification, Part I" because of Leonard Nimoy's schedule. Spock's presence on Romulus would later be mentioned in "Face of the Enemy" [TNG], even though Spock himself wasn't seen in that episode.* SEE: ***Aktuh and Melota;*** **Amarie; Andorian blues; Bardakian pronghorn moose;**

Barolian freighter; "cowboy diplomacy"; D'Tan; Dulisian IV; Galorndon Core; *jolan true;* **Krocton Segment; K'Vada, Captain; "Melor Famagal"; Neral; Omag's girls; Omag; Pardek, Senator; Proconsul; progressive encryption lock; Romulan Star Empire; Romulus; Rutian archaeological vessel; Sela; Spock; suck salt; Uhlan; Vulcan nerve pinch.**

Uniform Code of Justice. Federation legal guidelines governing the administration of justice. Chapter 4, article 12 granted a witness the right to make a statement before being questioned in a trial or hearing. ("The Drumhead" [TNG]). SEE: **Seventh Guarantee.**

uniforms, Starfleet. *A variety of Starfleet uniforms have been featured throughout the various incarnations of* Star Trek. *The original Starfleet uniforms were created by original* Star Trek *costume designer William Ware Theiss, who also designed the original version of the arrowhead-shaped Starfleet emblem. Theiss's work included the original versions designed for the two pilot episodes, as well as the various black-collared costumes used during the series itself, and the dress uniforms. Starfleet uniforms seen in the first four* Star Trek *movies were designed by Robert Fletcher. The variations added in* Star Trek V *were designed by Nilo Rodis, and in* Star Trek VI *by Dodie Shepherd. Bill Theiss also designed the original versions of the uniforms for the first season of* Star Trek: The Next Generation, *while Robert Blackman and Durinda Rice Wood designed additional versions and modifications in subsequent seasons. Blackman also designed the Starfleet jumpsuits seen in* Star Trek: Deep Space Nine. SEE: **insignia, Starfleet.** *Illustrations on pages 359 and 360.*

United Earth Space Probe Agency. Early operating authority for the first *Starship Enterprise.* ("Charlie X" [TNG]). Kirk mentioned the UESPA to **Captain John Christopher** when Christopher asked if the *Enterprise* had been built by the Navy. Kirk answered that they were a combined service stating that their authority was the United Earth Space Probe Agency. ("Tomorrow Is Yesterday" [TOS]). *The term United Earth Space Probe Agency was actually devised by story editor John D. F. Black early during the show's first season. It was only used a couple of times before being replaced with Starfleet by "Court Martial" (TOS). (It was once abbreviated as UESPA, pronounced YOU-SPAH). Later episodes have suggested that Starfleet existed even before the first pilot episode, and we assume that Starfleet existed as far back as 2161, when the Federation was founded.*

United Federation of Planets. An alliance of approximately 150 planetary governments and colonies, united for mutual trade, exploratory, scientific, cultural, diplomatic, and defensive endeavors. Founded in 2161 ("The Outcast" [TNG]). Federation members include Earth, Vulcan, and numerous other planetary

(Continued on page 361.)

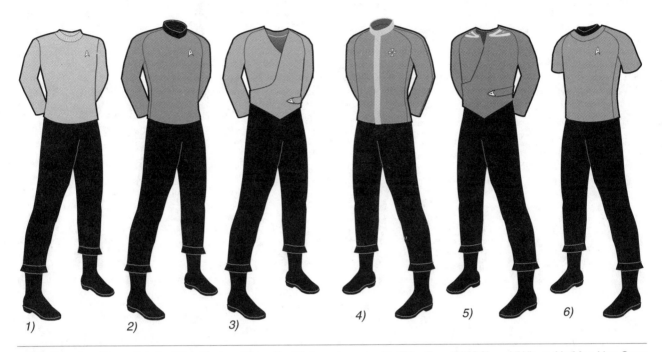

Uniforms, Starfleet - Original Star Trek series. *1) Pilot version, used in "The Cage" (TOS) and "Where No Man Has Gone Before" (TOS). 2) Duty uniform used throughout most of the Original Series. 3) Wraparound variation occasionally worn by Kirk. 4) Dress uniform. 5) Variation of Kirk's wraparound. 6). Dr. McCoy's medical tunic.*

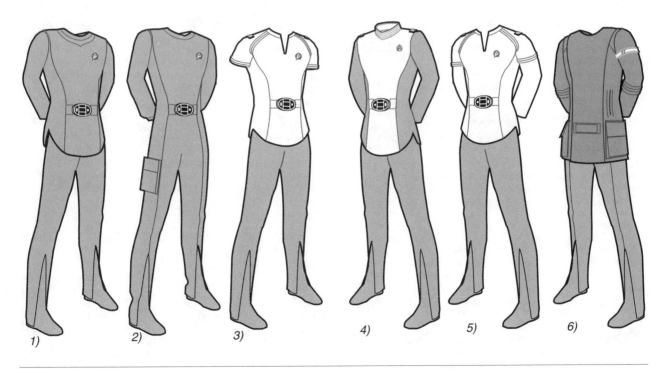

Uniforms, Starfleet - Star Trek: The Motion Picture. *1) Starfleet duty uniform. 2) Utility jumpsuit. 3) Short sleeve fatigue variant. 4) Admiral's uniform worn by Kirk. 5) Long-sleeve fatigue. 6) Field jacket.*

(Continued on next page.)

(Continued from previous page.)

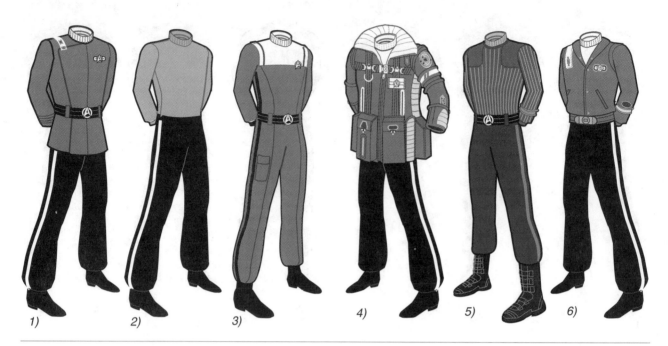

Uniforms, Starfleet - **Star Trek II** - **Star Trek VI.** *1) Officer's duty uniform. 2) Duty uniform without jacket. 3) Cadet jumpsuit. 4) Field jacket. 5)* Star Trek V *variation worn on landing party duty. 6) Officer's "bomber jacket."*

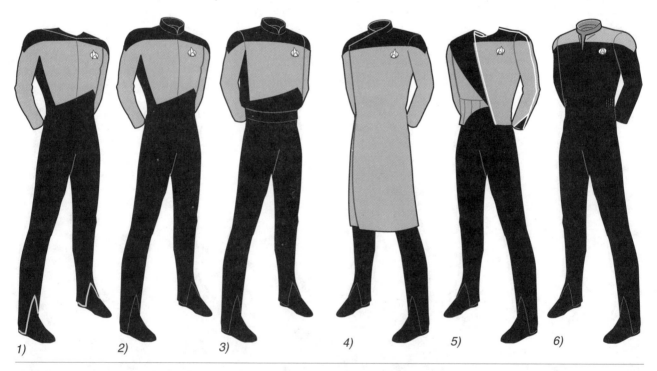

Uniforms, Starfleet - **Star Trek: The Next Generation** *and* **Star Trek: Deep Space Nine.** *1) First- and second-season duty uniform. 2) Third-season duty uniform. 3) Third-season uniform variation, used primarily for lead characters, still in use. 4) Officer's dress uniform. 5) First-season admiral's uniform. Several variations of this uniform were used. 6) Starfleet jumpsuit from* Star Trek: Deep Space Nine.

(Continued from page 358.)
states. The Federation is governed by the **Federation Council**, composed of representatives from the various member planets, that meet in the city of San Francisco on Earth. The Council itself is led by a **Federation Council President**, whose office is in the city of Paris on planet Earth. (*Star Trek IV: The Voyage Home*, *Star Trek VI: The Undiscovered Country*). Although the Federation and its Starfleet have done an extraordinary job of maintaining a generally peaceful climate in this part of the galaxy (*Star Trek II: The Wrath of Khan*), the Federation and its member planets have been involved in a number of armed conflicts over the years. Notable among these are the tensions with the **Klingon Empire** that lasted almost a century until the **Organian Peace Treaty**, and later the **Khitomer** conference of 2293. Still unresolved are conflicts with the **Romulan Star Empire** and the **Tholian Assembly**. The Federation was involved in a protracted, bitter war with the **Cardassians** that dated back to the 2350s. An uneasy peace treaty with the Cardassian Union was reached in 2366. ("The Wounded" [TNG]). Conflict with the Cardassians continued at lower levels for years. One particular hot spot was **Bajor**, after the end of Cardassian occupation of the planet in 2369, when the Federation took over operation of the old Cardassian mining station **Deep Space 9** in the Bajoran system near the newly discovered stable wormhole. ("Emissary" [DS9]). *There is no definitive list of members in the Federation, since the shows' writers need the freedom to invent new members as specific stories require. The 150-member figure was deliberately chosen to approximate the members in Earth's present United Nations.* SEE: **Constitution of the United Federation of Planets**.

United Nations, New. An organization of nation-states on planet Earth, formed during the 21st century. In 2036, the New United Nations declared that no Earth citizen could be made to answer for the crimes of their race or forebearers. The New United Nations had ceased to exist by the year 2079 in the aftermath of **World War III**. ("Encounter at Farpoint, Part I" [TNG]).

United States Constitution. Legal document providing the foundation for the representative government system of the **United States of America** on Earth. The United States Constitution provided for extensive protection of individual rights, including the right to face one's accuser. ("Court Martial" [TOS]). The **Yangs** of planet **Omega IV** adopted the United States Constitution and an American flag as symbols of their fight against their enemies the **Kohms**. ("The Omega Glory" [TOS]).

United States of America. Nation on planet Earth, founded in 1776, that world's first large-scale experiment in representational democratic government. The United States was responsible for many of Earth's early achievements in space exploration.

The United States' flag of 2033 had 52 stars, a number that was maintained until 2079. ("The Royale" [TNG]). *It is not known if the United States ceased to exist in 2079 or if a 53rd state was added then. That year does appear to coincide with the end of the World War III nuclear holocaust.*

units of measure. SEE: **AU; denkirs; kellicams; kellipates; kilodyne; kiloquad; kolem; kph; melakol; millicochrane; onkians; terrawatt; tessipate; trisec; warp factor**.

universal translator. Device used to provide real-time two-way translation of spoken languages. It operated by sensing and comparing brain-wave frequencies, then selecting comparable concepts to use as a basis for translation. Kirk used a handheld universal translator to communicate with the life-form known as the **Companion** in 2267. ("Metamorphosis" [TOS]). A software version of the universal translator was programmed into the *Enterprise*-D's main computer. This enabled real-time communications with such life-forms as the **nanites**. ("Evolution" [TNG]). *Actually, we figured that Paramount somehow managed to install universal translators in everyone's television receivers, which could explain why so many of the galaxy's life-forms seem to be speaking English.*

universe, parallel. SEE: **mirror universe**.

University of Betazed. Educational institution at which **Deanna Troi** studied psychology prior to her joining Starfleet. As a student at the university, she helped care for **Tam Elbrun**. ("Tin Man" [TNG]).

• **"Unnatural Selection."** *Next Generation* episode #33. Written by John Mason & Mike Gray. Directed by Paul Lynch. Stardate 42494.8. *First aired in 1989. Scientists who have genetically designed their children for superior immune systems find themselves aging incredibly fast, the victims of that improved immunity.* SEE: **Darwin Genetic Research Station; Gagarin IV; Gamma 7 Sector; Kingsley, Dr. Sara; *Lantree, U.S.S.*; "Linear Models of Viral Propagation"; marker beacon; Pulaski, Dr. Katherine; quarantine transmitter; *Repulse, U.S.S.*; *Sakharov, Shuttlecraft*; security access code; Star Station India; styrolite; Taggert, Captain; Telaka, Captain L. Isao; Thelusian flu; transporter ID trace**.

• **"Up the Long Ladder."** *Next Generation* episode #44. Written by Melinda M. Snodgrass. Directed by Winrich Kolbe. Stardate 42823.2. *First aired in 1989. Captain Picard must persuade two vastly dissimilar colonies, each doomed, that they can only survive by living together.* SEE: **Bringloid V; Bringloidi; *chech'tluth*; clone; Dieghan, Liam; European**

Hegemony; Ficus Sector; firefighting; Granger, Wilson; love poetry, Klingon; Mariposa (planet); *Mariposa, S.S.*; Moore, Admiral; Neo-Transendentalism; Odell, Brenna; Odell, Danilo; replicative fading; *rop'ngor*; Starbase 73; tea ceremony, Klingon; Vallis, Elizabeth; World War III; Yoshimitsu computers.

user code clearance. A code required to access the control systems of a starship. ("Hero Worship" [TNG]). SEE: **security access code.**

U.S.S. Identifying prefix used as part of the names of Federation starships, as in *U.S.S. Enterprise. There is some question as to what* U.S.S. *actually stands for. Captain Pike once identified the* Enterprise *as a United Space Ship, while it was called a United Star Ship in other episodes. We assume that ships with an* S.S. *prefix are usually vessels of Federation registry, but not part of the Federation starfleet.*

Utopia Planitia Fleet Yards.
Starfleet shipyards in orbit around the planet Mars and on the surface of the planet. The *Enterprise*-D was built there. Members of the Galaxy class Starship development project included Dr. **Leah Brahms** ("Booby Trap" [TNG]). The actual construction of the *Enterprise*-D was supervised by Commander **Orfil Quinteros**. ("11001001" [TNG]).

    Lieutenant Commander **Benjamin Sisko** was assigned to Utopia Planitia for some three years following the tragic death of his wife aboard the *U.S.S. Saratoga* in early 2367, prior to his assignment to station **Deep Space 9** in mid-2369. ("Emissary" [DS9]).
    Part of the Utopia Planitia Fleet Yards on the surface of Mars was very briefly glimpsed as a view from deep space in "Parallels" (TNG), while Brahms's drafting room (presumably in the orbital part of the yards) was re-created in "Booby Trap" (TNG) and "Galaxy's Child" (TNG).

Utopia Planitia. Location on planet Mars first explored by the automated space probe *Viking 2,* which soft-landed there on September 3, 1976, part of Earth's first attempt to employ spaceflight in the search for extraterrestrial life. It is also the site of the **Utopia**

Planitia Fleet Yards where the *Starship Enterprise*-D was built in the mid-24th century.
    The fact that the Enterprise-D *was supposed to have been built at Utopia Planitia was inscribed on the* **dedication plaque** *for the ship located on the main bridge. A copy of the dedication plaque was included in a CD-ROM collection of art and literature scheduled to be sent to the surface of Mars aboard the Russian* Mars '94 *space probe, definitely a case of life imitating art.*

uttaberries. A blueberry-like fruit found on **Betazed**. ("Ménage à Troi" [TNG]).

Ux-Mal. Star system from which a group of noncorporeal criminal life-forms were exiled to a moon of planet **Mab-Bu VI** during the 21st century. The criminals remained at Mab-Bu VI for four centuries before they made an unsuccessful attempt to escape aboard the *Starship Essex* in 2167. A century later, they made a second attempt to escape their prison when the *Starship Enterprise*-D visited that moon. ("Power Play" [TNG]).

Uxbridge, Kevin. (John Anderson). The last survivor of the **Delta Rana IV** colony. Though colony records showed him in 2366 to be an 85-year-old human botanist, the crew of the *Enterprise*-D discovered him to be a **Douwd**, who had masqueraded as a human for more than 50 years. Uxbridge survived the **Husnock** attack at Delta Rana IV, and in retribution used his enormous powers to annihilate the entire Husnock race. Uxbridge later felt profound regret over his act of destruction and remained in self-imposed isolation on the planet along with an image of his human wife, **Rishon Uxbridge**, who had perished in the Husnock attack. ("The Survivors" [TNG]). *Photo: Kevin Uxbridge and the re-created image of his wife, Rishon.*

Uxbridge, Rishon. (Anne Haney). Botanist and composer of tao-classical music; the wife of **Kevin Uxbridge**. She was 82 years old when she was killed in the **Husnock** attack on the **Delta Rana IV** colony. ("The Survivors" [TNG]). *Anne Haney later played a Bajoran judge in "Dax" (DS9).*

Vaal. Sophisticated computer god-machine that controlled planet **Gamma Trianguli VI**. The inhabitants of the planet worshipped Vaal as a god, providing it with fuel. In exchange, Vaal provided an idyllic, Eden-like environ-

ment. Vaal maintained a powerful planetary defense system that crippled the *Enterprise* when the ship orbited the planet in 2267. Vaal nearly destroyed the *Enterprise* before a barrage of phaser fire succeeded in destroying the computer. ("The Apple" [TOS]). SEE: **Akuta**.

Vadosia. (Jack Shearer). Bolian ambassador who visited **Deep Space 9** in 2369 on a fact-finding mission to the **Bajoran wormhole**. ("The Forsaken" [DS9]).

Vadris III. Planet where the natives think they're the only intelligent life in the universe. **Q** offered to take archaeologist **Vash** to Vadris III, but she declined. ("Q-Less" [DS9]).

Vagh. (Ed Wiley). The Klingon governor of the **Kriosian system**. When the Kriosian population under his control began to rebel and demand independence in 2367, Vagh accused the Federation of aiding their cause. The crew of the *Enterprise*-D was able to show that it was the Romulans who were supporting the rebels. Governor Vagh became the target of an assassination attempt by Geordi La Forge, acting under Romulan control. The Romulans hoped by having La Forge murder the governor, a rift would be formed in the Federation/Klingon alliance. ("The Mind's Eye" [TNG]).

Vagra II. Planet in the Zed Lapis Sector. Now nearly deserted, Vagra II was the home to life-forms who left the planet to become creatures of dazzling beauty. In doing so, they left behind a creature called **Armus**, which still lives on the planet. *Enterprise*-D shuttlecraft 13 crashed there in 2364, and Security Chief **Natasha Yar** was killed there by **Armus** while on a rescue mission to the planet's surface. ("Skin of Evil" [TNG]).

valerian root tea. A favored beverage of Deanna Troi. ("Second Chances" [TNG]).

Valerians. Alien race that supplied extremely pure weapons-grade **dolamide** to the **Cardassians** during the occupation of Bajor. A Valerian transport vessel requested permission to dock at Deep Space 9 in 2369 for repairs. Major Kira Nerys asked that their request be denied because of their history with the Cardassians, but Commander Sisko refused. ("Dramatis Personae" [DS9]).

Valeris. (Kim Cattrall). Starfleet officer who played a pivotal role in the conspiracy to assassinate Klingon **chancellor Gorkon** in 2293. Valeris had been mentored by Spock, and was the first Vulcan to graduate at the top of her class at Starfleet Academy. Although fiercely logical, Valeris feared the changes that would be wrought when a new era of peace came upon the Federation. She was arrested at the Khitomer peace conference for her role in the assasination of Gorkon. (*Star Trek VI: The Undiscovered Country*).

Valiant, S.S. Early interstellar vessel, embarked on exploratory mission in 2064 and was lost when it was swept out of the galaxy, into the energy barrier. Shortly after contact with the barrier, at least one crew member mutated into a godlike being, forcing the ship's captain to order the *Valiant* destroyed to prevent the escape of the mutated crew member. ("Where No Man Has Gone Before" [TOS]). SEE: **barrier, galactic**.

Valiant, U.S.S. Federation starship that contacted planet **Eminiar VII** in 2217 and was destroyed. The *Valiant* was declared a causality in the 500-year-old war between planets Eminiar VII and **Vendikar**. ("A Taste of Armageddon" [TOS]). *We assume this is a different ship from the* S.S. Valiant *that disappeared around 2065.*

Valkris. (Cathie Shirriff). Klingon operative who obtained then-secret **Project Genesis** data from the Federation, providing it to the Klingon government. Valkris was killed by Klingon commander **Kruge** because she had read the Genesis material, but her death was an honorable one. (*Star Trek III: The Search for Spock*).

Valley of Chula. Scenic valley on planet Romulus. Data recreated the Valley of Chula on the *Enterprise*-D holodeck for the benefit of **Alidar Jarok**, but Jarok found the spectacular sight to be of little comfort. ("The Defector" [TNG]).

Valley. Area on planet **Beta III** where the *Enterprise* landing party claimed to be from. ("Return of the Archons" [TOS]).

Vallis, Elizabeth. One of five survivors of the crash of the **S.S. Mariposa** on the planet of the same name. Vallis and the other four survivors turned to cloning technology to populate their world. ("Up the Long Ladder" [TNG]).

Valo system. A solar system located in neutral space near the **Cardassian** border. Many **Bajorans** settled in the Valo system following the annexation of their homeworld by the Cardassians. Bajoran leader **Keeve Falor** resided in a settlement camp on the southern continent of Valo II. Another

Bajoran leader, **Jas Holza**, lived in a settlement camp on Valo III. The third moon of Valo I had a composition that made sensor reading impossible. The Bajoran terrorist leader **Orta** maintained a base on this moon. ("Ensign Ro" [TNG]).

Valt Minor. Star system neighboring **Krios**, which takes its name from Valt, one of the two brothers who once ruled a vast empire. Valt was at war for centuries with neighboring system Krios (named after Valt's brother), until the historic **Ceremony of Reconciliation** in 2368. ("The Perfect Mate" [TNG]).

Valtane, Mr. Science officer aboard the **U.S.S. Excelsior** under the command of Captain Sulu in 2293. (*Star Trek VI: The Undiscovered Country*).

Valtese horns. A musical instrument native to the **Valt Minor** star system. Though the horns sounded like braying Targhee moonbeasts, they were said to soothe the nerves of Valtese males, at least according to the empathic metamorph Kamala. ("The Perfect Mate" [TNG]).

Valtese. Humanoid race inhabiting the star system of **Valt Minor**. ("The Perfect Mate" [TNG]). SEE: **Krios**.

Van Doren, Dr. Cardiologist who developed a **cardiac replacement** technique used in the replacement of **Jean-Luc Picard**'s heart in 2327. By 2365, the mortality rate for the procedure had been reduced to 2.4%. ("Samaritan Snare" [TNG]).

Van Gelder, Dr. Simon. (Morgan Woodward). Director of the **Tantalus V** penal colony in 2266. Van Gelder became dangerously insane from testing an experimental **neural neutralizer** device, after which **Dr. Tristan Adams** took control of the colony, using the neural neutralizer to further his own goals. Van Gelder recovered and returned to his duties as director after Adams died from exposure to the neutralizer. ("Dagger of the Mind" [TOS]). *Actor Morgan Woodward would later portray Captain Ron Tracey in "The Omega Glory" (TOS).*

Van Mayter, Lieutenant. An *Enterprise*-D crew member and part of the engineering staff. Van Mayter was killed when she was caught in a section of the ship that phased out of existence when exposed to dark matter in the **Mar Oscura** nebula in 2367. The phasing caused the lieutenant to be trapped in the deck itself. ("In Theory" [TNG]).

Vanderberg, Chief Engineer. (Ken Lynch). Leader of the **pergium** mining station on **Janus VI** in 2267. Vanderberg summoned the *Enterprise* when 50 of his men were mysteriously killed by an entity later learned to be an intelligent subterranean life-form known as the **Horta**. ("The Devil in the Dark" [TOS]).

Vandor IX. Planetoid in the Vandor star system, the location

of **Dr. Paul Manheim**'s laboratory, where he conducted studies into the relationships between time and gravity. Manheim lived there with his wife, **Jenice Manheim**. ("We'll Always Have Paris" [TNG]).

Vandor star system. Remote binary star system consisting of B-class giant with an orbiting companion pulsar. Location of **Dr. Paul Manheim**'s laboratory. ("We'll Always Have Paris" [TNG]).

Vanna. (Carlene Polite). One of the leaders of the **Troglyte** underground on planet **Ardana**, known as the **Disrupters**, who won early reforms for the Troglyte working class in 2269. ("The Cloud Minders" [TOS]).

Vanoben transport. Vessel from which a valuable, ornately carved sphere was stolen in 2369. An item looking very much like this artifact was subsequently brought to Deep Space 9 by the **Miradorn** twins **Ah-Kel** and **Ro-Kel**, who were seeking a buyer for their prize. ("Vortex" [DS9]).

Vantika, Rao. (James Harper). **Kobliad** scientist and criminal who fled Kobliad authorities for twenty years before finally being killed on station Deep Space 9 in 2369. Vantika had been using illegal means to obtain **deuridium**, a substance needed to prolong his life, when he was captured by Kobliad security officer **Kajada**. Vantika transferred his consciousness to Dr. Julian Bashir, using a **microscopic generator** device, intending to escape in Bashir's body. His plan failed when Kajada trapped his consciousness in an energy containment cell, then destroyed the cell. ("The Passenger" [DS9]).

Varel. (Susanna Thompson). Romulan officer. She was an assistant to Mirok during the testing of a **Romulan interphase** generator in 2368. ("The Next Phase" [TNG]).

Varis Sul. (Gina Phillips). Leader, or **tetrarch,** of the **Paqu** village on planet **Bajor**. Varis Sul came to Deep Space 9 in 2369 to negotiate land boundaries with representatives of the rival **Navot** village. Varis, who was only 15 years old at the time of the negotiations, had become the leader of the Paqu when her parents were killed by the **Cardassians**. While on the station, Varis became friends with **Nog** and **Jake Sisko**, who gave her the idea of turning the border dispute into an opportunity. She decided to compromise by offering free trade access to both sides of the river in exchange for giving the Navot back their land. ("The Storyteller" [DS9]). SEE: **Ferengi Rules of Acquisition; Glyrhond**.

Varley, Captain Donald. (Thalmus Rasulala). Friend to Jean-Luc Picard and commander of the **U.S.S. Yamato** at the time of its destruction in 2365. *Two of Varley's officers, unseen but referred to on Varley's computer-screen logs, were Commander Steve Gerber and Lieutenant Commander*

Beth Woods, named for the episode's writers. ("Contagion" [TNG]).

Varon-T disruptor. A small pistol, banned in the Federation. Only five of these devices were manufactured; **Zibalian** trader **Kivas Fajo** reportedly owned four of them. A vicious weapon, the Varon-T disrupted the body from the inside out, causing a slow and painful death. Fajo used one of the disruptors to kill his assistant, **Varria**, in 2366. ("The Most Toys" [TNG]).

Varria. (Jane Daly). A female humanoid assistant to Zibalian trader **Kivas Fajo**. Varria came into Fajo's employ as a young adult and served him for fourteen years during which the amoral Fajo delighted at the gradual loss of her ideals. In 2366, when Fajo kidnapped Data, Varria attempted to help Data escape. Varria was murdered by Fajo during the escape attempt. ("The Most Toys" [TNG]).

Vash. (Jennifer Hetrick). Archaeologist and adventurer whom Jean-Luc Picard first met on the resort planet **Risa** in 2366. Vash, an attractive human female, had been an assistant to scientist **Dr. Samuel Estragon** as he searched for the fabled *Tox Uthat*. After Estragon's death, in 2366, Vash used his notes to locate the *Uthat*, buried on the resort planet of Risa. Vash had

competitors in her search, including Estragon's ex-associate **Sovak** and two **Vorgon** criminals from the future. Picard, vacationing on Risa at the time, assisted Vash. Although the *Uthat* was later destroyed by Picard, he and Vash parted friends, after having become romantically involved during their adventure. ("Captain's Holiday" [TNG]). Vash returned to the *Enterprise*-D to attend a **Federation Archaeology Council** symposium held there in 2367. She was abducted, along with Picard and other *Enterprise*-D personnel, by **Q**, who cast them all into an elaborate re-creation of Earth's ancient **Robin Hood** legends. Despite this, Vash later agreed to join Q in exploring unknown parts of the galaxy. ("QPid" [TNG]). She explored the Gamma Quadrant for two years with Q, but eventually left him to explore on her own. In 2369, Vash was discovered in the Gamma Quadrant by the runabout *U.S.S. Ganges* and brought back to Deep Space 9, bringing with her several artifacts from her travels. Vash attempted to raise money by auctioning some of her treasures at **Quark's bar**, but one of the artifacts contained a life-form from the Gamma Quadrant that generated a **graviton field** that nearly destroyed the station. Having been away from Earth for 12 years, Vash was tempted to accept an invitation from the **Daystrom Institute** to speak on her travels, but she ultimately declined. ("Q-Less" [DS9]).

Vassbinder, Dr. Speaker at the deep-space psychology seminar attended by members of the *Enterprise*-D crew in 2369. Vassbinder gave what Picard described as a "hypnotic" lecture on the ionization effect of warp nacelles before realizing he was supposed to be talking about psychology. ("Timescape" [TNG]).

Vault of Tomorrow. Subterranean chamber on planet **Janus VI** where the **silicon-based life**-form known as the **Horta** kept the eggs from which would be born their next generation. Federation miners on Janus VI broke into the Vault of Tomorrow in 2267, thereby accidentally threatening the future of the Horta race. ("The Devil in the Dark" [TOS]).

Vaytan. Star with a superdense corona. Vaytan was chosen as site for the first test of a new **metaphasic shield** device in 2369. ("Suspicions" [TNG]).

Vedek Assembly. Influential congress of 112 **Bajoran** spiritual leaders on planet **Bajor**. Among the members of the assembly in 2369 were **Vedek Bareil** and **Vedek Winn**, two leading contenders to become the next **Kai**, following the departure of **Kai Opaka**. Vedek Bareil told Commander Sisko he longed for the simplicity of his arboretum after listening to 112 vedeks speaking at once. ("In the Hands of the Prophets" [DS9]).

vedek. Title given to a Bajoran religious leader who was a member of the powerful **Vedek Assembly**. ("In the Hands of the Prophets" [DS9]).

Vega Colony. The *U.S.S. Enterprise*, under the command of Captain Christopher Pike, was en route to the Vega Colony at the time it picked up a distress call from the *S.S. Columbia* in 2254. ("The Cage," "The Menagerie, Part I" [TOS]). *Vega is the brightest star in the constellation Lyra (the harp) as seen from Earth.*

Vega IX probe. A long-range automated Starfleet probe that was sent to record the collapse of **Beta Stromgren** in 2366. The probe discovered the living spacecraft code-named **Tin Man** in orbit of the star. ("Tin Man" [TNG]).

Vega-Omicron Sector. Patrol assignment of the *U.S.S. Aries* at the time Riker declined the opportunity to command that ship in 2365. ("The Icarus Factor" [TNG]).

Vegan choriomeningitis. Rare and deadly disease that almost killed James Kirk in his youth. The disease remained dormant in his bloodstream and in 2268 was used by people of planet Gideon to infect volunteers willing to die to solve their overpopulation crisis.

Symptoms include high fever, pain in the extremities, delirium, and death if not treated within 24 hours. ("The Mark of Gideon" [TOS]).

VeK'tal response.   A measure of Klingon physiological condition. ("Ethics" [TNG]).

Vekma. (Laura Drake). Klingon warrior, female. Crew member aboard the Klingon vessel *Pagh* during Riker's tenure as first officer on that ship in 2365. Vekma had fun at Riker's expense, wondering out loud if Riker would have the stamina to endure a Klingon female. It is not known if she had the chance to satisfy her curiosity. *Vekma was not identified by name in the episode; her name appears only in the script.* ("A Matter of Honor" [TNG]).

Velara III.   Non-class-M planet that was the object of a terraforming project under the direction of **Kurt Mandl** in 2364. Previously believed to be uninhabited, Velara III was discovered to be the home of subsurface crystalline life-forms called "microbrains." Mandl attempted to conceal the existence of these life-forms because part of his project involved raising the water table on the planet, a move that would threaten the life-forms. Acting in self-defense, the microbrains seized control of the *Starship Enterprise*-D, and the planet was eventually quarantined by Federation order at the request of the microbrains. ("Home Soil" [TNG]).

Velos VII Internment Camp. Cardassian prison camp where **Dr. Dekon Elig** was imprisoned. He was killed there in 2360 while trying to escape from the facility. ("Babel" [DS9]).

Veltan sex idol. A rare objet d'art. Twenty-fourth century collector **Palor Toff** boasted of owning a Veltan sex idol; his friend **Kivas Fajo** owned four. ("The Most Toys" [TNG]).

vendarite.   Valuable mineral on planet **Ligos VII**. The renegade Ferengi who invaded the *Enterprise*-D in 2369 used the science team stationed on the planet as slave laborers to mine the vendarite. ("Rascals" [TNG]).

Vendikar. Planet in **Cluster NGC 321** that had been at war with its neighbor **Eminiar VII** for 500 years, ending in 2267. Vendikar was originally settled by people from Eminiar VII, but they turned against their homeworld. The two planets developed an agreement whereby they would conduct their war by computers only. Attacks would be launched mathematically, and those individuals designated as casualties would have 24 hours to report to disintegration chambers so that their deaths could be recorded.

   The arrangement lasted until 2267 when Captain Kirk broke the subspace radio link between the two worlds, forcing them to the bargaining table for peace talks. ("A Taste of Armageddon" [TOS]).

• "Vengeance Factor, The." *Next Generation* episode #57. Written by Sam Rolfe. Directed by Timothy Bond. Stardate 43421.9. *First aired in 1989. A beautiful young woman is actually an old weapon of death whose mission is to win revenge on a rival clan. The late Sam Rolfe was the developer of* The Man From U.N.C.L.E. *television series in the early 1960s.* SEE: **Acamar III; Acamar system; Acamarians/ Gatherers; Artonian lasers; Brull; Chorgan; Gamma Hromi II; *Goddard, U.S.S.*; Hromi Cluster; Marouk; microvirus;** noranium alloy; parthas á la Yuta; Penthor-Mul; Starbase 343; Temarek; Tonkian homing beacons; Tralesta; Volnoth; Yuta.

Ventanian thimble.   An archeological artifact from the Lapeongical period of Ventanian history. Captain Picard kept one on his ready-room desk. He was impressed that **Kamala**, the **empathic metamorph** from Krios, recognized it, just as she knew he would be. ("The Perfect Mate" [TNG]).

Ventax II. A class-M planet that, a millennium ago, suffered from terrible wars and environmental havoc. According to Ventaxian legend, this dark age was ended by the Contract of Ardra, in which the mythic figure **Ardra** agreed to grant a thousand years of peace and prosperity in exchange for the population delivering itself into slavery at the end of the millennium. Federation anthropologist **Dr. Howard Clark** issued a distress call from Ventax II in 2367 when a con artist identifying herself as Ardra attempted to collect on that contract. First contact with the Ventaxians had been made in 2297 by a Klingon expedition. ("Devil's Due" [TNG]).

Venus drug. An illegal substance believed to make women more beautiful and men more handsome and attractive to the opposite sex. Although the drug appeared to be highly effective when used to enhance the appearance of Mudd's women, it was later noted that a placebo dose (consisting of inert gelatin) had a similar effect when ingested by **Eve McHuron**, suggesting that belief in oneself remains the most effective enhancement of all. ("Mudd's Women" [TOS]).

Verath. A statue from the Verath solar system was auctioned off at Quark's bar by archaeologist **Vash** in 2369. Vash explained that the civilization of the Verathans reached its height 30,000 years ago and conducted trade through an interconnected communication network to other systems. ("Q-Less" [DS9]).

Veridium Six. A slow-acting, cumulative poison used to kill Klingon High Council leader **K'mpec** in 2367. Administered in small doses in K'mpec's favorite wine, the poison had no antidote. ("Reunion" [TNG]).

vermicula.   A food consisting of small wormlike animals, consumed by the humanoid inhabitants of planet **Antide III**. ("Manhunt" [TNG]).

vertazine. Medication used by Federation medical personnel to combat vertigo. ("Cause and Effect" [TNG]).

verterons. Subatomic particles that allow a vessel on impulse power to pass through the **Bajoran wormhole** unharmed. A lesson on the subject taught by **Keiko O'Brien** at her classroom in Deep Space 9 in 2369 explained this fact to her students, despite **Vedek Winn**'s objections that such teaching constituted blasphemy to the Bajoran religion. ("In the Hands of the Prophets" [DS9]).

veruul. A Romulan expletive. Riker used this term to counter Alidar Jarok's insults to Lieutenant Worf. ("The Defector" [TNG]).

V'Ger. Contraction for "Voyager." A massive machine lifeform built around **NASA**'s ancient *Voyager VI* space probe. *Voyager*, which launched from Earth in the late 20th century, had fallen into a black hole and emerged on the other side of the galaxy, near a planet of

living machines. The inhabitants of the machine planet found the robot *Voyager VI* to be a kindred spirit, and gave it the ability to carry out what they believed to be *Voyager*'s prime directive: To learn all that is learnable, and to return that knowledge to its creator. Unfortunately, in doing so, they gave *Voyager*, now called V'Ger, the ability to destroy the objects being studied. Upon reaching Earth, where V'Ger believed its creator resided, V'Ger joined with **Willard Decker** and **Ilia**, and departed for parts unknown. (*Star Trek: The Motion Picture*).

Vians. Advanced humanoid race of unknown origin. The Vians rendered aid to the **Minaran star system** in 2268 when the star went nova. Due to limited resources, the Vians had the ability to save the inhabitants of only one of the Minaran planets. The Vians

therefore conducted an elaborate experiment to determine which planet's inhabitants would be saved. The extraordinary self-sacrifice of the **Minaran empath**, Gem, caused the Vians to choose to save **Gem**'s people. ("The Empath" [TOS]).

Vico, S.S. Federation research vessel, *Oberth* class, registry number NAR-18834. In 2368, the *Vico* was assigned to explore the interior of the **Black Cluster**. Inside the cluster, the *Vico* encountered severe gravitational wavefronts that were amplified by the

Vico's shields, destroying the ship. There was only one survivor, a young boy named **Timothy**, who was rescued by the *Enterprise*-D. ("Hero Worship" [TNG]). *Because the* Vico *had an S.S. designation and it did not have an NCC registry prefix, we assume it was not a Starfleet vessel, even though it was of Federation registry.*

Victory, H.M.S. Ancient British sailing ship. Geordi La Forge built a large model of the oceangoing vessel as a gift for

Starship *Victory* **captain Zimbata**. The *H.M.S. Victory* was Lord Horatio Nelson's (1758-1805) flagship during the battle of Trafalgar, in which he was killed. Prior to the **Borg** encounter of 2366-2367, Captain Jean-Luc Picard drew inspiration from Nelson's courage at Trafalgar. *Geordi's* Victory *model still graces the late Gene Roddenberry's office in the home of his widow, Majel Barrett Roddenberry.* ("Elementary, Dear Data" [TNG], "The Best of Both Worlds, Part I" [TNG]).

Victory, U.S.S. Federation *Constellation*-class starship, registry number NCC-9754. Commanded by **Captain Zimbata**. Geordi La Forge served as an ensign aboard this vessel prior to his assignment to the *Enterprise*-D. ("Elementary, Dear Data" [TNG]).

In 2362, a *Victory* away team was sent to the surface of planet **Tarchannen III** to investigate the disappearance of 49 Federation personnel. It was not realized at the time that all five members of that team (including Geordi La Forge) were infected with an alien DNA strand that would compel them to return to Tarchannen III five years later. ("Identity Crisis" [TNG]). *The* Victory *was a re-use of the* **U.S.S. Stargazer** *model originally built for "The Battle" (TNG).*

victurium alloy. Metal used in the superstructure of some space vehicles. The *Enterprise*-D transporters were unable to penetrate the large amount of alloy in the hull of the **S.S. Vico**. ("Hero Worship" [TNG]).

viewer. Generic term used to describe visual display screens used aboard Federation starships. Some viewers include holographic screen matrices, enabling them to display three-dimensional images. Viewers can be small desktop devices intended for personal use, or can be large

wall-mounted units as in a main viewer on a starship's bridge. *Illustration: desktop viewer from original series.*

Vigo. Weapons officer aboard the **U.S.S. Stargazer** during the **Battle of Maxia** in the year 2355 under the command of Captain Jean-Luc Picard. ("The Battle" [TNG]).

viinerine. Traditional Romulan food. Troi, masquerading as a Romulan officer, misidentified another Romulan dish as *viinerine*, but managed to bluff her way out of the situation. ("Face of the Enemy" [TNG]).

Vilmor II. Planet in the Vilmoran system covered by dry ocean beds but little life. Billions of years ago, Vilmor II was covered by oceans full of life that had been seeded by ancient humanoids some four billion years ago. The genetic codes from fossils on Vilmor II provided the last pieces of an interstellar puzzle left behind by those humanoids in the genes of life on planets across the galaxy. ("The Chase" [TNG]). SEE: **humanoid life**.

Vina. (Susan Oliver). A crew member aboard the **S.S. Columbia**, and the only survivor of the expedition when it crashed on planet **Talos IV** in 2236. The **Talosians** cared for her and attempted to mend her wounds, but had no idea what a human being should look like. As a result, Vina was restored to health, but was severely disfigured. ("The Cage," "The Menagerie, Parts I and II" [TOS]).

• **"Violations."** *Next Generation* episode #112. Teleplay by Pamela Gray and Jeri Taylor. Story by Shari Goodhartz and T. Michael and Pamela Gray. Directed by Robert Wiemer. Stardate 45429.3. *First aired in 1992. A researcher visiting the* Enterprise-D *commits a number of hideous telepathic rapes.* SEE: **antimatter containment; Circassian cat; CPK levels; Crusher, Jack R.; Davis, Ensign; diencephalon; hippocampus; histamine; Hurada III; Inad; Iresine Syndrome; Japanese brush writing; Jev; Kaldra IV; Keller, Ensign; La Forge, Geordi; Martin, Dr.; Melina II; Nel System; O'Brien, Keiko; Obachan; Starbase 440; Tarmin; telepathic memory invasion; thalamus; Ullians.**

VISOR. Acronym for Visual Instrument and Sensory Organ Replacement. A remarkable piece of bioelectronic engineering that allowed **Geordi La Forge** to see, despite the fact that he was born blind. A slim device worn over the face like a pair of sunglasses, the VISOR permitted vision in not only visible light, but across much of the electromagnetic spectrum including infrared and radio waves. The VISOR, while giving La Forge better-than-normal sight, also caused him continuous pain. ("Encounter at Farpoint, Part II" [TNG]). A device called a **Visual Acuity Transmitter** was once used with Geordi's VISOR in an attempt to allow transmission of Geordi's visual perceptions, but the device proved unreliable and the images were extremely difficult to interpret. To the untrained eye, the VISOR output resembled a crazy collage of swirling colors and vague shapes. ("Heart of Glory" [TNG]). **Dr. Katherine Pulaski** once proposed to Geordi a

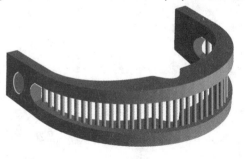

surgical procedure which would have replaced his VISOR with optical implant devices offering nearly the same visual range. Geordi declined the opportunity. ("Loud as a Whisper" [TNG]). *At the time this scene was written and shot, the show's producers were indeed considering the possibility of giving Geordi "normal" sight, but both Gene Roddenberry and actor LeVar Burton eventually realized that a "miracle" cure would weaken Geordi as a role model to disabled people in our audience.* La Forge and Centurion **Bochra** linked La Forge's VISOR with a tricorder to form a device capable of detecting neutrino emissions, since a standard tricorder was incapable of detecting this phenomenon. This improvisation saved both men's lives because they were trapped on planet **Galorndon Core** at the time. ("The Enemy" [TNG]). SEE: **neural output pods.** La Forge's VISOR provided the Romulans with a unique opportunity to use his neural implants to provide direct input to his visual cortex, giving them the ability to program La Forge's mind to commit criminal acts. The Romulans tried unsuccessfully to use La Forge to murder Klingon governor **Vagh** in 2367 with this technique. ("The Mind's Eye" [TNG]). *Geordi's VISOR was modeled on a hair clip donated to the show by UCLA researcher Kiku Annon.*

Visual Acuity Transmitter. Small device that permitted the short-range transmission of visual images recorded by the **VISOR** worn by **Geordi La Forge**. This device was used when La Forge participated in a rescue mission to a crippled **Talarian** freighter in 2364, but the unit failed after a short time because of complexity of the signal exceeded the ability of the unit to handle. The image displayed by the Visual Acuity Transmitter contained an enormous amount of information, but was difficult for an untrained human to view. ("Heart of Glory" [TNG]).

Vixis. (Spice Williams). First officer of the Klingon Bird-of-prey commanded by **Captain Klaa**. (*Star Trek V: The Final Frontier*).

voice-transit conductors. Telecommunications system used by the now-vanished civilization on planet **Kataan**. ("The Inner Light" [TNG]).

Volchok Prime. Planet where Ferengi Hoex bought out his rival **Turot's** controlling interest in a cargo port. ("The Nagus" [DS9]).

Volnoth. (Marc Lawrence). Elderly **Gatherer** and member of the clan **Lornack**. He died suddenly during the negotiations on **Gamma Hromi II** in 2366. Investigation revealed him to have been murdered by **Yuta** in vengeance for the Lornaks' massacre of the **Tralesta** clan in 2286. ("The Vengeance Factor" [TNG]).

Voltaire, Shuttlepod. Shuttlepod #03, attached to the *Starship Enterprise-D*. Captain Picard piloted the *Voltaire*, using the shuttlepod to fly ahead of the *Enterprise-D*, guiding the starship out of the **Mar Oscura** nebula in 2367. The *Voltaire* was destroyed, although Picard was beamed to safety. ("In Theory" [TNG]). *The* Voltaire *was named for the 18th-century French writer and philosopher.*

Volterra Nebula. A stellar "nursery" in which proto-stars are in the process of coalescing from nebular material. The *Enterprise*-D conducted a survey mission in the Volterra Nebula in 2369. ("The Chase" [TNG]).

***Vor'cha*-class attack cruiser.** SEE: **Klingon attack cruiser.**

Vorch-doh-baghk, Kahless! Translates as "All hail Kahless." The ritual greeting for the Klingon historical figure. ("Rightful Heir" [TNG]).

Vorgons. A humanoid race, capable of time travel. Two Vorgon criminals, **Ajur** and **Boratus**, traveled back some 300 years from the 27th century to locate Jean-Luc Picard, in hopes of locating the powerful *Tox Uthat*. Ajur and Boratus were thwarted when Picard destroyed the object to prevent it from falling into the wrong hands. ("Captain's Holiday" [TNG]).

Vorn, I.K.C. Klingon Bird-of-Prey that transported **Klingon High Council** member **Duras** to a rendezvous with the *Enterprise*-D in 2367. Duras was aboard the *Vorn* when Lieutenant **Worf** discovered that Duras had murdered **K'Ehleyr**. Worf, claiming the right of vengeance, killed Duras aboard the *Vorn*. ("Reunion" [TNG]).

Vorta Vor. In Romulan mythology, the source of all creation. (*Star Trek V: The Final Frontier*). SEE: **Sha Ka Ree.**

• **"Vortex."** *Deep Space Nine* episode #12. Written by Sam Rolfe. Directed by Winrich Kolbe. *No stardate given. First aired in 1993. A fugitive bargains with Odo for his safety.* SEE: **Ah-Kel; Chamra Vortex; changeling; Croden; Exarch; *Ganges, U.S.S.*; Miradorn; Nehelik Province; Odo; Rakhar; Rakhari; Rigelian freighter; Ro-Kel; *T'Van*; *toh-maire*; Vanoben transport; Yareth.**

Voyager VI. Early automated interplanetary space probe launched from Earth in the late 1990s. Upon leaving the Solar System, *Voyager VI* fell into a black hole and emerged on the other side of the galaxy, near a planet of living machines. (*Star Trek: The Motion Picture*). SEE: **V'Ger.** *Voyager I and II, actual space probes launched by NASA in the early 1970s, were among the first to explore Jupiter, Saturn, and the outer Solar System.*

V'sal. SEE: **Mot.**

Vulcan death grip. There is no such thing as a Vulcan death grip, but Spock claimed to have used it when he apparently killed Kirk during their spy mission aboard a Romulan vessel in 2268. The ruse allowed Kirk to escape back to the *Enterprise*. ("The *Enterprise* Incident" [TOS]).

Vulcan harp. Stringed musical instrument from planet Vulcan. Spock enjoyed playing the instrument during his off-duty

hours. *The Vulcan harp was first seen in "Charlie X" (TOS), then later used in "The Conscience of the King" (TOS), in which he accompanied Uhura's song "Beyond Antares"; "Amok Time" (TOS); and "The Way to Eden" (TOS). A replica of the original prop, borrowed from Gene Roddenberry's office, was used in Star Trek V: The Final Frontier.*

Vulcan Master. (Edna Glover, Paul Weber, Norman Stuart). Elder mentors who guided Vulcan aspirants through the *Kohlinar* ritual. (*Star Trek: The Motion Picture*).

Vulcan mind-meld. An ancient Vulcan ritual in which two persons are telepathically linked, sharing each other's consciousness. To Vulcans, mind-melding is a deeply personal experience, providing an intense intimacy. **Spock** used a mind-meld in 2266 to determine the truth of **Dr. Simon Van Gelder**'s apparently wild claims that he was the director of the **Tantalus V** penal colony. ("Dagger of the Mind" [TOS]). Spock occasionally used his mind-melding skills to provide a telepathic distraction to an adversary, as at **Eminiar VII** ("A Taste of Armageddon" [TOS]). Mind-melding can be performed with intelligences as diverse as humans, the robot space probe **Nomad** ("The Changeling"), the **Horta** ("The Devil in the Dark" [TOS]), and the **Kelvans.** When mind-melding with the Kelvan named **Kelinda**, Spock was able to glimpse the apparently humanoid creature's true form: an immense being with hundreds of tentacles. ("By Any Other Name" [TOS]). A mind-meld was used to permit **Jean-Luc Picard** to provide emotional support to Ambassador **Sarek** in 2366 when the ambassador was suffering the debilitating effects of terminal **Bendii Syndrome.** Sarek benefited from the captain's emotional control, but Picard had to endure the fierce onslaught of the ambassador's unleashed emotions. ("Sarek" [TNG]). *The Vulcan mind-meld was first used in "Dagger of the Mind" (TOS). Mind-melds were also performed in "Spectre of the Gun" (TOS), "The Omega Glory" (TOS), Star Trek III: The Search for Spock, and Star Trek VI: The Undiscovered Country.* SEE: *katra*; **synaptic pattern displacement.**

Vulcan nerve pinch. A Vulcan technique in which finger pressure is applied to certain nerves at the base of the neck, instantly and nonviolently rendering that individual unconscious. Although the technique appears to work on nearly all humanoid species (and several nonhumanoids as well), few non-Vulcans have been able to master the nerve pinch. ("The Enemy Within" [TOS]). Spock tried, unsuccessfully to teach the nerve pinch to Kirk, but many years later, Data was able to master the technique. ("Unification, Part II" [TNG]). *The Famous Spock Nerve Pinch (as it became known to* the show's production staff) was invented by actor Leonard Nimoy, who devised it because he thought Spock would not stoop to rendering an opponent unconscious with a karate chop. SEE: **FSNP**.

Vulcan Science Academy. Institute of higher learning on planet Vulcan. **Spock** chose to apply to Starfleet in 2249 rather than stay on his homeworld and study at the Academy. That decision was the cause of a rift between Spock and his father, **Sarek**, that lasted for 18 years. ("Journey to Babel" [TOS]). The director of the Academy from 2354-2369 was subspace theoretician **Dr. T'Pan.** ("Suspicions" [TNG]).

Vulcan. Class-M planet, homeworld to the Vulcan race. Hot and arid, Vulcan is a member of the United Federation of Planets. Vulcan was the homeworld of Spock and Sarek. The planet has no moon. ("The Man Trap" [TOS]). *The original* Starship Enterprise *visited Vulcan in "Amok Time" (TOS) and "Journey to Babel" (TOS). We also saw Vulcan (curiously with several moons — or at least nearby planets) in* Star Trek: The Motion Picture*, then again in* Star Trek III *and* Star Trek IV. *The* Enterprise-D *visited Vulcan in "Sarek" (TNG) and "Unification, Part I" (TNG).* SEE: **Vulcans**.

Vulcana Regar. City on planet **Vulcan**, home to **T'Shanik**. ("Coming of Age" [TNG]).

Vulcanis. Alternate name for planet **Vulcan**. *Vulcanis was used in the first few episodes of the original* Star Trek *series before Spock's homeworld was changed to Vulcan.*

Vulcans. Humanoid race native to planet Vulcan, of which Mr. Spock is a member. Vulcans were once a passionate, violent people whose civilization was torn by terrible wars ("Let That Be Your Last Battlefield" [TOS], "All Our Yesterdays" [TOS]). The ancient philosopher **Surak**, revered as the father of Vulcan civilization, led his people some 2,000 years ago to reject their emo-

tions in favor of a philosophy that embraced pure logic. ("The Savage Curtain" [TOS]). Vulcan society is now based entirely on logic and any trappings of emotion are considered to be in extremely poor taste.

One group did not accept Surak's teachings and instead left Vulcan to found the warrior **Romulan Star Empire.** ("Unification, Part I" [TNG]).

In the distant past, Vulcans killed to win their mates. Even in the present, Vulcans revert to ancient mating rituals, apparently the price these people must pay for totally suppressing their natural emotions. When Vulcan children are about seven, their parents select a future mate, and the two children are joined in a ceremony that links them telepathically. When the two children come of age, they are compelled to join together for the marriage rituals. The time of mating, **Pon farr**, is when the stoically logical Vulcans pay for their rigid control by experiencing a period of total emotional abandon. In Vulcan adults, *Pon farr* comes every seven

years. ("Amok Time" [TOS]). SEE: **Koon-ut-kal-if-fee**.

Because planet Vulcan has a higher gravity than Earth, and its atmosphere is thinner, Vulcans in an Earth-normal environment demonstrate greater physical strength and more acute hearing than humans. The intensity of the Vulcan sun caused the Vulcans to evolve a secondary eyelid to protect the retina. This inner eyelid involuntarily closes when the eye is exposed to extremely intense light. Spock's **inner eyelid** protected him in 2267 against powerful light used in an experiment to eradicate the **Denevan neural parasite** in 2267. ("Operation— Annihilate!" [TOS]). A Vulcan's heart is where a human's liver is. When injured, Vulcans concentrate their strength, blood, and antibodies onto the injured organs in a type of self-induced hypnosis. ("A Private Little War" [TOS]).

Certain elements of Vulcan prehistory suggest that the Vulcan race may have originated with colonists from another planet, possibly humanoids from **Sargon's planet** 500,000 years ago. ("Return to Tomorrow" [TOS]). Vulcans have telepathic capacity, as practiced in the **Vulcan mind-meld**. Although the telepathic ability is quite limited, Spock once felt the death screams of the 400 Vulcan crew members of the Starship **Intrepid** across inter-stellar distances. ("The Immu- 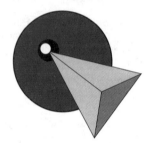 nity Syndrome" [TOS]). *Illustration: Vulcan* **IDIC** *symbol.* SEE: **fal-tor-pan; katra; Kohlinar; Plak-tow;** *plomeek* **soup; Sarek; Spock; Stonn; Tal-shaya; T'Pau; T'Pring; T'plana-Hath; Vulcan nerve pinch.**

W-particle interference. Commander Data used ship's sensors to scan for W-particle interference to confirm the presence of gaps in normal space within the **Mar Oscura** in 2367. ("In Theory" [TNG]).

Wadi. Humanoid species discovered by a Vulcan ship in the Gamma Quadrant in 2369. A Wadi diplomatic delegation was the first formal first contact from the **Gamma Quadrant** to visit the Alpha Quadrant through the **Bajoran wormhole**. Tall in stature, the Wadi were interested mostly in games and went straight to **Quark's bar** upon arriving at station Deep Space 9. When Quark cheated them at **Dabo**, the leader of the Wadi, **Falow,** forced him to play an elaborate game they called **Chula**. The stakes were hight, and involved the involuntary participation of key members of the Deep Space 9 crew. ("Move Along Home" [DS9]).

Wagner, Professor. A speaker at the deep-space psychology seminar attended by members of the *Enterprise*-D crew in 2369. Counselor Troi spent a great deal of time at the professor's lecture, but later admitted she found it less than stimulating. ("Timescape" [TNG]).

Wagnor. (Andrew Bicknell). Pilot of the Angosian police vessel that **Roga Danar** commandeered after his escape from the *Enterprise*-D in 2366. ("The Hunted" [TNG]).

Wallace, Dr. Janet. (Sarah Marshall). Expert in endocrinology. Dr. Wallace was aboard the original *Starship Enterprise* in 2267 when a radiation-induced hyper-accelerated aging disease struck several of the *Enterprise* crew members. She and James Kirk had been romantically involved in 2261 but decided to go their separate ways, pursuing different careers.  She later met and married **Dr. Theodore Wallace**, a man 26 years her senior, when they were working on a project together on planet Aldebaran III. ("The Deadly Years"[TOS]).

Wallace, Dr. Theodore. Late husband to endocrinologist **Janet Wallace**. He met his wife on Aldebaran III, where the couple worked together. ("The Deadly Years" [TOS]).

Wallace. *Enterprise*-D crew member, part of the engineering staff. Wallace was one of two engineers left at the command post set up on a remote planet. The command post was used to coordinate the teams searching for Commander **Data**, following his disappearance in late 2369. ("Descent, Part I" [TNG]).

Walsh, Captain Leo Francis. Name assumed by **Harry Mudd** when he came aboard the *Enterprise* in 2266. According to Mr. Mudd, Leo Walsh was to be the captain on his transport vessel but suddenly died, making it necessary for Mudd to take charge. ("Mudd's Women" [TOS]).

Wanoni tracehound. Predatory animal that pursued its prey with enthusiastic vigor. **Odo** likened **Lwaxana Troi** to a Wanoni tracehound when she expressed interest in the **shape-shifter**. ("The Forsaken" [DS9]).

Warbird, Romulan. SEE: **Romulan Warbird**.

warning beacons. Transmitter intended to inform nearby space vehicles of a potential hazard. Warning beacons were placed around planet **Tarchannen III** in 2367 after it was discovered that one of the life-forms on the planet reproduced by mutating unsuspecting visitors. ("Identity Crisis" [TNG]).

Warnog. Klingon ale. ("Rightful Heir" [TNG]).

warp field. The "bubble" of subspace in which a starship travels when using **warp drive**. A low-level warp field can have the effect of reducing the local **gravitational constant** within the field itself. This is because a subspace field resembles the time-space distortion of a gravitational field. The effect is that a low-level warp field can be used to temporarily reduce the apparent mass of an object (with relationship to the outside universe). This technique was used by Geordi La Forge in an unsuccessful attempt to prevent the moon of planet **Bre'el IV** from crashing into the planet in 2366. ("Deja Q" [TNG]). O'Brien was able to use a low-level warp field to reduce the mass of Deep Space 9 sufficiently for the station's maneuvering thrusters to move the station to the **Denerios Belt** following the discovery of the Bajoran Wormhole in 2369. ("Emissary" [DS9]).

warp bubble. An enclosed **subspace** field. A starship at warp speeds exists within a warp bubble, essentially its own universe. A **static warp bubble** was accidentally created by Wesley Crusher in 2367 during a warp drive experiment aboard the *Enterprise*-D. ("Remember Me" [TNG]).

warp core breach. SEE: **antimatter containment**.

warp drive. Primary propulsion system used by most faster-than-light interstellar spacecraft. Warp drive systems used by Federation **starship**s employ the controlled annihilation of matter and **antimatter** ("The Naked Time" [TOS]), regulated by dilithium crystals, to generate the tremendous power required to warp space and travel faster than light. Warp drive was invented in 2061 by noted scientist **Zefram Cochrane** of Alpha Centauri. ("Metamorphosis" [TOS]). SEE: **antimatter containment; Cochrane distortion; Cochrane, Zefram; dilithium; matter/antimatter reaction chamber; nacelle; subspace; transwarp; warp factor.**

For more detailed information regarding warp drive and other technical matters, please refer to the Star Trek: The Next Generation Technical Manual *by Rick Sternbach and Michael Okuda, published by Pocket Books.*

Next page: Warp-speed chart as recalibrated for Star Trek: The Next Generation. *Note that the indication of warp 5 as the "new" normal cruising speed was established in* "Force of Nature" (TNG).

Warp speed chart for Starship Enterprise, NCC-1701D

SPEED	Kilometers per hour	Number of times speed of Light	APPROXIMATE TIME TO TRAVEL						NOTES
			Earth to moon 400,000 kilometers	Across Sol system 12 million kilometers	To nearby star 5 light-years	Across one sector 20 light-years	Across Federation 10,000 light-years	To nearby Galaxy 2,000,000 light-years	
Standard orbit	9600	less than 0.00001 SUBLIGHT	42 hours	142 years	558,335 years	2 million yrs	1.12 billion years	223.33 billion years	Synchronous orbit around Class-M planet
Full impulse (1/4 lightspeed)	270 million	0.25 SUBLIGHT	5.38 seconds	44 hours	20 years	80 years	400,000 years	8,000,000 years	Normal maximum impulse speed
Warp factor 1	1078 million	1	1.34 seconds	11 hours	5 years	20 years	100,000 years	2,000,000 years	Warp One= SPEED OF LIGHT
Warp factor 2	11 billion	10	0.13 seconds	1 hour	6 months	3 years	9,921 years	198,425 years	
Warp factor 3	42 billion	39	0.03 seconds	17 minutes	2 months	1 year	2,568 years	51,360 years	
Warp factor 4	109 billion	102	0.013237 seconds	7 minutes	18 days	2 month	984 years	19,686 years	
Warp factor 5	230 billion	214	0.006291 seconds	3 minutes	9 days	1 month	468 years	9,357 years	New cruising speed
Warp factor 6	423 billion	392	0.003426 seconds	2 minutes	5 days	19 days	255 years	5,096 years	Old normal cruising speed
Warp factor 7	707 billion	656	0.002049 seconds	1 minute	3 days	11 days	152 years	3,048 years	
Warp factor 8	1103 trillion	1,024	0.001313 seconds	39 seconds	2 days	7 days	98 years	1,953 years	
Warp factor 9	1.63 trillion	1,516	0.000886 seconds	26 seconds	1 day	5 days	66 years	1,319 years	
Warp factor 9.2	1.78 trillion	1,649	0.000815 seconds	24 seconds	1 day	4 days	61 years	1,213 years	old normal maximum speed
Warp factor 9.6	2.06 trillion	1,909	0.000704 seconds	21 seconds	23 hours	4 days	52 years	1,048 years	maximum rated speed, can be maintained for 12 hours
Warp factor 9.9	3.29 trillion	3,053	0.000440 seconds	13 seconds	14 hours	2 days	33 years	655 years	auto-shutdown of engines after 10 minutes
Warp factor 9.99	8.53 trillion	7,912	0.000169 seconds	5 seconds	6 hours	22 hours	13 years	253 years	nearly infinite power required
Warp factor 9.9999	215 trillion	199,516	0.000006 seconds	0.2 seconds	13 minutes	53 minutes	6 months	10 years	maximum subspace radio speed (with booster relays)
Warp factor 10	<infinite>	<infinite>	0	0	0	0	0	0	Warp 10 **cannot** be reached

<infinite> This speed is meaningless – a starship at Warp 10 would occupy all points in the universe simultaneously.

(Use these estimates for comparison only – your actual mileage may vary).

warp factor. Unit of measure used to measure faster-than-light warp velocities. Warp factor one is c, the speed of light, while higher speeds are computed geometrically under one of two different formulae. The original *Starship Enterprise* had a cruising speed of **warp factor** 6, and could reach warp 8 only with significant danger to the ship itself. ("Arena" [TOS]). The ship nevertheless reached warp 11 in 2267 when modified by **Nomad** to increase engine efficiency by 57%. ("The Changeling" [TOS]). The **Kelvans** were also successful in modifying the ship's engines to rech warp 11. ("By Any Other Name" [TOS]). The ship reached warp 14.1 in 2268 when the warp engines were sabotoged by **Losira**. ("That Which Survives" [TOS]). By the 24th century, a new warp-factor scale was in use that employed an asymptotic curve, placing warp 10 as an infinite value. Under the new scale, the *Galaxy*-class *Enterprise*-D had a normal cruising speed of warp 6 (392 times light speed, about warp 7.3 under the old system), and a maximum normal velocity of warp 9.2 (about 1649 times light speed, equivalent to about warp 11.8 in the "old" system). *The original* Star Trek *series occasionally had ships and other objects traveling at warp 10 or faster. At the beginning of* Star Trek: The Next Generation, *Gene Roddenberry said he wanted to change the warp-speed scale to put warp 10 at the absolute top of the scale. We therefore assume that the warp scale has been recalibrated so that all the speeds shown in the original show are "actually" less than warp 10. Interestingly, the original* Star Trek *series never established actual speeds for warp factors in any episode or movie, although the old warp factor cubed formula has come to be generally accepted. A new upper limit for warp speed travel was established in "Force of Nature" (TNG), when speeds exceeding warp 5 were found to cause dangerous damage to the space-time continuum. Illustration: Warp field diagram for* Galaxy-*class starship.*

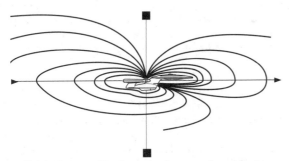

warp field phase adjustment. A procedure used to suppress the subspace interference generated by a starship's warp engines. By adjusting the field phase of the Ferengi ship *Krayton*, Commander Riker was able to send a surreptitious signal to the *Enterprise*-D when he was held captive on that ship in 2366. ("Ménage à Troi" [TNG]).

Warren, Dr. Mary. (Lois Hall). Scientist assigned to the Federation anthropological field team on planet **Mintaka III**. Warren died from injuries she sustained in a failure of the anthropologists' "**duck blind**" in 2366. ("Who Watches the Watchers?" [TNG]).

Warrior/Adonis. (Leo Damian). A member of the interpretive chorus of mediator **Riva** from planet **Ramatis III**. Each member of the Chorus represented a different part of Riva's personality. Warrior/Adonis represented passion, the libido, and the anarchy of lust. He also said he was the romantic and the definition of honor. ("Loud As a Whisper" [TNG]). SEE: **Scholar/Artist**; **Woman**.

Washburn. (Richard Compton). *Enterprise* engineering officer who was part of the boarding party to the derelict *U.S.S. Constellation* in 2267. ("The Doomsday Machine" [TOS]). *Richard Compton went on to become a television director who directed "The Last Outpost" (TNG). Compton's first assistant director on that episode was Charles Washburn.*

Watkins, John B. (Kenneth Washington). *Enterprise* Engineer killed by **Losira**, near the **Kalandan outpost** in 2268. ("That Which Survives" [TOS]).

• **"Way to Eden, The."** Original Series episode #75. Teleplay by Arthur Heinemann. Story by Michael Richards and Arthur Heinemann. Directed by David Alexander. Stardate 5832.3. *First aired in 1969. The* Enterprise *is hijacked by a group of renegades who have rejected modern technological life to search for the mythical planet Eden. An early version of this episode, originally titled "Joanna," written by D. C. Fontana, was a love story between James Kirk and Joanna McCoy, daughter of* **Dr. Leonard McCoy**. *In the aired version, the Joanna character became Irina Galliulin, Chekov's love interest. Michael Richards is the pseudonym of D. C. Fontana.* SEE: **Adam**; *Aurora*; **Auxiliary Control Center**; **Catuallan**; **Chekov, Pavel A.**; **Eden**; *Galileo II*, **Shuttlecraft**; **Herbert**; **Irina Galliulin**; **One**; **Palmer, Lieutenant**; **Sevrin, Dr.**; *Synthococcus novae*; **Tiburon**; **Tongo Rad**; **Vulcan harp**.

• **"We'll Always Have Paris."** *Next Generation* episode #24. Written by Deborah Dean Davis and Hannah Louise Shearer. Directed by Robert Becker. Stardate 41679.9. *First aired in 1988. While responding to a distress call from a noted scientist, Picard encounters a woman he once loved, now the wife of that scientist.* SEE: **Blue Parrot Cafe**; **Cafe des Artistes**; **Coltar IV**; **Dean, Lieutenant**; **Edouard**; **fencing**; **Gabrielle**; **Herbert, Transporter Chief**; **Ilecom system**; *Lalo, U.S.S.*; **Manheim Effect**; **Manheim, Dr. Paul**; **Manheim, Jenice**; **Paris**; **Pegos Minor**; **Picard, Jean-Luc**; **Sarona VII**; **Vandor IX**; **Vandor star system**.

weather modification net. System used to detect and dissipate dangerous meteorological disturbances in a planetary atmosphere. A weather modification net did not detect the tornado that killed **Amanda Rogers'** biological parents on one of the planets in the **Bilaren system**. ("True-Q" [TNG]).

Webb. (Richard Merrifield). Radar monitor technician with Earth's 20th-century United States Air Force in Omaha, Nebraska, when the *Starship Enterprise* was picked up as a UFO. The starship had been propelled back to 20th-century Earth and was low in the atmosphere when it was detected. ("Tomorrow Is Yesterday" [TOS]).

wedding. In many humanoid cultures, a ceremony celebrating the joining of two individuals into a family unit. Specific rituals varied widely. In 2367, Lieutenant Worf observed that Human bonding rituals "involve a great deal of talking and dancing and crying." Following the long-standing human tradition of a ship's captain officiating at weddings, *Enterprise* captain Kirk conducted the Martine/Tomlinson wedding in 2266. Unfortunately, this wedding was interrupted by a Romulan attack. ("Balance of Terror" [TOS]). Weddings held aboard the *Enterprise*-D included the Ishikawa/O'Brien wedding in 2367 ("Data's Day" [TNG]) and the Lwaxana Troi/Campio wedding of 2368 ("Cost of Living" [TNG]), though the latter wedding was not completed because the groom abruptly left the ceremony. There were

also the 2364 nuptials planned for Deanna Troi and Wyatt Miller, but this ceremony was canceled after the groom left the ship ("Haven" [TNG]). *Given the* Enterprise *history for weddings, Keiko and Miles were pretty lucky to make it to the altar after all.*

Wellington, U.S.S. Federation starship, *Niagara* class, Starfleet registry number NCC-28473. The *Wellington* underwent a computer system upgrade by **Bynar** technicians at **Starbase 74** in 2364. ("11001001" [TNG]). The *Wellington* was in the vicinity of Starbase 123 in early 2367. It reported no unusual readings after a warp field experiment aboard the *Enterprise*-D by Wesley Crusher. ("Remember Me" [TNG]). Ensign **Ro Laren** served aboard the *Wellington* until she was held responsible for an incident in which eight people were killed on **Garon II** because of Ro's failure to obey orders. ("Ensign Ro" [TNG]).

Wesley, Commodore Robert. (Barry Russo). Commander of the *Starship* **Lexington** in 2268 and officer in charge of the disastrous **M-5** computer tests. A friend of James Kirk, Bob Wesley had the courage not to attack the *Enterprise* after the M-5 **multitronic** unit malfunctioned seriously. ("The Ultimate Computer" [TOS]). *Bob Wesley was named for* Star Trek

creator Gene Roddenberry, whose middle name was Wesley. Roddenberry used Robert Wesley as his pen name on his television scripts in the 1950s while he was still working for the Los Angeles Police Department. Barry Russo also played **Commander Giotto** *in "The Devil in the Dark" (TOS).*

West, Colonel. (Rene Auberjonois). Starfleet officer who conspired with **Admiral Cartwright** and Klingon **General Chang** to obstruct **Chancellor Gorkon**'s peace initiatives in 2293. West was the trigger man who, disguised as a Klingon, unsuccessfully attempted to assassinate the **Federation Council President** at the **Khitomer** conference. (*Star Trek VI: The Undiscovered Country*). SEE: **Operation Retrieve.** *Colonel West's scenes in* Star Trek VI *were cut prior to the theatrical release of that film, but they were restored in the*

videocassette and laserdisk versions. Actor Rene Auberjonois also played **Odo** *in* Star Trek: Deep Space Nine.

whale song. A beautiful, mournful sound produced by the **humpback whale**s of planet Earth. It is not known what purpose these songs serve, but it is believed by some scientists that they are a form of communication for these highly intelligent cetaceans. Whale song was also the medium of communication between humpback whales and an alien space probe of unknown origin.. (*Star Trek IV: The Voyage Home*). SEE: **Probe, the**

Whalen. (David Selburg). Literature historian and 20th-century specialist aboard *Enterprise*-D. Whalen was injured in a **Dixon Hill** holodeck simulation when the system was damaged by a **Jaradan** probe in 2364. ("The Big Goodbye" [TNG]).

• **"What Are Little Girls Made Of?"** Original Series episode #10. Written by Robert Bloch. Directed by James Goldstone. Stardate 2712.4. *First broadcast in 1966. Nurse Chapel's missing fiancé is discovered, living in a "perfect" android body.* SEE: **Andrea; android; Brown; Chapel, Christine; Earth Colony 2; Exo III; Kirk, George Samuel; Kirk; Korby, Dr. Roger; Mathews; Midos V; Old Ones; Rayburn; Ruk.**

• **"When the Bough Breaks."** *Next Generation* episode #18. Written by Hannah Louise Shearer. Directed by Kim Manners. Stardate 41509.1. *First aired in 1988. An advanced race offers to trade scientific information in exchange for the children of* Enterprise-D *crew members.* SEE: **Accolan; Aldea; Aldeans; Bernard, Dr. Harry, Sr.; Bernard, Harry, Jr.; calculus; cloaking device; Aldean; Custodian, The; Duana; Epsilon Mynos system; Melian; Neinman; ozone; Progenitors; Radue; Rashella; Xerxes VII; Zadar IV.**

• **"Where No Man Has Gone Before."** *Original Series* episode #2. Written by Samuel A. Peeples. Directed by James Goldstone. Stardate 1312.4. *First aired in 1966. An energy barrier at the edge of the galaxy mutates Kirk's friend, Gary Mitchell, into a godlike being. This was the second pilot episode for the original* Star Trek *series. It was the first episode in which most of the regular original cast (including Captain Kirk) appear. Spock was, in fact, the only character to be carried over from the first pilot. The designs of the costumes and many sets were changed somewhat between this episode and "The Corbomote Maneuver" (TOS), the first regular series episode. "Where No Man Has Gone Before" prompted NBC to buy* Star Trek *as a weekly series.* SEE: **Aldebaran; barrier, galactic; Canopus Planet; Dehner, Dr. Elizabeth; Delta Vega; Dimorus; extrasensory perception; Kaferian apples; Kelso, Lieutenant Lee; Kirk, James T.; Leslie, Mr.; lithium cracking station; lithium crystals; Mitchell, Gary; "Nightingale Woman"; phaser rifle; Piper, Dr. Mark; recorder marker; Scott, Montgomery; Smith, Yeoman; Sulu, Hikaru; Tarbolde, Phineas; three-dimensional chess; turbolift;** *Valiant, S.S.*

• **"Where No One Has Gone Before."** *Next Generation* episode #6. Written by Diane Duane & Michael Reaves. Directed by Rob Bowman. Stardate 41263.1. *First aired in 1987. A warp drive experiment gone awry sends the Enterprise-D into another galaxy. This episode was loosely based on Diane Duane's Star Trek novel, The Wounded Sky. This was the first appearance of the Traveler, who would be seen again in "Remember Me" (TNG).* SEE: **Ajax, *U.S.S.*; Argyle, Lieutenant Commander; Crusher, Wesley; *Fearless, U.S.S*; Galaxy M33; intermix formula; Kosinski; Picard, Jean-Luc; Picard, Yvette Gessard; *targ*; Tau Alpha C; Traveler; Yar, Natasha.**

• **"Where Silence Has Lease."** *Next Generation* episode #28. Written by Jack B. Sowards. Directed by Winrich Kolbe. Stardate 42193.6. *First aired in 1988. The* Enterprise-D *is trapped in a "hole in space" by a life-form named Nagilum trying to understand the concept of death. This episode was the first time we saw Worf's holodeck Klingon exercise program.* SEE: **Autodestruct; calisthenics program, Klingon; Class 1 sensor probe; Cornelian Star System; "hole in space"; Morgana Quadrant; Nagilum; *Yamato, U.S.S.***

whip, Ferengi. SEE: **Ferengi whip.**

White Rabbit. Character from Lewis Carroll's book ***Alice in Wonderland.*** The White Rabbit was a sentient biped who was very late for an important date when he appeared to Dr. McCoy on the **amusement park planet**. McCoy had noted that the planet looked like something out of *Alice in Wonderland.* ("Shore Leave" [TOS]).

white rhinos. Extinct animal species from planet Earth. White rhinoceros were known by the zoological name *Ceratotherium simum.* The species was hunted to extinction in the 22nd century. ("New Ground" [TNG]). *Given the continued poaching of the rhinoceros, it is unfortunately very possible that this Star Trek prediction will come true much sooner than the 22nd century.*

• **"Who Mourns for Adonais?"** Original Series episode #33. Written by Gilbert Ralston. Directed by Marc Daniels. Stardate 3468.1. *First aired in 1967. The* Enterprise *is captured by a powerful alien who was once worshipped on planet Earth as the Greek god Apollo.* SEE: **A&A officer; Antos IV; Apollo; Beta Geminorum system; Chekov, Pavel A.; dryworm; gods, Greek; Kyle, Mr.; Palamas, Lieutenant Carolyn; Pollux IV; Pollux V; Starbase 12.**

• **"Who Watches the Watchers?"** *Next Generation* episode #52. Written by Richard Manning & Hans Beimler. Directed by Robert Wiemer. Stardate 43173.5. *First aired in 1989. A cultural observervation team is accidentally discovered by a planet's native humanoids who decide that Captain Picard is their god.* SEE: **Barron, Dr.; duck blind; Fento; Hali; hologram generator; Liko; Mintaka III; Mintakan tapestry;** Mintakans; Nuria; Oji; Palmer, Dr.; proto-Vulcan; Warren, Dr. Mary.

• **"Whom Gods Destroy."** Original Series episode #71. Teleplay by Lee Erwin. Story by Lee Erwin and Jerry Sohl. Directed by Herb Wallerstein. Stardate 5718.3. *First aired in 1969. Kirk and Spock are held captive in an insane asylum by a former Starfleet hero.* SEE: **Antos IV; Axanar; cellular metamorphosis; Cochrane deceleration maneuver; Cory, Governor Doland; Elba II; environmental suits; fleet captain; Garth of Izar; Kirk, James T.; Marta; Tau Ceti; Three-dimensional chess.**

Wilkins, Professor. Member of the **Starnes Expedition** to planet **Triacus** in 2268. ("And the Children Shall Lead" [TOS]).

Williams, Ted. Famous **baseball** player who was an outfielder for the Boston Red Sox from 1939-1960 on Earth. Williams twice won the Triple Crown and was elected to Baseball's Hall of Fame in 1966. A holographic version of Williams was available in a baseball **holosuite** program enjoyed by Jake and **Benjamin Sisko** on station Deep Space 9. ("If Wishes Were Horses" [DS9]). SEE: **Bokai, Buck.**

Wilson, Transporter Technician. (Garland Thompson). *Enterprise* crew member under the command of Captain James Kirk in 2266. Wilson surrendered his phaser pistol to a partial duplicate of Kirk created in a transporter malfunction. ("The Enemy Within" [TOS]).

Winchester. Brand name for a rifle used on 19th-century Earth. Deanna Troi's holodeck character, Durango, carried a Winchester in the program ***Ancient West.*** ("A Fistful of Datas" [TNG]).

• **"Wink of an Eye."** Original Series episode #68. Teleplay by Arthur Heineann. Story by Lee Cronin. Directed by Jud Taylor. Stardate 5710.5. *First aired in 1968. The* Enterprise *is commandeered by aliens who exist in a hyperaccelerated time frame.* SEE: **Compton; Deela; hyperacceleration; Rael; regrigration unit; Scalos; Scalosians.**

Winn, Vedek. (Louise Fletcher). Politically ambitious **Bajoran** religious leader who sought to succeed **Kai Opaka**, following Opaka's disappearance in 2369.

Winn, a member of an orothodox order, engineered conflict on station Deep Space 9, claiming that the teaching of scientific theories on the origins of the **Bajoran wormhole** was inconsistent with Bajoran religious faith. Winn was, in fact, plotting to draw her political rival, **Vedek Bareil**, to the station, where Winn's co-conspirator attempted to assassinate him; an unsuccessful effort to eliminate Bareil as candidate for Kai. ("In the Hands of the Prophets" [DS9]). SEE: **Neela.**

Wise Ones. Race of beings also known as the **Preservers**. ("The Paradise Syndrome" [TOS]).

Woban. (Jordan Lund). Leader of the **Navot** village on planet Bajor. Woban came to Deep Space 9 in 2369 to negotiate a land dispute with representatives of the rival **Paqu** nation. ("The Storyteller" [DS9]). See: **Glyrhond; Varis Sul.**

Woden Sector. Region of space where the **Talarian** warship *Q'Maire* was located when it responded to a distress call from a **Talarian observation craft** in 2367. ("Suddenly Human" [TNG]). *The sector was named as an homage to the ship of the same name that was destroyed in "The Ultimate Computer" (TOS).*

Woden. Old-style ore freighter that was automated and carried no crew. The *Woden* was destroyed by the **M-5** mutitronic unit in 2268 when that experimental computer malfunctioned seriously. ("The Ultimate Computer" [TOS]). *The* Woden *was a re-use of the* S.S. Botany Bay *model from "Space Seed" (TOS).*

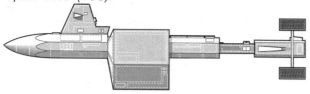

Wogneer creatures. Life-forms that lived in the Ordek Nebula. Captain Picard played a part in protecting them. ("Allegiance" [TNG]).

Wolf 359. The site of a terrible battle in which some 40 Federation starships tried in vain to prevent a Borg invasion of Earth in early 2367. Commanded by **Admiral J. P. Hanson**, the Starfleet armada was decimated by the Borg ship, resulting in the loss of 39 ships and 11,000 lives. Among the vessels lost were the *Starships* **Tolstoy, Kyushu, Melbourne,** and **Saratoga.** ("The Best of Both Worlds, Part II" [TNG]). *Casualty figures from "The Drumhead" (TNG). Saratoga established in "Emissary" (DS9). The aftermath of the battle of Wolf 359 was shown in "The Best of Both Worlds, Part II" (TNG), but three years after that episode was made, "Emissary" (DS9) had a dramatic flashback that showed some of the battle itself, in which **Ben Sisko**'s wife, **Jennifer Sisko**, was killed in the destruction of the* Saratoga. *Wolf 359 is a real star. Located 7.8 light-years away in the constellation Leo, it is the fourth-closest star to Earth.*

• **"Wolf in the Fold."** Original Series episode #36. Written by Robert Bloch. Directed by Joseph Pevney. Stardate 3614.9. *First aired in 1967. Scotty is accused of murdering two women, but the culprit is Jack the Ripper.* SEE: **Alpha Carinae V; Alpha Majoris I; Alpha Proxima II; Argelians; Argelius II; Argus River region; Beratis; Deneb II; Drella; Hengist, Mr.; Jack the Ripper; Jaris; Kara; Kesla; Mellitus; Morla; psychotricorder; Redjac; Rigel IV; Scott, Montgomery; Sybo; Tark; Tracy, Lieutenant Karen.**

Woman. (Marnie Mosiman). A member of the interpretive chorus of mediator **Riva** from planet **Ramatis III**. Each member of the chorus represented a different part of Riva's personality. Woman represented harmony, wisdom, and the balance that bound together passion and intellect. ("Loud as a Whisper" [TNG]). SEE: **Scholar/Artist; Warrior/Adonis.** *Actor Marnie Mosiman is in real life the wife of John DeLancie, better known as **Q**.*

wompat. Animal often kept as a pet by **Cardassian** children. ("Chain of Command, Part II" [TNG]).

Woo, Dr. Professor at the **Daystrom Institute**. Benjamin Sisko told **Vash** that Professor Woo was especially eager for her to return to the institute to speak on her travels through the Gamma Quadrant. ("Q-Less" [DS9]).

Worf, Colonel. (Michael Dorn). Klingon official who unsuccessfully defended Kirk and McCoy in 2293 when the two Starfleet officers were placed on trial for the assassination of **Chancellor Gorkon**. (*Star Trek VI: The Undiscovered Country*). *Publicity materials for* Star Trek VI *(and the evidence of the character name and the actor) suggest that Colonel Worf was the grandfather of* Enterprise-D *security officer* **Worf**, *and father of* **Mogh**.

Worf. (Michael Dorn). The first Klingon warrior to serve in the Federation Starfleet and an influential figure in Klingon politics. ("Encounter at Farpoint, Part I" [TNG]).

<u>Childhood and family.</u> Worf, son of **Mogh**, was born on the **Klingon Homeworld** in 2340. As a young child, Worf accompanied his parents to the **Khitomer** Outpost in 2346.

Worf was orphaned later that year in the brutal **Khitomer massacre**, a Romulan attack in which 4,000 Klingons were killed. Worf was rescued by **Sergey Rozhenko**, a human crew member from the **U.S.S. Intrepid**. Sergey and his wife, **Helena Rozhenko**, adopted Worf and raised him as their own son, because it was believed that Worf had no remaining family on the Homeworld. ("Sins of the Father" [TNG]).

With his new family on the farm world of **Gault** ("Heart of Glory" [TNG]) and later on Earth, Worf found it difficult to fit into the alien world of Humans and was a bit of a hell-raiser. ("Family" [TNG]). Worf was raised along with an adoptive brother, Nikolai Rozhenko, the biological son of the Rozhenkos. ("Homeward" [TNG]). Nikolai entered Starfleet Academy at the same time as Worf, but later dropped out because he found Starfleet not to his liking. ("Heart of Glory" [TNG]).

Worf's hobbies include the building of ancient Klingon ocean sailing vessels in a bottle, considered difficult handiwork. ("Peak Performance" [TNG]).

Worf's adoptive parents remained close to him over the

years, and made it a point to visit him in early 2367 when the *Enterprise*-D was docked at **Earth Station McKinley** for repairs. ("Family" [TNG]).

Worf had a son, **Alexander Rozhenko**, in 2367, with Ambassador **K'Ehleyr**, with whom he had been romantically involved. When K'Ehleyr was murdered by Klingon high council member **Duras**, Alexander returned to Earth to be cared for by Sergey and Helena. ("Reunion" [TNG]).

For some reason, Worf's experiences on Earth never included drinking prune juice. When given a taste of it by Guinan in 2365, Worf pronounced it "a warrior's drink" ("Yesterday's *Enterprise*" [TNG]).

The first Klingon in Starfleet. Following his graduation from **Starfleet Academy** in 2361, Worf held the rank of Lieutenant, Junior Grade, and served as flight control officer (conn) aboard the *U.S.S. Enterprise*-D. ("Encounter at Farpoint" [TNG]). *(There is a three-year period between his graduation and the start of* Star Trek: The Next Generation *that is still unaccounted for.)*

Worf was promoted to acting chief of security and made a full lieutenant following the death of Lieutenant **Natasha Yar** at planet **Vagra II** in late 2364 ("Skin of Evil" [TNG]). Worf felt intense guilt when Lieutenant **Marla Aster** was accidentally killed on an away mission in 2266, orphaning her son **Jeremy Aster**. Worf later took Jeremy into his family through the Klingon *R'uustai*, or bonding, ceremony. ("The Bonding" [TNG]).

In 2368, Worf's spinal column was shattered in an accident when several cargo containers collapsed onto him. Worf was left paralyzed, and his prognosis indicated little hope for a full recovery. In accordance with Klingon tradition, Worf refused medical treatment and opted for the *Hegh'bat* form of ritual suicide. He was dissuaded from taking his life when **Dr. Toby Russell** performed a dangerous experimental surgical procedure called **genetronic replication**, in which a new spinal column was generated to replace the damaged organ. The surgery was successful, in part because Klingon physiology includes redundancy for nearly all vital bodily functions. ("Ethics" [TNG]). SEE: *brak'lul*.

Worf once investigated a claim that his father had not died at Khitomer, but was instead being held prisoner at a secret Romulan prison camp in the **Carraya System**. Although the report was false, Worf did indeed find a prison camp where survivors of the Khitomer massacre and their families were being held. At the camp, Worf fell in love with a half-Romulan, half-Klingon woman named **Ba'el**. Worf led some of the prisoners to freedom, but the majority (including Ba'el) chose to remain, regarding the Carraya prison as their home. ("Birthright, Parts I and II" [TNG]). *Worf and the freed prisoners all promised never to reveal the story of the prison camp at Carraya, so we assume Starfleet has no knowledge of it.*

In Klingon politics. Worf was thrust into high-level Klingon politics in 2366 when he discovered that he had a biological brother, **Kurn**. The **Klingon High Council** had ruled that their father, **Mogh**, had committed treason at **Khitomer**. Worf and Kurn challenged this judgment, but found the High Council unwilling to hear evidence that the politically powerful **Duras** family had falsified the charges against Mogh. Although Worf was willing to die in the challenge to protect his family honor, he eventually chose to accept a humiliating discommendation rather than allow his brother to be killed. ("Sins of the Father" [TNG]). Worf later killed Duras for having murdered **K'Ehleyr**. ("Reunion" [TNG]).

Worf was once again dragged into high-level Klingon politics in late 2367 and early 2368 when a challenge to the **Gowron** regime by the Duras family triggered a **Klingon civil war**. Worf and Kurn agreed to support the Gowron regime in exchange for the rightful restoration of honor to the Mogh family. During the conflict, Worf was forced to resign his Starfleet commission because he would not otherwise be permitted to take sides in that internal political matter. ("Redemption, Parts I and II" [TNG]).

In 2369, Worf experienced a crisis of faith, and requested a leave of absence to visit the Klingon monastery on **Boreth**. While meditating to invoke visions of **Kahless the Unforgettable**, Worf met a very real vision of Kahless. It was discovered that this Kahless was in fact a clone of the original, created by the clerics of Boreth. At Worf's suggestion, and with the support of High Council leader Gowron, the new Kahless was installed as the ceremonial Emperor of the Klingon people in 2369. ("Rightful Heir" [TNG]). *Worf's first appearance was in "Encounter at Farpoint" [TNG].*

The character was conceived by Gene Roddenberry and Bob Justman, who wanted a Klingon on the bridge as a reminder to the audience that today's enemies can become tomorrow's friends. Although Worf was originally intended to be little more than a costumed extra with elaborate makeup, he has since grown into one of the most complex and interesting of Star Trek *characters.*

Work Bee. Small one-person extravehicular craft used for orbital construction and similar work. The Work Bee employed a modular design and could be equipped with robotic waldoes or it could be used as a control cab for a cargo sled. (*Star Trek: The Motion Picture*). *The Work Bee was designed by Andrew Probert. The model was built at Magicam.*

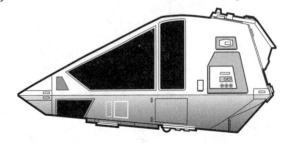

World Series. Championship baseball games formerly played each year on Earth. The World Series was an event meriting planetary interest, but gradually declined in popularity until 2042, when only 300 spectators attended the last game of the final World Series, won by **Buck Bokai** of the **London Kings**. ("If Wishes Were Horses" [DS9]). SEE: **Newson, Eddie.**

World War III. A nuclear war that devastated much of Earth during the mid-21st century. Some 37 million people died in the conflict. ("Bread and Circuses" [TOS]). In the post-atomic horror after this conflict (around 2079), much of Earth reverted to a barbaric state, and legal systems were adopted that ended many individual rights including the right to legal counsel. ("Encounter at Farpoint, Part I" [TNG]) Earth was still recovering from World War III in the early 22nd century. One philosopher of the time was Liam Dieghan, founder of the Neo-Transcendentalist movement. Dieghan advocated a return to a simpler life, one more in harmony with nature. ("Up the Long Ladder" [TNG]).

wormhole, Bajoran. SEE: **Bajoran wormhole.**

wormhole. A subspace bridge (or tunnel) between two points in "normal" time and space. Most wormholes are extremely unstable and their endpoints fluctuate widely across time and space. An improperly balanced warp-drive system can create an artificial wormhole that can pose a serious danger to the ship and its crew. (*Star Trek: The Motion Picture*). SEE: **Bajoran wormhole; Barzan wormhole; quantum fluctuations;** *Trieste, U.S.S.* Illustration: Schematic diagram of wormhole, used in Keiko O'Brien's schoolroom in "In the Hands of the Prophets" (DS9).

• **"Wounded, The."** *Next Generation* episode #86. Teleplay by Jeri Taylor. Story by Stuart Charno & Sara Charno and Cy Chermax. Directed by Chip Chalmers. Stardate 44429.6. *First aired in 1991. A renegade Starfleet captain threatens the fragile peace between the Federation and the Cardassian Union. This episode introduces the Cardassians, a new race of adversaries for our Federation heroes that would appear frequently in* Star Trek: Deep Space Nine. *SEE:* **Cardassia; Cardassians; Cardies; coded transponder frequency; Cuellar system; Daro, Glinn;** *Galor*-**class Cardassian warship; glinn; gul; Haden, Admiral; Kanar; Kayden, Will; Kelrabi system; Macet, Gul; Maxwell, Captain Benjamin; "Minstrel Boy, The";** *Nebula*-**class starship; O'Brien, Miles;** *Phoenix, U.S.S.*; **plankton loaf; potato casserole; prefix code;** *Rutledge, U.S.S.*; **Sector 21503; Sector 21505; Setlik III; Starbase 211;** *Stargazer, U.S.S.*; *Trager*; **United Federation of Planets.**

Wrenn. (Raye Birke). Commander of the last **Tarellian** vessel carrying survivors of the Tarellian plague. Wrenn was attempting to land his ship on planet **Haven** when the physician **Wyatt Miller** joined his people in an effort to seek a cure for their disease. Father to **Ariana**. ("Haven" [TNG]).

Wrigley's Pleasure Planet. *Enterprise* crew member **Darnell** saw the last surviving **M-113 creature** in the form of a woman he had left behind on that planet. ("The Man Trap" [TOS]).

written languages. SEE *illustration next page.*

Wu. (Lloyd Kino). **Kohm** inhabitant of planet **Omega IV**. At the time of the *Enterprise* visit to Omega IV in 2268, Wu was 462 years old. Wu's ancestors had survived a terrible biological war and their descendants inherited powerful antibodies that protected against disease, prolonging life. ("The Omega Glory" [TOS]).

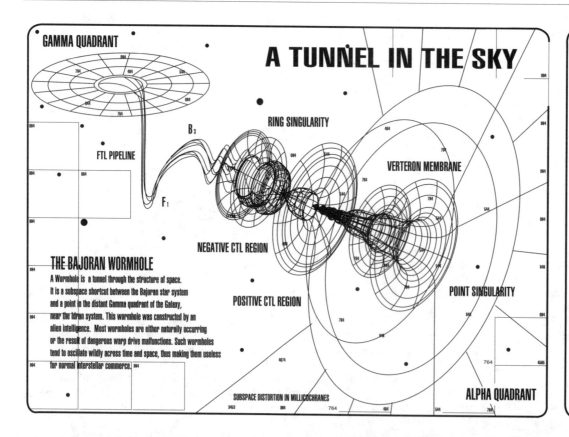

GAMMA QUADRANT

A TUNNEL IN THE SKY

RING SINGULARITY

FTL PIPELINE

VERTERON MEMBRANE

NEGATIVE CTL REGION

THE BAJORAN WORMHOLE

A Wormhole is a tunnel through the structure of space. It is a subspace shortcut between the Bajoran star system and a point in the distant Gamma quadrant of the Galaxy, near the Idran system. This wormhole was constructed by an alien intelligence. Most wormholes are either naturally occurring or the result of dangerous warp drive malfunctions. Such wormholes tend to oscillate wildly across time and space, thus making them useless for normal interstellar commerce.

POSITIVE CTL REGION

POINT SINGULARITY

SUBSPACE DISTORTION IN MILLICOCHRANES

ALPHA QUADRANT

VOCABULARY WORDS
SUPERLUMINAL
SPACE WARP
WORMHOLE
SINGULARITY
HAWKING, STEPHEN
EVENT HORIZON
SCHWARZSCHILD
EINSTEIN-ROSEN
KERR NEWMAN
NEGATIVE SPACE
MILLICOCHRANE
WARP FACTOR
POSITIVE CTL
NEGATIVE CTL
KERR OBJECT
GODEL UNIVERSE
SYNC SHIFT
TIME DILATION

Written languages. Specimens of writing from several cultures: 1) Federation standard English. 2) Klingon. 3) Bajoran. 4) Ferengi. 5) Romulan. 6) Ancient Vulcan calligraphy from Spock's book of Vulcan wisdom in "Unification, Part II" (TNG). Note that in most cases, we have deliberately refrained from developing a translation for written alien languages. The reason is that if the words or symbols have English equivalents, it is much more difficult to organize the patterns of the writing in an alien fashion. This is why most written alien languages on Star Trek don't have "normal" word groupings or paragraph blocks. For example, Ferengi is based on a branching flow chart, using lots of 60-degree angles, whereas ancient Vulcan seems to be based on some kind of musical scales.

1)

TO EXPLORE STRANGE, NEW WORLDS.
TO SEEK OUT NEW LIFE, AND NEW CIVILIZATIONS.
TO BOLDLY GO WHERE NO ONE HAS GONE BEFORE.

2)

3)

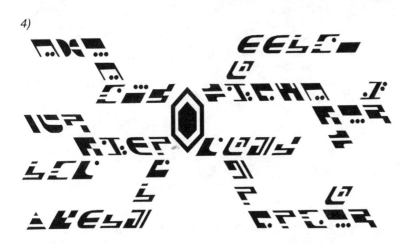

4)

5)

6)

Xanthras III. Destination of the *Enterprise*-D following its mission in the Gamma Erandi nebula in 2366. The *Enterprise* was to rendezvous with the ***U.S.S. Zapata***. ("Ménage à Troi" [TNG]).

Xelo. Valet to **Lwaxana Troi** prior to Mr. **Homn**. Mrs. Troi said she terminated Xelo's employment because he was strongly attracted to her. ("Haven" [TNG]).

Xendi Sabu star system. Solar system where the *Enterprise*-D rendezvoused with a Ferengi vessel in 2364 when **DaiMon Bok** offered Captain Picard the extraordinary gift of Picard's old vessel, the ***Stargazer***. ("The Battle" [TNG]).

Xendi Starbase 9. Starbase where the ***U.S.S. Stargazer*** was towed after the *Enterprise* received the old vessel from the Ferengi in 2364. ("The Battle" [TNG]).

xenopolycythemia. Disease characterized by an abnormal proliferation of red blood cells causing varied symptoms including weakness, fatigue, enlarged spleen, and pain in the extremities. **Dr. Leonard McCoy** was diagnosed with terminal xenopolycythemia in 2268. He was cured, thanks to advanced medical information from the spaceship **Yonada**. Prior to that time, xenopolycythemia was considered to be incurable. ("For the World Is Hollow and I Have Touched the Sky" [TOS]).

Xerxes VII. Planet on which legend says a mythical land called Neinman may be found. ("When the Bough Breaks" [TNG]).

Yadozi Desert. A legendary dry environment. Odo compared the possibilty of Dax being infatuated with the Quark as being as likely as finding a drink of water in the Yadozi Desert. ("A Man Alone" [DS9]).

Yale, Mirasta. (Carolyn Seymour). Minister of Science on planet **Malcor III**. Yale supervised her planet's development of warp-drive technology and was a strong advocate of her people's space exploration programs in 2367. Prior to the construction of the first warp-powered spacecraft, the discovery of a covert Federation presence on Malcor III led the conservative Malcorian government to delay the planet's space program. Yale chose to leave her planet and explore space aboard the *Enterprise*-D. ("First Contact" [TNG]). SEE: **first contact.** *Carolyn Seymour has not only played a Malcorian, but two Romulans. She portrayed **Subcommander Taris** in "Contagion" (TNG) and **Commander Toreth** in "Face of the Enemy" (TNG).*

Yamato, U.S.S. *Galaxy*-class Federation starship commanded by **Captain Donald Varley**. Starfleet registry number NCC-71807. A sister ship of the *Enterprise*-D. ("Where Silence Has Lease" [TNG]). The *Yamato* was destroyed in 2365 by an ancient **Iconian** computer software weapon that caused the failure of the ship's antimatter containment system, resulting in the ship's explosion and the loss of all hands. The software weapon had also been responsible for a series of other malfunctions aboard the *Yamato* including the failure of a shuttlebay forcefield. ("Contagion" [TNG]).

Although the Yamato's *registry number was established in "Contagion" to be NCC-71807, an earlier, incorrect number was given in "Where Silence Has Lease," when an illusory version of that ship was seen. An early draft for that episode gave the number as NCC-1305E, which didn't fit into the numbering scheme developed for starships in* The Next Generation. *Mike Okuda wrote a note to the producers, requesting the number be changed, but didn't send the memo because a later draft of that script dropped the reference to the* Yamato's *registry number. Mike wasn't aware that an even later draft of the script restored the scene and the incorrect number. By the time he found out (when he saw the completed episode on the air), he had already prepared the markings for the U.S.S. Yamato saucer, for the scene when that ship blew up in the episode "Contagion" (TNG). Named for the Japanese World War II battleship. The dedication plaque for the bridge of the* Yamato *bore a motto from Thomas Jefferson: "I have sworn eternal hostility against every form of tyranny over the mind of man."*

yamok sauce. Cardassian foodstuff and condiment. On stardate 46844, **Ferengi** tradesman **Quark** had 5,000 wrappages of *yamok* sauce, a considerable surplus since his

Cardassian clientele had fallen off sharply when station **Deep Space 9** was taken over by Starfleet. Quark didn't know what to do with the stuff, so his nephew **Nog** used it in a business venture ("Progress" [DS9]). The Cardassian **Aamin Marritza**, liked *yamok* sauce on his **sem'hal stew**. ("Duet" [DS9]).

Yanar. (Rosalind Ingledew). Daughter of **Debin** from the planet **Altec**. Yanar had been secretly engaged to marry **Benzan** of Straleb, and nearly triggered a breakdown of the **Coalition of Madena** when she accepted the Jewel of Thesia from Benzan as a pledge of marriage. ("The Outrageous Okona" [TNG]).

Yangs. One of two ethic groups on planet **Omega IV** who, centuries ago, fought a terrible bacteriological war. The few survivors of the conflict lived because they happened to have powerful natural immunity, and had extraordinarily long life spans. In 2268, Starfleet captain **Ronald Tracey** of the **U.S.S. Exeter** sided with the **Kohms**, ancient enemies of the Yangs, supplying the Kohms with phasers that proved devastating in their technologically primitive conflict. *Enterprise* personnel, investigating the disappearance of the *Exeter*, theorized that the Yangs were culturally similar to Earth's 20th-century "Yankees," based on their worship of such icons as the American flag and the United States' Constitution. ("The Omega Glory" [TOS]).

Yangtzee Kiang, U.S.S. Starfleet *Danube*-class **runabout**, registry number NCC-72453, one of three runabouts assigned to station **Deep Space 9**. ("Emissary" [DS9], "Past Prologue" [DS9]). The *Yangtzee Kiang* was destroyed in a crash on a penal-colony moon in the Gamma Quadrant. Bajoran religious leader **Kai Opaka** was killed in the crash, although artificial microbes in the moon's environment later restored her to life, for as long as she remained there. ("Battle Lines" [DS9]). The *Yangtzee Kiang* was replaced on Deep Space 9 by the *U.S.S. Orinoco*. ("The Siege" [DS9]).

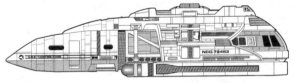

Yar, Ishara. (Beth Toussaint). The younger sister of *Enterprise*-D security chief **Natasha Yar**. Born in the failed **Turkana IV** colony in 2342, Ishara was orphaned just after birth. Ishara was raised by her sister, Tasha, until she became a loyal member of the **Coalition** cadre, one of the factions fighting for control of the colony. When Natasha Yar left Turkana IV in 2352, Ishara chose to remain behind be-

cause she felt her cadre was her family. Ishara regarded her sister as a coward for leaving Turkana. When the *Enterprise*-D arrived at Turkana IV in 2367, Ishara acted as liaison between the *Enterprise*-D crew and the Coalition. The *Enterprise*-D crew and Data in particular were eager to accept her as a friend, but Ishara used this trust in an unsuccessful attempt to gain a tactical advantage over the rival **Alliance** cadre. ("Legacy" [TNG]).

Yar, Natasha, (alternate). (Denise Crosby). In the alternate timeline created when the **Enterprise-C** vanished from its "proper" place in 2344 into a temporal rift, *Enterprise*-D security officer Tasha Yar did not die at planet **Vagra II** in 2364. Instead, she remained as security chief aboard that ship during a war between the Federation and the Klingons. The alternate Yar was on duty when the *Enterprise*-C emerged from a temporal rift, and she served as liaison between the two ships, working closely with **Lieutenant Richard Castillo**, with whom she became romantically involved. When it was learned that the *Enterprise*-C had to return to the past, the alternate Yar volunteered to return with that ship, despite the knowledge that the mission meant virtually certain death. ("Yesterday's *Enterprise*" [TNG]). No direct evidence survived of the existence of the alternate Yar (or the emergence of the *Enterprise*-C) after the return of the *Enterprise*-C to the past. However, in 2367, a Romulan operative named **Sela** began a series of covert operations against the Klingon government. Sela was apparently the child of Yar and a Romulan general who had captured the *Enterprise*-C bridge crew at **Narendra III**. The Romulan general agreed to spare the bridge crew if Yar agreed to become his consort. Sela was born a year later, in 2345. Sela claimed that the alternate Yar was killed trying to escape when Sela was four. ("Redemption, Part II" [TNG]).

Yar, Natasha. (Denise Crosby). *Enterprise*-D chief of security under the command of Captain **Jean-Luc Picard**. ("Encounter at Farpoint, Part I" [TNG]).

Ukrainian in descent, Yar was born on a failed Federation colony on planet **Turkana IV**. Her parents were killed when she was only five, and she spent much of her childhood in a bitter struggle for survival, evading marauding rape gangs and caring for her younger sister, Ishara Yar. One of the few "normal" aspects of her childhood was her ownership of a pet kitten that she protected. ("Where No One Has Gone Before" [TNG]). Tasha escaped from Turkana IV at the age of 15, choosing to join Starfleet. ("The Naked Now" [TNG]).

As a Starfleet officer, she impressed Captain Picard with her courage in rescuing a wounded colonist, making her way through a Carnellian mine field. Thus, Picard requested that she be transferred to the *Enterprise*-D in early 2364. ("Legacy" [TNG]). While under the inhibition-stripping effects of the **Psi 2000 virus**, Tasha apparently became intimate with fellow *Enterprise*-D crew member **Data**. ("The Naked Now" [TNG]).

Yar was killed in late 2364 while participating in a rescue mission on planet **Vagra II**. SEE: **Armus**. Tasha, knowing her line of work entailed considerable risk, left a holographic farewell to her comrades in which she thanked her shipmates for being part of her life. ("Skin of Evil" [TNG]). Data kept a small holographic portrait of Tasha, and he considered it one of his most precious personal possessions. ("The Measure of a Man" [TNG]).

Tasha Yar was first seen in "Encounter at Farpoint" (TNG). Although her character died in "Skin of Evil" (TNG), we saw her holographic portrait in "The Measure of a Man" (TNG), and her alternate-timeline version (SEE: Yar, Natasha [alternate]) in "Yesterday's Enterprise" (TNG). The alternate Tasha's daughter, Sela, was also played by Denise Crosby.

Yareena. (Karole Selmon). Wealthy land owner and wife of leader **Lutan** on planet **Ligon II**. Yareena was nearly killed in ritual combat with *Enterprise*-D security chief Yar in 2364 when both became involved in a local power struggle. ("Code of Honor" [TNG]).

Yareth. (Leslie Engelberg). The daughter of the **Rakhari** fugitive **Croden**. When Croden was convicted of crimes against the Rakhari state, Croden hid her in a stasis chamber on an asteroid in the **Chamra Vortex** so that she would not be executed with the rest of his family. She remained in stasis until 2369, when with the assistance of Odo, she was freed. ("Vortex" [DS9]).

Yarnek. (Janos Prohaska, voice of Bart LaRue). Rock creature from planet **Excalbia** who, in 2269, conducted an experiment to examine the human philosophies of "good" and "evil." The **Excalbians** created replicas of several historical figures falling into either category, placed them into a conflict, then observed the results. Included among the combatants were *Enterprise* officers Kirk and Spock. Good eventually did triumph over evil, allowing the *Enterprise* to be set free, but Yarnek promised other cultures would be tested in the same manner. ("The Savage Curtain" [TOS]). *Yarnek's name was never mentioned in the aired episode and was obtained from the script. Janos Prohaska also played the **Horta** in "Devil in the Dark" (TOS) and the **mugato** in "A Private Little War" (TOS). Bart LaRue supplied the voice of the **Guardian of Forever** in "City on the Edge of Forever" (TOS) and played the Roman television announcer in "Bread and Circuses" (TOS).*

Ya'Seem. Archaeological discovery first uncovered by the renowned scientist **M'Tell**. ("The Chase" [TNG]). *Unfortunately, the episode does not make clear what Ya'Seem is or why it was so important.*

Yash-El, night blessing of. "Dream not of today." This ancient saying was a question that **Jean-Luc Picard** missed on his final archaeology exam under **Professor Richard Galen**. ("The Chase" [TNG]).

Yeager loop. An aerobatic maneuver executed by five single-pilot spacecraft. Starting in a Diamond Slot formation, the five ships would perform an Immelmann turn in concert. The Yeager loop was used as a demonstration of piloting prowess by cadets at **Starfleet Academy**. ("The First Duty" [TNG]). *Named for one of Chuck Yeager's most famous flight maneuvers, see next entry.*

Yeager, Chuck. Aircraft test pilot on planet Earth, the first human to fly faster than the speed of sound. Yeager accomplished this feat on October 27, 1947, in a rocket-powered craft called the *Glamorous Glennis*. Commander La Forge likened **Dr. Ja'Dar**'s revolutionary **soliton wave** rider experiment in 2368 to Yeager's historic achievement. ("New Ground" [TNG]).

Yellow Alert. A state of significantly increased readiness aboard Federation starships and other vessels. In the event of an actual or imminent emergency, the commanding officer can order the state of readiness increased even further to **Red Alert**.

"Yesterday's *Enterprise*." *Next Generation* episode #63. Teleplay by Ira Steven Behr & Ronald Manning & Hans Beimler & Ronald D. Moore. From a story by Trent Christopher Ganino & Eric Stillwell. Directed by David Carson. Stardate 43625.2. *First aired in 1990. A Starship Enterprise from the past emerges into the present, and the shape of time becomes badly distorted.* SEE: **Ambassador-class starship; Archer IV (alternate); Archer IV; Castillo, Lieutenant Richard; class-1 probe; *Enterprise*-C, U.S.S.; Garrett, Captain Rachel; gravimetric fluctuations; Guinan; K'Vort-class battle cruisers; Klingon War (alternate); Military Log; Narendra III (alternate); Narendra III; prune juice; Romulans; Selar, Dr.; Starbase 105; Starfleet monitor stations; temporal rift; TKL ration; Warbird, Romulan; Worf; Yar, Natasha (alternate).**

yIntagh. A Klingon expletive. ("Redemption, Part I" [TNG]).

yominium sulfide. Chemical compound with the molecular formula $K_4Ym_3(SO_7^3Es_2)$. The makeup of this substance was a question in Spock's memory test during his reeducation in 2286. (*Star Trek IV: The Voyage Home*). *Yominium was the "invention" of Star Trek IV associate producer Kirk Thatcher, who named it for Leonard Nimoy (spell it backward). Yes, we know the formula is inconsistent with a sulfide.*

Yonada. Multigeneration spaceship built by the **Fabrini** civilization 10,000 years ago. *Yonada*, which was built inside a large asteroid, was a slower-than-light ship designed to transport part of the Fabrini civilization to a "promised world" when their home sun went nova ten millennia ago. ("For the World Is Hollow and I Have Touched the Sky" [TOS]). SEE: **Natira**. *Yonada was expected to reach its final destination in late 2269. Kirk*

promised McCoy that they would be there for the arrival, but since this would have been just after the end of the original Star Trek *series, we do not know if they made it.*

Yorktown, U.S.S. Federation starship, *Constitution* class, Starfleet registry number NCC-1717. The *Yorktown* was scheduled to rendezvous with the *Enterprise* in 2268 to transfer critically needed vaccines for planet **Theta VII**. The *Enterprise* was unable to make the rendezvous with the *Yorktown* until the investigation and destruction of the **dikironium cloud creature** was complete. ("Obsession" [TOS]).

The *Yorktown* was disabled by an alien space probe approaching Earth in 2286. The ship's chief engineer rigged a makeshift solar sail to provide emergency power. (*Star Trek IV: The Voyage Home*). SEE: **Probe, the**.

Yorktown *was the original name of* Star Trek*'s spaceship, before the ship was called* Enterprise, *from Gene Roddenberry's first draft of the series outline written in 1964. Roddenberry reportedly suggested that the second Starship* Enterprise, NCC-1701-A, *launched at the end of* Star Trek IV, *had previously been named the* Yorktown, *since it seems unlikely that Starfleet could have built a new* Enterprise *so quickly. If this was the case, the* Yorktown *may have made it safely back to Earth and been repaired and renamed, or perhaps there was a newer, replacement* Yorktown *already under construction at the time of the probe crisis.*

Yosemite National Park. One of the most beautiful places on planet Earth, set aside as a nature preserve in 1890. Yosemite was a favored shore-leave spot for Captain Kirk, and he was joined by there by shipmates Spock and McCoy for a camping expedition in 2287. (*Star Trek V: The Final Frontier*).

Yosemite, U.S.S. Federation starship, *Oberth* class, registry number NCC-19002. The *Yosemite* was severely damaged while conducting a study of the **plasma streamer** between a binary star pair in the **Igo Sector** in 2369. During transport of plasma samples to the ship, **quasi-energy microbes** caused an explosion of a sample container, resulting in severe damage to the ship and the death of at least one crew member. ("Realm of Fear" [TNG]). *The ship was named for Yosemite National Park.*

Yoshimitsu computers. Some 225 of these devices were carried on board the *S.S. Mariposa* when it set out for the **Ficus Sector** in 2123. ("Up the Long Ladder" [TNG]).

Yridians. Race of humanoids known as interstellar dealers of information. Yridian agents, working for Cardassian interests, were responsible for the murder of archaeologist **Richard Galen** in 2369, an effort to steal his research data. The Romulans intercepted communications between the Yridians and the Cardassians, making the Romulans aware of the importance of Galen's work. ("The Chase" [TNG]). SEE: **humanoid life**. **Jaglom Shrek**, who sold **Worf** information about **Mogh**, was an Yridian. ("Birthright, Part I" [TNG]).

Yuta. (Lisa Wilcox). An **Acamarian** and member of the clan **Tralesta**, she was Sovereign **Marouk**'s chef and chief food taster. Yuta was the last surviving member of the Acamarian Tralesta clan that had been massacred in 2286 by the rival **Lornak** clan. Though she appeared to be a woman in her twenties, her body had been altered to dramatically reduce her rate of aging so that she could exact revenge against the Lornaks. Her body was infused with a genetically engineered **microvirus** that was harmless to all except the members of the Lornak clan.

Over the next century, Yuta was successful in murdering nearly all members of the Lornak clan by exposing them to this microvirus. Commander Riker was attracted to her, but after determining her true purpose, he was forced to kill her to prevent her from assassinating **Chorgan**, the Gatherer Leader and the last member of the Lornak clan. Yuta's victims included **Volnoth** and **Penthor-Mul**. ("The Vengeance Factor" [TNG]).

Yutan. (Gary Pillar). Member of the **hill people** tribe on **Tyree**'s planet. ("A Private Little War" [TOS]).

zabathu, Andorian. An animal similar to a terrestrial horse. Holographic simulations of this animal were available for riding on the *Enterprise*-D holodeck. ("Pen Pals" [TNG]).

Zabo. (Steve Marlo). One of **Jojo Krako**'s henchmen on planet **Sigma Iotia II** in 2268. ("A Piece of the Action" [TOS]).

Zadar IV. Planet on which oceanographer **Dr. Harry Bernard, Sr.,** once lived with his son prior to their residence aboard the *Enterprise*-D. ("When the Bough Breaks" [TNG]).

Zaheva, Captain Chantal. (Deborah Taylor). Commanding officer of the *U.S.S. Brattain*. Zaheva died violently along with most of her crew when *Brattain* personnel suffered severe dream deprivation when the ship was trapped in a **Tyken's Rift** in 2367. ("Night Terrors" [TNG]).

Zakdorn. Humanoid race reputed to be formidable warriors and regarded for over nine millennia as having the greatest strategic minds in the galaxy. So strong was this reputation that as of 2365, it had not been tested in actual conflict within recent memory. ("Peak Performance" [TNG]). SEE: **Kolrami, Sirna.** Zakdorn official **Klim Dokachin** was the administrator of the Starfleet surplus depot in orbit of planet **Qualor II**. ("Unification, Part I" [TNG]).

Zaldans. Humanoid race characterized by webbed hands. Zaldan cultural values reject human courtesy as a form of dishonesty, so the proper (and courteous) way to address a Zaldan is with brutal honesty. ("Coming of Age" [TNG]). SEE: **Rondon.**

Zalkon. Homeworld of the **Zalkonians.** The government of this planet claimed the **Zeta Gelis Cluster** as part of their space. ("Transfigurations" [TNG]).

Zalkonians. A humanoid race distinguished by multiple horizontal facial ridges. Sometime prior to 2366, a few members of the Zalkonian race began suffering from painful isoelectrical bursts and exhibiting strange mutations of their tissues. The Zalkonian government, fearful of these new beings, persecuted and attempted to kill everyone who experienced these mutations. One Zalkonian, who became known as **John Doe,** escaped his homeworld, and was successful in allowing the metamorphosis aboard the *Enterprise*-D in 2366, becoming the first of his race to transmute into a noncorporeal being. ("Transfigurations" [TNG]).

Zambrano, Battle of. Historic conflict on planet **Solais V,** location of which later became the site of peace talks mediated by **Riva** of planet **Ramatis III.** ("Loud as a Whisper" [TNG]). *The Battle of Zambrano, identified only in a computer graphic map seen on the bridge, was named for "Loud as a Whisper" writer Jacqueline Zambrano.*

Zan Periculi. Species of flower native to Lappa IV, a Ferengi world. **DaiMon Tog** presented some of these flowers to Lwaxana Troi. ("Ménage à Troi" [TNG]).

Zapata, U.S.S. Starship that the *Enterprise*-D was scheduled to meet following the mission to the Gamma Erandi nebula in 2366. ("Ménage à Troi" [TNG]).

Zarabeth. (Mariette Hartley). Citizen from planet **Sarpeidon** who was banished after two of her family conspired to kill planetary leader **Zor Khan.** Zarabeth was sent some 5,000 years into her planet's past, into a brutal ice age, where she lived in total isolation. Her loneliness was broken only briefly when Spock and McCoy were accidentally sent into Sarpeidon's past by

the **atavachron,** before returning to their present. While there, Spock became emotionally involved with Zarabeth, who loved him, too. ("All Our Yesterdays" [TOS]). *Mariette Hartley also played the mutant Lyra'a in Gene Roddenberry's pilot film,* Genesis II.

zark. Klingon riding animal, somewhat similar to an Earth horse. ("Pen Pals" [TNG]).

Zaterl emerald. A semi-mythical gemstone, reputed to be located in the ruins of Ligillium. Captain Picard offered to take **Ardra** there to try to convince her to accept arbitration in the matter of the **Contract of Ardra.** ("Devil's Due" [TNG]).

Zaynar. (J. Michael Flynn). An aide to Angosian prime minister **Nayrok.** ("The Hunted" [TNG]).

Zayra IV. Planet on which can be found an arachnid known as the **Talarian hook spider. Miles O'Brien** was called in to reroute an emitter array at a starbase on that planet, some time prior to his assignment to the *Enterprise*-D. ("Realm of Fear" [TNG]).

Zayra. (Edward Albert). Bajoran who operated the Transit Aid center on station Deep Space 9, he accused **Odo** of murdering **Ibudan** in 2369. Zayra incited others to form a lynch mob to harass the shape-shifter. ("A Man Alone" [DS9]).

Zed Lapis Sector. Region where planet Vagra II is located. ("Skin of Evil" [TNG]).

Zee-Magnees Prize. Prestigeous scientific award. **Dr. Richard Daystrom** won the Zee-Magnees Prize for his invention of **duotronics** in 2243. Daystrom was only 24 years old at the time. ("The Ultimate Computer" [TOS]). *A framed certificate on the wall of **Dr. Ira Graves**'s laboratory in "The Schizoid Man" (TNG) indicated that Graves had also won the coveted award for his work in positronic neural networks, although the certificate wasn't clearly visible in the final cut of the episode.*

Zek. (Wallace Shawn). Wizened leader of Ferengi commerce who served as **Grand Nagus.** Zek had enormous ears and carried a cane of his likeness made from gold-pressed **latinum.** Zek convened a major trade conference on Deep

Space 9 in 2369 to announce the appointment of his successor as Grand Nagus. Zek named Quark as his successor, and apparently died shortly thereafter. In fact, Zek's death was a ruse intended to test the suitability of his son, **Krax**, to one day assume the mantle as Nagus. Zek came out of hiding when he realized that his son was not as mercenary as Zek would

have liked. Zek therefore decided not to retire and remained the Grand Nagus a bit longer. ("The Nagus" [DS9]).

zenite. Rare mineral substance found on planet **Ardana** used to combat botanical plagues such as that which occurred on planet **Merak II** in 2269. Zenite is mined, and in its raw state produces hazardous zenite gas, which was found to impair mental functions in unprotected mine workers. ("The Cloud Minders" [TOS]). SEE: **filter masks; Troglytes.**

Zeon. Outer planet in star system M43 Alpha that had crude interplanetary capabilities that was the victim of a campaign of genocide by the Nazi-style government on planet **Ekos** in 2268. ("Patterns of Force" [TOS]).

Zeta Alpha II. Planet that was the departure point of the **U.S.S. Lalo**, just before that ship was lost to the **Borg** in 2366. ("The Best of Both Worlds, Part I" [TNG]).

Zeta Gelis Cluster. Region charted by the *Enterprise*-D in 2366. While mapping this area, the crew discovered the **Zalkonian** known as **John Doe** on one of the planets there. The *Enterprise*-D continued to map the Zeta Gelis Cluster during the seven-week period of Doe's recovery. ("Transfigurations" [TNG]).

Zetar. Planet where all corporeal life was destroyed millennia ago. ("The Lights of Zetar" [TOS]). SEE: **Zetarians.**

Zetarians. Mysterious **non-corporeal life**-forms, the last survivors of the planet **Zetar**. The Zetarians wandered through space for millennia, searching for a body in which they could live again. They thought they had found such a body when they discovered *Enterprise* crew member **Mira Romaine**

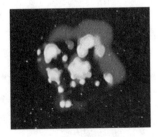

in 2269. When Romaine's fellow crew members discovered that her mind had been invaded by the Zetarians and that she was in danger of losing her identity, Romaine was placed into a decompression chamber where the Zetarians were driven from her body. ("The Lights of Zetar" [TOS]).

Zhukov, U.S.S. Federation starship, *Ambassador* class, Starfleet registry number NCC-62136. The ship was commanded by **Captain Gleason**. The *Zhukov* was **Reginald Barclay**'s assignment prior to his being transferred to the *Enterprise*-D in 2366. ("Hollow Pursuits" [TNG]). The starship met the *Enterprise*-D again in 2367 for the transfer of Federation ambassador **T'Pel**. ("Data's Day" [TNG]). The *Zhukov* transfered several science teams to the *Enterprise*-D in preperation for the *Enterprise*-D's mission at the **Phoenix Cluster** in 2368. ("The Game" [TNG]). *The Zhukov was named for Russian General Grigori Konstantinovich Zhukov (1896-1974).*

Zibalians. Life-forms, largely humanoid, with distinctive tattooing in the temporal areas of the face. Some Zibalians were traders, including the notorious **Kivas Fajo**. ("The Most Toys" [TNG]).

Zimbata, Captain. Commander of the *Starship* **Victory**. Geordi La Forge served under Zimbata aboard the *Victory* in 2363 prior to La Forge's assignment to the *Enterprise*-D. Geordi presented Zimbata with a gift of a model of the ancient sailing ship *Victory* in 2365. ("Elementary, Dear Data" [TNG]).

Zlangco. (Paul Collins). Leader of the **Nol-Ennis,** who fought his eternal enemies, the **Ennis**, on a penal-colony moon in the Gamma Quadrant. ("Battle Lines" [DS9]).

Zor Khan. Tyrant on planet **Sarpeidon** who banished **Zarabeth** 5,000 years into the past because two of her kinsmen were involved in a conspiracy to kill him. ("All Our Yesterdays" [TOS]).

Zora. (Carol Daniels Derment). Notorious scientist who conducted cruel experiments of the body chemistries of living beings on the planet **Tiburon**. A replica of Zora was created by the inhabitants of planet **Excalbia** in 2269, part of their study of the human concepts of "good" and "evil." ("The Savage Curtain" [TOS]). SEE: **Yarnek.**

Zorn, Groppler. (Michael Bell). A leader of the **Bandi** people of planet **Deneb IV**. Zorn had participated in the capture of a spaceborne shape-shifting life-form, coercing it to assume the form of a starbase. ("Encounter at Farpoint, Parts I and II" [TNG]).

Zweller, Cortin. (Ned Vaughn). Aka Corey Zweller. Academy friend of Ensign **Jean-Luc Picard**. Following their graduation from Starfleet Academy in 2327, Ensigns Corey Zweller, **Marta Batanides,** and Jean-Luc Picard were assigned to **Starbase Earhart** to await their first deep-space assignments. During this layover, Corey was challenged to a game of **dom-jot** by a **Nausicaan**, leading to a fight in which Picard was impaled by one of the Nausicaans and his heart was damaged beyond repair. Zweller was later assigned to the *Starship* **Ajax**. ("Tapestry" [TNG]).

zylo eggs. Alien life-form that Data chose as a subject for his first attempt at **painting**. ("11001001" [TNG]).

Zytchin III. Planet where Captain Picard once spent a four-day vacation. He told Dr. Crusher that he enjoyed his time there, but later said he had lied. ("Captain's Holiday" [TNG]).

APPENDIX A: HISTORICAL EVENTS IN THE *STAR TREK* UNIVERSE

This timeline is drawn from the *Star Trek Chronology: The History of the Future* by Denise Okuda and Michael Okuda. For further historical information, as well as for information on how this timeline was derived, we refer you to the Chronology.

1957: First artificial satellite launched from Earth. *Sputnik I* is orbited by the Soviet Union, marking the dawn of Earth's Space Age.

1969: Neil Armstrong becomes the first human to walk on Earth's moon, proclaiming the historic *Apollo 11* flight to be "one small step for a man, one giant leap for mankind."

1992: Eugenics Wars begin when a group of genetically bred "supermen" seize control of one-quarter of Earth, plunging the planet into a terrible conflict.

1996: Eugenics Wars end. The genetic tyrants are overthrown. One "superman," Khan Noonien Singh, escapes into space aboard the *S.S. Botany Bay.*

2026: Joe DiMaggio's hitting record is broken by Buck Bokai, a shortstop from the London Kings.

2061: Warp drive is invented by Zefram Cochrane. The development of the faster-than-light is a crucial milestone in spaceflight.

2065: *S.S. Valiant* lost near galaxy's edge.

2079: Earth recovers from World War III, a terrible conflict in which some 37 million people are killed.

2117: Zefram Cochrane disappears and is believed dead.

2156: Romulan Wars begin between Earth forces and the Romulan Star Empire.

2160 Romulan Wars ended by the Battle of Cheron. The Treaty of Algeron establishes the Romulan Neutral Zone.

2161: United Federation of Planets incorporated.

Starfleet established with a charter "to boldly go where no man has gone before."

2165: Sarek of Vulcan is born.

2218: First contact with the Klingon Empire. The incident is a disaster, leading to nearly a century of hostilities between the Klingons and the Federation.

2222: Montgomery Scott is born.

2227: Leonard H. McCoy is born.

2230: Spock is born, son of Sarek and Amanda.

2233: James T. Kirk is born in Iowa on Earth.

2237: Hikaru Sulu is born in San Francisco on Earth.

2239: Uhura is born on Earth.

2243: Dr. Richard Daystrom invents duotronics, the basis for the computer systems used aboard the *Enterprise.*

2245: The first *Starship Enterprise*, NCC-1701, is launched. Captain Robert April commands the ship's first five-year mission of exploration.

2245: Pavel A. Chekov is born.

2250: Kirk enrolls in Starfleet Academy. As a cadet, he serves aboard the *U.S.S. Republic.*

2251: Christopher Pike assumes command of the *Starship Enterprise.* He leads two five-year missions of exploration into the unknown.

2252: Spock, a cadet at Starfleet Academy, begins serving aboard the *Enterprise* under Captain Pike.

2253: Spock graduates from Starfleet Academy.

2254: Kirk graduates from Starfleet Academy, the only cadet ever to beat the infamous "no-win" *Kobayashi Maru* training scenario. Kirk is assigned to *U.S.S. Farragut.*.

2254: *Starship Enterprise* at planet Talos IV. ("The Cage" [TOS]).

2261: David Marcus, son of James Kirk and Carol Marcus, is born.

2264: James T. Kirk begins historic five-year mission on *Enterprise.*

2266: **First season of the original *Star Trek* series.** (Continues into 2267).

Romulans violate the Neutral Zone for the first time in over a century.

Captain Christopher Pike, severely injured in a training accident, returns to Talos IV to live.

2267: *S.S. Botany Bay*, Khan's sleeper ship, is discovered adrift near the Mutara Sector. Khan and his followers are exiled to planet Ceti Alpha V.

Relations with Klingon Empire deteriorate; open warfare is averted by establishment of the Organian Peace Treaty.

Second season of the original *Star Trek* series. (Continues into 2268).

Spock returns to his homeworld to take T'Pring as his bride, but he is spurned in favor of Stonn.

Coridan is admitted to the Federation after the Babel Conference.

2268: Third season of the original *Star Trek* series. (Continues into 2269).

Romulan/Klingon alliance established, permitting the exchange of spacecraft designs and military technology, including the cloaking device.

Kirk and Spock arrested by Romulan authorities on a covert mission to steal an improved Romulan cloaking device.

2269: Kirk's five-year mission ends; *Enterprise* returns to Spacedock for major upgrade.

Kirk promoted to admiral, Spock and McCoy retire from Starfleet.

2271: *Star Trek: The Motion Picture*.

Enterprise successfully defends Earth from V'Ger probe. Spock and McCoy return to Starfleet.

2284: Spock becomes an instructor at Starfleet Academy. *U.S.S. Enterprise* assigned to training duty at the Academy.

2285: *Star Trek II: The Wrath of Khan*.

Khan escapes from Ceti Alpha V, hijacks *U.S.S. Reliant*, tries to steal Project Genesis.

Spock dies defending the *Enterprise*.

***Star Trek III: The Search for Spock*.**

Original *Starship Enterprise* destroyed while Kirk and crew rescue Spock's body, which was later reunited with his *katra*.

Spock is reborn at Genesis Planet.

2286: *Star Trek IV: The Voyage Home*.

Kirk and company save Earth from an alien probe by bringing two humpback whales to the 23rd century.

U.S.S. Enterprise-A, the second starship to bear the name, is launched. Kirk demoted from admiral to captain, and placed in command of the new ship.

2287: *Star Trek V: The Final Frontier*.

Starship Enterprise-A is hijacked by Spock's half-brother, Sybok, who pursues his visions of God.

2290: Hikaru Sulu promoted to captain of the *Starship Excelsior*.

2293: *Star Trek VI: The Undiscovered Country*.

Klingon moon Praxis explodes, crippling the Klingon economy, forcing major cutbacks in military expenditures, culminating in the Khitomer peace accords.

2295: Captain Scott retires, is missing en route to the Norpin Colony aboard the *U.S.S. Jenolen*.

2305: Jean-Luc Picard is born.

2311: The Tomed Incident. The Romulans enter an extended period of isolationism that lasts until 2364.

2324: Beverly Howard, the future Beverly Crusher, is born.

2327: Jean-Luc Picard graduates from Starfleet Academy.

2328: Cardassian Union annexes Bajor.

2333: Jean-Luc Picard assumes command of the *U.S.S. Stargazer*.

2335: William T. Riker is born in Valdez, Alaska, on Earth.

2336: Deanna Troi is born on Betazed.

2337: Natasha Yar is born on Turkana IV.

2338: Data is discovered on planet Omicron Theta.

2340: Worf is born on the Klingon Homeworld.

2344: *Starship Enterprise*-C is destroyed at Narendra III.

2346: Worf's parents are killed by Romulans at the Khitomer massacre. Worf is adopted by a human Starfleet officer, Sergey Rozhenko.

2355: *U.S.S. Stargazer* is nearly destroyed in the Battle of Maxia.

2357: Riker graduates from Starfleet Academy. His first assignment is the ill-fated *U.S.S. Pegasus*.

2361: Riker, now aboard the *Starship Potemkin*, participates in a rescue mission at planet Nervala IV. A transporter malfunction creates an exact duplicate of Riker who remains undiscovered on the planet until 2369.

2363: *Starship Enterprise*-D, the fifth starship to bear the name, is launched under the command of Jean-Luc Picard.

William Riker serves as Executive officer aboard the *U.S.S. Hood* prior to his assignment to the *Enterprise*-D.

2364: First season of *Star Trek: The Next Generation*.

First known contact with the Ferengi. First contact with Q.

Natasha Yar is killed at planet Vagra II.

Extragalactic conspiracy uncovered attempting to infiltrate Starfleet Command.

2365: Second season of *Star Trek: The Next Generation*.

Dr. Katherine Pulaski serves as *Enterprise*-D chief medical officer.

First known contact with the Borg.

2366: Third season of *Star Trek: The Next Generation*.

Enterprise-C briefly enters this time from the past.

Worf accepts discommendation for acts his late father did not commit against the Klingon Empire.

Captain Jean-Luc Picard is captured by the Borg, becoming Locutus of Borg.

2367: Fourth season of *Star Trek: The Next Generation*.

Thirty-nine starships destroyed by the Borg in the battle of Wolf 359.

Alexander Rozhenko, son of Worf and K'Ehleyr, is born.

Wesley Crusher is accepted to Starfleet Academy.

Jean-Luc Picard serves as arbiter of succession to determine the new leader of the Klingon High Council.

2368: Fifth season of *Star Trek: The Next Generation*.

Duras family attempts to seize control of the Klingon High Council, plunging the Empire into a brief civil war.

Ambassador Spock is sighted on Romulus, supporting reunification of the Romulan and Vulcan peoples.

Ambassador Sarek of Vulcan dies at age 203.

Wesley Crusher admits helping to cover up a fatal accident at Starfleet Academy and is held back for a year.

2369: Sixth season of *Star Trek: The Next Generation*.

Captain Scott is discovered alive, suspended in a transporter beam aboard the *U.S.S. Jenolen*.

Cardassians withdraw claim to Bajor, withdraw from Bajoran space, and abandon station Deep Space 9.

First season of *Star Trek: Deep Space Nine*.

Federation Starfleet assumes control of station Deep Space 9 at the request of the Bajoran provisional government.

Benjamin Sisko assigned to command Deep Space 9. First stable wormhole discovered near planet Bajor.

Kai Opaka is killed in the Gamma Quadrant, resulting in a political power struggle to determine her successor.

2370: Seventh season of *Star Trek: The Next Generation*.

Lore is dismantled while attempting to lead the Borg on a new campaign of conquest.

A Federation-wide "speed limit" of warp 5 is imposed after discovery of evidence that excessive use of warp drive may damage the fabric of space.

Second season of *Star Trek: Deep Space Nine*.

A Bajoran religious extremist group called the Circle attempts to overthrow the Bajoran provisional government.

APPENDIX B: TIMELINE OF *STAR TREK* PRODUCTION

Early 1960s: Ex-police officer and noted Western writer Gene Roddenberry begins developing ideas for an new adventure television series. One of his concepts involves a 19th-century dirigible, á la Jules Verne. His ideas eventually evolve into *Star Trek*, which Roddenberry refers to as "Wagon Train to the Stars."

1964: Roddenberry submits a series proposal for *Star Trek* to MGM, where he receives the first of many rejections. Conventional wisdom in the television industry holds that science fiction is too expensive, too difficult to produce, and that it cannot work with continuing characters.

Desilu Studios agrees to develop *Star Trek*, and signs Roddenberry to a development deal. Desilu attempts to sell the series concept to CBS, which initally expresses interest, but instead develops a series called *Lost in Space*. NBC agrees to fund the pilot.

"The Cage" (TOS) begins filming. Jeffrey Hunter plays the part of *Enterprise* captain Christopher Pike.

1965: The completed episode is delivered to NBC, which subsequently rejects the pilot, calling it "too cerebral" for television.

NBC makes the highly unusual move of ordering a second pilot, requesting that several changes be made in the series format. Among these is the elimination of a woman second-in-command and the alien Mr. Spock. Roddenberry accedes to the first request, but refuses on the second. NBC also requests that the series be more solidly action-adventure-based. Three new scripts are developed for the second pilot. These include "Mudd's Women," "The Omega Glory," and "Where No Man Has Gone Before."

July 19. "Where No Man Has Gone Before" (TOS) begins filming with William Shatner in the role of Captain James T. Kirk. Leonard Nimoy as Mr. Spock is the only character retained from the first pilot.

1966: NBC accepts the second *Star Trek* pilot episode and places the show in its upcoming Fall schedule. Production begins on the first regular episode, entitled "The Corbomite Maneuver" (TOS).

September 8: The first episode of *Star Trek* airs on the NBC television network. The episode is "The Man Trap" (TOS), which was actually the fifth segment filmed.

1967: Desilu Studios and Paramount Pictures are acquired by Gulf & Western Corporation, which combines the two facilities under the Paramount name.

Star Trek is renewed for a second season by NBC. Although the show is far from a ratings hit, it develops a loyal viewership.

1968: Prompted by low ratings, NBC cancels *Star Trek* at the end of the second season. An extraordinary outburst of fan support, including a massive letter-writing campaign spearheaded by Bjo Trimble, reportedly results in a million letters being received by the network. NBC bows to viewer pressure and makes an on-air announcement that *Star Trek* is renewed for a third year.

In the aftermath of the dramatic renewal announcement, NBC schedules *Star Trek*'s third year for Friday nights at 10:00, considered at the time to be the "death slot" because of low viewership. Roddenberry subsequently resigns as show producer (retaining the title of executive producer), and Fred Freiberger produces the show's third season.

1969: *Star Trek* is canceled after its third season, at almost the same time as Neil Armstrong becomes the first human to walk on the moon. The last episode to be produced and aired is "Turnabout Intruder" (TOS).

Star Trek immediately returns to television in syndicated reruns across the country, frequently in more favorable timeslots than it had during its original network run. This extensive exposure wins many new viewers for *Star Trek*.

1972: *Star Trek*'s popularity continues to grow, and the first *Star Trek* convention is held in New York. The organizers expect a couple of hundred attendees but are surprised to find the final count exceeds 3,000. NBC considers a *Star Trek* revival, possibly as a TV movie, although the project never comes to fruition.

1973: An animated version of *Star Trek* airs on NBC, produced by Filmation Associates. Gene Roddenberry and D. C. Fontana are both actively involved in writing and producing the series, which eventually runs for some 22 half-hour episodes. Original Series actors contribute their voice talents to the Emmy Award-winning show.

1976: Paramount attempts to develop a low-budget feature-film version of *Star Trek*. Numerous big-name writers are invited to pitch story ideas, but nothing comes of the project, although *James Bond* production designer Ken Adam and *Star Wars* illustrator Ralph McQuarrie are engaged to design a new version of the *Enterprise*.

1977: Paramount announces plans to produce a new weekly series entitled *Star Trek II* for syndication, bypassing the existing networks. This show would be the flagship of a studio attempt to create a "fourth network." The proposed series would feature the adventures of a second five-year mission of the *Enterprise* under the command of Captain Kirk. All of the Original Series actors agree to return, except for Leonard Nimoy, whose character is slated to be replaced by a full-Vulcan officer named Xon.

1978: Spurred by the unprecedented success of *Star Wars*, as well as lackluster interest in Paramount's fourth network project, Paramount cancels *Star Trek II* just two weeks before the scheduled start of principal photography. Instead, the studio announces plans to expand the first episode into a major feature film to be directed by Robert Wise. In a surprise last-minute move, Leonard Nimoy agrees to return as Mr. Spock.

1979: *Star Trek: The Motion Picture* is released. The film is a resounding financial success, although fan and critical reaction is mixed.

1980: Based on the success of *Star Trek: The Motion Picture*, a second *Star Trek* feature is placed in development under the supervision of Harve Bennett. The project eventually becomes *Star Trek II: The Wrath of Khan*, a sequel to "Space Seed" (TOS). Some members of the *Star Trek* fan community react negatively to plans for the film to feature the death of Spock.

1982: *Star Trek II: The Wrath of Khan* is released to critical and financial success. Just prior to release, the film's ending is slightly modified to make Spock's death more ambiguous, leaving the door open for his return in a sequel.

Shortly after *Star Trek II*'s release, Leonard Nimoy indicates a willingness to return for such a sequel, and plans are announced for *Star Trek III* to be directed by Nimoy.

1984: *Star Trek III: The Search for Spock* is released, featuring the return of Spock from the dead and the destruction of the original *Starship Enterprise*.

1986: *Star Trek IV: The Voyage Home* is released. Leonard Nimoy also directs this story of time travel back to the 20th century.

Paramount announces plans to produce a new syndicated series entitled *Star Trek: The Next Generation*, to be produced by Gene Roddenberry, featuring an all-new cast. Roddenberry recruits a staff including

Original Series veterans Bob Justman, Dorothy Fontana, David Gerrold, Eddie Milkis, and John Dwyer to get the show underway.

1987: *Star Trek: The Next Generation* debuts as a syndicated weekly series featuring Patrick Stewart as Captain Jean-Luc Picard aboard the *Starship Enterprise-D*. The first episode is "Encounter at Farpoint" (TNG). Although Roddenberry is actively involved in the show's early production, he soon steps back into a more supervisory role, leaving day-to-day operations in the hands of Rick Berman.

1988: William Shatner takes a turn at directing the fifth feature, *Star Trek V: The Final Frontier*.

Star Trek: The Next Generation is renewed for a second season. Whoopi Goldberg joins the *Star Trek* cast as Guinan, and Diana Muldaur plays *Enterprise-D* chief medical officer Katherine Pulaski.

1989: Gates McFadden as Dr. Beverly Crusher returns to the *Star Trek* cast at the beginning of the show's third season.

1990: *Star Trek: The Next Generation* is renewed for an unprecedented fourth season. Wil Wheaton, as Wesley Crusher, departs the *Star Trek* cast midway through the year. The last segment of the season, "Redemption, Part I" (TNG), is the show's 100th episode.

1991: Gene Roddenberry dies at the age of 70, shortly after the 25th anniversary of his creation, which has become more popular than ever.

Star Trek VI: The Undiscovered Country is released, touted as the final voyage of the original crew.

1993: A new *Star Trek* series entitled *Star Trek: Deep Space Nine* premieres, featuring Avery Brooks as Commander Ben Sisko in charge of station Deep Space 9. The show is created by Rick Berman and Michael Piller.

Star Trek: The Next Generation begins its 7th season, expected to be the show's final year. *Star Trek*'s ratings are stronger than ever. Paramount announces plans to do a feature-film version of the series for release in late 1994.

Paramount announces plans to produce yet another *Star Trek* television series, tentatively entitled *Star Trek: Voyager* for airing in early 1995.

And the adventure continues...

APPENDIX C: EPISODE LISTS AND WRITER CREDITS

The authors of this book wish to acknowledge the writers of the Star Trek *television episodes and motion pictures, from whose work this document has been derived.*

Star Trek: The Original Series Year 1 (first aired 1966-67)

1. "The Cage." Written by Gene Roddenberry.
2. "Where No Man Has Gone Before." Written by Samuel A. Peeples.
3. "The Corbomite Maneuver." Written by Jerry Sohl.
4. "Mudd's Women." Teleplay by Stephen Kandel. Story by Gene Roddenberry.
5. "The Enemy Within." Written by Richard Matheson.
6. "The Man Trap." Written by George Clayton Johnson.
7. "The Naked Time." Written by John D. F. Black.
8. "Charlie X." Teleplay by D. C. Fontana. Story by Gene Roddenberry.
9. "Balance of Terror." Written by Paul Schneider.
10. "What Are Little Girls Made Of?" Written by Robert Bloch.
11. "Dagger of the Mind." Written by S. Bar-David.
12. "Miri." Written by Adrian Spies.
13. "The Conscience of the King." Written by Barry Trivers.
14. "The *Galileo* Seven." Teleplay by Oliver Crawford and S. Bar-David. Story by Oliver Crawford.
15. "Court Martial." Teleplay by Don M. Mankiewicz and Steven W. Carabatsos. Story by Don M. Mankiewicz.
16. "The Menagerie, Parts I and II." Written by Gene Roddenberry.
17. "Shore Leave." Written by Theodore Sturgeon.
18. "The Squire of Gothos." Written by Paul Schneider.
19. "Arena." Teleplay by Gene L. Coon. From a story by Fredric Brown.
20. "The Alternative Factor." Written by Don Ingalls.
21. "Tomorrow Is Yesterday." Written by D. C. Fontana.
22. "The Return of the Archons." Teleplay by Boris Sobelman. Story by Gene Roddenberry.
23. "A Taste of Armageddon." Teleplay by Robert Hamner and Gene L. Coon. Story by Robert Hamner.
24. "Space Seed." Teleplay by Gene L. Coon and Carey Wilber. Story by Carey Wilber.
25. "This Side of Paradise." Teleplay by D. C. Fontana. Story by Nathan Butler and D. C. Fontana.
26. "The Devil in the Dark." Written by Gene L. Coon.
27. "Errand of Mercy." Written by Gene L. Coon.
28. "The City on the Edge of Forever." Written by Harlan Ellison.
29. "Operation— Annihilate!" Written by Steven W. Carabatsos.

Star Trek: The Original Series Year 2 ((first aired 1967-68)

30. "Catspaw." Written by Robert Bloch.
31. "Metamorphosis." Written by Gene L. Coon.
32. "Friday's Child." Written by D. C. Fontana.
33. "Who Mourns for Adonais?" Written by Gilbert Ralston.
34. "Amok Time." Written by Theodore Sturgeon.
35. "The Doomsday Machine." Written by Norman Spinrad.
36. "Wolf in the Fold." Written by Robert Bloch.
37. "The Changeling." Written by John Meredyth Lucas.
38. "The Apple." Written by Max Ehrlich.
39. "Mirror, Mirror." Written by Jerome Bixby.
40. "The Deadly Years." Written by David P. Harmon.
41. "I, Mudd." Written by Stephen Kandel.
42. "The Trouble with Tribbles." Written by David Gerrold.
43. "Bread and Circuses." Written by Gene Roddenberry and Gene L. Coon.
44. "Journey to Babel." Written by D. C. Fontana.
45. "A Private Little War." Teleplay by Gene Roddenberry. Story by Jud Crucis.
46. "The Gamesters of Triskelion." Written by Margaret Armen.
47. "Obsession." Written by Art Wallace.
48. "The Immunity Syndrome." Written by Robert Sabaroff.
49. "A Piece of the Action." Teleplay by David P. Harmon and Gene L. Coon. Story by David P. Harmon.
50. "By Any Other Name." Teleplay by D. C. Fontana and Jerome Bixby. Story by Jerome Bixby.
51. "Return to Tomorrow." Written by John Kingsbridge.
52. "Patterns of Force." Written by John Meredyth Lucas.
53. "The Ultimate Computer." Teleplay by D. C. Fontana. Story by Laurence N. Wolfe.
54. "The Omega Glory." Written by Gene Roddenberry.

55. "Assignment: Earth." Teleplay by Art Wallace. Story by Gene Roddenberry and Art Wallace.

Star Trek: The Original Series Year 3 (first aired 1968-69)

56. "Spectre of the Gun." Written by Lee Cronin.

57. "Elaan of Troyius." Written by John Meredyth Lucas.

58. "The Paradise Syndrome." Written by Margaret Armen.

59. "The *Enterprise* Incident." Written by D. C. Fontana.

60. "And the Children Shall Lead." Written by Edward J. Lakso.

61. "Spock's Brain." Written by Lee Cronin.

62. "Is There in Truth No Beauty?" Written by Jean Lisette Aroeste.

63. "The Empath." Written by Joyce Musket.

64. "The Tholian Web." Written by Judy Burns and Chet Richards.

65. "For the World Is Hollow and I Have Touched the Sky." Written by Rick Vollaerts.

66. "Day of the Dove." Written by Jerome Bixby.

67. "Plato's Stepchildren." Written by Meyer Dolinsky.

68. "Wink of an Eye." Teleplay by Arthur Heinemann. Story by Lee Cronin.

69. "That Which Survives." Teleplay by John Meredyth Lucas. Story by Michael Richards.

70. "Let That Be Your Last Battlefield." Teleplay by Oliver Crawford. Story by Lee Cronin.

71. "Whom Gods Destroy." Teleplay by Lee Erwin. Story by Lee Erwin and Jerry Sohl.

72. "The Mark of Gideon." Written by George F. Slavin and Stanley Adams.

73. "The Lights of Zetar." Written by Jeremy Tarcher and Shari Lewis.

74. "The Cloud Minders." Teleplay by Margaret Armen. Story by David Gerrold and Oliver Crawford.

75. "The Way to Eden." Teleplay by Arthur Heinemann. Story by Michael Richards and Arthur Heinemann.

76. "Requiem for Methuselah." Written by Jerome Bixby.

77. "The Savage Curtain." Teleplay by Gene Roddenberry and Arthur Heinemann. Story by Gene Roddenberry.

78. "All Our Yesterdays." Written by Jean Lisette Aroeste.

79. "Turnabout Intruder." Teleplay by Arthur H. Singer. Story by Gene Roddenberry.

Star Trek movies (originally released 1979-1991)

1. *Star Trek: The Motion Picture.* Screenplay by Harold Livingston. Story by Alan Dean Foster.

2. *Star Trek II: The Wrath of Khan.* Screenplay by Jack B. Sowards. Story by Harve Bennett and Jack B. Sowards.

3. *Star Trek III: The Search for Spock.* Written by Harve Bennett.

4. *Star Trek IV: The Voyage Home.* Story by Leonard Nimoy and Harve Bennett. Screenplay by Steve Meerson & Peter Krikes and Harve Bennett & Leonard Nimoy.

5. *Star Trek V: The Final Frontier.* Story by William Shatner & Harve Bennett & David Loughery. Screenplay by David Loughery.

6. *Star Trek VI: The Undiscovered Country.* Story by Leonard Nimoy and Lawrence Konner & Mark Rosenthal. Screenplay by Nicholas Meyer & Denny Martin Flinn.

Star Trek: The Next Generation Year 1 (first aired 1987-88)

1. "Encounter at Farpoint, Part I." Written by D. C. Fontana and Gene Roddenberry.

2. "Encounter at Farpoint, Part II." Written by D. C. Fontana and Gene Roddenberry.

3. "The Naked Now." Teleplay by J. Michael Bingham. Story by John D. F. Black and J. Michael Bingham.

4. "Code of Honor." Written by Katharyn Powers & Michael Baron.

5. "Haven." Teleplay by Tracy Tormé. Story by Tracy Tormé & Lan Okun.

6. "Where No One Has Gone Before." Written by Diane Duane & Michael Reaves.

7. "The Last Outpost." Teleplay by Herbert Wright. Story by Richard Krzemien.

8. "Lonely Among Us." Teleplay by D. C. Fontana. Story by Michael Halperin.

9. "Justice." Teleplay by Worley Thorne. Story by Ralph Wills and Worley Thorne.

10. "The Battle." Teleplay by Herbert Wright. Story by Larry Forrester.

11. "Hide and Q." Teleplay by C. J. Holland and Gene Roddenberry. Story by C. J. Holland.

12. "Too Short a Season." Teleplay by Michael Michaelian and D. C. Fontana. Story by Michael Michaelian.

13. "The Big Goodbye." Written by Tracy Tormé.

14. "Datalore." Teleplay by Robert Lewin and Gene Roddenberry. Story by Robert Lewin and Maurice Hurley.

15. "Angel One." Written by Patrick Barry.

16. "11001001." Written by Maurice Hurley & Robert Lewin.

17. "Home Soil." Teleplay by Robert Sabaroff. Story by Karl Guers & Ralph Sanchez and Robert Sabaroff.

18. "When the Bough Breaks." Written by Hannah Louise Shearer.

19. "Coming of Age." Written by Sandy Fries.

20. "Heart of Glory." Teleplay by Maurice Hurley. Story by Maurice Hurley and Herbert Wright & D. C. Fontana.

21. "The Arsenal of Freedom." Teleplay by Richard Manning & Hans Beimler. Story by Maurice Hurley & Robert Lewin.

22. "Skin of Evil." Teleplay by Joseph Stefano and Hannah Louise Shearer. Story by Joseph Stefano.

23. "Symbiosis." Teleplay by Robert Lewin and Richard Manning and Hans Beimle. Story by Robert Lewin.

24. "We'll Always Have Paris." Written by Deborah Dean Davis and Hannah Louise Shearer.

25. "Conspiracy." Teleplay by Tracy Tormé. Story by Robert Sabaroff.

26. "The Neutral Zone." Television story & teleplay by Maurice Hurley. From a story by Deborah McIntyre & Mona Glee.

Star Trek: The Next Generation Year 2 (first aired 1988-89)

27. "The Child." Written by Jaron Summers & Jon Povill and Maurice Hurley.

28. "Where Silence Has Lease." Written by Jack B. Sowards.

29. "Elementary, Dear Data." Written by Brian Alan Lane.

30. "The Outrageous Okona." Teleplay by Burton Armus. Story by Les Menchen & Lance Dickson and David Landsberg.

31. "The Schizoid Man." Teleplay by Tracy Tormé. Story by Richard Manning & Hans Beimler.

32. "Loud as a Whisper." Written by Jacqueline Zambrano.

33. "Unnatural Selection." Written by John Mason & Mike Gray.

34. "A Matter of Honor." Teleplay by Burton Armus. Story by Wanda M. Haight & Gregory Amos and Burton Armus.

35. "The Measure of a Man." Written by Melinda M. Snodgrass.

36. "The Dauphin." Written by Scott Rubenstein & Leonard Mlodinow.

37. "Contagion." Written by Steve Gerber & Beth Woods.

38. "The Royale." Written by Keith Mills.

39. "Time Squared." Teleplay by Maurice Hurley. Story by Kurt Michael Bensmiller.

40. "The Icarus Factor." Teleplay by David Assael and Robert L. McCullough. Story by David Assael.

41. "Pen Pals." Teleplay by Melinda M. Snodgrass. Story by Hannah Louise Shearer.

42. "Q Who?" Written by Maurice Hurley.

43. "Samaritan Snare." Written by Robert L. McCullough.

44. "Up the Long Ladder." Written by Melinda M. Snodgrass.

45. "Manhunt." Written by Terry Devereaux.

46. "The Emissary." Television story and teleplay by Richard Manning & Hans Beimler. Based on an unpublished story by Thomas H. Calder.

47. "Peak Performance." Written by David Kemper.

48. "Shades of Grey." Teleplay by Maurice Hurley and Richard Manning & Hans Beimler. Story by Maurice Hurley.

Star Trek: The Next Generation Year 3 (first aired 1989-90)

49. "The Ensigns of Command." Written by Melinda M. Snodgrass.

50. "Evolution." Teleplay by Michael Piller. Story by Michael Piller and Michael Wagner.

51. "The Survivors." Written by Michael Wagner.

52. "Who Watches the Watchers?" Written by Richard Manning & Hans Beimler.

53. "The Bonding." Written by Ronald D. Moore.

54. "Booby Trap." Teleplay by Ron Roman and Michael Piller & Richard Danus. Story by Michael Wagner & Ron Roman.

55. "The Enemy." Written by David Kemper and Michael Piller.

56. "The Price." Written by Hannah Louise Shearer.

57. "The Vengeance Factor." Written by Sam Rolfe.

58. "The Defector." Written by Ronald D. Moore.

59. "The Hunted." Written by Robin Bernheim.

60. "The High Ground." Written by Melinda M. Snodgrass.

61. "Deja Q." Written by Richard Danus.

62. "A Matter of Perspective." Written by Ed Zuckerman.

63. "Yesterday's *Enterprise*." Teleplay by Ira Steven Behr & Richard Manning & Hans Beimler & Ronald D. Moore. From a story by Trent Christopher Ganino & Eric A. Stillwell.

64. "The Offspring." Written by Rene Echevarria.

65. "Sins of the Father." Teleplay by Ronald D. Moore & W. Reed Moran. Based on a teleplay by Drew Deighan.

66. "Allegiance." Written by Richard Manning & Hans Beimler.

67. "Captain's Holiday." Written by Ira Steven Behr.

68. "Tin Man." Written by Dennis Putman Bailey & David Bischoff.

69. "Hollow Pursuits." Written by Sally Caves.

70. "The Most Toys." Written by Shari Goodhartz.

71. "Sarek." Television story and teleplay by Peter S. Beagle. From an unpublished story by Marc Cushman & Jake Jacobs.

72. "Ménage à Troi." Written by Fred Bronson & Susan Sackett.

73. "Transfigurations." Written by René Echevarria.

74. "The Best of Both Worlds, Part I." Written by Michael Piller.

Star Trek: The Next Generation Year 4 (first aired 1990-91)

75. "The Best of Both Worlds, Part II." Written by Michael Piller.

76. "Suddenly Human." Teleplay by John Whelpley & Jeri Taylor. Story by Ralph Phillips.

77. "Brothers." Written by Rick Berman.

78. "Family." Written by Ronald D. Moore.

79. "Remember Me." Written by Lee Sheldon.

80. "Legacy." Written by Joe Menosky.

81. "Reunion." Teleplay by Thomas Perry & Jo Perry and Ronald D. Moore & Brannon Braga. Story by Drew Deighan and Thomas Perry & Jo Perry.

82. "Future Imperfect." Written by J. Larry Carroll & David Bennett Carren.

83. "Final Mission." Teleplay by Kasey Arnold-Ince and Jeri Taylor. Story by Kasey Arnold-Ince.

84. "The Loss." Teleplay by Hilary J. Bader and Alan J. Alder & Vanessa Greene. Story by Hilary J. Bader.

85. "Data's Day." Teleplay by Harold Apter and Ronald D. Moore. Story by Harold Apter.

86. "The Wounded." Teleplay by Jeri Taylor. Story by Stuart Charno & Sara Charno and Cy Chermax.

87. "Devil's Due." Teleplay by Philip Lazebnik. Story by Philip Lazebnik and Willian Douglas Lansford.

88. "Clues." Teleplay by Bruce D. Arthurs and Joe Menosky. Story by Bruce D. Arthurs.

89. "First Contact." Teleplay by Dennis Russell Bailey & David Bischoff and Joe Menosky & Ronald D. Moore and Michael Piller. Story by Marc Scott Zicree.

90. "Galaxy's Child." Teleplay by Maurice Hurley. Story by Thomas Kartozlan.

91. "Night Terrors." Teleplay by Pamela Douglas and Jeri Taylor. Story by Sheri Goodhartz.

92. "Identity Crisis." Teleplay by Brannon Braga. Based on a story by Timothy DeHaas.

93. "The Nth Degree." Written by Joe Menosky.

94. "QPid." Teleplay by Ira Steven Behr. Story by Randee Russell and Ira Steven Behr.

95. "The Drumhead." Written by Jeri Taylor.

96. "Half a Life." Teleplay by Peter Allan Fields. Story by Ted Roberts and Peter Allan Fields.

97. "The Host." Written by Michel Horvat.

98. "The Mind's Eye." Teleplay by René Echevarria. Story by Ken Schafer and René Echevarria.

99. "In Theory." Written by Joe Menosky & Ronald D. Moore.

100. "Redemption, Part I." Written by Ronald D. Moore.

StarTrek:The Next Generation Year 5 (first aired 1991-92)

101. "Redemption, Part II." Written by Ronald D. Moore.

102. "Darmok." Teleplay by Joe Menosky. Story by Philip Lazebnik and Joe Menosky.

103. "Ensign Ro." Teleplay by Michael Piller. Story by Rick Berman and Michael Piller.

104. "Silicon Avatar." Teleplay by Jeri Taylor. From a story by Lawrence V. Conley.

105. "Disaster." Teleplay by Ronald D. Moore. Story by Ron Jarvis and Philip A. Scorza.

106. "The Game." Teleplay by Brannon Braga. Story by Susan Sackett & Fred Bronson and Brannon Braga.

107. "Unification, Part I." Teleplay by Jeri Taylor. Story by Rick Berman and Michael Piller.

108. "Unification, Part II." Teleplay by Michael Piller. Story by Rick Berman and Michael Piller.

109. "A Matter of Time." Written by Rick Berman.

110. "New Ground." Teleplay by Grant Rosenberg. Story by Sara Charno and Stuart Charno.

111. "Hero Worship." Teleplay by Joe Menosky. Story by Hilary J. Bader.

112. "Violations." Teleplay by Pamela Gray and Jeri Taylor. Story by Shari Goodhartz and T. Michael and Pamela Gray.

113. "The Masterpiece Society." Teleplay by Adam Belanoff and Michael Piller. Story by James Kahn and Adam Belanoff.

114. "Conundrum." Teleplay by Barry Schkolnick. Story by Paul Schiffer.

115. "Power Play." Teleplay by Rene Balcer and Herbert J. Wright & Brannon Braga. Story by Paul Ruben and Maurice Hurley.

116. "Ethics." Teleplay by Ronald D. Moore. Story by Sara Charno & Stuart Charno.

117. "The Outcast." Written by Jeri Taylor.

118. "Cause and Effect." Written by Brannon Braga.

119. "The First Duty." Written by Ronald D. Moore & Naren Shankar.

120. "Cost of Living." Written by Peter Allan Fields.

121. "The Perfect Mate." Teleplay by Gary Perconte and Michael Piller. Story by René Echevarria and Gary Perconte.

122. "Imaginary Friend." Teleplay by Edithe Swensen and Brannon Braga. Story by Jean Louise Matthias & Ronald Wilkerson and Richard Fliegel.

123. "I, Borg." Written by René Echevarria.

124. "The Next Phase." Written by Ronald D. Moore.

125. "The Inner Light." Teleplay by Morgan Gendel and Peter Allan Fields. Story by Morgan Gendel.

126. "Time's Arrow, Part I." Teleplay by Joe Menosky and Michael Piller. Story by Joe Menosky.

Star Trek: The Next Generation Year 6 (first aired 1992-93)

127. "Time's Arrow, Part II." Teleplay by Jeri Taylor. Story by Joe Menosky.

128. "Realm of Fear." Written by Brannon Braga.

129. "Man of the People." Written by Frank Abatemarco.

130. "Relics." Written by Ronald D. Moore.

131. "Schisms." Teleplay by Brannon Braga. Story by Jean Louise Matthias & Ron Wilkerson.

132. "True-Q." Written by René Echevarria.

133. "Rascals." Teleplay by Allison Hock. Story by Ward Botsford & Dana Dru Botsford and Michael Piller."

134. "A Fistful of Datas." Teleplay by Robert Hewitt Wolfe and Brannon Braga. Story by Robert Hewitt Wolfe.

135. "The Quality of Life." Written by Naren Shankar.

136. "Chain of Command, Part I." Teleplay by Ronald D. Moore. Story by Frank Abatemarco.

137. "Chain of Command, Part II." Written by Frank Abatemarco.

138. "Aquiel." Teleplay by Brannon Braga & Ronald D. Moore. Story by Jeri Taylor.

139. "Face of the Enemy." Teleplay by Naren Shankar. Story by René Echevarria.

140. "Tapestry." Written by Ronald D. Moore.

141. "Birthright, Part I." Written by Brannon Braga.

142. "Birthright, Part II." Written by René Echevarria.

143. "Starship Mine." Written by Morgan Gendel.

144. "Lessons." Written by Ronald Wilkerson & Jean Louise Matthias.

145. "The Chase." Story by Ronald D. Moore & Joe Menosky. Teleplay by Joe Menosky.

146. "Suspicions." Written by Joe Menosky and Naren Shankar.

147. "Rightful Heir." Teleplay by Ronald D. Moore. Story by James E. Brooks.

148. "Second Chances." Story by Mike Medlock. Teleplay by René Echevarria.

149. "Timescape." Written by Brannon Braga.

150. "Descent, Part I." Teleplay by Ronald D. Moore. Story by Jeri Taylor.

Star Trek: Deep Space Nine Year 1 (first aired 1993)

1. "Emissary, Part I." Teleplay by Michael Piller. Story by Rick Berman & Michael Piller.

2. "Emissary, Part II." Teleplay by Michael Piller. Story by Rick Berman & Michael Piller.

3. "A Man Alone." Teleplay by Michael Piller. Story by Gerald Sanford and Michael Piller.

4. "Past Prologue." Written by Kathryn Powers.

5. "Babel." Teleplay by Michael McGreevey and Naren Shankar. Story by Sally Caves and Ira Steven Behr.

6. "Captaive Pursuit." Teleplay by Jill Sherman Donner and Michael Piller. Story by Jill Sherman Donner.

7. "Q-Less." Teleplay by Robert Hewitt Wolfe. Story by Hannah Louse Shearer.

8. "Dax." Teleplay by D. C. Fontana and Peter Allan Fields. Story by Peter Allan Fields.

9. "The Passenger." Teleplay by Morgan Gendel and Robert Hewitt Wolfe & Michael Piller. Story by Morgan Gendel.

10. "Move Along Home." Teleplay by Frederick Rappaport and Lisa Rich & Jeanne Carrigan-Fauci. Story by Michael Piller.

11. "The Nagus." Teleplay by Ira Steven Behr. Story by David Livingston.

12. "Vortex." Written by Sam Rolfe.

13. "Battle Lines." Teleplay by Richard Danus and Evan Carlos Somers. Story by Hilary Bader.

14. "The Storyteller." Teleplay by Kurt Michael Besmiller and Ira Steven Behr. Story by Kurt Michael Bensmiller.

15. "Progress." Written by Peter Allan Fields.

16. "If Wishes Were Horses." Teleplay by Nell McCue Crawford & William L. Crawford and Michael Piller. Story by Nell McCue Crawford & William L. Crawford.

17. "The Forsaken." Teleplay by Don Carlos Dunaway and Michael Piller. Story by Jim Trombetta.

18. "Dramatis Personae." Written by Joe Menosky.

19. "Duet." Teleplay by Peterr Allan Fields. Story by Lisa Rich & Jeanne Carrigan-Fauci.

20. "In the Hands of the Prophets." Written by Robert Hewitt Wolfe.

BIBLIOGRAPHY

Alexander, David: *Roddenberry, the Authorized Biography* (Roc Books, 1994). In-depth biography of the creator of *Star Trek*.

Asherman, Allan: *The Making of Star Trek II* (Pocket Books, 1982). Interviews with key production personnel and the cast of the second feature film.

Asherman, Allan: *The Star Trek Compendium* (Pocket Books, rev. ed. 1993). Episode-by-episode guide to the original *Star Trek* series and the feature films.

Asherman, Allan: *The Star Trek Interview Book* (Pocket Books, 1988). Interviews with cast and key creative personnel from the original *Star Trek* television series and feature films.

Clarke, Arthur C.: *Profiles of the Future* (Bantam Books, 1958). Clarke's classic exploration into the limits of technology; fascinating reading, even to see where real science has bypassed Clarke's predictions.

Gerrold, David: *The Trouble with Tribbles* (Ballantine Books, 1974). Gerrold's experiences in the writing and production of the classic Original Series episode.

Gerrold, David: *The World of Star Trek* (Ballantine Books, 1974; Bluejay Books, 1984). Overview of the original *Star Trek* phenomenon by one of the writers of the original *Star Trek* series.

Koenig, Walter: *Chekov's Enterprise: A Personal Journal of the Making of Star Trek: The Motion Picture* (Pocket Books, 1980; Intergalactic Press, 1991). Anecdotes from the actor's personal diary.

Nemecek, Larry: *Star Trek: The Next Generation Companion* (Pocket Books, 1992). Episode-by-episode guide to the series.

Okrand, Marc: *The Klingon Dictionary* (Pocket Books, 1985). Authentic reference to the spoken Klingon language by the linguist who invented it for the films and show.

Okuda, Michael and Okuda, Denise: *Star Trek Chronology: The History of the Future* (Pocket Books, 1993). Information from the episodes and movies woven into a definitive timeline of the *Star Trek* universe.

Reeves-Stevens, Judith and Garfield: *The Making of Star Trek: Deep Space Nine* (Pocket Books, Fall, 1994). Behind the scenes of *Star Trek: Deep Space Nine*.

Sackett, Susan and Roddenberry, Gene: *The Making of Star Trek: The Motion Picture* (Pocket Books, 1980). Behind the scenes of the first feature film.

Shatner, William with Kreski, Chris: *Star Trek Memories* (Harper Collins, 1993). Anecdotes from the making of the original series.

Sternbach, Rick and Okuda, Michael: *Star Trek: The Next Generation Technical Manual* (Pocket Books, 1991). Just about everything you ever wanted to know about the *Starship Enterprise*-D, in far more technical detail than you *ever* wanted to know it.

Toffler, Alvin: *Future Shock* (Random House, 1970). Toffler's treatise on the impact of technology and accelerating change on our society.

Trimble, Bjo: *On the Good Ship Enterprise, My 15 Years With Star Trek* (Donning Company, 1982). Trimble's adventures in and around *Star Trek* production, fandom, and conventions.

Trimble, Bjo: *The Star Trek Concordance* (Ballantine Books, 1976). Trimble's original comprehensive reference to the first *Star Trek* series and the animated *Star Trek*. (A revised and updated edition of this book, which will include the *Star Trek* feature films, is scheduled for publication soon.)

Whitfield, Stephen E. and Roddenberry, Gene: *The Making of Star Trek* (Ballantine Books, 1968). Behind the scenes of the first *Star Trek* television series.